THE BIG BOOK OF ADVENTURE STORIES

Edited and with an introduction by

OTTO PENZLER

Foreword by
DOUGLAS PRESTON

VINTAGE CRIME/BLACK LIZARD
Vintage Books
A Division of Random House, Inc.
New York

A VINTAGE CRIME/BLACK LIZARD ORIGINAL, MAY 2011

Library of Congress Cataloging-in-Publication Data
The big book of adventure stories / edited and with an introduction by Otto Penzler;
foreword by Douglas Preston.
p. cm.
ISBN 978-0-307-47450-6
1. Adventure stories, English.   2. Adventure stories, American.   I. Penzler, Otto.
PR1309.A38B54 2011
823'.08708—dc22
2011002226

Book design by Christopher M. Zucker

www.blacklizardcrime.com

Printed in the United States of America
10 9 8 7 6 5 4 3 2

FOR BULLET BOB CRAIS—

AN ADVENTURE HERO FOR OUR TIME

CONTENTS

CONTENTS

THINGS HAPPEN

DOUGLAS PRESTON

READING IS NEVER quite the same after the age of sixteen. The adventure books I devoured as a child remain with me to this day more fiercely than the "superior" works of literature I read later on, when I was (allegedly) an educated and sophisticated reader.

I was an avid consumer of adventure literature, good, bad, and ugly. Partly that was because I grew up in the deadly boring suburb of Wellesley, Massachusetts, in an age before Xbox, World of Warcraft, and Facebook. When we got home from school, there were only two ways for us kids to entertain ourselves: terrorize the neighborhood with pyrotechnic devices purchased from the back of comic books, or hunker down in some quiet corner reading an adventure story.

By the age of nine or ten I had run through the Hardy Boys books and had gone on to the harder stuff: John Buchan, Arthur Conan Doyle, Jack London, Rudyard Kipling, H. G. Wells, Jules Verne, Sax Rohmer. At some point I discovered H. Rider Haggard and was captivated by *King Solomon's Mines*. And so I picked up a second novel by Haggard, *She*. The title was unpromising. I did not like books that had women in them, and I had an especial horror of any sort of romance.

But it turned out the "she" in the novel was no romantic heroine. She was an evil, two-thousand-year-old murderous queen who lived in catacombs beneath an extinct volcano in darkest Africa, where she ruled over a race of subhuman degenerates. Now that was my kind of woman.

In some books, there are passages that affect you so powerfully that you remember exactly where you were when you read them. That happened to me with *She*. I will never forget the horrifying climax, when the beautiful but wicked queen regresses to her real age. I read that passage while in bed, in my attic room, late one winter's night, the wind rattling the windowpanes. I was reading under the covers and the batteries in my flashlight were dying. As I struggled to see, I had to keep tapping it, the beam flickering and dulling and sometimes blinking out entirely to my enormous frustration.

Smaller and smaller she grew; her skin changed colour, and in place of the perfect whiteness of its lustre it turned dirty brown and yellow, like a piece of withered parchment. She felt at her head: the delicate hand was nothing but a claw now, a human talon like that of a badly-preserved Egyptian mummy, and then she seemed to realize what kind of change was passing over her, and she shrieked—ah, she shrieked!—she rolled upon the floor and shrieked! Smaller she grew, and smaller yet, till she was no larger than a monkey. Now the skin was puckered into a million wrinkles, and on the shapeless face was the stamp of unutterable age. I never saw anything like it; nobody ever saw anything like the frightful age that was graven on that fearful countenance, no bigger now than that of a two-months' child, though the skull re-mained the same size, or nearly so, and let all men pray they never may, if they wish to keep their reason.

I kept my reason, just barely, but I never forgot the sheer excitement of reading that passage. Having read (and even loved) such novels as *Ulysses, War and Peace*, and *A Farewell to Arms*, I must admit that nothing ever quite equaled the sheer excitement of the ten-year-old boy reading *She* under covers. Perhaps this is why I became a writer of adventure stories myself.

She was first published in 1886 and 1887 (as a magazine serial) and became one of the best-selling books in the English language. It's a terribly flawed novel, crammed with odious racial stereotypes, fusty Victorian ideas about women, jejune characters, and histrionic prose. And yet *She* still manages to be a wonderful book, even a great book, an exemplar of the adventure novel at its finest. It is a cracking good story, astonishingly inventive, with vivid settings and scenes of hair-raising action. The novel introduced a wide range of thriller elements that would be used, reused, and eventually debased by lesser authors in the century to follow. Through its pages, I escaped my humdrum suburban childhood existence for a brief shining moment.

Adventure literature is, at its core, escapist. It is not a genre but a category, and a broad one at that. Adventure fiction is not realistic. Its aim is not to mirror life. It moves fast. Things happen. People die. *To the Lighthouse*, it is not. It transports the reader to the ends of the earth or into outer space. In adventure fiction the characters are larger than life. They are blazingly heroic or raging with malevolence; they are brutally repulsive or stunningly beautiful. Nobody is average. The settings are dramatic: impenetrable jungles, burning deserts, erupting volcanoes, earthquakes, lost cities, measureless caverns, mountains beyond mountains. And yet, even in these exotic locales, the adventure story never fails to uphold society's values. *She* is a veritable encyclopedia of Victorian prejudices, attitudes, and beliefs. Tarzan, raised by an unknown tribe of apes in deepest Africa, is at the same time an exemplar of utterly conventional American morality.

That partly explains, in my view, the appeal of adventure fiction. The risk is comfortable. Filled with excitement, exoticism, mystery, and violence, and set in the farthest corners of the world, these stories nevertheless reaffirm the safest values of home. They tell us who we are and what we believe, and they suggest such values are universal, even twenty thousand leagues under the sea.

Many of the stories in this volume date from the golden age of adventure literature, which stretches from the Victorian era to the 1920s. Specifically, I would bracket the golden age from the establishment of the British Indian Empire in 1858 to the discovery of King Tut's tomb in 1922. The one opened the Anglo-American (and French) age of colonial rule, while the other was the last great discovery of that age.

That sixty-five-year period forms an astonishing record of real adventure and discovery, when the last blank places on the world map were filled in. Explorers penetrated the interiors of Africa and the Amazon. They discovered astonishing ruins and lost civilizations in Peru, Mexico, and Central America. Mind-boggling temples were found in the jungles of French Indochina. Vast diamond mines were unearthed in South Africa. The Nile was traced to its source. Expeditions opened up the polar regions, the Himalayas, and the deserts of outer Mongolia. In America, the West was being "won," with Indian wars, headline-grabbing massacres, cattle drives, gold and silver strikes.

This explosion of discovery gave birth to the modern literature of adventure. Many of the writers in this volume took part in this grand opening of the world, as colonial administrators, soldiers, journalists, or adventurers themselves.

Haggard spent much time in colonial South Africa, as did John Buchan and Edgar Wallace; Kipling, P. C. Wren, and others served in the British Raj in India; Talbot Mundy was for a while a big-game hunter in East Africa; Jack London joined the Yukon gold rush; L. Patrick Greene was a civil servant in Rhodesia. As you will see from the many stories in this volume, they mined their own striking life experiences to marvelous effect.

After 1922, especially with the advent of the airplane, terra incognita dwindled to nothing. The colonial powers found themselves in retreat and colonialism fell into disrepute. The world shrank and the natives became restless. There was little left to discover, no blank spot that couldn't be flown over. Today, adventure literature struggles with this lack of mystery. We know too much.

Nevertheless, the adventure story holds a cen-tral place in the human imagination. If you look at the very earliest examples of human literature, what do you find? Not novels of manners, not angst-ridden narratives of adulterous martini-sipping suburbanites, not Pynchonesque intellectual bricks. No, what you find are red-blooded adventure stories filled with heroes, villains, carnage and murder, narrow escapes, improbable coincidences and, of course, monsters. *Gilgamesh,* the *Odyssey, Beowulf,* the Norse sagas, the Ramayana, the Pentateuch—these ur-texts are all largely composed of classic adventure stories.

The love of such stories must run deep in human nature. Perhaps it is embedded in our very genes. This volume contains a brilliant selection of some of the finest adventure stories ever written, many rescued from undeserved obscurity and published in book form for the first time. Load your flashlight with fresh batteries and enjoy . . .

INTRODUCTION

OTTO PENZLER

THE VOLUME YOU HOLD in your hands is unlike any book you are likely to encounter in what has sneaked up on us to become the twenty-first century. It is a collection of stories—yes, real stories, with heroes and villains; with beginnings, middles, and ends; with conflict and excitement.

It is also a collection of extremes. There is violence of biblical proportions here. It does not approach the graphic descriptions of splatterpunk, thankfully, but be prepared for people to be beaten, tortured, and killed. There are exploits so extremely heroic that they defy reason, stretching one's ability to suspend disbelief. Go with it. Characters on these pages often possess powers and traits of mythical stature. They were largely created in a time when readers did not demand absolute realism—so the protagonists' brilliance, their physical strength, their talents, are of such an exceptional nature that sophisticated readers may be tempted to roll their eyes or guffaw at the impossibility of it all. Alternately, they can sit back and enjoy the kind of stories that prevailed throughout the world until the middle of the last century, when gods and heroes began to take a backseat to characters who weren't that different from the people reading about them. Instead of offering stories designed to create wonder, awe, and riotous entertainment, today's fiction often seeks to reflect the lives of ordinary folks. Outer space, the jungles of darkest Africa, the lawless open seas, fearsome deserts of sand or ice, and the American

frontier have been largely replaced by mundane suburbs, cities, and rural areas. This is not meant to suggest that the adventure story has disappeared. It hasn't, but it is now aimed more at young readers—whereas previously it had been written for everyone who appreciated a thrilling story.

It is impossible to avoid the subject of insensitivity in many of these stories. In a time when arbiters of social conscience frown on, or forbid, even the use of such words as *terrorist, blind, handicapped, American Indian*, and *jungle*, this collection cannot help but send the extremely politically correct screaming into the street. I have read hundreds of stories written in the nineteenth century and for twentieth-century pulp magazines, British as well as American, and these tales exhibit a near-universal insensitivity that one can forget existed not so long ago. Asians are almost uniformly described as yellow, and generally as evil, sneaky, and vicious. Black characters are often referred to as niggers, and casually racist remarks are unthinkingly used to describe both villains and accomplished figures who play important, heroic roles. Anyone who is not white and Anglo-Saxon is liable—no, make that *likely*—to be referred to with an insulting epithet, even if it is not necessarily regarded as insulting by the speaker or by the object of the denigrating term. While they are the most egregious examples, racial slurs are not the only examples of language unlikely to pass muster these days. A one-legged man is called a cripple, women are girls or dames, a very short person is a midget, and so on. Yet to attempt to judge authors who worked in a different era by the standard usages of today is both narrow-minded and silly, just as it would be to impart sinister motives or attitudes to them. It would make as much sense to bring today's sensibilities to these usages as to complain that a character is using a horse and buggy when he should be using a car, or that he uses a messenger to deliver news when he should simply use his cell phone. Words, not to mention concepts, that never arise in this fiction are *diversity* and *multiculturism*. That was then, this is now. If the differences are too hard to understand or accept, you may need to skip a lot of these stories, sticking mainly with those set in fictional ancient eras or in the future, so that ethnic slurs cannot offend—since one is unlikely to feel the pain of civilizations that have never existed.

Other extremes in this book include the wide array of settings and eras in which these stories take place, as well as the great variety of authors who produced them. There are famous writers (O. Henry, H. G. Wells) and little-known ones (Carl Stephenson, Georges Surdez); literary figures (Rudyard Kipling, Alexander Woollcott) and pulp wordsmiths (George F. Worts, Frank Packard); those who starved (Jack London, Clark Ashton Smith) and those whose success remains legendary (Edgar Wallace, Edgar Rice Burroughs).

Adventure fiction has the sound of a genre, but it isn't. It is a collection of genres, with the frequent inclusion of genre-defying stories that adhere to the requirements of the label: to be exciting and to follow primary characters engaged in bold and unusual activities. More often than not, these characters are larger than life—whether a quiet-spoken cowboy who is slow to take offense but then proves to have the fastest gun in the West, a swordsman who can attack a dozen foes and emerge unscathed, or a thief (usually an honorable one, as is de rigueur for most burglars and highwaymen in the pulps and literature of the nineteenth century) who has

escaped the clutches of the law during a long career.

Opportunities for adventure have decreased as the world has grown smaller in the past century. Radios, telephones, automobiles, and airplanes have turned regions formerly perceived as inaccessible and remote, filled with wild animals and terrifying tribes, into popular tourist attractions or booming, modern cities with swelling populations. It is hard to remember that at the turn of the previous century, just a hundred years ago, most people in Western Europe and the United States had never seen an elephant, and a rhinoceros was a wonder when showmen toured with one. If someone wanted to escape his past, he could join the French Foreign Legion or head to the South Seas, where no questions were asked or answered. Shooting large animals for fun was regarded as the act of a brave sportsman. Throwing a handful of coins to a ragged group of villagers in a far land identified someone as a kind and generous soul. Inventing or using an unusual scientific device elevated one to the level of fearless genius: many of these science-fictional machines, such as lasers, television, and rockets, are commonplace today.

Between these covers are heroes who do all of these things and more, and a fair number of villains as dedicated to ruling the world, or destroying it, as the good guys are to saving it or improving it. There is nostalgia here for a simpler time—when the difference between Good and Evil was less defined in shades of gray than in clear-cut black and white, and when stopping a madman took higher priority than understanding that his desire to wipe out an entire city might have been caused by a childhood trauma.

Names of the great characters in the history of popular culture abound on these pages, although many became more popular in media other than print. The giants of motion pictures, radio, television, and comic books often had their start in adventure books and magazines, though they might be hard to recognize apart from their names. And what names they are!

Here are Tarzan of the Apes and Sheena, Queen of the Jungle. Here are the Cisco Kid and Hop-along Cassidy. Here are Bulldog Drummond and the Scarlet Pimpernel. And here are Zorro, Conan, Beau Geste, and Allan Quatermain. Here are impossible escapes, victory against hopeless odds, damsels in distress rescued by brave warriors, and heinous evildoers thwarted by righteous lawmen. Here are unknown islands ruled by megalomaniacs, pirate ships, lost civilizations, and universes not part of our known reality.

Bring to these extraordinary worlds your young heart and you will be rewarded with some of the most thrilling stories invented by the great storytellers of the nineteenth, twentieth, and even twenty-first centuries. Here, adventure awaits!

SWORD AND SORCERY

FARNHAM BISHOP AND ARTHUR GILCHRIST BRODEUR

FARNHAM BISHOP (1886–1930) wrote several nonfiction books, including *Our First War in Mexico* (1916) and *The Story of the Submarine* (1916), before he wrote his most famous work, *The Altar of the Legion* (1926), a novel set in Roman Britain during its war against the invading Saxons, in collaboration with Arthur Gilchrist Brodeur (1888–1971). Brodeur, a professor for many years at the University of California, Berkeley, was a scholar most noted for *The Art of Beowulf* (1959).

Together, Bishop and Brodeur also wrote a series of novelettes about Lady Fulvia, one of the rare examples of a female protagonist in pulp adventure fiction.

During the time of the Second Crusade, Fulvia is the beautiful eighteen-year-old daughter of Count Arnulfo of Rocca Forte, a city in Sicily. This beautiful, fertile island in the middle of the Mediterranean had attracted fortune hunters and adventurers from every part of the world for hundreds of years, and various powers had ruled in turn until defeated by the next invaders. Sicily experienced little stability until a small but formidable band of Normans conquered it and Roger II was crowned king in 1130, bringing peace and justice to the land.

Even so, in the Lady Fulvia stories, certain greedy Norman barons fight among themselves for power and for the rich lands controlled by Arnulfo, as well as for the hand of his daughter, who spurns them all. The stories about Fulvia tell of her struggles to keep herself, her father, and her people safe in a savage time.

"The Golden Snare" was first published in the April 18, 1918, issue of *Adventure*.

THE GOLDEN SNARE

FARNHAM BISHOP AND

ARTHUR GILCHRIST BRODEUR

THE GALLEY-SLAVES, half-asleep over their oars, kept up a languid beat in time to their overseer's drowsy counting. The *Sea Nymph*'s nodding captain dreamed of iced wine and lettuce in the cool arcade of some shore tavern; there was no warning cry from the lookout or sleepy helmsman, no attempt to alter the course or sound a call to arms. No one saw the black, looming shadow that crept menacingly near.

Healthily asleep behind a curtain which, drawn across the forward end of the half-open cabin on the poop and laced to the railing, sheltered her from the eyes of her father's seamen, the Lady Fulvia lay without covering or garment on a gilded, deep-cushioned bed. A purple

awning kept off the dews of the hot Mediterranean night and screened her eyes from the glare of the masthead-light.

About her, on pallets, lay her maids, less lovely than she in spite of the beauty for which they had been chosen to her service. Like herself, like all the others of her time, they were innocent of night-clothing. All slept with the serenity of sinless pilgrims; for they were returning to Rocca Forte from a pilgrimage to the shrine of Santa Lucia di Celsi.

Like a huge monster striking in the dark, the triple-timbered, steel-shod ram of another galley tore through the *Sea Nymph*'s starboard side, throwing her over to port till she lay on her beam-ends, water spouting inboard in fountains through her oar-ports. In a moment she righted, rolled back on an even keel, then heeled to starboard, the great ragged hole in her timbers letting in a rush of hissing, gurgling seawater. Its ram withdrawn, the monster that had crushed her backed away. Swiftly the *Sea Nymph* filled and sank, while her startled, panic-stricken crew and passengers wailed and cried to heaven.

Fulvia woke with the crash of shattered timbers and the shrieks of mangled men ringing in her ears, and a strangling tingling that choked throat and lungs thickly. She could not see; she could only feel the black smother that pressed against and within her. With the energy of fear, she fought against it, lashing out with arms and legs, blinded and gasping. At last she shook it off, and with a final gulp of salt water, she found herself swimming instinctively and badly in the warm Mediterranean.

Hurled from her bed by the shock of the hostile ram, she had been shot out over the low, uncurtained port bulwark into the sea; she had not more than half waked till she went under and sank deep. Now, however, her courage restored with full consciousness, she launched out into a steady stroke through the black darkness. She had come up facing the galley. The mastheadlight, still burning, swung nearer and nearer the waves; the screams of the chained rowers beat horribly upon her ears.

Her heart convulsed with pity and horror, she turned and struck out with all her might, knowing that the suction of the sinking ship would drag her under if she waited. In her eighteen short years Fulvia had seen ships sink and men die often. As she fought her way past the growing eddies, a loud and terrible wail rang out behind her, and she knew the *Sea Nymph* was gone. She did not dare look to see.

As she swam, her numb mind wakened to more than normal activity. Thoughts rushed in upon her, questions surged into her brain, requiring immediate answer. Who had made the attack? Who had dared sink a ship of her father's? Not pirates, surely, for Count Arnulfo of

Rocca Forte had swept them far from his coast ten years before and held a broad strip of sea with his swift galleys. Where were the patrol-ships of her father's vassals, who were responsible even in ordinary times for the safety of the shores intrusted to them? Why were they not doubly on the watch now, when they knew that she was coming back from her pilgrimage?

Fierce anger swept over her. Arnulfo's only child, she had all the fierce Viking spirit of that iron-handed Norman adventurer, whose ancestors, like others of their race, had overrun all shores from the Baltic to Northern Africa, carving out kingdoms for themselves in the warm, rich South. Arnulfo's grandsire, half-Dane, half-Frenchman, adventuring from Normandy, had seized the land of Rocca Forte, with its motley, many-tongued towns, its abundant fields, its dark, rough mountains, and its deep harbor dominated by the grim cliff and ruinous fortress that had given the land its name.

That first Arnulfo, or Arinulf—"The Eagle-Wolf," as his Northern companions called him—had rebuilt the fortress out of hewn stones quarried long ago by Greeks, by the Carthaginian seamen who came after the Greeks, by the Romans who came after both, and by the fierce Saracens that raided the golden island ruled and loved in the dead past by those three vanished peoples. He, the Eagle-Wolf, had founded Rocca Forte's grandeur; his son strengthened that which the Dane had won; and the son's son, Fulvia's father, sent his trained warriors of the many bloods and his Norman captains over the sea, behind the mountains, along the coast, enriching and extending his domains.

Having acted as King Roger's champion when that monarch was crowned at Palermo in 1130, Arnulfo was high in favor with the court. His was a strong, savage house, given to hearty laughter, to fierce tempests of destructive anger, to unexpected anger, to unexpected kindness and unguessed ferocity. And he was just, even when most cruel.

From her father and his sires, Fulvia had inherited their tempestuous anger, their iron strength, their flaming blue eyes. But it was her mother who gave Fulvia her dark velvet skin, her mother's silken Italian grace that swayed Fulvia's strong, lithe body, her mother's patrician charm and soft ways that hid the Northern fire in Fulvia's heart. Roma Marcellini was a daughter of the proudest family in the Eternal City, a family that had given consuls and generals of legions to the Republic of the Seven Hills and the Empire of the Caesars. Yet Roma had given no son to Arnulfo; only a daughter more beautiful than herself, with all her Roman queenliness.

Born and matured in that Sicily which has been lovely from the dawn of time, growing up one of its children of a hundred races, Fulvia had found herself virtual queen over a motly, picturesque people whose Southern blood was strengthened by the infusion of wild Northern strains: Frank, Dane and Norman. She was the heritor of a land that sparkled and overflowed with beauty beneath a dazzling sky; a land of rock, sea, fiery mountains, and abundant rivers. All about her were the strongholds of her own folk, the temples and cities of dead races that had built grandly and grandly perished. She did not understand all these things, but they were part of her, part of her own strength and beauty, part of her own fire and grace.

And she, the daughter of Arnulfo of Rocca Forte, had been assailed in the waters which her own father ruled! She had seen her ship sinking and her people perishing, the victims of a hostile attack where no enemy should dare to show a sail! Who had been bold enough to do this thing? And above all, where were the watchful galleys of Fulk di Neri—Fulk the Black—and of Ricoberto, who held this part of the coast for her father?

Voices boomed across the water. Looking back over her shoulder as she swam, Fulvia saw the masthead-light of the *Sea Nymph*, still burning, a lance-length above the waves. The galley must have gone down in shallow water, she realized,

and now rested on the bottom. Some of her people—her maids, perhaps, who were on the high poop and such others as were not chained to benches like the wretched galley-slaves— might well have escaped the sea.

"Aid! Aid for the Lady Fulvia!" rang a stentorian voice; the voice, she knew, of Jaufré, the faithful captain of the escort. Lights flashed; in their shifting glare she saw that the *Sea Nymph*'s waist was barely awash. From the high forecastle came the clash and gleam of weapons.

"Aid! Who attacks Arnulfo's daughter?" Jaufré called again.

"Silence that fool with a knife!" a thick voice boomed in reply. "Cut him down!"

In sheer surprise, Fulvia stopped treading water, and swallowed a salt mouthful. He who had just spoken, who must have been the attacker, was Fulk di Neri himself! Traitors, not pirates, had sunk her ship!

"Let him live!" came across the water in a high-pitched, effeminate drawl. "Having lost two good men overpowering the fellow, it would be wasteful to kill him. Let Jaufré be put to use; the *Falcon* needs a new starboard stroke-oar. Chain him to the bench."

Fulvia grew hot with anger. This man who ordered her servant chained to a bench was Ricoberto, the second of the two vassals who should have guarded the shore and protected her with their lives.

"But I fear the Lady Fulvia is drowned," the languid voice resumed. "We have spent our pains for nothing."

"You thrice-accursed fool!" Fulk roared at him. "She would be safe in our hands now, if you had laid your ship aboard and seized her, as we had planned. Why in the name of Judas did you ram the *Sea Nymph* as if she had been full of Saracens?"

"You may speak to my helmsman about that, if it please you," Ricoberto answered sulkily. "But you will have to go to a dryer and warmer place to find him, for I gave him my point for his awkwardness. Light the rest of your cressets and let us search the wreck, which is not all under water. We may yet find the Lady Fulvia aboard her."

"Pray to your patron saint that you may!" Fulk retorted. "If she has been drowned, here in the waters intrusted to us, Arnulfo will boil us in blood. Her dead body would prove a poor hostage for us. Cressets, there!"

Between wrath and fear, Fulvia swam hastily away from the wreck. In a little, the cressets—iron baskets holding wreaths of tar-soaked rope—would blaze out over the water, and she would be seen. She knew now that the attack had been carefully planned by the very men whose duty it was to defend her, that they had purposed to seize her, either to facilitate the schemes of their own treacherous ambition, or for a worse purpose. In either case, they had touched the weak spot in Arnulfo's armor.

If they meditated revolt, planned to depose the old warrior-count and seize his possessions, they had only to capture her, and her father's hands would be tied. Dearly as he loved his power and his rich lands, he loved Fulvia more. With her in their hands, the traitors could play for what stakes they chose, set any terms they would.

Striking out swiftly and silently, she bore away from the wreck and the two galleys lying beside it. A glance at the waning stars gave her direction—land was straight before her—and told her that dawn was near. She must reach the shore and find hiding before the light betrayed her to the searchers' eyes.

She knew both men well. Indeed, both had sued for her hand. Fulk, a swarthy Norman giant of forty-odd years, was a famous fighter and a swaggering bully. He commanded five galleys and rendered homage to Arnulfo for a rocky strip of coast and a brace of fishing villages. His men were professional soldiers of all races. Like the soldier he was, he had gone direct to her father, asking to marry Fulvia. Arnulfo had laughed in his face, bade him wed with his equals, and given him another village. Preferring Arnulfo's laughter to his wrath, Fulk accepted the gift, with a poor pretense at content.

Ricoberto, a smooth, womanish Italian, was made in another mold. Proud of his girlish features, he wore his dark hair in long curls over his shoulders, delighted in rich garments and splendid Saracen armor, and perfumed himself noxiously. A splendid swordsman, a dancer and harper of great skill, he could be a charming companion, and talked well. But he was cruel: a serving-maid had once spilled a basin of water over his soft boots; Ricoberto had slapped the girl's face again and again with his open palm, till Fulvia's angry protest stopped him.

Ricoberto had brought his suit to Fulvia himself. Quite sure of himself he had been, maddeningly self-possessed. When she refused him, he smiled lightly, and replied, with all gaiety:

"There is time yet, lady; and there are other women. You will grow wiser as you grow older."

Arnulfo was getting gray; his arm was not as strong as it had been. It might be, Fulvia reflected, that these traitors planned to use her against the old count's power, to compel him to resign his lands to them. Or it might be that they meant to compel her to choose between them. Rather choose death, she resolved, and swam faster. The gray of dawn was already encroaching on and mingling with the black of night.

"They slew my people!" she muttered fiercely. "Their evil love, or their cursed ambition, sent good men to death! I will pay them for it if it costs me my life!"

Before her the shore was outlined against the growing light, as a low, black line. A few minutes more and she would be safely on the beach. Safely? What safety was there on land or water for a lovely, helpless, unclothed girl? Yet better far, she thought, to risk whatever might be in store for her ashore than to fall into the hands of men whose wicked purpose was proved by murder and treason. Besides, once ashore, she might lie hidden in some wood until chance sent a peasant woman to her rescue, or found her some escape, however hard, from the fate that capture meant.

Gradually the shore became clearer; it was near at hand now, and the light was bright enough to enable Fulvia to make out the country a little way behind it. It was low, with a long, sandy beach inclosed within the protecting arms of two headlands and split by the slow current of a brook. As the first red glory of sunrise broke upon the blue water, she could see that the brook was wide and clear. It came down to the beach through a high wilderness of salt grass, beyond which the ground rose slowly, the hills beyond inclosing its valley between their green sides.

Behind the salt grass, the edges of the brook were screened by high, thick brush, which ran straight back to the dense, shaggy forest clothing the lower hill-slopes. Here was shelter, here was concealment! Straight for the brook's mouth she headed, and scraped a little sand-bar at its entrance: the stream was much shallower than she had expected. The cold fresh water struck against her breast; the rays of the rising sun warmed her neck and sparkled on the tawny golden masses of her hair.

In the soft daylight she did not dare come out and cross the beach, where she would be in full sight of those on the galleys. So she swam steadily up the brook, in spite of weary limbs and aching lungs, till she reached and passed the line of the woods. Here they could not see her.

The cressets had gone out on the wreck and on its enemies lying beside it, a half-mile or so offshore. Hidden in the forest, Fulvia could still hear the brazen voice of Fulk exhorting his men to search every corner of the *Sea Nymph*, to find her body if she lay drowned in the hull, to comb the water around for her swimming, to dive down into the clear depths for her sunken corpse. She heard, too, the high-pitched voice of Ricoberto ring out in a shout of command, and she shrank instinctively into the shelter of the deeper woods.

Thorn-scratched, scraped by dry branches, exhausted with her efforts to push through the thick growth, she was forced to stop. Glancing about her, she found no path, no yielding of the

forest's dense green wall. Try as she would, she could not force a passage.

The brook, however, was more promising. Here in the woods, its course was often broken by ripples or little cascades, where the banks had caved and dead branches had choked it. But so far as she could see, it was not too wide to wade, and was nowhere impassable. She must follow its course upstream. As she waded, the birds sang with insistent merriment in the thickets, flew in dipping flight from tree to brook, or started up with sudden rush of wings from quiet pools at the plash of her feet.

At last she came to a cleared space on the right bank: cleared long ago, and now dotted with dwarf trees and brush. Huge old stumps, half-rotted, stood all around. Fulvia placed one foot on the shelving edge and mounted the bank, dripping in the dappled sunlight. Suddenly stopping still, she gazed intently ahead. There, its ruined court littered with moss-grown stones, stood a cluster of ivy-embowered Corinthian pillars, the lovely shard of what had been a Roman temple.

The capitals were still intact, and crowned with a broken pediment, the whole of stained, greenish marble. As by a miracle, the shrine below was preserved: a corner of the wall, sheltering the figure of an undraped, enthroned woman with a carven wreath on her brows, and a marble dove on one lovely wrist. The base of the pedestal bore, in letters filled with green moss, the legend:

VENUS ALMA VICTRIX

Wondering, Fulvia stared at the ruin, herself appearing like the nymph of the grove. There was a rich pagan beauty to the scene: the centuries-old forest, with its sylvan brook; the ancient temple, broken, but still beautiful; and the unclothed, awestruck girl before the shrine.

But Fulvia knew nothing of these things. To her, unlettered like all women of her time, the inscription meant no more than the temple. An enthroned woman in a shrine, however, meant something very definite and holy; and at the foot of the pagan goddess Fulvia kneeled, repeating her "Ave Maria" with fervent devotion. Then, her caution awakening, she realized that if she could climb to the lofty pediment she might be able to see the galleys on the water, and observe if she were followed.

The weathered stone afforded a few foot-holds, but it was slippery; the vines which cloaked it formed a safer ladder. Up them she dragged herself with lithe strength, till she could fling one arm over a splendid capital. Once at the top, she gazed out over the sea, now sparkling white-crested azure in the crisp morning breeze.

A choked cry burst from her. Fulk's galley lay as it had been, grappled to the wreck; but Ricoberto's was just outside the wide mouth of the brook! 'Round swung the long, graceful hull, as the port oars pulled and the starboard rowers backed water, till the bow pointed out to sea and the stern toward the shore; for the long ram made it inadvisable to dock a Mediterranean war galley bows-on to the beach. Skilfully her crew backed the *Falcon* in, brought her alongside a straight strip of mossy bank that looked like a quay-wall, and there made her fast to convenient trees.

The port quarter gangway was run out and a landing party of thirty men-at-arms disembarked. Dividing themselves into two parties, they deployed rapidly along the sea-beach on either side of the brook, halted, faced inland, and, at a signal from Ricoberto standing on the galley's poop, advanced, like a line of skirmishers, into the interior. Then Ricoberto himself landed and, to Fulvia's horror, came wading up the bed of the brook, alone.

Panic in her heart, Fulvia threw herself face-downward flat upon the pediment, clutching at the green vine-tendrils. Ricoberto knew! This was his country and he was a famous hunter, who knew every stream and trail of his own woods. And, having thrown beaters out on both sides, Ricoberto was leisurely wading up the brook be-

tween, waiting for his beaters to frighten and drive her toward him. And now Fulvia remembered the shout Ricoberto had given as she swam into the mouth of the brook. It was light then, and he must have caught the gleam of her hair in the rays of the rising sun. But why, in that case, was Fulk not pursuing her also? Why was he still searching the water and the wreck?

Then the truth flashed upon her. Ricoberto had not reported his discovery to Fulk; he was beguiling Fulk, was hunting her for himself! She shivered; come what might, she vowed, she would never fall alive into the hands of that womanish, cruel, double traitor.

Lying flat on the pediment, comfortably warmed by the morning sun, she resolved to stay on her rocky shelter. Its height concealed her from the brook; a long, crumbling slab of marble, carved deep with the story of Aeneas, formed a low parapet between her and the forest on either side. No one would dream of looking here for her. It was only when she stole a glance over the side that she saw how fatal it would be to stay.

Where she had climbed there were broken ivy-branches all along the column; and in the shadow, where no ray of the sun would dry it, her own wet foot-print, stained with the mold of the ruined court, pointed treacherously to her hiding-place. She must descend at once and find another refuge. She could not hope to keep ahead of Ricoberto's war-toughened rascals long; she must take cover in some spot so secluded that not one of the many keen eyes searching for her could find it.

A flash of color caught her eye. Close to her motionless elbow lay a six-inch lizard, the scarlet bag of his throat distending and emptying with his breath. The sight roused recollection, then anger. Once she had seen just such a jewel-throated creature chased and beaten to death by boys; now she, the Lady Fulvia, daughter of Arnulfo of Rocca Forte, was pursued with still more wanton cruelty!

Her fierce Northern blood roused at the

thought. Oh, if she had a weapon, she would face her pursuers, and show them how a conqueror's daughter could defend herself! Careless in her indignation, she raised her head, and a lock of her tawny hair fell across her eyes. The glint of it shone fierily golden in the sun.

"Ah!" she cried to herself, "with a hair of my head I will trap you, Ricoberto the Hunter!"

She glanced rapidly toward the brook, noted the creepers trailing in a brown-flecked pool, nodded eagerly, and clambered down the vine-covered column in haste.

"With a single hair!" she repeated, laughing softly.

Ricoberto, broad of shoulder and slender-waisted, made a splendid figure of handsome confidence, as he waded up the brook, heedless for once of his exquisite Cordovan hip-boots, now quite spoiled with the water. The light flashed upon his Moorish helmet, and on the arrow-proof corselet of Saracen plate, for which he had paid a golden fortune, abhorring the coarse ring-mail of the Normans. He gazed from bank to bank, peered up the brook, and searched the thick growth of the banks with a gaze whose eagerness was masked with apparent indifference. Sure that Fulvia could not escape his beaters, he dallied now and then to snatch a glowing flower from the brink, or to fling water at a bright-hued insect.

A butterfly fluttered down from a tall stalk, and spread out on a stone before him, lazily sunning its wings. Ricoberto stooped to admire its velvet black and crimson, scooped swiftly with one hand, and swept it up. Having looked his fill, he lazily tore the dainty insect to pieces, and scattered them on the water.

Suddenly he uttered a smothered cry. At the further end of the pool in which he stood thigh deep, a flat rock thrust up its gray surface; and, gleaming like amber across its dulness, lay a long hair of tawny gold. He waded carefully forward into the pool, taking heed not to trip on the creepers that thrust forth into the water, bent forward, and picked up the hair between thumb and forefinger of a dainty glove.

One of the dangling creepers, finger-thick, moved strangely up and back; just as he raised one dripping leg, it pulled sharply, and Ricoberto fell face-downward with a heavy splash. His trunk weighed down by his plate corselet, he lay churning in water three feet deep, choking and strangling. One leg, upthrust above the pool, was held high in air by a slip-noose of green creeper. He was more helpless than a trapped beast, for he was both trapped and drowning.

From behind a mossy rock, sheltered by almost tropical foliage, Fulvia thrust her eager face. Seeing, she stepped out from her cover, and ran forward, reeling the stem of the noosed creeper back in her hands, so that it should not slacken. From the bank she sprang, landing astride Ricoberto's plunging back. Down shot her left hand to where his left arm was flapping madly about, grasped his wrist and with a swift tug brought it up behind his shoulder-blade.

Before he could wrench it loose, her right hand had taken a turn about his wrist with a loop of the creeper; the next kick of his own trapped leg drew the line taut. Instinctively Ricoberto's right hand came up over his back to free his left; instantly Fulvia trapped that too, then bound both his wrists tightly together, tying knot upon knot as swiftly and deftly as any sailor. Then, placing one knee and both her hands on his back, with all her strength, she thrust the man deep down in the pool.

She waited until his free leg no longer splashed, until the bubbles ceased to well up from the water, and Ricoberto was limp and still. Then she set to work, dragging the body out over the gray rock, and laying it flat there. With flying fingers she unfastened the straps of his corselet and flung it off, stripped off his boots, his leather jerkin, Cordovan hose and gloves, and tore the helmet from his head.

Faint at first, then nearer and louder, she could hear the shouts of those hunting her through the woods on either hand. In feverish haste she flung on the dead man's outer garments, strapped on his armor, tugged on the wet hose and boots, and belted on his long, slender sword. Then, drawing her glorious hair tight back, she braided it swiftly, thrust it down under the collar of the jerkin, and put on the helmet.

The long curtain of flexible mail that hung behind it she flung over neck and shoulders; over her face she drew the velvet-lined mask of fine chain-mail, with little holes for eyes and nostrils, that formed the Saracen vizor of Ricoberto's helmet. She was now, to the outward eye, Ricoberto himself, with no feature showing, no sheen of hair to betray herself. Thrusting the body into the pool, she waded confidently downstream toward the dead man's galley.

On the long strip of mossy bank that looked like a quay—and which had been a quay in the ancient days when this wilderness had been a city—lounged and diced a sprawling half-dozen of Ricoberto's men-at-arms, left behind to guard the *Falcon*. At the sound of a high-pitched hail, they sprang to their feet with one accord, pouching dice and snatching up weapons. Down the brook waded the wet, but jaunty figure of their captain, his war-mask over his face. A spear-length off he halted, and addressed them in drawling, silken tones.

"Ah," he purred with menacing politeness, "so ye must rest from your hard labors while your betters are at work. I will find employment for you. Go, search the forest with your fellows, and it were better that ye do not return till ye have found the Lady Fulvia. Speed, for I am anxious for her."

With perfect mimicry Fulvia imitated the tones of perilous courtesy which always preceded one of Ricoberto's most violent outbursts of cruelty; and the men-at-arms, deluded by the voice, flew in swift apprehension toward the wood to carry out the order. Drawing sword, and plucking a tuft of dry grass from the bank,

she carefully wiped the glittering weapon, and advanced swaggeringly up the gangway, where she found herself confronted by the one fighting man who remained aboard: a stocky, swarthy fellow in steel cap and mail, and armed with a short broadsword. It was the overseer of the galley-slaves. Pointing to Jaufré, the captain of her escort, who, as she had heard Ricoberto command in the dark, sat shackled to the starboard stroke-oar, she commanded:

"Unshackle that fellow. I would have sport with him."

The imitation was perfect; but the overseer stood stock-still, the hair on his shaggy neck bristling like that of an angry dog. His eyes burned suspiciously, fixed on hers, which she concealed behind dark, lowered lashes, lest he see that they were blue.

"First raise that mask!" barked the overseer.

A sudden swift flash, and the man leaped back just in time to escape Fulvia's sword, dragging out his own as he sprang. Steel clashed on steel, the burly overseer parrying one fierce thrust after another, backing farther and farther before a hand and wrist more supple, if weaker than his own. Along the raised fore-and-aft bridge between and above the inboard ends of the rowers' benches he backed, fighting doggedly, his heavy blade chopping through Fulvia's guard again and again, only to be stopped by the plate of proof.

At last, as his panting opponent paused to draw breath, he heaved his sword on high, brandishing it with both hands for a mighty blow. The pretended Ricoberto suddenly dropped all appearances of weariness and leaped in, driving the point of her long blade through his throat from front to back.

Breathing fast, Fulvia walked swiftly aft between the rows of excited slaves, who were torn between their fear of the supposed Ricoberto and their delight at the death of the brutal overseer. Fulvia mounted the poop, faced them, wiped her dripping sword, and took off her helmet. The slaves burst into surprised shouts; the dying overseer recognized her through the film that clouded his eyes, and it became clear to him, too late, what it was that had made him suspicious of her: when she had drawn and wiped her sword the set and motion of her arms were not those of a man's. He cursed gaspingly and died.

Glancing from his body to the slaves, Fulvia addressed them in a calm, authoritative voice:

"Ricoberto also is dead. I slew him. When Fulk learns of it it will go hard with both you and me. Therefore you must stand by me and obey my orders. If ye are faithful I will give you freedom and much gold. Arnulfo's daughter does not break her word. Will ye obey?"

Grateful for the overseer's death, wild with joy at the promise of freedom and wealth, the slaves could hardly be restrained from giving loud voice to their emotion. With one accord they swore fidelity, clasping their chained hands and begging her to unfasten their shackles. But this was just what Fulvia knew better than to do.

These men were the scum of the Mediterranean: criminals from Palermo, working out the penalty of savage crimes; captured Greek and Saracen pirates; broken thieves and cutthroats from the African coast. She dared not free them until she should be safe in the harbor of Rocca Forte, lest they turn against her in the evil of their hearts. Therefore she bade them wait, and with the point of the overseer's hammer she knocked the pin from the chains that bound Jaufré alone.

The slaves, furious with disappointment, began to clamor. She shouted stern orders at them, but they roared her down. Seizing the dead overseer's whip, Jaufré cracked it menacingly at them; but Fulvia laid her hand on his arm.

"Let them be!" she commanded. "I have promised them their freedom and I will not begin by abusing them."

Jaufré pleaded with her, urging that their shouts would soon attract the suspicion of Fulk, whose galley would sweep down upon them.

"We are but two," he insisted; "we must beat these dogs into submission and force them to row while there is yet time to escape."

Fulvia shook her head, her white lips closed firmly.

Wrathful outcries from the wood rang through the shouts of the slaves. Turning Fulvia saw the flash of mail through the trees, heard the clamor of the men-at-arms who had just found Ricoberto's corpse, and knew that they would hasten to the shore to seize and kill his slayer.

"See!" she cried to the galley-slaves. "Behold the dogs of Ricoberto, who thirst for blood. Will mine alone satisfy them, do you think? Row for your lives!"

Smitten with cold fear, the slaves bent to their oars, striking and splashing in their confusion. Swiftly Fulvia cut through the bow and stern warps with her sword, while Jaufré's knotted arms strained at the gang-plank. With a grating rattle, he dragged it aboard single-handed. Taking the helm herself, Fulvia called the stroke in a well-simulated imitation of Ricoberto's voice; the oars began to pull together, and the *Falcon* shot out into deep water.

With loud shouts of rage, the landing-party raced down through the salt grass, waving their weapons and grimacing with fury. But they stopped at the water's edge, for they had no boats, and the *Falcon* was a good ship's-length from the shore.

Now Fulk heard, and his suspicions were roused indeed. Leaping from his seat in the cabin of his galley, where he was questioning Fulvia's rescued maids and the other survivors of the *Sea Nymph*, he ran to the rail and hailed the *Falcon*.

Now until that moment Fulvia had had no thought of doing anything but to head down the coast and run full speed for Rocca Forte. But, as Fulk hailed, an audacious thought shot through her brain; instead of coming about, she held straight on and brought her prize to within a cable-length of the other galley. There she spoke quickly and quietly to Jaufré, who put the overseer's whistle to his lips and blew "Rest oars!"

His brazen voice ringing out over the water, Fulk again demanded the cause of the uproar.

Her war-mask once more concealing her features, the girl answered—

"Fulvia!"

"Have you found her?" bellowed Fulk.

"She is here!" Fulvia replied.

The astonished slaves, not sensing her purpose, and in terrible fear of Fulk, began to claw with their oars; but a low command and a few swift sentences from Jaufré quieted them.

"Is she safe?" Fulk questioned.

With a convincing imitation of Ricoberto's falsetto laugh, Fulvia replied—

"Safe indeed, noble Fulk, and longing to pour her wrath into your ears."

Fulk sounded the silver whistle that depended from his neck; a small boat was put overside, and he lowered his huge frame into it. As the boat came alongside the *Falcon*, Jaufré, his face concealed under a wide-brimmed hat of plaited straw and averted from Fulk's gaze, caught and held its bow. With a bold smirk and a fine swagger, Fulk climbed aboard. Facing the figure which stood at the break of the poop, he asked—

"Where is she?"

"She is here!" Fulvia shouted, casting her helmet to the deck.

On the instant, Jaufré thrust his mighty arm and shoulder against the bow of the small boat, sending it half-way back to its parent galley.

"Give way!" he roared to the *Falcon*'s rowers, as he whipped out the overseer's sword and turned to follow Fulk. "Give way!"

A warning cry from the startled crew of the rowboat beat upon Fulk's ears; but he was too stunned with the sight of Fulvia's face above Ricoberto's armor to heed the cry; and when his keen Norman mind reasserted itself he had thoughts and eyes for Fulvia alone. Drawing his sword, he set foot on the steps leading up to the poop, bent on disarming and seizing her.

Just then the *Falcon*, urged suddenly by the obedient arms of the excited galley-slaves, bounded ahead, nearly flinging him to his knees. Hearing steps behind him, he looked back and saw Jaufré's menacing form, sword uplifted to

strike. Loudly Fulk shouted to his own ship's crew; but fully half his men were still searching the *Sea Nymph*, or sweeping the bottom with a drag stretched between the other two small boats. Hearing his cry, they pulled alongside as fast as they could; petty officers shouted, the trumpet blew, wreck and galley were in a riot of confusion.

But even with a fair start, his ship had no chance in a race with the *Falcon*, one of the swiftest ships on the coast; far less chance now, when Fulvia's galley-slaves were pulling for freedom. And Fulk himself was trapped, with the thirsty sword of an angered countess before him and the blade of a veteran soldier behind; while the *Falcon* bounded on to safety.

He had no choice, no chance; and he knew it. If he struck at Fulvia, Jaufré would hew him down from behind. If he turned to deal with Jaufré, Fulvia's blade would run him through the back. His courage oozed away. With a groan, Fulk flung his sword into the sea, and dropped to his knees before his injured lady.

"Mercy, most noble one! Mercy, gracious lady!" he begged.

"First bid your crew row quietly behind, without attempting a rescue; and command them to treat my servants and my maids with respect," Fulvia countered.

Obediently, Fulk roared his orders till one answered that they understood.

Then, in the silken tones of Ricoberto, Fulvia said to Jaufré—

"Let Fulk be put to use; chain him to a bench."

Eagerly Jaufré dragged the traitor to the nearest bench, freed the slave who tugged at the huge sweep, and chained Fulk in his place, thrusting the oar into his hand. The slaves burst into jeers and gibes at the fallen nobleman, taunting him till he cowered behind his oar; then mockingly they bade him pull strongly, lest he keep Arnulfo's gallows waiting.

Then, while Jaufré took the helm, and the liberated slave brought her meat and wine, Fulvia gazed down from the poop upon her prisoner, upon the captured *Falcon*, and upon the prize that followed laboriously astern. Setting down a quail's wing half eaten, she called—

"Fulk!"

The humbled traitor looked up, his face crimson with shame.

"Have you had enough of treason?"

He nodded ignominiously.

"Then," she laughed, "if Arnulfo spares your life, plot no more against him. Remember, he is the father of Fulvia of Rocca Forte!"

THE DEVIL IN IRON

ROBERT E. HOWARD

THE TERM "Sword and Sorcery" was virtually invented to describe the works of Robert Ervin Howard (1906–1936), whose most famous creation, Conan, has become an iconic figure in the world of adventure fiction and film. As a young man in Texas, Howard held numerous odd jobs—all of which he hated, knowing he was born to be a writer. He produced reams of stories and poems while still a teenager, and made his first sale to one of the greatest of all pulp magazines, *Weird Tales,* which published "Spear and Fang" in its July 1925 issue. Although he wrote in many genres, including boxing, westerns, horror, and detective and historical fiction, he is known today for his fantastic adventure series about the vengeful Solomon Kane, a Puritan swashbuckler in Africa; King Kull, who thrived in ancient Atlantis; Bran Mak Morn, a king of the Caledonian Picts, an ancient Scottish tribe that fought the Romans; and, most memorably, Conan the Barbarian, who lived in Cimmeria during the fictional Hyborian Age, about twelve thousand years ago. Even as a young man, Conan was a large, heavily muscled wandering warrior who loved food, drink, women, and battle. His powerful sword was as invincible as he was, and he was always ready to fight. Barbarism, he proclaimed, was the natural state of being. He battled hordes of enemies—whether human, monstrous, or magical—with a fearlessness that suggested an almost suicidal disregard of his own life. Such a worldview may reflect the author's own: A lifelong depressive, Howard was inordinately close to his mother. When her tuberculosis reached its final stage and a nurse told him she would never again be conscious, he put a gun in his mouth and killed himself at the age of thirty, by which time he had written an astounding number of books (more than fifty) and short stories (more than two hundred), mostly unpublished during his lifetime. Although Howard died young, Conan lives, in the pages of the stories and the two films about him. *Conan the Barbarian* made a star of bodybuilder Arnold Schwarzenegger, the future governor of California, who also starred in the sequel, *Conan the Destroyer* (1984).

"The Devil in Iron" was originally published in the August 1934 issue of *Weird Tales;* its first book publication was in *Conan the Barbarian* (New York: Gnome, 1954).

THE DEVIL IN IRON

ROBERT E. HOWARD

I

THE FISHERMAN LOOSENED his knife in its scabbard. The gesture was instinctive, for what he feared was nothing a knife could slay, not even the saw-edged crescent blade of the Yuetshi that could disembowel a man with an upward stroke. Neither man nor beast threatened him in the solitude which brooded over the castellated isle of Xapur.

He had climbed the cliffs, passed through the jungle that bordered them, and now stood surrounded by evidence of a vanished state. Broken columns glimmered among the trees, the straggling lines of crumbling walls meandered off into the shadows, and under his feet were broad paves, cracked and bowed by roots growing beneath.

The fisherman was typical of his race, that strange people whose origin is lost in the gray dawn of the past, and who have dwelt in their rude fishing-huts along the southern shore of the Sea of Vilayet since time immemorial. He was broadly built, with long, apish arms and a mighty chest, but with lean loins and thin, bandy legs. His face was broad, his forehead low and retreating, his hair thick and tangled. A belt for a knife and a rag for a loin-cloth were all he wore in the way of clothing.

That he was where he was proved that he was less dully incurious than most of his people. Men seldom visited Xapur. It was uninhabited, all but forgotten, merely one among the myriad isles which dotted the great inland sea. Men called it Xapur, the Fortified, because of its ruins, remnants of some prehistoric kingdom, lost and forgotten before the conquering Hyborians had ridden southward. None knew who reared those stones, though dim legends lingered among the Yuetshi which half intelligibly suggested a connection of immeasurable antiquity between the fishers and the unknown island kingdom.

But it had been a thousand years since any Yuetshi had understood the import of these tales; they repeated them now as a meaningless formula, a gibberish framed to their lips by custom. No Yuetshi had come to Xapur for a century. The adjacent coast of the mainland was uninhabited, a reedy marsh given over to the grim beasts that haunted it. The fisher's village lay some distance to the south, on the mainland. A storm had blown his frail fishing-craft far from his accustomed haunts, and wrecked it in a night of flaring lightning and roaring waters on the towering cliffs of the isle. Now in the dawn, the sky shone blue and clear; the rising sun made jewels of the dripping leaves. He had climbed the cliffs to which he had clung through the night because, in the midst of the storm, he had seen an appalling lance of lightning fork out of the black heavens, and the concussion of its stroke, which had shaken the whole island, had been accompanied by a cataclysmic crash that he doubted could have resulted from a riven tree.

A dull curiosity had caused him to investigate; and now he had found what he sought and

16

an animal-like uneasiness possessed him, a sense of lurking peril.

Among the trees reared a broken dome-like structure, built of gigantic blocks of the peculiar iron-like green stone found only on the islands of Vilayet. It seemed incredible that human hands could have shaped and placed them, and certainly it was beyond human power to have overthrown the structure they formed. But the thunderbolt had splintered the ton-heavy blocks like so much glass, reduced others to green dust, and ripped away the whole arch of the dome.

The fisherman climbed over the debris and peered in, and what he saw brought a grunt from him. Within the ruined dome, surrounded by stone-dust and bits of broken masonry, lay a man on a golden block. He was clad in a sort of skirt and a shagreen girdle. His black hair, which fell in a square mane to his massive shoulders, was confined about his temples by a narrow gold band. On his bare, muscular breast lay a curious dagger with a jeweled pommel, shagreen-bound hilt, and a broad crescent blade. It was much like the knife the fisherman wore at his hip, but it lacked the serrated edge, and was made with infinitely greater skill.

The fisherman lusted for the weapon. The man, of course, was dead; had been dead for many centuries. This dome was his tomb. The fisherman did not wonder by what art the ancients had preserved the body in such a vivid likeness of life, which kept the muscular limbs full and unshrunken, the dark flesh vital. The dull brain of the Yuetshi had room only for his desire for the knife with its delicate waving lines along the dully gleaming blade.

Scrambling down into the dome, he lifted the weapon from the man's breast. And as he did so, a strange and terrible thing came to pass. The muscular dark hands knotted convulsively, the lids flared open, revealing great dark magnetic eyes whose stare struck the startled fisherman like a physical blow. He recoiled, dropping the jeweled dagger in his perturbation. The man on the dais heaved up to a sitting position, and the fisherman gaped at the full extent of his size,

thus revealed. His narrowed eyes held the Yuetshi and in those slitted orbs he read neither friendliness nor gratitude; he saw only a fire as alien and hostile as that which burns in the eyes of a tiger.

Suddenly the man rose and towered above him, menace in his every aspect. There was no room in the fisherman's dull brain for fear, at least for such fear as might grip a man who has just seen the fundamental laws of nature defied. As the great hands fell to his shoulders, he drew his saw-edged knife and struck upward with the same motion. The blade splintered against the stranger's corded belly as against a steel column, and then the fisherman's thick neck broke like a rotten twig in the giant hands.

II

Jehungir Agha, lord of Khawarizm and keeper of the coastal border, scanned once more the ornate parchment scroll with its peacock seal, and laughed shortly and sardonically.

"Well?" bluntly demanded his counsellor Ghaznavi.

Jehungir shrugged his shoulders. He was a handsome man, with the merciless pride of birth and accomplishment.

"The king grows short of patience," said he. "In his own hand he complains bitterly of what he calls my failure to guard the frontier. By Tarim, if I can not deal a blow to these robbers of the steppes, Khawarizm may own a new lord."

Ghaznavi tugged his gray-shot beard in meditation. Yezdigerd, king of Turan, was the mightiest monarch in the world. In his palace in the great port city of Aghrapur was heaped the plunder of empires. His fleets of purple-sailed war galleys had made Vilayet an Hyrkanian lake. The dark-skinned people of Zamora paid him tribute, as did the eastern provinces of Koth. The Shemites bowed to his rule as far west as Shushan. His armies ravaged the borders of Stygia in the south and the snowy lands of the Hyperboreans in the north. His riders bore torch and sword westward into Brythunia and Ophir and Corinthia, even to the borders of Nemedia. His gilt-helmeted swordsmen had trampled hosts under their horses' hoofs, and walled cities went up in flames at his command. In the glutted slave markets of Aghrapur, Sultanapur, Khawarizm, Shahpur, and Khorusun, women were sold for three small silver coins—blonde Brythunians, tawny Stygians, dark-haired Zamorians, ebon Kushites, olive-skinned Shemites.

Yet, while his swift horsemen overthrew armies far from his frontiers, at his very borders an audacious foe plucked his beard with a red-dripping and smoke-stained hand.

On the broad steppes between the Sea of Vilayet and the borders of the easternmost Hyborian kingdoms, a new race had sprung up in the past half-century, formed originally of fleeing criminals, broken men, escaped slaves, and deserting soldiers. They were men of many crimes and countries, some born on the steppes, some fleeing from the kingdoms in the west. They were called *kozak,* which means wastrel.

Dwelling on the wild, open steppes, owning no law but their own peculiar code, they had become a people capable even of defying the Grand Monarch. Ceaselessly they raided the Turanian frontier, retiring in the steppes when defeated; with the pirates of Vilayet, men of much the same breed, they harried the coast, preying off the merchant ships which plied between the Hyrkanian ports.

"How am I to crush these wolves?" demanded Jehungir. "If I follow them into the steppes, I run the risk either of being cut off and destroyed, or of having them elude me entirely and burn the city in my absence. Of late they have been more daring than ever."

"That is because of the new chief who has risen among them," answered Ghaznavi. "You know whom I mean."

"Aye!" replied Jehungir feelingly. "It is that devil Conan; he is even wilder than the *kozaks,* yet he is crafty as a mountain lion."

"It is more through wild animal instinct than through intelligence," answered Ghaznavi. "The other *kozaks* are at least descendants of civilized men. He is a barbarian. But to dispose of him would be to deal them a crippling blow."

"But how?" demanded Jehungir. "He has repeatedly cut his way out of spots that seemed certain death for him. And, instinct or cunning, he has avoided or escaped every trap set for him."

"For every beast and for every man there is a trap he will not escape," quoth Ghaznavi. "When we have parleyed with the *kozaks* for the ransom of captives, I have observed this man Conan. He has a keen relish for women and strong drink. Have your captive Octavia fetched here."

Jehungir clapped his hands, and an impassive Kushite eunuch, an image of shining ebony in silken pantaloons, bowed before him and went to do his bidding. Presently he returned, leading by the wrist a tall handsome girl, whose yellow hair, clear eyes, and fair skin identified her as a pure-blooded member of her race. Her scanty silk tunic, girded at the waist, displayed the marvelous contours of her magnificent figure. Her fine eyes flashed with resentment and her red lips were sulky, but submission had been taught her during her captivity. She stood with hanging head before her master until he motioned her to a seat on the divan beside him. Then he looked inquiringly at Ghaznavi.

"We must lure Conan away from the *kozaks,*" said the counsellor abruptly. "Their war camp is at present pitched somewhere on the lower reaches of the Zaporoska River—which, as you well know, is a wilderness of reeds, a swampy jungle in which our last expedition was cut to pieces by those masterless devils."

"I am not likely to forget that," said Jehungir wryly.

"There is an uninhabited island near the mainland," said Ghaznavi, "known as Xapur, the Fortified, because of some ancient ruins upon it. There is a peculiarity about it which makes it perfect for our purpose. It has no shore-line, but rises sheer out of the sea in cliffs a hundred and fifty feet tall. Not even an ape could negotiate them. The only place where a man can go up or down is a narrow path on the western side that has the appearance of a worn stair, carved into the solid rock of the cliffs.

"If we could trap Conan on that island, alone, we could hunt him down at our leisure, with bows, as men hunt a lion."

"As well wish for the moon," said Jehungir impatiently. "Shall we send him a messenger, bidding him climb the cliffs and await our coming?"

"In effect, yes!" Seeing Jehungir's look of amazement, Ghaznavi continued: "We will ask for a parley with the *kozaks* in regard to prisoners, at the edge of the steppes by Fort Ghori. As usual, we will go with a force and encamp outside the castle. They will come, with an equal force, and the parley will go forward with the usual distrust and suspicion. But this time we will take with us, as if by casual chance, your beautiful captive." Octavia changed color and listened with intensified interest as the counsellor nodded toward her. "She will use all her wiles to attract Conan's attention. That should not be difficult. To that wild reaver she should appear a dazzling vision of loveliness. Her vitality and substantial figure should appeal to him more vividly than would one of the doll-like beauties of your seraglio."

Octavia sprang up, her white fists clenched, her eyes blazing and her figure quivering with outraged anger.

"You would force me to play the trollop with this barbarian?" she exclaimed. "I will not! I am no market-block slut to smirk and ogle at a steppes-robber. I am the daughter of a Nemedian lord—"

"You were of the Nemedian nobility before my riders carried you off," returned Jehungir cynically. "Now you are merely a slave who will do as she is bid."

"I will not!" she raged.

"On the contrary," rejoined Jehungir with studied cruelty, "you will. I like Ghaznavi's plan. Continue, prince among counsellors."

"Conan will probably wish to buy her. You will refuse to sell her, of course, or to exchange her for Hyrkanian prisoners. He may then try to steal her, or take her by force—though I do not think even he would break the parley-truce. Anyway, we must be prepared for whatever he might attempt.

"Then, shortly after the parley, before he has time to forget all about her, we will send a messenger to him, under a flag of truce, accusing him of stealing the girl, and demanding her return. He may kill the messenger, but at least he will think that she has escaped.

"Then we will send a spy—a Yuetshi fisherman will do—to the *kozak* camp, who will tell Conan that Octavia is hiding on Xapur. If I know my man, he will go straight to that place."

"But we do not know that he will go alone," Jehungir argued.

"Does a man take a band of warriors with him, when going to a rendezvous with a woman he desires?" retorted Ghaznavi. "The chances are all that he *will* go alone. But we will take care of the other alternative. We will not await him on the island, where we might be trapped ourselves, but among the reeds of a marshy point which juts out to within a thousand yards of Xapur. If he brings a large force, we'll beat a retreat and think up another plot. If he comes alone or with a small party, we will have him. Depend upon it, he will come, remembering your charming slave's smiles and meaning glances."

"I will never descend to such shame!" Octavia was wild with fury and humiliation. "I will die first!"

"You will not die, my rebellious beauty," said Jehungir, "but you will be subjected to a very painful and humiliating experience."

He clapped his hands, and Octavia paled. This time it was not the Kushite who entered, but a Shemite, a heavily muscled man of medium height with a short, curled, blue-black beard.

"Here is work for you, Gilzan," said Jehungir. "Take this fool, and play with her awhile. Yet be careful not to spoil her beauty."

With an inarticulate grunt the Shemite seized Octavia's wrist, and at the grasp of his iron fingers, all the defiance went out of her. With a piteous cry she tore away and threw herself on her knees before her implacable master, sobbing incoherently for mercy.

Jehungir dismissed the disappointed torturer with a gesture, and said to Ghaznavi: "If your plan succeeds, I will fill your lap with gold."

III

In the darkness before dawn an unaccustomed sound disturbed the solitude that slumbered over the reedy marshes and the misty waters of the coast. It was not a drowsy water-fowl nor a waking beast. It was a human who struggled through the thick reeds, which were taller than a man's head.

It was a woman, had there been anyone to see, tall, and yellow-haired, her splendid limbs molded by her draggled tunic. Octavia had escaped in good earnest, every outraged fiber of her still tingling from her experience in a captivity that had become unendurable.

Jehungir's mastery of her had been bad enough; but with deliberate fiendishness Jehungir had given her to a nobleman whose name was a byword for degeneracy even in Khawarizm.

Octavia's resilient flesh crawled and quivered at her memories. Desperation had nerved her climb from Jelal Khan's castle on a rope made of strips from torn tapestries, and chance had led her to a picketed horse. She had ridden all night, and dawn found her with a foundered steed on the swampy shores of the sea. Quivering with the abhorrence of being dragged back to the revolting destiny planned for her by Jelal Khan, she plunged into the morass, seeking a hiding-place from the pursuit she expected. When the reeds grew thinner around her and the water rose about her thighs, she saw the dim loom of an island ahead of her. A broad span of water lay between, but she did not hesitate. She waded out until the low waves were lapping about her waist; then she struck out strongly, swimming with a vigor that promised unusual endurance.

As she neared the island, she saw that it rose sheer from the water in castle-like cliffs. She reached them at last, but found neither ledge to stand on below the water, nor to cling to above. She swam on, following the curve of the cliffs, the strain of her long flight beginning to weight her limbs. Her hands fluttered along the sheer stone, and suddenly they found a depression. With a sobbing gasp of relief, she pulled herself out of the water and clung there, a dripping white goddess in the dim starlight.

She had come upon what seemed to be steps carved in the cliff. Up them she went, flattening herself against the stone as she caught the faint clack of muffled oars. She strained her eyes and thought she made out a vague bulk moving toward the reedy point she had just quitted. But it was too far away for her to be sure, in the darkness, and presently the faint sound ceased, and she continued her climb. If it were her pursuers, she knew of no better course than to hide on the island. She knew that most of the islands off that marshy coast were uninhabited. This might be a pirate's lair, but even pirates would be preferable to the beast she had escaped.

A vagrant thought crossed her mind as she climbed, in which she mentally compared her former master with the *kozak* chief with whom—by compulsion—she had shamefully flirted in the pavilions of the camp by Fort Ghori, where the Hyrkanian lords had parleyed with the warriors of the steppes. His burning gaze had frightened and humiliated her, but his cleanly elemental fierceness set him above Jelal Khan, a monster such as only an overly opulent civilization can produce.

She scrambled up over the cliff edge and looked timidly at the dense shadows which confronted her. The trees grew close to the cliffs, presenting a solid mass of blackness. Something whirred above her head and she cowered, even though realizing it was only a bat.

She did not like the looks of those ebony shadows, but she set her teeth and went toward them, trying not to think of snakes. Her bare feet made no sound in the spongy loam under the trees. Once among them, the darkness closed frighteningly about her. She had not taken a dozen steps when she was no longer able to look back and see the cliffs and the sea beyond. A few steps more and she became hopelessly confused and lost her sense of direction. Through the tangled branches not even a star peered. She groped and floundered on, blindly, and then came to a sudden halt.

Somewhere ahead there began the rhythmical booming of a drum. It was not such a sound as she would have expected to hear in that time and place. Then she forgot it as she was aware of a presence near her. She could not see, but she knew that something was standing beside her in the darkness.

With a stifled cry she shrank back, and as she did so, something that even in her panic she recognized as a human arm curved about her waist. She screamed and threw all her supple young strength into a wild lunge for freedom, but her captor caught her up like a child, crushing her frantic resistance with ease. The silence with which her frenzied pleas and protests were received added to her terror as she felt herself being carried through the darkness toward the distant drum which still pulsed and muttered.

IV

As the first tinge of dawn reddened the sea, a small boat with a solitary occupant approached the cliffs. The man in the boat was a picturesque figure. A crimson scarf was knotted about his head; his wide silk breeches, of flaming hue, were upheld by a broad sash which likewise supported a simitar in a shagreen scabbard. His gilt-worked leather boots suggested the horseman rather than the seaman, but he handled his boat

with skill. Through his widely open white silk shirt showed his broad muscular breast, burned brown by the sun.

The muscles of his heavy bronzed arms rippled as he pulled the oars with an almost feline ease of motion. A fierce vitality that was evident in each feature and motion set him apart from common men; yet his expression was neither savage nor somber, though the smoldering blue eyes hinted at ferocity easily wakened. This was Conan, who had wandered into the armed camps of the *kozaks* with no other possessions than his wits and his sword, and who had carved his way to leadership among them.

He paddled to the carven stair as one familiar with his environs, and moored the boat to a projection of the rock. Then he went up the worn steps without hesitation. He was keenly alert, not because he consciously suspected hidden danger, but because alertness was a part of him, whetted by the wild existence he followed.

What Ghaznavi had considered animal intuition or some sixth sense was merely the razor-edged faculties and savage wit of the barbarian. Conan had no instinct to tell him that men were watching him from a covert among the reeds of the mainland.

As he climbed the cliff, one of these men breathed deeply and stealthily lifted a bow. Jehungir caught his wrist and hissed an oath into his ear. "Fool! Will you betray us? Don't you realize he is out of range? Let him get upon the island. He will go looking for the girl. We will stay here awhile. He *may* have sensed our presence or guessed our plot. He may have warriors hidden somewhere. We will wait. In an hour, if nothing suspicious occurs, we'll row up to the foot of the stair and await him there. If he does not return in a reasonable time, some of us will go upon the island and hunt him down. But I do not wish to do that if it can be helped. Some of us are sure to die if we have to go into the bush after him. I had rather catch him descending the stair, where we can feather him with arrows from a safe distance."

Meanwhile the unsuspecting *kozak* had

plunged into the forest. He went silently in his soft leather boots, his gaze sifting every shadow in eagerness to catch sight of the splendid tawny-haired beauty of whom he had dreamed ever since he had seen her in the pavilion of Jehungir Agha by Fort Ghori. He would have desired her even if she had displayed repugnance toward him. But her cryptic smiles and glances had fired his blood, and with all the lawless violence which was his heritage he desired that white-skinned golden-haired woman of civilization.

He had been on Xapur before. Less than a month ago he had held a secret conclave here with a pirate crew. He knew that he was approaching a point where he could see the mysterious ruins which gave the island its name, and he wondered if he would find the girl hiding among them. Even with the thought he stopped as though struck dead.

Ahead of him, among the trees, rose something that his reason told him was not possible. *It was a great dark green wall, with towers rearing beyond the battlements.*

Conan stood paralyzed in the disruption of the faculties which demoralizes anyone who is confronted by an impossible negation of sanity. He doubted neither his sight nor his reason, but something was monstrously out of joint. Less than a month ago only broken ruins had showed among the trees. What human hands could rear such a mammoth pile as now met his eyes, in the few weeks which had elapsed? Besides, the buccaneers who roamed Vilayet ceaselessly would have learned of any work going on on such stupendous scale, and would have informed the *kozaks.*

There was no explaining this thing, but it was so. He was on Xapur and that fantastic heap of towering masonry was on Xapur, and all was madness and paradox; yet it was all true.

He wheeled to race back through the jungle, down the carven stair and across the blue waters to the distant camp at the mouth of the Zaporoska. In that moment of unreasoning panic even the thought of halting so near the inland sea was repugnant. He would leave it behind him, would quit the armed camps and the steppes, and put a thousand miles between him and the blue mysterious East where the most basic laws of nature could be set at naught, by what diabolism he could not guess.

For an instant the future fate of kingdoms that hinged on this gay-clad barbarian hung in the balance. It was a small thing that tipped the scales—merely a shred of silk hanging on a bush that caught his uneasy glance. He leaned to it, his nostrils expanding, his nerves quivering to a subtle stimulant. On that bit of torn cloth, so faint that it was less with his physical faculties than by some obscure instinctive sense that he recognized it, lingered the tantalizing perfume that he connected with the sweet firm flesh of the woman he had seen in Jehungir's pavilion. The fisherman had not lied, then; she *was* here! Then in the soil he saw a single track of a bare foot, long and slender, but a man's not a woman's, and sunk deeper than was natural. The conclusion was obvious; the man who made that track was carrying a burden, and what should it be but the girl the *kozak* was seeking?

He stood silently facing the dark towers that loomed through the trees, his eyes slits of blue bale-fire. Desire for the yellow-haired woman vied with a sullen primordial rage at whoever had taken her. His human passion fought down his ultra-human fears, and dropping into the stalking crouch of a hunting panther, he glided toward the walls, taking advantage of the dense foliage to escape detection from the battlements.

As he approached he saw that the walls were composed of the same green stone that had formed the ruins, and he was haunted by a vague sense of familiarity. It was as if he looked upon something he had never before seen, but had dreamed of, or pictured mentally. At last he recognized the sensation. The walls and towers followed the plan of the ruins. It was as if the crumbling lines had grown back into the structures they originally were.

No sound disturbed the morning quiet as Conan stole to the foot of the wall which rose sheer from the luxuriant growth. On the southern reaches of the inland sea the vegetation was almost tropical. He saw no one on the battlements, heard no sounds within. He saw a massive gate a short distance to his left, and had no reason to suppose that it was not locked and guarded. But he believed that the woman he sought was somewhere beyond that wall, and the course he took was characteristically reckless.

Above him vine-festooned branches reached out toward the battlements. He went up a great tree like a cat, and reaching a point above the parapet, he gripped a thick limb with both hands, swung back and forth at arm's length until he had gained momentum, and then let go and catapulted through the air, landing catlike on the battlements. Crouching there he stared down into the streets of a city.

The circumference of the wall was not great, but the number of green stone buildings it contained was surprising. They were three or four stories in height, mainly flat-roofed, reflecting a fine architectural style. The streets converged like the spokes of a wheel into an octagon-shaped court in the center of the town which gave upon a lofty edifice, which, with its domes and towers, dominated the whole city. He saw no one moving in the streets or looking out of the windows, though the sun was already coming up. The silence that reigned there might have been that of a dead and deserted city. A narrow stone stair ascended the wall near him; down this he went.

Houses shouldered so closely to the wall that half-way down the stair he found himself within arm's length of a window, and halted to peer in. There were no bars, and the silk curtains were caught back with satin cords. He looked into a chamber whose walls were hidden by dark velvet tapestries. The floor was covered with thick rugs, and there were benches of polished ebony, and an ivory dais heaped with furs.

He was about to continue his descent, when he heard the sound of someone approaching in the street below. Before the unknown person could round a corner and see him on the stair, he stepped quickly across the intervening space and dropped lightly into the room, drawing his simi-

tar. He stood for an instant statue-like; then as nothing happened he was moving across the rugs toward an arched doorway when a hanging was drawn aside, revealing a cushioned alcove from which a slender, dark-haired girl regarded him with languid eyes.

Conan glared at her tensely, expecting her momentarily to start screaming. But she merely smothered a yawn with a dainty hand, rose from the alcove, and leaned negligently against the hanging which she held with one hand.

She was undoubtedly a member of a white race, though her skin was very dark. Her square-cut hair was black as midnight, her only garment a wisp of silk about her supple hips.

Presently she spoke, but the tongue was unfamiliar to him, and he shook his head. She yawned again, stretched lithely, and without any show of fear or surprize, shifted to a language he did understand, a dialect of Yuetshi which sounded strangely archaic.

"Are you looking for someone?" she asked, as indifferently as if the invasion of her chamber by an armed stranger were the most common thing imaginable.

"Who are you?" he demanded.

"I am Yateli," she answered languidly. "I must have feasted late last night, I am so sleepy now. Who are you?"

"I am Conan, a *hetman* among the *kozaks*," he answered, watching her narrowly. He believed her attitude to be a pose, and expected her to try to escape from the chamber or rouse the house. But, though a velvet rope that might be a signal cord hung near her, she did not reach for it.

"Conan," she repeated drowsily. "You are not a Dagonian. I suppose you are a mercenary. Have you cut the heads off many Yuetshi?"

"I do not war on water rats!" he snorted.

"But they are very terrible," she murmured. "I remember when they were our slaves. But they revolted and burned and slew. Only the magic of Khosatral Khel has kept them from the walls—" She paused, a puzzled look struggling with the sleepiness of her expression. "I forgot," she muttered. "They *did* climb the walls, last night. There was shouting and fire, and people calling in vain on Khosatral." She shook her head as if to clear it. "But that can not be," she murmured, "because I am alive, and I thought I was dead. Oh, to the devil with it!"

She came across the chamber, and taking Conan's hand, drew him to the dais. He yielded in bewilderment and uncertainty. The girl smiled at him like a sleepy child; her long silky lashes drooped over dusky, clouded eyes. She ran her fingers through his thick black locks as if to assure herself of his reality.

"It was a dream," she yawned. "Perhaps it's all a dream. I feel like a dream now. I don't care. I can't remember something—I have forgotten—there is something I can not understand, but I grow so sleepy when I try to think. Anyway, it doesn't matter."

"What do you mean?" he asked uneasily. "You said they climbed the walls last night? Who?"

"The Yuetshi. I thought so, anyway. A cloud of smoke hid everything, but a naked, blood-stained devil caught me by the throat and drove his knife into my breast. Oh, it hurt! But it was a dream, because see, there is no scar." She idly inspected her smooth bosom, and then sank upon Conan's lap and passed her supple arms around his massive neck. "I can not remember," she murmured, nestling her dark head against his mighty breast. "Everything is dim and misty. It does not matter. You are no dream. You are strong. Let us live while we can. Love me!"

He cradled the girl's glossy head in the bend of his heavy arm and kissed her full red lips with unfeigned relish.

"You are strong," she repeated, her voice waning. "Love me—love—" The sleepy murmur faded away; the dusky eyes closed, the long lashes drooping over the sensuous cheeks; the supple body relaxed in Conan's arms.

He scowled down at her. She seemed to partake of the illusion that haunted this whole city, but the firm resilience of her limbs under his questing fingers convinced him that he had a living human girl in his arms, and not the shadow of a dream. No less disturbed, he hastily laid her on the furs upon the dais. Her sleep was too deep to be natural. He decided that she must be an addict of some drug, perhaps like the black lotus of Xuthal.

Then he found something else to make him wonder. Among the furs on the dais was a gorgeous spotted skin, whose predominant hue was golden. It was not a clever copy, but the skin of an actual beast. And that beast, Conan knew, had been extinct for at least a thousand years; it was the great golden leopard which figures so prominently in Hyborian legendry, and which the ancient artists delighted to portray in pigments and marble.

Shaking his head in bewilderment, Conan passed through the archway into a winding corridor. Silence hung over the house, but outside he heard a sound which his keen ears recognized as something ascending the stair on the wall from which he had entered the building. An instant later he was startled to hear something land with a soft but weighty thud on the floor of the chamber he had just quitted. Turning quickly away, he hurried along the twisting hallway until something on the floor before him brought him to a halt.

It was a human figure, which lay half in the hall and half in an opening that obviously was normally concealed by a door which was a duplicate of the panels of the wall. It was a man, dark and lean, clad only in a silk loin-cloth, with a shaven head and cruel features, and he lay as if death had struck him just as he was emerging from the panel. Conan bent above him, seeking the cause of his death, and discovered him to be merely sunk in the same deep sleep as the girl in the chamber.

But why should he select such a place for his slumbers? While meditating on the matter, Conan was galvanized by a sound behind him. Something was moving up the corridor in his direction. A quick glance down it showed that it ended in a great door which might be locked. Conan jerked the supine body out of the panel-entrance and stepped through, pulling the panel shut after him. A click told him it was locked in place. Standing in utter darkness, he heard a shuffling tread halt just outside the door, and a faint chill trickled along his spine. That was no human step, nor that of any beast he had ever encountered.

There was an instant of silence, then a faint creak of wood and metal. Putting out his hand he felt the door straining and bending inward, as if a great weight were being steadily borne against it from the outside. As he reached for his sword, this ceased and he heard a strange slobbering mouthing that prickled the short hairs on his scalp. Simitar in hand he began backing away, and his heels felt steps, down which he nearly tumbled. He was in a narrow staircase leading downward.

He groped his way down in the blackness, feeling for, but not finding, some other opening in the walls. Just as he decided that he was no longer in the house, but deep in the earth under it, the steps ceased in a level tunnel.

V

Along the black silent tunnel Conan groped, momentarily dreading a fall into some unseen pit; but at last his feet struck steps again, and he went up them until he came to a door on which his fumbling fingers found a metal catch. He came out into a dim and lofty room of enormous proportions. Fantastic columns marched about the mottled walls, upholding a ceiling, which, at once translucent and dusky, seemed like a cloudy midnight sky, giving an illusion of impossible height. If any light filtered in from the outside it was curiously altered.

In a brooding twilight Conan moved across the bare green floor. The great room was circular, pierced on one side by the great bronze valves of a giant door. Opposite this, on a dais against the wall, up to which led broad curving steps, there stood a throne of copper, and when Conan saw what was coiled on this throne, he retreated hastily, lifting his simitar.

Then, as the thing did not move, he scanned it more closely, and presently mounted the glass steps and stared down at it. It was a gigantic snake, apparently carved of some jade-like substance. Each scale stood out as distinctly as in real life, and the iridescent colors were vividly reproduced. The great wedge-shaped head was half submerged in the folds of its trunk; so neither the eyes nor jaws were visible. Recognition stirred in his mind. The snake was evidently meant to represent one of those grim monsters of the marsh which in past ages had haunted the reedy edges of Vilayet's southern shores. But, like the golden leopard, they had been extinct for hundreds of years. Conan had seen rude images of them, in miniature, among the idol-huts of the Yuetshi, and there was a description of them in the *Book of Skelos*, which drew on prehistoric sources.

Conan admired the scaly torso, thick as his thigh and obviously of great length, and he reached out and laid a curious hand on the thing. And as he did so, his heart nearly stopped. An icy chill congealed the blood in his veins and lifted the short hair on his scalp. Under his hand there was not the smooth, brittle surface of glass or metal or stone, but the yielding, fibrous mass of a *living* thing. He felt cold, sluggish life flowing under his fingers.

His hand jerked back in instinctive repulsion. Sword shaking in his grasp, horror and revulsion and fear almost choking him, he backed away and down the glass steps with painful care, glaring in awful fascination at the grisly thing that slumbered on the copper throne. It did not move.

He reached the bronze door and tried it, with his heart in his teeth, sweating with fear that he should find himself locked in with that slimy horror. But the valves yielded to his touch, and he glided through and closed them behind him.

He found himself in a wide hallway with lofty tapestried walls, where the light was the same twilight gloom. It made distant objects indistinct and that made him uneasy, rousing thoughts of serpents gliding unseen through the dimness. A door at the other end seemed miles away in the illusive light. Nearer at hand the tapestry hung in such a way as to suggest an opening behind it, and lifting it cautiously he discovered a narrow stair leading up.

While he hesitated he heard in the great room he had just left, the same shuffling tread he had heard outside the locked panel. Had he been followed through the tunnel? He went up the stair hastily, dropping the tapestry in place behind him.

Emerging presently into a twisting corridor, he took the first doorway he came to. He had a twofold purpose in his apparently aimless prowling: to escape from the building and its mysteries, and to find the Nemedian girl who, he felt, was imprisoned somewhere in this palace, temple, or whatever it was. He believed it was the great domed edifice in the center of the city, and it was likely that here dwelt the ruler of the town, to whom a captive woman would doubtless be brought.

He found himself in a chamber, not another corridor, and was about to retrace his steps, when he heard a voice which came from behind one of the walls. There was no door in that wall, but he leaned close and heard distinctly. And an icy chill crawled slowly along his spine. The tongue was Nemedian, but the voice was not human. There was a terrifying resonance about it, like a bell tolling at midnight.

"There was no life in the Abyss, save that which was incorporated in me," it tolled. "Nor was there light, nor motion, nor any sound. Only the urge behind and beyond life guided and impelled me on my upward journey, blind, insensate, inexorable. Through ages upon ages, and the changeless strata of darkness I climbed—"

Ensorcelled by that belling resonance, Conan crouched forgetful of all else, until its hypnotic power caused a strange replacement of faculties and perception, and sound created the illusion of sight. Conan was no longer aware of the voice, save as far-off rhythmical waves of sound. Transported beyond his age and his own individuality, he was seeing the transmutation of the

being men called Khosatral Khel which crawled up from Night and the Abyss ages ago to clothe itself in the substance of the material universe.

But human flesh was too frail, too paltry to hold the terrific essence that was Khosatral Khel. So he stood up in the shape and aspect of a man, but his flesh was not flesh; nor the bone, bone; nor blood, blood. He became a blasphemy against all nature, for he caused to live and think and act a basic substance that before had never known the pulse and stir of animate being.

He stalked through the world like a god, for no earthly weapon could harm him, and to him a century was like an hour. In his wanderings he came upon a primitive people inhabiting the island of Dagonia, and it pleased him to give this race culture and civilization, and by his aid they built the city of Dagon and they abode there and worshipped him. Strange and grisly were his servants, called from the dark corners of the planet where grim survivals of forgotten ages yet lurked. His house in Dagon was connected with every other house by tunnels through which his shaven-headed priests bore victims for the sacrifice.

But after many ages a fierce and brutish people appeared on the shores of the sea. They called themselves Yuetshi, and after a fierce battle were defeated and enslaved, and for nearly a generation they died on the altars of Khosatral.

His sorcery kept them in bonds. Then their priest, a strange gaunt man of unknown race, plunged into the wilderness, and when he returned he bore a knife that was of no earthly substance. It was forged of a meteor which flashed through the sky like a flaming arrow and fell in a far valley. The slaves rose. Their saw-edged crescents cut down the men of Dagon like sheep, and against that unearthly knife the magic of Khosatral was impotent. While carnage and slaughter bellowed through the red smoke that choked the streets, the grimmest act of that grim drama was played in the cryptic dome behind the great daised chamber with its copper throne and its walls mottled like the skin of serpents.

From that dome the Yuetshi priest emerged alone. He had not slain his foe, because he wished to hold the threat of his losing over the heads of his own rebellious subjects. He had left Khosatral lying upon the golden dais with the mystic knife across his breast for a spell to hold him senseless and inanimate until doomsday.

But the ages passed and the priest died, the towers of deserted Dagon crumbled, the tales became dim, and the Yuetshi were reduced by plagues and famines and war to scattered remnants, dwelling in squalor along the seashore.

Only the cryptic dome resisted the rot of time, until a chance thunderbolt and the curiosity of a fisherman lifted from the breast of the god the magic knife and broke the spell. Khosatral Khel rose and lived and waxed mighty once more. It pleased him to restore the city as it was in the days before its fall. By his necromancy he lifted the towers from the dust of forgotten millenniums, and the folk which had been dust for ages moved in life again.

But folk who have tasted of death are only partly alive. In the dark corners of their souls and minds death still lurks unconquered. By night the people of Dagon moved and loved, hated and feasted, and remembered the fall of Dagon and their own slaughter only as a dim dream; they moved in an enchanted mist of illusion, feeling the strangeness of their existence but not inquiring the reasons therefor. With the coming of day they sank into deep sleep, to be roused again only by the coming of night, which is akin to death.

All this rolled in a terrible panorama before Conan's consciousness as he crouched beside the tapestried wall. His reason staggered. All certainty and sanity were swept away, leaving a shadowy universe through which stole hooded figures of grisly potentialities. Through the belling of the voice which was like a tolling of triumph over the ordered laws of a sane planet, a human sound anchored Conan's mind from its flight through spheres of madness. It was the hysterical sobbing of a woman.

Involuntarily he sprang up.

VI

Jehungir Agha waited with growing impatience in his boat among the reeds. More than an hour passed, and Conan had not reappeared. Doubtless he was still searching the island for the girl he thought to be hidden there. But another surmise occurred to the Agha. Suppose the *hetman* had left his warriors near by, and that they should grow suspicious and come to investigate his long absence? Jehungir spoke to the oarsmen, and the long boat slid from among the reeds and glided toward the carven stairs.

Leaving half a dozen men in the boat, he took the rest, ten mighty archers of Khawarizm, in spired helmets and tiger-skin cloaks. Like hunters invading the retreat of the lion, they stole forward under the trees, arrows on string. Silence reigned over the forest except when a great green thing that might have been a parrot swirled over their heads with a low thunder of broad wings and then sped off through the trees. With a sudden gesture Jehungir halted his party, and they stared incredulously at the towers that showed through the verdure in the distance.

"Tarim!" muttered Jehungir. "The pirates have rebuilt the ruins! Doubtless Conan is there. We must investigate this. A fortified town this close to the mainland!—Come!"

With renewed caution they glided through the trees. The game had altered; from pursuers and hunters they had become spies.

And as they crept through the tangled gowth, the man they sought was in peril more deadly than their filigreed arrows.

Conan realized with a crawling of his skin that beyond the wall the belling voice had ceased. He stood motionless as a statue, his gaze fixed on a curtained door through which he knew that a culminating horror would presently appear.

It was dim and misty in the chamber, and Conan's hair began to lift on his scalp as he looked. He saw a head and a pair of gigantic shoulders grow out of the twilight gloom. There was no sound of footsteps, but the great dusky form grew more distinct until Conan recognized the figure of a man. He was clad in sandals, a skirt, and a broad shagreen girdle. His square-cut mane was confined by a circlet of gold. Conan stared at the sweep of the monstrous shoulders, the breadth of swelling breast, the bands and ridges and clusters of muscles on torso and limbs. The face was without weakness and without mercy. The eyes were balls of dark fire. And Conan knew that this was Khosatral Khel, the ancient from the Abyss, the god of Dagonia.

No word was spoken. No word was necessary. Khosatral spread his great arms, and Conan, crouching beneath them, slashed at the giant's belly. Then he bounded back, eyes blazing with surprise. The keen edge had rung on the mighty body as on an anvil, rebounding without cutting. Then Khosatral came upon him in an irresitible surge.

There was a fleeting concussion, a fierce writhing and intertwining of limbs and bodies, and then Conan sprang clear, every thew quivering from the violence of his efforts; blood started where the grazing fingers had torn the skin. In that instant of contact he had experienced the ultimate madness of blasphemed nature; no human flesh had bruised his, but *metal* animated and sentient; it was a body of living iron which opposed his.

Khosatral loomed above the warrior in the gloom. Once let those great fingers lock and they would not loosen until the human body hung limp in their grasp. In that twilit chamber it was as if a man fought with a dream-monster in a nightmare.

Flinging down his useless sword, Conan caught up a heavy bench and hurled it with all his power. It was such a missile as few men could even lift. On Khosatral's mighty breast it smashed into shreds and splinters. It did not even shake the giant on his braced legs. His face lost something of its human aspect, a nimbus of fire played about his awesome head, and like a moving tower he came on.

With a desperate wrench Conan ripped a whole section of tapestry from the wall and whirling it, with a muscular effort greater than that required for throwing the bench, he flung it over the giant's head. For an instant Khosatral floundered, smothered and blinded by the clinging stuff that resisted his strength as wood or steel could not have done, and in that instant Conan caught up his simitar and shot out into the corridor. Without checking his speed he hurled himself through the door of the adjoining chamber, slammed the door, and shot the bolt.

Then as he wheeled he stopped short, all the blood in him seeming to surge to his head. Crouching on a heap of silk cushions, golden hair streaming over her naked shoulders, eyes blank with terror, was the woman for whom he had dared so much. He almost forgot the horror at his heels until a splintering crash behind him brought him to his senses. He caught up the girl and sprang for the opposite door. She was too helpless with fright either to resist or to aid him. A faint whimper was the only sound of which she seemed capable.

Conan wasted no time trying the door. A shattering stroke of his simitar hewed the lock asunder, and as he sprang through to the stair that loomed beyond it, he saw the head and shoulders of Khosatral crash through the other door. The colossus was splintering the massive panels as if they were of cardboard.

Conan raced up the stair, carrying the big girl over one shoulder as easily as if she had been a child. Where he was going he had no idea, but the stair ended at the door of a round, domed chamber. Khosatral was coming up the stair behind them, silently as a wind of death, and as swiftly.

The chamber's walls were of solid steel, and so was the door. Conan shut it and dropped in place the great bars with which it was furnished. The thought struck him that this was Khosatral's chamber, where he locked himself in to sleep securely from the monsters he had loosed from the Pits to do his bidding.

Hardly were the bolts in place when the great door shook and trembled to the giant's assault.

Conan shrugged his shoulders. This was the end of the trail. There was no other door in the chamber, nor any window. Air, and the strange misty light, evidently came from interstices in the dome. He tested the nicked edge of his simitar, quite cool now that he was at bay. He had done his volcanic best to escape; when the giant came crashing through that door he would explode in another savage onslaught with his useless sword, not because he expected it to do any good, but because it was his nature to die fighting. For the moment there was no course of action to take, and his calmness was not forced or feigned.

The gaze he turned on his fair companion was as admiring and intense as if he had a hundred years to live. He had dumped her unceremoniously on the floor when he turned to close the door, and she had risen to her knees, mechanically arranging her streaming locks and her scanty garment. Conan's fierce eyes glowed with approval as they devoured her thick golden hair, her clear wide eyes, her milky skin, sleek with exuberant health, the firm swell of her breasts, the contours of her splendid hips.

A low cry escaped her as the door shook and a bolt gave way with a groan.

Conan did not look around. He knew the door would hold a little while longer.

"They told me you had escaped," he said. "A Yuetshi fisher told me you were hiding here. What is your name?"

"Octavia," she gasped mechanically. Then words came in a rush. She caught at him with desperate fingers. "Oh Mitra! What nightmare is this? The people—the dark-skinned people—one of them caught me in the forest and brought me here. They carried me to—to that—that *thing*. He told me—he said—am I mad? Is this a dream?"

He glanced at the door which bulged inward as if from the impact of a battering-ram.

"No," he said; "it's no dream. That hinge is giving way. Strange that a devil has to break down a door like a common man; but after all, his strength itself is a diabolism."

"Can you not kill him?" she panted. "You are strong."

Conan was too honest to lie to her. "If a mortal man could kill him, he'd be dead now," he answered. "I nicked my blade on his belly."

Her eyes dulled. "Then you must die, and I must—oh Mitra!" she screamed in sudden frenzy, and Conan caught her hands, fearing that she would harm herself. "He told me what he was going to do to me!" she panted. "Kill me! Kill me with your sword before he bursts the door!"

Conan looked at her, and shook his head.

"I'll do what I can," he said. "That won't be much, but it'll give you a chance to get past him down the stair. Then run for the cliffs. I have a boat tied at the foot of the steps. If you can get out of the palace you may escape him yet. The people of this city are all asleep."

She dropped her head in her hands. Conan took up his simitar and moved over to stand before the echoing door. One watching him would not have realized that he was waiting for a death he regarded as inevitable. His eyes smoldered more vividly; his muscular hand knotted harder on his hilt; that was all.

The hinges had given under the giant's terrible assault and the door rocked crazily, held only by the bolts. And these solid steel bars were buckling, bending, bulging out of their sockets. Conan watched in an almost impersonal fascination, envying the monster his inhuman strength.

Then without warning the bombardment ceased. In the stillness Conan heard other noises on the landing outside—the beat of wings, and a muttering voice that was like the whining of wind through midnight branches. Then presently there was silence, but there was a new *feel* in the air. Only the whetted instincts of barbarism could have sensed it, but Conan knew, without seeing or hearing him leave, that the master of Dagon no longer stood outside the door.

He glared through a crack that had been started in the steel of the portal. The landing was empty. He drew the warped bolts and cautiously pulled aside the sagging door. Khosatral was not on the stair, but far below he heard the clang of a metal door. He did not know whether the giant was plotting new deviltries or had been summoned away by that muttering voice, but he wasted no time in conjectures.

He called to Octavia, and the new note in his voice brought her up to her feet and to his side almost without her conscious volition.

"What is it?" she gasped.

"Don't stop to talk!" He caught her wrist. "Come on!" The chance for action had transformed him; his eyes blazed, his voice crackled. "The knife!" he muttered, while almost dragging the girl down the stair in his fierce haste. "The magic Yuetshi blade! He left it in the dome! I—" his voice died suddenly as a clear mental picture sprang up before him. The dome adjoined the great room where stood the copper throne—sweat started out on his body. The only way to that dome was through that room with the copper throne and the foul thing that slumbered in it.

But he did not hesitate. Swiftly they descended the stair, crossed the chamber, descended the next stair, and came into the great dim hall with its mysterious hangings. They had seen no sign of the colossus. Halting before the great bronze-valved door, Conan caught Octavia by her shoulders and shook her in his intensity.

"Listen!" he snapped. "I'm going into the room and fastening the door. Stand here and listen; if Khosatral comes, call to me. If you hear me cry out for you to go, run as though the devil were on your heels—which he probably will be. Make for that door at the other end of the hall, because I'll be past helping you. I'm going for the Yuetshi knife!"

Before she could voice the protest her lips were framing, he had slid through the valves and shut them behind him. He lowered the bolt cautiously, not noticing that it could be worked from the outside. In the dim twilight his gaze sought that grim copper throne; yes, the scaly brute was still there, filling the throne with its loathsome coils. He saw a door behind the throne

and knew that it led into the dome. But to reach it he must mount the dais, a few feet from the throne itself.

A wind blowing across the green floor would have made more noise than Conan's slinking feet. Eyes glued on the sleeping reptile he reached the dais and mounted the glass steps. The snake had not moved. He was reaching for the door. . . .

The bolt on the bronze portal clanged and Conan stifled an awful oath as he saw Octavia come into the room. She stared about, uncertain in the deeper gloom, and he stood frozen, not daring to shout a warning. Then she saw his shadowy figure and ran toward the dais, crying: "I want to go with you! I'm afraid to stay alone— *oh!*" She threw up her hands with a terrible scream as for the first time she saw the occupant of the throne. The wedge-shaped head had lifted from its coils and thrust out toward her on a yard of shining neck.

Then with a smooth flowing motion it began to ooze from the throne, coil by coil, its ugly head bobbing in the direction of the paralyzed girl.

Conan cleared the space between him and the throne with a desperate bound, his simitar swinging with all his power. And with such blinding speed did the serpent move that it whipped about and met him in full midair, lapping his limbs and body with half a dozen coils. His half-checked stroke fell futilely as he crashed down on the dais, gashing the scaly trunk but not severing it.

Then he was writhing on the glass steps with fold after slimy fold knotting about him, twisting, crushing, killing him. His right arm was still free, but he could get no purchase to strike a killing blow, and he knew one blow must suffice. With a groaning convulsion of muscular expansion that bulged his veins almost to bursting on his temples and tied his muscles in quivering, tortured knots, he heaved up on his feet, lifting almost the full weight of that forty-foot devil.

An instant he reeled on wide-braced legs, feeling his ribs caving in on his vitals and his sight growing dark, while his simitar gleamed above his head. Then it fell, shearing through the scales and flesh and vertebrae. And where there had been one huge writhing cable, now there were horribly two, lashing and flopping in the death throes. Conan staggered away from their blind strokes. He was sick and dizzy, and blood oozed from his nose. Groping in a dark mist he clutched Octavia and shook her until she gasped for breath.

"Next time I tell you to stay somewhere," he gasped, "you stay!"

He was too dizzy even to know whether she replied. Taking her wrist like a truant schoolgirl, he led her around the hideous stumps that still looped and knotted on the floor. Somewhere, in the distance, he thought he heard men yelling, but his ears were still roaring so that he could not be sure.

The door gave to his efforts. If Khosatral had placed the snake there to guard the thing he feared, evidently he considered it ample precaution. Conan half expected some other monstrosity to leap at him with the opening of the door, but in the dimmer light he saw only the vague sweep of the arch above, a dully gleaming block of gold, and a half-moon glimmer on the stone.

With a gasp of gratification he scooped it up, and did not linger for further exploration. He turned and fled across the room and down the great hall toward the distant door that he felt led to the outer air. He was correct. A few minutes later he emerged into the silent streets, half carrying, half guiding his companion. There was no one to be seen, but beyond the western wall there sounded cries and moaning wails that made Octavia tremble. He led her to the southwestern wall, and without difficulty found a stone stair that mounted the rampart. He had appropriated a thick tapestry rope in the great hall, and now, having reached the parapet, he looped the soft strong cord about the girl's hips and lowered her to the earth. Then, making one end fast to a merlon, he slid down after her. There was but one way of escape from the island—the stair on the western cliffs. In that direction he hurried, swinging wide around the spot from which had come the cries and the sound of terrible blows.

Octavia sensed that grim peril lurked in those leafy fastnesses. Her breath came pantingly and she pressed close to her protector. But the forest was silent now, and they saw no shape of menace until they emerged from the trees and glimpsed a figure standing on the edge of the cliffs.

Jehungir Agha had escaped the doom that had overtaken his warriors when an iron giant sallied suddenly from the gate and battered and crushed them into bits of shredded flesh and splintered bone. When he saw the swords of his archers break on that man-like juggernaut, he had known it was no human foe they faced, and he had fled, hiding in the deep woods until the sounds of slaughter ceased. Then he crept back to the stair, but his boatmen were not waiting for him.

They had heard the screams, and presently, waiting nervously, had seen, on the cliff above them, a blood-smeared monster waving gigantic arms in awful triumph. They had waited for no more. When Jehungir came upon the cliffs they were just vanishing among the reeds beyond earshot. Khosatral was gone—had either returned to the city or was prowling the forest in search of the man who had escaped him outside the walls.

Jehungir was just preparing to descend the stairs and depart in Conan's boat, when he saw the *hetman* and the girl emerge from the trees. The experience which had congealed his blood and almost blasted his reason had not altered Jehungir's intentions toward the *kozak* chief. The sight of the man he had come to kill filled him with gratification. He was astonished to see the girl he had given to Jelal Khan, but he wasted no time on her. Lifting his bow he drew the shaft to its head and loosed. Conan crouched and the arrow splintered on a tree, and Conan laughed.

"Dog!" he taunted. "You can't hit me! I was not born to die on Hyrkanian steel! Try again, pig of Turan!"

Jehungir did not try again. That was his last arrow. He drew his simitar and advanced, confident in his spired helmet and close-meshed mail. Conan met him half-way in a blinding whirl of swords. The curved blades ground together, sprang apart, circled in glittering arcs that blurred the sight which tried to follow them. Octavia, watching, did not see the stroke, but she heard its chopping impact, and saw Jehungir fall, blood spurting from his side where the Cimmerian's steel had sundered his mail and bitten to his spine.

But Octavia's scream was not caused by the death of her former master. With a crash of bending boughs Khosatral Khel was upon them. The girl could not flee; a moaning cry escaped her as her knees gave way and pitched her grovelling to the sward.

Conan, stooping above the body of the Agha, made no move to escape. Shifting his reddened simitar to his left hand, he drew the great half-blade of the Yuetshi. Khosatral Khel was towering above him, his arms lifted like mauls, but as the blade caught the sheen of the sun, the giant gave back suddenly.

But Conan's blood was up. He rushed in, slashing with the crescent blade. And it did not splinter. Under its edge the dusky metal of Khosatral's body gave way like common flesh beneath a cleaver. From the deep gash flowed a strange ichor, and Khosatral cried out like the dirging of a great bell. His terrible arms flailed down, but Conan, quicker than the archers who had died beneath those awful flails, avoided their strokes and struck again and yet again. Khosatral reeled and tottered; his cries were awful to hear, as if metal were given a tongue of pain, as if iron shrieked and bellowed under torment.

Then wheeling away he staggered into the forest; he reeled in his gait, crashed through bushes and caromed off trees. Yet though Conan followed him with the speed of hot passion, the walls and towers of Dagon loomed through the trees before the man came with dagger-reach of the giant.

Then Khosatral turned again, flailing the air with desperate blows, but Conan, fired to beserk fury, was not to be denied. As a panther strikes down a bull moose at bay, so he plunged under the bludgeoning arms and drove the crescent blade to the hilt under the spot where a human's heart would be.

Khosatral reeled and fell. In the shape of a man he reeled, but it was not the shape of a man that struck the loam. Where there had been the likeness of a human face, there was no face at all, and the metal limbs melted and changed. . . . Conan, who had not shrunk from Khosatral living, recoiled blenching from Khosatral dead, for he had witnessed an awful transmutation; in his dying throes Khosatral Khel had become again the *thing* that had crawled up from the Abyss millenniums gone. Gagging with intolerable repugnance, Conan turned to flee the sight; and he was suddenly aware that the pinnacles of Dagon no longer glimmered through the trees. They had faded like smoke—the battlements, the crenellated towers, the great bronze gates, the velvets, the gold, the ivory, and the dark-haired women, and the men with their shaven skulls. With the passing of the inhuman intellect which had given them rebirth, they had faded back into the dust which they had been for ages uncounted. Only the stumps of broken columns rose above crumbling walls and broken paves and shattered dome. Conan again looked upon the ruins of Xapur as he remembered them.

The wild *hetman* stood like a statue for a space, dimly grasping something of the cosmic tragedy of the fitful ephemera called mankind and the hooded shapes of darkness which prey upon it. Then as he heard his voice called in accents of fear, he started, as one awaking from a dream, glanced again at the thing on the ground, shuddered, and turned away toward the cliffs and the girl that waited there.

She was peering fearfully under the trees, and she greeted him with a half-stifled cry of relief. He had shaken off the dim monstrous visions which had momentarily haunted him, and was his exuberant self again.

"Where is he?" she shuddered.

"Gone back to hell whence he crawled," he

replied cheerfully. "Why didn't you climb the stair and make your escape in my boat?"

"I wouldn't desert—" she began, then changed her mind, and amended rather sulkily, "I have nowhere to go. The Hyrkanians would enslave me again, and the pirates would—"

"What of the *kozaks*?" he suggested.

"Are they better than the pirates?" she asked scornfully. Conan's admiration increased to see how well she had recovered her poise after having endured such frantic terror. Her arrogance amused him.

"You seemed to think so in the camp by Ghori," he answered. "You were free enough with your smiles then."

Her red lips curled in disdain. "Do you think I was enamored of you? Do you dream that I would have shamed myself before an ale-guzzling, meat-gorging barbarian unless I had to? My master—whose body lies there—forced me to do as I did."

"Oh!" Conan seemed rather crestfallen. Then he laughed with undiminished zest. "No matter. You belong to me now. Give me a kiss."

"You dare ask—" she began angrily, when she felt herself snatched off her feet and crushed to the *hetman*'s muscular breast. She fought him fiercely, with all the supple strength of her magnificent youth, but he only laughed exuberantly, drunk with the possession of this splendid creature writhing in his arms.

He crushed her struggles easily, drinking the nectar of her lips with all the unrestrained passion that was his, until the arms that strained against him melted and twined convulsively about his massive neck. Then he laughed down into the clear eyes, and said: "Why should not a chief of the Free People be preferable to a city-bred dog of Turan?"

She shook back her tawny locks, still tingling in every nerve from the fire of his kisses. She did not loosen her arms from his neck. "Do you deem yourself an Agha's equal?" she challenged.

He laughed and strode with her in his arms toward the stair. "You shall judge," he boasted. "I'll burn Khawarizm for a torch to light your way to my tent."

THE MIGHTY MANSLAYER

HAROLD LAMB

HAROLD ALBERT LAMB (1892–1962) graduated from Columbia University and immediately began writing for pulp magazines, most notably *Adventure* magazine, to which he contributed the majority of his fiction between 1917 and 1936. In addition to being fast-paced, clear, and told with a minimum of archaic language, his stories are exceptional for their time in being historically accurate. The characters are mostly imaginary, as are the stories, but they appear against a background of solid history. While Lamb is generally regarded as one of America's half-dozen greatest adventure writers, his nonfiction and historical biographies have been held in even higher esteem, often remaining in print for decades as the definitive works on their subjects. Among his most successful books are *Genghis Khan: The Emperor of All Men* (1927), *The Crusades* (1931), *Alexander of Macedon: The Journey to World's End* (1946), and *Charlemagne: The Legend and the Man* (1954).

A favorite screenwriter of Cecil B. DeMille's, Lamb collaborated on screenplays for such films as *The Crusades* (1935), starring Loretta Young and Henry Wilcoxon, and *The Plainsman* (1936), with Gary Cooper as Wild Bill Hickok, Jean Arthur as Calamity Jane, and James Ellison as Buffalo Bill Cody. He also contributed to such DeMille films as *The Buccaneer* (1938), a War of 1812 tale starring Fredric March as Jean Lafitte (Anthony Quinn, who had a minor role, directed a remake in 1958, with Yul Brynner, Claire Bloom, Inger Stevens, and Charlton Heston), and *Samson and Delilah* (1949), starring Hedy Lamarr, Victor Mature, George Sanders, and Angela Lansbury.

Lamb's adventure fiction is often set during the Crusades, or features Asian or Middle Eastern protagonists. His most famous works, however, are about sixteenth- and seventeenth-century Cossacks, frequently with his great hero Khlit, who is featured in eighteen adventures and appears in a nineteenth. A powerful swordsman deemed to have grown too old to remain in the Cossack army, Khlit goes out on his own to seek adventure and battle for worthy causes from Moscow to the Himalayas; in the later tales, he is mainly a sage old teacher and advisor to his grandson and other brave Cossacks. Khlit made his first appearance in the November 1, 1917, issue of *Adventure*. Eight adventures of Khlit were collected in *The Curved Saber* (1964) and five others in *The Mighty Manslayer*—a 1969 collection that, incidentally, does not include "The Mighty Manslayer."

"The Mighty Manslayer" was first published in the October 15, 1918, issue of *Adventure*.

THE MIGHTY MANSLAYER

HAROLD LAMB

The Wealth-Bearers are heavily burdened. Their burden is more precious than gold gleaming under enamel. The Wealth-Bearers are strong. Their burden is finer than the seven precious substances.

The faces of the Onon Muren are turned toward the mountains of Khantai Khan. The white faces of the Onon Muren are still. There is fear in the shadows of Khantai Khan. Yet the fear does not touch the Wealth-Bearers.

The five sons of Alan Goa have dried their blood in the earth. But the fear is still in the forests of Khantai Khan. Can another hand lift what One hand held? Nay, the fear is too great!

From the book of Chakar Noyon, the gylong *of the Uhoten Lamasery.*

CHAKAR NOYON WAS DEAD, long before the end of the sixteenth century, when Khlit, the Cossack called the "Wolf," he of the Curved Saber, rode into Samarkand. Yet the book of Chakar Noyon, who was very wise, was owned by Mir Turek, the merchant; and in the bazaars of Samarkand Khlit met with Mir Turek.

Truly, there are many books that are not to be believed. Yet did Mir Turek believe the book of Chakar Noyon, and Mir Turek was not only a shrewd merchant, but a scholar. And he thirsted for gold. Likewise there was the tale of the Leo Tung astrologer. The astrologer did not see the Bearers of Wealth, but he saw the white faces of the Onon Muren and he told of the terror of Khantai Khan.

Khlit could not read, not even the gold inscription on his famous curved sword. He was sick of the hot sands of Persia and the ruined towns of Turkestan. His dress had changed since he became an exile from the Cossack camps—he wore green leather pantaloons, topped by a wide purple sash, with a flowing cloak of crimson silk. He still had his sheepskin hat, and his burned pipe. As he rode through the sun-baked bazaars of Samarkand his eye fell on the booth of Mir Turek, and on the elephant in the booth.

It was a small elephant, or rather a pair of them, of ivory and gold. Khlit had never seen such a creature before, and the sight delighted him. He dismounted and sauntered slowly to the bazaar of the merchant, lest the latter suspect that he was anxious to buy.

Mir Turek was a stout man, with a broad nose and slant, bleared eyes. He was dressed in the white robe of a scholar, and he put down a parchment he was reading as the Cossack seated himself cross-legged on the rug before him. Mir Turek watched the stars with the astrologers, and the month was one when his star was ascendent. The ivory elephants, he said, in bastard Usbek which Khlit understood, were not to be sold. They were a talisman of good fortune.

Khlit took from his wallet the last of the gold

coins left from the sack of Alamut and laid them on the rug before the merchant. Likewise he drew his sword from its sheath and laid it across his knees. The sun, gleaming on the bright blade with its curious lettering, threw a pallid glow over the yellow face of Mir Turek.

The merchant glanced curiously from the sword to Khlit. His eyes widened as he scanned the inscription on the weapon. Long and steadfastly he looked at its owner. Truly, thought Mir Turek, his star was ascendent.

"Offspring of the devil's jackal!" growled Khlit. "Scouring of a beggar's pot! Where is there a merchant who will not sell his goods? Sell me the images or I will slit your fat belly for you."

Mir Turek turned a shade grayer and his eyes watered. Still, he could not tear his eyes from the inscription. He pointed to the sword.

"Is that, like the gold pieces, from Persia?" he asked.

"Nay, one without honor," replied Khlit carelessly, "a Cossack does not buy or steal his sword. It was my father's and his father's. I will take the images."

"Nay, lord," hastily broke in the merchant, "they are a talisman. I dare not sell." He glanced swiftly to each side down the bazaars. "But come to my house tonight—the house of Mir Turek, the merchant—in the alley at the south corner of the Registan, and we will talk concerning them, you and I."

When Khlit had gone Mir Turek drew together the silk curtains in front of his booth. Yet he did not leave the stall. He sat motionless, in thought. He fingered the parchment as one caresses a treasure. Carefully he read over a portion of the book and drew in his breath with a grateful sigh. Without doubt, his star was watching over him, as the astrologer had said. And the elephants were truly a potent talisman.

In the mind of Mir Turek was a picture. The picture was of a host of fighting men following their banners over the steppe. Also, of the oak trees of Khantai Khan where few men ventured. In the back of Mir Turek's mind, like the reflection in a pool of water, was a fear, an old fear, that had been his father's and his father's before him.

Khlit was weary of Samarkand and homesick for the wide plains of the steppe. Wherefore he drank much that night, many bowls of Usbek wine, that stirred his memories of the Ukraine and the Tatar land, but did not affect his head or the firmness of his step. He remembered that Mir Turek had invited him to come to his house. So Khlit sought and found the door of the merchant's home on the Registan, and, although he could not read, he came to know somewhat of the book of Chakar Noyon.

The door of Mir Turek opened at his touch and the Cossack swaggered through the antechamber and walked uninvited to a room in the rear. It was a chamber hung with yellow silk of a strange kind, and filled with ivory images of elephants and small pagodas. A girl who had been sleeping curled up on some rugs in one corner sprang to her feet and would have fled swiftly, but Khlit checked her.

She was a child of fourteen, slender and delicate of face with a mass of dark hair that descended over her shoulders. The small, olive face that turned up at the Cossack was frightened. So it was that Khlit met the girl Kerula, child of Mir Turek, whose mother, a Kallmark slave, was dead.

"Eh, little sparrow," chuckled Khlit, patting the girl's hair, "I will not hurt you. Tell your master, Mir Turek, the shrewd merchant, that Khlit, called the Wolf, is come to his house."

He seated himself on the rugs the girl had left. No sooner had he done so than she approached shyly and began to tug at one of his heavy boots.

"Truly, lord," she said softly, "when a lord is drunk it is hard to take off his high shoes. Yet I would show honor to the one who comes to buy me. Such is the will of my master, Mir Turek, who can cheat better than any other merchant of Samarkand."

"In the house of a stranger, little daughter,

they must slay me before my boots can be taken off, or my sword from my side." Khlit threw back his shaggy, white-haired head, with a roar of laughter that startled the girl. "So, I have come to buy you? Nay, devil take it, I have come for some ivory trinkets."

"I did not know, lord," the girl drew back and Khlit saw that she was trembling. "Mir Turek said that he would sell me, and that I should comb my hair, for men would come to look at me and feel my limbs. They have never seen my face in the streets of Samarkand, yet Mir Turek told Fogan Ultai, chief of the servants, that I would bring the price of two good horses. Fogan Ultai doubted, and for that Mir Turek beat me. Then Fogan Ultai struck me on the ears to ease his honor—"

A sound of shuffling steps caused the child to break off in alarm. Mir Turek stood before them, scowling.

"Chatterer! Slanderer of your master! Be off to the slaves' quarters. This is a Cossack lord, not a buyer of slaves, Kerula. Leave us."

The girl slipped from the room, and a smile replaced the scowl on the merchant's face as he seated himself by Khlit. The Cossack considered him in silence. He had never seen a man who resembled Mir Turek. The man's eyes slanted even more than those of a Turkoman; his black hair was straight, instead of curly, and his hands were long and carefully kept. The merchant proffered a cup of wine from an ebony stand, but Khlit shook his head.

"The Turkomans say," said Khlit grimly, "that when a sword is drawn, no excuse is needed. I have come for the trinkets, not wine."

"Yet I am no Turkoman," smiled Mir Turek, and his voice purred. "See, it is written that he who drinks from the cup need have no care. Can you read the words on the cup? The language is like that on your sword."

"Nay, it looks as if a dog had scratched it," responded the Cossack idly.

He could not read in books, but he was wise in the language of men's faces and he knew that Mir Turek had more in his mind than he spoke.

"Here is the money, I will take the trinkets."

He nodded at where the elephants stood on an ebony cabinet, but Mir Turek held up one hand.

"The men of Samarkand are fools—Usbeks— and are fit only to be slaves. The chief of my slaves, Fogan Ultai, has told me that there is a story in the bazaars that you are Khlit, the Cossack who outwitted Tal Taulai Khan, leader of the Golden Horde, and that your sword is as much to be feared as that of Kaidu, the warrior of the Tatars. Truly, I see that you are a man of valor. I have need of such a man."

"Aye, I am Khlit. Men call me the Wolf. Say what is on your mind, Mir Turek. The short word is best, if it is the truth."

Mir Turek's eyes half-closed. Through the narrowed lids they rested on Khlit's sword.

"Before the star Ortu descends from its zenith," he said slowly, "I am going from Samarkand to Karakorum, in the land of the Tatars far to the north. The journey will be over the mountains that these fools call the Roof of the World, past Kashgar, to the Great Desert of Gobi. There is no one in Samarkand who will go with me, yet the journey is not difficult, for my grandfather's father came over the route from Karakorum to Samarkand."

"Aye," said Khlit.

"I need a man who will lead the Turkomans who go with me as guard," pursued the other. "There are robbers in the Roof of the World and by the borders of the Great Desert the Tatar tribes fight among themselves, for Tal Taulai Khan is dead and the Jun-gar fight with the Kallmarks and the Boron-gar with both.

"The home of my family is in Altur Haiten, by the mountains of Khantai Khan. But the journey to the north is perilous, and I need a leader of fighting men. I am learned in the knowledge of books and trade, but I can not wield a sword. The name of Khlit, the Wolf, will protect my caravan."

"Aye," said Khlit. Something in his tone caused Mir Turek to glance at him sharply.

"Will you come to Karakorum, lord?" he asked. "Name what price you ask. It will be paid.

As a pledge, take, without payment, the twin elephants."

"I will come," said Khlit, "when your tongue has learned to speak the truth, Mir Turek. Truly, I am not a fool, like these of Samarkand. An Usbek chief could lead your men, and for little pay. My name is not known north of the Roof of the World. Cease these lies, Mir Turek—I like them little."

The slant eyes of the merchant closed, and he folded his arms into his long sleeves. He was silent for a space as if listening, and as he listened a change came over his face. Khlit heard the sound, too, a low murmur in an adjoining room. Mir Turek got to his feet without noise and vanished in the direction of the sound. Khlit waited watchfully, but in a moment the merchant reappeared, dragging Kerula by the arm. The girl's brown eyes were filled with tears.

"Busybody! One without honor!" He flung the slender form of the slave girl on the rugs, and planted his slippered toes in her ribs. "Blessed is the day when I can sell you and be bothered no longer by tears. Did I not say the lord was not a buyer of women? Fogan Ultai shall reward you for listening."

The girl sobbed quietly, rolling over to escape the assault of Mir Turek's broad feet. Khlit watched in silence. She was the merchant's property, and he was entitled to do with her as he chose. Still, the sight was not pleasant. Mir Turek continued his imprecations, mingled with promises that Kerula would be sold without fail, on the morrow. Khlit touched the girl's hair as if admiring its fine texture.

"Harken, Kerula," he said. "Is there no young Turkoman who looks upon you with favor and who would please you for a master?"

"Nay, lord," sobbed the girl, withdrawing beyond the merchant's reach, "why should I like a Turkoman? Without doubt, they are shaggy as mountain sheep."

"She can not come to Karakorum," put in Mir Turek. "The journey through the mountains is too hard, and she would die, without profit to me."

Khlit regarded his black pipe thoughtfully. It was long since he had seen the fresh face and clear eyes of a child. He reached into his wallet and drew out the coins he had offered for the elephants. These he laid before Mir Turek.

"You have named a price for the girl, Mir Turek," he said, "the price of two horses. Here it is. I will buy the child."

The merchant's slant eyes gleamed at sight of the gold, but he shook his head dubiously.

"I could get a better price in the bazaars. What do you want with the girl, Cossack? She can not come on the journey."

Khlit's beard wrinkled in a snarl.

"Take the money for the girl, Mir Turek. I will take Kerula. Nay, she will not come with us, one-without-understanding!" Turning to the slave, Khlit's tone softened. "Tomorrow, Kerula, you can beat the back of Fogan Ultai with a stick, for I will watch. Go where you will in Samarkand, for you are free. I have bought you of Mir Turek. And I say to go where you will."

The girl gazed at him wide-eyed. As if to convince herself she had heard aright she put out her hand and touched the Cossack's coat. The latter, however, took no more notice of her.

II

Khlit had said that Mir Turek lied. It was then that the merchant told Khlit the true cause of his journey to Karakorum. And this tale was strange, strange beyond belief. It was the fruit of Mir Turek's reading, and the tale of the Leo Tung astrologer who had gone, with Mir Turek's grandfather's father, to the mountains of Khantai Khan, to the tomb of Genghis Khan.

Yet in spite of the strangeness of the tale, Khlit did not say this time that Mir Turek lied. In Khlit's veins was the blood of the Cossack Tatar folk who had ruled the empire of the steppe, and taken treasure from their enemies. He wondered, but did not speak his thoughts.

It was a tale that began with the death of

Genghis Khan, called the "Master of the Earth," and ended with the death of Mir Turek's ancestor and the Leo Tung man from the vapor that lay among the trees of Khantai Khan. It was about a treasure such as Khlit had not thought existed in the world, the treasure of Genghis Khan.

There came a time, said Mir Turek, when the "Mighty Manslayer" paused in his conquest of the world. The beast Kotwan appeared to Genghis Khan in a vision and the ruler of the Tatar horde which had subjugated the world from Khorassan to Zipangu, and from Lake Baikal to the furthest city of Persia, returned home to die.

Genghis Khan was wiser than all other rulers. Knowing that he was dying, he gave orders that peace be made with his worthiest foes, the Chinese of Tangut and Sung, and that his death should not be disclosed. When his body was carried to the tomb in the mountains of Khantai, twenty thousand persons were slain to keep him company to the shades of the Teneri, among them those who built the tomb. So said the astrologer of Leo Tung. Thus none could say they had seen the spot where the Master of the Earth lay in the grip of the Angel of Death.

Twenty thousand souls accompanied Genghis Khan on his journey to the Teneri, and the treasure, spoils of a thousand cities, was placed in his tomb. This tomb was unmolested by the Tatars, until the coming of Leo Tung, who was a Chinaman and dared to look on the dead face of the leader of the Horde. Leo Tung had found the spot in the forests of Khantai Khan, with Mir Turek's ancestor. They had passed the gate of the Kukukon River; they had passed the Onon Muren; they had seen the starlight gleam on the Bearers of Wealth.

They had seen the treasure of Genghis Khan, said Mir Turek, his eyes gleaming as with fever, but the mists of Khantai Khan had closed around them. Mir Turek did not know just why they had left the tomb. He knew that a great fear came on them and they fled. The Leo Tung man

had died very quickly, and the other went from the Khantai Khan region to Samarkand.

Before he died he had told his son the way to the tomb of Genghis Khan. And so the tale had come to Mir Turek. The merchant of Samarkand knew that a change had taken place in the Tatar people. Their power had been broken by the Chinese, shortly after the death of Genghis Khan. With the assistance of Khlit, he might enter the tomb and find the treasure of Genghis Khan, Master of the Earth and leader of the Golden Horde.

Aye, said Mir Turek softly, he was a scholar, but he had searched in books for the wealth of Genghis Khan. There was the tale of Chakar Noyon, *gylong*, which told of the tomb. Chakar Noyon, being a priest, had said that the Onon Muren or spirits of the slain twenty thousand guarded the tomb; that was an idle story. Mir Turek did not believe it.

Nevertheless, when the other had finished, Khlit asked himself why the fathers of Mir Turek had not sought for the tomb of Genghis Khan. He found the answer in the fever that burned in the other's eyes and the restless movements of the white hands. Mir Turek felt in his heart a great fear of what he was to do, and this fear had been his fathers'.

Khlit was not the man to shrink from seizing gold. Even the gold of the tomb of Genghis Khan. Yet, with his desire for gold was mingled delight at the thought of returning to the steppe that had been his home, even in another part of the world.

III

Thus it happened that Khlit began the journey which was to take him over the mountains called the Roof of the World, above Ladak, or Tibet, north of Kashgar, past Issyuk Kul and Son Kul, the twin lakes of the clouds, to the desert of Gobi.

Concerning this journey and its ending there are few who believe the story of Khlit. Yet the

Cossack was not the man to say what was not so, for love of the telling. And there is the book of Chakar Noyon, to be found in one of the Samarkand mosques, and the annals of the chronicler of Hang-Hi, the great general of the Son of Heaven. Truly, belief is, after all, the fancy of the hearer and only the fool is proud of his ignorance.

When the sun gilded the top of the ruins of Bibi Khanum, the followers of Mir Turek had pitched their felt tents on the slope of Chupan Ata, on the way to the Syr River. Already the heat of the Samarkand valley had been replaced by the cool winds of the mountains and Khlit was glad to don his old sheepskin coat. He looked around with some satisfaction at the camp.

Mir Turek's following consisted of a dozen Turkomans and Fogan Ultai, master of the slaves. These had placed their small tents in a circle beside the donkeys, the pack-animals of the expedition.

Khlit's leadership had already instilled discipline into the sturdy but independent followers. Two stood as sentries near the caravan path. The Turkomans had tried rebellion against the Cossack, and had learned why he was called the Wolf. Fogan Ultai, however, as the servant of Mir Turek, was not under Khlit's orders. Twice during the day the leader of the slaves had refused obedience and Mir Turek had upheld him.

Fogan Ultai was a small man, pale in face, with dark hair like his master's, and the same slant eyes. Khlit did not like the man, who was watchful and silent, speaking occasionally to Mir Turek in a tongue the Cossack did not understand. As long as Fogan Ultai did not interfere with his authority over the Turkomans, Khlit was willing to leave the other in peace.

It was after the evening meal, and Khlit was smoking his pipe in front of the tent he had pitched for himself. He sat with his back to the tent, his sword over his knees, watchful of what went on. In the twilight gloom he could make out the figures of the men throwing dice by a fire.

Suddenly Khlit took his pipe from his mouth. He made no other movement, but his tall figure stiffened to alertness and his keen eyes searched the gloom. A shadow had appeared, slipping from tent to tent, making no sound. And the sentries had not given warning.

The shadow paused in front of him, and Khlit's hand went to his sword. The form approached him, and a small figure cast itself at his feet. A pair of white hands clasped his boots.

"Lord, you are my master—be merciful," the voice of Kerula came out of the darkness. "Lord, do not kick me, because I followed after you on a donkey that was lame, so it was not taken with the others, and slipped past the men who are watching. I followed because you would have sent me back if I had come sooner. But my hunger is very great now, and I am cold."

Khlit reached out his rough hand and took the girl by the shoulder. Kerula's white face looked up into his. He could feel the girl's warm breath against his cheek.

"I said you could not come, Kerula," he replied gruffly. "Why do you seek the hardship of the journey? It is no path for a girl. There are gallants in Samarkand who would buy you flowers and slaves—"

"Nay, lord. I am afraid of the men of Samarkand. I have no master but you, Khlit, lord. The others would bring shame on me, the women say. I will follow after the caravan, truly, on the lame donkey, and you will not know I am there. Perhaps I can prepare your food, or clean the mud from your boots. Do not let them send me to Samarkand."

Khlit shook his head, and the child gave a soft wail of distress.

"The way is too hard," he said. "The men will give you food, but tomorrow—"

The girl rose from her knees, with bowed head.

"You are my lord, and you send me to the bazaars of Samarkand. I have no home. If you would let me follow, I would sleep with your horse, and bring your wine cups, until we reach the land where Genghis Khan rules. My mother, before she died, told me of the land."

Khlit raised his head in surprise at the girl's speech. Before he could answer a shadow appeared beside Kerula, and Fogan Ultai's soft voice spoke.

"Get back where you came from, Kerula, or your palms will be well whipped! You have heard the word of the Cossack lord. Our master, Mir Turek, would let you off less easily if he knew you were here."

The master of the slaves caught the child roughly and shook her. She clasped his hand and sank her teeth into it viciously. Fogan Ultai gave a cry of pain. As he lifted his free hand to strike the girl she sprang free defiantly.

"Mir Turek shall know of this, offspring of the low-born," hissed the servant. "You say you have had no food for a day. Good! You will pray to me for food before you shall leave the camp."

"Who gave you authority, Fogan Ultai," said Khlit, "to give orders in the camp? If I say the child shall eat, you will bring her food."

"I?" Fogan Ultai shivered as if with cold. "I am no slave, and my caste—" he broke off— "nay, I heard you say she was to go, Khlit."

"I said that the men would give her food. You have keen ears, Fogan Ultai. Since you have come, like a dog at the scent of a carcass, you may bring the food to Kerula. She is hungry."

"Mir Turek would not allow that to come to pass, Khlit." The other's voice was smooth and sibilant. "He knows it is not for such as I to bring food, or for a Cossack to give me orders—"

Fogan Ultai's speech ended in a strangling gasp. Khlit had risen from his sitting posture, and as he rose his heavy fist crashed into the other's face. Fogan Ultai lay on the ground, his arms moving slowly, half-stunned. Slowly he got to his feet, staggering. The girl drew in her breath sharply and shrank back.

"Cossack," Fogan Ultai mumbled, for blood was in his mouth, "the girl is yours and if it is your wish—she shall eat. But a man is a fool who seeks an enemy. Let another bring the food."

"I said you, Fogan Ultai, not another."

The attendant was silent for a moment. He felt his injured face tenderly. Khlit waited for the flash of a dagger or the hiss of an imprecation but Fogan Ultai was silent. Surely, Khlit thought, he was a strange man.

"The food shall be brought, Cossack, if it is still your wish. Yet it would be well to say otherwise."

Receiving no response from Khlit, the man turned and disappeared into the darkness. Khlit turned to the girl roughly, for he knew that he had earned an enemy.

"Sit in my tent, Kerula," he said shortly. "The wind is cold. After you have eaten, roll yourself in my woolen robe. I shall sleep with my horse."

The next day saw Kerula mounted on her lame donkey riding behind Khlit and Mir Turek. The latter said nothing concerning the appearance of the girl, and Khlit thought that he had spoken with Fogan Ultai. The difficulty of the way grew, and cold gripped the riders. The Turkoman horses, wrapped in their felt layers, with their high-peaked wooden saddles seemed indifferent to the change in climate, but the donkeys shivered, and Mir Turek wrapped himself in a costly fur robe. Khlit saw to it that the girl had a sheepskin cloak that had been carried in the baggage.

The moon which had been bright at the start of the journey had vanished to a circlet of silver when the riders, under guidance of one of the Turkomans, passed the blue waters of the mountain lakes, Issyuk Kul and Son Kul, and reached the passes of the Thian Shan Hills. Here the Turkoman guide gave up the leadership, but Fogan Ultai declared that he could find his way among the passes with the aid of the merchantman's maps and the stars.

Khlit, who saw everything as he rode, noted that Mir Turek had fallen silent, and that the merchant spent much time in talk with Fogan Ultai in the *yurtas* in the evenings. So far, however, the master of the slaves had been content to keep out of Khlit's way. The Cossack paid no further attention to Fogan Ultai, other than to see to the loading and priming of the brace of Turkish pistols he carried in his belt. These were the only firearms of the expedition.

Mir Turek broke his silence, one day when the sunlight lay on the rock slopes of the mountains without warming the faces of the riders, to speak of Genghis Khan. It was through these passes, said the merchant, that the slaves of the Mighty Manslayer carried the wealth that had been taken from the cities of Damascus and Herat to Karakorum.

The fever burned in the man's eyes as he spoke. The wealth of Genghis Khan had been so great that his minister had never counted it. From the four corners of Asia slaves brought it to the Master of the Earth. Genghis Khan had kept a hoard of gold, the book of Chakar Noyon said, at his palace. One minister had given away jewels to his wives, until Genghis Khan had learned of it, when the minister had cut his own throat to avoid the wrath of the conqueror.

Khlit listened while Mir Turek told of the campaigns of Genghis Khan, and how victories had come to the standard of the Horde, the standard of yaks' tails that had traveled from Karakorum to Herat.

The merchant halted his words as the advance rider of the party came to them. The Turkoman, who had been some hundred paces in front of Khlit and Mir Turek, brought with him a slender man in a long robe who carried a pack. The man, Khlit saw, was clean-shaven, with the hair of his forehead cut to the skin.

The stranger spoke with Mir Turek, who shook his head to show that he did not understand. At the merchant's gesture Fogan Ultai rode up and addressed the newcomer. The two fell back among the attendants where Kerula was. But Mir Turek did not resume his conversation. He seemed impatient to halt, when before he had been eager to push on. As his reason, he gave the rising wind which seemed to promise snow. The star Ortu, said Mir Turek, was no longer above them, and they could not count on its protection.

Khlit accordingly called a halt. The felt tents were pitched, the *yurta* formed. Kerula was accustomed to see to the erecting of the Cossack's shelter, which was beside her own, and Khlit rode into the twilight to see to the posting of the sentries. Before he returned he saw a strange sight. For the Turkomans on watch had kneeled to the ground and laid their ears against the path.

Khlit brought the men to their feet with a hearty imprecation. The Turkomans were sullen, saying that they listened for signs of approaching danger. What this danger was, they would not say. But one, the less sullen of the two, muttered that danger might be met along the path that could be heard, and could not be seen.

Impatient of the men's superstition, Khlit returned to his tent where Kerula sat with his evening meal. Around the fire which blazed very brightly, the others of the party were gathered. And Khlit frowned as he watched. The stranger they had met that day stood in front of the fire, throwing grease from a pot upon it.

As the man with the shaven head did this, he read aloud from a small book he held. The words meant nothing to Khlit, but Mir Turek and Fogan Ultai listened intently. Truly, Khlit thought, Mir Turek was a man of double meanings. For the merchant had declared that the newcomer was a beggar. Khlit had never known a beggar who could read. As he turned this over in his mind, Kerula, who had crept near him spoke.

"Khlit, lord," she whispered, her eyes bright in the firelight, and all save her eyes covered by the fur cloak for the cold, "last night I dreamed a strange dream. It was that a falcon flew down on my wrist, and it held the sun and a star in its talons. The falcon had flown far, and was weary, but it held the sun. And I was glad."

"You have many dreams, little sparrow," smiled Khlit.

When he smiled, the bitterness faded from his hard face. Kerula loved to see him smile. More often of late she had coaxed him to do so.

"Am I a conjuror, to tell you what they mean?"

"Nay, Khlit, lord," she chattered, "you are too tall and big for a conjuror. See, the man who is reading prayers by the fire is such a one. I heard Fogan Ultai say he was a *gylong*, servant of the great lamas, and a man of wisdom."

Fogan Ultai had called the stranger a man of wisdom. Mir Turek had said he was a beggar. One had lied, and Khlit suspected it was Mir Turek.

"Did Fogan Ultai say more than that, Kerula?" he asked carelessly, watching the group by the fire.

"Aye, Khlit, lord. I heard him say to Mir Turek the man was a conjuror. Then he said to the man with the long robe that he was clever, he could conjure the two pistols away from you, and he—Fogan Ultai—would give him a donkey and some gold."

"Hey, little Kerula, he would have to be a very wise man to do that," chuckled Khlit. "Are you sure you did not dream that, too?"

"Nay, Khlit, lord," the girl looked at him strangely, "but I dreamed that we met an evil, two-headed snake, and that you buried it. After that, the snake was no longer evil."

Khlit said no more, but long after Kerula had crept into her tent, and the group around the fire had scattered, he sat in thought, his curved sword across his knees. What had prompted the Turkomans to turn sullen and lay their ears to the ground? Why had Mir Turek, who trusted him, lied that evening about the *gylong*? And why did Fogan Ultai desire his pistols?

IV

In a dream the beast Kotwan with the head of a horse and a horn in its forehead, that speaks all languages, came to Genghis Khan, the Mighty Manslayer. The beast Kotwan spoke as follows: "It is time for the Master to return to his own land." Whereupon Genghis Khan turned home-ward. And when he reached his home he died.

From the book of Chakar Noyon, gylong.

Concerning the events that came to pass when the party of Mir Turek crossed the desert of Gobi, Khlit is the only one who will tell. It is true that the narrative of the Hang-Hi chronicler mentions the sights and sounds which Khlit and Kerula heard in the night. But the Chinese historian ascribes the sounds to wind in the sand and the imagination of the Tatar travelers whose minds were filled with stories of Genghis Khan. Fools, said the Chinaman, walk unreflecting. Yet Khlit was not the man to be led astray by sounds that he imagined.

As for Kerula, Khlit found that the girl's tongue was eager to repeat stories of Genghis Khan that she heard from Mir Turek. The child had listened while the scholar read from his books. The books were all she knew, and so she supposed that Genghis Khan and his Tatar Horde were still alive, and might be met with on the sands of the Great Desert.

Khlit humored her in her fancies, and smiled at the dreams she repeated. He knew that the "dreams" of Kerula were her way of telling things that she thought he might not believe. The Cossack did not laugh at the girl for her fancies, because he was always ready to hear more of Genghis Khan, a conqueror more powerful than any Khlit had known. Even Tal Taulai Khan seemed a *mirza* beside the figure of the man who was called the Mighty Manslayer.

Mir Turek had ceased to talk with Khlit concerning their journey, and the tomb in the forest of Khantai Khan. The merchant and Fogan Ultai rode with the *gylong*. Neither interfered with his leadership, which was all Khlit asked. He was aware that since the coming of the *gylong*, a change had taken place in the party. The Turkomans became more sullen and had to be driven forward. And Mir Turek grew silent, seemingly waiting for something. Khlit took care to keep Kerula with him as much as possible. He had heard the Turkomans talking about her.

"Fogan Ultai says," he had heard them say, "that the girl Kerula has the ears of a skunk and the eyes of an ermine."

When the party descended the slope of the Thian Shan Hills and entered the desert, the Turkomans murmured further. This was natural, however, in face of the difficulties in front of them.

The desert, the first that Khlit had seen, was an ocean of sand, with wind ridges and gullies. In order to keep to a straight course by the sun, it was necessary to cut across the ridges, which varied from eight to some twenty feet in height. There were few springs to be met with, and the party was forced to keep an outlook for the coming of wind, which meant a halt and hurried preparation against sand-storms.

Although the country was new to Khlit, he did not give up his leadership of the party. On the advice of the *gylong*, Khlit exchanged their donkeys at a village on the edge of the desert, for a smaller number of camels. He kept his own horse, but the others gave up theirs. Thus the *gylong* gained a camel for his donkey.

After a rest at the village, Khlit ordered an advance into the desert, when the moon was again full. Mir Turek was content, as the star he regarded as his protection was now high in the heavens. Khlit rode at the rear of the little caravan where he could watch the Turkomans and where there was no one at his back.

The party had gone far into the desert and the Thian Shan summits had vanished on the horizon when the first of the strange events came to pass.

Khlit had been sleeping soundly in his felt tent, when he was awakened by Kerula crawling through the flap in early daylight. The girl's hair hung loose around her face, and Khlit saw that her eyes were wide and fixed. He had grasped his sword when the flaps of the tent moved, but now he released it, and sat up, wide awake on the instant. The girl crept close to him, shivering, yet it was not from cold of the night.

"I am frightened, Khlit, lord," she whispered. "For I have had a dream in the night. It

was that an animal crawled around my tent, crying my name. I heard it sniffing, and clawing at the tent. How could an animal call my name? I am afraid."

"A dream will not hurt you, little sparrow," answered Khlit cheerfully. "And the sun has come up to chase it away."

The girl, however, did not smile.

"When I came from my tent," she said softly, "I saw the marks of the beast. It had gone away. But how could it speak? I heard it calling, calling 'Kerula.' Animals can not speak, can they, unless—"

Khlit, to distract her, bade her gruffly prepare his morning meal. Later, however, when he left his shelter he took care to look at the ground around Kerula's tent which was beside his. He saw that there were actually marks on the ground.

Carefully, Khlit scanned them. They were marks of hoofs, and ran completely around the tent, clearly visible in the sand. When he tried to follow them away from the place he lost them in the tracks of the party. The hoof-marks, he saw, were smaller than those of a horse. He had heard that there were antelopes in the desert. Yet the tracks were larger than antelope hoofs. He said nothing of what he had seen to the girl.

The day's journey was short, and Mir Turek halted early, fearing a sand-storm, for the sun had gone behind clouds. The Turkomans gathered about the fire at dusk, and Khlit was obliged to drive one from the *yurta* to watch from a sand ridge. For his own satisfaction he placed a pointed stake firmly in the ground by his tent, indicating the direction they were to take in the morning. He had learned by experience that the ridges were often changed in appearance overnight.

As he sat over his evening meal with Kerula pensive beside him, the figure of Fogan Ultai detached itself from the group by the fire and approached him.

"Health to you, Khlit," said the master of the slaves with a bow. "The Turkomans have asked that I come as spokesman. It is not well to force a man to do what his habits forbid. They are murmuring against standing sentry during the night. The Turkomans have heard stories of the desert in the village we left. They think evil things may come to the sentries. You and I are wise—we know they are fools. Still, it is best to let a man do as he is accustomed."

"Does a sheep hide his head when the tiger hunts, Fogan Ultai?" said Khlit. "Shall the camp be blind during the night when there may be danger? Nay, a beast came last night and passed around Kerula's shelter."

Fogan Ultai shook his head, smiling.

"There are no beasts in the desert, Khlit. The evils the Turkomans fear are not to be seen. Let them sleep in their tents. It is not well," the man's voice dropped, "to tie the knot of hatred."

"Then, Fogan Ultai, you and I are wise. We do not fear the stories of evil. We two will watch, each taking half the night."

For a long moment Fogan Ultai's slant eyes gleamed into Khlit's. Then he turned away indifferently.

"Let the Turkomans stand watch. They are low-born."

Yet the Turkomans could not have watched well that night. Before dawn Kerula burst into Khlit's shelter and clung to him sobbing. The same animal, she said, had come close to her tent. She had not been asleep this time, and she had heard its claws on the felt. Its breath had smelled of musk, so strong that it sickened her.

When the beast had been on the other side of the tent, the girl had slipped out on the side nearest Khlit and had dashed into his shelter. She was shaken with sobs, pressing her hands against her face.

"It is the beast, Kotwan," she sobbed. "He has come to take me with him. Oh, do not let him take me, Khlit, lord. I am afraid of Kotwan, who smells of musk. He called my name and he wants me to follow him to the shades of the Teneri, up into the air over the desert."

Khlit tried to quiet the girl, saying that he heard nothing, but when he made a move to leave the shelter, she clung to him tearfully. It was

long before she dropped off to sleep, wrapped in some of his furs. Khlit listened, without moving for fear of disturbing her, and heard nothing more. Yet he fancied that an odor of musk filled the shelter.

V

The next day the girl had recovered somewhat from her fright. She refused to leave Khlit's side during the march over the shifting sands. Sleep overtook her at times on the camel, and she swayed in the cords that kept her in place. Each time this happened, she awoke with a start, and cried out for Khlit.

The Cossack did not like the look in the girl's face. She was pale and the lack of sleep added to the fatigue of the journey was beginning to tell on her. Khlit did not mention her experience of the night, for he found that she believed the strange beast Kotwan had come to her tent. The girl's brain was filled with idle fancies. His heart was heavy, however, at the look of dread in her eyes, for Kerula had endeared herself to him, as much as another person could win the affection of a man who counted his enemies by the thousand, and thirsted for fighting.

That night Kerula begged to be allowed to sleep in his tent, but the Cossack sternly ordered her to her own, and she went reluctantly. Contrary to his custom, he did not post a sentry, but retired early to his shelter, and his snores soon kept accompaniment to the monotonous reading of the *gylong* by the fire.

Before midnight, however, when the camp was quiet, Khlit's snores ceased. The flap of his tent was lifted cautiously and the Cossack crawled out on all fours. Noiselessly he made his way from his tent to the edge of the camp.

The *yurta* had been placed in a gully. Khlit, surveying his surroundings in the starlight, saw that the camels and the Turkoman shelters were some paces distant from the tents of the leaders.

Crawling down the gully, Khlit sought a depression where he could see the tent of Kerula against the skyline, within bowshot. He scooped out a seat for himself in the sand, with his back against the wind. Drawing his sheepskin *svitza* close about him, for the night was cold, he settled himself to watch, denying himself the comfort of a pipe. If an animal visited the tents between then and dawn, he was determined to have a look at it.

Khlit did not attach significance to the fears of the girl about the mythical animal she called Kotwan. He had seen, however, the tracks around the tent which were too large for an antelope, and he had caught the scent of musk, which Kerula declared came from the visitant of the night. No animal that Khlit knew smelled of musk, and had sharp hoofs. As far as he knew Fogan Ultai was right when he said there were no beasts in the desert, for the party had not met any since leaving the foothills of the Thian Shan. Wherefore Khlit was curious.

The Cossack was accustomed to watching, and he did not nod as he sat in the sand depression, with his scrutiny fixed on the horizon near the tents. The stars gleamed at him, and an occasional puff of wind stirred the sand about him. He must have watched for some hours, and the stars were not paler when he sat erect, gazing closely at the tents.

Something had moved near Kerula's shelter. The light was indistinct and Khlit could not make it out. He had heard nothing. Presently he felt that the thing was moving away from the tent and nearer him.

Khlit softly removed one of the pistols from his belt and got to his knees. Crouching low over the sand he could make out a dark object passing across the stars, moving down the gully toward him. For the first time he heard a sound, a low hiss that he could not place.

Then Khlit stiffened alertly. The wind had brought him the odor of musk. The scent clung to his nostrils and ascended to his brain. He felt the hair at the back of his neck stir, and a chill puff of wind sent tingles down his spine.

The black object was within a few paces, and he saw that it was something moving on all fours. Carefully he leveled the pistol, taking the best aim he could in the dark.

And then Khlit let the pistol fall to his side. The odor of musk that came to him so strongly was surely from the windward side. Yet the dark object came toward him from the *yurta* which was away from the wind. Khlit drew a deep breath and his eyes strained toward the moving form. His heart gave a leap as he recognized it. It was Kerula, moving over the sand on her hands and knees.

The child had crept from her tent out into the night that she feared. He could hear her labored breathing as she passed him slowly. The scent of musk could not have come from the girl. It had come from the windward side. Khlit turned quickly and searched the darkness with anxious glance.

On the further side of the gully, some distance in front of the girl was a larger object, defined against the sand. It moved in the same direction, away from the camp. Khlit heard a hissing sound come from it, and understood why he had smelled the musk. Watching the girl, he had not seen the other thing pass him. He made it out as an animal of powerful build, with horns, that seemed to drag its hind legs.

Quickly Khlit raised his pistol. Sighting it at the beast's head he pulled the trigger. The weapon clicked dully and he thrust it into his belt with a curse. The sand must have choked its flint and powder.

With a hasty glance at the moving forms, Khlit rose to his feet. Bending low, he trotted over the sand ridge at his side into the gully that ran beside the one he had been in. For some distance he ran, following the winding of the gully.

Fearful of losing trace of the girl and the animal, he turned back to the ridge, to find that he was running through an opening into the other gully. His heavy boots made no sound in the sand, and Khlit did not see that he was heading straight for the creeping animal until he heard a sharp hiss, and saw the object rise up before him.

He caught a brief glimpse of horns and long ears outlined against the sky, and felt a hot breath on his face. His hand leaped to his sword, and the curved blade was pulled from its sheath.

As Khlit's arm swept upward with the sword, it moved outward. The blade struck the beast where it was aimed, under the head. Khlit saw it stagger back and slashed it twice across the head as it fell to the sand. Moving back from the struggling object he called to the girl.

"Kerula! Here is Khlit, do not be afraid."

A moment more and Kerula was beside him, clinging to his coat, her head buried in his sleeve.

"It was the beast Kotwan," she cried, "calling me outside my tent. I heard it calling me and I came. Oh, it smelled of musk, and it kept calling. My legs would not hold me up and I crawled—where is the beast Kotwan?"

"Nay, little Kerula," laughed Khlit, "the beast Kotwan is a strange beast. But it will not come for you again. See!"

Drawing the girl after him, the Cossack stepped to the side of the dark object on the sand. He felt of it cautiously. It did not move. And when Khlit drew up his hand it held a beast's hide and horns. The hide seemed to be that of an antelope. The girl had bent over the figure that lay at their feet, fearfully. She tugged at Khlit's arm excitedly.

"Khlit, lord," she whispered, "it is the *gylong*. You have slain the *gylong*."

"Aye," said Khlit shortly. "The conjuror will conjure no more. I thought it was a strange animal that stood up on two legs when it saw you."

He felt in the sand and lifted two objects. One was a pony's hoof, cut off above the fetlock and dried. The other was a long dagger. He showed them to the girl.

"There is Kotwan's hoof, little Kerula. And the hide stinks of musk."

Khlit said nothing to Kerula, but he remembered the words of Fogan Ultai, and he guessed it was not wantonness, but the promise of a reward that had led the conjuror to terrify the girl and lure her into the desert. Also he began to understand why Fogan Ultai had coveted his pistols. Yet much was not clear to Khlit. He knew

that Fogan Ultai hated Kerula because Khlit had made him demean himself in bringing her food. Still, this did not seem a sufficient reason for the girl's death.

Khlit's détour into the other gullies had confused him as to the direction of the camp. Unwilling to run the risk of going further from the *yurta* in trying to find it, he took the girl a short distance from the dead man and sat down to wait for dawn, sheltering her with his *svitza*. Kerula, relieved of her fear, soon became sleepy.

"How is it, Kerula," he asked thoughtfully, "that this fellow Fogan Ultai is so trusted by Mir Turek? Hey, your father fears him—as he feared the *gylong*."

"I do not know, Khlit, lord," Kerula responded sleepily. "Mir Turek will not give orders to Fogan Ultai. When the master of the slaves came to Samarkand he showed Mir Turek a gold disk he wore. They thought I was sleeping, but I looked out at them, and the gold disk was made like a sun, with rays, with writing in the center. That was not long ago—and soon Mir Turek began to speak of the tomb of Genghis Khan to himself when he read the books."

The voice of the girl trailed off and she was soon sleeping. Khlit waited patiently for dawn. The stars had begun to fade and the fresh wind sprang up.

Khlit's thoughts were busy and he was not aware that he slept. Surely, he felt the wind on his face and heard the girl's calm breathing. They were sitting near the top of one of the ridges, and he could make out the nearest waves of sand.

The moon was high above him, and there was a faint line of scarlet to the east. No, Khlit could not have been asleep. He did not remember dozing, nor did he waken. And yet, as a mist comes from the mountains, the mystery of the desert of Gobi came from the dark wastes of sand and gathered around the Cossack, the girl, and the still figure that had been the *gylong*.

It came without warning, and gradually.

Khlit thought at first that the camels were stirring. He listened and he heard the wave of sound come from the east and close around him. This time he did not feel the fear that had gripped him for a space when he saw the strange beast in the dark.

Awe came upon Khlit as he listened. He strained his eyes, yet he could see nothing. With the wind the sounds swelled, and swept over him. Khlit marveled, as he listened, not moving. And something deep in him stirred at the sounds. He felt a swift exultation that rose with the sounds and left him when they had gone.

Out of the desert came the murmur of many horses' feet in the sand—the feet of thousands of horses that galloped with a clashing of harness. Surely, there were riders on the horses, for a chant rose from the sands, from thousands of throats, a low, wild chant that gripped Khlit's heart.

Came the creak of laden carts from the darkness. Carts that were drawn by oxen laboring under the *kang*. With them sounded the *pad-pad* of camels' feet. The chant of the riders died and swelled. When it swelled, it drowned the other sounds.

With it echoed the clash of arms, myriad of scabbards beating against the sides of horses. Another sound that Khlit knew was the flapping of standards came to his ears. In the darkness beside him a cavalcade was passing. No cavalcade, a host of mounted warriors. The chant was the song of the warriors and Khlit's throat trembled to answer it.

Mingling with the chant came a heavy tread that was strange to Khlit. The sands trembled under the tread. The sound neared Khlit and passed, not by him but over him. This was no tread of horses.

Khlit peered into the darkness, but the sand ridges were desolate. The stars were not obscured, and the line of crimson grew in the east. Louder swelled the chant of the horsemen, and the heavy tread of giant feet.

The clash of cymbals echoed faintly and with it the sound of distant trumpets. Then came the sound of a mighty trumpeting, not of horns, but of animals. The trumpeting drowned the chant of the riders. It ceased and silence descended suddenly on the desert.

Kerula stirred in his arms, and Khlit stood up to look over the sand ocean.

"Nay, Khlit, lord," the girl whispered, "you will not see them. I am not asleep. I am awake, and I heard it also. The passing of the *tumans*, with their standards of yaks' tails. I heard the wagons, and their oxen. And the creaking of the leather castles on the Bearers of Wealth. It was just as Mir Turek told me it would be. The chant of the mounted men was loudest of all, until the Bearers of Wealth gave the greeting of Dawn to the Master of the Earth."

Khlit rubbed his hand across his forehead and gazed at the dead *gylong*.

"I heard some sounds as of horsemen passing—" he began doubtfully.

"Aye, Khlit, lord. It was the army of Genghis Khan crossing the desert."

Then Khlit wondered if he had truly slept. The chant of the riders was still in his ears. But the rising sun showed the sands empty, and the camp at a little distance.

"Nay, little Kerula," he said finally, "you have dreamed another dream."

Yet when Khlit and Kerula returned to the *yurta*, they found only Mir Turek and Fogan Ultai with three camels. The Turkomans had gone, late in the night with the greater number of camels and most of the food. Fogan Ultai said that he had not been able to stop them, for they had heard sounds in the desert, and they were afraid.

VI

If a man despoils the tomb of a wise and just ruler he loses his virtue. Evil follows him and his sons. He is like a sal tree with a creeper o'ergrown.

Yen Kui Kiang, chronicler of Hang-Hi.

It was the beginning of Winter when Mir Turek and his companions left the desert of Gobi and reached a small village of mud huts to the north in the Tatar country of Karakorum, near the mountains of Khantai Khan.

The desert had taken its toll from the travelers. The Turkomans had not been seen after their departure. The *gylong* lay where he had fallen, covered by the shifting sands. Mir Turek believed the conjuror had gone with the attendants. Fogan Ultai said nothing, and Khlit wondered what the master of the slaves knew of the death of the *gylong*. Fogan Ultai had an uncanny way of getting information for himself. Before the party reached the village, the master of the slaves joined them with the tidings that all the surrounding country had been vacated by the Tatars.

From a herdsman, he said, he had learned that the Tatars were gathered within the walls of Altur Haiten where they had been besieged by the Chinese for a year. Altur Haiten was one of the strongholds of Tatary, to which the retreating hordes had been driven by Hang-Hi, the general of Wanleh, Emperor of China. Thus Mir Turek's prophecy that they would find the way to the mountains of Khantai Khan clear, was verified. Yet Khlit, wearied by the months of hardship in the desert, saw that if the way was clear, it was also barren of food and the supplies they needed.

They had come from the desert on the two surviving camels. Kerula and the remaining stock of grain and dates had been placed on the stronger of the beasts, and the three men took turns in riding the other. Khlit saw to it that Mir Turek and Fogan Ultai never rode on the other camel together. Since the affair of the *gylong* he had been wary of the two. Yet he had noticed two things.

One—Mir Turek feared Fogan Ultai more than at the start of the expedition. Two—Mir Turek was unwilling to part with Khlit, owing for some reason to his ownership of the curved sword. This, Kerula had told him, and Khlit had asked the girl if she could read the lettering on the sword. She could not do so, as the inscription was neither Chinese nor Usbek Tatar.

The girl had borne the journey bravely, yet she was very weak when they came to the village of mud huts. She was disappointed, too, because she had imagined that when they neared Karakorum they would find the Tatar country alive and flourishing as it had been in the days of Genghis Khan. Truly, thought Khlit, this was strange; for Kerula had learned of the old Tatars from Mir Turek, and she believed she lived in the land of the Master of the Earth. Khlit placed her in one of the mud huts of the empty village, and gave her fruit and water that he found near by.

He would not have left the girl if it had not been for Mir Turek. The merchant had been in a fever of excitement since he saw the summits of Khantai Khan. His fat figure was wasted by hardships, and his frame was hot with fever. He would not rest until he had left the girl with Fogan Ultai and set out, with Khlit and the two camels for the mountains.

"The girl will be safe, Khlit," he declared, "for Fogan Ultai can not leave the village without the camels. Come, we will go to the Kukulon gate, and the tomb of Genghis Khan while the way is open."

Khlit went reluctantly. He did not like to leave the girl with Fogan Ultai in the village. He liked even less the deserted appearance of the country. He knew what Mir Turek chose to forget, that they were at the end of their supplies, and must have food.

Yet he was not less eager than Mir Turek to go to the tomb of Genghis Khan. They were near a treasure which Mir Turek said was without equal in the world. Khlit had seen the treasure of the Turks, but he knew this would be greater, for the Tatars had despoiled the cities of the Turks. Lust of the gold gripped him.

The two set out at daybreak in the absence of Fogan Ultai and rode toward the mountains at the best pace of the camels. And as the slopes of Khantai Khan rose above them, Mir Turek's fever grew on him. He fastened his slant eyes greedily on the hills, and when they came in sight of a blue sheet of water, he gave a hoarse cry of triumph.

"The Lake Kukulon," he whispered. "The books told the truth. A river runs to the lake from the mountains. Aye, here we will find the Kukulon gate where my ancestor saw the Onon Muren."

But Khlit looked beyond the lake, and saw that where a river made its way down the slopes, the earth was a yellow and grayish color. He saw for the first time the forest of Khantai Khan. The trees, instead of the green verdure of pine and the brown foliage of oak, were bare of leaves. The forest of Khantai Khan was a dead forest. And Khlit's forebodings grew on him as he urged his camel after Mir Turek.

VII

Mir Turek skirted the edge of the lake, which was small, and followed an invisible path through the foothills, evidently finding his way by the instructions he had received from the man who had been there before. He headed toward a ravine that formed the valley between two crests of Khantai Khan. In this valley he could catch glimpses of the River Kukulon.

The merchant was gripped by the fever of gold. But Khlit kept his presence of mind, and watched carefully where they went. The Cossack was not superstitious; still, what he saw gave him misgivings. The ground they passed over was a dull gray in color, and the trees seemed withered as if by flames. The camels went ahead unwillingly. If he had been alone, Khlit might have gone no further. It was not fear of the mythical Onon Muren that oppressed him, or the fate of the others who had preceded them. A warning instinct, bred of the dead forests, held him back.

At the edge of the River Kukulon they dismounted from the camels, fastening the beasts to a blasted tree-trunk, and went forward on foot, Mir Turek keeping to the bank of the stream which now descended from the gorge in the valley. Mir Turek went more slowly, scanning his surroundings, especially the river. The din of the waters drowned conversation, but the merchant signified by a gesture that he was sure of the way. Above them the gorge changed to a rocky ravine, down which the Kukulon boiled, a succession of waterfalls and pools.

The sun was at its highest point when Khlit saw the first sign of what had struck the attention of their predecessors. He halted above a large pool and caught Mir Turek's shoulder, pointing down into the blue water. The sun struck through to the bottom of the pool.

Among the rocks which formed the bottom Khlit had made out a series of white objects. Round, and white, polished by the water and gravel, he saw dozens of human skulls, and the tracework of skeletons.

"Hey, Mir Turek," he shouted grimly, "here are the Onon Muren come to greet us. Did your ancestor say we would see them?"

The merchant gazed down into the pool, and stared at the skulls with watery eyes.

"Aye, Khlit," he cried, "these are the Onon Muren. Did not the books say that twenty thousand had been slain at the tomb? It is proof we are on the right path."

"That may be, Mir Turek," replied Khlit without stirring, "yet the books said the Onon Muren guarded the tomb. Are they not a warning to go back?"

Mir Turek laughed eagerly, but his hand was shaking as he pointed up the gorge.

"There is the Kukulon gate," he cried, "you and I are wise, Khlit. We do not fear the bones of dead men. The star Ortu is again high in its orbit, and you, Cossack, have the curved sword of—"

He broke off, and stumbled forward, raising a gray cloud of dust that choked Khlit. The latter followed, muttering. The curved sword, he grumbled, would not cut the throats of spirits. Why did Mir Turek remind him so often of his sword? Khlit wondered why there were no bones visible on the ground. He thought that they had been covered by the gray dust. In that,

Khlit was right. Yet, with all his wise knowledge, he did not guess the nature of the gray dust. If he had done so, he would not have followed Mir Turek further.

Khlit saw no gate, yet when they reached a pool larger than the others, at the bottom of a waterfall that fell between two pinnacles of rock, Mir Turek declared that they had come to the Kukulon gate. Here Khlit made his last protest, as Mir Turek informed him that the Kukulon gate was not to be seen. It lay, the merchant said, behind the waterfall, under the column of water. Khlit pointed to the skulls which gleamed at them again from the pool.

"In Samarkand," he said, "I swore that I would go with you, Mir Turek, to the tomb of Genghis Khan. If you go, I will go also. Yet I heard strange things in the desert of Gobi. The forest of Khantai Khan is not to my liking. I have a foreboding, Mir Turek. Men call me Wolf not because I have the courage of a fool. It would be well to turn back here."

Mir Turek thrust his lined face close to Khlit, and his smooth lips curled in a snarl, as of an animal that finds itself at bay.

"Do men truly call you Wolf, Khlit, or are you a jackal that whimpers at danger?"

"Nay, Mir Turek," said Khlit angrily, "you are a fool not to know fear from wisdom. Come!"

With this the Cossack jumped waist-deep into the pool. His heavy boots slipping and sliding over the skulls on the rocks, he crouched low and made his way along the rock at the rear of the waterfall. The force of the current carried the stream a yard out from the rock and Khlit was able to advance under the fall. Keeping his footing with difficulty he pressed forward in the semidarkness of the place.

He was wet through with the spray which rose from the rocks. Feeling the rock's surface carefully, he found that at a point it gave way. He could see a dark fissure where the rocks divided to the height of a man. Planting his feet cautiously he turned into the opening. For several yards he made his way forward until free of the spray from the waterfall.

"We are in the caverns now," the voice of Mir Turek echoed in his ear excitedly. "The books said that those who built the tomb changed the course of the Kukulon to cover the gate."

The gate of Kukulon! Beyond it lay the treasure of Genghis Khan. Mir Turek had spoken truly, Khlit thought as he sniffed the damp air of the cavern. And as he did so Khlit smelled danger as a hound smells a fox. A thin, strong odor came to him, not from the river but from the cavern. Was it dust from the gray earth?

"See," repeated Mir Turek, "there is the place where the sun comes in. The cavern leads to there. Come."

As Mir Turek ran stumbling ahead Khlit saw for the first time a circle of gray light, at some distance. Toward this the other headed, as fast as his weakened legs could carry him. The footing seemed smooth, as though prepared by men. As the gray light grew stronger Khlit saw that the cavern was littered with rusted arms and Tatar helmets. Here and there the skulls of the Onon Muren lay. Strange, thought Khlit, that the Tatars had been slain at the threshold of the tomb of Genghis Khan.

When he caught up with Mir Turek the other was standing at the end of the cavern, looking down into a chasm. Khlit glanced up and saw that the illumination was daylight, coming from an opening in the roof of the chasm. The opening was round, and as far as he could see, the chasm was round, descending straight into the heart of the mountain.

They stood at the entrance of the tunnel. The path, however, did not end here. A bridge of rock stretched across to the further side of the chasm. It was narrow and rose slightly, like a bent bow. Surely, thought Khlit, the hands of men had made this. He smelled the strange odor more strongly.

He saw also, why the light was dimmed. Up from the chasm thin streams of vapor rose, twining around the rock bridge. These streams of vapor did not eddy, as there was no wind. They wound upward in dense columns through which the further side of the gorge could be seen.

Mir Turek caught his arm and pointed to the further side.

"The Bearers of Wealth!" he screamed. "See, the Bearers of Wealth, and their burden. The tomb of Genghis Khan. We have found the tomb of Genghis Khan!"

The shout echoed wildly up the cavern, and Khlit thought that he heard a rumbling in the depths of the cavern in answer. He looked where Mir Turek pointed. At first he saw only the veil of smoke. Then he made out a plateau of rock jutting out from the further side. On this plateau, abreast of them, and at the other end of the rock bridge gigantic shapes loomed through the vapor. Twin forms of mammoth size reared themselves, and Khlit thought that they moved, with the movement of the vapor. These forms were not men but beasts that stood side by side. Between them they supported a square object which hung as if suspended in the air.

As he looked he saw that the twin shapes did not move—that it was the smoke which had deceived him. They faced him, tranquil and monstrous, and Khlit's heart quivered at the sight. He had seen similar beasts once before. His mind leaped back to the bazaars of Samarkand. Of giant size, the twin forms across the chasm were like the two elephants he had sought to buy from Mir Turek.

"The Bearers of Wealth!" chanted the merchant, stretching out both hands. "The golden elephants. All the treasure of Genghis Khan is melted into the Bearers of Wealth. So the books said and they did not lie. *Akh*, the star Ortu is truly a blessed omen. The followers of the dead Genghis Khan brought the treasure into the caverns of Khantai Khan. There they molded it into the elephant-forms and hung the casket of Genghis Khan between them. Yet none left the mountain alive."

Khlit stared across the chasm in wonder. If the forms of the Bearers of Wealth were gold, there must be tons of it. Even if jewels were not melted in the gold, the wealth was beyond measure. Lust of the gold surged over him, and at the same time another feeling.

Far below him the rumbling sounded in the mountain, and brought a fleeting thought of the rumbling he had heard on the desert of Gobi—the tread of the Bearers of Wealth. For the second time a sense of coming danger gripped him. Nothing moved in the chasm, and the rumbling might well be stones dropping in the depths. Khlit peered down and could not see the bottom.

"Aye," he said grimly, "it is the tomb of a hero."

As he spoke he caught the scent of the vapors and staggered back.

"The wealth of Genghis Khan," screamed Mir Turek, trembling. "I have found it and it is mine. Blessings to the Teneri and the great Buddha!"

With that he started across the rock bridge. Khlit ran after him.

The rumblings echoed in the depths below them, and the vapors twined around the form of Mir Turek. Khlit felt them close around him, with a warm touch. Mir Turek stumbled and threw up his arms with a choking cry.

"*Akh! Akh!* The Onon Muren—at my throat—"

Khlit leaped forward, dizzy with the stifling vapors. He caught Mir Turek as the merchant was falling to the rock bridge. For an instant both were poised over the side of the bridge, half-way across to the tomb of Genghis Khan.

With all the force of his powerful muscles, Khlit dragged Mir Turek back, and hauled the senseless form of the other to safety in the cavern where they had stood a moment before. His head was swimming and his throat burned with the touch of the vapors. He sat down on a rock near the suffering Mir Turek and tore open the fastenings of his coat, at the throat. It was many moments before his head cleared and he was able to see the gray forms of the Wealth-Bearers across the chasm.

Truly, thought Khlit, the Onon Muren watched over the tomb of Genghis Khan. And those who invaded the tomb must have earned the wrath of the Onon Muren.

As soon as his strength had returned, Khlit

lifted the form of the merchant to his shoulder and made his way back to the Kukulon gate, under the waterfall, to the hills of Khantai Khan.

VIII

Mir Turek had partly recovered when the two reached the village that night, but he was weak, and badly shaken by the experience in the chasm of the Wealth-Bearers. They found, however, that food was running low, and Khlit was anxious that Kerula should have medicines, for the girl was still suffering from her trip across the desert. She greeted Khlit joyfully, however, as he descended stiffly from his camel.

"Fogan Ultai has returned, Khlit, lord," she said, "and he has a plan. He has been to the edge of the Chinese camp around Altur Haiten, and he says that we can get to the city at night. The Tatars come through the Chinese lines. Then we can see the great Tatar warriors who are fighting there, and we can get plenty of food in the city."

Khlit considered this.

"Aye," he said, "it might be done. Yet you had better stay here with Mir Turek, Kerula."

"Nay, I would be frightened!" she exclaimed quickly. "Fogan Ultai says we can all go. And I do not want to be away from you, my lord, with the curved sword that every one fears. I dreamed last night that the two-headed snake you met and buried was not really buried, but it pursued me."

So it happened that when Mir Turek had recovered strength sufficiently, the four went with the camels to the outskirts of the Chinese camp, waiting there until darkness permitted a passage to the city. Khlit had agreed to this, after talking with Fogan Ultai. He did not trust the master of the slaves, who was sullen because Khlit and Mir Turek had gone to the mountains of Khantai Khan without him, yet he calculated that where his own safety was at stake, Fogan Ultai would act with them. The country around was stripped of provisions by the cavalry of the Chinese, and Fogan Ultai had promised that he knew a way to the city.

Mir Turek was eager to gain Altur Haiten, being shaken by his trip to the tomb of Genghis Khan. The merchant remained feverish, talking to himself often and startled by the slightest sound. While the party were waiting for darkness at the edge of a wood within sight of the tents and pavilions of the Chinese camp and the brown walls of the besieged city, Mir Turek laid a cloth on the ground and prayed earnestly. Kerula was in high spirits.

"Now we shall see the men of Genghis Khan," she sang, "the men of the Golden Horde. They will welcome us because Mir Turek is a man of wisdom and Khlit, lord, is a chieftain."

So Khlit went to the Chinese camp, not suspecting. With Kerula's hand in his he followed Fogan Ultai. In the darkness they followed ravines, keeping clear of the camp-fires. Seldom had Khlit, the Wolf, been trapped. Yet how should he suspect?

He heard Mir Turek murmuring prayers behind him, and turned to curse the merchant, with Kerula's hand still in his. For an instant the strange words of the other caused him suspicion. What language was the merchant speaking? Why had Mir Turek been so curious about his sword? And why had he given up thought of the treasure of Genghis Khan? The suspicion came too late.

They were threading a ravine within bowshot of the Chinese sentinels. Suddenly Khlit heard a quick cry from Kerula. His hand went to his sword. But the same instant a heavy blow fell across the back of his neck.

Khlit sank to his knees. Before he could rise, hands closed on him. The darkness seemed to give birth to forms that sprang at him. His arms were pinned, and bound to his sides. A cloth was thrown over his head, and he was picked up bodily by many men and borne off.

IX

One evening, early in the Winter which marked the first year of the siege of Altur Haiten, as related by Yen Kui Kiang, chronicler of Hang-Hi, the general of the Imperial forces sat in the Hall of Judgment in his pavilion. The pavilion was distant from the walls of Altur Haiten, but the sound of the cannon, and the roar of flame could be heard distinctly.

Hang-Hi, mandarin of a high order, master of literature, and favorite general of Wanleh, Son of Heaven, had been listening to Yen Kui Kiang, in company with his councillors and mandarins of the tribunal of ceremonies, as the chronicler read from the books of Confucius. Always, said Yen Kui Kiang, in his chronicles, Hang-Hi listened to words of the great Confucius before undertaking to judge cases that came to him for trial, in order that his mind might be open and just.

The man who commanded a Chinese army to the number of two hundred thousand was tall, with a portly figure, imposing in his robe of blue-and-gold silk embroidered with a miniature dragon and the likeness of Kwan-Ti, god of war. His eyes were dark and brilliant, and his arms crossed on his breast were the arms of a wrestler.

The ebony and lacquer Hall of Judgment was occupied only by Hang-Hi's advisors and lieutenants, seated in order of rank on each side of the carpet that ran up the center of the hall to the dais on which the viceroy of the Son of Heaven sat.

At Hang-Hi's side sat Chan Kieh Shi, old and wizened, a veteran of a hundred battles, who had no equal at chess play. It was Chan Kieh Shi who had brought the heavy cannon from Persia that were battering down the walls of Altur Haiten, and who had sworn an oath on his ancestral tablets to bury the last of the Khans of Tatary, the hereditary enemies of the Son of Heaven, before he died.

This evening, Yen Kui Kiang relates, only one case was brought to judgment. That was the case of a stranger, Khlit, called the Wolf, and Mir Turek, a resident of Samarkand whose great-grandfather had been a mandarin.

When the attendant of the Hall of Judgment brought in the two prisoners, the eyes of the Chinese council surveyed them impassively. Behind the slant eyes lurked the cruelty of a conquering race and the craft of the wisest men in Asia. Not once during the startling events of the evening, did the slant eyes open wide or the breath come faster in the thin lips.

They noted silently that while one prisoner, the man called Mir Turek, prostrated himself before the dais, the other, called Khlit, stood erect with folded arms, although heavily chained. Especially did Chan Kieh Shi watch Khlit, while the Chinaman's fan moved slowly before his face. The fan was inscribed with the battles he had won.

When the attendant had brought a curved sword to the dais and laid it at Hang-Hi's feet, Yen Kui Kiang bowed before Hang-Hi.

"Gracious Excellency," the secretary said softly, "the man at your feet is one called Mir Turek, although he has a Chinese name. He was found in Samarkand by one of our agents. Many times he has sworn that he would aid the cause of the Son of Heaven and remain true to the faith of his ancestors. The man called Mir Turek says that he has news for you, such news as will earn him absolution from his neglect. He swears that he has been working for Wanleh, and that he is ready to show the fruits of his work."

"And the other, Yen Kui Kiang," put in Chan Kieh Shi abruptly, "who is he?"

"I do not know, Excellency," the secretary said, "he was taken a few nights ago with Mir Turek, and he has twice tried to break free."

"Oh, gracious Excellency," said Mir Turek, eagerly, "give your servant leave to speak his news, and you shall know of this man."

Receiving a nod of assent from the general, the merchant hurried on, his voice trembling.

"This man, called Khlit, the Wolf, a Russian Cossack, came to my house in Samarkand. I was curious, for he speaks as one having high authority, yet he had no rank or wealth. When he showed me his sword I saw the answer. Knowing how valuable the man's secret would be to your Excellency, I hastened to bring him, unknowing, to the army before Altur Haiten. Truly, Khlit's secret is written on his sword. He can not read. And he can not understand what we are saying."

As one, the eyes of the council turned to Khlit. The Cossack stood erect without noticing them, gazing moodily at his curved sword which lay at the feet of Hang-Hi. It had been taken from him the night of his capture, and for the first time since he had received it from his father other hands had held the blade. And, Kerula, in spite of her prayers to be allowed to share his prison tent had been taken away, he knew not where.

Khlit had made two efforts to escape, without result other than the heavy chains he wore on wrists and ankles. He had shared his tent with Mir Turek. Fogan Ultai had disappeared. Khlit had not been slow to lay his seizure on Fogan Ultai and he had sworn an oath that the other should repent it. Now he waited proudly for what was to come.

"Gracious Excellency," Mir Turek went on, bowing, "I saw that the man's face resembled a Russian Tatar, and the message of the sword showed that I was right. Lo, I am a student of learned books, a humble follower in the path of Hang-Hi and his men of wisdom. The sword, Khlit said, had been handed down from father to son for many generations, and in truth the inscription is ancient.

"It says on the sword," Mir Turek pointed to the blade, "that it was the sword of Kaidu, great khan of the Kallmark Tatars, and descendant of Genghis Khan. Khlit, although he does not know it, is one of the few who are of the royal blood of the Grand Khans of Tatary."

The fan of Chan Kieh Shi paused for a second and resumed its sweep. Hang-Hi glanced impassively from Khlit to Mir Turek and bent over the sword, studying the inscription. It was the first time he had had a sword of the Grand Khans at his feet.

"Wherefore, Excellency," hastened Mir Turek, "I brought Khlit, called the Wolf, to the mountains of Khantai Khan on a pretense of finding treasure, hoping to yield him prisoner to your Graciousness, and atone for my absence from the empire, and perhaps earn a place among your men of wisdom."

Mir Turek bowed anxiously and stepped back at a sign from the attendant. His face was bathed in sweat but his eyes were gleaming with a feverish hope.

"Is this all you have to tell?" asked Hang-Hi.

"That is all, Excellency," responded Mir Turek.

But his eyes fell. For he thought of the mountains of Khantai Khan and the tomb of untold riches.

"Call the agent from Samarkand, who has taken the name of Fogan Ultai," said Hang-Hi.

Mir Turek's eyes swept the assembly in sudden fear. He had known of the mission of Fogan Ultai, but he had hoped he would not be confronted with the secret agent of all-powerful Wanleh. Fogan Ultai was very crafty.

Khlit stirred for the first time when he saw Fogan Ultai enter the tribunal. The erstwhile master of the slaves was dressed in the silken robe of a mandarin of caste. Around his neck was suspended a gold disk wrought in the likeness of a sun. The councillors who were of lesser rank than Fogan Ultai rose and bowed. The agent advanced to the dais, bowing low three times, and touched his forehead. Khlit's arms strained at the chains, then dropped to his side. The attendant was beside him with drawn sword, and he waited.

"Tell the one called Khlit," suggested Chan Kieh Shi softly, "the truth of his descent. Then he will suffer more greatly under our punishment."

Thus it was that Khlit, the Cossack named the Wolf, came to know in the tribunal of Hang-Hi, that he was descended from the Grand Khans, hereditary rulers of Tatary and enemies of China. No name was hated by the Chinese like the name of Tatar.

He listened to Fogan Ultai's words without change of countenance. His people had been of the same race as the Tatars. And he had won the respect of Tal Taulai Khan, his brother in blood, and of the Kallmarks. Khlit's only allegiance in life had been to his sword. He exulted in the knowledge that he had come of a royal line. It did not surprise him that the fact had not been known before. In the bloody warfare of Cossack and Tatar the man was lucky who could name his race beyond his grandfather. At the same time he was aware of the danger he stood from the Chinese.

"Ask him," said Hang-Hi curiously, "what he would say to us, now that he is our prisoner?"

Fogan Ultai spoke with Khlit and turned to the general thoughtfully.

"Excellency," he said slowly, "this man is no common man. He has the wisdom of a fox and the courage of a wounded wolf. He asks which should be honored, a royal prisoner or the man who betrayed him?"

X

Khlit's next act was to ask for Kerula. He had sought for information of the girl, but no one had told him where she was. Fogan Ultai bared his teeth as he answered, for he remembered how Khlit had made him, a mandarin of high caste, bring food to the girl.

Kerula, he told Khlit, had been offered the choice of two things, when she had come before him. She had been taken to the Chinese camp with the two others. And Fogan Ultai had given her the choice of becoming a slave with the captives who labored at the siege work, or of joining the household of Hang-Hi. The child, he said, was fair of face and body. She had chosen to become one of the women of the household when she was told that Khlit was a captive and his sword taken from him.

Khlit became silent at this, and moody. He could not blame the girl for her choice. She had chosen life instead of hardships and death. And she was young. Fogan Ultai turned to Hang-Hi with a low bow.

"Excellency, Almighty Commander of the Ming host, the man, Mir Turek, lied when he said he had told you all he knew. He knows a secret of great importance. This secret is what first took me to Samarkand, for I had heard that a scholar of that city had said that he knew the hiding-place of the treasure of Genghis Khan."

Mir Turek started and would have thrown himself prostrate before Hang-Hi, but the attendant restrained him.

"In Samarkand," went on Fogan Ultai, "I joined the household of Mir Turek, showing him, in order to avoid menial service, the gold-rayed sun which he recognized. I was not able to learn his secret, for Mir Turek was crafty and he suspected me. When he joined company with the Tatar, Khlit, descendant of Kaidu, I came with them across the desert to the mountains of Khantai Khan. From what I overheard and the words of the girl of Mir Turek, Kerula, I knew that they had come to find the tomb of Genghis Khan.

"One day Mir Turek and his companion visited the mountains in my absence, and it is certain they went to the place of the treasure. Knowing that Mir Turek planned to deliver Khlit a prisoner to you, I waited until they had come within our lines, when I took them with some men I had posted for that purpose. Thus Mir Turek lied, for he kept from you the secret of the treasure which is very great."

Fogan Ultai folded his arms into his silken sleeves and waited with bent head. Mir Turek's agonized gaze went from face to face that was turned to him and he tried to speak but could not.

"Your plan was excellent, Fogan Ultai," said Hang-Hi at length. Turning to his favorite general the commander asked: "What is your word concerning Mir Turek, Chan Kieh Shi?"

Chan Kieh Shi shrugged his bent shoulders slightly. He was the advisor of Hang-Hi. Sometimes he thought that the latter asked too often for his advice. He wondered what the famous commander would do without him.

"Pour molten silver into the ears of Mir Turek until he tells us the place of the treasure. Then we shall have the Tatar hoard of wealth, at the same time that we slay the Jun-gar khans in Altur Haiten, and your Excellency's wars will be over."

Mir Turek stretched out his arms imploringly.

"Oh, Gracious One—Viceroy of the Son of Heaven, harken. Truly I planned to take you to the place of the treasure of Genghis Khan. Yet is the place perilous. The Onon Muren watch over it—the gods allow no one to come there—"

"Even the gods," said Hang-Hi ominously, "pay homage to the victor in the conflict. So it says in the sacred book."

He lifted his hand to the attendant who stood beside the trembling merchant with bared sword.

"Strike once," he said, "and sever the sinews of the traitor behind the knees. Thus will he learn to kneel to me. Strike again and slit his mouth wide into both cheeks. Thus he may learn to speak the truth."

A shriek from the unhappy Mir Turek was silenced as the armed attendant swung his short sword, without hesitation, against the back of the man's legs. Mir Turek fell to his knees. Khlit, looking around in surprise, saw the man in armor take the face of Mir Turek in the hollow of his arm. In spite of the merchant's struggles, the other twice drew the sharp edge of his weapon against Mir Turek's mouth. A choking form, prostrate on the floor, hands pressed against his bleeding mouth, was all that remained of Mir Turek.

Khlit took a deep breath and his eyes sought Hang-Hi's. The commander bent over Mir Turek.

"You will not die until you have shown us the way to the tomb of Genghis Khan, Mir Turek," he said softly. "How am I to trust a man without honor?"

At a sign from him Khlit and the moaning Mir Turek were conducted to their tent. By signs the guard indicated that the crippled man was to remain in the tent, while Khlit must take his turn at labor with the other captives.

For several days while the merchant lay tossing on the floor of the tent, Khlit went out at night under guard to the siege works of the Chinese engineers. With other Tatar captives he hauled heavy stones for the Persian cannon, and dug earthworks opposite the walls of Altur Haiten under the arrows of the Tatar defenders.

Never had Khlit seen a battle like this, and his interest grew each night that he worked. The Chinese had pushed a network of earthen mounds, backed by leather and timbers to within a few feet of the crumbling walls where they planned to deliver their final assault. Beyond bowshot of the walls the giant Persian cannon were ranged which steadily enlarged the breaches in the brick ramparts to the east.

The Chinese were not content to demolish the walls which were breached at several points. A fire from a few muskets was kept up at the Tatars who sought to man the ramparts. Mangonels, formed of giant beams, cast buckets of unquenchable fire, prepared by the special firemakers of Hang-Hi over the walls. Into the city beyond, iron chests were dropped by the mangonels. These chests held powder, lighted by a fuse which exploded after they had fallen in the houses.

Against the Chinese the Tatars made only feeble efforts. Being naturally mounted fighters, accustomed to warfare on the plains, the defenders were at a disadvantage which was heightened by their lack of firearms. Arrows did little damage against the earthworks of the besiegers which lined the eastern side.

The Tatars, numbering about seventy thousand fighting men, Khlit discovered from the captives, had given up assaults against the Chinese. They still had their horses which subsisted on the fields between the walls and the city proper, but each sortie from the gates had been greeted by heavy musketry fire, and the terrible flames of the fire-makers.

Khlit saw that the plight of the defenders was near desperate. They awaited the day, with the fortitude of their race, when Hang-Hi should storm the walls. The Jun-gar khans, he heard, quarreled and drank their time away.

Khlit helped feed the cannon, toiling half-naked at the giant stones. He became silent, and made no effort to resent the whips of the Chinese overseers that scorched his back when he rested. Much he thought over the words of Fogan Ultai. His identity as a descendant of the Grand Khans, he knew, would earn him death with the fall of the city, or later at the court of Wanleh. The thought of dying a captive was bitter.

Kerula had gone from his existence. Khlit had not had many companions, but the girl had touched his heart—perhaps with her tales of the Tatar warriors. He took a grim satisfaction in the sufferings of Mir Turek. He had no hope of escape, chained and under guard. Yet Khlit counted the blows of the Chinese overseers and remembered them.

XI

It was one night when he was stumbling with fatigue, and had lost thought of everything except the stones he was hauling and the count of the blows he received that Khlit heard from Kerula. That night hope came to him again, and all his old craft.

One of his guards halted him abruptly by the cannon, and urged him back toward the tent. The guards habitually vented their fear of the followers of Genghis Khan on the prisoners.

"Come, Tatar," he said in broken Usbek, "there is a woman of the royal household that asks for you among the prisoners. Why does she want to see a dog? We must do her bidding, for she wears the clothes of a favorite."

The tent of the two prisoners was lighted by the glow from the fire caldrons near by. Khlit's heart leaped as he saw a cloaked, slender form standing beside the couch of Mir Turek. He had guessed who it was, before the girl had pushed the guards from the tent and closed the flap.

The cloak fell back from her face and Khlit stared. It was Kerula, but her cheeks were red with henna, and her eyebrows blackened and arched. Her long hair was tied in a close knot, and its scent came to his nostrils.

She gave a low cry as she saw the half-naked figure of Khlit, his body blackened with powder and dirt. She pointed inquiringly to where Mir Turek gazed at them helplessly from his couch.

"Tell me, Khlit, lord," Kerula whispered, her face close to his, tinged with the red of the flames outside, "will Mir Turek live? He told me how grievously he suffered. What have they done to you? I searched for two days and nights before I found you. Did you think I would forget you, Khlit, lord?"

Khlit crossed his powerful arms on his chest.

"The thought was mine, Kerula," he said quietly. "Yet I believed that you were the one to feel pain, not I. As for Mir Turek, he is dying of his hurts."

The girl raised her head proudly, although her cheeks flamed.

"Aye," she said, "I have suffered. I am your slave. It was my will to serve you. So I chose to go to the pavilion of Hang-Hi instead of the siege works."

"I do not understand," Khlit shook his head. "The household of the Chinese general will give you comforts and you will have honor—of a kind."

"Nay, Khlit, lord, it was for you."

The girl smiled at him eagerly. With a glance at Mir Turek she stepped closer.

"I saw them take your sword from you. Your curved sword. And my heart was heavy. Tell me, will not the noble Tatar khans come from Altur Haiten and break the power of Hang-Hi? I told them so at the pavilion, but they laughed, saying that Genghis Khan was dead."

"The noble khans," said Khlit bitterly, "will not attack."

"They will, they must. And you must join them, Khlit, lord, when they do so. See, this is why I went to the household of Hang-Hi. They watched it carefully, but I was too clever for them. I took it from them to give to you. See—"

The girl felt under her silk cloak and drew

out a weapon which she pressed into Khlit's hand. He stared at it dumbly.

"It is your curved sword, Khlit, the sword that makes men afraid of you. As soon as I had taken it I came to find you."

Khlit took his sword in his hand and touched it lovingly. He eyed the inscription curiously. Surely, Kerula had been faithful to him.

"If no one suspects you, Kerula," he said gruffly, for he was moved, "go whence you have come. The tent is dangerous, for Fogan Ultai is coming at dawn and he must not find you."

"I have made you glad," said the girl softly, "and my heart is light. I do not want to leave you, but if they found me they would suspect. Now that you have your curved sword they will not keep you prisoner, will they? Harken, Khlit, lord." She drew off a slender silken girdle that confined her cloak. "When one Tatar and another are true friends they become *andas*. Each helps and protects the other. Give me your girdle."

Puzzled, Khlit lifted his sash from the pile of his discarded clothing. At a sign from the girl he bound it around her slim waist under the cloak. She touched his hand shyly as he did so. Then she tied her own girdle around him.

"Now we are comrades, Khlit, lord, although I am still a slave. Truly the honor is great and I am happy. When two persons become *andas* both have one life; neither abandons the other, and each guards the life of his *anda*. Thus we strengthen our *anda* anew and refresh it."

"Aye," said Khlit gruffly, "I will protect you, little sparrow."

At a warning sound from the guards outside the tent Kerula slipped away, with a glance at Mir Turek, who turned his mutilated face away. No one else entered and Khlit seated himself in a corner of the tent. He took his sheepskin coat and tied the sword deftly in the lining. The coat he placed over his shoulders. Until the gray light of dawn lightened the tent he remained motionless. He did not sleep, nor did Mir Turek who lay moaning and gasping for breath. The fire that stood in a caldron by Mir Turek's bed was

smoldering to embers when Khlit arose, casting aside his coat and came to the bed of the other.

"Mir Turek," he said softly, "Hang-Hi has made you a cripple. Fogan Ultai is coming to get you to show the way to the tomb of Genghis Khan. Yet you will not do it. Do you fear greatly? I have no fear."

The merchant raised himself on his elbow and his ghastly face peered at Khlit.

"Mir Turek, Fogan Ultai would throw you down the chasm to the Muren, when you have shown him the path. You have bled much, and your heart is weakening until death stands near tonight. We two, Mir Turek, know of the tomb of Genghis Khan. You will not live to take him there at dawn."

A hoarse sound came from the throat of Mir Turek and his eyes sought Khlit's feverishly.

"Man, born to life is deathless, Mir Turek," resumed Khlit slowly. "He must go hence without home, without resting-place. So said the great Genghis Khan. A few days ago I saved your life. But now you are dying and I can not save you."

Mir Turek sank back upon his couch, shuddering. Khlit looked at him not angrily, but sadly, as at one who was no longer a man. Death, he thought, would be a good friend to Mir Turek. And he would watch until it had come, freeing him from his pain.

XII

The sentries were dozing on their spears outside the door of the tent in the early dawn when they were awakened by the crackle of flames. There was a crash as of the lacquer sides of the tent falling in and a burst of flames swirled up behind their backs.

The door of the tent was thrust open and Khlit staggered out, his garments smoking. Inside the door they could see a wall of flame that caught at the woodwork and hangings of the structure. The sentry who spoke Usbek shook Khlit by the shoulder.

"Where is the other?" he shouted, stepping back from the heat of the fire.

Khlit drew his long coat closer about him, so that the hidden sword could not be seen. "Go and bring him forth, dog!" he snarled. "How can a man in chains carry another?"

But he knew that no man could go into the flames. He had waited until the last moment before coming out, so that the flames might get to the remains of Mir Turek. Thus he had seen to it that the body was not dishonored. And now no one but Khlit knew the way to the tomb of Genghis Khan.

An angry shout caused them to turn. Several men had ridden up on camels, and Fogan Ultai dismounted. The agent of Wanleh caught the chief sentry by the throat furiously.

The unhappy man pointed to the burning tent and Fogan Ultai released him with a curse. He scanned the flames for a moment. Then he faced Khlit and the Cossack saw that his slant eyes were cold and hard as those of a snake.

"This is your doing, Khlit," he snarled. "Once before, in the desert you slew a man of mine. You have taken the life of Mir Turek. Your turn will not wait. The torture will be finer, and longer, for this."

"Aye, Khlit," said the voice of Chan Kieh Shi behind him, "you will see if the blood of Kaidu is truly in you. We will take your life slowly, so you will not die for three days."

Khlit threw back his head and laughed, and the sentries wondered.

"When you are dead," resumed Fogan Ultai with relish, "your head will be cast over the ramparts of Altur Haiten, and the Tatar dogs will know we have slain one of their breed."

"Nay," said Khlit grimly, "it is not I that am a dog! Was it I that made Mir Turek a beast that crawled to death? Did I send the *gylong* to murder a child in the desert? Men have not named me dog but Wolf. And the wolf knows well the ways of the dog."

"When Hang-Hi rides into the city of Altur Haiten," growled Chan Kieh Shi, pointing a withered finger at Khlit, "you shall bear him company, tied to his horse's tail. Thus will the Tatars know their kind."

"Truly, Fogan Ultai," said Khlit, "a man who is feared is greatly honored. You do me honor in spite of yourselves."

"Is this honor?" The agent struck him viciously across the face with his whip. "Or this?"

"Aye," laughed Khlit, "for the overseer has done me greater homage. He had struck me twenty-eight times."

Fogan Ultai fingered his sword longingly, but Chan Kieh Shi made a warning gesture.

"Then you can count the days until your death, which will be when Altur Haiten is sacked."

"Nay," replied Khlit, "I shall not die."

"Dog!" Fogan Ultai spat in his direction. "Hang-Hi has promised it me."

Khlit stepped to the camel's side.

"Fool!" he snarled, "blind jackal! If you kill me there will be no one to show you the way to the tomb of Genghis Khan. Mir Turek knew the secret, but he is dead."

Fogan Ultai's expression did not change but his eyes consulted Chan Kieh Shi. The old general stared long at Khlit. He spoke quickly to Fogan Ultai, and then turned to Khlit.

"We shall find the way to the tomb," he said. "The torture will make you take us there."

Khlit appeared to consider this.

"Will Hang-Hi give me my freedom if I take you to the tomb?"

"If you show us the treasure of Genghis Khan—" Fogan Ultai's slant eyes closed cunningly—"Hang-Hi may give you freedom."

"Aye," added Chan Kieh Shi, "he may do so."

Again, Khlit seemed to ponder their words. He raised several objections which Fogan Ultai met shortly. Finally he raised his manacled hands.

"How can I climb the mountains of Khantai Khan in chains?" he asked.

At a sign from Chan Kieh Shi the sentries unlocked Khlit's chains around his arms, and at his request from his feet. He was led to a camel and mounted, thrusting his arms into the sleeves of his coat and wrapping it about him. He hugged his sword fastened to the inside of his coat, over his chest, close to him as they started. Khlit rode in the center, with Fogan Ultai and Chan Kieh Shi one on either side and two spearmen to the rear. Khlit smiled grimly as he noted that they had given him the clumsiest camel.

He did not put trust in the promise of Fogan Ultai. More than once he caught the agent looking at him contemptuously, sidelong. But he said nothing.

They passed out of the Chinese encampment and gained the plain. Khlit headed toward the Kukulon Lake. The group rode without speaking, Khlit busied with his thoughts. There was no hope of breaking free from his guards, he saw, and he did not intend to try.

Khlit had been playmate with death for many years. He had never, however, planned to come so close to death as at the cavern of Khantai Khan, by the Onon Muren. He circled the lake in the path Mir Turek had taken. He thought of the dead merchant, and it occurred to him that he was the only survivor of the four who had ventured into the tomb of Genghis Khan. Verily, he marveled, the Onon Muren watched over the treasure well.

He noted grimly how his companions stared at the skeletons in the lake. But he did not pause when they dismounted from the camels, pressing onward over the gray soil, among the blasted trees. Fogan Ultai had fallen silent, and more than once the agent stopped and stared about him curiously as Khlit had done. Chan Kieh Shi, however, pushed ahead as fast as his bent legs could carry him.

At the Kukulon gate Khlit paused to explain to his companions how they must go under the waterfall. They followed him without hesitation, first the mandarins, then the guards. Khlit stood again in the cavern under the falls and smelled the strange odor that came from the chasm. Here he noted that Fogan Ultai spoke with Chan Kieh Shi but the old man replied impatiently and pushed on.

Still Khlit had not spoken. They felt their way to the light that came down the corridor, Chan Kieh Shi turning over with his foot the Tatar forms that lined the way. They came out into the light and stood on the ledge by the rock bridge.

Khlit pointed silently to the giant forms outlined in the vapor on the other side of the bridge. The Chinese stared curiously about them, at the gray vault overhead and the chasm.

For the second time Khlit stood before the tomb of his ancestor. He raised his hand as if in greeting to the casket that hung between the golden elephants. Then he drew his belt closer about him, and spoke for the first time.

"There is the tomb," he said, "come!"

Fogan Ultai stepped back cautiously, motioning for him to go ahead. As he advanced the Chinese followed closely, their eyes straining on the dim forms across the chasm through the mist.

Khlit bent his head low on his chest and raised the sleeve of his coat against his mouth and nose. He broke into a run as he stepped on the rock bridge. He felt the vapors warm his face and heard the rumbling below. On he ran, without looking back. He heard a sound that was not the rumbling of the mountain.

His brain was dizzy as the stifling fumes gripped him. Staggering forward he fell to his knees and crawled onward. Biting his lips to keep from breathing the poison he gained the further end of the bridge and the clearer air of the plateau. A cold breeze from some cavern drove the vapors back. Khlit had crossed the rock bridge in safety.

He climbed to his feet, supporting himself by one of the legs of the elephants. His hand touched a long pole, and he glanced at it. The pole supported a crest of horns hung with a hundred yaks' tails. Khlit knew that he held the standard of Genghis Khan.

Leaning on the standard for support he looked back the way he had come. On the rock bridge one man was crawling, choking and gasping. Khlit saw that it was one of the guards, the last to venture on the bridge. He watched the man draw himself forward. The Chinese, blinded and strangling, slipped to the side of the rock bridge. Vainly he tried to gain his balance, clutching at the smooth rock. His hold slipped, Khlit heard a hoarse cry, and a white figure dropped into the depths of the chasm, after the others.

Khlit was alone in the tomb of Genghis Khan.

The Cossack seated himself against the form of the Bearer of Wealth. His eyes wandered idly over the standard, gray with dust, above him. Then he stretched out at full length on the rock, and in a little while was asleep.

XIII

In times which are gone thou didst swoop
    like a falcon before us; today a car bears
    thee as it rumbles, advancing,
Oh thou, my Khan.
Hast thou left us; hast thou left wife and
    children, and the *kurultai* of thy na-
    tion?
Oh thou, my Khan.
Sweeping forward in pride, as sweeps for-
    ward an eagle, thou didst lead us afore-
    time,
Oh thou, my Khan.
Thou didst bring triumph and joy to thy
    people for sixty and six years; art thou
    leaving them now?
Oh thou, my Khan.
        Death chant of Genghis Khan.

The night sentries were dozing at the door of the *kurultai* hall where the Tatar chieftains of the Jun-gar were assembled. In the hall, where the sound of the Chinese cannon echoed at intervals, were the nine khans that ruled what was left of the Tatar race on the borderland of China. Here was the leader of the Kalkas horde, from Karakorum, the chief of the Chakars, whose people had been between the Great Wall and the desert of Gobi, the commander of the Eleuts, and others.

The ranks of the commanders of the Tatars were thinned. A Kallmark khan had left Altur Haiten with his followers when they deserted the ill-fated city. The leaders of the Hoshot and Torgot hordes had fallen in unsuccessful sallies. Evil was the plight of the chiefs of the Jun-gar, and they drank deeply, to forget.

They lay on benches around the long table of the *kurultai* council, swords and spears stacked against the walls, waiting for word of the expected attack of the army of Hang-Hi. For a year they had been directing the defense of the walls, leaders of horsemen penned in a citadel. They were veteran fighters, but they were weary and there had been many quarrels over the wine goblets.

They had been drinking deeply, these lords of Tatary, and few looked up when a man entered the hall. Yet these few did not again lay their heads upon the table. They stared in amazement and rose to their feet, feeling for swords.

The man who had come in was tall, with gray mustaches hanging to his broad shoulders. His face was scarred, and his eyes alert. His heavy boots were covered with gray dust, as was his *svitza*.

High was the ceiling of the hall, yet the standard of yaks' tails, which the man carried reached nearly to the ceiling. It was a standard like those of the Jun-gar, but of a different pattern. It bore a gold image of the sun and moon, tarnished by age.

Without speaking the man stood in the doorway and looked at the chiefs of the Jun-gar. Leaning on the stout pole of the standard, he watched them and his mouth curled in a snarl.

"Who are you, warrior, and what do you seek?" asked a khan whose head was clearer than the others. "What standard do you bring to the *kurultai*?"

One by one the sleepy warriors awakened, and fixed their eyes on the newcomer. A veteran, chief of the Chakars, gave a hoarse cry as he saw the standard of yaks' tails and rose dizzily fighting the wine fumes in his brain.

"Who are you, Standard-Bearer?" he asked.

Still the stranger did not speak. He leaned on the pole, and watched them until the last of the chieftains had risen.

"Evil is the day," he said in broken Tatar, "when the Jun-gar khans put aside their swords for the wine cup."

"Who is it that speaks thus to the Jun-gar chiefs?" asked the Chakar veteran. "These are not the words of a common man."

"My name is Khlit," said the newcomer, gazing at the circle of watchers, "and I am the Standard-Bearer of Genghis Khan. I have come from the tomb of the Master of the Earth with the banner of the sun and moon, because there will be a great battle, aye, such a battle as has not been for many years—since the Grand Khans were dead."

In the silence that followed the chieftains consulted each other with their eyes. The man who had appeared in the hall had startled them, and the Jun-gar khans felt a quick dread. The words of Khlit did not reassure them. The old Chakar leader stepped close to the standard and ran his eye over each detail of the design and emblems. He faced Khlit and his face was stern.

"Whence came this warrior?" he spoke in his gruff tones. "Answer truly, for a lie will earn death. The banner of Genghis Khan was like this, yet it has been buried for generations in the hills of Khantai Khan."

"From the tomb in the hills of Khantai Khan came this," said Khlit grimly. "From where the Onon Muren watch, by the Kukulon gate. I have slept at the tomb of Genghis Khan, among the twenty thousand slain. Have the chieftains of the Jun-gar forgotten the standard of a thousand battles?"

"Nay," said the old man, "it is truly the banner of Genghis Khan. For here, by the sun and moon are the emblems of the old hordes, the wolf of the Kallmarks, the doe of the Chakars—"

The other chieftains crowded around the two, and their slant eyes gleamed at Khlit. In the eyes he read amazement, suspicion, and uncertainty. Khlit saw that they but half-believed the words of the elder. He raised his hand for attention.

"Harken, lords of the Jun-gar," he said slowly. "You ask who I am. I am a fighter of the steppes and I follow the paths of battles. I found the road to the tomb of Genghis Khan, looking for treasure. Yet while I slept in the tomb a thought and a plan came to me. Genghis Khan is dead. Yet the thought came to me. It was to carry the standard that stood in the tomb to the chiefs of the Jun-gar, through the Chinese lines, so that they might have new heart for battle. If you truly believe this to be the standard of the Mighty Manslayer, I will tell you the plan, for words of wisdom should not fall on dead ears. Speak, do you believe?"

The chieftains looked at each other with bleared eyes. Then the Chakar lord raised both hands and bowed his head.

"Said I not this was the banner? Aye, it is an omen."

One by one the Jun-gar chiefs raised their hands and bowed. In their hearts was the dread of the name of the Mighty Manslayer. One of their number stepped forward.

"Aye," he said slowly, "this is the standard that was buried. But it belongs to the grave of the One. The man who brought it from the grave will die, for it is written that none shall come from the tomb of Genghis Khan and live. Shall we keep the standard for the men of Hang-Hi to carry to Liang Yang? Altur Haiten and all in it are doomed. How may we keep the standard, when it can not serve us, except to fall into the hands of the enemies of Genghis Khan and make their triumph greater?"

"Not so," said Khlit, "for there will be a great battle. And the standard of the dead Khan should be with the men who are the remnants of his power. There is fear in the hearts of the Chinese at the name of Genghis Khan."

He saw, however, that the Tatars had been impressed with the speech of their companion. Even the Chakar khan nodded his head in agreement to what the other had said.

"The battle," continued the khan, "will be the assault of the city. How can we prevent it? Hang-Hi has a quarter million men. We have a scant sixty-five thousand horsemen. The Chinese have driven us from the Wall of Shensi and across the desert to Altur Haiten. Many Tatars died in the desert. Those in Altur Haiten are deserting by night to go to their homes. The engines of the Chinese are breaching the walls. We have only spears and arrows to fight against gunpowder. Our food supplies are running out, and the men fight among themselves for what is left. We are shut in on four sides. The men are losing their strength from lack of food."

A murmur of assent went up. Khlit found no encouragement in the yellow faces that were lined with weariness and drunkenness.

"If we were in the plains," said the Chakar chief, "there might be hope. But our sallies have been repulsed. We are penned in the city. Truly, Hang-Hi is too great a general to outwit."

"Fools!" Khlit's lips curled in scorn. "Would Genghis Khan fear such a man as Hang-Hi? I have seen him, and he is like a fat woman. I have seen the fortifications of the Chinese and the cannon. They can be taken."

"The earthworks keep us from attacking on the east," returned the Chakar leader, "and the walls are breached so that an army can march through." He laid his hand on the pole. "What is the word of the *kurultai*, noble lords; shall we lay the standard of Genghis Khan in the flames, so that it will not be taken by the enemy? This man must not have it, for no low-born hand should touch it. Such is the law."

An assenting shout went up. Instantly Khlit snatched his sword from its sheath. The Chakar khan was quick, or his hand would have been severed from his arm. As it was, Khlit's sword slit the skin of his fingers which dripped blood. The others reached for their weapons angrily. Khlit raised his sword as they closed about him.

"Aye," he said gruffly, "no low-born hand shall touch the standard. I will keep it, for I am of the blood of the Grand Khans. My sword

which was my father's and his before him bears witness. Read the writings, dogs!"

Several of the Tatars scanned the inscription and wonder replaced the rage in their slant eyes. The Chakar chief broke the silence.

"I bear no grudge," he said, "for this man is of the royal blood. How otherwise could he come from the tomb and live? It is so written. Yet shall he burn the standard rather than let it fall into the hands of the Chinese."

"If I am the keeper of the standard," growled Khlit, "shall I burn what it is my duty to protect?"

He leaned on the pole and watched the Jungar chiefs. Khlit had brought the standard from the tomb with him with much difficulty, into Altur Haiten because he saw an opportunity to throw in his lot with the defeated Tatars. He counted on the banner restoring their spirit. He had not counted on the reception he met, but all his cunning was aroused to make the Jun-gar chiefs believe in the standard of the dead conqueror as an omen of victory.

He planned to place all his cunning, with the talisman of Genghis Khan, to the aid of the weakening chieftains. He understood the plan of the Chinese camp, thanks to his experience as a prisoner. And he was burning to seek revenge for the twenty-nine blows that had been given him. Kerula had named him her *anda*. The girl had sacrificed herself for him, and Khlit was determined to win her back alive or take payment for her death. And the prospect of the coming battle intoxicated him.

Already he had won the Jun-gar to acknowledgment of the standard and of his right to advise them. But he proceeded warily.

"As one of the royal blood, oh Khan," said the man shrewdly who had first objected, "you will take the command from us? We will yield you the command, for since Tal Taulai Khan died we have had no one of the blood of Kaidu on the frontier."

"As one of the royal blood, Chief," responded Khlit dryly, for he saw jealousy flame in the faces of the others, "I shall carry the standard of Genghis Khan. Is not that the greatest honor? You and your companions will lead the hordes, for I have come only to bring the banner, and to tell you the plan that came to me in the tomb of Genghis Khan. Do not insult my ears further by saying that the standard should be burned, however."

He saw understanding come into the faces of the Jun-gar, and they sheathed their swords.

"Did the spirit of Genghis Khan suggest this plan to you?" asked the Chakar.

But Khlit was not to be trapped.

"As I slept in the tomb the plan came to me," he said. "Who am I to say whence it came? I am not a man of wisdom, but a fighter."

"Harken, men of the Jun-gar," he went on, raising his voice, "you say that your men are deserting? Will they desert if the banner of Genghis Khan leads them? You say that the Chinese engines are breaching the walls. Are we prisoners, to stay behind walls? You say that your men are horsemen. Let them fight, then, as horsemen."

The Chakar khan bowed low. This time he kneeled and the others followed his example.

"Speak, warrior," he said, "for we will listen. Tell us your plan and our ears will not be dead. We, also, are fighters, not men of wisdom."

XIV

The day set for the capture of Altur Haiten by Hang-Hi dawned fair upon the activity of the Chinese camp. A pavilion of silk, supported by bamboo poles and hung with banners, was erected for the general of Wanleh on a rise fronting the eastern walls of the city which had been breached for the assault.

Hang-Hi's lieutenants had made final preparations for the attack the night before. Junks, moored at the river bank, had brought extra powder and supplies from China. Scaling ladders had been assembled in the earthworks. The ditch around the city had been filled in long ago by Chinese engineers. The cannon were loaded and primed for the salvo that was to start the attack.

Early in the day Hang-Hi took his station in the pavilion where he could see the eastern walls. Past the pavilion marched streams of bannermen with picked footmen and regiments in complete armor. Hang-Hi's advisors assembled by his chair. But the general wore a frown.

"Has no trace been found," he asked Yen Kui Kiang, impatiently, "of Chan Kieh Shi?"

The secretary bowed low and crossed his arms in his sleeves.

"Gracious Excellency," he explained, "riders have searched the surrounding country. They have been to the mountains of Khantai Khan. Chan Kieh Shi went with the agent, Fogan Ultai, to find the tomb of Genghis Khan, and since that day we have found no sign—"

"Fool!" Hang-Hi struck his ivory wand against his knee. "Tell me not what I know already. Have you learned that Chan Kieh Shi lives?"

"Nay, Excellency," muttered the secretary, "we know not."

"There are volcanos in the mountains of Khantai Khan," mused Hang-Hi, "and our men have been troubled by the sulfur fumes, which the Tatars fear, not knowing their nature. It is possible—"

He broke off, for some of his men were staring at him curiously. Hang-Hi did not desire to let them know how much he felt the loss of the wisest of the Chinese generals. Still, there was nothing to fear. The Tatars, his spies had reported, were weak with hunger and torn by divided leadership. Their number was small. And his preparations for the attack were flawless. It could not fail.

"Excellency," ventured Yen Kui Kiang, "new reports from spies have come in. They say that the people of Altur Haiten are talking much of Genghis Khan. Our spies heard mention of his tomb. It may be that they hope for a miracle to save them."

"There are no miracles, Yen Kui Kiang," said Hang-Hi softly, "and Genghis Khan is dead. Why should I fear a dead man? Yet the tomb—Mir Turek said that was where the treasure of the Tatars was hidden. It may be that one of them found the tomb—"

"Send me the girl Kerula, who was taken with Mir Turek," he said after a moment. "She may know something of the treasure. Still, the Tatar dogs can not eat gold, nor can they melt it into swords."

He waited when one of the mandarins of the court of ceremonies read to him the annals of the court, until the girl was brought.

Kerula, pale but erect, stood at the foot of Hang-Hi's chair, and the Chinese general surveyed her impassively. Women, he thought, were a toy, fashioned for the pleasure of men, unschooled in the higher virtues.

Yen Kui Kiang interpreted the questions of Hang-Hi. Then he turned to the general humbly.

"Oh, right hand of Wanleh, Son of Heaven, harken. The girl Kerula says that she has no knowledge of the tomb of Genghis Khan. She was a slave of Mir Turek, and he guarded his secret from her. She says that men who have gone to the tomb died within a short time. And she has a strange thought—"

"Speak, Yen Kui Kiang," urged the general as he hesitated. "It is written that heaven sometimes puts wise thoughts into the heads of children."

"It is strange, Excellency. The girl says that Genghis Khan still rides over Tatary. That he and his army are to be heard in the night."

Kerula caught the meaning of what the secretary was saying, and raised her head eagerly. Her eyes were swollen from weeping, and her thin hands were clasped over the splendor of her gold-embroidered garment.

"Aye, lord," she said quickly, "I have heard the army. It was in the desert. We heard the *tumans*, Khlit and I, and they were many. The Tatar horsemen sang their chant for us, and we heard the greeting to Dawn, by the elephants."

"Child's fancies," murmured Hang-Hi when the other interpreted. "Our travelers have reported that the Tatar herdsmen believe these tales of the desert. If a grown man believes, why should not a child?"

"She says further," added Yen Kui Kiang after a moment, "that what she heard was true. For Chinese sentries have reported armed men moving over the plains. The child thinks this is the army of Genghis Khan, coming to slay the Chinese. Then she says that last night she heard again the chant of the Tatar horsemen."

Hang-Hi smiled impassively. Well he knew that the Tatars Kerula had heard of were deserters slipping out from the doomed city at night. Many thousands had made their way past the sentries by the west walls, who had orders not to see them—for Hang-Hi wished to allow the number of defenders to dwindle. Since the loss of Chan Kieh Shi he had grown cautious.

"What was the chant Kerula heard?" he asked indifferently. "Perchance it was the dogs fighting among themselves. Although, so fast do they desert in the night, there are few to quarrel."

The cheeks of the girl flushed under the paint. All her fancies had been wound around the Tatar warriors and the great Genghis Khan. Even the beleaguered city and the imprisonment of Khlit had failed to convince the child that she did not live in the time of the Tatar conquerors. So much had the books of Mir Turek done.

She sang softly, her eyes half-closed:

"Oh lion of the Teneri, wilt thou come? The devotion of thy people, thy golden palace, the great Hordes of thy nation—all these are awaiting thee.

"Thy chiefs, thy commanders, thy great kinsfolk, all these are awaiting thy coming in the birth-land which is thy stronghold.

"Thy standard of yaks' tails, thy drums and trumpets in the hands of thy warriors of the Kalkas, the Torgots, the Jun-gar—all are awaiting thee."

"That is the chant," she said proudly, "I heard it over the walls last night when the cannon did not growl. It was the same that the riders sang in the desert."

Hang-Hi stared at her and shook his head. He looked inquiringly at Yen Kui Kiang.

"There was some revelry and shouting in the town, Excellency," declared the secretary. "Assuredly, the child has strange fancies."

"It was not fancy, Yen Kui Kiang," observed Hang-Hi thoughtfully, "when Kerula said that no men returned from the tomb of Genghis Khan. Take her back to the women's quarters and watch her. She may be useful as hostage."

He held up his hand for silence as a blast of trumpets sounded from the walls of Altur Haiten.

"Wait: our enemies sound a parley. Go, Yen Kui Kiang, and bring us their message. It may be the surrender of the city."

Hang-Hi and his councillors watched while the eastern gate in front of them swung back to allow the exit of a Tatar party. Yen Kui Kiang with some Chinese officers met them just outside the walls. After the brief conference the Chinese party returned to the silk pavilion, while the Tatars waited.

The secretary bowed very low before Hang-Hi and his face was troubled with the message he was to deliver.

"The Tatar dogs are mad, Excellency," he muttered, "truly their madness is great. They say that they will give us terms. If we yield all our prisoners, and the wealth our army has taken, with our arms and banners, they will allow us to return in safety to the Great Wall. They ask hostages, of half our generals. On these terms the Tatars, in their madness, say we can return safely. Otherwise they will give battle."

Hang-Hi rose from his throne, and his heavy face flamed in anger. He had not expected this.

"Hunger must have maddened them, Excellency," repeated Yen Kui Kiang, prostrating himself, "for they say Genghis Khan has taken command of their army. Their terms, they say, are the terms of Genghis Khan to his enemies—"

A joyous cry from Kerula interrupted him. The girl was looking eagerly toward the walls of the city, her pale face alight. Hang-Hi motioned her aside, and some soldiers grasped her, thrusting her back into the pavilion.

"This is our answer," cried Hang-Hi. He lifted his ivory wand. "Sound the assault. Our cannon will answer them."

"But, Excellency," remonstrated Yen Kui Kiang, who was a just man, "the envoys—"

He was interrupted by the blast of a hundred cannon. The walls of Altur Haiten shook under the impact of giant rocks, which had undermined their base. A volley of musketry followed, and few of the envoys reached the gateway in safety before the iron doors closed.

Trumpets rang out through the Chinese camp. The regiments of assault were set in motion toward the walls, led by men in armor with scaling ladders, and mercenaries with muskets. The attack on Altur Haiten had begun.

XV

Hang-Hi sank back in his chair and watched. Yen Kui Kiang took his place at the general's side. The chronicler of the Chinese saw all that took place that day. And the sight was strange. Never had a battle begun as this one did.

Hang-Hi saw the Chinese ranks advance in good order beyond the breastworks to the filled-in moat. Then, for the first time, he began to wonder. The walls of Altur Haiten, shattered by cannon, were barren of defenders. No arrows or rocks greeted the attackers who climbed to the breaches and planted their scaling ladders without opposition.

At a signal from one of the generals, rows of men in armor began to mount the scaling ladders. The columns that faced the breaches made their way slowly over the débris. Hang-Hi wondered if the defenders had lost heart. Truly, there could be few in the city, for his sentries had counted many thousand who fled from the place during the last few nights on horseback.

The Chinese forces mounted scaling ladders to the top of the walls without opposition. Not a shot had been fired. No one had fallen wounded. The men in the breaches were slower, for the Tatars had erected barricades.

A frown appeared on the smooth brow of Hang-Hi. It seemed as if the city was in his grasp. Yet he wondered at the silence. Suddenly he arose. Men on the walls were shouting and running about. The ranks under the walls swayed in confusion. Were the shouts an omen of victory?

Hang-Hi gripped his ivory wand quickly. His councillors stared, wide-eyed. Slowly, before their eyes the walls of Altur Haiten began to crumple and fall. They fell not inward, but outward.

The eastern wall, a section at a time, fell with a sonorous crash. Fell upon the ranks of the attackers, with the men who had gained the top. Hang-Hi saw men leaping desperately into space. The men under the walls crowded back in disorder. A moan sounded with the crash of bricks, the cry of thousands of men in pain. Then the space where the walls had been was covered by a rising cloud of dust and pulverized clay.

Through this smoke, Hang-Hi could make out giant beams thrusting. He guessed at the means which had toppled the walls on the attackers, after the Chinese cannon had undermined them.

The moans of the wounded gave place to a shrill battle-cry from behind the dust curtain. Hang-Hi saw ranks of Tatars with bared weapons surging forward. As the battle-cry mounted the oncoming ranks met the retreating attackers and the blended roar of a mêlée drowned all other sounds.

Hang-Hi glanced over the scene of conflict. Only a portion of the east walls facing him had fallen. The rest stood. But the sally of the Tatars carried them forward into the breastworks of the Chinese. There the disordered regiments of assault rallied, only to be pushed back further, among the guns and machines. In the dense mass of fighting men it was useless to fire a musket, and the cannon were silent.

Hang-Hi turned to his aides and began to give orders swiftly. Mounted couriers were sent to the other quarters of the camp for reinforcements. Reserve regiments were brought up and thrown into the mêlée. Chosen men of Leo Tung and the Sung commanders advanced from the junks in the river. The rush of the Tatars was stemmed in the rear of the cannon.

Then Hang-Hi addressed his generals. It was a stroke of fortune from heaven, he said, that levelled the walls. The Tatars were few and already they were retreating to the city, fighting desperately. The Chinese would be victorious, he said, for there was no longer any obstacle to their capture of Altur Haiten. Surely, the Tatars had become mad. Why otherwise should they speak of Genghis Khan, who was dead?

When the sun was high at mid-day Hang-Hi's meal was served in the pavilion and he ate and drank heartily. Messengers had informed him of all that was taking place. The Tatars, they said, were fighting with a courage which they had not previously shown. They had spiked the cannon, and thinned the ranks of the musketmen.

On the other hand, the sally had been by a few thousand, who had retired behind the mounds of brick and clay where the walls had been. A second assault by the Chinese, ordered for the afternoon, could not fail of success.

In the midst of Hang-Hi's meal, came a mounted courier from the west quarter of the camp.

"Oh, Excellency," he cried, bowing to the floor of the pavilion, "we have been attacked by mounted Tatars from the plains. They came suddenly, and many were killed. They came, many thousands, from the woods."

Other messengers confirmed this. Unexpectedly a strong force of mounted Tatars had appeared and defeated the weakened regiments who were stationed on the west side. These had retreated in confusion to the north and south.

"Dogs!" snarled the general of Wanleh. "Are you women to run from a few riders? Order the forces on the south and north to hold their ground. My men will be in Altur Haiten in a few hours. Whence came these new foemen?"

Yen Kui Kiang advanced and bowed.

"Favored of Heaven," he said, "they must be some of the deserters returned. They are fighting fiercely, but their number can not be great. Without doubt they can be easily checked during our assault."

But the secretary had not reckoned on the mobility and prowess of the Horde, fighting in their favorite manner, maneuvering on horseback against infantry. Before the assault could be ordered, Hang-Hi learned that a second column of the enemy, stronger than the first had struck the rear of the Chinese camp to the north and broken the ranks of the besiegers. Yen Kui Kiang declared that the latter were falling back in orderly manner on the masses of troops to the east, but the quick eyes of Hang-Hi saw crowds of his men pouring from the north side in rout.

By mid-afternoon the situation of the Chinese had not improved. They held two of the four sides of the city—the east and south. More than sixty thousand men had fallen in the destruction of the walls, and the defeat by the cavalry. Hang-Hi found that the river at his rear which had served as a means of communication from China, hindered movements of his troops and menaced him if he should retreat further.

Assembling his generals, Hang-Hi ordered the veteran Leo Tung men to take the first ranks on the east, facing the cavalry, between the town and the river, and the legions of the Sung generals to hold the southern camp. The other troops he had drawn up for the assault of the city he ordered to the breastworks facing the demolished walls.

The southern camp which had escaped attack, he ordered to be watchful. This portion of his troops faced both the city and the plains, without the support of the river. Hang-Hi was thankful in his heart that the Tatar cavalry had drawn off in the afternoon. His men feared the Tatars on horseback.

He wished vainly for Chan Kieh Shi. As evening fell he heard the chant of the defenders inside the walls. Whence had come the army of mounted men? They seemed to have sprung from the plains—Chakars and Tchoros, and even Kallmarks from the horde which had deserted early in the siege. And messengers brought him word that they had seen the standard of Genghis Khan among the Kallmarks.

The signal for the final assault of Altur Haiten was never given.

XVI

Kerula had taken refuge soon after the battle began in the household pagoda of Hang-Hi with the other women. Here she took her place at one of the windows looking toward the south, listening with all her ears to the reports that were brought to the pagoda.

Night had fallen and she could not see the flare of the flame caldrons, or the flash of cannon. The camp of the Chinese seemed thronged with soldiers in confusion who passed hither and thither with torches, and red lanterns. Mounted men fought to get through the throngs, trampling the infantry. Moaning of the wounded could be heard. Kerula's thoughts were busy as she watched.

She had heard of the Tatar army that attacked from the plains. The Chinese had told wild tales of the fierceness and daring of the riders. Kerula pressed her hands together and trembled with joy. She had no doubt that this army was the Horde of Genghis Khan that she had heard in the desert. Did not the messengers say they had seen the yaks'-tails banner and heard the name of the Mighty Manslayer shouted? She had told this to the women and they had cried out in fear, leaving her alone as one accursed. Kerula was glad of this.

She listened intently at the window. She had

caught the distant roar of battle in the dark. This time, however, it came from the south, in a new quarter. The sounds came nearer instead of receding. Kerula leaned far out and listened.

Truly, a great battle was being fought, unknown to the girl. Scarcely had nightfall come when the Chinese regiments to the south had been struck in the rear by successive phalanxes of Tatar horsemen that broke their ranks and threw them into confusion. For the second time the army of the plains had appeared, led by the banner of yaks' tails, and chanting their war-song. These were not the warriors who had waited for a year behind the walls of Altur Haiten. Who were they and whence had they come?

Messages began to reach the women's quarters. A rumor said that the Sung generals had been captured or killed with most of their men. Another reported that a myriad Tatars were attacking in the dark. Genghis Khan had been seen riding at the head of his men, aided by demons who gave no quarter.

The confusion in the streets below Kerula grew worse. Men shouted that Altur Haiten was empty of defenders—that the Tatars were all in the plains. Reinforcements hurrying to the south lost their way in the dark and were scattered by fugitive regiments.

A mandarin in a torn robe ran into the hall of the pagoda and ordered the women to get ready to take refuge in the junks.

"A million devils have come out of the plains," he cried, "and our doctors are pronouncing incantations to ward them off. Hang-Hi has ordered all his household to the boats."

A wail greeted this, which grew as the women surged toward the doors in a panic. Kerula was caught in the crowd and thrust through the gate of the pagoda into the street.

She could see her way now, for buildings in the camp were in flames some distance away. Beside the women hurried soldiers without arms. She saw one or two of the helmeted Leo Tung warriors strive to push back the mob.

"Fools and dogs!" growled one sturdy warrior. "Hang-Hi holds the southern camp with one hundred thousand men. The bannermen of Leo Tung are coming to aid him. There is no battle, save on the south. Blind, and without courage!"

But the women pushed past him, screaming and calling:

"The junks! We were told to go to the junks. There we will be safe!"

As often happens, the confusion of the Chinese camp was heightened by the frantic women, and their outcry caused further panic at a time when the Leo Tung warriors who were trying to win through the mob of routed soldiers, prisoners, camp-followers and women, might have restored order. It was an evil hour for Hang-Hi that he left his pavilion to go to the front, with great bravery. In his absence the terror of the unknown gripped the camp.

"The junks!" a fleeing soldier shouted. "We shall be safe there."

The spear of a Leo Tung pierced his chest but other voices took up the cry:

"The junks! The camp is lost."

The cry spread through the camp, and the crowds began to push toward the river front, carrying with them many of the Leo Tung men.

Kerula cast about for a shelter, for she did not wish to be carried to the river. Rather she hoped to be picked up by some of the Tatars who she knew were coming. An open archway invited her and she slipped inside, to find herself in the empty Hall of Judgment.

Lanterns of many colors were lighted along the walls of the hall, and banners of victory hung around the vacant chair of Hang-Hi. The Chinese general had planned to sit there that night with his councillors, after the fall of Altur Haiten.

Kerula ran up the silken carpet to the dais and crouched in some of the hangings where she was safe from observation.

"The junks!" she heard continually. "Hang-Hi is defeated. His men are running back from the south. To the river!"

Gradually the shouting diminished, and Kerula guessed that that part of the camp was deserted. She was about to venture out from her hiding-place for a look into the street when she heard the sound of horses' feet outside.

Her heart leaped, for she thought that the men of Genghis Khan had come. Surely, she felt, the horsemen must be Tatars, for the Chinese had no cavalry. She heard voices at the archway and listened. Her heart sank as she heard Hang-Hi's voice.

"Go to the Leo Tung men, Yen Kui Kiang, and order them to hold the other side of the river. Put the junks in motion and take the survivors of the Sung forces with my own Guard back along this side of the river. The flames of the camp will light the way. Go! The battle is lost, for those we let pass as deserters were not deserters, but an army, few at a time."

"Nay, Excellency," Yen Kui Kiang remonstrated, "my place is with you. Shall the viceroy of the Son of Heaven go unattended?"

"Does the viceroy of the Son of Heaven need the help of men?" Hang-Hi answered. "I give you this as a duty. Go!"

A brief silence followed, when the horses' hoofs sounded again down the street. A murmur of voices, and Kerula heard the doors of the Hall of Judgment close. She looked out from her hiding-place. Hang-Hi, gorgeous in his silken and gold robe, was walking up the carpet toward his seat.

XVII

Kerula did not move. It was too late to hide behind the hangings. A movement would have attracted the attention of the general, who advanced quietly to the dais. The girl wondered, for the appearance of the commander was not that of a conquered man.

He seated himself on his throne and spread his robe on his knee. Kerula watching him, saw the wide, yellow face bend over his robe thoughtfully. He was writing on the cloth with a brush dipped in gilt.

Hang-Hi's stately head turned and the slant eyes fastened on her. Kerula did not shrink back. Her eyes met the general's proudly, and the man smiled at her. Again Kerula marveled. Was this the man who had been defeated by Genghis Khan?

"Little captive," said the Chinese slowly, and she understood, for she had learned the language quickly, "why are you not with the other women? Have you come to die with your master, as an honorable woman should?"

"Nay, Hang-Hi, lord," Kerula answered proudly, "I am waiting for my *anda*—a warrior to protect me. He has promised. He is a great warrior—Khlit, the Wolf. He has been to the tomb of Genghis Khan."

Hang-Hi had finished his writing, and laid down his brush. He took a stout silk cord from the breast of his robe and fingered it curiously.

"Khlit said that the banner of Genghis Khan was at the tomb," added the girl. "He will come, for he has promised."

Hang-Hi lifted his head and pointed to the writing on the robe.

"This is an ode," he said slowly, "and it means that it is better to lose one's life than to lose honor by saving it. Little captive, you also will lose yours. We shall know the secrets of life and death, you and I. The banner of Genghis Khan?" His brow darkened moodily. "Could it have been brought from the tomb to the Tatars? If Chan Kieh Shi were here he could answer my question."

He listened, as a roar and crackling that was not of a mob came to his ears. He passed his hand over his forehead, seeming to forget the girl.

"Fools!" he murmured. "How could they believe—Tatars and Chinese—that Genghis Khan was alive? He is dead, and the dead can not live. Yet the name of Genghis Khan was on the lips of the Tatars, and my men feared. Fools! Their folly was their undoing."

The roar and crackling came nearer and Kerula thought she smelled smoke. She gazed in fascination at the silken cord.

"Nay," he said grimly, catching her glance,

"the cord is for me, little captive. It is easier than the flames. The flames are near us, for I ordered my men to set fire to the Hall. Listen—"

Kerula heard a crackling that soared overhead. Smoke dimmed the banners along the wall. She saw Hang-Hi lift his hands to his throat. Once they fell to his lap, and rose again with the silken cord. With a cry she sped down the aisle.

The heavy teak door at the further end was closed. She beat on it with her fists helplessly, and wrenched at the fastenings. Behind her the hall glowed with a new light.

She pulled at the door with all her strength and it gave a little. She squeezed through the opening, and ran under the archway into the street.

As she did so she threw up her hands with a cry. Rank upon rank of dark horsemen were passing. Their cloaked figures and helmets were not Chinese. She was struck by one of the horses and fell to the ground. Dimly she was aware that the horse which struck her had turned. Then the black mantle of night seemed to fall on her and her eyes closed.

When she opened her eyes again and looked around her she was in a very different place. She lay on a pallet, covered with straw, in a small hut. The sun was streaming into it from a window over her head.

Kerula turned her head. She felt weak. The darkness that had closed on her was very near, but the sun's rays heartened her. The hut was empty save for one man. She looked at him, and her pulse quickened.

Khlit was seated on a stool, watching her, his black pipe between his teeth, and his curved sword over one knee. His clothing was covered with dust, but his eyes were keen and alert. She put out one hand and touched the sword over his knee.

"Khlit, lord," she said happily, "you came to me as you promised you would. I told Hang-Hi you would come. But—"

A frown crossed her face as if she was striving to remember something.

"I dreamed such a dream, Khlit, lord. It seemed as if I was being carried on a horse by a warrior. I saw flames, and then darkness of the plains. Then I saw that he carried the standard of Genghis Khan that Hang-Hi feared. The standard of yaks' tails flapped over me as we went to the tomb in the mountains, and I cried with happiness. I dreamed it was Genghis Khan that carried me."

"It was a good battle," Khlit growled, "it was a battle such as I have never seen. Nay, little Kerula, was your dream anything but a dream?"

"Aye, Khlit, lord. But then the standard of Genghis Khan. Surely that was real, for the men of Hang-Hi saw it."

Khlit touched the lettering on his sword.

"Nay, Kerula," he said slowly, "the standard of Genghis Khan lies in his tomb where the Onon Muren watch. No man will go there. For the standard, and what is in the tomb belong to Genghis Khan."

In his eyes as he spoke was the look of a man who has looked upon forbidden things, unafraid. Yet when men asked him if he knew the way to the tomb where the treasure was he said that surely no man could find his way to the dead. And when Kerula told him again that her memory of the ride was real, he laughed and told her that it was a dream, among dreams.

THE SEVEN BLACK PRIESTS

FRITZ LEIBER

WHEN FRITZ REUTER LEIBER (1910–1992) sold his first short story, "Two Sought Adventure," for the August 1939 issue of *Unknown,* he introduced two of the most popular characters in the genre of "Sword and Sorcery"—a term that he coined. At nearly seven feet tall, with long, shaggy red hair, the giant Fafhrd carried an enormous broadsword and was one of the greatest swordsmen the world had ever seen. His friend and companion, the diminutive and accomplished thief Gray Mouser, was equally adept with "Scalpel," his shorter weapon. The two adventurers were jointly developed by Leiber and his friend Harry Otto Fischer, though Leiber was the sole author of nearly all the stories over a period of fifty years. The partners claimed that Fafhrd was based on Leiber and the Mouser on Fischer.

Sword and sorcery fantasy tales were only one element of Leiber's fiction. His early horror fiction had been heavily influenced by H. P. Lovecraft, and among his eight Hugo Awards and two Nebula Awards are such science-fiction classics as *The Big Time* (1957) and *The Wanderer* (1964). His best-known work is probably the voodoo-witchcraft novel *Conjure Wife* (1943), which has been filmed three times, most memorably in 1962 under the title *Burn, Witch, Burn!* (also known as *Night of the Eagle*). With a chilling script by George Baxt, Charles Beaumont, and Richard Matheson, the film starred Janet Blair and Peter Wyngarde. The novel was also the basis for *Weird Woman* in 1944, and for *Witches' Brew* in 1980.

"The Seven Black Priests" was originally published in the May 1953 issue of *Other Worlds Science Stories;* it was first collected in book form in *Two Sought Adventure* (New York: Gnome, 1957).

THE SEVEN BLACK PRIESTS

FRITZ LEIBER

EYES LIKE red lava peered from a face black as dead lava down the sheer mountainside at the snowy ledge that narrowed off into chilly darkness barely touched by dawn. The black priest's heart pounded its rib cage. Never in his life nor his priest-father's before him had intruders come by this narrow way that led from the Outer Sea across the mountains known as the Bones of the Old Ones. Never in three long returns of the Year of the Monsters, never in four sailings of the ship to tropic Klesh to get them wives, had any but he and his fellow-priests trod the way below. Yet he had always guarded it as faithfully and warily as if it were the nightly assault-route of blasphemy-bent spearmen and bowmen.

There it came again—and unmistakably!—the rumble of singing. To judge from the tone, the man must have a chest like a bear's. As if he had drilled for this nightly (and he had) the black priest laid aside his conical hat and stepped out of his fur-lined shoes and slipped off his fur-lined robe, revealing his skinny-limbed, sag-bellied, well-greased frame.

Moving back in the stony niche, he selected a narrow stick from a closely-shielded fire and laid it across a pit in the rock. Its unsputtering flame revealed that the pit was filled to a hand's breadth of the top with a powder that glittered like smashed jewels. He judged it would take some thirty slow breaths for the stick to burn through at the middle.

He silently returned to the edge of the niche, which was the height of three tall men—seven times his own height—above the snowy ledge. And now, far along that ledge, he could dimly distinguish a figure—no, two. He drew a long knife from his loincloth and, crouching forward, poised himself on hands and toes. He breathed a prayer to his strange and improbable god. Somewhere above, ice or rocks creaked and snapped faintly, as if the mountain too were flexing its muscles in murderous anticipation.

"Give us the next verse, Fafhrd," merrily called the foremost of the two snow-treaders. "You've had thirty paces to compose it, and our adventure took no longer. Or is the poetic hoot owl frozen at last in your throat?"

The Mouser grinned as he strode along with seeming recklessness, the sword Scalpel swinging at his side. His high-collared gray cloak and hood, pulled close around him, shadowed his swart features but could not conceal their impudence.

Fafhrd's garments, salvaged from their sloop wrecked on the chilly coast, were all wools and furs. A great golden clasp gleamed dully on his chest and a golden band, tilted awry, confined his snarled reddish hair. His white-skinned face, with gray eyes wide set, had a calm bold look to it, though the brow was furrowed in thought. From over his right shoulder protruded a bow, while from over his left shoulder gleamed the sapphire eyes of a brazen dragonhead that was the pommel of a longsword slung on his back.

His brow cleared and, as if some more genial mountain than the frozen one they traveled along had given tongue, he sang:

> *Oh, Lavas Laerk*
> *Had a face like a dirk*
> *And of swordsmen twenty-and-three,*
> *And his greased black ship*
> *Through the waves did slip—*
> *'Twas the sleekest craft at sea;*
> *Yet it helped him naught*
> *When he was caught*
> *By magic, the Mouser, and me.*
> *And now he feeds fishes*
> *The daintiest dishes,*
> *But—*

The words broke off and the Gray Mouser heard the hissing scuff of leather on snow. Whirling around, he saw Fafhrd hurtle over the side of the cliff and he had a moment to wonder whether the huge Northerner, maddened by his own doggerel, had decided to illustrate dramatically Lavas Laerk's plunge to the bottomless deeps.

The next moment Fafhrd caught himself with elbows and hands on the margin of the ledge. Simultaneously, a black and gleaming form hit the spot he had just desperately vacated, broke its fall with bent arms and hunched shoulders, spun over in a somersault, and lunged at the Mouser with a knife that flashed like a splinter of the moon. The knife was about to take the Mouser in the belly when Fafhrd, supporting his weight on one forearm, twitched the attacker back by an ankle. At this the small black one hissed low and horribly, turned again, and lunged at Fafhrd. But now the Mouser was roused at last from the shocked daze that he assured himself could never grip him in a less hatefully cold country. He dove forward at the small black one, diverting his thrust—there were sparks as the weapon struck stone within a finger's width of Fafhrd's arm—and skidding his greased form off the ledge beyond Fafhrd.

The small black one swooped out of sight as silently as a bat.

Fafhrd, dangling his great frame over the abyss, finished his verse:

> *But the daintiest dish is he.*

"Hush, Fafhrd," the Mouser hissed, stooped as he listened intently. "I think I heard him hit."

Fafhrd absentmindedly eased himself up to a seat. "Not if that chasm is half as deep as the last time we saw its bottom, you didn't," he assured his comrade.

"But what was he?" the Mouser asked frowningly. "He looked like a man of Klesh."

"Yes, with the jungle of Klesh as far from here as the moon," Fafhrd reminded him with a chuckle. "Some maddened hermit frostbitten black, no doubt. There are strange skulkers in these little hills, they say."

The Mouser peered up the dizzy mile-high cliff and spotted the nearby niche. "I wonder if there are more of him?" he questioned uneasily.

"Madmen commonly go alone," Fafhrd asserted, getting up. "Come, small nagger, we'd best be on our way if you want a hot breakfast. If the old tales are true, we should be reaching the Cold Waste by sunup—and there we'll find a little wood at least."

At that instant a great glow sprang from the niche from which the small attacker had dropped. It pulsed, turning from violet to green to yellow to red.

"What makes that?" Fafhrd mused, his interest roused at last. "The old tales say nothing of firevents in the Bones of the Old Ones. Now if I were to give you a boost, Mouser, I think you could reach that knob and then make your own way—"

"Oh no," the Mouser interrupted, tugging at the big man and silently cursing himself for starting the question-asking. "I want my breakfast cooked over more wholesome flames. And I would be well away from here before other eyes see the glow."

"None will see it, small dodger of mysteries," Fafhrd said chucklingly, letting himself be urged away along the path. "Look, even now it dies."

But at least one other eye had seen the pulsing glow—an eye as large as a squid's and bright as the Dog Star.

"Ha, Fafhrd!" the Gray Mouser cried gaily some hours later in the full-broken dawn. "There's an omen to warm our frozen hearts! A green hill winks at us frosty men—gives us the glad eye like a malachite-smeared dusky courtesan of Klesh!"

"She's as hot as a courtesan of Klesh, too," the huge Northerner supplemented, rounding the brown crag's bulging shoulder in his turn, "for she's melted all the snow."

It was true. Although the far horizon shone white and green with the snows and glacial ice of the Cold Waste, the saucer-like depression in the foreground held a small unfrozen lake. And while the air was still chilly around them, so that their breath drifted away in small white clouds, the brown ledge they trod was bare.

Up from the nearer shore of the lake rose the hill to which the Mouser had referred, the hill from which one star-small point still reflected the new-risen sun's rays at them blindingly.

"That is, if it is a hill," Fafhrd added softly. "And in any case, whether a courtesan of Klesh or hill, she has several faces."

The point was well taken. The hill's green flanks were formed of crags and hummocks which the imagination could shape into monstrous faces—all the eyes closed save the one that twinkled at them. The faces melted downward like wax into huge stony rivulets—or might they be elephantine trunks?—that plunged into the unruffled acid-seeming water. Here and there among the green were patches of dark red rock that might be blood, or mouths. Clashing nastily in color, the hill's rounded summit seemed to be composed of a fleshily pink marble. It too persisted in resembling a face—that of a sleeping ogre. It was crossed by a stretch of vividly red

rock that might be the ogre's lips. From a slit in the red rock, a faint vapor rose.

The hill had more than a volcanic look. It seemed like an upwelling from a more savage, primal, fiercer consciousness than any that even Fafhrd and the Gray Mouser knew, an upwelling frozen in the act of invading a younger, weaker world—frozen yet eternally watchful and waiting and yearning.

And then the illusion was gone—or four-faces-out-of-five gone and the fifth wavering. The hill was just a hill again—an odd volcanic freak of the Cold Waste—a green hill with a glitter.

Fafhrd let out a gusty sigh. He surveyed the farther shore of the lake. It was hillocky and matted with a dark vegetation that unpleasantly resembled fur. At one point there rose from it a stubby pillar of rock almost like an altar. Beyond the hairy bushes, which were here and there flecked with red-leafed ones, stretched the ice and snow, broken only occasionally by great rocks and rare clumps of dwarfed trees.

But something else was foremost in the Mouser's thoughts.

"The eye, Fafhrd. The glad, glittering eye!" he whispered, dropping his voice as though they were in a crowded street and some informer or rival thief might overhear. "Only once before have I seen such a gleam, and that was by moonlight, across a king's treasure chamber. That time I did not come away with a huge diamond. A guardian serpent prevented it. I killed the wriggler, but its hiss brought other guards.

"But this time there's only a little hill to climb. And if at this distance the gem gleams so bright, Fafhrd"—his hand dropped and gripped his companion's leg, at the sensitive point just above the knee, for emphasis—"think how big!"

The Northerner, frowning faintly at the violent squeeze as well as at his doubts and misgivings, nevertheless sucked an icy breath in appreciative greed.

"And we poor shipwrecked marauders," continued the Mouser raptly, "will be able to tell the gaping and envious thieves of Lankhmar that we not only crossed the Bones of the Old Ones, but picked them on the way."

And he went skipping gaily down the skimpy ledge that merged into the narrow, lake-edged, rocky saddle that joined this greater mountain with the green one. Fafhrd followed more slowly, gazing steadily at the green hill, waiting for it to turn back into faces again, or to turn to no faces at all. It did neither. It occurred to him that it might have been partly shaped by human hands and, after that, the notion of a diamond-eyed idol seemed less implausible. At the far end of the saddle, just at the base of the green hill, he caught up with the Mouser, who was studying a flat, dark rock covered with gashes which a moment's glance told Fafhrd must be artificial.

"The runes of tropic Klesh!" the Northerner muttered. "What should such hieroglyphs be doing so far from their jungle?"

"Chiseled, no doubt, by some hermit frost-bitten black, whose madness taught him the Kleshic language," the Mouser observed sardonically. "Or have you already forgotten last night's knifer?"

Fafhrd shook his head curtly. Together they pored over the deep-chopped letters, bringing to bear knowledge gained from the perusing of ancient treasure-maps and the deciphering of code-messages carried by intercepted spies.

"The seven black . . ." Fafhrd read laboriously.

". . . priests," the Mouser finished for him. "They're in it, whoever they may be. And a god or beast or devil—that writhing hieroglyph means any one of the three, depending on the surrounding words, which I don't understand. It's very ancient writing. And the seven black priests are to serve the writhing hieroglyph, or to bind it—again either might be meant, or both."

"And so long as the priesthood endures," Fafhrd took up, "that long will the god-beast-devil lie quietly . . . or sleep . . . or stay dead . . . or not come up . . ."

Abruptly the Mouser bounded straight into the air, fanning his feet. "This rock is hot," he complained.

Fafhrd understood. Even through the thick walrus-soles of his boots he was beginning to feel the unnatural warmth.

"Hotter than the floor of hell," the Mouser observed, hopping first on one foot and then the other. "Well, what now, Fafhrd? Shall we go up, or not?"

Fafhrd answered him with a sudden shout of laughter. "You decided that, little man, long ago! Was it *I* who started to talk about huge diamonds?"

So up they went, choosing that point where a gigantic trunk, or tentacle, or melted chin strained from the encasing granite. It was not an easy climb, even at the beginning, for the green stone was everywhere rounded off, showing no marks of chisel or axe—which rather dampened Fafhrd's vague theory that this was a hill half-formed by human-wielded tools.

Upward the two of them edged and strained, their breath blowing out in bigger white clouds although the rock was uncomfortably hot under their hands. After an inch-by-inch climb up a slippery surface, where hands and feet and elbows and knees and even toasted chin must all help, they stood at last on the lower lip of one of the green hill's mouths. Here it seemed their ascent must end, for the great cheek above was smooth and sloped outward a spear's length above them.

But Fafhrd took from the Mouser's back a rope that had once guyed the mast of their shipwrecked sloop, made a noose in it, and cast it up toward the forehead above, where a stubby horn or feeler projected. It caught and held. Fafhrd put his weight on it to test it, then looked inquiringly at his companion.

"What have you in mind?" the Mouser asked, clinging affectionately to the rock-face. "This whole climb begins to seem mere foolishness."

"But what of the jewel?" Fafhrd replied in pleasant mockery. "So big, Mouser, so big!"

"Likely just a bit of quartz," the Mouser said sourly. "I have lost my hunger for it."

"But as for me," Fafhrd cried, "I have only now worked up a good appetite."

And he swung out into emptiness, around the green cheek and into thin, brilliant sunlight.

It seemed to him as if the still lake and the green hill were rocking, instead of himself. He came to rest below the face's monstrously pouchy eyelid. He climbed up hand over hand, found good footing on the ledge that was the eyelid pouch, and twitched the end of the rope back to the Mouser, whom he could no longer see. On the third cast it did not swing back. He squatted on the ledge, bracing himself securely to guy the rope. It went tight in his hands. Very soon the Mouser stepped onto the ledge beside him.

The gaiety was back in the small thief's face, but it was a fragile gaiety, as though he wanted to get this done with quickly. They edged their way along the great eye-pouch until they were directly below the fancied pupil. It was rather above Fafhrd's head, but the Mouser, nimbly hitching himself up on Fafhrd's shoulders peered in readily.

Fafhrd, bracing himself against the green wall, waited impatiently. It seemed as if the Mouser would never speak. "Well?" he asked finally, when his shoulders had begun to ache from the Mouser's weight.

"Oh, it's a diamond, all right." The Mouser sounded oddly uninterested. "Yes, it's big. My fingers can just about span it. And it's cut like a smooth sphere—a sort of diamond eye. But I don't know about getting it out. It's set very deep. Should I try? Don't bellow so, Fafhrd, you'll blow us both off! I suppose we might as well take it, since we've come so far. But it won't be easy. My knife can't . . . yes, it can! I thought it was rock around the gem. But it's tarry stuff. Squidgy. There! I'm coming down."

Fafhrd had a glimpse of something smooth, globular and dazzling, with an ugly, ragged, tarry circlet clinging to it. Then it seemed that someone flicked his elbow lightly. He looked down. Momentarily he had the strangest feeling of being in the green steamy jungle of Klesh. For protruding from the brown fur of his cloak was a wickedly barbed little dart, thickly smeared with a substance as black and tarry as that disfiguring the diamond eye.

He quickly dropped flat on the ledge, crying out to the Mouser to do the same. Then he carefully tugged loose the dart, finding to his relief that, although it had nicked the thick hide of his cloak beneath the fur, it had not touched flesh.

"I think I see him," called the Mouser, peering down cautiously over the protected ledge. "A little fellow with a very long blowgun and dressed in furs and a conical hat. Crouching there in those dark bushes across the lake. Black, I think, like our knifer last night. A Kleshian, I'd say, unless he's one more of your frostbitten hermits. Now he lifts the gun to his lips. Watch yourself!"

A second dart pinged against the rock above them, then dropped down close by Fafhrd's hand. He jerked it away sharply.

There was a whirring sound, ending in a muted snap. The Mouser had decided to get a blow in. It is not easy to swing a sling while lying prone on a ledge, but the Mouser's missile crackled into the furry bushes close to the black blowgunner, who immediately ducked out of sight.

It was easy enough then to decide on a plan of action, for few were available. While the Mouser raked the bushes across the lake with sling shots, Fafhrd went down the rope. Despite the Mouser's protection, he fervently prayed that his cloak be thick enough. He knew from experience that the darts of Klesh are nasty things. At irregular intervals came the whirr of the Mouser's casts, cheering him on.

Reaching the green hill's base, he strung his bow and called up to the Mouser that he was ready in his turn to cover the retreat. His eyes searched the furry cliffs across the lake, and twice when he saw movement he sent an arrow from his precious store of twenty. Then the Mouser was beside him and they were racing off along the hot mountain edge toward where the cryptically ancient glacial ice gleamed green. Often they looked back across the lake at the dubious furry bushes spotted here and there with blood-red ones, and twice or thrice they thought they saw movement in them—movement coming their way. Whenever this happened, they sent an arrow or a stone whirring, though with what effect they could not tell.

"The seven black priests—" Fafhrd muttered.

"The six," the Mouser corrected. "We killed one of them last night."

"Well, the six then," Fafhrd conceded. "They seem angry with us."

"As why shouldn't they be?" the Mouser demanded. "We stole their idol's only eye. Such an act annoys priests tremendously."

"It seemed to have more eyes than that one," Fafhrd asserted thoughtfully, "if only it had opened them."

"Thank Aarth it didn't!" the Mouser hissed. "And 'ware that dart!"

Fafhrd hit the dirt—or rather the rock—instantly, and the black dart skirred on the ice ahead.

"I think they're unreasonably angry," Fafhrd asserted, scrambling to his feet.

"Priests always are," the Mouser said philosophically, with a sidewise shudder at the dart's black-crusted point.

"At any rate, we're rid of them," Fafhrd said with relief, as he and the Mouser loped onto the ice. The Mouser leered at him sardonically, but Fafhrd didn't notice.

All day they trudged rapidly across the green ice, seeking their way southward by the sun, which got hardly a hand's breath above the horizon. Toward night the Mouser brought down two low-winging arctic birds with three casts of his sling, while Fafhrd's long-seeing eyes spied a black cave-mouth in an outcropping of rock under a great snowy slope. Luckily there was a clump of dwarfed trees, uprooted and killed by moving ice, near the cave's mouth, and soon the two adventurers were gnawing tough, close-grained brown bird and watching the flickering little fire in the cave's entrance.

Fafhrd stretched hugely and said, "Farewell to all black priests! That's another bother done with." He reached out a large, long-fingered hand. "Mouser, let me see that glass eye you dug from the green hill."

The Mouser without comment reached into his pouch and handed Fafhrd the brilliant tar-circled globule. Fafhrd held it between his big hands and viewed it thoughtfully. The firelight shone through it and spread from it, highlighting the cave with red, baleful beams. Fafhrd stared unblinkingly at the gem, until the Mouser became very conscious of the great silence around them, broken only by the tiny but frequent crackling of the fire and the large but infrequent crackling of the ice outside. He felt weary to death, yet somehow couldn't consider sleep.

Finally Fafhrd said, in a faint unnatural voice, "The earth we walk on once lived—a great hot beast, breathing out fire and spewing molten rock. Its constant yearning was to spit red-hot stuff at the stars. This was before all men."

"What's that?" the Mouser queried, stirring from his half-trance.

"Now men have come, the earth has gone to sleep," Fafhrd continued in the same hollow voice, not looking at the Mouser. "But in its dream it thinks of life, and stirs, and tries to shape itself into the form of men."

"What's that, Fafhrd?" the Mouser repeated uneasily. But Fafhrd answered him with sudden snores. The Mouser carefully teased the gem from his comrade's fingers. Its tarry rim was soft and slippery—repugnantly so, almost as if it were a kind of black tissue. The Mouser put the thing back in his pouch. A long time passed. Then the Mouser touched his companion's fur-clad shoulder. Fafhrd woke with a swift shudder. "What is it, small one?" he demanded.

"Morning," the Mouser told him briefly, pointing over the ashes of the fire at the lightening sky.

As they stooped their way out of the cave, there was a faint roaring sound. Looking over the snow-rim and up the slope, Fafhrd saw hurtling down toward them a vast white globe that grew in size in the very brief time while he watched. He and the Mouser barely managed to dive back into the cavern before the earth shook and the noise became ear-splitting and everything went momentarily dark as the huge snowball thundered over the cave-mouth. They both smelled the cold sour ashes blown into their faces from the dead fire by the globe's passing, and the Mouser coughed.

But Fafhrd instantly lunged out of the cave, swiftly stringing his great bow and fitting to it an arrow long as his arm. He sighted up the slope. At the slope's summit, tiny as bugs beyond the wickedly-barbed arrowhead, were a half-dozen conical-hatted figures, sharply silhouetted against the yellow-purple dawn.

They seemed busy as bugs too, fussing furiously with a white globe as tall as themselves.

Fafhrd let out half a breath, paused, and loosed his arrow. The tiny figures continued for several breaths to worry the stubborn globe. Then the one nearest it sprang convulsively and sprawled atop it. The globe began to roll down the slope, carrying the arrow-pierced black priest with it and gathering snow as it went. Soon he was hidden in the ever-thickening crust, but not before his flailing limbs had changed the globe's course, so that it missed the cave-mouth by a spear's length.

As the thundering died, the Mouser peered out cautiously.

"I shot the second avalanche aside," Fafhrd remarked casually. "Let's be moving."

The Mouser would have led the way around the hill—a long and winding course looking treacherous with snow and slippery rock—but Fafhrd said, "No, straight over the top, where their snowballs have cleared a path for us. They're much too cunning to expect us to take that path."

However, he kept an arrow nocked to his bow as they made their way up the rocky slope, and moved quite cautiously as they surmounted the naked crest. A white landscape green-spotted with glacial ice opened before them, but no dark specks moved up it and there were no hiding places nearby. Fafhrd unstrung his bow and laughed.

"They seem to have scampered off," he said. "Doubtless they're running back to their little green hill to warm themselves. At any rate, we're rid of them."

"Yes, just as we were yesterday," the Mouser commented dryly. "The fall of the knifer didn't seem to worry them at all, but doubtless they're scared witless because you put an arrow into another of their party."

"Well, at all events," Fafhrd said curtly, "granting that there were seven black priests to begin with, there are now but five."

And he led the way down the other side of the hill, taking big reckless strides. The Mouser followed slowly, a stone rocking in his dangled sling and his gaze questing restlessly to every side. When they came to snow, he studied it, but there were no tracks as far as he could see to either side. By the time he reached the foot of the hill, Fafhrd was a sling's cast ahead. To make up the distance, the Mouser began a soft-footed, easy lope, yet he did not desist from his watchfulness. His attention was attracted by a squat hummock of snow just ahead of Fafhrd. Shadows might have told him whether there was anything crouched behind it, but the yellow-purple haze hid the sun, so he kept on watching the hummock, meanwhile speeding up his pace. He reached the hummock and saw there was no one behind it almost at the moment he caught up with Fafhrd.

The hummock exploded into a scatter of snow-chunks and a black sag-bellied figure erupted out of it at Fafhrd, ebony arm extended for a knife-slash at the Northerner's neck. Almost simultaneously the Mouser lunged forward, whirling his sling backhanded. The stone, still in the leather loop, caught the slasher high in the face. The curved knife missed by inches. The slasher fell. Fafhrd looked around with mild interest.

The attacker's forehead was so deeply indented that there could be no question of his condition, yet the Mouser stared down at him for a long time. "A man of Klesh, all right," he said broodingly, "but fatter. Armored against the cold. Strange they should have come so far to serve their god." He looked up and without raising his arm from his side, sharply twirled his sling—much as a bravo might in some alley as a warning to skulkers.

"Four to go," he said and Fafhrd nodded slowly and soberly.

All day they trod across the Cold Waste—watchfully, but without further incident. A wind came up and the cold bit. The Mouser pulled in his hood so that it covered his mouth and nose, while even Fafhrd hugged his cloak closer around him.

As the sky was darkening to umber and indigo, Fafhrd suddenly stopped and strung his bow and let fly. For a moment the Mouser, who was a bit bothered by his comrade's bemused air, thought that the Northerner was shooting at mere snow. Then the snow leaped, kicking four gray hooves, and the Mouser realized Fafhrd had brought down white-furred meat. He licked his numb lips greedily as Fafhrd swiftly bled and gutted the animal and slung it over his shoulder.

A little way ahead was an outcropping of black rock. Fafhrd studied it for a moment, then took an axe from his belt and struck the rock a careful blow with the back of the head. The Mouser eagerly gathered in the corner of his cloak the large and small chunks that flaked off. He could feel their oiliness and he felt warmed by the mere thought of the rich flame they would make.

Just beyond the outcropping was a low cliff and at its base a cave-mouth slightly sheltered by a tall rock perhaps two spears' lengths in front of it. The Mouser felt a great glow of anticipated content as he followed Fafhrd toward the inviting dark orifice. He had greatly feared, being numb with cold, aching with fatigue, famished, that they might have to camp out and content themselves with the bones of yesternight's birds. Now in an astonishingly short space they had found food, fuel, shelter. So wonderfully convenient. . . .

And then, as Fafhrd rounded the sheltering rock and strode toward the cave-mouth, the thought came to the Mouser: *Much too convenient*. Without further thought, he dropped the coal and sprang at his comrade, hurling the huge fellow flat on his face.

A dart hissed close over him and clicked faintly against the sheltering rock. Again without pause the Mouser darted into the cave-mouth, whipping his sword Scalpel from its sheath. As he entered the cave he zigged a bit to the left, then zagged suddenly to the right and flattened himself against the rocky wall there, slashing prudently at the darkness as he tried to pierce it with his gaze.

Across from him, on the other side of the mouth, the cave bent back in an elbow, the end of which, to the Mouser's amazement, was not dark but dimly lit by a pulsing light that seemed neither that of fire nor the outer twilight. If anything, it resembled the unnatural glow they had seen back in the Bones of the Old Ones.

But unnatural or not, it had the advantage of silhouetting the Mouser's antagonist. The squat fellow was now gripping a curved knife rather than a blowgun. As the Mouser sprang at him, he scuttled back along the elbow and dodged around the corner from behind which the pulsing glow came. To the Mouser's further amazement, he felt not only a growing warmth as he pursued but also moistness in the air. He rounded the corner. The black priest, who'd stopped just beyond it, lunged at him. But the Mouser was prepared for this and Scalpel took his adversary neatly in the chest, just off center, transfixing him, while the curved knife slashed only steamy air.

For a moment the fanatic priest tried to work

his way up along the thin blade and so get within striking distance of the Mouser. Then the nefarious glare died in the priest's eyes and he slumped, while the Mouser distastefully whipped out the blade.

The priest tottered back into the steamy glow, which the Mouser now saw came from a small pit just beyond. With a blood-choking gargling moan the black one stepped back into the pit and vanished. There was a scuff of flesh against rock, a pause, and then a faint splash, and then no sound at all, except for the soft, distant bubbling and seething that the Mouser now realized came steadily from the pit—that is, until Fafhrd came clumping up belatedly.

"Three to go," the Mouser informed him casually. "The fourth is cooking at the bottom of that pit. But I want broiled dinner tonight, not boiled, and besides, I haven't a long enough fork. So fetch in the black stones I dropped."

Fafhrd objected at first, eyeing the steam-and-fire vent almost superstitiously, and urged that they seek other lodging. But the Mouser argued that to spend the night in the now-empty, easily scanned cave was far better than to risk ambush in the outer dark. To the Mouser's relief Fafhrd agreed after peering down the pit for possible handholds that might help a live or boiled attacker. The small man had no desire to leave this pleasantly steamy spot.

The fire was built against the outer wall of the cave and near the mouth, so that no one could creep in without being revealed by its flames. After they had polished off some grilled liver and a number of tough, seared chops and had tossed the bones into the hot fire, where they sputtered merrily, Fafhrd settled back against the rocky wall and asked the Mouser to let him look at the diamond eye.

The Mouser complied with some reluctance, once again experiencing repugnance for the frostily-gleaming stone's tarry circlet. He had the feeling that Fafhrd was going to do something unwise with the stone—what, he didn't know. But the Northerner merely glanced at it for a moment, almost puzzledly, and then thrust

it away in *his* pouch. The Mouser started to object, but Fafhrd curtly replied that it was their common property. The Mouser could not but agree.

They had decided to stand watch by turns, Fafhrd first. The Mouser snuggled his cloak around him, and tucked under his head a pillow made of pouch and folded hood. The coal fire flamed, the strange glow from the pit pulsed wanly. The Mouser found it decidedly pleasant to be between the dry heat of the former and the moist warmth of the latter, both spiced by the chill air from outside. He watched the play of shadows through half-closed eyes. Fafhrd, sitting between the Mouser and the flames, bulked reassuringly large, wide-eyed, and alert. The Mouser's last thought as he drowsed off was that he was rather glad that Fafhrd had the diamond. It made his own pillow that much less bumpy.

He woke hearing an odd soft voice. The fire had burned low. For a frightening moment he thought that a stranger had somehow come into the cave—perhaps muttering hypnotic words to put a sleepspell on his comrade. Then he realized that the voice was the one Fafhrd had used last night, and that the Northerner was staring into the diamond eye as if he were seeing limitless visions there, and rocking it slowly to and fro. The rocking made the glittering beams from the gem synchronize with the pulsing glow in a way the Mouser didn't like.

"Nehwon's blood," Fafhrd was murmuring, his voice almost a chant, "still pulses strongly under its wrinkled rocky skin, and still bleeds hot and raw from wounds in the mountains. But it needs the blood of heroes before it can shape itself into the form of men."

The Mouser jumped up, grabbed Fafhrd by the shoulder and shook him gently.

"Those who truly worship Nehwon," Fafhrd went on entrancedly, as if nothing had happened, "guard its mountain-wounds and wait and pray for the great day of fulfillment when Nehwon shall wake again, this time in man's form, and rid itself of the vermin called men."

The Mouser's shaking became violent and

Fafhrd woke with a start—only to assert that he had been awake all the time and that the Mouser had been having a nightmare. He laughed at the Mouser's counter-assertions and would not budge from his own. Nor would he give up the diamond, but tucked it deep in his pouch, gave two huge yawns and fell asleep while the Mouser was still expostulating.

The Mouser did not find his watch a pleasant one. In place of his former trust in this rocky nook, he now scented danger in every direction and peered as often at the steamy pit as at the black entrance beyond the glowing coals, entertaining himself with vivid visions of a cooked priest somehow writhing his way up. Meanwhile the more logical part of his mind dwelled on an unpleasantly consistent theory that the hot inner layer of Nehwon was indeed jealous of man, and that the green hill was one of those spots where inner Nehwon was seeking to escape its rocky jacket and form itself into all-conquering man-shaped giants of living stone. The black Kleshite priests would be Nehwon-worshippers eager for the destruction of all other men. And the diamond eye, far from being a bit of valuable and harmless loot, was somehow alive and seeking to enchant Fafhrd with its glittering gaze, and lead him to an obscure doom.

Three times the Mouser tried to get the gem away from his comrade, the third time by slitting the bottom of the Northerner's pouch. But though the Mouser knew himself the most cunning cutpurse in Lankhmar, though perhaps a trifle out of practice, Fafhrd each time hugged the pouch tighter to him and muttered peevishly in his sleep and unerringly brushed away the Mouser's questing hand. The Mouser thought of taking the diamond eye by force, but was stopped by the unreasoning conviction that this would touch off murderous resistance in the Northerner. Indeed, he had strong misgivings as to the state in which his comrade would awake.

But when the cave-mouth finally lightened, Fafhrd roused himself with a shake and a morning yawn-and-growl as stentorious and genial as any the Mouser had ever winced at. Fafhrd

acted with such chipper, clear-headed enthusiasm that the Mouser's fears were quite blown away, or at least driven deep into the back of his mind. The two adventurers had a cold-meat breakfast, and carefully wrapped up and packed away the legs and shoulders that had been roasted during the night.

Then while Fafhrd covered him with arrow nocked to taut bowstring, the Mouser darted out and sprang to cover behind the outside of the stone sheltering the entrance. Bobbing up here and there for quick glances over its top, he scanned the cliff above the cave for any sign of ambushers. Holding his sling at the ready, he covered Fafhrd while the latter rushed forth. After a bit they satisfied themselves that there were at least no nearby lurkers in the pale dawn, and Fafhrd led off with a swinging stride. The Mouser followed briskly enough, but after a little while became possessed with a doubt. It seemed to him that Fafhrd was not leading them straight along their course, but swinging rather sharply off toward the left. It was hard to be at all sure, for the sun had still not broken through and the sky was filled with purplish and yellowish scarf-like clouds, while the Mouser could not tell for certain just which way they had come yesterday, since things are very different looking back than looking forward.

Nevertheless he voiced his doubts after a while, but Fafhrd replied with such good-humored assurance, "The Cold Waste was my childhood playground, as familiar to me as Lankhmar's mazy alleys or the swampways of the Great Salt Marsh to you," that the Mouser was almost completely satisfied. Besides, the day was windless, which pleased the Mouser no end, because of his worship of warmth.

After a good half-day's trudging they mounted a snowy rise and the Mouser's eyebrows rose incredulously at the landscape ahead: a tilted plain of green ice smooth as glass. Its upper edge, which lay somewhat to their right, was broken by jagged pinnacles, like the crest of a great smooth wave. Its lower slope stretched down for a vast distance to their left, finally losing itself in what looked like a white mist, while straight ahead there seemed to be no end.

The plain was so green that it looked like a giddily enchanted ocean, tilted at the command of some mighty magician. The Mouser felt sure it would reflect the stars on a clear night.

He was somewhat horrified, though hardly surprised, when his comrade coolly proposed that they walk straight across it. The Northerner's shrewd gaze had spotted a section just ahead of them where the slope leveled off briefly before sweeping down again. Along this level ribbon, Fafhrd asserted, they could walk with ease—and then the Northerner set out without waiting for a reply.

With a fatalistic shrug the Mouser followed, walking at first as if on eggs and with many an uneasy glance at the great downward slope. He wished he had bronze-cleated boots—even ones worn flat like Fafhrd's—or some sort of spurs to fix to his own slippery shoes, so that he'd have a better chance of stopping himself if he did start to slide. After a while he grew more confident and took longer and swifter, if still most gingerly steps, and the gap Fafhrd had put between them was closed.

They had walked for perhaps three bowshots across the plain, and still had no sight of an end to it, when a flicker of movement in the corner of his right eye made the Mouser look around.

Swiftly and silently sliding down toward them from some hiding place in the ragged crest, came the remaining black priests, three abreast. They kept their footing like expert skiers—and indeed they seemed to be wearing skis of some sort. Two of them carried spears improvised by thrusting dagger grips into the muzzles of their long blowguns, while the midmost had as lance a narrow, needle-sharp icicle or ice-shard at least eight feet long.

No time now for slings and arrows, and of what use to sword-skewer one who has already spear-skewered you? Besides, an icy slope is no place for dainty near-stationary maneuvering. Without a word to Fafhrd, so certain he was that

the Northerner would do the same, the Mouser took off down the dreaded leftward slope.

It was as if he had cast himself into the arms of a demon of speed. Ice whirred softly under his boots; quiet air became cold wind whipping his garments and chilling his cheeks.

But not enough speed. The skiing black priests had a headstart. The Mouser hoped the level stretch would wreck them, but they merely sailed out from it with squat majesty and came down without losing footing—and hardly two spears' lengths behind. Daggers and ice-lance gleamed wickedly.

The Mouser drew Scalpel and after trying fruitlessly to pole himself along to greater velocity with it, squatted down so as to offer the least resistance to the air. Still the black priests gained. Fafhrd beside him dug in his dragon-pommeled longsword so that ice-dust spouted up fountainwise, and shot off in a great swing sideward. The priest bearing the ice-lance swerved after him.

Meanwhile the two other priests caught up with the Mouser. He arched his hurtling body away from the spear-thrust of the first and knocked that of the second aside with Scalpel, and for the next few moments there was fought the strangest sort of duel—almost as if they weren't moving at all, since they were all moving at the same speed. At one point the Mouser was sliding down backward, parrying the nasty blowgun-spears with his shorter weapon.

But two against one always helps, and this time might have proved fatal, if Fafhrd had not just then caromed back from his great sideward swing full of speed from some slope he alone had seen, and whirled his sword. He passed just behind the two priests and then their heads were skidding along separately from their bodies, though all at the same speed.

Yet it would have been all up with Fafhrd, for the last black priest, perhaps helped by the weight of his ice-lance, came hurtling after Fafhrd at even greater speed and would have skewered him except the Mouser deflected the ice-lance upward, with Scalpel held in two hands, and the icy point merely ruffled Fafhrd's streaming red hair.

The next moment they all plunged into the white-icy mist. The last glimpse the Mouser had of Fafhrd was of his speeding head alone, cutting a wake in the neck-high mist. Then the Mouser's eyes were beneath the mist's surface.

It was most strange to the Mouser to skim swiftly through milky stuff, ice-crystals stinging his cheeks, not knowing each instant if an unknown barrier might wreck him. He heard a grunt that sounded like Fafhrd's, and on top of that a tingling crash, which might have been the ice-spear shattering, followed by a sighing, tortured moan. Next came the feeling of reaching bottom, followed by an upward swoop, and then the Mouser broke out of the mist into the purple-yellow day and skidded into a soft snowbank and began to laugh wildly with relief. It was some moments before he noticed that Fafhrd, also shaking with laughter, was likewise half buried in the snow beside him.

When Fafhrd looked at the Mouser, the latter shrugged inquiringly at the mist behind them. The Northerner nodded confirmingly.

"The last priest dead. None to go!" the Mouser proclaimed happily, stretching in the snow as if it were a featherbed. His chief idea was to find the nearest cave—he was sure there would be one—and enjoy a great rest.

But Fafhrd turned out to be full of other ideas and a seething energy. Nothing would do but they must press on swiftly until dusk, and he presented to the Mouser such alluring pictures of getting out of the Cold Waste by tomorrow, or even nightfall, that the small man soon found himself trotting along after the big one, though he couldn't help wondering from time to time how Fafhrd could be so supremely sure of his direction in this chaos of ice, snow, and churning, unpleasantly-tinted clouds. The whole Cold Waste couldn't have been his playground, surely, the Mouser told himself, with an inward shudder at child Fafhrd's notion of proper places to play.

Twilight overtook them before they reached the forests Fafhrd had promised, and at the Mouser's urgent insistence they began to hunt for a place to pass the night. This time a cave wasn't so easily come by. It was quite dark before Fafhrd spotted a rocky notch with a clump of stunted trees growing in front of it that promised at least fuel and passable shelter.

However, it appeared that the wood would hardly be needed, for just short of the tree-clump was a black rock outcropping resembling the one that had given them coal last night.

But just as Fafhrd joyfully lifted his axe, the outcropping came to life and lunged at his belly with a dagger.

Only Fafhrd's exuberant and undiminished energy saved his life. He arched his belly aside with a supple swiftness that amazed even the Mouser, and drove the axe deep into his attacker's head. The squat black body thrashed its limbs convulsively and swiftly grew stiff. Fafhrd's deep laughter rumbled like thunder. "Shall we call him the none black priest, Mouser?" he inquired.

But the Mouser saw no cause for amusement. All his uneasiness returned. If they had missed their count on one of the black priests—say the one who had spun down in the snowball or the one supposedly slain in the mist—why mightn't they have missed their count on another? Besides, how could they have been so convinced, simply from an ancient inscription, that there had been only seven black priests? And once you admitted there might have been eight, why mightn't there be nine, or ten, or twenty?

However, Fafhrd merely chuckled at these worries and chopped wood and built a roaring fire in the rocky notch. And although the Mouser knew the fire would advertise their presence for miles around, he was so grateful for its warmth that he found himself unable to criticize Fafhrd at all severely. And when they had warmed and eaten their roast meat from the morning, such a delicious tiredness came over the Mouser that he tucked his cloak around him and headed straight for sleep. However, Fafhrd chose that moment to drag out and inspect by firelight the diamond eye, which made the Mouser open his own a slit.

This time Fafhrd did not seem inclined to go into a trance. He grinned in a lively and greedy fashion as he turned the gem this way and that, as though to admire the beams flashing from it while mentally appraising its value in square Lankhmarian goldpieces.

Although reassured, the Mouser was annoyed. "Put it away, Fafhrd," he snapped sleepily.

Fafhrd stopped turning the gem and one of its beams blinked directly at the Mouser. The latter shivered, for he had for a moment the sharp conviction that the gem was looking at him with evil intelligence.

But Fafhrd obediently tucked the gem away with a laugh-and-a-yawn and cloaked himself up for sleep. Gradually the Mouser's eerie feelings and realistic fears were both lulled as he watched the dancing flames, and he drowsed off.

The Mouser's next conscious sensations were of being tossed roughly down onto thick grass that felt unpleasantly like fur. His head ached splittingly and there was a pulsing yellow-purple glow, shot through with blinding gleams. It was a few moments before he realized that all these lights were outside his skull rather than inside it.

He lifted his head to look around and agonizing pain shot through it. However, he persisted and shortly found out where he was.

He was lying on the hillocky, dark-vegetated shore across the acid-seeming lake from the green hill. The night sky was live with northern lights, while from the mouthlike slit—now open wider—in the green hill's pinkish top, a red smoke came in puffs like a man eagerly panting and heaving. All the hill's green flank-faces seemed monstrously alive in the mixed lights, their mouths twitching and their eyes flashing— as if every one of them held an eye-diamond. Only a few feet away from the Mouser, Fafhrd stood stiffly behind the stubby pillar of rock, which was indeed a carved altar of some sort, topped by a great bowl. The Northerner was

chanting something in a grunty language the Mouser didn't know and had never heard Fafhrd use.

The Mouser struggled to a sitting position. Gingerly feeling his skull, he found a large lump over his right ear. At the same time Fafhrd struck sparks—apparently with stone and steel—above the bowl, and a pillar of purple flame shot up from it, and the Mouser saw that Fafhrd's eyes were tight shut and that in his hand he held the diamond eye.

Then the Mouser realized that the diamond eye had been far wiser than the black priests who had served its mountain-idol. They, like many priests, had been much too fanatical and not nearly as clever as the god they served. While they had sought to rescue the filched eye and destroy the blasphemous thieves who had stolen it, the eye had taken care of itself very nicely. It had enchanted Fafhrd and deceived him into taking a circling course that would lead him and the Mouser back to the vengeful green hill. It had even speeded up the last stage of the journey, forcing Fafhrd to move by night, carrying the Mouser with him after stunning him in his sleep with a dangerously heavy blow.

Also, the diamond eye must have been more foresighted and purposeful than its priests. It must have some important end in view, over and beyond that of getting itself returned to its mountain-idol. Otherwise, why should it have instructed Fafhrd to preserve the Mouser carefully and bring him along? The diamond eye must have some use for both of them. Through the Mouser's aching brain reverberated the phrase he remembered Fafhrd muttering two nights before: "But it needs the blood of heroes before it can shape itself into the form of man."

As all these thoughts were seething painfully in the Mouser's brain, he saw Fafhrd coming toward him with diamond eye in one hand and drawn longsword in the other, but a winning smile on his blind face.

"Come, Mouser," Fafhrd said gently, "it is time we crossed the lake and climbed the hill and received the kiss and sweet suck of the topmost lips and mingled our blood with the hot blood of Nehwon. In that way we will live on in the stony rock-giants about to be born, and know with them the joy of crushing cities and trampling armies and stamping on all cultivated fields."

These mad phrases stung the Mouser into action, unintimidated by the pulsing lights of sky and hill. He jerked Scalpel from its scabbard and sprang at Fafhrd, engaging the longsword and making a particularly clever disarming thrust-and-twist guaranteed to send the longsword spinning from Fafhrd's hand—especially since the Northerner still had his eyes closed tight.

Instead, Fafhrd's heavy blade evaded the Mouser's swift one as easily as one avoids a baby's slap, and, smiling sorrowfully, he sent a rippling thrust at the Mouser's throat that the latter could escape only with the most fantastic and frantic of backward leaps.

The leap took him in the direction of the lake. Instantly Fafhrd closed in, attacking with scornful poise. His large face was a mask of blond contempt. His far heavier sword moved as deftly as Scalpel, weaving a gleaming arabesque of attack that forced the Mouser back, back, back.

And all the while Fafhrd's eyes stayed tight shut. Only when driven to the brink of the lake did the Mouser realize the reason. The diamond eye in Fafhrd's left hand was doing all the seeing for the Northerner. It followed every movement of Scalpel with a snaky intentness.

So, as he danced on the slippery black rim above the wildly-reflecting lake, with the skies throbbing yellow-purple above him and the green hill panting behind, the Mouser suddenly ignored Fafhrd's threatening blade and ducked and slashed unexpectedly at the diamond eye.

Fafhrd's cut whistled a finger's breadth above the Mouser's head.

The diamond eye, struck by Scalpel, exploded in a white burst.

The black furry ground beneath their feet heaved as if in despairing torment.

The green hill erupted with a vindictive red blast that sent the Mouser staggering and that shot a gush of molten rock twice the hill's height toward the bruised night-sky.

The Mouser grabbed hold of his bewilderedly-staring companion and rushed him away from the green hill and the lake.

A dozen heartbeats after they left the spot, the erupting molten rock drenched the altar and splashed wide. Some of the red gouts came even as far as the Mouser and Fafhrd, shooting fiery darts over their shoulders as they scampered. One or two gouts hit and the Mouser had to beat out a small fire they started in Fafhrd's cloak.

Looking back as he ran, the Mouser got a last glimpse of the green hill. Although still spouting fire and dribbling red streams, it seemed otherwise very solid and still, as though all its potentialities for life were vanished for a time, or forever.

When they finally stopped running, Fafhrd looked stupidly down at his left hand and said, "Mouser, I've cut my thumb. It's bleeding."

"So's the green hill," the Mouser commented, looking back. "And bleeding to death, I'm happy to say."

MEGALOMANIA RULES

LORING BRENT

GEORGE FRANK WORTS (1892–1962) used the pseudonym Loring Brent for many of his pulp stories, most notably his Peter the Brazen series, one of the most popular (and best) in the distinguished history of *Argosy*. Peter Moore is a wireless radio operator aboard ships plying the waters near China, where he finds himself in the midst of wild adventures and in confrontations with villains of epic proportions. The author, in addition to being a successful businessman, editor, and writer, had also worked as a ship's wireless operator as a young man, much like his greatest hero. The Peter the Brazen series ran in *Argosy* in 1918 and 1919, but by virtue of frequent demand, the character was revived in a superior series that ran from 1930 to 1935, also in *Argosy,* regarded by many pulp aficionados as the finest series of action-adventure stories of all time. In particular, the three novellas in which Peter faces the evil Chinese mastermind "the Blue Scorpion" are considered classics of pulp fiction. The three encounters with the Blue Scorpion, among other stories, were most recently reprinted in the impressive two-volume set *The Compleat Adventures of Peter the Brazen* (2003); another recent collection is 2007's *Peter the Brazen.* Both books were published using the author's real name, George F. Worts, rather than the Loring Brent pseudonym under which the Peter Moore stories were originally issued.

"The Master Magician" was first published in the February 25, 1933, issue of *Argosy.*

THE MASTER MAGICIAN

LORING BRENT

CHAPTER I
IN THE DARK

ICE HOUSE LANE has always been a dark, danger-ous little thoroughfare—the scene of quiet knif-ings innumerable. The nearest street lamp is well up the hill and around the bend, where Duddel and Zetland and Wyndham Streets and Albert Road, after twisting and writhing about among the hills, triumphantly merge.

Ice House Lane is a lonely little lane at best. It climbs steeply from Queen's Road and quickly loses itself in the hill that sweeps up so majesti-cally from Hongkong Harbor. Its unimportance is frowned upon by dingy houses and frowzy es-tablishments. Here are obscure merchants and traders who deal in third-rate opium and cam-phor and ginger.

Here, too, is Ice House Inn, a very obscure inn, which commends itself to the wayfarer be-cause of its very obscurity and many exits. In Ice House Inn a hunted man may rest his weariness, secure in the knowledge that he can make es-cape, if necessary, by any of thirteen exits.

Peter Moore had selected Ice House Inn as a temporary abode, while his enemies in northern

A scene was appearing in the crystal!

China forgot his existence, entirely because of its obscurity and its handy exits. He came and went very quietly, generally after dark. He did not relish the dankness and furtive air of Ice House Inn. But dankness and furtiveness are preferable to six inches of steel in the back.

Turning the corner into Ice House Lane on this particular night, he was totally unprepared for the surprise that awaited him. He collided with a stranger in the dark.

It was darker at that corner than the innermost passage in a Chinese Emperor's tomb, darker than the inside of a cow. Sometimes there was light from the stars. To-night there were no stars. Salty vapor was rolling in from the sea, and at higher altitudes this vapor formed billowing dark clouds.

There was no good reason to suppose that the collision was not an innocent accident. Afterward, Peter Moore realized that the fellow must

have been waiting there. There was a thump as the two men met. And while Moore could see nothing of him, his groping hands informed him that the man was heavy and muscular—a white man in white man's clothing.

Both men grunted, then laughed, then apologized. Moore's groping hand encountered the man's hand. On the instant, the hand of the invisible stranger slipped a small flat object into his hand. And he was promptly gone.

Peter Moore yelled after him, and started to follow. But he heard no footsteps or echoes of footsteps. He ran all the way back to Queen's Road. A ricksha coolie went clop-clopping down the moist pavement between the shafts of his empty vehicle. Against a moldy brick wall, a Sikh in a dirty red turban was broiling a fragment of fish at the end of chopsticks over the glowing coal of a brazier.

The American ran back to the intersection.

He peered into doorways, into likely lurking places. But the man with whom he had collided was nowhere to be seen.

Having satisfied himself that search was useless, he stepped into a deep doorway, made sure that he was unobserved, and struck a match. In the light of the match flame, he scrutinized the object which had been thrust into his hand by the mysterious stranger.

It looked at first like a thin, flat, red candy lozenge, about an inch square.

But the little red lozenge, unfolded, became a sheet of crackling red paper, similar to the paper in which, with tinfoil, camera films are wrapped. The match flame showed a row of tiny manikins drawn in white ink. There were five of them. Each was the symbol of a man. The three symbols at the left of the row were checked off.

Moore studied this unsigned cryptograph with eyes at first surprised and wondering, then incredulous. The flame of the match, forgotten, burned down to his fingers. He dropped the stub of the match, thrust the red paper into his pocket, and went up the hill to Ice House Inn at a lope.

In the dark and unwholesome reception room was an old-fashioned wall telephone. He nervously called a number. A man answered. Moore asked for Miss Susan O'Gilvie.

A clear, crisp young voice presently sounded in Moore's ear. When he spoke, Miss O'Gilvie gave a little shriek of delight.

"I've changed my mind," he said. "Do you still want to go to Roger Pennekamp's party?"

"I'd love to! I'm dying to!" she cried. Then, in a hushed voice, she added, "Has anything happened?"

"No," he said.

A lean gray shape like a starved rat slunk out between two blobs of darkness, which were fishing junks. It was a motor launch, low, lean, powerful. It was running without lights of any kind.

It crept out of the vaporous dark, whispered past under the glossy white stern of the yacht *Buccaneer*, and slipped off in the direction of Hunghom Bay, picking its way among the rusty-sided tramps and the sleeping sampans and junks with which Hongkong Harbor was littered.

As it passed, the man who stood smoking a cigarette at the stern rail of the *Buccaneer* became aware that a pair of green eyes were steadily staring up at him from one of the portholes. Nothing but the two eyes. No face. No mouth. No nose. They might have been set in the head of a man or a leopard or a gigantic snake. They were as cold as bits of glacier ice. Sparks of sly intelligence, they stared up at the young man in the dress suit with unwinking curiosity. As the porthole passed, the eyes slowly slid in invisible sockets.

These eyes were so cold and somehow so sinister that the young man in the dress suit felt a momentary uneasiness, as if a malignant will were reaching out and coming to grips with his own; and the sensation it gave him was that he had touched some creature that was ugly and slimy.

With a flick of his fingers, he sent his cigarette spinning down through the air. The glowing ruby spark dropped into the water beside the gray launch, missing the porthole by inches and giving him a fleeting glimpse of the face in which the green eyes were set—a face oily and square, the color of saffron.

Peter Moore had expected to recognize that face, but he was sure that he had never seen it before.

He watched the gray launch slink and vanish into the thin mist with a bubbling of exhaust from throttled engines, and he made sure once again that the automatic pistol in the holster strapped under his left armpit was there.

He was not aware that a Chinese deckhand had crept up behind him on silent felt soles and had held up two fingers of one yellow hand for the green eyes to see. Nor was he yet quite aware that the gray launch might prove to be the herald of an amazing adventure.

But he was suspicious.

Dance music, as soft and smooth as though filtered through silk, came from the *Buccaneer*'s ballroom, to mingle with the creakings and groanings of the shipping anchored and moored all about. Scents of expensive perfumes, too, mingled with the stench from these ageless hulks.

Roger Pennekamp was giving this party with his customary lavishness. There were over a hundred guests aboard—the cream of Hongkong's diplomatic and social circles. The Recourse Bay Hotel orchestra had been hired for the evening. There was an abundance of food and anything you wished to drink, from good German beer to vintage champagne.

Peter Moore was by way of being the guest of honor—a very belated guest of honor. Roger Pennekamp had sailed into "The Pearl of the Orient" this morning in his palatial yacht, had ferreted out Peter Moore and insisted on celebrating their reunion. They hadn't met in six years.

"I'm taking a look around the world, studying conditions," the American oil millionaire had explained, "and when I heard the rumor, in Singapore, that you were back in southern China, I came two thousand miles out of my way to say hello."

But there was more than that behind the *Buccaneer*'s visit. There was trouble. Peter Moore had detected it in the eyes of his old friend. They were the eyes of a man haunted by fear.

Moore now understood why. The lozenge of red paper explained why—with shocking eloquence.

He had been opposed to the party because he was systematically avoiding all social functions. He was living according to a Confucian proverb: What the eye does not see and the ear does not hear, the brain does not concern itself with.

His determination to avoid being seen in public had been shattered by the little crackling sheet of red paper. With troubled eyes on the mist into which the gray launch had slipped, he heard a girl's low, excited voice say, "Peter! The next dance is ours! Remember!"

.   .   .

He turned to find Susan, her eyes bright, her face pink with excitement, her dark sleek hair disarrayed. When she was excited she was beautiful.

Her new gown, of midnight-blue satin, was cleverly cut to reveal the beauty of her slim tanned shoulders and practically her entire and equally beautiful slim back. The matched pearls about her neck seemed to glow with inner fires against the rich golden brown of her skin.

There was something very warm, very vital, about Susan O'Gilvie. Moore had never seen the pearls before. They must be worth a quarter of a million. He would perhaps never see them again. He sometimes suspected Susan of wearing jewels once, then giving them away.

Once, a pair of diamond heels she had worn had almost cost both of them their lives. She scorned his warning that to wear costly jewels in China was to invite death. In fact, she scorned warnings of any nature.

Reputed to be the richest young woman in America, if not in the world, she could afford to indulge her whims. Susan was a thrill hunter—a girl with an insatiable hunger for adventurous excitement.

Time after time she had plunged herself into dangerous predicaments and had frantically called upon Peter Moore to help. Since the eventful night of their meeting on the trans-Pacific crossing, she had—always with the most innocent of intentions—drawn him into one dangerous Oriental complication after another, until he was now a hunted man, a refugee. It was as if she had deliberately spun a web of enchantment about the young man, a web with threads of gold. But he was not in love with Susan O'Gilvie.

Looking at her vivid loveliness now, he told himself so emphatically. He could not possibly love a girl with her thirst for excitement, her greed for thrills, and he certainly could not love a girl whose weekly income was greater than his yearly salary from the General Electric Company.

Yet her attitude, even when she was angry with him, was that he had always belonged to her, and always would.

Her eyes, not blue, but a deep, alluring violet, were trying to transmit an appeal, a message. She said, menacingly, almost growling it, "Remember! This is our dance!"

Moore looked about for an explanation. He suspected that she was up to more mischief. Then he saw the cause of her perturbation—a tall, slim, black-haired young man who was forging through a group of men and women near a doorway.

Jason Whitelaw had become, in the past month, something of a problem. He was the latest of Susan's endless procession of lovesick young men. Jason Whitelaw was taking a sightseeing trip through the Far East when, in Hongkong, he had met Susan—and condensed his sightseeing.

He was a cultured, suave young man from Boston, and he appeared to have an independent income. Susan treated him coldly; gave him no encouragement. She had been a target for too many fortune hunters.

It seemed to Peter Moore that Jason Whitelaw was eminently eligible, but when he said so to Susan, she had indignantly cried: "Stop throwing eligible young men at me! When I get around to thinking of marriage, you are going to be the victim. Besides, I think Jason Whitelaw is snaky."

He didn't, as he approached now, look snaky to Peter. He looked like a hurt and crestfallen young man. His dark eyes were liquidly appealing.

Susan, backing to the rail beside Peter, slipped her hand through his arm and seemed to snuggle against him.

"Mr. Moore asked me for this dance," she said sweetly.

The black-haired young man looked imploringly at Peter, and Peter, feeling very sorry for him, said, "We're going to sit it out. You'd better join us."

He winced as Susan pinched his arm. Then she quickly said, "Jason, I've lost my scarf. Will you see if I left it in the bows?"

Jason Whitelaw hesitated. He looked suspicious and even more hurt, as if he knew that she was merely trying to get rid of him.

"Will you wait here?" he said in his deep, melancholy voice.

"Of course we will!" Peter said heartily.

When the sorrowful young man had gone, Susan sighed impatiently. "He makes me furious! He's so damned meek! He said he'd jump off a dock with a piece of railroad iron tied to his neck if I didn't promise to marry him. I said I'd help him tie it on! It was dark and spooky up there. He tried to kiss me. It was like being kissed by a dying calf. And what's more," she said, working herself into a fine fury, "I'm going to do something violent to you if you tell me once more to be nice to him. I'm a one-man woman. And I've worn myself to a shadow being nice to him. I despise him!"

Moore chuckled. Susan indignantly removed her hand from his arm and stared balefully across the black water toward the lights of the Peak. The reflections of these lights on the misty water were dull blades like disused swords.

Susan shivered and, looking up contritely, said, "I'm sorry I got mad, Peter. But the truth is, I feel uneasy. I've had a premonition all evening that something ugly is going to happen."

Peter nodded, with a lazy grin.

"Yeah?" he drawled. "You're up to something, and you're breaking it gently."

"Not at all, my dear," she said crisply. "Ever since you telephoned me, I've felt uneasy. And I wish you would explain why you changed your mind about coming to this party."

A man's deep voice interrupted her with, "I hope I'm not intruding." It was their host. Roger Pennekamp was a heavy-set man of about fifty-five, with the keen eyes, the powerful chin, and the executive manner which are commonly ascribed to American business giants.

He gave Susan an admiring smile, but looked

at Peter grimly. "Pete," he said, "it's time for us to go into a huddle. I've got something on my mind that won't keep any longer. Let's go to my room where we can have privacy and I'll tell you my real reason for barging up to Hongkong to see you."

Susan started impulsively away, but the oil magnate said quickly, "No, no, Miss O'Gilvie. You're included. You're a clever young woman, and you may be helpful. It is a very disturbing mystery. We'll need your level head."

Susan darted a somewhat triumphant look at Peter as Mr. Pennekamp took her arm. She had seldom been accused of being level-headed, and she was seldom taken so seriously. She was flattered.

Moore followed them up the wide deck to the owner's suite. The door was opened upon an airy, spacious sitting room, as luxurious as the drawing room of an expensive apartment. Shelves along the walls were inviting with books. There was even a fireplace in which were fire-dogs supporting halved logs ready to be kindled.

Moore observed, in one corner, a low ebony taboret inlaid with mother-o'-pearl on which stood a carved ebony elephant. On the tusks and trunk reposed a sphere of crystal about four inches in diameter, as clear as a drop of rain water. He recalled that Roger Pennekamp had always been interested in occult phenomena, and he remembered that Roger Pennekamp had, in the old days, consulted a crystal ball. This one betrayed the value he placed on metaphysical paraphernalia. It was a museum piece, worth a small fortune.

Closing and bolting the door, the American millionaire said harshly, "Pete, I learned in Singapore that Hiram Coopwood vanished two months ago!"

Susan glanced quickly at Peter Moore. His eyes were lazily closed. He looked as if he were grinning. He wasn't grinning. It was a queer expression, instantly gone.

"Two of us left," he said quietly.

The millionaire gravely nodded. "You and I, Pete."

Susan excitedly cried, "How perfectly fascinating!"

CHAPTER II
THE MENACE

Roger Pennekamp took a rich-looking blond cigar from a bronze humidor, bit off the end, and lit it. His hand holding the match was trembling a little. Susan did not miss that detail, or that he looked pale and haggard.

He said, "Did you get one of these?"

And he removed from his vest pocket a little lozenge of red paper, similar to the one which the mysterious stranger had thrust into Moore's hand in the dark of Ice House Lane. It proved, when he unfolded it, to be identical. There were the five little figures of men, in white ink, with the three on the left checked off.

Moore nodded, and removed the cryptograph from his pocket.

"You didn't even mention it," Susan said indignantly. "What does it mean?"

"The five figures," Mr. Pennekamp replied, "stand for five men. The three that are checked off are John Kyle, Adam Brumpter, and Hiram Coopwood. The two unchecked figures are Peter and myself. John Kyle, Adam Brumpter, and Hiram Coopwood are checked off because they have one by one vanished. John Kyle disappeared in 1927 while prospecting for gold in New Zealand. Adam Brumpter vanished from a hotel in Buitenzorg, Java, in 1929. Hiram Coopwood walked out of his bungalow in Singapore one night two months ago and has not been heard from since. Pete, has anything happened to you?"

"Nothing so far."

"Then I must be slated for the next disappearance. Within the last few months, three attempts have been made. In Zanzibar, an ivory trader who happened to bear a close resemblance to me was murdered. He was my dinner guest. We were sitting in the stern with the lights out because of the mosquitoes. I went to fetch some fresh cigars. When I returned, he was gone. Next morning his body was found floating in the harbor, with a brass wire around his neck.

"In Ceylon, two Hindus were shot by members of my crew while attempting to pick the lock of that door. They were shot because, since these things began to happen, I've given orders to my crew to shoot first and ask questions afterward.

"In Sydney, a definite kidnap attempt was made. I was walking down a dark street, on my way to the waterfront from a hotel. Four men jumped me—threw a black cloak over my head. By pure luck, a policeman happened along; they whisked off the cloak—vanished!"

Susan uttered a small shriek. She looked excitedly from Pennekamp to Moore. She fired questions: "But why? What's at the bottom of it? What have you done? Who sent this message?"

"Zarlo."

"Who?" Susan bleated.

The millionaire looked surprised. "Hasn't Pete told you about Zarlo?"

"No!"

"It was a closed book," Peter said grimly. "I hoped it would stay closed."

"But who," Susan panted, "is Zarlo?"

"A human mystery," Pennekamp replied. "The most dangerous indivual in the Far East. A sorcerer. A magic worker—black magic! A master of the occult. A hypnotist. A mind reader. The only white man I ever knew who had thoroughly mastered the mysteries of Yoga. A man who can, with the crystal ball, twist your mind inside out—make you completely the slave of his will!"

Susan glanced quickly at Peter. She knew that he did not believe in such things. But Susan was always ready to believe anything that sounded thrilling.

She said breathlessly, "He sounds positively fantastic! He doesn't sound human!"

"He doesn't," Pennekamp said, "look human. He's tall, lean, and dark. Black cavernous eyes. A bony skull. The most sinister-looking man I've ever seen."

"Why does he want you and Peter to vanish?"

"We offended him," said Peter.

"We kicked him off a throne," Pennekamp amplified.

"And let a wild mob kick him around in the dust," Peter added with a wry grin.

Susan expelled her breath with an explosive sound. "Tell me about it!" she commanded.

"It happened," the millionaire said, "about six years ago in the sultanry of Tuzpan, in Luzon. Four of us—four Americans—were involved. I had an oil concession, John Kyle a copra concession, and Hiram Coopwood and Adam Brumpter, respectively, a tin mine and a gold mine."

"None of us was in Tuzpan when the trouble started—when Zarlo came to Tuzpan. Why he went there or where he came from no one knows. I heard a strange rumor that a white man—a tall, sinister white man—had become the king of Tuzpan.

"It didn't make sense. Tuzpan was ruled by a native girl, Queen Lali, the daughter of old Sultan Malava. Zarlo came to Tuzpan, evidently saw rich opportunities, and promptly dominated Lali's will.

"His first act was to order all Americans out of the sultanry. Actually, Queen Lali issued that ukase. Tuzpan, being in the Philippines, is supposed to be an American protectorate, and I don't have to mention the sinfully careless policy of the United States in dealing with her protectorates. She lets those old Philippine sultans do very much as they please.

"Zarlo did exactly as he pleased. What he wanted, apparently, was a clear field for practicing a fanatical religion. It was a horrible religion. It involved human sacrifice and bloodletting for the supposed purification of the soul. Briefly, his idea was general moral degradation. He was, of course, to be the god."

"He must have been mad," Susan said.

"No," Pennekamp disagreed, "he was only shrewd. There was something back of that religious idea. I mean, it was part of some plan. God knows what the plan was."

The millionaire mopped perspiration from his forehead with a billowing white handkerchief.

"He was such a striking devil. That was it! He did look like the devil—like the conventional portraits you've seen of Satan. All he lacked was horns. He had the deep-set eyes, the satanic smile, and he certainly had the devil's persuasiveness—and dark powers.

"When the Tuzpan trouble started, I was in Japan with John Kyle. I cabled Pete, in Shanghai, to go down and investigate. Because Pete has a greater practical knowledge of the Far East than any white man out here.

"Pete hadn't been in Tuzpan ten hours when Zarlo ordered his arrest. Pete escaped through the jungles, made his way to Manila, and cabled me his information. I chartered a tramp steamer, picked up Brumpter and Coopwood in Hongkong, and Pete in Manila. We went to Tuzpan.

"We went ashore—the five of us—armed to the teeth. It's always been my rule, in a surprise attack, to strike fast and hard. We struck hard. We went to the palmetto house where Zarlo was holding court—actually sitting on a throne—and before any one realized what we were up to, we unthroned Zarlo. I mean, we pulled and kicked him off his teakwood throne!

"The mob that had followed us from the waterfront and through the streets waited for lightning to strike us for our effrontery to the Great White God. But the only lightning striking that afternoon was in Pete's oratory.

"He used the throne as a soap-box. He made a speech in the native dialect while we held Zarlo. The mob seemed hypnotized."

"What," Susan breathlessly interrupted, "did you say to them, Peter?"

Moore grinned. "It began," he said: " 'Friends, Tuzpanians, and countrymen, lend me your ears. I come to bury Zarlo, not to praise him!' "

"You make me furious," Susan said. "Go on, Mr. Pennekamp."

"Whatever it was Pete said, it calmed them down. But it was a dangerous calm. They suddenly decided that Zarlo had tricked them. Before we could interfere, they ganged him.

"Mind you, we didn't want that. We didn't want his life. We simply wanted him to clear out of Tuzpan, and we were using the most effective method we knew. But it was too effective. Things were out of control—wild!

"They dragged him out of our hands. They tore off his clothes. They stoned him. They kicked him around in the dirt. He got away finally, in a dugout. But before he went, he sent us his compliments. He said he would get us all!

"We'd heard too many down-and-outers make such threats to worry. We forgot Zarlo. Queen Lali came out of her trance and ruled Tuzpan again. Every so often, you know, some ambitious white man finds himself on the beach and cooks up the scheme of becoming king of some native tribe. Generally, they don't last long. They blow up like toy balloons. I put Zarlo in that class. And that was where I made my mistake.

"When John Kyle disappeared in New Zealand, I wasn't alarmed. He had enemies. He led a dangerous life. But when Brumpter vanished similarly in Java, I was alarmed. And when Hiram Coopwood vanished in the identical manner of the others, I knew that Zarlo—somewhere—somehow—was making good on that threat of his.

"Any lingering doubts in my mind were dismissed when these mysterious occurrences I mentioned began happening to me. It appeared definitely that I was to be the next victim."

Susan's eyes were almost black with excitement. "But where is Zarlo?"

The oil magnate shook his head as if with weariness. And wearily said, "I don't know. No one knows. In the past two months, I've spent upwards of two hundred thousand—gold—trying to find out. I've hired the cleverest detectives in the Far East. I've had this part of the world combed for Zarlo—Japan, Mongolia, China, India, Cambodia, Malaya, the South Seas. It's no use. This minute, I'd give a cold million to know where he is!"

Mr. Pennekamp's cigar had gone out. He had chewed the end of it to shreds. He burst out savagely, "Damn him! He's laughing at me! He's playing with me! He's got me! Why do you suppose he sent this cryptograph? To show his contempt! He's failed three times, but sometime he won't fail—in spite of every precaution I can take! I can't lock myself up in a fort. I've got to keep on the go. My business demands it. And sooner or later he's going to succeed. And he's going to get you, too, Pete!"

Susan, shivering, cried, "Oh, please don't say such things! There must be some way."

Pennekamp said heavily, "I've exhausted all the ways there are. I've used the crystal. Pete laughs at such things. But I've got images in it. I know that Zarlo uses one. I know that if I just concentrate, if the vibrations are right, I can catch him by the use of the crystal.

"All right!" he shouted. "Go on and laugh!"

"I'm not laughing," Peter said.

"But you think it's a joke!"

"No. I've never been convinced. I'm willing to be convinced."

"All right. Wait until midnight. It always works best for me after midnight. I'll try to show you what I've seen every night for the past two weeks."

"The same image?"

"The same image—not clear enough to describe."

"Do you think," Susan breathed, "it has something to do with Zarlo?"

"I'm convinced of it!"

Susan looked at Peter with a certain hostility. "I suppose you don't agree with that, either."

He firmly shook his head.

"Or that Zarlo has the powers that Mr. Pennekamp says he has?"

"I don't believe that Zarlo has occult powers," Peter answered. "I concede him nothing but a tremendous personality—evil but tremendous—and powerful magnetism. And terrific will power." He grinned faintly. "You see, Susan, I'm one of the men who has never seen an Indian boy climb a rope suspended from nothing."

Susan snorted irefully. "But Mr. Pennekamp has made a study of such things. Look at those books!"

Peter had seen those books six years ago—many of them. He knew that Pennekamp had a library well stocked with works on Yoga, hypnotism, spiritism, demonology, crystal-gazing, mind reading, thought transference, astrology, and kindred subjects. Many of them Peter had studied.

"I suppose," Susan said, "that you don't think Zarlo used magical powers of some kind in making those three men vanish!"

Again Peter shook his head. "No, Susan. My humble opinion, since you've asked for it, is that Zarlo is comfortably entrenched, hidden, somewhere, and has sufficient means to pay handsomely for mysterious disappearances. But don't think that I underestimate his mentality. I simply believe that he is the brains, the so-called master mind, behind a very efficient organization."

Susan said stubbornly, "I think you're wrong. I agree absolutely with Mr. Pennekamp." And she looked at Mr. Pennekamp with shining eyes. Always, when given the choice, Susan decided on whatever would give her the greatest thrill.

The millionaire said, "Frankly, Pete, I came up here because I want to place myself in your hands. I want you to take charge of this horrible mess. I'll place unlimited funds at your disposal. The *Buccaneer* will go wherever you say. Only stay aboard. Match your wits with Zarlo's. I must return to my guests now. Don't go ashore to-night until I've given you the crystal demonstration. It may give us a clew of some sort."

Some one tapped discreetly at the bolted door. Peter, who was nearest, unbolted and opened it.

Jason Whitelaw was standing outside with

Susan's black-and-silver scarf draped over one arm. His eyes were liquidly appealing.

Beyond him, beyond the rail, Peter saw the gray launch sliding past, vanishing into the vaporous murk between the two junks.

CHAPTER III
KIDNAPPED

Susan said, in a voice of exasperation, "Oh, Lord."

"I thought you were going to wait," the sad-eyed young man said reproachfully. "You said you would."

Susan caught a sharp glance from Peter and said, "I'm awfully sorry, Jason, but I forgot all about it."

"You promised me another dance," Jason said mournfully, "and the orchestra is playing 'Good Night, Ladies.'"

Susan glanced again at Peter, a little uncertainly. His eyes said very plainly, "Be a good sport." And hers flashed back the equally plain retort, "I'm just fed up with being nice to him!"

But she went, thereby proving that Peter Moore exercised some slight control over that spirited young person.

A group of guests came up the deck, heading for this doorway. Among them Peter recognized Henshaw, the American consul to Hongkong. Peter was not precisely on speaking terms with Consul Henshaw. Consul Henshaw had made it very clear, in a brief conversation less than one week ago, that Peter Moore's continued presence in Hongkong was highly undesirable. And it seemed to Peter, at that moment, that American consuls, in cities up and down the China coast, had been murmuring such messages to him ever since he was a little boy.

He slipped out on deck. He wanted to keep an eye on that gray launch. And he wanted to be alone, to think.

The deck was almost deserted. The party was rapidly breaking up. A launch loaded with guests was just leaving the ship's ladder for Blake Pier. The orchestra, sobbing out "Good Night, Ladies," sounded as if it were dying.

Peter made his way up to the boat deck. From here he could see the harbor better. A square white excrescence amidships—just abaft the yellow funnel—he presumed was the wireless shack. It was dark. He tried the doorknob. Locked.

An amiable voice said, "Homesick, Mr. Moore?"

A tall, slender young man was lounging against a funnel guy. In the glow from the wheelhouse, Peter discerned a small black mustache in a hard, brown face, and the mild gleam of gold on collar and sleeves. The captain.

"My name's Tackaberry. I've seen you around. You used to be a wireless operator, didn't you, before you stood the coast on its ear?"

Peter Moore was always emphatic in his denials that he was a trouble hunter. He maintained that his escapades were always innocent enough, but his reputation was a case of the dog once given a bad name. It stuck.

But he wasn't feeling argumentative. Captain Tackaberry detached himself from the funnel guy and said, "I suppose the old man has called you in to help ride herd."

Peter wasn't giving out information, either. "Where did he sign you on?"

"Sydney. Or are you replacing Sparks?"

"No," said Peter. "I'm just prowling around, wondering about a gray launch I've seen standing off and on out there."

"Her?" the skipper said. "Isn't she a police boat?"

"No. The harbor police boats are black and carry an antenna. I'd keep an eye on her."

He had the feeling, as he continued aft, that the air was charged with a "Says you!" Captain Tackaberry was cocky, and, by the bulk at his hip, he was, Peter gathered, armed. Starting down an iron ladder into the stern, he reflected that Roger Pennekamp had no doubt turned his crew into an armed guard.

Reaching the main deck again, he started forward on the starboard side, watching the lights of Causeway Bay through the thin mist. He saw nothing of the gray launch.

The yacht had a deserted feeling. All the guests had left.

At the forward turn of the deck he almost collided with Jason Whitelaw, hurrying around from the other side. Susan's black-and-silver cloak hung over one arm. He looked surprised. He said sharply, "Where's Susan?"

"I thought you took her off to dance."

"I did! But when the music stopped she told me to get her cloak and meet her at Pennekamp's cabin. She said she was going there for you. She isn't there!"

Peter wasn't alarmed. "She's probably in the engine room," he said, "kidding the engineers, or in the pantry, having a sandwich. She'll turn up."

A wild scream put a period, so to speak, to that. It came from aft and was suddenly muffled.

Peter had heard Susan cry out in terror before. He knew the sound of her scream. He saw now that the stern was in darkness.

Jason cried, "Some one just switched those lights off! It's swarming with coolies!"

Peter, starting down the deck, could see figures churning about in the semidarkness back there.

He shouted, "Susan!" and started to run.

Roger Pennekamp, suddenly emerging from a corridor doorway, white with panic, cried, "What is it, Pete?"

"They've got Susan!" Peter, snatching out his automatic, ran on.

Just beyond the stern rail he saw the upper works of the gray launch. Two dim shapes at the rail were passing down what looked like a long, slim bundle into hands reaching up ghostlike from below.

The bundle was squirming and kicking.

He dared not fire yet. Jason, pounding down the deck beside him, panted, "Shoot! For God's sake, shoot!"

But Peter didn't shoot until the squirming bundle had vanished. His intention was to shoot his way to the rail, then to shoot into the engine compartment of the gray launch.

But his plan was frustrated. A mass of yellow men came charging toward him. Peter fired with deliberation. At his left elbow another pistol was roaring. More feet came pounding down the deck. Other feet were pounding overhead.

Then he was surrounded. His assailants were harbor *fokies*—the yellow scum of the Hongkong waterfront, half-naked, silent, armed with knives.

He emptied the pistol into them, then clubbed it and systematically hammered heads and faces and hands.

He found himself shoulder to shoulder with Captain Tackaberry. On his other side was Jason Whitelaw. Mr. Pennekamp was not to be seen.

The captain was wielding a revolver that looked, as its butt came clanking down on a skull, two feet in length.

Reinforcements came surging aft down both sides of the deck.

Harbor coolies were spilling over the rail like rats. Some of them reached the deck or the cabin roof of the gray launch. Others fell into the water and yelled.

A fist or knee caught Peter full and hard in his solar plexus. His breath and all desire to stand erect departed with a painful grunt.

He rolled over and tried to sit up. But his muscles were paralyzed. He could neither speak nor move.

Jason Whitelaw was a few feet away on his knees, with blood gushing out of a cut below his left eye.

The deck was littered with casualties, most of them yellow. Just behind Peter lay Roger Pennekamp, face down, clawing at the deck with his fingernails.

Some one turned on the lights as Peter got to his feet, with his breath painfully sobbing in his throat. He stiffened himself against an impulse to collapse. He wedged himself between two men at the rail who were yelling and firing into the mist with revolvers. He caught a glimpse of the gray launch vanishing into the vapors.

It disappeared with a muffled roar of powerful engines toward the open sea.

CHAPTER IV
IN THE CRYSTAL

Peter Moore, recovering his wind, heard Captain Tackaberry profanely barking orders. He discovered that the left sleeve of his coat was slit from shoulder to elbow, that the shirt sleeve under it was slit and soaked with blood from a knife slash of which he had been unaware.

The *Buccaneer* was to up-anchor and get under way immediately.

It was useless. Peter knew it was useless. There was only one possible hope. He pushed himself away from the rail and staggered to the iron ladder which ran to the boat deck. He was still painfully short of breath. He laboriously climbed the ladder and made his way to the wireless house. He braced his back against the bellying side of a lifeboat and kicked until the lock gave and the door flew inward.

He turned on lights, threw switches to the transmitting position, and rapped out, with the Morse key, the call letters of the Hongkong harbor police radio station.

When the central station answered, he tapped a message to the official in charge, briefly describing the gray launch, and requesting that it be overhauled and held with every one on board. He signed the message "Pennekamp."

Through the open door he heard the clanking of a heavy chain, the sound of men running to and fro, then the vibration of powerful engines.

The *Buccaneer* was under way. When Peter went below, the deck was crowded with harbor police officers. One of the police launches, attracted by the shooting, had come alongside to investigate.

The captain of the police boat wanted the *Buccaneer* to remain at her anchorage for an official inquiry. Roger Pennekamp was expostulat-

ing. The yacht was meanwhile picking her way through shipping.

Peter had no interest in that argument. He was sick with worry. He was furious at himself for having let Susan out of his sight.

Returning to the wireless cabin, he put on the ear phones and waited for an answer to the message. He heard, far away, the shrill yapping of a Jap freighter talking with the Formosa station. Closer at hand were the mosquito-like voices of the harbor police boats, reporting failure. Police boats stationed in Lyeemoon Pass, Tathong Channel and Quarry Bay made their reports. No launch of the description given had been seen.

Peter went out on deck, sick with disappointment. The wrangling on the deck below was still going on. Roger Pennekamp was shouting that he didn't give a damn about British police or admiralty red tape. A cold English voice was citing a list of penalties for leaving a port without clearance papers, and for disobeying police orders.

The *Buccaneer* was meanwhile slipping down Tathong Channel to the sea. The lights of Kowloon dwindled.

The central police radio station was calling when Peter returned to the instruments. He wondered where the *Buccaneer*'s radio operator was. There was an answer to the message, and it was a disheartening answer. The gray launch, unquestionably headed for the sea, had escaped with clean heels. One of the police boats had identified and hailed it, had ordered it to halt, had sent a shot across its bows; and the gray launch had fled at a speed estimated at forty-five knots!

No one could guess where the gray launch was heading. A tramp freighter, a junk, miles offshore, might be waiting at a rendezvous to receive its passenger. Or the launch might be, at this moment, hidden behind any one of the hundreds of small and large islands with which the China coast in this region is dotted.

A Chinese boy in white appeared in the doorway and said, "That masta, him wanchee you that side." He jabbed downward with a thumb.

Peter went below. He was heartsick and still

seething with self-recriminations. The police and their boat were gone. The deck had been cleared of dead and wounded.

Roger Pennekamp and the young man from Boston were waiting for him in the sitting room of the owner's suite. Both men showed evidences of frantic worry. The millionaire was pacing up and down, chewing distractedly at a dead cigar. Jason Whitelaw was slumped in a chair, his face as white as the bandage which had been applied to the gash in his cheek.

When Peter closed the door, Pennekamp said, "I've been telling Whitelaw about Zarlo. There's no question that Zarlo was behind this attack. Those men had instructions to get the three of us—Miss O'Gilvie, you, and me. They expected to overpower the crew. But we happened to strike too hard. Mark my word, Pete, this isn't the end. He'll keep on till he gets us. What have you been doing?"

Peter told him. Pennekamp nodded. "I thought you were up there. Once they got her, they were safe. And Lord knows where they're taking her!"

"To Zarlo," Peter said wearily.

Jason burst out frantically, "Good Lord, can't you find out where this fellow Zarlo is?"

Roger Pennekamp stopped pacing. "I may be able to. I think I've been on the right track for weeks. To-night, with so much in the air, I may have luck."

Peter realized where this was leading. The crystal ball! He knew that, in the crises of his life, Roger Pennekamp consulted that lucid sphere as some men, equally rational in all other respects, consulted astrologists or fortune tellers.

The millionaire was explaining that he could not possibly hope for results if there were skepticism or ridicule in the room. Would Peter promise to bring an open mind to the crystal? Would Whitelaw?

More to humor the distracted man than because he had the slightest faith in such things, Peter promptly assented.

"We will sit on the three sides, facing inward, facing it," Pennekamp said. "Kindly sit down, gentlemen. I will turn out all the lights save the one directly overhead."

When the two young men had seated themselves in chairs facing the crystal ball, the oil magnate switched off the lights, then pressed another button which controlled a pale green bulb overhead.

It gave a ghostly light. A pale-green spark seemed to float in the ball.

"I must ask you to help me as much as you can, gentlemen," Pennekamp said, seating himself in the third chair.

Peter, touching the table, had found that it was bolted to the deck, and that the little ebony elephant supporting the sphere was bolted, or fastened somehow, to the top of the taboret. And he supposed that this provision had been made in case of rough weather.

Pennekamp was crouched down, staring into the depths of the ball. "You must concentrate," he said tensely. "You realize that what we want to know is, where Miss O'Gilvie is being taken. Where that is, Zarlo is. *We—must— concentrate!*"

It was not hard for Peter to concentrate. He wanted the answer to that question more than he had ever wanted anything in his life. He stared into the crystal ball until his eyes ached. It underwent, in his imagination, curious changes of substance. It became a large, perfectly round drop of water. It became a soap bubble. It became a perfect sphere of colorless transparent jelly. The reflection of the pale green light overhead played strange tricks.

He thought he saw the ball growing luminous, filled with an aurora-like display of blue and green and yellow.

Pennekamp said hoarsely, "It's coming through!"

"Blue and green and yellow!" Jason Whitelaw whispered.

Peter started. Very definitely he saw the play of light now.

The colors shifted about. The green became a horizontal stripe, or streak, at the bottom of the ball. Above this, golden light shimmered. And above the yellow, blue—the blue of a tropical sky.

He could not, would not, believe this. His eyes were playing tricks on him!

The blue at the top of the ball was a soft burning blue. The green at the bottom had a shivering shifting quality. He caught a glimmer of white. It shocked him. That glimmer was exactly like the frothing white of a breaking wave!

Then he saw that the glowing yellow area between sky-blue at the top and sea-green at the bottom was a cliff.

"There it comes!" Pennekamp whispered.

Peter saw trees now, very clearly, as if they came out of this spectroscopic fog. They were at the base of the sandstone cliff.

Now the cliff shockingly changed. It was not a cliff but a yellow skull, with sockets where the eyes had been, a socket where the nose had been.

But it wasn't a skull. It was a cliff. Blue sky overhead. Deep-green sea beneath. With a cluster of palms along the beach at the base.

Peter's heart was hammering in his ears.

"Look! Look!" Pennekamp cried harshly. "Don't you see it? The sky? The sea?"

The young man from Boston whispered, "It's there! A cliff! And palm trees!"

The millionaire said tremulously, "Pete?"

Peter said heavily, as if he were speaking in spite of himself, "Yes. It's there. Clear."

"It's what I've been seeing every night for the past two weeks!" Pennekamp said triumphantly. "But never so clear!"

Jason Whitelaw said, in a desperate voice, "Is that where she is? Is that where she is?"

"You do see it, Pete?"—a gasp.

"Yes."

"Do you make it out?" Pennekamp cried. "I mean, have you seen it before? Does it mean anything? Is it any place you've seen?"

"Wait a minute," Peter said. It was all suddenly clear—almost clear. Once, on a moonlit night, he had seen that skull-like headland.

He exclaimed, "Skull Island—Sinanga—Borneo!" as the words, or pictures, flashed into his mind.

The image was fading. The vivid, intense colors swam, dimmed. Gradually the image vanished. The ball became empty.

The green spark, a reflection of the bulb overhead, seemed to swim back out of a rainbow haze.

Roger Pennekamp sprang up, switched on the lights. His face was flushed. His eyes were glittering with excitement.

"Don't lose it!" he said with a nervous laugh, and pressed a wall button. He opened the door. When a steward appeared, he said, "Tell Captain Tackaberry to come here at once." He swung around on Peter. "Where is this place?"

"South of Borneo."

"An island?"

"A large, wild island."

"Skull Island?"

"That's what sailors call it, because of that headland. I think the name on the charts is Sinonga, or Sinanga."

Pennekamp had trotted to a wall where hung a large chart of the western Pacific. Peter joined him.

"In the Java Sea?"

"Yes, I'm sure of that—almost due west of Makassar, almost due north of Soerabaya—I'd say where the lines meet. I know it's about midway between the Equator and ten south."

They were probing about among circles and squares and oblongs on the chart—the little known islands to the south of the great irregular mass which is Borneo.

Peter found it. It was spelled "Soononga."

Captain Tackaberry came in, with his white cap cocked on one side of his curly brown hair.

The owner said, "Have you ever heard of Skull Island?"

The skipper frowned, squinted, grimaced. "Yes, sir. I think so. It's familiar."

"Pete, is there any question in your mind that what you saw is the headland of Skull Island, or Soononga?"

"I'm sure."

Pennekamp jabbed his spatulate forefinger at the long rectangle labeled Soononga I.

"This is where we're going, captain. How long will it take?"

"About a week."

"Know those waters?"

"I've sailed through those islands in a windjammer. They're pretty tough waters. Bad currents."

"Well, that's where we're going. Now!"

CHAPTER V
SKULL ISLAND

The night when Skull Island was sighted was destined to be one of violent surprise. Roger Pennekamp, Peter Moore, and Jason Whitelaw were seated in steamer chairs on the port side amidships when the excitement began.

The night was hot and still. The stars, brilliantly rippling, gleamed on a sea as flat, as dark as a sheet of slate. There was no wind except that which was created by the *Buccaneer*'s passage. She was traveling slowly, because of uncharted reefs. At intervals a man in the bows heaved the lead and cried out the depth in fathoms to the bridge.

There was an air of tension aboard, a sense of unexpected exciting possibilities.

The three men, in deck pyjamas, were sipping long iced drinks. They spoke seldom. Out there in the darkness, they knew, was Soononga Island. Peter could all but feel the loom of it.

The moon rose at a little after ten thirty. There was a forewarning silky red gleam, like ruby light shining on a taut wire, along the east-ern horizon. Then the moon popped up out of the sea like a ripe red plum.

The night grew palely luminous as it rose. And as its brilliance became silver and reached out, the land they were skirting came into visibility like the image on a photographic film being developed.

Far ahead, off the port bow, was the headland—a ghostly, palely-glowing thing, even at this distance and in this wan light strikingly resembling a human skull. It seemed to glow eerily, with an inward light of its own.

Peter was standing at the rail, with Jason on his left, the millionaire on his right, when it happened. Looking across the strait at the dark mystery of the island, he was wondering if Susan was captive there. His face in the deck-light was haggard.

He had suddenly a curious illusion of sound. It was as if, from all around him, were the whispers of fingers, hands rubbing together.

Then the blow fell. It was, in a way, a repetition of that night in Hongkong, more than a week ago. Suddenly, the deck was swarming with silent, half-naked men, only these invaders were dark-brown, or black—not yellow.

Before he could cry out, a hot, salty wet hand was clapped down upon his mouth, and his neck was jammed in the crook of a powerful arm.

He kicked backward, caught a shin with the heel of his foot; struck again. His captor grunted deeply, slightly relaxed that strangle hold.

Peter, writhing, twisting with all his strength, caught a blurred glimpse of men struggling all over the deck. He saw Roger Pennekamp wriggle out of a black man's arms, reach for his pistol. Day and night since Hongkong that pistol had never been out of reach.

He fired it into the black man's mouth, and the black man went toppling back to the rail.

Peter struck out with both fists. He had the satisfaction of seeing one antagonist fall leadenly. Another. And another. But it was hopeless.

Some one dropped a black cloth down over his head. Mighty arms pinioned his arms. He was lifted. Stifling under the black hood, trying to extricate himself, he felt that he was being carried rapidly down the deck toward the stern. There were shouts and cries. Pennekamp was yelling for the crew. Evidently the invaders hadn't overpowered him.

A fist or club crashed down on Peter's head. The blow did not knock him out. It rendered him only partially unconscious. But it paralyzed his muscles, his very will to struggle. Limp, helpless, he felt himself being handed down and down.

A moment later, still held tightly by powerful hands, he heard an engine begin to purr.

More shouts and more shots.

Under him, some kind of craft gave a leap. He heard water hissing under a hull being propelled at tremendous speed.

A moment later, while his hands were held, the wrists were bound with rope, the black cloth was removed, and a strange voice said, "Take it easy, Moore."

Blinking, he looked into the sun-blistered face of a white man with red hair. The white man sat beside him. There was a German automatic pistol in one hand. The other hand was grasping the wheel, which was of the automobile type. His face was brightly lighted from the instrument board.

The red-headed man was grinning. Peter turned his head, looked aft. Directly aft was a covered compartment which housed the engines. Aft of the engine compartment was a large cockpit packed solid with black men—presumably the boarding party. And dwindling astern, like a vision, was the snowy white hull, with its diamond-sparkling lights, of the *Buccaneer*.

Some one groaned on the other side of him. He looked quickly and gave a grunt of surprise. Slumped down in a corner of the seat was the young man from Boston, wrists likewise bound. A lump over Jason's left eye looked as large as a

hen's egg. He was still groggy from the blow which had raised that bump.

Peter looked back at the redhead.

"Any sense asking you questions?" he said grimly.

"Not unless you want to get hoarse," was the answer. "You better save your strength, fella."

This had a sinister sound. Peter presently learned that it had a sinister meaning.

"But you didn't get Pennekamp," he said.

"No," the redhead said harshly. "But we will. He won't leave now. He won't run out on his pals!"

The speedboat, Peter saw, was of the most modern and luxurious type. It was traveling over the smooth water of the strait at a speed of at least thirty-five knots.

He looked apprehensively toward land. Soononga Island appeared to be a solid wall of jungle growing at the foot of high dark cliffs; a sinister island, dark with sinister possibilities.

The cliff magically opened. The boat entered a zone of rich, sickly sweetness—the mingled odors of nameless jungle flowers, which, opening in the dark, were spilling their cloying sweetness into the faint breeze that drew offshore.

A river flowed out through the opening in the cliff. Beyond was a small round lake. The redhead switched on a searchlight. The boat crossed this lake with unabated speed and charged up a black river not more than twenty feet in width, arched over by the branches of trees and snake-like vines.

The tunnel thus formed echoed with the reverberations of the speedboat's exhaust. The sides of the tunnel were a tangled, slimy mass of mangrove trunks.

At a distance which Peter estimated to be approximately a mile from the lake, the redhead throttled the engines. There was a crude wharf of logs on the port side. He maneuvered the boat alongside the wharf and said curtly, "Come on, you guys."

Peter climbed out. Groaning, Jason followed. They looked about them. There was only a small clearing carved out of the jungle by the wharf—no evidences of human habitation.

"This way," the redhead said. "Step lively."

"How far?" groaned the young man from Boston.

"Plenty far."

He started ahead along a narrow trail with a flashlight in one hand. Peter observed that there were other flashlights in his pockets—one protruding from each hip pocket. They must mean a long trek.

As they advanced along a thin, twisting trail, which had been hacked through the jungle, the blacks began to vanish. Other trails, like tributaries, led off from it, and from time to time, a handful of the natives would slip off along one of these "feeders," presumably toward their villages.

It was a night of horror. Baleful eyes glowed at them from thickets. Insects assailed them in swarms. The trail wound and twisted through the densest jungles Peter had ever seen, through swamps, through immense fields of parched cactus grass, higher than a man's head.

Time after time, Peter stumbled over an unseen root or a slippery stone and fell. And the redhead evidently had a sense of humor. When Peter or Jason fell, the redhead laughed. He laughed when they floundered through a fast stream, waist-deep, with slimy banks tangled with alligator grass. He laughed when they cursed at unseen thorns which tore at their flesh.

The sky was filling, like a dark sphere, with the pale suffusion of tropical dawn when the three white men, followed by a half-dozen blacks, entered an immense field of the parched cactus grass. They fought their way through it, Peter judged, for a quarter of an hour. The sky was pink-stained when, reaching the other side of it, they entered another stretch of dense jungle. Monkeys chattered and shrieked at them.

The trail was well traveled here. And the night of horror came abruptly to an end. The trail ended at their objective—a towering mass of dark stone—a castle built in a clearing hewn from the jungle! It reached at least a hundred feet into the air. High up were windows. The structure had the air of an impregnable fortress.

Peter, running his eyes up the dark, moss-grown wall, reflected with sardonic humor, "Journeys end in lovers' meetings." Perhaps Susan was still alive in this grim edifice. Knowing Zarlo, knowing how the mind of that monomaniac ran, he could picture the fate in store for him. Death by cruel torture, with Susan standing helplessly by. Zarlo had had six years in which to prepare for this triumphant moment.

They reached a heavy door of some dark tropical wood studded with the heads of bronze spikes.

The red-headed man hammered on it with the butt of his pistol. The door opened. A middle-aged man with ferret's eyes stood in a small hallway, from which a flight of stone steps ran upward. He wore the white livery of a servant in the tropics. His smile was suave and oily.

"Come in, gentlemen," he whispered.

The red-headed man was evidently not a gentleman, for he did not come in. He turned about and walked down the trail. Peter wondered where. That trail, he believed, was the only means of escape.

The man in white re-bolted the great door and said unctuously, "If you will follow me, gentlemen, I will show you your quarters."

He might have been a butler in any American or English mansion.

The two tired young men, their faces swollen from insect bites, their deck pyjamas bloody and tattered from thorns and repeated falls, followed him up the stone stairway to another bronze-studded door.

He unlocked the door, and locked it after them, pocketing the key.

The hall which they had entered might have been the reception hall in any luxurious American or English country house. A living room and a library gave from it. All the floors were of a light-hued hard wood like oak. Rich Oriental rugs covered them. Tapestries and fine canvases hung on the walls.

It was incredible—impossible to believe that this castle, with its luxuries, existed in the heart of a savage jungle island.

Since landing on this island, Peter's mind had been occupied with little else but thoughts of escape, provided he could rescue Susan. Such hopes as he had were fading. As he progressed through this fantastic castle, he saw no one but the servant, yet he had the sense that his every step was spied on.

The two prisoners were conducted up a wide, handsome stairway. The bannister was of mahogany or nara-wood, beautifully inlaid with mother-o'-pearl.

Their escort led them down a long wide hall, with doors on either side. All were closed. Beyond each was mystery. Was Susan behind one of them?

At one of the doors the servant paused. He opened a small, pearl-handled pocket knife, and carefully cut the cords binding Jason's wrists. He gave the same service to Peter, then said, in his suave manner, "Gentlemen, you are the guests of Zarlo. Anything you wish is yours. This is your room, Mr. Whitelaw."

Jason gave Peter a bewildered look from sick, bloodshot eyes and limped into the room.

"This way, Mr. Moore."

"Don't we bunk together?"

"Hardly, sir! We have accommodations here for sixty guests and you are practically our only ones."

"Practically?"

"Practically," said the man with his unctuous smile.

He had stopped at another door, six beyond Jason's.

"I am instructed to say that when you are bathed and dressed, my master has requested that you go to the green room on the floor above this. You will find clothing to fit you in the wardrobe."

With his somewhat sinister smile, he withdrew. Peter opened the door and entered a room which might have been a guest room in any rich man's house in almost any civilized country. It was tastefully, even magnificently, furnished. The furniture—bed, chairs, chest of drawers, dressing table—looked European.

Adjoining the bedroom was a luxurious bathroom in white tile. If Peter had not been so apprehensive about Susan's fate and his own future, he would have marveled at all this luxury—marveled at the patience, the money which must have been expended so lavishly to erect this remarkable retreat.

He conducted a brief tour of exploration. From two windows on one side, he looked down upon the dark green roof of the jungle. He went to the closet. It seemed to be full of men's clothes, all sizes, but not new.

Curiously, he looked in the inner coat pockets at tailors' labels, to ascertain who had worn these clothes.

A cold thrill proceeded down his spine as he read the first name. Hiram Coopwood! Hiram Coopwood, who had left his Singapore bungalow for a walk two months ago and had never been seen again! In another coat was the name of John Kyle, written in indelible ink in the label of a New York tailor. John Kyle had vanished in New Zealand in 1927. In another coat, he found the name of Adam Brumpter, who had disappeared so mysteriously in Java in 1929.

Peter wondered why Zarlo had captured Jason. Was Jason to be an innocent victim?

All logical thought was at that moment driven from Peter's head by a sound. It was like the roar of a jungle beast, but it resembled the roar of no beast that Peter had ever heard. A snarling, half-human roar, it was blood-chilling.

Peter ran to the window. He threw it open and looked down. He saw nothing.

He had the hopeless, desperate feeling that a relentless fate was closing in on him.

CHAPTER VI
JASON'S TRUE COLORS

The servant had returned to Jason Whitelaw's room. Without knocking, he turned the knob and walked in. He quickly closed the door.

The young man from Boston, exhausted, was stretched out on the bed. He sprang up now and cried hoarsely, "Where is she, Hascomb?"

The servant did not seem at all surprised that Whitelaw knew his name.

"Across the hall, sir, the third door down—left."

"Oh, my God!" the young man groaned. "Why? Why wasn't she put on another floor?"

"What difference does it make? Moore won't live long enough to bother."

Whitelaw said angrily, "That isn't the point. She must not know about him. My whole scheme is ruined if she knows he is here."

"I'm sorry, sir." Hascomb did not look sorry. He looked surly.

Impatiently, Whitelaw said, "Well, give me the key."

Hascomb forked a key out of his pocket. "I don't think you need have any alarm, Mr. Whitelaw. She is completely under the master's power."

Whitelaw snatched the key out of his hand and snapped, "Clear out of here!"

He did not wait for the door to close. He stripped off his tattered garments, ran into the bathroom, and shaved and showered. Then he ran back, threw open the closet, took down a white linen suit. From a chest of drawers he removed a shirt, socks, underwear, a necktie. All these clothes fitted him perfectly.

With a glance at his bruised, swollen face in a mirror, he picked up the key and let himself out. He went to the door Hascomb had specified, inserted the key, and opened it.

A girl's voice mumbled, "Peter!"

Whitelaw put his finger to his mouth, said "Sh!" warningly, and closed the door. Susan got up from a chair in which she had been sitting by a window. She wore a white linen dress which obviously had not been made for her. Her face was gaunt and colorless. Her eyes had a dazed, leaden look. They were the eyes of a person drugged.

Whitelaw eagerly took her hands. She stared up at his face, blinking her eyes, as if trying hard to think.

"Jason!" she whispered. Her hands were cold and limp. She seemed inert, lifeless.

"Listen!" he said. "We must be very quiet. If I am discovered here, my life won't be worth a cent. Darling, I've come here—fought my way here through the jungles—to rescue you. I've got a ship, a schooner, waiting. Somehow, I'll get you out of here. I love you, and, if necessary, I'll die fighting for you!"

This somewhat grandiose speech did not seem to impress Susan. She was staring into his face. She whispered, thickly, "Where—is he?"

"Who?"

"Peter!"

Jason averted his eyes and compressed his lips. He frowned. His shoulders seemed to sag. "In Japan," he muttered.

"Oh!" Susan said softly.

"I'm sorry, Susan. He was scared out. The night they got you in Hongkong, he simply went all to pieces. He knew Zarlo was after him. He—he decided he would be safest in Japan."

"Peter?" the girl said incredulously. "Peter did that?"

"I'm horribly sorry. There was nothing for me to do but my best, single-handed. I found from one of the men we captured in that Hongkong attack, where Zarlo lives. I came here. Now, listen carefully! Zarlo thinks I was shipwrecked here. He suspects nothing. I'm going to get you out of here somehow."

Susan, looking at him, whimpered. Her dazed eyes were glistening with tears. "I can't believe that Peter did that!"

"I know how you feel, darling. I'm sorry—horribly sorry."

She seemed to go limp. He caught her into

his arms. He had not intended to do that. He had intended to be cautious. But the sight of her destroyed his careful intentions. Holding her almost savagely, he kissed her. Limp in his arms, Susan made no protest—nor did she respond.

Panting, trembling, he put her away from him finally and attempted to cover his mistake. "Susan, you must trust me. You know I love you enough to give up my life for you."

Susan looked at him tragically. "I can't believe that Peter—"

"Forget him!" Jason snapped. "He's yellow!"

He went to the door, trying to control his anger. He had been doing that for so many months that now, after his recent hardships, it threatened to blow up.

But her drugged eyes contained neither surprise nor suspicion. Still hungry for the touch of her slim body, he rejected the impulse to return to her. He must be more restrained. He must make her realize what he had suffered to save her. She would, in time, love him. She must love him.

Quietly, he let himself out. He went swiftly down the hall and down the stairs. Crossing the library, he opened a door at the far end of it, and said sharply, "Zarlo! Are you here?"

He did not feel as courageous as his voice sounded, or as he tried to look.

The room he had entered was almost totally dark. High on the side of a wall, a pin-point of light gleamed. Out of the darkness emerged, slowly, the bulk of a figure seated before a table. About eight inches above this table, the pin-point of light was repeated.

Whitelaw knew that Zarlo was occupied with his crystal. He was afraid of Zarlo, of his dark powers.

"Zarlo!" he said sharply.

A deep voice, crackling as with an electrical discharge, came from the invisible face above the crystal.

"You have failed," the voice said.

Stifling his fear of this man, Whitelaw cried angrily, "That's not true!"

"Your agreement was that you were to bring both of them."

"Was it my fault that the men you sent fumbled their chance? Pennekamp had a gun. I thought they'd overwhelm them. If they'd stayed any longer, the crew would have driven them off, and you wouldn't even have Moore."

He was breathing hard, indignantly. "And you haven't lived up to your agreement. You were to take every precaution that Miss O'Gilvie did not become aware of Moore's being here."

"Is she aware of it?" the crackling voice said.

"She may become aware of it! Why couldn't she have been put in another part of the house?"

The magician said, "Whitelaw, you are a fool. You are a harebrained fool. You will never get away with this. Just what is your plan?"

"Is that schooner waiting on the other side of the island?"

"It is."

"Then my plan is unchanged. I will go through all the motions of rescuing her from here. I will take her through the jungle to the schooner."

"And then—?"

"I will marry her!"

"What a fool you are, Whitelaw! What good will marriage do? She is infatuated with Moore. You can never get him out of her head. Once you reach civilization, she will be through with you."

"No. I'm counting on her gratitude. With Moore dead, she'll turn to me, love me, in time."

"No, Whitelaw. I have seen into her brain. There will never be another man in her brain but Moore. With her wealth, she'll stop at nothing to find out what's become of him."

"How can she find out anything? He will be dead. He left Hongkong secretly. No one knows how or when or why he left Hongkong. I told her he went to Japan."

"Yes. You are so infatuated with her beauty, and so greedy to have her money, that you aren't thinking at all. How about the crew of the *Buccaneer*?"

"They'll be scattered all over the world. You're going to get Pennekamp within a few days. His yacht will go to the nearest port. The crew will disband."

"You're not only a fool, you're a dangerous fool. The Chinese say, 'A man burning with passion follows the undulations of a thought.' You think neither to left nor to right of it. You think of nothing but this girl's body—and her wealth. Don't you realize she will hunt the world for the crew of the *Buccaneer*? And will find out from them that you lied—that Moore came here?"

"I have it all worked out," Whitelaw said angrily. "We are not going immediately to civilization. We are going to be wrecked conveniently on one of the Javanese Islands, where a ship never calls. A renegade missionary is there—waiting there. I may keep Susan there years—until she falls in love with me."

"I still say you are a harebrained fool! You are exposing me needlessly to danger. I have not yet decided that I will let you carry out your farcical rescue of the young lady. I have taken a fancy to her. I may decide to keep her for myself."

Whitelaw said harshly, "Zarlo, if you go back on our agreement, hell will bust!"

The shapeless figure over the crystal ball chuckled.

CHAPTER VII
THE SKULLS

Refusing to wear dead men's clothes, Peter rummaged about in drawers and presently found a gray flannel shirt and a pair of white duck pants which fitted him fairly well.

He went down the hall, pausing at Whitelaw's door. He knocked, waited, tried the knob. He called softly, but there was no answer. Presuming that the young man from Boston was asleep with exhaustion, Peter proceeded to the staircase, looked up, hesitated, then went down.

He wanted to investigate. He wanted to look for avenues of escape and, generally, to get the lay of the land.

He returned to the hall through which he and Whitelaw had been conducted by the servant. The door at the top of the stone steps, which led down to the great studded entrance door, was locked. To the left of it was another door, closed but not locked. Opening it, Peter discovered another flight of steps, likewise of stone. He walked cautiously down. The steps led to the cellars. In various rooms, quantities of food were stored here, as if for a siege. He wondered where the servants were, the guards. So far he had not seen any one but the butler.

A tunnel ran between rooms and vanished into distant murkiness. He walked down it a hundred feet. It was, possibly, an underground passage to some exit in the jungle. He came to a heavy door which was locked.

He turned about and retraced his steps, climbed the stairs and again entered the hall. He had the feeling that, while he saw no one, he was under constant observation. He entered a spacious drawing room, filled with beautifully carved furniture.

A familiar exotic perfume attracted him. He went to the end of the room and entered a large hall of white stone. It was a kind of reception hall—an immensity of white stone. A fountain gurgled and splashed in the center of it. This room was at least a hundred and fifty feet square. Along the walls were placed at regular intervals carved chests, the chests, perhaps, of early Spanish explorers. Above them hung great tapestries.

On a small table, he found, with other items, a full box of Japanese safety matches. He thrust the box into a pants pocket.

The room was sickly sweet with the odor of the frangipani blossom. Looking about for the source of the smell, he saw that it emanated from a large stone trough, filled with the waxy white flowers, on a balcony.

Peter climbed a narrow stairway to the balcony, which ran all about the great room. Here were other wall ornaments—actually a museum collection: trophies of all kinds from the southern seas, brilliant old grass tapestries from

Tahiti, Papuan lances, spears, bows and arrows, shields, blowguns, Brunei bronze war gongs. In one corner stood a suit of medieval Japanese armor, reddish-brown.

Peter examined the balcony and its appurtenances with great interest, but was disappointed in what he found. There was no way of escape. All the windows on the lower floor were heavily barred.

He went to the stone trough. It was a Papuan chieftain's coffin, brilliantly decorated in a savage pattern of reds and greens and blues, resembling the sarcophagus of an Egyptian king. It stood on two pedestals near the edge of the balcony. Peter went close and sniffed the blossoms.

He went to the rail and looked down. The rail was a thick blue velvet rope, strung along posts, affixed to the top of each post with heavy blue velvet cord. Just below him was a stone table about twelve feet in length. On either end of it stood a Satsuma vase, gold, red, and white. Each of these vases was six or seven feet high.

This great room was, in short, very much like a museum room. Its deathly silence, and the feeling that he was being watched, added to his apprehension. He tried one of the doors near the stone coffin. It opened, to his surprise, into the hall not far from his bedroom.

An idea was tugging at his imagination, but it was not yet ripe. He proceeded down the hall to the stairs again and this time went up. He climbed one flight and found himself on the top floor.

At one end of the hall was a large room of many windows, bright with the early-morning sunlight. At the other end was a locked door. A steep flight of steps led to a trapdoor, which, he supposed, opened upon the roof.

He walked into the green room, alert with suspicion and curiosity. The walls were tinted green; the rugs and hangings had been selected to carry out the green color scheme.

This was evidently a game room. There was a billiard table at one end. Here, too, the walls were adorned with trophies of the southern seas—spears, shields, blowguns. In one corner were several glass cases which he did not notice until later, because they were against the glare of the morning sun.

He made a tour about the windows. A door gave upon a balcony. He went out and inspected the scene. Below him the jungle extended in great waves of green in all directions. The horizons consisted of hills. The sea was not visible.

Zarlo, he realized, had constructed this castle with the intention of making it absolutely inaccessible. Certainly, no one would have suspected its existence.

Looking over the edge of the balcony, Peter saw, close to the side of the house, a walled inclosure. The walls, of stone, looked high. Down low on one wall, a large iron ring had been set into the masonry, and from this ring a heavy rusted chain led into a small structure of bamboo and palm thatch built in one corner of the inclosure. He supposed that a large dog was at the other end of the chain, asleep in the thatched structure.

He returned to the green room and for the first time saw the glass cases. There were five of them. Each case was about a foot square, neatly built of plate glass with nickeled metal bindings. Each case stood on a stone pedestal. They looked like exhibition cases in a museum.

He walked swiftly over to them, with his heart suddenly thumping in his throat.

Of the five cases, the two at the right were empty. Each of the other three contained a human skull!

With fists gripped at his sides, Peter stared at the three grinning death's heads, and felt the color ebbing from his face.

Then he saw that on each case was affixed a neatly lettered placard. He read the first.

Number One
JOHN KYLE
In Memoriam

This gentleman bravely met his death on Soononga Island while chained to a tree in the jungle on the night of August 7, 1927. Leopards, attracted by the smell of rancid meat with which his naked body was smeared, devoured him.

Feeling more than slightly ill, Peter moved to the next case and read the placard.

Number Two
ADAM BRUMPTER
In Memoriam

This gentleman courageously embraced death on Soononga Island while swimming in Shark Cove on the afternoon of October 15, 1929. With hands and feet tied, he was floated out into the cove, supported by corks. Sharks, attracted by the blood flowing from the stump of his severed hand, devoured him.

Shuddering, Peter glanced at the grinning skull. He saw that the top of the skull had been crushed and skillfully repaired with cement. Deep gouges in the bone over the left eye socket were probably made by sharks' teeth.

He moved to the next case, revolted yet attracted by a morbid, terrible curiosity. The placard read:

Number Three
HIRAM COOPWOOD
In Memoriam

This gallant gentleman gladly greeted death during the night of May 4, 1932, while staked out on an anthill which housed army ants. The ants, disturbed by his presence, marched out in columns of eight and, fleck by fleck, plucked the skin from his flesh and the flesh from his bones.

Scientific Note: Mr. Coopwood screamed for 48 minutes, before he lapsed into unconsciousness. The last shred of flesh was picked from his skeleton 2 hours and 37 minutes from the time the ants attacked.

Sick with faintness, Peter glanced at the two empty cases. There was a placard on each. Each bore only a name, and, beside the name, a large, neat question mark. Number Four was Roger Pennekamp. Number Five was Peter Moore.

He looked dully at the question mark by his name. He was all but nauseated. What horrible form of death was Zarlo planning for him?

He was conscious of a sensation of shrinking in his flesh, as if every fiber of his body were protesting at the threat of some unimaginably horrible torture.

Panic invaded him. He knew that escape—alive—from this fantastic place was impossible. Yet he could die in his own way, if he wished. He could leap to his death from that balcony. Cornered, it was his only choice—death painlessly rather than by some fiendish prolonged torture. Yet, alive, there was always the slim hope that he might somehow contrive to escape—find Susan and deliver her to safety.

He took a desperate grip on his panic-stricken thoughts. Zarlo had, of course, reckoned on that—his hoping until the end. Then torture, undoubtedly more hideous than that to which either of these three poor devils had been subjected.

"Wondering?" a crackling voice behind him said.

CHAPTER VIII
RONGA

Peter wheeled about. Zarlo, tall and dark and sinister, stood there with his arms folded on his chest. In the white satin robe he wore, he gave the effect of great height. His black eyes, set in their darkly blue cavernous sockets, were burning with a light of malignant mirth.

Peter did not, for a moment, see the man

standing beside him, a personal guard. A black man, naked except for a loin cloth, staring at Peter with a gummy grin. There was a curved sword, a *parang*, gleaming in the black hand.

In his harsh, deep, crackling voice, Zarlo said, "Mr. Moore, it gives me the greatest pleasure to welcome you to my house. After so many years!" His manner was gravely courteous. "Are you wondering how you will meet your death? Don't wonder, Mr. Moore. Leave that in my hands!"

Peter controlled an impulse to leap on him, but he knew that the grinning black man would have his head split open before he could reach Zarlo's throat.

"We have come a long, long way, Mr. Moore, from the beach at Tuzpan," Zarlo said. His tone was amiable. He was solicitous of Peter's comfort. Did Mr. Moore find things to his liking?

Peter made no answers. He realized that he was the mouse being toyed with by the cat. His faculties seemed to become sharpened. Every nerve seemed to grow taut, as if preparing for some violent contingency.

"You were examining my pretty skulls. Interesting specimens, aren't they? I think your skull will be a handsome addition to the collection, Mr. Moore."

It was, to Peter, utterly incredible. And his amazement was due not to Zarlo's grotesque threats, but to the fact that he was not a madman. His mania was only that of revenge—revenge for that old blow to his pride, his vanity and his ambition.

"I want to show you something, Mr. Moore." It was the conversational tone of a genial host, showing a guest through his house.

Peter followed him out onto the balcony. The sun on his face was friendly, warming. He had seen that sun rise in far-away places and under remarkable circumstances. Would he live to see it rise once more?

He went to the end of the balcony. How quickly, how easily he could end this panicky suspense!

From where he stood he could look along the side of the house, down past windows to the roof of the jungle.

Zarlo was talking affably. "Perhaps you are curious about my castle, Mr. Moore. It hasn't always been mine. It's really a fascinating story. It carries out my philosophy of life—dog eat dog. That is the philosophy of all wise men. Take what you want!" He paused, cupped hands to his mouth, and called in a deep, ringing tone:

"Ronga!"

Peter, looking down, saw the heavy chain move. Then a shaggy brown head appeared. A creature looked up. A man, it was! An immense man. His head and face were a mat of tangled brown hair. His body was naked except for a loin cloth. He stared up at the balcony with squinting eyes. His eyes, even at that distance, looked dead.

Peter glanced at Zarlo, who was smiling crookedly.

"Mr. Moore, that man was once the owner of this castle. His name is Fulton D. Agnor. You may have heard of him. He was a New York banker. He grew to hate modern civilization. He had no wife, no family, no relatives, and his friends had betrayed him. He converted his wealth into cash. He looked the world over for a refuge, where he could spend the rest of his life isolated. He found, in this spot, his paradise. At incredible expense he built this castle. When you and your friends drove me out of Tuzpan, I heard of this place. I came. With the power of my will, I drove the soul out of Mr. Fulton D. Agnor, making him the snarling, ravening beast you now see. And I gave him his present name by simply reversing the letters of Agnor—Ronga. A fitting name for such a creature!

"I keep him chained there, an animal. A strange kind of pet, eh? If you should escape from here, I would simply turn Ronga loose."

Peter stared at the thing in the inclosure. Zarlo's voice rose again in that ringing shout: "Ronga! Damn you! Ronga!"

The man-beast, staring up, raised his arms. He snarled.

Zarlo called, "Ronga wants his breakfast. Feed him." And to Peter, "Watch the gate."

A barred gate at the end of the pit opened. A white goat was pushed in by unseen hands. The beast roared. The goat bleated in terror. Ronga rushed, in a great leap, to the end of his chain. The goat danced back beyond his reach, bleating.

The beast rushed again. Peter saw him close his hands, like talons, about the goat's neck. He heard, but did not see, the helpless animal die. Its scream, as its neck was snapped, was like that of a human in agony.

Peter, sickened, had looked away. He was filled with loathing, with fury. His senses suddenly cleared. Looking away from the pit, he had glanced down along the wall of the castle. There was a curly brown head protruding from one of the windows, and a small white hand hung limply down over the sill.

It was Susan. She had perhaps seen that bloody affair, and had fainted. Peter saw that her window was on the floor below. He counted the windows from where he stood, estimated where her room was. Just down the hall from his, on the other side!

He glanced quickly at Zarlo. That human monster had not seen. He was staring down with glowing eyes into the pit where the man-beast was savagely devouring the goat.

Jason Whitelaw came out onto the balcony. He was still scowling over his disappointment at the hands of Susan. He glanced at Peter, and his scowl darkened.

Peter stared at him. He had thought that he knew Jason fairly well. And he expected now, not that petulantly scowling young man, but a young man white and quaking with fear.

He expected some kind of signal from Jason, and when the young man scowled at him, as if he did not see him, Peter was puzzled. And his puzzlement became confusion when Jason said, in a surly voice, "Zarlo, what are you going to do with this fellow?"

An unfinished gesture with his thumb indicated Peter. And even then Peter did not comprehend the import of it. It was necessary for him to shift his whole point of view. Jason was an innocent victim of a conspiracy the intention of which was to trap Peter Moore and Roger Pennekamp. At least, Peter had taken that for granted.

His first slow intimation of trouble was the tone with which Jason had addressed Zarlo. It was both petulant and familiar. It clearly indicated, if not a friendship, at least an acquaintance of some standing.

And he realized the shocking truth. Jason had asked Zarlo, in this petulant, familiar tone, what he was going to do with "this fellow"—with him, Peter!

It was hard to grasp all of that at once. Harder still to believe what was a natural, an inevitable conclusion. For a moment, he felt hollow—an "all gone" feeling. Then he was furious. He was murderously furious at this "young man from Boston" who had so heartlessly, so cold-bloodedly betrayed and double crossed him. If it was his last act alive, he would settle that—now!

"You rotten little rat!" he said, and lunged at Whitelaw. His savagely swinging right fist smashed into Whitelaw's jaw. The left fist followed it.

Whitelaw's head snapped up and back. His shoulders swung back. His legs gave way at the knees. He went over and down with a thump.

On his shoulder blades, limp, eyes glassy, he became suddenly invisible. Everything was suddenly invisible. Something heavy and hard had struck Peter forcibly on the back of his head . . .

When Peter recovered consciousness he was lying on the bed in his room. Hascomb was seated on the edge of the bed with a whisky bottle in one hand, an empty glass in the other. He still wore his oily grin. He walked over to a table, placed the glass and bottle on it, and returned to the bed.

"In this house," he said, "it is wise to cultivate self-control."

"In any house," Peter dryly amended, and deeply meant it.

His head ached—a painful pulsing behind his eyes. But strength was flowing back into him. His arms and legs tingled. He wanted to get off this bed, but realized the wisdom of utmost caution. He must take it easy. He must think. And when he had thought, he must act.

His plan for his and Susan's escape was ready. But there must be no more mistakes. He must keep his head.

Lying there, with that sneering servant staring at him, he reviewed his plan of action. It must go off smoothly, without a hitch. He fumbled at his pocket, to make sure the box of safety matches was still there. He gripped his hands, to make sure there was ample strength in fists and arms.

And lying there, trying to take it easy, making sure he had overlooked no contingencies which it might lie within his power to anticipate or prevent, he estimated the servant's strength. He must, first of all, put this fellow out of commission.

Hascomb was, obviously, suspicious of him. Obviously, he had been stationed here as a guard. He looked and acted as if he were prepared for trouble. His eyes did not once shift from Peter's eyes. He was clever. He knew that when a man plans trouble, his eyes give the signal. And if Peter's eyes gave the signal, Hascomb would act before he could act.

Peter lowered his lids as if he were sleepy. Hascomb sat down again, still staring at him. Peter waited. Seeming to drowse, he watched Hascomb's eyes. Perhaps five minutes passed. Then Hascomb's eyes, tiring, perhaps, of Peter's face, went for a moment to the window.

Peter seized that chance. He sat up suddenly, threw his right arm about Hascomb's neck, and held it in a hammer-lock.

Hascomb leaped up, pulling Peter with him, as Peter had hoped he would. The servant tried to kick Peter in the shins, but Peter had anticipated that, too.

Peter slugged him twice, once with each fist, and Hascomb's interest in conflict evaporated. He sagged, a dead weight, in Peter's arms.

Peter laid him on the bed and strode to the door. He was now going to execute his difficult and dangerous program. There must be no hitch, there must be no hesitation.

At the door, with his hand on the knob, he took a deep breath. He let himself out, ran to the door down the hall which gave upon the balcony of the great white stone room, and fell swiftly to work. He took down a magnificent battle-ax from its bronze hooks, and quickly chopped the cords which bound the thick velvet rope, serving as a balcony rail, to the posts. He chopped through the rope at each end. Then he coiled up approximately one hundred feet of the rope and threw the coil down near the Papuan coffin.

He now snatched a stout Marquesan lance from the wall and addressed himself to the coffin. He hated to destroy such a beautiful specimen, but it was necessary to his plans. He was, so to speak, working in the dark. He did not know what his enemies' plans were, and he was working on the theory that fire is best fought with fire, surprises with surprises.

It took all his strength to move the handsome stone coffin, with its sickly-smelling blossoms, but he did move it. He moved it a fraction of an inch, with the lance as a lever. Another fraction. Another. As it toppled, he put his shoulder against it, and gave a Herculean shove.

The coffin began to fall. Peter snatched up the coil of velvet rope in one hand, the battle-ax in the other, and went to the door. He waited just long enough to be sure the job was done. With a lurch, the coffin fell.

Peter opened the door, ran into the hall and to the door which he believed was Susan's. Pressing his mouth into the corner formed by door and jamb, he called her name.

And at that instant, the castle of Zarlo was

filled with a roaring, as of a mighty explosion. Even Peter, who had caused that terrific din, was surprised by the volume, the intensity of it. It sounded as if a charge of dynamite had gone off.

The Papuan coffin, weighing upwards of a ton, had toppled over the balcony; had fallen with a mighty impact on the twelve-foot stone table below, shattering it. The two enormous Satsuma vases, one at either end of the table, had joined in the tumult. Each had fallen to the marble floor, a second apart, and to the mighty echoing reverberations of the falling coffin were added the new crashing as the uproar of the smashing vases was added to the wild tumult. It was terrific.

And it worked. Surprise fought surprise. There were shouts, hoarse cries from all directions as men from all over the house surged to the scene of demolition.

And Peter, with the battle-ax, was chopping through a door. When the door gave, he ran inside and propped the battle-ax under the knob to prevent invasion.

Susan, with frantic arms about his neck, was sobbing, "Peter! Darling!"

She began babbling questions. Peter was too busy to answer. He seized a long bench and dragged it to the window, making sure that the ends considerably overlapped the window. About the middle of this he knotted one end of the velvet rope.

Men were hammering at the door. Peter climbed over the sill, grasped the rope in both hands, told Susan to hang to his neck.

When she was hanging there, he started sliding down. The velvet rope burned through his hands.

Then he discovered that he was, so to speak, midway between the frying pan and the fire. Above him a black hand containing a knife began to hack at the rope. Below him was the pit containing the man-beast, looking up at them, with claws distended.

Peter, making his plans an inch at a time, slid down faster. When he was dangling just above the pit, he braced his feet against the wall and pushed with all his strength. He and Susan swung out. When they were poised, for a breathless moment, beyond the outer wall of the pit, he let go, just as the knife at the window above cut through the rope.

They fell perhaps a dozen feet into a thick tangle of bushes, starred with bright-red small flowers. Peter would remember those flowers. Like innumerable little red stars, they welcomed him and Susan.

Susan screamed and Peter had suddenly the sensation of being stabbed in a million places. The bushes cushioned their fall. But the bushes stabbed and raked them with thorns.

With the breath almost knocked out of him, Peter pushed through the thorns, dragging Susan after him by the hand, toward a path. Down this path they ran. It presently joined the jungle trail up which Peter and Whitelaw and the red-headed man had come a few hours previously.

They would, of course, be followed. He had anticipated that, but he had planned, with the confusion resulting from the crashing of the coffin, to gain a few precious seconds. Granted those seconds, he had another plan to insure their escape.

Still running, they reached the end of the jungle path which then entered the high, parched cactus grass. And behind them, as they ran, they heard the snarling roar of Ronga.

Zarlo had threatened that. Evidently, he had acted immediately on the sounding of the alarm, had turned the man-beast loose.

Peter, looking back, from the middle of the great field of tall grass, saw the waving of it as the beast entered the field behind them.

He told Susan to run on to the end of the field. Then he extracted the box of Japanese safety matches from his pocket and began swiftly to ignite them and toss them behind him as he followed her. He threw flaming matches to left and right.

The cactus grass burned swiftly. Wherever a flaming match fell, it ignited, and the flames fiercely spread. As Peter ran to overtake Susan, flames roared behind him. Already, black smoke was gushing up from the highly inflammable grass, and so swiftly did the fire spread that Peter was himself in danger of being trapped.

He ran for it. At the edge of the jungle he paused beside Susan and looked back. In all directions the fire he had started was spreading. Dense black smoke, shot with leaping flame, gushed and roared upward. And above this uproar he could hear the roaring of the beast, frustrated, driven back and back by the flames.

Peter was laughing with relief and elation. His whole plan of action had carried through without a hitch. The explosive crash of the coffin and the two great vases had sufficiently demoralized the household for him to get Susan safely away. And the firing of the cactus grass would withhold pursuit, would give Susan and him at least a half hour's head start.

"We're safe!" he exulted. "Now we've got to travel fast."

The rest of the way was, he believed, comparatively simple. The trek back to the river. The only possible contingency was that the boat might be guarded. He did not believe it would be guarded. Certainly, the redhead would have been too exhausted from the trip to return and guard it.

But Peter was not worrying about that. Luck had so far been with him. And luck, once it began to smile, had a way of continuing to smile.

Yet his plans were wrecked by a source from which he would have least expected it. Susan! Susan was tired. Susan was dazed. Stimulated for a time by the excitement of their getaway, she was now suffering a kind of relapse.

A hundred yards beyond the edge of the burning field, she declared she could go no farther. She felt dizzy, sick, strange. Peter offered to carry her.

She cried, "Don't touch me! Keep away from me!"

He said, incredulously, "Good Lord, what's the matter?"

"You don't understand! Keep away from me!"

He stopped and stared at her, with fists planted on hips. He said impatiently, "Stop this nonsense. We've got away to a fine start. We're going to push on. Come on!"

"No, no! I can't go with you."

He was now thoroughly perplexed. "What's the matter? What's got into you?"

She shrank away from him, took a few steps back toward the castle. "I can't go! I've got to go back! He's ordering me to go back. He's willing me! I can't stop him. I've got to go!"

Before Peter could prevent her, she had started to run back down the path toward the smoking field.

He shouted to her to stop. She ran like a deer. He was too astonished for a moment to move. What she had said had fairly paralyzed his muscles.

Then, realizing, he started after her. By the time he had reached the field she had vanished. He shouted at the top of his lungs. And ran harder, into the smoke.

A root tripped him. He fell, sprawling upon the embers of smoldering roots.

He dragged himself wearily to his feet. He could not catch her now. She had gone back to the castle. Bitterly, he started walking through the smoke. His plan of escape had worked perfectly—every detail had worked so perfectly! He felt sick with disappointment. And he appreciated, as he had never done before, the diabolical cleverness of Zarlo.

CHAPTER IX
END OF A FOOL

When Susan reached the castle, the bronze-studded door was open. She ran fairly into the arms of a half-dozen black men, all armed with knives, who were starting out.

They took her to Zarlo, in his study. Looking at her with expressionless eyes, he ordered them to lock her in the room next to her old room. His voice was lazy, but he looked dangerous.

Susan, locked in this room, came partially to her senses. In stark terror she realized what she had done. Fighting down an impulse to scream, she seated herself on the edge of the bed and tried to compose herself. She was seated there, twisting her hands in her lap, softly whimpering, when Jason Whitelaw came in. His face was white and grim. There was a dark, raw bruise on his chin from the blow Peter had given him on the balcony, and there was ugliness in his eyes.

Closing the door, he advanced on her. He said thickly, "Susan, you've got to listen to me. I love you. I'm going to get you out of this."

Susan, utterly unnerved, sprang up. She struck him in the face with her fist. They were futile blows, but they accomplished one object. They caused Whitelaw to drop the key. He forgot the key. He forgot caution, too. He forgot how careful he was going to be.

He caught Susan in his arms, held her so tightly that she could not move. He began hungrily to kiss her. He kissed her mouth, her throat.

Susan realized, perhaps for the first time, just what his intentions were. And the realization transformed her into a young human wildcat. She twisted out of his arms. She doubled up her small fists and threw herself at him.

Whitelaw, surprised by the very fury of her attack, gave ground. They were not far from the open door now. And before the savagery of her attack, he backed away until he was in the hall.

And before he could prevent her, she had slammed the door and dragged a chair under the knob. She was, for the moment, safe. But only, she realized, for the moment.

She understood perfectly the thorough perfidy of Jason Whitelaw. He would, she knew, stop at nothing now.

And he proved this by his immediate actions. Recovering from the fury of that attack, faced by the shut door, Whitelaw lost all hold on his self-restraint. He battered at the door with his fists. He shouted. He implored, he entreated, he threatened.

The door remained closed. He kicked at it, and again he hammered on it. He shouted until he was hoarse.

Backed into a corner, white with terror, Susan listened.

In a frenzy of frustration, the disappointed lover kicked and beat at the door until his fists and feet were throbbing with pain.

There was another way! He would get into that room! He ran into the room adjoining—the room Susan had previously occupied. There was a cornice about eight inches in length which ran along the outside wall. He would enter the room in which she was now barricaded by means of this cornice!

Only a man half mad with fury would have considered such a dangerous route.

Zarlo's jeering criticism of him occurred to him as he started along the cornice: "A man burning with passion follows the undulations of a thought. You are a harebrained fool!"

Susan was at the open window and heard his harsh breathing, and the scuffle of his shoes on that narrow ledge of stone. She tried frantically to close the window, but it was jammed and would not move.

Sobbing, she thought, "I'll push him off! I'll kill him!"

Below her, as she glanced down, she saw the beast. He had evidently been returned to his inclosure by Zarlo. The hair of his face and head was singed. He lifted his hairy arms and snarled.

She looked back at Whitelaw, and tried again to pull the window down.

Then she heard Whitelaw yell. She looked out in time to see him clawing desperately at the smooth wall above him, to see him lose his balance and plunge downward.

And she saw the beast lift his arms to catch Whitelaw. Her heart seemed to stop. Whitelaw was plunging down toward those hairy upraised arms.

The beast uttered a snarling roar as Whitelaw fell into his powerful arms. Whitelaw had been saved from a dreadful death for a fate even more dreadful.

As Susan stared, Whitelaw screamed out in agony. The beast was crushing, tearing him to death! Through a mist of faintness, Susan heard the snapping of bones. Then the beast picked up the broken carcass in his arms and hurled it against a wall.

Then Zarlo leaped into the inclosure and the beast became quiet.

A hammering at her door distracted Susan. She heard Peter's voice and she ran to open it. As she unlocked and opened the door, another man plunged down the hall—a red-headed man.

Susan screamed a warning. As Peter came into the room, she tried to shut the door, but the red-headed man had wedged his foot in the crack. Before Peter could help her, the door smashed open and the redhead charged in with automatic pistol drawn.

But Peter had a chair ready, in his hands. He brought the chair swinging down on the charging redhead. He dropped the pistol, but he came right on. Peter lifted the chair again for another swing, but the redhead came in under it, and grabbed his throat in powerful fingers.

Peter dropped the chair. His breath was cut off. Susan's screams seemed to come from far away.

In a twisting lunge, he carried the redhead to the floor. For just a moment, the fingers at his throat slipped away. And Peter drove his fists like battering rams into the distorted face. In a space of seconds he struck a dozen tremendous blows before the red-headed man could reach his throat again.

The fingers relaxed, fell limply at the ends of limp arms.

Peter picked up the pistol and staggered to the door, which Susan had closed.

He said hoarsely, "Come on. It's our last chance!" and flung the door open.

The hall outside was, at a glance, a solid, packed mass of black bodies, black men waiting.

Peter fired into them. A man fell. Another. He aimed deliberately. They fell back, turned to rush him, but they wilted before that deadly fire. Some ran. Peter dropped the pistol when the hammer fell, finally, with a click, and picked up a *parang*. With this, he ran one black man through the throat.

Those who remained were too terrified to touch him. He took Susan's hand and ran with her down the hall to the stairs. And down the stairs.

And at the bottom of the stairs Zarlo and the beast were waiting!

Black men, recovered from their terror at his savage counter-attack, were following Peter and Susan down the stairs. Except for the *parang*, he was unarmed. And against such odds he was helpless.

Zarlo, standing with his arms folded across his chest, said in his crackling voice, "Ronga! Get him! Kill him! Kill the girl!"

And Ronga started up the stairs toward him, with glittering bloodshot eyes.

Peter was, for a moment, unable to move. The beast was like some horrible apparition. The singed hair of his head and face was matted, dripping with blood—Whitelaw's blood. His hands and arms to the shoulders were red and gleaming with the wet blood. His chest was slimy with gore.

"Get him, Ronga!" Zarlo cried ringingly.

The beast snarled. Susan screamed. She backed against the wall and screamed again and again.

Peter, knowing the superhuman strength of those bloody arms, lifted the *parang* and leaped. He was eight or ten steps above Ronga when he leaped. His intention was to strike the blade into the beast's throat.

But Ronga anticipated that. The blade snapped out of Peter's hand as the beast's paw flicked up and clamped down on his wrist. With a snarling roar, he grabbed Peter against his chest.

But before he could encircle him with the other arm, Peter struck with his left fist with every ounce of power he possessed. And there was science behind that blow.

It might have killed an ordinary man. It shocked and dazed Ronga only for a moment. But that moment gave Peter an advantage. It gave him the chance to free his other hand, and this, too, he sent swiftly and savagely into action.

He slugged Ronga in the jaw a second time, and followed with another sledgehammer blow from his left.

Zarlo was calling upon Ronga to kill him.

The beast was backing down the stairs. He seemed to sag. The bloodshot eyes were swimming.

"Go back there!" Zarlo thundered. "Get him! Kill him, I tell you!"

Ronga, with a muttered groan, collapsed at Zarlo's feet.

Peter ran back up the stairs. He grasped Susan's hand and pulled her down into the hall.

Before Zarlo could prevent him he had pulled Susan past and to the other end of the hall. The door leading into the small hall was locked. The door adjoining it was a few inches ajar.

There remained only one possible avenue of escape—the cellars!

Peter yanked open that door and half carried Susan down the long flight of stairs. He felt utterly exhausted. His legs would hardly support him. His breath was like fire in his lungs. Only the vital necessity of prompt, swift action sustained him.

Susan, sobbing, gasping, cried:

"What are we going to do?"

He answered wearily:

"There may be an underground passage. If there isn't, we're done for."

They reached the door of the tunnel. Peter searched for a tool; found a sledgehammer in a near-by room. He swung it down on the lock. His arms ached so that he could hardly stand the pain of lifting the sledgehammer, bringing it down. The cellar seemed to fill with a mist. He blinked sweat out of his eyes and swung and swung. Almost senseless with exhaustion, it seemed to him that all of his life he had been swinging the sledgehammer at this obstinate lock.

But the lock presently disintegrated. Peter dropped the sledgehammer, and with the little strength that remained, opened the door.

Beyond was an empty room, approximately twelve feet square. No doors led from it. It was comprised of solid walls of masonry.

"Ronga!" Zarlo cried. "Get up! Damn you, get up! Get after them!"

He kicked the recumbent figure in the ribs.

The beast shuddered. He rolled slowly over onto his back and sat up. He looked up at Zarlo with strange eyes. He bent forward until he was crouched on his haunches, and his eyes stared and stared at Zarlo.

"Damn you! Get up!"

The beast slowly got up, pushing himself up as a gorilla might. He stood a moment, swaying, still staring at Zarlo, never, in fact, for an instant taking his eyes from Zarlo.

And Zarlo grew alarmed. Once again he shouted, "Ronga! Damn you, follow them! Get them! Get that man! I want them killed—both of them!"

Ronga shook his head slightly, in the gesture of one dazed. Swiftly he reached out and pinioned Zarlo's arms to his sides.

Zarlo cried sharply for help. But there was no help. The black men had fled. The castle echoed emptily to his cries. With a savage lunge he broke away from the beast and started up the stairs, a few steps at a time, backing up, shouting.

And step by step Ronga followed him.

Halfway up, Zarlo ran to the top of the stairs, and the beast, agile as an orang-utan, followed. Still shouting, Zarlo ran up the next flight of stairs and into the green room, the beast only a few feet behind him, deathly silent, menacingly alert.

"Go back!" Zarlo shouted.

The beast followed him, eyes staring, until Zarlo backed against the glass cases containing the skulls of his three victims. He stepped aside. The beast, swinging his arms, swept the cases from their pedestals. Glass crashed. Three skulls rolled onto the floor.

The beast picked up the nearest. He hurled it at Zarlo. The skull missed, crashed through a window. He picked up another, and hurled it. Zarlo yelped with pain as it cracked his elbow. He picked up the skull as it fell and savagely threw it back at Ronga.

Ronga warded it off with the palm of one hand. He kicked the third skull aside with his naked foot. Then he sprang on Zarlo. Once again he pinioned his arms to his sides. He lifted him easily over his head.

The master magician kicked and yelled and struggled. The beast, carrying him, walked to the balcony door and kicked it open.

Zarlo, realizing his intention, began to implore.

"Ronga! Put me down! I will give you anything! Ronga, listen! I will set you free! I will go! This place will be yours again! Ronga! Good God—"

It ended in a shriek of agonized terror. Ronga had stopped at the railing.

Sounds of his terror, not intelligible words, flowed in a thick, shrill stream from the lips of the master magician.

Ronga cast him down carelessly, as though he were casting away something utterly worthless. And he watched until the falling man struck the wall of the inclosure and rebounded, a shapeless thing in a white robe, to lie across the heavy iron chain.

CHAPTER X
THE BEAST

In the small cellar room into which Peter's optimism had led him, Susan was bandaging the wound in Peter's arm. He had not known he was stabbed there.

He was sitting on the floor with his back, in more senses than one, against the wall. His head had sagged down onto his chest. The loss of so much blood had done for him. He had not the strength to stand.

And Susan was whimpering her contriteness. She had been impelled, against her will, to return to the castle. Zarlo had willed her to return.

A sound of heavy, harsh breathing arrested her apology. Some one was coming down the tunnel toward them. Susan could not see who it was. A short flight of steps intervened. And suddenly she screamed, thinly.

"Peter!" she gasped. She was frantically squeezing his hand. "Look! What will we do?"

A shadow, cast by one of the electric bulbs in the arched ceiling of the tunnel, came toward them. A head—shoulders. A long, black, sinister shadow.

"The beast!" Susan screamed.

She cowered down against Peter. The beast came slowly toward them. They could hear his bare feet, his heels, softly thudding on the stone, in a measured beat. It was like the approach of an automaton.

Peter tried to rise. There was no strength left in him. He tried twice. The third time he came weakly, swaying, to his feet. But if his back had not been against the wall, he would have collapsed.

Slowly the beast walked down the steps. Susan, clinging to Peter, shuddered as his feet, then his legs, appeared.

Peter drew a deep breath. The sledgehammer was lying near the door, where it had slipped out of his limp hands.

He could support himself, he believed, but he knew he could not reach the sledgehammer in time. Once again mist seemed to be rising about him.

Then it was too late. The beast entered the room. He looked at them, from one white face to the other.

He said quietly, in a voice of unutterable weariness, "Don't be alarmed. Please don't be alarmed. There has been some terrific confusion—like a horrible nightmare. I don't know what has happened. I—I wish you'd help me to understand. My name is Fulton Agnor. This is supposed to be my house, yet something has happened. I wonder—would you be so good—would you explain?"

Peter, in that swimming mist, felt strength return with hope restored. He heard Susan laugh with hysterical relief. Fulton Agnor's soul had been restored to him when Zarlo plunged to his death. That, at least, was Susan's emphatic explanation, and she would listen to no other.

They returned that evening, Peter on a stretcher, to the river and the speedboat, and at dusk they boarded the *Buccaneer*. Fulton Agnor had proved to be a solicitous host. He had urged them to remain, and Susan had wanted to remain, but Peter, perhaps, did not put too much faith in Mr. Agnor's sanity.

Roger Pennekamp met them as they came up the ship's ladder, a haggard man, aged by worry. Peter's first question was, "What have you done with Tackaberry?"

"I did what you said. He is in irons."

Later, refreshed by a bath, a shave, clean clothes, and a stiff drink of excellent Bourbon, Peter joined Mr. Pennekamp and Susan on deck. The yacht was slipping through moonlit jade water and the headland of Skull Island was fading astern.

Susan had been relating the day's excitement to Mr. Pennekamp. She was already seeing her experience as a thrilling, a "perfectly fascinating" adventure.

Peter seated himself on the wicker settee beside her, and Susan snuggled against him and looked into his face with shining eyes. He wondered if her appetite for adventurous thrills would ever be satisfied. Evidently not. Her attitude—and he was convinced of its sincerity—was that she would, by tomorrow morning, be delighted to embark on another adventure, if a sufficiently thrilling adventure should happen along. And he was tired of adventuring. And the thought of marrying Susan became, once again, too dismaying to contemplate.

She cuddled her warm little hand into his and sighed. Then she asked how Mr. Pennekamp and Peter had found their way to Zarlo's hideout.

"A crystal ball," Peter said dryly. "That night in Hongkong we saw the headland of Skull Island in the crystal ball—and I recognized it."

She straightened up and said triumphantly:

"There! And you won't believe in occult demonstrations!"

"Not in that one," Peter said, and grinned. "The day after we'd seen it, I investigated the crystal. I found a pair of fine wires leading from the taboret, down through the deck and eventually into Captain Tackaberry's room. Under the crystal was a clever little arrangement—a small electric bulb, a lens, and a beautifully hand-colored transparency—a tiny colored film of the headland.

"When the skipper knew that Mr. Pennekamp or anybody else wanted to see an image in the ball, the skipper generously obliged. In his cabin, he turned on current through a rheostat, so that the image, at first dim and weak, became clearer and brighter. And, when the demonstration was over, smoothly faded out.

"Knowing then that Tackaberry was a tool of Zarlo's I would have had him put in irons immediately. But I wanted to see him play his game out. I wanted to go to Skull Island, because I believed you were there."

"You're wonderful!" Susan marveled.

"No," he said. "Dumb. Very dumb. I waited too long. I didn't expect that surprise attack so soon."

The look she gave him was a curious mixture of admiration and defiance.

"I don't care," she complained. "There is something in such things. Zarlo had Mr. Agnor and me completely under the control of his will."

"With the aid of drugs," Peter said. "And post-hypnotic suggestion. He kept Mr. Agnor drugged—therefore soulless, for six years—a slave to his will. I still maintain that occultism, mysticism, is the bunk."

A protesting murmur from Mr. Pennekamp indicated that the oil millionaire's faith in occultism was by no means shaken. And Susan's mouth was already open, to protest and argue.

"Zarlo," Peter said, "had a remarkably magnetic personality."

"How," Susan cried, "did he make me return? He did! I know he did!"

"He had drugged you," Peter argued. "While you were drugged, he easily hypnotized you. I grant that. He planted ideas—orders—in your head. One idea was that, in case you tried to escape, you were to return."

"Is that what you mean by post-hypnotic suggestion?"

"Yep."

"And you say that that is why I returned to the castle?"

Peter grinned. "That's right, Susan."

"Then I think it's perfectly ridiculous. I absolutely believe I was enslaved by that monster's will. I absolutely believe in all sorts of occultism! And I think it's perfectly fascinating!"

RICHARD CONNELL

RICHARD EDWARD CONNELL (1893–1949) was a successful and prolific short-story writer who also enjoyed some success in Hollywood. At the age of eighteen, he became the city editor of the *New York Times,* then went to Harvard, where he edited both the *Harvard Lampoon* and the *Harvard Crimson.* Upon graduation, he returned to journalism, but was then offered a lucrative job writing advertising copy. Soon after serving in World War I, however, Connell sold several short stories and swiftly established himself as one of America's most popular and prolific magazine writers; he also produced four novels. Many of his stories served as the basis for motion pictures, notably *Brother Orchid* (1940), starring Edward G. Robinson, Ann Sothern, and Humphrey Bogart, and based on his 1938 short story of the same name. Connell wrote original stories for several films, including *F-Men* (1936), with Jack Haley, and *Meet John Doe* (1941), directed by Frank Capra and starring Gary Cooper and Barbara Stanwyck—the latter of which earned him a nomination for an Academy Award. He was nominated for another Oscar for his screenplay for *Two Girls and a Sailor* (1944), with June Allyson, Gloria DeHaven, and Van Johnson. He also wrote the screenplay for *Presenting Lily Mars* (1943), which starred Judy Garland and Van Heflin and was based on Booth Tarkington's novel.

Connell is known today mainly for "The Most Dangerous Game," one of the most anthologized stories ever written. It has also inspired numerous cinematic versions, including the classic 1932 RKO film of the same title (called *The Hounds of Zaroff* in England), with Joel McCrea, Fay Wray, and Leslie Banks; *A Game of Death* (1945), with John Loder, Edhar Barrier, and Audrey Long; and *Run for the Sun* (1956), with Richard Widmark, Jane Greer, and Trevor Howard. The story has also sparked a number of looser adaptations in other media, especially radio and television—sometimes credited and sometimes not.

"The Most Dangerous Game" was first published in the January 19, 1924, issue of *Collier's;* it won the O. Henry Memorial Prize and was soon thereafter published in Connell's collection *Variety* (New York: Minton, 1925).

THE MOST DANGEROUS GAME

RICHARD CONNELL

"OFF THERE TO THE RIGHT—somewhere—is a large island," said Whitney. "It's rather a mystery—"

"What island is it?" Rainsford asked.

"The old charts called it Ship-Trap Island," Whitney replied. "A suggestive name, isn't it? Sailors have a curious dread of the place. I don't know why. Some superstition—"

"Can't see it," remarked Rainsford, trying to peer through the dank tropical night that pressed its thick warm blackness in upon the yacht.

"You've good eyes," said Whitney with a laugh, "and I've seen you pick off a moose moving in the brown fall bush at four hundred yards, but even you can't see four miles or so through a moonless Caribbean night."

"Nor four yards," admitted Rainsford. "Ugh! It's like moist black velvet."

"It will be light enough in Rio," promised Whitney. "We should make it in a few days. I hope the jaguar guns have come from Purdey's. We should have some good hunting up the Amazon. Great sport, hunting."

"The best sport in the world," agreed Rainsford.

"For the hunter," amended Whitney. "Not for the jaguar."

"Don't talk rot, Whitney. You're a big-game hunter, not a philosopher. Who cares how a jaguar feels?"

"Perhaps the jaguar does."

"Bah! They've no understanding."

"Even so, I rather think they understand one thing—fear. The fear of pain and the fear of death."

"Nonsense," laughed Rainsford. "This hot weather is making you soft, Whitney. Be a realist. The world is made up of two classes—the hunters and the huntees. Luckily you and I are hunters. Do you think we have passed that island yet?"

"I can't tell in the dark. I hope so."

"Why?"

"The place has a reputation—a bad one."

"Cannibals?"

"Hardly. Even cannibals wouldn't live in such a God-forsaken place. But it's gotten into sailor lore, somehow. Didn't you notice that the crew's nerves seemed a bit jumpy today?"

"They were a bit strange, now you mention it. Even Captain Nielsen."

"Yes, even that tough-minded old Swede, who'd go up to the devil himself and ask him for a light. Those fishy blue eyes held a look I never saw there before. All I could get out of him was: 'This place has an evil name among seafaring men, sir.' Then he said, gravely: 'Don't you feel anything?' Now you mustn't laugh but I did feel a sort of chill, and there wasn't a breeze. What I felt was a—a mental chill, a sort of dread."

"Pure imagination," said Rainsford. "One superstitious sailor can taint a whole ship's company with his fear."

"Maybe. Sometimes I think sailors have an extra sense which tells them when they are in danger . . . anyhow I'm glad we are getting out of this zone. Well, I'll turn in now, Rainsford."

"I'm not sleepy. I'm going to smoke another pipe on the after deck."

There was no sound in the night as Rainsford sat there but the muffled throb of the yacht's engine and the swish and ripple of the propeller.

Rainsford, reclining in a steamer chair, puffed at his favourite briar. The sensuous drowsiness of the night was on him. "It's so dark," he thought, "that I could sleep without closing my eyes; the night would be my eyelids—"

An abrupt sound startled him. Off to the right he heard it, and his ears, expert in such matters, could not be mistaken. Again he heard the sound, and again. Somewhere, off in the blackness, someone had fired a gun three times.

Rainsford sprang up and moved quickly to the rail, mystified. He strained his eyes in the direction from which the reports had come, but it was like trying to see through a blanket. He leaped upon the rail and balanced himself there, to get greater elevation; his pipe, striking a rope, was knocked from his mouth. He lunged for it; a short, hoarse cry came from his lips as he realized he had reached too far and had lost his balance. The cry was pinched off short as the blood-warm waters of the Caribbean Sea closed over his head.

He struggled to the surface and cried out, but the wash from the speeding yacht slapped him in the face and the salt water in his open mouth made him gag and strangle. Desperately he struck out after the receding lights of the yacht, but he stopped before he had swum fifty feet. A certain cool-headedness had come to him, for this was not the first time he had been in a tight place. There was a chance that his cries could be heard by someone aboard the yacht, but that chance was slender and grew more slender as the yacht raced on. He wrestled himself out of his clothes and shouted with all his power. The lights of the boat became faint and vanishing fireflies; then they were blotted out by the night.

Rainsford remembered the shots. They had come from the right, and doggedly he swam in that direction, swimming slowly, conserving his strength. For a seemingly endless time he fought the sea. He began to count his strokes; he could do possibly a hundred more and then—

He heard a sound. It came out of the darkness, a high, screaming sound, the cry of an animal in an extremity of anguish and terror. He did not know what animal made the sound. With fresh vitality he swam towards it. He heard it again; then it was cut short by another noise, crisp, staccato.

"Pistol shot," muttered Rainsford, swimming on.

Ten minutes of determined effort brought to his ears the most welcome sound he had ever heard, the breaking of the sea on a rocky shore. He was almost on the rocks before he saw them; on a night less calm he would have been shattered against them. With his remaining strength he dragged himself from the swirling waters. Jagged crags appeared to jut into the opaqueness; he forced himself up hand over hand. Gasping, his hands raw, he reached a flat place at the top. Dense jungle came down to the edge of the cliffs, and careless of everything but his weariness Rainsford flung himself down and tumbled into the deepest sleep of his life.

When he opened his eyes he knew from the position of the sun that it was late in the afternoon. Sleep had given him vigour; a sharp hunger was picking at him.

"Where there are pistol shots there are men. Where there are men there is food," he thought; but he saw no sign of a trail through the closely knit web of weeds and trees; it was easier to go along the shore. Not far from where he had landed, he stopped.

Some wounded thing, by the evidence a large animal, had crashed about in the underwood. A small glittering object caught Rainsford's eye and he picked it up. It was an empty cartridge.

"A twenty-two," he remarked. "That's odd. It must have been a fairly large animal, too. The hunter had his nerve with him to tackle it with a light gun. It is clear the brute put up a fight. I suppose the first three shots I heard were when the hunter flushed his quarry and wounded it. The last shot was when he trailed it here and finished it."

He examined the ground closely and found what he had hoped to find—the print of hunting boots. They pointed along the cliff in the direction he had been going. Eagerly he hurried along, for night was beginning to settle down on the island.

Darkness was blacking out sea and jungle before Rainsford sighted the lights. He came upon them as he turned a crook in the coast line, and his first thought was that he had come upon a village, as there were so many lights. But as he forged along he saw that all the lights were in one building—a château on a high bluff.

"Mirage," thought Rainsford. But the stone steps were real enough. He lifted the knocker and it creaked up stiffly as if it had never before been used.

The door, opening, let out a river of glaring light. A tall man, solidly built and black-bearded to the waist, stood facing Rainsford with a revolver in his hand.

"Don't be alarmed," said Rainsford, with a smile that he hoped was disarming. "I'm no robber. I fell off a yacht. My name is Sanger Rainsford of New York City."

The man gave no sign that he understood the words or had even heard them. The menacing revolver pointed as rigidly as if the giant were a statue.

Another man was coming down the broad, marble steps, an erect slender man in evening clothes. He advanced and held out his hand.

In a cultivated voice marked by a slight accent which gave it added precision and deliberateness, he said: "It is a great pleasure and honour to welcome Mr. Sanger Rainsford, the celebrated hunter, to my home."

Automatically Rainsford shook the man's hand.

"I've read your book about hunting snow leopards in Tibet," explained the man. "I am General Zaroff."

Rainsford's first impression was that the man was singularly handsome; his second, that there was a bizarre quality about the face. The general was a tall man past middle age, for his hair was white; but his eyebrows and moustache were black. His eyes, too, were black and very bright. He had the face of a man used to giving orders. Turning to the man in uniform, he made a sign. The fellow put away his pistol, saluted, withdrew.

"Ivan is an incredibly strong fellow," remarked the general, "but he has the misfortune to be deaf and dumb. A simple fellow, but a bit of a savage."

"Is he Russian?"

"A Cossack," said the general, and his smile showed red lips and pointed teeth. "So am I.

"Come," he said, "we shouldn't be chatting here. You want clothes, food, rest. You shall have them. This is a most restful spot."

Ivan had reappeared and the general spoke to him with lips that moved but gave forth no sound.

"Follow Ivan if you please, Mr. Rainsford. I was about to have my dinner, but will wait. I think my clothes will fit you."

It was to a huge beam-ceilinged bedroom with a canopied bed large enough for six men that Rainsford followed the man. Ivan laid out an evening suit and Rainsford, as he put it on, noticed that it came from a London tailor.

"Perhaps you were surprised," said the general as they sat down to dinner in a room which suggested a baronial hall of feudal times, "that I recognized your name; but I read all books on hunting published in English, French and Russian. I have but one passion in life, and that is the hunt."

"You have some wonderful heads here," said Rainsford, glancing at the walls. "That Cape buffalo is the largest I ever saw."

"Oh, that fellow? He charged me, hurled me

against a tree and fractured my skull. But I got the brute."

"I've always thought," said Rainsford, "that the Cape buffalo is the most dangerous of all big game."

For a moment the general did not reply, then he said slowly: "No, the Cape buffalo is not the most dangerous." He sipped his wine. "Here in my preserve on this island I hunt more danger-ous game."

"Is there big game on this island?"

The general nodded. "The biggest."

"Really?"

"Oh, it isn't here naturally. I have to stock the island."

"What have you imported, General? Tigers?"

The general grinned. "No, hunting tigers ceased to interest me when I exhausted their possibilities. No thrill left in tigers, no real dan-ger. I live for danger, Mr. Rainsford."

The general took from his pocket a gold ciga-rette case and offered his guest a long black ciga-rette with a silver tip; it was perfumed and gave off a smell like incense.

"We will have some capital hunting, you and I," said the general.

"But what game—" began Rainsford.

"I'll tell you. You will be amused, I know. I think I may say, in all modesty, that I have done a rare thing. I have invented a new sensation. May I pour you another glass of port?"

"Thank you, General."

The general filled both glasses and said: "God makes some men poets. Some he makes kings, some beggars. Me he made a hunter. But after years of enjoyment I found that the hunt no longer fascinated me. You can perhaps guess why?"

"No—why?"

"Simply this: hunting had ceased to be what you call a 'sporting proposition.' I always got my quarry . . . always . . . and there is no greater bore than perfection."

The general lit a fresh cigarette.

"The animal has nothing but his legs and his instinct. Instinct is no match for reason. When I realized this, it was a tragic moment for me."

Rainsford leaned across the table, absorbed in what his host was saying.

"It came to me as an inspiration what I must do."

"And that was?"

"I had to invent a new animal to hunt."

"A new animal? You are joking."

"I never joke about hunting. I needed a new animal. I found one. So I bought this island, built this house, and here I do my hunting. The island is perfect for my purpose—there are jun-gles with a maze of trails in them, hills, swamps—"

"But the animal, General Zaroff?"

"Oh," said the general, "it supplies me with the most exciting hunting in the world. Every day I hunt, and I never grow bored now, for I have a quarry with which I can match my wits."

Rainsford's bewilderment showed in his face.

"I wanted the ideal animal to hunt, so I said, 'What are the attributes of an ideal quarry?' and the answer was, of course: 'It must have courage, cunning, and, above all, it must be able to reason.' "

"But no animal can reason," objected Rains-ford.

"My dear fellow," said the general, "there is one that can."

"But you can't mean—"

"And why not?"

"I can't believe you are serious, General Zaroff. This is a grisly joke."

"Why should I not be serious? I am speaking of hunting."

"Hunting? Good God, General Zaroff, what you speak of is murder."

The general regarded Rainsford quizzically. "Surely your experiences in the war—"

"Did not make me condone cold-blooded murder," finished Rainsford stiffly.

Laughter shook the general. "I'll wager you'll forget your notions when you go hunting with me. You've a genuine new thrill in store for you, Mr. Rainsford."

"Thank you, I am a hunter, not a murderer."

"Dear me," said the general, quite unruffled, "again that unpleasant word; but I hunt the scum of the earth—sailors from tramp ships—lascars, blacks, Chinese, whites, mongrels."

"Where do you get them?"

The general's left eyelid fluttered down in a wink. "This island is called Ship-Trap. Come to the window with me."

Rainsford went to the window and looked out towards the sea.

"Watch! Out there!" exclaimed the general, as he pressed a button. Far out Rainsford saw a flash of lights. "They indicate a channel where there's none. Rocks with razor edges crouch there like a sea-monster. They can crush a ship like a nut. Oh, yes, that is electricity. We try to be civilized."

"Civilized? And you shoot down men?"

"But I treat my visitors with every consideration," said the general in his most pleasant manner. "They get plenty of good food and exercise. They get into splendid physical condition. You shall see for yourself tomorrow."

"What do you mean?"

"We'll visit my training school," smiled the general. "It is in the cellar. I have about a dozen there now. They're from the Spanish bark San-lucar, which had the bad luck to go on the rocks out there. An inferior lot, I regret to say, and more accustomed to the deck than the jungle."

He raised his hand and Ivan brought thick Turkish coffee. "It is a game, you see," pursued the general blandly. "I suggest to one of them that we go hunting. I give him three hours' start. I am to follow, armed only with a pistol of smallest calibre and range. If my quarry eludes me for three whole days, he wins the game. If I find him"—the general smiled—"he loses."

"Suppose he refuses to be hunted?"

"I give him the option. If he does not wish to hunt I turn him over to Ivan. Ivan once served as official knouter to the Great White Tsar, and he has his own ideas of sport. Invariably they choose the hunt."

"And if they win?"

The smile on the general's face widened. "To date I have not lost."

Then he added, hastily: "I don't wish you to think me a braggart, Mr. Rainsford, and one did almost win. I eventually had to use the dogs."

"The dogs?"

"This way, please. I'll show you."

The general led the way to another window. The lights sent a flickering illumination that made grotesque patterns on the courtyard below, and Rainsford could see a dozen or so huge black shapes moving about. As they turned towards him he caught the green glitter of eyes.

"They are let out at seven every night. If anyone should try to get into my house—or out of it—something regrettable would happen to him. And now I want to show you my new collection of heads. Will you come to the library?"

"I hope," said Rainsford, "that you will excuse me tonight. I'm really not feeling at all well."

"Ah, indeed? You need a good restful night's sleep. Tomorrow you'll feel like a new man. Then we'll hunt, eh? I've one rather promising prospect—"

Rainsford was hurrying from the room.

"Sorry you can't go with me tonight," called the general. "I expect rather fair sport. A big, strong black. He looks resourceful—"

The bed was good and Rainsford was tired, but nevertheless he could not sleep, and had only achieved a doze when, as morning broke, he heard, far off in the jungle, the faint report of a pistol.

General Zaroff did not appear till luncheon. He was solicitous about Rainsford's health. "As for me," he said, "I do not feel so well. The hunting was not good last night. He made a straight trail that offered no problems at all."

"General," said Rainsford firmly, "I want to leave the island at once."

He saw the dead black eyes of the general on

him, studying him. The eyes suddenly brightened. "Tonight," said he, "we will hunt—you and I."

Rainsford shook his head. "No, General," he said, "I will not hunt."

The general shrugged his shoulders. "As you wish. The choice rests with you, but I would suggest that my idea of sport is more diverting than Ivan's."

"You don't mean—" cried Rainsford.

"My dear fellow," said the general, "have I not told you I always mean what I say about hunting? This is really an inspiration. I drink to a foeman worthy of my steel at last."

The general raised his glass, but Rainsford sat staring at him. "You'll find this game worth playing," the general said, enthusiastically. "Your brain against mine. Your woodcraft against mine. Your strength and stamina against mine. Outdoor chess! And the stake is not without value, eh?"

"And if I win—" began Rainsford huskily.

"If I do not find you by midnight of the third day, I'll cheerfully acknowledge myself defeated," said General Zaroff. "My sloop will place you on the mainland near a town."

The general read what Rainsford was thinking.

"Oh, you can trust me," said the Cossack. "I will give you my word as a gentleman and a sportsman. Of course, you, in turn, must agree to say nothing of your visit here."

"I'll agree to nothing of the kind."

"Oh, in that case—but why discuss that now? Three days hence we can discuss it over a bottle of Veuve Cliquot, unless—"

The general sipped his wine.

Then a business-like air animated him. "Ivan," he said, "will supply you with hunting clothes, food, a knife. I suggest you wear moccasins; they leave a poorer trail. I suggest, too, that you avoid the big swamp in the southeast corner of the island. We call it Death Swamp. There's quicksand there. One foolish fellow tried it. The deplorable part of it was that Lazarus followed him. You can't imagine my feelings, Mr. Rainsford. I loved Lazarus; he was the finest hound in my pack. Well, I must beg you to excuse me now. I always take a siesta after lunch. You'll hardly have time for a nap, I fear. You'll want to start, no doubt. I shall not follow until dusk. Hunting at night is so much more exciting than by day, don't you think? Au revoir, Mr. Rainsford, au revoir."

As General Zaroff, with a courtly bow, strolled from the room, Ivan entered by another door. Under one arm he carried hunting clothes, a haversack of food, a leathern sheath containing a long-bladed hunting knife; his right hand rested on a cocked revolver thrust in the crimson sash about his waist. . . .

Rainsford had fought his way through the bush for two hours, but at length he paused, saying to himself through tight teeth, "I must keep my nerve."

He had not been entirely clear-headed when the château gates closed behind him. His first idea was to put distance between himself and General Zaroff and, to this end, he had plunged along, spurred by the sharp rowels of something approaching panic. Now, having got a grip on himself, he had stopped to take stock of himself and the situation.

Straight flight was futile for it must inevitably bring him to the sea. Being in a picture with a frame of water, his operations, clearly, must take place within that frame.

"I'll give him a trail to follow," thought Rainsford, striking off from the path into trackless wilderness. Recalling the lore of the foxhunt and the dodges of the fox, he executed a series of intricate loops, doubling again and again on his trail. Night found him leg-weary, with hands and face lashed by the branches. He was on a thickly wooded ridge. As his need for rest was imperative, he thought: "I have played the fox, now I must play the cat of the fable."

A big tree with a thick trunk and outspread branches was near by, and, taking care to leave no marks, he climbed into the crotch and stretched out on one of the broad limbs. Rest brought him new confidence and almost a feeling of security.

An apprehensive night crawled slowly by like a wounded snake. Towards morning, when a dingy grey was varnishing the sky, the cry of a startled bird focussed Rainsford's attention in its direction. Something was coming through the bush, coming slowly, carefully, coming by the same winding way that Rainsford had come. He flattened himself against the bough and, through a screen of leaves almost as thick as tapestry, watched.

It was General Zaroff. He made his way along, with his eyes fixed in concentration on the ground. He paused, almost beneath the tree, dropped to his knees and studied the ground. Rainsford's impulse was to leap on him like a panther, but he saw that the general's right hand held a small automatic.

The hunter shook his head several times as if he were puzzled. Then, straightening himself, he took from his case one of his black cigarettes; its pungent incense-like smoke rose to Rainsford's nostrils.

Rainsford held his breath. The general's eyes had left the ground and were travelling inch by inch up the tree. Rainsford froze, every muscle tensed for a spring. But the sharp eyes of the hunter stopped before they reached the limb where Rainsford lay. A smile spread over his brown face. Very deliberately he blew a smoke ring into the air; then he turned his back on the tree and walked carelessly away along the trail he had come. The swish of the underbrush against his hunting boots grew fainter and fainter.

The pent-up air burst hotly from Rainsford's lungs. His first thought made him feel sick and numb. The general could follow a trail through the woods at night; he could follow an extremely difficult trail; he must have uncanny powers; only by the merest chance had he failed to see his quarry.

Rainsford's second thought was more terrible. It sent a shudder through him. Why had the general smiled? Why had he turned back?

Rainsford did not want to believe what his reason told him was true—the general was playing with him, saving him for another day's sport. The Cossack was the cat; he was the mouse. Then it was that Rainsford knew the meaning of terror.

"I will not lose my nerve," he told himself, "I will not."

Sliding down from the tree, he set off into the woods. Three hundred yards from his hiding-place he stopped where a huge dead tree leaned precariously on a smaller, living one. Throwing off his sack of food, he took his knife from its sheath and set to work.

When the job was finished, he threw himself down behind a fallen log a hundred feet away. He did not have to wait long. The cat was coming back to play with the mouse.

Following the trail with the sureness of a bloodhound came General Zaroff. Nothing escaped those searching black eyes, no crushed blade of grass, no bent twig, no mark, no matter how faint, in the moss. So intent was the Cossack on his stalking that he was upon the thing Rainsford had made before he saw it. His foot touched the protruding bough that was the trigger. Even as he touched it, the general sensed his danger, and leaped back with the agility of an ape. But he was not quite quick enough; the dead tree, delicately adjusted to rest on the cut living one, crashed down and struck the general a glancing blow on the shoulder as it fell; but for his alertness he must have been crushed beneath it. He staggered but he did not fall; nor did he drop his revolver. He stood there, rubbing his injured shoulder, and Rainsford, with fear again gripping his heart, heard the general's mocking laugh ring through the jungle.

"Rainsford," called the general, "if you are within sound of my voice let me congratulate you. Not many men know how to make a Malay man catcher. Luckily for me I, too, have hunted in Malacca. You are proving interesting, Mr. Rainsford. I am now going to have my wound dressed; it is only a slight one. But I shall be back. I shall be back."

When the general, nursing his wounded shoulder, had gone, Rainsford again took up his flight. It was flight now, and it carried him on for some hours. Dusk came, then darkness, and still he pressed on. The ground grew softer under his moccasins; the vegetation grew ranker, denser; insects bit him savagely. He stepped forward and his foot sank into ooze. He tried to wrench it back, but the mud sucked viciously at his foot as if it had been a giant leech. With a violent effort he tore his foot loose. He knew where he was now. Death Swamp and its quicksand.

The softness of the earth had given him an idea. Stepping back from the quicksand a dozen feet, he began, like some huge prehistoric beaver, to dig.

Rainsford had dug himself in, in France, when a second's delay would have meant death. Compared to his digging now, that had been a placid pastime. The pit grew deeper; when it was above his shoulders he climbed out and from some hard saplings cut stakes, sharpening them to a fine point. These stakes he planted at the bottom of the pit with the points up. With flying fingers he wove a rough carpet of weeds and branches and with it covered the mouth of the pit. Then, wet with sweat and aching with tiredness, he crouched behind the stump of a lightning-blasted tree.

By the padding sound of feet on the soft earth he knew his pursuer was coming. The night breeze brought him the perfume of the general's cigarette. It seemed to the hunted man that the general was coming with unusual swiftness; that he was not feeling his way along, foot by foot. Rainsford, from where he was crouching, could not see the general, neither could he see the pit. He lived a year in a minute. Then he heard the sharp crackle of breaking branches as the cover of the pit gave way; heard the sharp scream of pain as the pointed stakes found their mark. Then he cowered back. Three feet from the pit a man was standing with an electric torch in his hand.

"You've done well, Rainsford," cried the general. "Your Burmese tiger pit has claimed one of my best dogs. Again you score. I must now see what you can do against my whole pack. I'm going home for a rest now. Thank you for a most amusing evening."

At daybreak Rainsford, lying near the swamp, was awakened by a distant sound, faint and wavering, but he knew it for the baying of a pack of hounds.

Rainsford knew he could do one of two things. He could stay where he was. That was suicide. He could flee. That was postponing the inevitable. For a moment, he stood there thinking. An idea that held a wild chance came to him, and, tightening his belt, he headed away from the swamp.

The baying of the hounds drew nearer, nearer. Rainsford climbed a tree. Down a watercourse, not a quarter of a mile away, he could see the bush moving. Straining his eyes, he saw the lean figure of General Zaroff. Just ahead of him Rainsford made out another figure, with wide shoulders, which surged through the jungle reeds. It was the gigantic Ivan and he seemed to be pulled along. Rainsford realized that he must be holding the pack in leash.

They would be on him at any moment now. His mind worked frantically, and he thought of a native trick he had learned in Uganda. Sliding down the tree, he caught hold of a springy young sapling and to it fastened his hunting knife, with the blade pointing down the trail. With a bit of wild grape-vine he tied back the sapling . . . and ran for his life. As the hounds hit the fresh scent, they raised their voices and Rainsford knew how an animal at bay feels.

He had to stop to get his breath. The baying of the hounds stopped abruptly, and Rainsford's heart stopped, too. They must have reached the knife.

Shinning excitedly up a tree, he looked back. His pursuers had stopped. But the hope in Rainsford's brain died, for he saw that General Zaroff was still on his feet. Ivan, however, was not. The knife, driven by the recoil of the springing tree, had not wholly failed.

Hardly had Rainsford got back to the ground when, once more, the pack took up the cry.

"Nerve, nerve, nerve!" he panted to himself as he dashed along. A blue gap showed through the trees dead ahead. The hounds drew nearer. Rainsford forced himself on towards that gap. He reached the sea, and across a cove could see the grey stone of the château. Twenty feet below him the sea rumbled and hissed. Rainsford hesitated. He heard the hounds. Then he leaped far out into the water.

When the general and his pack reached the opening, the Cossack stopped. For some moments he stood regarding the blue-green expanse of water. Then he sat down, took a drink of brandy from a silver flask, lit a perfumed cigarette and hummed a bit from *Madame Butterfly*.

General Zaroff ate an exceedingly good dinner in his great panelled hall that evening. With it he had a bottle of Pol Roger and half a bottle of Chambertin. Two slight annoyances kept him from perfect enjoyment. One was that it would be difficult to replace Ivan; the other, that his quarry had escaped him. Of course—so thought the general, as he tasted his after-dinner liqueur—the American had not played the game.

To soothe himself, he read in his library from the works of Marcus Aurelius. At ten he went to his bedroom. He was comfortably tired, he said to himself, as he turned the key of his door. There was a little moonlight, so before turning on the light he went to the window and looked down on the courtyard. He could see the great hounds, and he called: "Better luck another time." Then he switched on the light.

A man who had been hiding in the curtains of the bed, was standing before him.

"Rainsford!" screamed the general. "How in God's name did you get here?"

"Swam. I found it quicker than walking through the jungle."

The other sucked in his breath and smiled. "I congratulate you. You have won the game."

Rainsford did not smile. "I am still a beast at bay," he said, in a low, hoarse voice. "Get ready, General Zaroff."

The general made one of his deepest bows. "I see," he said. "Splendid. One of us is to furnish a repast for the hounds. The other will sleep in this very excellent bed. On guard, Rainsford. . . ."

He had never slept in a better bed, Rainsford decided.

THE MAN WHO WOULD BE KING

RUDYARD KIPLING

WRITTEN BY RUDYARD KIPLING (1865–1936) at the peak of England's colonial period under Queen Victoria, "The Man Who Would Be King" is one of the many stories the prolific and distinguished author set in India, where he was born. Raised in the care of Indians in Bombay until the age of six, Kipling learned Hindustani concurrently with English and developed a love for the region and its people. After English schooling, he returned to India at eighteen, becoming a journalist and short-story writer. By the turn of the twentieth century, he was one of the world's most popular and highly regarded authors, and was the first English-language author to win the Nobel Prize for Literature (1907). Many of his best-known works have been successfully filmed, such as his tales of "the soldiers three"—Ortheris, Mulvaney, and Learoyd—in *Plain Tales from the Hills* (1888) and *Soldiers Three* (1888), which formed the basis for the 1951 motion picture *Soldiers Three,* starring Stewart Granger, David Niven, and Walter Pidgeon. Kipling's 1894 *The Jungle Book,* and its 1895 sequel, yielded numerous films based on its stories, including two featuring Sabu, *Elephant Boy* (1937) and *The Jungle Book* (1942); the well-known 1967 Disney animated film; and several adaptations in the 1990s. *Kim* (1901) was filmed in 1950 with Errol Flynn and Dean Stockwell, then remade in 1984 with Ravi Sheth and Peter O'Toole. The familiar narrative poem "Gunga Din" also received cinematic treatment in the 1939 film starring Cary Grant, Victor McLaglen, and Douglas Fairbanks.

A dedicated colonialist, Kipling is credited with inventing the phrase "the white man's burden" with a poem of that title, meant to reflect the responsibility felt by the British for their perceived racial inferiors. Using settings outside of India, he produced such masterpieces as *The Light That Failed* (1890; filmed in 1939 with Ronald Colman, Ida Lupino, and Walter Huston) and *Captains Courageous* (1897; filmed in 1937 with Spencer Tracy, Lionel Barrymore, and Freddie Bartholomew, and unmemorably remade in 1995). When the motion-picture version of "The Man Who Would Be King," one of the greatest adventure films of all time, was released in 1975, its nonstop adventure and storytelling locomotion recalled the great swashbucklers of the 1930s and '40s; it was immediately described as the sort of movie that no one made anymore. Adapted and directed by John Huston, who had wanted to produce it for more than two decades, the movie starred Sean Connery as Daniel Dravot and Michael Caine as Peachey Carnehan, with Christopher Plummer as Rudyard Kipling, who narrates the tale (he is unnamed in the short story).

"The Man Who Would Be King" was originally published in *The Phantom Rickshaw and Other Tales* (Allahabad, India: A. H. Wheeler, 1888).

THE MAN WHO WOULD BE KING

RUDYARD KIPLING

"Brother to a Prince and fellow to a beggar if he be found worthy."

THE LAW, as quoted, lays down a fair conduct of life, and one not easy to follow. I have been fellow to a beggar again and again under circumstances which prevented either of us finding out whether the other was worthy. I have still to be brother to a Prince, though I once came near to kinship with what might have been a veritable King and was promised the reversion of a Kingdom—army, law-courts, revenue, and policy all complete. But, to-day, I greatly fear that my King is dead, and if I want a crown I must go and hunt it for myself.

The beginning of everything was in a railway train upon the road to Mhow from Ajmir. There had been a Deficit in the Budget, which necessitated travelling, not Second-class, which is only half as dear as First-class, but by Intermediate, which is very awful indeed. There are no cushions in the Intermediate class, and the population are either Intermediate, which is Eurasian, or native, which for a long night journey is nasty, or Loafer, which is amusing though intoxicated. Intermediates do not patronize refreshment-rooms. They carry their food in bundles and pots, and buy sweets from the native sweet-meat-sellers, and drink the roadside water. That is why in the hot weather Intermediates are taken out of the carriages dead, and in all weathers are most properly looked down upon.

My particular Intermediate happened to be empty till I reached Nasirabad, when a huge gentleman in shirt-sleeves entered, and, following the custom of Intermediates, passed the time of day. He was a wanderer and a vagabond like myself, but with an educated taste for whiskey. He told tales of things he had seen and done, of out-of-the-way corners of the Empire into which he had penetrated, and of adventures in which he risked his life for a few days' food. "If India was filled with men like you and me, not knowing more than the crows where they'd get their next day's rations, it isn't seventy millions of revenue the land would be paying—it's seven hundred millions," said he; and as I looked at his mouth and chin I was disposed to agree with him. We talked politics—the politics of Loafer-dom that sees things from the underside where the lath and plaster is not smoothed off—and we talked postal arrangements because my friend wanted to send a telegram back from the next station to Ajmir, which is the turning-off place from the Bombay to the Mhow line as you travel westward. My friend had no money beyond eight annas which he wanted for dinner, and I had no money at all, owing to the hitch in the Budget before mentioned. Further, I was going into a wilderness where, though I should resume touch with the Treasury, there were no tele-

THE MAN WHO WOULD BE KING

graph offices. I was, therefore, unable to help him in any way.

"We might threaten a Station-master, and make him send a wire on tick," said my friend, "but that'd mean inquiries for you and for me, and I've got my hands full these days. Did you say you are traveling back along this line within any days?"

"Within ten," I said.

"Can't you make it eight?" said he. "Mine is rather urgent business."

"I can send your telegram within ten days if that will serve you," I said.

"I couldn't trust the wire to fetch him now I think of it. It's this way. He leaves Delhi on the 23d for Bombay. That means he'll be running through Ajmir about the night of the 23d."

"But I am going into the Indian Desert," I explained.

"Well and good," said he. "You'll be changing at Marwar Junction to get into Jodhpore territory—you must do that—and he'll be coming through Marwar Junction in the early morning of the 24th by the Bombay Mail. Can you be at Marwar Junction on that time? 'Twon't be inconveniencing you because I know that there's precious few pickings to be got out of these Central India States—even though you pretend to be correspondent of the *Backwoodsman*."

"Have you ever tried that trick?" I asked.

"Again and again, but the Residents find you out, and then you get escorted to the Border before you've time to get your knife into them. But about my friend here. I *must* give him a word o'mouth to tell him what's come to me or else he won't know where to go. I would take it more than kind of you if you was to come out of Central India in time to catch him at Marwar Junction, and say to him:—'He has gone South for the week.' He'll know what that means. He's a big man with a red beard, and a great swell he is. You'll find him sleeping like a gentleman with all his luggage round him in a Second-class compartment. But don't you be afraid. Slip down the window, and say:—'He has gone South for the

week,' and he'll tumble. It's only cutting your time of stay in those parts by two days. I ask you as a stranger—going to the West," he said, with emphasis.

"Where have *you* come from?" said I.

"From the East," said he, "and I am hoping that you will give him the message on the Square—for the sake of my Mother as well as your own."

Englishmen are not usually softened by appeals to the memory of their mothers, but for certain reasons, which will be fully apparent, I saw fit to agree.

"It's more than a little matter," said he, "and that's why I ask you to do it—and now I know that I can depend on you doing it. A Second-class carriage at Marwar Junction, and a red-haired man asleep in it. You'll be sure to remember. I get out at the next station, and I must hold on there till he comes or sends me what I want."

"I'll give the message if I catch him," I said, "and for the sake of your Mother as well as mine I'll give you a word of advice. Don't try to run the Central India States just now as the correspondent of the *Backwoodsman*. There's a real one knocking about here, and it might lead to trouble."

"Thank you," said he, simply, "and when will the swine be gone? I can't starve because he's ruining my work. I wanted to get hold of the Degumber Rajah down here about his father's widow, and give him a jump."

"What did he do to his father's widow, then?"

"Filled her up with red pepper and slippered her to death as she hung from a beam. I found that out myself and I'm the only man that would dare going into the State to get hush-money for it. They'll try to poison me, same as they did in Chortumna when I went on the loot there. But you'll give the man at Marwar Junction my message?"

He got out at a little roadside station, and I reflected. I had heard, more than once, of men personating correspondents of newspapers and bleeding small Native States with threats of exposure, but I had never met any of the caste before. They lead a hard life, and generally die with great suddenness. The Native States have a wholesome horror of English newspapers, which may throw light on their peculiar methods of government, and do their best to choke correspondents with champagne, or drive them out of their mind with four-in-hand barouches. They do not understand that nobody cares a straw for the internal administration of Native States so long as oppression and crime are kept within decent limits, and the ruler is not drugged, drunk, or diseased from one end of the year to the other. Native states were created by Providence in order to supply picturesque scenery, tigers, and tall-writing. They are the dark places of the earth, full of unimaginable cruelty, touching the Railway and the Telegraph on one side, and, on the other, the days of Harun-al-Raschid. When I left the train I did business with divers Kings, and in eight days passed through many changes of life. Sometimes I wore dress-clothes and consorted with Princes and Politicals, drinking from crystal and eating from silver. Sometimes I lay out upon the ground and devoured what I could get, from a plate made of a flapjack, and drank the running water, and slept under the same rug as my servant. It was all in the day's work.

Then I headed for the Great Indian Desert upon the proper date, as I had promised, and the Night Mail set me down at Marwar Junction, where a funny little, happy-go-lucky, native-managed railway runs to Jodhpore. The Bombay Mail from Delhi makes a short halt at Marwar. She arrived as I got in, and I had just time to hurry to her platform and go down the carriages. There was only one Second-class on the train. I slipped the window and looked down upon a flaming red beard, half covered by a railway rug. That was my man, fast asleep, and I dug him gently in the ribs. He woke with a grunt and I saw his face in the light of the lamps. It was a great and shining face.

"Tickets again?" said he.

"No," said I. "I am to tell you that he is gone South for the week. He is gone South for the week!"

The train had begun to move out. The red man rubbed his eyes. "He has gone South for the week," he repeated. "Now that's just like his impidence. Did he say that I was to give you anything?—'Cause I won't."

"He didn't," I said, and dropped away, and watched the red lights die out in the dark. It was horribly cold because the wind was blowing off the sands. I climbed into my own train—not an Intermediate Carriage this time—and went to sleep.

If the man with the beard had given me a rupee I should have kept it as a memento of a rather curious affair. But the consciousness of having done my duty was my only reward.

Later on I reflected that two gentlemen like my friends could not do any good if they foregathered and personated correspondents of newspapers, and might, if they "stuck up" one of the little rat-trap states of Central India or Southern Rajputana, get themselves into serious difficulties. I therefore took some trouble to describe them as accurately as I could remember to people who would be interested in deporting them: and succeeded, so I was later informed, in having them headed back from the Degumber borders.

Then I became respectable, and returned to an Office where there were no Kings and no incidents except the daily manufacture of a newspaper. A newspaper office seems to attract every conceivable sort of person, to the prejudice of discipline. Zenana-mission ladies arrive, and beg that the Editor will instantly abandon all his duties to describe a Christian prize-giving in a back-slum of a perfectly inaccessible village; Colonels who have been over-passed for commands sit down and sketch the outline of a series of ten, twelve, or twenty-four leading articles on Seniority *versus* Selection; missionaries wish to know why they have not been permitted to escape from their regular vehicles of abuse and swear at a brother missionary under special patronage of the editorial We; stranded theatrical companies troop up to explain that they cannot pay for their advertisements, but on their return from New Zealand or Tahiti will do so with interest; inventors of patent punkah-pulling machines, carriage couplings and unbreakable swords and axle-trees call with specifications in their pockets and hours at their disposal; tea-companies enter and elaborate their prospectuses with the office pens; secretaries of ball-committees clamor to have the glories of their last dance more fully expounded; strange ladies rustle in and say:—"I want a hundred lady's cards printed *at once,* please," which is manifestly part of an Editor's duty; and every dissolute ruffian that ever tramped the Grand Trunk Road makes it his business to ask for employment as a proof-reader. And, all the time, the telephone-bell is ringing madly, and Kings are being killed on the Continent, and Empires are saying—"You're another," and Mister Gladstone is calling down brimstone upon the British Dominions, and the little black copy-boys are whining, "*kaa-pi chay-ha-yeh*" (copy wanted) like tired bees, and most of the paper is as blank as Modred's shield.

But that is the amusing part of the year. There are six other months wherein none ever come to call, and the thermometer walks inch by inch up to the top of the glass, and the office is darkened to just above reading-light, and the press machines are red-hot of touch, and nobody writes anything but accounts of amusements in the Hill-stations or obituary notices. Then the telephone becomes a tinkling terror, because it tells you of the sudden deaths of men and women that you knew intimately, and the prickly-heat covers you as with a garment, and you sit down and write:—"A slight increase of sickness is reported from the Khuda Janta Khan District. The outbreak is purely sporadic in its nature, and, thanks to the energetic efforts of the District authorities, is now almost at an end. It is, however, with deep regret we record the death, etc."

Then the sickness really breaks out, and the less recording and reporting the better for the peace of the subscribers. But the Empires and the Kings continue to divert themselves as selfishly as before, and the Foreman thinks that a daily paper really ought to come out once in twenty-four hours, and all the people at the Hill-stations in the middle of their amusements say, "Good gracious! Why can't the paper be sparkling? I'm sure there's plenty going on up here."

That is the dark half of the moon, and, as the advertisements say, "must be experienced to be appreciated."

It was in that season, and a remarkably evil season, that the paper began running the last issue of the week on Saturday night, which is to say Sunday morning, after the custom of a London paper. This was a great convenience, for immediately after the paper was put to bed, the dawn would lower the thermometer from 96 degrees to almost 84 degrees for half an hour, and in that chill—you have no idea how cold is 84 degrees on the grass until you begin to pray for it—a very tired man could set off to sleep ere the heat roused him.

One Saturday night it was my pleasant duty to put the paper to bed alone. A King or courtier or a courtesan or a community was going to die or get a new Constitution, or do something that was important on the other side of the world, and the paper was to be held open till the latest possible minute in order to catch the telegram. It was a pitchy black night, as stifling as a June night can be, and the *loo,* the red-hot wind from the westward, was booming among the tinder-dry trees and pretending that the rain was on its heels. Now and again a spot of almost boiling water would fall on the dust with the flop of a frog, but all our weary world knew that was only pretence. It was a shade cooler in the press-room than the office, so I sat there, while the type ticked and clicked, and the night-jars hooted at the windows, and the all but naked compositors wiped the sweat from their foreheads and called for water. The thing that was keeping us back, whatever it was, would not come off, though the *loo* dropped and the last type was set, and the whole round earth stood still in the choking heat, with its finger on its lip, to wait the event. I drowsed, and wondered whether the telegraph was a blessing, and whether this dying man, or struggling people, was aware of the inconvenience the delay was causing. There was no special reason beyond the heat and worry to make tension, but, as the clock hands crept up to three o'clock and the machines spun their fly-wheels two and three times to see that all was in order, before I said the word that would set them off, I could have shrieked aloud.

Then the roar and rattle of the wheels shivered the quiet into little bits. I rose to go away, but two men in white clothes stood in front of me. The first one said:—"It's him!" The second said, "So it is!" And they both laughed almost as loudly as the machinery roared, and mopped their foreheads. "We see there was a light burning across the road and we were sleeping in that ditch there for coolness, and I said to my friend here, 'The office is open. Let's come along and speak to him as turned us back from Degumber State,' " said the smaller of the two. He was the man I had met in the Mhow train, and his fellow was the red-bearded man of Marwar Junction. There was no mistaking the eyebrows of the one or the beard of the other.

I was not pleased, because I wished to go to sleep, not to squabble with loafers. "What do you want?" I asked.

"Half an hour's talk with you cool and comfortable, in the office," said the red-bearded man. "We'd *like* some drink—the Contrack doesn't begin yet, Peachey, so you needn't look—but what we really want is advice. We don't want money. We ask you as a favor, because you did us a bad turn about Degumber."

I led from the press-room to the stifling office with the maps on the walls, and the red-haired man rubbed his hands. "That's something like," said he. "This was the proper shop to come to. Now, Sir, let me introduce to you Brother Peachey Carnehan, that's him, and Brother Daniel Dravot, that is *me*, and the less said about our professions the better, for we have been

most things in our time. Soldier, sailor, compositor, photographer, proof-reader, street-preacher, and correspondents of the *Backwoodsman* when we thought the paper wanted one. Carnehan is sober, and so am I. Look at us first and see that's sure. It will save you cutting into my talk. We'll take one of your cigars apiece, and you shall see us light."

I watched the test. The men were absolutely sober, so I gave them each a tepid peg.

"Well *and* good," said Carnehan of the eyebrows, wiping the froth from his moustache. "Let me talk now, Dan. We have been all over India, mostly on foot. We have been boiler-fitters, engine-drivers, petty contractors, and all that, and we have decided that India isn't big enough for such as us."

They certainly were too big for the office. Dravot's beard seemed to fill half the room and Carnehan's shoulders the other half, as they sat on the big table. Carnehan continued:—"The country isn't half worked out because they that governs it won't let you touch it. They spend all their blessed time in governing it, and you can't lift a spade, nor chip a rock, nor look for oil, nor anything like that without all the Government saying—'Leave it alone and let us govern.' Therefore, such as it is, we will let it alone, and go away to some other place where a man isn't crowded and can come to his own. We are not little men, and there is nothing that we are afraid of except Drink, and we have signed a Contrack on that. *Therefore,* we are going away to be Kings."

"Kings in our own right," muttered Dravot.

"Yes, of course," I said. "You've been tramping in the sun, and it's a very warm night, and hadn't you better sleep over the notion? Come to-morrow."

"Neither drunk nor sunstruck," said Dravot. "We have slept over the notion half a year, and require to see Books and Atlases, and we have decided that there is only one place now in the world that two strong men can Sar-a-*whack*. They call it Kafiristan. By my reckoning it's the top right-hand corner of Afghanistan, not more than three hundred miles from Peshawar. They have two and thirty heathen idols there, and we'll be the thirty-third. It's a mountainous country, and the women of those parts are very beautiful."

"But that is provided against in the Contrack," said Carnehan. "Neither Women nor Liquor, Daniel."

"And that's all we know, except that no one has gone there, and they fight, and in any place where they fight a man who knows how to drill men can always be a King. We shall go to those parts and say to any King we find—'D' you want to vanquish your foes?' and we will show him how to drill men; for that we know better than anything else. Then we will subvert that King and seize his Throne and establish a Dynasty."

"You'll be cut to pieces before you're fifty miles across the Border," I said. "You have to travel through Afghanistan to get to that country. It's one mass of mountains and peaks and glaciers, and no Englishman has been through it. The people are utter brutes, and even if you reached them you couldn't do anything."

"That's more like," said Carnehan. "If you could think us a little more mad we would be more pleased. We have come to you to know about this country, to read a book about it, and to be shown maps. We want you to tell us that we are fools and to show us your books." He turned to the bookcases.

"Are you at all in earnest?" I said.

"A little," said Dravot, sweetly. "As big a map as you have got, even if it's all blank where Kafiristan is, and any books you've got. We can read, though we aren't very educated."

I uncased the big thirty-two-miles-to-the-inch map of India, and two smaller Frontier maps, hauled down volume INF–KAN of the *Encyclopaedia Britannica*, and the men consulted them.

"See here!" said Dravot, his thumb on the map. "Up to Jagdallak, Peachey and me know the road. We was there with Roberts's Army. We'll have to turn off to the right at Jagdallak through Laghmann territory. Then we get

among the hills—fourteen thousand feet—fifteen thousand—it will be cold work there, but it don't look very far on the map."

I handed him Wood on the *Sources of the Oxus*. Carnehan was deep in the *Encyclopaedia*.

"They're a mixed lot," said Dravot, reflectively; "and it won't help us to know the names of their tribes. The more tribes the more they'll fight, and the better for us. From Jagdallak to Ashang. H'mm!"

"But all the information about the country is as sketchy and inaccurate as can be," I protested. "No one knows anything about it really. Here's the file of the *United Services' Institute*. Read what Bellew says."

"Blow Bellew!" said Carnehan. "Dan, they're an all-fired lot of heathens, but this book here says they think they're related to us English."

I smoked while the men pored over Raverty, Wood, the maps and the *Encyclopaedia*.

"There is no use your waiting," said Dravot, politely. "It's about four o'clock now. We'll go before six o'clock if you want to sleep, and we won't steal any of the papers. Don't you sit up. We're two harmless lunatics, and if you come, to-morrow evening, down to the Serai we'll say good-bye to you."

"You *are* two fools," I answered. "You'll be turned back at the Frontier or cut up the minute you set foot in Afghanistan. Do you want any money or a recommendation down-country? I can help you to the chance of work next week."

"Next week we shall be hard at work ourselves, thank you," said Dravot. "It isn't so easy being a King as it looks. When we've got our Kingdom in going order we'll let you know, and you can come up and help us to govern it."

"Would two lunatics make a Contrack like that?" said Carnehan, with subdued pride, showing me a greasy half-sheet of note-paper on which was written the following. I copied it, then and there, as a curiosity:

This Contrack between me and you persuing witnesseth in the name of God—Amen and so forth.

*(One) That me and you will settle this
matter together: i.e., to be Kings of
Kafiristan.*

*(Two) That you and me will not, while
this matter is being settled, look at any
Liquor, nor any Woman, black, white
or brown, so as to get mixed up with
one or the other harmful.*

*(Three) That we conduct ourselves with
dignity and discretion, and if one of us
gets into trouble the other will stay by
him.*

*Signed by you and me this day.
Peachey Taliaferro Carnehan.
Daniel Dravot.
Both Gentlemen at Large.*

"There was no need for the last article," said
Carnehan, blushing modestly; "but it looks regular. Now you know the sort of men that loafers
are—we *are* loafers, Dan, until we get out of
India—and *do* you think that we would sign a
Contrack like that unless we was in earnest? We
have kept away from the two things that make
life worth having."

"You won't enjoy your lives much longer if
you are going to try this idiotic adventure. Don't
set the office on fire," I said, "and go away before
nine o'clock."

I left them still poring over the maps and
making notes on the back of the "Contrack." "Be
sure to come down to the Serai to-morrow,"
were their parting words.

The Kumharsen Serai is the great four-
square sink of humanity where the strings of
camels and horses from the North load and unload. All the nationalities of Central Asia may be
found there, and most of the folk of India
proper. Balkh and Bokhara there meet Bengal
and Bombay, and try to draw eye-teeth. You can
buy ponies, turquoises, Persian pussy-cats,
saddle-bags, fat-tailed sheep and musk in the
Kumharsen Serai, and get many strange things
for nothing. In the afternoon I went down to see
whether my friends intended to keep their word
or were lying about drunk.

A priest attired in fragments of ribbons and
rags stalked up to me, gravely twisting a child's
paper whirligig. Behind him was his servant
bending under the load of a crate of mud toys.
The two were loading up two camels, and the inhabitants of the Serai watched them with shrieks
of laughter.

"The priest is mad," said a horse-dealer to
me. "He is going up to Kabul to sell toys to the
Amir. He will either be raised to honor or have
his head cut off. He came in here this morning
and has been behaving madly ever since."

"The witless are under the protection of
God," stammered a flat-cheeked Usbeg in broken Hindi. "They foretell future events."

"Would they could have foretold that my caravan would have been cut up by the Shinwaris
almost within shadow of the Pass!" grunted the
Eusufzai agent of a Rajputana trading-house
whose goods had been feloniously diverted into
the hands of other robbers just across the Border, and whose misfortunes were the laughing-
stock of the bazar. "Ohé, priest, whence come
you and whither do you go?"

"From Roum have I come," shouted the
priest, waving his whirligig; "from Roum, blown
by the breath of a hundred devils across the sea!
O thieves, robbers, liars, the blessing of Pir
Khan on pigs, dogs, and perjurers! Who will
take the Protected of God to the North to sell
charms that are never still to the Amir? The
camels shall not gall, the sons shall not fall sick,
and the wives shall remain faithful while they are
away, of the men who give me place in their caravan. Who will assist me to slipper the King of
the Roos with a golden slipper with a silver heel?
The protection of Pir Khan be upon his labors!"
He spread out the skirts of his gabardine and
pirouetted between the lines of tethered horses.

"There starts a caravan from Peshawur to
Kabul in twenty days, *Huzrut*," said the Eusufzai trader. "My camels go therewith. Do thou
also go and bring us good-luck."

"I will go even now!" shouted the priest. "I
will depart upon my winged camels, and be at
Peshawur in a day! Ho! Hazar Mir Khan," he

yelled to his servant, "drive out the camels, but let me first mount my own."

He leaped on the back of his beast as it knelt, and, turning round to me, cried:—"Come thou also, Sahib, a little along the road and I will sell thee a charm—an amulet that shall make thee King of Kafiristan."

Then the light broke upon me, and I followed the two camels out of the Serai till we reached open road and the priest halted.

"What d' you think o' that?" said he in English. "Carnehan can't talk their patter, so I've made him my servant. He makes a handsome servant. 'Tisn't for nothing that I've been knocking about the country for fourteen years. Didn't I do that talk neat? We'll hitch on to a caravan at Peshawur till we get to Jagdallak, and then we'll see if we can get donkeys for our camels, and strike into Kafiristan. Whirligigs for the Amir, O Lor! Put your hand under the camel-bags and tell me what you feel."

I felt the butt of a Martini, and another and another.

"Twenty of 'em," said Dravot, placidly. "Twenty of 'em, and ammunition to correspond, under the whirligigs and the mud dolls."

"Heaven help you if you are caught with those things!" I said. "A Martini is worth her weight in silver among the Pathans."

"Fifteen hundred rupees of capital—every rupee we could beg, borrow, or steal—are invested on these two camels," said Dravot. "We won't get caught. We're going through the Khaiber with a regular caravan. Who'd touch a poor mad priest?"

"Have you got everything you want?" I asked, overcome with astonishment.

"Not yet, but we shall soon. Give us a memento of your kindness, Brother. You did me a service yesterday, and that time in Marwar. Half my Kingdom shall you have, as the saying is." I slipped a small charm compass from my watch-chain and handed it up to the priest.

"Good-bye," said Dravot, giving me a hand cautiously. "It's the last time we'll shake hands with an Englishman these many days. Shake hands with him, Carnehan," he cried, as the second camel passed me.

Carnehan leaned down and shook hands. Then the camels passed away along the dusty road, and I was left alone to wonder. My eye could detect no failure in the disguises. The scene in the Serai attested that they were complete to the native mind. There was just the chance, therefore, that Carnehan and Dravot would be able to wander through Afghanistan without detection. But, beyond, they would find death, certain and awful death.

Ten days later a native friend of mine, giving me the news of the day from Peshawur, wound up his letter with:—"There has been much laughter here on account of a certain mad priest who is going in his estimation to sell petty gauds and insignificant trinkets which he ascribes as great charms to H. H. the Amir of Bokhara. He passed through Peshawur and associated himself to the Second Summer caravan that goes to Kabul. The merchants are pleased because through superstition they imagine that such mad fellows bring good-fortune."

The two, then, were beyond the Border. I would have prayed for them, but, that night, a real King died in Europe and demanded an obituary notice.

The wheel of the world swings through the same phases again and again. Summer passed and winter thereafter, and came and passed again. The daily paper continued and I with it, and upon the third summer there fell a hot night, a night-issue, and a strained waiting for something to be telegraphed from the other side of the world, exactly as had happened before. A few great men had died in the past two years, the machines worked with more clatter, and some of the trees in the Office garden were a few feet taller. But that was all the difference.

I passed over to the press-room, and went through just such a scene as I have already described. The nervous tension was stronger than it had been two years before, and I felt the heat more acutely. At three o'clock I cried, "Print off," and turned to go, when there crept to my chair what was left of a man. He was bent into a circle, his head was sunk between his shoulders, and he moved his feet one over the other like a bear. I could hardly see whether he walked or crawled—this rag-wrapped, whining cripple who addressed me by name, crying that he was come back. "Can you give me a drink?" he whimpered. "For the Lord's sake, give me a drink!"

I went back to the office, the man following with groans of pain, and I turned up the lamp.

"Don't you know me?" he gasped, dropping into a chair, and he turned his drawn face, surmounted by a shock of grey hair, to the light.

I looked at him intently. Once before had I seen eyebrows that met over the nose in an inch-broad black band, but for the life of me I could not tell where.

"I don't know you," I said, handing him the whiskey. "What can I do for you?"

He took a gulp of the spirit raw, and shivered in spite of the suffocating heat.

"I've come back," he repeated; "and I was the King of Kafiristan—me and Dravot—crowned Kings we was! In this office we settled it—you setting there and giving us the books. I am Peachey—Peachey Taliaferro Carnehan, and you've been setting here ever since—O Lord!"

I was more than a little astonished, and expressed my feelings accordingly.

"It's true," said Carnehan, with a dry cackle, nursing his feet, which were wrapped in rags. "True as gospel. Kings we were, with crowns upon our heads—me and Dravot—poor Dan—oh, poor, poor Dan, that would never take advice, not though I begged of him!"

"Take the whiskey," I said, "and take your own time. Tell me all you can recollect of everything from beginning to end. You got across the Border on your camels, Dravot dressed as a mad priest and you his servant. Do you remember that?"

"I ain't mad—yet, but I shall be that way

soon. Of course I remember. Keep looking at me, or maybe my words will go all to pieces. Keep looking at me in my eyes and don't say anything."

I leaned forward and looked into his face as steadily as I could. He dropped one hand upon the table and I grasped it by the wrist. It was twisted like a bird's claw, and upon the back was a ragged, red, diamond-shaped scar.

"No, don't look there. Look at *me*," said Carnehan. "That comes afterward, but for the Lord's sake don't distrack me. We left with that caravan, me and Dravot playing all sorts of antics to amuse the people we were with. Dravot used to make us laugh in the evenings when all the people was cooking their dinners—cooking their dinners, and . . . what did they do then? They lit little fires with sparks that went into Dravot's beard, and we all laughed—fit to die. Little red fires they was, going into Dravot's big red beard—so funny." His eyes left mine and he smiled foolishly.

"You went as far as Jagdallak with that caravan," I said, at a venture, "after you had lit those fires. To Jagdallak, where you turned off to try to get into Kafiristan."

"No, we didn't neither. What are you talking about? We turned off before Jagdallak, because we heard the roads was good. But they wasn't good enough for our two camels—mine and Dravot's. When we left the caravan, Dravot took off all his clothes and mine too, and said we would be heathen, because the Kafirs didn't allow Mohammedans to talk to them. So we dressed betwixt and between, and such a sight as Daniel Dravot I never saw yet nor expect to see again. He burned half his beard, and slung a sheep-skin over his shoulder, and shaved his head into patterns. He shaved mine, too, and made me wear outrageous things to look like a heathen. That was in a most mountainous country, and our camels couldn't go along any more because of the mountains. They were tall and black, and coming home I saw them fight like wild goats—there are lots of goats in Kafiristan.

And these mountains, they never keep still, no more than the goats. Always fighting they are, and don't let you sleep at night."

"Take some more whiskey," I said, very slowly. "What did you and Daniel Dravot do when the camels could go no farther because of the rough roads that led into Kafiristan?"

"What did which do? There was a party called Peachey Taliaferro Carnehan that was with Dravot. Shall I tell you about him? He died out there in the cold. Slap from the bridge fell old Peachey, turning and twisting in the air like a penny whirligig that you can sell to the Amir.— No; they was two for three ha'pence, those whirligigs, or I am much mistaken and woeful sore. And then these camels were no use, and Peachey said to Dravot—'For the Lord's sake, let's get out of this before our heads are chopped off,' and with that they killed the camels all among the mountains, not having anything in particular to eat, but first they took off the boxes with the guns and the ammunition, till two men came along driving four mules. Dravot up and dances in front of them, singing,—'Sell me four mules.' Says the first man,—'If you are rich enough to buy, you are rich enough to rob'; but before ever he could put his hand to his knife, Dravot breaks his neck over his knee, and the other party runs away. So Carnehan loaded the mules with the rifles that was taken off the camels, and together we starts forward into those bitter cold mountainous parts, and never a road broader than the back of your hand."

He paused for a moment, while I asked him if he could remember the nature of the country through which he had journeyed.

"I am telling you as straight as I can, but my head isn't as good as it might be. They drove nails through it to make me hear better how Dravot died. The country was mountainous and the mules were most contrary, and the inhabitants was dispersed and solitary. They went up and up, and down and down, and that other party, Carnehan, was imploring of Dravot not to sing and whistle so loud, for fear of bringing down the tremenjus avalanches. But Dravot says that if a King couldn't sing it wasn't worth being King, and whacked the mules over the rump, and never took no heed for ten cold days. We came to a big level valley all among the mountains, and the mules were near dead, so we killed them, not having anything in special for them or us to eat. We sat upon the boxes, and played odds and even with the cartridges that was jolted out.

"Then ten men with bows and arrows ran down that valley, chasing twenty men with bows and arrows, and the row was tremenjus. They was fair men—fairer than you or me—with yellow hair and remarkable well built. Says Dravot, unpacking the guns—'This is the beginning of the business. We'll fight for the ten men,' and with that he fires two rifles at the twenty men, and drops one of them at two hundred yards from the rock where we was sitting. The other men began to run but Carnehan and Dravot sits on the boxes picking them off at all ranges, up and down the valley. Then we goes up to the ten men that had run across the snow too, and they fires a footy little arrow at us. Dravot he shoots above their heads and they all falls down flat. Then he walks over them and kicks them, and then he lifts them up and shakes hands all round to make them friendly like. He calls them and gives them the boxes to carry, and waves his hand for all the world as though he was King already. They takes the boxes and him across the valley and up the hill into a pine wood on the top, where there was half a dozen big stone idols. Dravot he goes to the biggest—a fellow they call Imbra—and lays a rifle and cartridge at his feet, rubbing his nose respectful with his own nose, patting him on the head, and saluting in front of it. He turns round to the men and nods his head, and says,—'That's all right. I'm in the know too, and all these old jim-jams are my friends.' Then he opens his mouth and points down it, and when the first man brings him food, he says—'No'; and when the second man brings him food, he says 'No'; but when one of the old priests and the boss of the village brings him food, he says—'Yes'; very haughty, and eats it slow. That was how we came to our first village, without any trouble, just as though we had tumbled from the skies. But we tumbled from one of those damned rope-bridges, you see, and you couldn't expect a man to laugh much after that."

"Take some more whiskey and go on," I said. "That was the first village you came into. How did you get to be King?"

"I wasn't King," said Carnehan. "Dravot he was the King, and a handsome man he looked with the gold crown on his head and all. Him and the other party stayed in that village, and every morning Dravot sat by the side of old Imbra, and the people came and worshipped. That was Dravot's order. Then a lot of men came into the valley, and Carnehan and Dravot picks them off with the rifles before they knew where they was, and runs down into the valley and up again the other side, and finds another village, same as the first one, and the people all falls down flat on their faces, and Dravot says,—'Now what is the trouble between you two villages?' and the people points to a woman, as fair as you or me, that was carried off, and Dravot takes her back to the first village and counts up the dead—eight there was. For each dead man Dravot pours a little milk on the ground and waves his arms like a whirligig and 'That's all right,' says he. Then he and Carnehan takes the big boss of each village by the arm and walks them down into the valley, and shows them how to scratch a line with a spear right down the valley, and gives each a sod of turf from both sides o' the line. Then all the people comes down and shouts like the devil and all, and Dravot says,—'Go and dig the land, and be fruitful and multiply,' which they did, though they didn't understand. Then we asks the names of things in their lingo—bread and water and fire and idols and such, and Dravot leads the priest of each village up to the idol, and says he must sit there and judge the people, and if anything goes wrong he is to be shot.

"Next week they was all turning up the land in the valley as quiet as bees and much prettier, and the priests heard all the complaints and told Dravot in dumb show what it was about. 'That's just the beginning,' says Dravot. 'They think we're Gods.' He and Carnehan picks out twenty good men and shows them how to click off a rifle, and form fours, and advance in line, and they was very pleased to do so, and clever to see the hang of it. Then he takes out his pipe and his baccy-pouch and leaves one at one village and one at the other, and off we two goes to see what was to be done in the next valley. That was all rock, and there was a little village there, and Carnehan says,—'Send 'em to the old valley to plant,' and takes 'em there and gives 'em some land that wasn't took before. They were a poor lot, and we blooded 'em with a kid before letting 'em into the new Kingdom. That was to impress the people, and then they settled down quiet, and Carnehan went back to Dravot who had got into another valley, all snow and ice and most mountainous. There was no people there and the Army got afraid so Dravot shoots one of them, and goes on till he finds some people in a village, and the Army explains that unless the people wants to be killed they had better not shoot their little matchlocks; for they had matchlocks. We make friends with the priest and I stays there alone with two of the Army, teaching the men how to drill, and a thundering big Chief comes across the snow with kettledrums and horns twanging, because he heard there was a new God kicking about. Carnehan sights for the brown of the men half a mile across the snow and wings one of them. Then he sends a message to the Chief that, unless he wished to be killed, he must come and shake hands with me and leave his arms behind. The Chief comes alone first, and Carnehan shakes hands with him and whirls his arms about, same as Dravot used, and very much surprised that Chief was, and strokes my eyebrows. Then Carnehan goes alone to the Chief, and asks him in dumb show if he had an enemy he hated. 'I have,' says the chief. So Carnehan weeds out the pick of his men, and sets the two of the Army to show them drill and at the end of two weeks the men can manoeuvre about as well as Volunteers. So he marches with the Chief to a great big plain on the top of a mountain, and the Chief's men rushes into a village and takes it; we three Martinis firing into the brown of the enemy. So we took that village too, and I gives the Chief a rag from my coat and says, 'Occupy till I come'; which was scriptural. By way of a reminder, when me and the Army was eighteen hundred yards away, I drops a bullet near him standing on the snow, and all the people falls flat on their faces. Then I sends a letter to Dravot, wherever he be by land or by sea."

At the risk of throwing the creature out of train I interrupted, "How could you write a letter up yonder?"

"The letter? Oh!—The letter! Keep looking at me between the eyes, please. It was a string-talk letter, that we'd learned the way of it from a blind beggar in the Punjab."

I remember that there had once come to the office a blind man with a knotted twig and a piece of string which he wound round the twig according to some cypher of his own. He could, after the lapse of days or hours, repeat the sentence which he had reeled up. He had reduced the alphabet to eleven primitive sounds; and tried to teach me his method, but failed.

"I sent that letter to Dravot," said Carnehan; "and told him to come back because this Kingdom was growing too big for me to handle, and then I struck for the first valley, to see how the priests were working. They called the village we took along with the Chief, Bashkai, and the first village we took, Er-Heb. The priests at Er-Heb were doing all right, but they had a lot of pending cases about land to show me, and some men from another village had been firing arrows at night. I went out and looked for that village and fired four rounds at it from a thousand yards. That used all the cartridges I cared to spend, and I waited for Dravot, who had been away two or three months, and I kept my people quiet.

"One morning I heard the devil's own noise of drums and horns, and Dan Dravot marches down the hill with his Army and a tail of hundreds of men, and, which was the most amazing—a great gold crown on his head. 'My Gord, Carnehan,' says Daniel, 'this is a tremenjus business, and we've got the whole country as far as it's worth having. I am the son of Alexander by Queen Semiramis, and you're my younger brother and a God too! It's the biggest thing we've ever seen. I've been marching and fighting for six weeks with the Army, and every footy little village for fifty miles has come in rejoiceful; and more than that, I've got the key of the whole show, as you'll see, and I've got a crown for you! I told 'em to make two of 'em at a place called Shu, where the gold lies in the rock like suet in mutton. Gold I've seen, and turquoise I've kicked out of the cliffs, and there's garnets in the sands of the river, and here's a chunk of amber that a man brought me. Call up all the priests and, here, take your crown.'

"One of the men opens a black hair bag and I slips the crown on. It was too small and too heavy, but I wore it for the glory. Hammered gold it was—five pound weight, like a hoop of a barrel.

" 'Peachey,' says Dravot, 'we don't want to fight no more. The Craft's the trick so help me!' and he brings forward that same Chief that I left at Bashkai—Billy Fish we called him afterward, because he was so like Billy Fish that drove the big tank-engine at Mach on the Bolan in the old days. 'Shake hands with him,' says Dravot, and I shook hands and nearly dropped, for Billy Fish gave me the Grip. I said nothing, but tried him with the Fellow Craft Grip. He answers, all right, and I tried the Master's Grip, but that was a slip. 'A Fellow Craft he is!' I says to Dan. 'Does he know the word?' 'He does,' says Dan, 'and all the priests know. It's a miracle! The Chiefs and the priests can work a Fellow Craft Lodge in a way that's very like ours, and they've cut the marks on the rocks, but they don't know the Third Degree, and they've come to find out. It's Gord's Truth. I've known these long years that the Afghans knew up to the Fellow Craft Degree, but this is a miracle. A God and a Grand-Master of the Craft am I, and a Lodge in the Third Degree I will open, and we'll raise the head priests and the Chiefs of the villages.'

" 'It's against all the law,' I says, 'holding a Lodge without warrant from any one; and we never held office in any Lodge.'

" 'It's a master-stroke of policy,' says Dravot. 'It means running the country as easy as a four-wheeled bogy on a down grade. We can't stop to inquire now, or they'll turn against us. I've forty Chiefs at my heel, and passed and raised according to their merit they shall be. Billet these men on the villages and see that we run up a Lodge of some kind. The temple of Imbra will do for the Lodge-room. The women must make aprons as you show them. I'll hold a levee of Chiefs to-night and Lodge to-morrow.'

"I was fair run off my legs, but I wasn't such a fool as not to see what a pull this Craft business gave us. I showed the priests' families how to make aprons of the degrees, but for Dravot's apron the blue border and marks was made of turquoise lumps on white hide, not cloth. We took a great square stone in the temple for the Master's chair, and little stones for the officers' chairs, and painted the black pavement with white squares, and did what we could to make things regular.

"At the levee which was held that night on the hillside with big bonfires, Dravot gives out that him and me were Gods and sons of Alexander, and Passed Grand-Masters in the Craft, and was come to make Kafiristan a country where every man should eat in peace and drink in quiet, and specially obey us. Then the Chiefs come round to shake hands, and they were so hairy and white and fair it was just shaking hands with old friends. We gave them names according as they was like men we had known in India—Billy Fish, Holly Dilworth, Pikky Kergan that was Bazar-master when I was at Mhow, and so on and so on.

"The *most* amazing miracle was at Lodge next night. One of the old priests was watching us continuous, and I felt uneasy, for I knew we'd have to fudge the Ritual, and I didn't know what the men knew. The old priest was a stranger come in from beyond the village of Bashkai. The minute Dravot puts on the Master's apron that the girls had made for him, the priest fetches a whoop and a howl, and tries to overturn the stone that Dravot was sitting on. 'It's all up now,' I says. 'That comes of meddling with the Craft without warrant!' Dravot never winked an eye, not when ten priests took and tilted over the Grand-Master's chair—which was to say the stone of Imbra. The priest begins rubbing the bottom end of it to clear away the black dirt, and presently he shows all the other priests the Master's Mark, same as was on Dravot's apron, cut into the stone. Not even the priests of the temple of Imbra knew it was there. The old chap falls flat on his face at Dravot's feet and kisses 'em. 'Luck again,' says Dravot, across the Lodge to me, 'they say it's the missing Mark that no one could understand the why of. We're more than safe now.' Then he bangs the butt of his gun for a gavel and says:—'By virtue of the authority vested in me by my own right hand and the help of Peachey, I declare myself Grand-Master of all Freemasonry in Kafiristan in this the Mother Lodge o' the country, and King of Kafiristan equally with Peachey!' At that he puts on his crown and I puts on mine—I was doing Senior Warden—and we opens the Lodge in most ample form. It was an amazing miracle! The priests moved in Lodge through the first two degrees almost without telling, as if the memory was coming back to them. After that, Peachey and Dravot raised such as was worthy—high priests and Chiefs of far-off villages. Billy Fish was the first, and I can tell you we scared the soul out of him. It was not in any way according to Ritual, but it served our turn. We didn't raise more than ten of the biggest men because we didn't want to make the Degree common. And they was clamoring to be raised.

" 'In another six months,' says Dravot, 'we'll hold another Communication and see how you are working.' Then he asks them about their villages, and learns that they was fighting one against the other and were fair sick and tired of it. And when they wasn't doing that they was fighting with the Mohammedans. 'You can fight those when they come into our country,' says Dravot. 'Tell off every tenth man of your tribes for a Frontier guard, and send two hundred at a time to this valley to be drilled. Nobody is going to be shot or speared any more so long as he does well, and I know that you won't cheat me because you're white people—sons of Alexander—and not like common, black Mohammedans. You are *my* people, and, by God,' says he, running off into English at the end, 'I'll make a damned fine Nation of you, or I'll die in the making!'

"I can't tell all we did for the next six months because Dravot did a lot I couldn't see the hang of, and he learned their lingo in a way I never could. My work was to help the people plough, and now and again go out with some of the Army and see what the other villages were doing, and make 'em throw rope-bridges across the ravines which cut up the country horrid. Dravot was very kind to me, but when he walked up and down in the pine wood pulling that bloody red beard of his with both fists I knew he was thinking plans I could not advise him about, and I just waited for orders.

"But Dravot never showed me disrespect before the people. They were afraid of me and the Army, but they loved Dan. He was the best of friends with the priests and the Chiefs; but any one could come across the hills with a complaint and Dravot would hear him out fair, and call four priests together and say what was to be done. He used to call in Billy Fish from Bashkai, and Pikky Kergan from Shu, and an old Chief we called Kafuzelum—it was like enough to his real name—and hold councils with 'em when there was any fighting to be done in small villages. That was his Council of War, and the four priests of Bashkai, Shu, Khawak, and Madora was his Privy Council. Between the lot of 'em they sent me, with forty men and twenty rifles, and sixty men carrying turquoises, into the Ghorband country to buy those hand-made Martini rifles, that come out of the Amir's workshops at Kabul, from one of the Amir's Herati regiments that would have sold the very teeth out of their mouths for turquoises.

"I stayed in Ghorband a month, and gave the Governor there the pick of my baskets for hushmoney, and bribed the Colonel of the regiment some more, and, between the two and the tribespeople, we got more than a hundred hand-made Martinis, a hundred good Kohat Jezails, that'll throw to six hundred yards, and forty man-loads of very bad ammunition for the rifles. I came back with what I had, and distributed 'em among the men that the Chiefs sent to me to drill. Dravot was too busy to attend to those things, but the old Army that we first made helped me, and we turned out five hundred men that could drill, and two hundred that knew how to hold arms pretty straight. Even those corkscrewed, hand-made guns was a miracle to them. Dravot talked big about powder-shops and factories, walking up and down in the pine wood when the winter was coming on.

" 'I won't make a Nation,' says he, 'I'll make an Empire! These men aren't niggers; they're English! Look at their eyes—look at their mouths. Look at the way they stand up. They sit on chairs in their own houses. They're the Lost Tribes, or something like it, and they've grown to be English. I'll take a census in the spring if the priests don't get frightened. There must be a fair two million of 'em in these hills. The villages are full o' little children. Two million people—two hundred and fifty thousand fighting men—and all English! They only want the rifles and a little drilling. Two hundred and fifty thousand men, ready to cut in on Russia's right flank when she tries for India! Peachey, man,' he says, chewing his beard in great hunks, 'we shall be Emperors—Emperors of the Earth! Rajah Brooke will be a suckling to us. I'll treat with the Viceroy on equal terms. I'll ask him to send me twelve picked English—twelve that I know of—to help us govern a bit. There's Mackray, Sergeant-pensioner at Segowli—many's the good dinner he's given me, and his wife a pair of trousers. There's Donkin, the Warder of Tounghoo Jail; there's hundreds that I could lay my hand on if I was in India. The Viceroy shall do it for me. I'll send a man through in the spring for those men, and I'll write for a dispensation from the Grand Lodge for what I've done as Grand-Master. That—and all the Sniders that'll be thrown out when the native troops in India take up the Martini. They'll be worn smooth, but they'll do for fighting in these hills. Twelve English, a hundred thousand Sniders run through the Amir's country in driblets—I'd be content with twenty thousand in one year— and we'd be an Empire. When everything was shipshape, I'd hand over the crown—this crown I'm wearing now—to Queen Victoria on my knees, and she'd say: "Rise up, Sir Daniel Dravot." Oh, it's big! It's big, I tell you! But there's so much to be done in every place— Bashkai, Khawak, Shu, and everywhere else.'

" 'What is it?' I says. 'There are no more men coming in to be drilled this autumn. Look at those fat, black clouds. They're bringing the snow.'

" 'It isn't that,' says Daniel, putting his hand very hard on my shoulder; 'and I don't wish to say anything that's against you, for no other living man would have followed me and made me what I am as you have done. You're a first-class Commander-in-Chief, and the people know you; but—it's a big country, and somehow you can't help me, Peachey, in the way I want to be helped.'

" 'Go to your blasted priests, then!' I said, and I was sorry when I made that remark, but it did hurt me sore to find Daniel talking so superior when I'd drilled all the men, and done all he told me.

" 'Don't let's quarrel, Peachey,' says Daniel, without cursing. 'You're a King too, and the half of this Kingdom is yours; but can't you see, Peachey, we want cleverer men than us now— three or four of 'em, that we can scatter about for our Deputies. It's a hugeous great State, and I can't always tell the right thing to do, and I

haven't time for all I want to do, and here's the winter coming on and all.' He put half his beard into his mouth, and it was as red as the gold of his crown.

" 'I'm sorry, Daniel,' says I. 'I've done all I could. I've drilled the men and shown the people how to stack their oats better; and I've brought in those tinware rifles from Ghorband—but I know what you're driving at. I take it Kings always feel oppressed that way.'

" 'There's another thing too,' says Dravot, walking up and down. 'The winter's coming and these people won't be giving much trouble, and if they do we can't move about. I want a wife.'

" 'For Gord's sake leave the women alone!' I says. 'We've both got all the work we can, though I *am* a fool. Remember the Contrack, and keep clear o' women.'

" 'The Contrack only lasted till such time as we was Kings; and Kings we have been these months past,' says Dravot, weighing his crown in his hand. 'You go get a wife too, Peachey—a nice, strappin', plump girl that'll keep you warm in the winter. They're prettier than English girls, and we can take the pick of 'em. Boil 'em once or twice in hot water, and they'll come out as fair as chicken and ham.'

" 'Don't tempt me!' I says. 'I will not have any dealings with a woman not till we are a dam' side more settled than we are now. I've been doing the work o' two men, and you've been doing the work o' three. Let's lie off a bit, and see if we can get some better tobacco from Afghan country and run in some good liquor; but no women.'

" 'Who's talking o' *women*?' says Dravot. 'I said *wife*—a Queen to breed a King's son for the King. A Queen out of the strongest tribe, that'll make them your blood-brothers, and that'll lie by your side and tell you all the people thinks about you and their own affairs. That's what I want.'

" 'Do you remember that Bengali woman I kept at Mogul Serai when I was a plate-layer?' says I. 'A fat lot o' good she was to me. She taught me the lingo and one or two other things; but what happened? She ran away with the Station Master's servant and half my month's pay. Then she turned up at Dadur Junction in tow of a half-caste, and had the impidence to say I was her husband—all among the drivers in the running-shed!'

" 'We've done with that,' says Dravot. 'These women are whiter than you or me, and a Queen I will have for the winter months.'

" 'For the last time o' asking, Dan, do *not*,' I says. 'It'll only bring us harm. The Bible says that Kings ain't to waste their strength on women, 'specially when they've got a new raw Kingdom to work over.'

" 'For the last time of answering, I will,' said Dravot, and he went away through the pine-trees looking like a big red devil. The low sun hit his crown and beard on one side and the two blazed like hot coals.

"But getting a wife was not as easy as Dan thought. He put it before the Council, and there was no answer till Billy Fish said that he'd better ask the girls. Dravot damned them all round. 'What's wrong with me?' he shouts, standing by the idol Imbra. 'Am I a dog or am I not enough of a man for your wenches? Haven't I put the shadow of my hand over this country? Who stopped the last Afghan raid?' It was me really, but Dravot was too angry to remember. 'Who brought your guns? Who repaired the bridges? Who's the Grand-Master of the sign cut in the stone?' and he thumped his hand on the block that he used to sit on in Lodge, and at Council, which opened like Lodge always. Billy Fish said nothing and no more did the others. 'Keep your hair on, Dan,' said I; 'and ask the girls. That's how it's done at Home, and these people are quite English.'

" 'The marriage of the King is a matter of State,' says Dan, in a white-hot rage, for he could feel, I hope, that he was going against his better mind. He walked out of the Council-room, and the others sat still, looking at the ground.

" 'Billy Fish,' says I to the Chief of Bashkai, 'what's the difficulty here? A straight answer to a true friend.' 'You know,' says Billy Fish. 'How should a man tell you who knows everything? How can daughters of men marry Gods or Devils? It's not proper.'

"I remember something like that in the Bible; but, if, after seeing us as long as they had they still believed we were Gods, it wasn't for me to undeceive them.

" 'A God can do anything,' says I. 'If the King is fond of a girl he'll not let her die.' 'She'll have to,' said Billy Fish. 'There are all sorts of Gods and Devils in these mountains, and now and again a girl marries one of them and isn't seen any more. Besides, you two know the Mark cut in the stone. Only the Gods know that. We thought you were men till you showed the sign of the Master.'

"I wished then that we had explained about the loss of the genuine secrets of a Master-Mason at the first go-off; but I said nothing. All that night there was a blowing of horns in a little dark temple halfway down the hill, and I heard a girl crying fit to die. One of the priests told us that she was being prepared to marry the King.

" 'I'll have no nonsense of that kind,' says Dan. 'I don't want to interfere with your customs, but I'll take my own wife.' 'The girl's a little bit afraid,' says the priest. 'She thinks she's going to die, and they are a-heartening of her up down in the temple.'

" 'Hearten her very tender, then,' says Dravot, 'or I'll hearten you with the butt of a gun so that you'll never want to be heartened again.' He licked his lips, did Dan, and stayed up walking about more than half the night, thinking of the wife that he was going to get in the morning. I wasn't any means comfortable, for I knew that dealings with a woman in foreign parts, though you was a crowned King twenty times over, could not but be risky. I got up very early in the morning while Dravot was asleep, and I saw the priests talking together in whispers, and the Chiefs talking together too, and they looked at me out of the corners of their eyes.

" 'What is up, Fish?' I says to the Bashkai man, who was wrapped up in his furs and looking splendid to behold.

" 'I can't rightly say,' says he; 'but if you can induce the King to drop all this nonsense about marriage, you'll be doing him and me and yourself a great service.'

" 'That I do believe,' says I. 'But sure, you know, Billy, as well as me, having fought against and for us, that the King and me are nothing more than two of the finest men that God Almighty ever made. Nothing more, I do assure you.'

" 'That may be,' says Billy Fish, 'and yet I should be sorry if it was.' He sinks his head upon his great fur cloak for a minute and thinks. 'King,' says he, 'be you man or God or Devil, I'll stick by you to-day. I have twenty of my men with me, and they will follow me. We'll go to Bashkai until the storm blows over.'

"A little snow had fallen in the night, and everything was white except the greasy fat clouds that blew down and down from the north. Dravot came out with his crown on his head, swinging his arms and stamping his feet, and looking more pleased than Punch.

" 'For the last time, drop it, Dan,' says I, in a whisper. 'Billy Fish here says that there will be a row.'

" 'A row among my people!' says Dravot. 'Not much. Peachey, you're a fool not to get a wife too. Where's the girl?' says he, with a voice as loud as the braying of a jackass. 'Call up all the Chiefs and priests, and let the Emperor see if his wife suits him.'

"There was no need to call any one. They were all there leaning on their guns and spears round the clearing in the centre of the pine wood. A deputation of priests went down to the little temple to bring up the girl, and the horns blew up fit to wake the dead. Billy Fish saunters round and gets as close to Daniel as he could, and behind him stood his twenty men with matchlocks. Not a man of them under six feet. I was next to Dravot, and behind me was twenty men of the regular Army. Up comes the girl, and a strapping wench she was, covered with silver and turquoises but white as death, and looking back every minute at the priests.

" 'She'll do,' said Dan, looking her over. 'What's to be afraid of, lass? Come and kiss me.' He puts his arm round her. She shuts her eyes, gives a bit of a squeak, and down goes her face in the side of Dan's flaming red beard.

" 'The slut's bitten me!' says he, clapping his hand to his neck, and, sure enough, his hand was red with blood. Billy Fish and two of his matchlock-men catches hold of Dan by the shoulders and drags him into the Bashkai lot, while the priests howls in their lingo,—'Neither God nor Devil but a man!' I was all taken aback, for a priest cut at me in front, and the Army behind began firing into the Bashkai men.

" 'God A-mighty!' says Dan. 'What is the meaning o' this?'

" 'Come back! Come away!' says Billy Fish. 'Ruin and Mutiny is the matter. We'll break for Bashkai if we can.'

"I tried to give some sort of orders to my men—the men o' the regular Army—but it was no use, so I fired into the brown of 'em with an English Martini and drilled three beggars in a line. The valley was full of shouting, howling creatures, and every soul was shrieking, 'Not a God nor a Devil but only a man!' The Bashkai troops stuck to Billy Fish all they were worth, but their matchlocks wasn't half as good as the Kabul breach-loaders, and four of them dropped. Dan was bellowing like a bull, for he was very wrathy; and Billy Fish had a hard job to prevent him running out at the crowd.

" 'We can't stand,' says Billy Fish. 'Make a run for it down the valley! The whole place is against us.' The matchlock-men ran, and we went down the valley in spite of Dravot's protestations. He was swearing horribly and crying out that he was a King. The priests rolled great stones on us, and the regular Army fired hard, and there wasn't more than six men, not counting Dan, Billy Fish, and Me, that came down to the bottom of the valley alive.

"Then they stopped firing and the horns in the temple blew again. 'Come away—for Gord's sake come away!' says Billy Fish. 'They'll send runners out to all the villages before ever we get to Bashkai. I can protect you there, but I can't do anything now.'

"My own notion is that Dan began to go mad in his head from that hour. He stared up and down like a stuck pig. Then he was all for walking back alone and killing the priests with his bare hands; which he could have done. 'An Emperor am I,' says Daniel, 'and next year I shall be a Knight of the Queen.'

" 'All right, Dan,' says I; 'but come along now while there's time.'

" 'It's your fault,' says he, 'for not looking after your Army better. There was mutiny in the midst, and you didn't know—you damned engine-driving, plate-laying, missionary's-pass-hunting hound!' He sat upon a rock and called me every foul name he could lay tongue to. I was too heart-sick to care, though it was all his foolishness that brought the smash.

" 'I'm sorry, Dan,' says I, 'but there's no accounting for natives. This business is our Fifty-Seven. Maybe we'll make something out of it yet, when we've got to Bashkai.'

" 'Let's get to Bashkai, then,' says Dan, 'and, by God, when I come back here again I'll sweep the valley so there isn't a bug in a blanket left!'

"We walked all that day, and all that night Dan was stumping up and down on the snow, chewing his beard and muttering to himself.

" 'There's no hope o' getting clear,' said Billy Fish. 'The priests will have sent runners to the villages to say that you are only men. Why didn't you stick on as Gods till things was more settled? I'm a dead man,' says Billy Fish, and he throws himself down on the snow and begins to pray to his Gods.

"Next morning we was in a cruel bad country—all up and down, no level ground at all, and no food either. The six Bashkai men looked at Billy Fish hungry-wise as if they wanted to ask something, but they said never a word. At noon we came to the top of a flat mountain all covered with snow, and when we climbed up into it, behold, there was an Army in position waiting in the middle!

" 'The runners have been very quick,' says Billy Fish, with a little bit of a laugh. 'They are waiting for us.'

"Three or four men began to fire from the enemy's side, and a chance shot took Daniel in the calf of the leg. That brought him to his senses. He looks across the snow at the Army, and sees the rifles that we had brought into the country.

" 'We're done for,' says he. 'They are Englishmen, these people,—and it's my blasted nonsense that has brought you to this. Get back, Billy Fish, and take your men away; you've done what you could, and now cut for it. Carnehan,' says he, 'shake hands with me and go along with Billy. Maybe they won't kill you. I'll go and meet 'em alone. It's me that did it. Me, the King!'

" 'Go!' says I. 'Go to Hell, Dan. I'm with you here. Billy Fish, you clear out, and we two will meet those folk.'

" 'I'm a Chief,' says Billy Fish, quite quiet. 'I stay with you. My men can go.'

"The Bashkai fellows didn't wait for a second word but ran off, and Dan and Me and Billy Fish walked across to where the drums were drumming and the horns were horning. It was cold—awful cold. I've got that cold in the back of my head now. There's a lump of it there."

The punkah-coolies had gone to sleep. Two kerosene lamps were blazing in the office, and the perspiration poured down my face and splashed on the blotter as I leaned forward. Carnehan was shivering, and I feared that his mind might go. I wiped my face, took a fresh grip of the piteously mangled hands, and said:— "What happened after that?"

The momentary shift of my eyes had broken the clear current.

"What was you pleased to say?" whined Carnehan. "They took them without any sound. Not a little whisper all along the snow, not though the King knocked down the first man that set hand on him—not though old Peachey fired his last cartridge into the brown of 'em. Not a single solitary sound did those swines make. They just closed up tight, and I tell you their furs stunk. There was a man called Billy Fish, a good friend of us all, and they cut his throat, Sir, then and there, like a pig; and the King kicks up the bloody snow and says: 'We've had a dashed fine run for our money. What's coming next?' But Peachey, Peachey Taliaferro, I tell you, Sir, in confidence as betwixt two friends, he lost his head, Sir. No, he didn't neither. The King lost his head, so he did, all along o' one of those cunning rope-bridges. Kindly let me have the paper-cutter, Sir. It tilted this way. They marched him a mile across that snow to a rope-bridge over a ravine with a river at the bottom. You may have seen such. They prodded him behind like an ox. 'Damn your eyes!' says the King. 'D'you suppose I can't die like a gentleman?' He turns to Peachey—Peachey that was crying like a child. 'I've brought you to this, Peachey,' says he. 'Brought you out of your happy life to be killed in Kafiristan, where you was late Commander-in-Chief of the Emperor's forces. Say you forgive me, Peachey.' 'I do,' says Peachey. 'Fully and freely do I forgive you, Dan.' 'Shake hands, Peachey,' says he. 'I'm going now.' Out he goes, looking neither right nor left, and when he was plumb in the middle of those dizzy dancing ropes, 'Cut, you beggars,' he shouts; and they cut, and old Dan fell, turning round and round and round twenty thousand miles, for he took half an hour to fall till he struck the water, and I could see his body caught on a rock with the gold crown close beside.

"But do you know what they did to Peachey between two pine-trees? They crucified him, Sir, as Peachey's hand will show. They used wooden pegs for his hands and his feet; and he didn't die. He hung there and screamed, and they took him down next day, and said it was a miracle that he wasn't dead. They took him down—poor old Peachey that hadn't done them any harm—that hadn't done them any. . . ."

He rocked to and fro and wept bitterly, wiping his eyes with the back of his scarred hands and moaning like a child for some ten minutes.

"They were cruel enough to feed him up in the temple, because they said he was more of a God than old Daniel that was a man. Then they turned him out on the snow, and told him to go home, and Peachey came home in about a year, begging along the roads quite safe; for Daniel Dravot he walked before and said:—'Come along, Peachey. It's a big thing we're doing.' The mountains they danced at night, and the mountains they tried to fall on Peachey's head, but Dan he held up his hand, and Peachey came along bent double. He never let go of Dan's hand, and he never let go of Dan's head. They gave it to him as a present in the temple, to remind him not to come again, and though the crown was pure gold, and Peachey was starving, never would Peachey sell the same. You knew Dravot, Sir! You knew Right Worshipful Brother Dravot! Look at him now!"

He fumbled in the mass of rags round his bent waist; brought out a black horsehair bag embroidered with silver thread; and shook therefrom on to my table—the dried, withered head of Daniel Dravot! The morning sun that had long been paling the lamps struck the red beard and blind sunken eyes; struck, too, a heavy circlet of gold studded with raw turquoises, that Carnehan placed tenderly on the battered temples.

"You behold now," said Carnehan, "the Emperor in his habit as he lived—the King of Kafiristan with his crown upon his head. Poor old Daniel that was a monarch once!"

I shuddered, for, in spite of defacements manifold, I recognized the head of the man of Marwar Junction. Carnehan rose to go. I attempted to stop him. He was not fit to walk abroad. "Let me take away the whiskey and give me a little money," he gasped. "I was a King once. I'll go to the Deputy Commissioner and ask to set in the Poorhouse till I get my health. No, thank you, I can't wait till you get a carriage for me. I've urgent private affairs—in the south—at Marwar."

He shambled out of the office and departed in the direction of the Deputy Commissioner's house. That day at noon I had occasion to go down the blinding hot Mall, and I saw a crooked man crawling along the white dust of the road-side, his hat in his hand, quavering dolorously after the fashion of street-singers at Home. There was not a soul in sight and he was out of all possible earshot of the houses. And he sang through his nose, turning his head from right to left:

> *"The Son of Man goes forth to war,*
> *A golden crown to gain;*
> *His blood-red banner streams afar—*
> *Who follows in his train?"*

I waited to hear no more, but put the poor wretch into my carriage and drove him off to the nearest missionary for eventual transfer to the Asylum. He repeated the hymn twice while he was with me whom he did not in the least recognize, and I left him singing it to the missionary.

Two days later I inquired after his welfare of the Superintendent of the Asylum.

"He was admitted suffering from sun-stroke. He died early yesterday morning," said the Superintendent. "Is it true that he was half an hour bareheaded in the sun at midday?"

"Yes," said I, "but do you happen to know if he had anything upon him by any chance when he died?"

"Not to my knowledge," said the Superintendent.

And there the matter rests.

GRANT STOCKBRIDGE

ONE OF THE MOST popular and weirdest of all pulp heroes was The Spider, the nom de guerre of wealthy socialite Richard Wentworth. Hoping to emulate the staggering success of Street & Smith's The Shadow, the new pulp publisher Popular Publications hired R. T. M. Scott (1882–1996), who had achieved great popularity with his series about Aurelius Smith, Secret Service agent, to launch its own masked and caped crime fighter. The Spider series commenced with Scott's *The Spider Strikes* in September of 1933. Scott also wrote one more novel—though research and the memory of some old pulpsters have suggested that his son Robert, an associate editor at Popular and an occasional writer for the pulps, actually produced the first two novels. In any case, Scott was soon replaced by Norvell Page (1904–1961), a former journalist and prolific writer for *Black Mask, Dime Mystery,* and other pulps. Page continued the series under the house name Grant Stockbridge; the byline was also used for several other writers of the 116 novels that followed those by Scott. *The Spider* rivaled *The Shadow* and *Doc Savage* in its popularity as a hero pulp, but it was more graphically violent than its competitors, and its masked avenger more frightening.

Playboy and amateur criminologist Richard Wentworth is a handsome stalwart by day, but at night he battles the unflinchingly evil master criminals intent on destroying New York (and who later expand their horrors to include the entire country). The Big Apple is repeatedly bombed and burned, or set upon by diseases, death rays, and hordes of beasts, robots, or subhuman villains; after unimaginable destruction, only The Spider can save it. In his disguise of a mask—later replaced with a cape, wig, makeup, hunchback, and fangs—he is a fearsome avenger indeed. Although kind of heart, The Spider is ruthless in his protection of the weak, shooting to kill and branding the forehead of his victims with a Spider seal from a specially designed cigarette lighter. He is aided by his loyal servant, Ram Singh (a member of a Sikh royal family); Ronald Jackson, his chauffeur; Harold Jenkyns, his butler; Police Commissioner Stanley Kirkpatrick (Wentworth's close friend but a sworn enemy of The Spider); and his longtime girlfriend, Nita Van Sloan.

"The Wings of Kali" unfortunately lacks Wentworth's supporting cast of sidekicks, and has none of the accoutrements of his disguises. Nor are the villains of such colossal ambition that the fate of millions is at stake. But allowances have to be made, as this rare story is The Spider's first case. It was originally published in the May 1942 issue of *The Spider*.

THE WINGS OF KALI

The Spider's First Case

GRANT STOCKBRIDGE

FOREWORD: It occurred to me that many of the readers might be as interested as I was to learn about some of the early work of the SPIDER. The old readers know, of course, that it was during college that Richard Wentworth determined upon his career of service and that, thereupon, he undertook a strenuous mental and physical preparation for his work. In pursuit of this then, he came eventually to India . . . and it was there that the SPIDER performed his first mission. "Injustice has ever been a challenge to me," he said. "I really didn't consider myself prepared to begin work, but when I discovered the truth behind a small portion of hell in old Benares, I had to act." The truth is, of course, that all Wentworth's life he has "had to act" whenever he ran across injustice. He has found plenty to do. . . . AUTHOR.

THE VOICE of the woman was raised and desperate. No words were distinguishable but the tone was frantic. In the inner court of the Beano Club, nothing and no one moved. The woman and the man who mumbled answers at her were not visible. The multiple chaotic sounds of the Indian night were shut out by stone walls . . . and sounds within were trapped there. The Beano was not the best club in Benares, but it was discreet.

A man appeared suddenly in the main entrance of the Inner Court and stood looking, with a certain challenge, over the vegetation-choked patio. Pierced brass lanterns overhead emitted more shadow than light. Somewhere the creaking sway of a *punkah* fanned a faint metallic rustle from the palms. In the central basin, water plashed softly. The woman's voice lifted again, pleading.

The man in the entrance of the court, despite his youth, wore authority like a cloak. His face, too rugged to be called handsome, was keenly intelligent. His tropical evening dress was precise. Faultless. He struck his palms together softly.

From the shadows a bare-footed Hindu glided toward him and salaamed, his dark face incuriously submissive.

"Wentworth, *sahib*?" he murmured.

"I have certain instructions to give," Wentworth told him quietly, "which I am sure will require that all servants leave the inner court for an indefinite period. . . ." Gold glinted as their hands touched, and the Hindu salaamed again.

In a corner, among the motionless palms, a macaw screamed.

The corner where the woman sat was completely screened off, between columns, from the court. Her back was very straight and, under the dark sweeping wing of her hair, her eyes were bitter.

"I'm through with it, Walter," she said forcefully. "I tell you I'm through with all that! If I'd known you were in Benares, or even in India, I would not have come. But now I'm here I have to stay. It's my only chance, Walter. Listen to me! My only chance! I'm through with you and your kind!"

The man's face was yellow, rather than sun-browned, and there was heat only in his eyes. His lips moved in a faint smile and he reached out a powerful, thin hand and seized one of hers. "That's for me to say, Meliss," he drawled. "I tell you . . . we're just starting!"

The woman's hand struggled to escape, and it was futile. The man grinned as some men do,

when a bird is caught in a snare, and flutters at the approach of death. His face was ruthless, a mask of desire.

"You will obey," he said flatly, "or I will have you sent out of India, your passport revoked . . . *for moral turpitude!* You wouldn't have much chance then, would you?" He looked into her gray eyes steadily, hungrily. "Would you, Meliss?"

Melissa James ceased to struggle and slumped back in her chair. Her eyes were very wide. Her teeth set on her lower lip. It was with her right hand that she reached into the pocket of her coat, and suddenly presented a small and blunt-nosed revolver across the table.

"I don't want to do it," she gasped, "but as God is my witness. . . ."

Walter Bishop laughed harshly. He struck aside the gun, wrenched it from her and dragged the woman up out of her chair into his arms.

"You always were a spitfire, Meliss," he said, and kissed her.

The woman's fists beat futilely against his shoulders . . . and Richard Wentworth stepped into the alcove where they were. He reached out and tapped Walter Bishop on the shoulder.

"Beg pardon, Bishop," he said.

Bishop whipped about to face him; Melissa James staggered back into the chair. The gun remained in Bishop's fist.

Bishop said, harshly, "You've got a hell of a nerve, walking into a private party! Get out!"

Wentworth lifted his brows faintly. "One fancied an official was always on duty," he murmured. "Do you need any assistance, or are you quite able to take care of your . . . prisoner unaided? I'll be glad to take her in charge for you." He bowed to Melissa James. "If I may offer, madame? Glad to escort you anywhere. This chap, Bishop, has rather a reputation as a rotter, you know. Unsavory women and that sort of thing."

Bishop swore and took a choppy stride forward. The gun in his fist twisted into line. Wentworth looked at him. His firm mouth held its steady, polite smile, but the blue-gray depths of his eyes were like flame. Bishop winced at their direct slash. He stopped, uncertainly.

Melissa James's face was expressionless save for the fear that shone in her gray eyes. Her hands gripped the side of the table, and she shook her head jerkily.

"No, no," she whispered. "I am quite . . . safe . . . with Mr. Bishop."

Wentworth clicked his heels. "So sorry, madame," he said. "My apologies, Bishop." He marched out of the booth.

Bishop stood motionless for a half minute after Wentworth had left. "He's lying," he muttered at Melissa James. "The rotter! Telling stories like that."

"They might cost you your position at the consulate. Is that it, Walter?" Melissa James said steadily.

Bishop swore. "You open your mouth and you go out, the way I told you," he snapped. "Understand?"

Melissa James nodded in fear.

"I'll be back," Bishop snapped at her. "Stay here."

He went striding out of the booth, gun thrust into his pocket . . . and moments later, Wentworth slipped into the place again. He smiled into the woman's startled face.

"I rather fancied my remark would cause him to take punitive action against me," he murmured.

"Will he . . . revoke your passport?" Melissa James asked, slowly.

Wentworth threw back his head, but his laughter was soft. "I doubt it," he said. "I rather think he has gone to arrange for me to be assassinated!" He drew from his pocket an Indian bracelet of heavy, pierced silver, set with turquoise. He placed it on the table. "Frankly, Miss James, the man has outlived his usefulness as a government official, and as a human being. I have . . . heard about him. But you do not have to remove such creatures. They destroy themselves before very long, and I have a definite feeling that Bishop's time is about up." He gestured to the bracelet. "This bracelet was thrown to the table from the palms. You were afraid to investigate. Remember to say that."

Wentworth bowed and was instantly gone . . . but he did not go far. The palms offered ample concealment. Wentworth thought he would be *safer* near Bishop. He had not exaggerated to Melissa James when he had mentioned assassination. Walter Bishop had used the technique before, when his position was threatened.

He heard the man return, heard his sharp oath at sight of the bracelet. "You're playing with me, Melissa!" he rasped. "Where did you get that bracelet?"

Melissa followed instructions.

Wentworth smiled thinly and seized hold of the flutings of a slender column that lifted to the ceiling. He went up agilely and, presently, was crouched on the roof. He could look over the palms now to the table where Walter Bishop stood menacingly over the woman. Wentworth drew a knife carefully from his inner pocket. It was a slender knife of unmistakable Eastern workmanship. He held it by the tip, rose . . . and threw!

The knife flew in a silver streak and bit solidly into the center of the table. It quivered there and the thin note of its vibration reached to Wentworth's ears, even on the roof. Bishop stared at the thing as if it were a snake. He no longer threatened Melissa James. He stood, tense as a mongoose, crouched. His lips were snarled away from his teeth and his beady eyes flicked here and there over the palms about him.

He had the gun in his fist. Abruptly, he turned and fled!

Wentworth waited a space of minutes, then he dropped lightly to the floor beneath and once more bowed before Melissa James.

"I think, madame," he said gravely, "that I will offer you once more my escort to your hotel."

Melissa James looked at him curiously. She was older than he, a mature woman, and yet there was no sense of disparity between them. Wentworth was strong, sure, competent. His smile met hers.

"I'm not sure I understand you," the woman said. "What are you doing to Walter Bishop?"

Wentworth shrugged. "I am doing nothing. The man is eaten alive with fear. The bracelet was once worn by his slave girl, whom he had killed. The knife was the weapon used. It is very easy to learn these things, if the natives trust you." He did not add that scarcely one man in a thousand could win that trust; nor that the Hindus trusted him only because he was all man, good, trustworthy, selfless.

Melissa James's hand rested on his arm. "You are in danger, with me," she said.

Wentworth laughed. "No more with you than without you," he said. "I have a car outside."

They went out, and the shadowed entrances of the Beano Club were discreet as usual. The bougainvillea vines thrust their foliage between them and the light. There was a thick odor of Udumbarra blossoms. Wentworth handed Melissa James into the front seat of his convertible coupé, sprang in beside her. They swung down toward the Ganges, low and broad and dark between its mounting tiers of holy steps, the *ghats*. The skyline was dominated by the swollen dome and minarets of the mosque of the Mogul emperor of long ago . . . Aurangzer. The night blotted out the ugliness, left only the graceful silhouettes.

Melissa James leaned back and let the night creep into her, and Wentworth also looked casual, but his eyes stabbed alertly into the darkness. He was not deceived by Bishop's flight. The man would be back! For Bishop knew that Wentworth was behind the bracelet and the dagger . . . and he would know that he dared not permit Wentworth to live!

The attack came with the suddenness of an explosion. From a dark side street, a procession of donkeys plodded into their path. When Wentworth jerked the car to a halt, men swarmed at him from both sides of the street. They dropped from the overhanging eaves . . . a dozen of them.

With a quick agility, Wentworth sprang to his feet upon the seat, jerked open the rumble seat of his car. There were grunts and squeals and . . . a moment later . . . Wentworth was hurling young suckling pigs into the faces of the assailants! Mortal screams burst from the knifemen! With howling fright, they turned and fled into the darkness from which they had come! As quickly as it had begun, the attack was over, finished, destroyed.

Wentworth laughed and dropped back behind the wheel. "That's only the first step of the attack," he said as he drove steadily on. "Bishop has shown a fondness for Mohammedan assassins. They are very brave and very ruthless in the execution of their orders. The only thing is that the touch of a pig renders them unclean . . . and they dare not be killed while unclean. So they had to retreat. A little matter of their religious beliefs."

Melissa James was shivering. "Only the first step, you said?" she whispered in a frightened voice.

Wentworth's smile lingered, but it was there for the benefit of Melissa. "Why, yes," he said quietly. "Since his assassins have failed, Walter Bishop will have to attack himself. Would you care to walk for a while along the banks of the Ganges?"

He stopped the car. Below them, to the left, there was a dark and smoldering fire where some Hindu burned the body of a member of his family. The moon was drunken above the waters, lop-sided, yellow, unclean.

Melissa James said, "No, no. I'm going to stay in the car. Can't we hurry now? Can't we go to the hotel?"

Wentworth said, "Not quite yet." His words came out with strain. "Don't be afraid. I shall not be far away. And get down low in your seat."

Wentworth turned away . . . and the shadows swallowed him. It was very still. The river made faint washing, sucking noises against the steps. There was a sudden outbreak of dog-howling, but it died. Somewhere, a woman was wailing.

Melissa James crouched low in her seat and shivered. The shadows seemed to be in motion. There were at least three men, hooded and dark, slipping along the side of the street, she thought. She clamped her lips together. It was only when there was a footstep beside the car, the touch of a hand on her shoulder, that she screamed!

She twisted about and was staring into the face of Walter Bishop. His face was twisted into an angry mask. "Where is he?" he asked hoarsely. "Tell me, before I cut your throat!"

Melissa James shuddered and shrank away, but the fingers bit into her shoulder like talons. "He said he was going for a walk," she whispered. "Down by the river. I don't know."

From the night, there was a sudden sound of laughter. It was whispering laughter, flat and mocking . . . strangely sinister. Walter Bishop cursed and swung toward the sound. Half way up the front of a building, silhouetted against its white marble, was a curiously hunched figure. And suddenly, it sailed out into the night, straight toward them! From its shoulders a cape fluttered back like black wings!

"Death!" came a wailing cry in Hindustani. "Death . . . on the wings of Kali!"

Bishop shouted a fierce oath. He whipped out a gun and started to shoot. In the shadows where three hooded men had crouched, there was suddenly only scampering fright. Bishop yelled at the men. "It's a fake!" he shouted. "Come back here, I tell you. It's a fake!"

His gun blasted at the assassins who sought to flee him . . . and one of them paused for a brief instant. There was a silvery glint of steel in the night . . . and then Bishop coughed tearingly. He bent forward and took slow steps forward, three of them. Then his knees went lax and he pitched forward on his face.

Melissa James looked from the fallen man up into the night. The swooping black figure was gone as if it had never been. There was silence save for the fleeing soft feet of the terrified assassins . . . Melissa smothered a scream as a man spoke to her, gently.

"I've had a delightful walk," he said. "The moonlight on the Ganges . . . marvelous. The moonlight on the mosque . . . marvelous. The moonlight on Bishop . . . marvelous."

Melissa James looked at Richard Wentworth as he slid in under the wheel of the coupé and sent it rolling gently forward.

"Now, my dear," Wentworth said. "I'm sure you will be able to work out your life in harmony and peace, untroubled by the Walter Bishops of the world. He is quite dead. And his reputation will be untarnished, for in the morning they will say that he was attacked by assassins and died, bravely defending himself. Which is close enough to the truth. You won't be questioned. The Beano Club is very discreet."

Melissa shivered. "You . . . *you* are like fate," she whispered. "So sure of yourself! You destroyed him!"

Wentworth smiled, and his eyes were quite cold. "No, madame," he said. "I did not destroy him. It is not necessary that anyone should destroy a man who has lived by murder and by fear, for that which a man does will surely destroy him! I only gave fate . . . a little help!"

THE WHITE SILENCE

JACK LONDON

NO AMERICAN WRITER has ever written adventure fiction about the frigid and remote regions of Alaska and Canada as evocatively and successfully as Jack London (1876–1916). Born John Chaney, he was the illegitimate son of William Chaney, an itinerant astrologer; eight months after his birth, his mother married John London. His impoverished youth in the San Francisco area was also marked by vagabond periods: going on the road as a hobo, riding freight trains, and landing in jail for a month of hard labor—which deepened both his sympathy for the working-class poor and his distaste for the drudgery of that life. London became enamored with socialism after reading the *Communist Manifesto*, though he was so eager to be rich that he joined the Klondike gold rush in Canada's Yukon Territory in 1896. He returned to Oakland without having mined an ounce of gold, but with the background knowledge for the classic American novel *The Call of the Wild* (1903), which would become one of the bestselling novels of the early twentieth century, with more than 1.5 million copies sold in London's lifetime. Prior to his book-writing career, however, he sold stories to *Overland Monthly*, *Black Cat*, and *Atlantic Monthly* in the 1890s. He was also hired as a journalist by Hearst to report on the Russo-Japanese War for the unheard-of fee of $4,000, and it soon became an international bestseller, earning over a million dollars. By 1913, having produced such adventure classics as *The Sea Wolf* (1904), *White Fang* (1906), and the autobiographical *Martin Eden* (1909), he was regarded as the highest-paid and most popular author in the world. London, however, had become a heavy drinker while still a teenager, and alcoholism, illness, financial woes, and overwork may have induced him to commit suicide at the age of forty, though the official cause of death was listed as uremic poisoning.

"The White Silence" was originally published in the February 1899 issue of *Overland Monthly;* it was first published in book form in *The Son of the Wolf* (Boston: Houghton Mifflin, 1900).

[handwritten margin notes: "stepdad", "wrote call of the wild", "committed suicide due to alcohol"]

THE WHITE SILENCE

JACK LONDON

(handwritten margin note: the dog bit out the frozen ice in her toes)

"CARMEN WON'T LAST more than a couple of days." Mason spat out a chunk of ice and surveyed the poor animal ruefully, then put her foot in his mouth and proceeded to bite out the ice which clustered cruelly between the toes.

"I never saw a dog with a highfalutin' name that ever was worth a rap," he said, as he concluded his task and shoved her aside. "They just fade away and die under the responsibility. Did ye ever see one go wrong with a sensible name like Cassiar, Siwash, or Husky? No, sir! Take a look at Shookum here, he's—"

Snap! The lean brute flashed up, the white teeth just missing Mason's throat.

"Ye will, will ye?" A shrewd clout behind the ear with the butt of the dog whip stretched the animal in the snow, quivering softly, a yellow slaver dripping from its fangs.

"As I was saying, just look at Shookum here—he's got the spirit. Bet ye he eats Carmen before the week's out." "I'll bank another proposition against that," replied Malemute Kid, reversing the frozen bread placed before the fire to thaw. "We'll eat Shookum before the trip is over. What d'ye say, Ruth?"

The Indian woman settled the coffee with a piece of ice, glanced from Malemute Kid to her husband, then at the dogs, but vouchsafed no reply. It was such a palpable truism that none was necessary. Two hundred miles of unbroken trail in prospect, with a scant six days' grub for themselves and none for the dogs, could admit no other alternative. The two men and the woman grouped about the fire and began their meager meal. The dogs lay in their harnesses for it was a midday halt, and watched each mouthful enviously.

"No more lunches after today," said Malemute Kid. "And we've got to keep a close eye on the dogs,—they're getting vicious. They'd just as soon pull a fellow down as not, if they get a chance."

"And I was president of an Epworth once, and taught in the Sunday school." Having irrelevantly delivered himself of this, Mason fell into a dreamy contemplation of his steaming moccasins, but was aroused by Ruth filling his cup. "Thank God, we've got slathers of tea! I've seen it growing, down in Tennessee. What wouldn't I give for a hot corn pone just now! Never mind, Ruth; you won't starve much longer, nor wear moccasins either."

The woman threw off her gloom at this, and in her eyes welled up a great love for her white lord—the first white man she had ever seen—the first man whom she had known to treat a woman as something better than a mere animal or beast of burden.

"Yes, Ruth," continued her husband, having recourse to the macaronic jargon in which it was alone possible for them to understand each other; "wait till we clean up and pull for the Outside. We'll take the White Man's canoe and go to the Salt Water. Yes, bad water, rough water,—great mountains dance up and down all the time. And so big, so far, so far away,—you travel ten sleep, twenty sleep, forty sleep" (he graphically enumerated the days on his fingers), "all the time water, bad water. Then you come to great village, plenty people, just the same mosquitoes next summer. Wigwams oh, so high,—ten, twenty pines. Hi-yu skookum!"

He paused impotently, cast an appealing glance at Malemute Kid, then laboriously placed the twenty pines, end on end, by sign language. Malemute Kid smiled with cheery cynicism; but Ruth's eyes were wide with wonder, and with pleasure; for she half believed he was joking, and such condescension pleased her poor woman's heart.

"And then you step into a—a box, and pouf! up you go." He tossed his empty cup in the air by way of illustration and, as he deftly caught it, cried: "And biff! down you come. Oh, great medicine men! You go Fort Yukon. I go Arctic City,—twenty-five sleep,—big string, all the time,—I catch him string,—I say, 'Hello, Ruth! How are ye?'—and you say, 'Is that my good husband?'—and I say, 'Yes'—and you say, 'No can bake good bread, no more soda'—then I say, 'Look in cache, under flour; good-by.' You look and catch plenty soda. All the time you Fort Yukon, me Arctic City. Hi-yu medicine man!"

Ruth smiled so ingenuously at the fairy story that both men burst into laughter. A row among the dogs cut short the wonders of the Outside, and by the time the snarling combatants were separated, she had lashed the sleds and all was ready for the trail.

"Mush! Baldy! Hi! Mush on!" Mason worked his whip smartly and, as the dogs whined low in the traces, broke out the sled with the gee pole. Ruth followed with the second team, leaving Malemute Kid, who had helped her start, to bring up the rear. Strong man, brute that he was, capable of felling an ox at a blow, he could not bear to beat the poor animals, but humored them as a dog driver rarely does—nay, almost wept with them in their misery.

"Come, mush on there, you poor sore-footed brutes!" he murmured, after several ineffectual attempts to start the load. But his patience was at last rewarded, and though whimpering with pain, they hastened to join their fellows.

No more conversation; the toil of the trail will not permit such extravagance. And of all deadening labors, that of the Northland trail is the worst. Happy is the man who can weather a day's travel at the price of silence, and that on a beaten track.

And of all heart-breaking labors, that of breaking trail is the worst. At every step the great webbed shoe sinks till the snow is level with the knee. Then up, straight up, the deviation of a fraction of an inch being a certain precursor of disaster, the snowshoe must be lifted till the surface is cleared; then forward, down, and the other foot is raised perpendicularly for the matter of half a yard. He who tries this for the first time, if haply he avoids bringing his shoes in dangerous propinquity and measures not his length on the treacherous footing, will give up exhausted at the end of a hundred yards; he who can keep out of the way of the dogs for a whole day may well crawl into his sleeping bag with a clear conscience and a pride which passeth all understanding; and he who travels twenty sleeps on the Long Trail is a man whom the gods may envy.

The afternoon wore on, and with the awe, born of the White Silence, the voiceless travelers bent to their work. Nature has many tricks wherewith she convinces man of his finity,—the ceaseless flow of the tides, the fury of the storm, the shock of the earthquake, the long roll of heaven's artillery,—but the most tremendous, the most stupefying of all, is the passive phase of the White Silence. All movement ceases, the sky clears, the heavens are as brass; the slightest whisper seems sacrilege, and man becomes timid, affrighted at the sound of his own voice. Sole speck of life journeying across the ghostly wastes of a dead world, he trembles at his audacity, realizes that his is a maggot's life, nothing more. Strange thoughts arise unsummoned, and the mystery of all things strives for utterance.

And the fear of death, of God, of the universe, comes over him,—the hope of the Resurrection and the Life, the yearning for immortality, the vain striving of the imprisoned essence,—it is then, if ever, man walks alone with God.

So wore the day away. The river took a great bend, and Mason headed his team for the cutoff across the narrow neck of land. But the dogs balked at the high bank. Again and again, though Ruth and Malemute Kid were shoving on the sled, they slipped back. Then came the concerted effort. The miserable creatures, weak from hunger, exerted their last strength. Up— up—the sled poised on the top of the bank; but the leader swung the string of dogs behind him to the right, fouling Mason's snowshoes. The result was grievous. Mason was whipped off his feet; one of the dogs fell in the traces; and the sled toppled back, dragging everything to the bottom again.

Slash! the whip fell among the dogs cruelly, especially upon the one which had fallen.

"Don't, Mason," entreated Malemute Kid; "the poor devil's on its last legs. Wait and we'll put my team on."

Mason deliberately withheld the whip till the last word had fallen, then out flashed the long lash, completely curling about the offending creature's body. Carmen—for it was Carmen— cowered in the snow, cried piteously, then rolled over on her side.

It was a tragic moment, a pitiful incident of the trail,—a dying dog, two comrades in anger. Ruth glanced solicitously from man to man. But Malemute Kid restrained himself, though there was a world of reproach in his eyes, and, bending over the dog, cut the traces. No word was spoken. The teams were double-spanned and the difficulty overcome; the sleds were under way again, the dying dog dragging herself along in the rear. As long as an animal can travel, it is not shot, and this last chance is accorded it—the crawling into camp, if it can, in the hope of a moose being killed.

Already penitent for his angry action, but too stubborn to make amends, Mason toiled on at the head of the cavalcade, little dreaming that danger hovered in the air. The timber clustered thick in the sheltered bottom, and through this they threaded their way. Fifty feet or more from the trail towered a lofty pine. For generations it had stood there, and for generations destiny had had this one end in view—perhaps the same had been decreed of Mason.

He stooped to fasten the loosened thong of his moccasin. The sleds came to a halt, and the dogs lay down in the snow without a whimper. The stillness was weird; not a breath rustled the frost-encrusted forest; the cold and silence of outer space had chilled the heart and smote the trembling lips of nature. A sigh pulsed through the air—they did not seem to actually hear it, but rather felt it, like the premonition of movement in a motionless void. Then the great tree, burdened with its weight of years and snow, played its last part in the tragedy of life. He heard the warning crash and attempted to spring up but, almost erect, caught the blow squarely on the shoulder.

The sudden danger, the quick death—how often had Malemute Kid faced it! The pine needles were still quivering as he gave his commands and sprang into action. Nor did the Indian girl faint or raise her voice in idle wailing, as might many of her white sisters. At his order, she threw her weight on the end of a quickly extemporized handspike, easing the pressure and listening to her husband's groans, while Malemute Kid attacked the tree with his ax. The steel rang merrily as it bit into the frozen trunk, each stroke being accompanied by a forced, audible respiration, the "Huh!" "Huh!" of the woodsman.

At last the Kid laid the pitiable thing that was once a man in the snow. But worse than his comrade's pain was the dumb anguish in the woman's face, the blended look of hopeful, hopeless query. Little was said; those of the Northland are early taught the futility of words and the inestimable value of deeds. With the temperature at sixty-five below zero, a man cannot lie many minutes in the snow and live. So the sled lashings were cut, and the sufferer, rolled in furs, laid on a couch of boughs. Before him roared a fire, built of the very wood which wrought the mishap. Behind and partially over him was stretched the primitive fly,—a piece of canvas, which caught the radiating heat and threw it back and down upon him,—a trick which men may know who study physics at the fount.

And men who have shared their bed with death know when the call is sounded. Mason was terribly crushed. The most cursory examination revealed it. His right arm, leg, and back were broken; his limbs were paralyzed from the hips; and the likelihood of internal injuries was large. An occasional moan was his only sign of life.

No hope; nothing to be done. The pitiless night crept slowly by—Ruth's portion, the despairing stoicism of her race, and Malemute Kid adding new lines to his face of bronze.

In fact, Mason suffered least of all, for he spent his time in Eastern Tennessee, in the Great Smoky Mountains, living over the scenes of his childhood. And most pathetic was the melody of his long-forgotten Southern vernacular, as he raved of swimming holes and coon hunts and watermelon raids. It was as Greek to Ruth, but the Kid understood and felt,—felt as only one can feel who has been shut out for years from all that civilization means.

Morning brought consciousness to the stricken man, and Malemute Kid bent closer to catch his whispers.

"You remember when we foregathered on the Tanana, four years come next ice-run? I didn't care so much for her then. It was more like she was pretty, and there was a smack of excitement about it, I think. But d'ye know, I've come to think a heap of her. She's been a good wife to me, always at my shoulder in the pinch. And when it comes to trading, you know there isn't her equal. D'ye recollect the time she shot the Moosehorn Rapids to pull you and me off that rock, the bullets whipping the water like hailstones?—and the time of the famine at Nuklukyeto?—when she raced the ice-run to bring the news? Yes, she's

been a good wife to me, better 'n that other one. Didn't know I'd been there? Never told you, eh? Well, I tried it once, down in the States. That's why I'm here. Been raised together, too. I came away to give her a chance for divorce. She got it.

"But that's got nothing to do with Ruth. I had thought of cleaning up and pulling for the Outside next year,—her and I,—but it's too late. Don't send her back to her people, Kid. It's beastly hard for a woman to go back. Think of it!—nearly four years on our bacon and beans and flour and dried fruit, and then to go back to her fish and caribou. It's not good for her to have tried our ways, to come to know they're better 'n her people's, and then return to them. Take care of her, Kid,—why don't you,—but no, you always fought shy of them,—and you never told me why you came to this country. Be kind to her, and send her back to the States as soon as you can. But fix it so she can come back,—liable to get homesick, you know.

"And the youngster—it's drawn us closer, Kid. I only hope it is a boy. Think of it!—flesh of my flesh, Kid. He mustn't stop in this country. And if it's a girl, why, she can't. Sell my furs; they'll fetch at least five thousand, and I've got as much more with the company. And handle my interests with yours. I think that bench claim will show up. See that he gets a good schooling; and Kid, above all, don't let him come back. This country was not made for white men.

"I'm a gone man, Kid. Three or four sleeps at the best. You've got to go on. You must go on! Remember, it's my wife, it's my boy,—O God! I hope it's a boy! You can't stay by me,—and I charge you, a dying man, to pull on."

"Give me three days," pleaded Malemute Kid. "You may change for the better; something may turn up."

"No."

"Just three days."

"You must pull on."

"Two days."

"It's my wife and my boy, Kid. You would not ask it."

"One day."

"No, no! I charge—"

"Only one day. We can shave it through on the grub, and I might knock over a moose."

"No,—all, right; one day, but not a minute more. And, Kid, don't—don't leave me to face it alone. Just a shot, one pull on the trigger. You understand. Think of it! Think of it! Flesh of my flesh, and I'll never live to see him!

"Send Ruth here. I want to say good-by and tell her that she must think of the boy and not wait till I'm dead. She might refuse to go with you if I didn't. Good-by, old man; good-by.

"Kid! I say—a—sink a hole above the pup, next to the slide. I panned out forty cents on my shovel there.

"And, Kid!" He stooped lower to catch the last faint words, the dying man's surrender of his pride. "I'm sorry—for—you know—Carmen."

Leaving the girl crying softly over her man, Malemute Kid slipped into his parka and snow-shoes, tucked his rifle under his arm, and crept away into the forest. He was no tyro in the stern sorrows of the Northland, but never had he faced so stiff a problem as this. In the abstract, it was a plain, mathematical proposition,—three possible lives as against one doomed one. But now he hesitated. For five years, shoulder to shoulder, on the rivers and trails, in the camps and mines, facing death by field and flood and famine, had they knitted the bonds of their comradeship. So close was the tie that he had often been conscious of a vague jealousy of Ruth, from the first time she had come between. And now it must be severed by his own hand.

Though he prayed for a moose, just one moose, all game seemed to have deserted the land, and nightfall found the exhausted man crawling into camp, light-handed, heavy-hearted. An uproar from the dogs and shrill cries from Ruth hastened him.

Bursting into the camp, he saw the girl in the midst of the snarling pack, laying about her with an ax. The dogs had broken the iron rule of their masters and were rushing the grub.

He joined the issue with his rifle reversed, and the hoary game of natural selection was played out with all the ruthlessness of its primeval environment. Rifle and ax went up and down, hit or missed with monotonous regularity; lithe bodies flashed, with wild eyes and dripping fangs; and man and beast fought for supremacy to the bitterest conclusion. Then the beaten brutes crept to the edge of the firelight, licking their wounds, voicing their misery to the stars.

The whole stock of dried salmon had been devoured, and perhaps five pounds of flour remained to tide them over two hundred miles of wilderness. Ruth returned to her husband, while Malemute Kid cut up the warm body of one of the dogs, the skull of which had been crushed by the ax. Every portion was carefully put away, save the hide and offal, which were cast to his fellows of the moment before.

Morning brought fresh trouble. The animals were turning on each other. Carmen, who still clung to her slender thread of life, was downed by the pack. The lash fell among them unheeded. They cringed and cried under the blows, but refused to scatter till the last wretched bit had disappeared,—bones, hide, hair, everything.

Malemute Kid went about his work, listening to Mason, who was back in Tennessee, delivering tangled discourses and wild exhortations to his brethren of other days.

Taking advantage of neighboring pines, he worked rapidly, and Ruth watched him make a cache similar to those sometimes used by hunters to preserve their meat from the wolverines and dogs. One after the other, he bent the tops of two small pines toward each other and nearly to the ground, making them fast with thongs of moosehide. Then he beat the dogs into submission and harnessed them to two of the sleds, loading the same with everything but the furs which enveloped Mason. These he wrapped and lashed tightly about him, fastening either end of the robes to the bent pines. A single stroke of his hunting knife would release them and send the body high in the air.

Ruth had received her husband's last wishes and made no struggle. Poor girl, she had learned the lesson of obedience well. From a child, she had bowed, and seen all women bow, to the lords of creation, and it did not seem in the nature of things for woman to resist. The Kid permitted her one outburst of grief, as she kissed her husband,—her own people had no such custom,—then led her to the foremost sled and helped her into her snowshoes. Blindly, instinctively, she took the gee-pole and whip, and "mushed" the dogs out on the trail. Then he returned to Mason, who had fallen into a coma, and long after she was out of sight crouched by the fire, waiting, hoping, praying for his comrade to die.

It is not pleasant to be alone with painful thoughts in the White Silence. The silence of gloom is merciful, shrouding one as with protection and breathing a thousand intangible sympathies; but the bright White Silence, clear and cold, under steely skies, is pitiless.

An hour passed,—two hours,—but the man would not die. At high noon the sun, without raising its rim above the southern horizon, threw a suggestion of fire athwart the heavens, then quickly drew it back. Malemute Kid roused and dragged himself to his comrade's side. He cast one glance about him. The White Silence seemed to sneer, and a great fear came upon him. There was a sharp report; Mason swung into his aerial sepulcher; and Malemute Kid lashed the dogs into a wild gallop as he fled across the snow.

SAKI

BORN IN BURMA of Scottish parents, H. H. Munro (1870–1916), better known as Saki, was sent to England at the age of two when his mother died. After traveling abroad with his father, he returned to Burma to join the police force, but he was always sickly and soon returned to London. There, he had a successful career as a journalist, writing Lewis Carroll–like political sketches for the *Westminster Gazette* (collected in book form in 1902 as *The Westminster Alice*) and short stories for the same newspaper (collected in book form in 1904 as *Reginald*). He also worked for several other papers, including six years as a foreign correspondent in Russia, the Balkans, and Paris, before joining the British Army at the outset of World War I. Munro was killed in France in 1916.

Although he was known personally for his humor, and much of his work has a satirical bite, the author is best remembered today for his short horror stories, which are often told in a witty yet cruel manner. His most famous stories are "Sredni Vashtar" and "The Open Window."

Munro never made clear how he came to choose the pseudonym of Saki. It may have been taken from the character of the cupbearer in the *Rubáiyát of Omar Khayyam*. The name may also refer to the saki, a small South American monkey featured in Munro's short story "The Remoulding of Groby Lington" (contained in *The Chronicles of Clovis*, 1912).

"Sredni Vashtar" was first published in *The Chronicles of Clovis* (London: John Lane, The Bodley Head, 1912).

SREDNI VASHTAR

SAKI

CONRADIN WAS TEN YEARS OLD, and the doctor had pronounced his professional opinion that the boy would not live another five years. The doctor was silky and effete, and counted for little, but his opinion was endorsed by Mrs. De Ropp, who counted for nearly everything. Mrs. De Ropp was Conradin's cousin and guardian, and in his eyes she represented those three-fifths of the world that are necessary and disagreeable and real; the other two-fifths, in perpetual antagonism to the foregoing, were summed up in himself and his imagination. One of these days Conradin supposed he would succumb to the mastering pressure of wearisome necessary things—such as illnesses and coddling restrictions and drawn-out dulness. Without his imagination, which was rampant under the spur of loneliness, he would have succumbed long ago.

Mrs. De Ropp would never, in her honestest moments, have confessed to herself that she disliked Conradin, though she might have been dimly aware that thwarting him "for his good" was a duty which she did not find particularly irksome. Conradin hated her with a desperate sincerity which he was perfectly able to mask. Such few pleasures as he could contrive for himself gained an added relish from the likelihood that they would be displeasing to his guardian, and from the realm of his imagination she was locked out—an unclean thing, which should find no entrance.

In the dull, cheerless garden, overlooked by so many windows that were ready to open with a message not to do this or that, or a reminder that medicines were due, he found little attraction. The few fruit-trees that it contained were set jealously apart from his plucking, as though they were rare specimens of their kind blooming in an arid waste; it would probably have been difficult to find a market-gardener who would have offered ten shillings for their entire yearly produce. In a forgotten corner, however, almost hidden behind a dismal shrubbery, was a disused tool-shed of respectable proportions, and within its walls Conradin found a haven, something that took on the varying aspects of a playroom and a cathedral. He had peopled it with a legion of familiar phantoms, evoked partly from fragments of history and partly from his own brain, but it also boasted two inmates of flesh and blood. In one corner lived a ragged-plumaged Houdan hen, on which the boy lavished an affection that had scarcely another outlet. Further back in the gloom stood a large hutch, divided into two compartments, one of which was fronted with close iron bars. This was the abode of a large polecat-ferret, which a friendly butcher-boy had once smuggled, cage and all, into its present quarters, in exchange for a long-secreted hoard of small silver. Conradin was dreadfully afraid of the lithe, sharp-fanged beast, but it was his most treasured possession. Its very presence in the tool-shed was a secret and fearful joy, to be kept scrupulously from the knowledge of the Woman, as he privately dubbed his cousin. And one day, out of Heaven

175

knows what material, he spun the beast a wonderful name, and from that moment it grew into a god and a religion. The Woman indulged in religion once a week at a church near by, and took Conradin with her, but to him the church service was an alien rite in the House of Rimmon. Every Thursday, in the dim and musty silence of the tool-shed, he worshipped with mystic and elaborate ceremonial before the wooden hutch where dwelt Sredni Vashtar, the great ferret. Red flowers in their season and scarlet berries in the winter-time were offered at his shrine, for he was a god who laid some special stress on the fierce impatient side of things, as opposed to the Woman's religion, which, as far as Conradin could observe, went to great lengths in the contrary direction. And on great festivals powdered nutmeg was strewn in front of his hutch, an important feature of the offering being that the nutmeg had to be stolen. These festivals were of irregular occurrence, and were chiefly appointed to celebrate some passing event. On one occasion, when Mrs. De Ropp suffered from acute toothache for three days, Conradin kept up the festival during the entire three days, and almost succeeded in persuading himself that Sredni Vashtar was personally responsible for the toothache. If the malady had lasted for another day the supply of nutmeg would have given out.

The Houdan hen was never drawn into the cult of Sredni Vashtar. Conradin had long ago settled that she was an Anabaptist. He did not pretend to have the remotest knowledge as to what an Anabaptist was, but he privately hoped that it was dashing and not very respectable. Mrs. De Ropp was the ground plan on which he based and detested all respectability.

After a while Conradin's absorption in the tool-shed began to attract the notice of his guardian. "It is not good for him to be pottering down there in all weathers," she promptly decided, and at breakfast one morning she announced that the Houdan hen had been sold and taken away overnight. With her short-sighted eyes she peered at Conradin, waiting for an outbreak of rage and sorrow, which she was ready to

rebuke with a flow of excellent precepts and reasoning. But Conradin said nothing: there was nothing to be said. Something perhaps in his white set face gave her a momentary qualm, for at tea that afternoon there was toast on the table, a delicacy which she usually banned on the ground that it was bad for him; also because the making of it "gave trouble," a deadly offence in the middle-class feminine eye.

"I thought you liked toast," she exclaimed, with an injured air, observing that he did not touch it.

"Sometimes," said Conradin.

In the shed that evening there was an innovation in the worship of the hutch-god. Conradin had been wont to chant his praises, tonight he asked a boon.

"Do one thing for me, Sredni Vashtar."

The thing was not specified. As Sredni Vashtar was a god he must be supposed to know. And choking back a sob as he looked at that other empty corner, Conradin went back to the world he so hated.

And every night, in the welcome darkness of his bedroom, and every evening in the dusk of the tool-shed, Conradin's bitter litany went up: "Do one thing for me, Sredni Vashtar."

Mrs. De Ropp noticed that the visits to the shed did not cease, and one day she made a further journey of inspection.

"What are you keeping in that locked hutch?" she asked. "I believe it's guinea-pigs. I'll have them all cleared away."

Conradin shut his lips tight, but the Woman ransacked his bedroom till she found the carefully hidden key, and forthwith marched down to the shed to complete her discovery. It was a cold afternoon, and Conradin had been bidden to keep to the house. From the furthest window of the dining-room the door of the shed could just be seen beyond the corner of the shrubbery, and there Conradin stationed himself. He saw the Woman enter, and then he imagined her opening the door of the sacred hutch and peering down with her short-sighted eyes into the thick straw bed where his god lay hidden. Perhaps she would prod at the straw in her clumsy impatience. And Conradin fervently breathed his prayer for the last time. But he knew as he prayed that he did not believe. He knew that the Woman would come out presently with that pursed smile he loathed so well on her face, and that in an hour or two the gardener would carry away his wonderful god, a god no longer, but a simple brown ferret in a hutch. And he knew that the Woman would triumph always as she triumphed now, and that he would grow ever more sickly under her pestering and domineering and superior wisdom, till one day nothing would matter much more with him, and the doctor would be proved right. And in the sting and misery of his defeat, he began to chant loudly and defiantly the hymn of his threatened idol:

Sredni Vashtar went forth,
His thoughts were red thoughts and his teeth
    were white.
His enemies called for peace, but he brought
    them death.
Sredni Vashtar the Beautiful.

And then of a sudden he stopped his chanting and drew closer to the window-pane. The door of the shed still stood ajar as it had been left, and the minutes were slipping by. They were long minutes, but they slipped by nevertheless. He watched the starlings running and flying in little parties across the lawn; he counted them over and over again, with one eye always on that swinging door. A sour-faced maid came in to lay the table for tea, and still Conradin stood and waited and watched. Hope had crept by inches into his heart, and now a look of triumph began to blaze in his eyes that had only known the wistful patience of defeat. Under his breath, with a furtive exultation, he began once again the paean of victory and devastation. And presently his eyes were rewarded: out through that doorway came a long, low, yellow-and-brown beast, with eyes a-blink at the waning daylight, and dark wet stains around the fur of jaws and throat. Conradin dropped on his knees. The great polecat-ferret made its way down to a small brook at the foot of the garden, drank for a moment, then crossed a little plank bridge and was lost to sight in the bushes. Such was the passing of Sredni Vashtar.

"Tea is ready," said the sour-faced maid; "where is the mistress?" "She went down to the shed some time ago," said Conradin. And while the maid went to summon her mistress to tea, Conradin fished a toasting-fork out of the sideboard drawer and proceeded to toast himself a piece of bread. And during the toasting of it

THE SEED FROM THE SEPULCHER

CLARK ASHTON SMITH

GENERALLY REGARDED as one of the three greatest contributors, along with Robert E. Howard and H. P. Lovecraft, to the revered *Weird Tales* magazine, Clark Ashton Smith (1893–1961) was a Californian and a prodigy, educating himself by reading an unabridged dictionary and the *Encyclopaedia Britannica* several times. In his teens, he sold short stories to *Overland Monthly* and *Black Cat,* but soon turned his attention to poetry, and published *The Star-Treader and Other Poems* in 1912. Reviewers hailed him as "the Keats of the Pacific Coast" and "the boy genius of the Sierras." Despite the accolades, his next two collections of poetry were self-published; in order to earn a living, he went back to writing fiction. An early and enduring correspondence with the great horror writer Lovecraft encouraged Smith to write dark fantasy, which he did prolifically during the 1920s and '30s for *Weird Tales* (more than a story per month from 1929 to 1937), *Amazing Stories,* and *Strange Stories,* thus establishing himself as one of the masters of the form. When the people closest to him died—his mother in 1935, his friend Howard in 1936, and both his father and Lovecraft in 1937—Smith went into a deep depression and wrote almost nothing for the rest of his life. He might have faded into obscurity but for the fact that Arkham House, the publishing company founded by August Derleth to keep Lovecraft in print, began expanding in the 1960s to publishing similar authors. The Arkham editions of Smith's stories and poems are all avidly collected today.

Smith's stories are almost universally grisly, macabre, and grotesque—and the present story, perhaps his most famous, is no exception. "The Seed from the Sepulcher" was originally published in the October 1933 issue of *Weird Tales*; it was first collected in *Tales of Science and Sorcery* (Sauk City, WI: Arkham House, 1964).

THE SEED FROM THE SEPULCHER

CLARK ASHTON SMITH

"YES, I FOUND the place," said Falmer. "It's a queer sort of place, pretty much as the legends describe it." He spat quickly into the fire, as if the act of speech had been physically distasteful to him, and, half averting his face from the scrutiny of Thone, stared with morose and somber eyes into the jungle-matted Venezuelan darkness.

Thone, still weak and dizzy from the fever that had incapacitated him for continuing their journey to its end, was curiously puzzled. Falmer, he thought, had undergone an inexplicable change during the three days of his absence; a change that was too elusive in some of its phases to be fully defined or delimited.

Other phases, however, were all too obvious. Falmer, even during extreme hardship or illness, had heretofore been unquenchably loquacious and cheerful. Now he seemed sullen, uncommunicative, as if preoccupied with far-off things of disagreeable import. His bluff face had grown hollow—even pointed—and his eyes had narrowed to secretive slits. Thone was troubled by these changes, though he tried to dismiss his impressions as mere distempered fancies due to the influence of the ebbing fever.

"But can't you tell me what the place was like?" he persisted.

"There isn't much to tell," said Falmer, in a queer grumbling tone. "Just a few crumbling walls and falling pillars."

"But didn't you find the burial pit of the Indian legend, where the gold was supposed to be?"

"I found it . . . but there was no treasure."

Falmer's voice had taken on a forbidding surliness; and Thone decided to refrain from further questioning.

"I guess," he commented lightly, "that we had better stick to orchid-hunting. Treasure trove doesn't seem to be in our line. By the way, did you see any unusual flowers or plants during the trip?"

"Hell, no," Falmer snapped. His face had gone suddenly ashen in the firelight, and his eyes had assumed a set glare that might have meant either fear or anger. "Shut up, can't you? I don't want to talk. I've had a headache all day; some damned Venezuelan fever coming on, I suppose. We'd better head for the Orinoco tomorrow. I've had all I want of this trip."

James Falmer and Roderick Thone, professional orchid hunters, with two Indian guides, had been following an obscure tributary of the upper Orinoco. The country was rich in rare flowers; and, beyond its floral wealth, they had been drawn by vague but persistent rumors among the local tribes concerning the existence of a ruined city somewhere on this tributary; a city that contained a burial pit in which vast treasures of gold, silver, and jewels had been interred together with the dead of some nameless people. The two men had thought it worth while to investigate these rumors. Thone had fallen sick while they were still a full day's journey from the site of the ruins, and Falmer had gone on in a canoe with one of the Indians, leaving the other to attend to Thone. He had returned

179

at nightfall of the third day following his departure.

Thone decided after a while, as he lay staring at his companion, that the latter's taciturnity and moroseness were perhaps due to disappointment over his failure to find the treasure. It must have been that, together with some tropical infection working in the man's blood. However, he admitted doubtfully to himself, it was not like Falmer to be disappointed or downcast under such circumstances.

Falmer did not speak again, but sat glaring before him as if he saw something invisible to others beyond the labyrinth of fire-touched boughs and lianas in which the whispering, stealthy darkness crouched. Somehow, there was a shadowy fear in his aspect. Thone continued to watch him, and saw that the Indians, impassive and cryptic, were also watching him, as if with some obscure expectancy. The riddle was too much for Thone, and he gave it up after a while, lapsing into restless, fever-turbulent slumber from which he awakened at intervals, to see the set face of Falmer, dimmer and more distorted each time with the slowly dying fire and the invading shadows.

Thone felt stronger in the morning: his brain was clear, his pulse tranquil once more; and he saw with mounting concern the indisposition of Falmer, who seemed to rouse and exert himself with great difficulty, speaking hardly a word and moving with singular stiffness and sluggishness. He appeared to have forgotten his announced project of returning toward the Orinoco, and Thone took entire charge of the preparations for departure. His companion's condition puzzled him more and more: apparently there was no fever and the symptoms were wholly ambiguous. However, on general principles, he administered a stiff dose of quinine to Falmer before they started.

The paling saffron of sultry dawn sifted upon them through the jungle tops as they loaded their belongings into the dugouts and pushed off down the slow current. Thone sat near the bow of one of the boats, with Falmer in the rear, and a large bundle of orchid roots and part of their equipment filling the middle. The two Indians occupied the other boat, together with the rest of the supplies.

It was a monotonous journey. The river wound like a sluggish olive snake between dark, interminable walls of forest, from which the goblin faces of orchids leered. There were no sounds other than the splash of paddles, the furious chattering of monkeys, and petulant cries of fiery-colored birds. The sun rose above the jungle and poured down a tide of torrid brilliance.

Thone rowed steadily looking back over his shoulder at times to address Falmer with some casual remark or friendly question. The latter, with dazed eyes and features queerly pale and pinched in the sunlight, sat dully erect and made no effort to use his paddle. He offered no reply to the queries of Thone, but shook his head at intervals with a sort of shuddering motion that was plainly involuntary. After a while he began to moan thickly, as if in pain or delirium.

They went on in this manner for hours. The heat grew more oppressive between the stifling walls of jungle. Thone became aware of a shriller cadence in the moans of his companion. Looking back, he saw that Falmer had removed his sun-helmet, seemingly oblivious of the murderous heat, and was clawing at the crown of his head with frantic fingers. Convulsions shook his entire body, the dugout began to rock dangerously as he tossed to and fro in a paroxysm of manifest agony. His voice mounted to a high un-human shrieking.

Thone made a quick decision. There was a break in the lining palisade of somber forest, and he headed the boat for shore immediately. The Indians followed, whispering between themselves and eyeing the sick man with glances of apprehensive awe and terror that puzzled Thone tremendously. He felt that there was some devilish mystery about the whole affair; and he could not imagine what was wrong with Falmer. All the known manifestations of malignant tropical diseases rose before him like a rout of hideous fantasms; but, among them, he could not recognize the thing that had assailed his companion.

Having gotten Falmer ashore on a semicircle of liana-latticed beach without the aid of the Indians, who seemed unwilling to approach the sick man, Thone administered a heavy hypodermic injection of morphine from his medicine chest. This appeared to ease Falmer's suffering, and the convulsions ceased. Thone, taking advantage of their remission, proceeded to examine the crown of Falmer's head.

He was startled to find, amid the thick disheveled hair, a hard and pointed lump which resembled the tip of a beginning horn, rising under the still unbroken skin. As if endowed with erectile and resistless life, it seemed to grow beneath his fingers.

At the same time, abruptly and mysteriously, Falmer opened his eyes and appeared to regain full consciousness. For a few minutes he was more his normal self than at any time since his return from the ruins. He began to talk, as if anxious to relieve his mind of some oppressing burden. His voice was peculiarly thick and toneless, but Thone was able to follow his mutterings and piece them together.

"The pit! the pit!" said Falmer—"The infernal thing that was in the pit, in the deep sepulcher! . . . I wouldn't go back there for the treasure of a dozen El Dorados . . . I didn't tell you much about those ruins, Thone. Somehow it was hard—impossibly hard—to talk.

"I guess the Indian knew there was something wrong with the ruins. He led me to the place . . . but he wouldn't tell me anything about it; and he waited by the riverside while I searched for the treasure.

"Great gray walls there were, older than the jungle—old as death and time. They must have been quarried and reared by people from some lost planet. They loomed and leaned, at mad, unnatural angles, threatening to crush the trees about them. And there were columns too: thick, swollen columns of unholy form, whose abominable carvings the jungle had not wholly screened from view.

"There was no trouble finding that accursed burial pit. The pavement above had broken through quite recently, I think. A big tree had pried with its boa-like roots between the flagstones that were buried beneath centuries of mold. One of the flags had been tilted back on the pavement, and another had fallen through into the pit. There was a large hole, whose bottom I could see dimly in the forest-strangled light. Something glimmered palely at the bottom; but I could not be sure what it was.

"I had taken along a coil of rope, as you remember. I tied one end of it to a main root of the tree, dropped the other through the opening, and went down like a monkey. When I got to the bottom I could see little at first in the gloom, except the whitish glimmering all around me, at my feet. Something that was unspeakably brittle and friable crunched beneath me when I began to move. I turned on my flashlight, and saw that the place was fairly littered with bones. Human skeletons lay tumbled everywhere. They must have been removed long ago . . . I groped around amid the bones and dust, feeling pretty much like a ghoul, but couldn't find anything of value, not even a bracelet or a finger ring on any of the skeletons.

"It wasn't until I thought of climbing out that I noticed the real horror. In one of the corners—the corner nearest to the opening in the roof—I looked up and saw it in the webby shadows. Ten feet above my head it hung, and I had almost touched it, unknowing, when I descended the rope.

"It looked like a sort of white lattice work at first. Then I saw that the lattice was partly formed of human bones—a complete skeleton very tall and stalwart, like that of a warrior. A pale, withered thing grew out of the skull, like a set of fantastic antlers ending in myriads of long and stringy tendrils that had spread upward till they reached the roof. They must have lifted the skeleton, or body, along with them as they climbed.

"I examined the thing with my flashlight. It must have been a plant of some sort, and apparently it had started to grow in the cranium. Some of the branches had issued from the cloven crown, others through the eye holes, the mouth, and the nose holes, to flare upward. And the roots of the blasphemous thing had gone downward, trellising themselves on every bone. The very toes and fingers were ringed with them, and they drooped in writhing coils. Worst of all, the ones that had issued from the toe ends *were rooted in a second skull,* which dangled just below, with fragments of the broken-off root system. There was a litter of fallen bones on the floor in the corner. . . .

"The sight made me feel a little weak, somehow, and more than a little nauseated—that abhorrent, inexplicable mingling of the human and the plant. I started to climb the rope, in a feverish hurry to get out, but the thing fascinated me in its abominable fashion, and I couldn't help pausing to study it a little more when I had climbed half way. I leaned toward it too fast, I guess, and the rope began to sway, bringing my face lightly against the leprous, antler-shaped boughs above the skull.

"Something broke—possibly a sort of pod on one of the branches. I found my head enveloped in a cloud of pearl-gray powder, very light, fine, and scentless. The stuff settled on my hair, it got into my nose and eyes, nearly choking and blinding me. I shook it off as well as I could. Then I climbed on and pulled myself through the opening. . . ."

As if the effort of coherent narration had been too heavy a strain, Falmer lapsed into disconnected mumblings. The mysterious malady, whatever it was, returned upon him, and his delirious ramblings were mixed with groans of torture. But at moments he regained·a flash of coherence.

"My head! my head!" he muttered. "There must be something in my brain, something that grows and spreads; I tell you, I can feel it there. I haven't felt right.at any time since I left the burial pit . . . My mind has been queer ever since . . . It must have been the spores of the ancient devil-plant . . . The spores have taken root . . . The thing is splitting my skull, going down into my brain—a plant that springs out of a human cranium—as if from a flower pot!"

The dreadful convulsions began once more, and Falmer writhed uncontrollably in his companion's arms, shrieking with agony. Thone, sick at heart, and shocked by his sufferings, abandoned all effort to restrain him and took up the hypodermic. With much difficulty, he managed to inject a triple dose, and Falmer grew quiet by degrees, and lay with open glassy eyes, breathing stertorously. Thone, for the first time, perceived an odd protrusion of his eyeballs, which seemed about to start from their sockets, making it impossible for the lids to close, and lending the drawn features an expression of mad horror. It was as if something were pushing Falmer's eyes from his head.

Thone, trembling with sudden weakness and terror, felt that he was involved in some unnatural web of nightmare. He could not, dared not, believe the story Falmer had told him, and its implications. Assuring himself that his companion had imagined it all, had been ill throughout with the incubation of some strange fever, he stooped over and found that the horn-shaped lump on Falmer's head had now broken through the skin.

With a sense of unreality, he stared at the object that his prying fingers had revealed amid the matted hair. It was unmistakably a plant-bud of some sort, with involuted folds of pale green and bloody pink that seemed about to expand. The thing issued from above the central suture of the skull.

A nausea swept upon Thone, and he recoiled from the lolling head and its baleful outgrowth, averting his gaze. His fever was returning, there was a woeful debility in all his limbs, and he heard the muttering voice of delirium through the quinine-induced ringing in his ears. His eyes blurred with a deathly and miasmal mist.

He fought to subdue his illness and impotence. He must not give way to it wholly; he must go on with Falmer and the Indians and reach the nearest trading station, many days away on the Orinoco, where Falmer could receive aid.

As if through sheer volition, his eyes cleared, and he felt a resurgence of strength. He looked around for the guides, and saw, with a start of uncomprehending surprise, that they had vanished. Peering further, he observed that one of the boats—the dugout used by the Indians—had also disappeared. It was plain that he and Falmer had been deserted. Perhaps the Indians had known what was wrong with the sick man, and had been afraid. At any rate, they were gone, and they had taken much of the camp equipment and most of the provisions with them.

Thone turned once more to the supine body of Falmer, conquering his repugnance, with effort. Resolutely he drew out his clasp knife, and, stooping over the stricken man, he excised the protruding bud, cutting as close to the scalp as he could with safety. The thing was unnaturally tough and rubbery; it exuded a thin, sanguinous fluid; and he shuddered when he saw its internal structure, full of nerve-like filaments, with a core that suggested cartilage. He flung it aside, quickly, on the river sand. Then, lifting Falmer in his arms, he lurched and staggered towards the remaining boat. He fell more than once, and lay half swooning across the inert body. Alternately carrying and dragging his burden, he reached the boat at last. With the remainder of his failing strength, he contrived to prop Falmer in the stern against the pile of equipment.

His fever was mounting apace. After much delay, with tedious, half-delirious exertions, he pushed off from the shore, till the fever mastered him wholly and the oar slipped from oblivious fingers. . . .

He awoke in the yellow glare of dawn, with his brain and his senses comparatively clear. His illness had left a great languor, but his first thought was of Falmer. He twisted about, nearly falling overboard in his debility, and sat facing his companion.

Falmer still reclined, half sitting, half lying, against the pile of blankets and other impedimenta. His knees were drawn up, his hands clasping them as if in tetanic rigor. His features had grown as stark and ghastly as those of a dead man, and his whole aspect was one of mortal rigidity. It was this, however, that caused Thone to gasp with unbelieving horror.

During the interim of Thone's delirium and his lapse into slumber, the monstrous plant bud, merely stimulated, it would seem, by the act of excision, had grown again with preternatural rapidity, from Falmer's head. A loathsome pale-green stem was mounting thickly, and had started to branch like antlers after attaining a height of six or seven inches.

More dreadful than this, if possible, similar growths had issued from the eyes, and their stems, climbing vertically across the forehead, had entirely displaced the eyeballs. Already they were branching like the thing from the crown. The antlers were all tipped with pale vermilion. They appeared to quiver with repulsive animations, nodding rhythmically in the warm, windless air . . . From the mouth, another stem protruded, curling upward like a long and whitish tongue. It had not yet begun to bifurcate.

Thone closed his eyes to shut away the shocking vision. Behind his lids, in a yellow dazzle of light, he still saw the cadaverous features, the climbing stems that quivered against the dawn like ghastly hydras of tomb-etiolated green. They seemed to be waving toward him, growing and lengthening as they waved. He opened his eyes again, and fancied, with a start of new terror, that the antlers were actually taller than they had been a few moments previous.

After that, he sat watching them in a sort of baleful hypnosis. The illusion of the plant's visible growth and freer movement—if it were illusion—increased upon him. Falmer, however, did not stir, and his parchment face appeared to shrivel and fall in, as if the roots of the growth were draining his blood, were devouring his very flesh in their insatiable and ghoulish hunger.

Thone wrenched his eyes away and stared at the river shore. The stream had widened and the current had grown more sluggish. He sought to recognise their location, looking vainly for some familiar landmark in the monotonous dull-green cliffs of jungle that lined the margin. He felt hopelessly lost and alienated. He seemed to be drifting on an unknown tide of madness and nightmare, accompanied by something more frightful than corruption itself.

His mind began to wander with an odd inconsequence, coming back always, in a sort of closed circle, to the thing that was devouring Falmer. With a flash of scientific curiosity, he found himself wondering to what genus it belonged. It was neither fungus nor pitcher plant, nor anything that he had ever encountered or heard of in his explorations. It must have come, as Falmer had suggested, from an alien world: it was nothing that the earth could conceivably have nourished.

He felt, with a comforting assurance, that Falmer was dead. That, at least, was a mercy. But, even as he shaped the thought, he heard a low, guttural moaning, and, peering at Falmer in a horrible startlement, saw that his limbs and body were twitching slightly. The twitching increased, and took on a rhythmic regularity, though at no time did it resemble the agonized and violent convulsions of the previous day. It was plainly automatic, like a sort of galvanism; and Thone saw that it was timed with the languorous and loathsome swaying of the plant. The effect on the watcher was insidiously mesmeric and somnolent; and once he caught himself beating the detestable rhythm with his foot.

He tried to pull himself together, groping desperately for something to which his sanity could cling. Ineluctably, his illness returned: fever, nausea, and revulsion worse than the loathliness of death. But, before he yielded to it utterly, he drew his loaded revolver from the holster and fired six times into Falmer's quivering body . . . He knew that he had not missed, but, after the final bullet, Falmer still moaned and twitched in unison with the evil swaying of the plant, and Thone, sliding into delirium, heard still the ceaseless, automatic moaning.

There was no time in the world of seething unreality and shoreless oblivion through which he drifted. When he came to himself again, he could not know if hours or weeks had elapsed. But he knew at once that the boat was no longer moving; and lifting himself dizzily, he saw that it had floated into shallow water and mud and was nosing the beach of a tiny, jungle-tufted isle in mid-river. The putrid odor of slime was about him like a stagnant pool; and he heard a strident humming of insects.

It was either late morning or early afternoon, for the sun was high in the still heavens. Lianas were drooping above him from the island trees like uncoiled serpents, and epiphytic orchids, marked with ophidian mottlings, leaned toward him grotesquely from lowering boughs. Immense butterflies went past on sumptuously spotted wings.

He sat up, feeling very giddy and lightheaded, and faced again the horror that accompanied him. The thing had grown incredibly: the three-antlered stems, mounting above Falmer's head, had become gigantic and had put out masses of ropy feelers that tossed uneasily in the air, as if searching for support—or new provender. In the topmost antlers, a prodigious blossom had opened—a sort of fleshy disk, broad as a man's face and white as leprosy.

Falmer's features had shrunken till the outlines of every bone were visible as if beneath tightened paper. He was a mere death's head in a mask of human skin; and beneath his clothing the body was little more than a skeleton. He was quite still now, except for the communicated quivering of the stems. The atrocious plant had sucked him dry, had eaten his vitals and his flesh.

Thone wanted to hurl himself forward in a mad impulse to grapple with the growth. But a strange paralysis held him back. The plant was like a living and sentient thing—a thing that watched him, that dominated him with its unclean but superior will. And the huge blossom, as he stared, took on the dim, unnatural semblance of a face. It was somehow like the face of Falmer but the lineaments were twisted all awry, and were mingled with those of something wholly devilish and nonhuman. Thone could not move—he could not take his eyes from the blasphemous abnormality.

By some miracle, his fever had left him; and it did not return. Instead, there came an eternity of frozen fright and madness, in which he sat facing the mesmeric plant. It towered before him from the dry, dead shell that had been Falmer, its swollen, glutted stems and branches swaying gently, its huge flower leering perpetually upon him with its impious travesty of a human face. He thought that he heard a low, singing sound, ineffably sweet, but whether it emanated from the plant or was a mere hallucination of his overwrought senses, he could not know.

The sluggish hours went by, and a gruelling sun poured down its beams like molten lead from some titanic vessel of torture. His head swam with weakness and the fetor-laden heat, but he could not relax the rigor of his posture. There was no change in the nodding monstrosity, which seemed to have attained its full growth above the head of its victim. But after a long interim Thone's eyes were drawn to the shrunken hands of Falmer, which still clasped the drawn-up knees in a spasmodic clutch. Through the ends of the fingers, tiny white rootlets had broken and were writhing slowly in the air—groping, it seemed, for a new source of nourishment. Then, from the neck and chin, other tips were breaking, and over the whole body the clothing stirred in a curious manner, as if with the crawling and lifting of hidden lizards.

At the same time the singing grew louder, sweeter, more imperious, and the swaying of the great plant assumed an indescribably seductive tempo. It was like the allurement of voluptuous sirens, the deadly languor of dancing cobras. Thone felt an irresistible compulsion: a summons was being laid upon him, and his drugged mind and body must obey it. The very fingers of Falmer, twisting viperishly, seemed beckoning to him. Suddenly he was on his hands and knees in the bottom of the boat. Inch by inch, with terror and fascination contending in his brain, he crept forward, dragging himself over the disregarded bundle of orchid-plants—inch by inch, foot by foot, till his head was against the withered hands of Falmer, from which hung and floated the questing roots.

Some cataleptic spell had made him helpless. He felt the rootlets as they moved like delving fingers through his hair and over his face and neck, and started to strike in with agonizing, needle-sharp tips. He could not stir, he could not even close his lids. In a frozen stare, he saw the gold and carmine flash of a hovering butterfly as the roots began to pierce his pupils.

Deeper and deeper went the greedy roots, while new filaments grew out to enmesh him like a witch's net. . . . For a while, it seemed that the dead and the living writhed together in leashed convulsions . . . At last Thone hung supine amid the lethal, ever-growing web; bloated and colossal, the plant lived on; and in its upper branches, through the still, stifling afternoon, a second flower began to unfold.

CARL STEPHENSON

CARL STEPHENSON (1893–1967?) was born in Vienna and spent most of his life in Germany. Although he was well known as a writer, editor, and publisher in his own country, "Leiningen Versus the Ants" appears to be the only story he ever published for an English-language audience. This thrilling adventure tale, set in the heart of the Brazilian jungle, has been frequently anthologized and was adapted for the dramatic radio program *Escape* in 1948, then again for CBS Radio's *Suspense* in 1959.

The story also inspired the 1954 motion picture *The Naked Jungle*, which starred Charlton Heston as Christopher Leiningen (though the character's first name does not appear in the story); Eleanor Parker as his wife, Joanna (a character added for the film); and William Conrad, who had acted in one of the radio adaptations. The film was directed by Byron Haskin.

"Leiningen Versus the Ants" was first published in English in the December 1938 issue of *Esquire*. It was originally published as a novella in Germany in 1937.

LEININGEN VERSUS THE ANTS

CARL STEPHENSON

"**UNLESS THEY ALTER** their course, and there's no reason why they should, they'll reach your plantation in two days at the latest."

Leiningen sucked placidly at a cigar about the size of a corn cob and for a few seconds gazed without answering at the agitated District Commissioner. Then he took the cigar from his lips, and leaned slightly forward. With his bristling grey hair, bulky nose, and lucid eyes, he had the look of an aging and shabby eagle.

"Decent of you," he murmured, "paddling all this way just to give me the tip. But you're pulling my leg of course when you say I must do a bunk. Why, even a herd of saurians couldn't drive me from this plantation of mine."

The Brazilian official threw up lean and lanky arms and clawed the air with wildly distended fingers. "Leiningen!" he shouted. "You're insane! They're not creatures you can fight— they're an elemental—an 'act of God'! Ten miles long, two miles wide—ants, nothing but ants! And every single one of them a fiend from hell; before you can spit three times they'll eat a full-grown buffalo to the bones. I tell you if you don't clear out at once there'll he nothing left of you but a skeleton picked as clean as your own plantation."

Leiningen grinned. "Act of God, my eye! Anyway, I'm not an old woman; I'm not going to run for it just because an elemental's on the way. And don't think I'm the kind of fathead who tries to fend off lightning with his fists either. I use my intelligence, old man. With me, the brain isn't a second blindgut; I know what it's there for. When I began this model farm and plantation three years ago, I took into account all that could conceivably happen to it. And now I'm ready for anything and everything— including your ants."

The Brazilian rose heavily to his feet. "I've done my best," he gasped. "Your obstinacy endangers not only yourself, but the lives of your four hundred workers. You don't know these ants!"

Leiningen accompanied him down to the river, where the Governrnent launch was moored. The vessel cast off. As it moved downstream, the exclamation mark neared the rail and began waving its arms frantically. Long after the launch had disappeared round the bend, Leiningen thought he could still hear that dimming imploring voice, "You don't know them, I tell you! *You don't know them!*"

But the reported enemy was by no means unfamiliar to the planter. Before he started work on his settlement, he had lived long enough in the country to see for himself the fearful devastations sometimes wrought by these ravenous insects in their campaigns for food. But since then he had planned measures of defence accordingly, and these, he was convinced, were in every way adequate to withstand the approaching peril.

Moreover, during his three years as a planter, Leiningen had met and defeated drought, flood, plague, and all other "acts of God" which had come against him—unlike his fellow-settlers in the district, who had made little or no resistance. This unbroken success he attributed solely to the observance of his lifelong motto: *The human brain needs only to become fully aware of its powers to conquer even the elements.* Dullards reeled senselessly and aimlessly into the abyss; cranks, however brilliant, lost their heads when circumstances suddenly altered or accelerated and ran into stone walls, sluggards drifted with the current until they were caught in whirlpools and dragged under. But such disasters, Leiningen contended, merely strengthened his argument that intelligence, directed aright, invariably makes man the master of his fate.

Yes, Leiningen had always known how to grapple with life. Even here, in this Brazilian wilderness, his brain had triumphed over every difficulty and danger it had so far encountered. First he had vanquished primal forces by cunning and organization, then he had enlisted the resources of modern science to increase miraculously the yield of his plantation. And now he was sure he would prove more than a match for the "irresistible" ants.

That same evening, however, Leiningen assembled his workers. He had no intention of waiting till the news reached their ears from other sources. Most of them had been born in the district; the cry "The ants are coming!" was to them an imperative signal for instant, panic-stricken flight, a spring for life itself. But so great was the Indians' trust in Leiningen, in Leiningen's word, and in Leiningen's wisdom, that they received his curt tidings, and his orders for the imminent struggle, with the calmness with which they were given. They waited, unafraid, alert, as if for the beginning of a new game or hunt which he had just described to them. The ants were indeed mighty, but not so mighty as the boss. Let them come!

They came at noon the second day. Their approach was announced by the wild unrest of the horses, scarcely controllable now either in stall or under rider, scenting from afar a vapor instinct with horror.

It was announced by a stampede of animals, timid and savage, hurtling past each other; jaguars and pumas flashing by nimble stags of the pampas; bulky tapirs, no longer hunters, themselves hunted, outpacing fleet kinkajous; maddened herds of cattle, heads lowered, nostrils snorting, rushing through tribes of loping monkeys, chattering in a dementia of terror; then followed the creeping and springing denizens of bush and steppe, big and little rodents, snakes, and lizards.

Pell-mell the rabble swarmed down the hill to the plantation, scattered right and left before the barrier of the water-filled ditch, then sped onwards to the river, where, again hindered, they fled along its bank out of sight.

This water-filled ditch was one of the defence measures which Leiningen had long since prepared against the advent of the ants. It encompassed three sides of the plantation like a huge horseshoe. Twelve feet across, but not very deep, when dry it could hardly be described as an obstacle to either man or beast. But the ends of the "horseshoe" ran into the river which formed the northern boundary, and fourth side, of the plantation. And at the end nearer the house and outbuildings in the middle of the plantation, Leiningen had constructed a dam by means of which water from the river could be diverted into the ditch.

So now, by opening the dam, he was able to fling an imposing girdle of water, a huge quadrilateral with the river as its base, completely around the plantation, like the moat encircling a medieval city. Unless the ants were clever enough to build rafts, they had no hope of reaching the plantation, Leiningen concluded.

The twelve-foot water ditch seemed to afford in itself all the security needed. But while awaiting the arrival of the ants, Leiningen made a further improvement. The western section of the ditch ran along the edge of a tamarind wood, and the branches of some great trees reached over the water. Leiningen now had them lopped so that ants could not descend from them within the "moat."

The women and children, then the herds of cattle, were escorted by peons on rafts over the river, to remain on the other side in absolute safety until the plunderers had departed. Leiningen gave this instruction, not because he believed the non-combatants were in any danger, but in order to avoid hampering the efficiency of the defenders. "Critical situations first become crises," he explained to his men, "when oxen or women get excited."

Finally, he made a careful inspection of the "inner moat"—a smaller ditch lined with concrete, which extended around the hill on which stood the ranch house, barns, stables and other buildings. Into this concrete ditch emptied the inflow pipes from three great petrol tanks. If by some miracle the ants managed to cross the water and reach the plantation, this "rampart of petrol" would be an absolutely impassable protection for the beseiged and their dwellings and stock. Such, at least, was Leiningen's opinion.

He stationed his men at irregular distances along the water ditch, the first line of defence. Then he lay down in his hammock and puffed drowsily away at his pipe until a peon came with the report that the ants had been observed far away in the South.

Leiningen mounted his horse, which at the feel of its master seemed to forget its uneasiness, and rode leisurely in the direction of the threatening offensive. The southern stretch of ditch—the upper side of the quadrilateral—was nearly three miles long; from its center one could survey the entire countryside. This was destined to be the scene of the outbreak of war between Leiningen's brain and twenty square miles of life-destroying ants.

It was a sight one could never forget. Over the range of hills, as far as eye could see, crept a darkening hem, ever longer and broader, until the shadow spread across the slope from east to west, then downwards, downwards, uncannily swift, and all the green herbage of that wide vista was being mown as by a giant sickle, leaving only the vast moving shadow, extending, deepening, and moving rapidly nearer.

When Leiningen's men, behind their barrier of water, perceived the approach of the long-expected foe, they gave vent to their suspense in screams and imprecations. But as the distance began to lessen between the "sons of hell" and the water ditch, they relapsed into silence. Before the advance of that awe-inspiring throng, their belief in the powers of the boss began to steadily dwindle.

Even Leiningen himself, who had ridden up just in time to restore their loss of heart by a display of unshakable calm, even he could not free himself from a qualm of malaise. Yonder were thousands of millions of voracious jaws bearing down upon him and only a suddenly insignificant, narrow ditch lay between him and his men and being gnawed to the bones "before you can spit three times."

Hadn't this brain for once taken on more than it could manage? If the blighters decided to rush the ditch, fill it to the brim with their corpses, there'd still be more than enough to destroy every trace of that cranium of his. The planter's chin jutted; they hadn't got him yet, and he'd see to it they never would. While he could think at all, he'd flout both death and the devil.

The hostile army was approaching in perfect formation; no human battalions, however well-drilled, could ever hope to rival the precision of that advance. Along a front that moved forward as uniformly as a straight line, the ants drew nearer and nearer to the water ditch. Then, when they learned through their scouts the nature of the obstacle, the two outlying wings of the army detached themselves from the main body and marched down the western and eastern sides of the ditch.

This surrounding maneuver took rather more than an hour to accomplish; no doubt the ants expected that at some point they would find a crossing.

During this outflanking movement by the wings, the army on the center and southern front remained still. The besieged were therefore able to contemplate at their leisure the thumb-long, reddish-black, long-legged insects; some of the Indians believed they could see, too, intent on them, the brilliant, cold eyes, and the razor-edged mandibles, of this host of infinity.

It is not easy for the average person to imagine that an animal, not to mention an insect, can *think*. But now both the European brain of Leiningen and the primitive brains of the Indians began to stir with the unpleasant foreboding that inside every single one of that deluge of insects dwelt a thought. And that thought was: Ditch or no ditch, we'll get to your flesh!

Not until four o'clock did the wings reach the "horseshoe" ends of the ditch, only to find these ran into the great river. Through some kind of secret telegraphy, the report must then have flashed very swiftly indeed along the entire enemy line. And Leiningen, riding—no longer casually—along his side of the ditch, noticed by energetic and widespread movements of troops that for some unknown reason the news of the check had its greatest effect on the southern front, where the main army was massed. Perhaps the failure to find a way over the ditch was persuading the ants to withdraw from the plantation in search of spoils more easily attainable.

An immense flood of ants, about a hundred yards in width, was pouring in a glimmering-black cataract down the far slope of the ditch. Many thousands were already drowning in the sluggish creeping flow, but they were followed by troop after troop, who clambered over their sinking comrades, and then themselves served as dying bridges to the reserves hurrying on in their rear.

Shoals of ants were being carried away by the current into the middle of the ditch, where gradually they broke asunder and then, exhausted by their struggles, vanished below the surface. Nevertheless, the wavering, floundering hundred-yard front was remorselessly if slowly advancing towards the beseiged on the other bank. Leiningen had been wrong when he supposed the enemy would first have to fill the ditch with their bodies before they could cross; instead, they merely needed to act as steppingstones, as they swam and sank, to the hordes ever pressing onwards from behind.

Near Leiningen a few mounted herdsmen awaited his orders. He sent one to the weir—the river must be dammed more strongly to increase the speed and power of the water coursing through the ditch.

A second peon was dispatched to the outhouses to bring spades and petrol sprinklers. A third rode away to summon to the zone of the offensive all the men, except the observation posts, on the near-by sections of the ditch, which were not yet actively threatened.

The ants were getting across far more quickly than Leiningen would have deemed possible. Impelled by the mighty cascade behind them, they struggled nearer and nearer to the inner bank. The momentum of the attack was so great that neither the tardy flow of the stream nor its downward pull could exert its proper force; and into the gap left by every submerging insect, hastened forward a dozen more.

When reinforcements reached Leiningen, the invaders were halfway over. The planter had to admit to himself that it was only by a stroke of luck for him that the ants were attempting the crossing on a relatively short front: had they assaulted simultaneously along the entire length of the ditch, the outlook for the defenders would have been black indeed.

Even as it was, it could hardly be described as rosy, though the planter seemed quite unaware that death in a gruesome form was drawing closer and closer. As the war between his brain and the "act of God" reached its climax, the very shadow of annihilation began to pale to Leiningen, who now felt like a champion in a new Olympic game, a gigantic and thrilling contest, from which was determined to emerge victor. Such, indeed, was his aura of confidence that the Indians forgot their stupefied fear of the peril only a yard or two away; under the planter's supervision, they began fervidly digging up to the edge of the bank and throwing clods of earth and spadefuls of sand into the midst of the hostile fleet.

The petrol sprinklers, hitherto used to destroy pests and blights on the plantation, were also brought into action. Streams of evil-reeking oil now soared and fell over an enemy already in disorder through the bombardment of earth and sand.

The ants responded to these vigorous and successful measures of defence by further developments of their offensive. Entire clumps of huddling insects began to roll down the opposite bank into the water. At the same time, Leiningen noticed that the ants were now attacking along an ever-widening front. As the numbers both of his men and his petrol sprinklers were severely limited, this rapid extension of the line of battle was becoming an overwhelming danger.

To add to his difficulties, the very clods of earth they flung into that black floating carpet often whirled fragments toward the defenders' side, and here and there dark ribbons were already mounting the inner bank. True, wherever a man saw these they could still be driven back into the water by spadefuls of earth or jets of petrol. But the file of defenders was too sparse and scattered to hold off at all points these landing parties, and though the peons toiled like madmen, their plight became momentarily more perilous.

One man struck with his spade at an enemy clump, did not draw it back quickly enough from the water; in a trice the wooden haft swarmed with upward-scurrying insects. With a curse, he dropped the spade into the ditch; too late, they were already on his body. They lost no time; wherever they encountered bare flesh they bit deeply; a few, bigger than the rest, carried in their hind-quarters a sting which injected a burning and paralyzing venom. Screaming, frantic with pain, the peon danced and twirled like a dervish.

Realizing that another such casualty, yes, perhaps this alone, might plunge his men into confusion and destroy their morale, Leiningen roared in a bellow louder than the yells of the victim: "Into the petrol, idiot! Douse your paws in the petrol!" The dervish ceased his pirouette as if transfixed, then tore off his shirt and plunged his arm and the ants hanging to it up to the shoulder in one of the large open tins of petrol. But even then the fierce mandibles did not slacken; another peon had to help him squash and detach each separate insect.

Distracted by the episode, some defenders had turned away from the ditch. And now cries of fury, a thudding of spades, and a wild trampling to and fro, showed that the ants had made full use of the interval, though luckily only a few had managed to get across. The men set to work again desperately with the barrage of earth and sand. Meanwhile an old Indian, who acted as medicine-man to the plantation workers, gave the bitten peon a drink he had prepared some hours before, which, he claimed, possessed the virtue of dissolving and weakening ants' venom.

Leiningen surveyed his position. A dispassionate observer would have estimated the odds against him at a thousand to one. But then such an onlooker would have reckoned only by what he saw—the advance of myriad battalions of ants against the futile efforts of a few defenders—and not by the unseen activity that can go on in a man's brain.

For Leiningen had not erred when he decided he would fight elemental with elemental. The water in the ditch was beginning to rise; the stronger damming of the river was making itself apparent.

Visibly the swiftness and power of the masses of water increased, swirling into quicker and quicker movement its living black surface, dispersing its pattern, carrying away more and more of it on the hastening current.

Victory had been snatched from the very jaws of defeat. With a hysterical shout of joy, the peons feverishly intensified their bombardment of earth clods and sand.

And now the wide cataract down the opposite bank was thinning and ceasing, as if the ants were becoming aware that they could not attain their aim. They were scurrying back up the slope to safety.

All the troops so far hurled into the ditch had been sacrificed in vain. Drowned and floundering insects eddied in thousands along the flow, while Indians running on the bank destroyed every swimmer that reached the side.

Not until the ditch curved towards the east did the scattered ranks assemble again in a coherent mass. And now, exhausted and half-numbed, they were in no condition to ascend the bank. Fusillades of clods drove them round the bend towards the mouth of the ditch and then into the river, wherein they vanished without leaving a trace.

The news ran swiftly along the entire chain of outposts, and soon a long scattered line of laughing men could be seen hastening along the ditch towards the scene of victory.

For once they seemed to have lost all their native reserve, for it was in wild abandon now they celebrated the triumph—as if there were no longer thousands of millions of merciless, cold and hungry eyes watching them from the opposite bank, watching and waiting.

The sun sank behind the rim of the tamarind wood and twilight deepened into night. It was not only hoped but expected that the ants would remain quiet until dawn. But to defeat any forlorn attempt at a crossing, the flow of water through the ditch was powerfully increased by opening the dam still further.

In spite of this impregnable barrier, Leiningen was not yet altogether convinced that the ants would not venture another surprise attack. He ordered his men to camp along the bank overnight. He also detailed parties of them to patrol the ditch in two of his motor cars and ceaselessly to illuminate the surface of the water with headlights and electric torches.

After having taken all the precautions he deemed necessary, the farmer ate his supper with considerable appetite and went to bed. His slumbers were in no wise disturbed by the memory of the waiting, live, twenty square miles.

Dawn found a thoroughly refreshed and active Leiningen riding along the edge of the ditch. The planter saw before him a motionless and unaltered throng of besiegers. He studied the wide belt of water between them and the plantation, and for a moment almost regretted that the fight had ended so soon and so simply. In the comforting, matter-of-fact light of morning, it seemed to him now that the ants hadn't the ghost of a chance to cross the ditch. Even if they plunged headlong into it on all three fronts at once, the force of the now powerful current would inevitably sweep them away. He had got quite a thrill out of the fight—a pity it was already over.

He rode along the eastern and southern sections of the ditch and found everything in order. He reached the western section, opposite the tamarind wood, and here, contrary to the other battle fronts, he found the enemy very busy indeed. The trunks and branches of the trees and the creepers of the lianas, on the far bank of the ditch, fairly swarmed with industrious insects. But instead of eating the leaves there and then, they were merely gnawing through the stalks, so that a thick green shower fell steadily to the ground.

No doubt they were victualing columns sent out to obtain provender for the rest of the army. The discovery did not surprise Leiningen. He did not need to be told that ants are intelligent, that certain species even use others as milch cows, watchdogs, and slaves. He was well aware of their power of adaptation, their sense of discipline, their marvelous talent for organization.

His belief that a foray to supply the army was in progress was strengthened when he saw the leaves that fell to the ground being dragged to the troops waiting outside the wood. Then all at once he realized the aim that rain of green was intended to serve.

Each single leaf, pulled or pushed by dozens of toiling insects, was borne straight to the edge of the ditch. Even as Macbeth watched the approach of Birnam Wood in the hands of his enemies, Leiningen saw the tamarind wood move nearer and nearer in the mandibles of the ants. Unlike the fey Scot, however, he did not lose his nerve; no witches had prophesied his doom, and if they had he would have slept just as soundly. All the same, he was forced to admit to himself that the situation was far more ominous than that of the day before.

He had thought it impossible for the ants to build rafts for themselves—well, here they were, coming in thousands, more than enough to bridge the ditch. Leaves after leaves rustled down the slope into the water, where the current drew them away from the bank and carried them into midstream. And every single leaf carried several ants. This time the farmer did not trust to the alacrity of his messengers. He galloped away, leaning from his saddle and yelling orders as he rushed past outpost after outpost: "Bring petrol pumps to the southwest front! Issue spades to every man along the line facing the wood!" And arrived at the eastern and southern sections, he dispatched every man except the observation posts to the menaced west.

Then, as he rode past the stretch where the ants had failed to cross the day before, he witnessed a brief but impressive scene. Down the slope of the distant hill there came towards him a singular being, writhing rather than running, an animal-like blackened statue with shapeless head and four quivering feet that knuckled under almost ceaselessly. When the creature reached the far bank of the ditch and collapsed opposite Leiningen, he recognized it as a pampas stag, covered over and over with ants.

It had strayed near the zone of the army. As usual, they had attacked its eyes first. Blinded, it had reeled in the madness of hideous torment straight into the ranks of its persecutors, and now the beast swayed to and fro in its death agony.

With a shot from his rifle Leiningen put it out of its misery. Then he pulled out his watch. He hadn't a second to lose, but for life itself he could not have denied his curiosity the satisfaction of knowing how long the ants would take—for personal reasons, so to speak. After six minutes the white polished bones alone remained. That's how he himself would look before you can—Leiningen spat once, and put spurs to his horse.

The sporting zest with which the excitement of the novel contest had inspired him the day before had now vanished; in its place was a cold and violent purpose. He would send these vermin back to the hell where they belonged, somehow, anyhow. Yes, but how was indeed the question; as things stood at present it looked as if the devils would raze him and his men from the earth instead. He had underestimated the might of the enemy; he really would have to bestir himself if he hoped to outwit them.

The biggest danger now, he decided, was the point where the western section of the ditch curved southwards. And arrived there, he found his worst expectations justified. The very power of the current had huddled the leaves and their crews of ants so close together at the bend that the bridge was almost ready.

True, streams of petrol and clumps of earth still prevented a landing. But the number of floating leaves was increasing ever more swiftly. It could not be long now before a stretch of water a mile in length was decked by a green pontoon over which the ants could rush in millions.

Leiningen galloped to the weir. The damming of the river was controlled by a wheel on its bank. The planter ordered the man at the wheel first to lower the water in the ditch almost to vanishing point, next to wait a moment, then suddenly to let the river in again. This maneuver of lowering and raising the surface, of decreasing then increasing the flow of water through the ditch was to be repeated over and over again until further notice.

This tactic was at first successful. The water in the ditch sank, and with it the film of leaves. The green fleet nearly reached the bed and the troops on the far bank swarmed down the slope to it. Then a violent flow of water at the original depth raced through the ditch, overwhelming leaves and ants, and sweeping them along.

This intermittent rapid flushing prevented just in time the almost completed fording of the ditch. But it also flung here and there squads of the enemy vanguard simultaneously up the inner bank. These seemed to know their duty only too well, and lost no time accomplishing it. The air rang with the curses of bitten Indians. They had removed their shirts and pants to detect the quicker the upward-hastening insects; when they saw one, they crushed it; and fortunately the onslaught as yet was only by skirmishers.

Again and again, the water sank and rose, carrying leaves and drowned ants away with it. It lowered once more nearly to its bed; but this time the exhausted defenders waited in vain for the flush of destruction. Leiningen sensed disaster; something must have gone wrong with the machinery of the dam. Then a sweating peon tore up to him—

"They're over!"

While the besieged were concentrating upon the defence of the stretch opposite the wood, the seemingly unaffected line beyond the wood had become the theatre of decisive action. Here the defenders' front was sparse and scattered; everyone who could be spared had hurried away to the south.

Just as the man at the weir had lowered the water almost to the bed of the ditch, the ants on a wide front began another attempt at a direct crossing like that of the preceding day. Into the emptied bed poured an irresistible throng. Rushing across the ditch, they attained the inner bank before the slow-witted Indians fully grasped the situation. Their frantic screams dumbfounded the man at the weir. Before he could direct the river anew into the safeguarding bed he saw himself surrounded by raging ants. He ran like the others, ran for his life.

When Leiningen heard this, he knew the plantation was doomed. He wasted no time bemoaning the inevitable. For as long as there was the slightest chance of success, he had stood his ground, and now any further resistance was both useless and dangerous. He fired three revolver shots into the air—the prearranged signal for his men to retreat instantly within the "inner moat." Then he rode towards the ranch house.

This was two miles from the point of invasion. There was therefore time enough to prepare the second line of defence against the advent of the ants. Of the three great petrol cisterns near the house, one had already been half emptied by the constant withdrawals needed for the pumps during the fight at the water ditch. The remaining petrol in it was now drawn off through underground pipes into the concrete trench which encircled the ranch house and its outbuildings.

And there, drifting in twos and threes, Leiningen's men reached him. Most of them were obviously trying to preserve an air of calm and indifference, belied, however, by their restless glances and knitted brows. One could see their belief in a favorable outcome of the struggle was already considerably shaken.

The planter called his peons around him.

"Well, lads," he began, "we've lost the first round. But we'll smash the beggars yet, don't you worry. Anyone who thinks otherwise can draw his pay here and now and push off. There are rafts enough to spare on the river and plenty of time still to reach 'em."

Not a man stirred.

Leiningen acknowledged his silent vote of confidence with a laugh that was half a grunt. "That's the stuff, lads. Too bad if you'd missed the rest of the show, eh? Well, the fun won't start till morning. Once these blighters turn tail, there'll be plenty of work for everyone and higher wages all round. And now run along and get something to eat; you've earned it all right."

In the excitement of the fight the greater part of the day had passed without the men once pausing to snatch a bite. Now that the ants were for the time being out of sight, and the "wall of petrol" gave a stronger feeling of security, hungry stomachs began to assert their claims.

The bridges over the concrete ditch were removed. Here and there solitary ants had reached the ditch; they gazed at the petrol meditatively, then scurried back again. Apparently they had little interest at the moment for what lay beyond the evil-reeking barrier; the abundant spoils of the plantation were the main attraction. Soon the trees, shrubs, and beds for miles around were hulled with ants zealously gobbling the yield of long weary months of strenuous toil.

As twilight began to fall, a cordon of ants marched around the petrol trench, but as yet made no move towards its brink. Leiningen posted sentries with headlights and electric torches, then withdrew to his office, and began to reckon up his losses. He estimated these as large, but, in comparison with his bank balance, by no means unbearable. He worked out in some detail a scheme of intensive cultivation which would enable him, before very long, to more than compensate himself for the damage now being wrought to his crops. It was with a contented mind that he finally betook himself to bed where he slept deeply until dawn, undisturbed by any thought that next day little more might be left of him than a glistening skeleton.

He rose with the sun and went out on the flat roof of his house. And a scene like one from Dante lay around him; for miles in every direction there was nothing but a black, glittering multitude, a multitude of rested, sated, but none the less voracious ants: yes, look as far as one might, one could see nothing but that rustling black throng, except in the north, where the great river drew a boundary they could not hope to pass. But even the high stone breakwater, along the bank of the river, which Leiningen had built as a defence against inundations, was, like the paths, the shorn trees and shrubs, the ground itself, black with ants.

So their greed was not glutted in razing that vast plantation? Not by a long chalk; they were all the more eager now on a rich and certain booty—four hundred men, numerous horses, and bursting granaries.

At first it seemed that the petrol trench would serve its purpose. The besiegers sensed the peril of swimming it, and made no move to plunge blindly over its brink. Instead they devised a better maneuver; they began to collect shreds of bark, twigs and dried leaves and dropped these into the petrol. Everything green, which could have been similarly used, had long since been eaten. After a time, though, a long procession could be seen bringing from the west the tamarind leaves used as rafts the day before.

Since the petrol, unlike the water in the outer ditch, was perfectly still, the refuse stayed where it was thrown. It was several hours before the ants succeeded in covering an appreciable part of the surface. At length, however, they were ready to proceed to a direct attack.

Their storm troops swarmed down the concrete side, scrambled over the supporting surface of twigs and leaves, and impelled these over the few remaining streaks of open petrol until they reached the other side. Then they began to climb up this to make straight for the helpless garrison.

During the entire offensive, the planter sat peacefully, watching them with interest, but not stirring a muscle. Moreover, he had ordered his men not to disturb in any way whatever the advancing horde. So they squatted listlessly along the bank of the ditch and waited for a sign from the boss. The petrol was now covered with ants. A few had climbed the inner concrete wall and were scurrying towards the defenders.

"Everyone back from the ditch!" roared Leiningen. The men rushed away, without the slightest idea of his plan. He stooped forward and cautiously dropped into the ditch a stone which split the floating carpet and its living freight, to reveal a gleaming patch of petrol. A match spurted, sank down to the oily surface— Leiningen sprang back; in a flash a towering rampart of fire encompassed the garrison.

This spectacular and instant repulse threw the Indians into ecstasy. They applauded, yelled, and stamped, like children at a pantomime. Had it not been for the awe in which they held the boss, they would infallibly have carried him shoulder high.

It was some time before the petrol burned down to the bed of the ditch, and the wall of smoke and flame began to lower. The ants had retreated in a wide circle from the devastation, and innumerable charred fragments along the outer bank showed that the flames had spread from the holocaust in the ditch well into the ranks beyond, where they had wrought havoc far and wide.

Yet the perseverance of the ants was by no means broken; indeed, each setback seemed only to whet it. The concrete cooled, the flicker of the dying flames wavered and vanished, petrol from the second tank poured into the trench—and the ants marched forward anew to the attack.

The foregoing scene repeated itself in every detail, except that on this occasion less time was needed to bridge the ditch, for the petrol was now already filmed by a layer of ash. Once again they withdrew; once again petrol flowed into the ditch. Would the creatures never learn that their self-sacrifice was utterly senseless? It really was senseless, wasn't it? Yes, of course it was senseless—provided the defenders had an *unlimited* supply of petrol.

When Leiningen reached this stage of reasoning, he felt for the first time since the arrival of the ants that his confidence was deserting him. His skin began to creep; he loosened his collar. Once the devils were over the trench there wasn't a chance in hell for him and his men. God, what a prospect, to be eaten alive like that!

For the third time the flames immolated the attacking troops, and burned down to extinction. Yet the ants were coming on again as if nothing had happened. And meanwhile Leiningen had made a discovery that chilled him to the bone—petrol was no longer flowing into the ditch. Something must be blocking the outflow pipe of the third and last cistern—a snake or a dead rat? Whatever it was, the ants could be held off no longer, unless petrol could by some method be led from the cistern into the ditch.

Then Leiningen remembered that in an outhouse nearby were two old disused fire engines. Spry as never before in their lives, the peons dragged them out of the shed, connected their pumps to the cistern, uncoiled and laid the hose. They were just in time to aim a stream of petrol at a column of ants that had already crossed and drive them back down the incline into the ditch. Once more an oily girdle surrounded the garrison, once more it was possible to hold the position—for the moment.

It was obvious, however, that this last resource meant only the postponement of defeat and death. A few of the peons fell on their knees and began to pray; others, shrieking insanely, fired their revolvers at the black, advancing masses, as if they felt their despair was pitiful enough to sway fate itself to mercy.

At length, two of the men's nerves broke: Leiningen saw a naked Indian leap over the north side of the petrol trench, quickly followed by a second. They sprinted with incredible speed towards the river. But their fleetness did not save them; long before they could attain the rafts, the enemy covered their bodies from head to foot.

In the agony of their torment, both sprang blindly into the wide river, where enemies no less sinister awaited them. Wild screams of mortal anguish informed the breathless onlookers that crocodiles and sword-toothed piranhas were no less ravenous than ants, and even nimbler in reaching their prey.

In spite of this bloody warning, more and more men showed they were making up their minds to run the blockade. Anything, even a fight midstream against alligators, seemed better than powerlessly waiting for death to come and slowly consume their living bodies.

Leiningen flogged his brain till it reeled. Was there nothing on earth could sweep this devil's spawn back into the hell from which it came?

Then out of the inferno of his bewilderment rose a terrifying inspiration. Yes, one hope remained, and one alone. It might be possible to dam the great river completely, so that its waters would fill not only the water ditch but overflow into the entire gigantic "saucer" of land in which lay the plantation.

The far bank of the river was too high for the waters to escape that way. The stone breakwater ran between the river and the plantation; its only gaps occurred where the "horseshoe" ends of the water ditch passed into the river. So its waters would not only be forced to inundate into the plantation, they would also be held there by the breakwater until they rose to its own high level. In half an hour, perhaps even earlier, the plantation and its hostile army of occupation would be flooded.

The ranch house and outbuildings stood upon rising ground. Their foundations were higher than the breakwater, so the flood would not reach them. And any remaining ants trying to ascend the slope could be repulsed by petrol.

It was possible—yes, if one could only get to the dam! A distance of nearly two miles lay between the ranch house and the weir—two miles of ants. Those two peons had managed only a fifth of that distance at the cost of their lives. Was there an Indian daring enough after that to run the gauntlet five times as far? Hardly likely; and if there were, his prospect of getting back was almost nil.

No, there was only one thing for it, he'd have to make the attempt himself; he might just as well be running as sitting still, anyway, when the ants finally got him. Besides, there *was* a bit of a chance. Perhaps the ants weren't so almighty, after all; perhaps he had allowed the mass suggestion of that evil black throng to hypnotize him, just as a snake fascinates and overpowers.

The ants were building their bridges. Leiningen got up on a chair. "Hey, lads, listen to me!" he cried. Slowly and listlessly, from all sides of the trench, the men began to shuffle towards him, the apathy of death already stamped on their faces.

"Listen, lads!" he shouted. "You're frightened of those beggars, but you're a damn sight more frightened of me, and I'm proud of you. There's still a chance to save our lives—by flooding the plantation from the river. Now one of you might manage to get as far as the weir—but he'd never come back. Well, I'm not going to let you try it; if I did I'd be worse than one of those ants. No, I called the tune, and now I'm going to pay the piper.

"The moment I'm over the ditch, set fire to the petrol. That'll allow time for the flood to do the trick. Then all you have to do is wait here all snug and quiet till I'm back. Yes, I'm coming back, trust me"—he grinned—"when I've finished my slimming-cure."

He pulled on high leather boots, drew heavy gauntlets over his hands, and stuffed the spaces between breeches and boots, gauntlets and arms, shirt and neck, with rags soaked in petrol. With close-fitting mosquito goggles he shielded his eyes, knowing too well the ants' dodge of first robbing their victim of sight. Finally, he plugged his nostrils and ears with cotton-wool, and let the peons drench his clothes with petrol.

He was about to set off, when the old Indian medicine-man came up to him; he had a wondrous salve, he said, prepared from a species of chafer whose odor was intolerable to ants. Yes, this odor protected these chafers from the attacks of even the most murderous ants. The Indian smeared the boss's boots, his gauntlets, and his face over and over with the extract.

Leiningen then remembered the paralyzing effect of ants' venom, and the Indian gave him a gourd full of the medicine he had administered to the bitten peon at the water ditch. The planter drank it down without noticing its bitter taste; his mind was already at the weir.

He started off towards the northwest corner of the trench. With a bound he was over—and among the ants.

The beleaguered garrison had no opportunity to watch Leiningen's race against death. The ants were climbing the inner bank again—the lurid ring of petrol blazed aloft. For the fourth time that day the reflection from the fire shone on the sweating faces of the imprisoned men, and on the reddish-black cuirasses of their oppressors. The red and blue, dark-edged flames leaped vividly now, celebrating what? The funeral pyre of the four hundred, or of the hosts of destruction?

Leiningen ran. He ran in long, equal strides, with only one thought, one sensation, in his being—he *must* get through. He dodged all trees and shrubs; except for the split seconds his soles touched the ground the ants should have no opportunity to alight on him. That they would get to him soon, despite the salve on his boots, the petrol in his clothes, he realized only too well, but he knew even more surely that he must, and that he would, get to the weir.

Apparently the salve was some use after all; not until he reached halfway did he feel ants under his clothes, and a few on his face. Mechanically, in his stride, he struck at them, scarcely conscious of their bites. He saw he was drawing appreciably nearer the weir—the distance grew less and less—sank to five hundred—three—two—one hundred yards.

Then he was at the weir and gripping the ant-hulled wheel. Hardly had he seized it when a horde of infuriated ants flowed over his hands, arms and shoulders. He started the wheel—before it turned once on its axis the swarm covered his face. Leiningen strained like a madman, his lips pressed tight; if he opened them to draw breath . . .

He turned and turned; slowly the dam lowered until it reached the bed of the river. Already the water was overflowing the ditch. Another minute, and the river was pouring through the near-by gap in the breakwater. The flooding of the plantation had begun.

Leiningen let go the wheel. Now, for the first time, he realized he was coated from head to foot with a layer of ants. In spite of the petrol his clothes were full of them, several had got to his body or were clinging to his face. Now that he had completed his task, he felt the smart raging over his flesh from the bites of sawing and piercing insects.

Frantic with pain, he almost plunged into the river. To be ripped and splashed to shreds by piranhas? Already he was running the return journey, knocking ants from his gloves and jacket, brushing them from his bloodied face, squashing them to death under his clothes.

One of the creatures bit him just below the rim of his goggles; he managed to tear it away, but the agony of the bite and its etching acid drilled into the eye nerves; he saw now through circles of fire into a milky mist, then he ran for a time almost blinded, knowing that if he once tripped and fell . . . The old Indian's brew didn't seem much good; it weakened the poison a bit, but didn't get rid of it. His heart pounded as if it would burst; blood roared in his ears; a giant's fist battered his lungs.

Then he could see again, but the burning girdle of petrol appeared infinitely far away; he could not last half that distance. Swift-changing pictures flashed through his head, episodes in his life, while in another part of his brain a cool and impartial onlooker informed this ant-blurred, gasping, exhausted bundle named Leiningen that such a rushing panorama of scenes from one's past is seen only in the moment before death.

A stone in the path . . . too weak to avoid it . . . the planter stumbled and collapsed. He tried to rise . . . he must be pinned under a rock . . . it was impossible . . . the slightest movement was impossible. . . .

Then all at once he saw, starkly clear and huge, and, right before his eyes, furred with ants, towering and swaying in its death agony, the pampas stag. In six minutes—gnawed to the bones. God, he *couldn't* die like that! And something outside him seemed to drag him to his feet. He tottered. He began to stagger forward again.

Through the blazing ring hurtled an apparition which, as soon as it reached the ground on the inner side, fell full length and did not move. Leiningen, at the moment he made that leap through the flames, lost consciousness for the first time in his life. As he lay there, with glazing eyes and lacerated face, he appeared a man returned from the grave. The peons rushed to him, stripped off his clothes, tore away the ants from a body that seemed almost one open wound; in some paces the bones were showing. They carried him into the ranch house.

As the curtain of flames lowered, one could see in place of the illimitable host of ants an extensive vista of water. The thwarted river had swept over the plantation, carrying with it the entire army. The water had collected and mounted in the great "saucer," while the ants had in vain attempted to reach the hill on which stood the ranch house. The girdle of flames held them back.

And so imprisoned between water and fire, they had been delivered into the annihilation that was their god. And near the farther mouth of the water ditch, where the stone mole had its second gap, the ocean swept the lost battalions into the river, to vanish forever.

The ring of fire dwindled as the water mounted to the petrol trench, and quenched the dimming flames. The inundation rose higher and higher: because its outflow was impeded by the timber and underbrush it had carried along with it, its surface required some time to reach the top of the high stone breakwater and discharge over it the rest of the shattered army.

It swelled over ant-stippled shrubs and bushes, until it washed against the foot of the knoll whereon the besieged had taken refuge. For a while an alluvium of ants tried again and again to attain this dry land, only to be repulsed by streams of petrol back into the merciless flood.

Leiningen lay on his bed, his body swathed from head to foot in bandages. With fomentations and salves, they had managed to stop the bleeding, and had dressed his many wounds. Now they thronged around him, one question in every face. Would he recover? "He won't die," said the old man who had bandaged him, "if he doesn't want to."

The planter opened his eyes. "Everything in order?" he asked.

"They're gone," said his nurse. "To hell." He held out to his master a gourd full of a powerful sleeping draught. Leiningen gulped it down.

"I told you I'd come back," he murmured, "even if I am a bit streamlined." He grinned and shut his eyes. He slept.

THE SEA RAIDERS

H. G. WELLS

ALONG WITH JULES VERNE, Herbert George Wells (1866–1946) was one of the first and greatest of all writers of science fiction, though he disliked being thought of as such, claiming that the works were merely a conduit for his social ideas. Wells began his adult life as a scientist, and might, with a bit more encouragement, have made a successful career as a biologist, but instead was offered work as a journalist and quickly began to produce fiction. His prolific writing career was loosely divided into three eras, but it is only the novels and short stories of the first, when he wrote fantastic and speculative fiction, that are much remembered today. Such early titles as *The Time Machine* (1895), *The Island of Doctor Moreau* (1896), *The Invisible Man* (1897), and *The War of the Worlds* (1898) are all milestones of the genre; they also all feature Wells's dim view of mankind, a perspective that led him to join the socialist Fabian Society. He turned to more realistic fiction after the turn of the century with such highly regarded (at the time) novels as *Kipps* (1905), *Ann Veronica* (1909), *Tono-Bungay* (1909), and *Marriage* (1912). The majority of his works over the last three decades of his life were both fiction and nonfiction books reflecting his political and social views—as dated, unreadable, and insignificant as they are misanthropic.

More than two dozen films have been based on Wells's novels, with countless others using them as uncredited sources. Among the most famous are the classic *The Invisible Man* (1933), *Things to Come* (1936), *The First Men in the Moon* (1919 and 1964), *The Island of Dr. Moreau* (1977 and 1996, more capably filmed as *Island of Lost Souls* in 1932), *The War of the Worlds* (1953 and 2005), and *The Time Machine* (1960 and 2002), among many others.

"The Sea Raiders" was originally published in the December 6, 1896, issue of the *Weekly Sun Literary Supplement;* it was first collected in book form in *The Plattner Story and Others* (London: Methuen, 1897).

THE SEA RAIDERS

H. G. WELLS

I

UNTIL THE EXTRAORDINARY affair at Sidmouth, the peculiar species *Haploteuthis ferox* was known to science only generically, on the strength of a half-digested tentacle obtained near the Azores, and a decaying body pecked by birds and nibbled by fish, found early in 1896 by Mr. Jennings, near Land's End.

In no department of zoölogical science, indeed, are we quite so much in the dark as with regard to the deep-sea cephalopods. A mere accident, for instance, it was that led to the Prince of Monaco's discovery of nearly a dozen new forms in the summer of 1895, a discovery in which the before-mentioned tentacle was included. It chanced that a cachalot was killed off Terceira by some sperm whalers, and in its last struggles charged almost to the Prince's yacht, missed it, rolled under, and died within twenty yards of his rudder. And in its agony it threw up a number of large objects, which the Prince, dimly perceiving they were strange and important, was, by a happy expedient, able to secure before they sank. He set his screws in motion, and kept them circling in the vortices thus created until a boat could be lowered. And these specimens were whole cephalopods and fragments of cephalopods, some of gigantic proportions, and almost all of them unknown to science!

It would seem, indeed, that these large and agile creatures, living in the middle depths of the sea, must, to a large extent, forever remain unknown to us, since under water they are too nimble for nets, and it is only by such rare, unlooked-for accidents that specimens can be obtained. In the case of *Haploteuthis ferox*, for instance, we are still altogether ignorant of its habitat, as ignorant as we are of the breeding-ground of the herring or the sea-ways of the salmon. And zoölogists are altogether at a loss to account for its sudden appearance on our coast. Possibly it was the stress of a hunger migration that drove it hither out of the deep. But it will be, perhaps, better to avoid necessarily inconclusive discussion, and to proceed at once with our narrative.

The first human being to set eyes upon a living *Haploteuthis*—the first human being to survive, that is, for there can be little doubt now that the wave of bathing fatalities and boating accidents that travelled along the coast of Cornwall and Devon in early May was due to this cause—was a retired tea-dealer of the name of Fison, who was stopping at a Sidmouth boarding-house. It was in the afternoon, and he was walking along the cliff path between Sidmouth and Ladram Bay. The cliffs in this direction are very high, but down the red face of them in one place a kind of ladder staircase has been made. He was near this when his attention was attracted by what at first he thought to be a cluster of birds struggling over a fragment of food that caught the sunlight, and glistened pinkish-white. The tide was right out, and this object was not only far below him, but remote across a broad waste of rock reefs covered with dark seaweed and interspersed with silvery shining tidal pools. And he was, moreover, dazzled by the brightness of the further water.

In a minute, regarding this again, he perceived that his judgment was in fault, for over this struggle circled a number of birds, jackdaws and gulls for the most part, the latter gleaming blindingly when the sunlight smote their wings, and they seemed minute in comparison with it. And his curiosity was, perhaps, aroused all the more strongly because of his first insufficient explanations.

As he had nothing better to do than amuse himself, he decided to make this object, whatever it was, the goal of his afternoon walk, instead of Ladram Bay, conceiving it might perhaps be a great fish of some sort, stranded by some chance, and flapping about in its distress. And so he hurried down the long steep ladder, stopping at intervals of thirty feet or so to take a breath and scan the mysterious movement.

At the foot of the cliff he was, of course, nearer his object than he had been; but, on the other hand, it now came up against the incandescent sky, beneath the sun, so as to seem dark and indistinct. Whatever was pinkish of it was now hidden by a skerry of weedy boulders. But he perceived that it was made up of seven rounded bodies distinct or connected, and that the birds kept up a constant croaking and screaming, but seemed afraid to approach it too closely.

Mr. Fison, torn by curiosity, began picking his way across the wave-worn rocks, and finding the wet seaweed that covered them thickly rendered them extremely slippery, he stopped, removed his shoes and socks, and rolled his trousers above his knees. His object was, of course, merely to avoid stumbling into the rocky pools about him, and perhaps he was rather glad, as all men are, of an excuse to resume, even for a moment, the sensations of his boyhood. At any rate, it is to this, no doubt, that he owes his life.

He approached his mark with all the assurance which the absolute security of this country against all forms of animal life gives its inhabitants. The round bodies moved to and fro, but it was only when he surmounted the skerry of boulders I have mentioned that he realised the horrible nature of the discovery. It came upon him with some suddenness.

The rounded bodies fell apart as he came into sight over the ridge, and displayed the pinkish object to be the partially devoured body of a human being, but whether of a man or woman he was unable to say. And the rounded bodies were new and ghastly-looking creatures, in shape somewhat resembling an octopus, with huge and very long and flexible tentacles, coiled copiously on the ground. The skin had a glistening texture, unpleasant to see, like shiny leather. The downward bend of the tentacle-surrounded mouth, the curious excrescence at the bend, the tentacles, and the large intelligent eyes, gave the creatures a grotesque suggestion of a face. They were the size of a fair-sized swine about the body, and the tentacles seemed to him to be many feet in length. There were, he thinks, seven or eight at least of the creatures. Twenty yards beyond them, amid the surf of the now returning tide, two others were emerging from the sea.

Their bodies lay flatly on the rocks, and their eyes regarded him with evil interest; but it does not appear that Mr. Fison was afraid, or that he realised that he was in any danger. Possibly his confidence is to be ascribed to the limpness of their attitudes. But he was horrified, of course, and intensely excited and indignant, at such revolting creatures preying upon human flesh. He thought they had chanced upon a drowned body. He shouted to them, with the idea of driving them off, and finding they did not budge, cast about him, picked up a big rounded lump of rock, and flung it at one.

And then, slowly uncoiling their tentacles, they all began moving towards him—creeping at first deliberately, and making a soft purring sound to each other.

In a moment Mr. Fison realised that he was in danger. He shouted again, threw both his boots, and started off, with a leap, forthwith. Twenty yards off he stopped and faced about, judging them slow, and behold! the tentacles of their leader were already pouring over the rocky ridge on which he had just been standing!

At that he shouted again, but this time not threatening, but a cry of dismay, and began jumping, striding, slipping, wading across the uneven expanse between him and the beach. The tall red cliffs seemed suddenly at a vast distance, and he saw, as though they were creatures in another world, two minute workmen engaged in the repair of the ladder-way, and little suspecting the race for life that was beginning below them. At one time he could hear the creatures splashing in the pools not a dozen feet behind him, and once he slipped and almost fell.

They chased him to the very foot of the cliffs, and desisted only when he had been joined by the workmen at the foot of the ladder-way up the cliff. All three of the men pelted them with stones for a time, and then hurried to the cliff top and along the path towards Sidmouth, to secure assistance and a boat, and to rescue the desecrated body from the clutches of these abominable creatures.

II

And, as if he had not already been in sufficient peril that day, Mr. Fison went with the boat to point out the exact spot of his adventure.

As the tide was down, it required a considerable detour to reach the spot, and when at last they came off the ladder-way, the mangled body had disappeared. The water was now running in, submerging first one slab of slimy rock and then another, and the four men in the boat—the workmen, that is, the boatman, and Mr. Fison— now turned their attention from the bearings off shore to the water beneath the keel.

At first they could see little below them, save a dark jungle of laminaria, with an occasional darting fish. Their minds were set on adventure, and they expressed their disappointment freely.

But presently they saw one of the monsters swimming through the water seaward, with a curious rolling motion that suggested to Mr. Fison the spinning roll of a captive balloon. Almost immediately after, the waving streamers of laminaria were extraordinarily perturbed, parted for a moment, and three of these beasts became darkly visible, struggling for what was probably some fragment of the drowned man. In a moment the copious olive-green ribbons had poured again over this writhing group.

At that all four men, greatly excited, began beating the water with oars and shouting, and immediately they saw a tumultuous movement among the weeds. They desisted to see more clearly, and as soon as the water was smooth, they saw, as it seemed to them, the whole sea bottom among the weeds set with eyes.

"Ugly swine!" cried one of the men. "Why, there's dozens!"

And forthwith the things began to rise through the water about them. Mr. Fison has since described to the writer this startling eruption out of the waving laminaria meadows. To him it seemed to occupy a considerable time, but it is probable that really it was an affair of a few seconds only. For a time nothing but eyes, and then he speaks of tentacles streaming out and parting the weed fronds this way and that. Then these things, growing larger, until at last the bottom was hidden by their intercoiling forms, and the tips of tentacles rose darkly here and there into the air above the swell of the waters.

One came up boldly to the side of the boat, and clinging to this with three of its sucker-set tentacles, threw four others over the gunwale, as if with an intention either of oversetting the boat or of clambering into it. Mr. Fison at once caught up the boathook, and, jabbing furiously at the soft tentacles, forced it to desist. He was struck in the back and almost pitched overboard by the boatman, who was using his oar to resist a similar attack on the other side of the boat. But the tentacles on either side at once relaxed their hold, slid out of sight, and splashed into the water.

"We'd better get out of this," said Mr. Fison, who was trembling violently. He went to the tiller, while the boatman and one of the workmen seated themselves and began rowing. The other workman stood up in the fore part of the boat, with the boathook, ready to strike any more tentacles that might appear. Nothing else seems to have been said. Mr. Fison had expressed the common feeling beyond amendment. In a hushed, scared mood, with faces white and drawn, they set about escaping from the position into which they had so recklessly blundered.

But the oars had scarcely dropped into the water before dark, tapering, serpentine ropes had bound them, and were about the rudder; and creeping up the sides of the boat with a looping motion came the suckers again. The men gripped their oars and pulled, but it was like trying to move a boat in a floating raft of weeds. "Help here!" cried the boatman, and Mr. Fison and the second workman rushed to help lug at the oar.

Then the man with the boathook—his name was Ewan, or Ewen—sprang up with a curse and began striking downward over the side, as far as he could reach, at the bank of tentacles that now clustered along the boat's bottom. And, at the same time, the two rowers stood up to get a better purchase for the recovery of their oars. The boatman handed his to Mr. Fison, who lugged desperately, and, meanwhile, the boatman opened a big clasp-knife, and leaning over the side of the boat, began hacking at the spiring arms upon the oar shaft.

Mr. Fison, staggering with the quivering rocking of the boat, his teeth set, his breath coming short, and the veins starting on his hands as he pulled at his oar, suddenly cast his eyes seaward. And there, not fifty yards off, across the long rollers of the incoming tide, was a large boat standing in towards them, with three women and a little child in it. A boatman was rowing, and a little man in a pink-ribboned straw hat and whites stood in the stern hailing them. For a moment, of course, Mr. Fison thought of help, and then he thought of the child. He abandoned his oar forthwith, threw up his arms in a frantic gesture, and screamed to the party in the boat to keep away "for God's sake!" It says much for the modesty and courage of Mr. Fison that he does not seem to be aware that there was any quality of heroism in his action at this juncture. The oar he had abandoned was at once drawn under, and presently reappeared floating about twenty yards away.

At the same moment Mr. Fison felt the boat under him lurch violently, and a hoarse scream, a prolonged cry of terror from Hill, the boatman, caused him to forget the party of excursionists altogether. He turned, and saw Hill crouching by the forward rowlock, his face convulsed with terror, and his right arm over the side and drawn tightly down. He gave now a succession of short, sharp cries, "Oh! oh! oh!—oh!" Mr. Fison believes that he must have been hacking at the tentacles below the water-line, and have been grasped by them, but, of course, it is quite impossible to say now certainly what had happened. The boat was heeling over, so that the gunwale was within ten inches of the water, and both Ewan and the other labourer were striking down into the water, with oar and boathook, on either side of Hill's arm. Mr. Fison instinctively placed himself to counterpoise them.

Then Hill, who was a burly, powerful man, made a strenuous effort, and rose almost to a standing position. He lifted his arm, indeed, clean out of the water. Hanging to it was a complicated tangle of brown ropes, and the eyes of one of the brutes that had hold of him, glaring straight and resolute, showed momentarily above the surface. The boat heeled more and more, and the green-brown water came pouring in a cascade over the side. Then Hill slipped and fell with his ribs across the side, and his arm and the mass of tentacles about it splashed back into the water. He rolled over; his boot kicked Mr. Fison's knee as that gentleman rushed forward to seize him, and in another moment fresh tentacles had whipped about his waist and neck, and after a brief, convulsive struggle, in which the boat was nearly capsized, Hill was lugged overboard. The boat righted with a violent jerk that all but sent Mr. Fison over the other side, and hid the struggle in the water from his eyes.

He stood staggering to recover his balance for a moment, and as he did so he became aware that the struggle and the inflowing tide had carried them close upon the weedy rocks again. Not four yards off a table of rock still rose in rhythmic movements above the in-wash of the tide. In a moment Mr. Fison seized the oar from Ewan, gave one vigorous stroke, then, dropping it, ran to the bows and leapt. He felt his feet slide over the rock, and, by a frantic effort, leapt again towards a further mass. He stumbled over this, came to his knees, and rose again.

"Look out!" cried someone, and a large drab body struck him. He was knocked flat into a tidal pool by one of the workmen, and as he went down he heard smothered, choking cries, that he believed at the time came from Hill. Then he found himself marvelling at the shrillness and variety of Hill's voice. Someone jumped over him, and a curving rush of foamy water poured over him, and passed. He scrambled to his feet dripping, and without looking seaward, ran as fast as his terror would let him shoreward. Before him, over the flat space of scattered rocks, stumbled the two workmen—one a dozen yards in front of the other.

He looked over his shoulder at last, and seeing that he was not pursued, faced about. He was astonished. From the moment of the rising of the cephalopods out of the water he had been acting too swiftly to fully comprehend his actions. Now it seemed to him as if he had suddenly jumped out of an evil dream.

For there were the sky, cloudless and blazing with the afternoon sun, the sea weltering under its pitiless brightness, the soft creamy foam of the breaking water, and the low, long, dark ridges of rock. The righted boat floated, rising and falling gently on the swell about a dozen yards from shore. Hill and the monsters, all the stress and tumult of that fierce fight for life, had vanished as though they had never been.

Mr. Fison's heart was beating violently; he was throbbing to the finger-tips, and his breath came deep.

There was something missing. For some seconds he could not think clearly enough what this might be. Sun, sky, sea, rocks—what was it? Then he remembered the boatload of excursionists. It had vanished. He wondered whether he had imagined it. He turned, and saw the two workmen standing side by side under the projecting masses of the tall pink cliffs. He hesitated whether he should make one last attempt to save the man Hill. His physical excitement seemed to desert him suddenly, and leave him aimless and helpless. He turned shoreward, stumbling and wading towards his two companions.

He looked back again, and there were now two boats floating, and the one farthest out at sea pitched clumsily, bottom upward.

III

So it was *Haploteuthis ferox* made its appearance upon the Devonshire coast. So far, this has been its most serious aggression. Mr. Fison's account, taken together with the wave of boating and bathing casualties to which I have already alluded, and the absence of fish from the Cornish coasts that year, points clearly to a shoal of these voracious deep-sea monsters prowling slowly along the sub-tidal coastline. Hunger migration has, I know, been suggested as the force that drove them hither; but, for my own part, I prefer to believe the alternative theory of Hemsley. Hemsley holds that a pack or shoal of these creatures may have become enamoured of human flesh by the accident of a foundered ship sinking among them, and have wandered in search of it out of their accustomed zone; first waylaying and following ships, and so coming to our shores in the wake of the Atlantic traffic. But to discuss Hemsley's cogent and admirably-stated arguments would be out of place here.

It would seem that the appetites of the shoal were satisfied by the catch of eleven people—

for, so far as can be ascertained, there were ten people in the second boat, and certainly these creatures gave no further signs of their presence off Sidmouth that day. The coast between Seaton and Budleigh Salterton was patrolled all that evening and night by four Preventive Service boats, the men in which were armed with harpoons and cutlasses, and as the evening advanced, a number of more or less similarly equipped expeditions, organised by private individuals, joined them. Mr. Fison took no part in any of these expeditions.

About midnight excited hails were heard from a boat about a couple of miles out at sea to the south-east of Sidmouth, and a lantern was seen waving in a strange manner to and fro and up and down. The nearer boats at once hurried towards the alarm. The venturesome occupants of the boat—a seaman, a curate, and two schoolboys—had actually seen the monsters passing under their boat. The creatures, it seems, like most deep-sea organisms, were phosphorescent, and they had been floating, five fathoms deep or so, like creatures of moonshine through the blackness of the water, their tentacles retracted and as if asleep, rolling over and over, and moving slowly in a wedge-like formation towards the south-east.

These people told their story in gesticulated fragments, as first one boat drew alongside and then another. At last there was a little fleet of eight or nine boats collected together, and from them a tumult, like the chatter of a marketplace, rose into the stillness of the night. There was little or no disposition to pursue the shoal, the people had neither weapons nor experience for such a dubious chase, and presently—even with

a certain relief, it may be—the boats turned shoreward.

And now to tell what is perhaps the most astonishing fact in this whole astonishing raid. We have not the slightest knowledge of the subsequent movements of the shoal, although the whole south-west coast was now alert for it. But it may, perhaps, be significant that a cachalot was stranded off Sark on June 3rd. Two weeks and three days after this Sidmouth affair, a living *Haploteuthis* came ashore on Calais sands. It was alive, because several witnesses saw its tentacles moving in a convulsive way. But it is probable that it was dying. A gentleman named Pouchet obtained a rifle and shot it.

That was the last appearance of a living *Haploteuthis*. No others were seen on the French coast. On the 15th of June a dead body, almost complete, was washed ashore near Torquay, and a few days later a boat from the Marine Biological station, engaged in dredging off Plymouth, picked up a rotting specimen, slashed deeply with a cutlass wound. How the former had come by its death it is impossible to say. And on the last day of June, Mr. Egbert Caine, an artist, bathing near Newlyn, threw up his arms, shrieked, and was drawn under. A friend bathing with him made no attempt to save him, but swam at once for the shore. This is the last fact to tell of this extraordinary raid from the deeper sea. Whether it is really the last of these horrible creatures it is, as yet, premature to say. But it is believed, and certainly it is to be hoped, that they have returned now, and returned for good, to the sunless depths of the middle seas, out of which they have so strangely and so mysteriously arisen.

ISLAND PARADISE

LESTER DENT

WHILE WORKING as a Western Union telegraph operator, Lester Dent (1904–1959) sold his first story to a pulp magazine for the small fortune (by the standards of the time) of $450; it was published in the September 1929 issue of *Top-Notch Magazine*. An action-adventure story titled "Pirate Cay," it has no relation to "Hell Cay" other than the similarity of title. Soon after that first sale, Dent moved to New York for a full-time job writing for Dell Publishing. When Street & Smith planned to replicate the success it had had with *The Shadow*, it hired Dent to develop *Doc Savage* under the house name Kenneth Robeson. Dent could have been cast to play the "Man of Bronze" himself—he was over six feet two inches tall, weighed more than two hundred pounds, and was a polymath who had acted variously as a pilot, radio operator, architect, plumber, electrician, and draftsman. *Doc Savage*, first published in March 1933, lasted for seventeen years and 181 issues, of which Dent wrote 159. He wrote for other pulp magazines as well, most famously the two stories about Oscar Sail published in *Black Mask* in 1936. In addition to the Doc Savage adventure series and his other short stories for the pulps, Dent later wrote a handful of novels, including *Lady to Kill* (1946), *Lady Afraid* (1948), *Lady So Silent* (1951), and *Lady in Peril* (1959).

A draft of "Hell Cay" was produced as early as 1930, but it remained unsold. After spending two years sailing in the Caribbean and among the Florida Keys on his schooner, the *Albatross*, Dent rewrote the story in 1939. While it bears some similarities to "The Frozen Buddha," a pulp story he published in 1930, "Hell Cay" has never before been published.

HELL CAY

LESTER DENT

CHAPTER I

IT WAS JANUARY in the Caribbean, with tropical days like brazen brass in Jamaica, when Carse paid off his parachute jumper and his ticket seller and watched them take the next boat north. Carse stayed. He hadn't thought it necessary to tell the boys he didn't have enough money left to buy himself a ticket.

Carse had no idea he was waving a red flag in front of a bull called disaster. He merely thought he'd stay and try to sell his planes. Try to salvage a little out of failure.

For three weeks, he kept the two planes on an empty stretch of Jamaican beach while he vainly hunted for buyers. It was a little lonesome. Fortunately, there was food to be had—you just fished or climbed trees for it. And it didn't cost anything to sleep on the beach.

It was a good chance to catch up on his swimming, and he did a lot of that. Pete Carse, in swimming trunks, was somewhat startling, so much so that he had always been reluctant to take a dip on a public beach. People stared at him. He disliked being stared at. His torso was tremendously muscled; there were sinews that stood out in knots on his arms and in ridges across his stomach. They were the muscles of an exhibitionist. Carse had made his living, at one time, in that fashion. He had made as high as a thousand a week in vaudeville. But there were tough times, so he went with a circus for less—much less—

money. Then burlesque houses. And finally carnivals. A muscle-head in a carnival. Carse had sense enough to quit. His few thousand dollars, saved by the frugal, clean living to which a professional acrobat must submit, had been expended piling up hours for a transport pilot's license and flying two elderly planes. He was going to establish an inter-island air line in the Caribbean.

So now he was broke.

One night he went to sleep feeling depressed.

He awakened suddenly, thinking at first that he had an ache in the back of his neck. Then he sensed what the ache was.

The man holding the gun muzzle against Carse's neck was a wizened Carib dressed in a dirty cotton shirt and the remains of blue denim dungarees.

The Carib said: "Sit still! Take her easy!"

Carse swallowed twice, not without difficulty. Several more men stood nearby.

"Shall I shoot 'im now, Cap'n Largo?" asked the Carib.

"Ain't safe," growled Captain Largo. "Pot him when we take off."

Captain Largo was a colossus; his weight must have been close to three hundred pounds. His head was a dwarfed tangerine that squatted on his bulging shoulders without the formality of much neck, and he had no eyebrows, beard, or hair. A tangled brush of black hair covered his bare arms and crowded up around his neck like fur. His dirty flannel trousers bulged alarmingly at the leg seams, and his sagging paunch was additionally propped up by two huge revolvers thrust inside his belt.

If I was casting a pirate for a play, Carse thought, I would hire him.

Suddenly a gust of profanity erupted nearby.

"Damn your black hides!" the voice gasped. "You can't get away with this."

Carse turned his head. Back under the royal palms which fringed the beach, two ragged Carib blacks were dragging the writhing figure of a white man toward the water.

Carse concluded they were going to put the man on his amphibian. The craft had been cut loose from its mooring buoy and run close inshore. Four men held her there. The plane's tail structure was a high spidery shadow between Carse and the reefs where the surf squashed.

Carse turned his head again. There was no movement about the *Widow*, the little three-place biplane that had been converted into a seaplane by the substitution of pontoons. The *Widow* was snubbed to an anchor buoy a hundred yards down the beach, fifty yards out from shore.

The captive cursed, lashed out suddenly. The Carib with the gun shifted his gaze momentarily. Carse took hold of the native's arms and made them break, with crunching sounds.

Carse came to his feet, levered the screeching Carib upward, and threw him with the same movement. The Carib struck Largo, who sat down heavily.

Carse knocked Largo prone, then fell on him. He felt Largo's muscles, like big snakes, writhing under him.

"Steal my plane, will you!" Carse gritted.

The prisoner—the man they had been going to put on the plane—wrenched free. He bolted for the fringe of silver-boled royal palms with their girdles of oleanders and poinsettias. The man was little more than an emaciated scare-crow, with a face burned a faded black by the tropical sun.

A Carib tugged at a sheathed knife thrust under his belt, got it free, flexed his arm to throw.

Carse grabbed the gun which had dropped from Largo's nerveless fingers and hurled it. The weapon struck the woolly head of the native and exploded. Native and gun fell to the sand.

Carse got up and charged, and his fist caught the remaining native as the fellow sought to dodge. The man fell. Carse went on after the scuttling figure of the white man, pausing only to scoop up the revolver.

Suddenly shots made hollow sounds in the hot, steam-filled night. They came in a procession, spewing, vicious. A submachine gun or one of those new auto-rifles.

The fleeing prisoner made a coughing noise and became a flailing mess of arms and legs on the ground.

"Damn!" Carse groaned.

He caught up the fallen captive, dragged him under cover. Lead tore at leafage like savage hail. Bullets made flute noises, ricocheting off the ivory boles of the royal palms.

Carse waited with the revolver he had picked up. At length he fired, once. He didn't get the man named Largo, but he must have scared the fellow badly, for Largo barked out orders, and they ran to Carse's amphibian.

Carse emptied his gun at them, but got no satisfaction except a great deal of profanity.

Blades of amphibian propellers jerked spasmodically, vanished in whirling speed. The auto-rifle kept emitting its gobbling roar.

The amphibian left the surface of the bay, volleyed along gathering flying speed; then the pilot banked recklessly, courted disaster with one wing tip almost cutting the water.

Carse nudged the stridently breathing form of the prisoner. "They're gettin' away!" he complained. "With my plane."

The other made no answer. Carse peered at

him, then caught the man under the arms and dragged him to moonlight.

That the man had been shot through the lungs was indicated by scarlet bubbles breaking out of the bullet hole. The man listened to the fleeing amphibian, tried to curse, and gagged on a bubbling crimson flood.

"Easy," Carse warned.

The wounded man pulled himself to his knees. He plunged two thin, parchment-skinned fingers deep inside his mouth, deliberately making himself be sick. Carse tried to stop him.

"Cut it out," the man said. "This is important."

After a while, he was holding a small rubber-covered lump that had come out. He mumbled something about "lucky to get it out that way."

"Never occurred to 'em to pump out my stomach," he added.

"Take it easy," Carse said. "I'll get you to the Port Royal hospital. Only a few miles."

He ripped off his shirt, with some misgivings about its sanitary qualities, and set about stemming the flow of blood. There was only one bullet hole, in front, which meant the slug had hung somewhere in the other man's scrawny chest. The wounded man was gagging repeatedly, making horrible gurgling sounds.

"Blasted bullet felt like a dum-dum," the man gasped.

He had the small rubber-covered lump clenched in his talon-like right hand. He eyed Carse intently.

He said, "You're a queer-lookin' chap. Who—what are you?"

"Nobody important," Carse said.

The man said, "I think I'm gonna die in a minute. Who are you?"

"A flier," Carse told him. "Name of Peter Carse."

"That your plane they got?"

Carse said, "Yes," and swore bitterly.

"I'm Agile Sharp," gasped the wounded man. "You ain't never heard of me." He began coughing again. The spasm lasted for fully a minute. Then he extended his hand.

"Take it," he said.

Peter Carse took the rubber-covered lump. It was perhaps three-quarters of an inch square. The covering of rubber resembled a piece torn from a child's toy balloon, and it was tied round with silk thread.

"You'll be in a hospital before long," Carse began. "Better keep this yourself."

"You want your plane back?"

"Well—hell yes."

"Place where they'll take it is in here." Agile Sharp's voice was all whispering agony now. He tried to cough again, sounding strangled.

Carse dropped beside the man and discovered he could barely hear words off the taut lips.

Later, Carse stood up and stared at the line of surf that glowed weirdly with sea fire. The man had died.

Several times he turned the diminutive rubber-covered packet in his hands. He took out matches and lighted a small fire of dry stuff that gave light. Then he took the packet and opened it.

CHAPTER II
THE UNEXPECTED

Carse circled the *Widow* over the island. As he looked downward, he suspected his eyes had grown big. It was a strange island. As he had flown toward the place, he had noticed a wide strip of dazzling white beach, and back of that a narrow band of mangrove swamp. Sitting in the middle of the swamp was a formation startlingly like a great block of stone—cliffs that rose steep and forbidding to vanish into a blanket of fog. The fog—it might have been termed a low-lying cloud—covered island and sea. Carse had been flying under it.

He got out the chart that had been inside the rubber-covered packet. The chart was hardly six inches square. He studied it.

There was not much doubt that this was the

island depicted on the chart; the latitude and longitude figures were the same.

There were really two drawings on the chart, which puzzled Carse. The first design was that of this island, an ordinary island, the only distinguishing feature being a greatly oversized bay that was completely landlocked except for an entrance that was winding and extremely narrow.

The second drawing was the peculiar one. It looked unlike any island Carse had ever seen, being an intricate bunch of marks, all straight lines, terminating in a square black patch. It was more like a geometrical figure than anything else. For a while, Carse had thought someone must have merely taken a pen and doodled on the corner of the map. Yet the thing was so carefully done that it must have some meaning.

Carse frowned. The whole affair was mysterious and he could not understand any of it, except that his plane had been stolen. As a matter of fact, the plane theft was the only item that really concerned him. He wanted his plane back. He couldn't afford to lose it.

He began searching the island, hoping to locate his ship.

It was growing dark. The heavy fog seemed to be closing down, and it was dangerous to prowl around over the sea with night coming on. He would have to land.

The decision to land was hardly made when he discovered the first sign of life about the place. Directly below! A human figure! Sprawled on the beach, an arm waving feebly.

Carse yanked the *Widow* about in a second circle. It was hard to be certain by the fleeting glimpse he had been able to get, but he did not believe the form sprawled on the beach was one of those involved in the theft of the amphibian. Not Largo. Nor any of the Caribs.

He determined again to land. The gesturing of the figure on the beach unmistakably had been a summons for help.

The *Widow*'s eggshell-thin floats smacked the surface a little too solidly; spray poured over the cockpit in a cloud. "Damned nervousness!" Carse growled as he hauled spasmodically on the

stick and the throttle. He got the ship back on even keel, then shut off the ignition and clambered out on the pontoons.

The figure on the beach did not move now. It lay grotesquely. A small form, pitifully twisted.

Carse dropped overside in water waist deep. He paused only to fish an automatic pistol out of a map pocket.

Then he walked up on the beach—and found himself looking into the twin maws of a double-barreled shotgun.

The hands that held the gun were small, and looked capable. She had been lying on the gun.

"Drop it!" she ordered sharply.

Pete Carse let the automatic fall, tried not to blink his astonishment.

She was a small girl, curved delectably in the right places, it was obvious, even though she wore a man's white ducks, which were torn and stiff with black mud. Around her waist was a web hunting belt that was knotty with shotgun shells.

Just how pretty she was, Carse could not tell. Her face was horribly sunburned. On her forehead and cheeks the skin had blistered, and was peeling off in papery, ragged patches. Her lips were cracked. But her eyes were large and a fascinating shade of brown.

She jammed the barrel of the big weapon into his back and began to search him.

"I could be a friend," Carse said.

The girl set her cracked lips grimly, answered nothing. She flicked open his billfold, saw the pilot's license and four one-dollar bills, then replaced it. Then she found the map in the pocket of his shirt. She jumped as though hit.

"You're one of them!" The girl's voice was filled with loathing.

Carse said hotly, "Somebody stole my plane. A man named Largo!"

"I don't fool easy," the girl said.

Carse eyed her. She thought he was an enemy, and apparently her opinions did not change easily.

"Suppose you tell me what it is all about," he suggested.

Her stare was scornful. "So now Largo changes his methods," she said grimly. "He sends around an innocent to softsoap me."

"But—"

"Back up!" the girl said. "Get the motor of your plane started. You're taking me away from here!"

Carse did not move; he was thinking. The girl knew Largo, so his amphibian might have touched this island, and the place would therefore be the island shown on the chart. But all the rest of it baffled him.

"Who is Agile Sharp?" Carse asked.

He was not prepared for the change in the girl—the way her eyes widened and her lips quivered suddenly.

At this juncture, a shot crashed, the bullet coming so close that Carse could not tell whether bullet snap or gun report was louder.

A man plunged out on the beach, a hulking monster of a man. Largo! He fired at them again, and there was no question about the bullet snap being louder.

Largo's rifle smacked a third time. The bullet dug up a vortex of sand under the girl's feet. She screamed, whirled, dived for the wall of jungle. She vanished in the heavy growth of foliage.

Carse snatched up the automatic she had made him drop, and headed for the fringe of jungle. He saw Largo fumble wildly at his pockets, evidently for cartridges. Carse halted and emptied the clip in his automatic at Largo. The big man lunged headlong for the bush and gained it, apparently unharmed.

Carse bolted for the jungle himself.

A dozen yards into the green tangle, Carse halted and listened. There was no sound; the calm was intense and oppressive, with no chatter of tropical life, none of the splashes of gaudy feathered color and raucous birdcalls usually so profuse. Heat was bringing perspiration through his skin in sticky beads.

The surrounding undergrowth was unbelievably thick, nests of gnarled mangroves being as thick as water grass and laced together with creepers, while the branches were webbed with lianas and grotesque aerial roots. Plant life underfoot was lush, fulsome, with tremendous leaves and stems that broke with rotten, squishy sounds.

Carse waited and nothing happened. It was getting much darker, the fog dropping lower. The jungle was becoming uneasy. And suddenly, somewhere out to sea, there was a rumble and lightning crawled jaggedly across the sky, not reaching the earth.

Rain came, a few drops at first, then in sheets and beating torrents. It poured down the steep slopes in floods, beating the fronds of the palms and the overlarge leaves wildly. Carse placed the automatic under his armpit to protect it from the water.

He stumbled over mangrove roots, became entangled in the branches. He tried to climb up higher among the boughs and progress through them in that fashion. It was almost impossible going. Once he fell and hung like a netted fish in the lianas and vines, struggling furiously to free himself.

The downpour of rain ended as suddenly as it had begun.

Carse turned back toward the beach, covering the last hundred feet on all fours, crawling a few feet at a time, pausing to listen. And then he lay very still.

There was a stranger on the beach. A big dark negro who stood at the edge of the tangle of mangroves and stunted palms. The man was big only as far as his bones went, Carse discovered when he peered more intently in the pale light. The fellow was dissolute-looking, flabby, and he wore only a pair of ragged dungarees. He had taken off his shirt and was wringing it.

The man's damp slick skin glistened like greasy ebony as he worked with his shirt.

There was a very modern-looking submachine gun cocked in the crotch of a mangrove near where he stood.

Carse maneuvered, then lunged for him and arrived before the fellow could reach the submachine gun. He tripped the big Carib, fell on him. They swapped some blows and Carse discovered his foe had almost no strength, and no will to use what little power he had. The man made mewing sounds of fright.

"Where's my plane?" Carse demanded. "And where's that girl?"

The Carib gulped, rolled eyes that were set in puffy sacs. Carse eased up on the man's throat.

"How I know?" the man gulped. "The *muchacha*? I not see her—or her devil! She scream—perhaps her devil get her and Largo both!"

"What were you doing?"

"Me? I am watchman, *señor*."

"How many others on guard?"

"None."

"Where's my plane?"

The prisoner rolled his eyes. "*Quién sabe!* Maybe the devil get it."

"What's this talk about a devil?"

The prisoner only shuddered and gurgled. He was very scared.

The little monoplane, the *Widow*, had survived the storm unharmed. Carse climbed onto the float and removed the main cable leading to each magneto, and placed the cables in a trouser pocket. Not a very effective attempt at putting the motor out of commission, he thought grimly, but it would take time for anyone to make repairs.

He secured the rifle and took the remaining automatic out of the forward cockpit.

"You're taking me to my plane!" he informed his prisoner. "And I'd be damn careful not to meet any friends if I was you."

The fellow stared at Carse and licked his lips. Finally he nodded without any enthusiasm whatever. "You gonna wish you hadn't," he mumbled.

Carse got the submachine gun from the mangrove fork.

"Let's make tracks," he said.

Now that the rain had ceased entirely, the calm was dead and oppressive. They covered several hundred yards and Carse began to take notice of something that was puzzling.

"The birds—why no birds?" he asked.

The prisoner peered about uneasily. "*Señor*, much here you do not know!" He looked at Carse and shuddered violently. "Smell, *señor*!"

Carse sniffed. He could detect an odor, or rather a stench; it was nauseating despite the fact that it was vague.

"Something dead," Carse said.

The prisoner turned and tried to go back. Carse jabbed him with the muzzle of the submachine gun.

"Little smell won't hurt you," he said grimly. "But a dose of lead might!"

"*Dios!*" muttered the Carib.

Carse said suspiciously, "Back up against that palm. Now—what's this all about?"

The Carib shrugged. "I am not know, *señor*. I have been work on boat that carry liquor to coast of your Florida. Smuggler you call him, no? Largo is own thees boat. One day he come here. I am stay on boat and cook while Largo ashore. *Dios!* I know nothing of what go on."

Carse said, "You're pretty dumb, or you're a damned liar."

They went ahead until abruptly the ground ceased to rise, and they stood on the rim of a downward slope that was almost a cliff. The canopy of leafage overhead was thick, making it impossible to see what lay beyond. The strange odor was stronger, oppressive.

Suddenly, the prisoner gave a loud moan of horror. He raised one arm, pointed. His eyes protruded. "*Dios!*" he moaned. "*Dios mío!*"

The captive whirled and bolted back the way they had come.

CHAPTER III
THE LAGOON OF DEAD SHIPS

The big native screamed shrilly as his bare toe hooked a vine, and he flopped headlong. Carse leaped, caught him in a flying tackle as the fellow tried to gain his feet. The fellow's fright was very real!

Carse muzzled his prisoner with a hand. "Cut that!"

Then Carse peered in the direction they had been headed, searching for the cause of the sudden outburst. Through an irregular opening, laced with blade-like palm fronds, he saw a bay. And it was the bay shown on the chart that had been rubber-wrapped.

Outwardly, it seemed just an ordinary island bay.

The strange, nauseating stench was reaching his nostrils in more overpowering volume. Carse wrinkled his nose. It had the sickening quality of decomposition. He became aware of another strange fact. Nowhere was there a sign of an insect. No humpbacked spiders, no land leeches that gorged themselves on blood and rolled aside like fat grubs, no red ants with bites that burned like electric sparks.

The prisoner shuddered again and his teeth chattered. Carse forced him forward, half dragging him, keeping the cold steel of the gun pressed against his neck. They reached the bay.

Mangroves grew out into black, unclean-looking water. Inches at a time, Carse worked ahead. The prisoner began moaning and Carse tightened his grip.

It became evident that the bay was what had ages ago been the interior of a volcanic cone. The steepness of the sides, the lava-like quality of the stone, the formation of the lagoon all contributed to that theory. A volcanic cone with a part of one side eroded away by the sea.

The prisoner broke into mumbling.

"Devil in the bay!" the fellow gasped.

But everything had vanished from Carse's mind, wiped away by his astonishment at what was protruding about the expanse of stinking water. Ships! There must have been scores of vessels. They lay in the shallows where they had sunk to the bottom near shore; some floated farther out. Here and there a rotting mast tip of a submerged craft protruded above the glazed surface.

Not fifty yards from where Carse crouched there was a sailing vessel, its masts standing gaunt and spidery, rigging draped in frayed ends and yards a-sag. Sails had been furled, but the rolls of fabric had rotted free and fallen to the decks. The hull timbers were weathered and agape. Paint was gone, woodwork cracked and twisted by exposure to the brazen tropical sun.

Alongside her lay a steel-hulled vessel, undoubtedly a yacht, for her lines were trim, masts slanting and obviously intended for appearance rather than service. Some paint still clung to her hull and superstructure, gray, with a banding of vermilion.

Carse ran his gaze swiftly over the lagoon. He was having difficulty in breathing the steam-filled air with its overpowering stench of decaying ships and rotting rigging. His amazement grew. Some of these ships were of other centuries! There were old square-riggers of the nineteenth century, even a fat high-pooped galleon or two.

Then he saw his amphibian. The plane lay in the bay, not far from the opening itself.

"Get going," Carse ordered the black. They began to skirt the lagoon, toward the spot where the amphibian lay.

Carse changed his course abruptly, got close to the hull of a dead craft that seemed to be of the sixteenth century. He worked along the lagoon edge. It had occurred to him that there might be danger of being seen.

He was curious about the weird ghostly wrecks. He waded out, the water coming up gradually under his arms and around his neck, water that was foul and loathsome. He settled the problem of the prisoner by tearing strips from the black's own shirt to bind the man's hands.

A dozen strokes with one hand, other hand holding the submachine gun and automatic pistol over his head to clear the water, carried Carse and his prisoner to the rust-eaten sides of the yachty-looking craft. It lay low in the water, so very low that Carse could close one hand over the rail. He hauled himself up the rust-scabbed hull.

The prisoner sputtered, gasped, got up a little water, and peered about. Horror spread over his face. Carse had to clamp a hand on the fellow's throat to stifle a scream.

On the decks of the yacht was a picture of long-dead violence and sudden death. Skeletons were scattered on the moldy deck. They lay with no regard to order, twisted into knots or with outstretched arm bones. Shoes, bits of cloth, a few finger bones, were strewn where they had been washed by tropical downpour. There were diving suits splayed grotesquely on the sun-blistered planking, like spectral monsters in the half-light of oncoming darkness. The round glass window in one of the domed helmets faced them, twisted horribly to one side. Something gleamed grisly and yellow behind the glass. Carse squinted. It was the skull of a man.

"But what on earth killed 'em?" Carse exploded.

The prisoner moaned; his words were almost incoherent. "Devil get us!"

In spite of himself, a shiver ran down Carse's spine.

"The devil with your devil!" he gritted. "I'm gonna look into this!"

He gagged the captive, then tied him to the rail of the boat, using his own shirt and the other's belt. Then he moved for the superstructure, stepping gingerly to avoid the grisly relics underfoot.

It was then that he made another curious discovery: there was no evidence of violence visible upon the skeletons. Nothing to show what had killed them. No smashed skulls, no broken bones.

The deck house hatch gaped, an opening that was black and malodorous. Carse glanced about, then stepped gingerly inside. Planking groaned, made a shrill rasping that riffled the short hairs along the back of his neck and edged his teeth. Gradually his eyes became accustomed to the dark.

The cabin was large and had evidently been a lounge. Beyond there was a corridor, with doors at intervals, some open, others closed. Carse tested one of the latter. The panel stuck stubbornly. He raised his fist to drive it through the rotting wood, then lowered it. There had come the sudden realization that he had strayed from the object which had brought him to the lagoon. His amphibian. Why was he wasting time exploring?

He retraced his steps, came up on deck again, felt glad to get away from the atmosphere of death that impregnated the foul interior.

"I'm beginning to feel like you do about this place," he announced. He walked over to remove the gag.

Then he jumped convulsively. His skin went icy.

The prisoner was now dead.

The man hung loose over the rail, his thick lips twisted into a grimace of stark horror, the eyes with their enormous whites distended. Fingers which had done the garroting had torn and compressed the rubbery flesh like a machine.

Carse looked away in horror, then stared incredulously. His other plane, the *Widow*, was now inside the lagoon!

CHAPTER IV
JOOL WAS SCARED

The little monoplane was beached not a score of fathoms from the huge amphibian. It could not—positively could not—have been there when Carse had gone below. The thing was weird, fantastic.

There had been no sound.

It was on a par with the rest of the things which had happened since he had been awakened so unpleasantly on the beach.

Carse took a step forward and a terrific weight struck him in the middle of the back. The impact bore him headlong to the deck. The submachine gun left his hand, bounced against the rotten rail, and dropped over the side. Carse twisted and landed on his side.

A huge, dark-skinned, beam-sized arm slid around his neck with deadly speed, shut off his wind.

Carse almost grunted with relief. There was only one assailant.

The fellow was a gigantic native, far larger than the flabby Carib whom Carse had just found throttled. The man's weight was a great deal more; he was taller, his frame more angular, without the blubbery layers of fat which had covered the muscles of the other.

The big fellow looked supremely confident as he got a grip on Carse's throat and clamped down. Carse shifted; his fingers, tapering and squarely blunt on the ends, clamped about the thick wrists. The big native's face instantly went stark. Tardily, he tried to drive a knee into the flier's middle. He groaned loudly as Carse struck him, and landed like a huge ebony spider on the weathered deck planks.

Carse did not again flail the flint-like hulk with his fists; a quick twist, into which he put every ounce of effort, and the black groveled on the deck under the combined agony of a double arm lock.

"Behave," he advised the black, "or I'll break both your arms."

He eased the pressure and the writhing subsided. Without relaxing vigilance, he searched the big form. There were no weapons.

The big native stared at him, muttered, "Never thought Ah'd have no trouble handlin' you."

The fellow wore worn belted duck trousers and a cotton shirt. Carse loosened the belt, jerked it off, and snugged it about the man's powerful wrists. The leather was as thick as a harness tug, fairly sure to hold.

"Now—who're *you*?" Carse asked sharply.

The native sawed his bound hands from side to side to ease the aching after-effects of the arm lock.

"Yassuh," he mumbled uneasily. "Dey calls me Jool."

"I don't mean that," Carse said impatiently. "Why did you jump me?"

Jool opened his thick-lipped gash of a mouth, seemed to reconsider, and abruptly closed it.

"You killed this fellow on deck?" Carse accused.

The other made no answer.

"How did my little plane get in here so suddenly?"

The other was an ebony mask of silence.

"How did all these ships get here?"

When the other did not answer, Carse jerked the prisoner to his feet.

Immediately, and for no apparent reason, the black looked toward shore, then emitted a hoarse bellow of terror. At the same time he flashed into life and ran. Carse collared him just as he rounded the deck house and sought to dive headlong over the rail.

"Leggo!" the fellow gasped.

"You stay right here!" Carse said grimly. "What's wrong with you?"

"Dis debbil place!" Jool mumbled.

"How you mean?"

Jool's not unintelligent features displayed mingled doubt and uncertainty, but mostly stark, undiluted fear.

"White boy, we both goin' kick bucket if we stays."

"Why?"

"Debbil comin'!"

Carse snorted, said, "You talk like you'd spent some time in the United States."

Jool looked at Carse's automatic and groaned. "Gun ain't gwine do you no good."

"Do you know where that girl is?" Carse demanded.

The man opened his mouth, a denial obviously on the tip of his tongue. He said nothing. Yet it was very plain that he knew something.

"If you'll take me to the girl, we'll leave this place," Carse offered after a moment's thought.

"Yassuh!"

The assent was explosive. The man was on his feet instantly.

The native bounded up on the rail, leaped sprawling into the water. He vanished, but was on the surface at once and swimming powerfully for the mangroves in spite of his bound arms, kicking up a great, boiling maelstrom with his big feet. He seemed to care nothing for the amount of noise he made.

Watching suspiciously, Carse ran along the rail to the bow, keeping abreast of the native. A glance overside showed him the yacht had been anchored; the thick chain, warty with rust, was in place. He lowered himself, hand over hand, then stroked in the wake of the prisoner.

Jool went through the tangle of mangroves with a terrific splashing of mud. He was breathing heavily, mumbling to himself and paying not the slightest attention to the amount of noise he made.

"Slow up!" Carse barked warningly. "And *quiet!*"

The moaned response came without a slackening in pace. "Nobody gonna hear us. And we gotta go 'way from this place mighty sudden! Debbil almost heah!"

They came out of the tangled mangroves to firmer ground, and Carse increased his pace and caught up with the lumbering native.

CHAPTER V
CAMP RAID

There was a loud rustling and ripping of leafage, and the increasing darkness rained half-naked, striking, clutching figures. Jool, who had been whimpering, now surprisingly made not a sound. He dived wildly into the brush and was gone. Someone, a white man, began striking at

Carse with the stock of a rifle. Then Largo's voice roared out, bellowing orders.

"Hell—it's that flier!" Largo yelled. "Get 'im!"

Carse fought furiously, but the steaming, odorous darkness seemed alive with grasping figures. The beam of a flashlight licked out, the incandescent glare hitting Carse in the eyes with agony that was intolerable. Somebody kicked him on the chin with a boot; flame came into his eyes, turned red and then purple.

He was stunned the barest instant, but the moment was his undoing. His arms were pinned and handcuffed. The men apparently had the steel bracelets ready.

"That damn native got away!" Largo's voice rumbled. "Why in hell didn't somebody drill him?"

So the native who talked Alabama English and who had fled was no friend of Largo's. Carse was surprised.

Largo was an American, Carse decided; the man's slang smacked of the States.

Carse was searched. They removed his automatic and found the wires he had removed from the magnetos of the *Widow's* motor; a loud grunt told him that someone recognized the cables for what they were.

"Walk!" Largo ordered. "To the beach. We'll talk as we go. What're you doing here?"

"Hunting for my plane."

"You find it?"

"Yes."

"The hell you did!" The big man's explosion was startled.

"The plane," Carse said grimly, "is in the lagoon."

"Hell—so that's where it went!" Largo's mutter was so genuinely amazed that Carse decided the fellow hadn't known the amphibian was inside the lagoon.

Carse said, "A native was murdered in the bay a few minutes ago."

Largo stared and swore. Obviously he hadn't known that, either.

Largo's amazement did not explain the mystery. What was Largo after? Where did the girl figure in the puzzle? And most baffling of all—what was the mystery of the dead ships? Carse scowled over the complications.

"The dead ships," Carse began, "what—"

"Shut up!" Largo snarled.

They worked downward through the steaming labyrinth of jungle, approaching the bay. They made glaring blades of light from powerful flashlights penetrate yards ahead and to the sides; the light disclosed an unbelievable maze of contorted jungle growth.

As for the men themselves, they were an unsavory crew. Seven of them, and Largo. Two had mahogany-hued skins and were short but incredibly wide and stocky. One was a mulatto, a tall and surly-looking thug. Two were flabby islanders. The remaining two were white men. The dark, brick-red flush of their faces ending in a sharply defined semicircle just above their eyes could have but one meaning—they had recently worn flying helmets. They must be Largo's plane pilots. Carse noted one of them carried the ignition cables in his pocket.

The little cavalcade reached the flat beach, turned sharply to the right. Largo's camp was less than a hundred yards farther on, under the frowning heights of the cliff face. Nearby, the glassy, squirming water seemed quite deep.

Two of the men scuttled into the bush, later to emerge with a bundle of rolled blankets and some cooking utensils.

"What has become of the girl?" Carse demanded.

Largo burst into a low rage of oaths and smashed the flier Carse a terrific blow with his fist. Carse fell, head and shoulders striking the brittle lava with a thudding jolt. Largo gurgled curses until he ran out of breath, then angrily tore up an armload of foliage from the nearby jungle and made himself a bed on the edge of the open space. All of the others followed his exam-

ple, with the exception of the man who was to stand guard.

The watchman snapped a pair of manacles on Carse's ankles, then lounged about, armed with an auto-rifle and two automatics.

The two men whom Carse had taken for fliers had bedded down apart from the others, not far from where Carse lay. Carse strained his ears in the jungle stillness, and after a time he heard the fliers whispering.

"When do we make the break, Spang?" one of them breathed.

The other flier whispered, "Not until midnight."

"You think Largo suspects anything?"

"He will," muttered the other, "if you don't stop blattin'."

The first flier turned restlessly. After that, there was only the moist, hot silence of a tropical night.

Carse went to work cautiously and tugged his handkerchief out of his hip pocket. He tore it in half—ripping a thread at a time to avoid attracting the guard's attention—and worked the pieces around the metal circlet, padding it so it would not cut into his flesh. In an emergency, he felt fairly certain he could snap the links. He had done a handcuff-breaking act once while muscle-heading with a carnival, and the cuffs had been real.

He had just finished the padding when the guard gave a faint, hissing gasp. The next instant his body vanished mysteriously into the thick wall of the jungle.

Carse stiffened. Then his tendons bunched and strained. The handcuff links broke with a sound that was brittle, like splintering glass. The sleeping men did not stir.

Carse waited for what seemed an age, though the interval was probably only a minute, before the body of the guard sank quietly into view, being lowered by a pair of immense arms that were as black as ebony. The guard had obviously been choked to unconsciousness. Carse watched. He made out a shadow, a great bulk of a shadow, crouched at the edge of the jungle.

He distinguished, after a time, a second crouching figure. When a pale streak of moonlight fell across the figure, he knew it was the girl. With her was Jool, the big dark native who spoke with an Alabaman accent. The girl and Jool were preparing to raid the camp, Carse decided.

Carse prepared to snatch the handcuff links and doubled up, muscles cording spasmodically. One of the steel circlets crackled loudly and snapped, but not before both rings had cut into his flesh. He lost no time. He came to his feet, running.

He heard the girl rap something that was angry. Jool, a hulking black giant, tore out of the wall of jungle, charging like a tornado. Largo and his sleeping men came to life. The clearing became a roaring vortex of noise and motion. Largo seemed to be squalling orders even before his little hairless eyes were open.

"Shoot that damn black!" Largo yelled. He did not wait for somebody else to execute the order but jerked out a huge revolver and fired from his hip. The bullet either hit the black giant and shocked him backward, or scared him so that he took flight. Jool stumbled a few yards and went into the sea, great arms and legs jerking horribly. A loud splash was audible as he struck the water.

Carse took advantage of the confusion to run to the edge of the jungle, grab the girl, and continue his flight.

"Shoot 'em!" Largo bawled. "Shoot 'em all!"

A submachine gun spewed; the hollow popping of automatics and revolvers joined in. Lead cut through the growth with deadly squealing.

Carse stumbled repeatedly, for the terrain was unbelievably rough. Soft, mushy earth and great, jagged fragments of upended lava made treacherous footing.

"We'll be out of range in a minute," he puffed after a time. "I'll head for the bay."

The slender form in his arms stiffened, then writhed, exhibiting a surprising amount of lithe strength. "No! It's certain death to do that!" the girl cried.

"Eh?"

"Not into the cove! We're already too close to it. We're in danger even now!"

"We stand a better chance if we head for the bay," he argued. "The planes are there."

"No, you don't understand! We would never make it!" The girl's words were an incoherent rush. "Turn to the right. Jool showed me a place where we will be safe."

Carse placed the girl on her feet.

"All right," he growled. "I'll trust you."

"You don't need to sound so skeptical!" the girl snapped. "We came to that camp in hopes of rescuing you. You bungled it—and caused the death of Jool, the only person who knows this horrible island."

Carse said, "I'm sorry. And I don't think Jool was killed."

Her tone changed. "We can't talk now," she whispered hurriedly. "Come on."

Carse remembered that nocturnal trip through the jungle for a long time, and it was something he would rather have forgotten. He was amazed at the quantity of clothing and hide he managed to leave hanging on thorns and sharp branches before they came to a cave.

The cave had probably been formed by a giant air bubble when the lava was in a molten state, Carse concluded. The walls and arched ceiling were smooth-glazed, although there was a pile of rubble at the entrance.

By the wavering, sickly flame of a ship's lantern which the girl had lit, Carse looked about him. Near one wall, he saw a blanket, and there were smoke-stained cooking utensils and a pine box which probably held provisions. Two rifles leaned against the stone walls.

The girl pointed at the rifles and said, "My father's guns. I have no ammunition for them."

"Your father?" Carse eyed her.

"Why, I'm Theresa Sharp," the girl said. "You knew that, didn't you?"

Carse shook his head. "I didn't know who you were. I don't know anything that goes on around here."

She stared at him. "You don't know my father?"

Carse started to shake his head, then considered. "What was his name—his first name?"

"Elman Sharp," the girl said. "But they called him Agile."

"Agile!" Carse winced, then wondered if his expression had showed what he felt. Evidently it had, for the girl stared at him.

"You *have* heard of him!" She stepped forward suddenly and grasped his arm. "What has happened to him?"

Carse didn't like the job, but he told her what had happened, from the moment of his rude awakening on the beach. He made the death of her father seem less gory than it had been. Because it was necessary to round out the story and convince Theresa Sharp that his own motives were good, he brought in enough of his own troubles to convince her that he was here because he had been following his stolen plane. The girl heard him through in dry-eyed silence, her face gradually draining of color.

CHAPTER VI
THE DARK COVE

Theresa Sharp's tense suffering silence lasted for some time. Then she wiped her eyes on the soiled, tattered sleeves of her white shirt. "I believe your story." She looked up wearily at Carse. "Probably more than you will believe mine."

Carse frowned. "I don't get that."

"The whole affair is almost as much a mystery to me," she said. The startled disbelief that registered on Carse's face must have been complete, because she went on hurriedly. "I'll tell you the story behind it, and maybe you'll understand. You see, I was a comparative stranger to my own father. I had not seen Dad since I was a baby—almost twenty years ago. Mother died when I was a few months old. I was placed in charge of a nurse and later I went to exclusive schools, and I graduated from one of the most exclusive in upstate New York this spring."

She got up and paced nervously.

"I always thought my father was extremely wealthy, but I never knew where he got his money."

Outside there was the stillness of the tropical night, but no sound of bird life whatever except that once, far out to sea somewhere, a gull made an excited noise. A little breeze had sprung up, too, so they could hear the surf sucking at the coral cove.

Theresa Sharp said, "All those years, I never saw Dad. Letters came, and bank drafts for large sums of money. They were mailed from many different ports—always ports in the Caribbean or the Gulf of Mexico. This spring I got the idea of coming down here. At first, Dad was against it, but I wrote him I was coming anyway."

She bowed and moved closer so that her words, pitched in a low murmur, could reach Carse's ears.

"He cabled me to come to Kingston," she went on. "I arrived three days ago. Dad acted strangely, it seemed to me, so that I felt I hardly knew him. You know what surprised me most? His refusal to tell me what kind of business he was engaged in."

She shivered.

"Dad seemed scared, or something," she continued. "He had a fast seagoing cabin cruiser, and we got aboard and came to this island. As soon as we got here, Dad did a strange thing. He took me aside and warned me not to visit the bay at the other end of the island. He said it would be certain death to do so."

Carse frowned. "He didn't give any explanation?"

"None whatever." The girl's hands were clenching and unclenching with emotion. "I insisted he tell me, but it did no good. I just know that it is dangerous around the bay. I don't know why. But Dad told me there was death there, and I believe him."

"What about Largo?" Carse asked.

"I don't know. But Jool was scared of him. I think Largo has been an enemy of my father for a long time. Dad left two days ago in the cabin cruiser," the girl explained. "I was left here with Jool. I was getting worried, and it didn't help my peace of mind any when Largo showed up in the amphibian and immediately shot at us. We have been hiding since."

"The amphibian," Carse explained, "was the plane they stole from me."

"How did they happen to get hold of your plane?" the girl asked.

"Well, it was simple. I advertised both crates for sale and stated that they were lying on the beach. All they had to do was come and get the one they wanted."

Carse was thoughtful for a long time. Then he started. "You know what I think?"

The girl stared at him.

"That's hokum about the bay being dangerous," Carse said. "I've been there. I found derelict ships. It's an amazing place, and I wandered around over it, and nothing happened to me. I think we should go there and get one of the planes and clear out of here and find the Coast Guard—if they have a Coast Guard down in this neck of the woods."

The girl shook her head slowly. "I would advise against it. At first, I didn't trust Jool, but now I do. And he was deathly afraid of the bay. I'm sure there's something terrible there."

"My planes are there," Carse said stubbornly. "That's one way to escape."

"You said something about derelict ships?" the girl inquired.

Carse told her about the strange bay of lost craft. The recital took some time, and the awe and stark incredulity which he had felt when he saw the place must have crept into his voice, because the girl watched him with breathless amazement. He described the yacht to her and explained that in his opinion it had lain there many years, judging from the rust upon the hull.

He told her of the galleon, a great ponderous craft with high stern and ridiculously unseaworthy hull, vessels of another century lying in a curious cove of dead ships.

"Why, that's unbelievable," the girl muttered.

"That's what I thought."

There was silence for a while, and as they were thinking, there came a soft thudding sound outside the cave entrance and a fluttering. A bird had fallen, Carse saw. It was some kind of night-flying seabird, and it went through a sort of convulsion lying there in front of the cave until finally it was still in death.

"I don't like this place," Carse said suddenly. "You say my father gave you a map?"

"Yes."

"Maybe it will tell us something about the lagoon."

"I have it here." Carse fumbled in the watch pocket of his trousers, produced the folded square of the map. He spread the wrinkled sheet out, moving close to the wobbling, scarlet glow of the ship's lantern.

"Great grief!" he exploded in stark wonder.

"What is it?" gasped the girl.

"There are two designs. One of them is a chart of the island." Carse's voice was excited. "But the other—why, it's . . ."

At this point, a gun muzzle poked into the cave and a voice said, "Hate to distract your attention, friends."

Carse dropped the chart, came half-erect. A harsh order crackled out of the square of darkness framed in the aperture. There was no weapon in reach. A pair of ugly, ribbed snouts of blued steel—automatic rifle muzzles—darted into the aurora of lamplight.

"Quiet!" Carse warned the girl. "I think it's Largo."

It was not Largo. It was two gangling, hard-faced figures who entered behind darting flashlight beams. Carse eyed them, hit by a dawning understanding. Largo's aviators. They must be double-crossing their chief.

The pair held automatic rifles on Carse and the girl.

"That bald-headed toad is suspicious," one said. "He may be following."

Evidently he referred to Largo.

One held a gun on them. The other set about binding them hand and foot. They used their belts and snubbed them tight about Carse's arms, and strips ripped from blankets completed the tying job. The man doing the binding fingered Carse's shattered handcuff links in awe.

"Cripes!" he muttered.

When the job was done, he backed off with a relieved alacrity that showed he was scared of Carse.

Both of them sidled to the feeble luminance of the kerosene flame. They spread the chart out on the rough planks.

"This is it," one growled.

The other chuckled, "Shows the exact spot!"

"Think we've tied 'em well enough to hold?"

"Sure."

A moment later they spun about, one with the chart in his hands, and left. The beams of their flashlights licked out as they disappeared. Their footsteps clattered hollowly for a few minutes, abruptly subsided, and there was silence.

CHAPTER VII
BLAZING DARKNESS

Four or five minutes later, when the two men returned, they were lugging an ordinary steel safe perhaps two feet square, which looked fairly modern. They dropped this in the middle of the chamber, glanced hastily at Carse and the girl to make sure they had no prospect of getting free, then left again.

Their two captors reappeared, more noisily this time, perspiring and tumbling a heavy steel-bound chest end over end ahead of them. The chest was upended in the middle of the cave.

They raked the two prisoners carelessly with the beam of a flashlight, and were satisfied.

"Damn Largo!" one said. "The bald ape would burn if he could see us now, wouldn't he?"

"Shut up!" said the other. "It's nearly morn-

ing. Come on! We'll lam with what we got. We can cripple one crate and fly the other out. Later we can hire a gang and come back for the rest before Largo gets off the damn island!"

The other man grunted from his effort to extract the contents of the steel safe. An object came free, an ordinary leather handbag, badly worn.

"Whatcha get?"

"Dunno. It's heavy as hell. What's wrong?"

The other had been straining his ears.

"Listen!" he rasped. They listened intently. "Somebody coming. Bring the rifles."

In a moment they had gone.

"Now!" Carse breathed frantically. He went to work on the bonds, and although what he accomplished in splits of seconds might have seemed like a miracle, it was nothing of the sort. He was a man with a naturally insatiable curiosity, so that his interval spent with carnival and circus had not been unprofitable, although it had seemed very much so at the time. He had observed rope escape artists, had even thought enough about learning the trade at one time that he had acquired a considerable knowledge of the tricks involved.

Once Carse was free, he untied the astounded girl.

They heard a shout outside, sharp and angry. Largo's voice. He had discovered the two fliers. There were shots, two or three of them that blasted the stillness, and after that a frantic noise of men fighting to get through the jungle.

"This way!" Carse whispered. "Largo is following the two fliers."

Carse led the way, and the girl followed, as they traveled with speed and quiet until they reached the spot on the beach where Largo's men had been camped. They found the place deserted. The darkness was not as intense, so dawn must be approaching. Carse searched the thicket.

"Come here," he called softly. "What do you make of this?"

He was referring to a case of dynamite, high-test stuff that had been concealed under bushes.

The girl said, "They must have intended to

use it to dynamite their way into some of the derelicts."

"My guess too," Carse said grimly. "And it's going to be some help."

Carse shouldered the case of dynamite. There was a rifle concealed with the dynamite, an old gun that was large and ancient, so clumsy that doubtless no one had wanted to lug it through the brush.

"Take that gun," Carse advised the girl.

She jacked the lever back and examined the cartridge chamber. The weapon was loaded.

Carse worked along the beach, moving with infinite care. They could hear Largo conducting his pursuit on the other side of the island somewhere. When Carse reached the little bay, he made a grim explanation.

"The important thing," he said, "is to keep them from leaving the island with either of my planes."

He moved out to the mouth of the cove, searched for a while, then placed the case of dynamite in a crack in the rock. He left one end of the dynamite case exposed, but carefully piled boulders over the other end.

The girl said, "If that explodes, it will block the mouth of the bay." She waved her arm. "The stone walls are high, the bay mouth narrow, and a blast would certainly dislodge enough stone to close it."

"That," Carse said, "would be too bad." He showed his teeth grimly. "But not as bad as having them get away with my planes."

They withdrew and took up a position on the lip of the crater where Carse could watch the spot where he had concealed the dynamite. He could distinguish the box faintly, so there was a chance of his hitting it with the old rifle, although the light was as yet very poor.

The eastern horizon had colored with the pale scarlet of approaching day. The enflamed eye of the sun would soon slide into view.

It was then that Carse's jaw sagged in angry defeat. The brief tropical night was fading and the bay was bathed in a flood of mellow, yellow-ish light. The small plane, the *Widow,* was where

he had last seen it. The two fliers had reached the craft, splashing through the shallows. They were working over the motor, replacing the ignition cables. They accomplished the job in a startlingly short time.

The motor was equipped with a hand-inertia starter. One flier braced himself against the side of the fuselage, struggling with the crank until the engine stuttered and made a sickly rattle. Instantly the flier was overside and rocking the pontoons free of the beach mud. The water was glassy, lifeless, like glazed black onyx, with a stretch in the center of the tiny lagoon that was clear.

Carse made an angry strangled noise and reached for the old rifle. If the mouth of the bay was blocked, there was very little chance of the plane taking off. He aimed deliberately. There was enough light now that he could see the dynamite case concealed in the stone crevice. He fired.

He didn't need the girl's whispered "You missed" to know that the bullet had gone wide. He fired again. A third time. He began to realize why the old rifle had been left behind at camp. It would take a wizard to hit the broadside of a barn with it.

The plane was darting forward like a teal, gathering speed. Halfway across the lagoon, the pilot began bobbing the light ship, hoping to get it on step. It whipped past close against the rail of a crumbling galleon that had a carved figurehead, queer masts, and a high penthouse at bow and stern which marked it as of sixteenth-century vintage.

The plane was slow getting off. It would have to pass through the mouth of the bay and out to sea before it acquired sufficient momentum.

Carse had been calculating carefully and aiming with the utmost care. He stroked the trigger. This time the bullet struck.

There was a sudden blinding scarlet glare. Their eardrums throbbed under the terrific explosion. The shock, the crash, made the earth quake, and for scores of yards the waters of the lagoon flattened under the blast pressure.

A great section of the cliff face tumbled outward, upset, fell into the water, and carried the plane under. The ship caved like a swatted fly, and lost resemblance to its former shape just before it sank beneath the surface. With a continued roaring, the slide took a huge portion of the crater rim into the bay.

"You helped your plane a lot," the girl said.

"Didn't I!" Carse muttered grimly.

Largo and his men appeared suddenly. They floundered out of the mangroves near the rotting hulk of a two-masted schooner. Largo made a prodigous scream, grasped the rail, and hauled himself aboard with one hand, holding a submachine gun in his other fist. He held the weapon ready to fire should either of the two unlucky fliers appear on the boiling surface of the bay.

Largo continued his savage demonstration by lumbering along the deck of the wreck toward the bow. Abruptly he wavered, seemed to stumble.

"Watch!" the girl whispered.

Carse was staring.

What followed was weird, ghastly, uncanny. The bald-headed giant ran about, screaming shrilly, horribly. He sprang toward the bow, trying to reach the sweltering mangroves that grew on the shore of the bay, but he began to stagger, and finally he sank into a shapeless bundle of thick arms and legs and huge spider-round body. He thrashed there for two or three minutes before he became still. By that time, his companions had also gone down. One of them did quite a bit of screaming, his shrieks echoing from the steep sides of the cove, but afterward there was no sound. Sepulchral, oppressive quiet had settled over the lagoon of death once more.

CHAPTER VIII
VANISHED TREASURE

A startled sound from Theresa Sharp broke the moribund silence. "Look," she breathed. Carse followed her pointing finger and said in a surprised voice, "Jool!"

The huge native saw them. He had been resting against the oars of the tiny dory which he was rowing well out to sea while he stared toward the bay, apparently trying to discover what was happening.

He stood up, waved his great, capstan-sized arms like a windmill, and pointed with both hands, then brought the dory leaping toward the narrow beach with a series of mighty strokes from the long oars. Carse stared at the lagoon, the strange place that reeked of death and menace.

"Come on!" he grunted. "Feel safer if we clear out."

Together, they ploughed headlong through the tangled, sweating jungle that grew like moss on the abrupt sides of the ancient crater. Jool was shivering with impatience as they reached the white beach. There was a bandage about his ribs, held in place by a strip of sailcloth. He seemed weak. Evidently the bullet from Largo's gun which had hit him earlier in the night had nicked his side, perhaps shattered a rib or two.

"Us gotta go!" he rumbled. "Dat debbil loose."

Carse pushed the girl unceremoniously into the dory, then shoved the big native, who was suddenly very weak and helpless, down into it as well. He took the oars and rowed well offshore before he voiced a question. "You took my plane and towed it into the bay, didn't you. You could do that because your devil—only came out with low tide, didn't it?" he asked Jool.

"Yassuh!" The native peered at Carse. "So you done got him all figured out."

The girl looked puzzled, incredulous.

Carse said, "Gas."

The girl said, "What?"

"Natural gas. A particularly poisonous type, vapor coming from deep in the earth where this ancient volcano is still active, escaping through a vent in the side of the crater. At high tide the opening is underwater, shutting off the gas. The aperture was exposed and the gas flowed only when the tide was low."

He paused to backstroke and get the dory bows pointed into the sea.

"The explosion of the dynamite against the side of the crater must have opened the vent above the surface, so that the gas came out and killed Largo and the others."

"Yassuh," mumbled Jool. "She did."

Carse stared at the island. "Ships were trapped there for ages," he grunted. "Low tide and the gas did for them. Greed probably had something to do with it."

Jool had collapsed into an upholstered seat. "Yassuh!" he puffed heavily. "Yassuh."

"How much treasure is left back there?" Carse demanded.

Jool jerked his kinky head sadly. "Dar ain't but a little left. Marse Sharp take mos' all of it to a bank in New O'leans, sah. Dar was jus' one load. Dan he was goin' take Missy an' go 'way to Geo'gia!"

Carse said, "We can rig up some kind of a thatched sail and make another island. It won't be safe to go around that death trap now. Masks would give protection from that gas, but we haven't got any."

Theresa Sharp looked at him. Her face was raw, blistered. Skin, loosened by the brazen heat of the sun, hung in ragged patches from her tilted nose and symetrical cheeks. Carse grinned reassuringly, conscious that his own person was the worse for wear and that the handcuff links still jangled musically at his wrists.

"I'll come back another time, with gas masks," he said.

The girl nodded, but corrected, "*We'll* come back."

Carse looked at her, and noted a private impression that had been growing, an impression that she was a very attractive bit of feminity even in her present weather-beaten condition, so that once she underwent repairs she probably would be something devastating.

She smiled at him. He liked her smile. He was aware of a number of things he liked, and he had a feeling that the rest of this thing would be rather pleasant.

LOUIS L'AMOUR

AS ONE OF the most famous and best-loved writers of western fiction who ever lived, Louis L'Amour (1908–1988) was a prolific producer of novels and short stories. Less known is that L'Amour wrote in other genres as well, especially early in his career. His first published short story was "Death, Westbound," a Depression-era tale of train-hopping, which appeared in *10 Story Book* (March 1933); it was followed by "Anything for a Pal" in *True Gang Life* (October 1935). Thereafter he wrote sports stories, mysteries, and adventure fiction, mostly for the pulps, as well as poetry and nonfiction.

L'Amour published his first western (though he preferred the appellation "frontier story"), "The Town No Guns Could Tame," in the March 1940 issue of *New Western Magazine*. Then came a deluge of western fiction, some of it under the pseudonym of Jim Mayo, Sam Brant, or, for a series of contracted Hopalong Cassidy novels in 1950 and 1951, Tex Burns. L'Amour's first novel under his own name, *Westward the Tide*, also appeared in 1950. In 1952, his novella "The Gift of Cochise" was published in *Collier's* magazine. When he sold the rights to Hollywood (for $4,000), the protagonist's name was changed from Ches Lane to Hondo Lane, thereby providing one of John Wayne's greatest film roles as the titular character of *Hondo* (1953).

Born Louis Dearborn LaMoor, the hardworking author eventually produced eighty-nine novels and fourteen short-story collections. At the time of his death, all were in print, with several posthumous collections still to come. Some years after L'Amour died, a large cache of additional stories was discovered—mainly western and adventure fiction written later in his life. (Although he had become a more accomplished writer than in his pulp days, the competition to sell stories to the highest-paying "slick" magazines was fierce, and these had failed to sell.) The stories were found in two large boxes originally made to hold carbon paper that L'Amour, as an officer, had "liberated" from a German aluminum factory at the end of World War II. The "carbon paper box stories" produced more than half a dozen new collections, beginning with *West of Dodge* (1996).

"Off the Mangrove Coast," one of these stories, was first published in *Off the Mangrove Coast* (New York: Bantam, 2000).

OFF THE MANGROVE COAST

LOUIS L'AMOUR

THERE WERE FOUR of us there, at the back end of creation, four of the devil's own, and a hard lot by any man's count. We'd come together the way men will when on the beach, the idea cropping up out of an idle conversation. We'd nothing better to do, all of us being fools or worse, so we borrowed a boat off the Nine Islands and headed out to sea.

Did you ever cross the South China Sea in a forty-foot boat during the typhoon season? No picnic certainly, nor any job for a churchgoing son; more for the likes of us, who mattered to no one, and in a stolen boat, at that.

Now, all of us were used to playing it alone. We'd worked aboard ship and other places, sharing our labors with other men, but the truth was, each was biding his own thoughts, and watching the others.

There was Limey Johnson, from Liverpool, and Smoke Bassett from Port-au-Prince, and there was Long Jack from Sydney, and there was me, the youngest of the lot, at loose ends and wandering in a strange land.

Wandering always. Twenty-two years old, I was, with five years of riding freights, working in mines or lumber camps, and prizefighting in small clubs in towns that I never saw by daylight.

I'd had my share of the smell of coal smoke and cinders in the rain, the roar of a freight and the driving run-and-catch of a speeding train in the night, and then the sun coming up over the desert or going down over the sea, and the islands looming up and the taste of salt spray on my lips and the sound of bow wash about the hull. There had been nights in the wheelhouse with only the glow from the compass and out there beyond the bow the black, glassy sea rolling its waves up from the long sweep of the Pacific . . . or the Atlantic.

In those years I'd been wandering from restlessness but also from poverty. However, I had no poverty of experience and in that I was satisfied.

It was Limey Johnson who told us the story of the freighter sinking off the mangrove coast; a ship with fifty thousand dollars in the captain's safe and nobody who knew it was there anymore . . . nobody but him.

Fifty thousand dollars . . . and we were broke. Fifty thousand lying in a bare ten fathoms, easy for the taking. Fifty thousand split four ways. A nice stake, and a nice bit of money for the girls and the bars in Singapore or Shanghai . . . or maybe Paris.

Twelve thousand five hundred dollars a piece . . . if we all made it. And that was a point to be thought upon, for if only two should live . . . twenty-five thousand dollars . . . and who can say what can or cannot happen in the wash of a weedy sea off the mangrove coast? Who can say what is the destiny of any man? Who could say how much some of us were thinking of lending a hand to fate?

Macao was behind us and the long roll of the sea began, and we had a fair wind and a good run away from land before the sun broke upon the waves. Oh, it was gamble enough, but the Portuguese are an easygoing people. They would be slow in starting the search; there were many who might steal a boat in Macao . . . and logically, they would look toward China first. For who, they would ask themselves, would be fools enough to dare the South China Sea in such a boat; to dare the South China Sea in the season of the winds?

She took to the sea, that ketch, like a baby to a mother's breast, like a Liverpool Irishman to a bottle. She took to the sea and we headed south and away, with a bearing toward the east. The wind held with us, for the devil takes care of his own, and when again the sun went down we had left miles behind and were far along on our way. In the night, the wind held fair and true and when another day came, we were running under a high overcast and there was a heavy feel to the sea.

As the day drew on, the waves turned green with white beards blowing and the sky turned black with clouds. The wind tore at our sheets in gusts and we shortened sail and battened down and prepared to ride her out. Never before had I known such wind or known the world could breed such seas. Hour by hour, we fought it out, our poles bare and a sea anchor over, and though none of us were praying men, pray we did.

We shipped water and we bailed and we swore and we worked and, somehow, when the storm blew itself out, we were still afloat and somewhat farther along. Yes, farther, for we saw a dark blur on the horizon and when we topped a wave, we saw an island, a brush-covered bit of sand forgotten here in the middle of nothing.

We slid in through the reefs, conning her by voice and hand, taking it easy because of the bared teeth of coral so close beneath our keel. Lincoln Island, it was, scarcely more than a mile of heaped-up sand and brush, fringed and bordered by reefs. We'd a hope there was water, and

we found it near a stunted palm, a brackish pool, but badly needed.

From there, it was down through the Dangerous Ground, a thousand-odd miles of navigator's nightmare, a wicked tangle of reefs and sandy cays, of islands with tiny tufts of palms, millions of seabirds and fish of all kinds . . . and the bottom torn out of you if you slacked off for even a minute. But we took that way because it was fastest and because there was small chance we'd be seen.

Fools? We were that, but sometimes now when the fire is bright on the hearth and there's rain against the windows and the roof, sometimes I think back and find myself tasting the wind again and getting the good old roll of the sea under me. In my mind's eye, I can see the water breaking on the coral, and see Limey sitting forward, conning us through, and hear Smoke Bassett, the mulatto from Haiti, singing a song of his island in that deep, grand, melancholy bass of his.

Yes, it was long ago, but what else have we but memories? For all life is divided into two parts: anticipation and memory, and if we remember richly, we must have lived richly. Only sometimes I think of them, and wonder what would have happened if the story had been different, if another hand than mine had written the ending?

Fools . . . we were all of that, but a tough, ruddy lot of fools, and it was strange the way we worked as a team; the way we handled the boat and shared our grub and water and no whimper from any man.

There was Limey, who was medium height and heavy but massively boned, and Long Jack, who was six-three and cadaverous, and the powerful, lazy-talking Smoke, the strongest man of the lot. And me, whom they jokingly called "The Scholar" because I'd stowed a half-dozen books in my sea bag, and because I read from them, sometimes at night when we lay on deck and watched the canvas stretch its dark belly to the wind. Smoke would whet his razor-sharp knife and sing "Shenandoah," "Rio Grande," or "High Barbaree." And we would watch him cautiously and wonder what he had planned for that knife. And wonder what we had planned for each other.

Then one morning we got the smell of the Borneo coast in our nostrils, and felt the close, hot, sticky heat of it coming up from below the horizon. We saw the mangrove coast out beyond the white snarl of foam along the reefs, then we put our helm over and turned east again, crawling along the coast of Darvel Bay.

The heat of the jungle reached out to us across the water and there was the primeval something that comes from the jungle, the ancient evil that crawls up from the fetid rottenness of it, and gets into the mind and into the blood.

We saw a few native craft, but we kept them wide abeam wanting to talk with no one, for our plans were big within us. We got out our stolen diving rig and went to work, checking it over. Johnson was a diver and I'd been down, so it was to be turn and turn about for us . . . for it might take a bit of time to locate the wreck, and then to get into the cabin once we'd found it.

We came up along the mangrove coast with the setting sun, and slid through a narrow passage into the quiet of a lagoon where we dropped our hook and swung to, looking at the long wall of jungle that fronted the shore for miles.

Have you seen a mangrove coast? Have you come fresh from the sea to a sundown anchorage in a wild and lonely place with the line of the shore lost among twisting, tangling tentacle roots, strangling the earth, reaching out to the very water and concealing under its solid ceiling of green those dark and dismal passages into which a boat might make its way?

Huge columnar roots, other roots springing from them, and from these, still more roots, and roots descending from branches and under them, black water, silent, unmoving. This we

could see, and beyond it, shutting off the mangrove coast from the interior, a long, low cliff of upraised coral.

Night then . . . a moon hung low beyond a corner of the coral cliff . . . lazy water lapping about the hull . . . the mutter of breakers on the reef . . . the cry of a night bird, and then the low, rich tones of Smoke Bassett, singing.

So we had arrived, four men of the devil's own choosing, men from the world's waterfronts, and below us, somewhere in the dark water, was a submerged freighter with fifty thousand dollars in her strongbox.

Four men . . . Limey Johnson—short, powerful, tough. Tattooed on his hands the words, one to a hand, HOLD—FAST. A scar across the bridge of his nose, the tip of an ear missing . . . greasy, unwashed dungarees . . . and stories of the Blue Funnel boats. What, I wondered, had become of the captain of the sunken ship, and the others who must have known about that money? Limey Johnson had offered no explanation, and we were not inquisitive men.

And Long Jack, sprawled on the deck looking up at the stars? Of what was he thinking? Tomorrow? Fifty thousand dollars, and how much he would get of it? Or was he thinking of the spending of it? He was a thin, haggard man with a slow smile that never reached beyond his lips. Competent, untiring . . . there was a rumor about Macao that he had killed a man aboard a Darwin pearl fisher . . . he was a man who grew red, but not tan, with a thin, scrawny neck like a buzzard, as taciturn as Johnson was talkative. Staring skyward from his pale gray eyes . . . at what? Into what personal future? Into what shadowed past?

Smoke Bassett, powerful tan muscles, skin stretched taut to contain their slumbering, restless strength. A man with magnificent eyes, quick of hand and foot . . . a dangerous man.

And the last of them, myself. Tall and lean and quiet, with wide shoulders, and not as interested in the money. Oh, yes, I wanted my share, and would fight to have it, but there was more than the money; there was getting the money; there was the long roll of the ketch coming down the China Sea; there was the mangrove coast, the night and the stars . . . there were the boat sounds, the water sounds . . . a bird's wing against the wind . . . the distant sounds of the forest . . . these things that no man can buy; these things that get into the blood; these things that build the memories of tomorrow; the hours to look back upon.

I wanted these more than money. For there is a time for adventure when the body is young and the mind alert and all the world seems there for one's hands to use, to hold, to take. And this was my new world, this ancient world of the Indies, these lands where long ago the Arab seamen came, and where the Polynesians may have passed, and where old civilizations slumber in the jungles; awaiting the explorations of men. Where rivers plunge down massive, unrecorded falls, where the lazy sea creeps under the mangroves, working its liquid fingers into the abysmal darkness where no man goes or wants to go.

What is any man but the total of what he has seen? The sum of what he has done? The strange foods, the women whose bodies have merged with his, the smells, the tastes, the longings, the dreams, the haunted nights? The Trenches in Shanghai, Blood Alley, Grant Road in Bombay, and Malay Street in Singapore . . . the worst of it, and the best . . . the temples and towers built by lost, dead hands, the nights at sea, the splendor of a storm, the dancing of dust devils on the desert. These are a man . . . and the solid thrill of a blow landed, the faint smell of opium, rubber, sandalwood, and spice, the stink of copra . . . the taste of blood from a split lip.

Oh, yes, I had come for things other than money but that evening, for the first time, no man gave another good night.

Tomorrow there would be, with luck, fifty thousand dollars in this boat . . . and how many ways to split it?

No need to worry until the box was aboard, or on the line, being hoisted. After that, it was every man for himself. Or was I mistaken?

Would we remain friends still? Would we sail our boat into Amurang or Jesselton and leave it there and scatter to the winds with our money in our pockets?

That was the best way, but with such men, in such a place, with that amount of money . . . one lives because one remains cautious . . . and fools die young.

At the first streaks of dawn, I was out of my blankets and had them rolled. While Smoke prepared breakfast, we got the diving outfit up to the side. We were eating when the question came.

"I'll go," I said, and grinned at them. "I'll go down and see how it looks."

They looked at me, and I glanced up from my plate and said, "How about it, Smoke? Tend my lines?"

He turned to me, a queer light flicking through his dark, handsome eyes, and then he nodded.

A line had been drawn . . .

A line of faith and a line of doubt . . . of the three, I had chosen Smoke Bassett, had put in him my trust, for when a man is on the bottom, his life lies in the hands of the man who tends his lines. A mistaken signal, or a signal ignored, and the diver can die.

I had given my life to Smoke Bassett, and who could know what that would mean?

Johnson was taking soundings, for in these waters, chart figures were not to be trusted. Many of the shores have been but imperfectly surveyed, if at all, and there is constant change to be expected from volcanic action, the growth of coral, or the waves themselves.

When we anchored outside the reef, I got into the diving dress. Limey lent me a hand, saying to me, "Nine or ten fathoms along the reef, but she drops sharp off to fifty fathoms not far out."

Careful . . . we'd have to be careful, for the enemies of a diver are rarely the shark or the octopus, but rather the deadline and constant danger of a squeeze or a blowup. The air within the suit is adjusted to the depth of the water and its pressure, but a sudden fall into deeper water can crush a man, jamming his entire body into his copper helmet. Such sudden pressure is called a squeeze.

A blowup is usually caused by a jammed valve, blowing a man's suit to almost balloon size and propelling him suddenly to the surface where he lies helpless until rescued. While death only occasionally results from a blowup, a diver may be crippled for life by the dreaded "bends," caused by the sudden change in pressure, and the resulting formation of nitrogen bubbles in the bloodstream.

When the helmet was screwed on, Limey clapped me on the top and I swung a leg over to the rope ladder. Smoke Bassett worked the pump with one arm while he played out the hose and rope. Up—down. *Chug-chug.* A two-stroke motion like a railroad hand car. It didn't take much energy but each stroke was a pulse of oxygen . . . like a breath, or the beating of your heart. The big mulatto grinned at me as he worked the handle.

Clumsy, in the heavy shoes and weighted belt, I climbed down and felt the cool press of water rise around me. Up my body . . . past my faceplate.

It was a slow, easy descent . . . down . . . down . . . and on the bottom at sixty feet.

In the dark water, down where the slow weeds wave in the unstirring sea . . . no sound but the *chug-chug-chug* of the pump, the pump that brings the living air . . . down in a green, gray, strange world . . . cowrie shells . . . a big conch . . . the amazing wall of the reef, jagged, broken, all edges and spires . . . a stone fish, all points and poison.

Leaning forward against the weight of the water, I moved like some ungainly monster of the deep, slowly along the bottom. Slowly . . . through the weeds, upon an open sand field beneath the sea . . . slowly, I walked on.

A dark shadow above me and I turned

slowly . . . a shark . . . unbelievably huge . . . and seemingly uninterested . . . but could you tell? Could one ever know?

Smell . . . I'd heard old divers say that sharks acted upon smell . . . and the canvas and rubber and copper gave off no smell, but a cut, a drop of blood in the water, and the sharks would attack.

Chug-chug-chug . . . I walked on, turning slowly from time to time to look around me. And the shark moved above me, huge, black, ominous . . . dark holes in the reef where might lurk . . . anything. And then I saw . . . something.

A blackness, a vast deep, opening off to my right, away from the reef. I looked toward it, and drew back. Fifty fathoms at some places, but then deeper, much deeper. Fifty fathoms . . . three hundred feet.

A signal . . . time for me to go up. Turning, I walked slowly back and looked for the shark, but he had gone. I had failed to hold his interest . . . and I could only hope that nothing in my personality would induce him to return.

When the helmet was off, I told them. "Probably the other way. But when you go down, Limey, keep an eye open for that shark. I don't trust the beggar."

On the third day, we found the hulk of the freighter. At the time, I was below, half asleep in my bunk. Bassett was in the galley cooking, and only Long Jack was on deck, handling the lines for Limey. Dozing, I heard him bump against the vessel's side and I listened, but there was nothing more, only a sort of scraping, a sound I could not place, as if something were being dragged along the hull.

When I heard the weighted boots on the deck, I rolled over and sat up, kicking my feet into my slippers. Johnson was seared on the rail and his helmet was off and Long Jack was talking to him. When they heard my feet on the deck, they turned. "Found it!" Limey was grinning his broken-toothed smile. "She's hanging right on the lip of the deep. She's settin' up fairly straight. You shouldn't have much trouble gettin' the box."

There was a full moon that night, wide and white; a moon that came up over the jungle, and standing by the rail, I looked out over the lagoon and watched the phosphorescent combers roll up and crash against the outer reef. When I had been standing there a long time, Smoke Bassett walked over.

"Where's Limey?"

"Fishin'," he said, "with a light."

"Tomorrow," I said, "we'll pick it up."

"Anson Road would look mighty good now. Anson Road, in Singapore . . . an' High Street. You know that, Scholar?"

"It'll look better with money in your pocket."

"Look good to me just anyway." Smoke rolled a cigarette. "Money ain't so important."

We watched the moon and listened to the breakers on the reef. "You be careful down there," Smoke Bassett told me suddenly. "Mighty careful." He struck a match and lit his cigarette, as he always did, one-handed.

Lazily, I listened to the sea talking to the reef and then listened to the surf and to the jungle beyond the line of mangroves. A bird shrieked, an unhappy, uncanny sound.

"Them two got they heads together," Smoke Bassett said. "You be careful."

Long Jack . . . a queer, silent man around whom one never felt quite comfortable. A taciturn man with a wiry strength that could be dangerous. Only once had we had words and that had been back in Macao when we first met. He had been arrogant, as if he felt he could push me around. "Don't start that with me," I told him.

His eyes were snaky, cold, there were strange little lights in them, and contempt. He just looked at me. I didn't want trouble so I told him, "You could make an awful fool of yourself, Jack," I said.

He got up. "Right now," he said, and stood there looking at me, and I know he expected me to take water.

So, I got up, for this was an old story, and I knew by the way he stood that he knew little about fistfighting, and then a fat man, sitting in a dirty singlet and a blue dungaree coat, said, "You *are* a fool. I seen the kid fight in Shanghai, in the ring. He'll kill you."

Long Jack from Sydney hesitated and it was plain he no longer wanted to fight. He still stood there, but I'd seen the signs before and knew the moment was past. He'd had me pegged for a kid who either couldn't or wouldn't go through.

That was all, but Long Jack had not forgotten, I was sure of that. There had been no further word, nor had we talked much on the trip down the China Sea except what was necessary. But it had been pleasant enough.

The next morning when I got into the suit, Limey came up to put on the copper helmet. There was a look in his eyes I didn't like. "When you get it out of the desk," he said, "just tie her on the line and give us a signal."

But there was something about the way he said it that was wrong. As I started into the water, he leaned over suddenly and stroked his hand down my side. I thought he wanted something and turned my faceplate toward him, but he just stood there so I started down into the water.

When I was on the deck of the freighter, I started along toward the superstructure and then saw something floating by my face. I stepped back to look and saw it was a gutted fish. An instant, I stood there staring, and then a dark shadow swung above me and I turned, stumbled, and fell just as the same huge shark of a few days before whipped by, jaws agape.

On my feet, I stumbled toward the companionway, and half fell through the opening just as the shark twisted around and came back for another try.

And then I knew why Limey Johnson had been fishing, and what he had rubbed on my arm as I went into the water. He had rubbed the blood and guts of the fish on my suit and then had dumped it into the water after me to attract the shark.

Sheltered by the companionway, I rubbed a hand at my sleeve as far around as I could reach, trying to rub off some of the blood.

Forcing myself to composure, I waited, thinking out the situation.

Within the cabin to the right, I had already noticed the door of the desk compartment that held the cash box stood open to the water. That meant the money was already on our boat; it meant that the bumping I'd heard along the side had been the box as it was hoisted aboard. And letting me go down again, rubbing the blood and corruption on my sleeve had been a deliberate attempt at murder.

Chug-chug-chug . . . monotonously, reassuringly, the steady sound of the pump reached me. Smoke was still on the job, and I was still safe, yet how long could I remain so under the circumstances?

If they had attempted to kill me they would certainly attempt to kill Smoke, and he could not properly defend himself, even strong as he was, while he had to keep at least one hand on the pump. Outside, the shark circled, just beyond the door frame.

Working my way back into the passage, I fumbled in the cabin, looking for some sort of weapon. There was a fire ax on the bulkhead outside, but it was much too clumsy for use against so agile a foe, even if I could strike hard enough underwater. There was nothing . . . suddenly I saw on the wall, crossed with an African spear of some sort, a whaler's harpoon!

Getting it down, I started back for the door, carefully freeing my lines from any obstructions.

Chug . . . chug . . . chug . . .

The pump slowed, almost stopped, then picked up slowly again, and then something floated in the water, falling slowly, turning over as I watched, something that looked like an autumn leaf, drifting slowly down, only much larger.

Something with mouth agape, eyes wide, blood trailing a darkening streamer in the green water . . . it was Long Jack, who had seen the last of Sydney . . . Long Jack, floating slowly down,

his belly slashed and an arm cut across the biceps by a razor-edged knife.

An instant I saw him, and then there was a gigantic swirl in the water, the shark turning, doubling back over, and hurling himself at the body with unbelievable ferocity. It was my only chance; I stepped out of the door and signaled to go up.

There was no response, only the *chug-chug-chug* of the pump. Closing my valve only a little, I started to rise, but desperately as I tried, I could not turn myself to watch the shark. Expecting at any moment that he would see me and attack, I drifted slowly up.

Suddenly the ladder hung just above me although the hull was still a dark shadow. I caught the lower step and pulled myself slowly up until I could get my clumsy feet on the step. Climbing carefully, waiting from moment to moment, I got to the surface and climbed out.

Hands fumbled at the helmet. I heard the wrench, and then the helmet was lifted off.

Smoke Bassett had a nasty wound over the eye where he had been struck by something, and where blood stained his face it had been wiped and smeared. Limey Johnson was standing a dozen feet away, only now he was drawing back, away from us.

He looked at the harpoon in my hands and I saw him wet his lips, but I said nothing at all. Bassett was helping me out of the helmet, and I dared not take my eyes from Johnson.

His face was working strangely, a grotesque mask of yellowish-white wherein the eyes seemed unbelievably large. He reached back and took up a long boat hook. There was a driftwood club at my feet, and this must have been what had struck Bassett. They must have rushed him at first, or Long Jack had tried to get close, and had come too close.

When I dropped the weight belt and kicked off the boots, Smoke was scarcely able to stand. And I could see the blow that had hit him had almost wrecked the side of his face and skull. "You all right? You all right, Scholar?" His voice was slurred.

"I'm all right. Take it easy. I'll handle it now."

Limey Johnson faced me with his new weapon, and slowly his courage was returning. Smoke Bassett he had feared, and Smoke was nearly helpless. It was Limey and me now; one of us was almost through.

Overhead the sun was blazing . . . the fetid smell of the mangroves and the swamp was wafted to the ketch from over the calm beauty of the lagoon. The sea was down, and the surf rustled along the reef, chuckling and sucking in the holes and murmuring in the deep caverns.

Sweat trickled into my eyes and I stood there, facing Limey Johnson across that narrow deck. Short, heavy, powerful . . . a man who had sent me down to the foulest kind of death, a man who must kill now if he would live.

I reached behind me to the rail and took up the harpoon. It was razor sharp.

His hook was longer . . . he outreached me by several feet. I had to get close . . . close.

In my bare feet, I moved out away from Smoke, and Limey began to move warily, watching for his chance, that ugly hook poised to tear at me. To throw the harpoon was to risk my only weapon, and risk it in his hands, for I could not be sure of my accuracy. I had to keep it, and thrust. I had to get close. The diving dress was some protection but it was clumsy and I would be slow.

There was no sound . . . the hot sun, the blue sky, the heavy green of the mangroves, the sucking of water among the holes of the coral . . . the slight sound of our breathing and the rustle and slap of our feet on the deck.

He struck with incredible swiftness. The boat hook darted and jerked back. The hook was behind my neck, and only the nearness of the pole and my boxer's training saved me. I jerked my head aside and felt the thin sharpness of the point as it whipped past my neck, but before I could spring close enough to thrust, he stepped back and bracing himself, he thrust at me. The curve of the hook hit my shoulder and pushed me off balance. I fell back against the bulwark,

caught myself, and he lunged to get closer. Three times he whipped the hook and jerked at me. Once I almost caught the pole, but he was too quick.

I tried to maneuver . . . then realized I had to get *outside* of the hook's curve . . . to move to my left, then try for a thrust either over or under the pole. In the narrow space between the low deckhouse and the rail there was little room to maneuver.

I moved left, the hook started to turn, and I lunged suddenly and stabbed. The point just caught him . . . the side of his singlet above the belt started to redden. His face looked drawn. I moved again, parried a lunge with the hook, and thrust again, too short. But I knew how to fight him now . . . and he knew, too.

He tried, and I parried again, then thrust. The harpoon point just touched him again, and it drew blood. He stepped back, then crossed the deck and thrust at me under the yard; his longer reach had more advantage now, with the deckhouse between us, and he was working his way back toward the stern. It was an instant before I saw what he was trying to do. He was getting in position to kill Bassett, unconscious against the bulwark beside the pump.

To kill . . . and to get the knife.

I lunged at him then, batting the hook aside, feeling it rip the suit and my leg as I dove across the mahogany roof of the deckhouse. I thrust at him with the harpoon. His face twisted with fear, he sprang back, stepped on some spilled fish guts staining the deck. He threw up his arms, lost hold of the boat hook, and fell backward, arms flailing for balance. He hit the bulwark and his feet flew up and he went over, taking my harpoon with him . . . a foot of it stuck out his back . . . and there was an angry swirl in the water, a dark boiling . . . and after a while, the harpoon floated to the surface, and lay there, moving slightly with the wash of the sea.

There's a place on the Sigalong River, close by the Trusan waters, a place where the nipa palms make shade and rustle their long leaves in the slightest touch of wind. Under the palms, within sound of the water, I buried Smoke Bassett on a Sunday afternoon . . . two long days he lasted, and a wonder at that, for the side of his head was curiously crushed. How the man had remained at the pump might be called a mystery . . . but I knew.

For he was a loyal man; I had trusted him with my lines, and there can be no greater trust. So when he was gone, I buried him there and covered over the grave with coral rock and made a marker for it and then I went down to the dinghy and pushed off for the ketch.

Sometimes now, when there is rain upon the roof and when the fire crackles on the hearth, sometimes I will remember: the bow wash about the hull, the rustling of the nipa palms, the calm waters of a shallow lagoon. I will remember all that happened, the money I found, the men that died, and the friend I had . . . off the mangrove coast.

THE GOLDEN ANACONDA

ELMER BROWN MASON

LIKE MANY of the best pulp writers of adventure fiction, Elmer Brown Mason (1877–?) is largely forgotten today, except by serious aficionados of pulp magazines. With no novels to his credit, he was not prolific by the standards of his pulp-writing colleagues, though his brief (five-story) series about Wandering Smith is justly revered by devotees of a kind of fiction seldom written today, when the globe has shrunk in almost every way. Born in Deer Lodge, Montana, Mason was the son of the surveyor-general of Montana and the grandson of the mayor of Chicago during the time of the Great Fire of 1871. He studied abroad, at Yale, then at Princeton, where he received his BA in 1903. A variety of jobs and careers followed, beginning with employment at two prominent publishing houses, Dodd, Mead and Harper & Brothers, then as a New York City real estate broker and a lumberman, before he returned to Yale for graduate work in botany and entomology. Mason's interest in and knowledge of earth sciences are featured in most of his short stories. His many journeys throughout America, often undertaken as part of his work for the U.S. Bureau of Entomology, and to such exotic destinations as Borneo and Patagonia, also provided colorful backgrounds for his fiction. He fought in both the Spanish-American War, in the Philippines, and in World War I, after which the effects of poison gas left him debilitated (to an unknown degree).

Mason's most significant contribution to adventure fiction was the character Isaiah Ezekiel Smith, whose extensive travels have given him the nickname "Wandering." His job, such as it is, is to help anyone "who wants to go after something unusual in a strange place." He usually may be found at Père Guerrin's, a very rough restaurant in New Orleans. "If I happen to be there," he says, "and feel like going, I wire back: *Come a-hooting.*" And off he goes with a new best friend in search of moths and butterflies, orchids and snakes, fish, iguanas, or a rare black flamingo, to wherever he needs to go—whether the Louisiana bayous, the Everglades, Colombia, or the Amazon—for romance and adventure.

"The Golden Anaconda" was first published in the February 20, 1916, issue of *Popular Magazine*.

THE GOLDEN ANACONDA

ELMER BROWN MASON

THE PROFESSOR cautiously raised his flaming red head above the side of the boat, reached back, picked up a felt-wrapped wire loop attached to a thick cord, and lunged over the bow.

"Got him!" he yelled, and I threw my weight on the cord. Instantly there was a terrific splashing. The jungle awoke to the chatter of monkeys, shrieks of gorgeously colored macaws, and the clear-toned clang of a bell bird's voice. From a lather of foam emerged the head of an anaconda, the great water boa of South America, lashing the river with its sides as it swam from us. The professor calmly began to row against the great snake, while I dragged at the rope, using one of the seats as a lever. The boat slid over the captive, and the prof, dropping his oars, imprisoned its tail in another felt-protected loop. Then we caught the wicked head in a steel mesh net, hauled it on board, and tied it up—it was a little one, only about ten feet long.

Easy, wasn't it? But it didn't always work out that way. Nothing on earth has a worse disposition than an anaconda, save, perhaps, an angry bee. The day before, we had hooked on to an eighteen-foot monster and not been able to gain an inch on it. Reddy finally gave me a little slack by rowing with its pull. The anaconda decided to come into the boat of its own accord, mouth wide open, looking as though it didn't need a dentist. I shot its head to pieces and a leg of the prof's pants, with a load of No. 6, and we spent some time plugging up the bullet holes in the forward part of the skiff.

Nevertheless I liked the excitement, and the whole proposition was certainly a sporting one. Professor Ritchie McKee had blown into Père Guerrin's café in New Orleans, red head and all, with three hundred dollars, orders from every zoological garden in America covering several tons of snakes, and the proposition that I help finance an expedition up the Magdalena River into Colombia. He was a little middle-aged Scotchman, with china-blue eyes, the flaming red hair I have already mentioned, and an argument that he needed the money.

Somehow he hit me just right, and we were calling one another Reddy and Wandering within the hour while quarreling over the respective merits of different brands of canned goods in a tropical climate. The upshot of the matter was that I now found myself in the upper reaches of the Magdalena River, navigating, with the assistance of three mestizos and Mose, my cook, a flat-bottomed, broad-beamed, wood-burning thing built like a house boat and loaded with snake cages.

Don't think for a moment that we got where we were without the slightest difficulty, just paddled along, fanned by tropic breezes. We didn't. And the worst of our troubles began and never ended when we picked up the orchid hunter.

There was nothing much doing until we were well up the Magdalena, past where you take the overland route for Bogotá. The river, before that point, had been alive with alligators, which made it unhealthy for anacondas, and, as anacondas were our main objective, we did not waste time on shore looking for other kinds of snakes. Once beyond the Bogotá connection, however, we anchored and put off in a skiff to explore a small tributary. There we took our first big water snake, right at the mouth, and a pretty struggle we had, too. After carrying it aboard our flatboat, we went up farther, and, a mile from the main river, came upon the most incongruous craft, deserted and tied to the bank, that you can possibly imagine in the middle of South America. It was a thirty-foot launch, decked over, brave with white paint and brass fittings, the simple engine built to burn wood, and the most perfectly appointed thing I have ever seen.

Hardly had we finished examining it and got back into our own boat when there was a wild chorus of yells from the jungle, the spat-spat-spat! of an automatic, and a lanky white man jumped on deck, cast off the line, and, dodging into the cabin, let the launch go down with the current. The air was instantly full of that sharp whistling sound that I had learned, on a previous trip, to associate with the tiny poisoned arrows the natives shoot from their bamboo blowguns, and I promptly yanked our boat around under the protection of the bulwarks of the larger craft. For five minutes, as we were carried swiftly down the stream, we all lay low, and then the white man put his head over the side of the launch.

He had about as disagreeable a face as I have ever looked upon: very high forehead, long pointed nose, thin lips, and the longest curved white teeth I have ever seen in a human being's mouth—they were more like an animal's than a man's—and his first remark was quite in keeping with his appearance:

"Who in the devil are you, pray?"

It made me mad, of course. White men are not only polite to one another in the jungle through motives of policy, but also because they are generally really glad to see a face of their own color.

"This is King Robert Bruce, late of Scotland," I answered, "and if you include me in your polite inquiry, allow me to present myself as the Archbishop of Canterbury."

"None of your nonsense!" he snarled. "I want to know who you are," and he actually threw an automatic on us.

There was not one thing to do. I just ached to get my hands on him, but you can't rush a twelve-shoot gun from a skiff onto a launch. I swallowed my mad as best I could, and was just beginning to tell him our entire family history when there was a whistling whir in the air, the automatic clattered to the deck, and a pretty little poisoned arrow was sticking in his wrist. He grabbed up the gun with his left hand, turning it loose into the jungle, and by that time we were both on board.

In a few moments the wounded man turned a sickly green, and we certainly had one time over him! Reddy was always loaded up with snake-bite dope, and we treated him with the dissolved purple crystals of permanganate of potash and injections of strychnine, praying, at the same time, that the arrow was tipped only with snake poison, and not the deadly *wourali* for which there is really no antidote. We pulled him through finally, but only after five hours' work; and meanwhile we put several long miles between ourselves and that unhealthy locality, the launch towing behind our flat-bottomed side-wheeler.

When our involuntary guest came to, he was frankly distrustful, but somewhat more polite. He volunteered the information that his name was Hiram Jones—Hiram Jones nothing! I know a John Doe when I see one, and he certainly belonged to that indefinite family—that he was collecting orchids, had discovered what he recognized as a new species—all collectors are nuts over new species—on a tree of a native graveyard, and that the natives had jumped him when he tried to get it. Also that he was rather obliged to us, hoped to make it all right, would do as much for us under the same circumstances. We were collecting reptiles, were we not? Reptiles *exclusively*, hey, what!

I disliked the man exceedingly, felt that he

was lying in other ways than about his name, and piously looked forward to getting rid of him as soon as possible. At that time he was too weak to turn off, however, and during the night his launch blew up and burned to the water's edge.

The man positively had a fit! He raved of *Cattleya mendelli, Dowiana aurea, Odoratum coronarium*—I know something of orchids, and these certainly were valuable ones if he had 'em—and beat at the fire with his one good hand. We finally had to drag him away, and all that we saved was a little ammunition, some clothes, and a bunch of English bank notes. The orchids were between decks forward, where the fire was hottest.

At first he suggested that we take him back to the Bogotá connection, which, of course, was out of the question; and then, much to my disgust, made a deal with McKee to go with us and have the privilege of the extra skiff to carry on his work.

The neighborhood where we took the ten-footer I began this yarn with was a fine place for the big snakes. There were many little tributaries running into the river, and each one seemed to have its pair of anacondas. Sometimes we missed them when they were stretched out along a branch over the water, their rich olive-green bodies with the two alternate rows of large oval spots along the back and small white-eyed spots on the sides blending perfectly with the lichen-decked limb of some giant tree. Mostly, however, they lay with just a fraction of their heads above water; and the prof was a wonder at picking out, from yards away, just the ripple that showed where a great snake was patiently waiting for what the current might bring. Then, with a few cautious oar strokes, we'd drift down on it, and the rest was purely mechanical.

Reddy, who was a cheerful, even-tempered little cuss, grew happier with each successive captive, and the one of which I have just spoken making our sixth sizable snake, we rowed back contentedly toward the main river. At the mouth of the tributary, a chorus of wild yells broke on our ears, and, quickening our stroke, we shot out

into the river to see Hiram Jones climbing onto the steamer, the opposite shore lined with furiously gesticulating savages.

"We'll have to go from here!" I exclaimed angrily. "That imitation English boob has been monkeying around the graveyards of the simple peasantry again."

"He shouldn't have done it," complained Reddy. "Now we have lost a good hunting ground. You had better speak to him, Wandering, while I am stowing away the snake. I'm not big enough to quarrel with him, and two men shouldn't jump on one."

Very tactfully put, I call it. The hint wasn't lost on me. I rolled my sleeves up as I got on board, and the prof dove down the companionway, dragging his net full of snakes.

"Look here, alias 'Iram Jones," I said, taking care to get close enough to him so he couldn't use his gun, "we've had enough of this graveyard work, and of stirring up the natives."

What I was aiming to do was obvious, and I'll give him credit for being no coward. The fight lasted several minutes. He was a better boxer than I, but hadn't been through the school of lick-'em-or-get-half-killed I had been brought up in. When he yelled, " 'Nough!" I got off him rather pleased with myself and willing to listen to what he had to say. It proved to be the same story. Native cemetery—you tell 'em by rags tied to sticks—rare orchid on tree, niggers popping out from every direction when he went for it. The only difference was that this time he had brought away what he was after, and it certainly was a marvelous thing! The flower, already fading, was about a foot across, olive-green, regularly blotched with black, while the stamens were pure gold color and gave off a musky odor.

"It looks for all the world like an anaconda," said the prof, who had come on deck as soon as the noise was over.

"Just the ticket! I'll call it *Oncidium anacondae*, Barlow"—Barlow, mind you!—said the so-called Hiram Jones, and, unconscious of the name he had let slip, picked up the tangle of aerial rootlets among which the strange flower bloomed. Something round, about the size of a tennis ball, fell thumping from the mass to the deck, and, making sure it was not a reptile, I picked it up while the other two men crowded nearer. Pulling away a few dead leaves, I held in my hand an infinitesimal mummy head, too small to be even that of a baby, looking as though it must have belonged to the tiniest of pygmies or else a gnome. The features, absolutely perfect in every detail, though shrunken beyond belief, were those of an old, old man, and in place of eyes were two crimson crystals sunk deep beneath the parchment-covered forehead. The whole thing was hard, like a lump of rubber, without a sign of a bone in it.

For several moments we gazed, astounded, at this gruesome object; and then Barlow, alias Hiram Jones, spoke:

"Look here, you blokes, do you know what this means—a fortune for every one of us! I saw hundreds of heads hanging to this one tree— thought they were weaver birds' nests. My word! *Look* at those bloody stones! They are rubies!"

The nearest I have ever come to engaging in the ghoul business was when I helped an old scientist to dig up the bones—and part of the skin and fur—of gigantic antediluvian lizards and mammoths in a salt marsh of the Brazilian coast. They say that rubies affect people's brains, however, and I'll admit for a moment I was tempted. Not so the little Scotchman.

"You dirty Sassenach!" he roared. "Do you think I'm going to turn corpse robber for all the red crystals in the world? I—I have a good mind to feed you to my anacondas. Don't you dare open your mouth to make such a suggestion again!"

"No, don't you dare!" I echoed shamefacedly, and there the matter rested.

Of course I had heard of the little mummy heads. Everybody who has been south of Panama hears the tale. But I had never seen one before, hardly believed in them. The tribes along the Magdalena are reputed to remove the skull from the heads of their own dead as well as their enemies, and shrink them to the size of small or-

anges by some mysterious process that keeps the features in proportion and as clear cut as in life, preserving them indefinitely. Why they were hung in trees, and how they were protected from bird and beast, was still an unwritten chapter.

II

While all this was going on, there was an awful hullabaloo from the shore, yells, beating of native drums, and the ear-splitting bray from a bamboo horn. The river was at least a mile broad there, however, and we were anchored in the middle of it; so I did not fear an attack in the daytime—savages don't come out after steamers when it is light; they have learned better. We had loaded up with wood for fuel the day before, and I didn't propose to stop again until we reached the Rio de Sucuriú—native for River of the Anaconda—a fork of the Magdalena about which I had some rather vague information, and which was really our ultimate destination.

After the crew had piled enough wood under the boilers to get up steam, I left Mose to tend them, and went forward to see what I could pick up from the mestizos in regard to local burial customs. It was little enough. They knew of the mummy heads, of course, and of the substitution of bright crystals for eyes, the standing in the community of the preserved deceased being indicated by the kind of stone, but they could tell me nothing of where these same stones came from—they were sacred things in possession of the priests alone.

I had only been forward about ten minutes when a yell from Reddy told me something was wrong below.

At the door of one of the cabins I found the little Scotchman hauling the unconscious Englishman out by the legs. The olive-green orchid lay on the floor, and from it emanated an odor of musk, only muskier, that caught you by the throat and simply choked you. We soused the senseless man over the side, and by the time he took in coming to he certainly must have been pretty near to cashing in. Then we fished out the deadly orchid on the end of a long pole, and should have thrown it overboard had the sick man not begged with actual tears that we save it. Later he tied it to the end of a stick and fixed it firmly over the bow. Outdoors, the odor was not so oppressive, but we came stern, nevertheless, where we could not smell it.

Steam was up by that time, but another factor upset our calculations. The wind and river began to rise, both coming straight down on us, and finally I had to steer our unwieldy craft into the backwater near the shore to avoid being rammed by the trees that came booming down the current; and just as we anchored, the black tropic night shut down like a curtain.

You can't fool with a storm in that latitude. The river lashed into foam, great sheets of water were bodily torn from the surface and whipped to shreds in the air, whole trees came whirling down, rearing and plunging as though alive, while the heavens were rent with lightning and shaken by thunder. The worst of it was over in thirty minutes, but the river rose and rose till our anchor began to drag. With full steam I could just keep head to it, but no more, and I had to feel around for hours before I could find bottom where the anchor would hold. Thankfully my crew then turned in, and I went forward to take one last look to see we were not drifting, when through the blackness I saw what appeared to be a large log coming swiftly down on us. It struck the anchor chain, split, and I had only time to recognize it as a native dugout before a naked savage described a parabola over the bow into my arms.

After a brief struggle—he was slippery as an eel—I caught his wrists and escorted him down to the light of the main cabin, calling to McKee and the Englishman.

Of course the naked wild man must have been scared to death, but he gave no sign of it, just stood up swaying with the pitch of the boat, and waited, apparently unperturbed, for what was to come, his eyes fixed on Reddy's flaming topknot. He was only about four and a half feet tall, gracefully formed, with features so far from being negroid that they appeared as clear cut as a young girl's, and he was not black, but a clear light chocolate. Through his elaborately arranged hair were stuck several of the tiny poisoned arrows, though he seemed to have lost his bamboo blowgun.

We all stared at him with nothing to say. As a matter of fact, he was much more at ease than were we, and then I bethought myself of asking some questions about the Rio de Sucuriú.

There are about twelve different and distinct languages spoken along the Magdalena, but there also exists a kind of *lingua franca* common to all the tribes of the river banks. I called in one of my mestizos and through him began to interrogate my captive.

The Rio de Sucuriú was only three canoe days farther up—he had come from there himself, caught by and driven before the storm. Yes, there were many serpents there, but they harmed not man since man was their brother and the son of "she who was married to the golden one, queen of all serpents."

I gave him food, which he wolfed down ravenously; and then, just as the mestizo turned to leave, a strange thing happened. From a shelf where the Englishman had placed it, the tiny mummy head fell to the floor and bounced to the savage's feet. He made a quick grab for it, but Barlow was before him, snatching it to himself with a fierce: "It's mine!" The speech was unintelligible to the naked man, but the gesture was unmistakable. He flew to his feet and pointed with two quick words.

"He says 'dead stealer,' " translated my interpreter at my look of interrogation; and then, listening to a stream of passionate sibilants, continued: "He has heard of the white man, and death is waiting for him as a slave who murders his master. At once he must give him the head that it may hang again on the sacred tree, lest another head he dreads come to him. He wants it now."

"Give him the thing!" I ordered. "We can't afford to quarrel with the natives, especially with one who comes from where we are going. He'd put us in wrong at once."

"I won't!" snarled the Englishman. "Kill him and throw him overboard. Dead men tell no tales."

And he actually meant it. Just as cold-blooded as that. I made a snatch for the mummy head, missed it, then struck it out of his hand, and the prof picked it up and gave it to the savage.

He took it into his cupped hands and made a kind of a salaam, turning it face upward, and we saw that the rubies were gone from the eye sockets, gouged out.

I believe I should have killed Barlow, alias Hiram Jones, then and there had we been alone. As it was, I turned and struck him across the mouth.

"Get out of my sight, you unclean ghoul!" I shouted, and he slunk quietly away.

I presented the little naked savage with a square of red cloth—it pleased him immensely—to wrap the head in, which he did with the greatest reverence; and, while he squatted on the floor, one hand on the bundle to keep it from rolling with the pitch of the boat, I made him a regular oration.

I told him we were capturing snakes, which, strangely enough, did not seem to astonish him, and that we hoped to find many big ones in the Rio de Sucuriú. I also tried to convey to him that the Englishman was quite mad, and that in no way had we been parties to the taking of the head. He made no comment, except to ask why we didn't burn the madman to drive the wickedness out of him; and then, after a parting look of admiration at the professor's red head, tactfully terminated the interview by curling around his precious bundle and going to sleep.

Reddy and I talked till daylight, and the upshot of our conversation may be epitomized into two paragraphs.

Though we had no intention of gouging rubies out of the mummy heads of the native dead, we hadn't the slightest objection to negotiating with the priests for them.

He wished to Heaven there was some way of getting rid of our English incubus without handing him over to the vengeance of the savages.

III

The river sank as quickly as it had risen, and we skirted the current for two whole days before we came to the fork that had been dubbed the Rio de Sucuriú. Our savage pointed out the channel all the way, and we thus avoided the usual hang-ups on sand bars.

Rather strange and most self-contained person, that naked wild man! He was outwardly quite unimpressed by the boat and its contents, all of which must have been new and very wonderful to him, but he seldom took his eyes from the prof's red head. Me, he evidently considered Reddy's subordinate, despised the Englishman, and classed the mestizos as slaves. Mose, my cook, who was a very black, black man, plainly puzzled him. The orchid stuck up in the bow was familiar to him, and he looked on it with mingled feelings of fear and disgust.

At the mouth of the Rio de Sucuriú, our guest left us, taking along the mummy head in its red wrapping, and promising to return after two darknesses to show us where we might capture more snakes. I for one was glad to see him go. He would put us in right with his tribe, and it would not be necessary to keep constantly on the alert for the vicious little poisoned arrows. Neither did the Englishman grieve over this departure. We hadn't treated that gentleman with undue consideration these last days, had hardly spoken to him at all in spite of his attempt at an apology. He had tried to explain his eccentric behavior in regard to the mummy head on the grounds that he did not know what he was doing from the time the deadly orchid overcame him—even claimed that he did not know what had become of the rubies. All this was mixed in with whining over the loss of his launch and orchids—at least a thousand pounds' worth—and, after talking interminably, he ended up by borrowing some clothes from me with the excuse that his own we had saved were so shrunk by the water he could not get into them. I let him have some, of course, but I'll be dog-goned if I wanted to.

Opposite where we anchored, a spit of rock, some twenty feet broad, ran out into the water, so perfectly reproducing in shape the head of an anaconda that had the idea not been ridiculous I should have called it the work of man. Also the Rio de Sucuriú was well named. We took three anacondas the first day, one sixteen feet long, and located a pair of monsters that we simply did not dare to tackle alone. Reddy was crazy to get them, and suggested wild scheme after wild scheme for their capture. Having no desire to trouble the digestion of a thirty-foot snake, I turned all his plans down, urging that we wait until the natives appeared and then enlist their assistance. In the meantime, Barlow hunted orchids by himself, and he certainly brought in a heap of them.

At sunrise of the third day, we were awakened by a most infernal din, the throbbing beat of native drums, the savage braying of bamboo horns, accompanied by the splashing of paddles. Before the mist had gone, we found ourselves surrounded by dugouts, and, as the sun rose, a state craft paddled underneath the stern of our side-wheeler. Hewn out of a single log, it was fifty feet long, with thirty paddlers, and in the bow stood the savage whom we had picked up farther down the river.

"Grab your guns!" gasped Barlow.

"Guns nothing!" I answered, and I was scared. "There are hundreds of them. We'd be torn to pieces in ten minutes. Wits alone will get us out of this."

I summoned my mestizo interpreter, and the savage in the bow of the state canoe began to speak.

I can't give his exact words, but the substance was as follows: The Red God with his friend and slaves was welcome in the territory of the Sucuriú people, though not the one with him who slew from behind and respected not the dead.

There would be feasting, and many serpents would be bestowed upon us that we might be honored.

Plainly the prof was the Red God, and our best card, so I shoved him up on the bulwarks, meanwhile orating all I knew through the mestizo. I said we much appreciated the honor done us and should be tickled to death to have the snake donation—we'd make some donation on our own side; that we had only six days to linger, then the Red God and us, his servants, must return whence we had come; that the wicked one among us had been driven temporarily mad by the flower of death and was not responsible for his actions, but would be punished when we returned to our own land.

Then we permitted—indeed, I don't see how we could have hindered—the naked savages to swarm all over the boat. Not one thing on board was taken or even touched, however, and we all rowed to shore feeling as though we were part of some fantastic dream.

The feast was no worse or better than others of its kind, and liberally watered with palm wine. The entertainment following consisted of the customary savage dances. Our party and our former guest, now host, sat, or rather squatted, a little apart from the rest of the Sucuriú people, and were served by young slaves of whom there seemed to be a large number. The entire performance was something new to the prof, and he enjoyed it all hugely, also the palm wine—until I had to warn him. You see, I had been up against it before, and knew it was not to be trusted. Like all Scotchmen, he knew best, however, and when I discovered, in the gloom, that he had his arm around an attractive but more than lightly clad brown girl, the party broke up. Savages believe in love at first sight, rapid wooings, and absolute sincerity. Besides, I'm darned if the girl wasn't extremely good-looking.

The prof was cross as a bear the next morning, and took occasion to insult me seventeen separate and distinct times. I took it all gracefully, though; I've had palm-wine heads myself and know what they mean. Finally, however, he accused me of being jealous of his "way with the weemen," and myself having an eye on "yon mud-colored lassie" of the night before. This was too much. I'm a respectable widower—twice—and couldn't afford to have my name scandalously coupled with a brown girl—Père Guerrin might hear of it—so I soused him over the side until he told me he felt good-humored again. Reddy had come on the trip with a single crash suit, so we routed out some of Barlow's shrunken clothes. They surely had shrunk, fitted the little Scotchman exactly, and he was just half the size of the orchid hunter.

By this time several dugouts were alongside, and we prepared a dozen or so of the felt-wrapped wire loops and explained their use to the natives. They caught on at once, and we started toward where Reddy and I had seen the snakes that were too large for us to tackle alone. Anacondas, in addition to their devilish bad temper, are about as shy as you make 'em; but the savages paddled along, singing and whooping as though the game was a deaf stone idol instead of the alertest reptile that swims. The mestizo interpreter could not check them, and they did not seem to understand my signs for silence—on the contrary, whooped the louder. As we pushed into the backwater, where we had seen the monsters, the reason for this lack of caution was apparent. Far from being alarmed, a thirty-foot anaconda undulated swiftly toward us. A native rose in the bow of the leading canoe, and, holding a dead capybara above his head, began a kind of a chant. I got the translation later. Here it is:

> "Brother, thy brothers come,
>   An offering bear to thee.
> With fear the jungle is dumb,
>   Sucuriú people are we.
> Brother, the golden one
>   Watches, where crowned with gold,
> She sits and basks in the sun,
>   Wrapped in HIS golden fold.
> Brother, we bind you free,
>   Bitter though be your strife,

> Though you our brother be,
>   We pay the debt for a life."

The anaconda raised five feet of its body out of the water, and the singer cast the capybara into the waiting jaws. Before the snake could dive, a felt-wrapped wire loop circled it, then another. The dugouts swarmed about it, the lashing tail was imprisoned, and, in less time than I can tell, Reddy slipped the steel-mesh net over the wicked head. The female was not so easily captured, one savage losing a large chunk of his shoulder; but, within two hours, both reptiles were safely ensconced within our damp hold—and they measured respectively thirty-one and a half and twenty-eight feet.

In three days we had as many big snakes as we could cram into the large cages, while the savages were eager to catch more, and delighted with our gifts. It had been necessary to establish a tariff, so rapidly were serpents brought us; not only anacondas, but the gentler, beautifully marked boas that reach a length of ten feet and take the place of our own domestic cat as rat catchers in the native huts. We paid so many yards of cloth, according to length, and added an alarm clock when an especially fine specimen was taken. Reddy became jubilant and more jubilant with every addition to our collection, forgot all about the "mud-colored lassie," and I was pretty well pleased myself. Barlow alone of our party was not happy, and with cause. No sooner was he out of sight of our side-wheeler than *ping!* a little arrow would stand up, quivering, on the side of his skiff. These missiles were not poisoned, but this did not prove that the next one might be harmless. The Englishman took the hint and spent his time morosely moping on board, and begging us to go farther down the river. Selfish ugly brute he was—though, I grant him, brave enough; he had fought me—and I heartily wished us well rid of him.

The professor now began to think of smaller reptiles, and was specially desirous of grabbing onto a few fer-de-lances. These are pleasant snakes, known by the Spaniards as *rabos de hueso*—bone tails—from the curiously colored and spike-like tip at the end of the body, about the deadliest things in the reptile line, and so temperamental that only one ever survived to reach the New York zoo, where it died of excitement.

We tried a hunt on dry land, equipped with wire loops and very close mesh metal nets. Only three specimens resulted from the entire day's tramp, and these did not amount to anything, were as common as savages, Reddy said. An attempt to enlist the natives in this new sport, something we had shied away from at first for fear of being deluged with the commoner reptiles, was entirely unsuccessful. Our former guest, who seemed to be the chief of the Sucuriú people in spite of his youth, lucidly explained that all the lesser snakes had been captured long ago and taken to the place of the dead. Requests for information as to the location of said place of the dead met with the same chilling silence that I well remember having had from a fat lady at the only ball I ever went to in my life, when I apologized for tearing a yard off the rear end of her dress.

Not only did we fail to make a single capture the next day, but, in addition, the prof got badly stung by a large blue wasp, and the savages plainly looked with disfavor on our land expeditions. Furthermore, on the boat, the Englishman exhibited three tiny arrows, distinctly tipped with poison this time, that had been shot on board during our absence. He asserted, with unnecessary profanity, that he was going wherever we did from that time on.

Oddly enough, not one of us suggested moving on, and, when you come to think of it, it wasn't so odd, after all. You see, we were all fundamentally fighting men, and the fact that the savages obviously wanted us to pull out just got our dander up. Besides, I was mighty curious to see that place of the dead to which all the land reptiles had been transported, and unquestionably the prof felt the same way. That little red-headed devil had something else on his mind, however, as I was to find out later.

Before I forget it, since you always hear Scotchmen spoken of as hard-headed, I should like to state right here that the man who says Scotchmen aren't at the same time sentimental is a liar—they invented sentiment.

Barlow, of course, really wanted to stay, because he was crazy for another shy at the orchids, with which the woods in that neighborhood seemed to be crammed.

Each of us kept strictly to himself that night. The Englishman took the poisonous orchid from the bow of the boat—it smelled worse during the darkness, too—and boxed it up carefully. The professor got into a skiff and went ashore. I turned in and dreamed of thirty-foot anacondas, their heads covered with flaming red hair and their mouths full of long curved teeth.

IV

Before sunrise, the mestizo interpreter woke me with the news that there was a canoe alongside with some savages in it who wanted to talk to me. I stacked up the pillows under McKee's head; he was breathing heavily and had a way of sleeping flat that invited heat apoplexy—and went on deck. It was just getting light as I looked down into the native boat, and what I saw there came near to doubling me up with mirth at the same time that I recognized its seriousness. In the bow sat the young chief, simply trembling with rage; the paddler was an old white-wooled brown man, evidently the father of the pretty chocolate-colored girl in the stern. For her part, she had been weeping, held her head very high, and wore, by a string around her neck—and indeed she wore little else—an unmistakable red object, an ample lock of the professor's auburn—by courtesy—hair.

The young savage shot out a stream of *sssss*'s that sounded like an angry anaconda, and the interpreter elucidated. Briefly the substance was that Reddy was trying to steal his girl, that she was ready and anxious to be stolen, and that we were therewith ordered to beat it at once, if not sooner. Through the mestizo I promptly told his nibs to forget it; we'd stay as long as we pleased.

The answering flow of sibilants was less virulent and shorter, and translated into a query as to what we would take to go away.

Then I had an inspiration. Slowly, word by word, I had my man impart to this autocratic savage a promise that we would leave the moment the Red God had secured all the land reptiles he wanted, and there must be many; that he wished to visit the place of the dead and see what crawling things he could find there; and that if both these requirements were met he would shake the girl.

For a long time the savage hesitated, and when he finally spoke I could only gather from the rendering of his words that we were to go with him that morning, prepared to stay several days, and with everything we owned that would hold reptiles. The rest of his speech was a jumble to me: The Golden One might blast us— breath of death—sacred road—

The dugout sheered off, and, going below, I beat a brisk tattoo with a pair of military brushes on the side of the cabin.

"Awake, my red-haired Lothario!" I yelled. "Awake! I have good news. Jump into your clothes, and don't wait to brush your hair; you've ruined your beauty, anyhow, by that gob you cut out of your bang. Come and catch little snakelets; we're going where there are oodles of them."

Reddy sat up, somewhat blear-eyed; then, scrambling out, looked at himself in the four-inch mirror on the wall.

"I dinna see it has changed my appearance," he remarked. "I mind some palm wine—What were you saying about wee snakes?"

I told him. The serpent made Eve forget her Adam. The mere promise of venomous reptiles made Reddy forget his Eve. The little Scotchman turned into a whirlwind, and, when the dugouts arrived, had enough collecting paraphernalia piled up to load three of them to the guards. Every one of us, except Mose, whom I

left behind in charge of the boat, mestizos as well as the Englishman, went ashore at the anaconda-head-shaped outcrop, where we found the young chief awaiting us with a dozen slaves for porters.

For an hour we followed a jungle trail, single file, the chief evidently steering by a lofty peak in the distance. Then the trail broadened out, and we found ourselves walking upon rock the like of which I have never before seen. It was a road, or rather causeway, thirty feet broad, built of ten-foot-square blocks of stone, and winding back and forth up to the highlands. No twenty men could have lifted one of those square blocks; no, not fifty men; and there were millions of 'em. Furthermore, the middle of the stoneway was worn smooth by the footsteps of thousands, exactly like the flagstone in front of the swinging doors of Père Guerrin's café.

Not one of us said a word until we had passed along the two half-mile undulations, and then the Scotchman spoke the conclusion of his thoughts:

"We-el, 'tis Aztec. I'll say no more."

"It's a bloomin' snake miles long," said Barlow; "miles, miles long, with its head in the river."

I had nothing to say. To tell the truth, it kind of made me feel religious, awed me, especially the wearing away of the solid rock by those countless feet. They must have been bare feet, too, and their owners dead for the Lord knows how many tens, hundreds, even thousands of years!

We followed the great sweeping curves of this mighty road till noon, now to the right, now to the left, always rising, until finally the mountain loomed above us, and just then the causeway broke off short in a chaos of tumbled blocks of stone. On either side were acre-large enclosures that looked as though they might once have been water tanks, terraced one above the other to the base of the mountain, two miles away. Above the ruins of this ancient road a way of more recent origin had been fashioned. Zigzagging from tall forest tree to tall forest tree were a pair of thick long bamboos, one above the other, the lower a path to which bare feet might cling, the upper a handrail.

Where the road broke off, the chief halted, pointing to the splintered and shattered blocks of stone below. My eyes followed his gesture, and, ten feet beneath me, a yellow serpent was stretched out in the sun; another, crawling lazily from a fissure in the rocks; a third lay coiled. There were snakes large, snakes small, snakes of every hue of the rainbow. The place was alive with reptiles.

"This is heaven," stated the professor positively, picking out a wire loop and collecting box and preparing to climb down to the jumbled bowlders.

"This is the nearest to hell I have ever seen," I remarked, getting ready to follow him.

We could not stay among the ruins; the reptiles were too thick about us. And, after Reddy had come within a hair's breadth of being struck by a fer-de-lance whose head I shot off, we climbed back again. The broad walls of the tank furnished us with a four-foot path, however, and from it we angled, trapping snakes in a loop on the end of a bamboo pole exactly as you snare suckers with a copper wire. It was unpleasant, but exciting, sport. I, for one, was perfectly willing to land my snake on the wall, perfectly unwilling from that time on to have anything to do with it. Barlow limited his activities to toting the collecting boxes and swearing. He cursed the savages, the snakes, the sky, the earth, Reddy, and me, until the Scotchman, after a few moments' deep thought, told him such language was "fair weeked" and it would be no sin to tip him over into the reptile den.

We took fifty snakes, ten of which were the dreaded fer-de-lances, a German flag—immortalized in Kipling's tale—three species of coral snakes, a green racer, two bush masters, and others whose names I simply can't remember. Then night came.

As the light went, a strong breeze blew down from the mountain onto our camp; but, far from

being laden with the scent of flowers, it brought an aroma that to me suggested ten thousand alligators. The Englishman recognized it, however, from the first whiff.

"Death orchids!" he exclaimed. "There must be a hundred burial trees near here, and perhaps rubies—"

"Which you will leave alone," I interrupted, "or I'll give you a licking that will make the last one seem like love taps, and hand you over to the savages afterward."

Of course Reddy was primarily a snake collector, and that was his dominant interest, but he was all of a man besides, and, as such, crazy to see what was at the end of the long bamboo road. It was obvious the chief did not intend that we should go farther, and so we made our plans without consulting him. The wall of the next tank was five feet higher than the one in which we had done our strange fishing, and on it grew a tree to which ran the bamboo bridge. We decided that the next morning we three—the Englishman being unwilling to leave us for a moment—would climb this tree and follow the swaying airway to the mountain. With this purpose in view, we turned in early, after sending back the mestizos and some porters with our boxes of snakes.

V

In the morning, our project was simplified by the withdrawal of the savages farther down the stone causeway. Very evidently they did not at all care for that neighborhood. Immediately after breakfast, we set out, taking a few snakes first in case any one might be spying; and then, scrambling up the five-foot wall, looked down into the next tank—and stood transfixed.

For a moment—as had the Englishman— I thought the dead trees of which the enclosure was full held an enormous colony of weaver birds' nests. On every branch and twig hung a tiny mummy head, the sunlight glinting here and there on jeweled eyes, and an odor of musk floating up to us—though more faintly than during the night—from the foot-wide, olive-green flowers of the death orchids, the only living thing, save reptiles, that flourished in that gruesome place.

"Let's go back," Barlow begged, in a whisper; "not even rubies are worth it!"

"I'm afeered," simply stated the Scotchman.

"We're in for it now; let's go on," I urged; and then I added, since I saw both of my companions were scared to death, and so, indeed, was I: "*I'm* not afraid!"

"You're a le-er!" promptly responded Mc-Kee, and began to climb the tree we had selected the night before.

From the fragile bamboo bridge we looked down for a full two miles on enclosure after enclosure full of dead trees hung with the shrunken heads. There were thousands; and, as we progressed, they became unquestionably more ancient, had fallen to the ground—even the trees themselves had sometimes fallen—and lay heaped like the debris of blackened combs and litter beneath a century-old wild bees' hive. On one tree I counted two hundred heads; there were fifty trees in that section, thirty separate sections in all, making, at a low, *low* estimate, three hundred thousand of these tiny relics of what had once been human beings. It was the vast graveyard of a mighty race, a race dwindled to the few poor survivors of the present day—the Sucuriú people.

From the swaying bamboos we stepped at last onto solid rock, a continuation of the great causeway, but narrowing like the tail of an anaconda. At its very tip lay a fifty-yard, sand-bordered pool from which it seemed the twelve-mile-long stone serpent might have emerged.

Tired and breathless, we sat gazing into the clear water that backed up against a sheer cliff, and then from a small cave across from us, its top just above water level, came a ripple. Something split the surface of the water, and there emerged a head as red as Reddy's own, followed by a woman's face and arm, her hand resting lightly on the neck of a nine-foot anaconda, and her body swaying from side to side through the water with the undulations of the swimming serpent.

"I'm going crazy!" gasped Barlow. "Do *you* see it, you blokes?"

" 'Tis extraordeenary," vouchsafed the prof.

The swimmers struck shallow water, the girl stood up, and the anaconda curled about her till its head rested on her shoulder. Snake and woman, save for her flaming hair, were both a golden yellow, and it would have been hard to say which was the more beautiful.

Quite unafraid, she approached us, her eyes on the prof's glowing head, and then stopped. I rose and bowed, which was ridiculous; couldn't think of anything else to do; but she never even looked at me.

One arm she raised and pointed at McKee, and in some mysterious way the gesture asked a question as plainly as though she had traced an interrogation point on the smooth white sand. For a moment she stood pointing, and then, raising both her hands, pressed two fingers across her lips. Again the gesture needed no interpretation, was as clear as though she had put it into words—the woman was dumb.

"Puir, puir lassie!" said the prof, with infinite pity. "Puir bonnie lassie!"

And I felt my own heart go out to the beautiful voiceless thing standing like some goddess of the olden days, the golden snake coiled about her golden form.

"Let me talk to her," said the little Scotchman, and, beckoning her nearer, began to trace pictures on the sand.

The Englishman may have thought he was crazy, but I *knew* I was as I watched Reddy drawing the story of our voyage. According to his pictures, we came from the rising sun— "rising" indicated by a series of dashing rays— she glanced at his hair—then came up a broad river in a great canoe—

It was a fine series of drawings, and covered ten yards of sand. When it was finished, the woman put her hand up to her hair and drew from among the thick tresses a small skin bag. This she opened, and took out a pear-shaped stone, with which she began to mark on the sand, and that stone was an inch-long ruby!

Barlow made the sign of the cross and rose to his feet.

"Let's look around a bit, Wandering," he begged, "while the children draw pictures. Perhaps we'll find a ten-headed lion with a basket of diamonds in each mouth. I'm in for what there is to see before I'm locked up in the dippy house."

I needed a chance to collect my thoughts myself, so followed him, leaving Reddy and the girl bent absorbingly over their tracings.

To the left of the stone snake's tail, rude steps were cut in the living rock, and up these we scrambled. They led to a small platform, and again in the rock was hollowed out a little house, with windows and doors, stuck there on the cliff like a swallow's nest. Inside were jars of pottery, hammers and knives fashioned from flint, and wood evidently stacked for burning that went into dust at our touch. No human could have dwelt there for years and years; everything was too quiet, too motionless, too covered with the dust of ages. We stole silently out into the sunlight again, and, by the doorstep, the Englishman picked up a ruby carved in the likeness of a coiled snake.

More steps led to another rock-hollowed house, differing in no respect from the first, and we climbed up from terrace to terrace, exploring the countless long-abandoned dwellings of a dead race. The sun was well to the west when we reached a shelf broader and longer than the others with no doors or windows cut in the rock, only a long line of bathtub-shaped depressions. Each depression held the crumbling bones of a skeleton, and every skeleton was headless! Our faces turned from this row of open graves, we walked to the far end of the shelf and came to a great hole on the brink of which, scattered among flint knives, hatchets, and little round balls of clay, were small rubies, red snakes' eyes they looked like, which Barlow eagerly gathered up. Together we peered into this pit, and mixed

with the clay balls were thousands upon thousands of skulls each split neatly in half, while here and there, adhering to the clay balls, was a piece of parchment-like skin.

"I'm sick!" I whispered. "Let's get out of here."

"I'm dead with thirst," Barlow answered through parched lips, his face pasty white in spite of the heat.

No nightmare could be more awful than our descent from those endless silent terraces. We slipped and clung to the edge of thousand-foot precipices, slid down the rude steps, skinning hands and knees, and our throats were full of the dead dust of long-forgotten peoples, our lips swollen, our tongues thick. Twice the Englishman abandoned his bag of rubies; twice, sobbing, he went back for it. The sweetest music I have ever heard was Reddy's voice from near below, calling and cursing by turns. And then the sun sank, leaving the world bitter cold.

It was darker than pitch down by the pool, the only sign of light a sheen from the still water that made our faces look like white blurs in a big splash of ink. By groping around rather at haphazard, we collected a few pieces of wood for a fire, and, shivering, huddled over it. As the flames rose, picking our faces out of the gloom, it became more than apparent that the prof had somehow acquired a black eye. It was a beaut, covered all one side of his face, and very naturally I asked how he got it.

" 'Tis nothing," Reddy answered; "a wee bump against yon stone."

"It's a right-handed swat," I insisted. "You got fresh and the lady biffed you."

"You're a le-er," he flared; "the lassie no laid hands on me; 'twas the snake."

It isn't the easiest thing in the world to get a Scotchman to tell what he doesn't want to; but I finally gathered in his story, what there was of it.

The girl had understood his drawings, but hers were quite unintelligible to him, a series of snakes, fishes, triangles, and complicated geometrical figures. More by gesture than anything else, he gathered that food was brought her over the bamboo bridge by the savages; that she dwelt in a cave rising from the other side of the pool, and that she had been there for fifteen complete sun revolutions. " 'Tis then an unfortunate thing happened," he continued. "To encourage the lassie, I put me hand on her shoulder. 'Twas by no means a caress, ye'll understand; more like a pat. And then the snake struck me with his head on the side of me face. The lassie was fair angry and drove it into the water. I dinna blame her; it spoiled the pleasure of the whole day for both of us. At sundown she became greatly agitated, pushing me toward yon bamboo bridge, and then, when I would not go, swimming back and forth from me to the cave across the pool, making signs for me to follow her. I would have humored the puir lassie had ye two not been away pleasuring all the day."

"Pleasuring?" repeated Barlow. "A peach of a lot of pleasure we had while you were philandering, and we've brought back a fortune."

Come to think of it, so we had. The rubies simply slipped my mind. Things get kind of out of proportion in the wilderness. We had out the bag and felt and hefted it—it was too dark to look at the stones—and it weighed all of ten or twelve pounds. Quite a hunk of jewels, and yet somehow it failed to impress me. I couldn't think of the little red things in terms of money; only as eyes of the horrible shrunken mummy heads. Reddy didn't show any undignified amount of joy over them, either, refused to commit himself to any undue enthusiasm until he knew exactly what the stones would bring "within a thousand dollars, say," a question on which we naturally could not enlighten him. With the Englishman it was quite different. He fair lusted over the bag in the darkness. They would buy him a boat of his own, brass fittings and all, air-tight compartments that would preserve orchids forever. He'd travel in Borneo, Brazil, India; there should be money enough to go everywhere. His thoughts took a sudden twist—

"Look here, you blokes," he whined, "at least half of what they bring belongs to me. I was the

one that found them. Any court of law would uphold me."

"We-el, let's submit it to a court of law," suggested McKee.

"We'll divide these rubies into three parts when we get back to the boat," I stated positively. "Meanwhile, since you found 'em, you can carry 'em."

The moon rose, and at the same moment we saw the golden maiden swimming toward us, the anaconda in her wake. She came straight to Reddy and tried to lead him into the water, carrying her hands to her nostrils, pointing out into the darkness, and beckoning imploringly. Never have I seen anything more tragic than the look of agony on her face, of striving to make the Scotchman understand.

"Puir lassie!" he said pityingly. "I'll be back. She canna bear to have me leave her."

"And you're going now," I insisted; "it won't be the easiest thing in the world to travel that thread of bamboo by moonlight, and the sooner we reach our flat scow the better."

The woman followed us, the great snake coiled about her body—she must have been as strong as an ox as well as impervious to cold—and importuned Reddy with imploring gestures to return. He shook his head, however, and, slipping off our shoes and tying them around our necks, we fitted our stockinged feet to the slippery bridge.

Hardly had we gone a hundred yards, with me leading, when I stopped and held up my hand.

"Nothing doing!" I shouted. "Beat it back as quick as you can, praying that the wind doesn't change!"

And I had reason! From beneath me came the indescribable odor of the death orchids, only a hundred times stronger than I had ever smelled it before, forming a deadly barrier that no breathing thing could hope to penetrate. Already I felt my head reeling as I climbed back toward the mountain, and that with the breeze blowing from us. We reached firm ground none too soon, the girl clinging to the prof's hand and striving to drag him into the pool, for at that very moment the wind changed.

"To the pool for your lives!" I yelled, plunging in and wading out until only my face was above the surface. The poisonous miasma from the death orchids was blowing down on us like mist above a marsh, and lay suspended not six inches above the water, sinking lower and lower every second.

"We're all done for," sang the Englishman, "just as I was rich, too. I'm no coward, but I refuse to die with my sins unconfessed. Listen to me, Wandering! I intended to murder you and that fool of a snake-collecting Scotchman so I could keep all the rubies. I shot the top of the man's head off who hired me for this trip. He knew nothing about orchids; intended to claim all the credit for what we found; and, besides, I wanted that launch. Two years ago—"

"Can your childish babble!" I screamed. "Who cares a hoot for what you were going to do or have done? Where's Reddy? Hey, Reddy! Reddy! Reddy!" I yelled.

The water swirled; I felt a hand clutch my arm, and the golden woman rose beside me.

"Where's Reddy?" I screamed in her face, and the poor dumb thing actually smiled at me, pulling my hand.

"They say drowning's easy," droned the Englishman. "I'll just take a whiff of that corpse flower and flop over into deep water."

He stuck his head out into the grayness, and I saw it drop forward just as I caught him beneath the arm. Following the pull of the girl's hand, I swam with her, towing the senseless man after me. Once the lash of the anaconda's body touched my leg, and then there was darkness. I felt, rather than saw, rock above me; next was conscious of space, inky blackness, but room all about me. My feet touched bottom. Hauling Barlow with me, I staggered forward and fell face downward on smooth dry sand.

It was Reddy's voice that brought me back.

"Are ye there, Wandering?" he whispered.

"Yes. Are you all right, Reddy?"

"Yes, the lassie saved me. Feel around till ye find me; I'd like to touch something human."

Barlow's body across my knees quivered, and I raised him to an upright position. He groaned and slid down against me. My groping hand found the little Scotchman, pulled him to me, and I threw an arm over his shoulder. Once my other hand touched the smooth wet body of the anaconda, and I snatched it quickly away. And then—wonder of wonders!—I slept dreamlessly, beautifully, blissfully!

VI

The moment of waking brought with it a full consciousness of all that had taken place. The morning came filtering in through the water that blocked the entrance to the cave, lighting it with the dim gray quietness of an empty church. Pressed against my right side lay Barlow, breathing naturally. McKee's red head was pillowed on my left shoulder, and crouching near by, her fiery hair spread on the sand, slept the girl. There was someone else, or, rather, something else, awake beside me. The golden anaconda lay curled about the golden woman, its diamond eyes fixed unflinchingly on mine.

I shook Barlow, and he sat up while slowly the meaning of his surroundings came over him.

"I say, this isn't hell, after all!" he ejaculated, getting to his feet. "Now ain't this a rum go! I say, Wandering, I was out of my head last night. You mustn't pay any attention to what I said. I'm really very fond of you and Reddy." And he smiled at me, showing all his long curved teeth.

My hand on McKee's forehead made him open his eyes, and at the same time his teeth began to chatter.

"The lassie saved us," was the first thing he said. "Wake up, bonnie one!" But she was already awake, looking up at him with adoring eyes.

"The sunlight for mine!" I chortled. "Never expected to see it again. You first, prof!"

Teeth chattering, the little Scotchman waded into the water and dove under the arch of rock, the girl and snake following him.

"Now you!" I directed Barlow.

"We'd better look around and see if she hasn't some rubies hidden here," he answered, and then splashed into the water just in time to avoid a vigorous kick.

Never did sunshine seem so blessed as that shining upon us outside; never did the whole world seem more joyous or beautiful! I just gave myself up to breathing and soaking in the warmth, gazing up at the sun till my eyes blurred.

When I finally turned to my companions, Barlow was coming out of the pool with the bag of rubies that he had dropped there the night before, and the look on his face as he gloated over the open sack was that of a demon.

Then Reddy claimed my attention. He was leaning against the golden woman, her arm about him, and, though his face was red as fire, he was shivering like a leaf. It didn't take a second glance for me to realize what was the matter. The *calentura* fever had him, and it behooved us to get back to the boat and quinine, lots of quinine, as swiftly as possible. The knowledge of his condition was in the girl's eyes as she looked anxiously at me. Indeed she raised her hand, palm down, moving it, shaking, in front of her face; and if that is not a good symbol for fever I have never seen one.

Had Reddy been less far gone, that two miles of climbing would have been agony for him. As it was, he moved along the slippery bamboo as only a drunkard of a man spurred on by fever could have done. At times he was delirious, shouted and sang, apologized to several imaginary "weemen" for making them love him. The girl kept her hand beneath his elbow, indeed carried him the last quarter of a mile, looping the anaconda around him to ease her burden. Barlow and I kept one bamboo length to the rear. The weight of snake and woman plus Reddy must have been considerable, and we did not dare put too severe a strain on any one section of the seemingly slender bridge. Down our tree we climbed at last, first the girl with her now raving burden, which she laid tenderly on the wall to draw breath, then yours truly, and last Barlow.

From behind me came his voice:

"Great heavens, Wandering, look below you to the right!"

I glanced over the edge of the wall, and immediately beneath me lay coiled a fer-de-lance that must have been all of twelve feet long—the most absolutely venomous object I have ever seen.

"Glad Reddy doesn't want—"

My words were drowned by the bang of an automatic, and I felt a sear of fire along my side. Spinning on my heel, and at the same time ducking low, I dodged the second bullet and caught Barlow's gun arm at the wrist in both of my hands. He snapped his left hand to my throat while I strove to twist away his weapon. Deeper sank his fingers in my flesh, deeper and deeper. I felt my eyes popping from my head, my tongue protruding, and swung him in front of me in a last furious effort to break free. From the girl's lips that I had never before heard utter a sound came three distinct hisses. Dimly I saw the anaconda uncoil from her body, writhe forward, and, quicker than light, cast a coil around Barlow's neck, while I wrenched from him, falling face over the edge of the wall. There was a mighty crunch of breaking bones, and man and snake went over me inextricably mixed, straight down upon the fer-de-lance below. The poison reptile struck three times, sinking its fangs once in the body of the anaconda and twice in the Englishman's thigh.

We did not even attempt to retrieve the dead man; left him where he lay. Reddy was our first care. Turn by turn that wonderful golden woman and I half carried, half led him on the mile-long undulations of that mighty causeway, until we finally reached the stone snake's head jutting out into the river. There the golden anaconda joined us, apparently none the worse for the venom from its poison cousin, and wrapped itself around its mistress. Not a savage had shown the tip of his nose all the way, and at my hail Mose came ashore in the skiff unmolested.

For ten days the girl and I fought off death from the little Scotchman, and at dawn of the eleventh day the fever broke.

Reddy was a good little man, but "weemen" were his weakness. I had pieced together disconnected fragments of his ravings with rather astonishing results. Not only did he have a wife in Scotland, but also one on the Continent. The upshot of my cogitations was, again, that Reddy was a good little man, but that was no reason why he should take all the goddess of a golden woman had to give. At present his plan was to settle down in the wilderness with her and forget the world—I was to deliver his snakes. I knew, however, that sooner or later he would return to civilization—they all do—and then what would she have left?

My mind was slowly made up, and, though I hated the plan worse than death, I began to put it into execution at once. Under my direction, the mestizos got up steam, and then I went to the woman and told her by signs to go ashore and get Reddy wild grapes, a thing she had often done before. Like a child she obeyed me.

No sooner was she out of sight than up came the anchor and we steamed away. Just in time, too, for as we rounded from the Rio de Sucuriú into the main river, the girl's crimson head showed above the water, coming swiftly after us. It was impossible for any swimmer to catch our side-wheeler, however, when it was going with the current, and the last I saw of her was her beautiful nude golden body, with its crown of flaming hair raised half out of the water, her arms held out imploringly while her dumb lips worked, the head of the great snake making an arrow-shaped ripple by her side.

Reptiles and all, we reached New Orleans without adventure. It was not a pleasant trip for either of us, though. Reddy refused to speak to me when he learned what I had done while he was sick and helpless. He expressed himself as absolutely certain that the "puir dumb lassie" would pine away and die for love of him. God help me, but I can never be sure that he was not right!

Back in civilization, I took the bag of rubies—Barlow had dropped it on the wall during his last fight—to a jeweler to get them valued. However well the Englishman may have known orchids, he was distinctly not up on precious stones. His fortune in rubies proved to consist of garnets—very fine ones, it is true, but nevertheless nothing more than garnets.

One last word in connection with Barlow. The day after Reddy's fever broke, the chief of the Sucuriú people paddled out to us and threw something on board. It proved to be a package done up in the identical red cloth which I had given him to wrap the mummy head. Inside were two objects. First Barlow's head, shrunken the size of a small orange, all the teeth gone save two that overlapped the wrinkled mouth like the curved tusks of a peccary, while from each socket protruded the fang of a fer-de-lance; second, also a tiny mummy head, its top blown away, leaving it roughly flat, the features unmistakably those of a high-bred Englishman, rubies—garnets I now know them—for eyes, and attached to it by a slender gold chain was a monocle.

We had given back the savage his dead; he returned ours to us.

I heard indirectly, one month after our return, of Reddy's marriage, in New York, to a widow with four children. Wonder if he sent cards to his other wives? I know none came for me. Could I have foreseen this, I never should have taken him from the golden woman, but left him in the wilderness with the pious hope that the golden anaconda might make a meal of him some dark night, mistaking him for a hog.

FRANK L. PACKARD

BORN IN MONTREAL of American parents, Frank Lucius Packard (1877–1942) was a civil engineer who began his writing career as an expert about and lover of railroads and rail travel, producing numerous short stories (some collected in 1911's *On the Iron at Big Cloud*) and several novels, including *Running Special* (1925) in that milieu. He also made numerous trips to the Far East and elsewhere in search of adventure material, resulting in such popular works as *Two Stolen Idols* (1927), *Shanghai Jim* (1928), and *The Dragon's Jaws* (1938). Packard's greatest success, however, came with his Jimmie Dale series, which sold more than two million copies in book form. Dale, like his namesake, O. Henry's Jimmy Valentine, is a safecracker who learned the skill in his father's safe-manufacturing business. A wealthy member of one of New York's most exclusive clubs, Dale also has multiple alter egos: He is the Gray Seal, the mysterious thief who leaves his eponymous mark at the scene of his crimes; Larry the Bat, a member of the city's underworld; and Smarlinghue, a fallen artist. In the "Raffles" tradition of literary cracksmen, Dale's burglaries are illegal, of course, but they are benevolently committed in order to right wrongs, and involve no violence. Initially serialized in *People's*, the Dale stories yielded five books, beginning with *The Adventures of Jimmie Dale* in 1917 and concluding with *Jimmie Dale and the Missing Hour* in 1935. Seven films were made from Packard's novels and short stories, most notably *The Miracle Man* (1932), starring Sylvia Sidney and Chester Morris; this story of a con man was also filmed as a silent picture in 1919.

"Shanghai Jim" was first published in magazine form in 1912; its first book appearance was in *Shanghai Jim* (Garden City, NY: Doubleday, Doran, 1928).

SHANGHAI JIM

FRANK L. PACKARD

CHAPTER I
THE THREE PEARLS

UNDER THE LIGHTED, swinging lamp in the cuddy of a small two-masted schooner, two men sat facing each other at the table. Bob Kenyon, black-haired, clean-shaven, big across the shoulders, and displaying an enviable muscular development of chest where his shirt was open at the neck against the tropical heat, was a young American of perhaps twenty-eight or -nine; the other, Captain David Watts, master and owner, was a wiry, weather-beaten, blue-eyed, bearded little New Zealander of fifty.

"Old Isaacs ought to be along any minute now," said Captain David Watts significantly.

Bob Kenyon thrust one hand into his trousers pocket, extracted therefrom a little cloth sack that had once done duty as a container for cigarette tobacco, loosened the drawstring, and rolled three pearls of great size into the hollow of his other hand.

"I thought you said, when you sent for him, that this chap Isaacs was to be trusted," he observed.

"And so he is," returned the older man coolly. "That's the reason I picked him out. He's the best of the brokers ashore, which may not be saying much, but it's a safe bet he knows more about pearls than all the rest of them put together. He's been at it now for a number of years here, and I've never heard a word said about him except that he was on the square."

Bob Kenyon, still rolling the three pearls in the hollow of his hand, smiled a little quizzically.

"Why all the precaution, then?" he inquired.

"I'll tell you why," said Captain David Watts, a sudden grim earnestness in his voice. "It ain't that I'm afraid of Isaacs, except that, like every other human being, he's got a tongue. If he buys the pearls, all right; but we ain't likely to come to any bargain off-hand to-night, and, for your own sake, it ain't a wise thing to have anybody know where they're kept in the meantime. We're partners in 'em in a way, but my share is small compared with yours according to the bargain when you staked the schooner for the trip, and, except for this little bit of by-play that we're going to pull off, I ain't going to have it any other way than that they stay in your possession—and right in your pocket, which is the safest place for 'em. But the world don't need to know it! I'm an old-timer here, and you ain't even been ashore yet, and I know what I'm talking about. The minute the word's out, it's a question of keeping your weather eye skinned. The lagoon's filling up with pearlers coming in, and some of 'em, so far as morals go, don't belong anywhere except in hell; and, furthermore, the town itself, to say nothing of the whole island of Illola, ain't unanimous in its church attendance in spite of the missionary stations. There's a British Resident here, and native police, and all that, but—" He ended with an expressive shrug of his shoulders.

"You've put an enormous price on these

pearls," remarked Bob Kenyon speculatively. "Don't you think you're a bit high?"

"It ain't a question of thinking," Captain David Watts answered tersely. "I know they're worth all and more'n I've said they are!"

"All right, then," said Bob Kenyon quietly. He pushed the pearls across the table. "I must say it seems a little unnecessary to me—but go as far as you like."

Captain David Watts picked up the pearls, opened a locker, and took out a leather wallet. He placed the pearls inside the wallet, returned the wallet to the locker, and closed the locker again. He nodded his head in self-approval.

"Now," said he, "let's go up and take a look-see if he's coming."

Bob Kenyon rose from his seat and followed the other up the little companionway to the deck, and for a moment both stood at the schooner's rail staring out over the black, mirror-like, un-rippled surface of the lagoon. It was a quiet night, the moon just rising, the scented odor of tropical vegetation in the air. Off to the extreme right of the bay in which the schooner was anchored, scores of scintillating little gleams, denoting the position of the town, broke through the palms that fringed the beach, but, growing fewer and fewer as the eye followed the shore line, finally dwindled out until, opposite where the little vessel lay within not more than two hundred yards from the shore, a point, closing this end of the bay, exhibited only a lonely and deserted stretch of sand. Here and there in the lagoon, some quite close at hand, some farther off, singly and in little groups, the riding lights of other vessels twinkled like stars against the sky line. But there was no sign of any approaching boat.

"What the devil's keeping him!" exclaimed Captain David Watts impatiently.

"Oh, it's early yet," said Bob Kenyon unconcernedly. "It's scarcely eight o'clock." He pointed suddenly to two or three little dots of light that came from the windows of a house high up on a hill and almost abreast of the schooner's position. "What place is that up there?" he asked.

The question was apparently irrelevant to Captain David Watts's thoughts. He answered with a grunt:

"That's the British Residency—Colonel Willetts's place." And then: "Damn that man, Isaacs!"

Bob Kenyon made no comment. He was still staring at the lights on the hill when Captain David Watts, after an impatient turn or two along the schooner's deck, finally halted again beside him at the rail.

"Look here!" said Captain David Watts abruptly. "A thing like this don't happen in the lifetime of many men—one pearl maybe—but not three of 'em. I don't go off half-cocked as a general rule, not me; but though my stake don't amount to one-two-three alongside of yours, I've been as excited as a kid ever since we found 'em, and you've never even batted an eyelash. What's the idea? Is it because you just don't and won't believe they're worth what I've kept on telling you they were day after day?"

Bob Kenyon's eyes shifted from the lights on the hill to the rugged, honest face beside him. He brushed his hand across his forehead as though, fogged, he sought to clear his mental vision.

"Why, I don't know," he said slowly. "To tell you the truth, I haven't thought much about them—sort of all in the day's work, you know."

"Good Lord!" ejaculated Captain David Watts helplessly. "Listen to that! Well, answer me this, then. Granting those pearls are worth all I say they are, and that's a fortune, and a whopping big one, what are you going to do with yourself from now on?"

Bob Kenyon shook his head.

"Same answer," he said. "I haven't thought about it, but I don't think it would change anything."

Captain David Watts stuck a square-ended cigar in his mouth and sucked on it unlighted.

"Well, then, you're wrong!" said Captain David Watts, a sudden sharpness in his voice.

"I'm going to say something to you because I like you, my lad—and, damme, you can take it or leave it! When you and I met up a while ago at MacDonald's in Suva, I was broke, and you said you had enough to pay the expenses of a trip, including a fair screw for me, and take your chances on the luck. So I fancy you weren't exactly rolling in wealth, and, on that score, I don't blame you for the sort of pillar-to-post life, I take it, you've led up to now. I can't think of anything much, according to the stories you've let slip, that you haven't done, from plantation work to the present fling at pearl fishing, or any place in this lower half of the world where you haven't been during the last five years. But you keep that up and it gets to be a habit that ends, if you live long enough, in a whining, gin-begging, stinking beachcomber. You think it over, my boy. You know the islands well enough to know what they can do to any white man who lets himself drift. There's no excuse for you doing that any more. You're a rich man to-night whether you believe it or not."

In the flare of a match there was a queer tightening of Bob Kenyon's lips, as he bent his head to light a cigarette.

"What would you suggest?" he asked, without inflection in his voice.

"Settle down and get married," replied Captain David Watts promptly. "Yes, and"—his seriousness became suddenly mellowed by a quiet chuckle—"blimy, I'll show you the girl! You see those lights on the hill you were asking about? Well, there's a girl for you! As fine a looker as ever you clapped your eyes on is Marion Willetts, and none of those new fancy notions about her, either! She's the kind of a wife for a man— kept the Residency going like one o'clock for her father ever since her mother died a number of years ago."

"And, of course," said Bob Kenyon facetiously, "the British Resident's first choice for a son-in-law would be an embryonic beachcomber, and naturally the lady's preference would—"

Bob Kenyon stopped abruptly, as a low hail came across the water.

"Hello!" exclaimed Captain David Watts. "What's that?"

The hail was repeated.

And now both men, staring shoreward, made out the white figure of a man on the sandy beach of the point.

"That'll be old Isaacs now," said Captain David Watts in a puzzled way. "But it's blamed queer. He's walked out from the town instead of taking a boat."

"Well, you know him and I don't," said Bob Kenyon; "so you'd better take the dinghy and fetch him aboard. I'll take him back, and that'll be turn about; besides, as I haven't been ashore yet, I'd like to stretch my legs and take a look at the town when this business is over."

"Right you are!" agreed Captain David Watts, and, hurrying aft to where the dinghy floated astern, he pulled the boat alongside and clambered in.

Bob Kenyon watched the other for a moment; then, his elbows on the rail, his chin cupped in his hands, his eyes fastened and held on the window lights on the hill again. The cigarette fell with a little hiss into the water. There came again that queer tightening of his lips, and with it now, slowly, a strange whiteness came creeping into his face. So Marion Willetts had never married! Of course, he had supposed that she was somewhere here on this island, but that had had no bearing on his coming. She would never know he was here. He would see to that. Besides, when he had seen her last, five years ago, he had been Mr. John Hingston—he was Bob Kenyon now.

Strange! Life was strange—a strange, queer thing! So was love! Why hadn't she married? She couldn't have cared—not that much. She had been a very beautiful girl of eighteen then.

His hands, clenching, bit into the folds of his cheeks. Well, *he* had cared, and—God help him!—he still cared. But he hadn't come here to this island expecting to torture himself with the might-have-been—or to sell pearls either! He broke into a sudden, low, mirthless laugh. The pearls! There seemed to be something mockingly ironical in the fact that stupendous luck of this kind, which he neither needed nor cared about, should come his way, when luck of another, if grimmer, sort had persistently eluded him for five futile years!

He roused himself, conscious that he was still staring at the window lights on the hill, as the splash of oars alongside warned him that the dinghy had returned. And then, a moment later, Bob Kenyon smiled to himself in the moonlight at the sight of a curious little personage who was coming toward him along the deck in the wake of Captain David Watts. The man was bent-shouldered and stooped as he walked; he had a patriarchal beard and wore sun glasses; his white duck suit had long since lost any claim to intimacy with the washtub; and his head was crowned with an oversized pith helmet, also incredibly dirty and much the worse for wear, and which, obviously to keep it from resting on his ears, was cocked a little askew, giving its owner a ludicrously jaunty air.

"Bob," said Captain David Watts, "this is Mr. Isaacs. Mr. Isaacs, this is Bob Kenyon, my partner in this deal."

"I'm glad to meet Mr. Isaacs," said Bob Kenyon pleasantly, shaking hands.

"Humph!" grunted Mr. Isaacs ungraciously. "Well, I'll tell you right now, young man, I don't like this business."

Bob Kenyon, taken a little aback, stared at the other; but, before he could speak, Captain David Watts interposed.

"He says our crew of black-skinned rascals, that we let go ashore and warned to keep their mouths shut, have been talking," said Captain David Watts. "So Mr. Isaacs walked."

"I don't understand," said Bob Kenyon.

"You don't, eh?" said Mr. Isaacs crustily. "Well, I think I can make it clear. The whole town is buzzing like a hornets' nest over your pearls. I don't believe for a moment you've got anything much out of the ordinary, but the town

does—the damned things have grown to the size of hens' eggs already." He turned irritably on Captain David Watts. "Why the devil didn't you bring them ashore to me yourself as soon as you dropped anchor this afternoon, instead of sending that black fool with a message to me to come out this evening?"

"Let's go down to the cabin," suggested Captain David Watts placatingly. "We'll get it all straightened out down there."

He led the way. The others followed. Mr. Isaacs sat down at the table. And then Bob Kenyon, leaning negligently against a bulkhead, smiled again as Captain David Watts produced a bottle and set it down in front of the visitor from shore.

"I don't drink," said Mr. Isaacs testily, "and you know it." He shoved the bottle away. "Why don't you answer my question, and where are those pearls?"

"You know why," said Captain David Watts mildly. "It was on your account. I gave the crew shore leave until to-morrow because I thought you could come off here to-night with nobody the wiser about anything. Nobody else knew anything about the pearls. Some friends of mine from that schooner there nearest us came aboard this afternoon to ask what luck we'd had, and have a drink, but they didn't go away burdened with information. I thought I could trust those fellows of mine, and it looked like the best thing to do—they must have got hold of liquor somewhere to loosen up like that."

"A nice mess!" said Mr. Isaacs tartly. "As much as my life is worth! I wouldn't have come at all if I hadn't done business with you for the last few years. Blast it! Don't you understand? I'm seen coming out to your schooner. And then they say old Isaacs has bought the pearls, old Isaacs has got them. And old Isaacs stands the best chance he ever had in his life of getting his throat cut before morning. I'd have had to have some one row me if I'd taken a boat out here from the town, and that would have given the show away. So I slipped out back of the town, and walked. Two miles!" He pushed the pith helmet nervously back on his head—and nervously snatched at it again to save it from falling to the floor as the rear brim of it bumped against his shoulders. "I hope to God I haven't been seen even as it is!"

Bob Kenyon leaned a little forward toward the other.

"You don't mean that literally, do you?" he asked.

"Mean it!" Mr. Isaacs gulped distressingly as though something had caught in his throat. "Of course, I mean it! With the stories going around now that those pearls are the greatest find that has ever been made at one time in the Pacific, there's any one of a dozen men in the riff-raff of the town that wouldn't ask for anything better than a chance to stick a knife into you for them. You ask Captain Watts."

Captain David Watts nodded.

"Yes; that's true," he said. "I've already told Kenyon so."

"Yes," said Mr. Isaacs caustically, "and I suppose what you've really got is worth maybe somewhere around twenty or thirty quid or so!" He jerked his battered pith helmet forward on his head again. "Well, well!" he ejaculated impatiently. "Let's see 'em! Let's see 'em! I want to get back."

"Twenty quid!" repeated Captain David Watts with a quiet chuckle. "Oh, right-o!" He opened the locker, produced the wallet, and from the wallet took out the three pearls. These he laid on the table in front of Mr. Isaacs. "Well, there you are!"

Mr. Isaacs did not move, he simply sat and stared at the pearls; but there was a sudden, sibilant little sound as Mr. Isaacs sucked in his breath.

Captain David Watts hung eagerly over the table. Bob Kenyon, watching, lighted a cigarette.

And then Mr. Isaacs adjusted his amber-colored sun spectacles, and, picking up the pearls one at a time, examined each in turn. Finally, he pushed the three of them away from him, and, with a shake of his head, leaned back in his chair.

"I can't do any business with you," he said brusquely.

Captain David Watts wiped his forehead with his sleeve.

"What's the matter?" he said hoarsely. "I know they're good."

"That's the matter," said Mr. Isaacs. "They're too good for a little island broker like me. I've never seen anything like them before. I tell you frankly I could not even value them. They're worth thousands of pounds."

"Well, make us an offer," suggested Bob Kenyon.

Mr. Isaacs shook his head again.

"I haven't got money enough," he said. "I've got to be honest with you. The run of pearls that are brought in here from the surrounding islands are one thing—these are another. I haven't got money enough, and all the brokers here put together haven't got money enough to buy them."

Captain David Watts laughed boisterously.

"What did I tell you!" he exclaimed gleefully.

Bob Kenyon whistled softly.

"What's to be done, then?" he asked.

Mr. Isaacs reached out for the pearls again, stared at them again, and once more, but with extreme reluctance this time, pushed them away from him.

"Get out of here with them," said Mr. Isaacs bluntly. "With that story going around, and with more than a fair share of the scum of the Pacific here at any time and worse now during the pearling season, it's the only safe thing to do. Besides, the only place to sell these is in the big market, and then to special buyers. My advice to you is to get what stores you need aboard the first thing in the morning and pull out at once for Auckland or Sydney. And, when you get there, clap those pearls in a bank for safe-keeping. They may have to be sent to New York, or Paris, or London. I don't know. Anyway, that's my advice."

"And I'll say it's not bad," said Captain David Watts after a moment. "And I'll say, as I've always said, that you're a square man, Isaacs."

"I'm not so square," said Mr. Isaacs with sudden irascibility. "It's only because I've got to be. You don't think I'm a fool, do you? You don't think I wouldn't like to get my hands on those pearls, do you? Only I wouldn't have any chance of putting anything over on you even if I tried, for sooner or later everybody from Hongkong to the other end of the world will know the price they brought. But I'm not philanthropic either, and business is business, and before you sail, if you like, I'll get some letters ready for you to take along to the right people in Auckland and Sydney who can start things going for you, and I'll leave it to you to say if you think there's a bit of commission coming to me when you've made your sale."

"Fair enough!" said Bob Kenyon promptly.

Captain David Watts gathered up the pearls, replaced them in the wallet, and returned the latter to the locker.

"Aye," he agreed. "And no more than proper, I say."

Mr. Isaacs stood up.

"All right, then," he said. "I'll get back." He secured his pith helmet firmly askew by means of a little corkscrew twist, and headed for the companionway. "One of you will have to take me ashore."

"I'm going ashore," said Bob Kenyon. "I'll take you."

He followed the pearl broker on deck, and started aft behind the other toward where the dinghy was made fast. Halfway along the deck he glanced back. Captain David Watts was just emerging from the companionway. A moment later the other joined him, and, as Mr. Isaacs clambered over the side into the dinghy, Bob Kenyon felt the wallet pressed into his hand. He pocketed it with an amused smile. The old skipper was as fine as they made them—but at times, perhaps, a bit old-womanish. From the day the pearls had been found, Captain David Watts had steadfastly refused any share in their custodianship. Oh, well! What difference did it make? If the old man was the more contented to have it

that way, there was no reason why it should be otherwise.

"I'm going to turn in," said Captain David Watts. "I think you said you were going to take a look at the town, Bob; but I'm not so sure you'd better. You heard what Mr. Isaacs here said."

"Nonsense!" Bob Kenyon laughed. "To begin with, nobody knows who I am except perhaps those chaps who came aboard from that schooner over there this afternoon. I'm not a marked man, even if what Mr. Isaacs says is true. Besides, it isn't even nine o'clock yet, and I shan't be gone more than an hour or two."

"Well, maybe that's so," admitted Captain David Watts. "And anyway, I fancy you can look out for yourself. Good-night, Mr. Isaacs, and many thanks to you!"

Bob Kenyon dropped into the dinghy, shipped the oars, and began to pull away from the schooner.

"You don't want to be landed at that point again, do you, Mr. Isaacs?" he inquired. "I'm rowing over to the town anyway, and it isn't, as you said, as though there was any one to talk who had brought you out here. It'll save you a long walk."

Mr. Isaacs grunted his affirmation.

"I'm not anxious to walk," he said. "There are plenty of places on the beach in front of the town to land without being seen. Just keep away from the rest of the schooners on the way in, that's all."

"Right!" said Bob Kenyon, and settled down to the pull across the lagoon.

And thereafter, apart from the fact that Mr. Isaacs gratified his curiosity with a question or two as to how and where the pearls had been found, the conversation languished. At the expiration of some ten minutes, the distance being but perhaps a quarter of that traversed by Mr. Isaacs in following the windings of the road ashore, the dinghy grounded on the beach at a spot a hundred yards or so away from the town's wharf.

Here, there appeared to be no one about, and,

as they stepped ashore, Mr. Isaacs tapped Bob Kenyon on the shoulder.

"It's none of my business, young man," said he gruffly; "but, unless you're looking for trouble, don't drink with every one you meet. And if you're not sure you can keep your mouth shut, my advice to you is to go straight back to the schooner."

Bob Kenyon smiled quietly.

"I guess I'll be all right," he said.

"Humph!" grunted Mr. Isaacs—and, turning abruptly, trudged off across the sand.

CHAPTER II
THE CRIME

Bob Kenyon pulled the dinghy a little higher up on the beach, and stood for a moment taking stock of his surroundings. Across the beach itself was a fringe of palms. Through these he could see numerous window lights stretching out for quite a distance to right and left. From directly in front of him the strumming of a banjo, the squeak of a fiddle, and the rattle of a tin-pan piano made a riotous, if unmusical, medley of sound, and presently he stepped out in that direction.

He made his way through the trees, and, coming out on the road, found himself in front of a rambling, two-story, wooden structure, every window alight, and which from its sign proclaimed itself to be the Southern Cross Hotel. He did not, however, enter here immediately, but began to stroll leisurely along the street which, though quite dark in spots where the stores and copra agents' offices were closed for the night, was by no means deserted. Natives in *lava-lavas*, that looked like abbreviated aprons of gaudy hue, meandered, never hurrying, here and there. Mingling with these was a sprinkling of East Indian coolies, and, now and then, monarchial in his importance and immensely conscious of his uniform, most polite to the whites and equally brusque with the less for-

tunate of his own color, stalked a native policeman. But to all these Bob Kenyon paid little or no attention. His interest was centered on the whites, little groups of whom—for the most part a rough-and-ready-looking lot and the majority evidently from the pearling fleet—congregated outside the lighted windows of various other public houses of the same ilk as the Southern Cross. And though once or twice he caught snatches of their conversation—"the luck of Captain David Watts" . . . "the greatest find ever made in the Pacific"—he spoke to no one, save to return an occasional good-night that was flung with easy camaraderie in his direction. But into each of these men's faces he looked, not offensively, but steadily and with a disarming smile, as he passed by. It had become a habit of long standing.

And then Bob Kenyon began to enter the various bars. But, though he ordered much, he drank little. He scanned the faces at the bars, and at the gaming tables that were invitingly easy of access. At the end of an hour, apparently a little unsteady on his feet, he found himself again in front of the Southern Cross Hotel. The banjo, the fiddle, and the piano were still in discordant evidence. This time he stepped inside, looked around a little owlishly, lurched toward a table in the corner that was shadowy in the ill-distributed lighting from the oil lamps, subsided somewhat heavily into a chair, and ordered a gin and tonic. The drink, though it was surreptitiously spilled upon the floor, appeared to be the last straw in his bout with sobriety, for presently he sprawled across the table, his head down on his out-flung arms.

The long bar was well patronized. There was constant coming and going. No one paid any attention to the lone figure in the corner.

Bob Kenyon's face, hidden in his arms, was hard-set as he watched. Somehow it was different to-night from all the nights that had gone before. To-night there were *two* faces instead of the one that usually visualized itself before him. To-night there was the face of a girl whose eyes were blue, and whose hair, when the sunlight was on it, was like glinting gold, a sweet, wistful face that kept rising before him, living its way into his life again. And she was here. He knew where *she* was. And the temptation grew strong upon him to go out to where those lighted windows on the hill were because, perhaps, unseen himself, he might obtain a stolen glimpse of her, perhaps see her smile, perhaps hear her voice again.

He half raised his head—and let it drop again. He snarled savagely, contemptuously at himself under his breath. Had he not promised himself that if he came to this island here he would not torture himself with memories of her? Hers was not the face he sought; it was the face of a *man* he searched for amongst those faces there at the bar, as he had searched at other bars, in other islands, in the lowest holes of vice below the equator, along the waterfronts of the shipping centers from China to Honolulu—a face with a close-cropped bullet head, with thick, sensual lips, with slightly slanting eyes, with a complexion that was darkened with a tinge of Malay blood—the face of Shanghai Jim.

Bob Kenyon's white helmet slid a little farther over his forehead, covering still more his eyes as he scrutinized those who came, and went, and lounged about the doors. It was five years since he had seen that face—a year after his elder brother's strange disappearance in Bombay—and he had not even known then that his brother had been murdered, much less that he had stood face to face with—in the person of Shanghai Jim—the murderer himself. And then, after that year, when he had given up hope of ever solving his brother's disappearance, he had made a trip home to New York via England, and in England had met Marion Willetts, who, though she lived on the island of Illola where her father was the Resident, was on a visit to what she too called "home"—as all out-post families of the Empire called the motherland. They had seen a great deal of each other in a very little while. He had returned to Bombay—and then that sinister sequence of events: The murder of a

young Englishman committed by and brought home to Shanghai Jim; Shanghai Jim's flight and disappearance; the night that he, Bob Kenyon, had listened to the tale of his brother's murder told by Shanghai Jim's "runner," Dublin Mike; his meeting again with Marion Willetts as she passed through Bombay on her return to Illola—and his own arrest.

Bob Kenyon's face was as white as the pipe-clayed helmet on his head. Everything had culminated—and ended—that night. He was left with only one aim, one object, one desire in life—to find Shanghai Jim.

And so he had searched for Shanghai Jim, and the years had gone by without sign or trace or vestige of the man. And to-night he still searched—searched each face as it came up there to the bar, not because he had more reason to believe Shanghai Jim was in Illola than anywhere else in this quarter of the world, but because he searched as he always searched—everywhere.

There was a grim tightness to Bob Kenyon's lips. The years stood for futility. The man might be dead. How did he know? It was admittedly astounding that a man like Shanghai Jim, known in his day from end to end of the southern world, the mention of whose sailors' boarding-house in Bombay was an "open sesame" to a flood of fervent and virile blasphemy by seamen wherever ships were found, and the measure of whose iniquity ran the gamut of the decalogue, had succeeded in covering his tracks to such an extent that he had been able to defy discovery. But Shanghai Jim was clever; in his mixed blood he coupled the cunning of the Malay with the diabolical ingenuity of the degenerate white—that was the only way to account for it. It would be more astounding still if a man so widely known as Shanghai Jim, besides being wanted by the police, should have died anywhere unrecognized, his death unreported. No; Shanghai Jim was not dead! Shanghai Jim was alive; not here perhaps, but somewhere, somewhere on this side of the world, because the chances were a thousand to one that the Malay in the man would deny the north—and somewhere, some day, a year or ten from now, he and Shanghai Jim would meet.

Illola—this island here—Marion! Again he was back to that! He had not come here following any clew. In his search he had long since surrendered himself blindly into the hands of fate. His meeting with Captain David Watts in Suva had been purely a matter of chance. He had never seen the man in his life before. But money being no object to him, he had hired the old skipper and his schooner simply because the pearl fisheries offered as hopeful a field as any other.

Bob Kenyon lifted a hand suddenly and brushed it heavily across his eyes. Faces! Faces! Faces! Like mocking ghosts! Not one of them at the bar there was the one he sought. And tonight, as never before, he had become tired of watching them. He was full of disquiet and unrest. He knew why. He had overrated his immunity from the memories that *her* presence here on the same island with him, her nearness to him, might bring.

He lurched up from his chair, and, stumbling in simulated intoxication, made his way out to the street. It was still early, not much more than ten o'clock, and he had been ashore but little over an hour, but his spirit rebelled against any further vigil that night—and it seemed as though he had become mentally fatigued almost to the point of exhaustion. He crossed the road, went down to the beach, and, pushing off the dinghy, began to row back to the schooner.

He rowed leisurely, and presently a quiet born of the serenity of the night fell upon him; and at moments he rested on his oars, allowing the little craft to glide forward under the impetus of his last strokes until, its way quite gone, he pulled on again for a little while. It was very silent out here on the lagoon, but dark now because the moon had gone under a cloud. Elsewhere a sky, wonderfully blue even in the night, sparkled with a thousand stars. And he lost count of time. And finally, drifting silently past the schooner anchored nearest to his own some few hundred yards away, he rounded the counter of

his own vessel, stood up, and, making fast, prepared to clamber aboard.

And then suddenly, half over the rail, he hung for an instant motionless, robbed of all power of movement, as a scream of agony, a horrible sound out of the silence that sent the blood cold in his veins, rang through the night, and, repeated, rang again.

But now Bob Kenyon was in action. The glow from the skylight showed that the lamp was burning in the cabin. The cries had come from there. He leaped across the deck and flung himself down the companionway. And here for an instant again, because it seemed as though his reason had fled and his brain refused its functions, he stood still, save that he swayed upon his feet like a man stunned.

Upon the floor, dead, stabbed, lay Captain David Watts.

A mist seemed to swim before Bob Kenyon's eyes, but out of this mist there loomed another figure—the figure of a man, naked but for the cotton trousers that clung to the flesh as though they had recently been immersed in water—the figure of a man, head lowered, knife in hand, and crouched to spring. And Bob Kenyon's eyes fastened on the other's face—on a face with slightly slanting eyes, with thick, sensual lips, half open now like those of a snarling beast with teeth displayed. And slowly out from his body went Bob Kenyon's great muscular arms reaching toward the other, his fingers wide apart, curved inward like claws, trembling with an unholy eagerness. And from his lips there came a choking sound.

"Shanghai Jim!" he whispered.

"Yes, you damned fool!" snarled the other. "And you're young Hingston. So you've found me, have you? And maybe you thought I didn't know what you've been after for the last five years! Well, you'll have a chance to give my chin-chin to your brother to-night before I'm through with you, and—"

The man stopped abruptly—listening. Subconsciously Bob Kenyon was aware that sounds were coming across the water from the direction of the near-by schooner.

And then Bob Kenyon sprang. There was a flicker of light on the knife blade as Shanghai Jim struck with a swift, full-arm, downward blow, but Bob Kenyon caught the other's wrist, and, as he turned the thrust aside, the blade gashed a cut across Shanghai Jim's own chin. And Bob Kenyon laughed now and grappled with the other, and for a moment, hugged close in each other's embrace, the two men lurched and swayed around the little cabin carrying destruction in their path, and the blood flowing from Shanghai Jim's chin made great crimson blotches on Bob Kenyon's shirt.

Shouts, the sound of oars, came nearer from across the water now. And these sounds seemed to lend an added frenzy to Shanghai Jim's struggles, for the man with a quick, sudden twist broke almost free, and Bob Kenyon, as he sought to tighten his hold on the other, felt his hands slipping on the naked flesh of the man's back and chest. He could not get his grip again. He dug with his fingers mercilessly, with untamed fury, into the man's flesh, making a fold of it, but the fold flattened out, and with a bound Shanghai Jim disappeared up the companionway.

It threw Bob Kenyon off his balance and he stumbled to the floor. Then with a bound he, too, was up the companionway and on the deck after the other. It was dark here, the moon still obscured, but he saw Shanghai Jim, like a black shadow, streak forward across the deck, and, reaching the shore rail, swing himself overboard.

Bob Kenyon whirled in the other direction, and, racing aft, jumped into the dinghy. His jaws were clamped now like a vise. The man had taken the water with scarcely a splash in the hope, no doubt, that he had gained the rail quickly enough to avoid having been seen, and that he, Bob Kenyon, would still be searching the schooner's deck for him. Well, it would not do the other any good! The man could not escape now. Shanghai Jim! The years of it! He knew where Shanghai Jim was now—in the water somewhere. The reckoning would come to-night.

He stood up, staring at the black surface of the water. There was nothing to be seen—not a ripple. The man was swimming under water, of course, but certainly he would also be swimming in the direction of the shore. That was obviously how the man had come out to the schooner—swimming—his cotton drawers had been wet.

Bob Kenyon sat down and began to row the dinghy away from the schooner. He was cool now—almost abnormally cool—but there was something deadly and remorseless in his composure. He kept staring around in all directions at the surface of the water. If the cursed moon would only break free of that cloud! It was just on the edge of it! The trouble was that, curving from the point, the shore line was semi-circular, making a long stretch of beach that was everywhere equidistant from the schooner, and there was no telling just where the man might head for.

It was only two hundred yards. He was halfway in now, and still he had seen nothing. He heard voices from the schooner as the boat's crew from the neighboring craft boarded her. He kept scanning the surface intently until his eyes ached with the strain. Nothing! Shanghai Jim, to give him his due, was a magnificent swimmer.

And then well over to the left, just barely discernible, he saw something dark emerge from the water and disappear quickly in the black shadows of the trees. With a low cry, he spun the boat's head in that direction, and rowed with all his strength. That was Shanghai Jim. He couldn't be mistaken. It wasn't imagination—not just a shadow. They had seen it too from the schooner. They were shouting, and the boat was coming. But there was neither time to wait for them to come up, nor any good to be accomplished by it. Shanghai Jim in the woods there already had too big a lead. Besides, somehow—and a strange laugh came into Bob Kenyon's throat—he preferred to reckon with Shanghai Jim alone.

The boat smashed its nose upon the shore, and leaping from it, Bob Kenyon dashed across the beach. The moon was coming out again. He smiled through grim lips. That would help. He was running now, dodging the trees in his path.

The road ought to be ahead here somewhere. The man couldn't be very far away—he hadn't had that much start.

Bob Kenyon halted for an instant to listen—and faintly, in front of him, he heard the rustle of undergrowth and the snap of a twig. He plunged on once more. But now suddenly he found himself laboring and making progress with difficulty. The ground was rising sharply under his feet. He hadn't noticed that before. And now, too, he was aware of the crashing of branches behind him, the sound of men running, stumbling, tripping, the sound of hoarse shouting. He swore savagely to himself under his breath. Why didn't they spread out fan-wise?

He ran on. Shanghai Jim was in front of him. He was sure of it. He had heard the man that time when he had stopped to listen. The trees seemed to be growing thinner and thinner, with the spaces between all moon-flecked now; but also now, immediately in front of him, what seemed to be a thick wall of foliage blocked his path. Strange! He plunged at it, tore and broke his way through it—and suddenly, on the other side, stood still, panting for his breath, amazed, and for a moment wholly bewildered. A stretch of lawn confronted him. A few yards away there twinkled the lights of a house; and, nearer still, the slim figure of a girl in white, the glint of gold in her hair under the moonlight, the blue eyes wide and startled, stood facing him.

He drew in his breath. He felt the color come and go from his face. He heard himself cry out in a low, inarticulate way. And mechanically he reached his hand to his hat. But he had no hat.

"Mar—Miss Willetts!" he stammered.

She came forward, staring into his face.

"Mr. Hingston!" she said almost inaudibly; and then, with a quick little cry: "What is the matter? There is blood all over you! You are hurt!"

Marion! This was Marion! This was really Marion! But there was something else—there *must* be something else, only his brain seemed all in turmoil. Yes, that was it—Shanghai Jim!

"No, I am not hurt," he blurted out.

"But what are you doing here?" she cried. "Where did you come from? How did you get here? What does it all mean? And who are those men coming there now through the shrubbery?"

He turned as she spoke. Three men were on the lawn, and were running toward him. A voice bawled out:

"You damned hound! We've got you!"

They were upon him, battering at him, striking at him. He heard Marion Willetts scream. He tried to speak—and then, stung to fury by the rain of blows being showered upon him, he struck right and left with all his strength. And then the butt of a revolver crashed against his skull, he felt his knees sag under him—and consciousness was blotted out.

CHAPTER III
WITHOUT ALIBI

When Bob Kenyon regained his senses he found himself in a lighted room, and stretched out on a settee of some kind. There was a buzz of voices around him. His head throbbed and ached miserably, and he blinked suddenly with pain as the reflected light from a mirror on the opposite wall seemed to stab at his eyes. He struggled up on his elbow. Three men were grouped around a flat-topped desk, at which a fourth man, elderly, gray-haired, stern-faced, military in bearing, was seated. At the elderly man's elbow stood Marion Willetts, and in front of her on the desk was a basin and some cloths. What was it all about? Marion's face over there was as white as chalk. And she wouldn't meet his eyes. He raised his hand in a puzzled way to his forehead. His head was swathed in a bandage.

The elderly man at the desk spoke now.

"I have been waiting for you to regain consciousness," he said. "Are you well enough to understand what I say now?"

"Yes, quite all right," Bob Kenyon answered a little jerkily.

"I am Colonel Willetts, and this is the British Residency," said the other. "I am ready to hear anything you have to say, but at the same time I must warn you that any statement you make may be used against you. You are accused of the murder of Captain David Watts."

For an instant the room seemed to swim around Bob Kenyon as he lurched suddenly to his feet. And then, with a grip on himself, his hands clenched, he stood rigid.

"What utter rot!" he said contemptuously.

Colonel Willetts held up the leather wallet and the three pearls.

"These were found on your person when you were brought in here from the lawn a few minutes ago," he stated coldly. "Captain Watts was stabbed to death in the cabin of his schooner. Your clothing is covered with blood, and—"

"Wait a minute!" Bob Kenyon cried out sharply. His brain had cleared now—cleared as in a flash. "This is all some ghastly mistake—and while you're sitting here the man you want is escaping. You've heard of Shanghai Jim, haven't you? You must have heard of him! He was wanted for a murder in Bombay some five years ago. His description was published everywhere."

"I will answer your question," replied Colonel Willetts curtly; "though I do not see what bearing it can have on the matter. I have heard of Shanghai Jim. I know something of his record, and, for that matter, I also know that his description has been for a long time in the hands of the police here, just as it probably has been elsewhere."

"Well, then," said Bob Kenyon tersely, "it was Shanghai Jim who murdered Captain Watts to-night in the cabin, and I—"

"You're a liar!" broke in one of the three men savagely, stepping abruptly forward from the desk. "You know me, don't you? I'm from the schooner that's anchored next to Captain Watts's. You saw me when we came aboard you this afternoon. And I saw you this evening boozing at every bar in town. You're a bad one and a rotter, that's what you are! It wasn't long after I'd got back on board to-night when we heard the screams from Captain Watts's schooner, and

went over there as fast as we could. There wasn't anybody on board except old Dave, dead in the cabin—and then as the moon came out we spotted you in the dinghy making for the shore, and the moment you saw us coming you rowed like mad and tried to make your escape in the woods. If it was this Shanghai Jim that you're so glib about, what became of him? There wasn't any boat but yours on the beach."

"He swam ashore. It was Shanghai Jim I was after," said Bob Kenyon.

"And he swam out to the schooner to begin with to do his dirty work, I suppose?" rasped the man.

"Yes," said Bob Kenyon.

"Hell!" jerked out the man furiously. And then, facing quickly around to Marion Willetts: "I beg your pardon, Miss, but Captain David Watts was one of the oldest friends—and the best—I ever had."

Colonel Willetts turned to his daughter.

"I have allowed you to stay, Marion," he said quietly, "because you said you knew this man; but I think it will be just as well now if you go to your room."

Bob Kenyon's eyes shifted to the girl. She was toying with the basin and cloths—bandages he knew they were now—that lay on the corner of the desk. And now she picked these up, and, without raising her head, started silently away across the room—but, near the door, she paused for an instant as the spokesman of the three men spoke again.

"And that's another point against him, if any more are needed," snapped the man. "He's sailing under two names, if your daughter knew him as Hingston. Captain Watts introduced him to us as Bob Kenyon, his partner. The swine evidently wasn't satisfied with a *share*—he wanted all!"

Bob Kenyon's eyes were still on the girl. She had paused, but she had not looked up, and now she went on again, and the door was closed behind her. He bit his lips. They didn't believe him—but, worse still, they were letting Shanghai Jim escape. They were letting Shanghai Jim escape—the thought brought him to the verge of madness. They must believe him—he must make them—so that they would do something.

"I can explain the names!" he cried out sharply. "Shanghai Jim murdered my brother in Bombay nearly a year before that other murder for which the police want him now. Since then I have been trying to find him. To have kept the name of Hingston would only have been playing into his hands. I took the name of Bob Kenyon."

There was silence for a moment in the room. Bob Kenyon flushed. He was conscious that it had sounded lame.

Colonel Willetts cleared his throat.

"Is there anything more you wish to say?" he demanded.

"Yes!" said Bob Kenyon, a sudden rush of bitterness and passion upon him. "To beg you, for God's sake, not to sit here and let the man escape! I tell you it was Shanghai Jim. When I went aboard to-night I found him in the cabin, a knife in his hand, and Captain Watts dead on the floor. We fought for a minute, but Shanghai Jim broke away from me—we had heard these men coming from their schooner, you understand? Shanghai Jim ran up on deck, and I ran after him. He jumped overboard. I jumped into the dinghy; but he was swimming under water, and I did not catch sight of him again until just as he landed and ran into the woods. I was still out on the lagoon, and that is the reason why at that moment I suddenly, as these men say, began to row like mad."

Again Colonel Willetts cleared his throat.

"As I understand you, then," he said, "when you went aboard, this Shanghai Jim was already in the cabin. You fought for a minute, and, as he broke away, you immediately gave chase, first to the deck, and then at once jumped into your dinghy. Is that correct?"

Bob Kenyon nodded his head.

"Yes," he said.

Colonel Willetts once more held up the wallet and pearls.

"How, then," he asked severely, "do you account for these being in your possession?"

"Why," said Bob Kenyon readily, "they—" He stopped abruptly, a cold sense of disaster seeming suddenly to numb his tongue. To say that they were always kept in his possession through a whim of Captain David Watts! It wasn't only that this, too, might sound lame—it was far worse than that! It was to stamp him both as guilty and a liar. To-morrow, old Isaacs would testify that the wallet and pearls had been taken from a locker by Captain Watts—and had been *replaced* in the locker before he, Bob Kenyon, and Isaacs had left the cabin to go ashore. The truth sounded like a damning lie on the face of it.

His lips tightened. He was in a hole—a bad hole. The evidence was overwhelmingly against him. Those three men there, glaring at him with unfriendly, angry eyes, honestly believed him guilty—as he, in their place, would have believed any man under like circumstances, and with like evidence against him, to be guilty. There was only one chance for him—Shanghai Jim. To find Shanghai Jim again! That was his only chance. It seemed to plumb the depths of irony. It was sardonic. They wouldn't do anything because they didn't believe him. They wouldn't let him do anything. It was as though Hell, on the side of Shanghai Jim, laughed in mockery—while the prey escaped.

He clenched and unclenched his hands, and yet he heard himself speaking now quietly and steadily:

"I haven't answered your question. It's no good my trying to answer it now—or perhaps ever. But I tell you again that it was Shanghai Jim who murdered Captain Watts; that it was Shanghai Jim to-night, who, on account of the stories floating around the town, no doubt, tried to get those pearls; that Shanghai Jim is on this island. I know the evidence is all against me, and that probably the only thing that would clear me, prove my story, is to find Shanghai Jim. In that case, you'd believe me, wouldn't you?"

"Oh, yes, undoubtedly," replied Colonel Willetts a little wearily; "but it is a good many years since this Shanghai Jim disappeared, and, according to your own version, though well known and readily recognizable, he has ever since eluded the police. It is hardly likely that he could have come here without being recognized."

"He has to be *somewhere*," said Bob Kenyon tersely.

"The police theory, I believe," said Colonel Willetts, "is that the man is long since dead."

"He's not dead!" Bob Kenyon cried fiercely. "I saw him to-night. And if you want an additional mark of identification, there's a long gash across his chin that he got in the fight with me for possession of his knife in the cabin. That's where the blood on my clothes came from. You admit that finding him will prove my story. Then it's only fair play that you do something. I've a right to demand that."

There was a mingling of snarls, oaths, and contemptuous laughter from the three men at the desk. Colonel Willetts, with a frown and a wave of his hand, silenced them.

"Yes," he said after a moment's hesitation, "I suppose you are entitled to that. I will order a search made for him in the morning, and, though I say quite frankly that I put little credence in your story, the search will be a thorough one."

"But to-night—now! Between now and morning!" exclaimed Bob Kenyon passionately.

Colonel Willetts shook his head.

"Apart from the town itself and the vessels in the lagoon, which I will attend to to-night, it would be utterly impracticable to beat the miles of bush and woodland on the island in the darkness, where, if anywhere, according to your story, he is most likely to be. That is the best I can do for you."

Bob Kenyon squared his shoulders. It was all he could expect—more, perhaps, than another man in Colonel Willetts's place would have done. There was nothing more to be said.

"Thank you," he said hoarsely.

He sat down on the settee. His head was throbbing brutally. He buried it in his hands, half to ease the pain of it, half because he wanted to try to think, to try to think clearly. There wasn't a loophole—save Shanghai Jim. Unless Shanghai Jim were found now, he, Bob Kenyon, was as good as dead—on the end of a rope. Shanghai Jim! The man seemed to have brought a curse into his life that was to carry through even to an ignominious and hideous end. Shanghai Jim! He could see that face now—the gloating, slanting eyes, the thick, half-parted lips, and—yes, this was queer!—something white around the chin as though a piece of cloth had been tied there.

A sudden cry rose to his lips. He choked it back. He wasn't mad, was he? That *was* Shanghai Jim! Not imagination—Shanghai Jim in the flesh, with a cloth tied around the wound on his chin! And the soul of Bob Kenyon laughed; and the brain of the man, virile, fighting for him as it had never fought before, beat down the promptings of impulse that bade him leap to his feet and fling himself across the room. Through his fingers, as they covered his face, he had been staring at that mirror over there; and in that mirror, from diagonally across the room, was reflected an open window with the face of Shanghai Jim peering in over the sill—both mirror and window out of the range of vision of the men at the desk.

He became aware that Colonel Willetts was speaking to the three men who were grouped around him.

"I shall keep these pearls here to-night," he heard Colonel Willetts say.

Bob Kenyon made no movement save that, still looking through his fingers, he turned his eyes toward the desk. Colonel Willetts was unlocking a drawer. Into this he put the wallet and the pearls, and, closing the drawer, locked it again.

Bob Kenyon's eyes reverted to the mirror. The face was still there—and it seemed to grin now horribly, triumphantly, maliciously.

And now Bob Kenyon was conscious that Colonel Willetts was addressing him directly.

"I sent for the police when you were brought

into the house. They should be here presently. I have no choice but to give you into custody."

Bob Kenyon made no reply. Was he a fool, a blind, mad fool to have flung away his chance of life? The face was gone now! Shanghai Jim was gone! No—he was right, sure of it, certain of it! Something in his inner consciousness assured him he had made the one play that could save him. Long before any one could have got outside, had he given the alarm, Shanghai Jim would have vanished, and in the darkness almost certainly have made his escape; and in that case, knowing he had been seen, Shanghai Jim would not dare to come back. As it was now, Shanghai Jim *would* come back—for those pearls. The window was open—the man had both seen the pearls and had heard Colonel Willetts say they would be kept in that desk there to-night. Yes, in that, he, Bob Kenyon, was right—logically it was without a flaw.

But now—what now? For a moment bitter regret, a stinging, jeering, self-mockery for this very act of his that logic indorsed, swept over him again. Everything that he had told these men to-night in his own defense had seemed flimsy and but to make his case worse. To tell them now that Shanghai Jim *had* been at that window there, and that he had let the man go without a word! He had not thought of that. And he had just been demanding as his right that something be done to catch Shanghai Jim! The position was untenable. They would not believe him, of course. The story was all of a piece—the mythical Shanghai Jim!

And then suddenly there fell upon Bob Kenyon a sort of grim exhilaration. There was one way left, desperate perhaps, but, if it succeeded, sure. After all, this was between Shanghai Jim and himself, all the years of it—and the end was between Shanghai Jim and himself! There was no other end. There could be no other end. He wanted it that way.

Slowly Bob Kenyon raised his head, and as though in a helpless way looked around the room. The police, on their way out from the town, would be here any minute now—Colonel Willetts over there had said so. The settee on which he sat was a light wicker affair of the kind usually in vogue in the tropics. Just within a yard or so of him was a door—not the door through which Marion had gone out and which obviously led into the interior of the house, but a door which quite likely opened on the lawn.

He put his hands to his head again as though in sudden pain, staggered to his feet, swayed unsteadily, and, as if to save himself from falling, reached out to grasp the back of the settee—and then, quick as the winking of an eye, the settee in air above his head, he sent it hurtling toward the group of men at the desk, and with a leap reached the door, flung it wide, and found himself in the open.

Cries, shouts, excited exclamations, and a shot rang out behind him. Bob Kenyon, running at top speed, vaulted the hedge and gained the shelter of the trees. And then he paused to get his breath. It wasn't a question of putting distance between himself and the Residency—that was what they would expect him to do—and that was precisely what he neither wanted nor intended to do. He couldn't afford to go far away. He smiled now a little grimly as he swung himself silently into the branches of a tree that was almost on the fringe of the woods. They couldn't *hear* him up here—and if they couldn't hear him, the chances of finding him in the darkness, as he realized now his chances of finding Shanghai Jim had been when he had chased after the latter, were comparatively nil. Through the foliage he could see the lights of the house. He heard cries from various directions around him—men thrashing through the bushes and undergrowth. Then these sounds grew more indistinct, and finally only reached him faintly from the distance.

And then another moment of disquiet came. Suppose that in view of all this hubbub Shanghai Jim, for the very reason that he, Bob Kenyon, had refrained from giving the alarm when the other was at the window, might not return!

No! He shook his head decisively. It was not at all the same thing as though Shanghai Jim had had to run for it knowing that he had been discovered at the window. As a matter of fact, having heard probably the greater portion of the conversation that had taken place in the room, and having heard, if still in the immediate neighborhood, the sounds of sudden excitement and a shot from the house, Shanghai Jim would put two and two together, and would arrive pretty accurately at the truth of who was really the quarry—and in that case Shanghai Jim's position, in Shanghai Jim's mind, would be immeasurably bettered, for, if he then returned and stole the pearls, the theft would naturally be laid at Bob Kenyon's door. True, those out on the man-hunt now might stumble upon Shanghai Jim—but the possibility was very remote.

Bob Kenyon eased his cramped position as best he could. Shanghai Jim would be back there to-night when the way was clear and the lights were out and the Residency was asleep—and so would he, Bob Kenyon! He must believe in that, cling to that belief—if not, he might as well chuck up the sponge. It was no longer a matter alone of bringing his brother's murderer to account; his own life depended on it now, and . . . and . . . He felt the sudden twitching of his lips though they were tight pressed together. Something within him was fighting stubbornly for expression. Why hold it back? Why not admit it? There was no one to see or hear. Marion! She had not looked at him. She had refused to meet his eyes. She might not care—she could not care now. It was too long ago. But, deny it if he would, however little it might mean to her, vindication in her eyes meant more to him to-night, now, since he had seen her again, than the mere fact that he should go free. His hands clenched upon the branches that supported him until the knuckles stood out like knobs under the tight-drawn skin. The years had been very empty without her.

"Marion!" Bob Kenyon whispered out into the night.

CHAPTER IV
WHAT THE TRAP CAUGHT

The lights still burned in the Residency. Bob Kenyon sat there in the tree for a long time—sat there until there was no longer any sound in the woods around him save only the sounds of the insects, and the soft flutter of the leaves in their thousands stirred by the gossip of the night breeze in the branches of the trees; sat there until the lights yonder began to go out one by one, and until by and by the Residency was all in darkness.

And then Bob Kenyon lowered himself to the ground, and began to make his way cautiously toward the house. There should be little trouble in gaining entry into the Residency. In the heat of the tropics, save in a storm, windows were not closed and bolted; and the shutters that served for privacy were obstacles of a far lesser nature. He reached the edge of the lawn, and, moving now with still greater caution than before, skirted the hedge until he arrived at a position opposite to the door by which, as nearly as he could judge, he had made his escape. And then on hands and knees he crawled across this portion of the lawn, and stood up finally against the wall in the shadow of the house. Yes, here was the door! He tried it. It was locked. He moved then to the window beside it. By the aid of a little force, but with scarcely a sound, he got the shutters open—and the next minute he had swung himself over the sill, and dropped silently to the floor inside the room.

He listened now. There was not a sound—no movement apparently anywhere in the house. This was the room, wasn't it? He could hardly have made a mistake—but he must make sure. He began to grope around him. It was very dark in here. He could see nothing. He dared not light a match—it might give warning to Shanghai Jim. His lips twisted in the darkness. Shanghai Jim! How did he know that Shanghai Jim had not already been here? How sure was he now, after all, that he still had not played the fool? He snarled at himself irritably under his breath. Was it the darkness and the silence that conjured up doubts and fancies and disturbing theories in his mind? Shanghai Jim wouldn't have come until the lights were out, that was certain—and since he, Bob Kenyon, had come the moment the last light had been extinguished, Shanghai Jim could not reasonably have been here ahead of him. As a matter of fact, the household could but barely have retired by now. What time was it? He had no means of telling. He could not see his watch. At a guess it might be one o'clock—perhaps two.

His hands groping out before him touched a piece of furniture—felt over it. It was the flat-topped desk. So far, so good! He moved a little away from it, and, finding a chair, sat down. He had nothing to do now but wait.

The time dragged itself by. Bob Kenyon sat without movement. The silence seemed to become more and more profound with each passing moment, save that after a while it began to possess *noises* of its own—to beat and palpitate against his ear-drums, startling him every now and then into the belief that some actual sound had been made. It brought his nerves to tension, like tight-drawn bow strings; it peopled the darkness with imaginary and flitting shadows.

Suppose Shanghai Jim didn't come?

The phrase began to repeat itself over and over in his brain, and in a sing-song way kept tempo and rhythm with that throb, throb, throb of the silence in his ears.

Suppose Shanghai Jim didn't—

It sounded like a faint footfall. He derided himself viciously under his breath. He had heard dozens of footfalls in the last—how long was it, anyway?—half hour, or hour, that he had sat here. It was gone now like all the rest. There remained just that damnable pounding in his ears again, and—

No! Not this time! This was not imagination! A door into the room was being quietly opened. And now his eyes, straining, made out what seemed like a black shadow even against the sur-

rounding darkness. It came nearer and nearer. Shanghai Jim! Shanghai Jim! Bob Kenyon's shoulders drew forward until his body was crouched to spring. It seemed as though every emotion he possessed were culminating in one vast upheaval of his soul—that he gloated in this moment which through all the years he had waited for. Nearer—still nearer! The shadow was opposite to him now, not a yard away—and Bob Kenyon, laughing in a low, choked way, sprang from the chair and launched himself upon it.

Something yielding, something without resistance, something that crumpled to the floor, carrying him with it, met his attack. Bob Kenyon in a blind way gained his knees, and for an instant it seemed as though his heart had stopped its beat. And then like a man crazed and distraught he leaned forward again touching the soft, clinging garment that enveloped the form upon the floor—and lifting up a woman's head, he pillowed it on his shoulder. He whispered her name over and over again. He did not need to see. It mattered nothing if the darkness hid her face. He knew.

"Marion! Marion!" he whispered wildly. "Have I hurt you?"

She stirred a little.

"Who is that?" she said faintly. "What—what has happened? I could not sleep to-night, and so—"

"It's John Hingston," Bob Kenyon broke in hoarsely. "Are you badly hurt? Have I hurt you?"

"No," she said—and then suddenly with a low, startled cry as full consciousness seemed to return to her, she drew herself sharply away and struggled to her feet. "You—you here?" she faltered. "It was bad enough before—in Bombay. But I did not want to believe to-night. And now you are back here—that desk—those pearls. Have you already got them? If not, I—I think you had better go before I call out. If you have already taken them, you must put them back."

Bob Kenyon, too, was on his feet now. He fought to steady his voice.

"Would you take my word for it?" he asked. "How would you know whether I had them or not?"

"I know where the key is. I shall look," she replied evenly.

It was a moment before Bob Kenyon spoke again. Vindication in her eyes, his own life, depended not only on the fact that he should stay here, but that Shanghai Jim should have no warning.

"No," he said deliberately at last; "you are not going to look. Nor are you going to raise any alarm. You are either going to return to your own room with the promise that you will say nothing of my presence in the house, or you are going to sit down in that chair there and not make a sound—I only hope we haven't made too much noise already. You must make your choice."

"My *choice*! Do you realize what you are saying?" she flashed out instantly. "Do you think that you can frighten me? You would not dare—"

"Oh, yes, I would!" interrupted Bob Kenyon in a strangely dogged way. "And I must ask you not to speak above a whisper. When one is desperate, one dares anything. I would dare anything to-night. I've got to make you understand that. I would even dare to tell you what I am sure you once knew—that I love you."

He heard her draw in her breath with a sudden gasp—as though anger and amazement struggled for the supremacy.

"Which will you do?" he demanded.

"Neither!" she exclaimed sharply.

"It would be safer if you went back to your room." He spoke in low, steady tones now. "You would be out of danger. I am waiting for Shanghai Jim."

"Shanghai Jim?" She repeated the words with a curious little note of interrogation, as though she were not sure she had heard aright.

"I saw him in that mirror on the wall over there when they were grilling me here in this room to-night," he said. "He was standing outside the window."

"And you said nothing?" Her voice was flat, dull.

"Because, before anybody could have reached him, he would have made his escape in the woods, just as I did—and he would not have come back. As it is, he saw the pearls placed in that desk. It's his one chance to get them, for Heaven knows where they'll be to-morrow—and so I am waiting for him now."

There was a slight rustle of her garments.

"I—I am sitting down in the chair," she said.

It was very quiet in the room now—and it was a long minute before Bob Kenyon broke the silence. He moved closer to the chair—and suddenly impulse stronger than himself surged upon him, and he knelt beside it.

"Marion!" he said.

She did not answer.

He felt his pulse quicken, the blood pound through his veins. He had called her Marion—and she had not rebuked him. And then the great shoulders of the man squared. Did it mean that there was a chance—a chance for *more* than vindication? A chance to fight for more than life? He scarcely dared trust his voice to hold to the low, guarded whisper that it must not exceed.

"Will you listen?" he said huskily. "It has been wrong, all wrong, between us—since that night. You know that when I first met you in England my brother had disappeared for over a year, and that I had given up all hope of ever discovering what had happened to him. You know that my brother and I were the last of our family and fairly well off—too well off, perhaps, for my brother's sake. His commission business in Bombay was merely a side issue with him. He lived there because he liked the place, and I'm afraid he went the pace and had a bit of a reputation. When I left college I went out to join him, and it was then, almost immediately after my arrival, that he mysteriously disappeared. I had made very few acquaintances; in fact, I was scarcely known at all. I let the clerk run the business, such as it was, and spent months trying to find my brother. I went everywhere, I think, in that quarter of the globe—and then, as I said, when I had given up all hope of ever hearing anything about him, I went to America and England for a change, before returning to Bombay to wind up the business there, as I had no intention of living in Bombay myself."

Bob Kenyon paused for an instant. The figure in the chair beside him did not move, did not speak.

He went on again:

"I returned to Bombay. You will remember that you expected to come out that way on your return home to Illola here a month or so later, and—and you were to let me know what ship you were coming on."

She spoke now for the first time.

"I wrote you two weeks before I sailed—as soon as I knew myself," she said almost inaudibly.

"I never got the letter," said Bob Kenyon with a quick intake of his breath.

"Would it have mattered?" she said dully. "I can not see that it would."

"But I can—now!" There was something suddenly vibrant in Bob Kenyon's whispering tones. "Marion! Marion! Listen! A week or so after I got back to Bombay, this Shanghai Jim, whom I knew well by sight because in my previous search for my brother I had been several times in his dive as I had been in many others seeking information, murdered a young Englishman in a fit of his diabolical Malay rage, and badly wounded his own 'runner' who had tried to interfere. He just barely managed to make his escape from the police, and fled no one knew where. Then, a few days before you arrived, though I did not know then that you were on the ship, I received a message to go to the hospital where Shanghai Jim's 'runner,' a man known everywhere on the waterfront as Dublin Mike and who had been there in hospital for weeks with his wounds, was dying and wanted to see me. I went; and to revenge himself, of course, on Shanghai Jim, Dublin Mike told me the story of my brother's death."

Again Bob Kenyon paused. It seemed as though the form in the chair before him, indis-

tinct as it was, had changed position and was leaning a little forward toward him.

"Shanghai Jim," said Bob Kenyon after a moment, "besides his sailors' boarding-house, ran a low gambling dive. My brother went in there one night and foolishly displayed a large sum of money. Between them, Shanghai Jim and Dublin Mike drugged him and took the money; and then, to get rid of him, they shanghaied him. They put him on board a sailing ship that night—and got their commission for it, too, out of the ship's captain. But before they put him on board, they doped him again, and this time gave him a deliberate overdose of the drug. They couldn't afford to have him come back on them with his story. The result was that the ship's captain got what he thought was the ordinary run of drunken sailor; but what he really got was a man, under whatever fictitious name Shanghai Jim had seen fit to ship him, who never regained consciousness, and who died and was buried two days later at sea."

"Yes," she said a little tremulously.

"I asked Dublin Mike where he thought Shanghai Jim had gone, and Dublin Mike, dying though he was, cursed Shanghai Jim as I had never heard a man cursed before. He said Shanghai Jim was too clever for the police, that the police would never find him, and that there was only one way, one chance—to pick up a clew in some of the dives where Shanghai Jim might have made a confidant of some one, and especially in a famous dope joint run by a Chinaman named Ling Su, and so—"

A sudden, half-choked sob came from the chair.

"Don't!" she interrupted in a quick, low, broken way. "I—I know now. I understand. That night when we had made up a little slumming party from the ship, and I—I saw you coming out of that miserable doorway looking the way you did! I—I thought you had forgotten me and my letter in—in a debauch."

Bob Kenyon's hand felt out before him almost as though it were afraid, and found and lay over the back of hers.

"Yes," he said, "I had been nearly two days in Ling Su's. As I told you, hardly any one in Bombay knew me. I was dressed for the part. I had got the entrée there through Dublin Mike. I—I saw you—I see you now—standing outside that doorway with all those chaps and girls. I had forgotten what I looked like, unshaven, filthy, unkempt, disreputable. I had forgotten my part at sight of you. I don't blame one of those chaps who was with you for doing what he did. I should have done the same. I looked exactly what he called me—a drunken bum. But I had forgotten all that for the moment when I jumped toward you and caught your hand; and when he struck me in front of you, I—I lost my head. The other men who were with your party naturally joined in when I knocked that first chap down, and just as naturally the hangers-on in that locality, the habitués of the dives, believing me to be one of themselves, sided in with me. In the mêlée that followed, besides being arrested, I was rather badly hurt by one of the police. I was off my head for several days, and when I got around again, you had left Bombay, and—and you had left no word."

She was crying softly in the darkness.

"Oh, I didn't know, I didn't know you had been hurt like that! They told me that your brother had had a very bad record, and that you, as much as was known of you, were like him—spending most of your time in places like that. I know why now, but I didn't understand then. That was why I went and left no word. I thought that my arrival in Bombay was of far less consequence to you than a night in your usual haunts. And—and I think that night when I saw you like that I wanted to die, because—because—" Her voice broke.

"Because—because you cared?" he whispered eagerly. "Was it that?"

There was no answer.

His arms reached out to her, encircled her, drew her close to him.

"Marion! Marion—was it that?" he urged hoarsely.

Her voice was so low he could barely catch her words.

"I have always cared," she said. "Always, always, always."

A great tenderness, and a great awe, and a great glory were upon him. And his lips found hers, and found the tear-wet eyelids; and his hand caressed her hair and brushed it back from her forehead.

And for a time neither spoke.

And then she stirred in his arms, and suddenly her hands were lifted to cling passionately to his shoulders, and she was whispering wildly:

"Oh, I am afraid! I am afraid! If he doesn't come what will you do? They will hunt you—catch you—and—and without this Shanghai Jim the evidence is all against you. Even I was a witness against you—your name. I waited outside the door and heard you explain that, but—but without Shanghai Jim you would never be believed."

"He will come," Bob Kenyon answered. He laid his hands over hers on his shoulders. He was strangely sure now. He *knew*. "He will come," he said again.

"But he may not dare—even for the pearls," she said fearfully. "If he is clever enough to be here in a small place like this and the police not know it, even though they have his description, he is too clever to run any risk of falling into a trap."

Bob Kenyon drew her cheek against his own.

"That's just it," he said reassuringly. "He has no reason to think there is the slightest risk of a trap; and, besides that, if he knows that I escaped, which I am pretty sure he does, he knows that if he gets the pearls to-night the theft will be attributed to me, and so contribute another link in the evidence against me for the murder of Captain Watts. I don't know how he has evaded the police. He may only have put in here on one of the pearling schooners. He may have been living here harbored and sheltered by some confederate. I don't know. I've been trying to answer that question for five years all over this part of the world. But I will know to-night. He will come. I saw it in his eyes and I saw it in his face at the window. He will come." His hands tightened suddenly, warningly, upon her. "He is coming now! Do you hear that? At the door over there—the outside door!"

"Yes," she breathed.

He drew her silently away from the chair, and, retreating back along the wall, crouched down behind what, in the darkness, seemed to him to be a bookcase of some sort.

"Don't make a sound until I tell you," he cautioned; "then run instantly for your father and any other men who may be in the house. Do you understand?"

"Yes," she answered; "but—but you?"

"There is absolutely nothing to be afraid of," he whispered back. "Now quiet—don't move—don't stir! He's got the door open now."

There was a faint, low, creaking sound from across the room. Then utter silence. It seemed to last interminably. Then there came the soft *pad* of a footfall treading warily; and, peering out, Bob Kenyon could discern a blur of white in the darkness. It came on, a shadowy, filmy thing, crossing the room; and now it reached the position where the desk stood, and seemed to hover there. Shanghai Jim—Shanghai Jim at last! Quietly Bob Kenyon released his arm from the girl's grasp, and crept silently a few steps forward in the direction of the desk.

And then he stood still.

A match crackled and spurted into flame. The figure at the desk, holding the little torch, back turned, was bending over and examining the lock on the drawer.

And upon Bob Kenyon there descended a sudden sense of utter hopelessness, of dismay, of disaster. Everything, far more now than when he had stolen into this room, far more than mere life itself, the love that he knew now was his, its promise and the wondrous vista of the years that only a little while ago he had glimpsed ahead, were all, as though by a single, mocking stroke of fate, shattered and destroyed. That wasn't

Shanghai Jim there. It was a man who wore a ridiculously large pith helmet. It wasn't even necessary to see the other's face, though he had, indeed, caught a side view of it. It was old Isaacs, the pearl broker—old Isaacs with a revolver dangling in his free hand.

The match went out. There came a sound much like the gnawing of a rat. The man was working at the drawer.

And then the numbness following, as it were, a blow that had been struck him, began to clear from Bob Kenyon's brain. It wasn't Shanghai Jim—but it wasn't hopeless either. He understood now. It was clear—even childishly clear. He had evidently hit the nail on the head when he had said that Shanghai Jim was protected and helped by some confederate ashore. That confederate was old Isaacs. Old Isaacs was the only one who had been shown the pearls and had reason to believe they were in Captain Watts's locker; and, pretending they were beyond his reach financially, had said so with specious honesty—and had sent Shanghai Jim to get them *for nothing*. Yes, he saw it all now. Shanghai Jim was in turn the only one, apart from those then present in the room here, who knew the pearls had been placed in the drawer of the desk. But Shanghai Jim had also *heard* what had been said—and with that knife gash across his chin which was proof of his, Bob Kenyon's, story, and which would instantly attract attention and mark his identity to even a casual glance, had not dared venture out any more in person. And so it had been old Isaacs's turn again.

Grim-lipped, his jaws clamped, Bob Kenyon was creeping silently on again toward the desk. It wasn't Shanghai Jim there—but old Isaacs must know where Shanghai Jim was hiding. That was enough—because old Isaacs would tell all he knew! There wouldn't be any mercy. With his fingers once on old Isaacs's throat, the man would *talk*!

The attack upon the desk drawer went on, and in the stillness it seemed to sound thunderously loud. Bob Kenyon crept nearer—still nearer. He was close enough now to spring, and he crouched a little, poised.

"*Now*, Marion! Quick!" he called, and launched himself forward.

He heard a sharp, startled oath; he heard Marion's footsteps racing from the room; he heard her calling wildly for her father; and then, even as he closed with the man in front of him, there was a blinding flash, the roar of the report, and the flame-tongue of a revolver shot scorched his face. And now, locked together, they lurched and staggered here and there in the darkness, Bob Kenyon's left arm hooked like a vise around the man's neck, his fingers feeling, searching, clawing for a throat-hold, while his right hand grasped at the other's wrist, struggling for possession of the weapon.

A minute passed—another. The man, old as he was, seemed to possess a maniacal strength; he tore and struck and battled like a demon, snarling oaths with hot, panting breath, raving in a fury as ungovernable as the fury with which he fought. But tighter and tighter now Bob Kenyon's fingers fastened themselves in the flesh of the man's throat; and his other hand, though it slipped again and again in the struggle for the ugly prize, still pinioned the wriggling, twisting wrist.

This way and that about the room they reeled, and then suddenly as they smashed against the wall and rebounded from it, a chair in their path crashed to the floor entangling their legs, and for an instant they hovered erect, swaying, straining to maintain their balance, then, tottering, pitched downward. Bob Kenyon, uppermost, was conscious of a great, roaring sound in his ears, of a revolver flash that was strangely obscured beneath his body, and of a sudden relaxation in the other's struggles—a sudden stillness in the form under him. It did not move any more. It did not snarl.

In a half-dazed way he rose to his feet. And subconsciously now he was aware that there was light in the room, and that others were there too—Colonel Willetts amongst them, clad in pyjamas. But he was staring down at the floor where a man with a revolver, still smoking, still clasped in his hand, lay dead. And there was a pith helmet there on the floor too, a ridiculously large one and most outrageously dirty; and moreover there was something very strange about the man's face—as though the beard were all lop-sided, as though it had been torn away from one side and had flopped over on the other, and where there was no beard a great strip of surgeon's plaster showed across the chin.

There was a stir in the room—voices—some one touched his arm.

But Bob Kenyon did not move. He was staring down into the face of Shanghai Jim.

THE PYTHON PIT

GEORGE F. WORTS

GEORGE FRANK WORTS (1892–1962) was a prolific short-story writer and novelist, both under his own name and as Loring Brent. Although a frequent contributor to the top-paying slick magazines of the time, such as the *Saturday Evening Post, Ladies' Home Journal, Everybody's,* and *Collier's,* he is best remembered today for his numerous contributions to pulp magazines in the 1920s and '30s. He wrote in many different genres, but his best work was in the realm of adventure fiction. Six films were made from Worts's stories and novels, most notably *The Phantom President* (1932), based on the 1932 novel of the same title, which starred Claudette Colbert and George M. Cohan in his first speaking role.

In addition to Peter the Brazen, whom he created under the pen name Loring Brent, perhaps Worts's most famous character is Samuel Larkin Shay, a.k.a. Singapore Sammy, who appeared in numerous pulp stories in the pages of *Argosy.* Sammy is an American citizen from the Midwest who has spent the past six years as a restless rover of the South Seas. He is searching for his rogue stepfather, who deserted him and his mother when Sammy was two years old, absconding with the family will that would have left Sammy a fortune. To collect his rightful inheritance, Sammy will endure virtually any hardship or danger.

"The Python Pit" was originally published as a serial in the May 6, May 13, and May 20, 1933, issues of *Argosy.*

THE PYTHON PIT

GEORGE F. WORTS

Lucky stayed where Singapore propped him.

WHETHER IT HELD FABULOUS PEARLS, OR CANNIBALS, SINGAPORE SAMMY WAS GOING TO THAT FORBIDDEN SOUTH SEAS ISLE—TO KILL A MAN.

CHAPTER I
BATTLE ROYAL

IT WAS New Year's Eve in the Sailors Delight, and Singapore Sammy was going to be rolled. He knew he was going to be rolled. And he suspected that he was going to be murdered. And he was reasonably sure that his partner Lucifer—"Lucky"—Jones was about to lose his luck and become vulture fodder unless something was speedily done about it.

Singapore Sammy saw the blue bottle spinning lazily through the air toward Lucky Jones's head, spilling its white contents as it came. Lucky was so occupied that he did not see the bottle. With his eyes gleaming with the love of battle, his wild black hair flying, his big jaw outthrust, he was driving his fists into the face of a Japanese sailor. The Jap went down.

Lucky evidently saw the bottle now but was unable to move—like a man in a nightmare rooted to a railroad track down which a train is thundering.

"Duck!" Singapore Sammy roared.

But Lucky Jones was incapable of ducking. As if he were hypnotized, he stood there and let

"Where is he?"
Singapore demanded.

the half-empty arrack bottle go twirling to its destination, which was a spot on his forehead just above the left eye. He sagged from sight— and the brawl went on.

With the best of intentions, Singapore Sammy had started it, when a Malay with one eye reached up and snatched at the copper wire encircling his neck. He had swiftly closed the Malay's other eye, and had recognized in the Malay's fat, brown, oily companion a man he was extremely anxious to have speech with.

But the oily one had evaded him. And every man in the room had wolfishly fallen upon the two Americans, proving that it does not pay to be an American in a foreign port these days when a brawl starts.

Singapore Sammy, who hated brawls, had acted promptly, however, upon experience. He wrenched a leg from a table and, using it as a club, battered every head that came within reach. And in the forty or fifty seconds which elapsed

from the brawl's beginning to Lucky's terminating the flight of the blue bottle, Singapore Sammy had accounted for three Malays, two Japanese sailors, two Chinese coolies and a tall unknown white man who now sat on the floor in a corner mourning a broken nose.

Tobacco smoke hung in creamy layers under the ceiling. Mingling upward were the sour fumes of alcohol from broken glasses and over-turned bottles. Shrill curses and yells in many tongues rounded off an impression of great confusion.

Singapore Sammy deftly knocked a gun out of one hand and a gleaming *parang* out of another. The police would be here any moment. What would the judge say?

"Ah-ha!" the judge would say. "So you're back again, Mr. Shay! I thought you were told to keep out of Singapore."

And Singapore Sammy—otherwise, Samuel Larkin Shay, American-born but at present citizen of the world—would enjoy the doubtful hospitality of Singapore Town for thirty or, maybe, sixty days.

One of the red-headed American's eyes was turning purple. Blood trickled in a thick red stream from a cut under the other one. His carrot-colored eyebrows moved in agitated jumps. When he was angry, they always did that—wriggling around on his sun-baked forehead like dancing red mice.

A Chinese, biding his time, leaped up unexpectedly and tried to snatch the soft copper wire from Singapore Sammy's neck. Some one else locked arms around his knees. He felt hands pawing at his hip pockets. That was where he carried his bankroll. And the Jap sailor was rushing at him with a three-legged stool in his hands.

Sammy saw that fat, oily, little Malay sliding along the wall toward a door. He couldn't reach him. But he must reach him. He laid about him with the table leg. The Chinese sat down and began to moan. The unseen enemy who had tackled his knees now sank his teeth into the calf of Sammy's left leg. Sammy bounced his club off the Jap's head, and the Jap also went into a flat spin.

But Sammy couldn't wield that club much longer. His throat was as dry as gunsmoke. His heart had become a throbbing ache. His muscles were striking for a five-hour day. He brought the club crunching down on an upturned ear above his left foot, and the teeth disengaged themselves from his calf.

A woman screamed. Her voice penetrated the uproar thinly, like the voice of a locust in a noisy jungle. There was a sudden hush, a sudden cessation of hostilities. And through the doorway surged a dozen—or a score—of Japanese sailors, looking very businesslike and anti-American in their trim blue uniforms.

Sammy saw the dark head of Lucky Jones rise up as if from the dead and waver like a wind-blown poppy. He shouted, "Out the back door!" But Lucky apparently heard nothing but birds.

The oily one was running for the door. Singapore overtook him, drove a sledgehammer fist into the brown jaw, and hooked his hand under his belt as the Malay dropped. He grabbed Lucky by the elbow with his free hand and, carrying the Malay as if he were a scuttle of coal, managed to escape as the Japanese invaders turned the Sailors Delight into another Manchuria.

He even managed, handicapped as he was, to break into a trot in the narrow alley at the far end of which the lights of the roadstead twinkled.

A cool breeze blew refreshingly into his hot face. With his burdens, Singapore Sammy trotted down the alley, never pausing, in spite of bursting lungs, until he reached the breeze-swept park that is known as Raffle's Reclamation. Here, a dog of war might pause to lick his wounds.

It seemed to him that he could still hear the clamor of the Sailors Delight, could still smell the fumes of alcohol. He was exhausted and still disgruntled.

With a faint grunt, Lucifer Jones slid to the ground and back into unconsciousness. Singapore arranged him on a bench under a date palm, then propped up his captive in a sitting position beside it and waited for him to come around. While waiting, he took inventory.

His disgust was violently intensified by the discovery that he had, in spite of his efforts, been robbed of $1200 in American banknotes. A quick inspection of the soft copper wire encircling his tough brown neck left him slightly comforted. The little chamois sack dangling at the end of the copper loop had not been looted. The blue fire pearl was still there.

But his money, his share in the proceeds of four months of sweat, toil and haggle with Chinos and Malays and black-skinned savages under broiling tropical suns, was lost forever. Some clever hand had plucked it out of his pocket, back there in that hellhole. An investigation of Lucky's pockets revealed that he, too, had been relieved of his personal fortune.

All gone! And it remained for this fat, oily,

unconscious Malay to say whether it had gone in a good cause. Would he talk, or would he refuse to talk?

He presently opened his eyes and blinked at the red-haired man. Sammy gave him a decent interval in which to pull himself together, then said, curtly, "Stand up, scum!"

The Malay groaned again. His hand swiftly went to where his knife had been. His eyes narrowed. The white man lifted one foot. The Malay, squealing, sprang up.

Hitching up his belt in a businesslike manner, the red-headed man growled, "Are you gonna tell me where my old man is, or do I have to shove your nose down between your shoulder blades?"

The Malay, with terror in his eyes, backed against the rough bole of the date palm. He was panting. His mouth hung ajar in an awful grimace, revealing his betel-blackened gums. His teeth were red.

The American shot a hand to the oily brown throat and held him rigidly against the tree.

"Spit it out!"

"*Tuan*, I do not know!"

Singapore banged the frizzly black head against the tree. The Malay repeated that he did not know until a muscular thumb was applied to his Adam's apple. Then he whimpered, "He will keel me, *tuan*, if I tell!"

"I'll kill you quicker if you don't! Where is he?"

He accented each word with increased pressure on the Malay's Adam's apple. The brown man's eyes were bulging.

"He is not in Singapore, *tuan*!"

"Ah!" Sammy breathed. "Where is he?"

"I do not know, *tuan*. I swear to you—" He gasped for breath now. He wriggled and kicked out with his feet. But the relentless hand of the white man held his head immovable.

"Konga!" he gasped.

Singapore Sammy relaxed the pressure. "What's that?"

"Konga!"

"Where is Konga?"

"East of Celebes! Please, *tuan*, let me go!"

"When did he leave?"

"Last night, *tuan*, on the bark *Bangalore*. She sailed on the ebb-tide!"

CHAPTER II
THE GIRL

Singapore Sammy stared at him with the aid of a remote arc light, saw the terror which made the Malay's eyes look sick, and dropped his hand. "Lam," he growled.

The Malay lammed. At a safe distance he panted threats and curses, then dived into the shrubbery.

For the past two weeks, since his return to the Straits Settlements, it had been Singapore Sammy's regular habit to prowl among the water-front dives, either alone or with Lucky, and to browse through the Chinese and Burmese districts, where pearl and elephant men foregathered, peering into bright shop windows, peering into faces, searching, always searching for an old man who might or might not be wearing the yellow rags of a Buddhist begging priest.

This man was Sammy's stepfather, and for seven years Sammy had been trailing him. When Sammy was a child of two, Bill Shay had deserted him and Sammy's mother, to answer the siren call of the Orient, taking with him all of Sammy's mother's savings and the will of Sammy's grandfather, which bequeathed to Sammy a fortune upward of a million dollars. Without the will, Sammy could not claim that fortune. And he could not secure the will until he had found his father.

The chase had taken him up and down and back and forth across Asia from Vladivostok to the Red Sea, from Darjeeling to Papeete. Always, that old rogue was one jump ahead of him. For Bill Shay was as clever as he was unscrupulous. He was a thief, a murderer, and, on occasions, a polished man of the world.

This time the trail had led from Bangkok to Singapore. And if Sammy had not encountered that Malay, whom a friendly bartender had informed him was Bill Shay's number one boy, the trail would have vanished again.

Now it led to Konga. Why Konga? Pearls, no doubt. Well, he would follow the trail to Konga. He must have that will. With the money to which it rightfully entitled him, he and Lucky could buy a small fleet of coasting steamers, now available at a rock-bottom figure. They reasoned that the depression would soon be over. And with business on the upgrade, that small fleet of steamers would make them a fortune.

Lucky Jones was groaning. His eyes presently opened. He sat up and clapped both hands to the seat of his pants.

"They got my roll!" he cried hoarsely.

"Happy New Year," Singapore said. "We've both been rolled. We're clean. But I've picked up the old man's trail again."

Lucifer Jones came, swaying, to his feet. He emitted a trumpet-like yell. "Come on!" he panted. "Back we go!"

"Cool down," Singapore said. "It's all over. It's a closed book. We start to-day with a brand-new calendar."

A heated argument began. Lucifer wasn't going to let that gang walk off with his fortune. Singapore argued that the Japs had taken possession of the Sailors Delight and would give them a welcome they would never forget.

"Listen," he said. "Listen, I've picked up the old man's trail."

Lucky eventually listened. "He's on his way," Singapore explained, "to Konga. It's an island eastward of Celebes, and it must be in the Arafura Sea. Did you ever hear of Konga?"

The reiteration of the word brought Lucky Jones completely, sharply, to his senses. He ran the fingers of both hands through his wild black hair. His gleaming dark eyes, one open wide, the other partly obscured by a mouse, gave him the look of a rampant buccaneer. With his hawk's nose, his sun-blackened skin, his sledgehammer jaw, he looked dangerous. He smacked one fist into the palm of the other hand.

"Konga!" he echoed. "How do you get that way, Redhead? I wouldn't put foot on that island for a million bucks! It's haunted!"

"Yeah?" Singapore growled.

"I mean haunted," the buccaneer said, almost savagely. "No man who goes ashore there is ever seen again."

"There you go!" the redhead said, with a deep sigh. "Always seein' spooks. Always throwin' salt over your left shoulder. Always gettin' goose pimples when you see a black cat. Always havin' hysterics when you see a rat swimmin' away from the ship. We're goin' to Konga!"

"And be et by them cannibals?"

"A minute ago they were ghosts."

"They're the Kongans. They might as well be ghosts. Nobody ever sees 'em. When these Kongans catch you, they lop off your head and scoop out your brains. Oh, no; you won't catch me goin' to Konga. In all the years I've been sailin' these waters I've heard of just two men who put foot on that island and lived to tell about it!"

"Yeah? What do they tell about it?"

"Just what I'm tellin' you! They call it the Island o' Dark Figures because, moonlight nights, you can sail in close and see their shadows jumpin' and dancin' on a bleached sandstone cliff inland. These shadows are seventy-five to a hundred feet high!"

Singapore grunted skeptically and said, with sarcasm, "Must be a race of pygmies. What do people go there for if these headache eaters are so hostile?"

"Pearls! A lagoon full of 'em! Lousy with pearls. Big pearls! Fancy numbers!"

"It's all clear now," Singapore interrupted.

"What's all clear now?"

"Why my old man's headin' for there."

"A fat chance he has of gettin' them pearls! That lagoon lays under a cliff five hundred foot sheer up. The Kongans stand up there and throw spears and rocks. If your old man's goin' to Konga, he's dumber than I thought."

"He left on the bark *Bangalore* last night. And we're followin' him. We can outsail that old boneyard easy."

The buccaneer vigorously shook his head. "I ain't goin' to Konga. I've got a better use for my brains."

Still arguing, they limped through streets graying with the new year's dawn toward Tanjong Pagar, toward the pier off which their schooner, the *Blue Goose,* was anchored, taking back streets and alleys to avoid the police, for they were a sorry-looking pair indeed. Each of them possessed a black eye, and numerous cuts and bruises. Their shore-going whites were ruined. One sleeve was missing from Lucifer's white duck coat. One leg of the redhead's pants dangled from the knee by a thread or two. Their faces were bruised, swollen and streaked with blood. There was a goose-egg over Lucky's left temple so large that the mouse under the eye looked like a shadow. They were stiff, sore and quarrelsome. Lucifer steadily and stubbornly refused to entertain any idea bearing remotely upon the suggestion of a trip to Konga, to "smoke out that old rat."

"Just to look at it, sailin' past, is plenty," he said. "It lays there lookin' like one of these prehistoric monsters, all hunched up and scaly and ready to jump. It's all mountains and jungles, and the mountain tops are always full of black clouds. I sailed around it once, a mile offshore. That was enough for me!"

"Who does it belong to?"

"The Dutch, but they don't bother. They sent an expedition in thirty years ago, account of a Dutch trader who went ashore there and got gobbled up, and not a man came out. They found one body floatin' in the lagoon, with the top of his head lopped clean off. They figure it ain't worth the trouble. And if the Dutch don't want it, we don't want it."

"Maybe the old man has figured out a way."

"He'll get his head lopped off!"

"No," Singapore said. "Bill Shay is too foxy. If he's goin' there, he knows it's safe to go there. He's got some dope. The trouble with you is, you believe in witches and bat's milk."

"No," Lucky said, with the air of a man weighing himself judicially, "I ain't superstitious. I'm just sensible. I don't want my brains dished up."

"You're goin' to Konga," Singapore said grimly, "and like it!"

"Is zat so?" the buccaneer inquired.

They limped along in silence. Twin sighs were unawarely released when the schooner they jointly owned hove into view. She was like a phantom riding in the mist rising from the water in the first coral-hued rays of the sun. Her slim blue hull might have been carved from the mist itself. But her spars, snowy white, were sharp and clean against the deep mysterious blue of the night sky. Sunlight glittered on bright-work. And then a miracle happened. The mist in which the *Blue Goose* rode was suddenly shot with gold, and the schooner became a gilded ship with spars of amethyst.

Neither of the men put into words the thoughts that this vision provoked. She was, even without those sunrise trimmings, the prettiest thing afloat on the Pacific. Faithful and fleet, she had borne them gallantly through the dirtiest kinds of weather. In light or heavy winds, she was as fast as she was practical, as staunch as she was beautiful. They don't build them like that any more. Her auxiliary kicked her along at an easy ten knots. Trim and glistening as a millionaire's yacht, she was the envy of every sailing man's eye.

"That little schooner ain't for sale, by any chance, is she, mister?"

Some one was bound to put that question to them in almost every port. Even in these hard times.

· · ·

As they walked out on the pier they perceived that the outshore end of it was stacked with a miscellany of crates and boxes.

On one of the crates sat a girl in a pale-green dress, golden silk stockings, white shoes. She was softly weeping into a wisp of green chiffon.

Singapore Sammy's eyes suddenly narrowed and turned to jade.

Lucky said cheerfully, "Oh, lady!"

The girl looked up from her woeful occupation as the two battered seafarers approached. They hesitated. A young and lovely girl, attired as if for a tea party, is not a familiar sight on the Singapore water front at dawn.

She looked about nineteen. Large brown eyes in a flushed face contemplated them with forlorn misery and doubt.

The rising sun etched out the soft, alluring line of her chin. Yes, she was very young and as forlorn as a lost kitten, perched there on that large crate.

As if tacitly agreeing that something ought to be done about it, the two young men stopped and uncomfortably waited.

Green chiffon fluttered in her hand. She cleared her throat, looked wonderingly from one bruised, blood-streaked face to the other, and said in a meek little voice, stammering: "Wh-which one of you is the cap-captain of that sc-sc-schooner?"

"The handsome one," Singapore Sammy gravely replied, jabbing his thumb in the direction of his partner's swollen, discolored face.

"Is—is she for charter?" the girl asked with wistful eagerness. The tip of her cute nose seemed to twitch. She softly, plaintively sniffled.

The joint owners of the *Blue Goose* ran speculative eyes over the assortment of boxes, crates and bundles.

"Who wants to charter?" the redhead briskly inquired.

"I do."

"You—yourself—personally?"

"Y-yes!" Without warning, the lovely unknown caught the six-inch square of chiffon to her mouth and burst into fresh weeping.

Eying her, Singapore Sammy said calmly, "Why the rainy season, sister?"

She looked up again, this time with hurt and defiance.

"Because you won't charter!" she wailed. "Because nobody wants to charter! I've been trying for five days to charter a ship, and nobody will charter."

"Yeah?" Captain Jones said incredulously. "If I got a dollar for every ship I could charter before noon, I could retire on the interest. There must be a catch in it somewhere. What is this—nitroglycerin?"

"It's because of where it's going," the girl cried. "My father's sick. He was mauled by a tiger. He's there all alone. I must get back to him!"

"Where?" Singapore said softly.

"Konga!"

CHAPTER III
MISSING

Tears made a blur of her eyes. Her nose was pink and shiny.

Her mouth was making little gulping grimaces. Her grief was as shameless as a child's. Here, if one could rely on his senses, was a girl all at odds with the designs of fate, a girl upon whom last straws had been relentlessly piled.

"Sure," Lucky said. "We're goin' to Konga."

"Since when?" Singapore inquired.

"Since now. Sister, if you'll just step up to the ticket office and buy your ticket, we'll be gettin' right under way. The *Blue Goose* has every modern convenience—hot and cold running doorknobs, courteous elevator boys, dancing from nine every evening until seven the next morning by our eleven-piece stringed orchestra—"

"Stow it," Singapore growled.

The girl looked bewildered.

"Don't mind him," the redhead went on. "He hit a bottle and a bottle hit him. Let's get this straight, sister. You mean you and your dad live on Konga?"

"Yes!"

"How long you been livin' there?"

"Almost a year."

"And you got out alive," Lucky cried, "to tell about it?"

"I'm not superstitious," the girl said.

"Neither are we," Lucky said promptly. "But we've changed our minds. We ain't for charter. You see, we're pearlers."

"But there are pearls there!" the girl cried. "The most wonderful lagoon of pearls in the archipelago!"

"You heard me wrong, sister. We're whalers."

"Aw, pipe down!" Singapore growled.

But it was too late. The girl slipped down and indignantly faced them. She was smaller than she looked; a half-pint of a girl, not more than five feet, high heels and all. Her eyes were wrathful. Glaring at Lucky, then at Singapore, she said, "You two big hulking brutes ought to be ashamed of yourselves! You're traders. I looked you up. If my father hadn't been mauled by that tiger, I wouldn't be in such a hurry. I'd wait till I found somebody who wasn't yellow!"

"You sure," Singapore drawled, "it was a tiger? Sure it wasn't one of them brain-scoopers?"

She looked at him unflinchingly. "I said tiger."

"Yellow," he said, "is a pretty safe color, though. I'm sorry, sister," he said firmly. "We ain't for charter. Come on, Lucky."

The two young men started on toward the end of the pier.

"I'll make it very well worth your while," the girl called after them. "I'll give you a thousand dollars for the freight and my passage."

Without turning, Singapore called, "Not to-day!"

The two young men exchanged a long glance and walked on toward the pierhead. But they said nothing. At the pierhead, Lucky placed his fingers between his lips and gave utterance to a whistle that resembled a siren's shriek.

No response from the *Blue Goose*.

There was, or should have been, a Malay *serang* and a deckhand out there. A Malay in a sampan, attracted by the whistling, came along-side the small boat landing stage below the pier-head. The two young men engaged him to ferry them out to the schooner.

Seated in the sampan's stern, they exchanged another long, puzzled look before either spoke.

"What's goin' on?" Lucky asked.

"I'd like to know," Singapore said.

"She's phony as hell."

"Sure! And where's our *serang*?"

"She sure looked sweet, though," Lucky said.

The sampan had reached the schooner. Singapore paid off the Malay, and the two young men climbed aboard. They went forward and looked into the fo'c's'le. No one was there. They called. No one answered. The *serang*'s and the island boy's belongings had not been disturbed. A tour of the ship disclosed nothing missing. They were about to abandon the search when Singapore noticed a spot on the holystoned deck about two feet abaft the wheel.

It was a faintly pink spot about eight inches in diameter, with a faint but darker ring around it. The discovery sent them looking for similar spots, which they found—a trail of them about eighteen inches apart, leading to the rail amid-ships on the port side.

The two men, reaching the rail, exchanged a long, probing look and each gave a grunt. Comment was hardly necessary. They knew that those pink spots were washed-up blood spots. Scratches in the recently varnished rail at the spot where the trail ended furthered the theory that they must obviously accept.

The *serang* or deckhand—or both—had been killed or fatally injured and thrown overboard. Those were fingernail scratches on the rail. Some one had clawed desperately at that rail.

Had the *serang* killed the island boy and thrown him to the harbor sharks? Or was it the other way around? No—in each case. Both were too amiable, and they had got along like brothers.

The spots where the blood had been washed

up were not damp. Sometime last night, then, some one had come aboard the schooner and killed the two men. Who? Why?

Sammy started forward with the evident intention of making a more thorough investigation, but thought better of it. Reason informed him that it was useless to look for further evidence. Killers who mopped up blood spots did not leave clews.

"We'll ship a new crew," Lucky said quietly, "as soon as we know what our plans are."

These two young men knew their East amazingly well. They had glimpsed a few of its hair-stirring mysteries. They knew that any attempt to track down the killers would be as futile as trying to find an original hair of Buddha. This mystery, like so many they had glimpsed, had neither beginning, middle, nor end. Two men about whom they knew little or nothing had vanished forever. They would never know who had killed the *serang* and the island boy, or why they had been killed. They knew only that something—some chain of darkly obscured events—had come to an end. It was as if they had glimpsed a vague, malignant face receding swiftly into a fog.

It did not occur to them that the ending of an Oriental mystery often cannot be distinguished from the beginning.

CHAPTER IV
DOROTHY BORDEN'S TALE

They searched their cabins and the gun lockers and the galley.

Nothing had been taken. Nothing was disturbed. A handful of silver and small gold coins on the desk in Lucky's cabin had not been touched. The mystery was complete.

The two young men, having shaved and showered and applied court plaster patches where they were most needed, were in their respective cabins getting into clean white clothes when their ship was hailed. A girl's clear voice cried, "*Blue Goose*—ahoy!"

Singapore looked out of the porthole and soberly answered, "Ahoy yourself, sister."

She was seated in the stern of the same sampan in which they had been ferried out, and her eyes were large and forlorn. She reminded him more than ever of a lost kitten.

"May I come aboard?"

"Sure! But you're wastin' your time."

When he went on deck, she was seated in a Bombay chair under a gently waving khaki canopy, with her hands clasped about her knees. He had never seen eyes so large, so tragic. It was as if all the woes, all the unhappiness in the large unhappy world shone out of them. He observed that she had trim little feet and trim pretty ankles. There was a fresh young loveliness about her which, combined with her wistful smile and the hopelessness in her eyes, gave her a terrific appeal. Automatically, Singapore Sammy steeled himself against it. She was as innocent as a rose drenched with morning dew. That kind was the most dangerous, Singapore reflected.

He more than half suspected that she and his father were somehow in league against him. It wouldn't be the first conspiracy that old rogue had rigged up for him, for, according to the terms of that will, in the event of Sammy's death Bill Shay would inherit the money. Wherefore, Sammy was wary of this girl.

Lucky was talking to her when he went on deck, and he was evidently in a similar frame of mind. Lucky's one useful eye was no longer playful; it was hard and unfriendly. He curtly· introduced her to Singapore as Miss Dorothy Borden.

"And I just told her," Lucky said, "that she was wastin' her time comin' out here. This schooner ain't for charter."

Miss Borden was quite pale. Her eyes looked as though they might cry again at any moment, and her mouth was tremulous.

She said huskily, "After all, I'm an American. You can't very well let down one of your countrywomen who is in trouble, can you? You must give me a chance. You'll listen to me, won't you?"

"We won't throw you overboard," Singapore said dryly. "Sure, we'll listen to you."

"But it won't do any good," Lucky said with a flash of his wolfish teeth.

The girl's eyes had grown desperate again.

"My father and I have lived on Konga nearly a year," she said in a breathless rush of words. "None of those stories about Konga are true. I know they aren't true. Why won't you believe me? Why should I lie to you? If those stories were true, I'd be dead. There's nobody on Konga except my father and me."

"Yeah?" Lucky said.

"But if there were cannibals there, I'd know about it. I'd have to know about it," Miss Borden said helplessly.

"If it's so safe," Singapore put in, "why hasn't somebody gone after those pearls?"

"Pearl divers are the most superstitious men in the world!"

"What's your old man doin' there?" Lucky asked.

Miss Borden's eyes were miserable. Her hands were clenched in her lap in desperation. She was obviously trying very hard to get herself under control. She nipped her lower lip between her small white teeth, and Singapore saw that her lip was raw and bleeding.

"The only way I can show you how untrue all those old legends are is to tell you the whole story. Will you let me?"

"Shoot the works," Singapore said lazily.

"But I'm warnin' you," Lucky added, "you're wastin' your time."

Miss Borden seemed to pull herself together. She gripped her hands in her lap, drew a deep, resolute breath.

"You men are Americans. Nobody who isn't an American could possibly understand. That's why I've been counting so on you two men to help me. Because you've got to help me. You've got to take this shipment to Konga—and me, too!"

It suddenly occurred to Sam Shay that she might be telling the truth. His father had left Singapore for Konga last night on the bark *Bangalore*. Was he headed for Konga because there were pearls in Konga—or because he had some diabolical scheme in mind with this girl and her father as his prospective victims? Or both?

Looking at Miss Borden, he felt suddenly uncomfortable. He could see now that the poor kid was worried pink, but he sensed, under her trembling dismay, a fighting determination to convince them of her sincerity. He was anxious to hear her story, and he wondered if her eyes always looked so tragic.

"My father is Daniel Borden. You've heard of him, haven't you?" she asked.

"The name's familiar," Singapore encouraged her. "What's his business?"

"He was the chairman of the board of the American Rod and Wire Corporation—the wire trust. They called him the Wire King. He lost practically his entire fortune—almost a hundred million—in the panic. The bankers called his notes and forced him to resign. They stripped him almost clean. He managed to salvage about a million. It almost killed him. I suppose you think that's terribly funny—a man almost dying because his fortune shrinks to a million dollars!"

"Nope," Sammy soberly denied. "Our fortune shrank down about the same proportion in the past two hours, and we know just how he would feel about it."

"He'd worked," Miss Borden went on, "all his life to accumulate that hundred million. He said a man needed a new philosophy to face the world these days. He was going to devote the rest of his life to enjoying himself. He had always had the dream of living in the South Seas. He asked me to go with him, and I did, because he was practically a nervous wreck. In Surabaya he heard of Konga from a drunken beachcomber."

"What did this beachcomber look like?" Lucky interrupted.

"I don't know. I didn't meet him. But Dad talked to him for hours. The beachcomber told him all about Konga. He called it the Haunted Island. He said no white man had ever come out of there alive except himself. Dad checked him up, and substantiated some of what he had said. He decided that we were going there to live."

"In spite of the brain-scoopers?" Lucky demanded.

"You don't know my father!" Miss Borden replied.

Sammy said, "How about you?"

"I was afraid to go. But the minute he began planning he changed so that I didn't have the heart to say I didn't want to go. He was happy for the first time since the stock market crash."

"How did you get there?" Lucky asked.

"At first no one would take us. Government officials tried to dissuade us from going. He had almost decided to buy a schooner when an old Chinese offered to charter him one at a fabulous rate on the condition that the schooner would anchor well offshore and that dad would arrange to land the stuff."

"Wait a minute," Lucky interrupted. "What was this Chink's name?"

"Wan Gow Sung."

"What was the schooner's name?"

"The *Lotus*."

"Okay. Go on." For the first time since she had begun her amazing narrative, Lucky seemed to believe that there might be a germ of truth in what Miss Borden was saying.

"So we went to Konga," she continued. Her voice still shook a little. "We anchored offshore, and dad took every box and bag and crate and plank and keg ashore in a small boat."

"How far?" Singapore wanted to know.

"A half mile row in and a half mile row back. I went in with the first load with my rifle and some ammunition. I stood guard all day long."

"What side of the island did you land on?" Lucky asked.

"The north side. It's the only side where the cliffs don't drop off sheer to the sea. It's a sandy table land, or plateau, with a few scattered palms, beefwood, jackfruit and mahogany trees—not jungle."

"Big?" Lucky asked.

"It's about two miles long and a half mile wide. A stream comes down from the mountains and runs along the edge of it into a small cove. Back up that ravine, where the stream flows down, is thick jungle. But the flat place was quite open—an ideal place to build a house."

Singapore Sammy darted a glance at Lucky. That young man was nodding his approval of the girl's description.

"One of the conditions Wan Gow Sung had made before we left Surabaya was that the schooner be unloaded by dark. I mean, he wouldn't lie off Konga longer than from dawn to dark. When darkness came, he would sail out to sea and stand off and on eight or ten miles offshore until the next morning. But dad was so enthusiastic over what he'd seen of Konga that he was determined to get everything ashore by nightfall. I lost count of the number of trips he made. Back and forth—back and forth all day long under that horrible sun. His hands were almost solid water blisters from the oars, and he was a physical wreck. He made the last trip just at dusk."

"With you," Singapore Sammy said, "watchin' for brain-scoopers!"

She nodded. "Yes. I thought any minute they'd come swooping down on us. I was petrified."

"What happened?"

"Nothing. I didn't see a living soul. And in all the months I've been there, I haven't seen a human being. There's nothing but birds and animals. Those stories of head hunters on Konga belong to South Seas folklore. There aren't any savages there, or I'd know about it. I've been over practically every square foot of that island." Her eyes pleaded with them to believe her.

Lucky Jones shook his head somewhat dubiously, but he didn't interrupt.

Sammy said, "What are you living in?"

"We built a little house and put up shelves and made tables and chairs."

"How about food?"

"We brought along crates and crates of canned goods. We had some vegetable seeds. I planted a garden. We have loads of fresh things."

"Wasn't it pretty lonesome?"

"I didn't mind, because dad was so contented. He looked years younger."

"Didn't it ever strike him," Singapore asked, "that it was pretty selfish of him, pennin' you up in a place like that?"

"It wasn't," she answered, "very hard to convince him that I was perfectly happy there. And I got used to it."

Singapore, watching her soft lips, was trying unsuccessfully to visualize a girl as delicately feminine as Miss Borden living such a life.

"How," Lucky said, "about this row you said your old man had with a tiger?"

"It was terrible," Miss Borden said. She shivered, and her lips trembled a little. "We had arranged with Wan Gow Sung to come back to Konga in six months with mail and supplies. One of the items was hunting dogs—the black skinny kind that are used for game hunting in Sumatra.

"He was absolutely punctual, but he said he hadn't expected to see us alive. He'd brought everything—books and mail and magazines and supplies and dogs."

"What were the dogs for?" Sammy asked. "Cats?"

"No; deer. But dad didn't know how to train them. They'd start off on a deer trail, but when a cat trail crossed it, they'd go off after the cat. We didn't want cats. We wanted deer. It was the only meat we had. One day about six weeks ago he took the dogs hunting. They started off on a deer trail, but they found tiger tracks. They trailed the tiger up a narrow box cañon.

"It was in a cave six or eight feet up the side of the cañon. Dad could smell the tiger, but he didn't realize it was so close."

Miss Borden's face was white.

"The first warning he had that it was so near was when it came rushing out of the cave. Dad backed down the cañon and fired as the tiger rushed, and when he pulled the trigger, nothing happened. The firing pin was jammed."

Miss Borden gulped a little and went on in a shaky voice,

"He scrambled up the side of the cañon. The tiger reached up and raked his left leg below the knee with its claws. It would have killed him if the dogs hadn't distracted it. Dad hooked his feet around a rock and worked away at the bolt until it worked. But the tiger had killed one dog and wounded another before he could start pumping bullets into it.

"Dad fainted from loss of blood about a mile from the house. I heard the dogs barking and found him lying there with his leg practically in ribbons.

"He ran a temperature of a hundred and five for almost a week. And not a single ship passed by.

"But he pulled through. And when I left him, about two weeks ago, he was able to hobble around and get his own meals. But one of the gouges isn't healed yet. We were running short of antiseptics. I wanted him to come up to Singapore or Surabaya and have proper medical attention, but he wouldn't. So I came."

"How'd you come?" Singapore asked quickly.

"I waited for the weekly steamer from Darwin to Singapore, rowed out and waited for it to pass. I got here about a week ago. I spent one day getting supplies, and the past five days I've been trying to charter a ship. And when I mention Konga, people say they don't want to charter. Last night I heard about you two men. When I heard you were Americans, I almost cried. I was so sure you'd help!"

She paused. Her hopeful young eyes went from Lucky Jones's face to Singapore Sammy's.

Singapore stole a glance at Lucky, and wondered if Lucky was actually listening to what she was saying. His one useful eye was moist and glowing.

It wasn't difficult to understand. Singapore was inclined to feel that way himself. He had been, he realized, seeing himself as the third inhabitant of that island paradise, and there was no room in the picture for Lucifer Jones. He was being swayed by pity. He mustn't, he grimly advised himself, let his seasoned judgment be warped by a foolish desire to take Miss Borden on his lap and comfort her.

He said harshly, "What makes you sure there are pearls in that lagoon? Maybe that's just another old beachcomber yarn, too."

Her answer was to open her small green suède handbag. From it she removed a lipstick, a tiny gold mirror, a gold compact, a gold pencil, a jade cigarette holder and three hairpins.

She extricated a wad of white tissue paper. Carefully, she removed the wrapping, and rolled into the palm of one hand a pale pink, spherical object, which gleamed with a satiny sheen. It was the size of a small pea.

The two young men bent close and peered at that fine pink pearl.

"Did this," Singapore asked, suppressing his excitement, "come out of that lagoon?"

"Yes."

"Any others?"

She seemed to hesitate. "N-no," she said reluctantly.

"You don't mean," Sammy said, "you found this and didn't look for others?"

"I didn't dare. It's a sharks' nest. Thousands of them. And they're absolutely savage."

CHAPTER V
SINGAPORE AGREES

The red-headed American, looking at the pearl, thought of a lagoon infested with tiger sharks.

"Sharks!" Lucky said softly.

"The first time I rowed around into the lagoon," Miss Borden said, "I dropped anchor in about the middle of it. A half dozen giant sharks struck at the anchor as it dropped. I've never seen sharks so savage. I hate them. I've stood on the beach and shot them until my rifle was too hot to hold. I've thrown meat in, and they come

rolling up, and when they roll, I shoot. The other sharks pounce on the wounded one, and tear him to shreds. Fights start. They're nothing but cannibals. I've seen that lagoon so pink with blood you couldn't see bottom. And when it cleared, there'd be more sharks than ever!"

"Any octopuses?" Lucky grunted.

She hesitated. "Yes. Big ones. And I've seen fights between sharks and octopuses that sent shivers down my spine. You can see the shells down there so plainly. Big ones! It must be one of the richest beds in the archipelago."

Both Singapore and Lucky were unaware that their expressions had subtly changed. Here was an eye witness to the existence of that fabled lagoon. And here was a pearl from it!

Pearls! A virgin bed of them!

With careful carelessness, Singapore Sammy said, "Why hasn't your old man done anything about those sharks?"

"I don't think he ever gave them a thought," the girl answered. "He isn't interested in the pearls—in making money in any way. The million he saved from the panic he put into a trust company. It pays him around forty thousand a year, and he doesn't need that. He isn't interested in pearling."

Sammy quietly said, "Has anybody been ashore on Konga since you and your father have been there?"

Miss Borden shook her head.

"Didn't Wan Gow Sung come ashore?"

"No, he wouldn't. We see ships pass, from Java to New Guinea and between Darwin and Singapore—five miles or so offshore. But no one has put a foot on Konga since we came."

She paused again and bit her lip.

"Why are you so doubtful about what I say? Why is every one so doubtful? Do I look like a liar or a thief?"

"You get us wrong," Singapore said gently. "Out here in this part of the world you learn to be hard-boiled."

"Perhaps you're too hard-boiled."

"Yeah. Perhaps we are."

"But it's so queer," Miss Borden said. "What

object could I have in lying to you?" Her eyes flitted from one dark, bruised face to the other. Singapore learned now that her eyes did not always have that tragic look. They were sparkling with indignation.

"All I'm asking you to do is to take this shipment and me to Konga. And all you have to do is to say that you will and I'll go get the thousand dollars at the bank this very minute. Isn't it a fair proposition?"

She went on: "I looked you up. I went to the harbormaster and made inquiries about you. He said you were a pair of very adventurous young men. You're the first men I've really tried hard to convince that Konga isn't what the rumors say it is." Her voice was suddenly pleading. "If you aren't interested in the money—aren't you interested in those pearls?"

"We haven't turned down your proposition yet," Lucky said. "But supposin' we went after those pearls, just for the sake of the argument. Your dad has a prior claim on that bed. What would he do?"

"He isn't interested in them."

"It must be funny to be that rich. But wouldn't he step in and say we were poachin'?"

"I'll guarantee he won't. If you can find a way to beat the sharks, he'd like to have you there just for the company."

Singapore and Lucky exchanged glances that gleamed with excitement.

"We'll find a way to beat the sharks," the redhead said. "How big is that lagoon?"

"About three quarters of a mile in diameter."

"How wide," Lucky barked, "is the inlet?"

"About five hundred feet—at high tide."

"How deep," Singapore wanted to know, "is the water in it at low tide?"

"Not more than a foot or so."

"What's the bottom like?"

"It's a sort of clay-like sand."

"Do you get it?" Singapore said to Lucky.

"Bottle it up?"

"Sure! Bottle it up! We go out there at low

tide and drive stakes close together across the inlet."

"Then," Lucky took him up, "we string eight or nine rows of barbed wire along the stakes to keep the sharks out at high tide!"

"Check! Then we dynamite the lagoon. Forty or fifty sticks will send every shark and octopus to the top belly-up. How are we hooked for dynamite?"

"We've got plenty in the lazarette. And all the divin' suit needs is a little patchin'."

Singapore got up. "Okay. We want to be pullin' out of here by four this afternoon."

Miss Borden said hesitantly, "Am I—am I going, too?"

"Can you cook?" Lucky said sharply.

"Of course I can! Do I have to cook?"

"Can you scrub decks? Can you heave an anchor? Can you shinny up a mast?"

She didn't know whether to take him seriously or not.

"Do I have to do all those things?"

"Don't pay any attention to him," Singapore said. "His brain is all crippled up from that bottle. It was lame enough before. Sure, you can go along. Maybe you'll bring us luck. We need plenty. You can use my cabin and I'll bunk in with Cap'n Jones. Let's go!"

They arranged that Lucky and Miss Borden were to go ashore while Singapore stayed aboard and warped the *Blue Goose* alongside the pier. While Miss Borden went to the bank and checked out of her hotel, Lucky would attend to clearance papers, supplies and signing up a new deckhand and *serang*.

CHAPTER VI
SINGAPORE'S PEARL

Considering their natures, it was remarkable that Singapore Sammy and Lucky Jones got along so well. They had been shipmates for upwards of two years, and had never had a serious disagreement. Perhaps it was because they were birds of a feather. Tough birds. Their histories were strangely alike. Neither knew what a home was. Each had been on the go since he was a youngster. Each had fought, begged, stolen and bummed his way all over the world. And each was as hard as flint.

Having no means of measuring his own hardness, Singapore was convinced that Lucky Jones was the hardest individual in the Far East. And the longer he knew him, the surer of this he became. It was not merely that he looked hard; Lucky was hard clean through. But this was, to Singapore, the right kind of hardness. It was the hardness of a diamond, clear and fine and honest.

He privately admired Lucky for looking so hard. With his thick bristling black hair, his eagle's eyes, his leathery complexion, his thin mouth, his sledgehammer jaw and his big muscular frame, Lucky looked his hardness. Singapore had never seen him in a situation, aboard ship or ashore, above water or below, in which Lucky had betrayed the slightest fear. You could depend on Lucky Jones to meet trouble with courage and decision, with all his brawn and all his brains.

It was accordingly painful to the point of being sickening when Lucky Jones started falling in love with Dorothy Borden. It was the first time Singapore had ever seen him betray softness in any degree. And the softness he was betraying over Dorothy was of the consistency of custard.

Almost from the moment he met her, Lucky became a different man. It reminded Sam of a character in Biblical times he had been told about as a kid—some strong man who was softened up because he fell in love with a woman.

While the *Blue Goose* slipped southward over the Equator, through the Rhio Archipelago, and into the blazing blue of the Karimata Sea, Singapore Sammy had that painful experience of seeing a good tough man fall hopelessly in love.

There was no question, of course, that Dorothy would have tempted almost any man. Her seagoing togs consisted of snug-fitting An-

tibes sweaters and snug-fitting white duck sailor pants, both sweaters and pants more or less innocently betraying the fact that she had a perfect little figure.

Lucky would follow her around the deck or sit and gaze at her with love-struck eyes. He sighed frequently. He lost his appetite. He couldn't sleep. He began to take the most elaborate pains with his personal appearance. He shaved every day, sometimes twice. He kept his boots lustrous. He even trimmed his shaggy black eyebrows. It would have been sidesplittingly funny if it had stopped there. But it didn't stop there.

He began to talk about getting married, settling down and giving up the sea. He appealed to Singapore. Wasn't she wonderful? Wasn't she a little honey?

Singapore disgustedly advised him to snap out of it. "Take a look at yourself in the mirror," he urged.

Singapore could, of course, understand Dorothy's falling for Lucky. Plenty of them had, but never before had Lucifer given any girl a tumble. At first it was something of a question whether or not Dorothy was meeting him halfway, or any part of the way. She had seemed to Singapore to be a collected, level-headed young woman. She had seemed to bestow as many glances and smiles on him as on Lucky.

Then Singapore came upon them one moonlit night. They were seated on a hatch cover. They were clasped in each other's arms. Their mouths were joined in what appeared to be an eternal kiss. Separating, they each said one word.

"Sweetness!" said Dorothy.

"Booful!" said Lucky.

Unseen, unheard, Singapore departed. There were twitchings in the vicinity of his stomach. He retired to the stateroom which he and Lucky shared. He took the pillow off Lucky's bunk and kicked it until it burst. Feathers exploded and, floating, settled upon everything in the room.

When Lucky came in, an hour or two later, and glimpsed the scene, he grunted, "What's this?"

"Horsefeathers—booful!" Singapore jeered.

"You can lay off that," the buccaneer said, projecting his lower jaw and planting his fists on his hips. "This is serious. Get it?"

Singapore, lying on his back stark naked in his bunk, with the ashes from half a dozen cigarettes strewn over his hairy chest, leered and said, "Sure I get it—booful. You're hooked."

He ate his breakfast the following morning in the galley, because he didn't want to see the two of them at the table. He avoided Dorothy the rest of the morning. He was in the bows, smoking and watching porpoises playing, when Dorothy came forward and settled down beside him.

She said bluntly, "You don't like me, do you, Sam?"

He grinned at her. "Kid," he said, "I haven't much use for women, no. But I haven't anything personal against you. You've got a good bean, you're a good-looker, and you've got class. A man would have to travel a long way to improve on what you've got."

"Then why are you so opposed to having Lucky like me?"

"A seagoing man who gets married is a sucker," the redhead answered. "Lucky's been at sea since he was old enough to wash behind his own ears. The sea's in his blood. I know that guy, sister. You can't any more take the sea out of his blood than you can out of a shark. If you marry him, what happens? He thinks it'll be easy to give up this life. But sooner or later, he feels the sea tuggin' at him. And then what? He loves you and he loves the sea. If he gives up the sea, he'll be sunk. If he gives up you, he'll be sunk."

"Why can't he combine the best features of each?"

"Sister, it's been tried. You can't stay at sea. That means you see him a few days each year. That's the bunk."

Dorothy was smiling mysteriously. "Is that your only objection to marriage, Sam—I mean, where you're concerned?"

"Nope. I am the guy the fellow meant when he said, 'The bird travels fastest who travels alone.' "

"Why do you want to travel so fast? Running away from something?"

"Nope. Lookin' for a guy."

Dorothy's eyes sparkled with interest. "Who?"

"My old man," he said. And told her about Bill Shay, about his craftiness, about the will, about that seven-year chase. But he omitted mentioning that Bill Shay was now on his way to Konga, because he knew it would worry her.

"Every time I get ready to close my hands around his neck—he's gone! Like a puff of smoke. Did you ever try to kill a krait adder by jumpin' on him, sister? The faster you jump, the easier he slips away from you. It's that way with my old man."

"How old are you, Sam?"

"Twenty-five. I've been on his trail since I was eighteen."

"Ever seen him?"

"Just once. In Siam. He was dressed up like an English lord. I talked to him for two hours, never suspectin'. When he got through kiddin' me, he lifted out his monocle and two huskies trussed me up to the post I was leanin' against. It was the first and last time I ever saw him. But I'll get him! And when I get him, I'll kill him!"

Dorothy shivered. "It seems horrible to hear any man talk like that about his own father."

"He ain't my father; he's my stepfather."

"But why is your name the same?"

"When my mother married him, I was a year old. She had my name legally changed from Larkin to Shay. The next time I'm in the States I'm gonna have it legally changed back to Larkin."

The girl was looking at the porpoises. When she looked back, the grimness in his face had relaxed. Dorothy dropped her eyes to his powerful brown neck, to the soft copper wire which encircled it.

"Why do you wear that?"

The fingers of one large brown hand fumbled at the copper wire. Singapore quickly lifted the copper loop over his head. Dangling from this strange neckpiece was a small chamois sack. He grinned at Dorothy and loosened the cord at the throat of the sack with his strong white teeth. Then, holding up the bottom of the sack and watching the girl's eyes, he shook down into his palm a blue pearl that gathered fire unto itself from the burning blue sky.

The blue pearl rolled about in his cupped palm, a bubble of magic flame. As blue as a Chantaboun sapphire, as big around as the end of its owner's forefinger, as full of fire as the eye of a charging leopard, that blue pearl was fit to grace the finger or the throat of a princess.

"Notice how it seems to burn?"

"Yes!" she gasped.

"This pearl, sister, is famous. It's the blue fire pearl of Malobar!"

"It's glorious!"

"Yeah. But don't let it hypnotize you. It's hypnotized richer girls than you, sister. It ain't for sale."

"Where'd you get it?"

"I won it in a fight. An up-country Malay sultan put it up for a ten-round go between me and another guy. Winner take all. Loser go to the sultan's black leopards for breakfast."

Dorothy's eyes were straining at him; her mouth was like a credulous child's.

"Did he?"

"Did he what?"

"Go to the—the leopards?"

The redhead lazily grinned. "No, sister. We started a riot, and while the riot was on we blew."

Dorothy expelled her breath in a panting sigh.

"It must be worth a fortune!"

"It's worth fifteen thousand in Paris—American gold—as it is. If I could ever find the mate I wouldn't take a hundred thousand for the pair."

"Aren't you afraid of carrying it around like that?"

He shook his head. "Nope. Because I'd die before anybody got it away. That's pretty safe insurance. They've tried to dope me. They've tried to trick me. They've tried to kill me, half a dozen different ways. But they haven't got it yet."

"Who?"

"Just about everybody who sees it."

"May I—hold it?"

Grinning, the redhead dropped the Malobar pearl into the chamois sack, drew the throat cord tight, and dropped the sack inside his shirt. The girl looked blank, as if she had been staring overlong at some dazzlingly bright object in the dark.

"Nobody," Singapore said, "has touched this pearl since I won it in that fight."

"Superstitious?"

"You can call it that."

She shivered. "There's something evil about that pearl. It's like looking at something from another world, something that you never thought existed. I never saw anything so blue or so luminous. It's weird—terrifying."

"Yeah. It gets you."

"It must," she breathed, "if you'd rather part with your life. Don't show it to dad!"

"That's a promise, sister."

She went aft to join Lucky, and the blue fire pearl wasn't mentioned again that day. But the subject wasn't dropped. Singapore woke up that night with the eerie feeling that he wasn't alone. He sat up and lit the gimballed lamp at the head of his bunk. Lucky was not in his bunk. He automatically fumbled at his throat. The copper wire was there. His hand dropped, groping for the chamois skin pouch. *Gone!*

CHAPTER VII
THE PHANTOM

Singapore had turned in that night in pants and shirt. Without pausing for shoes, he ran

*His cutthroat captors
seemed to be Mexicans.*

out into the corridor. He observed that Dorothy's stateroom door was open, that the light was on in there, but that her bedding was not disturbed.

He ran through the dining room and up the stairs to the deck.

The new *serang* was at the wheel. His eyes were luminous in the ghostly light from the binnacle. His dark body, naked to the waist, glistened in the light of the moon.

Singapore barked, "Where is she?"

"For'd, *tuan.*"

The red-headed man ran forward and found them sitting on their favorite hatch, Dorothy's small curly head close to Lucky's.

Dorothy was holding one hand before her. The fingers were bunched and pointing upward. In the nest formed by their tips lay a fantastic, luminously blue bubble.

Singapore swooped down on them. Panting, he snatched the Malobar pearl out of its nest.

"Somebody," he said harshly, "has a hell of a nerve!"

Lucky slowly stood up.

"Keep your shirt on, Red. She wanted to see it!"

"She saw it this mornin'!"

"Well, she wanted to hold it in her hand."

"Yeah? So you sneaked into my cabin and cut it off this wire!"

Lucky's eagle eyes were level with his. His thin lips were parted slightly. He looked ugly.

Dorothy wailed, "Oh, please, please!"

Lucky said quietly, "You trust me, don't you, Red?"

"You know I don't trust anybody with this pearl."

"Not even me?"

"You heard me!"

The buccaneer drew a deep breath. "Are you sayin' I'd steal your lousy bead?"

"When you're this way, you're not responsible."

He saw Lucky double up his fist, and he saw the fist start toward him. But he did not believe, until it was too late, that Lucky would go

297

through with that punch. He was sure Lucky would pull it at the last moment.

But Lucky didn't pull it.

The punch didn't do much damage. It was a blunt one on the chin, and Singapore had a tough chin. But he wasn't prepared for it. He staggered back, and brought up against the rail, which he gripped hard, one hand on either side of him.

Lucky, with both fists ready, came toward him. He waited. But Singapore, with his tongue wedged against his teeth, held onto the rail. If he didn't hang onto the rail, one of them was going to be killed. His chin burned from the punch, and his forehead felt like ice. His heart was going like a triphammer.

He held onto the rail until he was sure he had himself under control. Then, without a word, he turned and walked aft.

He was lying in his bunk smoking a cigarette when Lucky came in. The buccaneer slid a quick glance at him, then skinned off his coat.

He hung up the coat and walked over to the bunk and looked down into Singapore's face.

"Didn't feel like sparrin' to-night," he said, with a rising intonation, but he gave the effect of shoving out the words with his under lip.

Singapore looked up at him with a slightly curling upper lip.

"It would look that way," he answered. "I guess maybe I'm gettin' yellow—or something."

"Nuts. I got you. Red, I want to take that back."

"Go right ahead!"

Lucky lowered his sledgehammer chin. "Sock it."

Singapore reached up with his ham-like hand and dealt him an open-handed blow that sounded like a pistol shot. Lucky stepped back with a grin, rubbing his jaw.

"Okay?" he said.

"Next time, keep your shirt on."

This was the nearest to an apology and an acceptance of the same that these two were capable of. It should have cleared the air. But it didn't. Something was missing.

•   •   •

This occurred on the fifth night out of Singapore Town. The *Blue Goose* crossed the Emperor of China reef the next day, and that night, as if bearing out the vague foreboding of disaster with which Singapore Sammy had been visited on sailing day, the phantom stowaway was seen.

It was the kind of night that only the Malayan seas can brew for such occasions. The moon had a green cast to it. There was a thin greasy mist lying on all horizons, and this mist was shot with green. Even the sea, so blazingly blue by daylight, was tinted palely green. A night for ghosts to walk indeed!

Singapore had turned in early. Eight bells—midnight—had been struck perhaps ten minutes previously by the *serang* when Lucky lurched into the stateroom, striking a match along the wall with a sound like ripping cloth.

In the light of it, Singapore, coming fully awake, saw that Lucky's face, ordinarily a rich mahogany, was lemon-colored. And the buccaneer's eyes were pale and large. Sweat gleamed on his forehead, nose and cheeks. He was breathing rapidly through loosely parted lips.

"There's something on board!"

With agitated hands, Lucky lighted the gimballed lamp. The chimney danced out of his hand, fell to the floor with a small splintering crash. The flame licked up, orange and smoking.

"Something?"

"I saw it!"

"What the hell are you talkin' about?"

"It was a face. That's all! A white face, but it had a green tinge. Do you remember that dead guy we hauled out of Hongkong Harbor? Remember how white and green and glowy his face was from the phosphorus?"

"When did this happen?" Singapore growled.

"Right now, I tell yuh! I was up there on that forward hatch, smokin', when this face came right up over the bows—all white and green and glowy. You couldn't see its eyes. You couldn't see any hands. Nothin' but the face. It floated right up out of the sea!"

"You been hittin' that arrack again?"

Lucky said explosively, "Will you listen? I *saw* it! By the time I got for'd it was gone!"

"Where was Dorothy?"

"She turned in a half hour before I saw it."

"You're always seein' things. You saw the deckhand. He's a pale guy."

"How," Lucky cried, "do you think I got this way? The deckhand was asleep in his bunk. The *serang* was right there at the wheel."

"He see anything?"

"How could he when he was 'way aft?"

"Did it look like Biyong?" Biyong was their old *serang*, who had vanished so mysteriously, leaving so little trace, in Singapore.

"No. It was a thin face."

"Like whose?"

"A lifer's. Remember those lifers we saw in the solitary cells at New Hebrides? Moldy-skinned from bein' stir bugs so long? Kind of a green glow to them?"

"Maybe we've got an escaped convict aboard," Singapore said dryly.

"But it wasn't alive!"

"Things can look mighty funny when you're not expectin' them. How good a look did you take for'd?"

"I went over every inch. There wasn't any water. There wasn't any sign of a thing." His eyes dilated. He panted, "You know what it means, don't you, when you can count one more on board than there is? Somebody on board has his number up!"

Singapore said seriously, "If you didn't find it, then there can't be one extra aboard."

"Not findin' it don't mean it ain't aboard!"

"You mean," Singapore said sardonically, "you didn't bother to look below."

"I wanted my gun and a flash light."

"Okay. Take your gun. I'll take the flash light."

Singapore got out of his bunk and slipped his pants on. He was skeptical and a little bored. This wasn't the first ghost Lucky had seen.

The two men went into the corridor. Dorothy was standing in the door of her stateroom. She looked pale and anxious.

"What's happened?" she gasped. "What were you shouting about?"

"Your boy friend says he saw a ghost."

Dorothy said, "Where?"

"Up forward. About half an hour after you turned in."

She seemed relieved. Half smiling, she said, "What did you see, Lucky?"

"A greenish-white face," he said. "It floated up out of the sea."

"With seaweed hanging on it?"

"No."

Singapore, yawning, said that it must have been an optical illusion, perhaps caused by the checkered play of moonlight and shadow on sails or rigging.

Lucky insisted that it had been a human face, a man's face.

"Hair?"

"Tangled dark hair," Lucky said promptly.

"We'll take a look between decks," Singapore said wearily.

"Be careful!" Dorothy wailed.

"Better go in and lock your door," Lucky advised.

Sammy was extremely skeptical of the green-faced apparition, but when your pal has a weakness and you can't cure it, the only thing to do is cater to it. It would make Lucky feel better if they searched the ship, so they would search the ship. Systematically.

Sammy led the way, with the flash light in his hand, down a scuttle hatch into the forward hold. It was empty except for a few scraps of coconut shell—relics of their last copra cargo. The shipment of crates and boxes for which Dorothy had chartered the *Blue Goose* to Konga was stowed in the 'midships hold. The two men entered this hold through a bulkhead door. They looked thoroughly, examining every space where a man might be hiding. They shifted crates and boxes and threw the beam of the flash light into every crevice. And they found no stowaway.

They next searched the forward end—the chain locker, the paint locker, the fo'c's'le. They searched the galley. They even unlocked and peered into the small closet in which their store of liquor was kept—trade gin, arrack, whisky and beer. They searched the lazarette and the locker in which they stored their deep-sea diving gear—suits, pumps, shell baskets.

Singapore prodded with the flash light into the folds of the heavy tarred fishnet which they had picked up cheap in Guam and carried, not for any possible emergency, but in hope that they might some day sell it at a fat profit. There was no stowaway hiding in or under the folds of the heavy net.

They concluded the search by looking into the engine compartment and exploring the spaces about water tanks, oil tanks and gasoline tanks.

At the end of an hour of microscopic search Singapore was still convinced that Lucky had been the victim of an optical illusion. Yet what, Lucky argued, could have caused such an illusion? Both he and the *serang* insisted that none of the sails or rigging had moved for hours. The schooner was ghosting along under the lightest and steadiest of breezes. Unless you looked at the water and saw the passing of an occasional fleck of foam or spark of phosphorescence or clump of seaweed, you would have sworn that the *Blue Goose* was motionless upon a lifeless sea. The water, except in the path of the moon, was as still as glass. Slipping along at no more than two knots on an even keel, the schooner cut through the water with hardly a sound.

Yet while Singapore took no stock in Lucky's ghost, he felt suddenly uneasy, and he wondered if this was due to the superstitious fear that had gotten Lucky. Was this ghost Lucky's way of intuitively knowing that something was wrong? For Sam was convinced that something was wrong.

He was not superstitious, but he had developed to a remarkable degree the primitive trait of intuition. When he first came to the Far East, seven years previously, he had been fascinated by the Indian fakirs; had marveled at their ability to walk and dance unharmed on the sharp points of spikes, on knives, on coals of fire; at their ability to go for months without food.

What he had seen turned his point of view topsy-turvy. These things had paved the way to his development of a "sixth sense"—the primitive sense of intuition, particularly his intuition that danger was present when none of his material senses could possibly give him an alarm.

This sense was sounding an alarm now. Something was wrong. Something had been wrong, some danger had been threatening, from the day the *Blue Goose* sailed out of the Singapore roadstead. But he could not localize it.

The next appearance of the "phantom stowaway" occurred two nights later—on the night of the day that they passed the bark *Bangalore*, some ten miles to starboard, in the northwestern bight of the Banda Sea. The *Blue Goose* would, if these light steady winds held, reach Konga at least a day ahead of the *Bangalore*, so Lucky estimated.

It was the *serang*, at his post at the wheel, who saw the "phantom stowaway," moving about in the black shadow cast by the mainsail about an hour before dawn. The *serang* hailed him, but the ghostly figure did not answer the hail. It simply vanished. It was, the *serang* babbled, a thin, dark figure, showing no trace of white.

Singapore, Lucky Jones and Dorothy were in their cabins when the *serang* saw the apparition. He hastened below and awakened the men. He was so frightened that he was gibbering. Every one on board was accounted for. The deckhand, a half-caste Malay boy, had been sleeping in the stern, curled up on the deck near the wheel, because the fo'c's'le was so hot that night. Dorothy was asleep in her cabin. It was so quiet that when Singapore went to her door he could hear, through the varnished latticework, her regular breathing.

Singapore and Lucky went to the wheel with the *serang* and heard his stuttering, chattering account of what he had seen. He was looking forward, he said, when suddenly he saw the tall dark figure of a man moving about in the space between foremast and mainmast. The figure looked terrifically tall and thin. It made no sound. It moved about in the great shadow of the mainsail like a blacker shadow.

"Just like a tall black shadow, *tuan*!"

It was Singapore's opinion that the *serang* had seen nothing. He was sure that the *serang*, alone there at the wheel, had let his imagination get the better of him. Doubtless, he had been thinking of the ghost that Lucky had reported, and his imagination had played tricks on him.

But Lucky insisted on searching the ship again, this time thoroughly. Singapore realized that Lucky wanted desperately to prove, for his own peace of mind, that there was a creature of substance, not of uncanny shadow, on the *Blue Goose*.

"We're goin' over this ship," Lucky said grimly, "with a fine-tooth comb. This time we'll organize."

Brani, the *serang*, and Rochor, the deckhand, were to go aloft, Brani up the foremast, Rochor up the mainmast. Singapore and Lucky undertook to search the hull. They covered identically the territory they had gone over last night, but with greater thoroughness.

Singapore said to Lucky, "We're not going to find anything. There isn't any stowaway."

Lucky's face was a yellow-white. "I know it," he said hoarsely. But he would not stop searching.

They went over the *Blue Goose*, inch by inch. The sun was up to aid their search by the time Lucky admitted defeat. There was no stowaway!

CHAPTER VIII
AMBUSH

Lounging in a Bombay chair later that day, Singapore was angered over the elusiveness of a hunch. He had had a hunch right along, but he could not lay a finger on it. It was as elusive as a breath of vapor. His intuition was trying to warn him—but against what? Or was he uneasy because of all this talk of ghosts?

They were passing through islands which were jewels in a jade sea—the tropical isles of men's dreams. Off to the north, bestriding the Equator like a great cat with arched back and fluffed-out tail, loomed the island of Celebes, tropical stronghold of mysteries not yet solved by any white man.

They flew, under a fresh wind, over the invisible line that divides the Java Sea from the Arafura Sea. Lucky said that they would reach an anchorage off Konga sometime shortly after sunset.

By two in the afternoon, the island began to rise, a dark and mysterious mass, from the southern horizon. And the closer they approached, the more forbidding Konga became. Even in the glare of the equatorial sun, Konga looked as sinister, as menacing as it was, in those old legends, reported to be. It seemed to crouch there, a dark and waiting monster.

At a little after eight bells in the evening watch, Singapore, still lounging in the Bombay chair, darkly thinking and wondering, heard Lucky's sharp voice issuing orders.

"Stand by to lower your jibs! Lower away! Stand by to let go your anchor! Let go!"

There was a splash, a large greenish explosion as the phosphorescent water was agitated. Sails came fluttering down—ghosts in the starlight. There was no moon. It would not come up for another hour.

The *Blue Goose* was no more than a quarter of a mile offshore. The night was warm and sticky. Singapore smelled the odors of frangipani and pepper trees in blossom. They swept out from the land on an almost visible vapor. The effect was an illusion. It was as if cobwebs were stretching across his face. He went so far as to wipe his face with one hand, to get rid of the sensation. He didn't like it at all. Something, something, something was wrong.

He could see the white gleam of the beach, and the dark sinister loom of the mysterious island against the sparkling fat white stars. The Island of Dark Figures!

Dorothy came up from below, garrulous with excitement, like a girl preparing to go to her first dance. He couldn't see her, but he knew how bright her eyes, how flushed her cheeks must be.

She came and stood close to him. "Can you see the light of the bungalow?"

"No," he said. He had seen no lights. He wondered if Lucky planned to stay on this island. Lucky was a little dubious about his reception by her father. What would this millionaire say to his daughter—the apple of his eye—marrying a man who looked like a buccaneer all of the time and acted like one on the slightest provocation? Yet any man but a fool would know that Lucky was solid gold; would be tickled stiff to get him for a son-in-law.

But it was a great mistake. Dorothy was cute and young and pretty. She was smart, too. Just the same, it was a great mistake. Lucky wasn't the marrying kind. You might shore up a ship on dry land, but it was wrong. That ship belonged in the water. Its job was to travel. Singapore knew Lucky well enough to predict that he was paving the way to lifelong discontent and unhappiness. He would never get the sea and the lust for adventure out of his blood. On top of all this, it grieved Singapore more than he would have admitted under torture to see their friendship headed for the rocks.

Lucky came over. Singapore heard the sound of a kiss in the dark.

He stirred uncomfortably.

Dorothy said, excitedly, "When are we going ashore?"

"In the morning," Singapore answered.

"Oh," she wailed. "Not till then? Oh, please, please, please let's go ashore now. Look! There's the bungalow! Through those trees!"

Singapore looked and saw a lone light gleaming.

"I'm going to fire a salute," Dorothy said. She stepped to the rail. A random ray of light from the cabin picked bright glints from the weapon in her hand—a little pearl-handled twenty-five automatic which she wore in a snakeskin holster attached to a snakeskin belt.

Dorothy fired three shots, paused, fired two more. She said: "It's our private signal. It means 'All's well.'"

Singapore, watching the dark loom of the shore, first saw, then heard, the five shots in answer—five little spurts of blue-red fire, then the reports, which some cañon, far away, picked up and sent rattling off until the stuttering echoes subsided to a purr.

"Lucky!" the girl cried. "Sam! Oh, come on! Let's go. Dad'll have fits if we don't come. He'll be worried green. I know!" she said. "You're afraid, Lucky. You're afraid to look my father in the eye. And I thought you were so brave!"

"It isn't that," Lucky murmured.

"What is it?" she demanded.

"I'll tell you," Singapore said. "We're funny that way, kid. We've been cruisin' and tradin' among these islands for a long time. We like to see our noses in front of our faces. That's all."

It didn't seem, to Dorothy, to stand up as an argument. She pleaded with them. She bullied. She wheedled. She grew impatient.

Singapore knew it was ridiculous of him to feel as he felt. It was like a vague bristling, an unreasoning aversion to landing on that infamous island in the darkness. But it was two to one now; Lucky had decided to side with Dorothy.

"I'll just take my toilet things," she said. "The rest can wait until morning."

The *serang* and the deckhand lowered a boat. They were, Lucky said, to stay aboard.

"We may not be back until morning. Keep a good watch."

"*Aie, tuan!*"

Singapore rowed, with Lucky and Dorothy in the stern seat, holding hands and whispering. Occasionally he caught a word. But he wasn't much interested. He felt pretty sick about it. He was trying to decide what he would do. He would sell his half interest in the *Blue Goose*. He would make that dangerous journey, long-postponed, through jungles and swamps and mountains, into the northern part of Siam, where, he had been reliably informed, lived a Karen chieftain who possessed a mate to the blue fire pearl. He would, of course, wait here on Konga for the *Bangalore*—and Bill Shay. Then on to Siam!

The skeg of the dinghy grated on sand. He got out and pulled the bow up on the beach, then gave Dorothy a hand out onto the sand. He could just see the pale blur of her face in the starlight. Behind her, Lucky loomed tall and mysterious.

"There's a path through these trees," Dorothy said, and led the way across the beach to a grove. They were scrub palms. Their fronds hung motionless in the still air. Looking above them, Singapore saw the evening star like a dazzlingly bright incandescent light poised on the rim of the mountain. It gave the illusion of being so close that he could almost pick it out of the air.

With Dorothy showing them the way to the path, Singapore followed and Lucky brought up the rear. He was suddenly silent. If Singapore knew anything about it, Lucky was dreading this meeting with Dorothy's father.

"This way." She was walking rapidly. She disappeared into the shadows fifty feet ahead of Singapore.

Singapore wished he knew why he felt so uneasy. There was something in the air, an inaudible rhythm, like that of very distant drums to which the skin may be sensitive but the ears are not yet responsive.

The feeling persisted. His uneasiness grew. Something was wrong. He did not know why he wished they had waited until morning, but he did. The queer sense of a rhythm in the air persisted; in fact, became more pronounced. Was it in his imagination? It was, or seemed to be, beating in three-point time, like the blood-drums of the voodoos, like the sacrifice and death drums of savage tribes the world over.

He was certain that it was in his imagination. But the hair at the base of his head stirred a little.

Tumpatum-tump! Tumpatum-tump!

His skin tingled to the remote—or imagined—vibration. His ears strained. Nothing there. Or—not yet? A ghost of breeze, cool as fog, slid through the palm grove. His nerves were jiggling. Behind him, Lucky sighed heavily. Love-drunk!

Once you heard that measured beat, you kept on hearing it. An hour of it was enough to keep it beating in your brain for days. It could come back years later at the rustling of a dry leaf.

Tumpatum-tump! Tumpatum-tump!

A saddle in the hills was silvered with the rising moon. It was as if the saddle along its edges were magically white-hot. Vapors were even rising, as if from a demon's caldron. Singapore saw them with astonishment. Vapors or smoke? Or steam from jungles? No. Too high up for jungles, and the vapor was centered in one spot. Why one spot?

An edge of the moon jumped up, and suddenly illuminated a high wall, a cliff or mountainside, of bleached stone. Bleached sandstone. He stumbled over a root, gathered himself together. The ghostly little breeze carried strongly to his nostrils the sweet pungence of pepper tree blossoms.

He looked back at the mountainside—and suddenly saw something else. The chalky surface glowed not only with the stainless silver of the moon, but there were red-glowing patches, too. They shivered over the silvered wall. Incredulously staring, he saw the shadows of two human giants, crouching. Those shadows must have been hundreds of feet tall.

And seeing them, his ears distinctly heard, for the first time, the rhythm that faintly tapped against his skin.

Instantly, the uneasiness that had been weighing on him since the *Blue Goose* left Singapore sharply focused. His hunch became clear. His intuition, picking at his consciousness, showed him in shocking clarity a pattern formed of seemingly unrelated events.

The girl was perhaps fifty feet ahead of him, hurrying. He could hear the thump of her feet on the packed dark sand. He ran to her, clapped a hand on her shoulder and spun her around. He snatched the pistol out of her holster, and said through his teeth, "You dirty, double-crossing little—"

The girl screamed: "Alvarado! Martinez!"

He closed his hand about her neck, throttling her voice. He panted, "Lucky! Beat it!"

The girl struck at his face, kicked his shins and screamed.

The grove was swarming with giants. They must have been flattened against every palm bole, waiting to pounce.

CHAPTER IX
"WELCOME TO KONGA!"

Two of these giants fell savagely on Singapore, one from either side. A fist smashed into his left cheek, sending him spinning into a fist that came thumping up into his jaw. This jarred him back on his heels. He had lost the girl's pistol and his own. He straightened up; lashed out into reeling blackness. His knuckles buried themselves in bare flesh.

He fought with the fury of a surprised wild cat, yet he knew he had no chance. There seemed to be dozens of them. A man who must have been a head taller than Sammy threw himself on him and bore him, kicking and struggling, to the ground. Feet thumped into his ribs. A heel ground into the back of his hand. Fists were rising and falling, beating his face into a pulp.

With a superhuman effort, Singapore twisted his body, threw off the giant who lay on him. He writhed free. He was on his knees when a fist exploded on his chin like a bomb. He collapsed. He struggled up again. He struck out in every direction. Men, dimly seen, panted and grunted and closed in on him again.

Again he went down under the sheer weight of their hurtling bodies. He fought until he had

no strength left, until he could hardly suck in his breath.

Then they kicked him to his feet. He threw his arms about a palm bole and clung to it, gasping for breath. Blows fell on his head, his shoulders. His legs were kicked.

It was as unreal as the awful visions of a drowning man. He could not move but fists and feet thudded into him. He fell again and was again kicked to his feet. He struck a man in the face. An oath in Spanish was spat at him. Another man, in the same tongue, demanded to know where "the other one" was. And a third man gave, in Spanish—the Spanish of Mexico—the answer, "Back there."

Through a brain haze, Singapore wondered what Spaniards—Mexicans—were doing here. Spaniards—or Mexicans—on Konga! Stars reeled. He glimpsed, far away, those giant figures dancing crazily against the pink-and-silver glow on the white mountain and panted, "Lucky! Where are you?"

The answer, from a dozen feet behind him, was a coughing, spluttering series of oaths. Then came the distinct crashing of fist upon bone. A softer crash. Lucky was down again.

A hand applied between his shoulder blades gave Singapore a shove. He stumbled and spat out, "Who the hell are you?"

The harsh answer, in English: "You'll find out soon enough!"

So furious that he shook, he muttered, "That dirty, double-crossing little—" A fist smashed into his jaw.

"Move along!" A machete was waved threateningly before his face—yet no steel had been used in the fight!

He moved along, and the stars jiggled in their places. Blood was running out of his nose and mouth. One leg felt paralyzed—it hardly supported his weight. He could hardly see, because both eyes were almost swollen shut already. He was beaten—and sick with rage.

"Damn him—damn him!" It was all so clear. That lying Malay he had grabbed in the Sailors

Delight. Behind him, that lying bartender. How far back did it go, all fixed, all ribbed?

"Damn him—damn him!"

The murder of the *serang* and the island boy. That mysterious stowaway! Why, Singapore wrathfully asked himself, hadn't he opened those crates in the 'midships cargo hold? He'd have put white-hot pokers against that phantom's feet until he shrieked the whole truth!

He should have suspected the girl from the moment he saw her, wiping off crocodile tears with that green handkerchief.

"Move along, you rat!"

He stumbled on. Oh, it was all so clear now. Why hadn't it been just as clear days ago? But how convincingly the bartender had lied! How convincingly that Malay had lied! And that girl! She had clouded the whole situation just as an octopus clouds up the water to fool an enemy, a victim. Smoother than silk, the way she'd played up to Lucky, luring him, hypnotizing him, throwing their minds off the track!

The light through the trees came nearer. And the moon was up over the mountain now, drenching the little plateau with silver brightness. He was so bruised, so breathless, so sick he could hardly stand. At intervals, a hand in the small of his back gave him a shove. They were laughing about it, babbling in Spanish, flourishing weapons. Now and then a man kicked the calves of his legs.

He tried to pull himself together. It was a time for fast, clear thinking. What were Mexicans doing on Konga? Six thousand miles from Mexico. The tropical moon showed their faces plainly enough. He had, in all his life, never seen such a collection of brutal, villainous faces. There was a man with only one eye. There was a man with a livid scar, as if a horse had kicked him, curving under his mouth—a man with a double grin!

They swaggered and lurched along behind him. They kicked up sand with their shoes.

They laughed and roared and cursed. It was like a procession of madmen.

The door of the bungalow was open. He was still under the spell of that clever delusion. Not a bungalow. It was the roughest of rough shacks, roofed with ragged nipa—nothing but a shelter against the rains.

There was a rough plank table inside, and on this table burned the stump of a candle. Its orange flame licked up and fell back.

A thin-faced man with clipped gray hair, a man of perhaps fifty-one or -two, with keen blue eyes, sat behind the table. His complexion was beef-red from myriads of tiny ruptured veins and the tip of his large nose was faintly a telltale purple. It was a hard face, a brutal face, and the eyes were those of a predatory bird.

Singapore's heart was thumping. His face was suddenly wet with sweat.

The man at the table watched him with a mockingly grave and sympathetic interest. His mouth began to twitch. Suddenly he laughed; great booming laughter.

The laughter stopped. Old Bill Shay, elephant man, pearler, Buddhist priest, master of trickery, robber, murderer, vagabond extraordinary, bent forward and regarded his stepson with shimmering blue eyes.

"Welcome to Konga!" he chuckled. And added, with mocking sentimentality, "Sonny boy!"

CHAPTER X
BILL SHAY LAUGHS

There was a dirty old khaki sun helmet on the table before him.

And at his hand lay a Luger automatic pistol.

The two captives were pushed roughly into the shanty.

Old Bill Shay looked very well pleased with himself. As the result of the most ingenious trickery, he had lured his red-headed stepson into a trap from which there was no escape.

He said amiably, "Well, Alvarado, we seem to have done a nice clean job."

The giant who had first leaped on Singapore stood just beside him, with arms folded on massive chest. He looked like a cutthroat, a murderer, a pirate. He must have been six feet eight inches tall.

His face was so brown it was almost black. He had a hawklike beak. His teeth were bared in a wolfish grin.

" *'Sta bueno!*" he said, and launched into profane Spanish. Singapore gathered that Alvarado and his men had found the task a very pleasant one. When the two unsuspecting Americanos had come along that path, they had simply slapped them down.

"It was child's play. A little love tap—like this—and we had them."

In an excess of good humor, he slapped Singapore lightly on the jaw. The redhead brought up his fist swiftly to Alvarado's mouth. The Mexican staggered and roared. Men fell upon Singapore; punched and kicked him. His arms were held. Alvarado rubbed blood from his mouth, then spat into Singapore's face.

Old Bill Shay sat at the table with his chin cushioned on a palm, contemplating Sammy with an amiable grin.

He said now, judicially, "That's the trouble with you, Sammy. You don't use your nut. You're a born sucker. You think you're a wise guy. You're nothing but a sap. Alvarado, you'd better get your gang on board that hooker. I have some business to discuss with these two sea wolves. Vamoose!"

Glaring at him and cursing himself, the redhead tried to put his thoughts in order. It was all his fault. He should have seen through that lying bartender and lying Malay. He should have known that that little siren who called herself Dorothy Borden was a double-crossing liar. He should have opened up every box and crate in the 'midships hold and found that "phantom stowaway."

He had, through carelessness, fallen into the trap they had sprung, and dragged Lucky in with him.

Bill Shay picked up the automatic pistol. He released the safety catch and placed the pistol on the table again. His blue eyes were bright with good humor.

"We are going to have a little talk, sucker. But don't forget yourself again. I want my son to behave himself like a perfect little gentleman. If he doesn't, he gets spanked. Just keep in mind, Sam, that your dear old dad isn't dumb. It would break my heart to have to hurt you, Sam, but business is business. And that goes for your pal, too."

He took out of a pocket of his tunic a white Burmese cheroot. This he lighted at the candle flame, watching them over it with alert blue eyes. He puffed comfortably and said, "Do you remember what I told you in that letter when you were in the Singapore hospital a couple of years ago? 'The hand is faster than the naked eye. A wise man knows the aim of a bottle.' I guess you didn't get what daddy meant. That's the trouble with me. I give you credit for some intelligence. Well, I used to. But you're not smart. You're just a boob."

"You louse!" Sammy panted.

His stepfather gazed at him with a look of hurt surprise.

"That's right," Sammy snarled. "Grab yourself an eyeful of the guy who's some day gonna make you drink your own blood and like it! You wife beater! You baby robber! You lousy thief! I'll do it! I've sworn to do it. And I will."

His stepfather lifted one eyebrow. "Sammy, I'm surprised at you. I'm hurt, Sammy. Don't you remember what Confucius said? 'When early dawn unseals my eyes, before my mind my dad does rise.' Does a nice boy call his daddy names? And I've tried so hard to be proud of you. I've wanted to see you smart—like I am. And once or twice I kidded myself into thinking you were on the right track.

"I thought so that time when you fought your way out of the Maharaja of Malobar's jail—and got away with that fine blue fire pearl. I thought so again when you threw the live cobra into that crooked jeweler's cage in Singapore—and got away with the jack he'd stolen from you. And when you swam through that nest of sharks in Pemanggil Passage and outsmarted Big Nick Stark, the toughest crook south of Shanghai, I thought your brain was beginning to develop a little."

Bill Shay sighed and shook his head. "I admit, Sammy, that I was a little bit irritated at the way you stole the pink pig away from me in Siam, and I was mildly annoyed when you sneaked that sunken treasure out from under my nose up there in Sapahalu Strait. And there was another time when you got a lucky break, when you tricked me out of that salted sapphire mine, up on the Chantaboun River. I was just a mite provoked—I confess it freely, Sam. But I was pleased, too, because I thought you were working and studying hard to become, in time, and with breaks, a half-wit. But I was wrong again. Once a lamebrain, always a lamebrain."

"Listen, tough guy," Sammy interrupted. "I don't like the way your nose grows. I don't like the way you brush your hair. Let's stop slicing boloney and get places. You've got that will of my grandfather's, and you've got me where you want me. You're going to knock me off and get that million. What are we waiting for?"

His stepfather slowly shook his head. "Sammy," he said sadly, "don't you realize that when you say things like that it brings big pearly tears into my eyes? Why should I kill you? Why should I rob myself of the only real fun I have in life? You don't seem to get my point. Of course, you don't get most points. But couldn't you, if you banged your head against a wall, get your brain to working just a little? Can't you grasp that the thing that makes life worth while for me is the laughs I get out of you?

"If I knocked you off, what would be left? Nothing but pearls and elephants. It's laughing that keeps a man young, Sammy. And the reason I don't look my age is the laughs I get out of you. Of course, I ought to be ashamed for picking on such a mental cripple, but I'm human, Sammy, and the temptation is too great."

"You rat!" Sammy said.

His stepfather contemplated him with mocking reproach. There was a little pucker between his eyes, as if he were thoughtfully turning that epithet over in his mind.

"Perhaps you've never heard the old Siamese saying, 'Rats know the ways of rats.' Why don't you take lessons from me, Sammy? Of course, you wouldn't grasp the fine points, but if you really applied yourself we might filter a little useful light into that dim, echoing corridor between your ears."

Sammy, breathing hard, involuntarily took a step forward. The pistol was instantly in his stepfather's hand. And Singapore knew that Bill Shay would not hesitate to use that pistol, if the issue were forced. He knew that Bill Shay didn't want to use that pistol unless he was compelled to. He wanted to see Sammy squirm.

And Sammy was certain that, sometime tonight, he was going to be killed. Somehow this man was going to put him to death. How? By turning him over to the Kongans? It didn't really matter. Bill Shay was playing with him now as a cat plays with a captured sparrow. The kill would occur when Bill Shay tired of playing.

CHAPTER XI
SHANGHAI SALLY

The beat of the Kongan drums, up there on the hilltop, created a mad rhythm in Singapore Sammy's nerves. *Tumpatum-tump! Tumpatum-tump!* The flame of the candle on the rough plank table licked up. Smoke from the point of it was a black string reaching up to the palm-thatched roof of the shack. There was no wind. He heard the ticking sound of a scorpion crawling in the thatch. The odor of pepper tree blossoms was sickeningly sweet. Mingled with it was the acrid smell of old Bill Shay's white Burmese cheroot.

From the corner of his eye he saw Lucky Jones, beside him, sway a little. How long would the buccaneer preserve his self-control? Only that Luger in Bill Shay's hand was holding him back. But how long would it hold him back?

Careful, Lucky! Hold onto yourself.

Singapore's heart was beating heavily. He had that desperate feeling of helplessness enjoyed, perhaps, by an insect on a pin. He knew that the sweat of desperation was streaming off his forehead and running with the blood down his face, because he could feel it dribbling off his chin.

His stepfather tilted his head a little and lifted his eyes, as if he were weighing the meaning of the Kongan drums. Then he lowered the pistol. He was amiably smiling again and his eyes were twinkling.

"A father's duty," he said, "is to prepare his son to cope with life. The question is, are you too dumb to learn how? My opinion is that you are. Yet I owe it to you to make you learn a few things, no matter how painful it may be to that poor pulpy mass of confusion back of your eyes.

"We will take the present situation, and how it came about, as the first lesson. It was a neat trick, and it was smart. I know I ought to illustrate this lesson with diagrams and crayon drawings, so that that last year's bird nest inside your skull will grasp the points, but I'll do my best.

"First of all, Sammy, I kept in mind that I was dealing with a very low order of intelligence. So I said to myself, 'Bill,' I said, 'keep your tricks simple and childish. The simpler they are, the quicker that poor sap will fall for them.' So I primed that bartender, and I primed that Malay so that you would, being so simple-minded, go hot-footing it down my trail. Then I put a pretty girl into the picture, knowing, of course, how big dumb punks like you fall for any line a pretty girl hands out.

"It's going to be hard for you to get the purpose of these simple little gags, but I'll try hard and I'll promise to be patient, knowing how backward you are. The purpose, Sammy, was to get hold of your schooner. These friends of mine needed a good fast schooner and your schooner is good and fast."

Bill Shay paused, his eyes shimmering at the moonlit night behind Sammy and Lucky. Singapore glanced quickly at Lucky. The buccaneer looked dazed. He was in a semi-stupor—out on his feet from the beating he'd taken and the realization that that girl was a lying little cheat, the lowest kind of hypocrite. When Lucky came out of that daze, he was very apt to start wrecking things.

A girl's sweet, clear voice behind him said, "Well, here I am, Bill!"

And the girl who called herself Dorothy Borden serenely walked in with her hand lightly resting on the little pistol in her holster. Singapore had snatched it out of that holster, and the Mexicans, in their rush, had knocked it out of his hand. He supposed she had been all this time looking for it.

She bent down and kissed old Bill Shay lightly on the mouth. Straightening up, she turned toward the two men she had so thoroughly hoodwinked, and her eyes were softly aglow. She was even smiling. It was a sweet, rather gay little smile.

Glaring at her, Singapore found it hard to believe, even now, that she was not what she had professed to be. Her loveliness, her air of fresh innocence, would have deceived any man. It was utterly incredible that a girl who looked so innocent, so sweet, could be what this girl had proved herself to be.

He sent another glance in Lucky's direction, and saw that the buccaneer's jaw muscles were bulging, that that sledgehammer jaw was outthrust, that every muscle and tendon of Lucky's big frame was straining forward with an almost irresistible inclination to destroy her.

The smile the girl wore was, to Singapore, as fantastic as if she had suddenly changed color. How many times had she smiled at him in just that way? So sweet, so innocent, so lovable! It would have been easy to understand, now that her deception was revealed, if she had somehow changed, had turned hard-boiled. But she hadn't changed in the least.

Old Bill Shay asked, "Did these two tough eggs give you any trouble, Sally?"

"Oh, no," she said in her clear, sweet voice. "They were very nice."

"Say," Lucky burst out harshly, "who is this snake?"

Singapore said bitterly, "And that's a compliment."

Bill Shay slowly, with an air of defeat, shook his head. "Is this polite?" he said. "Haven't you even any manners? Don't you know that nice little gentlemen don't call ladies naughty names? I'm shocked. Talking like that about the smartest and loveliest girl in Asia!"

"I'll say this for her," Sammy said grimly. "She makes a corkscrew look straighter than a fishline with a shark on it." And he said to himself, "Keep cool!" But he wasn't keeping cool. A few more of these insults, and he'd ram a fist down that old crook's throat. It would almost be worth getting shot to do it.

Controlling himself with a great effort, he said, "She ought to have quite a reputation."

Old Bill Shay was fondling the girl's hand. "Why?" he said. "Because she made suckers of you two mental midgets? But you're right, Sammy. She has a reputation. She has the reputation of being the most beautiful, the cleverest and the most dangerous woman in the Far East. Sally Lavender—the girl from Shanghai! She turned Shanghai business and diplomatic circles into a pinwheel. You really started the Chino-Japanese war, didn't you, baby?"

Sally Lavender laughed softly. "Did I?"

"You see?" old Bill Shay cried. "Sally's modest. That's why I'm going to marry her. With her brains and my beauty, we expect to own Asia in about six months. Am I right, baby?"

"Aren't you always?"

"Spoken like a pal!" he chuckled. Then his face became grave. He solemnly regarded his red-headed stepson. His left eyebrow twitched. Then one corner of his mouth twitched. Then the other corner twitched. And he burst into roars of laughter.

"How," he asked, "are you going to like baby for a stepmother, Sam? Of course, it's a shame you can't come to the wedding. You and your pal would make a couple of cute flower girls. How about it, baby?"

Miss Lavender smiled. Her large beautiful eyes shimmered at Sammy. He was still finding her incredible. The fact of her was still so fantastic, so difficult to accept, that his face must have betrayed it. For his stepfather again burst into roars of laughter.

"Shanghai Sally!" he gurgled. "It almost rhymes with Singapore Sammy, doesn't it? Said Singapore Sam to Shanghai Sal, 'Momma, you are quite a gal.' Said Shanghai Sal to Singapore Sam, 'You bet your half-baked brain I am!' "

The girl said quietly, "Alvarado's men are on the schooner now. They took most of their things, and they're coming right back for the rest. I waited."

"Attababy! Did they take the gold?"

She laughed. "Did you think they'd give us a chance at it?"

"We'll get it," he said. "I like nice raw gold nuggets. I was just telling the boys, Sally, how to be smart like we are. Not that it will do any good, because there seem to be natural laws which prevent any one from driving nails with sponges. I was telling them about Alvarado's *caballeros*. I want Sammy to learn how things are done. Where was I? I was telling you why Alvarado's *caballeros* needed a good fast schooner.

"I realize, Sammy, that you are far too busy being the dumbest guy in the Far East to read the newspapers. If you were abreast of the times, you would know that, about five months ago, nineteen convicts, mostly murderers, made a break from a Mexican island penitentiary. It's in the Pacific, off San Blas. What's the name of it, baby?"

"Las Tres Marías," the girl said.

"That's it. They got away on a raft. A forty-foot sloop picked them up, thinking they were shipwrecked sailors. They killed off the crew of the sloop and sailed west. Two were drowned or eaten on the way. Three more were killed when the sloop cracked up on the reef out there. They've been here a couple of months. Sheer, downright providence—the same kind of providence that works for seagoing gnat brains like yours—got them this far without capture. There were two full moons, weren't there, baby?"

The girl from Shanghai nodded. She was gazing, with her wistful smile, at the copper wire encircling Singapore's neck.

"It seems that these cannibals," Bill Shay went on, "hold a festival every full moon. Like to-night. They dance themselves nutty. Then, if there are any strange brains around, they come down these hills and eat 'em." He chuckled. "It's just an old Konga custom."

He puffed leisurely at his white cheroot. And Singapore wondered if his stepfather was in league with these savages. He had an amazing way with the natives of all countries. It would not have surprised him to hear that Bill Shay was on good terms with the chieftain of the tribe.

"Each moon festival," Bill continued, "while these convicts have been here, the Kongans have come down and grabbed themselves a Mex. The convicts got pretty desperate. They got busy and carved a canoe out of a breadfruit log, and Pete Lopez, the most respectable-looking one of the lot—it happens he speaks several languages—was picked to go to Singapore and somehow get hold of a boat big enough to take them all off. Lopez paddled all the way to Timor Laut and took passage on a trading schooner. He inquired around for the smartest man in the Far East. That's how he came to find me. He wanted a good, fast schooner. Naturally, I thought of your schooner.

"Do you see, Sammy, how nicely it all dovetails? Are you learning this lesson? Try hard! Wrinkle your brow if it will help. Would you like to gnaw your thumb? Keep on trying to concentrate. Do you begin to see, through the fog, how smart your daddy is? For delivering them your schooner, I get all the money they found on the sloop when they pirated it, and, before I'm through, I'll get all the gold they found here.

"Did I mention the gold? They've been placer mining, Sammy, and they have a box of big shiny nuggets which they think they're going to keep. But they aren't going to keep them, Sammy. Because they are half-wits, just like you and your pal. Before I'm through with them, I'll have all the nuggets they mined. See how nicely it all fits together, Sammy? You simply play all the ends on the middle. They get a schooner. I get all their money and I get all your money. And Sally gets the Malobar pearl. That was the price she put on her services, and that's the price she gets. Is it clear to you now how a pair of smart brains work? Or is it completely over that genuine ivory ball you carry on the end of your neck? Don't you want to ask any questions? Teacher will gladly answer any questions. Don't be ashamed of being curious. Even rabbits are curious."

"Who killed my *serang* and deckhand?" Lucky hoarsely asked.

"I don't know. Who killed 'em, baby?"

"Lopez."

"And Lopez stowed away," Lucky snarled. "And when that cargo came aboard, he hid in an empty crate."

Bill Shay nodded indulgently. "That was my idea, too. He goes to the head of the class, doesn't he, baby? That cargo was also my idea, Sammy. In case you didn't investigate, it contains enough food to last the *caballeros* six months, or at least until they reach Madagascar."

Sally Lavender said quietly, "Bill, aren't those drums closer?"

Bill Shay leisurely stood up, with the Luger in his hand. He walked around the table with his eyes on Sammy.

"Yes," he said, "they're pretty close. Sammy, it's taken me some time to get around to the point of this talk, but I've had to explain myself in language that that crock of liverwurst under your hair could grasp. The point is, as Confucius says, 'The superior man will gladly lay down his life for his father.' Of course, you's not a superior man, but you'll do. Comfort yourself with the reflection that you aren't fit to spend your own money anyway. You can go to hell happy, knowing that your grandfather's money is going to be spent by a clever man."

"You lousy, cold-blooded murderer!"

His stepfather clicked his tongue in gentle reproof, then he smiled indulgently.

"I understand," he said. "You're joking with daddy. Where would you be, Sammy, without your sense of humor? It's nice to have a sense of humor, isn't it, baby? It takes a good, practical sense of humor to laugh when you learn you're going to have the top of your head lopped off and your brains scooped out and eaten like beans within the next few hours!"

"You rat!" Lucky rasped through puffed and bleeding lips.

"So that's how we get it?" Singapore said.

His stepfather seemed amazed. His eyes were large and round. He softly exclaimed, "Did you think I was going to kill you unless you forced me to? Don't you know, Sammy, that it's against the law to kill a man? I'm not going to kill you. I'm going to let the snakes or the Kongans do it. Then I'm going to take what's left of you to Surabaya as fast as I can—before it spoils—for purposes of identification. The law compels that, and I wouldn't dream of violating the law.

"Easy, Sammy! Don't lose your temper! Maybe a Konga queen will fall in love with your red hair and marry you. Being a queen's husband is a job that doesn't require any intelligence. Or maybe you'll get an idea and save yourself. I don't know what your brain would do with an idea if one got lost and strayed in there, but mistakes do happen. While there's life, isn't there always hope? Or, as Confucius says, 'The superior man has neither fear nor anxiety.' "

Singapore's eyes flicked to the girl. Her face was calm, not alarmed. Her eyes were large, round and watchful. The little pistol was in her hand. He heard Lucky groan with suppressed fury.

"Will you two men," the girl said in her deceptively sweet, gentle voice, "move over to the wall, facing it, with your hands above your heads?"

The two adventurers hesitated. But Singapore was more in fear of what she might do if he hesitated too long than he was of Bill Shay's cold-blooded ruthlessness. This girl, he knew, would not hesitate to shoot him in the back. So he raised his hands above his head and moved to the wall, facing it. And Lucky Jones did likewise.

Singapore felt fingers fumbling at the copper loop, felt the wire slip over his head.

Then the girl softly exclaimed, "Bill! It's gone! It was there when we came ashore. I made sure—felt it in the pouch when he helped me out of the dinghy. The pearl and the pouch are gone!"

CHAPTER XII
INTO THE PIT

Singapore felt his stepfather's hot breath on the back of his neck. Then Bill Shay prodded him in the backbone with the muzzle of a Luger.

"Sonny boy," he said softly, "where's Sally's pearl?"

"That's funny," Singapore jeered. "You two are so smart. You're the smartest pair of thieves in the Far East. Two people as smart as you are shouldn't have any trouble findin' Sally's pearl."

Old Bill Shay said sadly, "Sammy, I'm afraid I'm going to have to hurt you a little."

And Sammy answered, "Go to it."

"Search them both," Miss Lavender suggested.

"Okay. Keep them covered." Very thoroughly and systematically the old elephant man conducted that search. The pearl was, very evidently, not concealed on either man.

"He got rid of it," the girl said, "when the Mexicans attacked. He couldn't have hidden it very well. He didn't have time."

The Luger gently prodded Singapore in the backbone again.

"Sam," Bill Shay said, "that pearl is your wedding present to your stepmother. Am I going to have to be rough?"

"I was figurin'," Singapore said grimly, "on givin' it to her at the weddin'."

The pistol jabbed him in the spine again. This time it hurt so that he winced.

"I'll give you just ten seconds, sucker."

"It's in the ocean," Sam said.

"That's a lie."

"I can't get away with anything with you, can I, big shot? Sure it's a lie. I buried it in the sand while I was rasslin' with your boy friends."

"That's another lie!"

"Sure it is! When I'm in Rome, I go Roman all over!"

Bill Shay laid a powerful hand on his neck. With his other he jammed the muzzle of the Luger once again into Sammy's sore backbone. A fury that he could not control swept in a kindling wave through the redhead. He could restrain his urge to fight back no longer.

Within a space of time immeasurable, so swiftly did he go into action, he spun about. By some trick of mental telepathy, some electrically transferred nerve impulse, Lucky Jones went into action at the same split-second.

Both men whirled simultaneously. The pistol's muzzle raked along Sammy's ribs as he whirled. His right fist, on a crooked stiff arm, smashed into Bill Shay's face at a spot along the jaw midway between point of chin and ear. Lucky's left-handed punch brushed the pistol out of the girl's hand in passing and thumped into Bill Shay as his head rebounded from Singapore's punch.

The old elephant man was caught, as it were, between two hurricanes of bone and flesh. For a moment, his large red face remained stationary, a target like a half moon. Before it could waver, Singapore's fist struck one eye, the nose and the mouth with savage and beautifully timed precision. Bill Shay fell back with such violence against Sally Lavender that she sprawled backward, bringing up against the opposite wall. She slid down to the dirt floor. A shower of palm leaf splinters rattled down.

Bill Shay, continuing his precipitate backward flight, struck the table. It disintegrated. The elephant man went down noisily in its collapse. The candle flame vanished. The Luger sent three stabbing red-blue flames toward the roof in the immediate darkness.

There was silence, disturbed only by the distant beat of the drums.

The success of their unpremeditated attack was so startling that neither the redhead nor the buccaneer could, for a moment, speak.

Then: "Lucky!" Singapore croaked.

"Right here!"

"Hit?"

"No! You?"

"No! Breeze!"

They breezed, going through the narrow door shoulder to shoulder. Through the trees, they saw the gleam of the moon on wavelets. This was the shortest way to the ocean, and the ocean was their objective.

A path led from the shanty to the beach in a direct line—half again shorter than the way they had come.

They started down this path at a hard run, side by side. What their plan was, Heaven only knew. An uproar of men's voices over the water told them that the convicts had taken possession of the *Blue Goose*. Behind them, up on the hill, the Kongan drums sent down their pagan rhythm. *Tumpatum-tump! Tumpatum-tump!*

And suddenly, as he raced for the beach, Singapore realized that the drums had stopped; that his ears, so attuned to the beat, were merely repeating the rhythm. He guessed this meant that the Kongans were on their way.

"We should have grabbed them guns," Lucky panted, as he ran.

"What good would guns do?" Singapore answered.

"What do you figure we're gonna do?"

"Swim!"

"Where?"

"Anywhere! We'll find heavy enough driftwood on the beach to hang onto. We'll kick out and wait for a ship to pass."

"And get et by sharks!"

"Better than havin' our brains et like beans!"

They plunged through a scraggly grove of beefwood trees. One of two dark oblong patches, set close together, each perhaps ten feet wide by twenty in length, lay in their path. Nothing about those patches suggested treachery. They were such patches as fallen leaves might make.

The two sprinting fugitives dashed out upon the oblong patch directly in the path. The oblong patch gave way. It simply collapsed. The two men, in mid-stride, went down with it. Down, down and down a rectangular pit ten feet wide and twenty feet long, and perhaps fifteen feet deep. It might have been a grave dug for a giant's burial.

The bottom was soft wet clay. Striking it, the two adventurers skidded and fell, splashing.

"What the hell is this?" Lucky panted as he struggled up.

Singapore did not answer at once. He had fallen on his back, and the wind was knocked out of him.

He gasped, "Help me up!" And the buccaneer yanked him to his feet.

The moon rode high overhead and sent sufficient light into the pit to illuminate it perfectly. It plainly showed the stratified earth into which the pit had been dug. The upper stratum was white sand. Below that was a gray layer, of darker sand. Under that for five or six feet stretched black earth. Then came clay—slippery, slimy gray clay.

"Did they," Lucky panted, "expect us to fall into this if we made a get-away?"

Singapore didn't know. He was busy looking for a way out. He leaped up, tried to dig fingers and toes into the wall and claw up the side. But the sides were perpendicular. He fell back, with lumps of black dirt raining down upon him.

They both tried. But the top of the pit was a full nine feet above their heads. It was almost impossible to maintain a footing in the watery clay. It was like a mixture of lubricating oil and grease, strewn with the light branches and leaves which had camouflaged the pit. There was no strength in these branches. They broke like straw stems.

"There's only one way out of here." Singapore said. "We've got to kick down enough clay to make a ramp up to where we can claw out the dirt. Got a knife?"

"Nope. They took it."

"Let's get busy and kick. Look here!"

He indicated, with his foot, a square dark patch of earth on the side of the pit, perhaps two feet square, and about a foot from the bottom.

"What do you suppose that's for?"

"It blocks a tunnel!" Lucky cried. "It's the way out!"

This seemed logical—so logical, indeed, that Singapore disregarded the sudden sharp warning of his intuition. He had, in the excitement, forgotten about the pits dug in Malaysia and Sumatra for the trapping of wild animals; forgotten that these pits were dug side by side with only a thin layer of earth between the two, so that, with the animal in one pit, a cage could be lowered into the other, and the animal transferred from the one pit to the cage, merely by knocking out the thin separating wall of earth.

When Lucky kicked the square dark patch, his foot went cleanly through. That blow loosened all the earth, and a two-foot square aperture was revealed.

Lucky cried jubilantly, "It's a tunnel all right! Hey! Hold on! Maybe the Kongans use this tunnel! Maybe this is how they snuck up on them greasers!"

Singapore was staring suspiciously at the square, black hole.

Suddenly, he shouted, "Plug up that hole! Quick!"

He picked up clumps of clay in his hands, tearing them from the walls, hurling these heavy clumps at the opening. He had glimpsed two pairs of luminous, cold green eyes shining like emeralds in the blackness of the adjoining pit. They danced from side to side. They advanced. They retreated.

A sickening stench poured out of the hole.

"Pythons!" he yelled.

Hoarsely sucking in his breath with the sound of a sob, Lucky clawed out a lump of clay and hurled it at the hole. The lump struck the wall perhaps six inches above the hole. The force of it dislodged a thin slab of clay eighteen inches square, enlarging the aperture to that extent.

"Lower!" Singapore shouted.

"Why," Lucky panted, "didn't you let me get them guns?"

The two adventurers were working furiously, scooping up handfuls of clay and hurling them at the hole, raking it down from the sides in great wads with hooked fingers.

The head of the largest snake Singapore had ever seen suddenly darted out of the hole. The scaly dark body attached to the head was as thick as his forearm.

He hurled a ball of clay at it. The head darted aside, and the body behind it came sliding out of the adjoining pit, writhing and twisting like a huge and horrible cable of black steel.

Unawarely, the two men were shouting and cursing in the frenzied panic that this monster provoked. Sammy clearly understood now old Bill Shay's reference to snakes—the alternative to being bound to trees for the Kongans to capture. Bill Shay had planned to cast them into this pit! And Singapore Sammy knew that these pythons must be starved.

A large loop of the snake, cold and wet and slimy, went around him. The head of the reptile plunged down to within an inch of his eyes. Its eyes were green and coldly murderous. The loop settled about his shoulders, slipped down until it encircled his waist.

He struck at the head with his clenched fist. The emerald eyes slid away. A forked tongue darted out at him. The loop was tightening about him just above his hip bones; closing down, preparing to crush the life out of him.

He struck and clawed and pulled at the cable-like loop across his stomach; saw Lucky go stumbling past him, with a fold of the other python entwined three times about his chest and middle. A twitching black tail, blunt as the end of a club, caught at first one leg, then the other. It was pulling Sammy off his feet. He could not stand up. His hand went blindly out. He was lifted into the air, half-way to the top of the pit. He clawed at the side. He was filled with a desperate futility. The exertion of his utmost strength made absolutely no impression on the python.

He could hardly breathe now. The great black loop about his waist was tightening, tightening. He could feel the mad thumping of his heart against the awful irresistible pressure of it. He knew that his eyes were bulging from their sockets.

And now that they had subdued their victims, the two pythons proceeded more slowly. Another fold of the slimy black body slowly slipped over Singapore's head. For many seconds his nose was pressed flat by the white belly of the snake, and his nostrils were full of the awful stench of it. Then the coil slipped down to his neck, slid over his shoulders and joined the other convolution, tightening, always tightening.

He felt the pressure of blood against the sides of his head, pounding in his throat and ears, as the constriction about his chest and stomach increased. He was so weak now he could hardly struggle. He tried to speak. He knew this was the last act—curtains! He wanted to say so-long to Lucky. But the breath was squeezed out of him, and the coils of the python prevented him from swelling the walls of his chest to inhale. He felt ribs beginning to buckle, to crack. The pain where they joined his backbone was unbearable.

He was helpless. He knew he was going to die. This hideous pressure would continue to increase until death came, until he was crushed to a pulp. Then the huge jaws of the python would dislocate, and he would be forced into the monster's stomach.

His ears were full of a roaring, like that of a torrent of water. But there was no sound in the pit, except the sharp, short gasps of the doomed men and the slithering sound of the pythons settling down to their destruction.

His eyes, blinded by pain and blood, did not see a rope fall into the pit; nor was he aware of a small, slim figure sliding down the rope.

Perhaps his tortured senses registered flashes of blue-red; crashes of pistol fire. Next moment he was unconscious.

CHAPTER XIII
SALLY LAVENDER ACTS

Singapore Sammy's return to this life was signalized by a faint glow before his eyes and the sensation of fresh air being sucked into aching, fiery lungs.

He lay on his side, with his back to a wall of the pit. Close to his face lay a black thick loop of the python. It was quivering.

Sammy could not move. Intelligence informed him that the python must be quivering in its death agonies. The pit was very quiet. Some distance away, at the opposite end, he heard a faint gasping and gurgling. He managed to sit up.

Lucky was sitting at the far end, feebly wiping blood from his face.

Singapore said, weakly, "What—happened?"

A girl's clear voice answered, "I killed them. I shot them both through the head. They nearly killed you in their death struggles. I had to take the chance. There wasn't any choice."

He looked around. Sally Lavender was standing over him with her automatic pistol in one hand, a *parang* dripping with blood in the other.

"After I shot them," she said, "I hacked their heads off. Can you stand up? You'd better try."

Singapore tried. It called for all the strength he possessed to lift and push himself up. Then he had to cling to the slimy clay wall to keep himself erect. His legs were numb. His head whirled. His lungs burned and ached. But the bones of neither arms nor legs were broken. There was, however, a sharp, persistent pain where his ribs joined his backbone.

Dazed, he wondered why this girl had risked her life to save his and Lucky's. He staggered across the slippery clay to Lucky Jones and pulled him up.

"Where's the old man?" Singapore asked.

"He flew," the girl told him. "We've got to get out of here. Can you make it?"

"I can try."

She said breathlessly, "The other end of this rope is tied to a tree. Pull yourself up, then get us out."

"Okay. But I don't think I can make it."

He grasped the rope and tried. His bruised and torn muscles rebelled. He sank his teeth into his lower lip, breathed deep and tried again. Digging into the slippery wall with his toes, he kicked and pulled himself up to within four feet of the top. There he hung. Sweat oozed out on his forehead, ran into his eyes. Lucky, under him, was trying to help.

"Stand on my shoulders."

Sammy's feet found the buccaneer's wide shoulders. He took another deep breath and reached up on the rope. His mouth tasted salty with blood from his lip. He put all his strength into it. Slowly, slowly, his head rose up until his eyes were level with the gray stratum. Up! On up! The gray layer inched past his eyes, turned white. His eyes came level with the ground. He kicked, clawed, heaved; swung his body up over the edge. He rolled over and lay on his back, feebly gasping, utterly exhausted.

A voice said, "Hurry! Oh, hurry!"

He could not hurry. He could not move. He tried to get his breath. He tried to command his worn-out muscles to further effort.

Sammy succeeded in rolling over. A man was lying beside him. The man was Alvarado. His eyes, not two inches away, stared coldly into Singapore's. There was a wolfish grin at his lips.

Singapore grunted with dismay, then sucked in his breath with horror. The eyes of the Mexican were cold indeed—cold in death. Something was wrong with his face—worse than mere death. Above his thick, bristling black eyebrows, it ceased entirely to be.

"Hurry!" the girl's voice said.

Sammy got up on his elbows. Alvarado's head had been cut off cleanly just above the eyebrows, so cleanly that there was only a little blood smeared along the edge of the bone.

Singapore looked closer. Alvarado's head was as empty as an eggshell! The brains had been cleanly removed!

Had this, Sammy frantically wondered, happened while he and Lucky were in the pit? Or had Alvarado been lying here, in this shadow, when they ran down the path?

Struggling to his knees, panting for breath, more than half sick, the redhead looked about him. Each tree, it seemed to him, was thicker than it should normally be. Distorted imagination—or did every tree shield a silent, bloodthirsty savage?

There was no sound, except, distantly, the uproar from the schooner. Cold waves of horror squirmed down Sammy's spine. He sweated with the realization that he could not move.

"Hurry!" The girl's voice was a thin wail.

He felt his flesh tingling, tightening, with an awful terror. But he forced himself to move. He crawled to the edge of the pit, with his head hanging drunkenly. He looked down.

Moonlight flooded the upturned faces of Lucky and the girl from Shanghai.

"Pull her up!" Lucky panted.

Singapore automatically spat on his hands and grasped the rope. His actions, the response of protesting muscles, were as automatic as the beating of a heart. His body was a pulse of pain. His brain was sick—chaotic with fear of the unseen dark figures which he thought hysterically must be all about him, creeping toward him.

But he hauled on the rope. The girl slid up into view, pawed at the white sand and pulled herself up the rest of the way. She had fastened the rope about herself, under her arms. She untied it and dropped it back into the pit. With herself and Singapore pulling, Lucky was brought up.

His breath whistled with a horrid sound in his lungs. He tottered, saw Alvarado, and fell to hands and knees. He looked at the dead man's empty skull and groaned.

"How long—" he began thickly.

The girl cried softly, "Hurry! Oh, hurry!"

Lucky clawed feebly at the air; got to his feet and staggered.

"What's that?"—a thin whisper. Sally Lavender was pointing a shaking hand toward the thicket nearest the dark shack. Singapore, staring, was sure he saw a shadowy figure flit from one tree to another. He could not be sure enough. His eyes were playing tricks. First the moonlight was green-tinged, then it was red-tinged. No one ever had seen a Kongan and lived to tell about it!

Were there dark figures behind all these trees? The very air seemed alive with the imperceptible rustlings they made, with their breathing, with the beating of their hearts, with the very heat of their naked black bodies.

Lucky seemed too sick to grasp the danger. The girl seemed paralyzed. Sammy heard her whisper, like a faint echo, "Oh, hurry!" He would hear her saying that in his dreams, he believed, forever. Hurry! Oh, hurry!

He clutched Lucky by the arm. He made himself move and dragged Lucky with him. They stumbled along. Lucky lurched out of the path like a drunken man. Sammy tottered with him, fought for balance, pulled him back into the path. Sally Lavender was trying to run. She tripped and almost fell. Sammy heard her frightened sobs. He looked back. His scalp prickled. Were those shadows moving?

They plunged from the palm thicket onto the beach. "There!" the girl panted. The dinghy had been left high and dry on the white coral beach.

Staggering and stumbling, the two men pulled, lifted, pushed. They inched the boat into the water. The girl scrambled into the stern. Gasping, they tumbled in after her. Lucky dragged himself to the forward seat. Singapore snatched up the oars, dropped one, grabbed it as it slid into the water, began frantically to row. His lungs felt white-hot. The muscles of his back were a gnawing ache.

"Oh, hurry!" Sally whispered. Her eyes, enormous with fright, were on the black mass of trees.

With burning back and agonized lungs, Sammy bent forward and strained back. Forward, dip, pull. Forward, dip, pull. He rowed, it seemed, forever, keeping on a line mid-way between the schooner and the shore. He did this automatically, obeying his intuitions. Cannibals on the shore—murderers on the ship! Forward—dip—pull! Forward—dip—*pull!*

The beach blurred. The trees jigged. A million white-hot suns swam across his vision.

Sally's voice seemed to float to him from a great distance.

"Maskee! We're out of range."

He dropped the oars, crumpled forward until his head thumped down on his drawn-up knees. Presently he sat up and wiped his hand across his eyes. He stared at the shore. He stared at the girl's face. There was something uncanny, unreal about their being here.

"Where were they?" he said.

She whispered, "Why did they let us go?"

Their eyes were fixed hypnotically on each other's.

"Because you're a woman."

"Because you have red hair. Perhaps they've never—"

"Oh, no," Sammy said. "Oh, no." He paused. "Alvarado—" He stopped again. "Maybe they're still—"

She shivered; determinedly made the effort to pull herself together. Sighing, she said, "But, we're safe, Sam; we're safe."

He turned and looked out at the schooner, then back at her slim hand, resting on the pistol in her holster. Raucous laughter came in bursts from the *Blue Goose*. There was a soft, peaceful gurgling under the stern of the dinghy. Moonlight made crinkling silk of the sea. Singapore was suddenly conscious of a feeling of relief. He and Lucky were out of that trap. Or were they?

He looked back at her hand on the pistol. He knew that she was as cold-blooded, as ruthless as those pythons. And he wondered if this was another trap into which she was leading them. Was she still acting under Bill Shay's orders, or was she carrying on an enterprise of her own? Yet if Bill Shay had wished them killed, why had she risked her life, leaping into that pit?

"Yeah," he said sourly. "Yeah, we're safe, all right."

"But they're bound to go ashore! On account of Alvarado."

"And what makes you think they won't spot us?"

"I don't think they can see us from the schooner. Aren't we in the reflection of the mountains and those trees? We've got to take that chance. When they go ashore, we go aboard."

Sammy glanced at her hand again. Still on the pistol.

"Suppose," he said, "they decide to double-cross Alvarado. They've got that gold on board, haven't they?"

"Yes," she said, "but they'll go ashore. They want your blue pearl. They'll be sure Bill has it by now—they'd know he was going to double-cross me. They'll try to double-cross him for the pearl just as he planned to double-cross them for their gold."

"And you're bettin' they'll all go ashore."

"I am."

"Not leavin' a single man on guard?"

"I know them, Sam. They wouldn't leave one man aboard—he'd double-cross them and run off with the ship and the gold. And they'll all want to be on hand to get the pearl from your stepfather. And they planned to watch the pythons eat you. They wouldn't miss that."

"Maybe Alvarado was gonna double-cross them and get the pearl off the old man."

"No. He was going to be talking to him when they came and ganged him."

"Yeah. Listen, sister. You want to watch out you don't get balled up and double-cross yourself."

"I've managed," she said serenely, "to think fairly clear so far."

Singapore pondered that. "Yeah," he said, and wondered what she was thinking now.

The dinghy rose and fell gently with an almost imperceptible ground swell. The waves, breaking on the beach, made a soft whisper occasionally blotted out by the tumult from the schooner.

Sally Lavender said, "It's our only hope of escape. We three can handle the schooner— can't we, Lucky?"

The buccaneer answered in a thick, gritty voice, "I haven't a thing to say to you."

There were savage undercurrents in his voice. A sound of dull thumping floated from the *Blue Goose.*

"Red," he panted, "we've got to get aboard. You hear what they're doin'?"

"Yes, but we've gotta wait."

"The lousy scum're tearin' her apart!"

Sally said, "Don't you see, Lucky, if we're going to outwit those cutthroats and get away alive, we must pull together?"

"You heard me," Lucky said.

The girl made no answer. Her expression was serene. Sammy knew she didn't regret what she'd done to Lucky. She was like platinum. Nothing evidently touched her emotions. She was as impervious and as cold as that moonlike metal. Singapore had encountered her kind before, but never one so clever, so finished. He knew she was still after the blue fire pearl. But what was her scheme?

He drawled, "Where's your sweetie now?"

"You don't mean Bill Shay!"

"Why don't I?"

"I told you. You knocked him unconscious. The instant he came around, he left. He was almost strangling with rage. When I told him the drums had stopped, he simply flew."

Sammy gazed at her with a pucker between his puffed and swollen eyes. In the moonlight, her face was like new ivory—softly white and somehow luminous. Her eyes were enormous. Her mouth was a shadow. It was a tragic and a beautiful face. It was like a deadly flower of the jungles. It was as mysterious as a whisper heard in the night. As long as he lived, he would never answer her riddle. He was utterly fascinated by her contradictory blending of beauty and evil, of girlish innocence and diabolical cleverness. The devil disguised as a virgin!

"It beats me," he said, "how you fell for an old cobra like him."

"I wouldn't trust that man any farther than I can see around a corner!"

"Yeah? And he trusts you as far as he could throw that schooner by the bowsprit. How's he gettin' off the island?"

"He had a whaleboat hidden in some mangroves around on the south side. If the natives haven't grabbed him, he's well at sea by this time, cursing. How he must be cursing!"

Sammy smiled for the first time in hours. "He ran out on you!"

He had picked up the oars again, was slowly rowing. He wanted to be on the seaward side of the schooner when the Mexicans went ashore— if they went ashore. He wondered how long it would take them to drink up the contents of the liquor chest.

"No," the girl said. "I had three possible choices of getting away. With him. With Alvarado's men. And with you. I knew your chances were better than either his or theirs. You're resourceful and you're absolutely unafraid."

"You mean, you take us for a pair of suckers. What makes you think we'll save you? What makes you think we won't toss you to the sharks?"

She waited for the echoes of a splintering crash aboard the schooner to die away.

Lucky growled, "Those lousy wreckers—"

The girl said, "Neither of you would hurt a woman."

"Then why keep your hand on that gun?"

"I'm taking no chances."

Contemplating this false madonna with the most intense curiosity, Sammy slowly, with a baffled air, shook his head.

"How did you get to Konga in the first place?"

"Your stepfather and Lopez and I sailed from Timor Laut in the whaleboat."

"Why Lopez?"

"We had to have a pilot."

"You mean, you didn't trust Bill Shay?"

"I don't trust anybody but you, Sam."

"Boloney. Isn't Lopez the real brains of that outfit?"

She hesitated. "Yes."

"Who is Lopez?"

"He's the assassin of President Ortiba, but the Mexican authorities didn't find it out until after his escape from Las Tres Marías."

"How much reward they offerin'?"

"Twenty-five thousand pesos."

Sammy softly whistled. "Ten thousand gold! I thought you were a smart girl. When you were both in Singapore, why didn't you turn him in and collect that ten grand?"

"Because I'd given my word to help."

"Horsefeathers! You figured the blue pearl was worth five thousand more than he was. You haven't stopped thinkin' about that pearl once!"

She said, "I'm thinking exclusively about our get-away. What are we going to do if those cut-throats come back aboard before we can get under way?"

"We've got plenty of guns aboard," Sammy said. "We can start the kicker. She makes ten knots under power."

He was staring across the water at the *Blue Goose*. Men were swarming over the deck. One fell overboard. There were shouts of drunken laughter, then a sudden commotion alongside. They had lowered the longboat and were tumbling into it. The man in the water climbed in.

The longboat moved away from the side of the schooner. Oars flashed silver in the moonlight. The longboat moved toward the beach.

"How many do you count?" Sally whispered.

"Eleven," Sammy said.

"They're all there! Hurry!"

CHAPTER XIV
THE NET

When the dinghy reached the schooner, the longboat was just reaching shore. The girl from Shanghai seized the rail and swung herself up on deck. Lucky climbed up and Singapore, making the painter fast to a shroud, followed.

He slipped and almost fell in a pool of blood. Lucky was standing, with one hand grasping a shroud, staring down at the *serang*. The Malay was dead. His throat had been slit.

"God!" Lucky said.

The girl had gone aft. She called, "Hurry!" It was, to Sammy, like the beat of those drums. Hurry! Oh, hurry!

The two men went aft. On the deck, just forward of the wheel, the deckhand lay crumpled, with his face pillowed in the crook of his elbow, his legs drawn up under him. His head had been crushed in. His *parang* was lying beside his lifeless hand.

Lucky groaned, then slowly turned away. He sat down heavily and dropped his face in his hands. He lifted his head and said tonelessly to the girl, "You did this. You might as well have done it with your own hands."

She said evenly, "Do you realize that if we don't get out of here, or make some preparations, they'll kill all of us? Aren't you going to start the engine?"

"Don't talk to me," Lucky said hoarsely. "For God's sake, don't talk to me."

"Sam!" she cried. "They're coming back!"

He looked at the beach. The uproar of the

eleven men came loudly across the quarter mile of water. It was too far to see them clearly, but what he saw indicated that the Mexicans were launching their boat, and that the greatest confusion prevailed.

The longboat was moving slowly out from shore. Oars appeared to be in a tangle. And as he looked he saw a flash of phosphorescence streak through the water alongside the boat. There was another flash. Then another.

The girl cried, "They're throwing spears at them!"

Sammy saw more phosphorescent streaks, but he could see no one ashore. The Kongans, in the black shadows under the trees, were hurling spears but, true to those legendary accounts, were remaining invisible.

Some sort of order, however, had been established in the longboat. Those nearest the stern were blazing away at the trees with pistols and rifles. The others were working the oars with greater unison, but they were still obviously panic-stricken. Singapore could now occasionally see the flash of moonlight on a spear before it struck the boat or the water beside it. One oar suddenly ceased to move and slipped overboard.

The convicts were firing steadily and rowing furiously, and the gap between them and the shore was perceptibly widening.

There was now not time enough to get the schooner under way. Time only to drive off the returning convicts. With the same inspiration, Sammy and Lucky rushed for the cabin. Lucky reached it first.

It was in the wildest disorder. Furniture was overturned and smashed. Charts, letters, papers, empty bottles and broken glasses were strewn over the floor. The nara-wood panelling was splintered and scratched and dented where bottles and other objects had been hurled at it.

And the firearms were gone. The locker in which rifles and side arms were kept was empty except for some cleaning rods, some gun oil and a tube of gun grease.

The girl, waiting on deck, cried, "They're almost here! Hurry!"

The two men returned to the deck. The longboat was within two hundred yards of the schooner.

Sally wailed, "Where are the guns?"

"Gone!"

She stared at them in sudden terror. "What are we going to do? I've only two bullets left in my pistol—and the rest of my ammunition's ashore. They'll kill us all!"

"Lucky!" Singapore barked. "Dynamite! Come on!"

They ran and stumbled back to the cabin. Singapore opened the little door into the lazarette, where their dynamite was stored. But other things were stored here, too. Coils of rope. Bales of oakum. Spare sails. Oars. Odds and ends.

The dynamite, fuses and percussion caps were hidden under sails. They frantically removed the sails. Singapore pried off the top of a box of dynamite and snatched out several sticks.

Lucky cursed and said, "Red! There's only one cap! We were gonna get more caps in Singapore and forgot!"

"Come on!" Sammy snapped.

When they returned to the deck, the longboat was less than two hundred feet away. The Mexicans, still unaware that the schooner was occupied, were staring at the shore, still blazing away at the trees.

Singapore snatched up the dead deckhand's *parang* and swiftly cut a short length of fuse. He fitted the cap to a stick of dynamite, and the fuse to the cap. Bending low, he struck a match and lighted the fuse.

Sally Lavender's serenity had completely deserted her. Watching him, she beat her hands together and whispered hysterically, "Throw it!"

But Singapore gravely watched the fuse burn and Lucky, familiar with the habits of fuses and dynamite, gravely watched, too. He stepped back. At that moment, Singapore stood up and threw the dynamite.

It left a filmy thread of cream-colored smoke,

an arc, as it rose and fell. One of the Mexicans saw it; shouted a warning.

The stick of dynamite fell short of its target. It struck the water five feet ahead of the oncoming longboat.

Sally burst out, "Oh, you fool! Why didn't you throw it harder?"

Sammy drawled, "It's waterproof fuse, sister."

The men in the longboat, suddenly aware of their danger, were in an uproar again. A rifle cracked. The bullet ploughed across the rail, ricocheted, screaming. Splinters flew. Another bullet went past within inches of Singapore's left ear with a sound like savagely ripping canvas.

Then, just under the bows of the longboat, there was a terrific turbulence. No more than three seconds had actually elapsed since that stick of explosive had struck the water. A mass of water ten feet in diameter surged up from the ocean's surface to the accompaniment of a brief red flash, a tremendous muffled detonation.

The longboat vanished in spray. The girl from Shanghai staggered across the deck, clutched frantically at a spoke of the wheel as she went past, and fell into a Bombay chair. The two men had dropped to their knees.

Sammy watched the mass of water spring into the air, solid and green, and calmly waited for it to tumble back.

When it did, what remained of the longboat became visible. It had been shattered to a point half-way aft. The stern was down. Men were kicking and struggling. One of them sank. Two must have preceded him to the bottom, for only eight remained. These eight were in the water, swimming confusedly, evidently stunned.

The shattered longboat was slowly drifting aft with a litter of oars and splintered strakes. The eight survivors, in a cluster a hundred feet away, were now swimming toward the schooner. The shock of their immersion, coupled with the awareness of their danger, seemed to restore their strength. They came floundering through the water.

The girl screamed, "Stop them! Do something!"

Singapore panted, "Lucky! Come on! That fishnet!"

"What?"

"Come on!"

They dived into the cabin and ran to the locker where their diving gear was stored. They pulled and yanked and cursed at the heavy fishnet. But they succeeded in dragging it out of the locker, through the cabin, and up on deck. It had seemed to take ten minutes, yet only seconds had been consumed, and the eight swimmers were still twenty feet away.

They had spread out, were swimming in a line toward the schooner. Evidently they had agreed on a plan—to swarm up over the side as one man. Three of them had knives in their teeth.

Sally Lavender had her pistol in her hand. Two bullets! A disengaged corner of Sammy's mind wondered if she intended to shoot herself with the second one.

Working swiftly, the two men spread the heavy, tarred net along the deck. When completely unfolded, it was about a hundred feet long by fifty in width. But they did not require all of it. They unfolded and stretched out only half of it.

With Lucky at one end and Singapore at the other, they lifted it clear of the deck and started to swing it like a giant hammock.

Singapore panted, "Let go at three! One!"

"Okay!"

"—Two!—Three!"

The eight swimmers snarled and shrieked curses in Spanish. Some of these were as picturesque as they were blood-chilling. They would nail the Americanos by their tongues to the mainmast! They would hold them in the water for sharks to devour!

One snatched the knife from his teeth and hurled it. The knife skittered across the deck.

The heavy net swung outward and down upon their heads.

And the water under the net was quickly white with the efforts of the trapped eight to escape. Hands frantically pushed up against the net. Fingers clawed at it. Faces appeared momentarily to gasp; rolled over, disappeared, came up again. One man with a knife hacked desperately at the thick web. But the net sank upon him before he could hack a hole large enough.

Two of them dived down in an attempt to swim under and beyond the net. The outer fringe of it had sunk deep. There was a sudden churning phosphorescence where one of them was trapped.

But the other dived and swam deeper. He came up gasping, free of the net. He spat out water and curses and struck out for the schooner.

Sally Lavender breathed, "Lopez!"

Lucky snatched up a boathook. Lopez saw the galvanized iron end of it sweeping down on him and began to babble.

Lucky thrust the hook under the half-drowned Mexican's belt, and, "Gimme a hand, Red," he said.

Singapore laid hold of the handle, and they hauled Lopez aboard. Before Lucky could disengage himself from the clumsy handle, Lopez sprang at him. From a sheath at his hip he snatched a knife.

The redhead rushed at him as the knife went up; struck Lopez stiff-armed in the jaw. The knife rattled to the deck and rolled into a scupper. Lopez staggered back. One foot descended on the gleaming blade. The foot slipped. In a frantic effort to right himself, Lopez caught his other foot in a bight of the main sheet. In another instant his precipitate backward flight had taken up all the slack in the rope, and it brought him to a violent halt. He plunged, twisting, to the deck. There was a sharp, brief snapping sound, a yelp of agony.

The Mexican rolled over and moaned with the pain of that broken leg. Singapore looked over the side, to where the net had been. He saw nothing at first but green luminous bubbles. Then, deep down, he saw a large formless mass like a shadow, slowly, slowly sinking.

His recent strenuous demands on muscles already overtaxed had left him faint and cold and sick. The glimpse of that dark formless mass slowly sinking sent an icy chill up his spine.

He said huskily, "Come on, bozo. Let's get that anchor up. Let's get to hell out of this place."

"Okay."

Behind them, the clear, sweet voice of the girl from Shanghai said, "Both of you—stand where you are. Put your hands up."

CHAPTER XV
"COME AND GET IT!"

The two adventurers slowly turned. With small feet planted apart, with automatic pistol in hand, the girl from Shanghai resembled, in her snug blue-and-white striped sweater, and her mud-spattered sailor pants, a small boy playing pirate. Her expression was calm.

"Sam," she said, "I want—"

"Yeah," he interrupted. "You want the pearl."

"And I'm going to get it."

"Sure," he said. "Sure, you're gonna get it, baby. Step right up and take it."

"It's no use, Sam," she said sweetly. "I've got you on a spot. I know that pearl isn't on the island. It's handy. I want it and I'm going to have it. If I don't get it there is going to be one dead man on this ship—perhaps two. Now—just a moment. You don't have to tell me that pearl is insured with your life. I know you're stubborn enough to let yourself be killed before you'll give it up. If you don't give me the pearl I'm not going to kill you. No! I'm going to kill your pal! If either of you takes one step toward me you're both going to get it. I've got two bullets. And I'm a good shot."

Sammy, contemplating her, so innocent-looking in that boyish get-up, felt cold sweat prickling out on his forehead. He heard Lopez thinly moaning.

"I know you won't sacrifice Lucky's life," she

went on. "And you know I mean what I'm saying. You know I'm utterly ruthless. You know I haven't a heart. You know I'll kill him—or you—without an instant's hesitation. I will count five. If that pearl isn't lying at my feet by then, I will kill Lucky. *One!*"

"You can stop counting," Singapore said. "You're dead wrong, sister. I ain't on a spot. It's you that's on the spot."

"Two!"

"If you kill Lucky," Sam went on, in the same steady voice, "who gets you out of here? Who sails this ship? Lopez—with that broken leg?"

"Three!"

"If you kill Lucky, it leaves you and me alone on this ship. You can't kill me with any twenty-five-calibre bullet. Not unless you shoot me straight through the heart or brain. And I'll be on you like a hawk the minute you pull that trigger on Lucky!"

"Four!" But it wasn't certain. Her voice wavered.

"If you kill Lucky, two minutes from now you'll have a broken back. Three minutes from now you'll be where those Mexicans are. Give me that gun."

He walked toward her with his hand outstretched, as if he were about to shake her hand. He took the pistol. She offered not the slightest resistance. Her fingers were limp. She all but dropped the pistol into his hand.

She said wearily, "It was empty. I used the last bullets in the clip to kill those pythons. And you aren't going to hurt me." She was looking up unflinchingly, but without a trace of defiance, into his eyes. "Because I saved your life."

Singapore dropped the pistol into his pocket and drew a long breath of relief.

"You're smart," he said slowly, in a marveling voice. "You're the smartest woman I ever met. I guess I've given you a lot of laughs. Now I'm gonna give you another laugh. When those greasers jumped us to-night, the first thing that struck me was how smart you are. I knew you

were so smart that you always manage to land butter-side up. I knew you were so smart that, no matter what happened, you would wiggle out of this with a whole skin. I knew that, and I had a hunch you were gonna keep after me till you got that pearl."

Sally Lavender was looking up at his eyes steadily.

"I don't know what you're getting at," she said.

"No," he said, "you don't. That's why I'm givin' you this explanation. When we went ashore and I saw those big shadows dancin' on the cliff, I knew you had double-crossed us plenty. So I ran to you and grabbed your gun out of your holster."

"Yes," she said. "Alvarado knocked it out of your hand. What are you driving at?"

He reached for her holster, tilted it up. A small dark object slid out of the holster and into his palm. It was the little chamois skin pouch. He opened it and rolled out into his hand a glittering blue bubble which seemed to absorb the cold white light of the moon and give it back in a fiery iridescence.

The girl from Shanghai stared at it. She sucked in her breath through tight lips. For a moment, Sammy believed he saw stark murder in her eyes, but perhaps he imagined that; for she was sweetly smiling.

"Sammy," she said, "you're a smarter man than I am."

"Thank you, Sally," he replied, "for takin' such good care of my luck piece. Well, Lucky," he said, "what are we gonna do with this little cobra? You've taken the beatin'. What do we do with her? It's up to you."

Lucky turned away and started forward, as if he did not intend to answer. He paused and partly turned his head.

"No," he said. "It's your job. As far as I care, she don't exist and she never did exist. I don't want to see her again, dead or alive. I don't want to hear her again."

He walked away, limping.

Sally Lavender's eyes were large as they

stared up into the battered mask that was Singapore Sammy's face. She was taking little quick breaths. One hand was pressed up under her heart, as if she were trying to subdue its tumult. Her slim, small figure was rigid with terror.

She whispered, "What are you going to do with me?" Then, in a panic: "Don't look at me like that!"

He grinned at her. "Sister, you were dead right. That guy and I are a pair of soft-hearted suckers when it comes to hurtin' any woman. But, sister—how I wish you were a man!"

Sammy folded his arms on his chest and tightened his mouth.

"Sometime to-morrow," he went on, "we'll be droppin' anchor off the *kampong* at Timor Laut. That's where we say so-long. Until then—stay in your cabin."

The girl walked slowly to the cabin door. Reaching it, she slowly turned and looked at him. Her lips were smiling. Her eyes sparkled with tears, as they had that morning when Sammy first saw her, as forlorn as a lost kitten, perched on a crate on the Tanjong Pagar dock.

Her mouth suddenly made a little gulping grimace. The fingers of one small white hand were still outspread against the blue and white stripes across her left breast. She looked like a little girl, a heartbroken little girl who wanted to be assured and comforted. She looked delicate and fragile and hopelessly innocent. There was something childlike about her shameless grief. It was pathetic and appealing. She sniffled.

"Sammy," she said softly. "Oh—Sammy!"

"Listen, sister," Sammy said, "if you pull any fast ones, like tryin' to sink this ship, I'm gonna wring your doggoned little neck! Get into your cabin. Scram!"

A shout from Lucky hailed him forward. The buccaneer was on hands and knees before an opened box near the anchor winch. Other objects—machetes and piles of men's clothing—were nearby.

A match flame sputtered in Lucky's hand. He was staring into the box, which was about ten inches square and of about the same depth.

The match flame was dancing.

"Red!" he yelled. "Look! Gold!"

Singapore looked, just for an instant, before the flame expired, into the boxful of glowing yellow metal. He caught the expression, in the same fleeting instant, on Lucky's face. The match went out, leaving the expression sharp and clear in Sammy's mind. It was excited and jubilant.

"Four thousand dollars' worth o' nuggets!" Lucky said enthusiastically. "And listen, bo. That cargo down there is ours, too. Say, boy, we haven't done so bad for a pair o' suckers. A thousand cash for the charter. Four thousand for the gold. Another two thousand, anyhow, for the cargo. And ten thousand more when we turn Lopez over to the cops in Singapore! That's seventeen thousand bucks, Red! We sure cleared a pretty profit on this cruise. We're set, fella! We start tradin' again!"

"We sure do," Singapore said. "S'posin' you get this anchor chain up and down while I start up the engine."

He went aft and opened the engine hatch. He didn't quite share Lucky's enthusiasm. He couldn't get the picture of Sally Lavender out of his mind, standing there in the cabin doorway, shamelessly crying like a little girl. And he didn't have his grandfather's will. He'd been outsmarted once again by old Bill Shay. But if the Kongans hadn't killed Bill Shay they'd meet again, sometime, somewhere. And it was a great relief to know that Lucky's heart was on the road to convalescence.

SAND AND SUN

THE SOUL OF A TURK

ACHMED ABDULLAH

ACHMED ABDULLAH was the preferred pseudonym of Alexander Nicholayevitch Romanoff (1881–1945), who was born in Yalta, Russia. Romanoff was the son of Grand Duke Nicholas Romanoff (a cousin of the last czar) and Nourmahal Durani, an Afghan princess; originally Russian Orthodox, he was raised Muslim after his parents divorced, and later in life became a Roman Catholic. Clad in his turban and earring, Romanoff was a colorful element at Eton, and then studied at Oxford and the University of Paris. He joined the British army in 1900, and served as an officer for seventeen years in every part of the world, including India, China, Tibet, the Middle East, France, and Africa—much of the time as a spy, with a full year undercover in the Turkish army. His extensive knowledge of the languages, religions, and customs of these foreign cultures provided experiences and background for the next phase of his life, as a writer of pulp fiction and Hollywood screenplays.

The prolific Abdullah produced more than a hundred short stories and thirty books between 1915 and 1939, as well as several screenplays, the most famous of which was the cowritten *The Lives of a Bengal Lancer* (1935), starring Gary Cooper and Franchot Tone, for which he received an Academy Award nomination. The author's exotic adventure stories were already very popular when he wrote the novelization of his screenplay for *The Thief of Bagdad* (1924), the spectacularly successful Douglas Fairbanks film based on *Tales of the Arabian Nights*. Thereafter, he was undisputedly one of the most sought-after writers in America. Women, especially, adored Abdullah's romantic tales of Arabians, Persians, and other swarthy heroes, and popular demand elevated him from the pulps to the princely fees of the top "slick" magazines. He also wrote frequently of New York's Chinatown and the secrets of its opium dens, Tong wars, and slave traders. He adapted his most famous story, "The Hatchetman," for Broadway as *The Honourable Mr. Wong;* it in turn became a motion picture starring Loretta Young, Leslie Fenton, and, in the titular role, Edward G. Robinson. The film, with the action moved to San Francisco, was directed by William Wellman; it was released in the United States in 1932 as *The Hatchet Man*, and in Britain as *The Honourable Mr. Wong.*

"The Soul of a Turk" was first published in Abdullah's collection *Alien Souls* (New York: McCann, 1922).

THE SOUL OF A TURK

ACHMED ABDULLAH

THAT NIGHT, with no hatred in his heart but with a Moslem's implacable logic guiding his hand, he killed the Prussian drill sergeant who, scarlet tarbush on yellow-curled, flat-backed skull, was breveted as major to his regiment, the Seventeenth Turkish Infantry.

His comrades saw him creep into the tattered, bell-shaped tent where the Prussian was sleeping the sleep of utter exhaustion. They heard the tragic crack of the shot, and saw him come out again, smoking revolver in his right hand. Calmly squatting on their haunches, they watched him go to the commissary, help himself to slabs of spongy, gray bread, dried apricot paste, and a bundle of yellow Latakia tobacco leaves, fill his water canteen, and take the road toward the giant breast of the Anatolian mountains, studded here and there with small, bistre-red farms, like brooches clasping a greenish-black garment.

"Allah's Peace on you, brother Moslems!" he said piously, turning, the fingers of his left hand opening like the sticks of a fan, then closing them again, to show the inevitability of what he had done.

"And on you Peace, Mehmet el-Touati!" came their mumbled reply, tainted by just a shade of envy, because they told themselves that soon Mehmet el-Touati would be in his own country while their homes were far in the South and West, and they did not know the roads.

They were neither astonished, nor shocked. They understood him, as he understood them.

For, like himself, they were simple Turkish peasants, bearded, middle-aged, patient, slightly rheumy, who had been drafted into the army and thrown into the frothy, blood-stained cauldron of European history in the making, by the time-honored process of a green-turbaned priest rising one Friday morning in the mosque pulpit and declaring with melodious unction that the Russian was clamoring at the outer door of the Osmanli house, and that Islam was in danger.

The Russian—by Allah and by Allah, but they knew him of old!

He would ride over their fields, over the sown and the fallow. He would cut down the peach trees. He would pollute their mosques, their harems, and their wells. He would stable his horses in their cypress-shaded graveyards. He would enslave the women, kill the little children, and send the red flame licking over byre and barn thatch.

Therefore:

Jehad!—Holy War! Kill for the Faith and the blessed Messenger Mohammed!

Thus, uncomplaining, ox-eyed, they had pressed their wives and their children to hairy, massive chests, had adjusted the rawhide straps of their sandals, had trooped to district military headquarters, had been fitted into nondescript, chafing, buckram-stiffened uniforms, had been given excellent German rifles, wretched food, brackish water; and had trudged along the tilting roads of stony, bleak Anatolia.

Moslems, peasants, pawns—they had gone forth, leaving their all behind, stabbed on the horns of Fate; with no Red Cross, no doctors, no ambulances, to look after their wounded or to ease the last agonies of their dying; with sleek, furtive-eyed Levantine government clerks stealing the pittance which the war office allowed for the sustenance of the women and children and feeble old men who tilled the fields and garnered meagre crops with their puny arms while the strong, the lusty, the bearded, were away battling for the Faith; with none to praise their patriotism or sing epic paeans to the glory of their matter-of-fact courage; with neither flags waving nor brasses blaring; with no printed or spoken public opinion to tell them that they were doing right, that they were heroes; with nobody back home to send them encouragement or comforts or pitiful little luxuries.

They had gone forth, unimaginative, unenthusiastic, to kill—as a matter of duty, a sending of Kismet.

For Islam was in danger. The Russian was clamoring at the outer gate, beyond Erzeroum.

Turks, they. Cannon fodder. Bloody dung to mulch the fields of ambition.

Had come long months of fighting and marching and fighting again. Victories, soberly accepted. More marching, through a hot, sad land speckled with purple shadows.

And they had wondered a little, and one day Mehmet el-Touati, as spokesman of his company, had asked a question of his colonel, Moustaffa Sheffket Bey, who, in time of peace, was the civilian Pasha of his native district.

The colonel had smiled through white, even teeth.

"Yes, Mehmet el-Touati," he had replied. "We are going South."

"But Russia is in the North, Effendina, beyond the snow range."

"I know. But—have you ever hunted?"

"Often, Effendina."

"Good. You stalk deer against the wind, don't you, so that it may not scent you and bolt?"

"Yes, Effendina."

"It is the same with warfare, with hunting men. We are traveling South—for a while. We do not want the Russian to smell the Turkish scent."

"But—" Mehmet el-Touati had pointed at a corpse that lay curled up in the middle of the road, like a dog asleep in the sun. "These people are not—"

"No. They are not Russians. They are the Armenian jackals who accompany the Russian lion in search of carrion. They are the Russian's allies. They, too, are the enemies of the Faith. Kill them. Kill the jackals first. Presently, with the help of Allah, the All-Merciful, we shall nail the lion's pelt to the door of our house."

"*Alhamdulillah!*"

He, and the others, had accepted the explanation. They had marched—South. They had fallen on the Armenian villages with torch and rope and scimitar. They had killed.

It was an order.

Many of his regiment died. Others took their places, Turkish peasants like himself, middle-aged, bearded, solemn—but from districts farther South and West.

They, too, had heard that Islam was in danger, that the Russian was at the door.

Came more fighting, through many weary months. Then a defeat, a rout, a debacle; the ground littered with their dead and dying, amongst them the colonel of the Seventeenth, Moustaffa Sheffket Bey; and talk of treason in exalted places, of a renegade Saloniki Jew by the name of Enver Bey throttling the ancient Osmanli Empire and handing it over, tied hand and foot, to a Potsdam usurper.

Greeks and Syrians and Druses had spread the hushed, bitter tale through the ranks of the retreating army. But the grave Turkish peasant soldiers had slowly shaken their heads.

Leaky-tongued babble, that!

They had never heard of either Enver Bey or

the Potsdam usurper. Their very names were unknown to them. They were fighting because Islam was in danger.

Had not the green-turbaned priests told them so?

They had been defeated. What of it? That, too, was Fate—Fate, which comes out of the dark, like a blind camel, with no warning, no jingling of bells.

At first they had won, and presently they would win again. They would conquer as of old. It was so written.

They would return to their quiet, sleepy villages and once more till the fields. Once more they would harrow on the strips of fallow, shouting to their clumsy, humped oxen. Once more they would hear the creaking song of the water wheels, the chant of the mullahs calling the Faithful to prayer, and the drowsy zumming of the honey bees. Once more, on Friday, the day of rest of all God's creatures, they would stroll out with their women and children into the sloping hills and smoke their pipes and eat their food and sip their coffee and licorice water beneath the twinkling of the golden crab apples that clustered high up in the hedges and the greenish elderberries on their thick, purple-blue stalks.

Meanwhile more fighting, marching, suffering.

Torch and rope and scimitar had done the work. The Armenians had died by the thousands.

The land was a reeking shambles.

And—what of the Russian?

With the Armenians strung up in front of their own houses, or buried in shallow graves, there was only the Russian left to fight.

And he did fight, with long-range guns and massed machine-gun fire and airplanes and blazing white shells that screamed death from afar.

Daily he took toll, gave toll.

"But," said Mehmet el-Touati, voicing the sluggish, gray doubts of the Seventeenth Infantry which, in its turn, voiced the doubts of the army—"why is the Russian here, in the South? How did he come down from behind the snow ramparts of the Caucasus and is facing us here, in the flat lands, the yellow lands, the fertile lands? Also, I fought the Russian, twenty, thirty years ago, when I was a youth, with no gray in my hair and never a crack in my heart. Then the Russian was heavy and bearded and dressed in green. Now he is tall and lithe and slim and ruddy of skin and"—he pointed at an English prisoner—"dressed in khaki brown. I cannot understand it. Is there then truth in the bazaar babble that treason has crept into the Osmanli house on silent, unclean feet?"

Thus he spoke to the new colonel of the Seventeenth, Yakub Lahada Bey.

The latter was a monocled, mustached dandy from Stamboul, who had learned how to ogle and speak German and misquote Nietzsche and drink beer in the Berlin academy of war. Too, he had learned, nor badly, certain rudiments of strategy and tactics. But he had paid a bitter price for his lessons. For he had forgotten the simple, naïve decencies of his native land, the one eternal wisdom of the Koran which says that all Moslems are brothers, equal.

He dropped his eyeglass, twirled his mustache, and turned on Mehmet el-Touati with a snarl.

"Shut up, son of a dog with a dog's heart," he cried. "Get back—or—"

He lifted his riding crop significantly, and Mehmet el-Touati salaamed and walked away. He shrugged his shoulders. A beating from a master and a step in the mud, he said to himself, were not things one should consider in times of stress. Nor did he mind the killing, the dying, the wounds, the bleeding toes, the wretched food.

But what of Islam? What of the Russian? What of—treason?

Still, the priests had told them that Islam was in danger, that they must fight. And they did. Though not as well as before.

For doubt had entered their hearts.

Came another defeat; another retreat; another disgrace hushed up, followed by hectic clamorings from Stamboul, the seat of the Caliph, the Commander of the Faithful, and thunderous, choleric, dragooning orders zumming South from Berlin along the telegraph wires.

Then, one day, a red-faced, blue-eyed, white-mustached, spectacled giant, eagle-topped silver helmet on bullet head, stout chest ablaze with medals and ribbons, rode into headquarters camp and addressed the soldiers, who were lined up for parade review, in halting Turkish with a strange, guttural accent.

Mehmet el-Touati did not understand the whole of the harangue. But he caught a word here and there: about Islam being in danger, and the Russian at the door; too, something about a great Emperor in the North, Wilhelm by name, who, like themselves, was a good Moslem and coming to their rescue.

Thus Mehmet el-Touati cheered until he was hoarse. So did the others. And hereafter foreigners—Prussians, they called themselves—took the places of the Osmanlis as officers and drill sergeants in many of the regiments, including the Seventeenth. They said that they were Moslems—which was odd, considering that their habits and customs were different from those of the Turks. But—said the priests—they belonged to a different sect, and what did that matter in the eyes of Allah, the All-Knowing?

On and away, then!

Kill, kill for the Faith!

For days at a time they were loaded on flat, stinking cattle cars pulled by wheezy, rickety, sooty engines, until they lost all ideas as to direction and time and distance. East they were shipped—and fought, losing half their effectives, quickly replaced by raw village levies, until the Seventeenth was like a kaleidoscope of all the many provinces of the Turkish Empire, with Mehmet el-Touati the last surviving soldier of the Anatolian mountain district in his company.

Again they were loaded on flat cars, then unloaded, rushed into battle, bled white. Back on the cars once more—South, East, North, West!

The Russian—Mehmet el-Touati wondered—was he then all around them? Was he attacking the house of the Osmanli from all sides?

Hard, hard Fate! But—fight for the Faith! Islam was in danger—and on, on, along the neverending road of suffering and death!

Followed days of comparative quiet while the engines rushed their armed freight to the North; and Mehmet el-Touati, who had not complained when the food was wormy and the water thick with greenish slime, who had not complained when bits of shrapnel had lacerated his left arm and when a brutal German student-doctor had treated the wound, with no anesthetics, no drugs, with just his dirty fingers and dirtier scalpel—Mehmet el-Touati complained to the Prussian officer in charge of his company while they were camping on both sides of the railroad track.

"*Bimbashi!*" he said, salaaming with outstretched hands. "We are clean men, being Moslems. There is no water with which to make our proper ablutions before prayer."

"*Schnauze halten, verdammter Schweinehund!*" came the reply, accompanied by the supreme Teutonic argument: kicks and cuffs; and a detailed account in halting, guttural Turkish of what he, himself, brevet-major Gottlieb Krüger, thought of the Moslem religion, including its ablutions and prayers.

"Go and make your ablutions in—"

Then a frightful, brutal obscenity, and the soldiers who had accompanied Mehmet el-Touati drew back a little. They questioned each other with their eyes. They were like savage beasts of prey, about to leap.

"*Bashi byouk, begh; ayaghi byouk, tchobar—*" purred one of them, in soft, feline, minatory Turkish.

A knife flashed free.

The Prussian paled beneath his tan. . . .

A tight, tense moment of danger. A little moment, the result of a deed—brutal, though insignificant, except in the final analysis of national psychology that might have spread into gigantic, fuliginous conflagration, that might have sent the whole German-Turkish card house into a pitful, smoldering heap of ruins!

But a Turkish staff officer, fat, pompous, good-natured, his eyes red and swollen with too much hasheesh smoking, played the part of the *deus ex machina*. He stepped quickly between the Prussian and the Turks and talked to them in a gentle, soothing singsong, winding up with the old slogan, the old fetish, the old lie:

"Patience, brother Moslems! Patience and a stout heart! For Islam is in danger! The Russian is at the door!"

Yet, deep in the heart of Mehmet el-Touati, deep in the hearts of the simple peasant soldiers, doubt grew, and a terrible feeling of insecurity.

It was not alone that the Russian seemed to have many allies—Armenians yesterday, to-day Arabs and Syrians, to-morrow Greeks and Druses and Persians. All that could be explained, was explained, by the green-turbaned priests who accompanied the army. But they had been told that the Emperor of the North who was coming to their rescue was a Moslem, like themselves. Why then did these Prussian officers—for the case of brevet-major Gottlieb Krüger was not an isolated one—kick and curse their brother Moslems, the Turks? Why did they spit on Islam, the ancient Faith, their own Faith?

Mehmet el-Touati shrugged his shoulders resignedly.

The Russians must be beaten. Nothing else mattered. So, half an hour later, with his company, he was entrained once more and under way, toward the East this time, until one day the railroad tracks ended suddenly in a disconsolate, pathetic mixture of red-hot sand, twisted steel, and crumbling concrete.

They marched, horse, foot, and the guns, North, Northwest.

"Where to?" ran the question from regiment to regiment.

Then the answer:

"To Russia!"

And cheers. For, while they had heard vaguely of England and France and America, Russia alone expressed to them all they hated and feared; and, gradually, their doubts and misgivings disappeared as time and again they passed long columns of prisoners in the familiar bottle-green of the Tsar's soldiery, and as day after day the road tilted higher and the sharp scent of the foot hills boomed down on the wings of the morning wind and the ragged crags of Anatolia limned ghostly out of the purplish-gray welter.

Mehmet el-Touati was kept busy explaining to the men in his company, Southern and Western Turks all but himself.

"It's the North," he said. "It's my own country. Russia is over yonder—" sweeping a hairy, brown hand toward the hills that rolled down in immense, overlapping planes, blue and orchid and olive green, while the high horizon was etched with the lacy finials of spruce and fir and dwarf oak.

"My own country," he went on. "I can smell it, feel it. My heart is heavy with longing."

A terrible nostalgia was in his soul. Too, day after day, as the weeks of fighting had grown into the drab, sad cycle of years, he felt more old and lonely and tired. There was something ludicrously pathetic, something almost tragic, in the picture of this middle-aged, bearded, rheumy peasant shouldering a musket and fighting and killing.

But he did not complain, not even in his own heart. He marched on, patient, stolid. First there must be a victory. The Russian must be vanquished, the house of the Osmanli made safe.

Then peace—and the creaking of the water wheels, the chant of the mullahs, the happy laughter of the little children playing in the sun.

By this time, since the roads were narrow, mere trails made by stray cattle and wild beasts, the army corps had split into a number of columns, each composed of a half company with its complement of light mountain guns, taken into pieces and carried on the backs of small, mouse-colored mules; and the half company to which

Mehmet el-Touati belonged was the rearmost column, winding along hot, jagged roads where occasional thickets threw fleeting moments of shade, up steep hillsides where thick, purplish-gold sun shafts cleft the black rags of the fir trees, through valleys sweating with brassy, merciless heat, past fields of young corn that spread beneath the pigeon-blue sky like dull, sultry summer dreams.

On, while their feet chafed and bled, while the knapsacks cut their shoulders, and the rifles felt like hundredweights!

A few of the Seventeenth, Kurdish tribesmen mostly, nomads drafted on the way from amongst the black felt tents, had tried to desert.

Why fight any more, had been their sneering comment, since their pockets were lined with Syrian and Armenian gold and they had their fill of Syrian and Armenian blood?

So they had snapped their fingers derisively and had glided into the night shadows like ghosts, relying on the hereditary, kindly negligence of their Osmanli overlord. But they had reckoned without the fact that the latter was no longer master in his own house—that the brevet-major of the company was a Prussian drill sergeant, reared and trained with the Prussian ramrod, the Prussian code.

"*Rücksichtslos*—inconsiderate of everything except duty!" was his watchword, and his slogan was:

"I shall make an example—for the sake of discipline!"

He had halted the marching column—he drove them afterwards to make up for the time he had lost—until the deserters, one by one, had been recaptured, courtmartialed, sentenced to death.

The melancholy Turkish staff officer who was attached to the Seventeenth to act as a sort of philosophic, good-natured yeast, had tried to argue the point, to reason; had said that Brevet-Major Krüger was making a slight error, that he did not know these people.

"They are like homing birds, these tribesmen," he had said. "If a few of them want to go,

let them. We can always get more, and you cannot catch the winds of heaven with your bare hands. These deserters are Kurds, nomads, unreliable cattle, while the bulk of the army is Turkish. You know yourself that the real Turk is patient and obedient."

"Makes no difference! *Schlechte Beispiele verderben gute Sitten*—bad examples spoil good morals! If we let the Kurds do what they please, some day, when we least expect it, these stolid Turks of yours will take the bit between their teeth, and then there'll be the devil to pay! No! I am a Prussian. I will have discipline. Discipline is going to win this war. I shall make an example of these fellows!"

Then a firing squad. Blood stippling the dusty ground.

And Gottlieb Krüger was right. Perhaps, as the months dragged along on weary, bleeding feet and there was no end to suffering and dying, it was his slogan of discipline—with its obbligato accompaniment of courtmartial and death—which kept the Seventeenth as a fighting unit fully as much as the ancient fear and hatred of the Russian.

Then, one day, Mehmet el-Touati overheard a few words not meant for his ear; and, with a suddenness that to a Westerner would have seemed dramatic, even providential, but that to him, Turk, Moslem, was merely a prosy sending of Kismet to be accepted as such and used, a veil slipped from his eyes and slowly, in his grinding, bovine mind, he dovetailed what he overheard into relationship with himself, his own life, his past and present and future.

It was late in the afternoon and the company was camping in a little grove, spotted with purple lilac trees and walled in with the glowing pink of the horse-chestnut. The soldiers had loosened the collars of their tunics and lay stretched in the checkered, pleasant shade, sipping quickly brewed coffee, smoking acrid Latakia tobacco, talking of home, and Mehmet el-Touati, on the way to a little spring to fill his water canteen, happened to pass the tent where the Prussian brevet-major was sharing the contents of his brandy flask with the Turkish staff officer.

As he passed, a few words drifted through the tent flap, flew out on the pinions of Fate, buffeted against the stolid mind of Mehmet el-Touati with almost physical impact—caused him to tremble a little, then to drop to the ground, to creep close, to listen, tensely, with breath sucked in, lungs beating like trip hammers.

"Russia is smashed!" the Prussian was saying in his halting, guttural Turkish. "The Russians have signed a peace treaty with us, with Austria, with Bulgaria, with your country—Turkey. There'll be a little desultory border fighting— but all danger is past. The Russian is out of the running."

"You are sure of that?" asked the other.

"Absolutely. Remember the despatches I received this morning?"

"Yes."

"They were from headquarters. The peace treaty at Brest-Litovsk had been signed. Russia is out of the running—as harmless as a bear with his teeth and claws drawn. And now—"

"And now?" breathed the staff officer.

"And now?" came the silent echo in Mehmet el-Touati's heart, as he glued his ear against the tent.

"And now you Turks are going to see some real fighting. Of course I am only guessing. But I lay you long odds that your crack troops—like this regiment, the Seventeenth—are going to be sent to the Western front, brigaded with Prussians—and used against the French and British. Or perhaps they'll be sent to Albania to fight with the Austrians against the Italians, or to Macedonia to stiffen the Bulgarians a little."

"You mean to say the war is not over—with the Russian beaten?" asked the Turkish staff officer.

"Your war? Yes. It is over. But *our* war is not! And you are going to fight for us, my friend— and you are going to toe the mark and fight well. For—" he laughed unpleasantly, "remember our Prussian slogan—Discipline! Discipline!"

Mehmet el-Touati crept away, into the shadow of a horse-chestnut tree, to think. But he did not have to think long.

Only one fact stood out: the Russian was beaten; Islam was safe—and the house of the Osmanli.

Nothing else mattered.

The West front? Albania? Macedonia?

The French and British and Italians?

No, no! He shook his head. He knew nothing about them. They were not in his life, his world. Russia was beaten. Islam was safe, and he had done his duty, and now he must go home and look after his fields and his wife and his children. They had been neglected so long.

He must go soon. To-day. This very night. For here he was in the foot hills of his own country, where he knew the roads.

But—how?

He remembered the Kurds who had tried to desert, who had been caught, courtmartialed, shot, by orders of—

Yes! By orders of the Prussian, the foreigner!

The Turkish staff officer would not care. He would argue that one man more or less in the company was not worth the trouble of halting the column, of searching the surrounding valleys and mountains with a fine-tooth comb.

Thus—there was just one way—

And so, that night, with no hatred in his heart but with a Moslem's implacable logic guiding his hand, Mehmet el-Touati killed the Prussian officer and took the road toward his own country.

H. BEDFORD-JONES

KNOWN AS the "King of the Pulps" for his prodigious output and popularity, Henry James O'Brien Bedford-Jones (1887–1949) wrote about 1,400 short stories and approximately eighty books. In addition to using his own name, he deployed at least seventeen pseudonyms, including Allan Hawkwood, Gordon Keyne, and Michael Gallister, as well as various house names for publishers of boys' books and pulps. He customarily wrote between five thousand and ten thousand words a day, but on occasion he would write a complete twenty-five-thousand-word novella in a single day. He was the ultimate writer of historical adventure fiction and all its subgenres, including stories about pirates, the French Foreign Legion, big-game hunting, sports, and aviation, while also producing an enormous body of work in the science-fiction and fantasy fields. Although largely unremembered today except by historians and fans of the pulps, he was highly regarded in his time and sold to all the top magazines, including *Argosy, Adventure, Blue Book, Munsey's,* and *All-Story Weekly.*

Born in Ontario, Canada, Bedford-Jones became an American citizen in 1908, living mostly in New York and California. As one of the highest-paid writers in America, even during the Great Depression, he owned several homes and enjoyed a flamboyant lifestyle, hindered in no way by his good looks—he was compared to the dashing Errol Flynn. His story "Garden of the Moon," cowritten with Barton Browne and published in the *Saturday Evening Post* in 1937, was the basis for the musical comedy *Garden of the Moon* (1938), which was directed by Busby Berkeley, and starred Pat O'Brien, Margaret Lindsay, and John Payne.

"Peace Waits at Marokee" was originally published in the November 1940 issue of *Adventure*.

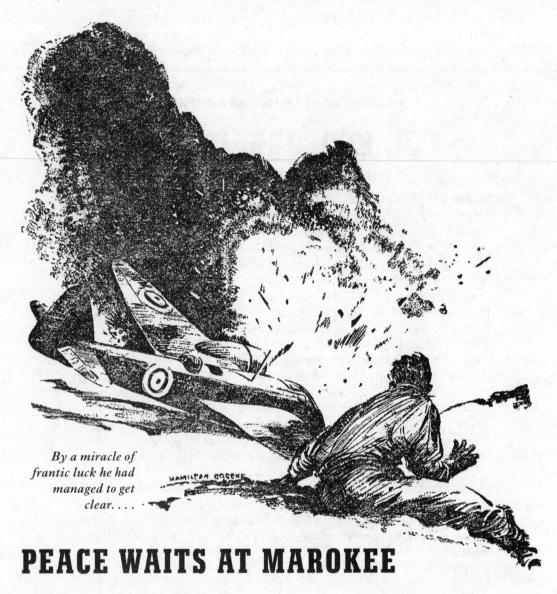

By a miracle of frantic luck he had managed to get clear....

PEACE WAITS AT MAROKEE

H. BEDFORD-JONES

DAWN WAS imperceptibly lifting above the marble hills of hell that lie between the Nile Valley and the Red Sea.

The Breguet two-seater, crumpled on its nose in the gravelly flat, was now a roaring pillar of flame; Essarts, the dead pilot, was at the bottom of that noble funeral pyre. Jean Facini, assistant pilot and gunner, had managed to bring the burning plane to a blind landing. By a miracle of frantic luck, he got clear before the fire touched him.

He had never expected to land alive. He was

still numb and shaken by it all, as he sat at a safe distance from exploding tanks and cartridges, drearily watching the prodigious burst of smoke and flame. The symbols of France on the body and wings of the Breguet vanished while he stared.

Suddenly a speck overhead caught Facini's eye, and he looked up. Dawn was mounting the eastern sky. The speck glinted like silver. It was a bomber, touched by the sunlight as yet denied to the world below. It glinted again and then vanished. He sighted it anew, but now as a dark descending object whose perfect silence startled him.

He moved farther from the heat of the blaze, staring. One of those big English craft, he perceived; a Blenheim, carrying a regular crew. Several of them had taken part in the raid on the Italian East Africa bases.

His first thought was that it had sighted the flames and was making for him, perhaps with intent to land on this strip of gravel and sand and cruel boulders, perhaps to send rescue later. But was it making for him? Was any human hand guiding this approaching ship? Fresh fear laid hold upon him, and a frightful wild surmise. A phantom, perhaps—a phantom plane!

He could hear no motors at all. There was no exhaust. The Blenheim was abnormally and horribly silent. He could even make out the motionless propellers as she came sweeping down, leveling out to make a landing.

Jean Facini crossed himself and swallowed hard, staring up with distended eyes. He was a shrewd, capable man, usually well-poised, unmoved by peril or risk; but now his steady, blithe efficiency was sapped by terror of the unknown.

The wings and fuselage of the Blenheim were bullet-torn, riddled, shot through and through. Next instant she was down, down a hundred yards away—down with a terrific crunch and crash, nosing up and over as the Breguet had done, only to fall back again, her left wing tearing clear away. Facini saw her settle motionless, silent as death itself. He sat there, horror distending his eyes.

Abrupt relief seized him, when her door opened and three men tumbled out of her. They looked about the empty skies and started toward him. He rose and went to meet them.

Three men; introductions were simple. Jock Erne, Anzac co-pilot, gaunt and loose-hinged and cheerful. Lance, observer and photographer, a quiet, deep-eyed, older man. Gunner Hawkins, stubby-nosed, rabbit-toothed, Cockney by his tongue.

"Saw your flame and nosed down for it," said Erne. "Alone?"

"Alone now." Facini's dark, mobile features were composed now. He pointed to the flames and told of Essarts, and the Caproni that had done for him. "It was wonderful of you to chance the landing."

Erne grinned. "No choice. Must have been the same Caproni that nailed us, but we got her. We were riddled. Petrol tanks emptied. Pilot riddled too. Poor Boddy! He was a grand pilot—Wellington chap. Well, he's gone. We touched up the jackals rather well, eh? Got those petrol tanks at Massowa, if I'm any judge. You speak English well."

Facini smiled. "I had an importing business at Mentone. I was often in London."

He saw blood dripping down over Erne's left hand, as the other turned.

"Lance, old chap! You know the orders. Take out everything we may need, then let her go. All the maps, and the water, especially the water. Hawkins, my lad, get your first-aid packet and go after this arm."

Erne sat down and bared his left arm; a bullet had torn the flesh badly. Hawkins fell to work on it. Lance went stumbling back toward the Blenheim.

Facini sat and waited, wearily. He looked the picture of despair; in reality, he was gloriously happy from the reaction. Happy to be alive, to have wads of money in his belt, to be rid of the French service forever. He cloaked the hatred in his eyes, as he met a quick glance from Erne.

"Facini, eh?" said the Anzac. "Odd names you French chaps have, to my notion."

"In Italian, it would be Fa*chi*ni." He pronounced the name in Italian fashion. "Yes, once our people were Italian in Savoy, long ago. I am a Savoyard, you see. Now we're all French, of course."

"You heard the radio reports last night, before we left the base?"

Facini nodded. He got out a packet of *jaunes* and lit one, to hide the savage exultation that shook him. France broken, crushed, done for! And now the army in Syria, of which his squadron formed part, would cease hostilities. He had been in the last French air raid of the war! Savoy would be Italian once more—and these English called the Italians jackals! Well, let them wait a bit, these English who had ceased to rule the world!

With cynical eye he watched Lance unload necessities from the crippled Blenheim; he asked Erne about her wireless and found it, too, had been riddled. They were preparing to fire her, dead pilot and all, lest her secrets fall into enemy hands.

Facini smiled inwardly, thinking of the information and photos he had given the Italian agent in Port Said; the new bomb racks and sights developed by the English, the new guns and mountings—everything! Italy, thanks to him, knew as much about these Blenheims as England did.

 The sun came up, red and scorching. Lance started his bonfire. The three Britons saluted the dead pilot; Facini rose and saluted also, quite sincerely. A brave man deserved this gesture, irrespective of nationality. Wiry, swarthy, alert, Facini looked what he was: one who could risk danger with calm and lucid gaze. A fifth columnist, whether spy or traitor, need not be a rascal.

"In case anyone's looking for us," said Erne, "take half an hour to give 'em a chance to spot the smoke. Get a bit of sleep while waiting, if you can."

Facini scooped hollows in the sand, only too glad to let someone else take charge. As he fell asleep, he wondered for the first time where the hell he was. Nothing about here except wild hills, touches of desert, utter emptiness. The crackling roar of the Blenheim was his last memory.

He wakened to find the sun high. Sitting up, he saw the other three grouped close by, and a pile of salvaged material, canteens and food. He fumbled in his jacket pocket and drew out a thick package of chocolate.

"All I can contribute," he said, and tossed it on the pile. Erne, who held a map open on his knees, beamed gauntly.

"Good. Know any Arabic? Neither do we. Before we left, I was given verbal bearings of a place whose name sounded like Marokee. Ever hear of it?"

"Oh, yes! I was there three weeks ago, landing supplies." Facini knuckled his eyes. "It's a spot near the Italian East, being secretly equipped as emergency landing field and advanced base for air operations. I understand it's to be kept a secret until the defenses are complete and it can be placed in use."

Erne nodded. "I see. You know more about it than we do, eh?"

"By good luck. We escorted some of your bombers landing guns there."

"Well, it's forty miles from here, roughly." Erne glanced around. "No chance now of our being picked up. We've food, and perhaps enough water to last three days. These hills are desert rock piles, inhabited only by a few Arabs and goats. There are no roads that we'll come upon; the existing tracks date from Roman times. We're close to Eritrean territory and can easily make it, surrendering to the first Italian outpost; or, if you choose, we can head for Marokee, or whatever the dashed name is. It lies to the north."

"So does the Red Sea," said Lance, his quiet eyes filled with anxiety. "Let's not waste time. We head north?"

"If you chaps decide," replied Erne amiably.

"I warn you, it'll be tough work! It'll take days. All blank hills and gorges, you know, blistering rock, a climb the whole blessed way. Either that, or turn ourselves in to the jackals."

"We'd bloody well best be abaht it," spoke up Gunner Hawkins. "I've reasons of me own for wanting to get there. Marokee, I sye!"

Three pairs of eyes went to Facini.

"Marokee," he said simply, and it was settled.

"Due north by compass." Erne folded his map. "We'll ready the loads and get started. Later we can find some shelter against the sun and rest until the worst heat of the day has passed."

They went to work. Facini, scornful of these English, hating them in his heart, set himself to match their efficiency and stamina and good cheer; he was savagely resolved to prove himself just a trifle better at everything than they were.

They got off at last. Pistols, binoculars, food and water. Nothing else. The water was the worst to carry, even in slung canteens, for it weighed like lead. Striking away from the gravel flat, Erne led into a narrow valley that trended north and east. It was a shallow gorge of naked rock and sand. The heat was consuming and terrible.

Facini laughed and talked as he swung into step. To himself, his laughter was more cynical. They were sorry for him. The enormous fact of France's utter collapse had stunned the army in Syria, but it had brought Facini wild exultation. And they were sorry for him, a Frenchman! They might better be sorry for themselves, he reflected.

Laughter surged again in him as he marched along the rocky defile. These others wanted to reach Marokee—well, so did he, and with far more reason! Not for the sake of rescue alone, but for what awaited him there. For he would be "Fachini" there, and no longer "Facini"; honor and decorations, an officer's uniform, a black shirt and the coveted emblem of the Fasces, would be awaiting him. For, by this time, the flag of Italy was waving over Marokee.

More than two weeks ago, he himself had sent through word about this place, and had received a reply. By the 20th, they had assured him, Marokee would be captured. Not destroyed, but surprised in the night and captured bodily, by a column of blackshirts and askaris from Italian East. Captured, to serve Italy against Egypt and the British base headquarters. He had suggested the clever scheme himself. Have a column in readiness, unsuspected. Loose a rain of bombs, destroy the wireless, rush the place; no word of its capture would reach the British until too late. And Italy would be solidly established there—forever!

They had assured him it would be done before the 20th. And today, he remembered, was the 22nd. Yes, thought Facini, he could well afford to smile!

No wonder he wanted with all his heart to reach Marokee, and what awaited him there.

"Cheerful blighter, ain't 'e?" observed Gunner Hawkins.

It was mid-afternoon and they were stirring. The shade of a rocky overhang had given shelter; packs off, boots off, they had slept well. Never better, thought Hawkins to himself, eyeing the strange naked walls of the ravine and the blazing rocks around.

A meal polished off, they were re-forming the loads. Hawkins nudged Lance and jerked his thumb at Facini, who was humming a brisk, gay air as he worked. Lance nodded carelessly.

"Yes, a good sort. By the way, Hawkins, why are you so anxious to reach Marokee?"

"Oo, me? Oh, I 'ave reasons!" Hawkins evaded, deliberately, showing his rabbit-teeth in a cheerful grin. Lance asked no more, but relapsed into his air of worried anxiety.

The loads were finished. Erne was poring over his map, Facini was lazily at stretch, still humming. The bloke had a rare good voice, thought Hawkins, stuffing his pipe and smoking with fair content. Aside from the heat and the things that irked him, and his desire to reach Marokee as soon as possible, Hawkins had no particular worry. They would pull through somehow. This was no worse than the blinding mid-summer camp. He had been scared to the quick at dawn, and the solid earth felt good.

"Gor! To think 'ow the cap'n spouted blood, and the ruddy crate spouted petrol!" he muttered. "Fair makes me sick, it does. And us not knowing if we'd find a landing place, and 'aving to keep up speed or fall plop! But 'ere we are, safe and sound."

Surreptitiously, he adjusted the pad under the collar of his tunic; handkerchief and torn shirt-tail were pinned there, out of sight. Pipe in teeth, he buckled his belt and hitched his shoes on swollen feet, then rose and strolled over to the Frenchman.

Facini was smoking one of his vile cigarettes and easing his position. He moved a flat rock with stockinged feet, shoving it aside. A strangled word escaped Hawkins.

"Look aht!"

With the word, he kicked frantically. From Facini broke a howl of pain and fury; the hobnailed boot struck his feet and ankles, so violently as to slew him about. He rolled over and came erect, agile as a cat, his swarthy features convulsed with rage.

Hawkins pointed. "You 'ad your ruddy feet fair on top of 'em!"

Looking down, Facini turned a sickly white. Hawkins grinned, amused by the man's sudden terror. Exposed by the overturn of the flat stone, two immense black scorpions were circling, tails aloft. Erne darted in and hammered them with a sharp bit of rock.

"Well done, gunner!" he exclaimed. "Damned well done!"

Hawkins glowed happily to the praise. Then he found Facini clasping him, embracing him in a fervor of comprehension and gratitude. He broke away and wiped his cheeks.

"Come, now, none o' that!" he gasped. "Too bloody thick, I calls it—"

"You saved my life," Facini was saying earnestly. "*Mon ami*, with all my heart I thank you, I thank you! It is something not easily forgotten."

Hawkins, abashed, grinned and turned this unwelcome emotion into a jest. They loaded up and were off, Erne and Lance in the lead, the other two following.

Unexpectedly, Hawkins found himself warming to the Frenchman; they had been drawn together by that sharp claw of chance. They tramped along and exchanged intimacies; each found the other a person of interest. Hawkins heard about the girl who was waiting in Mentone. He, broadly wistful, told of the missus and the two kids back home; by the last letter received, they had been evacuated to a farm in Sussex, away from the threatened bombs and agony of London.

Hawkins had knocked about in the army for a dozen years. He was ambitious to retire and raise, of all things, cabbages; they appealed to him, and he expatiated solemnly on their merits. Facini, who was in the perfume business or had been, talked of scent extraction and blending; Hawkins found this new and fascinating. Cabbages and perfumes alike had been knocked off their pins by the war, but Hawkins was consoling.

"The 'ole world's a bit screwy," he said complacently. "Soon's we clean up the Jerries, it'll swing back again. I'll 'ave me cabbages yet."

"No." Facini shook his head. "It's we who must change, my friend. The old order of things has gone forever. The world we knew will never come back again. If we're clever, we'll recognize the fact and profit by it. Now that France has collapsed, Hitler is supreme."

"Oo, 'im?" Hawkins laughed the derision he felt. It was good to be an Englishman, he reflected; a person with complete surety of heart and soul, a man not to be changed or bowled over like the froggies. "You wyte and see. Steady does it, me lad, steady does it! This 'ere plyce we're makin' for—wot's its bloody name?"

"Marokee," said Facini. "I've not seen it written, but that's the way it sounds."

"I 'ope to 'ell we get there soon."

He was aware of a curious glance from the darkly alert eyes. "Yes? Why?"

"Never you mind, lad. I 'ave me reasons."

Facini smiled. "So your feet are hurting, eh? Yes, these rocks are sharp; they're hard on boots and feet alike."

Hawkins merely snorted. He had no intention whatever of imparting his private reasons to anyone; but he certainly wanted to see Marokee ahead. He was jolly glad of that pad beneath the edge of his collar.

"Bet you didn't tyke it so cool when your ship was afire!" he observed.

"Cool? *Mon Dieu!* I was too frightened to know what I did," Facini confessed gravely. "After I got clear of her, I sat there shaking all over."

"Comin' down unexpected-like does grip at you." Hawkins shook his head. He liked this

frank admission of fear. "Don't mind sying that I 'ad the wind up meself when we got ripped wide open and the cap'n killed. Gor! What a perishin' sight 'e was!"

The afternoon blaze died down into grateful shadows here in the ravine. This road, however, was swinging too much eastward.

With his binoculars, Erne climbed the hillside on their left. Presently came his voice bidding them join him. It was a half hour's climb. At the crest they found more daylight, but evening was close just the same; the gorges to right and left were bluish and vague with shadow.

Hawkins, panting, cursed luridly to himself and inched his tunic back. He had left it unbuttoned; discipline did not exist here, and no one noticed or cared. He glowered at the endless sea of hills ahead.

"We must get down to that valley on the left," Erne was saying. "We can do it before darkness comes. Apparently it cuts straightaway northward, and that's our direction. Might come upon a Roman road or track, but I'm afraid it'd run east and west."

"Roman?" said Lance in some surprise. "Here in this desolation?"

Erne grinned faintly. "The finest stone and marble on earth used to come from here. Rome quarried these hills to form her most beautiful buildings. Then the barbarians swallowed up the world and those things were forgotten; same as they'll

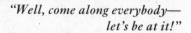

"Well, come along everybody— let's be at it!"

be a thousand years from now when somebody walks over Westminster and tells how Hitler had bombed it."

"Oh!" said Lance. "You mean, over Auckland and Wellington, after the Japs have taken New Zealand!"

Erne chuckled, and put away his binoculars.

"Score one for you, Canuck! Still, the Japs are closer to Vancouver than they are to Auckland, glory be! Well, come along everybody; let's be at it!"

The descent was long and hard. Hawkins and Lance gradually fell behind.

"Funny 'im knowing so blasted much about this 'ere country!" Hawkins jerked a thumb toward Erne, ahead. "Rare good sort, for a colonial. Anzac, ain't 'e?"

"Yes; New Zealand." Lance nodded and grimaced. "Damn! That's what I get for not wearing issue boots. These are light ones for hot weather. Hope they'll hang together."

Hawkins sucked at his pipe to fend off thirst. He had no particular use for toffs like Lance. Too bloody good for issue boots, was he? And some sort of colonial into the bargain; Canuck or something. The colonials were all right, of course; but still colonials.

Assuredly the rocks were bad. By the time the four men had won to the floor of the ravine Erne wanted to follow, they had had their fill of climbing and it was full dark. Luckily the moon was waxing and sat high overhead to help light the way.

The hours dragged wearily by. Hawkins cursed Jock Erne and admired him vastly; a pusher, he was, who kept them going at all costs, without mention of his own hurt. Midnight found them dead beat, for the floor of this gorge was all loose tumbled rock. Erne halted for an hour's rest. Hawkins flung himself down and was asleep before he knew it.

He wakened to Erne's touch and low voice; the pilot was at his side, rousing him. The wounded arm was hurting like blazes and needed a fresh dressing; and no sparing the io-dine either, said Erne. Hawkins got out his kit, bared the wound, and worked while Erne struck a match or two to help him see.

"Looks a bit of all right," he observed and fumbled in the obscurity. "'Arf a mo', now; there we are. Feel better?"

"Lord, man! It's wonderful!" Erne relaxed, with a sigh. "What did you put on it?"

"Secret, sir." Hawkins furtively screwed down the top of his canteen again. "Bit of a secret my missus taught me."

"Look here!" Erne gripped his wrist. "Not water? You didn't put water on it?"

"Wot? Wyste good water? Bli' me, sir, I wouldn't go and do that!" Hawkins declared indignantly.

"All right. Remember, that water means life to us! I doubt if we've covered ten miles. May find better going ahead. Lord! I certainly want to see Marokee in a hurry!"

"No more'n I do. Not by 'alf!" said Hawkins fervently. He hitched back his tunic and swore afresh. Erne peered at him.

"Here, what's wrong with you? Speak up! Why are you so damned anxious to get there?"

Hawkins felt himself yield by force of habit to the voice of authority. The others were asleep; he might as well be frank about it. After all, it was an order.

"Because o' me ruddy neck, sir," he replied uncomfortably.

"Well, what's wrong with your neck?" snapped Erne.

"Two boils a-comin' on fast." Hawkins felt injured at having to make such an admission. "Faster than I looked for. If we don't get there soon, I'll go fair mad, that's wot!"

"Oh!" Erne paused. "That's bad. I had one, three or four years back; couldn't lie abed nursing it, either. Frightfully bad! Well, steady on! We'll reach Marokee all right."

With a warm handclasp, he went to waken the others. Hawkins sat in a glow, his heart surging, his fingers cramming the final crumbs of tobacco into his pipe.

"Might ha' knowed 'e wouldn't laugh. Not 'im!" he reflected. "Gor! I'm sorry as I didn't put twice as much water on that 'ere bandage!"

 After another short halt at dawn, Erne kept pushing ahead until the morning was partly gone, and then made camp. High time, too. Lance was making heavy weather of it.

Lance had imagination plus, and now it was most desperately needful that he reach Marokee, for anxiety and terror spurred him each hour. Shortly before dawn they heard planes heading eastward, high up, on another raid; this touch with life cheered Lance tremendously. That cablegram burned in his pocket and was burned into his brain.

The message had arrived at the very last moment, as he was going out to take his place in the Blenheim. There was no chance to reply then. An hour or two would not matter, he had thought; they would be back shortly after sunrise. But they were not back; and now time was mattering most horribly. The lines graven in the quiet, poised, intellectual features were not from physical suffering; it is not our own hurts that bite the deepest.

Behind Lance lay Canada and a college universe of small horizons. In that forgotten past he had been a professor of Romance Languages. He was spending a sabbatical year in Paris, with his wife, when the war flared. He went into the air force, was sent out here to the near east. And now the French had collapsed, Paris was being bombed, and time would not wait for him.

He must have groaned unconsciously, for Facini glanced around and turned to him.

"Feet bad?" he asked. They had left the morning's camp behind. The gorge was a blaze of refracted heat. Lance straightened and tried to wipe the haunted look from his eyes.

"Oh, they might be worse. I'm all right, really," he said in French.

"*Tiens!*" Facini's face lit up. "Sit down and let me show you a trick, comrade. This accursed uniform jacket—glad to be rid of it." He called to Erne and Hawkins. "Go ahead, we'll catch up. I'm going to help his feet a bit."

The others went on. Facini chattered away gaily; Lance, who could think in French, made answer. A fine chap, this, Lance thought; the best type of southern Frenchman. Facini was slitting up his jacket while Lance got out of his footgear, cut and mangled by rocks.

"We'll fix that. Ah!" Facini, beginning to bandage the right foot with a strip of cloth, paused. "Blood, eh? Your feet are cut."

"No matter. Some things hurt worse than cuts."

Facini shrugged gravely and continued his work. The boots, replaced over the bandaged feet, had to be left unlaced. Lance stepped out and spoke joyously.

"Why, it's like having new feet! Facini, you're a miracle worker!"

He pressed the other's arm. Facini looked into his eyes and smiled. Lance could feel the friendly, intimate thrill that passed between them; it pleased him enormously.

"What can hurt worse?" queried Facini, as they took up the rugged way.

"Inability to help those dependent on us." Lance knew what most gratifies the Latin heart: to be told inner things and reasons, to be admitted to the precincts of the heart. So, striding onward, he confided in Facini. It helped him to do so, too; he held nothing back.

"The cable came just as we were leaving. My wife, you see, in Paris. I thought it announced the birth of a son, a daughter—we were sure it would be a boy. Instead, it said that she needed money desperately, that I must cable her some, so she could reach England. I can do it by wireless from Marokee, if we get there, if it's not too late, too late! God knows what's happening in Paris! She had funds. Something must have gone wrong."

"It is sad," Facini said very soberly. "Worse than sad, for a woman pregnant. But I do not think Paris will be bombed. Captured, yes—bombed, no. The news last night said it had been declared an open city."

"That does not lighten my burden," replied Lance. Still, talking things over did help tremendously. He showed Facini her picture, in the black, skin-soft money belt a friend had sent him from Toronto.

Although he perfectly comprehended the process, he was astonished at how deeply this confidence impressed Facini and awakened a warmth of responsiveness. Facini went into rather intimate detail about the girl in Mentone, about the family; and in the course of this let slip his feelings in a way Lance was too astute to miss.

"Good heavens, man! You're not a communist, surely?"

"No, but I might well be a fascist," Facini said drily. "Do you think Savoy is French? Far from it. We were annexed to France by force. Socially, industrially, civilly, we are bedeviled by the French. They strangle us with embraces."

"I didn't know France was an oppressor," Lance rejoined.

"Any undesired ruler is an oppressor," said Facini. Lance gave him a curious glance, then stumbled and a cry of pain escaped him. A jagged bit of rock, needle-sharp, had ripped half the left boot away and gashed his instep.

They halted again. Facini made a remarkably efficient job of the bandaging, using the last fragments of his jacket. Against these rocks, he observed, the tough cloth was more enduring than the soft leather. When these bandages were worn through, the English tunics would replace them.

"Marokee can't be more than a few miles away," said Jock Erne. "We'll reach it before night. Damn it, we must! Too much depends on it. We must!"

Since mid-morning of the third day, they had been camped here amid the ancient walls. Lance slept; even in repose his face was worn and haggard. Gunner Hawkins slept with uneasy stirrings; fever was in his blood, his neck was anguished, and lack of water had hit him cruelly. Erne's gaze touched them anxiously, then went to Facini, who shrugged.

"So it's not far, eh?"

"Only a few miles." Erne stabbed at the map with a finger. "This must be the Roman station of Mons Alba, indicated here. Look at the walls! You can trace the enclosure for animals, the cisterns, the defense wall. Marble from here built the monuments of antiquity; now it's empty desolation, even the roads forgotten. Well, wake 'em up, will you? I've one cigarette all around, before we get off."

Erne's gaunt, hard-chiseled features were blurred with beard, as were all four faces. He knew the others were suffering. He had driven them mercilessly, had driven himself as well. He was suffering more; his bullet-ripped arm, inflamed, was plaguing him with a thirst that could not be quenched.

Facini wakened the others. They joined him; he held his cigarette case open, mutely. A final smoke all around. Facini produced vestas, tiny waxed slivers. Cigarettes alight, the four relaxed, and Erne tossed his empty cigarette case away with a clatter.

"Odd matches," he said, inspecting one of the tiny vestas.

"Kind you see in Italy," said Lance. "Nowhere else, as a rule."

Erne wondered at Facini's startled expression, then forgot the matter.

"Not too far to go, lads," he announced. "We'll see Marokee before dark. We must!" He saw they were too far gone for any enthusiasm. He tried to spur them, in vain. A hard, quick ring came into his voice. "I want to get there more than any of you; I must, I shall get there! Nothing on this damned earth can stop me, either! So up and at it."

They staggered up obediently and were off anew. Erne was devoutly thankful that the ravine led northward and had a slight down grade. Twice this morning they had crossed the rocky slopes, to keep direction; to do it again would be impossible.

Left arm in its sling, he strode on without a limp, though his feet were badly cut. Facini, with a burst of energy, caught up and spoke thickly, rolling a pebble in his mouth.

"You're confident nothing can stop you. Why? Why must you reach Marokee?"

"Destiny!" Erne's thin lips curved. He liked this wiry, gay-hearted man who had kept abreast of them and never a word of grousing or complaint. "Life, for one thing; I mean to live. Then I must reach there to send a wireless message. It's imperative."

"Oh!" said Facini. "A woman, eh?"

"Hell, no!" Erne laughed harshly. "To the air ministry. They've been working on an idea of mine; an entirely new system of gun sighting and mounting, with a basic structural design that'll permit the use of long-range guns, accurately! You'll see a two-seater sit on the clouds well beyond range and blow hell out of Messerschmitts and Capronis. They'll be so far outranged that they'll be helpless!"

"*Dieu!*" Facini's eyes widened. "It's perfected?"

"One thing wrong about the sighting mechanism; it's held the whole thing back. Well, I've got the answer! It came to me night before last. I've worked it over in my mind. I've got it, absolutely! Twenty words wirelessed to the air ministry will change the whole war in the air. That's why I must get to Marokee . . . I must, I shall! I can't be stopped!"

It was unusually bad, even for this frightful road. They had come to patches of fallen stone and rubble that filled the bottom of the gorge, choking the way. One had to climb along. Thank the lord it was not upgrade! Erne glanced back at Lance and Hawkins; they were dragging themselves along with a horrible wavering effort. His voice pealed cheerily and bravely to encourage them.

The words ended in a gasp. A stone turned under his foot; his foot went down; he went down. Up again, only to stagger and catch himself, and stand on one foot. He knew instantly what it was; a bad twist of the ankle. Facini knew, too. He caught Erne's arm.

"Down! Sit down, quickly! Every instant counts!"

Erne obeyed and Facini knelt, fumbling at the boot, at the laces; already the ankle was swelling enormously, Erne perceived. He looked up, as Hawkins and Lance came weaving along like sleepwalkers. His voice stabbed at them.

"On you go, lads; keep moving! We'll overtake you presently. Nothing but a turned ankle." He watched them plod on and away. Then he spoke to Facini, a quiver in his words. "Off with you!" he said softly. "I'll rest a bit, then come along. You keep going."

Facini laughed a little. "You know better; so do I. You'll go with me. Too bad we've no water to reduce the inflammation. Nothing broken. Now I'll have to hurt you, but that's the only way to spread the blood and help the foot."

The sun was blazing down. The afternoon heat, in this little world of naked rock, was terrific. Both men were heat-parched, incapable of perspiration. None the less, Erne felt sweat gather on his brow as Facini worked shrewdly, gently manipulating ankle and leg.

Erne was close to panic; his boast that nothing could stop him had been shattered, for he was stopped. He no longer kept up the front that had driven them all so relentlessly; his willpower was futile. Then he realized that Facini was looking up at him and smiling, and speaking again.

"You'll get there. You think you can't touch foot to ground, but you will. We'll leave your boot and use your tunic to build up a bandage. Same as Lance."

He kneaded and massaged while he spoke. Erne, feeling weak and sick, shed his tunic. Facini slit the cloth and made it into a huge pad about the foot and ankle.

"May find a stick later to help you hobble," he said. "None around here. Up you get, now!

Hang on to my arm. You'll do famously. You must!"

Erne suppressed a groan as he came erect; then his iron will reacted. He was himself again. Grimly silent, he hobbled on, step upon step, his head swimming.

Ahead, the gorge widened and swung in a sharply angled curve. There they came upon the other two men. Lance had dropped and was shaking with helpless sobs. Hawkins was sitting beside him, and looked up at them with fever-bright eyes.

"Gimme a 'and wif 'im," he croaked.

Erne's brain cleared; he felt Facini press his hand and heard the composed voice.

"Stay here, Erne; they need you. I'll go on; it can't be far now. I'll get there and send back help."

Erne lowered himself to the stones. His breath came in a wheeze of futility; he was done.

 New vigor filled Facini as he strode down the gorge, alone. It widened, but it also curved again. His weariness fell away; exultation surged and surged upon him.

He knew what lay ahead, for today was the 24th. No later than the 20th, they had promised him; Marokee was now in Italian hands. And what a tremendous thing he had accomplished, all unexpectedly! Erne was helpless, was safe for gathering in; this man, and the thing he had invented . . . all useless to England now!

Eagerness grew in his soul. The blackshirts and askaris would welcome him; his name would be known to the officers. In Marokee, in Italian East, back in Italy, he would be a man famed and . . .

He halted abruptly, motionless, staring. The gorge had opened. There, half a mile away, he saw Marokee on its little flat-topped plateau.

He could see masses of men at work. No flag was flying; too bad he had not brought Erne's binoculars! However, there was no need. Below the plateau, other squads were going back and forth. Somewhere, a machine-gun rattled. His breath leaped in a gusty shout; taken, taken! Italy was here!

Facini broke into a flurried, stumbling run. Down the gorge, amid huge piled rocks, something moved; a man stepped out. Facini saw the black features. An askari! Wild with jubilation, he whipped up his revolver and fired again and again, in the air, saluting.

"*Viva!*" The hoarse shout burst from him. "*Viva Italia! Viva Italia!*"

Half a dozen rifle-shots cracked from among the rocks. Pealing metallic echoes filled the gorge; Facini spun about and fell.

He opened his eyes, flutteringly. He lay bandaged; a white officer knelt beside him. His brain cleared. A blank, terrible look came into his face; incredulity overwhelmed him. English! Black men, yes, but not askaris; King's African Rifles . . . he knew the uniform.

"Hell! Do you speak English?" the officer was saying.

"Yes, yes, of course," murmured Facini. The officer looked startled.

"Damned sorry; what made you shoot at us and yell in Italian? You're not one of them? We're mopping up, you know. The jackals jumped us last night. Damned near got us, but we've settled their hash. I say, where d'ye come from?"

Facini looked up, tried to speak; he could only groan.

"You're passing out," said the officer gently. "Deuced sorry. Tell me what I can do for you. Anything we can do. . . ."

Facini's brain reacted to the words in a startling flash. Dying! Then, even dying, he could still strike back at England!

They were done, back there; Erne was done and could not struggle on. With him would perish the thing he had invented.

Victory, even in defeat! There was the greatest blow that could be struck for Italy; struck without a word, struck in silence. Even a dying man could strike such a blow—it would mean the war won for Italy!

Then it was like the opening of a gate in his mind, and sunlight flooding in. What matter the war? Hawkins was in a bad way, would perish back among the rocks; Hawkins, who had saved his life. Poor Hawkins! Still, it was war.

And Lance. Ah, that was different! Lance must send that message; Lance, his friend, the brave and gentle fellow who suffered for love of those he could not help. Yes, Lance must be helped, for the sake of that woman and unborn child in Paris. Hawkins must be helped—it was the least a man could do.

"Pray for us, now and in the hour of our death . . ." Facini clutched the officer's sleeve with convulsive fingers. His voice gathered strength. "Three men—English, a mile or two—up the ravine. Bomber crashed—get help to them—all hurt. . . ."

He sighed, and his head lolled. Peace stole into his haggard, blurred features.

GABRIEL HUNT

AS THE mild-mannered founder and CEO of Juno, an Internet service provider, Charles Ardai (1969–) seems an unlikely candidate to be the creator of Gabriel Hunt, a swashbuckling adventure hero in the mold of Indiana Jones—that is, reminiscent of a pulp figure from the 1930s. Hunt lives in Manhattan, and enjoys the ability to engage in adventures in every part of the world due to the fabulous $100 million fortune of the Hunt Foundation. The first novel in the series, *Hunt at the Well of Eternity,* was published in 2009, and was followed by *Hunt Through the Cradle of Fear* (2009), *Hunt at World's End* (2009), and *Hunt Beyond the Frozen Fire* (2010). Ardai wrote all the books in the series under the name of his adventurer, Gabriel Hunt.

Ardai also founded the publishing company Hard Case Crime, a paperback house dedicated to reprinting classic pulp novels of the 1950s by authors such as Peter Rabe, Gil Brewer, David Dodge, and Cornell Woolrich; somewhat more modern thrillers by the likes of Donald E. Westlake, Max Allan Collins, and Lawrence Block; and original novels by Stephen King, Mickey Spillane, Jason Starr, and Ken Bruen, plus three by Richard Aleas, another pseudonym of Ardai himself. The first of the Aleas-signed novels, *Little Girl Lost* (2004), was nominated for both an Edgar Award and a Shamus Award; the second, *Songs of Innocence* (2007), was called one of the best books of the year by *Publishers Weekly*. The third, *Fifty-to-One* (2008), was a tribute to the books and authors of the publishing house's first fifty releases—a tour de force of fifty chapters, each titled with a Hard Case Crime book. Ardai won an Edgar for his short story "The Home Front" in 2007.

"Nor Idolatry Blind the Eye" was first published under the Gabriel Hunt pseudonym in *Hunt Through the Cradle of Fear* (New York: Leisure, 2009).

NOR IDOLATRY BLIND THE EYE

GABRIEL HUNT

I

THE HEEL of the bottle cracked against the bar on the first swing and then shattered on the second. The few conversations in the room died. In the silence Malcolm could hear glass crunching under his feet. He felt his legs shake and put out his other hand to steady himself.

There were three of them, and a broken bottle wouldn't hold them off long enough for him to get to the door. Assuming he could even make it to the door without falling on his face. There was a time when he could have made it in a dead sprint, turning over tables as he went to slow them down, but then there was a time when he wouldn't have had to run from a fight in the first place, not if it were a whole regiment facing him. A time when he'd been able to hold his liquor, too. But that was all part of the past—the dead past, buried three winters ago in a cold Glasnevin grave.

He shook his head, but it didn't get any clearer. He remembered coming to the pub, he remembered taking his first few drinks, and he remembered the three men taking up positions around him, reaching over his shoulder to collect their pints from the barman. Was that how the argument had started? Or had one of them said something? That he couldn't remember. He supposed it didn't matter.

The one in the middle was younger than the other two—just a kid, really. He was wearing a navy peajacket, probably his brother's or fa-

ther's, since he looked too young to have served himself. The others were dressed in denim windbreakers and dungarees, like they'd just stepped off a construction site. Which maybe they had—there was still plenty of rebuilding going on. The one on the left had the crumpled features of a boxer who'd taken too many trips to the mat. The one on the right looked almost delicate, his thin nose and long chin giving him the appearance of a society lad slumming in a tough neighborhood. Malcolm knew which one he'd prefer to face in a fight. Unfortunately, it didn't look like he'd get to choose.

All three had their hands up, palms out, but it was a gesture of mocking deference, not fear. Malcolm swung the bottle by the neck and they didn't even bother to step back.

"Go on, old man," the one in the middle said. "Just try it."

"Leave me alone," Malcolm said, or tried to—the words sounded strange to his ears, like he was talking through cotton. He forced himself to enunciate. "I don't want to fight you."

"Bugger that," the society boy said. "You're bloody well going to."

Malcolm feinted toward the boy's face with the jagged edge of the bottle, then dodged around him. The door was open and the way before him was clear, but he felt himself stagger as he ran, felt his head spin and the floor lurch up to meet him. He fought to catch his balance and then lost it again. He fell to one knee and the bottle spilled out of his hand.

The first kick caught him in the side as he was standing up, and it laid him out flat on the floor. After that, Malcolm couldn't say who was kicking him or even what direction the blows came from. He covered his head with one arm and tried to back up against the bar.

One boot heel caught him in the chest. By some old reflex, he snaked an arm out and pinched the foot in the crook of his elbow. He twisted violently and its owner came crashing to the floor.

"That's it," one of them said. Malcolm felt a fist bunched in the fabric of his shirtfront, felt himself lifted bodily from the floor and pressed back against the bar. It was the boxer's meaty fist at his throat, the boy in the peajacket looking on angrily over his shoulder. So the society lad must be the one laid out on the floor, groaning curses into the sawdust. Well, he had taken one down, anyway.

"You're going to wish you hadn't done that," the boxer said.

Malcolm swung a fist at him, but it was hardly a punch at all, and the man holding him deflected it lightly with his forearm. In return, he threw a right cross that snapped Malcolm's head violently to the side. Malcolm felt blood on his cheek where the man's ring had scraped a ragged groove, and he tasted bile when he swallowed. He tried to raise a knee toward the man's groin, but he couldn't—they were standing too close together, and anyway his legs felt like lead. He groped behind him on the bar, hoping his fingers would find something—a glass, an ashtray, anything—but all they found was another hand that pinned his firmly against the wood.

"Teach him a lesson," the boy in the peajacket said. He pressed down, grinding Malcolm's knuckles into the wood. "Teach him good."

He felt a thumb and forefinger at his chin, positioning his head, saw the man's fist cock back, saw it snap forward. After that, he didn't see anything, just felt the punches landing from the darkness.

One punch split his lip against his front teeth and he gagged from the taste of blood. He felt the night's liquor coming up and he made no effort to stop it. Vomit poured out of him, a day's worth of food and drink expelled in foul batches. The men holding him yanked their hands away and Malcolm slid to the floor.

"*Fucking narrowback lush—*" Another kick dug deep into his belly. From somewhere off to one side, Malcolm heard the click of a switchblade opening.

"Cut the sorry bastard—"

He forced his eyes open, rolled out of the way as the blade descended. It was the boy in the peajacket holding it. He swung again, and Malcolm lifted an arm to block it. He felt the blade slice through the sleeve and streak across the flesh beneath it.

"*Stop that!*"

It was a woman's voice. Malcolm hugged his bleeding arm to his chest and looked for the source of the voice. A pair of legs approached, clad in nylons, a tan skirt ending just below the knee. The shoes were brown leather and scuffed, with low heels, the sort a certain type of girl would call "sensible." On either side, a pair of paint-smeared dungarees turned in her direction.

"Leave him alone, or I'll bring the police."

"Stay out of this, love. It's not your fight."

"Oh, yes? And what do you call it when my husband is getting himself mauled by the likes of you?"

"You're married to . . . this?"

"He may not be much," she said, "but I'd just as soon not have him skewered over some tiff in a pub. Now would you be kind enough to help him up so I can bring him home?"

A tense moment passed, the blade still shining under the room's lights. Then a pair of rough hands folded the switchblade shut. It disappeared into the long slash pocket of the peajacket. "He's your problem, love. Help him yourself."

"Jaysus," one of the others said, "bird like

you and an old harp like him. No bleeding justice, is there?"

"Bastard." One of them got in a final kick, wiped the sole of his work boot on Malcolm's shirt. Then the men's legs went away. The woman's stayed.

Malcolm wanted to raise his eyes, to look at the woman's face, but his arm had started to throb and he found himself slipping in and out of consciousness.

The stockings took two steps forward, skirting the smear of filth beside him. The woman lowered herself to a crouch. The light was behind her and Malcolm could only faintly make out her features. She had a sharp widow's peak and fair skin, and the largest, saddest eyes he could remember seeing.

"You're Malcolm Stewart?" she said.

He nodded. She looked as though she'd been hoping he'd say no.

"Look at you," she said. "I can't take you to him like this."

"To whom?" he said. He felt dizzy. "Do I know you?"

"My employer. He asked me to bring you to him. He has—" She paused to look him over again, and the disappointment in her voice was undisguised when she spoke. "He has an assignment for you, Mr. Stewart."

". . . an assignment?"

"I told him it wasn't a good idea. I told him the reports he had were years old. But Mr. Burke's not one to be put off." She took him by his undamaged arm, pulled him not too gently to his knees. "Come along, Mr. Stewart. Let's get you bandaged up and bathed, what do you say?"

"I say," he mumbled, trying to think of the words. "I say 'thank you'?"

"Well," she said, "it's a start."

The iodine stung and the bandage smarted. He'd burned his tongue on the coffee she'd given him, and his chest was erupting with colorful bruises. His head was still ringing. But he'd showered (carefully, leaning against the wall) and he could feel sobriety returning to him, timidly, like a husband tiptoeing back into the house after an evening's debauch.

"Have you got a name?" he said. "Or would you rather I just thought of you as an anonymous benefactor?"

She was watching him from one of the bedroom chairs, legs crossed primly at the ankles, hands laced in her lap. She had an admirable figure and a face just this side of beautiful. And she was young, too—still in her early twenties, Malcolm guessed, which would make her less than half his age. He could understand why the lads in the bar might have had a hard time picturing them as man and wife.

"My name is Margaret Stiles. But that's not important. Only Mr. Burke is, and what he wants to talk to you about."

"And what is that?"

"He'll want to tell you himself."

"I see."

"Please choose a shirt and get dressed," she said. "We shouldn't keep Mr. Burke waiting."

There were three shirts laid out on the bed. Malcolm selected the softest of them, a red flannel, and drew it on over his bandaged arm. He winced as he buttoned it.

He was still wearing his own pants—they hadn't been spattered as badly. And the boots were his as well. A quick dunk under the tap had restored them to whatever prior vitality they might have claimed. His shirt had been ruined. He imagined it was now being incinerated in some hidden chamber of this house.

"Your Mr. Burke knows I'm here?"

"I spoke to him while you were in the shower."

"And he wants to see me now?"

"In a manner of speaking."

"Why 'in a manner of speaking'?"

"Come on," she said, standing up. "We've lost enough time."

"I want to know what you meant. He doesn't want to see me?"

"I imagine," she said, "that he would like to see you more than anything. But that's hardly an option."

"Any why is that?"

"His eyes, Mr. Stewart. He was blinded in North Africa."

North Africa. The words brought a rush of painful memories. The press toward Libya, the desert winds in his throat, the baking heat, and in the middle of it all, between spells of tortured boredom, the moments of utter chaos: the mortar rounds tearing great gouts out of the sand, and out of the men who sped across it. So Burke had been an 8th Army man? And had paid for it dearly, though not so dearly as some.

"I'm sorry," Malcolm said. "I was in that campaign myself."

"I know you were," she said. "It's one of the reasons he selected you, though perhaps he'll think better of it once he meets you."

"That's rather harsh, my dear."

"Harsh? Look at you. And what he'll ask of you, Mr. Stewart . . . it's ever so much worse than dealing with those three in the pub."

"I've dealt with worse."

"Yes, but recently?" She waited, but he had no answer for her. "Now will you please follow me?"

He stepped out into the hall. She led him down to the main floor on a staircase wide enough to hold four men abreast. The building was deceptive: From the front as they'd come in, it hadn't looked nearly as big as it turned out to be once you were inside. There was money behind this Burke, generations of it. It didn't show in ostentatious ways—no chandeliers dripping with crystal or gold leaf on the picture frames. But the pictures themselves looked like they'd fetch a pretty sum at auction, and the carpeting was the sort that costs as much as most people spend to furnish their entire homes.

They passed from the entry hall into a library, and on through a short connecting corridor into the kitchen, where a woman in a cook's smock stood cutting potatoes into a copper ket-tle. She looked up as they passed. He thought he spied a look of pity in her eyes.

"Another, Miss Stiles?"

Margaret moved them along without slowing.

Malcolm looked back over his shoulder. The woman was still watching, knife at the ready, supper temporarily forgotten.

Malcolm didn't say anything till they were out of earshot. "What did she mean, 'another'?"

"Never mind her." Margaret stopped at a closed door. She tugged on a brass pull set into the doorframe at eye level. He could hear a bell ring within and, moments later, a man's voice called out. "Miss Stiles?"

"Yes."

"Have you got Mr. Stewart with you?"

"Yes."

"Bring him in." It was a deep voice, muffled by the door, but strong, Malcolm thought, and self-confident. He was put in mind of his commanding officers from the army—it was the sort of voice you were trained to use when marshalling troops for a charge across a no-man's-zone. Some men didn't need to be trained, of course. They'd learned it in the nursery or had it bred into them from birth.

Margaret swung the door open. He was surprised to see no light behind it. She made no move to turn one on.

"Come in, Mr. Stewart," the voice intoned. "Don't let the darkness bother you. Miss Stiles will show you to a chair." She took him by the arm and steered him through the room, navigating obstacles he could see only dimly. It was oddly damp in the room, as though a window had been left open, but the only windows he could make out appeared to be shut and heavily curtained.

"It's for my eyes, you understand," Burke said. "Dark, cool, moist—I'm afraid it's the only way for me to be comfortable any longer."

"I'm sorry," Malcolm said.

"Come," Burke said. "Sit by me, and Miss Stiles will join us."

She put his hand on the arm of a chair, and he sat. Now that his eyes had begun to adjust, Malcolm could make out the outlines of Burke's face where he sat two feet away. He wore a beard, and his hair curved up from his forehead in uneven curls. The man leaned forward with his left hand out. Malcolm took it. Burke's grip was firm.

"What happened?" Malcolm said. "To your eyes, I mean. Shrapnel? Or fire?"

For a moment, Burke didn't say anything, and Malcolm thought perhaps he'd crossed a line. But for Christ's sake, the man had brought the subject up himself. And after all, hadn't Malcolm served in the same campaign, hadn't he seen plenty of friends lose eyes and worse—?

"No," Burke said. "Not shrapnel, nor fire, nor any of the other causes you'd imagine. I'll tell you what happened, Mr. Stewart, but that is the end of the story, not the beginning. Miss Stiles, could you turn up the fan? Thank you."

Malcolm heard Margaret's footsteps retreat and return. A mechanical hum he hadn't noticed before got louder, and he felt the air stir.

Burke leaned forward with his forearms on his knees. Malcolm could see he wasn't wearing anything over his eyes—no dark glasses, no patch. He didn't seem to blink, either. Of course, perhaps he had glass eyes . . . but no, that wouldn't explain the need to sit in the dark and keep things as damp and cool as a cellar.

"Mr. Stewart, I want to thank you for hearing me out. I need your help. Or to put it another way, I need the help of someone who knows his way around a part of the world I understand we have in common. Someone who's not easily frightened or put off the scent. I've asked around and people think highly of you."

"You must not have asked anyone in town," Malcolm said. "You'd have gotten a different picture."

"Yes, Miss Stiles told me about the scene in the pub. Most regrettable. You drink too much, Mr. Stewart."

"Or not enough."

"More and you'd be dead of it, and no use to me. Let's not fence with each other, shall we? You were a good man once. I heard it from men I trust. Until your wife died, I gather, and since then it's been one long bender, hasn't it?"

Malcolm flinched. "Not so long."

"Three years, man. And you once a good soldier. Where's your backbone?"

"I left it behind in the sand," Malcolm said, "where you left your eyes."

"Nonsense. You've still got a spine, man, you've just let it soften in that embalming fluid you insist on pouring into yourself. If you're to work for me, you'll do it dry, you understand?"

The voice of command—Malcolm almost felt himself sitting up straighter in response, against his will. "And am I to work for you?"

"I hope to God you are—I've exhausted everyone else."

"What is it you want done? I don't see you as the type to raise a private army, and I'm out of the soldiering business anyway."

"No. I've never been a soldier myself. What I have been—what I am, Mr. Stewart—is a student of history. When I went to North Africa it was not because of the war but in spite of it. I wasn't part of the military action, I was there on my own, pursuing one of the greatest mysteries of the ancient world."

Greatest mysteries of the ancient world? The man sounded like a radio programme. But he had a job to offer, apparently, and such offers were not plentiful these days.

"I understand," Malcolm said. "You were in Africa hunting something, but instead of finding it, you came across the military action instead?"

"No, Mr. Stewart. I found what I was looking for. I found it exactly where I thought it would be. I saw it with my own eyes. I'd searched for a decade and more, and by God, I found it." He fell silent.

"What happened?" Malcolm said.

"Some antiquities, Mr. Stewart, are hidden by time alone—a cave's entrance is covered in a sandstorm and forgotten, and no one sees its contents again for a thousand years. But others are kept hidden deliberately, passed from generation to generation in secret. The price for learning the secret is a vow to preserve it, and the penalty for revealing it is death. It is antiquities of this sort that are the harder to find. They aren't lost, you see, and the people who know where they are have an interest in keeping them from you."

"But you did find . . . whatever it was."

"I did, and I did it the hard way. You wouldn't know it to look at me now, but I was a stronger man than you, and faster, and better with a gun. I knew what I was after. I hunted it and the men who kept it, I hunted it through nine countries on three continents, and I found it, Mr. Stewart." His voice broke. "I found it. But I couldn't keep it. They caught me, and for several days they held me while they discussed what to do with me. Then they cut off my right hand—I'd touched it with that hand, you see. And of course I'd seen it, Mr. Stewart. I'd seen it."

Burke leaned over the side of the chair and pressed a switch on the desk beside him. A shaded light went on—low wattage, but enough to illuminate one side of Burke's face. The other side remained in shadow until he turned to face Malcolm full-on. Burke's eyes were wide open and leached of all color, only the faintest outline of concentric circles to hint where pupil and iris had once shown.

"They cut off my eyelids, Mr. Stewart. With the sharpest of knives, and gently, so gently, holding my head so I couldn't scream or injure myself. They wiped the blood from my eyes with silk. With silk, Mr. Stewart—I'll never forget the touch. Then they carried me out into the desert west of the Gattara Depression, left me in the Great Sand Sea, completely naked, left me to go blind and mad and then die—and I would have, surely, if I hadn't been found by a pair of soldiers from a British regiment who had wandered off course. They saved me from madness and death, Mr. Stewart. But it was too late to save me from blindness."

He switched off the light, but the image of the lidless, sun-bleached eyes hung between them. "The touch of light is quite painful still," he said. "But I wanted you to see. There should be no mystery between us."

It took a moment for Malcolm to find his voice. "What is it that you want me to do?"

"I've found it again," Burke said. "It has taken me years, and more money than you can imagine. It's cost several good men their lives. But I've found it, and this time it won't get away from me. Not with your help."

"And why should I help you?"

"There will be money, of course—quite a lot. But I know what you're going to say: Of what use is money if you're not around to spend it? And that's so. But there's more. This is your chance to be a part of something much greater than yourself, greater than me, greater than all of us. You will play a role in unraveling one of the greatest unsolved riddles of all time."

"Is that what you told the other men? The ones who died helping you?"

"Yes, Mr. Stewart, it is. It was the truth."

"And they took the job."

"I pay extremely well. And the men I chose had something in common with you."

"What's that?"

"Nothing to lose," Burke said.

It stung, but only because it was true. He had no family and no employment. His army pension kept his glass full as long as his tastes were cheap, and occasional under-the-table assignments paid the rest of his bills. He'd fetched and carried for some of London's worst, had ridden shotgun for questionable deliveries, had taken part in labor actions on whichever side cared to have him. It was a life, but only in the barest sense. Even when he'd had reason to, he'd never shrunk from risking it. Why would this be the assignment to make him put his foot down at last? And yet the image of Burke's lidless eyes was a hard one to rid himself of.

"Tell me, Mr. Burke, what it is that I'd be collecting for you, and how much you would pay me for it."

"I'd pay enough that you'd never need work again," Burke said.

"If you please, I'd prefer a number."

"Fifty thousand pounds, or its equivalent in any currency you choose. Gold, if you like."

Malcolm's mouth went dry. "You can't be serious. What are you asking me to do, steal the crown jewels?"

"Oh, something much more valuable than that. Do you remember your Bible, Mr. Stewart?"

"Not too well."

"There's a story in it about a man called Moses," Burke said. "You may recall he went up into the mountains for forty days, leaving his people behind. We're told they grew restless, that when he didn't return as promised, they called on his brother, Aaron, to make them an idol to protect them. A figure of a calf fashioned from the melted-down gold of their earrings and wristlets and such. When Moses returned and saw them worshipping this golden calf, the Bible says his anger was terrible. He smashed the tablets he was carrying, ordered the calf destroyed—ground to powder—and then mixed the powder with water and made his people drink it."

"And?"

"Like most of what's in the Bible, there are elements of historical truth to this story, but there is also much that's unreliable. Moses existed, surely, and so did the golden calf, and when he saw the thing being venerated at the foot of Sinai, it's very likely he did order it destroyed. Perhaps he even thought it had been, that the powder he was forcing down his people's throats was the residue of its destruction. But he was just a man, after all, and easily deceived.

"The golden calf was not destroyed, Mr. Stewart. I've *seen* it. I've touched it, I've held it in my hand. For three thousand years, it's been hidden, preserved by a priestly sect that moves it from place to place at two-year intervals. They'll kill any outsider who gets close to it. They tried to kill me, and they'll try to kill you. But they won't succeed—not if you're as good as people say."

"I was once," Malcolm said.

"And you shall be again. No more wine, man. You have a job to do." Burke extended his hand again, his left hand, and Malcolm watched it hang in the darkness, drawing him into a covenant that could cost him his life or worse.

Lydia, he thought, *if you were here, I'd spurn the offer and not think twice. But you're gone, my darling, in heaven or in sod, and I'm left behind to end my days alone. What harm if they end quickly?*

He took Burke's hand, felt it tighten around his own.

From the darkness, he heard Margaret's breath catch and felt a flicker of anger. She was the one who'd brought him here. What had she expected him to do?

Malcolm strode purposefully through the rooms, retracing their steps to the entry hall. Margaret had to run to keep pace.

"So, how many of us have there been?"

"Four. Unless you count the ambassador. He refused the offer."

"Probably the only time anyone has refused that man anything."

"He's a great man, and he's suffered greatly," Margaret said.

"And made others suffer."

"He's not made anyone do anything. He's offered the opportunity—"

"Four men have died chasing his opportunity."

"Then why did you say yes?" She wheeled on him and grabbed his arm. "No one forced you to."

"Maybe I just want the money."

She held his eyes, searched in them for something.

"I don't think so," she said. "I don't think you expect to see the money."

"Well, then, maybe I just need something to do, something that will get me out of this town."

She shook her head.

"So tell me, Miss Stiles, why am I doing it?"

"I don't know. I'd like to think it's because you recognize the importance of what he's discovered. But I don't think that's it at all. I think maybe it's the danger that attracts you. I think maybe you want to die."

"You're wrong," Malcolm said. "If that's what I wanted, this city's got no shortage of roofs to jump from."

"And pubs, where you can get yourself stuck by a boy with a knife."

"I didn't start that fight," Malcolm said.

"None of you ever starts a fight. But somehow you end up in so many. And eventually one of them's the death of you."

"Eventually. But not today."

"Only because I was there."

"And I've thanked you for it," Malcolm said.

"Who will you thank in North Africa, Mr. Stewart? When you're crossing the Jebel Akhdar, who will you lean on for support?"

"Maybe you'll come with me," he said, with a small smile. "And watch my back for me on the Jebel Akhdar."

She released his arm and he started toward the front door. She called out after him.

"You know what the difference is between you and the other four?"

He looked back. "What?"

"They had a chance," Margaret said.

II

He needed a drink in the worst way. It wasn't just the heat, nor the deprivation—he'd gone without for longer when he'd had to. It was the touch of the familiar he yearned for. A bit of the house red might have dimmed the sun and cooled the air; most of all, it would have made the place feel less alien.

Six years had gone unnoticed here. The flags of the Reich were gone, but no new standard had taken their place—the few flagpoles still standing were bare. The harbor hadn't been enlarged: two ships of modest size still filled it to capacity.

And bullet holes of various vintages scarred the walls of every building, silent reminders of the place's violent history.

Malcolm carried his bag into the center of town, waved off the attempts of two locals to take it off his hands for a couple of dirham. The papers Margaret had given him directed him to the hostel by the souq, and Malcolm picked his way to it through the crowded, listless streets. There were tradesmen bargaining, displaying their wares from hooks driven into the walls a century earlier. Reed baskets and hammered metal copils, cloth woven with traditional Arab motifs hanging side by side with war booty, bits of parachute silk and laceless boots, bayonet blades brown with rust and blood. Who would buy these things, Malcolm wondered, and with what money? But the merchants were there, and they didn't look like they were starving.

He palmed some folded dinars to the man behind the front desk at the hostel and was taken to a third-floor suite. The bed was low to the ground, and other than a mat and a basin the room had no furnishings, but it would do. It would have to. At least the elevation put it off limits to all but the more adventurous burglars—there was no balcony outside the window, and a thirty-foot fall to the cobblestones would end a man's career even if it were not fatal.

The call of the muezzin sang out and Malcolm closed the shutters of the window to muffle it. He'd have to get used to it—he'd be hearing it five times every day. But he was still tired from his trip, his healing arm was still sore, and he figured he could start getting used to it tomorrow.

He unpacked his revolver, wiped it down, sighted along the barrel and practiced firing a few times before loading it and sliding it into the holster on his hip. With his jacket on, all but the bottom of the holster was covered. Anyone looking for it would spot it, but a casual passer-by might not.

He folded Margaret's tidy pages of notes and tucked them into one of his shirt's breast pockets. He'd committed the information to memory during the crossing, but these names—he couldn't always remember which was the person's, which the street's.

The currency Burke had supplied went into his other breast pocket. Malcolm buttoned this one closed.

The rest? His clothing could stay here. It would be pawed through by the management, but as long as they expected another night's stay from him, they'd be unlikely actually to take any of it. He slung a small leather satchel over his shoulder and around his neck. The two paperbacks he'd brought as shipboard reading he wrapped in one of his shirts and shoved to the bottom of the bag. One was the new James M. Cain, the other a copy of the Christian Bible, and both would excite comment if left lying around.

Finally, he unfolded the crushed Borsalino he'd bought just before leaving, patted it back into shape. Every soldier knew you couldn't get by in the desert without a decent hat. It didn't have to be a Borsalino, but for God's sake, it was Burke's money he was spending, this might well be the last hat he'd ever own, and damn it, he'd bought the Borsalino.

He put it on and headed down to the street. He didn't bother to lock the door.

Dr. Ettouati's rooms were in the old quarter, where the buildings were smaller and the streets tighter. Standing with your arms out, you could almost touch the walls on either side. Malcolm consulted the notes, tucked them back into his pocket, and made his way to the building Burke had named.

It was a low, terraced building done in the Andalusian style, with rounded arches supported on the backs of narrow columns. There were fewer bullet holes here, and fewer people. One old woman watched from a nearby corner, leaning on a whiskbroom she'd been using to stir the dust between the cobblestones. He felt her eyes on him as he climbed the exposed staircase to the building's second story.

The doctor came to the door wiping his hands, and wiped them again after closing it behind them. He was a short man, no more than shoulder height to Malcolm, but solid, as though he'd be awfully hard to tip over. Malcolm was reminded of the statues he'd seen in Derna's museum when he'd passed through in '43, the heavy-featured stone guardians and gods, carved and unmovable.

"Burke wired me to expect you. You are the American, eh?"

"Hardly," Malcolm said.

"British?"

"That depends who you ask."

"Well. Which of us is not a citizen of the world, yes?" He waited for a response, got none, and went on. "Burke indicated that he wanted me to give you certain information I have collected for him about the Ammonites and their descendents. He seemed to think there was a modern sect carrying on their practices. This is, of course, highly unlikely.

"But there are ruins. Aren't there always? And there are records, and you're welcome to my notes on both." He pushed a notebook across the table between them. Malcolm thumbed through it briefly.

"Mr. Burke said you'd be able to point me toward a particular temple," Malcolm said. "North of Mechili."

"The Mechili find? Oh, I wouldn't call that a temple—really just a way station for travelers. And it's in poor condition. But if you want to see it . . ." He took the notebook back, paged through it, found what he was looking for and handed it back, tapping a forefinger on an illustration. The pencil sketch showed a stone altar, crudely carved with figures that might have been animals or people, or perhaps a bit of both.

"The Ammonites were a sacrificing people, and they missed no opportunity to provide their gods with a tribute. See this surface here?" He pointed to a flat rock protruding from the wall in the illustration. "That's where they would slaughter the lamb, or goat, or bullock, or what have you, and then burn it as an offering. There are channels here and here for the blood to run. You'll have to forgive the drawing, I am a poor draftsman . . ."

Malcolm thought the drawing was quite clear, actually. A grooved stone surface just large enough to hold a small animal, posts on either side to bind the struggling creature, channels to catch its blood.

Dr. Ettouati went on. "Young infants were also sometimes sacrificed, in times of—"

"Infants?"

"Yes," Ettouati said. "Is that the wrong word? I mean to say children, boy children. In times of crisis. Is this not what the word means, 'infant'? How do you say a boy child in English?"

"You say infant," Malcolm said. "Nothing wrong with your English."

"Good. Good. They would sometimes sacrifice an infant, although this was rare."

"It would more or less have to be, wouldn't it?"

"Well, a woman had more children then, but yes, they were not so plentiful as goats."

Malcolm turned the page. A hand-drawn map showed the approach to the temple—the way station, whatever it was—through a mountain pass. It was on the other side of the great Green Mountain, the Jebel Akhdar, with its sheer rock faces and endless twisting paths. Getting there wouldn't be an easy journey for a fully equipped party, much less a man traveling alone. But according to Burke, that's where he had to go.

"Tell me," Dr. Ettouati said, "has Burke told you what you are looking for?" He was wiping his hands again, Malcolm noticed, perhaps unconsciously but quite eagerly.

"No," Malcolm said. "Did he tell you?"

"Not a word. I don't imagine Burke as the type to root around in ancient sites for purely scholarly purposes, but he's said nothing about what he hopes to find. Ah, well. 'Ours not to reason why,' as your poet had it. Do you mean to go to Mechili?"

Malcolm nodded.

"I can come with you if you like," Ettouati said.

What would Burke say? He hadn't brought Ettouati into his confidence, and presumably he wouldn't want Malcolm to do so either. On the other hand, having a local to guide him through the mountains would make the journey easier.

"I'd appreciate it," Malcolm started to say—but before he could get the words out, a spray of blood covered his hands.

Everything seemed to happen in an instant, and in reverse: first the blood, streaking across his hands, then Ettouati's face crumpling as a bullet passed through it, and finally Malcolm became conscious of the sound, the thundercrack of gunfire echoing from wall to wall inside the small room. It took him longer than it should have to react: a bullet clipped his shoulder as he tipped over his chair and fell to the floor in front of the desk.

Where? How? He fought to call the layout of the room to mind as he jammed the bloody notebook into his pocket and fumbled his gun out of its holster. There had been two windows behind Ettouati, both shut. And beyond them a balcony? Probably—he'd seen a door in the other room.

He heard the rapid slap of running footsteps, chanced a look up over the top of the desk. The shutters of one window had been blown away, and through it he caught a glimpse of the shooter's arm, his back, as he sprinted for the door. Malcolm raced to the window, stuck first his gun and then his head through, but the man was already off the balcony, in the other room. Malcolm slid along the wall to the corner by the door with his gun raised in both hands. His hands were shaking, damn it, and it wasn't the shoulder wound doing it—the bullet had only grazed him. It was the shock of seeing a man killed just inches from his face. You thought you'd put it behind you, and in an instant it all comes back: the blood, the smell of a body suddenly opened to the air, the sick feeling in the pit of your stomach, the helplessness—

Damn it, pull yourself together. He gripped the gun tighter, swung around to face the door and kicked it open. He was firing before his foot touched the floor. There were two men, one in a sand-colored jalabaya, one in western-style khakis. A pair of red stains bloomed on the jalabaya and the man fell backward, the gun tumbling from his hand. Malcolm swung to face the other man, saw a curved blade flashing as the man raced toward him. He pulled the trigger twice. The first shot went wide, took a chunk out of the far wall and ricocheted off. The second caught the man in the gut. The dagger clattered to the floor as the man doubled over.

The front door was open, and through it he saw the old woman, now at the top of the stairs, the broom still in one hand, the doorknob in the other. She let the broom fall and took off, screaming for help.

Malcolm stepped around a low table to where the second man lay, gasping, struggling for breath. The knife was within the man's reach, and he saw the man go for it. Malcolm kicked it away, placed the sole of his boot on the man's hand, and leveled his gun at the man's face. "Who sent you?" Malcolm said.

The man was going into shock: his skin was gray and his face was shaking. The look of rage on his face was replaced by one of despair as the pain intensified. He spoke in a child's singsong whisper, the same words over and over: *"Molekh sh'ar liyot bein tekhem."*

"Who sent you?" Malcolm put more pressure on the man's hand. "Were you after Ettouati or me?"

". . . sh'ar liyot bein tekhem," the man whispered. *"Molekh sh'ar . . ."*

There wasn't time for this. The woman's screams had faded, but she'd be back any minute, together with whatever passed for the authorities in this town. They'd find him with a half-empty revolver in an apartment where three men had just been shot. He didn't want to find out what the inside of a Libyan prison was like.

He returned the gun to his holster and stepped off the man's hand. It wasn't mercy: the man would die of his gut wound, probably quite painfully as his stomach acids leaked out to poi-son his body. Shooting him now might have been more merciful. But Malcolm couldn't spare the bullet.

He took the stairs two at a time. In the alley behind the building, he found the transportation the men had used: a BMW R12, left over from the Wehrmacht. The sidecar was dented, the kickstand missing, the carriage streaked with rust. The glass cover of the headlamp was smashed in and one of the rubber handle grips had been torn off. But the engine was purring softly and when he gunned it, it responded instantly.

He pushed off against the wall with one leg and drove along the narrow alley as quickly as he dared, taking a sharp right when it became clear that continuing straight would take him to a dead end.

There was no time to return to the hostel, even assuming he could find it again. Between buildings, he could see the mountain in the distance and he used that to orient himself. He prayed the motorcycle's saddlebags held some water. It would be a short expedition if they didn't.

From behind him, he heard the roar of another motorcycle engine, and further back the throatier growl of a truck. He shot a look back over his shoulder and after a second saw the second cycle round a corner. The man driving it held a machine gun in one hand, the barrel resting on the handlebars. He shouted something in Arabic, raised the gun.

Malcolm took another corner, skirting the stone wall of the building by inches. The whine of his pursuer's engine grew higher-pitched as he accelerated. Malcolm turned his handgrip to match and felt the cobblestones streak by beneath him, jolting him, forcing him to hold on tighter than his wounds would allow. His sleeve was wet where his shoulder had bled, and his forearm still ached from the slash he'd received in the pub. He struggled to keep the machine upright, to find the end of this maze of alleys, to keep at least one turn between him and the men behind him.

Was this how the others had died, shot from

behind or smashed against a wall? He tried not to think about it, forced himself to concentrate on steering.

He was glad now that he hadn't taken a drink. His heart was racing and his reflexes, he knew, weren't what they once had been, but his hands were relatively steady and his vision clear. He heard Margaret's voice again—*The other four . . . they had a chance*—and gunned the engine.

They shot out from the old quarter, first Malcolm, then, some distance back, the man on the cycle, and finally what looked, at the edge of the circular mirror mounted on his handlebar, like an American jeep. There were no more turns to make: just the city's wide southern gate and, past it, the open desert. A spray of bullets shot in his direction, missing him narrowly. He grabbed the gun out of his holster. Only two shots left and no way to reload while driving, but it was still better than facing a machine gun unarmed. He sped through the gate, then took a hard left and braked to a stop behind the city wall. He turned back, lay low against the chassis, and waited for the other cycle to burst past.

But it didn't. The other cycle braked just inside the gate, idled as the jeep pulled up. He couldn't see them from where he was hidden, but he could hear their voices, the old woman and several men, all speaking in a tongue of which he understood only a few words. Among the words he recognized were "desert" and "death." It sounded as though they were deciding whether it was worth pursuing him. Why bother? One man alone in the desert would get all the justice he deserved. The night was coming; it was growing dark and cold. Let the man enjoy his victory—it would be brief.

Only don't allow him to seek refuge by sneaking back in. With alarm, Malcolm saw the heavy doors draw shut and heard the wooden bolt slide into place. Derna was off-limits to him now.

The foothills of the Jebel Akhdar were distant, and who knew how long his petrol would

last—but that was the only direction open to him.

Could he make it? He'd have to; there was no choice.

He drove off. Within minutes it was dark. Fortunately, the headlamp still worked, shattered glass or no, and he used it to cut a narrow path through the night. The light illuminated a trail of hard-packed sand and scrub, just a few feet at a time. He couldn't see the mountains any longer, but he took it on faith that he was still pointed in the right direction. In the morning he would check Ettouati's map, would correct his course. For now, all he had to do was drive— that, and stay awake.

The strange silence lulled him. Rarely, he would hear the cry of a distant bird, some nocturnal hunter calling to others of its kind; otherwise, the only sounds were those of his tires scouring the sand and his engine tearing through the night.

In his mind, he saw Burke's face, the naked eyes bulging in the half-light. He heard Margaret's voice: *Why did you say yes? No one forced you to.*

And he saw Lydia's face, too, remembered her as he'd seen her last, breathing shallow breaths in the hospital bed, delirious from the pain but clinging tightly to his hand, until all at once she wasn't any longer, all at once her face was still and her suffering was over. It had only been four months since he'd returned from the army. Four years he'd spent away, always a sea or an ocean or a continent between them, and then when he'd been able to return home at last, she'd been just a few months away from death.

When he'd been here last, in the desert, with tanks and munitions and men eager to kill for their masters, she'd kept him alive. He'd see her face when his eyes were closed, would whisper her name at night, would kiss the one snapshot he had of her when other men kissed crucifixes. He used to imagine that she'd protect him in battle, keep bullets from his path. He'd prayed to her: *Darling, let me come home to you, safe and sound, let no man take me from you.* And no man had.

But the reverse—that he had never considered, that she might be taken from him. In the prime of life, in peacetime, in a clean, quiet room overlooking a shaded yard, she'd died holding his hand, and he'd been able to do nothing to prevent it.

He found the road before him blurred and realized he was weeping. He wiped the tears away on the back of his sleeve and didn't slacken his pace. His only hope was to reach the mountains before the heat of day, and he found himself praying to her again. *Darling, stay with me now. The drive ahead is long; I need your help.*

Why had he said yes to Burke? He couldn't have answered Margaret honestly at the time; he hadn't known. But now he knew. Here in the desert again, more alone than he'd ever been, rocketing through the night with nothing but carrion birds for company, he felt closer to her than he had at any time since she'd died. She was there in the night, wrapping her arms about him and whispering softly in his ear. There was nothing left of her back home, nothing but a headstone and fading memories, but here he felt her presence as he hadn't in a very long time.

He wiped his eyes once more and bent low over the handlebars.

The dawn, when it came, broke suddenly. Malcolm saw the first shadings of gray light against the rocks, and within minutes the light had turned from the cool of early morning into the harsh, hostile glare it would remain for the rest of the day. Malcolm pulled over into the shadow of a boulder to rest the overheated engine.

He took his bearings. Somehow he'd managed not to stray too far from the path he'd meant to follow. The mountain was still some distance away, looming lush and green like a mirage. The Jebel Akhdar got its name from the trees and vegetation it supported, and he imagined he could find water once he got there. But until then, he was limited to whatever he had with him.

He searched through the saddlebags hanging on either side of the rear wheel. There was a goatskin canteen in one, half-full. He sniffed its contents and took a careful sip. It tasted stale, but it was water. He allowed himself two swallows before he recapped the canteen and put it back.

He stripped off his jacket and shirt, looked sideways at the trail of dried blood that ran across his left shoulder and disappeared down his back. He flexed his shoulder, stretched his arm, massaged the muscle. It wasn't a deep wound, and he didn't think it had gotten infected, but good God, he'd forgotten how much it hurt to get shot.

He put his shirt back on, folded the jacket and laid it in the bottom of the sidecar. From his shoulder pouch he took his ammunition case and reloaded his revolver. Then he got back on the cycle.

The fuel gauge showed the tank as nearly empty. It wouldn't last all the way to the mountain, that was certain, but it would take him a few more miles, and then he'd walk. He glanced at the map from Ettouati's notebook—the sketch wasn't as clear as he'd have liked, but it looked like he wanted to be west of where he was. He oriented himself against the sun, kicked the engine to life and settled in for the ride.

The heat grew, and his fatigue grew with it, till at midday he found himself drifting, felt his head jerk as he caught himself on the verge of sleep. It was tempting: Pull off, take a few hours to recuperate. But there was no shade here, and lying down in the open sun was suicide. He took another swig from the canteen, and drove on.

The foothills were in sight when the engine finally coughed and died. Malcolm took his jacket, slung the canteen across his chest, and started out on foot. The sand was hot, and soon the soles of his boots were, too. But there was nothing to be done for it. The hat kept the worst of the glare out of his eyes; and if it was hot, well, this was the desert, what did you expect? He bulled forward, keeping the base of the mountain in sight.

By the time he reached it, the canteen was

empty, his throat was parched, his legs ached, and his head swam. He kept moving forward mechanically, putting one foot in front of the other, hardly feeling the soreness in his shins, his shoulder, his sunburned neck. The hours in the sun had turned him into a desert creature, shambling forward without a thought other than the desire to get out of the heat. When he reached the first tree, he sank to his knees in its shade.

He didn't intend to sleep, and wasn't conscious of having done so, but when he next opened his eyes, the sun had shifted. He dug out the map. It showed a stream nearby and after searching for a bit, he found it. The water level was low, but it was fresh water and clean. He drank and refilled the canteen, then did the best job he could of washing his wound.

There were perhaps two hours of daylight left. The last thing Malcolm felt like doing was beginning the climb, but it had to be done. He set off. At first, the paths were nearly flat, but they grew steeper as he climbed, and the sparse vegetation of the mountain's base turned into something more like a forest as he rose, with ample undergrowth to trap his feet and make progress difficult. When the sun went down, what had been merely difficult became impossible, and finally Malcolm allowed himself to stop. He was hungry, but since he didn't know what around him was edible, he didn't take any chances. He wedged himself between a tree and the rock wall against which it had grown, tipped the hat forward over his face, and slept.

The next day's climb was easier, as the mountain leveled out for a stretch. To either side, he saw the curving paths along the rock walls slope upward alarmingly, but he stuck to Ettouati's map and followed the shallower course of the pass. He found a tree that resembled a date palm and took a chance on its fruit. He filled his pouch and when, several hours later, he still felt no ill effects from the first piece, he allowed himself a few more. Only a few—even edible fruit could give you the runs if you ate too much of it. But at least he wasn't ravenous any more, just hungry.

The path meandered, and he ached to cut across it, to attempt to find a shorter route, but he didn't dare. The mountains were treacherous here, famous for sudden drop-offs into gorges five hundred feet deep. If Ettouati had been there, he'd probably have known some better paths, but he wasn't, except in the form of his map. Malcolm had no choice but to treat the map as scripture.

He thought about Ettouati as he climbed, thought about the men who'd killed him. They'd looked more Egyptian than Libyan. Broader features, for one thing, and then there was the knife with its scalloped blade, the sort you'd find in Cairo sooner than in Tripoli. But he wasn't sure they'd been Egyptian, either. The language the second one had been speaking certainly hadn't sounded like Arabic.

He thought, too, of Burke and the assignment he'd accepted from him. Even if Malcolm made it to the Mechili temple, what was he supposed to do when he got there? Burke hadn't said, and Margaret's notes held no clues. There were dangerous men about, that much was clear—the ones who'd caught and mutilated Burke were presumably also the ones who'd sent the assassins to Ettouati's home. They'd seen to it that the other men Burke had put on their trail hadn't returned home, and they'd do what they could to add Malcolm to the list. So his first priority was staying out of their hands. But supposing he succeeded at that, how was he to find the bloody statue he was being paid to recover? He could hardly expect the thing to be sitting out in the open.

All Burke had said was that the statue was protected by a sect that moved it from place to place. The last word he'd had suggested it was at the Mechili site: Margaret had shown him the telegram. The man who'd sent it had been killed the next morning, strongly suggesting that he'd been on the right track. But that didn't mean he'd actually found the thing. And if he had, wouldn't they have moved it since?

No, Burke had insisted, they only moved it once every two lunar years. It's a practice they'd observed since Biblical times, and they wouldn't deviate from it just because someone located the site. They might not even know Lambert had sent a telegram—they might think they'd silenced him before he could tell anyone what he knew. And even if not, they'd have confidence in their ability to silence anyone else who came looking. In addition to the four men he'd sent, Burke had turned up stories of a dozen other men over the past century who'd gone looking for the calf and never returned.

Hearing that, Malcolm had very nearly backed out. A dozen other men—why think he'd fare better? The only man who'd made it out alive was Burke himself, and look what had happened to him.

But he'd already bought the damned hat. And he'd shaken hands on the deal. And what was the alternative, drinking himself to death slowly in a succession of West London pubs? Burke had been right: what did he have to lose?

Malcolm spent the second night between the roots of a giant acacia and woke with water on his face. It didn't rain often in this part of the world, and you took advantage of it when it did. He stripped off his clothing, put his gun under his jacket to keep it dry, and stood with his head tilted back. It was a brief shower, not even enough to wash all the dust off him, but its touch invigorated him. The morning sun dried him rapidly and he climbed back into his clothes before he could burn. He ate the last of his dates and started downhill.

He could see the way off the mountain by noon and set foot on level ground before nightfall. The southern desert stretched out before him, flat and featureless. Near the coast there had been frequent patches of vegetation and signs of animal life; here there was nothing except for the occasional jird scuttling ratlike across the sand. And the sand itself—it wasn't the rolling dunes you saw in Foreign Legion pictures, just a parched surface that had been bleached the color of bone and packed so hard it barely took footprints. He remembered a line from a poem they'd made him recite in grade school: *Boundless and bare, the lone and level sands stretch far away.* He'd had a mental image of the desert, he remembered, as a sort of giant beach. The reality, of course, drove such images out of your mind forever. You couldn't imagine the size of it, the emptiness, till you were standing inside it.

He started walking, setting a roughly southwesterly course. Traveling by night would be less arduous than trying to cross to Mechili with the sun beating down. He had a full canteen and he'd packed his pouch with whatever bits of fruit he'd been able to find on the way down the final slope. He could do the seven miles before dawn if he pushed himself. He'd be tired when he got there, which was not the best condition in which to face whoever might be waiting for him at the temple, and worst of all, if the landscape didn't change along the way, they'd be able to see him coming for the better part of a mile, but that was just all the more reason to approach at night. He pocketed the hat, shifted the strap of his bag so it cut into a different part of his back, and pushed forward.

At a certain point, the dusk gave way to total darkness. He had a tin of matches in his bag, but it wasn't worth using them up for the few instants of light they'd provide. His eyes adjusted, though it hardly mattered: there was nothing to see by day, less still at night. There was a hot wind that blew past from time to time, stirring the sand around him. He listened to his footsteps landing rhythmically. There was nothing else to do.

Was this what it was like to be blind? He couldn't imagine what Burke must have gone through, wandering the desert with the sun searing his unprotected eyes until at last they were burnt out like useless candle stumps. How he must have treasured the night! Until all he had was night.

It was strange, Malcolm thought, how the man burned to recover the least of what he'd lost—not his sight, not his hand, not the normal life he'd had, but that thing, that useless, useless thing he'd lost his sight pursuing. Oh, it was valuable, no doubt—priceless even—and Malcolm imagined that archaeologists and museum docents could jabber about it for a thousand years, but what good could it possibly do Burke? A three-thousand-year-old statue—was this worth a dozen men's lives? Or even one man's? There would be a certain satisfaction for Burke in recovering it, Malcolm supposed, in victoriously closing a chapter that had opened in bloody defeat. But in the clear light of day, what was that really worth?

In the clear light of day. Look at me, Malcolm thought, walking through the night at the arse end of nowhere, talking about the clear light of day. Who am I to take potshots at Burke for chasing some relic out of his past, when at least he has the good sense to do it from his armchair at home, with his fan blowing cool breezes on his brow? I'm the one on a trek through a desert I never thought I'd come back to. How's that for useless?

Fifty thousand pounds. That's not useless.

It is when you're wandering in the desert, Malcolm reminded himself. Nothing more useless then.

He drank a bit of his water, recapped the canteen, and kept going.

Ettouati's map had shown the temple as hidden inside the curve of a rocky outcropping, and in the half-light preceding sunrise Malcolm caught sight of a craggy shape in the distance, listing at an angle like a ship run aground. He was perhaps forty meters off to one side, but that was just as well: he'd be able to approach it from the side instead of straight on.

He crept up to the rocks slowly, revolver in hand, circled around the long way. He saw no one. There was an opening in the rocks where Ettouati had indicated, and he stepped in with his gun raised, but no one seemed to be inside either.

It was cool inside, and dark—stepping in from the desert was not unlike entering Burke's room back home, only less damp, and with the whirring of the electric fan replaced by the skit-tering of rodent feet. Malcolm lit a match, saw the carvings on the walls jump in the flickers of orange light. Animal-headed men in rows, some kneeling, some upright—the Egyptian influence was clear. But there was also an unfamiliar quality. These weren't ordinary hieroglyphs.

The images converged on the altar, which was larger than he'd thought it would be. You could fit a fairly large animal between the posts, and the drainage channels ran deep enough to catch quite a lot of blood without spilling over.

The match went out, and Malcolm decided not to light another. It wasn't bright in here, but enough light leaked in from outside that he could see what he needed to. He ran his hand along the surface of the altar and its underside, bent low to look closely at the wall. The carvings continued all the way around the altar and were framed by a rectangular groove extending from the ground on either side and meeting across the top. Malcolm felt along this groove, tried to fit the tips of his fingers inside it. It looked almost like the outline of a doorway, but when he pushed against the wall, it felt like pushing against solid rock.

He ran his index fingers along the length of the channels on the altar and at the far end of each, near the wall, he felt a pea-sized hole. This surprised him—it implied that the altar itself was hollow. He leaned forward and blew into one of the holes. A puff of dust rose and slowly settled.

He looked around. There had to be more here. Lambert's telegram had referred to a temple—an altar in a cave was not a temple. If there was a temple in this cave, it was somewhere deeper inside, but how were you supposed to get there from here? He tried to put himself in the place of the men who had built and used this place. If there was another area, what would they have done to gain access to it?

What, indeed. Ettouati's words came back to him. *The Ammonites were a sacrificing people. They missed no opportunity to provide their gods with a tribute.*

He lit another match, watched the ground as

a handful of jirds scattered. They were not large animals, about the size of rats, but—

Three or four, he imagined, might be equal in size to a small kid. Goat, that is. A small goat.

He dug through his shoulder pouch until he found his pocketknife and unfolded the longer of its blades. Then he took a few pieces of fruit—two dates, a wild fig—and cut them each in half. He pocketed the knife, placed half a fig on the ground and stood as close to perfectly still as he could. After a few seconds, he saw the dim shape of a jird nosing up to it.

He dropped his hat over the animal and scooped it up, pinning the sides of the brim between his fingers to trap it. It struggled violently and he almost lost his grip, but with his other fist he bunched the hat closed and smashed it twice against the cave wall. The jird went limp inside the hat.

He poured the body out onto the altar. It wasn't dead, he didn't think, but it was out cold and would stay where he left it. He put the other half of the fig on the ground and stepped back to wait.

In all, he managed to catch four. After that, though he still heard tiny claws clattering in the shadows, he wasn't able to lure any more into the trap. He looked over the bodies arranged in a row on the altar. They were smaller than he'd thought. Would four be enough?

There was only one way to know. He picked up one of the animals, held it firmly by its hindquarters above the left channel, and with one stroke of his knife sliced its head off. Its blood flowed freely, if not for long. He held it upside down directly over the hole at the end of the channel, watched as the flow drained off into the body of the altar. He pushed against the wall, but there was no movement. He tried using the posts for leverage, gripping one in each fist and straining. Nothing.

He decapitated the second jird, holding this one over the right-hand channel. Then he did the third and fourth. His hands were greasy from their fur and sticky with their blood. He wiped his hands roughly against the seat of his pants and took hold of the posts again. This time he thought he could feel something as he strained, some small shifting of the stone. But no more than that.

He cast about for something else he could use. Could he catch more jirds? It didn't seem likely, and even if he could, the blood from the first four would have dried up by the time he did, so he'd be starting over from scratch. There had to be another way.

He hefted the canteen. It was better than half full. He hated the idea of using any of his water this way, but—

He uncapped the canteen and carefully poured a thin stream into each channel. This time, when he pushed, he could hear the stones shift, some heavy internal counterweight slowly turning. He poured in some more, closed the canteen, took hold of the posts and pushed with all his strength.

The wall moved—slowly, with a grinding of stone against stone, but it moved, the altar and the section of the wall behind it both turning on some invisible, freshly lubricated axis.

There was light behind the wall, first a narrow orange crack and then an expanding glow like the flames of a thousand candles. And as the wall continued to turn, more smoothly now, more easily, Malcolm saw that there was also a man there, a man in a gold skullcap and patterned robe, standing with one arm crossed over his chest. The other arm was extended toward Malcolm, and held a gun.

III

Malcolm now regretted having holstered his own revolver, but there was nothing to be done for it. His couldn't outdraw a man who already had the drop on him, never mind doing so when his hands were sticky with blood.

His mind raced. The man hadn't pulled the trigger yet, but neither had he lowered the gun. He seemed to be weighing which would be more appropriate.

Malcolm dropped to his knees, held his bloody palms out. *"Molekh sh'ar liyot bein tekhem,"* he said.

Slowly, the gun lowered. *"Molekh sh'ar,"* the man said.

The room behind the altar stretched on for some distance and the ground sloped steeply downward. By the time Malcolm had followed the man to the far end, he suspected they were past the edge of the outcropping entirely and standing beneath the desert floor. The man slipped the gun inside the pocket of his robe and took out a ring of keys, one of which fit the lock set into the wrought-iron gate that barred their way. He swung the gate open and passed through without speaking a word.

Which was just as well, since Malcolm had used up all the words he knew in the man's language. If he'd tried to start a conversation, Malcolm would have had to make an attempt for the gun, however hopeless it might have been.

The room on the other side of the gate was several times the size of the entryway, a hollowed-out octagon with shallow alcoves carved into the walls, each containing a dish of tallow and a dancing flame. The center of the room held a freestanding stone altar in the shape of a giant hand, palm pointing toward the ceiling, fingers slightly curled.

There was one man kneeling in front of the altar and one standing behind it; on the altar itself was a pile of stones that looked as if they might have been chipped from the walls, only glowing, like the embers of a fire. It wasn't clear what the source of heat was, if indeed there was one—maybe it was just a source of light. The man behind the altar was short and wore the same sort of robe and skullcap the other man had on, while the one on his knees wore only a breechclout, a twisted strip of cloth knotted around his waist and between his legs. He swayed from side to side in time with a wordless chant, sometimes bowing forward to touch his head to the ground.

The robed men stood in silence, waiting, and Malcolm stood silently as well, but he used the time to steal glances around the room. There were openings in several of the walls leading off to dark corridors. Was the idol down one of them? If so, which one? And for how much longer could he maintain the charade of being a fellow worshipper? If he hadn't walked in on a ceremony in progress, surely they would have spoken to him already, and would instantly have found him out.

The kneeling man was swaying faster now as his chant grew louder. He reached out toward the altar, toward the stones, and jammed his hands in among them. Malcolm recoiled as the air filled with the stink of burning flesh. The man was howling now, screaming, in transports of pain and ecstasy.

Perhaps there would be a better opportunity later—perhaps. But it didn't seem likely.

Malcolm stepped up close to the man who had let him in, darted his hand into the pocket of the robe and grabbed the pistol. It was a German gun, heavy and cold to the touch. He whipped an arm around the man's neck and held the gun to his temple. The other robed man started forward.

"Take one more step and he dies," Malcolm said. "Do you understand me?"

The kneeling man rose to his feet. Malcolm saw that he still held a hot stone in each of his hands. His cheeks were covered with tears. His chest was scarred, long welts running haphazardly across his breastbone and along his ribs. Even barefoot as he was, he stood well over six feet tall, and his frame was formidable. But when he spoke, his voice was soft, calm.

"No, he doesn't understand you. Neither of them speaks English."

Malcolm found the man's voice unnerving. It was the furthest thing imaginable from the wordless howl it had been just moments before.

"He understands this," Malcolm said, gesturing with the pistol.

"You may shoot him if you want," he said. "It is what he deserves for letting you in."

Malcolm unwound his arm from around the robed man's throat and shoved him away. He re-oriented the Luger's sight so that it pointed squarely at the giant's naked chest. "And what about you, brother? Are you as ready to throw your own life away?"

Slowly and with a casual stride he came forward. "I am not afraid of pain. If it is Molekh's will that I die, I shall die."

"It's *my* will you need to be concerned about right now," Malcolm said. "The good news is I'm just here to do a job and leave—"

"You will never leave."

"We'll see. Why don't you back up against the wall, and tell the other two to do the same thing." The man paid no attention. Malcolm cocked the gun. "Now, or I swear to God I'll shoot you where you stand."

A voice spoke from behind him, a reverberant voice that rang from the stones. *"You swear to God?"*

Malcolm spun to find its source, but there was no one there.

"And which god is it that you swear to? When you are in my temple, do you swear to me?"

Malcolm saw movement in the corner of his eye and turned back, but the giant was suddenly beside him, and then the stones, still hot, were pressed against his gun hand, one on either side. He strained to pull the trigger, but the man had his hand firmly pinned. He felt his skin starting to sear.

Malcolm reached under his jacket left-handed, drew his own gun from its holster, jammed it into the man's gut and fired. The force of the gunshot sent the man stumbling back, freeing Malcolm's hand. He leveled the Luger at the man's head and pulled the trigger. A bloody spray stained the chamber floor.

The other two men were fleeing awkwardly in their cumbersome robes, heading for corridors on opposite sides of the room. To raise an alarm? To get reinforcements? He couldn't take the chance. One bullet apiece—left hand, right hand—and they were down.

Malcolm's heart was hammering, his head reeling. He heard the sound of laughter all around him, echoing louder as the thunder of gunfire died down. *"Blood!"* The voice was exultant. *"You do swear to me—you swear in blood, the blessed offering."*

"Who's talking?" Malcolm said, turning in a circle, scanning the shadows, a gun in each fist. "Where are you?"

"I am the Lord of this place and this people. I am brothergod to the Lord you worship, and have been since men first spoke of gods. I am many-named: men call me Melech, and Molekh, and Moloch; I have been called Legion, and Horror, and Beast, in fifty tongues and fifty times fifty, but men also call me Father, and Master, and Beloved. There is no end to the names men have given me."

"Enough," Malcolm said. "Save the booga-booga for the natives. Come out and face me."

"No man may look upon me and live."

Malcolm worked his way along one wall of the room, scanning the rock for a concealed loudspeaker, or some other mechanism that might explain where the voice was coming from. "Let's get one thing straight, Charley," he said. "I'm not here for the sermon. I'm not here for your fifty tongues or any of the rest of it. A man sent me here to collect a statue—either you have it or you don't. You leave me in peace and I'll leave you in peace."

"Peace!" The laughter was explosive. *"You talk of peace? Look about you. The blood of my servants stains my altar and you speak to me of peace?"*

Malcolm completed his circuit of the room. There was nothing—just rock and flame and the voice, shouting in his ear. The entrance to one of the dark corridors was next to him, and he stepped into it, but the voice followed him, chasing him along its length until he came out into a room much like the first. Only this one's altar was shaped like a pedestal, and where the other had held stones, this one held—

He couldn't see clearly what it held. There was a shape, but Malcolm could only see it through a haze, as though of smoke. Could it be the outline of a calf? It could be anything, he realized. And as he watched, the smoke closed up around the altar, obscuring the figure.

"You say you seek a statue. If so, your quest is doomed, for the statue you mean was destroyed a hundred generations ago."

"But—"

"But a man told you he saw it. You are not the first he has sent to me, this blind man. And you, so quick to believe, you take the word of a blind man over that of your own Scripture?"

"He wasn't blind when he saw it."

"You are all blind." The voice was now a guttural whisper, cold and insinuating. *"You see only what you wish to see. Each man who faces my altar sees that which he most desires and, addressing it with impure heart, gains only what he most dreads."*

The smoke began to thin, as though blown by a breeze.

"Your blind man spent a lifetime searching for my mount, the figure they made for me at the foot of Sinai, so when he came before me, that is what he saw.

"Look closely, child. What do you see? Like your ancestors before you, you have wandered in the desert and climbed the mountain's slopes. You did not bear this burden in pursuit of another man's quest."

Malcolm could make out the altar again, and upon it he saw a form, a human shape, but it was still indistinct.

"Do you even know what you are searching for?"

And the smoke vanished, in an instant, leaving the figure behind it bare. She was naked and pale and trembling, and Malcolm fell to his knees before her.

"Each man worships at the idol of his choosing."

"No," Malcolm said, shaking his head. "She's dead. I buried her." He turned to the woman seated on the altar. "You're dead, three years dead."

Lydia stepped down, came toward him, one arm outstretched. "My love, my poor love," she said.

He shrank from her. "It's impossible," he said. He shouted it: "It's impossible! This is a lie!"

"Why impossible? Do you doubt my power?" From the corridor, Malcolm heard the echo of footsteps approaching, and then one by one the men he'd killed entered the room, the two in robes and the third in his loincloth, his bloody trunk and head still bearing their horrible, fatal wounds. *"Over certain among the living I have influence, but over the dead—over the dead, I have utter command."*

"No," Malcolm said. But he couldn't deny the evidence of his eyes. These men—they had died, he had struck them down himself, had seen them fall. Yet here they were. And here she was, looking exactly as he remembered. His mind recoiled at the thought. And yet—

She reached out for him again, but the dead men in priestly robes each took one of her arms and between them they pulled her back toward the altar. The third man followed, his naked back gleaming in the candlelight, bloody and torn where the first bullet had emerged above his hip.

Malcolm launched himself to his feet, threw himself at the three men, but while the priests secured Lydia to the altar, the giant swatted him away, sent him reeling to the floor with one swipe of his scarred palm. Malcolm drew his gun and fired, twice, three times, till the chambers were all empty, but this time the bullets had no effect.

The priests stood back, and he saw that they had shackled Lydia to the stone, ankles and wrists encircled with iron bands. From the folds of his robe, one of them drew a knife with a curved and scalloped blade and handed it to the third man, the barebacked giant who had so casually fended off Malcolm's charge. The second priest positioned himself behind Lydia's head and placed one hand firmly on either side of her face.

"Close your eyes," the giant said. His voice was soft and calm and Malcolm's blood froze at the sound of it.

"Malcolm!" Lydia's cry took him back in an instant to her bedside at the hospital. "Help me."

"It's not real," Malcolm said. He shouted it to the ceiling of the cavernous room. "It's not real!"

"Your arrogance is awesome," the voice intoned, *"if you presume to state what is and is not real."*

"My wife is dead. You cannot change that. No one can."

"Perhaps. But can the dead not also suffer?"

And from the altar came a shriek of purest terror, of anguish beyond measure. He saw only the giant's broad back, stooped over the bound figure, saw the hugely muscled arms, streaked with sweat, rock as he gently worked the knife.

"Stop it," Malcolm said. "Please stop."

"Why, if it is not real?"

Malcolm had to struggle to keep his voice under control. "Why are you doing this?"

"Because I can, child, and because it is my pleasure. It is my pleasure that my power be revealed, that men may know a god of might still walks among them, that they may bend their knees in supplication."

"You want me to kneel?" He dropped to his knees, spread his arms out. "Please."

"Kneeling is more than a matter of being on your knees. I will spare her for you—and then you will kneel to me in earnest, you will bow to me and do my bidding, as your blind man does in spite of himself. And in time you will speak my name with true reverence rather than with deceit in your heart."

The men surrounding the altar stepped away, and Malcolm saw that Lydia was still bound to it, her face smeared with blood. He ran to the altar. She was shaking and pale, her torso covered with sweat, and he took her hand gently. One of the priests held a square of silk out to him. He took it and carefully wiped the blood around her eyes.

"My darling," she whispered. "Don't leave me."

So, Burke, he thought, here's your golden calf. I understand now. There's a thing you love and crave, and you had it once, too briefly, and now you ache to have it back. Yes, I know how you ache. There is no way you could leave it behind in the desert: you're bound to it for life, you are its slave. Even if it no longer exists outside your imagination.

I crave, too, Malcolm thought. You're not the only one; my imagination is no less troubled. But I am not blind, Burke, and I have not your capacity for blind faith.

"I left my wife in Glasnevin," he said softly, "and I'm going back to her there."

He let go of her hand, stepped back from the altar, and walked as rapidly as he could toward the corridor through which he'd entered. Behind him, the voice thundered.

"If you go, you will never see her again."

He kept walking.

"You will never speak to her, touch her, hear her voice."

He bit back tears.

"She will suffer torments you cannot conceive!"

And then she screamed, a shattering, curdled scream that seemed to contain more pain in it than any body could bear. Malcolm ran from it, tore through the first chamber and the iron gate and the entry hall, pursued by the sound of it. The flames of the candles lining the walls all at once were snuffed out, and at the far end of the corridor he saw the stone wall slowly swinging closed.

"Coward! You will curse the day you abandoned her to me."

The hall seemed endless, the band of light beyond the wall shrinking as he ran toward it. He bent forward and strained for extra speed, for the last desperate dregs of energy that would carry him through, and he reached the wall at last when only inches remained. He squeezed through sideways, scraping against the rock on either side. From inside, a final angry whisper came, one he could only barely make out.

And then the wall slammed shut.

He leaned against it, breathing heavily, sobbing freely. What have I done, he thought. What have I done?

It was twilight outside and dry and hot. He had little water and less food, and seven miles between him and the nearest source of either. There was nothing for it. He started walking.

I'll make it, he told himself. I'll make it home. I'll tell Burke nothing—let him think I died, let him send other men after me, I don't care. Just let me make it back.

An image came unbidden into his mind: the shackles, the altar, the woman writhing upon it.

It wasn't her, he told himself. It wasn't. The dead don't walk, or speak, or feel pain, or beg you not to leave.

But it looked—her touch, her voice, it was all—

Rubbish. It was an illusion, a dream, a bit of desert madness.

In his jacket pocket, where he'd crammed it as he ran, he felt the crumpled square of silk, still damp. He took it out, turned it this way and that in the fading light. It was real, and the blood on it was real—not a dream, not an illusion. But what did that mean? Something had happened in the temple, something terrible; but not to Lydia. That wasn't possible.

Are you certain? a voice in the back of his mind whispered.

Yes, damn it. I am certain.

Then why are you so frightened?

Because—because—

Because you saw her with your own eyes, you held her in your hand, and now you've gone and left her behind . . .

It wasn't her. It couldn't have been.

No, no, of course not. It couldn't. But you'll never know that for sure, will you?

And he remembered Molekh's final, whispered imprecation, the words hissed out at him just before the stone walls ground together. *"You may leave this place,"* the voice had said, *"but you will never escape it."*

The Jebel Akhdar was barely visible at the horizon. He marched on, and the night closed in around him.

THE SOUL OF A REGIMENT

TALBOT MUNDY

THE MOST prestigious of all the pulp magazines specializing in adventure fiction was titled, appropriately, *Adventure*, and its star contributor was Talbot Mundy, the pseudonym of William Lancaster Gribbon (1879–1940). Born in London, Gribbon sought a life of exotic adventure that took him to various jobs in England and Germany, and, at the age of twenty-one, to India and Africa. Although he described himself as a warrior and big-game hunter, he was, in fact, a con man, bigamist, serial adulterer, and convict with the Swahili nickname of Makundu Viazi—meaning "white arse." He eventually settled down, however, married, and moved to America in 1909, whereupon he began writing articles for English and American publications. After he sold a piece about boar hunting in India to the February 1911 issue of *Adventure,* he went on to write scores of novels, serials, stories, and articles for the pulps until the end of his life.

Gribbon's forte was stories set in India under British rule, the most famous of which was *King—Of the Khyber Rifles* (1916). The story came to the big screen in 1929 as *The Black Watch,* starring Victor McLaglen and Myrna Loy; it was famously remade in 1953 with Tyrone Power, Terry Moore, and Michael Rennie. Apart from his India-set works, Gribbon also wrote tales set in the Middle East, the latter mostly about James Schuyler Grim, a British Intelligence operative known as Jimgrim, as well as two books totaling five hundred thousand words—serialized in *Adventure*—about Tros of Samothrace, a Greek adventurer who aids the Britons and Druids in their battles with Julius Caesar. *Tros of Samothrace* (1934) and *Purple Pirate* (1935) are regarded by many as the apotheosis of pulp adventure fiction and were powerful influences on such "sword and sorcery" writers as Robert E. Howard and Fritz Leiber. Late in life, Mundy became a devoted believer in Theosophism, and, unpredictably, spent much of his last five years writing for the long-running (1933–1951) radio serial *Jack Armstrong, the All-American Boy.*

"The Soul of a Regiment," Mundy's most famous story, was also voted one of the most popular stories in the long, distinguished history of *Adventure* by its readers; it was first published in the February 1912 issue. It was first published in book form as a single story, *The Soul of a Regiment* (San Francisco: Dulfer, 1925).

THE SOUL OF A REGIMENT

TALBOT MUNDY

I

SO LONG AS its colors remain, and there is one man left to carry them, a regiment can never die; they can recruit it again around that one man, and the regiment will continue on its road to future glory with the same old traditions behind it and the same atmosphere surrounding it that made brave men of its forbears. So although the colors are not exactly the soul of a regiment, they are the concrete embodiment of it, and are even more sacred than the person of a reigning sovereign.

The First Egyptian Foot had colors—and has them still, thanks to Billy Grogram; so the First Egyptian Foot is still a regiment. It was the very first of all the regiments raised in Egypt, and the colors were lovely crimson things on a brand-new polished pole, cased in the regulation jacket of black waterproof and housed with all pomp and ceremony in the mess-room at the barracks. There were people who said it was bad policy to present colors to a native regiment; that they were nothing more than a symbol of a decadent and waning monarchism in any case, and that the respect which would be due them might lead dangerously near to fetish-worship. As a matter of cold fact, though, the raw recruits of the regiment failed utterly to understand them, and it was part of Billy Grogram's business to instill in them a wholesome respect for the sacred symbol of regimental honor.

He was Sergeant-Instructor William Stan-ford Grogram, V. C., D. S. M., to give him his full name and title, late a sergeant-major of the True and Tried, time expired, and retired from service on a pension. His pension would have been enough for him to live on, for he was unmarried, his habits were exemplary, and his wants were few; but an elder brother of his had been a ne'er-do-well, and Grogram, who was of the type that will die rather than let any one of his depend on charity, left the army with a sister-in-law and a small tribe of children dependent on him. Work, of course, was the only thing left for it, and he applied promptly for the only kind of work that he knew how to do.

The British are always making new regiments out of native material in some part of the world; they come cheaper than white troops, and, with a sprinkling of white troops in among them, they do wonderfully good service in time of war—thanks to the sergeant-instructors. The officers get the credit for it, but it is the ex-non-commissioned officers of the Line who do the work, as Grogram was destined to discover. They sent him out to instruct the First Egyptian Foot, and it turned out to be the toughest proposition that any one lonely, determined, homesick fighting-man ever ran up against.

He was not looking for a life of idleness and ease, so the discomfort of his new quarters did not trouble him overmuch, though they would have disgusted another man at the very beginning. They gave him a little, white-washed, mud-walled hut, with two bare rooms in it, and a lovely view on three sides of aching desert sand; on the fourth a blind wall.

It was as hot inside as a baker's oven, but it had the one great advantage of being easily kept clean, and Grogram, whose fetish was cleanliness, bore that in mind, and forebore to grumble at the absence of a sergeant's mess and the various creature comforts that his position had entitled him to for years.

What did disgust him, though, was the unfairness of saddling the task that lay in front of him on the shoulders of one lone man; his officers made it quite clear that they had no intention of helping him in the least; from the Colonel downward they were ashamed of the regiment, and they expected Grogram to work it into something like shape before they even began to take an interest in it.

The Colonel went even further than that; he put in an appearance at Orderly Room every morning and once a week attended a parade out on the desert where nobody could see the awful evolutions of his raw command, but he actually threw cold water on Grogram's efforts at enthusiasm.

"You can't make a silk purse out of a sow's ear," he told him a few mornings after Grogram joined, "or well-drilled soldiers out of Gyppies. Heaven only knows what the Home Government means by trying to raise a regiment out here; at the very best we'll only be teaching the enemy to fight us! But you'll find they won't learn. However, until the Government finds out what a ghastly mistake's being made, there's nothing for it but to obey orders and drill Gyppies. Go ahead, Grogram; I give you a free hand. Try anything you like on them, but don't ask me to believe there'll be any result from it. Candidly I don't."

But Grogram happened to be a different type of man from his new Colonel. After a conversation such as that, he could have let things go hang had he chosen to, drawing his pay, doing his six hours' work a day along the line of least resistance, and blaming the inevitable consequences on the Colonel. But to him a duty was

something to be done; an impossibility was something to set his clean-shaven, stubborn jaw at and to overcome; and a regiment was a regiment, to be kneaded and pummelled and damned and coaxed and drilled, till it began to look as the True and Tried used to look in the days when he was sergeant-major.

So he twisted his little brown mustache and drew himself up to the full height of his five feet eight inches, spread his well-knit shoulders, straightened his ramrod of a back and got busy on the job, while his Colonel and the other officers did the social rounds in Cairo and cursed their luck.

The material that Grogram had to work with were fellaheen—good, honest coal-black negroes, giants in stature, the embodiment of good-humored incompetence, children of the soil weaned on raw-hide whips under the blight of Turkish misrule and Arab cruelty. They had no idea that they were even men till Grogram taught them; and he had to learn Arabic first before he could teach them even that.

They began by fearing him, as their ancestors had feared every new breed of task-master for centuries; gradually they learned to look for instant and amazing justice at his hands, and from then on they respected him. He caned them instead of getting them fined by the Colonel or punished with packdrill for failing at things they did not understand; they were thoroughly accustomed to the lash, and his light swagger-cane laid on their huge shoulders was a joke that served merely to point his arguments and fix his lessons in their memories; they would not have understood the Colonel's wrath had he known that the men of his regiment were being beaten by a non-commissioned officer.

They began to love him when he harked back to the days when he was a recruit himself, and remembered the steps of a double-shuffle that he had learned in the barrack-room; when he danced a buck and wing dance for them they recognized him as a man and a brother, and from that time on, instead of giving him all the trouble they could and laughing at his lectures when his back was turned, they genuinely tried to please him.

So he studied out more steps, and danced his way into their hearts, growing daily stricter on parade, daily more exacting of pipe-clay and punctuality, and slowly, but surely as the march of time, molding them into something like a regiment.

Even he could not teach them to shoot, though he sweated over them on the dazzling range until the sun dried every drop of sweat out of him. And for a long time he could not even teach them to march; they would keep step for a hundred yards or so, and then lapse into the listless shrinking stride that was the birthright of centuries.

He pestered the Colonel for a band of sorts until the Colonel told him angrily to go to blazes; then he wrote home and purchased six fifes with his own money, bought a native drum in the bazaar, and started a band on his own account.

Had he been able to read music himself he would have been no better off, because of course the fellaheen he had to teach could not have read it either, though possibly he might have slightly increased the number of tunes in their repertory.

As it was, he knew only two tunes himself—"The Campbells Are Coming," and the National Anthem.

He picked the six most intelligent men he could find and whistled those two tunes to them until his lips were dry and his cheeks ached and his very soul revolted at the sound of them. But the six men picked them up; and, of course, any negro in the world can beat a drum. One golden morning before the sun had heated up the desert air the regiment marched past in really good formation, all in step, and tramping to the tune of "God Save the Queen."

The Colonel nearly had a fit, but the regiment tramped on and the band played them back to barracks with a swing and rhythm that was new not only to the First Egyptian Foot; it was new to Egypt! The tune was half a tone flat maybe, and the drum was a sheepskin business bought in the bazaar, but a new regiment marched behind it. And behind the regiment—two paces right flank, as the regulations specify—marched a sergeant-instructor with a new light in his eyes—the gray eyes that had looked out so wearily from beneath the shaggy eyebrows, and that shone now with the pride of a deed well done.

Of course the Colonel was still scornful. But Billy Grogram, who had handled men when the Colonel was cutting his teeth at Sandhurst, and who knew men from the bottom up, knew that the mob of unambitious countrymen, who had grinned at him in uncomfortable silence when he first arrived, was beginning to forget its mobdom. He, who spent his hard-earned leisure talking to them and answering their childish questions in hard-won Arabic, knew that they were slowly grasping the theory of the thing—that a soul was forming in the regiment—an indefinable, unexplainable, but obvious change, perhaps not unlike the change from infancy to manhood.

And Billy Grogram, who above all was a man of clean ideals, began to feel content. He still described them in his letters home as "blooming mummies made of Nile mud, roasted black for their sins, and good for nothing but the ashheap." He still damned them on parade, whipped them when the Colonel wasn't looking, and worked at them until he was much too tired to sleep; but he began to love them. And to a big, black, grinning man of them, they loved him.

To encourage that wondrous band of his, he set them to playing their two tunes on guest nights outside the officers' mess; and the officers endured it until the Colonel returned from furlough. He sent for Grogram and offered to pay him back all he had spent on instruments, provided the band should keep away in future.

Grogram refused the money and took the hint, inventing weird and hitherto unheard-of reasons why it should be unrighteous for the band to play outside the mess, and preaching respect for officers in spite of it. Like all great men he knew when he had made a mistake, and how to minimize it.

His hardest task was teaching the Gyppies what their colors meant. The men were Mohammedans; they believed in Allah; they had been taught from the time when they were old enough to speak that idols and the outward symbols of religion are the sign of heresy; and Grogram's lectures, delivered in stammering and uncertain Arabic, seemed to them like the ground-plan of a new religion. But Grogram stuck to it. He made opportunities for saluting the colors—took them down each morning and uncased them, and treated them with an ostentatious respect that would have been laughed at among his own people.

When his day's work was done and he was too tired to dance for them, he would tell them long tales, done in halting Arabic, of how regiments had died rallying round their colors; of a brand-new paradise, invented by himself and suitable to all religions, where soldiers went who honored their colors as they ought to do; of the honor that befell a man who died fighting for them, and of the tenfold honor of the man whose privilege it was to carry them into action. And in the end, although they did not understand him, they respected the colors because he told them to.

II

When England hovered on the brink of indecision and sent her greatest general to hold Khartum with only a handful of native troops to help him, the First Egyptian Foot refused to leave their gaudy crimson behind them. They marched with colors flying down to the steamer that was to take them on the first long stage of their journey up the Nile, and there were six fifes and a drum in front of them that told whoever cared to listen that "The Campbells were coming—hurrah! hurrah!"

They marched with the measured tramp of a real regiment; they carried their chins high; their tarbooshes were cocked at a knowing angle and they swung from the hips like grown men. At the head of the regiment rode a Colonel whom the regiment scarcely knew, and beside it marched a dozen officers in like predicament; but behind it, his sword strapped to his side and his little swagger-cane tucked under his left arm-pit, inconspicuous, smiling and content, marched Sergeant-Instructor Grogram, whom the regiment knew and loved, and who had made and knew the regiment.

The whole civilized world knows—and England knows to her enduring shame—what befell General Gordon and his handful of men when they reached Khartum. Gordon surely guessed what was in store for him even before he started, his subordinates may have done so, and the native soldiers knew. But Sergeant-Instructor Grogram neither knew nor cared.

He looked no further than his duty, which was to nurse the big black babies of his regiment and to keep them good-tempered, grinning and efficient; he did that as no other living man could have done it, and kept on doing it until the bitter end.

And his task can have been no sinecure. The Mahdi—the ruthless terror of the Upper Nile who ruled by systematized and savage cruelty and lived by plunder—was as much a bogy to peaceful Egypt as Napoleon used to be in Europe, and with far more reason. Mothers frightened their children into prompt obedience by the mere mention of his name, and the coal-black natives of the Nile-mouth country are never more than grown-up children.

It must have been as easy to take that regiment to Khartum as to take a horse into a burning building, but when they reached there not a man was missing; they marched in with colors flying and their six-fife band playing, and behind them—two paces right flank rear—marched Billy Grogram, his little swagger-cane under his left arm-pit, neat, respectful and very wide awake.

For a little while Cairo kept in touch with them, and then communications ceased. Nobody ever learned all the details of the tragedy that followed; there was a curtain drawn—of mystery and silence such as has always veiled the heart of darkest Africa.

Lord Wolseley took his expedition up the Nile, whipped the Dervishes at El Teb and Tel-el-Kebir, and reached Khartum, to learn of Gordon's death, but not the details of it. Then he came back again; and the Mahdi followed him, closing up the route behind him, wiping all trace of civilization off the map and placing what he imagined was an insuperable barrier between him and the British—a thousand miles of plundered, ravished, depopulated wilderness.

So a clerk in a musty office drew a line below the record of the First Egyptian Foot; widows were duly notified; a pension or two was granted; and the regiment that Billy Grogram had worked so hard to build was relegated to the past, like Billy Grogram.

Rumors had come back along with Wolseley's men that Grogram had gone down fighting with his regiment; there was a story that the band had been taken alive and turned over to the Mahdi's private service, and one prisoner, taken near Khartum, swore that he had seen Grogram speared as he lay wounded before the Residency. There was a battalion of the True and Tried with Wolseley; and the men used methods that may have been not strictly ethical in seeking tidings of their old sergeant-major; but even they could get no further details; he had gone down fighting with his regiment, and that was all about him.

Then men forgot him. The long steady preparation soon began for the new campaign that was to wipe the Mahdi off the map, restore peace to Upper Egypt, regain Khartum and incidentally avenge Gordon. Regiments were slowly drafted out from home as barracks could be built for them; new regiments of native troops were raised and drilled by ex-sergeants of the Line who never heard of Grogram; new men took charge; and the Sirdar superintended everything and laid his reputation brick by brick, of bricks which he made himself, and men were too busy under him to think of anything except the work in hand.

But rumors kept coming in, as they always do in Egypt, filtering in from nowhere over the illimitable desert, bourne by stray camel-drivers, carried by Dervish spies, tossed from tongue to tongue through the fish-market, and carried up back stairs to Clubs and Department Offices. There were tales of a drummer and three men who played the fife and a wonderful mad feringhee who danced as no man surely ever danced before. The tales varied, but there were always four musicians and a feringhee.

When one Dervish spy was caught and questioned he swore by the beard of the prophet that he had seen the men himself. He was told promptly that he was a liar; how came it that a feringhee—a pork-fed, infidel Englishman—should be allowed to live anywhere the Mahdi's long arm reached?

"Whom God hath touched—" the Dervish quoted; and men remembered that madness is the surest passport throughout the whole of Northern Africa. But nobody connected Grogram with the feringhee who danced.

But another man was captured who told a similar tale; and then a Greek trader, turned Mohammedan to save his skin, who had made good his escape from the Mahdi's camp. He swore to having seen this man as he put in one evening at a Nile-bank village in a native dhow. He was dressed in an ancient khaki tunic and a loin-cloth; he was bare-legged, shoeless, and his hair was long over his shoulders and plastered thick with mud. No, he did not look in the least like a British soldier, though he danced as soldiers sometimes did beside the camp-fires.

Three natives who were with him played fifes while the feringhee danced, and one man beat a drum. Yes, the tunes were English tunes, though very badly played; he had heard them before, and recognized them. No, he could not hum them; he knew no music. Why had he not spoken to the man who danced? He had not dared. The man appeared to be a prisoner and so were the natives with him; the man had danced that evening until he could dance no longer, and then the Dervishes had beaten him with a koorbash for encouragement: the musicians had tried to interfere, and they had all been beaten and left lying there for dead. He was not certain, but he was almost certain they were dead before he came away.

Then, more than three years after Gordon died, there came another rumor, this time from closer at hand—somewhere in the neutral desert zone that lay between the Dervish outpost and the part of Lower Egypt that England held. This time the dancer was reported to be dying, but the musicians were still with him. They got the name of the dancer this time; it was reported to be Goglam, and though that was not at all a bad native guess for Grogram, nobody apparently noted the coincidence.

Men were too busy with their work; the rumor was only one of a thousand that filtered across the desert every month, and nobody remembered the non-commissioned officer who had left for Khartum with the First Egyptian Foot; they could have recalled the names of all the officers almost without an effort, but not Grogram's.

III

Egypt was busy with the hum of building—empire building under a man who knew his job. Almost the only game the Sirdar countenanced was polo, and that only because it kept officers and civilians fit. He gave them all the polo, though, that they wanted, and the men grew keen on it, spent money on it, and needless to say, grew extraordinarily proficient.

And with the proficiency of course came competition—matches between regiments for the regimental cup and finally the biggest event of the Cairo season, the match between the Civil Service and the Army of Occupation, or, as it was more usually termed, "The Army vs. The Rest." That was the one society event that the Sirdar made a point of presiding over in person.

He attended it in mufti always, but sat in the seat of honor, just outside the touch-line, half-

way down the field; and behind him, held back by ropes, clustered the whole of Cairene society, on foot, on horseback and in dog-carts, buggies, gigs and every kind of carriage imaginable. Opposite and at either end, the garrison lined up—all the British and native troops rammed in together; and the native population crowded in between them and wherever they could find standing-room.

It was the one event of the year for which all Egypt, Christian and Mohammedan, took a holiday. Regimental bands were there to play before the game and between the chukkers, and nothing was left undone that could in any way tend to make the event spectacular.

Two games had been played since the cup had been first presented by the Khedive, and honors lay even—one match for the Army and one for the Civil Service. So on the third anniversary feeling ran fairly high. It ran higher still when half time was called and honors still lay even at one goal all; to judge by the excitement of the crowd, a stranger might have guessed that polo was the most important thing in Egypt. The players rode off the pavilion for the half-time interval, and the infantry band that came out on to the field was hard put to it to drown the noise of conversation and laughter and argument. At that minute there was surely nothing in the world to talk about but polo.

But suddenly the band stopped playing, as suddenly as though the music were a concrete thing and had been severed with an ax. The Sirdar turned his head suddenly and gazed at one corner of the field, and the noise of talking ceased—not so suddenly as the music had done, for not everybody could see what was happening at first—but dying down gradually and fading away to nothing as the amazing thing came into view.

It was a detachment of five men—a drummer and three fifes, and one other man who marched behind them—though he scarcely resembled a man. He marched, though, like a British soldier.

He was ragged—they all were—dirty and unkempt. He seemed very nearly starved, for his bare legs were thinner than a mummy's; round his loins was a native loin-cloth, and his hair was plastered down with mud like a religious fanatic's. His only other garment was a tattered khaki tunic that might once have been a soldier's, and he wore no shoes or sandals of any kind.

He marched though, with a straight back and his chin up, and anybody who was half observant might have noticed that he was marching two paces right flank rear; it is probable, though, that in the general amazement, nobody did notice it.

As the five debouched upon the polo ground, four of them abreast and one behind, the four men raised their arms, the man behind issued a sharp command, the right-hand man thumped his drum, and a wail proceeded from the fifes. They swung into a regimental quickstep now, and the wail grew louder, rising and falling fitfully and distinctly keeping time with the drum.

Then the tune grew recognizable. The crowd listened now in awe-struck silence. The five approaching figures were grotesque enough to raise a laugh and the tune was grotesquer, and more pitiable still; but there was something electric in the atmosphere that told of tragedy, and not even the natives made a sound as the five marched straight across the field to where the Sirdar sat beneath the Egyptian flag.

Louder and louder grew the tune as the fifes warmed up to it; louder thumped the drum. It was flat, and notes were missing here and there. False notes appeared at unexpected intervals, but the tune was unmistakable. "The Campbells are coming! Hurrah! Hurrah!" wailed the three fifes, and the five men marched to it as no undrilled natives ever did.

"Halt!" ordered the man behind when the strange cortège had reached the Sirdar; and his "Halt!" rang out in good clean military English.

"Front!" he ordered, and they "fronted" like a regiment. "Right Dress!" They were in line already, but they went through the formality of shuffling their feet. "Eyes Front!" The five men faced the Sirdar, and no one breathed. "General salute—pre-sent arms!"

They had no arms. The band stood still at attention. The fifth man—he of the bare legs and plastered hair—whipped his right hand to his forehead in the regulation military salute—held it there for the regulation six seconds, swaying as he did so and tottering from the knees, then whipped it to his side again, and stood at rigid attention. He seemed able to stand better that way, for his knees left off shaking.

"Who are you?" asked the Sirdar then.

"First Egyptian Foot, sir."

The crowd behind was leaning forward, listening; those that had been near enough to hear that gasped. The Sirdar's face changed suddenly to the look of cold indifference behind which a certain type of Englishman hides his emotion.

Then came the time-honored question, prompt as the ax of a guillotine—inevitable as Fate itself:

"Where are your colors?"

The fifth man—he who had issued the commands—fumbled with his tunic. The buttons were missing, and the front of it was fastened up with a string; his fingers seemed to have grown feeble; he plucked at it, but it would not come undone.

"Where are—"

The answer to that question should be like an echo, and nobody should need to ask it twice. But the string burst suddenly, and the first time of asking sufficed. The ragged, unkempt longhaired mummy undid his tunic and pulled it open.

"Here, sir!" he answered.

The colors, blood-soaked, torn—unrecognizable almost—were round his body! As the ragged tunic fell apart, the colors fell with it; Grogram caught them, and stood facing the Sirdar with them in his hand. His bare chest was seared with half-healed wounds and crisscrossed with the marks of floggings, and his skin seemed to be drawn tight as a mummy's across his ribs. He was a living skeleton!

The Sirdar sprang to his feet and raised his hat; for the colors of a regiment are second, in holiness, to the Symbols of the Church. The watching, listening crowd followed suit; there was a sudden rustling as a sea of hats and helmets rose and descended. The band of four, that had stood in stolid silence while all this was happening, realized that the moment was auspicious to play their other tune.

They had only one other, and they had played "The Campbells Are Coming" across the polo field; so up went the fifes, "Bang!" went the drum, and, "God save our gracious Queen" wailed the three in concert, while strong men hid their faces and women sobbed.

Grogram whipped his hand up to the answering salute, faced the crowd in front of him for six palpitating seconds, and fell dead at the Sirdar's feet.

And so they buried him; his shroud was the flag that had flown above the Sirdar at that ever-memorable match, and his soul went into the regiment.

They began recruiting it again next day round the blood-soaked colors he had carried with him, and the First Egyptian Foot did famously at the Atbara and Omdurman. They buried him in a hollow square formed by massed brigades, European and native regiments alternating, and saw him on his way with twenty-one parting volleys, instead of the regulation five. His tombstone is a monolith of rough-hewn granite, tucked away in a quiet corner of the European graveyard at Cairo—quiet and inconspicuous as Grogram always was—but the truth is graven on it in letters two inches deep:

HERE LIES A MAN

THEODORE ROSCOE

THEODORE ROSCOE (1906–1992) was a popular and prolific author for many of the great adventure and fantasy pulps, including *Wings, Flying Stories, Far East Adventure Stories, Fight Stories, Action Stories,* and the prestigious *Adventure* and *Argosy* magazines. Born in Rochester, New York, he wrote his first story when he was eight years old, published it himself, and sold copies, he once wrote, "for two pins each." His parents were world travelers and so was he; his childhood excursions would help to provide the exotic locales for many of his stories. Roscoe's first book was a mystery novel, *Murder on the Way!* (1935), followed by the cult classic *I'll Grind Their Bones* (1936). (Several of his pulp novels were published in book form in the 1980s and '90s, in very limited editions.) Roscoe also wrote several books about naval history, most notably the standard texts *United States Submarine Operations in World War II* (1949) and *United States Destroyer Operations in World War II* (1953), both published by the U.S. Naval Institute and still in print. His naval expertise was instrumental in his being named to a special presidential commission in the 1950s. Roscoe also penned the critically acclaimed nonfiction title *The Web of Conspiracy: The Complete Story of the Men Who Murdered Abraham Lincoln* (1959). In addition to his other work, he was a television writer for some years.

One of the staples of adventure pulps was romanticized stories of the French Foreign Legion, though they are seldom as humorous as the following retelling of the Medusa myth.

"Snake-Head" was first published in the January 7, 1939, issue of *Argosy*.

Let me live to be ten million, and I will not forget that creature like a living nightmare.

SNAKE-HEAD

THEODORE ROSCOE

PERHAPS, *MESSIEURS,* YOU DO NOT BELIEVE IN GORGONS WHOSE GLANCE TURNS MEN TO STONE. BUT HAVE YOU HEARD HOW THIBAUT CORDAY FACED A MODERN MEDUSA, WHILE HER SERPENTS SANG THEIR DEATH SONG?

I

"THAT IS a great story!" Old Thibaut Corday shut the book he had been reading with an enthusiastic bang. "It is a pity Monsieur Bulfinch could not give to the characters their right names. And of course he has exaggerated in the American fashion, and added a little here and there. But in general it is true, and told in picturesque style. I must write to the author and ask him how he found out about me."

I said, bewildered, "How he found out about *you?*"

"I am surprised to see the story in print, because I never told anybody. *Eh bien,* perhaps the Arab girl has told it. In one way or another it must have reached America, for here it is in a book. An adventure in which I figured, you comprehend."

I stared at Old Thibaut Corday in astonishment. I stared at the book in Old Thibaut Corday's hand in astonishment. There was the blue-eyed, cinnamon-bearded veteran of the French Foreign Legion, eighty-five years old at the most, and not looking a day over sixty. There was the book in his hand (some scholarly tourist must have left it by accident on the café table)— *Bulfinch's Mythology*!

"Is it not"—he misread my look—"an unusual coincidence? I have never told it to anybody, I repeat, for who would believe it? Then it crops up in a book which somebody chances to leave on our table here. Yes, the author must have heard it from the Arab girl, and he has given her version; had I told it to him, he could have been more accurate as to details. This woman he calls Medusa—she was a snake charmer. He has failed to explain about the victims she turned into stone. Also I do not quite understand the American colloquialisms: the writer describes me as having wings on my heels; I suppose that is a way of saying I ran very fast. *Enfin*, he says I flew. Another American way of saying I ran with great speed, I suppose."

I cried, "You—you think that story is about you?"

He stiffened at my incredulity. "Certainly it is about me! He has given me the fiction-name of Perseus. The princess he calls Andromeda. Or perhaps those are the names the Arab girl gave him. At any rate, here is the whole amazing account—the snake charmer, the people turned into marble and all the rest of it—even to the fight I put up at the last. There could not have been two such remarkable adventures in the world!"

"But that book is *Bulfinch's Mythology*!" I blurted out. "The story you've been reading is a classic. Every high-school student knows the story about Perseus and the Gorgon's head. Medusa was a Gorgon—a beautiful woman who had snakes growing out of her scalp instead of hair, and terrible eyes that turned everyone she saw into stone. The princess Andromeda was carried off into captivity, and Perseus, the young warrior, went to rescue her. But to save her he first had to kill the Gorgon. He appealed to Minerva, the Goddess of Wisdom, and Minerva gave him winged heels so that he could fly. So he flew to the Gorgon's cave and killed Medusa— didn't look at her face, but watched her reflection in his polished shield, and cut off her head at one whack!"

"Only it was a mirror!" Old Thibaut Corday corrected fiercely. "Instead of a shield, I used a mirror. The mirror the old Kabyle woman gave me!"

"But I'm trying to explain," I cried, "that the story about Perseus and Medusa is a myth. It isn't an American story. You've been reading the translation of an ancient Greek legend that was told in Athens two thousand years ago!"

"Greek legend? Athens? Two thousand years ago?" The old Legion veteran brought his fist down on the table. "But it happened with me not ten years ago when I was in the *Premièr Régiment* of the French Foreign Legion, and it was right here in North Africa on the border of Algiers! This woman you call—what?—a Gorgon?—this Medusa! Well, she lived in a cave in the mountains not far from the pass of El Kantara in the territory of the Kabyles. This princess Andromeda was an Arab princess taken captive by an enemy tribe. And I cut off the head of that snake charmer, too—I, Old Thibaut Corday—in that very cavern full of people turned into stone!"

A two-thousand-year-old fable come to life in the French Foreign Legion! This leathery old French soldier of fortune in the role of Perseus, hero of ancient Greek mythology! An Arab princess as Andromeda, and a snake charmer living in a cave full of people turned to stone! There was a story behind the shine in the old veteran's eyes, and I wanted to hear it. I had an idea it would beat the translation in *Bulfinch's Mythology* a mile!

And Old Thibaut Corday had hardly begun before I knew Professor Bulfinch and the ancient

Greek story-teller who invented the myth were going to be left far behind. Because they told the yarn as a fairy tale, and Old Thibaut Corday told it as truth—and just when I was about to call him a liar, he gave me a guarantee.

I do not know anything about Greece or Athens (Old Thibaut Corday began, with a suspicious look at the book at his elbow). There was a Greek in my Legion company once, but he did not last long. His name was Rosenapopolous, and he was killed in a surprise attack his first week on campaign. An Arab crept up behind him, and the sergeant bellowed, "Look out, Rosenapopolous!", but before the sergeant could get out the name, the Greek was hamstrung.

Come to think of it, that was the very campaign of which I speak. On the border of Algeria near Tunis. In the territory of the Kabyles. These Kabyles are one of the fiercest of Arab tribes, which means they are the most backward and most superstitious—another way of saying the most holy. They are Mohammedans, and they are mountaineers, as fanatical as maniacs, as tough as the barren ranges they occupy, as merciless as vultures. When they are not fighting the other Arab tribes, they are fighting the French, and they keep in practice for both by fighting among themselves. *Alors*, now that France has pacified and cleaned up Tunis, Mussolini has decided that he wants Tunis for himself. The Romans once conquered Algeria and Tunis, and Mussolini likes to call himself a Roman. With this intent, he announces himself as a friend of the Arabs. Ha! The only Arabs who will associate with him are these renegade Kabyles. It seems Mussolini has forgotten it was the Arabs who threw out the Romans to begin with; it is only the Foreign Legion of France that can control North Africa.

So it is the usual uprising. Mussolini sends his secret agents among the Kabyle renegades, and tells them to fight a holy war. Do you think those mountain tribesmen need any urging? *Bang!* A train is dynamited. *Slash!* A French girl

who has gone into the mountains to teach school has her throat cut. All this is very modern, our new diplomacy. Remains only for the War Department in Paris to put in a hurry call for the Foreign Legion.

Our detachment marched across Algeria, and we reached the mountain country of the Kabyles on the double quick. There the modern aspect of the campaign ended. Those mountains were old when the rest of this North African coast was cooling. They were old and burned-out and worn to the bone long before the Romans or the Arabs or Monsieur Mussolini or myself were ever heard of. Red iron crags and wind-swept ranges without a tree. Cliffs where the sun is a furnace by day, and one freezes at night. Peaks and canyons and boulders and rocks, and behind every rock a red-eyed Kabyle waiting to get a Foreign Legionnaire in the target sights of his gun.

Non, it was not the country to go marching in with a name like Rosenapopolous. Those Kabyle devils could strike like lightning and beat the echoes of their rifles on a disappearance. They jumped around on those rocky crags like goats. They vanished in the canyons like lizards going down a crack. We chased them, and we might as well have been chasing puffs of wind. We pursued them across precipices and into gorges, and we might as well have been pursuing shadows and ghosts. Rosenapopolous was not our only casualty on that expedition. Those Kabyle murderers made it hot for us from morning to night.

Even a name like Corday was too long. In a skirmish somewhere near the pass of El Kantara, I was captured. That was a hell of a thing, letting myself be captured by the Kabyles. We had been scouting up a canyon, and along in the middle of the afternoon I spotted one of those sharpshooting devils perched on a ledge up the canyon-wall like a hawk waiting for the mice to come along. The *salopard*! I let him have it. Lay on my stomach and trained my Lebel rifle on the speck of him visible up there, and let fly. *Bang!* That is war in the mountain country. What is it I have seen the children play in America—hide and seek? War in the mountain country is a game of hide and seek in which you must tag the enemy without ever giving him a chance to tag you.

But I did not kill the scoundrel. Instead of dying like a sportsman and a gentleman, he lay up there on that ledge and howled. Our heroes who stay home and draw the recruiting posters do not picture the enemy you have just shot as lying out in the sun somewhere, badly wounded and suffering. That Kabyle up there began to scream. He kept it up. I could see him sprawled as if his back were broken, and about every three minutes he uncorked a wail that did something to the muscles under my scalp.

I tried to walk away. I told myself that the devil deserved it. Besides, I had become separated from the rest of my companions, who had gone around a bend in the canyon and were busy with snipers around there. I could hear a lot of firing, and I started to join the skirmish, but the screams from the ledge came after me and held me back. *Dieu!* the fellow howled like a cat on a fence. It was hot up there on that cliff. He wanted a drink of water. Stuffing my fingers in my ears did not do any good. The trouble with me is, I am soft. *Non,* I am not a good soldier. I do not mind shooting at an enemy if he dies right away as he is supposed to. But if he lies down and screams from a broken back it hurts my conscience. At least I must return and finish the job.

So I started across the canyon to finish the job, but that Kabyle scoundrel was not reasonable. He had fallen with his head behind a boulder, and I could not arrange him in my gun-sights. I had to climb the canyon-wall to reach him, and I did not like that. *Sacré!* I had to climb all the way to his ledge.

Now I am this kind of a fool. I can shoot a man from a half a mile away, but at fifteen feet it is something else again. At fifteen feet a man is no longer a target. Wounded with a bullet in his ribs and his rifle tumbled into a crevice, he is not even an adversary. *Non,* he is not even an Arab Kabyle. He is a man.

Worse than that, this brigand I had shot was a youth. Hardly with a beard on his chin. It did not matter if he had intended to murder me— *enfin,* he did not know any better. His parents had brought him up wrong, and his religion promised him a front seat in Paradise for every Unbeliever that he killed, and the agents of Mussolini had given him good Christian advice by telling him to dislike the French. For this he lay with his ribs broken by a bullet. Here was the result of his family training, his politics and his religion. He looked up at me with his big brown Arab eyes, and he begged in the Kabyle dialect for a drink of water.

"All right, here is a drink," I told him. "Also here is a bottle of iodine and a bandage, although I know very well that when you are back on your feet next month you will repay this silly sentimentalism by trying to kill me. I am sorry I did not shoot you through the head. With better luck I may be able to bring down your father."

I brought down his father, all right. *Sacré nom de Dieu!* Scarcely had I uttered the hope, when his father, his brothers, his uncles and about sixteen cousins came down from a rocky overhang above like an avalanche of demons on my head. Those infernal relatives of that Kabyle boy had heard his caterwauling, and they had come hot-footing to the rescue. *Thumpety-thump-thump-thump* their sandals landed on the ledge around me. I had no time to aim or even swing my gun. Those sheeted brigands jumped on me like spiders, and before I could budge a finger I was bound neck to foot in a web of leather rope.

I was sorry, then, I had pulled that little Red Cross stunt. You bet I was! That boy's father did not appreciate it. All he could figure was that I had shot his son, and he had a gleam in his eye as nasty as a tarantula. I was slung up and carried off like a trussed pig. Old Man Kabyle—he was a big black-whiskered pirate—carried his wounded boy in his arms, and off we went across the cliff-tops. I do not know where we went, but when evening came down we were still traveling. Up and down and over the rocky crags; in and out through narrow canyons; across a burned-out valley of huge boulders, and up a mountain wall as steep as the side of a building.

That was the hell of a trail. At every mile the mountains became more desolate, more barren, more like the middle of nowhere. Those tribesmen were taking me beyond any hope of rescue; taking me off the map. They were traveling like the wind, and pulling in their shadows behind them. And all the way along that trail, that black-whiskered Kabyle with his son in his arms kept turning his head to look at me. Sacred stove! what looks. His forehead knotted with rage. His black eyes coated with a shining enamel of hate. Ah, but there was a speculation in those black eyes, too. A thoughtfulness. An inspired cunning. I knew what he was doing, and the sweat poured out on my forehead like creme-de-menthe. He was inventing tortures, you understand. He was thinking up all the nice things he would do to me because I had put a bullet in his son. I knew it was going to go mighty hard with my arms and legs and nervous system when we got to that Kabyle camp.

You have heard the first rule of the French Foreign Legion? Never allow yourself to be taken alive by an Arab! Especially if that Arab happens to be a Kabyle. When it comes to torturing an enemy, a Kabyle can be twice as cruel as a Spanish aristocrat, and a Spanish aristocrat is the sort of man who can bomb a kindergarten and do it with a prayer. Only a Kabyle can be more cunningly savage. It was the Kabyles who invented burying a man up to his neck in sand and covering his head with honey to bring the ants. It was the Kabyles who invented stuffing a man's mouth with sticks of dynamite and lighting a long fuse that he could watch for three hours. I could see that my black-bearded captor was thinking up something new for my particular case. I was not wrong about it, either.

We reached the Kabyle camp at moonrise, and it was a picture I will not soon forget. The black felt tents of the Arabs pitched on a bare plateau. Purple mountains ringed around. Goats and mangy dogs and a collection of old hags waiting to see the show. My heart went through the bottom of my boots, I can tell you. When those old women saw that wounded Kabyle boy they set up a wailing that turned my blood to icewater. You know how Arab women can wail? *Hoo-hoo-hooooo!* Well, I found out something. Old Blackbeard was the sheik of this tribe! I had shot the son of the sheik! Not only that, it had been that boy's wedding day. His bride-to-be was the princess of a neighboring Kabyle tribe, and she was on her way through the mountains even then, due to arrive in camp for the marriage ceremony around midnight.

Figure to yourself what was going to happen to me for shooting the son of a Kabyle sheik on his wedding day! *Non!* but you could not figure it. The unconscious boy was carried into a tent, and then the lamentations of those women turned into foamings at the mouth. They wanted to claw me to pieces, but the sheik had a better idea. I must be saved for the wedding party that was coming over the mountains—the bride-to-be would doubtless enjoy stabbing me through the heart. Meantime I was to be made as uncomfortable as possible. Ah, yes. The sheik had thought up a number of ways to make me regret I had shot his son.

Presently I was pinned to the ground. Flat on my back with my hands and feet fastened to stakes. I believe the term is spread-eagled. My shirt was torn off, and in the process I had been scratched up a bit. Not fatally, of course, for the idea was to keep me fairly alive. With this in view, I was revived every time I fainted, and I fainted pretty often. I fainted when I realized my Legion comrades were miles away and never in the world could find this isolated mountain hide-out. I fainted when an old woman came out of a tent with a big brass bowl in her hands, followed by the sheik arrived with a squeaking, biting rat in his grip. The bowl was placed upside-down on my stomach, and the rat was put under the bowl, and a little fire was built on top of the bowl. The invention was most ingenious. When the fire heated the bowl, it would get pretty hot inside, and the rat would start to dig. You will pardon me for fainting again.

Now you are probably wondering what all this has to do with a snake charmer and a beheading accomplished by a mirror and a cave full of people turned into stone. You are wondering what this has to do with this story of Medusa and Perseus. *Oui,* I see you are wishing I would get to that part of the adventure, and at last I am there. I do not like to talk of that rat-and-bowl incident, either.

To say the less of it, the bowl was just growing warm and the rat was spitting on his hands preparatory to picking up the shovel when there was an explosion of yells in the night, and the bridal party arrived. *You-wow!* They came into camp like that. Robes swirling, beards disheveled, the whole crowd hollering and leaping into the scene like a hurricane.

I was having my own troubles, but it came to me that something was wrong with this wedding bunch, something abnormal. The local Kabyles began to run around hollering to Allah, and Blackbeard the Sheik, who had been supervising my delicate operation, went over me with a bound, and rushed around in wild confab with the leader of the bride's crowd. Lucky for me, that tumult! In leaping my carcass, Old Blackbeard kicked over the fiery bowl on my stomach. In the dust and excitement and uproar, Monsieur Rat scampered off hickory-dickory-dock. Sacred stove! but that was a close call for me. A terrible calamity had befallen this wedding party, it seemed. Through the bedlam I managed to learn that the bride had been kidnapped.

Perhaps you think I did not bless those kidnappers. Trooping through the mountains, the wedding party had been ambushed by an enemy tribe. Those Kabyles had more feuds on their social calendar than they could keep track of, and these enemy Arabs had shot up the procession and waltzed off with the bride. But this was something more than your ordinary kidnapping. I gathered it was a whole lot more. The captive bride was a princess, but she was not being held for ransom. The Arabs who had grabbed her were pretty sore at this particular Kabyle clan, and they were taking her to a witch of some kind—a sorceress who was going to give her the evil eye.

"The Snake-Woman! The Snake-Woman!"

II

That is what the bride's party called her, and didn't those Kabyles howl to Allah at the mention of her name. *Dieu!* the whole camp got down and slammed their foreheads on the ground, and Old Blackbeard ran in a circle with his hands in the air, wailing to Allah.

"She is lost! The princess is lost! One look from the Snake-Woman's eye, and the princess will be turned into stone!"

Mon ami, I was just about done at that point, but when I heard Old Blackbeard yell that, I pricked up my ears. I told you those Kabyles were a superstitious bunch. So! And when Blackbeard yelled that business about the princess being turned into stone, there came to me a rumor I had heard in the Arab bazaars—one of those North African rumors that go whispering around the mosques and up the alleys of the Kasbah and in and out of the coffee dens to keep the population in a stew. What? A rumor about a wizardess who lived in a cave and had a stare that turned every man she saw into marble. A legend, of course. A yarn on the tongue of cameleers. But there was a little one-eyed rug merchant in Bou Saada who told me he had seen one of the victims this sorceress had petrified, and he swore by the three-fingered hand of Mohammed's wife that the story was true. I did not believe him, that liar! And I did not believe Old Blackbeard, the night of the kidnapping. But Blackbeard believed the business, I could see that, and I was mighty glad he did believe it. Running around in circles, he forgot about me. Those other Kabyles forgot about me, too.

"The princess will be turned into stone! Merciful Allah! The princess will be turned into stone!"

What a lament those devils set up. The women came out of their tents and tore their hair. The men ran up and down in their dirty robes, praying. In a sweat of terror and relief, I lay there spread-eagled, and I thanked heaven for this *brouhaha* which had thrown my captors into a panic.

"Save her!" The bride's father was leader of the ambushed party, and he howled at Blackbeard to do something. "How can we save her?"

"It is the custom to leave gold at the entrance to the Snake-Woman's cave!" Blackbeard moaned. "Much gold to appease the witch!"

"But it will leave me poverty-stricken," the bride's father wailed. "And when my brothers left such tribute at the mouth of the Snake-Woman's lair, their kidnapped children were never returned. Much gold have our tribesmen bestowed on this demoness. In the past to no avail!" He lifted his arms, squalling at his warriors in despair. "Five camels and ten hairs from the Beard of Mohammed to the man who rescues my daughter from the Snake-Woman's cave!"

"And I double the reward!" Blackbeard thundered. "Let the bravest of the Kabyles stand forward. As father of the warrior to whom the princess was betrothed, I double the reward for her rescue!"

Ten camels and all those sacred relics of Mohammed must have been a fortune to those mountain pariahs, but it did not bring the bravest of them forward. Those tribesmen swore and groaned and brandished their rifles, but I saw no volunteers. I began to comprehend that this Snake-Woman was a bugaboo of a pretty high order.

Alors, the father of the bride was on the verge of epilepsy. "By the Flames of Gehenna! is there no warrior among the Kabyles willing to chance his life for a princess of the blood of Mohammed? Is my daughter to pass into eternity accursed, spellbound in a bondage of stone? You!" he flung at Blackbeard, raving. "Where is this son of whom you boast? Where is this warrior to whom I gave my daughter in marriage—

aaaah, that she was on her way to the wedding this very night! Is he son of a sheik or son of a jackal that he does not come forward to attempt his bride's deliverance!"

"Halouf ben halouf!" Blackbeard roared. "Father of a pig! Is my son to be blamed because he lies close to death with the bullet of an Unbeliever in his breast? The calamity on your house is only equaled by that on mine! If your daughter remains bewitched in stone, it is only for the wounding of my son—Allah save him—by the Infidel you see captive over there!"

Holy Saint Catherine! That black-whiskered sheik pointed a finger at me, and the maddened crowd piled at me to shred me to pieces. "It is he! The Infidel, who has brought disaster upon us!" . . . "Allah's curse on this *Roumi* who has caused us this blight!" . . . "Butcher the French dog!" . . . "Cut out his eyes!"

Can you see me staked out on the ground, and that blood-thirsty wedding mob coming at me? Bones of the Little Corsican! I might have known those Kabyles would hold me responsible for everything. They had to wreak their vengeance on somebody, and I was it. If I wanted to live thirty more seconds I had to do some fast thinking, and I never thought faster in my life.

"Wait!" I screamed at Blackbeard, who was nearly on top of me with his knife. "I can save the kidnapped princess for you! I am not afraid of this Snake-Woman who turns your people into stone! Let me go to her cave, and I will return the princess to your tribe unharmed!"

How I ever got that out of my mouth, and in the Kabyle dialect besides, I do not know. But I screeched like a steam whistle, and the cry took effect. Those wolves stopped in their tracks, and Blackbeard came up short, his dagger not six inches from my nose.

"Pig!" he spat down at me. "Dog of a Christian, what do you know of this sorceress who changes men into rock with one look of her eye?"

"Only that the magic has no effect on a soldier of true courage! Behold!" I gave him. "I am unafraid! Tell me the lair of this witch, and I will go there single-handed where all your warriors fear to go. No woman as yet has been able to put the evil eye on me! Lead me to her, and I will return the lost princess to the tent of your son, in reward for which I ask only my life!"

That was a bold speech, was it not? The boldest I ever made. Also it was the sheerest bluff, one hundred percent bluff without a card in my hand to support it. But in a corner like that one must bid as if he held five aces. Too, I know Arabs. A plea for mercy is as useless before an Arab as a missionary's prayer would be on a tiger. Bluffers themselves, they are always surprised when they are met with bluff.

But surprised was not the word for it that night. They were stunned. There I was staked out on the ground like a carcass ready to be skinned alive, yet squalling that I was braver than they, offering to slay their witch-woman. It worked. By the very insolence, the unexpectedness of it, it worked.

"Hold!" That black-whiskered sheik flung up his hand. Rage on his face struggled with unbelief. "You hear what the Infidel has said?" he wheeled on the crowd. "Ha!" he flung at me. "You are willing, then, to face the Snake-Woman? By Allah's holy word! If you are as brave as you boast, perhaps we will give you this chance. Return the Princess Naja to her father unharmed, and my son's forgiveness for his injury will be assured. Attempt now to withdraw this bold offer, and you will be sorry!"

There was a glitter in his eye that convinced me I would be more than sorry if I backed down. And at the same time there was a gleam behind the glitter that suggested I was going to be sorry, anyway. That tarantula was accepting my offer a little too readily for my comfort. *Oui,* he was a little too quick on granting me this reprieve, and I had an idea that perhaps I had jumped from the frying pan into the fire.

But I had no time for subtleties, just then. All I wanted was to regain my feet from that spread-eagled posture. My stomach was on the verge of collapse from that rat-and-bowl business, and I was ready to grab at any straw to delay the murder that was waiting to pounce on me.

"Free me that I may start at once!" I bluffed, and louder. "Direct me to this evil-eyed spellbinder. But give me a weapon with which to slay her, and I will rid your people from her curse."

Old Blackbeard grinned at that. "You shall have my own scimitar," he assured me in a suddenly sweetened voice. "Up, dog of a Christian, and you will start at once!" Just to show me he was not quite my best friend, he spat in my face before giving his brigands the order to untie me.

I felt pretty blue when I was standing upright, however. Not for a minute could I stop bluffing, and I wanted to collapse from the strain. Picture me bare to the belt, my britches torn to rags, my torso covered with welts, and a big red circle on my stomach where that brass bowl had branded me. I was plastered with dirt and my chin was bleeding. *Non,* I was hardly this hero called Perseus in the account which you say is a Greek fairy tale, but I will wager I outbluffed any Greek in any fairy tale that night.

"Lead me on!" I cried in the voice of a stage actor volunteering his life for Napoleon. "Where is this wizardess to be found?" I tell you, I swaggered in such a way that those Moslem devils stared at me in awe.

But Old Blackbeard suspected a trick, and he was not going to give me a chance for any escaping act. He looped a rope around my neck, and clung to me as if I were a poodle on a leash. Never for a second was he forgetting I had put a bullet in his son.

"The Snake-Woman," he told me in that softened voice that was like poisoned sugar— "the Snake-Woman lives on the mountain, half a night's march distant. Do not think to evade us on the trail, for you go there as our captive until we reach the mouth of the cave. It is there I will give you my scimitar, and only for the sake of the Princess Naja will you proceed into the cave with Allah's blessing."

His black eyes glittered into mine as he gave me these instructions, and he concluded with a whisper that crawled into my ear like a cobra, "But I do not think Allah's blessing will avail. No man has ever returned alive from the Cave of the Petrified People."

Well, that was encouraging, not so? To learn I had offered to visit a place from which no man had ever returned alive! It was a not cheerful prospect, just when I was trying to pump up a little courage. I did not like Blackbeard for telling me about the Cave of the Petrified People.

Even less did I like the looks of awe those other ruffians were giving me. There was a lot of whispering and hobnobbing, and a big murmur went through the crowd as Blackbeard gave a yank on my leash to signal the start. There was no doubt those devils thought I had taken the worse of two evils in choosing this Snake-Woman instead of ordinary death.

"The ignorant curs!" I said to myself. "They fear this woman, whoever she is, more than death, itself. Am I—a soldier of the Legion—to be unnerved by this superstitious Arab nonsense?"

Sacred pipe! I was lucky to be alive right then. It was no time to worry about witches. I told myself there was no such thing as witchcraft and men being turned into stone. North Africa was full of fake wonder-workers and hoodoo men, and some hag in a cave had fooled these primitive brigands into believing she had supernatural power.

Enfin, I must fool them, myself, and I squared my shoulders and tried to look like Saint George on his way to fight the Dragon. But as I stumbled off through the moonlight, on the end of Blackbeard's rope, I had a qualm. I was glad to be leaving that camp. You bet I was. Only it came to me that if there were such things as vampires, hoodoos and witch-women, all of them inhabited those Kabyle mountains in North Africa.

Dead in daylight, those mountains at night were ghosts. In the moonlight the cliffs stood up white and sheer, while the canyons below were bottomless seas of ink. Pale peaks made a caravan of spectres under the stars; misshapen boulders were ghostly sentinels guarding the trail; fantastic black crags leaned down to watch us, like giants ready to pounce. A tremendous silence wrapped those mountains. As if every rock and stone and granite slab were holding its breath, listening. Once in Egypt I felt that same kind of hush come out of the Sphinx, and I would have given a thousand dollars to hear a bugle call in the middle of it as we marched from that camp that night.

But I did not hear any bugle calls, *mon gar'*. All I heard was the scuff of sandals, the whisper of Arab cloaks, the puffy breathing of my captors stealing along beside me, half invisible in the dark. That entire wedding crowd had come along to see the fun, and with Blackbeard tugging that rope around my neck, I staggered up the trail like a lost soul on his way to Hades with an escort of apparitions.

I did not like the walk Old Blackbeard took me on that night. At places the trail followed the rim of a precipice, an abyss so black and deep that when a pebble went over the edge it was absorbed as if by a vacuum. There was a canyon barely wide enough to squeeze through, and a ladder of jagged crags where a misstep would have plunged one into an ocean of nothing. We saw no goats or jackals on that trip—they had all been killed by falling off those cliffs. It was a nasty piece of mountain-climbing with a rope around my neck and that mob of cutthroats clinging to my heels. I began to wonder if I would not have been safer on the ground with my arms and legs tied to stakes.

"Where are the fiends taking me?" I groaned in my mind. "I can believe no man has returned alive from this witch's cave; what man could get there alive to begin with?"

The altitude was making me dizzy up there under the moon, and at the same time the silence was working on my imagination. Suppose this Snake-Woman did have some evil power? I had boasted a little when I declared that no woman had ever put the eye on me. Now that I was nearing the cave of the hag, my counterfeit confidence was failing me. I remembered how the little one-eyed rug merchant in Bou Saada had rolled his eye, describing the powers of this witch. Certainly the creature must have had something up her sleeve to frighten these bandits. As we neared her lair, my escort began to stare and peer as if they saw all the spectres of Tophet in the moonlight ahead.

"Slowly!" Blackbeard wheeled suddenly with uplifted finger. "We are almost there. Should the Snake-Woman be out of her hole, she might turn us all into marble at a glance."

Another time I might have laughed at the way those Kabyle gunmen hung back on the path. But I did not laugh that night. There was a witchery in the silence of those mountains, something that made me break out in goose pimples. I could hear the father of the kidnapped bride moaning prayers to Allah. Around me my captors muttered in fear. Blackbeard gave a jerk on my halter, and ordered me to walk ahead of him. I walked ahead, and the sheeted crowd came creeping at my heels like hunters moving up on a lion's den behind a decoy. I was the decoy, and I did not like the part. The trail climbed on and up through a jungle of silent rocks, and every few feet Blackbeard would give me a kick to hurry me up. I cursed myself for having sniped at his son, I can tell you. I cursed myself double for the Red-Cross-nurse act that had invited my capture.

Alors, the path made a sudden upward twist, and Blackbeard gave a yank on the leash. "There is the place!" he snarled from behind me. "Go up the mountainside and look in, you dog. Demonstrate the courage of which you brag." He was paying out the rope in his hands to let me go forward, and I saw in the mountain ahead an opening that looked like the door of a coal mine. If you think I wanted to look into that opening, you are wrong. But it was either that or Blackbeard, so I took the opening.

Do you know how the entrance of a coal mine looks at night? Well, that mouth in the mountainside was like a mine-shaft. A square door shored up with slabs of granite, and then a shaft that dipped down into the mountain at an angle of ninety degrees. Moonlight fell down into the shaft as far as darkness at the bottom, and there was a tunnel down there, and the blackness in that tunnel was the darkest black I had ever seen. I got a whiff of air that smelled as though it had been buried about ten thousand years, and I pulled back my head with a gasp of fear.

"The tunnel," Blackbeard called to me, "leads into the Cave of the Petrified People. Lucky for you the Snake-Woman was not out."

"But how can I go down and kill her?" I asked hopefully. "There are no steps to descend."

"We will let you down on the rope," Blackbeard snarled. "That is how the Snake-Woman's victims are brought to her. They are let down on a rope, and then the rope is cut so they cannot climb out. Shots drive them into the tunnel where the Snake-Woman seizes them. They never return."

That black-mawed cave sucked in his words and echoed them. A hundred voices seemed to mumble, "Never—"

The father of the kidnapped girl wrung his hands. "Hurry, hurry!" he cawed at me. "There is yet a chance the Snake-Woman has not transformed my daughter. It is written that one is safe while the Snake-Woman sleeps, for the magic is in her eye. *Mektoob!* It may be she is still asleep."

"The shots always wake her up," Blackbeard said grimly. "She catches her victims in the tunnel and turns them to stone. I have gone down to spy in the tunnel, and I have seen."

"And how am I to get out when the witch is slain?" I asked.

Blackbeard nodded fiercely. "We will wait for you. I have given my oath, and we will wait until sunrise. Return with the Princess Naja, and we will haul you out. Fail, dog, and you remain here to eternity."

Nom de Dieu! It was either remaining in that

hole until eternity, or going to eternity then and there on the mountainside. Any way I looked at it, eternity was staring me in the face, but I decided I would rather be petrified than chopped to pieces. So I went down.

III

I did not go on winged heels as in the Greek legend. The wings on my heels came later. I went down that moonlit mine-shaft on a strong piece of hemp, and when I reached the bottom I learned where that expression comes from—to be at the end of one's rope. I was at the end of my rope when I faced that black tunnel, I can tell you. All the way up the mountain I had been wildly planning how I might hack my way out of the mob at the moment Blackbeard gave me his scimitar, as promised. But that sheik was too smart for me again. He told me I would receive the blade when I reached the bottom of the mine-shaft and the rope was hauled up, and he went on to add that some day he would come down and get it out of my marble hand.

He was afraid to go near that mine-shaft, you comprehend. The rope was looped under my arms; twenty feet from the mine-mouth, Blackbeard and his crowd stood back to pay it out; I went down with a series of jerks that almost broke my neck. Then when the rope was hauled up, Blackbeard sent his wife to throw down to me the scimitar.

Picture me at the bottom of that shaft—when I looked up and saw the wrinkled face of an Arab woman peering down at me. *"Roumi,"* she called in a low, hoarse voice. "Here is the blade!"

That did not surprise me, for I know how Arabs treat their wives. But instead of a blade, she was clutching a piece of glass in her down-stretched hand. A little round piece of glass that reflected the moonray. I thought Old Blackbeard was playing me some trick, and my heart went through the soles of my boots. Then I heard the old woman's whisper.

"Catch the mirror, *Roumi*. Do not let it break. You tried to help my son after you shot him, and now I will try to help you. A mirror is your only chance against the Snake-Woman."

Well, that surprised me a bit. I had been cursing myself for that Red Cross stunt, and I was staggered by the old Arab woman's gratitude. I was so surprised that I caught the little mirror as she let it fall. I gripped it tight and tilted my face to hear her speak again.

"Do not look at the Snake-Woman," came her low-voiced call. "Do not look at her face, but watch her in the mirror. One stare from her eye would change you into stone." She pulled up her face-cloth hurriedly. "The Black Sheik would kill me for helping you, but you saved the life of our son."

Then she threw down the scimitar. The big blade struck near my boots with a clang, and I snatched it up and spun at the tunnel-mouth, expecting God knew what to rush out at me. Nothing rushed out. Nothing but blackness and a silence that made the hush on the mountainside din-like in comparison. I lifted my eyes to the opening overhead, but the old Arab woman was gone. Can you see me at the bottom of that moony shaft, scimitar clutched in one hand, mirror in the other, staring up at a little patch of night and stars? In front of me was that tunnel, a black throat breathing stale air. I did not want to go into that tunnel after a kidnapped Arab princess, my friend.

But if I was not back with the princess by sunrise, I would stay in that hole till eternity. Clutching scimitar and mirror, I said good-bye to Thibaut Corday, and I crept into the tunnel.

Now that tunnel was a detail they left out in the story of Perseus. Me, I think this Perseus had it soft. There was no time-limit set on Perseus, and he did not go through a tunnel. I wish I could describe to you my feelings as I went into that corridor in the earth, but it would take a nerve specialist to describe them. Consider what I had been through before I started that underground stroll. But that rat-and-bowl incident and the close shave from being flayed to death—those were pleasantries compared to the nerve-strain of that tunnel.

I do not suppose they had tunnels like that in Greece. Only in North Africa would you find such a thing. They talk of the St. Goddard Tunnel in the Alps. Well, that subway in the Kabyle mountains was dug a few years before the St. Goddard job. Quite a few years before! My boots in that passage stirred a dust as thick as smoke, and the air was staler than the atmosphere in a pharaoh's tomb.

Black? It was so black in that passage that I thought I had gone blind. I put out a hand and groped along the wall, moving like a mole. The tunnel zigzagged and bent, and at each successive bend I expected something terrible to happen. But nothing happened. Every few seconds I would stop to listen. I could hear nothing. A few steps farther on I would halt to peer. I could see nothing. There are times, my friend, when nothing is worse than something, and that was one of the times. The suspense was terrific. Sweat poured down my forehead, and blood pounded in my ears. After about twenty minutes of creeping along like a blind man in a haunted catacomb, I would have welcomed anything. A dozen times I started to turn back, but the thought of seeing sunrise over that mine-shaft pushed me on.

"There is no such thing as witchcraft!" I kept saying to myself. "There is no such thing as a woman's eye which changes men to stone."

And another thought bolstered my bluff. Perhaps I could find a side-passage, an exit, an escape from this subterranean hole. Hope springs eternal in the human breast, not so? I grabbed at that idea as a drowning man at a straw. *Dieu!* I fumbled along that invisible wall praying for an exit like one of those drainage mains which are offshoots of the Paris sewers. Funny how the wish is father to the thought. The more I wished for it, the more I became convinced I would find such an exit. The hope stiffened my legs. I hurried my pace. Presently I was walking faster. In that blind tunnel of zigzags and bends, I began to run. I was getting away! I had bluffed myself out of the Black Sheik's clutches, and I was going to get out of this tunnel.

Perhaps I even laughed a little at how easy it would be, for I have a memory of laughter that mocked the blank walls. The scimitar sweated in my hand and I told myself, "You'll find the way, Corday!"

Then, *bump!* Headlong I ran into an obstacle that hurled me backward in the dark. Solid rock that got in my way. A wall? Blindly I put out my hand, groping. The passage made a bend, there, and I had collided with a projecting boulder. The thing jutted out to block my path like a knee. Cursing, I ran my hand over the smooth curve of stone, trying to squeeze my way around. My blind hand went over the stone, and froze. It *was* a knee!

My friend, I jerked my hand away and stood there in the dark with every hair at attention on my head. In the blackness I had palmed a woman's knee! Do you think a soldier of the French Foreign Legion could mistake such an article? But no Legionnaire had ever come across a knee like that one! That was a stone knee—a marble knee! There was a woman there in that black tunnel, and her short skirt was blown back above her knee, and she was running. Only she wasn't running. In that pose she did not move an inch. She was frozen in stone.

And for the wink of an eye, I, too, was petrified.

Who wouldn't be?

Monsieur believes that I collided with a stone woman there in that tunnel? Too polite, *monsieur*. I see you are skeptical, but I tell you I am speaking the truth. I was skeptical, too, at first. Recovering from shock, I groped out again, and caught an arm. I figured this was my imagination, also. Until I put my hand on her face. That convinced me, on my oath! She had been running in my direction, and she was running still—in rock.

"The princess!" All the breath leaked out of me at that. The woman was wearing an Arab robe, and that was stone, too. "It must be the Arab princess, and the Snake-Woman caught her trying to escape."

Can't you hear me mumbling those words as I jittered there?

Now we are coming to the part where I had wings on my heels. The panic that came over me gave me wings. *Oui*, I flew. But in terror I failed to realize that I had squeezed past the woman and was running in the wrong direction. That tunnel had so many twists and bends I did not realize I was going toward the Snake-Woman's cave. The shock of that woman in the passage had put out of commission the compass in my head. I had not gone fifteen bounds before I ran into another obstacle. *Slam!* Head-on, I collided with a fat man.

He was dressed in Arab robes, too, and he was carrying a spear and he had a curly beard. I know he had a beard, because I tried to grab it. But it was not a beard of hair, my friend, and his stomach was not soft like the stomachs of other fat men. It was a beard of stone and a stomach as hard as concrete, and he was standing there at the side of the passage as stiff and stupid as a Prussian guardsman on parade.

I leaped back from him with a yell that made the echoes a hundred wailing banshees. I leaped and ran.

I do not know what direction I went after that. Terror robbed me of my senses. That tunnel was a black, insane nightmare, and I fled like a sightless idiot through a crowd. *Oui*, there were other figures in that passage. Men and women running, crouching, doubled in postures of agony or standing rigid in fear. I collided with them at the turns; brushed past them on the straightaway. They did not move, those creatures in that tunnel. They were so much stone. I ran full-tilt into a child, and my blade clanged sparks against his face as if I had struck an anvil.

I went mad with fright in that tunnel. It is bad enough bumping into people in the dark, but when you know those people are not flesh

and blood, it is something else. *Mère de Dieu!* I rushed on in a daze of terror, and then suddenly I was in a place where I almost lost what remained of my sanity.

The tunnel made a sharp leftward bend, and I rushed out into the middle of it before I could stop. Into the middle of what? Into the middle of a great domed cavern, a vast underground room as big as the interior of Notre Dame. It was lighted like a cathedral, too—which is to say, dim and shadowy with hushed blue shafts of light slanting down from above, corners shrouded in darkness, arches indistinct in gray dusk. But there were no gentle candles to relieve this gloom. The illumination was moonlight sifting through a great crack in the ceiling, an eerie incandescence from half a million miles overhead. And, as in a cathedral, the cavernous hush was broken by a low, murmurous buzzing; but the sound did not come from people telling their beads.

Non, the people in that cavern were not saying their prayers. They were not saying anything. There must have been a hundred of them there in the dimness, and their silence was the silence of the deaf and dumb and dead. It was a silence more extraordinary than death, for those people were posed in attitudes of life. Robed warriors there were, poised to throw uplifted spears. Women hugging children in their arms. A nude girl with an urn on her shoulder, looking sideways in fear. An old man bent on a staff, peering near-sightedly over an upraised lantern. In a far, dark corner a half-naked man—a porter evidently—in the act of escaping around a pillar with a huge round bundle on his back. A staring fellow with a pitchfork in his hands.

All these and more, a company frozen in dread, stood guard in that whispering chamber of horrors.

Word of honor, there were animals in it, too. A deer had somewhere wandered into that place, and the huntress who had followed the beast had just laid her hand on the animal's neck. It had happened a long time ago, I could see. The huntress carried a bow and arrow, and judging from the cobwebs, she looked as if she had been there for ten thousand years. All those people were covered with cobwebs, coated with dust. *Oui*, they leaped and crouched and ran and brandished spears in a hundred different poses of action, but their gestures were motionless; dust coated their bulging muscles and straining thighs. They had been caught, you comprehend. Like Lot's wife who had looked back and been turned into salt, those people had been petrified. Only they had been turned into stone.

Seeing those stone corpses, I almost turned into stone, myself. No such thing as witchcraft? Well, I wish you could have seen those people posed there in the gloom, their expressions fixed in marble, their gestures trapped in stone. *Dieu!* it needed but a key to unlock that spell—a magic word to bring them back to life, the spearmen throwing, the huntress catching that deer, the women running with their babes. A terrible sorcery had mummified those people into solid rock. You would have believed in sorcery, too, had you seen that crowd in the moon-shadowed dimness of that vast, eerie cavern, *monsieur*.

And the murmuring buzz that was like the muffled droning of prayer? Well, that murmuring buzz was the warning signal of a congregation of reptiles. Listen! That cavern was alive with snakes. As my vision cleared a little from the first daze of shock, I saw the floor of that cave was crawling. Did this fiction character, Perseus, have anything like that? He did not! The only snakes he had to contend with were in the Gorgon woman's hair; me, I saw a whole den of reptiles, hundreds of snakes. Fat snakes and thin snakes. Long snakes and short snakes. Rattlesnakes, *monsieur*! Everywhere! That rock-walled cavern was a perfect breeding ground for the things; they hung from every cornice, coiled in corners, writhed out of cracks in the wall, wriggled around the ankles of the stone people.

I tell you, that cave was humming and droning like a beehive, and those snakes were getting angrier by the second. Something in a distant corner had disturbed them. Heads up and buzzing, they were swarming around a stone

pedestal like a mass of cooking spaghetti, and when I saw what was on that pedestal the last bit of bluff leaked out of me. There was a figure on that pedestal, a white-robed woman standing rigid with her hands up over her face. At first I thought she was stone like the other figures in the dimness; then I saw the figure was alive.

A girl! A flesh and blood girl, in a pose of terror, too frightened to move. *Ventre bleu!* when I saw the gleam of moonlight on her dark young hair, I could feel my own limbs numbing. About sixty snakes had surrounded her pedestal, and there was enough poison in that stewing batch to have killed every girl in North Africa.

IV

"Jump!" I screamed in Kabyle. "The snakes are climbing up the pedestal! Jump!" That was a fool thing to do because it woke up every snake in the place. The murmur became a tremendous rattling, as if a horde of unseen voodoo doctors were shaking their skeletal beads.

The Arab girl's scream, smothered by her fingers, hardly reached me. "I cannot jump!" she wailed. "I dare not take my hands from my face. The Snake-Woman will see me!"

That gave me something to choke on. You bet it did. I was not afraid of those rattlesnakes. I had on my elephant-hide Legion *brodequins*—those big nail-studded marching boots that come up to the calf and are thick enough to ricochet a bullet. Snakes were something within my experience. What I could not cope with were those people of stone, the wizardry that had petrified them.

"Where is the Snake-Woman?" I bawled. Believe me, I was peering into the gloom ahead of me, expecting any second to be stacked up in marble. I did not see any demoness there, and the anticipation was something I could not stand. "Where is she hiding? Where?"

Then, before the Arab girl could answer, I saw her. I saw her in the mirror which I was clutching in my numbed left hand. She was behind me, you comprehend. Emerging from an aperture in the cavern wall; stepping through a curtain of gray cobwebs out onto a big marble platform furnished with a marble throne. *Oui*, she came out through the spiderwebs like a queen from behind a portiere, but the wickedest ruler in history never made such an entrance. Never!

Let me live to be ten million, and I will not forget the creature who walked out on that platform. Just the sight of her in a mirror made me wish I was back in that Kabyle camp with a bowl-prisoned rat on my appendix. That witch was twice the bulk of an ordinary woman. Built like an Amazon. But then, from throat to ankles cloaked in an evil purple mantle, a billowing shapeless robe that might have been robbed from the shoulders of a long-dead monarch, heavy with mildew and green decay.

This Gorgon called Medusa in the story of Perseus—at least she had a figure. My North African witch was a bloated monstrosity. Only in her face was there the semblance of anything feminine—a dead white face expressionless as a plaster death mask save for bulging, cruel eyes that rolled between hooded white lids like the eyes of a crocodile. Then around her neck, like a fur, a coiled rattlesnake! Another looped over her left shoulder, and a third wrapped around her left arm. But those were nothing to the viperous mass of her coiffure, the writhing tangle of little rattlesnakes that hissed out of her scalp, wriggled around her ears, hung down over her brow like a tumble of curls. *Dieu!* that creature was a figment of delirium tremens. The Gorgon of Perseus was a beauty alongside the one I saw. And the Gorgon of Perseus was fiction, whereas the one I beheld that night was real!

I could see her coming across that platform like a living nightmare. I could see the vipers coiling in her scalp. I could feel the penetration of her eyes on the back of my neck. That hoodoo did not know I could see her. Stealthily she moved, skirting the marble throne, down the stone steps of the platform, toward me on soundless feet. *Brrrrrr!* I was freezing. There was a flash reflected in the mirror—a scimitar coming out of her cloak. Silently she produced the blade. Crept up on me to do murder.

Now I know you will not believe this, but I could feel the marrow stiffening in my skeleton, the muscles hardening in my heart, the cement setting in the arteries of my arms and legs. The cement of terror, you will say. Perhaps. I am still not sure. I have an idea that if the Arab girl had not screamed when she did, I might today be rooted in that cavern, a mummy in stone, petrified and dust-covered like those fossilized figures which stood around me.

But the Arab girl screamed. That saved me. That, and the mirror.

One of those snakes had oozed up on the pedestal where the girl was perched, and she gave a scream that would have broken the spell on the Sphinx. It kicked me out of paralysis just in time. *Oui*, I whirled just in time to dodge the Gorgon's blow, and that monster, not realizing I had seen it in the mirror, was taken by surprise. The scimitar aimed at my skull missed me by a hair. I do not like to recall that big blade slicing past my face. If it had sliced down on my skull, it would have halved me like a sausage, and I would not be here to tell you what happened after that in the Cave of the Petrified People.

But I am not exactly certain of what happened after that. That blade zipped by me like a streak of dark lightning, and something snapped in my head. I do not know what it was that snapped, but the human mind can stand only a certain amount of terror. Go beyond that point, and a man begins to laugh. I laughed when that butcher-blade missed my skull. I shrieked a laugh to match the hideous death-mask look on that Gorgon's face, and I cut at that snaky head with my own scimitar—*zaff!*—a slash which missed, but made that snake charmer scream.

That Gorgon screamed and drove a blow at my middle that would have felled a pine tree. I can show you the scratch made by that Gorgon's scimitar where it was aimed to cut me in two. It bisects the circle branded on me by Blackbeard's heated bowl. My stomach had a bad time of it that night, my friend. A very bad time. *Slash, slash, slash,* that Gorgon's blade took three cuts at me before I could recover my wind, and each slash made me jump backward like a frog in reverse.

The last jump sent me crashing into one of those stone figures, and then I went berserk. Do you understand why? Well, there were a hundred people in that cavern around me turned into rock, but that Gorgon had not petrified me at first glance. Rushing me, its eyes were glaring like the eyes of a charging rhinoceros, but something had gone wrong with the magic, and that monster knew it. I knew it, too. Clutching my scimitar in both hands, I sprang to meet the rush. Blade for blade, I met the fiend. Slash for slash, the scimitars clashing together in midair. Sparks showering. Steel ringing on steel. Step by step, I drove the Snake-Woman back. In the center of that cavern we fought like maniacs, *monsieur*.

Can you visualize such a battle in that gloomy crypt? The smashing moon-curved blades? That snaky-haired Gorgon whirling, dodging in a swirl of purple robes? One Legionnaire mad as a hatter, swinging wildly to decapitate that monster? That silent audience of stone people standing around? Snakes hissing from every crevice in the floor? The Arab princess screaming on her pedestal? That Arab girl's screams got into my heart, *mon ami*, and pumped new blood into my exhausted arms. I was fighting for two lives in that terrible cave, and I battled as that hero in this fiction story never did.

Oui, I could see that Arab girl from the corner of my eye, a big hamadryad inching its scaly length up the pedestal to reach her. I fought the Snake-Woman then! Lashing criss-cross with my scimitar, I made the monster dance. I saw fear come into those sorcerous, cruel eyes. Heard the wheeze and whistle of the creature's tiring breath. Screeching, she dodged behind

the stone huntress with the deer, and I hurdled the animal to get at her. In and around the petrified people we duelled, circling the frightened girl with the urn on her shoulder, the staring fellow with the pitchfork, the motionless mothers hugging their children, the posed warriors immovably gesturing with their spellbound weapons.

It was one of those poor stone creatures that came to my aid in the end. A kneeling woman whose outstretched supplicating hand caught a fold of the Gorgon's robe and held the creature fast in a grip of granite. For a piece of wizardry, I give you that, *monsieur*. That a woman of stone should have captured and tripped the Gorgon! Yanked backward, the monster thought I had caught hold of the robe. Whirling with a squall, she slashed out wildly and whanged the stone woman a tremendous cut across the face. Sparks blazed as the ringing weapon shivered out of the Gorgon's grasp. At one bound I was on her. I drove a cut at that viper-wigged woman which would have sheared the head from an ox. All the fury of madness was behind that swipe, and I did not miss that time. The Gorgon did not have time to duck, and I did not have time to miss.

Blood sprayed in a geyser, and when I opened my eyes to look, I saw the Snake-Woman salaaming, headless. Never will I forget that headless, bending body, or the thing that rolled around on the floor at my feet. I give you my word, the basket-robber who attends the guillotine would have blanched at sight of that head.

Can you guess what had happened to that Gorgon's head, *monsieur*? There is nothing similar in this tale translated by Bulfinch. What had happened to that Gorgon's head was something extraordinary, even for a Gorgon! On the shoulders of that Snake-Woman it had been the head of a female. In leaping from those shoulders it had sprouted a man's beard. It had sprouted a set of black whiskers, I tell you, and when it hit the floor that woman's face had come off like a leaf shucked off of a cabbage. The white, plaster face and the coiffure of curly snakes had shucked off, and underneath that woman-faced death mask was another, a black-whiskered death mask—the face of a man!

I got out of that cavern then. I kicked that black-whiskered Gorgon's head under the stone woman who had captured him, and I grabbed up the woman-mask and rushed to rescue the Arab girl. The snake-headed thing in my clutch was merely plaster, but the snakes attacking the Arab princess were not, and I snatched her off that pedestal only in the nick of time.

"The Snake-Woman!" she screamed when she saw that thing in my hand. "Name of Allah! you have slain the Snake-Woman!"

I did not bother to disillusion her, you comprehend. I carried her across that cave of rattlesnakes and stone people; raced her through the tunnel. Wings on my heels? Airplane propellers, *monsieur*! Dawn was pink and blue in the mine-shaft when I got there, and how those Kabyle brigands shouted when they hauled me out with the Gorgon's head and the girl.

I did not bother to disillusion them, either. They carried me down the mountain on their shoulders, whooping and dervishing and firing salutes with their rifles, and promising me a great celebration as soon as the Black Sheik got back.

"And where is the Black Sheik?" I asked.

"He went off scouting by himself in the night," the bride's father told me. "He wanted to trail the kidnappers who ambushed our wedding party. He did not believe you would return from the Cave of the Petrified People."

The Kabyles were sorry when I explained that I could not wait for Blackbeard to come back and celebrate. I wish you could have seen my triumphal return to civilization. They carried me on their shoulders to within sight of a Legion outpost—me, clutching that snake-headed plaster mask aloft—and when they set me down, the kidnapped bride wanted to kiss me.

"Conqueror!" she called me. "Warrior of warriors! Killer of the Snake-Woman!"

Who was I to tell her I had merely slain her father-in-law? Far be it from me to disillusion a Kabyle tribe about their sheik. Ah, that black-whiskered rascal! Many a pot of gold he must have gathered as tribute for his Snake-Woman act, sneaking down into that cavern by means of some secret entry, collecting the offerings of his superstitious tribesmen, consigning his kidnapped victims to the rattlesnakes. Do you think an Arab might not order the kidnapping of his intended daughter-in-law? But those Kabyles had banded in friendship with Mussolini—all men are known by the company they keep.

Neither did I explain to the colonel how I had managed my escape. There is an insane hospital for Legionnaires, and I was not anxious to be stationed there. When the colonel asked me how I had escaped, I told him a snake charmer had sneaked me through the Kabyle lines.

"You must have used your head," the colonel guessed.

But he did not guess which one. Only one other person saw that Gorgon's head, and quite by accident. You recall the Greek, Rosenapopolous, who had been killed at the start of that campaign? His father. The father of Rosenapopolous, came to Algiers seeking word of his son. He wanted the boy to return to Athens, and when the colonel informed him I had been at the action where his son was killed, he came wandering into the barracks to question me. I was alone in the billet. Unpacking that plaster mask to hide it in my blanket roll. That Greek spied it with a yell.

"Praxiteles!"

"What is that?" I asked.

"It means I will give you five thousand dollars, *monsieur*, if you will take me to the place where you found that mask!"

I looked at him drearily. Not for fifty thousand dollars would I have gone back to that cave. Not for fifty million. Besides, the father of the kidnapped bride had ordered his tribesmen to blow up the place with dynamite, and on reaching the Legion outpost where those Kabyles had delivered me, I had heard somewhere in the distance a tremendous explosion. So I did not go back there with that Greek who was so quick to forget all about his dead son. I have never been able to find out what he meant by *Praxiteles*, but if he meant all the gold in the world, I would not have returned to that Cave of the Petrified People.

There was witchcraft in that cavern, my friend. Perhaps Blackbeard the sheik was a fake, but the wizard who had transformed those people into stone was no fake. I wish you could have seen those figures coated by the dust of centuries, spellbound in the midst of action. Instead of calling me a liar, as your eyes are calling me now, you would believe every word of this story. That it did not happen in Greece two thousand years ago does not signify that it did not happen ten years ago to me in the country of the Kabyles.

Old Thibaut Corday brought his hand down, *whack!* on *Bulfinch's Mythology*, and reared to his feet in stiff-shouldered indignation. My apologetic, "Wait!" was answered by a snort, and the old Legion veteran was through the door and gone in the Algerian twilight before I could salve his wounded feelings.

But presently he was back—having marched the distance to his *pension* in a surprisingly short time for his rheumatic legs—back grim-eyed, panting, a bundle wrapped in newspaper under his arm.

He surveyed me with a glance that had scorn and triumph burning in it to fry away my feeble grin. Upon the drink-ringed table he placed the bundle, and stood back with a gesture that Salome might have used.

"Skeptic!" he snapped at me. "You Americans! Always skeptic! Well, here is something for your skepticism, my friend. Regard that!"

I regarded it, all right. Wrappings torn off, it stared up at me with its sightless, empty-slitted eyes. Medusa's snaky head. A plaster mask in perfect preservation. A livid, life-like beauty!

I expelled a fervent breath.

Old Thibaut Corday was right; he *had* seen witchcraft in that cavern. The sorcery of a wizard who could, indeed, capture men and women in stone. But I did not tell the old Frenchman that the Romans (as boasted by Mussolini) had once conquered those mountains of North Africa. That the Romans had carried with them the looted treasures, the culture, the legends of a previously conquered Greece. That among those legends was the story of Perseus and the Gorgon (which must have been incorporated in Arab lore), and among the treasures were those figures he had seen in that underground cave: the marble Gods of ancient Athens—Diana the Huntress—Poseidon with his tines—Atlas weighted by the world upon his shoulders—Dionysus and Aphrodite and Hermes.

"There is no mistake about it," I agreed, staring at the plaster mask. "You are right, Old Thibaut Corday. It is sorcery."

But I did not tell him it was the sorcery of Praxiteles, greatest sculptor of all time. I did not want to disillusion the old Frenchman. When those Kabyles dynamited that cave he had discovered, they blew to pieces about ten million dollars' worth of ancient Greek statuary.

GEORGES SURDEZ

THE MOST famous member of the French Foreign Legion was Beau Geste, but the most consistently popular author of Legion stories was not P. C. Wren, the creator of the Geste brothers, but the Swiss-born Georges Surdez (1889–1949). After emigrating to Brooklyn, Surdez began writing fiction and sold his first story, the Foreign Legion–themed "The Yellow Streak," to the prestigious pulp *Adventure*, which published it in the issue of October 10, 1922. He apparently had firsthand knowledge of the Foreign Legion, as his numerous stories have been universally lauded for their verisimilitude and attention to accurate detail. One of the most highly regarded stylists of all the pulp magazine writers of the 1920s and '30s, Surdez quickly became a favorite contributor to the pages of *Adventure*, which also boasted the hugely popular Talbot Mundy.

The prolific Surdez also wrote for such top pulps as *Argosy* and *Blue Book,* as well as for America's most distinguished fiction magazines, including *Liberty,* the *Saturday Evening Post,* and *Collier's.* For the January 30, 1937, issue of the latter, he wrote the story "Russian Roulette." In this piece, Surdez invented the story's titular term to describe a dangerous game in which a partially loaded handgun is placed to the head and fired. Although the story primarily explores a suicidal version of the game in which only a single cartridge is removed, it also mentions the one-bullet version more commonly thought of today. The phrase was apparently inspired by the reputation that Russian soldiers and officers had for reckless behavior.

Surdez's novel *The Demon Caravan* (1927) was very loosely adapted for the 1953 film *Desert Legion,* starring Alan Ladd, Arlene Dahl, Richard Conte, and Akim Tamiroff. While the novel is about a nearly utopian society in a lost city in the mountains of North Africa, the motion picture is a fairly standard French Foreign Legion adventure.

"Suicide Patrol" was originally published in the August 1934 issue of *Adventure.*

A GRIPPING NOVEL OF THE LEGION—AND THE
HONOR OF MEN OF WAR.

SUICIDE PATROL

GEORGES SURDEZ

THE FRENCH expedition operating from Kasbah–
Tadla, in the Moroccan Middle-Atlas, had
reached the pass through the hills known as
Fom-el-Metmor. In preparation for the attack to
open the trails to the south, the infantry companies dislocated into small combat groups, and
deployed to face the rocky slopes flanking the
passage.

The units of the Foreign Legion could be distinguished from all others at a glance. There was
no need to look at the uniforms. Legionnaires in
formation move with that unmistakable, confident, cocky precision peculiar to the Corps, the
result more of a mental attitude than military
training. For Legionnaires are professionals of
war, and they face action with the alert, graceful
poise of a great actress facing her public.

The battalion was moving toward the firing
line without a wasted step, without a man out of
place, supple as a blade of steel, powerful as a
battering-ram. As the sections took open order,
to offer a poorer target to the whining lead
poured down by snipers lurking among bushes
and boulders on the slopes, there were short,
shrill whistled signals, few words, few gestures.
It was a Legion show.

Suddenly, this orderliness was marred by an
extraordinary interruption.

At the extreme left of the Fourth Company, there was confusion. Two men had started to fight, and to fight with fists. They forgot regulations, discipline, danger. The sergeant in charge of their group, a large, bulky German, ran to one of them in time to catch him as the fellow dropped back from a terrific jolt to the chin.

"Carroll!" the sergeant barked.

The man who brought up the rear of the combat group, a tall, rangy Legionnaire who wore the single green chevron of first-class private and the ribbons of two decorations on the breast of his faded khaki tunic, stepped forward. He was twenty-six; his shaven face was so deeply tanned that his light brown hair showed golden against his flesh below the rim of the képi.

"Take care of the other."

"Right, Sergeant."

And as Sergeant Kulhman shook the dazed man to consciousness, shoved him back into place, Legionnaire Carroll stood before the other. Dacorda, thirty years old, short, with very broad shoulders, was powerful, sure of himself. He had a swarthy, round Roman face, and sleek black hair. His lips twitched furiously, as he tried to dodge Carroll and get at his opponent.

"Take it easy," Carroll said in English. He knew why Kulhman had selected him. Dacorda, thought to be an American, although enlisted as Italian, must learn quickly and firmly what was best for him. An officer was coming to see what the trouble might be, and it was important to close the incident before he arrived.

"Let me at him," Dacorda pleaded.

"You'll get all the fighting you can handle in a few minutes."

"He can't call me that and get away with it."

Carroll shoved him back with his left hand. Then Dacorda swung for his jaw. With the officer on the way, haste was needed. Carroll calmly reversed the Lebel rifle he held and the iron-shod butt swung upward, caught the angry man in the belly. Dacorda sat down.

"That's that!" Carroll helped him to his feet, pushed him into the rank. "Keep your mouth shut, now. Everything can be settled later."

When Sub-Lieutenant d'Argoval, slim and aristocratic, reached the spot, Kulhman's group was on the move again.

"Well, Kulhman?"

"A man slipped, Lieutenant. New chap, not used to climbing. Nothing important, Lieutenant."

D'Argoval stared at the sergeant, at the men. He was young, twenty-one or -two, but he had experience. He saw that something had happened and that he would not be told. A novice might have asked questions. The sub-lieutenant shrugged and walked away.

"You're lucky the sergeant's a good guy," Carroll said scathingly to Dacorda. "That was fourteen days in the jug for you, eight of them solitary, if he reported you. What the hell was the matter?"

"That lousy wop, Gianella, has been riding me all morning because I can't talk good Italian," Dacorda grumbled. "I said I'd sock him if he kept it up. He did, and I did."

"Well, you enlisted as an Italian, didn't you?"

"That's nobody's business."

"Gianella was just kidding."

"Me too, I was just kidding! And I'll kid some more, see? And what about you socking me in the gut? What do they take a guy for? A slave?"

The tall Legionnaire ahead of Dacorda turned a lean, wrinkled face framed by gray hair to peer over a bony shoulder. A clipped, dingy red mustache showed under his hooked nose. He was forty or more.

"Carroll's all right. He had to do it. Didn't I tell you that temper would get you into a jam?"

"Sure, you told me, grandpop." Dacorda laughed. His anger vanished and he was smiling.

The First and Third Companies of the Battalion were in line, the groups huddled about the automatic rifles, forming a long, grim, crouching row. The Second and Fourth Companies were placed in support, sheltered by a low ridge of dark stone. The gunners tinkered with their weapons, and the others, having nothing to do, waited, sprawling or squatting on the ground. The officers gathered, ten yards behind the troopers, to consult the map a last time.

"We're attacking in half an hour," Sergeant Kulhman told Carroll. "It'll take that long for the artillery preparation. Say, maybe you had better talk to those new fellows—the lieutenant who brought up the replacements told me the short one must be a bit crazy. He fights all the time."

Carroll nodded. The two recruits, Dacorda and Zerlich, had joined the expedition the preceding afternoon, with a reinforcement draft from Tadla. It was easy to recognize them as newcomers. The other men, who had been campaigning for almost seven weeks, wore faded, lacerated khaki and boots mended with strings and wire. Both Dacorda and Zerlich had been issued new clothing and footgear before being sent to the front. Carroll found the two talking together, away from their companions.

"Have a smoke?" he offered. "They're American cigarettes."

"We got our own butts," Dacorda snapped.

"Thanks," Zerlich replied. He accepted a cigarette, lit it. "So you're American? What's your name?"

"James Carroll. They call me Jacques around here."

"Been in this outfit long?"

"Six months. Before that, with the First Regiment, in the Sahara. When did you enlist?"

"We've been in nine months. In training, Bel-Abbès and Saida."

"Like it?"

"It's all right," Zerlich commented.

"It's lousy," Dacorda grumbled. "Nothing doing most of the time. And stew every day. Don't the saps know you can roast meat?"

"They feed you better on active service. Plenty of game."

The three went still as the mountain batteries crashed into action. Yellow billows of smoke curled on the slopes. The black infantry was launching the first drive to break through the Pass, and the sharp, bloodcurdling war shouts of the Senegalese could be heard above the noise of the explosions.

Zerlich paled a little, smiled in apology.

"Guess I am pretty old for this game," he said. "But I had a tough break. I went to the States from Austria when I was a kid, ten or eleven. I was clerking in a hardware store, in Toledo, for years and had some money saved. I wanted to see the old country. Turned out there was some question about my old man's citizenship papers; they went through after I was twenty-one or something, and I was caught without a re-entry permit. I was trying to get in on the quota, got stranded in France, joined the Legion in Dijon, ran into Dacorda in Lyons, on the train. He was coming from Paris, where he had signed up. You see—"

"Shut up," Dacorda put in.

"Why? Carroll's here, ain't he? I was saying, Dacorda was born in Jersey. He had a share in a speak in Newark. Was making out all right, only he got himself a wife too many. The first one got wise, and he had to beat it."

"Hell, they said I'd get five years in the pen," Dacorda explained. "What's your out, Big Boy?"

"Nothing fancy," Carroll assured him. "Thought it was a broken heart at first. But the longer I stay here, I think it was indigestion. Can hardly think what the girl looked like. I suppose I really wanted to move around—"

"Soldier of fortune stuff, like in a book?" Dacorda wondered. "You're the first I ever seen." His dark eyes kindled, he indicated the battlefield. "What's this racket we're working at? Going to be tough? A real fight?"

"Wouldn't be surprised," Carroll informed him. "See, this bunch was supposed to throw a scare into the tribes around here. Make them behave, and say it's peace. But they called in a gang from down south to help them. They can fight, all of them, don't kid yourself. They have plenty of Spanish Mauser rifles, smuggled to them across the French Zone, from the Riff."

"Any chance of beating it?"

"You mean desert?" Carroll shook his head.

"Not in the mountains. These guys chop a guy up unless he talks their lingo. You might try it from Meknes, when we get back, if you have money. Hard to make, though. The Spanish turn you over to the French if they spot you on their territory. And it's eight years in the penal camp if you're gone more than a week. Ever see—"

He was interrupted by the shrill summons of metal whistles.

"Better get going."

 They ran to their places. The company moved, marched some distance left, swung and advanced toward the enemy. Carroll noted that his new acquaintances were nervous, but nervous in different fashions.

Dacorda strode, gripping his rifle so tightly that his knuckles were white. His face was grinning, tense with excitement. Zerlich was shaking, loose-kneed, shuffling, ready to drop or run. However, Carroll did not worry. He knew by past experience that it was easier to keep with the rest than to run alone.

"Is the small one troublesome?" Kulhman asked Carroll, in German.

"No. He'll be a good man when he learns what this is all about."

"That's good."

Kulhman spread his arms wide, as the whistles blew, and the group sank down. The automatic rifle went into action instantly, jerking on its metal fork. Carroll had handled an automatic in the past, and watched the firing with professional interest. Corporal Gottlieb, an expert, grouped his bullets masterfully. He was not hitting anyone, but he cleared the zone before his group of snipers.

Somewhere to the right, an officer was chanting the range.

"Two-fifty, two-fifty, up fifty . . . three hundred, three hundred . . ."

Four feet from Carroll, Zerlich stretched out full length, pushing his musette bag forward as if to shield his face. He did not enjoy the occasional prolonged twang of a passing missile. But Dacorda was grinning, fingering the bolt of his Lebel rifle.

"Hey, Jack—see the guys way up there? Two of them? Can I take a crack at them?"

"Wait for the order."

"They're not hitting nobody on our side."

"Never mind, they will," Carroll predicted, grimly.

Kulhman was on his feet. "Come on, come on!"

The ground was open before the company. Tiny geysers of dirt marked the impacts of bullets dropping short. Some distance to the right, Captain Barbaroux strolled, stick under one arm, pipe between his teeth.

"That guy's good," Dacorda said, with grim admiration.

Legionnaire Chuckleit, a gigantic, sandy-haired rifle-grenadier, sat down bruskly. He tried to rise, managed to gain one knee. Then, very slowly, as if a mighty hand pressed the nape of his neck, his massive shoulders arched, his right fist was propped on the earth, his head swinging lower and lower. He slithered sideways, stretched out. His face was oddly calm, as if with intense satisfaction.

Carroll felt stark cold along his spine.

"Wouldn't touch booze because of his health," Legionnaire Fenmayer shouted. "Look at him now! Posthumous citation for him!" Fenmayer was barely nineteen, a strong German boy, reckless and spirited, probably the toughest lad in the whole section.

Carroll steadied. The feverish calm of action came to him. He saw, heard, sensed everything, yet he felt as if in a dream. And he knew this sensation of unreality would last until he dropped, or began to suffer from fatigue and thirst.

"Rifle fire at will," Kulhman relayed the order. "Don't burn cartridges for nothing. They cost money."

"Go ahead and shoot now," Carroll told Dacorda.

The tough recruit promptly emptied his magazine. Then he turned a rueful face to Carroll. He had believed that his every shot would hit, that enemies would tumble like nine-pins. And he discovered that a stretch of three hundred meters gave eight bullets much space to miss in.

"You aim too high," Carroll advised.

Dacorda nodded, fired again.

A runner came from the captain. He howled, "Sergeant—the old man says your group's too far left. Work it right, right. Got it?"

"Sure. Tell him to come and show me himself, eh?" But Kulhman addressed his men, "Keep to the right."

It seemed simple enough for the combat group to keep in touch with the bulk of the company. But a rise of soil divided the slope they were climbing, the enemy's line appeared to make a right angle, and try as they would the Legionnaires were drawn to the left if they wished to face the firing. No man likes to offer his flank to the enemy. Carroll knew that this was a planned maneuver of the hillmen. Kulhman knew it, too.

"Right, I said, right!" the sergeant yelled. "Fix bayonets!"

The long blades glistened. Swinging right would bring some of the hillmen near enough for a sudden rush with the steel. Unnoticed, the Chleuhs had left a wedge of resistance at that point of their front.

Running with the velocity of frightened deer, half-naked riflemen, gaunt legs flitting, were darting down among the boulders. At a shouted signal, a number of them dove into a thicket of bushes, to fire on the other sections of the Fourth Company, while the rest concentrated on Kulhman's group. The whole stunt consumed less than fifteen seconds, and the combat group was neatly isolated. A runner saw this, started off, circling down the slope to report.

A well-aimed shot brought him down. Carroll saw him crawl into a hole near a large rock. It was impossible to know whether he had been seriously hurt.

Kulhman tried to lead the way across the slope, to regain contact as ordered. But the knot of Legionnaires had already lost touch with the engagement as a whole, and was fighting an isolated skirmish, one against five.

Carroll scowled, then laughed. Captain Barbaroux would be furious. The trick was perhaps the simplest used in the hills. The natives figured that even if beaten in the main encounter they could score several minor victories such as this, and make the French pay for their success. Not infrequently a half-score isolated men became ten corpses.

The experienced Legionnaires knew they were in a nasty plight. Zerlich's attitude had not changed. He was trying to bring his belly lower than his ankles. Dacorda was blissfully unaware of the danger. He enjoyed the fighting, sweated, panted. Even the tensely worried Kulhman caught Carroll's eye and nodded. Dacorda would be all right in action. Fenmayer was tossing grenades, which fell short but scared the hillmen back.

"Looks very bad," Kulhman suggested mildly.

His face, ordinarily brick-red, was almost white. Whether he escaped alive or not, he would suffer. Captain Barbaroux would blame him for having allowed his group to be isolated. And after the event, excuses would be hard to make.

"Come on, come on!" he begged.

But the Legionnaires were forced to take cover, literally pinned to the ground by a hot, accurate fire. Another man was killed, another wounded. Which left only eight in action.

Having brought their opponents to a halt, the natives started a concentric maneuver, slowly and surely backing the survivors to the edge of a sheer drop of thirty feet into a ravine thickly overgrown with bushes. Their intention was clear: if both tips of the human crescent managed to attain the brink of the pit, the Legion group would be crushed as if in a vise.

But they still respected the handful before them. They kept at long range now. From time to time, Carroll saw a head and shoulder appear, the pale flicker of a flaming rifle in the sunlight.

"We've got to break through before they rush us," Kulhman said.

Dacorda moved a few feet from his comrades, and hoisted himself on a boulder. He was as agile as a goat, deliberate and confident. Crouching, his rifle propped, he picked off man after man as if he had done nothing else all his life. Carroll knew that he was witnessing a rare spectacle: the first engagement of a born fighting man. Dacorda did not like drill, did not like routine. But he would go far in the Legion, if he lived.

"Get that fool off there," Kulhman howled. "You, Dacorda, come here! We've got to get going—can't leave you there—"

Dacorda, who did not understand French well, half-rose to listen. Suddenly, he slipped, tumbled from the boulder. His body struck the edge of the pit, slid off and vanished.

Kulhman stepped to the edge, gripped the branches of a bush for support and peered down. He gestured in discouragement, shook his head:

"He doesn't move. Done for, I guess." Then his attention snapped back to his job. "Gottlieb, you'll have to fire as you walk. But we'll be in the clear in a couple of hundred yards."

"Suits me," the corporal agreed.

He passed the broad leather sling of the automatic over his shoulder, braced the stock of the weapon against his right hip, barrel supported by the left hand. Thus, it was possible for a powerful man to walk some distance, firing the gun as he went, with only brief pauses to insert new magazines.

Legionnaire Panailoff, a tall, blond Russian, veteran of several wars, retrieved Chuckleit's bag of rifle-grenades. He ascertained the location of the nearest natives, laid the rifle almost horizontally on the ground to obtain maximum range, and fired four grenades in quick succession.

The metal missiles whirred through the air with a ruffling sound; there followed dull, smashing explosions. Carroll and the others were ready, and when the hillmen broke cover to avoid the splinters, the automatic and the Lebel rifles started to shoot. Kulhman was firing a very long-barreled German pistol, shooting wrist supported by the left hand.

Several Chleuhs fell.

"Come along, now!" the sergeant ordered.

 Carroll had not forgotten Dacorda. But Kulhman reported him dead. He had not even cried out as he fell. Moreover, although it was the tradition to pick up casualties when possible, the chief concern of all now must be for the automatic rifle and its ammunition. The capture of such a weapon meant many deaths on the Legion's side. Carroll started off with the rest.

But Zerlich, who had gone to look down at his comrade, raced up to him, clasped his arm. Carroll shook himself loose, and the old fellow caught at his garrison belt from behind.

"I must get to him, I must get to him!"

"We can't do him any good. The slobs won't bother going after him down there. Maybe they didn't even see him drop." Carroll felt that the wild-eyed Zerlich thought him a coward, a renegade, to leave an American lying exposed to mutilation, and he concluded lamely, "The ambulance men will pick him up before long."

"No, no! I must get to him!"

"Well, ask the sergeant."

Zerlich released Carroll, rushed to Kulhman. He spoke in very fluent German: "Please, kindly please, let me find my comrade. Please!"

"No time. Must save the machine rifle first. Orders."

"You just let me go. Legionnaire Carroll will help me. He's an American, too. I came so far with Dacorda that you cannot understand, Sergeant. For nine months, I have been with him every day, watching him. I can't leave him now."

Kulhman lost his temper.

"Shut up and get going, you blockhead! Want to get your throat cut? He doesn't move. The fall killed him."

"Please, I must get to him!"

"You're crazy. Get out of my way!" And as Zerlich did not obey, Kulhman's heavy hand rose, struck him squarely in the face, knocked him down.

He could not be blamed. His group now consisted of but seven men and two wounded. There was the automatic to save, which represented other lives. Zerlich was arguing with a superior in action, and Kulhman had the right to blow out his brains.

"You don't understand," Zerlich picked himself up, desperate. "It's millions, I'm telling you, millions! I must get to him now, help me, please! If I delay, all will be lost!"

"Maybe you could let us try," Carroll put in, trotting up.

He was touched by the old man's devotion to the surly Dacorda. The poor fool had gone mad, shouting of millions when he had enlisted in the Legion for a bonus of twenty dollars and the royal pay of five cents a week!

"Go ahead! Only we can't wait for you. If your throat's slit, you can't blame me!"

Carroll nodded. "Come on, Zerlich, we'll get to him."

There was an unexpected volunteer, Legionnaire Gianella, who had fought with Dacorda some time before. He was considered a humorous fellow, something of a clown, but a brave man in action. During the World War, he had been a sergeant in the famous Alpini.

"I quarrel with him," he said in his lilting French. "But he's almost Italian, and a good, strong fellow. Even if he struck me so hard, I do not wish him harm. I must help."

Kulhman was some distance away already, followed only by the gun crew and the wounded. Carroll knew that he was reluctant to leave one of his men in the lurch, for there were few as kind and courageous as the German. But responsibility for the automatic weighed on his mind.

Zerlich appeared to have lost all his fear. He strode, heedless of the bullets vibrating about him, gesturing, excited. At last, he crouched at the exact spot from which Dacorda had dropped. He pointed.

"There's the body."

Dacorda was face down, motionless, and blood covered a flat stone on which his head rested.

"How will we get down?" Carroll said aloud.

"Easily," Gianella spoke.

He produced a rope, thin and strong, which was used for fetching waters from deep wells. He tied it to the handle of his entrenching tool, wedging the small spade between the boulder and the ground, blade sunk in the earth.

"Wait until I call, then come down one after the other."

Without further conversation, he slid over the edge, grinned briefly, his teeth glittering white in his dark face, and dropped from sight. He yelled that the line was clear, and Zerlich followed him. Carroll was last, after a rapid glance about him. He noted with satisfaction that the hillmen were concentrating on the retreating group. The automatic was the prize they sought, and they felt sure that they could rake in the strays later.

"Let's go!"

"A moment," Gianella suggested. "Maybe we better take the stairs with us."

He jerked on the rope skilfully, until rope and entrenching tool tumbled down.

They knew approximately where Dacorda had dropped. But they had to hack their way through thick bushes to find the spot.

Carroll turned the body over, saw a wound on the forehead. Zerlich unbuttoned the tunic, removed a thick wallet with shaking fingers from an inside pocket. Carroll did not wonder at this. He would have done the same to obtain means of identification, the address of the man's relatives and friends. A man did not rob a comrade before two witnesses whom he had not known more than a day.

Gianella unscrewed the plug of his canteen, and was gingerly dabbing at Dacorda's forehead with a handkerchief. "Not hurt much. If he's a good man, he'll wake up when he smells this wine."

Carroll felt the torso, the legs, looking for wounds other than the shallow, if ugly-looking gash. Zerlich, who had been so eager to help Dacorda, was doing nothing except rustle papers, somewhere behind the group. The Italian shoved the spout of the canteen between the unconscious man's teeth. The wine spilled over the chin at first, then after a gurgling grunt and a cough, Dacorda opened his eyes.

"What the hell?" he challenged, sitting up suddenly. Then he recognized Gianella and spoke in Italian. While he was perhaps not too fluent, he knew many curses.

"Shut up," Carroll snapped, "he came with us to help you."

"Yeah?" Dacorda rubbed his eyes with his knuckles. Then his hand went to the pocket where he kept the wallet. Instantly, he was excited, tearing at his undershirt. Carroll saw a scapular strung around his muscular throat with a slender chain of gold beads.

"Who's got my dough, eh? Somebody snitched it!"

"Here," Zerlich said, handing back the wallet. "I got this to write to your folks in case—"

"You keep your dirty fingers off my stuff!"

"Listen," Carroll advised, "keep your shirt on, fellow. Without this guy, we wouldn't be here."

Dacorda opened the wallet, glanced into it. He slipped it back in the pocket. He still looked like a badly mangled man, with the blood smearing his face, spotting his clothes. But he was evidently unhurt. He rose awkwardly, staggered, then looked up.

"Baby! What a drop! Say, Jack, I must be lucky."

"You said it! And you'll have to be lucky to get out of here, too. So far as I know, we're right in the thick of them. They counter-attacked around here."

"Hell," Dacorda said carelessly, "they ain't so tough!"

But the remark reminded him of his present and most pleasing occupation. He picked up his rifle, examined the magazine. His gestures were soft, caressing.

Carroll, first-class Legionnaire, was automatically in charge.

"We'll work our way to the right. This ravine probably opens up on the plain, where the French are."

 The mountain artillery was pounding hard. The detonations of rifles, the hammering of automatics, and at intervals, the distant crashing of grenades could be heard. But the ravine itself seemed deserted. The four stopped to take a long drink, then started off.

But the moment they left the spot where they found Dacorda, directly beneath a slight overhang of the brink, two or three shots slapped out at short range, lead slashed through the twigs and foliage. The Legionnaires leaped back to hug the cliff.

"They can't lean over far enough to shoot us here," Carroll remarked. "We're safe enough."

"But *we* can't shoot at them from this place," Dacorda protested.

"That's too bad," Carroll agreed sarcastically, and he looked at the recruit. "Say, you're a queer guy. You were talking about deserting, a while back, and now you seem to like it."

"Sure, I do." Dacorda was candid. "I was glad when my regiment was kept in America during the war. And they had to draft me in the first place. What a sucker I was. Don't seem to make sense, but it gives me a kick."

"You must be one man in a thousand," Carroll suggested.

"Maybe," Dacorda agreed without false modesty.

For several hundred yards, the four walked without interference. The natives had given up trying to shoot them from above. And they conversed in four languages. Carroll used English with Dacorda and Zerlich, French with Gianella. Dacorda and the former Alpini spoke in Italian. Zerlich employed German with Gianella, who had picked up that language in the Legion. Yet not one of the four felt any wonder. It seemed the most natural thing for them to be grouped in the ravine, fleeing from foes with whom they had no quarrel, and serving a foreign power.

"Look out," Dacorda spoke suddenly.

Some distance away, the cliff became a steep slope, which would be easy to scale. Carroll nodded. The natives were fighting on their own soil, must know this place, and had probably reached it first. The four Legionnaires were silent, walked cautiously.

When the expected shots came, they dropped to the ground.

After returning the first volley, Carroll counted the reports, singling them out by position and sound. For it is easy to distinguish the sharp report of a Mauser, for example, from the thudding detonation with a slapping echo of an old-fashioned Chassepot rifle.

"Seven, maybe eight," he declared. "Let's go ahead."

For several minutes, the affair became a desultory duel. The Legionnaires moved from cover to cover in rapid rushes, while the natives waited in hiding.

Then the reports were very close, within a few yards. But the thick undergrowth made accurate aim almost impossible. One merely caught a glance of a fleeting cloth, the rustling of leaves.

"They're damned close," Dacorda breathed.

"Yes. Better fix your bayonet, fellow."

The stocky Legionnaire obeyed. Zerlich was pale as cream cheese, and appeared about to be ill. Gianella was sweating, and the drops beaded his thick, black mustache.

Carroll, the spearhead of the group, was attacked at close quarters first.

A Chleuh, nude save for the loin-cloth girdling his slim waist, materialized from a bush less than three feet away, leaping out from the side, knife brandished. Carroll hopped away, and the blade aimed at his chest caught his tunic over the left shoulder, rent the sleeve to the elbow, where it slashed into the flesh.

The Legionnaire dropped toward the hillman, shoulder forward, knocked him down and fell with him. The other was as tall as Carroll, but many pounds lighter. He squirmed and struggled; his free hand clawed at the soldier's throat, scraping his cheek. He contrived to clear his blade, sought to strike again. But Carroll's left hand circled his slender, sinewy wrist, and clung grimly.

They whirled over and over, the native on top, trying to bring his knees on the Legionnaire's chest. Carroll brought the point of his bayonet against the lean, brown side. For an instant, the hillman seemed about to break free and save himself, then the long steel shaft sank in.

Carroll shook himself free, scrambled upright, and clubbed at the head with the Lebel's butt, like a man clubbing a snake. A couple of blows were enough.

Carroll panted. Again, he felt as if dreaming; an odd, fierce drunkenness, the intoxication of extreme danger and of panic, urged him on. His comrades were struggling with the other natives.

There was a Chleuh kneeling on Zerlich. The skinny chap had been borne down easily; a ripping thrust had torn the front of his tunic. His hands were hampered by the tangle of loose cloth and severed straps.

Carroll lunged with the bayonet, caught the attacker in the flank. He heaved upward, literally pitched the hillman aside. Then the blade broke off.

Gianella was keeping off three men, whirling his rifle about his head in a *moulinet* as perfect as in a fencing room. They dodged and leaped away from the swinging butt with comical agility. Carroll's gun crashed in the small of the back of the nearest mountaineer. The steel stump dug in, and the man dropped and writhed, like a worm cut in two by a spade.

Carroll lost his grip on the weapon, closed on the next man with bare hands. A frenzy possessed him. Just what he did, he never recalled. But the Chleuh's wiry but light body was soon inert in his grasp.

Shots crashed out very near. Dacorda leaped back from his assailants, and fired, half-crouched. Carroll looked for his rifle, found it, straightened and sought for new foes. But the brief combat was over; three survivors were crashing madly through the bushes. They left six corpses behind.

"Ugly brutes, ain't they?" said Dacorda.

A number of Legionnaires were trotting down into the ravine. There were Kulhman, Fenmayer and Gottlieb with the automatic rifle, and Sub-Lieutenant d'Argoval. The latter grasped Carroll's shoulder impulsively and shook him.

"Thought we might be too late. Glad to see you, my friend!" He turned to Dacorda and spoke in French, "Your sergeant is very satisfied with your conduct." He added in English, "Good soldier!"

"You tell 'em," Dacorda admitted.

II

The pass through the hills at Fom-el-Metmor had been cleared of its defenders. The French column marched on and reached the plain beyond, the cavalry brushing away the scattered stragglers of the mountaineers.

But before the general in command could follow up his success and attain the next range of hills to the south, a terrific rain storm, accompanied by thunder, turned the plain into a lake of mud, the trails to bogs in which trucks and cannon were mired to the hubs. The roads between Kasbah-Tadla and Fom-el-Metmor were impassable for wagons. With the arrival of supplies problematic, it was foolhardy to keep on across a strange and hostile region.

The expedition encamped around the small native town of Ras-Metmor, a picturesque hud-dle of low, flat-roofed houses surrounded by a crenelated defensive wall which was buttressed by high towers at regular intervals, and resembled somewhat the medieval strongholds of the robber barons. There was no attempt to quarter the troops in the abandoned buildings. Health conditions were most unsatisfactory. So a small city of tents and light shacks rose on a hillock to the southwest, and the troops settled down with grim patience to wait until the sun dried the soil.

Carroll worked at the construction of trenches and dugouts, with the Legionnaires. And life was tolerable, for if the roads were not good enough for military convoys, a swarm of traders, such as always follows any armed expedition in primitive lands, found them passable. These people were avid for profit, and found in their greed for money the courage to risk themselves. They hailed from the ports of the Eastern Mediterranean mostly, Greeks, Maltese and Syrians. And they charged gold-rush prices for their goods. A bottle of poor wine, such as sold for three francs on the Coast, was handed out for fifteen francs.

Carroll received some money from home. Both Zerlich and Dacorda were well-supplied with cash. Men who are liable to be slain at any time are seldom thrifty. And they visited the town at night. When off-duty in the afternoons, they strolled in the zone protected by the outpost, and fished the streams with home-made lines.

"What do you intend to do when you get through here?" Zerlich asked Carroll.

"Newspaper work if I can get it," the younger man replied. "And you, Dacorda?"

"Think I could get to be sergeant if I stuck in the Legion?"

"Sure. You've got to learn French well enough to talk and to write it a little. What they want for a non-com is a guy who has guts and isn't too dumb. You're all right, except for the French. You can be sergeant inside three years. That means eight hundred francs a month in Morocco, too."

Dacorda smiled. "Then I guess I'll stick

around a while. I think I have a pull with that young guy, d'Argoval. He said he'd put me on the corporals' list as soon as I could talk French more. What do we do tonight?"

"The Moulin Rouge is open."

"Okay by me."

An odd incident marred that afternoon. The three had left camp for a walk and a swim in the narrow stream crossing the valley. Carroll produced a small pocket-camera, which immediately infuriated Dacorda. Even Zerlich did not appear overjoyed.

"Who'll see them?" Carroll protested. "Maybe I'd send them to my folks in Pennsylvania, that's all."

"You never can tell who sees what," Dacorda insisted.

"What are you worried about? Who cares out here how many janes you married? If it was a murder, you might be taken out, or if you were a big time crook. But bigamy? Marriage laws are different in France, anyway."

"Do me a favor?" Dacorda was stubborn. "Don't even mention me. I'm under another name, but somebody might get wise."

"What about you, Zerlich?"

"Don't want my picture taken, either."

Carroll shrugged and pocketed the camera. His years in the Legion had given him a broad tolerance for the sins of men. What Dacorda had done, what Zerlich feared, was their own business. But he was beginning to suspect deeper motives than those they were willing to allow.

They went to the Moulin Rouge that night. It was a night of strange portent.

In other surroundings, the Moulin Rouge would have seemed shabby, miserable. Thirty-six hours after the town was occupied, a Syrian trader opened it, with stuff brought on a couple of mule-drawn vans. He brought a few girls, some of them lazy, dull Algerians, some Spanish wenches from the Riff ports. They sang and danced. They were frontier town girls.

The officers did not frequent the town. The sergeants had their own resort, somewhat more pretentious and expensive. The Moulin Rouge catered to privates. Prices had been regulated at a meeting of the officers so as to be fair to the traders and to the troopers. The rules and regulations applied in garrison cities were not upheld. Men who fought were separated and not punished, unless serious harm was done.

The armed patrol which policed the town visited the establishment once every hour. There was a permanent guard on duty, a man picked for strength, who acted as official bouncer. The Moulin Rouge occupied a deserted residence of ample size, and tables overflowed from rooms into stables and cotes. The Syrian presided behind his plank bar, shutting off the angle of the largest room.

When Carroll and his comrades entered, the place was crowded. There were pink-cheeked young Frenchmen serving their regular term of military service in the artillery; solid, muscular infantrymen of the native regiments, who resembled Hindus in their khaki uniforms and turbans. There were Legionnaires; there were grinning, jovial Senegalese negroes; and even a few Indo-Chinese, mostly officers' servants. The various types did not mix much and occupied different corners of the rooms.

The bouncer had used his privileged position to become very drunk, and was asleep in a corner. It was obvious that the three had arrived immediately after some excitement. A girl was sweeping broken glass from the dirt floor. And a Russian Legionnaire was playing an accordion.

Young Fenmayer was seated with Gianella and a husky, silent German at the table next to theirs. He explained that the Legionnaires had wished the accordion to be played, that the owner had insisted on supplying music with his old phonograph, and that the machine had been smashed. The Syrian had added a tax to the price of drinks, to pay for his wrecked property. It was judged fair, and no one was to report him for increasing his rates.

"It's my treat tonight," Dacorda announced. "Cognac!"

The cognac was vile, Carroll thought. But Dacorda was not a connoisseur and drank greedily. In a few minutes, the bottle was nearly empty. Zerlich pretended to drink, but Carroll noticed that he put away little.

Fenmayer was full of red wine and aggression. Perhaps because he was jealous of Dacorda's quickly acquired reputation for toughness, he had taken a dislike to him. He started to peer threateningly at Dacorda, like a young bull challenging a rival in a pasture. He made remarks in German, which Dacorda did not understand, and which amused his friends. Carroll leaned over and warned him in a low voice, with ill result.

"I'm scared of nobody," Fenmayer said. He rose, unbuckled his belt, slipped off his tunic. He stood before Dacorda, fists clenched, parading his powerful arms and massive shoulders.

"What's eating him?" Dacorda wondered.

"Nothing, he's soused," Carroll put in.

"Says he wants to fight you," Zerlich explained.

"He's just a kid." Dacorda smiled.

"All the Germans think he's pretty good," said Zerlich. "Gianella told him you hit harder than anyone he knew of, and he said he'd take you on and lick you."

"That's only his side of the story," said Dacorda.

Very deliberately, he deposited his képi on the table, pushed his chair back to give himself room, stood up.

"All right, buddy. Come and get it!"

Fenmayer did not understand the words, but he could not mistake the challenge. His eyes blazed fiercely, his lips drew back on strong teeth, and he stepped forward. Dacorda did not move until he dodged a swinging right that would have cracked an oak beam. Then his feet parted, his torso swayed.

The punch was not a swing, and it was not a hook. But it caught Fenmayer on the side of the chin, a half-inch from the tip. It did the trick. Dacorda was seated and had replaced the képi on

his head before Fenmayer hit the floor. Gianella, laughing, hoisted him on his chair. Dacorda rubbed his right knuckles with the tip of his fingers after casually dipping them in the brandy.

"Wide open," he commented.

 The momentary hush ended; the conversation, the music and the singing resumed. Fenmayer opened his eyes, and Gianella made him understand that he had had his chance and lost. The big boy cried with humiliation. Dacorda reached over and patted his knee.

"Say, Jack, tell him he doesn't need to feel so bad. Say he's a good kid, and I'll show him how it's done later. Tell him I used to be a pro."

Carroll nodded, and consoled Fenmayer with a glamorous yarn concerning Dacorda. As it cost him not a thing, he declared that his friend had been middleweight champion of the world. And Fenmayer, very flattered, shook hands.

After an hour, some of the customers began to leave, to make it to camp before nine o'clock. The others trusted to the speed of their legs to get in under the wire before the bugle sounded. Another bottle of cognac followed the first. Dacorda was very happy.

"I'm going out for a minute," he said. "I'll be back for a last swig, then we'll lam back to camp."

Carroll saw him weave his way between the tables, go into the yard. He noted that Zerlich was staring after him. The accordion was playing "Volga," and the Legionnaires sang the German verses written for that tune in the Corps. Carroll was uneasy.

"I'm going to look for Dacorda," he said.

"He's all right," Zerlich said. "Have a drink."

"In a minute," Carroll retorted. He went out.

At first, the yard appeared pitch black, then the glow cast by the open door permitted Carroll to discern men moving, milling, in a corner of the enclosure. Dacorda was in the middle of the group. Carroll rushed to his help.

His friend's face had been covered with a

cloth, to stifle his shouts, and he was kicking savagely at the men holding him. Moroccan Tirailleurs. There were five of them. Obviously intending to rob the Legionnaire, they were careful not to hurt him to avoid investigation. No attention would be paid to a theft, but a murder would arouse resentment.

Carroll kicked the nearest Moroccan. He spun the next one, and punched him. A tingle of pain ran up his elbow; he knew he had struck solidly. The man howled, staggered and raced after his companions, already through the gate and in the street.

Then all was quiet in the yard, and the music and singing came loud and clear from inside. Dacorda was pulling off the sack on his head.

"Told you not to flash your roll," Carroll snapped.

"So you did, so you did!" Dacorda struck a match, scanned the ground. "First thing I did was to toss my pocketbook back here somewhere. Here it is!" He replaced the wallet in his pocket. "They hung on to me like dogs—" He swore. "They got it, they got it!"

"What?"

"My scapular. That's why they tore my shirt open." Dacorda was silent a moment, then blurted out, "You know damn well what they got! How did they know I had it if you didn't tell them? You dirty skunk!"

"Me? I told them you had—"

"Who else?"

"Are you calling me a thief?"

"You know damn well what you are!"

Carroll lost his head. He had helped Dacorda and was insulted in return. He moved instantly. He struck the other across the mouth, and the fight was started.

Neither of them could see clearly; they shifted for position in the dim light. This probably saved Carroll from a quick and ignominious knockout like Fenmayer's. He outweighed Dacorda by twenty-five or thirty pounds and was taller and had inches of reach on him. But the short man was a sheaf of springy muscles and knew his business.

When Dacorda grew accustomed to the poor light, his blows began to come more precisely, mostly to the body. Carroll was neither soft nor timid, could box as well as the average. But he was growing sick and dizzy from stomach punishment.

Fortunately for him, a flashlight swept on them from a few feet away. Behind it gleamed the brass buttons and gold chevrons of the patrol sergeant.

"Attention!"

Carroll obeyed instantly. So did Dacorda.

"What's going on?"

"Just a friendly argument, Sergeant," said Carroll.

"Oh, it's you! And Dacorda? I wondered when you Americans would come to blows. It never fails. A tradition, eh?"

"Sure, Sergeant."

"Well, Carroll, you've done enough to him." The sergeant swept the light on Dacorda's face. It was cut and bleeding. His own blows, more efficient and dangerous, had left few visible bruises on his opponent. "Now, you two, shake hands."

Dacorda shook his head.

"I'm through with you, Carroll. And if you think you got anything, you're wrong. That scapular was blessed for luck, that's all."

"I tell you I had nothing to do with this."

"You tried to take my picture this afternoon. Then this happens. I'm wise to you."

"He won't make peace, Sergeant," Carroll declared.

"All right. Carroll, you come back to camp with us. I'll inform the captain, who'll see that you don't get to town together. Dacorda, see that you're in time to answer the roll. After the start you made, it would be foolish to get punished."

Carroll marched back with the patrol, puzzled and angry.

The following morning, Carroll was assigned to a special chore, the shaping of heavy stones into blocks for the construction of a blockhouse. He watched for a chance to speak privately to Zerlich, who was on a wheelbarrow detail.

"Did Dacorda tell you anything about what happened last night?"

"He said you double-crossed him."

"How? What about?"

"He didn't explain."

"He thinks I got those natives to rob him? Is that what you mean?"

"He does."

"And what did you say to him?"

"Nothing, I kept my mouth shut."

"You're a friend!" Carroll said sarcastically.

"Well, Dacorda's scapular was stolen. Three of us saw it. Gianella is out of the question, so am I."

"Why would I want it?"

"Dacorda thinks you believe he's hidden something inside. He asked me a lot of questions, told me that as I spoke good German I should find out whether you had been in the Legion as long as you claim, and if you had had communications with the American Consulate. I asked. You did get a couple of letters."

"I lost my passport, reported it and they wrote me."

"All I could tell Dacorda was that you had received official mail. That seemed to worry him a lot. He says that they thought a guy fresh from America would make him suspicious so they got you, already in the Legion, to investigate him."

"Who's 'they' that hired me?"

"The cops, I guess."

"Do you think I'm a stool pigeon, too?"

"That's none of my business."

Zerlich was off with his load, and Carroll plied hammer and chisel a while. Zerlich suspected him of being an informer. It was a stupid mess. The attack on Dacorda must have been a coincidence, because he flashed his money so often. Carroll decided to test Zerlich's friendship.

"We're off-duty this afternoon. Want to go for a swim?"

"No. I'm going with Dacorda." Zerlich wiped his face, shrugged. "Listen, you're a nice enough guy, but I've been a friend of Dacorda's almost a year. You know plenty of people."

"I get it," Carroll concluded. "You're off me, he's off me. That makes it unanimous."

He turned indifferently, resumed work. But he was irritated. The insult was double: first, to accuse him of betraying a friend; second, to suspect him of being disloyal to a Legionnaire. The suspicion that he was a police informer, willing to sell a comrade for blood-money, was serious. If the rumor spread in the company, he wouldn't be very popular.

He was off-duty after lunch.

He found a man he had known in a hill station north of Midelt, a Spahi, regular cavalryman, named Moulai ben Brahim. Carroll and he had hunted together, and had become good friends. Ben Brahim listened to his relation of the robbery, nodding several times, his lean, brown fingers tugging at his black beard thoughtfully.

"And what can I do for you, Brother?"

"The man I hit must have a mark on his face today. All of them belonged to the Second Battalion of the Sixty-Eighth Moroccan Regiment. I noticed their collar badges. Maybe you could locate him, and give me a chance to talk it over."

"I'll find him, Allah willing."

Ben Brahim reported back by two o'clock. He had found a man with a bruised face among the Tirailleurs who admitted that he had been struck by a Legionnaire during a row. Ben Brahim explained that he had thought it best not to reveal that Carroll wished to see him, for in that case, Moktar ou Hannoun would have become suspicious.

Therefore, he had suggested that if Moktar had any money to spend, he should join Ben Brahim and two other cavalrymen to play cards. To avoid interference, the game would be held in a small deserted hut a couple of miles away from camp, almost on the line of the advanced posts. Moktar accepted. Carroll could follow, and in the isolated building, no one would come to disturb them.

"He will not talk easily," Ben Brahim warned.

Carroll gathered a few friends, among them

Gianella and Fenmayer. One never knew. They would serve as aids if needed, as witnesses otherwise.

"I'll try to get the scapular back, if I can," Carroll outlined. "In any case, I'll get him to say before all of you that the attack was his own idea and not planned by me."

"Dacorda's crazy!" Fenmayer said.

"He's worried sick. I better prove to him that he's all right."

 It was nearly three o'clock when Ben Brahim and two of his comrades left camp with a Tirailleur who sported a magnificent black eye. The Legionnaires followed at a distance, and found the four squatted around a folded blanket. Moktar was shuffling the cards. A brass kettle in which tea was being brewed was on a small fire in a corner of the room.

When he saw Carroll, whom he probably recognized, Moktar sought to rise. Ben Brahim restrained him, and spoke in Arabic.

"There will be no threats of police and jail. The Legionnaires want to speak as between men and man."

Fenmayer stood in the doorway. The Spahis went and sat against a far wall, unconcerned. Carroll sat down facing Moktar, who was a young chap about twenty-eight years old, with a brown, resolute face and steady, fearless eyes.

"You understand French?"

"Yes. I've been in the Army seven years."

"That's fine. Now, where did you get that eye?"

"You know."

"Last night, in the yard of the Moulin Rouge?"

"Yes," Moktar admitted. "But I've been promised there would be no police and no prison."

"That's right. We'll handle that ourselves. But we want the truth. Who was with you?"

"I cannot talk about others."

"You're right," Carroll conceded. He liked

Moktar's refusal to betray his accomplices. "Why did you attack the Legionnaire? To rob him, eh?"

"Yes."

"What did you take from him?"

"We could not find his bills, although we knew he had a lot. But we took change from his trouser pockets, and a little gold chain with a Christian amulet at one end. Here it is." Moktar produced the slender chain.

Carroll took it with a smile. He examined the cross hanging from the chain, which formed a small box. He opened it with a thumb nail. Inside was a minute white sliver, which Gianella said was a holy relic.

"There was nothing else in this?"

"No."

"You've heard, all of you? Now, Moktar, did you know me to speak to?"

"No. I know you are the one who hit me last night. Before that, I had seen you once or twice, at the cafe, with other men. But I never spoke."

"Did I tell you my friend had money, a gold chain? Did I suggest that you rob him?"

"Never."

"You swear it by Allah?"

"By Allah, I swear it."

"That's a good oath, and settles the matter," Carroll declared. "You fellows come to see Dacorda with me."

"A minute," Gianella broke in. "I'd seen that chain, too. We might as well find out who told this chap what Dacorda had under his shirt."

"Answer, Moktar."

"Somebody told me."

"Who?"

"I promised to keep quiet."

Ben Brahim drew Carroll aside, whispered for a few minutes. The American shook his head. "I wouldn't go as far as that—"

"But Moktar would in your place, and he doesn't know you wouldn't. It'll frighten him. Tell him, anyway."

"Take off your boots," Carroll ordered, returning to Moktar.

"There's nothing hidden in them."

"Take them off!"

Moktar removed his army boots. He wore no socks.

"Unless you tell us who gave you the tip about the gold chain, two of us will hold you, while one pours boiling water from that kettle over your feet. Make up your mind within two minutes."

"I'll report to my officer!"

"Your feet will be boiled, anyway. And there's only your word against us five. We'll swear you did it yourself while drunk." He wondered what he would do if Moktar called his bluff. But torture is not unusual to a Moroccan, and Moktar did not think it was a joke.

"The Syrian who runs the cafe told me."

"How did he know?"

"He didn't tell me."

"Tell us how the Syrian happened to speak to you about robbing my friend. Tell all from beginning to end."

Moktar nodded.

"It came about this way: I and a few friends went to the cafe last night. The Syrian has known me a long time. He called me behind the bar and asked me if I wanted to make some easy money.

"I said I did. He said all we had to do was gang on a Legionnaire he would point out, when we got a chance. Even as he spoke, you came in. You sat down, there were three of you, next to the young Legionnaire who now stands at the door, who got up and tried to fight your friend. He was stunned immediately.

"When the Syrian told us it was that man we had to attack, we hesitated. Then he said we could keep all the money on him for ourselves, if we only gave him a chain of gold which the man had around his neck. He would give us two hundred and fifty francs for it.

"We were a little scared of your friend, because he fought so well. But there was the money, and we were five. We followed him into the yard. We could not find his wallet, but we did find the chain and some loose change. Then you came, and we fled into the street.

"When you quarreled later, we entered the cafe—through the rear door. I showed the Syrian the gold chain, and he said it was what he wanted. He gave me the two hundred and fifty francs."

"How do you happen to have the chain to-day?"

"The Syrian was not acting for himself. A Legionnaire came over, and looked at the chain. He opened the locket, as you just did, and there was nothing there except what you saw. He seemed very disappointed, asked us if we had not opened it before and lost something. We said no, which was the truth.

"So the fellow gave the Syrian five hundred francs and said he might use him again. We understood then that we had taken all that risk for half the money promised. But there was nothing we could do against the Syrian thief.

"The Legionnaire looked at the chain a long time, then said he didn't want to keep it. The Syrian wouldn't have it in his place, because it might cause trouble if found. So they gave it to me. I didn't dare to try to sell it so soon after the robbery. That's all."

"The Legionnaire wasn't me?" Carroll insisted.

"No."

"Which was he?"

"He paid for my silence."

Carroll by this time would have gone any length to satisfy his curiosity. Dacorda had been partly right, there was a traitor in the company, spying on him. A suspicion he had dimly felt for several days was taking shape.

"Who was he?"

"He is tall and pretty old."

"Do I know him?"

"He sat with you and the man we robbed, last night."

"Zerlich!" Carroll turned to the others. "Dacorda will kill him!"

Fenmayer shrugged, Gianella smiled.

"Take your shoes and beat it," Carroll ordered Moktar. When the Moroccan had gone, happy to get off so easily, the American turned to Ben Brahim.

"Thank you, Brother. I offer nothing for the

service. But ask when needed." The cavalryman understood, and he took his friend away.

"Those men will not talk about what happened here," Carroll resumed, as the Legionnaires grouped around him. "Now, what do we do?"

"What's there to be done?" Fenmayer wondered, "except clear yourself and let the punk take what's coming. I never liked that old fellow."

"You're very young," Gianella said gently.

Carroll said, "Whatever Dacorda is hiding must be important. He'll be sore because he had trusted Zerlich like a brother. Sure, we can talk to him and we're not responsible for anything that happens. But is it doing a good turn to Dacorda to tell him something that'll drive him crazy and get him into a lot of trouble?"

"No," Fenmayer admitted. "But what's right's right."

"How do we know what's right? Sure, we have Dacorda's story of what he did. He says he married a couple of times. But what we just found out about Zerlich changes everything. He's followed Dacorda to the Legion, evidently, and didn't arrest him, even if the fellow admits the crime. That bigamy story must be a fake, and it may be murder."

"He's a Legionnaire. That's all we have to know."

"And what do you call Zerlich? Isn't he a Legionnaire?"

"He's a rat, that's what he is."

"And Dacorda may be a murderer."

"He's a Legionnaire." Fenmayer was stubborn.

"Looks to me as if it wasn't an ordinary crime," Carroll pointed out. "It costs a lot of money to cross the ocean, and it takes a lot of determination for a man to enlist in the Legion to keep track of another. Somebody supplied that money and Zerlich showed that determination. It's all right to say Zerlich's a stool pigeon, but maybe not. He may be doing his job."

"Carroll's right, Fenmayer," the other German put in.

"I'll agree to whatever he says," Fenmayer said. "What's the plan now?"

"The four of us will take Zerlich aside and tell him what we found out. If he has a satisfactory explanation, we keep out of his business. If not, we tell Dacorda."

The four went back to camp. In a street of the Legion sector, they saw Zerlich and Dacorda walking aimlessly. While the others kept some distance away, Carroll went up to them. Dacorda looked at him, turned his head aside and spat on the ground.

"I want to speak to you, Zerlich."

"I have nothing to say to you, Carroll. I told you where we stood."

"I have a message from a friend of yours."

"Why doesn't he come himself?"

"He's busy. You made a deal with him yesterday." Carroll held the older man's eyes. "And he claims it's now worth more than five hundred francs to him."

Zerlich's glance did not waver, he did not start. But a greenish pallor spread slowly over his sallow face. Carroll was forced to admire him for the careless laugh he contrived.

"I should have expected this," he said casually.

"Doing business with this bum?" Dacorda challenged.

"I seem to be. Sorry. Explain later." Zerlich fell in step with Carroll. "Don't mention names, places. It's important. I'd sooner have you find out than some foolish fellow who'd talk."

They stopped by the three others, who had joined a group of Legionnaires gathered before a notice fastened to the facade of the company's office shack, a large sheet, handsomely written by a prideful clerk.

The Legionnaires whose names are listed below will report tonight, immediately after mess, to Sub-Lieutenant d'Argoval's quarters, for special duty.

Carroll glanced at the dozen names as far down as "C," saw that he was not included. The written announcement, somewhat unusual in the field, aroused much curiosity.

"Zerlich's on there, the last listed," Gianella observed. "You have any idea of what it's about?"

"No."

"We better hurry. Mess is at five." Carroll led the way outside the barbed-wire enclosure surrounding the tents.

"Well, what's the idea of the four?" Zerlich smiled grimly. "A court-martial?"

"Call it that. Here's what we found out." Carroll related his interview with Moktar tersely. "I've got witnesses and the scapular to prove it. Before we tell Dacorda, we thought we'd listen to your side of it. Fair enough?"

"Fair, but awkward," Zerlich nodded.

"Can't be helped. After all, you encouraged him to suspect me. That's a dirty trick."

Zerlich lighted a cigarette. He was very cool, poised, and did not appear shamed. He replied in German, not the colloquial tongue he had employed until then, but the language of a cultured man. It was a moment, and somehow a dignity touched it.

"Gentlemen, I understand your suspicions. I must thank you for consulting me before informing Legionnaire Dacorda. I see that I have an explanation to supply if I do not wish to be exposed. As I am among you, it is most natural that I should be under your rules and traditions. Later, I shall be glad to have all know why I am here. You have guessed part of the truth. In the meanwhile, would you oblige me further by permitting me to reveal my intention to one of you only? A secret shared by four men is not a secret. It is evident that Carroll, whom I have most offended, should be the one picked. Will you rely on his judgment as to whether you should warn Dacorda or remain silent a while?"

The three glanced at Carroll, then nodded. Zerlich thanked them once more, and led the American aside. They walked slowly toward the river, across the naked plain where the afternoon sun was reflected redly in the drying puddles scattered on the drying red earth.

"My job's important enough, Carroll, to excuse any annoyance which I've inflicted upon you." Zerlich used English now. "I enlisted in the Legion to carry it out, taking the chance that I could legally get out as soon as my task was over. I'm Austrian born, brought up in America, that's true. Forget the rest of my story. It was cooked up for a purpose.

"Of course, Zerlich is no more my name than Dacorda is his. More or less unofficially, I'm an agent for the National Jewelers' Protective Association and a couple of insurance companies. Dacorda is a nice guy, but he is an accomplice of thieves and a receiver of stolen goods.

"Have you ever heard of James Barrister? You haven't, because you are not in my business. But I doubt that there's a plainclothes man anywhere who couldn't give you an oral portrait of the chap. He is, or was, a jewel thief, a genius in his line.

"About two years ago, he worked with a handsome young fellow, who interested a lady old enough to be his mother. That was Mrs. Tauberal. You read about that in the papers, didn't you? They took stuff from her—diamonds, emeralds, pearls, insured for more than five hundred grand. He waited for things to cool down, didn't need to hurry; he had plenty of other jack. We knew he had the stuff cached somewhere. But where?

"Old Man Tauberal reported the robberies. The gigolo squealed on Barrister. We found him in a hotel at Palm Beach, and picked him up for questioning. We locked him up until his lawyer got busy. We had a good case, with witnesses to crack his alibi. But we didn't want to jail him as much as we wanted to recover the stuff. So we pretended to have no proof, and he was released. That was to make him confident, understand?

"We had guys following him whom he spotted as we'd planned he should, because we had an agent working into his gang. We had to divert Barrister's attention. It took the fellow five months to get anywhere.

"One day, when Barrister pretended to be a stamp broker in a small office in New York, he managed to get away from the fellow tailing him. Our informer phoned that Barrister was in New Jersey, meeting some important people. We only checked on the facts, for we were certain he never took the stuff along on a first conference.

"Our spy then reported that another meeting had been arranged. Remember, it was serious business, not disposing of a dime's worth of peanuts. Nearly a million involved. There was a man from Amsterdam, another from London, big time fences come over on special business.

"We found the place, a big house once used as a fancy summer hotel back in the hills close to Pennsylvania. Barrister had rented it through a friend.

"On the day they met, we were on the job. We waited until Barrister had gone in, then counted his friends as they arrived. They all wore knickers and sweaters, had golf bags, and came in splendid cars. Looked more like a lot of Wall Street executives on a week-end than crooks. We had a field telephone rigged up in the woods for emergency. There were three New York detectives, and a couple of bulls from Newark, some State troopers, and a local cop who knew the grounds and the house.

"Barrister, we noticed, took in his golf bag. The others didn't. So we guessed what he carried in it. We were pretty excited, because Old Man Tauberal had offered a big reward, and there was money from other sources involved.

"We had taken care to have all the roads guarded in case somebody slipped out when we rushed in. A man would have to use a car to get clear, and the operative at the telephone had the license numbers of the cars and would report any car leaving to every trap along the roads.

"We were about to go ahead when an old delivery truck rattles into the yard. The local cop told us that the driver with a load of stuff in a big basket was Mike Melano, who ran a speakeasy. He was probably bringing up liquor for the party inside. He said that Melano's all right, had never done a crooked thing in his life except peddle booze.

"The cop said Melano fought professionally as Battling Melano, welterweight, and was good enough to be on four Madison Square Garden cards, in prelims. Everybody liked him. But we had something bigger to go after than a hicktown bootlegger. So we let him go in and out, carrying baskets, cases and crates, about four times.

"He stayed longer on the last trip, and we thought they were paying him for the junk he brought. He came out just when the guy at the telephone told us that everything's set all along the line, and that a mosquito couldn't get through unseen. We decided to let him go, because we wanted to keep things quiet. So, as he pulled away in his truck, we signaled the troopers to let him pass.

"As soon as he was out of sight, we walked in on them inside.

"There were nine men there, and not a gun in the place. Barrister smiled, asking us to have a drink. We pulled the place to pieces looking for the junk, and found nothing. Nobody was left except Melano, and we figured that Barrister was too smart to hand over a million to a man he doesn't know. We were *too* smart.

"There was no use stalling. Barrister was held for trial. We tried to sweat out of the others where the stuff was hidden. Barrister had told them the stuff was in the house, that they would see it. But they couldn't give us more dope than that. They said nothing whatever had happened.

"We had to make a deal with Barrister. We told him that he was due for a life stretch, if we bring out his former convictions. We told him we can get him ten to twenty, which means seven years with time off for good behavior, if it's worth a million to him not to stay inside for keeps. We showed him the proof we had, listed our witnesses. He's no damned fool; he knew we had him. He cracked and told us his story.

"Mike Melano had come in with a case, and although he seemed sort of stupid, he had noticed a lot of cops moving about on his way up.

He spoke of that to Barrister without knowing it meant a thing to him. Barrister guessed what was up. As we had let him go in Florida, he thought he could beat the case against him. Also, he knew he might make a deal if things got bad. Very few people hate a million dollars' worth.

"So he approached this Melano—to take five thousand dollars down and twenty thousand later, to take the stuff away. Barrister handed him a slip with the name of a safe-deposit vault, made him swear on the Cross that he won't squeal. And Melano took the stuff away under a cloth in his big basket. He walked right out under our noses—and we let him drive away!

"Barrister also told him who to tip off that he had carried out instructions. Must have been his lawyer, though we never found out, because Barrister had information, even in jail. Mike Melano had been scared to go to the place named on the slip, afraid it would be watched. So he had kept the stuff for a couple of days, and had it planted in a vault somewhere. He told Barrister that he had the password and the key, and wanted Barrister to tell him what to do with them, and asked about the twenty grand.

"Barrister told him not to talk to a soul, and suggested that Mike beat it abroad, in case we suspected him. That was before things got hot for Barrister.

"We got to Melano's place in a hurry. But he had been gone a couple of weeks. Barrister co-operated, and reported his address. Mike had gone to Italy. There, our agents found out that he had had some trouble. He was American born, his mother had been Irish, but his old man was Italian, so he could only stay a short time before being put in the army. We traced him to Lyons, France.

"One of our men in France went to him and made a proposition. Melano, he said, wouldn't be arrested, if he turned in the stuff. Then he promised him the twenty thousand if he would tell us where the stuff was kept. Of course, we had investigated on our side, looked up banks and storage-vaults for three hundred miles around New York, compared his signature with writing on thousands of cards. It was a tough job, and got us nowhere.

"Mike Melano told our man he wants to play square with Barrister, that he couldn't betray him. Raising the ante didn't help. Melano wasn't selling. In his way, he was being honest and that's a fact. He said he had sworn on the Cross to keep the secret.

"The next day, he slipped away from our man and went to Paris. I asked to be sent over to France, because I had my own idea of the job. One thing Melano must have kept with him right along was the key to the safe-deposit box he had hired. You can always trace a key. They have numbers, you know, and once you get hold of one, it's sure you'll find the lock it fits.

"I found Melano in Paris. He was like a kid with a new toy spending his money, what he had left. He'd given his grandmother in Italy two thousand dollars! I didn't let him see me, but I went through his baggage in the hotel. I found nothing important. I waited until he was taking a bath. He had nothing with him except a bathrobe, and I've been in the pockets three times. I searched his suit, his shirt, his tie, his collar, his socks, his shoes, everything. I even looked in his fountain pen and opened the case of his watch.

"But no key, although I knew he had it. A key worth a million to somebody, and fifty thousand to me, which means a house in the country, a fine car, retirement—the key to heaven, Carroll, the key to the sky!

"I get to thinking that he'd hid the key somewhere in Paris. Maybe in a bank, maybe at the Express Office, where he got mail from time to time, letters that Barrister wrote for us, asking him to come back and turn in the stuff. But Melano was wise that the cops were pressing Barrister, and swore not to obey any such orders. He didn't fall for the bait.

"I kept out of his sight, but never lost him. Then, one morning, he gets into a row with a big Swede living in the same hotel, over a girl. His size fooled the squarehead, who charged into him. Melano worked on him four or five seconds, split his eye, knocked out a few teeth, laid him like a hall rug. The Swede cracked his head when he dropped, and the police were called in.

"There were two of them, and Melano started on them. He knew he was in wrong, and beat it from the hotel without taking a thing. The police didn't know where to look for him, but I'd been following him days and I did. He was in a restaurant near Les Halles thirty minutes after. And he went from there and enlisted in the Foreign Legion. The owner of the place, an Italian, told him that was the safest place.

"All right, all I have to do is enlist in the Legion. I have come too far to lose him. Don't have to worry about my wife and three kids, my salary goes on, because that was the agreement when I left. And with official help from the States, I know that I can get out when the job's done. I didn't arrange anything in advance with the French, being afraid somebody would talk.

"I asked where and when that draft of recruits for the Legion was going. They told me Fort St. Jean, in Marseilles, in three days.

"So I decided not to enlist in the same place, which might make him suspicious. I took a train for Dijon and enlisted there. Almost had to cry my way in, too, because I'm no chicken and there are varicose veins on my legs. Well, our bunch went to Lyons, where it was put with the gang from Paris. I saw Melano, who calls himself Dacorda, right away.

"But I didn't talk to him. I talked to another man, about the States. And Melano, sort of homesick, started talking in English. He tried to explain why he was in, after my sad story, and without his knowing it, I made up that story about a couple of wives for him. The fellow knows how to fight, but he'll never be a good liar. Shows everything he feels, as you know.

"In the Legion, I nearly went crazy keeping in the same outfit with him. I didn't dare use official pull in asking for transfers. I've kept in the same company, but never in the same room, so I can't get a line on that key. Once or twice, I almost lost him, when he was sent to some other place. When the officers turned me down for a transfer, I slipped a hundred francs to this scribe, five hundred to another, fifty here and twenty there, until my name was on a list and I followed Dacorda.

"Then we were sent to Morocco, for fighting service. I didn't like the idea. And I was getting to like Dacorda. Except for not telling me his real story—he keeps his oath and shoots square with Barrister and his own soul—he loves me like a father. But there's fifty thousand dollars in it for me, and I'm a family man. And it's my job.

"When he went over the cliff, the other day, I was raving mad. I've been told those hillmen strip the bodies before chopping them up. I got scared that key would be lost where no one will ever find it. Lucky for me, you tagged along. You worked for nothing, and that risk was worth all I'm after, believe me. Then I saw that scapular and that cross. I thought right away that it's where he keeps it. You could, if you filed the guard down to fit. Even with part of the number missing, the make would help locate the box. They have records.

"So I used some more money, and got the Syrian to have him robbed. There's nothing in the scapular. When he suspects that it's a put-up job, what am I to do? Lose fifty thousand to play the hero for you?"

"No," Carroll admitted. He had listened to Zerlich with intense interest and growing admiration. The old chap spoke simply of the chances he had taken, of danger and fatigue accepted, to carry out the job. Service in the Legion was not easy for a man in the forties used to city life, fine hotels and good food. Sudden death for a married man with children and a comfortable home waiting for him was not a good prospect!

"What are you going to do, now, Carroll?"

"Tell the others to keep quiet, that your explanation is all right with me. And I'll take what's coming from Dacorda." He laughed. "He's a pretty good guy at that, isn't he?"

"That's what hurts," Zerlich admitted. "He was tempted by a lot of money and is no real crook. He'd die for me, he'd die for you, for anybody he likes. But I've got to get that key."

"I understand," Carroll granted. "Maybe you could speak to the captain and have him searched thoroughly."

"If that was all there was to it, we'd have done that in France. But suppose he has left it somewhere? He wouldn't tell. This way, he may give me a clue sometime, in a friendly talk. Or I may see the address when he writes to pay for the vault. See?"

"That may take a long time."

"I'll stick it out," Zerlich snapped. "Now, how can I square myself with him about this friend and the money you talked of?"

"Easily," Carroll pointed out. "You tell him you wanted to desert and propositioned a guy who wants more than you can give."

"That's a good idea," Zerlich admitted. "Listen, Carroll, I'll not forget what you're doing. When I collect—"

"Forget it, I'm not in your business," Carroll cut him short. He was sincere. Zerlich was a detective disguised as a Legionnaire, dealing with a man he judged a crook. It was all right for him to disregard the code. But he, Carroll, was a genuine Legionnaire. To prevent further temptation, for turning down a few thousand dollars which would have helped him considerably later was not easy, he changed the subject. "Better go back and eat. You have to report to d'Argoval after mess."

"Have you any idea what for?"

"No. One of the others on that list was a tinsmith. You're down on records as a dealer in hardware and a plumber in civilian life. Maybe you'll be asked to work on some job—pipe connections for the new blockhouse they're building, likely enough."

"That's probably it. Thanks and so long, Carroll."

 The "soup" bugle sounded. Carroll joined his friends, and as they ate he explained that Zerlich must be left alone. The matter was serious but concerned only the two involved. They stormed questions at him, and he promised that he would tell them as soon as he could, writing if they had separated.

After the meal, the Legionnaires summoned by d'Argoval were seen filing into the sub-lieutenant's tent. They remained inside for fifteen minutes, then emerged looking very important, very serious, and refusing information.

"Secret orders."

But they were inwardly elated and proud, with the exception of Zerlich, who looked worried. The others watched as the men busied themselves cleaning automatic pistols issued by the officer. Carroll guessed that they had been picked for a special and dangerous undertaking. Nettled that he had not been chosen, he felt that he would have been more use than Zerlich, a comparatively feeble novice.

He was startled when the detective, who had avoided him to show his sympathy to Dacorda, sought him out.

"I know you won't repeat this," Zerlich started. "I'm included on a job where there's ten chances of being bumped off for one of coming back. That young fellow gets us in there and smiles at us. He says, 'I've been selected for a dangerous mission. I knew that if I asked for volunteers, the whole company would stand up. I'd hurt somebody's feelings by not picking them. You are all Legionnaires, all ready for sacrifice and service. So I picked the names out of a hat!' And he looked as if he was being good to us."

"I'll replace you," Carroll said instantly.

He knew that d'Argoval was greedy for exciting jobs, and that following him tonight would be exciting. Carroll did not worry about danger. He had volunteered for several dangerous missions and come back alive. Moreover, he was on the list for sergeants, and had been held up because of a spree in Meknes. This stunt might wipe that from the slate.

"Can it be done?" Zerlich asked.

"Maybe. Let's talk to d'Argoval."

But the sub-lieutenant was asleep, resting for his trip that night, and the orderly would not allow them to enter. Zerlich suggested that they see the captain. Carroll, who knew Barbaroux, was doubtful. But he was eager to go, and there was a bare chance that it could be arranged.

The captain was in his office, the plank shack beside his tent. There were two clerks with him. The thick-set, red-faced officer was writing a report laboriously, fortifying himself with drinks of anisette from a bottle on his folding table. His massive face lifted. Carroll, who spoke excellent French, was spokesman. He gave the purpose of their call.

"No," Barbaroux snapped.

"Captain, I—"

"A thousand times, no!" The captain launched on a tirade. "When a Legionnaire has the honor to be selected for a dangerous mission, he should be pleased, by God, he should be pleased! If he isn't, he should have the decency not to admit it. Yes, you, the tall chap! You may be killed tonight. Why did you come to the Legion, if life was so dear?"

"I must explain—"

"This is the most preposterous request, the most ignoble scene I have heard of in seventeen years of Legion. Carroll, you have a right to take advantage of anything to obtain what you wish. I'm sorry I can't grant you the privilege you ask. But a Legionnaire does what he is asked. That's discipline. Dismissed!"

"Better tell him," Zerlich said.

"Legionnaire Zerlich has reasons to lay before you, Captain."

"A Legionnaire never reasons. He obeys."

"Yet—"

"Shut up and go, both of you."

"Tell him," Zerlich insisted.

"Legionnaire Zerlich is a police official on a mission, Captain."

"Following a man in my company?"

"It's his duty, Captain."

"Duty?" Barbaroux understood the weight of that word better than most. "Right, it's his duty. Zerlich, your credentials, please."

Zerlich produced two letters and a card.

"They're foreign papers," the captain declared. "I can't accept them."

"I haven't revealed my identity to the French police, Captain."

"That's too bad," Barbaroux said softly. "Officially, I can't recognize you as what you claim to be, on your mere word. You understand it would make it too easy to malinger. Any man could come to me and say he's on a mission and must be spared."

"Is there anything to be done, Captain?" Zerlich insisted.

"There's always something to be done about anything," Barbaroux was dangerously calm. "You must write me a letter outlining your mission, your reasons for deeming it more important than your duty as a Legionnaire. I shall transmit it to the battalion commander, who will send it to the colonel. In due course, it will reach Brigade Headquarters, then Divisional Headquarters, then Army Headquarters. You follow me?"

"Yes, Captain."

"It will be turned over to the Ministry of War. Which will dispatch it to the Police, who will send it to the Ministry of Foreign Affairs. The Embassy in Washington will handle it. I do not know the routine of your American offices, but ultimately, they will reply to our Embassy, and that reply will come back to me by the same route."

The Legionnaires understood that Barbaroux was joking.

"That will take time," Zerlich protested.

"Oh, no more than a year," Barbaroux assured him gently.

"I can wire the American Consulate in Casablanca."

"Can they identify you, confirm your statements, immediately?"

"They'll cable, and the answer will come tomorrow afternoon."

"Sorry, but you are on duty tonight. And you'll have to go. It would humiliate the whole company if a man hesitated." Barbaroux shrugged. "I don't like men in your trade in the Legion, Zerlich. I may be prejudiced, but I'm a Legionnaire, first and last. The answer was no and is no."

Outside, Zerlich stopped. "Who else can we see?"

"Nobody. You have to get the captain's permission to see the major, and all such requests must be asked a day in advance. There is no time."

"Then I've got to go."

"Sure. Barbaroux's nuts on the Legion, and all he cares is how a man acts while in it. He's shielded others before. And we like him for it."

"I'm sick to my stomach," Zerlich grumbled. "I was getting somewhere. Now, everything's spoiled. Those scribes will talk, and Dacorda'll be tipped off."

"Maybe you talked too soon."

"I don't want to get killed without him."

"You may come out alive."

"Small chance. Might as well tell you what the job is. They can't do more to me than is likely to happen. They found out that a big native chief is around here, a guy who deserted from a native regiment and has been training the forces we're fighting. Our bunch is to go inside the enemy's lines tonight, capture him. D'Argoval tells us that the Native Intelligence Service is not sure that this news wasn't given out purposely, to get us to do just what we're doing. We may be ambushed and massacred. Even if discovered accidentally inside their positions, we won't have a chance."

"Never can tell. I'll help you prepare."

The men in the small expedition had been instructed to take the bare bayonet, passed through the belt like a knife, six grenades in a bag, a pistol and a hundred cartridges, and also the two-quart canteen and a little hardtack. They were forbidden to wear képis, as the rigid outline of the peak might be spotted even in the darkness. Cloth wound like turbans would replace other headgear. The place chosen as a goal was a tiny hamlet in the hills, fifteen miles to the south.

Zerlich was like a man being made ready for the electric chair. Dacorda stood by and watched, but did not speak, sulking at Carroll's presence. It was evident he still suspected the wrong man. As he had no intimate friends other than Zerlich, he had not as yet heard the rumor spread through the camp by the scribes, to the effect that Zerlich was a detective.

They joined the little detachment assembling in the dusk. Dacorda stepped forward, offered his hard palm to his old friend.

"Wish I was going along with you, Pop," he said.

"So do I," Zerlich touched the hand and smiled in self-derision.

"Going to be tough, from the way you look."

"Plenty tough, Mike."

"Well, wish you luck."

"Thanks."

"Don't take any wooden nickels, Pop."

"I won't, Mike."

Dacorda's eyes moistened suddenly. He did not wait for the detachment to go, but left to hide his emotion. Carroll escorted Zerlich to the fringe of the camp. There, the old Legionnaire gave him an envelope. Around him, the majority of the group were asking a like service from their friends.

"In case—you know. Might add a couple of lines yourself. How it happened, why—might get her a small pension."

"I won't need to," Carroll said to console him.

Sub-Lieutenant d'Argoval called the roll, separated his followers from their friends to avoid last-minute substitutions or unwanted volunteers.

"Let's go!" he concluded.

Night fell. The stars were out. The camp fires glowed behind the detachment, and in the hills, very remote, blinked other flames, threatening, hostile. For a few minutes, Carroll stood with others who had escorted old comrades to the jumping-off place, and listened to the dwindling footsteps.

They grew fainter and fainter. Then they could be heard no longer.

III

The routine of the camp was not changed in any visible particular, probably to avoid discovery of the expedition by emissaries the hillmen sent to the city to glean information. Legionnaires and troopers of other units were permitted to go into the town as usual after sunset. But the men in Barbaroux's company were depressed and sullen, aware that their comrades were plunging deeper and deeper into unknown danger.

Carroll drifted into the Moulin Rouge. He noticed Dacorda, seated alone in a corner of the main room. He was not drinking much, and kept relighting the same cigarette, his eyes lost on space, his fingers drumming against the table.

It was easy to see that he was suffering from loneliness and worry, and Carroll had an impulse to join him. But he knew the man's temper, feared a public rebuff which might force him into a fight. He had several excellent reasons for not clashing with Dacorda. The first was that he liked the man in spite of what had happened, and he frankly admitted to himself that he did not want his body pounded again. When he took a deep breath, he could still feel the effects of the crushing blows inflicted on him.

"Why not call him over here and tell him the truth?" Gianella suggested. "The scribes have talked, and it's all over the battalion that Zerlich's from the police."

"That seems to be the simplest way," Carroll admitted. "But I know he likes the old chap, and somehow I don't want to be there when he finds out."

"Have it your way. Say, this isn't a cafe—it's a graveyard."

The Russian who had played the accordion the night before was present. But his heart was not in his music, and he soon tossed the instrument aside to settle down to steady drinking. Carroll was thinking, as they all were, of the Legionnaires following young d'Argoval in the darkness.

Fenmayer relieved his nervous strain by picking a fight with a big teamster from the artillery convoy. He beat him thoroughly in the courtyard. Only a half-dozen men went as far as the door to watch.

"When will they be back?" a Legionnaire asked.

"Should return to our outposts by dawn if they make it," a veteran replied. "If not—" He drew the edge of his hand across his throat.

"They must have reached the hills by now."

"Just about reached them."

In the section of the Moulin Rouge occupied by the Legionnaires, a dull, crushing silence fell. Card games petered out for want of attention.

It was a few minutes after seven when a sergeant of the Legion entered, the chin strap of his képi snug under his chin, to reveal that he was on duty. He barked for silence and made an announcement.

"Legionnaires of the Second and Fourth Company will report at once to their formations!"

They were on their feet instantly. Carroll buttoned up his tunic, buckled his belt and followed the rest. They started back to camp at a walk, but soon they were running.

The sergeants, already equipped, were waiting.

"Come on, get into full kit and make it snappy. Assembly in five minutes."

The Legionnaires found their guns and ammunition, formed on the esplanade left free between the rows of tents and the shallow defensive trench. In the light of a storm-lantern, they saw the general and a few staff-officers, the major commanding the battalion and the two captains, in animated conversation.

There was something dramatic and moving in this unexpected massing of armed men under the stars. All eyes turned south. But the night there was a black wall, and all the fires they had seen earlier had gone out.

Sergeant-chiefs called the roll. Barbaroux lighted his pipe. He shook hands with the general, with the major, who walked away slowly. Then he stepped to the front of his outfit.

"Attention!" ordered the oldest sergeant.

"Legionnaires!" Barbaroux uttered the word in a tone scarcely louder than the conversational. But there was so much feeling, so much affection in that word that they all stiffened when they heard it. "Legionnaires! Some of our comrades have gone out there. I know that you feel as anxious as I do. We have permission to move forward some distance, to be ready to support our men if they are threatened."

The two companies swung out of camp in columns by threes, at the supple, long pace of the Legion. In a very few minutes, camp and town were behind, the lights dwindling, the sounds muffled. There was an exhilaration in this march into the night, a keen sensation of danger and daring.

All understood the reason for the move. Doubtless, the belief that the report was false had been confirmed, and the high command already knew that Sub-Lieutenant d'Argoval and his group would be in trouble before morning.

The more sanguine among the Legionnaires hoped that they were to be the spearhead of a general night attack. But that was a vain supposition. Carroll understood what was expected of the half-battalion sent out. It was detached to station itself close to the hills, to be ready to greet survivors if any contrived to get back as far as the plain.

There could be no thought of marching nearly four hundred men into hostile hills at night, to fight, in the darkness, foes who knew the ground perfectly. The men of the supporting companies would be like men on a shore, standing by to throw out ropes and life preservers when called for, but forbidden to dive in even to effect rescues.

As a matter of fact, a halt was called two miles beyond the limits of the cavalry outposts that protected the camp from surprise during the day. The men were urged to sit down, ordered not to smoke.

The nervous strain was beginning. They must remain there and wait, wait until the firing started. Then they would have to wait until the survivors straggled in.

"It's ten o'clock," Sergeant Kulhman said.

The Legionnaires conversed in low voices. There was no laughter. Nothing to do except to wait. Squatted on his heels, gripping his rifle with both hands, Carroll was brooding when a hand touched his wrist.

"That you, Jack?"

"Dacorda?"

"Yeah. How's the kid, eh? I can't stand it hanging around like this, with nobody to talk to. It's awful, this here sitting around with your belly twisting inside of you and not allowed to do anything."

"You'll get used to that. Once, I spent a whole night sitting on my mess-kit, under a pouring rain. There were five of us, lost from a patrol."

"Oh, can that. This is bad enough without your saying it ain't so tough. Think they'll all be bumped off?"

"Some will get back, very likely."

"Think Zerlich will make it?"

"How do I know? I wouldn't bet on him. His legs aren't very strong, and he can't fight a lick, in close. You saw him the other day. The first guy had him down."

"Yeah. It's a crime he has to be a soldier. Nice guy, ain't he? What I mean is—sort of soft and refined, and wise. He makes me feel like I know nothing. He can explain machinery. Ever hear him tell about the stars? He could drive a ship across the ocean, I'll bet."

It wrung Carroll's heart a little to listen to him. Dacorda, a fearless man himself, did not admire courage in others. He did not scorn Zerlich for being timid in action. He was a loyal friend.

"He's smart, I guess."

"I'm sorry about last night, Jack. See, there's something been on my mind a long time, and anything that happens looks like it was a put-up job."

"Forget it."

"Since you've been in the Legion, you must have lost good pals."

"Plenty."

"Does a guy get, well, sort of used to it?"

"It hurts as much each time," Carroll said. "That's one thing you can't get used to. After a while, you get so you don't break down easy and do your grieving inside. That's all."

"Wish we could do something."

The hours dragged by, eventless. It was one in the morning, one-thirty. Almost at once, the Legionnaires startled. There was a muffled, remote cracking in their ears, scarcely more than a deep vibration in the air. But they all knew what it meant. Guns firing—the attack on their comrades was launched.

"Can't see flashes," Kulhman said. "They got jumped on in a ravine."

After that first rattling discharge, all was quiet for almost fifteen minutes. Then the vibration resumed, clearer, louder. The Legionnaires rose, stood tensely, necks craned.

The deeper reports of Chassepots rumbled through the sharp, lashing detonations of the Mausers. The sounds came from everywhere at once, deformed, prolonged and multiplied by echoes in the hills. More than fifty rifles were in action. D'Argoval and his men must have had their hands full.

Legionnaires were being massacred up there, and their comrades had to remain idle.

"You can see the flashes now!"

There were minute, blinking lights on the slopes, like fireflies darting about on a summer's night. At times, there were only a few, then they formed irregular streaks. Carroll sweated and grunted aloud. Dacorda pressed him with questions.

"Are they coming nearer, Jack? Can you tell the pistols from rifles? Was that a grenade busting?"

"Steady, Legionnaires," Barbaroux advised. "Nothing for us to do for a long time. Steady."

The sergeants took the cue, circulated in the groups, talked to their men. Even this slight illusion of activity eased the strain. But their helplessness weighed on them all like a ghastly burden. Their comrades were being killed, being killed—

Fenmayer started to sob from nervousness. He wept like a small child, with great heaves of his chest and convulsive gasps. He could face hand-to-hand fighting without flinching.

"There they are, *there they are!*"

The emplacement of the little detachment was now designated by the explosions of hand-grenades. The yellower, wider flashes appeared frequently, and could not be mistaken. Carroll knew that if grenades were used, the natives must be crowding the soldiers hard.

In his brain flitted tiny pictures, clear and sharp as etchings, of falling men screaming in the darkness, surrounded by fierce hillmen with knives, hacked and slashed.

It was impossible that some of the group had not succumbed. Maybe d'Argoval was gone, and he would never again see his grave, comforting smile, his boyish, rather awkward gestures. He would never hear the accented English when the sub-lieutenant believed preposterously that he was speaking the best American slang. Maybe Zerlich had dropped.

No, one never grew hardened to it.

The firing ceased abruptly.

"They're done for!"

"No, the natives have lost them in the dark."

The hills were silent and obscure for a long time. Kulhman said it was after four o'clock. The time had seemed to drag like eternity as it passed, but in retrospect, it fled by like a flash. Carroll stepped near the group of officers, listened.

"Intelligent fellow, d'Argoval," Captain Barbaroux was saying. "We studied the map together. On the way up, he must have picked out a couple of good hiding places in case there was a mishap. He's hiding until he can see his way clear. Probably figures we have done just as we did, moved supporting troops close to the hills to gather him in."

"They couldn't have been wiped out, Captain?"

"Nonsense. Legionnaires are not killed off with so little fuss."

He was right. The firing resumed at five. The grenades exploded only at wide intervals. Probably, they were saved for desperate encounters. Fighting from rock to rock, from bush to bush, hanging on doggedly, the isolated Legionnaires must be retreating faster. The flashes were followed by reports of corresponding intensity after a few seconds.

There was no light in the sky as yet, but the night felt somehow less thick. In the darkness, there floated a perceptible, grayish fog, rising like the breath of the soil. Carroll could see the crests of the hills dimly, stenciled across the paling sky. Fenmayer, worn out, had fallen asleep. He was snoring, his big body sprawled face down, face resting on a bent arm.

Dawn—

Faint light was sliding between the hills from the left, and a rose streak fused along the crests, which looked like rusty, nicked blades suddenly drenched with blood. The firing stopped again. There were vague sounds in the distance, faint shouts, calls. Jackals howled.

The Legionnaires stirred in the semi-obscurity, silhouetted in the fog. Faces showed, lined and haggard. A canteen filled with ration rum was passed from hand to hand.

"Are we going to stick here all day?" a man asked loudly. "Why don't we move forward?"

"I'll have the general explain when we return," Kulhman said.

The light increased; the sun was rising. Metallic glints were kindled on the rifles and the bayonets, sparkled on gold braid and brass buttons. Fenmayer awoke, stretched lingeringly, yawned. Then he was conscious of the situation, and his face grew hard.

"They're firing again!"

"Bah, they didn't make out so poorly," Sergeant Kulhman declared. "Sounds as if half of them were left."

The combat resumed on hillocks not very far inside the hostile zone. The companies were deployed, forming a long, tenuous skirmish line.

"Steady, steady," Barbaroux called.

He beckoned to Kulhman, spoke rapidly. The German returned, grinning cheerfully.

"I'm to take a couple of groups a little way into the hills, to try to help." He summoned Carroll. "Tell the American he needn't come. Wouldn't be right to risk himself for that guy out there."

" 'You stay here,' he says," Carroll translated.

"What's the matter with me? I ain't got smallpox."

"Zerlich's up there," Kulhman snapped.

"What about Zerlich?"

"Might as well tell you now," Carroll blurted out. "Zerlich is a cop. He told the captain last night. There are only two Americans here, and everybody knows he isn't after me."

Carroll expected an explosion of temper, oaths, a savage denunciation. But Dacorda surprised him anew. He scowled, as if the idea had difficulty seeping into his brain, then his face broke into a wide, cheerful smile.

"What do you know about that! It was him all the time, the son of a gun! Pop, I used to call him. Pop." He laughed. "Tell the squarehead it's okay, Jack, that I don't mind going."

"He's hardboiled," Carroll objected. "If he's alive, he'll pinch you."

"He can't collar me," Dacorda said, enjoying himself. "He don't dare! I know what he's after, and if he nabs me, he gets nothing. Listen, Jack, remember how he came after me when I fell over that cliff?"

"I remember he frisked you, sure."

"Never mind. I was as good as dead, without him. What do I care why he did it? How about it, Sergeant?"

"All right."

The sergeant went to obtain final instructions from Barbaroux.

 Carroll took a cartridge from his left pouch, slipped it into a breast-pocket. All Legionnaires fighting in Morocco save a cartridge for themselves. Without undue melodramatics, death is often better than capture in the hills. Carroll had never yielded to the superstition that the cartridge must be selected long in advance, and picked one at random when occasion called.

Dacorda saw the gesture, smiled.

"Mine's got a cross on it, so I can always tell it," he explained. He showed his "mercy cartridge." He had engraved a cross on it. The stocky man who had been known as Battling Melano smiled. "You never saw a cartridge like that, Jack. You think it's brass, but it's solid gold." He slipped the brass cylinder into a pocket, buttoned the flap securely. "Valuable!"

"Come on, come on!" Kulhman urged.

There were twenty men trotting behind him across the plain. They reached the slopes. The detonations were much nearer now. There was a halt, as Kulhman sought the position of the survivors. The automatic rifles opened up immediately. One raked right, the other left, of the Legionnaires' approximate location.

Although the sun was out, the mist still clung to bushes and grass like thin fleece. But they all knew that the sound of automatic firing would encourage their comrades to stick it out longer. Shorter flashes winked out from opposite slopes, bullets hummed, and the groups were under fire. The natives flung men to stem their advance.

"Fix bayonets. Forward!"

The groups made another long bound forward. Shadowy figures ran on the slopes to match their move. The hills were acrawl with riflemen, for the firing increased everywhere. A general engagement was starting. For four hundred yards, the Legionnaires raced, before opening fire anew.

Gianella was killed at the end of that run. The men of the old group were unlucky. Carroll removed the breech-bolt from the dead man's Lebel, slipped it in his musette bag.

Kulhman stood, heedless of the shots aimed at him, trying to locate the men he sought. And a bewildered fellow, in bloody undershirt and khaki breeches, broke cover from nearby bushes. He fell headlong among the groups.

"Hello, Corland," Kulhman greeted simply. "Know where we can find the others?"

"Bunched up, maybe three hundred yards to the right and down this slope. I came over because I'm the best runner."

"Why the hell didn't they come with you? Waiting for us to call them taxis?"

"They've got to stick with the officer."

"D'Argoval's wounded?"

"He's dead, Sergeant. They hit him last night, in the first attack. He kept walking until he died. We thought maybe we could save his head, so we've been carrying him since four."

Carroll's mind accepted the statement without surprise. He had felt the same as those men did. Dead officers are beheaded by the natives if the corpses are left behind, and the heads become trophies. In a way, leaving the head of one's officer in the enemy's possession was dishonorable. It was the most natural thing for those hard-pressed soldiers to carry that body most of the night, at the risk of their own lives.

"We'll bring them in," Kulhman stated.

With the private leading, there was no need to grope about. Kulhman tossed caution to the winds, and made a superb, headlong advance. The natives who had clung to the dwindling detachment all night long were unwilling to let go. They withstood the blasts of the automatics, and the bayonet was called into play.

Point and butt, point and butt—the Legionnaires drove through the hillmen like a steel wedge into soft pine. Fenmayer rose after an encounter with his face laid open from eye to chin. Carroll's long reach stood him in good stead. It was difficult to slip under his extended rifle with a knife. Once, a native who was only half-dead slashed at his legs as he hurdled over, and split the leather of his boot.

"There they are!"

The survivors of d'Argoval's expedition, six in number, were crouching among small boulders. The officer's corpse was a short distance behind them. They were so covered with blood and dirt that Carroll did not find Zerlich at once.

"You're all right now?"

"Sure. Got anything to drink? We've been at it all night."

Canteens were held out to them. Kulhman fired a smoke signal to indicate his position, organized its defense. It was up to the companies to rescue him now. It would have been madness to attempt a retreat through the swarming enemy.

"They jumped us about one-thirty. We fought all night," the rescued men repeated over and over. They seemed dazed, stunned to find themselves alive.

Then Carroll saw Zerlich. The detective was in bad shape. There was a gash under one eye; blood held his shirt glued to his skin. He started talking in a tense monotone as soon as Carroll hailed him.

"It's been going on all night, all night. They went crazy when the young officer was hit. I had to help carry him. He must weigh a ton. I was hit, too." He coughed with his hand against his mouth, showed it bloody. "Hit bad, in the lung."

"How you making out, Pop?" Dacorda asked, coming up.

"Lousy," Zerlich replied. His weary eyes sought Carroll, who read the mute question in them, and nodded. Yes, Dacorda had been told, Dacorda knew. "I'm sorry, Mike."

"That's all right," Dacorda said, patting the older man's shoulder reassuringly. "It's your racket, what the hell!"

Moroccan Spahis trotted by them, some firing from the saddle. Then long files of regular infantry followed. The firing reduced. A runner came to Kulhman, with instructions to remain where he was. The Legion units in action during the night would be allowed to rest before participating in the coming battle.

A military surgeon arrived, examined the wounded, applied first aid. He told Carroll that Zerlich was in no great danger.

"High and clean," he stated. "Six weeks in the hospital. Don't move him, the stretcher-bearers are on the way up."

"They'll get you back to camp," Carroll announced, "and from there you'll be flown in an ambulance plane to Meknes. What are you going to do? Get yourself out of the Legion or come back?"

"Go home. I've had enough!" Zerlich smiled weakly. "And my heart isn't in it anymore."

"What are you going to do about me, Pop?" Dacorda asked.

"Nothing, as long as they know you're here, anyway, and if they want you and can get you, there's nothing to stop them. No kidding, I hope they leave you alone."

Dacorda was nervous, as if ashamed of himself.

"See here, if it had to be anybody, I wish it was you. But I can't tell you. If you had got what you wanted so I couldn't help myself, I'd have been glad. Honest!"

"Mean that?" Carroll challenged.

"What do you think I am, a liar?"

Carroll thought the matter over. Dacorda had given an oath, which he had to keep. Reasoning coldly, his loyalty was doing no one any good. Barrister himself wanted the stuff found, to get clear. And Dacorda now said he wished he could settle the matter in some fashion.

"What's the matter with your jacket?" Carroll asked. "Here, I'll fix it." He rose, tipped the puzzled Dacorda's head back and jerked at his buttons. Then he sat down again. "Say, Zerlich, ever hear of the 'last cartridge,' the one you have for yourself?"

"Sure." Zerlich tried to shrug, winced with pain. "You'll find mine in my breast-pocket. Funny thing, when I thought I would need it, there it was, with my rifle back in camp and me with a pistol!"

Carroll found the cartridge.

"Dacorda wants to swap—sort of a souvenir. You take his, he gets yours."

"Say—" Dacorda broke off, as his hands felt his empty pocket.

"You haven't said a thing," Carroll reminded him.

He drew the bronze pellet with his teeth, shook the contents of the brass cylinder on his palm. With the particles of smokeless powder came a narrow strip of notched metal, showing brighter surfaces at one end, where the guard had been filed off.

"How did you know?" Dacorda wondered.

"Solid gold, solid gold. You just as good as told me."

"Well, that was a swell place for it, anyway," Dacorda said. "If I had had to use that cartridge, they could have looked for that key a long while. And I've been carrying it all the way from Rochester."

Zerlich and Carroll exchanged glances. There was small need for secrecy now!

"Listen, I'll say I made a deal with you, Dacorda, and send you fellows a cut."

An hour later, Dacorda and Carroll escorted the stretcher as far as the plain. They shook hands, exchanged few words. Their lives were separating. They stared at each other, smiled. Then the stretcher-bearers started toward the camp. The two who remained behind walked back slowly.

"If he does what he said, we'll be in soft," Dacorda suggested. "You'll have some dough to start out with when you finish your enlistment. Maybe, I'll be a sergeant then, and with high pay and a private income. Oh, baby! Think he won't change his mind?"

"He won't change his mind," Carroll concluded. "You see, when a man has seen and done certain things out here, dollars don't look so important anymore."

A GENTLEMAN OF COLOR

P. C. WREN

PERCIVAL CHRISTOPHER WREN (1885–1941) was born in Devonshire, England, and was a direct descendant of the great seventeenth-century architect Sir Christopher Wren. After graduating from Oxford, P. C. Wren joined the military and was posted to exotic corners of the world for several years. He wound up in India, where he worked as an educator, and then joined the Poona Volunteer Rifles as a captain. His biographers generally report that he also spent five years as a member of the French Foreign Legion, but there is no evidence to support this claim. It is more likely that he relied on his own military adventures, his association with former Legionnaires, and careful research to produce his books about the Legion—the most famous of which is *Beau Geste* (1924).

There were three Geste brothers: Michael (known as Beau due to his "remarkable physical beauty, mental brilliance, and general distinction") and Digby, who were twins, and their younger brother, John. When the honor of the brothers is questioned, each flees Britain to join the Foreign Legion in an attempt to deflect suspicion from the others. The first novel in which they appeared was an enormous success, and was adapted as a stage play in 1929, and a silent film starring Ronald Colman in 1926. The film was remade several times, most famously with Gary Cooper in 1939. Adventures of the French Foreign Legion became the rage during the 1920s and '30s, even inspiring a pulp magazine, *Foreign Legion Adventures*. Wren wrote additional books about the Geste brothers, including *Beau Sabreur* (1926), *Beau Ideal* (1928), and *Good Gestes* (1929), a short-story collection, as well as other Foreign Legion novels, including *Action and Passion* (1933), *Flawed Blades: Tales from the Foreign Legion* (1933), *Sinbad the Soldier* (1935), and *Fort in the Jungle* (1936).

Although Wren's tales of the Legion are romanticized, they carry a certain authenticity about life in that strange volunteer army of anonymous misfits, criminals, and adventurers who suffered and fought under horrific conditions for a country not their own. Written in a very different time, the stories display a chauvinism and a lack of political correctness that may offend some modern readers.

"A Gentleman of Color" was first published in *Good Gestes: Stories of Beau Geste, His Brothers and Certain of Their Comrades in the French Foreign Legion* (London: Murray, 1929).

A GENTLEMAN OF COLOR

P. C. WREN

I

LE LÉGIONNAIRE YATO was one of the quietest, most retiring and self-effacing men in the Company, and one of the most modest. It seemed to be his highest ambition—an ambition which he almost attained—to escape notice, to blush unseen, and to hide his light beneath a bushel.

And yet, to those who had the seeing eye, he was an extremely interesting person, and for many reasons. He greatly intrigued the Geste brothers, and in spite of his meek, self-effacing humility, they took note of him from the day he arrived, and watched him with interest.

At first sight, and to the casual eye, he was a poor specimen—small, narrow-shouldered, weedy, with yellowish face, a wiry scrub of short hair, and a silly sort of little straggling moustache, the loss of one hair of which would have made an obvious difference.

The mere look of him caused Sergeant-major Lejaune to feel unwell, and he made no secret of the fact. Indeed, he promised to stuff the little man into a slop pail and to be ill upon him.

Never had the Geste boys, who were watching the arrival of this batch of recruits, seen so hopelessly dull, stupid and apathetic a face in their lives, as that of this recruit, while Sergeant-major Lejaune regarded it; never had they seen one more acutely intelligent, expressive, spirited and observant as Sergeant-major Lejaune passed on.

"See that?" chuckled Digby to his brothers.

"Yes," replied Beau. "If I were Lejaune I think I'd let that gentleman alone. Wonder what brought him here."

"He's come 'for to admire and for to see,' I should think," said John, "and come a long way too." And as the line of recruits turned to their left and marched off, he added, "His shoulders have been drilled too, and I'll bet you any amount he's worn a sword and spurs."

Other interesting facts transpired later. The mild little man could cut your hair and shave you beautifully, and he could speak your language if you were English, French, Russian or German. He could also sketch rather marvellously, and do pictures of surpassing merit in watercolor and in oil. He preferred to do these drawings and pictures out in the open air—the more open the better—and he had done some beauties of the country round Quetta, for example, and the Khyber Pass, showing all the pretty forts and things.

His manners were delightful, and he gave offense to no man, least of all to those set in authority over him.

To their surprise, the Geste boys—who, during his early recruit days, went out of their way to help this lonely little stranger in a strange land—discovered that he knew England fairly well, particularly Portsmouth, Plymouth, Weymouth, Rosyth, Aldershot and Chatham.

For the most part, le légionnaire Yato's inoffensiveness, humility, excellent manners, and blameless conduct kept him out of almost all trouble, official or private—but not entirely. Although a man may camouflage himself with a protective coloring of drab dullness and uniformity, which does indeed protect him by hiding him from general notice, it may not always suffice to hide him from particular notice. His very quietness and mild meekness may be his undoing through attracting the eye of those who need a butt for their diversion, and even more urgently need long-suffering meekness and mildness in that butt.

Two such were Messieurs Brandt and Haff, men who, themselves the butt of their superiors for their stupidity, slovenliness, and general worthlessness, must find someone to be their butt in turn. Almost a necessity of their existence was someone upon whom they could visit the contumely heaped upon themselves. Subconsciously they felt that, for their self-respect's sake, they must stand upon something lower than themselves, or be themselves the lowest things of all.

And this recruit, Yato, seemed so suitable to their purpose, so dull and stupid, so unable to protect himself, so harmless, helpless and hopeless, so proper a target for the shafts of their wit.

So they put thornbush in his bed, and unpleasant matter in his *képi* and on his pillow; stole his kit; put a dead mouse in his coffee; arranged a booby trap for his benefit; fouled his white uniform after he had washed and ironed it; gave him false information, messages and orders, to his discomfiture and undoing; hid his brushes just before kit inspection; stole his soap; cut his bootlaces and generally demonstrated their own wit, humor and jocularity as well as his stupidity, harmlessness and general inferiority to themselves.

One day, Beau Geste and his brothers entered their barrack room and discovered the cringing Yato ruefully eyeing *les légionnaires* Brandt, Haff, Klingen and Schwartz—four huge and powerful men, who were proposing to toss him in a blanket, having first denuded him of all clothing. The bright idea had been that of Brandt. He had proposed it; Haff had seconded it; and the two, realizing with their wonted brilliance that a blanket has four corners, had impressed the services of the delighted and all-too-willing Schwartz and Klingen.

"Where shall we do it?" roared Schwartz, a great bearded ruffian, strong as a bull, rough as a bear, and sensitive as a warthog.

"You won't do it at all," said Beau Geste, advancing to where the four stood about Yato's disordered bed, from which they had dragged a blanket.

"I do not like to be touched and handled," said Yato quietly, in the silence that fell upon the surprised bullies. "Please leave me alone."

"They are going to leave you alone," said Beau Geste.

"Yes! Watch us!" shouted Brandt, and sprang at the cringing little Jap as the mighty Schwartz turned upon Michael Geste, his great hands clenched, his eyes blazing, and his teeth bared. But as he raised his fist to strike, he swung about as something, or someone, fell against him from behind.

It was Brandt.

Using his right arm as though it were an axe, of which the side of the hand from little finger to wrist was the edge, Yato had struck Brandt an extraordinary cutting chopping blow on the neck, below and behind the ear.

As Brandt fell against Schwartz and to the ground, apparently dead, the Jap seized Haff by the collar of his tunic, where it fastened at the throat, and jerked his head violently downward, at the same time himself springing violently upward, so that the top of his bullet-head struck Haff between the eyes with tremendous force.

The huge Schwartz, changing his line of attack as he turned about, sprang upon Yato, as might a lion upon a gazelle. The gazelle threw itself at the lion's feet—but not in supplication. Before the astonished Gestes could come to the rescue, they saw Yato fling his arms about Schwartz's ankles, causing the upper part of his body to fall forward. And as it did so, Yato astonishingly arose, hugging Schwartz's ankles to his breast.

The result of this lightning movement was

that the big man pitched upon his head so heavily that nothing but its thickness saved him from concussion of the brain, and it seemed impossible that his neck should not be broken. And, almost as the body of Schwartz reached the ground, Yato sprang at Klingen, who was in the act of drawing a knife.

Seizing the wrist of the hand that held this ugly weapon, the Japanese wheeled so that he stood beside Klingen, shoulder to shoulder, and facing in the same direction. As he did so, he thrust his left arm beneath Klingen's right, and across his chest, at the same time pulling Klingen's straightened right arm violently downward. There was a distinctly audible crack as the arm broke above the elbow.

Where four burly bullies had gathered about a cringing little man, three lay insensible and one knelt whimpering with pain.

"I do not like to be touched and handled," smiled Yato.

"I don't think you will be, to any great extent," smiled Digby Geste in return.

II

But a man may be touched without being handled, and it was the dominating desire of Klingen's life to "touch" Yato.

It became essential to his continued existence that he should avenge his broken arm, his humiliating defeat and utter overthrow.

For Klingen was a conceited man, devoid of pride, but filled with self-esteem.

He was handsome and he knew it. But "handsome is as handsome does," and Klingen had done most evilly. It was, in fact, by reason of his last and most treacherous love affair that he was hiding in the Legion.

He was big and strong and bold, and he had been made to grovel groaning at the feet of a man one-half his size. He hated pain, and he had been made to suffer agony unspeakable.

And so he was obsessed with thoughts of vengeance, and lived for the day when the Japanese should make full payment for the insult and the injury he had put upon the bold and brave, the hardy and handsome Klingen.

Meanwhile, a certain poor satisfaction could be obtained by lashing the unspeakable Oriental verbally; for, curiously enough, the Japanese did not resent such abuse—apparently. So when Klingen came out of hospital he poured forth upon his quiet shrinking enemy all the choice epithets, insults, and injurious foulness that he had perpetrated, polished and perfected during the miserable leisure of his enforced retirement.

He assured Yato that he was a yellow monkey, a loathsome "native," a *colored* man, if indeed he were a man at all. Klingen explained fully and carefully that he had always drawn the color line, and had drawn it straight and strong; also that it was, to him, the very worst aspect of life in the Legion that one was forced to herd with colored men, natives, that foul scum (or sediment) of humanity which is barely human. He explained that while he hated niggers, abhorred Arabs and detested Chinese, words utterly failed him to express the loathing horror with which he regarded Japs. Brown was bad, black was worse, but what could be said of yellow? That vile bilious color was disgusting in *anything*—but in human beings it was . . . !

One could be but dumbly sick, and whenever his revolted eye fell upon *le légionnaire* Yato, his revolting stomach almost had its way, and in crude pantomime Klingen would express his feelings.

And Yato would smile.

Furthermore, the good Klingen was at infinite pains to indicate the private and personal hideousness of Yato as distinct from his national bestiality. He would invite all present to contemplate the little man's unspeakable eyes, indescribable moustache, unmentionable nose, unbelievable hair, and unutterable ugliness.

And Yato would smile.

But it was noticed that Klingen never touched the Japanese, nor sought physical retaliation for his broken arm. Nor did Messieurs Haff, Brandt and Schwartz. In fact, these three

434

appeared to entertain feelings rather of reluctant admiration and sporting acquiescence than of hatred and vengeance, and when Klingen proposed various schemes for Yato's undoing, they would have none of them. They were quite content to regard him as a freak of nature and a human marvel.

Of him they had had quite enough, and it was their firm intention to leave him severely alone.

Not so Klingen. If Klingen were to live, Yato must die; or, better still—far, far better still—suffer some dire, ineffable humiliation, life-long and worse than death.

.   .   .

Seated in a row, on a bench in the Jardin Publique, Beau Geste in the middle, the three brothers contemplated the Vast Forever without finding life one grand sweet song.

Life was hard, comfortless, small and monotonous; but quite bearable so long as it yielded a lazy hour when they could sit thus, smoking their pipes in silent communion, or in idle and disjointed conversation about Brandon Abbas. Frequently Michael would speculate upon Claudia's doings; Digby and John upon those of Isobel.

"Here comes old Yato," murmured Digby. "I'm going to hit him, one day," he added.

"What for?" inquired John.

"Fun," replied Digby.

"Fun for whom—Yato?" inquired Michael.

"Yes," replied Digby. "I want to see what happens to me."

"You won't see," asserted Michael. "You'll only feel."

"Well, you two shall watch and tell me exactly what happens," said Digby. "Then I can do it to you two."

"Good evening, gentlemen," said Yato, with a courteous salute. "Excuse that I approach you."

The brothers rose as one, saluted the tiny man, and invited him to be seated with them.

"Excuse that I intrude with my insignificant presence, gentlemen, but I would humbly venture to do you the honor, and pay you the compliment, of asking a favor of you. You are *samurai*. If one of you gave assent with no more than a nod of his head, it would be a binding contract. . . . Will you do something for me?"

"Yes," replied Beau Geste.

"You do not stop to make conditions, nor to hear what the request may be. You do not fear that it may be something you would not like to do."

"No," replied Beau Geste.

"Ah," smiled Yato, "as I thought. Well, I'm going on a long walk one day soon, and I may want something done for me by a friend after I have gone. I do not *know* that I shall, but it is quite possible. . . ."

"We shall be delighted," said Beau Geste, and his brothers murmured assent.

Yato bowed deeply.

"Honorable sirs," he said.

"Better not tell us anything about your—er—long walk," said Beau Geste. "We shouldn't give you away, of course, but we're not good liars I'm afraid."

"Oh," smiled Yato, "tell them anything and everything that you know, should you be questioned. The honorable authorities will be entirely welcome to me—if they can catch me."

And he rose to go.

"I will leave a note under your pillow or in your *musette*," he continued, addressing Beau Geste. "Good-bye, gentle and honorable sirs. May I have the distinction of shaking the hands?"

"Queer little cove and great little gentleman," observed Digby when Yato had departed.

"Yes," agreed Michael. "A very good friend and a very dangerous enemy, I should say. I suppose he's in the Japanese Secret Service."

"I don't think I will hit him, after all," mused Digby.

III

Colonel the Baron Hoshiri of the Japanese General Staff, and of the French Foreign Legion (in the name of Yato), made his way along the Rue de Daya with, as he would have said, a song in his heart. There was no smile upon his grim lips, nor expression of joy in his eyes or upon his face. They were, in fact, utterly expressionless.

But he was very, very happy, for he was returning to his heaven upon earth, at the feet of Fuji Yama—the land of the cherry blossom, the chrysanthemum, the geisha, and the Rising Sun. He was leaving this land of barbarians devoid of manners, arts, graces and beauty.

Also, he had found a little friend, and she gave the lilt to the song that was in his heart.

A Flower from Japan.

Soiled and trodden and cast aside by these barbarian brutes, but still a Flower from Japan.

A pitiful little story—heartbreaking—but the little flower, picked up from the mud, dipped in pure cleansing dew, and set in a vase of fair water, was reviving.

He would take it back to Japan and it would bloom again and live, a thing of beauty and of joy.

Yes, a pitiful little tale.

Her parents had taken her to the *yoshiwara* to earn her dowry. There she had met her future husband, and thence she had been taken—rescued rather it seemed to her—by this man who so earnestly begged her to become his wife. He seemed a nice kind man, and her heart did not sink very much when he told her that they were going to travel to the wonderful West—for he was a merchant, and his business lay in Marseilles.

This was quite true, and in Marseilles, where his business lay, he sold her—in the way of business. Mr. Ah Foo (born in Saigon of a Chinese woman and a French Marine) did very well out of his little bride Sanyora—as he did out of all his other little brides, for he was what one might call a regular marrying man, and had entered the bonds of matrimony scores of times, and each of his wives had entered a bondage unescapable.

From Marseilles, Sanyora had been sold to a gentleman who travelled for his house, in Algiers, and had been taken to that house. Thence she had been appointed, without her knowledge or consent, to a vacancy (created by death—and a knife) in Oran. From there she had been sold into an even fouler bondage in Sidi-bel-Abbès.

Could she do nothing for herself? Yes—fight like a tiger-cat until drugged, and scream appeals for help—in Japanese, the only language she knew.

And, in that language, Colonel Hoshiri had heard her cry to God for death, as he passed below the open shutters of a house in a slum of the Spanish quarter. He had entered, asked for the Japanese girl, made his way to her room, addressed her in Japanese, and told her he only wished to be a friend and deliverer.

And now Sanyora had her own pretty room in a private house in a respectable quarter, and the Colonel had a haven of rest and peace—a refuge and quiet place in which he could take his ease and hear his own language from beautiful lips. Between them, they had made it a tiny corner of Japan, and, day by day, Sanyora grew more and more to be the dainty, charming and delightful geisha, wholly attractive mistress of the arts that delight and soothe and charm the eye and ear—and heart.

· · ·

As usual, *le légionnaire* Yato was watched and followed by his bitter and relentless enemy, Klingen. A stab in the back, as he passed through some dark alley, would be simple enough, but it would be *too* simple. To a devil like Yato, it would have to be a death-stroke, and he might die without knowing who had killed him. That would be a very poor sort of vengeance.

What Klingen wanted was to hurt him, and hurt him, and *hurt* him . . . humiliate him to the dust . . . disgrace and degrade and shame him . . . torture him to death . . . but a long, slow, lingering death. . . .

One night Yato might go to *le village Nègre.* Anything could happen there. There was no foul and fearful villainy that one could not buy, and a very little money went a very long way in *le vil-*

lage Nègre. One could certainly have a man way-laid, knocked on the head, gagged and bound and tied down on a native bedstead in a dark room in a native house. One could hire the room and have the key. One could visit one's victim nightly, and taunt him throughout the night. One could let him starve to death, or keep him alive for weeks.

The things one could do! What about that lovely trick of inverting a brass bowl on the man's bare stomach . . . a rat inside the bowl . . . some red-hot charcoal on top of the bowl. . . .

How long does it take the rat to eat his way into, and through, the man? Might it not be too quick a death? No, that was the whole point of it—a good sound slow torture.

Klingen licked his lips and followed the distant figure of Yato with his eyes.

Going to the same house again, was he? A pity he did not go to *le village Nègre*. What could be the attraction here? A woman, of course.

Klingen pondered the thought. There might be something in that . . . especially if he were fond of her. An idea—of dazzling brilliance. Jealousy! No vengeance like it—for a start. Get his woman from him. Was there a girl alive who would give a second glance at that hideous little yellow monkey when the fine big handsome swaggering swashbuckling Klingen was about? What an exquisite moment when the girl (seated on Klingen's knee, her head on Klingen's shoulder, her arms round Klingen's neck) turned languidly to Yato as Yato entered Yato's own room, and said to him in accents of extremest scorn, "Get to hell out of this, you dirty little yellow monkey. The sight and the smell of you make me feel sick in my stomach."

That would be a great moment. And these women could be bought.

·   ·   ·

Ah, yes . . . the little yellow devil was turning into the same house again. It *must* be a woman.

Klingen reconnoitered once again. The usual type of house with a common stairway leading up from a gloomy little basement hall to a rookery of rooms, apartments and flats occupied by hard-working poor people of the better sort.

Klingen hesitated, and for the first time entered the house and looked round the dingy entrance hall, stone-floored, stucco-walled, gloomily lit by a smoky oil lamp hanging against the wall, and by the rays that shone through iron-barred window spaces from a street lamp.

Should he climb the bare, wooden stair that led to the floors above? Why not? Anyone might enter the wrong house by mistake when searching for a friend. Still, it was a pity Schwartz, Haff and Brandt could not be persuaded to come along and have some fun at the expense of the yellow monkey.

Footsteps. . . . Someone coming down the stairs. . . . A little man in seedy European clothing. . . . An idea. . . .

"Excuse me, Monsieur," said Klingen, as the man reached the bottom of the stairs. "Can you tell me which is my friend's room? A *légionnaire*—a little fellow—Japanese."

The man shrugged his shoulders and made a gesture with his hands which showed that he was a Spaniard; also that he did not understand a word of what was being said to him.

Klingen mounted to the first floor, a bare landing, around three sides of which were closed, numbered doors. Should he tap at each in turn, and inquire for some nonexistent person? And what should he do if one of them were opened by Yato? Suppose the yellow tiger-cat attacked him again? His mended arm tingled at the thought. What was he doing here at all? This longing for vengeance was driving him mad. . . .

Klingen turned back, descended to the street, and took up his stand in a doorway from which he could keep watch upon the porch of the house in which was his enemy.

Another idea! . . . What about waiting until Yato left the house? He could then go in and knock at every door and ask:

"Is my friend *le légionnaire* Yato here—a little Japanese?" If one of the doors were opened by some woman who replied, "No, he has just gone," he would know that he had found what he sought, and would get to work forthwith. He would soon show her the difference between a Yato and a Klingen. And if Klingen knew anything of women, and he flattered himself that he most certainly did, there was a bad time coming for the yellow devil. . . . He could almost hear the very accents in which she should say:

"Get out of my sight, you filthy yellow cur. I've got a *man* now!"

Yes, and Klingen would have his knife ready too, and this time he'd throw it, if Yato made trouble. And he also flattered himself that he knew something of knife-throwing.

• • •

Ha! There he was. . . . Blister and burn him!

The retreating form of Yato turned the corner of the street, and Klingen darted across into the house. Running lightly up the stairs he knocked at the first door. No answer. He knocked again, and laid his ear against the wood. Silence.

He knocked at the next. A fat, slatternly woman, candle in hand, opened the door and eyed him hardily.

"Well?" she inquired, running her eye contemptuously over his uniform.

"Monsieur Blanc?" inquired Klingen.

The woman slammed the door in his face.

The third and fourth rooms were apparently empty.

A child opened the door of the fifth, and seeing a *légionnaire*, shut it instantly. Hearing a man's deep growling voice within, Klingen passed on.

To Klingen's inquiry, at the sixth room, as to whether Monsieur Blanc lived here, the woman who occupied it replied that he did, but was at the moment in the wine shop round the corner!

"Then may he sit there till he rots," observed Klingen, and climbed the second flight of stairs, and, arriving at a landing similar to the one below, repeated his strategy and tactics.

The first door was opened by a tiny dainty Japanese girl, and Klingen thrust his way into the room, closed the door behind him, locked it, and removed the key.

He had found what he wanted.

The girl stood staring, between terror and surprise. This man was in a similar uniform to that which her lover wore. He must be his friend, otherwise how would he have known she was here? But her beloved had only just gone. Had something happened to him, and why had this man thrust in so roughly, uninvited? But they were rough and rude, these Western barbarians. Why had he come? Did he think this place was like one of those dreadful houses in Marseilles, Algiers and Oran? And she shuddered at the thought.

Oh, if she could only understand what he was saying and make herself understood by him! He seemed to be speaking of someone named Yato. Was it conceivable that he might understand a word of Japanese?

"I am the servant of the Colonel Hoshiri. What do you want?" she said in her own tongue.

And, for reply, Klingen snatched her up in his arms and kissed her violently.

Well, this was a fine *affaire*! . . . This marched! . . . She might, or might not, be Yato's girl, but most certainly she was. A Japanese would hardly be visiting a house in a Sidi-bel-Abbès side street in which there was a Japanese woman, unless he were visiting her. Japs were not so common in the African hinterland as that. . . . But anyhow, and whoever she was, this was still a fine *affaire*, for here was Klingen the irresistible, locked up in a room with as pretty a little piece as he had ever clapped eyes on. And a very nice room, too, if a little bare. Bed, cushions, hangings, flowers in vase—yes, all very nice indeed.

And now for the little woman. A pity they could not understand each other's language, but the language of love is universal. He could soon make himself understood all right.

When *le légionnaire* Klingen let himself out of the room an hour or so later, he left a sobbing girl lying upon the bed weeping as though her heart would break; moaning as though it were already broken.

But Klingen, as he walked back to barracks, smiled greasily as he licked his lips, and encountering Yato in the barrack room, laughed aloud.

Yato was sitting on his bed engaged in *astiquage*—the polishing of his belts and straps.

Having whispered his story, punctuated with loud guffaws, to a little knot of his friends who evidently enjoyed the joke hugely, Klingen went over and stood in front of the Japanese, his hands on his hips, and, rocking himself to and fro, from heels to toes, leered exultingly. Without looking up, Yato continued waxing and polishing a cartridge pouch.

Suddenly he stopped—remained perfectly still, and stared at the floor between himself and Klingen.

Beau Geste drawing near, and watching carefully as he polished his bayonet, thought that Yato sniffed silently, as though trying to detect and capture an odor. Yes, decided Beau, Yato could smell something, and that something puzzled him. Rising to his feet, his hands behind him, and moving slowly, the Japanese approached Klingen, his head thrust forward, his nose obviously questing.

"What the hell!" growled Klingen, as Yato, his face not very much above the big man's sash, deliberately smelled at him.

Yato returned to his cot without remark.

But it seemed as though a shadow crossed his face. It was almost as though he changed color.

IV

Le légionnaire Klingen, smart in his walking-out kit, a red *képi*, dark-blue tunic with green red-fringed epaulettes, red breeches and white spats, tightened his belt a little, pulled his bayonet frog further back, and swaggered from the barrack room.

It was "holiday" (payday) and he intended to expend on wine the entire sum of 2½d. which he had received. Thereafter, being full of good wine and good cheer, it was his intention to see how the little Japanese girl was getting on, and to cheer her loneliness with an hour of his merry society. He would watch the yellow monkey go in, and wait till he came out, and if the girl had locked her door, he would tap and tap and knock and knock without saying anything until she did open it.

What a fighting little spitfire she was. But that was nine-tenths make believe, and the other tenth was ignorance of French.

From his seat on a barrel, in the corner of a dark wine shop which commanded a view of the street in which the girl's house stood, Klingen saw Yato approaching. Pulling down the visor of his *képi*, and bending his head forward, so that his face was concealed, he waited until the Japanese had passed, and then abandoned himself to the pleasures of drinking, anticipation, and thoughts of revenge.

He was absolutely certain that the girl was Yato's, and, as he rolled his wine upon his tongue, he rolled upon the debauched palate of his mind the flavor of the lovely vengeance that combined the enormous double gratification of deep enjoyment to himself and deep injury to Yato. He honestly agreed with Klingen that Klingen was a great man, and never greater than in this manifestation of his skill—that made his own pleasure his enemy's agony at a time when his enemy's agony was his own greatest pleasure.

On the whole, it had turned out to be quite a good thing that Schwartz, Brandt and Haff had declined to take any further hand in baiting Yato. Any vengeance, obtained with their help, could only have been crude and obvious, and have contained but the single satisfaction of injuring Yato.

But this was subtle, private, worthy of Klingen.

"Yes, my friend," he mused, sucking the wine drops from his moustache. "I hurt you by delighting myself, and you add immeasurably to that delight by being hurt."

And he laughed aloud.

A couple of thieves and their women, a fat person clothed from head to foot in brown corduroy, and an obese dealer in old clothes, who wore a tarboosh (or fez), a frock coat, a collarless blue shirt, football shorts, and a pair of curly-toed slippers, all turned to stare at the big soldier who laughed loudly at nothing.

"Mad," said a thief, and shrugged his shoulders.

"Drunk," growled the other.

"Mad *and* drunk," said a lady.

"*Que voulez-vous? C'est la Légion!*" observed her sister in joy, and drank to the health of *le légionnaire* Klingen, in methylated spirit. As his tenth *caporal* cigarette began to singe his moustache, and the last glass of his third bottle began to exhibit sediment, Klingen again pulled his cap over his eyes, and dropped his chin upon his chest. A small figure in the uniform of the Legion was passing on the other side of the road.

Two minutes later, Klingen was knocking at the door of the room in which dwelt the Japanese girl. To his first knock no answer was vouchsafed; to the second, a thin, high, childish voice replied unintelligibly. It might have been in invitation or prohibition.

Klingen turned the handle and, to his surprise, found that the door was not fastened. Entering the room, he saw a little figure on the remembered bed, its back toward him, its head and shoulders covered by a silken shawl. Turning, he locked the door, and slipped the key into his pocket.

The figure on the bed moved slightly and did not turn to him.

The little hussy! What was the game? Perhaps-I-will-perhaps-I-won't? Or was she pretending she hadn't heard him come in? Going to make a scene, perhaps, in the hope of extorting payment. Well, she'd be a clever girl if she got money out of Klingen! The other way about, more likely.

With quickened breathing, gleaming eye, and smiling lips, Klingen took a couple of steps in the direction of the bed, and from it, casting off shawl and covering, sprang Yato, lightly clad, his face devilish in its ferocity.

Klingen's right hand went to his bayonet and Yato's right hand, open, shot upward, so that the bottom of the palm struck Klingen beneath the chin. As it did so, Yato heaved mightily upward, as though hurling a sack of potatoes which was balanced on his hand. It was as if the Japanese lifted Klingen by the face, and flung him backward off his feet. But even as his enemy was in the act of falling, Yato flung his arm about him, and turning him sideways, fell heavily with him—Klingen being face downward. Instantly Yato, whose knee was in the small of Klingen's back, his right hand on his neck, seized Klingen's right wrist, and, dragging the arm upward and backward with a swift movement, dislocated his shoulder; and, as the prostrate man yelled in agony, Yato, with a similar movement of dexterous and powerful leverage, dislocated the other.

As Klingen again roared with pain, Yato hissed like a cat, and, with a grip of steel, dug his thumb and fingers into his victim's neck, with a grip that changed a howl to a broken whimper.

Five minutes later, Klingen's wrists were bound behind him with steel wire, his ankles were fastened together with a strap, and he was bound down upon the bed with a many-knotted rope, in such a manner that he could not raise his knees, nor his head, nor change his position by so much as an inch.

A large handkerchief or rag completely filled his mouth, and a piece of steel wire, passing round his face from beneath his chin to the top of his head, prevented him from ejecting it. In fact, the so recently active and joyous *légionnaire* Klingen could now move nothing but his eyes, could only see and hear—and suffer.

What was this yellow devil going to do with him? Mutilate him as the Arabs mutilate *les légionnaires* when they fall into their hands? And Klingen shuddered, as he thought of the photographs that hang in every Legion barrack room for the discouragement of deserters . . . photographs of the remains of things that have been men.

Was Yato going to carve and fillet him? Blind him? Cut his tongue out? Torture him with a red-hot iron? Cripple him for life? Destroy his hands, and so his livelihood? Or merely leave him there to die a dreadful lingering death of thirst and starvation?

He thought of what he himself had hoped and intended to do, if he could have had Yato waylaid in *le village Nègre*.

And he could not utter a word of supplication or remonstrance, nor make offer and promise of impossible reparation and bribe.

What was the cruel, wicked devil doing now? Heating an iron, sharpening a knife, boiling some water? These cursed Japs were artists at fiendish torture, and had a devilish ingenuity beyond the conception of simple, honest Westerners with their kindly hearts and generous natures.

What was he doing? *O God*, what *was* he doing? Something unthinkable . . . something unimaginable.

But, strangely enough, Yato was merely engaged in the exercise of one of his many peaceful and lawful pursuits. Seated comfortably beside *le légionnaire* Klingen, to whom he addressed no remark of any sort, he was making a selection from a number of small objects neatly packed in a sandalwood box. A faint, but pleasing odor came from this; also a small oblong cake of some black substance, in the powerful delicate fingers of the Japanese. Taking a tiny saucer from the box, he poured into it a little water from the flower vase, and in this placed the end of the black cake, that it might soak while he dispassionately studied the contorted face of his enemy. Anon, taking the cake in his fingers, he sketched broad lines of the deepest black upon Klingen's forehead and cheeks. Klingen, expecting either burn or slash, winced and shuddered as the substance touched his face. Settling down to his work, unhurried, methodical, and calm, Yato rubbed and dipped, rubbed and dipped, until the face of Klingen was

as black as soot—even to the eyelids, lips, ears, and throat.

Having completed this portion of his task to his satisfaction, Yato again considered the contents of the box, and selected another small stick. With this he most carefully continued his work, a keen and conscientious craftsman.

And then, changing his tools, Yato, with patient artistry, labored long and well to render indelible his striking effects. With a long-handled brush, whose bristles were needles of steel, he tapped and tapped and tapped at forehead, cheeks, and chin, until the blood began to ooze. With separate and single needles, he worked faithfully and well, in the places where the broader tools would fail of full effect. . . .

And at last he rose, an artist satisfied, fulfilled, and gazed upon the face of his enemy.

V

Le légionnaire Yato was not seen again in the barracks of the Legion. But, three days later, Beau Geste received a letter which reminded him of his promise to help his humble Japanese comrade. All the latter had to ask was that his honorable friend would proceed, forthwith, accompanied by his two honorable brothers, to a described house, and there, having asked a certain man for the key, go to room No. 7, and give freedom and assistance to an unfortunate man confined therein. Should they fail to do this, the poor fellow would starve to death. . . .

Michael, Digby and John did as they were asked.

"*Good God!* Yato!" ejaculated Michael, as they gazed upon Klingen.

"The wicked *devil*!" murmured John.

"What they call a 'gentleman of color,' " observed Digby,—for, until the worms devoured it, the whole face of Klingen would be a deep blue-black, save for the nose of glowing red.

AFTER KING KONG FELL

PHILIP JOSÉ FARMER

PHILIP JOSÉ FARMER (1918–2009) was born and raised and died in Indiana, although he also spent more than a decade elsewhere writing technical books and guides. While he sporadically produced work in other genres, Farmer was mainly a prolific science-fiction writer who was greatly admired by such colleagues as Isaac Asimov and Leslie Fiedler. Farmer won a contest in 1952 with his first novel, *Owe for the Flesh,* but the money was never paid, and the text remained unpublished until 1973. That work, however, contained the seed of the book series for which he is best known, *Riverworld* (1971–1983), about a river more than a million miles long on another planet, where everyone who ever lived on Earth is reborn at the peak of health and vitality and given a second chance. Farmer won the first of his three Hugo awards for a novella, *The Lovers,* published in the pulp magazine *Startling Stories* in 1952. The piece had previously been rejected by editors who found it repugnant because it broke several taboos by depicting a sexual relationship between a man and an alien with an unearthly reproductive system. In another series, *Dayworld* (1985–1990), Earth's unsustainable overpopulation is relieved by giving each person one day per week awake, and six in a state of suspended animation. In all, Farmer wrote more than seventy-five books, with works published in forty countries. Among other controversies in which he was involved, perhaps the most famous concerns *Venus on the Half-Shell* (1975). Farmer wrote the novel under the pseudonym Kilgore Trout, the name of an underappreciated science-fiction scribe who appears in many works written by Kurt Vonnegut. Vonnegut apparently was not pleased with the "homage."

The most famous animal character ever to appear onscreen is King Kong, the giant ape who falls for a pretty blond actress who comes to his domain—resulting in his capture. While being exhibited on a Broadway stage as "The Eighth Wonder of the World," Kong escapes, and famously carries the object of his affection up the side of the Empire State Building. Farmer's story gives a little background to these events and some other things that children are not meant to know.

"After King Kong Fell" was first published in *Omega*, an anthology edited by Roger Elwood (New York: Walker, 1973).

AFTER KING KONG FELL

PHILIP JOSÉ FARMER

THE FIRST half of the movie was grim and gray and somewhat tedious. Mr. Howller did not mind. That was, after all, realism. Those times had been grim and gray. Moreover, behind the tediousness was the promise of something vast and horrifying. The creeping pace and the measured ritualistic movements of the actors gave intimations of the workings of the gods. Unhurriedly, but with utmost confidence, the gods were directing events toward the climax.

Mr. Howller had felt that at the age of fifteen, and he felt it now while watching the show on TV at the age of fifty-five. Of course, when he first saw it in 1933, he had known what was coming. Hadn't he lived through some of the events only two years before that?

The old freighter, the *Wanderer*, was nosing blindly through the fog toward the surflike roar of the natives' drums. And then: the commercial. Mr. Howller rose and stepped into the hall and called down the steps loudly enough for Jill to hear him on the front porch. He thought commercials could be a blessing. They give us time to get into the bathroom or the kitchen, or time to light up a cigarette and decide about continuing to watch this show or go on to that show.

And why couldn't real life have its commercials?

Wouldn't it be something to be grateful for if reality stopped in mid-course while the Big Salesman made His pitch? The car about to smash into you, the bullet on its way to your brain, the first cancer cell about to break loose, the boss reaching for the phone to call you in so he can fire you, the spermatozoon about to be launched toward the ovum, the final insult about to be hurled at the once, and perhaps still, beloved, the final drink of alcohol which would rupture the abused blood vessel, the decision which would lead to the light that would surely fail?

If only you could step out while the commercial interrupted these, think about it, talk about it, and then, returning to the set, switch it to another channel.

But that one is having technical difficulties, and the one after that is a talk show whose guest is the archangel Gabriel himself and after some urging by the host he agrees to blow his trumpet, and . . .

Jill entered, sat down, and began to munch the cookies and drink the lemonade he had prepared for her. Jill was six and a half years old and beautiful, but then what granddaughter wasn't beautiful? Jill was also unhappy because she had just quarreled with her best friend, Amy, who had stalked off with threats never to see Jill again. Mr. Howller reminded her that this had happened before and that Amy always came back the next day, if not sooner. To take her mind off of Amy, Mr. Howller gave her a brief outline of what had happened in the movie. Jill listened without enthusiasm, but she became excited enough once the movie had resumed. And when Kong was feeling over the edge of the abyss for John Driscoll, played by Bruce Cabot, she got into her grandfather's lap. She gave a little scream and put her hands over her eyes when Kong carried Ann Redman into the jungle (Ann played by Fay Wray).

But by the time Kong lay dead on Fifth Avenue, she was rooting for him, as millions had before her. Mr. Howller squeezed her and kissed her and said, "When your mother was about your age, I took her to see this. And when it was over, she was crying, too."

Jill sniffled and let him dry the tears with his handkerchief. When the Roadrunner cartoon came on, she got off his lap and went back to her cookie-munching. After a while she said, "Grandpa, the coyote falls off the cliff so far you can't even see him. When he hits, the whole earth shakes. But he always comes back, good as new. Why can he fall so far and not get hurt? Why couldn't King Kong fall and be just like new?"

Her grandparents and her mother had explained many times the distinction between a "live" and a "taped" show. It did not seem to make any difference how many times they explained. Somehow, in the years of watching TV, she had gotten the fixed idea that people in "live" shows actually suffered pain, sorrow, and death. The only shows she could endure seeing were those that her elders labeled as "taped." This worried Mr. Howller more than he admitted to his wife and daughter. Jill was a very bright child, but what if too many TV shows at too early an age had done her some irreparable harm? What if, a few years from now, she could easily see, and even define, the distinction between reality and unreality on the screen but deep down in her there was a child that still could not distinguish?

"You know that the Roadrunner is a series of pictures that move. People draw pictures, and people can do anything with pictures. So the Roadrunner is drawn again and again, and he's

back in the next show with his wounds all healed and he's ready to make a jackass of himself again."

"A jackass? But he's a coyote."

"Now . . ."

Mr. Howller stopped. Jill was grinning.

"O.K., now you're pulling my leg."

"But is King Kong alive or is he taped?"

"Taped. Like the Disney I took you to see last week. *Bedknobs and Broomsticks*."

"Then *King Kong* didn't happen?"

"Oh, yes, it really happened. But this is a movie they made about King Kong after what really happened was all over. So it's not exactly like it really was, and actors took the parts of Ann Redman and Carl Denham and all the others. Except King Kong himself. He was a toy model."

Jill was silent for a minute and then she said, "You mean, there really *was* a King Kong? How do you know, Grandpa?"

"Because I was there in New York when Kong went on his rampage. I was in the theater when he broke loose, and I was in the crowd that gathered around Kong's body after he fell off the Empire State Building. I was thirteen then, just seven years older than you are now. I was with my parents, and they were visiting my Aunt Thea. She was beautiful, and she had golden hair just like Fay Wray's—I mean, Ann Darrow's. She'd married a very rich man, and they had a big apartment high up in the clouds. In the Empire State Building itself."

"High up in the clouds! That must've been fun, Grandpa!"

It would have been, he thought, if there had not been so much tension in that apartment. Uncle Nate and Aunt Thea should have been happy because they were so rich and lived in such a swell place. But they weren't. No one said anything to young Tim Howller, but he felt the suppressed anger, heard the bite of tone, and saw the tightening lips. His aunt and uncle were having trouble of some sort, and his parents were upset by it. But they all tried to pretend everything was as sweet as honey when he was around.

Young Howller had been eager to accept the pretense. He didn't like to think that anybody could be mad at his tall, blonde, and beautiful aunt. He was passionately in love with her; he ached for her in the daytime; at nights he had fantasies about her of which he was ashamed when he awoke. But not for long. She was a thousand times more desirable than Fay Wray or Claudette Colbert or Elissa Landi.

But that night, when they were all going to see the première of *The Eighth Wonder of the World*, King Kong himself, young Howller had managed to ignore whatever it was that was bugging his elders. And even they seemed to be having a good time. Uncle Nate, over his parents' weak protests, had purchased orchestra seats for them. These were twenty dollars apiece, big money in Depression days, enough to feed a family for a month. Everybody got all dressed up, and Aunt Thea looked too beautiful to be real. Young Howller was so excited that he thought his heart was going to climb up and out through his throat. For days the newspapers had been full of stories about King Kong—speculations, rather, since Carl Denham wasn't telling them much. And he, Tim Howller, would be one of the lucky few to see the monster first.

Boy, wait until he got back to the kids in seventh grade in Busiris, Illinois! Would their eyes ever pop when he told them all about it!

But his happiness was too good to last. Aunt Thea suddenly said she had a headache and couldn't possibly go. Then she and Uncle Nate went into their bedroom, and even in the front room, three rooms and a hallway distant, young Tim could hear their voices. After a while Uncle Nate, slamming doors behind him, came out. He was red-faced and scowling, but he wasn't going to call the party off. All four of them, very uncomfortable and silent, rode in a taxi to the theater on Times Square. But when they got inside, even Uncle Nate forgot the quarrel, or at least he seemed to. There was the big stage with its towering silvery curtains and through the curtains came a vibration of excitement and of delicious danger. And even through the curtains the hot hairy ape-stink filled the theater.

"Did King Kong get loose just like in the movie?" Jill said.

Mr. Howller started. "What? Oh, yes, he sure did. Just like in the movie."

"Were you scared, Grandpa? Did you run away like everybody else?"

He hesitated. Jill's image of her grandfather had been cast in a heroic mold. To her he was a giant of Herculean strength and perfect courage, her defender and champion. So far he had managed to live up to the image, mainly because the demands she made were not too much for him. In time she would see the cracks and the sawdust oozing out. But she was too young to disillusion now.

"No, I didn't run," he said. "I waited until the theater was cleared of the crowd."

This was true. The big man who'd been sitting in the seat before him had leaped up yelling as Kong began tearing the bars out of his cage, had whirled and jumped over the back of his seat, and his knee had hit young Howller on the jaw. And so young Howller had been stretched out senseless on the floor under the seats while the mob screamed and tore at each other and trampled the fallen.

Later he was glad that he had been knocked out. It gave him a good excuse for not keeping cool, for not acting heroically in the situation. He knew that if he had not been unconscious, he would have been as frenzied as the others, and he would have abandoned his parents, thinking only in his terror of his own salvation. Of course, his parents had deserted him, though they claimed that they had been swept away from him by the mob. This *could* be true; maybe his folks *had* actually tried to get to him. But he had not really thought they had, and for years he had looked down on them because of their flight.

When he got older, he realized that he would have done the same thing, and he knew that his contempt for them was really a disguised contempt for himself.

He had awakened with a sore jaw and a headache. The police and the ambulance men were there and starting to take care of the hurt and to haul away the dead. He staggered past them out into the lobby and, not seeing his parents there, went outside. The sidewalks and the streets were plugged with thousands of men, women, and children, on foot and in cars, fleeing northward.

He had not known where Kong was. He should have been able to figure it out, since the frantic mob was leaving the midtown part of Manhattan. But he could think of only two things. Where were his parents? And was Aunt Thea safe? And then he had a third thing to consider. He discovered that he had wet his pants. When he had seen the great ape burst loose, he had wet his pants.

Under the circumstances, he should have paid no attention to this. Certainly no one else did. But he was a very sensitive and shy boy of thirteen, and, for some reason, the need for getting dry underwear and trousers seemed even more important than finding his parents. In retrospect he would tell himself that he would have gone south anyway. But he knew deep down that if his pants had not been wet he might not have dared return to the Empire State Building.

It was impossible to buck the flow of the thousands moving like lava up Broadway. He went east on 43rd Street until he came to Fifth Avenue, where he started southward. There was a crowd to fight against here, too, but it was much smaller than that on Broadway. He was able to thread his way through it, though he often had to go out into the street and dodge the cars. These, fortunately, were not able to move faster than about three miles an hour.

"Many people got impatient because the cars wouldn't go faster," he told Jill, "and they just abandoned them and struck out on foot."

"Wasn't it noisy, Grandpa?"

"Noisy? I've never heard such noise. I think that everyone in Manhattan, except those hiding under their beds, was yelling or talking. And every driver in Manhattan was blowing his car's horn. And then there were the sirens of the fire trucks and police cars and ambulances. Yes, it was noisy."

Several times he tried to stop a fugitive so he could find out what was going on. But even when he did succeed in halting someone for a few seconds, he couldn't make himself heard. By then, as he found out later, the radio had broadcast the news. Kong had chased John Driscoll and Ann Redman out of the theater and across the street to their hotel. They had gone up to Driscoll's room, where they thought they were safe. But Kong had climbed up, using windows as ladder steps, reached into the room, knocked Driscoll out, and grabbed Ann, and had then leaped away with her. He had headed, as Carl Denham figured he would, toward the tallest structure on the island. On King Kong's own island, he lived on the highest point, Skull Mountain, where he was truly monarch of all he surveyed. Here he would climb to the top of the Empire State Building, Manhattan's Skull Mountain.

Tim Howller had not known this, but he was able to infer that Kong had traveled down Fifth Avenue from 38th Street on. He passed a dozen cars with their tops flattened down by the ape's fist or turned over on their sides or tops. He saw three sheet-covered bodies on the sidewalks, and he overheard a policeman telling a reporter that Kong had climbed up several buildings on his way south and reached into windows and pulled people out and thrown them down onto the pavement.

"But you said King Kong was carrying Ann Redman in the crook of his arm, Grandpa," Jill said. "He only had one arm to climb with, Grandpa, so . . . so wouldn't he fall off the building when he reached in to grab those poor people?"

"A very shrewd observation, my little chick-adee," Mr. Howller said, using the W. C. Fields voice that usually sent her into giggles. "But his arms were long enough for him to drape Ann Redman over the arm he used to hang on with while he reached in with the other. And to forestall your next question, even if you had not thought of it, he could turn over an automobile with only one hand."

"But . . . but why'd he take time out to do that if he wanted to get to the top of the Empire State Building?"

"I don't know why *people* often do the things they do," Mr. Howller said. "So how would I know why an *ape* does the things he does?"

When he was a block away from the Empire State Building, a plane crashed onto the middle of the avenue two blocks behind him and burned furiously. Tim Howller watched it for a few minutes, then he looked upward and saw the red and green lights of the five planes and the silvery bodies slipping in and out of the searchlights.

"Five airplanes, Grandpa? But the movie . . ."

"Yes, I know. The movie showed about fourteen or fifteen. But the book says that there were six to begin with, and the book is much more accurate. The movie also shows King Kong's last stand taking place in the daylight. But it didn't; it was still nighttime."

The Army Air Force plane must have been going at least 250 mph as it dived down toward the giant ape standing on the top of the observation tower. Kong had put Ann Redman by his feet so he could hang on to the tower with one hand and grab out with the other at the planes. One had come too close, and he had seized the left biplane structure and ripped it off. Given the energy of the plane, his hand should have been torn off, too, or at least he should have been pulled loose from his hold on the tower and gone down with the plane. But he hadn't let loose, and that told something of the enormous strength of that towering body. It also told something of the relative fragility of the biplane.

Young Howller had watched the efforts of the firemen to extinguish the fire and then he had turned back toward the Empire State Building. By then it was all over. All over for King Kong, anyway. It was, in after years, one of Mr. Howller's greatest regrets that he had not seen the monstrous dark body falling through the beams of the searchlights—blackness, then the flash of blackness through the whiteness of the highest beam, blackness, the flash through the next beam, blackness, the flash through the third beam, blackness, the flash through the lowest beam. Dot, dash, dot, dash, Mr. Howller was to think afterward. A code transmitted unconsciously by the great ape and received unconsciously by those who witnessed the fall. Or by those who would hear of it and think about it. Or was he going too far in conceiving this? Wasn't he always looking for codes? And, when he found them, unable to decipher them?

Since he had been thirteen, he had been trying to equate the great falls in man's myths and legends and to find some sort of intelligence in them. The fall of the tower of Babel, of Lucifer, of Vulcan, of Icarus, and, finally, of King Kong. But he wasn't equal to the task; he didn't have the genius to perceive what the falls meant, he couldn't screen out the—to use an electronic term—the "noise." All he could come up with were folk adages. What goes up must come down. The bigger they are, the harder they fall.

"What'd you say, Grandpa?"

"I was thinking out loud, if you can call that thinking," Mr. Howller said.

Young Howller had been one of the first on the scene, and so he got a place in the front of the crowd. He had not completely forgotten his parents or Aunt Thea, but the danger was over, and he could not make himself leave to search for them. And he had even forgotten about his soaked pants. The body was only about thirty feet from him. It lay on its back on the sidewalk, just as in the movie. But the dead Kong did not look as big or as dignified as in the movie. He was spread out more like an apeskin rug than a body, and blood and bowels and their contents had splashed out around him.

After a while Carl Denham, the man responsible for capturing Kong and bringing him to New York, appeared. As in the movie, Denham spoke his classical lines by the body: "It was Beauty. As always, Beauty killed the Beast."

This was the most appropriately dramatic place for the lines to be spoken, of course, and the proper place to end the movie.

But the book had Denham speaking these lines as he leaned over the parapet of the observation tower to look down at Kong on the sidewalk. His only audience was a police sergeant.

Both the book and the movie were true. Or half true. Denham did speak those lines way up on the 102nd floor of the tower. But, showman that he was, he also spoke them when he got down to the sidewalk, where the newsmen could hear them.

Young Howller didn't hear Denham's remarks. He was too far away. Besides, at that moment he felt a tap on his shoulder and heard a man say, "Hey, kid, there's somebody trying to get your attention!"

Young Howller went into his mother's arms and wept for at least a minute. His father reached past his mother and touched him briefly on the forehead, as if blessing him, and then gave his shoulder a squeeze. When he was able to talk, Tim Howller asked his mother what had happened to them. They, as near as they could remember, had been pushed out by the crowd, though they had fought to get to him, and had run up Broadway after they found themselves in the street because King Kong had appeared. They had managed to get back to the theater, had not been able to locate Tim, and had walked back to the Empire State Building.

"What happened to Uncle Nate?" Tim said.

Uncle Nate, his mother said, had caught up with them on Fifth Avenue and just now was trying to get past the police cordon into the building so he could check on Aunt Thea.

"She must be all right!" young Howller said. "The ape climbed up her side of the building, but she could easily get away from him, her apartment's so big!"

"Well, yes," his father had said. "But if she went to bed with her headache, she would've been right next to the window. But don't worry. If she'd been hurt, we'd know it. And maybe she wasn't even home."

Young Tim had asked him what he meant by that, but his father had only shrugged.

The three of them stood in the front line of the crowd, waiting for Uncle Nate to bring news of Aunt Thea, even though they weren't really worried about her, and waiting to see what happened to Kong. Mayor Jimmy Walker showed up and conferred with the officials. Then the governor himself, Franklin Delano Roosevelt, arrived with much noise of siren and motorcycle. A minute later a big black limousine with flashing red lights and a siren pulled up. Standing on the runningboard was a giant with bronze hair and strange-looking gold-flecked eyes. He jumped off the runningboard and strode up to the mayor, governor, and police commissioner and talked briefly with them. Tim Howller asked the man next to him what the giant's name was, but the man replied that he didn't know because he was from out of town also. The giant finished talking and strode up to the crowd, which opened for him as if it were the Red Sea and he were Moses, and he had no trouble at all getting through the police cordon. Tim then asked the man on the right of his parents if he knew the yellow-eyed giant's name. This man, tall and thin, was with a beautiful woman dressed up in an evening gown and a mink coat. He turned his head when Tim called to him and presented a hawklike face and eyes that burned so brightly that Tim wondered if he took dope. Those eyes also told him that here was a man who asked questions, not one who gave answers. Tim didn't repeat his question, and a moment later the man said, in a whispering voice that still carried a long distance, "Come on, Margo. I've work to do." And the two melted into the crowd.

Mr. Howller told Jill about the two men, and she said, "What about them, Grandpa?"

"I don't really know," he said. "Often I've

wondered . . . Well, never mind. Whoever they were, they're irrelevant to what happened to King Kong. But I'll say one thing about New York—you sure see a lot of strange characters there."

Young Howller had expected that the mess would quickly be cleaned up. And it was true that the Sanitation Department had sent a big truck with a big crane and a number of men with hoses, scoop shovels, and brooms. But a dozen people at least stopped the cleanup almost before it began. Carl Denham wanted no one to touch the body except the taxidermists he had called in. If he couldn't exhibit a live Kong, he would exhibit a dead one. A colonel from Roosevelt Field claimed the body and, when asked why the Air Force wanted it, could not give an explanation. Rather, he refused to give one, and it was not until an hour later that a phone call from the White House forced him to reveal the real reason. A general wanted the skin for a trophy because Kong was the only ape ever shot down in aerial combat.

A lawyer for the owners of the Empire State Building appeared with a claim for possession of the body. His clients wanted reimbursement for the damage done to the building.

A representative of the transit system wanted Kong's body so it could be sold to help pay for the damage the ape had done to the Sixth Avenue Elevated.

The owner of the theater from which Kong had escaped arrived with his lawyer and announced he intended to sue Denham for an amount which would cover the sums he would have to pay to those who were inevitably going to sue him.

The police ordered the body seized as evidence in the trial for involuntary manslaughter and criminal negligence in which Denham and the theater owner would be defendants in due process.

The manslaughter charges were later dropped, but Denham did serve a year before being paroled. On being released, he was killed by a religious fanatic, a native brought back by the second expedition to Kong's island. He was, in fact, the witch doctor. He had murdered Denham because Denham had abducted and slain his god, Kong.

His Majesty's New York consul showed up with papers which proved that Kong's island was in British waters. Therefore, Denham had no right to anything removed from the island without permission of His Majesty's government.

Denham was in a lot of trouble. But the worst blow of all was to come next day. He would be handed notification that he was being sued by Ann Redman. She wanted compensation to the tune of ten million dollars for various physical indignities and injuries suffered during her two abductions by the ape, plus the mental anguish these had caused her. Unfortunately for her, Denham went to prison without a penny in his pocket, and she dropped the suit. Thus, the public never found out exactly what the "physical indignities and injuries" were, but this did not keep it from making many speculations. Ann Redman also sued John Driscoll, though for a different reason. She claimed breach of promise. Driscoll, interviewed by newsmen, made his famous remark that she should have been suing Kong, not him. This convinced most of the public that what it had suspected had indeed happened. Just how it could have been done was difficult to explain, but the public had never lacked wiseacres who would not only attempt the difficult but would not draw back even at the impossible.

Actually, Mr. Howller thought, the deed was not beyond possibility. Take an adult male gorilla who stood six feet high and weighed 350 pounds. According to Swiss zoo director Ernst Lang, he would have a full erection only two inches long. How did Professor Lang know this? Did he enter the cage during a mating and measure the phallus? Not very likely. Even the timid and amiable gorilla would scarcely submit to this type of handling in that kind of situation. Never mind. Professor Lang said it was so, and so it must be. Perhaps he used a telescope with gradations across the lens like those on a submarine's periscope. In any event, until someone entered the cage and slapped down a ruler during the action, Professor Lang's word would have to be taken as the last word.

By mathematical extrapolation, using the square-cube law, a gorilla twenty feet tall would have an erect penis about twenty-one inches long. What the diameter would be was another guess and perhaps a vital one, for Ann Redman anyway. Whatever anyone else thought about the possibility, Kong must have decided that he would never know unless he tried. Just how well he succeeded, only he and his victim knew, since the attempt would have taken place before Driscoll and Denham got to the observation tower and before the searchlight beams centered on their target.

But Ann Redman must have told her lover, John Driscoll, the truth, and he turned out not to be such a strong man after all.

"What're you thinking about, Grandpa?"

Mr. Howller looked at the screen. The Road-runner had been succeeded by the Pink Panther, who was enduring as much pain and violence as the poor old coyote.

"Nothing," he said. "I'm just watching the Pink Panther with you."

"But you didn't say what happened to King Kong," she said.

"Oh," he said, "we stood around until dawn, and then the big shots finally came to some sort of agreement. The body just couldn't be left there much longer, if for no other reason than that it was blocking traffic. Blocking traffic meant that business would be held up. And lots of people would lose lots of money. And so Kong's body was taken away by the Police Department, though it used the Sanitation Department's crane, and it was kept in an icehouse until its ownership could be thrashed out."

"Poor Kong."

"No," he said, "not poor Kong. He was dead and out of it."

"He went to heaven?"

"As much as anybody," Mr. Howller said.

"But he killed a lot of people, and he carried off that nice girl. Wasn't he bad?"

"No, he wasn't bad. He was an animal, and he didn't know the difference between good and evil. Anyway, even if he'd been human, he would've been doing what any human would have done."

"What do you mean, Grandpa?"

"Well, if you were captured by people only a foot tall and carried off to a far place and put in a cage, wouldn't you try to escape? And if these people tried to put you back in, or got so scared that they tried to kill you right now, wouldn't you step on them?"

"Sure, I'd step on them, Grandpa."

"You'd be justified, too. And King Kong was justified. He was only acting according to the dictates of his instincts."

"What?"

"He was an animal, and so he can't be blamed, no matter what he did. He wasn't evil. It was what happened around Kong that was evil."

"What do you mean?" Jill said.

"He brought out the bad and the good in the people."

But mostly bad, he thought, and he encouraged Jill to forget about Kong and concentrate on the Pink Panther. And as he looked at the screen, he saw it through tears. Even after forty-two years, he thought, tears. This was what the fall of Kong had meant to him.

The crane had hooked the corpse and lifted it up. And there were two flattened-out bodies under Kong; he must have dropped them onto the sidewalk on his way up and then fallen on them from the tower. But how explain the nakedness of the corpses of the man and the woman?

The hair of the woman was long and, in a small area not covered by blood, yellow. And part of her face was recognizable.

Young Tim had not known until then that Uncle Nate had returned from looking for Aunt

Thea. Uncle Nate gave a long wailing cry that sounded as if he, too, were falling from the top of the Empire State Building.

A second later young Tim Howller was wailing. But where Uncle Nate's was the cry of betrayal, and perhaps of revenge satisfied, Tim's was both of betrayal and of grief for the death of one he had passionately loved with a thirteen-year-old's love, for one whom the thirteen-year-old in him still loved.

"Grandpa, are there any more King Kongs?"

"No," Mr. Howller said. To say yes would force him to try to explain something that she could not understand. When she got older, she would know that every dawn saw the death of the old Kong and the birth of the new.

ALEXANDER WOOLLCOTT

ALEXANDER WOOLLCOTT (1887–1943) was born near Red Bank, New Jersey, and graduated from New York's Hamilton College. Although not much read today, in his time "Aleck" Woollcott was a hugely influential critic, both of the theater and of literature, and helped make James Hilton's *Goodbye, Mr. Chips* and *Lost Horizon* bestsellers. He was a prolific drama critic for the *New York Times* before moving to the *New Yorker*, where he launched the "Shouts & Murmurs" column. His editor at the magazine was quoted as saying, "I guess he was one of the most dreadful writers who ever existed," although the great bookman Vincent Starrett selected Woollcott's 1934 novel, *While Rome Burns,* as one of the fifty-two "best-loved books of the twentieth century."

One of the founders of the Algonquin Round Table, he later became a charter member of the Baker Street Irregulars (and famously arrived at the inaugural banquet in a hansom cab). He loved the theater and wrote two plays with fellow Algonquin member George S. Kaufman, neither of which was successful. Kaufman, with Moss Hart, later wrote the play *The Man Who Came to Dinner* (1939), and based the titular character, Sheridan Whiteside, on Woollcott, exaggerating his best and worst characteristics. Less well known is that he also served as the inspiration for Waldo Lydecker in the film noir *Laura* (1944). Clifton Webb, who played Lydecker, also toured as Whiteside in *The Man Who Came to Dinner;* Woollcott also starred in a traveling company of the comedy. Although he didn't like Los Angeles, calling it "seven suburbs in search of a city," he liked being in films and had numerous small parts and cameos. There appears to be no corroboration for his claim that the Brandy Alexander cocktail was named after him.

"Moonlight Sonata" was first published in the October 3, 1931, issue of the *New Yorker.*

MOONLIGHT SONATA

ALEXANDER WOOLLCOTT

IF THIS REPORT were to be published in its own England, I would have to cross my fingers in a little foreword explaining that all the characters were fictitious—which stern requirement of the British libel law would embarrass me slightly because none of the characters is fictitious, and the story—told to Katharine Cornell by Clemence Dane and by Katharine Cornell told to me—chronicles what, to the best of my knowledge and belief, actually befell a young English physician whom I shall call Alvan Barach, because that does not happen to be his name. It is an account of a hitherto unreported adventure he had two years ago when he went down into Kent to visit an old friend—let us call him Ellery Cazalet—who spent most of his days on the links and most of his nights wondering how he would ever pay the death duties on the collapsing family manor-house to which he had indignantly fallen heir.

This house was a shabby little cousin to Compton Wynyates, with roof-tiles of Tudor red making it cozy in the noon-day sun and a hoarse bell which, from the clock tower, had been contemptuously scattering the hours like coins ever since Henry VIII was a rosy stripling. Within, Cazalet could afford only a doddering couple to fend for him, and the once sumptuous gardens did much as they pleased under the care of a single gardener. I think I must risk giving the gardener's real name, for none I could invent would have so appropriate a flavor.

It was John Scripture, and he was assisted, from time to time, by an aged and lunatic father who, in his lucid intervals, would be let out from his captivity under the eaves of the lodge to putter amid the lewd topiarian extravagance of the hedges.

The doctor was to come down when he could, with a promise of some good golf, long nights of exquisite silence, and a ghost or two thrown in—his fancy ran that way. It was a characteristic of his rather ponderous humor that, in writing to fix a day, he addressed Cazalet at *The Creeps, Sevenoaks, Kent.* When he arrived, it was to find his host away from home and not due back until all hours. Barach was to dine alone with a reproachful setter for companion, and not wait up. His bedroom on the ground floor was beautifully paneled from footboard to ceiling, but some misguided housekeeper under the fourth George had fallen upon the lovely woodwork with a can of black varnish. The dowry brought by a Cazalet bride of the mauve decade had been invested in a few vintage bathrooms, and one of these had replaced a prayer closet that once opened into this bedroom. There was only a candle to read by, but the light of a full moon came waveringly through the wind-stirred vines that half-curtained the mullioned windows.

In this museum, Barach dropped off to sleep. He did not know how long he had slept when he found himself awake again, and conscious that something was astir in the room. It took him a moment to place the movement, but at last, in a patch of moonlight, he made out a hunched figure that seemed to be sitting with bent, engrossed head in the chair by the door. It was the hand, or rather the whole arm, that was moving, tracing a recurrent if irregular course in the air. At first, the gesture was teasingly half-familiar, and then Barach recognized it as the one a woman makes when embroidering. There would be a hesitation as if the needle were being thrust through some taut, resistant material, and then, each time, the long, swift, sure pull of the thread.

To the startled guest, this seemed the least menacing activity he had ever heard ascribed to a ghost, but just the same he had only one idea, and that was to get out of that room with all possible dispatch. His mind made a hasty reconnaissance. The door into the hall was out of the question, for madness lay that way. At least he would have to pass right by that weaving arm. Nor did he relish a blind plunge into the thorny shrubbery beneath his window, and a barefoot scamper across the frosty turf. Of course, there was the bathroom, but that was small comfort if he could not get out of it by another door. In a spasm of concentration he remembered that he had seen another door. Just at the moment of this realization, he heard the comfortingly actual sound of a car coming up the drive, and guessed that it was his host returning. In one magnificent movement he leaped to the floor, bounded into the bathroom, and bolted its door behind him. The floor of the room beyond was quilted with moonlight. Wading through that, he arrived breathless, but unmolested, in the corridor. Far-

ther along he could see the lamp left burning in the entrance hall and hear the clatter of his host closing the front door.

As Barach came hurrying out of the darkness to greet him, Cazalet boomed his delight at such affability, and famished by his long, cold ride, proposed an immediate raid on the larder. The doctor, already sheepish at his recent panic, said nothing about it, and was all for food at once. With lighted candles held high, the foraging party descended on the offices, and mine host was descanting on the merits of cold roast beef, Cheddar cheese, and milk as a light midnight snack when he stumbled over a bundle on the floor. With a cheerful curse at the old goody of the kitchen who was always leaving something about, he bent to see what it was this time, and let out a whistle of surprise. Then, by two candles held low, he and the doctor saw something they will not forget while they live. It was the body of the cook. Just the body. The head was gone. On the floor alongside lay a bloody cleaver.

"Old Scripture, by God!" Cazalet cried out, and in a flash Barach guessed. Still clutching a candle in one hand, he dragged his companion back through the interminable house to the room from which he had fled, motioning him to be silent, tiptoeing the final steps. That precaution was wasted, for a regiment could not have disturbed the rapt contentment of the ceremony still in progress within. The old lunatic had not left his seat by the door. Between his knees he still held the head of the woman he had killed. Scrupulously, happily, crooning at his work, he was plucking out the gray hairs one by one.

GO WEST,
YOUNG MAN

THE CABALLERO'S WAY

O. HENRY

WILLIAM SYDNEY PORTER (1862–1910), whose pseudonym was O. Henry, wrote more than six hundred short stories. Often undervalued today because of their sentimentality, O. Henry's stories were once as critically acclaimed as they were popular. Many nonetheless remain iconic and familiar, notably such classics as "The Gift of the Magi," "The Furnished Room," "A Retrieved Reformation" (better known for its several stage and film versions as *Alias Jimmy Valentine*), and "The Ransom of Red Chief." Since 1918, the year's best short stories have been collected in a prestigious annual anthology named in his honor.

In "The Caballero's Way," O. Henry created a character who went on to become a beloved presence in motion pictures, radio, television, comic books, and comic strips—while undergoing a major change along the way. The Cisco Kid is not a heroic figure in the short story, but the exact opposite: a killer and multiple murderer. Yet by his third film, *In Old Arizona* (1929), he is transformed into a sartorially snappy turn-of-the-century Mexican hero who captures outlaws and rescues damsels in distress. Warner Baxter won the Oscar for best actor, the second ever given, for his portrayal of the revamped Cisco Kid. Nearly thirty films have been made about the character, plus 156 half-hour television episodes (among the first to be shot in color), produced between 1950 and 1956. On television, the Kid was played by Duncan Renaldo, and his sidekick, Pancho—not in the original story—was played for comic effect by Leo Carillo.

"The Caballero's Way" was first published in the July 1907 issue of *Everybody's Magazine;* its first book appearance was in O. Henry's *Heart of the West* (New York: McClure, 1907).

THE CABALLERO'S WAY

O. HENRY

THE CISCO KID had killed six men in more or less fair scrimmages, had murdered twice as many (mostly Mexicans), and had winged a larger number whom he modestly forebore to count. Therefore a woman loved him.

The Kid was twenty-five, looked twenty; and a careful insurance company would have estimated the probable time of his demise at, say, twenty-six. His habitat was anywhere between the Frio and the Rio Grande. He killed for the love of it—because he was quick-tempered—to avoid arrest—for his own amusement—any reason that came to his mind would suffice. He had escaped capture because he could shoot five-sixths of a second sooner than any sheriff or ranger in the service, and because he rode a speckled roan horse that knew every cowpath in the mesquite and pear thickets from San Antonio to Matamoras.

Tonia Perez, the girl who loved the Cisco Kid, was half Carmen, half Madonna, and the rest—oh, yes, a woman who is half Carmen and half Madonna can always be something more—the rest, let us say, was humming-bird. She lived in a grass-roofed *jacal* near a little Mexican settlement at the Lone Wolf Crossing of the Frio. With her lived a father or grandfather, a lineal Aztec, somewhat less than a thousand years old, who herded a hundred goats and lived in a continuous drunken dream from drinking *mescal*. Back of the *jacal* a tremendous forest of bristling pear, twenty feet high at its worst, crowded al-most to its door. It was along the bewildering maze of this spinous thicket that the speckled roan would bring the Kid to see his girl. And once, clinging like a lizard to the ridge-pole, high up under the peaked grass roof, he had heard Tonia, with her Madonna face and Carmen beauty and humming-bird soul, parley with the sheriff's posse, denying knowledge of her man in her soft *mélange* of Spanish and English.

One day the adjutant-general of the State, who is, *ex officio,* commander of the ranger forces, wrote some sarcastic lines to Captain Duval of Company X, stationed at Laredo, relative to the serene and undisturbed existence led by murderers and desperadoes in the said captain's territory.

The captain turned the color of brick dust under his tan, and forwarded the letter, after adding a few comments, per ranger Private Bill Adamson, to ranger Lieutenant Sandridge, camped at a water hole on the Nueces with a squad of five men in preservation of law and order.

Lieutenant Sandridge turned a beautiful *couleur de rose* through his ordinary strawberry complexion, tucked the letter in his hip pocket, and chewed off the end of his gamboge moustache.

The next morning he saddled his horse and rode alone to the Mexican settlement at the Lone Wolf Crossing of the Frio, twenty miles away.

Six feet two, blond as a Viking, quiet as a deacon, dangerous as a machine gun, Sandridge moved among the *jacales*, patiently seeking news of the Cisco Kid.

Far more than the law, the Mexicans dreaded the cold and certain vengeance of the lone rider that the ranger sought. It had been one of the Kid's pastimes to shoot Mexicans "to see them kick": if he demanded from them moribund Terpsichorean feats, simply that he might be entertained, what terrible and extreme penalties would be certain to follow should they anger him! One and all they lounged with upturned palms and shrugging shoulders, filling the air with *"Quién sabes"* and denials of the Kid's acquaintance.

But there was a man named Fink who kept a store at the Crossing—a man of many nationalities, tongues, interests, and ways of thinking.

"No use to ask them Mexicans," he said to Sandridge. "They're afraid to tell. This *hombre* they call the Kid—Goodall is his name, ain't it?—he's been in my store once or twice. I have an idea you might run across him at—but I guess I don't keer to say, myself. I'm two seconds later in pulling a gun than I used to be and the difference is worth thinking about. But this Kid's got a half-Mexican girl at the Crossing that he comes to see. She lives in that *jacal* a hundred yards down the arroyo at the edge of the pear. Maybe she—no, I don't suppose she would, but that *jacal* would be a good place to watch, anyway."

Sandridge rode down to the *jacal* of Perez. The sun was low, and the broad shade of the great pear thicket already covered the grass-thatched hut. The goats were enclosed for the night in a brush corral near by. A few kids walked the top of it, nibbling the chaparral leaves. The old Mexican lay upon a blanket on the grass, already in a stupor from his *mescal*, and dreaming, perhaps, of the nights when he and Pizarro touched glasses to their New World fortunes—so old his wrinkled face seemed to proclaim him to be. And in the door of the *jacal* stood Tonia. And Lieutenant Sandridge sat in his saddle staring at her like a gannet agape at a sailorman.

The Cisco Kid was a vain person, as all eminent and successful assassins are, and his bosom would have been ruffled had he known that at a simple exchange of glances two persons, in whose minds he had been looming large, suddenly abandoned (at least for the time) all thought of him.

Never before had Tonia seen such a man as this. He seemed to be made of sunshine and blood-red tissue and clear weather. He seemed to illuminate the shadow of the pear when he smiled, as though the sun were rising again. The men she had known had been small and dark. Even the Kid, in spite of his achievements, was a stripling no larger than herself, with black straight hair and a cold marble face that chilled the noonday.

As for Tonia, though she sends description to the poorhouse, let her make a millionaire of your fancy. Her blue-black hair, smoothly divided in the middle and bound close to her head, and her large eyes full of the Latin melancholy, gave her the Madonna touch. Her motions and air spoke of the concealed fire and the desire to charm that she had inherited from the *gitanas* of the Basque province. As for the humming-bird part of her, that dwelt in her heart; you could not perceive it unless her bright red skirt and dark blue blouse gave you a symbolic hint of the vagarious bird.

The newly lighted sun-god asked for a drink of water. Tonia brought it from the red jar hanging under the brush shelter. Sandridge considered it necessary to dismount so as to lessen the trouble of her ministrations.

I play no spy; nor do I assume to master the thoughts of any human heart; but I assert, by the chronicler's right, that before a quarter of an hour had sped, Sandridge was teaching her how to plait a six-strand rawhide stake-rope, and Tonia had explained to him that were it not for her little English book that the peripatetic *padre* had given her and the little crippled *chivo*, that she fed from a bottle, she would be very, very lonely indeed.

Which leads to a suspicion that the Kid's

fences needed repairing, and that the adjutant-general's sarcasm had fallen upon unproductive soil.

In his camp by the water hole Lieutenant Sandridge announced and reiterated his intention of either causing the Cisco Kid to nibble the black loam of the Frio country prairies or of hailing him before a judge and jury. That sounded business-like. Twice a week he rode over to the Lone Wolf Crossing of the Frio, and directed Tonia's slim, slightly lemon-tinted fingers among the intricacies of the slowly growing lariat. A six-strand plait is hard to learn and easy to teach.

The ranger knew that he might find the Kid there at any visit. He kept his armament ready, and had a frequent eye for the pear thicket at the rear of the *jacal*. Thus he might bring down the kite and the humming-bird with one stone.

While the sunny-haired ornithologist was pursuing his studies the Cisco Kid was also attending to his professional duties. He moodily shot up a saloon in a small cow village on Quintana Creek, killed the town marshal (plugging him neatly in the center of his tin badge), and then rode away, morose and unsatisfied. No true artist is uplifted by shooting an aged man carrying an old-style .38 bulldog.

On his way the Kid suddenly experienced the yearning that all men feel when wrong-doing loses its keen edge of delight. He yearned for the woman he loved to reassure him that she was his in spite of it. He wanted her to call his blood-thirstiness bravery and his cruelty devotion. He wanted Tonia to bring him water from the red jug under the brush shelter, and tell him how the *chivo* was thriving on the bottle.

The Kid turned the speckled roan's head up the ten-mile pear flat that stretches along the Arroyo Hondo until it ends at the Lone Wolf Crossing of the Frio. The roan whickered; for he had a sense of locality and direction equal to that of a belt-line street-car horse; and he knew he would soon be nibbling the rich mesquite grass at the end of a forty-foot stake-rope while Ulysses rested his head in Circe's straw-roofed hut.

More weird and lonesome than the journey of an Amazonian explorer is the ride of one through a Texas pear flat. With dismal monotony and startling variety the uncanny and multiform shapes of the cacti lift their twisted trunks and fat, bristly hands to encumber the way. The demon plant, appearing to live without soil or rain, seems to taunt the parched traveler with its lush gray greenness. It warps itself a thousand times about what look to be open and inviting paths, only to lure the rider into blind and impassable spine-defended "bottoms of the bag," leaving him to retreat, if he can, with the points of the compass whirling in his head.

To be lost in the pear is to die almost the death of the thief on the cross, pierced by nails and with grotesque shapes of all the fiends hovering about.

But it was not so with the Kid and his mount. Winding, twisting, circling, tracing the most fantastic and bewildering trail ever picked out, the good roan lessened the distance to the Lone Wolf Crossing with every coil and turn that he made.

While they fared the Kid sang. He knew but one tune and he sang it, as he knew but one code and lived it, and but one girl and loved her. He was a single-minded man of conventional ideas. He had a voice like a coyote with bronchitis, but whenever he chose to sing his song he sang it. It was a conventional song of the camps and trail, running at its beginning as near as may be to these words:

> *Don't you monkey with my Lulu girl*
> *Or I'll tell you what I'll do—*

and so on. The roan was inured to it, and did not mind.

But even the poorest singer will, after a certain time, gain his own consent to refrain from contributing to the world's noises. So the Kid, by the time he was within a mile or two of Tonia's *jacal*, had reluctantly allowed his song to die away—not because his vocal performance had become less charming to his own ears, but because his laryngeal muscles were aweary.

As though he were in a circus ring the speckled roan wheeled and danced through the labyrinth of pear until at length his rider knew by certain landmarks that the Lone Wolf Crossing was close at hand. Then, where the pear was thinner, he caught sight of the grass roof of the *jacal* and the hackberry tree on the edge of the arroyo. A few yards farther the Kid stopped the roan and gazed intently through the prickly openings. Then he dismounted, dropped the roan's reins, and proceeded on foot, stooping and silent, like an Indian. The roan, knowing his part, stood still, making no sound.

The Kid crept noiselessly to the very edge of the pear thicket and reconnoitered between the leaves of a clump of cactus.

Ten yards from his hiding-place, in the shade of the *jacal*, sat his Tonia calmly plaiting a rawhide lariat. So far she might surely escape condemnation; women have been known, from time to time, to engage in more mischievous occupations. But if all must be told, there is to be added that her head reposed against the broad and comfortable chest of a tall red-and-yellow man, and that his arm was about her, guiding her nimble small fingers that required so many lessons at the intricate six-strand plait.

Sandridge glanced quickly at the dark mass of pear when he heard a slight squeaking sound that was not altogether unfamiliar. A gun-scabbard will make that sound when one grasps the handle of a six-shooter suddenly. But the sound was not repeated; and Tonia's fingers needed close attention.

And then, in the shadow of death, they began to talk of their love; and in the still July afternoon every word they uttered reached the ears of the Kid.

"Remember, then," said Tonia, "you must not come again until I send for you. Soon he will be here. A *vaquero* at the *tienda* said to-day he saw him on the Guadalupe three days ago. When he is that near he always comes. If he comes and finds you here he will kill you. So, for my sake, you must come no more until I send you the word."

"All right," said the ranger. "And then what?"

"And then," said the girl, "you must bring your men here and kill him. If not, he will kill you."

"He ain't a man to surrender, that's sure," said Sandridge. "It's kill or be killed for the officer that goes up against Mr. Cisco Kid."

"He must die," said the girl. "Otherwise there will not be any peace in the world for thee and me. He has killed many. Let him so die. Bring your men, and give him no chance to escape."

"You used to think right much of him," said Sandridge.

Tonia dropped the lariat, twisted herself around, and curved a lemon-tinted arm over the ranger's shoulder.

"But then," she murmured in liquid Spanish, "I had not beheld thee, thou great, red mountain of a man! And thou art kind and good, as well as strong. Could one choose him, knowing thee? Let him die; for then I will not be filled with fear by day and night lest he hurt thee or me."

"How can I know when he comes?" asked Sandridge.

"When he comes," said Tonia, "he remains two days, sometimes three. Gregorio, the small son of old Luisa, the *lavandera*, has a swift pony. I will write a letter to thee and send it by him, saying how it will be best to come upon him. By Gregorio will the letter come. And bring many men with thee, and have much care, oh, dear red one, for the rattlesnake is not quicker to strike than is '*El Chivato*,' as they call him, to send a ball from his *pistola*."

"The Kid's handy with his gun, sure enough," admitted Sandridge, "but when I come for him I shall come alone. I'll get him by myself or not at all. The Cap wrote one or two things to me that make me want to do the trick without any help. You let me know when Mr. Kid arrives, and I'll do the rest."

"I will send you the message by the boy Gregorio," said the girl. "I knew you were braver than that small slayer of men who never smiles. How could I ever have thought I cared for him?"

It was time for the ranger to ride back to his camp on the water hole. Before he mounted his horse he raised the slight form of Tonia with one arm high from the earth for a parting salute. The drowsy stillness of the torpid summer air still lay thick upon the dreaming afternoon. The smoke from the fire in the *jacal*, where the *frijoles* blubbered in the iron pot, rose straight as a plumbline above the clay-daubed chimney. No sound or movement disturbed the serenity of the dense pear thicket ten yards away.

When the form of Sandridge had disappeared, loping his big dun down the steep banks of the Frio crossing, the Kid crept back to his own horse, mounted him, and rode back along the tortuous trail he had come.

But not far. He stopped and waited in the silent depths of the pear until half an hour had passed. And then Tonia heard the high, untrue notes of his unmusical singing coming nearer and nearer; and she ran to the edge of the pear to meet him.

The Kid seldom smiled; but he smiled and waved his hat when he saw her. He dismounted, and his girl sprang into his arms. The Kid looked at her fondly. His thick black hair clung to his head like a wrinkled mat. The meeting brought a slight ripple of some undercurrent of feeling to his smooth, dark face that was usually as motionless as a clay mask.

"How's my girl?" he asked, holding her close.

"Sick of waiting so long for you, dear one," she answered. "My eyes are dim with always gazing into that devil's pincushion through which you come. And I can see into it such a little way, too. But you are here, beloved one, and I will not scold. *Qué mal muchacho!* not to come to see your *alma* more often. Go in and rest, and let me water your horse and stake him with the long rope. There is cool water in the jar for you."

The Kid kissed her affectionately.

"Not if the court knows itself do I let a lady stake my horse for me," said he. "But if you'll run in, *chica*, and throw a pot of coffee together while I attend to the *caballo*, I'll be a good deal obliged."

Besides his marksmanship the Kid had another attribute for which he admired himself greatly. He was *muy caballero*, as the Mexicans express it, where the ladies were concerned. For them he had always gentle words and consideration. He could not have spoken a harsh word to a woman. He might ruthlessly slay their husbands and brothers, but he could not have laid the weight of a finger in anger upon a woman. Wherefore many of that interesting division of humanity who had come under the spell of his politeness declared their disbelief in the stories circulated about Mr. Kid. One shouldn't believe everything one heard, they said. When confronted by their indignant men folk with proof of the *caballero*'s deeds of infamy, they said maybe he had been driven to it, and that he knew how to treat a lady, anyhow.

Considering this extremely courteous idiosyncrasy of the Kid and the pride that he took in it, one can perceive that the solution of the problem that was presented to him by what he saw and heard from his hiding-place in the pear that afternoon (at least as to one of the actors) must have been obscured by difficulties. And yet one could not think of the Kid overlooking little matters of that kind.

At the end of the short twilight they gathered around a supper of *frijoles*, goat steaks, canned peaches, and coffee, by the light of a lantern in the *jacal*. Afterward, the ancestor, his flock corralled, smoked a cigarette and became a mummy in a gray blanket. Tonia washed the few dishes while the Kid dried them with the flour-sacking towel. Her eyes shone; she chatted volubly of the inconsequent happenings of her small world since the Kid's last visit; it was as all his other home-comings had been.

Then outside Tonia swung in a grass hammock with her guitar and sang sad *canciones de amor*.

"Do you love me just the same, old girl?" asked the Kid, hunting for his cigarette papers.

"Always the same, little one," said Tonia, her dark eyes lingering upon him.

"I must go over to Fink's," said the Kid, rising, "for some tobacco. I thought I had another sack in my coat. I'll be back in a quarter of an hour."

"Hasten," said Tonia, "and tell me—how long shall I call you my own this time? Will you be gone again to-morrow, leaving me to grieve, or will you be longer with your Tonia?"

"Oh, I might stay two or three days this trip," said the Kid, yawning. "I've been on the dodge for a month, and I'd like to rest up."

He was gone half an hour for his tobacco. When he returned Tonia was still lying in the hammock.

"It's funny," said the Kid, "how I feel. I feel like there was somebody lying behind every bush and tree waiting to shoot me. I never had mullygrubs like them before. Maybe it's one of them presumptions. I've got half a notion to light out in the morning before day. The Guadalupe country is burning up about that old Dutchman I plugged down there."

"You are not afraid—no one could make my brave little one fear."

"Well, I haven't been usually regarded as a jack-rabbit when it comes to scrapping; but I don't want a posse smoking me out when I'm in your *jacal*. Somebody might get hurt that oughtn't to."

"Remain with your Tonia; no one will find you here."

The Kid looked keenly into the shadows up and down the arroyo and toward the dim lights of the Mexican village.

"I'll see how it looks later on," was his decision.

At midnight a horseman rode into the rangers' camp, blazing his way by noisy "halloes" to indicate a pacific mission. Sandridge and one or two others turned out to investigate the row. The rider announced himself to be Domingo Sales, from the Lone Wolf Crossing. He bore a letter for Señor Sandridge. Old Luisa, the *lavandera*, had persuaded him to bring it, he said, her son Gregorio being too ill of a fever to ride.

Sandridge lighted the camp lantern and read the letter. These were its words:

Dear One: He has come. Hardly had you ridden away when he came out of the pear. When he first talked he said he would stay three days or more. Then as it grew later he was like a wolf or a fox, and walked about without rest, looking and listening. Soon he said he must leave before daylight when it is dark and stillest. And then he seemed to suspect that I be not true to him. He looked at me so strange that I am frightened. I swear to him that I love him, his own Tonia. Last of all he said I must prove to him I am true. He thinks that even now men are waiting to kill him as he rides from my house. To escape he says he will dress in my clothes, my red skirt and the blue waist I wear and the brown mantilla over the head, and thus ride away. But before that he says that I must put on his clothes, his pantalones *and* camisa *and hat, and ride away on his horse from the* jacal *as far as the big road beyond the crossing and back again. This before he goes, so he can tell if I am true and if men are hidden to shoot him. It is a terrible thing. An hour before daybreak this is to be. Come, my dear one, and kill this man and take me for your Tonia. Do not try to take hold of him alive, but kill him quickly. Knowing all, you should do that. You must come long before the time and hide yourself in the little shed near the* jacal *where the wagon and saddles are kept. It is dark in there. He will wear my red skirt and blue waist and brown mantilla. I send you a hundred kisses. Come surely and shoot quickly and straight.*

Thine Own Tonia

Sandridge quickly explained to his men the official part of the missive. The rangers protested against his going alone.

"I'll get him easy enough," said the lieutenant. "The girl's got him trapped. And don't even think he'll get the drop on me."

Sandridge saddled his horse and rode to the Lone Wolf Crossing. He tied his big dun in a clump of brush on the arroyo, took his Winchester from its scabbard, and carefully approached the Perez *jacal*. There was only the half of a high moon drifted over by ragged, milk-white gulf clouds.

The wagon-shed was an excellent place for ambush; and the ranger got inside it safely. In the black shadow of the brush shelter in front of the *jacal* he could see a horse tied and hear him impatiently pawing the hard-trodden earth.

He waited almost an hour before two figures came out of the *jacal*. One, in man's clothes, quickly mounted the horse and galloped past the wagon-shed toward the crossing and village. And then the other figure, in skirt, waist, and mantilla over its head, stepped out into the faint moonlight, gazing after the rider. Sandridge thought he would take his chance then before Tonia rode back. He fancied she might not care to see it.

"Throw up your hands," he ordered, loudly, stepping out of the wagon-shed with his Winchester at his shoulder.

There was a quick turn of the figure, but no movement to obey, so the ranger pumped in the bullets—one—two—three—and then twice more; for you never could be too sure of bringing down the Cisco Kid. There was no danger of missing at ten paces, even in that half moonlight.

The old ancestor, asleep on his blanket, was awakened by the shots. Listening further, he heard a great cry from some man in mortal distress or anguish, and rose up grumbling at the disturbing ways of moderns.

The tall, red ghost of a man burst into the *jacal*, reaching one hand, shaking like a *tule* reed, for the lantern hanging on its nail. The other spread a letter on the table.

"Look at this letter, Perez," cried the man. "Who wrote it?"

"*Ah, Dios!* it is Señor Sandridge," mumbled the old man, approaching. "*Pues, señor*, that letter was written by '*El Chivato*,' as he is called—by the man of Tonia. They say he is a bad man; I do not know. While Tonia slept he wrote the letter and sent it by this old hand of mine to Domingo Sales to be brought to you. Is there anything wrong in the letter? I am very old; and I did not know. *Valgame Dios!* it is a very foolish world; and there is nothing in the house to drink—nothing to drink."

Just then all that Sandridge could think of to do was to go outside and throw himself face downward in the dust by the side of his humming-bird, of whom not a feather fluttered. He was not a *caballero* by instinct, and he could not understand the niceties of revenge.

A mile away the rider who had ridden past the wagon-shed struck up a harsh, untuneful song, the words of which began:

Don't you monkey with my Lulu girl
Or I'll tell you what I'll do—

ZORRO DEALS WITH TREASON

JOHNSTON McCULLEY

ZORRO WAS NOT the only masked hero created by Johnston McCulley (1883–1958) but he was the most famous and endured the longest, both in printed form and on film. McCulley, born and raised in Illinois, worked as a journalist for the *Police Gazette* before becoming a popular and prolific pulp writer. His first costumed protagonist was Black Star, a master criminal who began appearing in magazines in 1916 and made his book debut five years later in *The Black Star*. McCulley also produced countless pulp serials about Robin Hood–like figures who wear costumes and take on melodramatic names, stealing from the corrupt rich and doling out the treasure to their victims or those in need. These early pulp heroes included The Thunderbolt, The Crimson Clown, The Avenging Twins, The Mongoose, The Green Ghost, and Thubway Tham, who steals wallets from people on the subway in nearly a hundred stories. McCulley's masked and costumed figures helped inspire such characters as The Shadow, The Green Lantern, Batman, and the Lone Ranger, among many others.

Yet it is Zorro (Spanish for *fox*), the nom de guerre of Don Diego Vega, that lives on in memory. By day, Zorro is a poetry-reading fop (much like the Scarlet Pimpernel); by night he is a righter of wrongs and protector of the poor—mostly Mexicans and Indians who are unjustly treated by the aristocratic Spaniards of Southern California in the late eighteenth and early nineteenth centuries. When trouble arises, he slips out of his mansion, dons his black clothes and mask, and rides his giant black stallion to defend the weak. An expert swordsman, he slashes a Z on the cheeks or foreheads of those he vanquishes. "I am the friend of the oppressed, *señor*," he informs a malefactor, "and I have come to punish you." He first rides onto the scene in *The Curse of Capistrano*, a five-part serial in *All-Story Weekly* in 1919 (it was published in book form under the title *The Mark of Zorro* in 1924). The serial caught the attention of Douglas Fairbanks, Jr., and Mary Pickford, who made it into *The Mark of Zorro* (1920), the first motion picture released by their new studio, United Artists. The film was instantly successful and induced McCulley to continue to write about his hero, with one modification: Zorro's black costume, an invention of Fairbanks, became a signature part of the more than sixty additional novels, stories, and novellas McCulley subsequently created. Over forty films about Zorro have been produced, and the Walt Disney television series was briefly but wildly successful in the late 1950s.

"Zorro Deals with Treason" is one of several tales in which an impostor appears; it was originally published in the August 18, 1934, issue of *Argosy*.

*"You seek
something,
señor?"*

ZORRO DEALS WITH TREASON

JOHNSTON McCULLEY

I

A NIGHT VISITOR

DOWN THE CAÑON and toward the temporary summer village of the Calientes rolled a tattoo of hoofbeats which grew rapidly in volume and echoed from the rocks.

The tribesmen at the fires sprang quickly and silently to their feet, reaching for their weapons, and some darted back out of the revealing moonlight to positions of advantage in the darkness. They knew that it was not a native's pony coming, but the mount of a white man, for the sounds told them clearly that the mount wore shoes.

But the unknown rider was not approaching furtively, like an enemy or a spy. So those about the fires relaxed, though they kept their weapons handy and curiosity remained with them. Down the narrow trail, presently, the rider came.

The horse he bestrode was a huge black, like a shadow in the bright moonlight. The rider wore a long black cloak which shrouded his form, and his face was covered with a black mask, and there was a blade at his side, moonlight glinting from its polished scabbard.

"You know me?" he shouted at them.

"Zorro . . . Zorro!" they cried in answer.

He lifted a hand in a demand for them to be silent, and they gave him instant attention. Then he spoke:

"I have done what little I could to protect and defend such as you. But it is impossible that one man do everything. Also, it is written that a

The rope jerked taut, pinning his arms to his sides.

"'Tis Señor Zorro!" somebody cried.

"Zorro . . . Zorro!" Those around the fires took up the cry, greeted him with wild shouts.

At the edge of the circle of amber light cast by the nearest fire, the rider drew rein. The tribesmen hurried toward him, to group and stand silently and respectfully, waiting for him to speak.

Here was Señor Zorro, the mysterious one, and their friend. In many ways, he had demonstrated his friendship. Here was the elusive rider who made fools of the soldiery who tried to catch him, who punished those who mistreated the natives and cheated them, crossing blades willingly with any and all, and leaving a jagged letter Z on the cheeks of those he fought, so marking them forever as men who had been vanquished by him.

man must help himself as well as take help from others."

They muttered at his words, but none of them made reply. They could not understand to what peroration his remarks were leading.

"You are being abused, cheated, wronged," the masked rider continued, his voice ringing back from the rocks. "You are treated worse than the flea-bitten dogs of the pueblo. You stand still and mute while the lash is being put across your backs. Are you men?"

They began muttering again, and sounds of rage rumbled from their throats as they remembered certain indignities and wrongs.

"Now, there is a plan afoot to make all of you slaves. Do you wish that?"

"No! . . . No!" they howled.

"Then you must band together, and strike!

Spare the few whites who are your friends, and slay the others. Use the torch on their buildings. Take what goods you wish from their houses. Drive your enemies from the land of your birth, and be free and happy again. You must prepare at once. The other tribes are preparing, and the Calientes must get ready also. I shall lead you to victory."

They cheered wildly when he said that, until the rock walls of the cañon rang with the echoes. The masked rider lifted a hand again in a demand for silence.

"Use care in your planning," he cautioned. "Do not let your enemies know what you do. The attack must be a complete surprise. Tomorrow night, at this same hour, I shall come to you again. That is all."

The shrill voice was still, and the echoes died away. A moment longer he remained there, looking down at them, then the black horse was turned. Hoofs spurned the flinty ground as he galloped back along the cañon trail, up to level country, back toward the little pueblo of Reina de Los Angeles.

Again, the tribesmen gathered around the fires, their heads bent forward. They talked in whispers until the dawn came stealing over the hills.

Señor Zorro would lead them against their enemies! They would use the torch and their knives, and be masters again in the land of their birth!

Wrongs, indignities would be avenged. They could not fail, for Señor Zorro himself would lead them. He would come again the following night to their camp, probably with complete plans for the uprising.

But Señor Zorro—which is to say Don Diego Vega—knew nothing of all this. He was not abroad this night, riding his big black horse, with a mask over his face and a blade ready at his side.

He was in his father's house in Reina de Los Angeles, reading the works of a poet, confined to his room, sneezing and sniffling inelegantly because of a cold in his head.

II
DON DIEGO SMELLS A PLOT

Don Diego Vega retained the cold the following afternoon when he went to take the air in the plaza, though his chest had been well greased with tallow, and he had eaten quantities of honey into which some evil-tasting drug had been mixed by good Fray Felipe of the chapel.

Don Diego strolled leisurely toward a mean hut wherein resided a certain Bardoso, a reformed and retired pirate. He could see Bardoso sitting on a bench on the shady side of his hut, the ever-present wine jug beside him.

Bardoso had one good eye, which lighted with interest when he beheld Don Diego's approach. The other orb had been lost during an affray on the high seas some years before, the man who had caused its loss having gone over the side an instant later to be food for sharks, and carrying Bardoso's cutlass with him in his breast.

Bardoso arose from the bench and bowed low, almost upsetting himself, for his legs were none too steady, due to the wine he had taken.

"A good day to you, pirate!" Don Diego said.

"The best day ever to you, Don Diego!" Bardoso replied. And, as he bowed low again, he added cautiously: "A private word with you, señor, if you don't mind."

"Do not stand to windward of me," Don Diego ordered, as he brushed a scented lace handkerchief delicately across his nostrils. "I have a bad cold in the head, but there are some odors so penetrating—"

"I trust that I do not offend you with a stench," Bardoso said. He grinned, for he knew that Don Diego was but jesting. Concerning odors, Bardoso felt secure, for he had taken a bath the last full moon, and there would not be another full moon for two or three days.

"How goes life with you, Bardoso?" Don Diego asked.

"I have some gossip which may amuse."

"Say on!"

A swift glance around assured Bardoso that

nobody was within earshot. "A certain tribesman of the Cocopahs, a neophyte known as José, who has listened to the *frailes* of the missions and has consented to adopt Christianity and work for them for nothing—"

"Enough!" Don Diego interrupted. "Use fewer words. I know José of the Cocopahs."

"This morning he told me a strange tale, repeating what had been told him by a friendly Caliente. It was that Señor Zorro appeared last night at the Caliente camp, and urged the tribesmen to an uprising."

"Indeed?" Don Diego said, brushing his nostrils with the scented handkerchief again.

"As the tale runs, Señor Zorro is to visit the camp again tonight at the same hour, in furtherance of the plan. It is in my mind that the troopers of the presidio may hear of it and lay a trap to catch him."

Don Diego blinked rapidly. Here was news.

"I cannot believe that the man was Zorro," Bardoso continued. "Zorro is not one to urge rebellion. Some rogue must be leading the natives astray."

"Possibly," Don Diego agreed.

"It is putting a stain upon the name of the real Zorro."

"I am wondering," Don Diego said, "who would go to the trouble of staining Zorro's name, and why."

"Ha, that is a thought! It is some deep plot, perhaps."

"No doubt," Don Diego agreed. "Is there more gossip, pirate?"

"It is rumored that the new officer at the presidio, this Capitán Marcos Lopez, is great friends with the person calling himself Don Miguel Sebastiano, lately come from San Francisco de Asís."

"I find nothing particularly strange in that," Don Diego remarked.

"As you say, Don Diego, there is nothing strange in it—birds of a breed fly together."

Don Diego chuckled and tossed Bardoso a coin. "Drink you my health, Señor Pirate," he said. And, in a lower voice, he added: "The health of Señor Zorro, also."

"With deep pleasure, Don Diego."

"Your one good eye sees much. But, which is better, you still have two good ears."

Don Diego chuckled again and strode on, glancing across the plaza toward the inn. He was thinking.

So a spurious Señor Zorro was abroad, stirring up the natives and getting the genuine Zorro a reputation for treason! No doubt, it was expected that the genuine Zorro would learn of it, and visit the camp of the Calientes to get at the truth, and there be captured.

Recently, there had been an exchange of officers at the presidio in Reina de Los Angeles, where Capitán Marcos Lopez was now in command. It was said that this Capitán Lopez stood high in the regard of His Excellency, the Governor. And His Excellency had some suspicion that Don Diego Vega was Señor Zorro, and would like to expose him as such, having an abiding hatred for Don Diego's father, who preferred honesty in affairs of state, and did not hesitate to say so.

Also, there had arrived some days before a certain Don Miguel Sebastiano, supposed to be touring through the country for pleasure. Don Diego knew him for a rogue with blade for sale. He would not be tarrying in Reina de Los Angeles did he not expect profit from the visit. And he was friendly with Capitán Marcos Lopez!

Don Diego's cold was not so bad but what he was able to smell a plot. No doubt, Don Miguel Sebastiano was the counterfeit Zorro. And the genuine Zorro was to be decoyed into a trap and destroyed.

Strolling slowly, Don Diego came presently to the shady side of the plaza and entered the inn. The fat landlord made haste to welcome him, bowing low, dusting off a bench, and bringing his best wine mug—a ponderous thing studded with semi-precious stones.

There was loud talk in a corner of the room, and Don Diego saw that Don Miguel Sebastiano was there. The fellow affected fine raiment, but carried it like a crow would the feathers of a pheasant.

He observed Don Diego in turn, and his eyes gleamed maliciously. He whispered to his companions of the bowl, and, as they watched, he lurched to his feet and reeled toward the table beside which Don Diego was sitting.

"Have I the rare honor of addressing Don Diego Vega?" he asked.

"As you have remarked, *señor*, it is an honor," Don Diego replied, his eyes like steel.

"I have been informed," Don Miguel said, with a sneer on his lips, and speaking loudly enough for all in the big room to hear, "that you waste time reading the works of poets."

"Time is not wasted in reading, *señor*, if one is intelligent enough to understand what one reads."

"And do you also do needlework?" Don Miguel asked, with a broad smile.

"When I do, *señor*, the needle I use has a sharp point," Don Diego replied.

"How is this—you grow angry? Your blood is hot? Are you not afraid of a stroke?"

"Nor of a thrust, *señor*!" Don Diego assured him.

"Ha! That remark would be creditable for a fighting man. But sweet love nonsense is more to your liking than fighting, is it not?"

The frantic landlord was hovering near, fearing for a tragedy in his place, but he could do nothing to prevent this. The others in the room enjoyed seeing the aristocratic, exclusive Don Diego Vega baited.

"I perceive," Don Diego said to his tormentor, "that you are trying to force a quarrel upon me. You have intimated that I am not a fighting man."

"I have, Don Diego."

"Perhaps, *señor*, that is why you are trying to pick a quarrel. Would you be so eager, if you thought that I had fighting ability?"

Don Miguel's face turned almost purple with wrath as somebody in the rear of the room laughed.

"Are you making an effort to be insulting, Don Diego?" Don Miguel roared.

"Making an effort? Alas, I thought that I had succeeded," Don Diego replied. "However, I am not adept at giving insults. It is a thing a *caballero* does not do well."

"*Señor!* Your words are almost beyond endurance!" Don Miguel cried.

He lurched forward angrily, and probably would have drawn blade, had there not been an interruption. But there entered from the plaza Capitán Marcos Lopez, and the *commandante*, understanding the scene at once, hastened forward with an arm upflung in warning.

"*Señores!*" he cried. "Let us have no serious trouble here! Don Miguel Sebastiano, you forget yourself! Perhaps you have taken too much wine."

Don Miguel acted like a man who suddenly remembers something of the utmost importance. He looked at the officer sheepishly, muttered some words that could not be understood, and lurched back to the corner to continue his wining and dicing with his companions.

"We have troubles enough already, with this confounded Señor Zorro planning an uprising of the natives," Capitán Lopez continued.

"What is this?" the landlord cried. "The natives are to trouble us again?"

"What did you expect? This Zorro pretends to right their wrongs to get a following, then turns renegade. It is always so. He should be hunted down like a mad dog," the *capitán* said. "But have no fear! My troopers will handle this precious Señor Zorro. For his treason, he shall hang!"

Don Diego Vega politely stifled a yawn with the back of his hand as he arose to leave. "I would not shape the noose, *capitán*, until I had caught him," he suggested.

"It might be only a waste of your valuable time."

III
A CHALLENGE TO FIGHT

At dusk that day, Sergeant Pedro Gonzales stood stiffly at attention in the presence of his commanding officer in the latter's quarters at the presidio.

Don Miguel Sebastiano was sitting beside the *capitán*, having dined with him, and he quaffed wine as he inspected the burly sergeant from hat to boots.

"Understand me well, Sergeant Gonzales, and make no errors," the *capitán* was saying. "You will take all the troopers except my orderly, and ride at once to the cañon, and go into hiding there, careful that you are not observed by the natives."

"It is an order, *capitán*."

"Don Miguel, as the bogus Zorro, will visit the camp again and utter treasonable words, which you and your men will remember if called on later to testify."

"Understood, *capitán*."

"Allow Don Miguel to ride away. The genuine Zorro may visit the camp. If he does, capture him. Then the treasonable words of the false Zorro may be fastened on the real Zorro, and he may be convicted of treason and hung. It will serve better than slaying him in a fight, for all will rise against him as a renegade, and it will mean disgrace for his proud family."

"It is understood, *capitán*," the big sergeant said. His countenance remained inscrutable, and did not betray what he thought of such tactics.

"You know the identity of the man we have under suspicion. His house is being watched. If he departs therefrom, when he returns he will be asked to explain his absence—that is in case you do not capture him."

"It is well, *capitán*," the sergeant said.

"A simple plot, and effective! He is decoyed to the cañon. Don Miguel utters treason, and you swear that Zorro said the words. You and your men will remember seeing only one Zorro."

"It is all understood, *capitán*."

"To your duty, then!"

Sergeant Pedro Gonzales saluted smartly and hurried to the barracks room to issue orders. Capitán Lopez turned to his companion.

"Miguel, you are supposed to be here all evening," he said. "I shall take my orderly and go to the inn, and talk there of Zorro's treason, inflaming men against him. And I shall say, also, that you took too much wine when you dined with me, and are sleeping."

"It is an excellent idea!" Don Miguel said.

"Slip out unseen now, and get into your Zorro garb, and get your black horse from the ravine. Give the troopers ample time to get into position before you appear at the camp of the natives."

Outside the window, crouching close to the adobe wall in the darkness, José of the Cocopahs heard all that. Now he continued to watch for a time, then hurried to the Vega house, and went to a servant's hut in the rear of the patio, as though on an ordinary visit to a friend.

But, a few minutes later, he was inside the house itself, through a secret entrance, explaining the entire affair to Don Diego.

Don Diego paced the floor, his head bent and his hands clasped behind his back, evidently thinking of a plan. Presently, he faced José.

"Zorro rides!"

"*Sí, señor!*" The native's eyes flashed.

"This time, good José, I need your help and that of some of your friends. And there is scant time to prepare."

"You have but to command, Don Diego."

"Listen carefully, then." Don Diego spoke at length, in hushed tones. "Now, go and prepare everything," he concluded. "And stand ready for me by the big rock on the San Juan Capistrano trail."

"It shall be as you say, Don Diego."

José departed. That the house might be watched by some of Capitán Lopez's spies worried Don Diego not at all, nor did the presence of family and servants. It was supposed that he had retired early because of his cold, and none of the latter would approach the chamber to trouble him.

He slipped silently along a corridor and down a rear stairway, and, unseen by any, came finally to the great cellar with its storerooms for food and drink. Candle in hand, he went to the rear, and got through the wall where there was false masonry at a tunnel's mouth.

He finally emerged in an adobe hut at the rear of the patio. Then, wrapping a black cloak around him, he darted from shadow to shadow until he was some distance from the house.

Half a mile out of town, in a depression not far from the highway, José of the Cocopahs had the black horse waiting. Don Diego changed garments swiftly, put on his mask and buckled on a blade. Then he muttered further instructions to José, and rode slowly away through the night.

For the present, Don Diego Vega did not exist. Señor Zorro was abroad.

Cautiously, he skirted the edge of the town and neared the inn, riding along the bottom of a ravine and keeping in the shadows. He tethered his horse to a clump of brush where it was quite dark.

Then he went forward afoot, continuing along the ravine, but leaving it presently and going toward the long, low building which housed the inn. José had informed him that the troopers had ridden away with Gonzales at their head, that Don Miguel Sebastiano had left the presidio. Capitán Lopez and his orderly servant should now be at the inn, the former making talk to carry on the plot.

The rear of the building was in darkness, save where a streak of light came through the partially opened door. Getting near, Zorro peered inside and saw the fat landlord dishing up food.

He slipped through the door like a shadow and glided forward. And suddenly the startled landlord found Señor Zorro standing there at his elbow, his manner threatening, his eyes gleaming through the holes in his mask.

"Silence, or you die!" Zorro hissed at him. "Speak only to answer, and then in whispers. Is Capitán Lopez now in the big room?"

"*Sí, señor!*" the landlord whispered, shaking with fear.

"What others?"

"One soldier with the *capitán*, and two travelers who have just come off El Camino Real. They are merchants."

"How is it that you have such scant company tonight?" Zorro demanded.

"There is a cock fight at a *hacienda* out the San Gabriel trail. Everybody has gone there."

"Go forward now, ahead of me, with your hands held high above your head," Zorro ordered.

The trembling landlord obeyed. They passed through the door and into the big room. Capitán Lopez sat at a table near the fireplace, and his orderly was on a bench in a corner. The two travelers were at another table not far away.

Señor Zorro pricked the fat landlord with the tip of his blade, so that the landlord gave a squeal of terror, and thrust him aside. Those in the room turned to look. By the light from the reeking torches and tallow dips, they saw Señor Zorro standing not far from the end of the fireplace.

Now he held a pistol in his left hand, as well as the blade in his right. He took a quick step forward, his eyes seeming to blaze through the holes in his mask.

"Against the wall, *capitán*!" he ordered. "You others remain as you are."

Capitán Lopez sprang to his feet. "What is this?" he cried. He had been caught at a disadvantage. He had removed belt and sword some time before, and loosened his clothing to be comfortable, and the weapon was on another table some distance from him. The trooper was not armed at all.

"It is Señor Zorro, as you know well, though you never have had sight of my face."

"And you dare come here and face me—you, an outlaw?" Lopez cried.

"As you see, *señor*."

"What is it you wish—to surrender and throw yourself on the mercy of His Excellency?"

"I am still in my right mind, Señor el Capitán. And His Excellency has no mercy."

"You have come here to murder me, perhaps?"

"I am not a murderer, *señor,* though you would have people think so of me. Sit on the end of that bench against the wall, and lend ear."

Capitán Lopez obeyed the order, moving slowly and with evident reluctance, thinking swiftly the while. His sword was on the table several feet away. He did not have a pistol in his sash, for he had come to the inn merely to drink and talk of Zorro's treason, anticipating no trouble or duty. And here was Zorro facing him— and he was supposed to be in the cañon inciting natives to rebellion.

Badly frightened, the two merchants were watching and listening. The landlord crouched trembling against the wall. The lone trooper made no move, not caring to advance upon Señor Zorro unless his officer so ordered.

"Capitán Lopez," Zorro said, "according to the learned doctors, it is impossible for a man to be in two places at the same time. It that not so?"

"Certainly."

"Señor Zorro is standing here before you, and in the plain eyesight of these others, so it is impossible for him to be elsewhere—say in the cañon toward the sea."

"I fail to make sense of what you say."

"Since Señor Zorro is here with you, the man who is busy stirring the natives to rebellion cannot be Zorro. Hence, if Zorro is accused of treason, you will know that the accusation is false."

"And who says Zorro is here?" Lopez asked.

"Have you not eyes, *señor*? Can you not see me?"

"You?" Capitán Lopez exclaimed. "Ha! I understand this affair now. Señor Zorro, while at his dark work of treason, has a friend appear here in a duplicate of Zorro's raiment, pretending to be he."

"That would, indeed, be a pretty subterfuge," Zorro admitted. "Your meaning is that I am unable to prove that I am the genuine Zorro?"

"Exactly, *señor*!"

"Ah! But I shall endeavor to leave behind me absolute proof of my identity, Señor el Capitán."

"And that—?" Lopez questioned.

"Is it not possible for you to guess? Have you no wit? Take up your blade from the table, *señor*," Zorro ordered. "And you others sit quietly as you are, else this pistol of mine will bark at you. I am about to cross blades with you, Señor el Capitán."

"You will give me fair fight?" Lopez cried, springing toward the table, hand open to grasp the hilt of his sword and tear it from its scabbard. "I welcome it!"

"I give you fair fight, *señor*, though I am at a loss to understand why you welcome it. After it is over, His Excellency will be compelled to send yet another officer to the presidio here."

"Ha! You are so certain you will slay me?"

"I have no intention of slaying you, *señor*. I am only going to leave proof that the real Zorro has been here, that he was not in the cañon preaching rebellion—and that your poor cat's-paw was."

Suddenly, Capitán Lopez understood. For an instant, something like fright swept through him. He reeled back against the wall and fought to gain control of himself.

"Zorro always leaves his mark, Señor el Capitán! Perhaps the bogus one could not do so much."

IV
ZORRO MAKES HIS MARK

There was nothing to do now but fight, Capitán Lopez knew. He was an officer, and one of his own troopers was in the room, as well as the fat landlord and two strange travelers, to tell the tale afterward. And there was a possibility that Señor Zorro would not win this combat. Capitán Lopez fancied himself as a master of fence.

But, when the blades crossed and clashed and rang, and he got the first feel of Zorro's wrist, he knew that this fight would be no light bout. He was facing a man who knew how to wield a blade. Caution came quickly to replace the rash rage with which he had at first attacked, and he fell back and fought carefully.

With bulging eyes, the others in the room watched the fighting, aware that Señor Zorro glanced their way frequently, and held pistol ready in his left hand as he fought. The merchants were not of fighting stock, nor was the landlord. The trooper made no move, nor would it have been the thing to do unless his officer called for help.

"Not bad, *capitán*!" Zorro cried, as he brushed aside a lunge. "A little too low, *señor*—" as he parried another. "It is a blade you hold, not a bludgeon."

"You'll not put mark on me!"

"'Tis scarce a fair time to make a wager, yet I am willing to do so," Zorro said. "If I mark you, let us say, you will leave Reina de Los Angeles, and save the Governor the trouble of recalling you in disgrace."

"I make no wager with an outlaw!" Lopez cried.

"Ha!" Señor Zorro's blade suddenly darted forward, and the *capitán* gave a cry and recoiled. Zorro dropped the point of his blade and stood waiting, laughing a little, scorning to follow up the advantage. "'Tis only the first cut, *señor*— the top bar of the Z."

"I shall kill you!"

"It is your rare privilege to try."

Capitán Lopez advanced to the attack again. It was a wild attempt, and for a moment Zorro was compelled to retreat, to sidestep, so that a man who did not know fence might have believed he was being hard pressed. But the soldier who sat on the bench in the corner knew that he was only being cautious and waiting for an opportunity.

Presently, it came. The sword of the *capitán* flashed out of his hand and clattered to the floor. In that same instant, Zorro's blade darted forward again.

"The lower bar of the Z, *capitán*," he said. "I join the two bars at my leisure. Pick up your blade, *señor*, and continue. Do your best, I beg of you, and at least make this combat interesting for me."

Capitán Lopez darted across the room and retrieved his blade from the floor. The flickering light from the nearest torch revealed that his face was ashen, save where blood trickled from his twice-wounded cheek. That Zorro had him at his mercy, he knew well.

But this was a time, Capitán Lopez told himself, when the rules of proper combat need not be observed to the letter. This Señor Zorro was an outlaw, and was not entitled to the treatment one should give a *caballero*. If he could slay Zorro now, or wound him and take him prisoner, there would be certain rich rewards from the Governor.

"Soldier!" Lopez cried. "Help me take this man! He is outlaw!"

As he finished his speech, Capitán Lopez charged wildly, his blade a flashing and erratic thing. He confused Zorro for an instant because of his utter disregard of proper method. As Zorro retreated, the trooper sprang off the bench.

The pistol Zorro held barked and flamed. A cloud of smoke swirled in the room. The trooper gave a cry and reeled back to the bench, to drop upon it weakly, clutching at a left shoulder that spouted blood.

Then Zorro pressed the fighting angrily.

"Craven!" he cried. "For that—"

"At him, man!" Lopez roared at the wounded trooper. "He has discharged his pistol. That stool—hurl it at him! Bring him down!"

The trooper lurched to his feet as Zorro compelled the *capitán* to retreat again. He picked up the heavy stool and hurled it, but Zorro sidestepped swiftly and jerked his head aside, and let the stool fly past him and crash against the wall.

"The door!" Lopez cried. "Get help!"

Weakened by the effort in throwing the stool, the wounded trooper staggered toward the door. But Zorro was before him. His blade bit lightly into the trooper's other shoulder, and the man reeled back.

"Now, Señor el Capitán!" Zorro cried.

He pressed forward again, a trace of anger in his manner. His blade was like a live thing, a flashing menace. Lopez could not stand against it. Again the point darted forward, and again the *capitán* felt a burn on his cheek. And his own blade was torn from his grasp once more, and clattered to the floor.

"Now you bear my mark, *señor*," Zorro said, as he leaned against the wall. "Sit down at that table. Be glad that I did not run you through!"

"This is not the end!" Lopez cried. "Though you know it not, Señor Zorro, I have you in a trap."

"I fear no traps." Zorro turned to the trembling landlord. "Get materials, and attend to that soldier's wound," he ordered. "Then bring supper for your two guests. I regret, *señores*, that necessity compelled me to interrupt your meal."

He looked again at the *capitán*, who was trying to stanch the flow from his wounded cheek, and darted swiftly to the kitchen door.

"*Señores, á Dios!*" he cried.

And then he was gone.

V

CAPTURE

Through the shadows he went, and got into the ravine where he had left his horse. He recharged his pistol, meanwhile listening for a din at the hostelry. But there came no outcry. The soldiers were out at the cañon. The majority of the younger townsmen were at the cock fight down

San Gabriel way. And Capitán Marcos Lopez, moreover, did not care to hasten the moment when knowledge of his discomfiture would become public.

Through the moon-drenched night Zorro rode again, unseen, and so came to a ravine which ran around the other side of the town. A soft hiss reached his ears. He stopped the horse.

"*Señor?*" José of the Cocopahs was before him.

"Everything is in readiness, José?"

"Everything, Señor Zorro. We shall do as you have ordered."

"I see nobody but you."

Soft words came from the lips of José. They penetrated the brush. From behind the shrubs and rocks crept men—furtive natives who approached Zorro as though awed.

"You understand fully?" Zorro asked them, speaking in low tones. "This false man would have led you into trouble. You would have been slain by the soldiers. Never would I counsel you to rebellion, for such a thing is wrong. Be prepared to do as José has instructed you."

They growled and muttered, trusting Zorro fully. José had explained the meaning of the affair to them. Now their hatred was against the man who would have used them for his purpose, though it caused the soldiery to slay them and burn their village.

"You have found his garments?" Zorro asked José.

"They are here, *señor*, where he changed."

"Send a man with them, far back among the rocks, so they cannot be found quickly. And now, go into hiding again, and wait for my signal."

They disappeared like so many shadows. Zorro held his head high, listening. From the far distance came the sounds of a horse's hoofs. Guiding his black deftly, Zorro rode back into the shadows.

The hoofbeats came nearer. The rider was making little speed, was moving with caution. Yet he wished speed above all else.

Don Miguel Sebastiano had visited the camp of the Calientes again, and had tried to stir them to war. Then he had ridden away, sure that the waiting troopers in ambush had heard him. He was eager now to change clothing, turn loose his horse, and get back to the presidio. For, only when he had done that, would he be safe. As long as he was abroad in the garb of Zorro, there was a chance of the masquerade being detected.

Into the ravine Don Miguel rode, piloting his horse to the place where he had left his clothes. He stripped saddle and bridle from the animal and turned him loose, and hid the gear behind some rocks. Then he went to the spot where he had left his garments behind a clump of shrubs.

A muttering of profanity came from his lips when he saw the clothes were not there. He began searching frantically behind other clumps of shrubs.

"You seek something, *señor*?" a soft voice asked.

Don Miguel Sebastiano sprang backward, his right hand diving toward the pistol he carried in his sash. But out of the darkness came a rope, hissing and coiling like a serpent, and it fell about him in a noose, and was jerked taut, pinning his arms to his sides.

Then an avalanche of men descended upon him out of the brush and from behind the rocks, natives who smothered him with their weight, who lashed his wrists behind his back.

They carried him to his horse, which they had caught. Saddle and bridle were brought from hiding and put on quickly, and Don Miguel was put into the saddle, and his ankles lashed beneath the mount's belly.

His mask had remained in place during all this. Nor did any one attempt to remove it now. Don Miguel cursed and howled, then began pleading and offered rewards for his freedom, but they answered him not at all.

From the darkness by the rocks came another horse, and he saw a replica of himself, as far as garments were concerned. From behind the mask of this second rider came a chuckle.

"So Señor Zorro has been captured at last! His end will be a pretty one, no doubt. For those who dabble in treason, there is always a rope waiting. There is a fine reward offered by His Excellency for Zorro's capture, too, I believe. These natives may claim it, and be right rich. They will be able to buy fine clothes, in which to dress when they attend your public hanging."

"Whoever you are—" Don Miguel began.

But Señor Zorro waved a hand at the men, and motioned to José of the Cocopahs, and then turned his horse and rode away through the darkness.

Now the natives put into effect the instructions they had received. Some rushed toward Reina de Los Angeles, shattering the calm night with their cries.

"Zorro is taken . . . Señor Zorro is captured! . . . They are taking him to the presidio!"

The din awoke those who slept, and brought out into the plaza men of substance and prominence, and a few ladies also. The mystery of Zorro had intrigued them. They wished to see the man's face.

Two natives rushed to the presidio, where Capitán Marcos Lopez had gone from the inn, to doctor his cut cheek. Their howls brought him forth.

"Zorro is captured—"

"One of you give me details!" he roared.

One stepped forward. "He was riding his black horse, and stopped where some men were talking. They bound him with ropes and are bringing him here. We share in the reward."

"Where was he caught?" Lopez asked.

"As he was leaving the town by the ravine. They are bringing him here."

Capitán Lopez was hoping that the genuine Zorro had been caught as he was riding away from the inn, but he was worried because Don Miguel had not returned. And another thing worried him—that this matter was to be so public.

Up the slopes from the plaza the men of the pueblo were coming. Among them were dons of importance, who had to be handled with velvet gloves. They would see his wounded face, and know that Zorro had bested him.

They gathered in front of the presidio, under the light of the torches which burned at either side of the entrance. Capitán Lopez retired quickly to his quarters. He bathed his face quickly again, but could not hide the wounds. And the swelling was extremely noticeable.

It was no disgrace to be marked by Zorro, however, so he would go out and face them. Zorro's capture offset everything. He would toss the natives a few coins, and take the huge reward to himself.

Capitán Lopez strolled through the corridor and to the front door, when he heard another din at the corner of the plaza. He greeted the important men of the community with professional dignity.

"The rogue has been preaching sedition," he explained. "My troopers rode out tonight to catch him. Undoubtedly he escaped them, only to be caught by others."

He could see a man on a black horse, with natives leading the mount and others walking on either side. The rider wore a black cloak, black mask. The shouting natives brought him on, screeching in their excitement.

They stopped the horse inside the light cast by the torches. Some of them rushed toward the *capitán*.

"Pay the reward to José, and he will share with us all," one said. "We are all Cocopahs."

"I thought Zorro was the friend of the Cocopahs," Lopez said, sneering a bit. "So you betray your friend for gold?"

"He planned an uprising and that is bad," José said, as he strode forward. "Many of us would have died. He escaped your soldiers, Señor el Capitán, but we captured him."

They brought the horse on, and then Capitán

Lopez knew the worst. This rider was garbed much as the real Zorro had been at the inn. But there were slight differences which Lopez noticed. They had captured Don Miguel Sebastiano.

Here was a predicament. Lopez must save this man, to save himself. He thought quickly. If he could get Don Miguel into the prison room without his mask being removed, if he could lock him in and drive all away, then let Don Miguel out and say that Zorro made an escape, all might be well.

"Untie the man!" Lopez ordered. "Take him from the horse. Leave the rope on his wrists. I'll take him to the prison room."

"Take off his mask!" somebody cried.

Lopez pretended not to hear. He began bellowing orders to the natives. He shouted for his orderly to take charge of the affair, and strode forward himself.

"Back, *señores*!" he cried. "We can take no chances here. The rogue may have friends among you, and there'll be no rescue!"

"Let us see his face!" some man cried again.

They had unfastened Don Miguel's feet, and helped him out of the saddle. They started leading him toward the door. Through the crowd, two men of prominence thrust their way.

"Capitán Lopez! We demand that this man's mask be removed. We would know the identity of Zorro."

"Presently—"

"Now!" one thundered.

The other reached out and whipped away the mask. "Don Miguel Sebastiano!" he cried.

VI

PUNISHMENT

There came a chorus of cries as the identity of the prisoner was made known. The crowd surged forward. Capitán Lopez was powerless to do more than bark at them. His one man could not help much, and Sergeant Gonzales and the troopers had not returned from the Caliente village.

"I'll get him into the prison room," Lopez cried. "Stand back, *señores*! This trooper of mine will help me."

An elderly don, who had some idea of his own regarding Zorro, stepped forward.

"This man is your friend," he accused. "It would be an easy thing for him to escape, under certain conditions."

"*Señor*, you dare intimate—" Lopez began.

"A few of us will go with you and the prisoner to your own quarters, *capitán*, and there have an understanding about this affair."

Lopez stormed, but it availed him nothing. They named a committee of men he dared not deny. They brushed aside his protests.

As they went down the corridor to the *capitán's* room, both Lopez and Don Miguel were trying desperately to think of some way out. The members of the committee kept them apart, so they could not talk. Lopez had some wild idea of disclaiming knowledge of Don Miguel, other than he had come recommended to him. Not trusting the *capitán* overmuch, Don Miguel expected that, and was preparing to off-set it.

They closed the corridor door, thrust Don Miguel on a bench against the wall. Capitán Lopez sat at his desk, and the men of the committee stood around him.

"There is some mistake," Lopez said.

"How is that, Señor el Capitán? Here is the man, dressed as Zorro always dresses. He had a mask on his face, and rode a black horse. He fought you in the inn, marked you—"

"Then how could he have been at the cañon talking to the tribesmen?" Lopez asked.

"We do not know. But here we have Zorro, who has done many good things, but who has wiped out them all by trying to create trouble with the natives. He will be guarded carefully, so he cannot escape. We demand, *capitán*, that you give him immediate military trial, and hang him at the corner of the plaza at sunrise."

"Perhaps it would be better to communicate first with His Excellency."

"His Excellency is in San Francisco de Asís at present, and it would take many, many days for him to be informed. Why bother the Governor with this? You have ample power to prosecute and punish under military law any highwayman or traitor, and this man seems to be both."

"But Don Miguel has but recently come to Reina de Los Angeles," Lopez protested, "and Señor Zorro has been committing his lawless acts hereabouts for more than a year."

"How do we know but what Don Miguel has been in this vicinity for that length of time, perhaps with a hiding place in the hills, or in some native village?"

Capitán Marcos Lopez glanced across the room at Don Miguel, and a look of hopelessness was in the face of each. The *capitán* decided to fight for time.

"What have you to say for yourself, Don Miguel?" he asked. "This charge is serious."

Don Miguel's eyes flashed. He had some idea that Capitán Lopez was about to desert him.

"Why not tell them the truth?" he asked. He looked at the committee. "*Señores*, it is easily explained. The joke is on me—"

"You consider treason a joke, *señor*?" one barked at him.

"It was a subterfuge, in an attempt to catch Señor Zorro. I was to play at being Zorro, visit the native camp and talk of an uprising. We believed that the real Zorro would hear of it, and go there, and the soldiers would catch him. That is all—except that by accident the natives caught me. And the genuine Zorro was there when they did it."

"He was there?" Lopez cried. "Then he knew of our scheme?"

"Evidently," Don Miguel said.

"I see it all now. He fought me at the inn, then hurried out and helped the natives catch you. The thing must be explained to the townsmen. Zorro laughs at us again. I'll take off your bonds, Don Miguel—"

"One moment, *señor!*" a committeeman protested. "You did not tell this tale at first. Now you are saying there are two Zorros—one false and one real. Let us question the natives who made the capture."

"They will lie," Lopez cried. "They adore this scamp of a Zorro. They will swear Don Miguel's life away."

"We have one Zorro here, and that is enough. If there is another, where is he?"

A voice from the corner answered: "Look this way, *señores!*"

There stood Zorro, blade in hand. He had ridden back to the presidio, and left his horse behind the building in the darkness. Through an open window he had crawled into the room adjoining the quarters of the *capitán*, and through an unlocked door he had entered.

"Do not compel me to violence, *señores*," he said, now. "Stand as you are, please. Keep that pistol from the hands of the *capitán!*"

Zorro held his own pistol in his left hand, they noticed now, and menaced them with it.

"You have heard the truth," he said. "Don Miguel is not Zorro. He and the *capitán* were trying to catch me by a trick. That is permissible in the game we play. But to try to make me out a renegade—ah, *señores*, that is too much!"

"You—" Lopez began.

"Silence, Señor el Capitán!" Zorro cried. "I have helped the natives at times, have punished those who mistreated them. But never have I counseled them to an uprising. I love them too much for that. They are but simple children, easy victims for unscrupulous men."

"You admit you are Zorro?" Lopez cried. "Seize him, you men!"

"Be warned!" Zorro cried in return, sweeping the pistol around in front of him. "*Señores*, this Don Miguel is not Zorro, and cannot be blamed for Zorro's acts. But the fact remains that he uttered treasonable words and tried to stir up the natives. So he is guilty of treason. And should he not be punished for that?"

"That is true," one of the committee said. "And this *capitán*, who abetted the plot—we shall see that the Governor recalls him."

"Are you all in league with this highwayman, this outlaw?" Lopez screeched. "You are lawbreakers yourselves if you do not aid me now in his capture."

"I am holding a pistol on them," Zorro observed. "And I have a task here. Don Miguel Sebastiano, we must have a settlement. A man cannot impersonate me and have me called renegade without being called on to account for it."

"You have pistol and blade, and I am unarmed," Don Miguel said.

"I give you fair fight, *señor*. I ask these *señores* to see that all is fair. Guard you the *capitán*, that he does not interfere. Unbind the man's wrists, and give him a blade. At the end of it, you may decide what is to be done with me."

The protests of Capitán Lopez were as nothing. Those of the committee liked the idea. There were some who had suspicion of Zorro's real identity. None liked Don Miguel and his tactics. Here was a chance, moreover, to see swordplay.

So Don Miguel was unbound and given a blade and a draft of wine for which he asked. Capitán Lopez was thrust into a corner and held there. More candles were lit, that the room would be bright with light.

Don Miguel's eyes gleamed strangely, and his tongue moistened his lips as though they suddenly had become parched. It was in his mind to slash at Zorro's mask and reveal the face of the man. It also was in his mind to run Zorro through, thus wiping out this stain and earning the reward of His Excellency.

Capitán Lopez could have told Don Miguel something of the way Zorro handled a blade, but he had no opportunity. Steel rang, and the fighting began.

They felt each other out cautiously. Don

Miguel had considerable skill, and Señor Zorro was a man who never made the mistake of underestimating an antagonist. But caution soon gave way to speed, spirited attack and defense.

Don Miguel found himself outgeneraled in an instant. Zorro's blade scratched his cheek. From the corner, Capitán Lopez gave a cry of warning:

"He's trying to carve his mark on you, Miguel!"

"The upper bar of the Z," Zorro said. "And here is the lower bar, *señor*!"

Don Miguel gave a great cry of rage as he felt the tip of the blade bite again. Zorro was prolonging the agony, as he had in the case of the *capitán*. Usually, that jagged Z was made by one stroke, by the tip of the blade playing over the cheek in a series of quick twists.

"And now, *señor*—" Zorro said.

But Don Miguel seemed to go insane. He rushed out, cut and slashed and lunged, like a man who knew nothing of fence, trying to overpower his enemy and bear him down. For a moment, Zorro was compelled to fight fiercely to save himself. His footwork accomplished this. Then Don Miguel, winded, his burst of passion spent, was off guard a moment, and again Zorro's blade bit.

"You wear the Z, *señor*!" he said; and disarmed his man.

The blade clattered to the floor. Panting, Don Miguel reeled against the wall, waiting for the end. A swift advance, a quick thrust, and it would be over.

But Zorro did not give the thrust. He stepped back, and motioned with the weapon he held.

"Pick up your blade, *señor*," he said.

Stepping away from the wall, Don Miguel Sebastiano went across the room and retrieved his sword. Again he faced Zorro, the point of his blade down.

"I have marked you, *señor*," Zorro said. "That is for daring to oppose me. Now, I shall deal with you for your treason, for having me

thought renegade, for upsetting the poor natives and almost getting them into serious trouble— and for some other things. You fight for life now, Don Miguel Sebastiano!"

Don Miguel had the feeling that it was so. Capitán Lopez made a last effort to stop this. He sprang off the bench and started forward.

"Enough!" he cried. "*Señores*, I call upon you to help me take this man!"

But they tossed him back upon the bench, and warned him to remain there, and turned to watch the fighting.

Perspiration stood out in great globules on the face of Don Miguel. He called upon all the science he knew. But there came to him the realization that he was no match for Zorro.

Every attempt he made was blocked. For every trick, Zorro had defense. Señor Zorro was but playing with him, wearing him down. Through the holes in his black mask, the eyes of Zorro glittered like those of a deadly serpent.

Then came a furious onslaught, and Don Miguel gave ground. His lower jaw was sagging, and a great fear was in his face. He brought up against the wall, called upon his remaining strength.

Another clash of steel, and Zorro's blade was thrust in the fatal stroke. Don Miguel dropped his sword and gave a sigh. He collapsed slowly to the floor.

Señor Zorro darted forward and bent over him.

"Needlework, *señor*!" he said, just loud enough for Don Miguel to hear.

"So!" Don Miguel was dying as he spoke. "*Capitán!* . . . *Señores!* This . . . this man . . . is—"

But Don Miguel did not speak the word.

Zorro faced the others. "*Señores*, my work here is done," he said. "Pardon me, if I now make my escape. Remember, *señores*, I still hold my pistol."

He backed to the door, watching them closely.

From somebody outside came a peculiar cry that made Zorro straighten slightly. And there was a sudden thunder of hoofbeats. Sergeant Gonzales and his troopers had returned from the cañon.

Capitán Marcos Lopez gave a glad cry and sprang off the bench again. He shouted orders for his orderly out in the corridor to hear.

"Warn Gonzales! Zorro is here! Make a capture!"

Señor Zorro darted into the adjoining room and closed and barred the door. He was through the window an instant later, and running to the rear of the presidio building, where he had left his horse.

"José!"

"*Señor?*"

"Into the saddle. Wait a moment, then ride. Decoy them for me."

"*Sí, señor!*"

There was a tumult in front of the presidio. Gonzales was howling to know what had happened. Capitán Lopez got past those of the committee and to the door, rushed into the corridor, and to the front.

"Zorro . . . here . . . escaping—" he cried. "Gonzales! Leave half your force, pursue with the others!"

At the rear of the building was a sudden clatter as a horse jumped into action. A black streak passed through the moonlight.

"There he goes!"

Troopers started in pursuit. But it was José of the Cocopahs in the saddle, though they knew it

not, and José feared not at all that any of the troopers could overtake the big black. He would outrace them, get to hiding—and Zorro would disappear again.

As for Señor Zorro, he was traveling cautiously from shadow to shadow, skirting the town, and coming down the slope toward his father's house. He got into the hut at the rear of the patio, through the tunnel, and into the house. Working swiftly, he hid his Zorro garb and blade, put on a dressing gown, and threw himself upon his couch.

Back at the presidio, the townsmen scattered. Capitán Marcos Lopez called to him the troopers left behind.

"We surround the Vega *casa* immediately," he said. "Any one who seeks to enter must be stopped. Perhaps we yet shall catch the fox, if Gonzales fails in the chase."

They galloped across the plaza and took up station, some in front, some in rear, and some on either side. In the moonlight, their movements were seen clearly. Word flashed through Reina de Los Angeles that the Vega house was being watched by the soldiery.

Capitán Marcos Lopez himself remained in front, watching and waiting. But he did not have long to wait. The big front door of the house was opened. Two servants appeared holding huge candelabra. And then, through the open door, came Don Diego's proud, white-haired father, and Don Diego himself was a step behind him.

"Capitán Lopez!" the proud head of the Vega house called. "Do me the kindness to take your

soldiers away. They are disturbing my household. We do not need their protection."

"Protection?" Lopez gasped.

"Could they possibly be here for any other reason?" Don Diego's father demanded. "If so, state that reason!"

Lopez hesitated only an instant. "They shall be removed, *señor*."

He was outwitted in some manner, he knew. There was Don Diego standing in the doorway.

No use to guard the house to catch him entering it, when he was inside already.

And now Don Diego delicately brushed his nostrils with a scented handkerchief, and sneezed a bit, and spoke:

"It appears, Señor el Capitán, that something has happened to your face. You have been playing roughly, perhaps, and got it scratched. But those who play roughly may expect to be hurt. That is the way of life. *Buenas noches, capitán!*"

CLARENCE E. MULFORD

CLARENCE EDWARD MULFORD (1883–1956) was born in Streator, Illinois, and had never set foot in the West when he began writing stories and novels about his iconic Hopalong Cassidy. The rough and dirty cowboy was twenty-three years old, the same age as the author, when he made his first appearance in "The Fight at Buckskin" (*Outing Magazine*, December 1905). This story, with seven additional ones, formed Mulford's first book, *Bar-20* (1907). As initially conceived by Mulford, Cassidy cut a very different figure than the clean-cut, always gentlemanly William Boyd, who would play him in sixty-six films (plus seven others made entirely from spliced together archival footage) and fifty-two television episodes.

Mulford also wrote a series about a rancher and deputy sheriff named Bob Colson, as well as stand-alone westerns, one of which, *The Orphan* (1908), was filmed in 1920 with William Farnum and remade in 1924 as *The Deadwood Coach* with Tom Mix. The first Cassidy movie was *Hop-Along Cassidy* (1935), which starred Boyd in the role that was to define his career. Mulford was always disappointed with the way Boyd portrayed his hard-drinking and combative creation, though when they finally met they became friends. Among the numerous differences between the fictional character and the celluloid one is that in the books, Cassidy works at the Bar-20 ranch and doesn't own it, and his best friend is the equally rough-and-ready Red Connors, who is replaced by the now familiar comic figure Gabby Hayes and, later, Andy Clyde. Also, after the very first film, Hopalong no longer limps. "Hopalong's Hop," while perhaps not the very best cowboy story ever written, tells the tale of how William Cassidy acquired his curious nickname, an incident rarely alluded to in the motion pictures or the television series. Although Mulford tired of his character late in life, Cassidy's enormous popularity continued. A publisher induced Louis L'Amour to write four more novels about him, but when L'Amour learned that he had to write the stories about the cleaned-up hero of the television series rather than a cowboy similar to Mulford's, he published them under the pseudonym Tex Burns.

"Hopalong's Hop" was originally published in the November 1912 issue of *Pearson's Magazine;* it was first published in book form in *The Coming of Cassidy* (Chicago: McClurg, 1913).

HOPALONG'S HOP

CLARENCE E. MULFORD

THE STORY OF THAT BULLY FIGHT WHICH GAVE TO COW-PUNCHER CASSIDY THE NAME HOPALONG—A STORY OF THE DAYS WHEN THE WEST BRED FIGHTING MEN.

HAVING SENT Jimmy to the Bar-20 with a message for Buck Peters, their foreman, Bill Cassidy set out for the Crazy M ranch, by the way of Clay Gulch. He was to report on the condition of some cattle that Buck had been offered cheap and he was anxious to get back to the ranch. It was in the early evening when he reached Clay Gulch and rode slowly down the dusty, shack-lined street in search of a hotel. The town and the street were hardly different from other towns and streets that he had seen all over the cow-country, but nevertheless he felt uneasy. The air seemed to be charged with danger, and it caused him to sit even more erect in the saddle and assume his habit of indifferent alertness. The first man he saw confirmed the feeling by staring at him insolently and sneering in a veiled way at the low-hung, tied-down holsters that graced Bill's thighs. The guns proclaimed the gun-man as surely as it would have been proclaimed by a sign; and it appeared that gun-men were not at that time held in high esteem by the citizens of Clay Gulch. Bill was growing fretful and peevish when the man, with a knowing shake of his head, turned away and entered the harness shop. "Trouble's brewin' somewheres around," muttered Bill, as he went on. He had singled out the first of two hotels when another citizen, turning the corner, stopped in his tracks

and looked Bill over with a deliberate scrutiny that left but little to the imagination. He frowned and started away, but Bill spurred forward, determined to make him speak.

"*Might* I inquire if this is Clay Gulch?" he asked, in tones that made the other wince.

"You might," was the reply. "It is," added the citizen, "an' th' Crazy M lays fifteen miles west." Having complied with the requirements of common politeness, the citizen of Clay Gulch turned and walked into the nearest saloon. Bill squinted after him and shook his head in indecision.

"He wasn't guessin', neither. He shore knowed where I wants to go. I reckon Oleson must 'a' said he was expectin' me." He would have been somewhat surprised had he known that Mr. Oleson, foreman of the Crazy M, had said nothing to anyone about the expected visitor, and that no one, not even on the ranch, knew of it. Mr. Oleson was blessed with taciturnity to a remarkable degree; and he had given up expecting to see anyone from Mr. Peters.

As Bill dismounted in front of the "Victoria" he noticed that two men farther down the street had evidently changed their conversation and were examining him with frank interest and discussing him earnestly. As a matter of fact they had not changed the subject of their conversation, but had simply fitted him in the place of a certain unknown. Before he had arrived they discussed in the abstract; now they could talk in the concrete. One of them laughed and called softly over his shoulder, whereupon a third man appeared in the door, wiping his lips with the back of a hairy, grimy hand, and focused evil eyes upon the innocent stranger. He grunted contemptuously and, turning on his heel, went back to his liquid pleasures. Bill covertly felt of his clothes and stole a glance at his horse, but could see nothing wrong. He hesitated: should he saunter over for information or wait until the matter was brought to his attention? A sound inside the hotel made him choose the latter course, for his stomach threatened to become estranged and it simply howled for food. Pushing open the door he dropped his saddle in a corner and leaned against the bar.

"Have one with me to get acquainted?" he invited. "Then I'll eat, for I'm hungry. An' I'll use one of yore beds tonight, too."

The man behind the bar nodded cheerfully and poured out his drink. As he raised the liquor he noticed Bill's guns and carelessly let the glass return to the bar.

"Sorry, sir," he said coldly. "I'm hall out of grub, the fire's hout, *hand* the beds are taken. But mebby 'Awley, down the strite, can tyke care of you."

Bill was looking at him with an expression that said much and he slowly extended his arm and pointed to the untasted liquor.

"Allus finish what you start, English," he said slowly and clearly. "When a man goes to take a drink with me, and suddenly changes his mind, why I gets riled. I don't know what ails this town, an' I don't care; I don't give a cuss about yore grub an' yore beds; but if you don't drink that liquor you poured out *to* drink, why I'll naturally shove it down yore British throat so cussed hard it'll strain yore neck. Get to it!"

The proprietor glanced apprehensively from the glass to Bill, then onto the businesslike guns and back to the glass, and the liquor disappeared at a gulp. "W'y," he explained, aggrieved. "There hain't no call for to get riled hup like that, stringer. I bloody well forgot hit."

"Then don't you go an' 'bloody well' forget

this: Th' next time I drops in here for grub an' a bed, you have 'em both, an' be plumb polite about it. Do you get me?" he demanded icily.

The proprietor stared at the angry puncher as he gathered up his saddle and rifle and started for the door. He turned to put away the bottle and the sound came near being unfortunate for him. Bill leaped sideways, turning while in the air and landed on his feet like a cat, his left hand gripping a heavy Colt that covered the short ribs of the frightened proprietor before that worthy could hardly realize the move.

"Oh, all right," growled Bill, appearing to be disappointed. "I reckoned mebby you was gamblin' on a shore thing. I feels impelled to offer you my sincere apology; you ain't th' kind as would even gamble *on* a shore thing. You'll see me again," he promised. The sound of his steps on the porch ended in a thud as he leaped to the ground, and then he passed the window leading his horse and scowling darkly. The proprietor mopped his head and reached twice for the glass before he found it. "Gawd, what a bloody 'eathen," he grunted. "'*E* won't be as easy as the lawst was, blime 'im."

Mr. Hawley looked up and frowned, but there was something in the suspicious eyes that searched his face that made him cautious: Bill dropped his load on the floor and spoke sharply. "I want supper an' a bed. You ain't full up, an' you ain't out of grub. So I'm goin' to get 'em both right here. Yes?"

"You shore called th' turn, stranger," replied Mr. Hawley in his Sunday voice. "That's what I'm in business for. An' business is shore dull these days."

He wondered at the sudden smile that illuminated Bill's face and half guessed it; but he said nothing and went to work. When Bill pushed back from the table he was more at peace with the world and he treated, closely watching his companion. Mr. Hawley drank with a show of pleasure and brought out cigars. He seated himself beside his guest and sighed with relief.

"I'm plumb tired out," he offered. "An' I ain't done much. You look tired, too. Come a long way?"

"Logan," replied Bill. "Do *you* know where I'm goin'? An' why?" he asked.

Mr. Hawley looked surprised and almost answered the first part of the question correctly before he thought. "Well," he grinned, "if I could tell where strangers was goin', an' why, I wouldn't never ask 'em where they come from. An' I'd shore hunt up a li'l game of faro, you bet!"

Bill smiled. "Well, that might be a good idea. But, say, what ails this town, anyhow?"

"What ails it? Hum! Why, lack of money for one thing; scenery, for another; wimmin, for another. Oh, h—l, I ain't got time to tell you what ails it. Why?"

"Is there anything th' matter with me?"

"I don't know you well enough for to answer that kerrect."

"Well, would you turn around an' stare at me, an' seem pained an' hurt? Do I look funny? Has anybody put a sign on my back?"

"You looks all right to me. What's th' matter?"

"Nothin', yet," reflected Bill slowly. "But there will be, mebby. You was mentionin' faro. Here's a turn you can call: somebody in this wart of a two-by-nothin' town is goin' to run plumb into a big surprise. There'll mebby be a loud noise an' some smoke where it starts from; an' a li'l round hole where it stops. When th' curious delegation now holdin' forth on th' street slips in here after I'm in bed, an' makes inquiries about me, you can tell 'em that. An' if Mr.—Mr. Victoria drops in casual, tell him I'm cleanin' my guns. Now then, show me where I'm goin' to sleep."

Mr. Hawley very carefully led the way into the hall and turned into a room opposite the bar. "Here she is, stranger," he said, stepping back. But Bill was out in the hall listening. He looked into the room and felt oppressed.

"No, she ain't," he answered, backing his intuition. "She is upstairs, where there is a li'l

breeze. By th' Lord," he muttered under his breath, "this is some puzzle." He mounted the stairs shaking his head thoughtfully. "It shore is, it shore is."

When Bill whirled up to the Crazy M bunkhouse and dismounted before the door a puncher was emerging. He started to say something, noticed Bill's guns and went on without a word. Bill turned around and looked after him in amazement. "Well, what th' devil!" he growled. Before he could do anything, had he wished to, Mr. Oleson stepped quickly from the house, nodded and hurried toward the ranch house, motioning for Bill to follow. Entering the house, the foreman of the Crazy M waited impatiently for Bill to get inside, and then hurriedly closed the door.

"They've got onto it some way," he said, his taciturnity gone, "but that don't make no difference if you've got th' sand. I'll pay you one hundred an' fifty a month, furnish yore cayuses an' feed you up here. I'm losin' two hundred cows every month an' can't get a trace of th' thieves. Harris, Marshal of Clay Gulch, is stumped, too. *He* can't move without proof; *you* can. Th' first man to get is George Thomas, then his brother Art. By that time you'll know how things lay. George Thomas is keepin' out of Harris's way. He killed a man last week over in Tuxedo an' Harris wants to take him over there. He'll not help you, so don't ask him to." Before Bill could reply or recover from his astonishment Oleson continued and described several men. "Look out for ambushes. It'll be th' hardest game you ever went up ag'in, an' if you ain't got th' sand to go through with it, say so."

Bill shook his head. "I got th' sand to go through with anythin' I starts, but I don't start here. I reckon you got th' wrong man. I come up here to look over a herd for Buck Peters; an' here you go shovin' wages like that at me. When I tells Buck what I've been offered he'll fall dead." He laughed. "Now I knows th' answer to a lot of things.

"Here, here!" he exclaimed as Oleson began to rave. "Don't you go an' get all het up like that. I reckon I can keep my face shut. An' lemme observe in yore hat-like ear that if th' rest of this gang is like th' samples I seen in town, a good gun-man would shore be robbin' you to take all that money for th' job. Fifty a month, for two months, would be a-plenty."

Oleson's dismay was fading, and he accepted the situation with a grim smile. "You don't know them fellers," he replied. "They're a bad lot, an' won't stop at nothin'."

"All right. Let's take a look at them cows. I want to get home soon as I can."

Oleson shook his head. "I gave you up, an' when I got a better offer I let 'em go. I'm sorry you had th' ride for nothin', but I couldn't get word to you."

Bill led the way in silence back to the bunkhouse and mounted his horse. "All right," he nodded. "I shore was late. Well, I'll be goin'."

"That gun-man is late, too," said Oleson. "Mebby he ain't comin'. You want th' job at *my* figgers?"

"Nope. I got a better job, though it don't pay so much money. It's steady, an' a hull lot cleaner. So long," and Bill loped away, closely watched by Shorty Allen from the corral. And after an interval, Shorty mounted and swung out of the other gate of the corral and rode along the bottom of an arroyo until he felt it was safe to follow Bill's trail. When Shorty turned back he was almost to town, and he would not have been pleased had he known that Bill knew of the trailing for the last ten miles. Bill had doubled back and was within a hundred yards of Shorty when that person turned ranch-ward.

"Huh! I must be popular," grunted Bill. "I reckon I will stay in Clay Gulch till t'morrow mornin'; an' at the Victoria," he grinned. Then he laughed heartily. "Victoria! I got a better name for it than that, all right."

When he pulled up before the Victoria and looked in the proprietor scowled at him, which made Bill frown as he went on to Hawley's. Putting his horse in the corral he carried his saddle and rifle into the barroom and looked around. There was no one in sight, and he smiled. Putting the saddle and rifle back in one corner under the bar and covering them with gunny sacks he strolled to the Victoria and entered through the rear door. The proprietor reached for his gun but reconsidered in time and picked up a glass, which he polished with exaggerated care. There was something about the stranger that obtruded upon his peace of mind and confidence. He would let someone else try the stranger out.

Bill walked slowly forward, by force of will ironing out the humor in his face and assuming his sternest expression. "I want supper an' a bed, an' don't forget to be plumb polite," he rumbled, sitting down by the side of a small table in such a manner that it did not in the least interfere with the movement of his right hand. The observing proprietor observed and gave strict attention to the preparation of the meal. The gun-man arose and walked carelessly to a chair that had blank wall behind it, and from where he could watch windows and doors.

When the meal was placed before him he glanced up. "Go over there an' sit down," he ordered, motioning to a chair that stood close to the rifle that leaned against the wall. "Loaded?" he demanded. The proprietor could only nod. "Then sling it acrost yore knees an' keep still. Well, start movin'."

The proprietor walked as though he were in a trance, but when he seated himself and reached for the weapon a sudden flash of understanding illumined him and caused cold sweat to bead upon his wrinkled brow. He put the weapon down again, but the noise made Bill look up.

"Acrost yore knees," growled the puncher, and the proprietor hastily obeyed, but when it touched his legs he let loose of it as though it were hot. He felt a great awe steal through his fear, for here was a gun-man such as he had read about. This man gave him all the best of it just to tempt him to make a break. The rifle had been in his hands, and while it was there the gun-man was calmly eating with both hands on the table and had not even looked up until the noise of the gun made him!

"My Gawd, 'e must be a wizard with 'em. I 'opes I don't forget!" With the thought came a great itching of his kneecap; then his foot itched so as to make him squirm and wear horrible expressions. Bill, chancing to glance up carelessly, caught sight of the expressions and growled, whereupon they became angelic. Fearing that he could no longer hold in the laughter that tortured him, Bill arose.

"Shoulder, ARMS!" he ordered, crisply. The gun went up with trained precision. "Been a sojer," thought Bill. "Carry, ARMS! About, FACE! To a bedroom, MARCH!" He followed, holding his sides, and stopped before the room. "This th' best?" he demanded. "Well, it ain't good enough for *me*. About, FACE! Forward, MARCH! Column, LEFT! Ground, ARMS! Fall out." Tossing a coin on the floor as payment for the supper Bill turned sharply and went out without even a backward glance.

The proprietor wiped the perspiration from his face and walked unsteadily to the bar, where he poured out a generous drink and gulped it down. Peering out of the door to see if the coast was clear, he scurried across the street and told his troubles to the harness-maker.

Bill leaned weakly against Hawley's and laughed until the tears rolled down his cheeks. Pushing weakly from the building he returned to the Victoria to play another joke on its proprietor. Finding it vacant he slipped upstairs and hunted for a room to suit him. The bed was the softest he had seen for a long time and it lured him into removing his boots and chaps and guns, after he had propped a chair against the door as a warning signal, and, stretching out flat on his back, he prepared to enjoy solid comfort. It was not yet dark, and as he was not sleepy he lay there thinking over the events of the past twenty-four hours, often laughing so hard as to shake the bed. What a reputation he would have in the morning! The softness of the bed got in its work and he fell asleep, for how long he did not know; but when he awakened it was dark and he heard voices coming up from below. They came from the room he had refused to take. One expression banished all thoughts of sleep from his mind and he listened intently. " 'Red-headed Irish gun-man.' Why, they means me! 'Make him hop into h—l.' I don't reckon I'd do that for anybody, even my friends."

"I tried to give 'im this room, but 'e wouldn't tyke *it*," protested the proprietor, hurriedly. "'E says the bloody room wasn't good enough for 'im, *hand* 'e marches me out hand makes off. Likely 'e's in '*Awley's*."

"No, he ain't," growled a strange voice. "You've gone an' bungled th' whole thing."

"But I s'y I didn't, you know. I tries to give 'im this werry room, George, but 'e would 'ave it. D'y think I wants 'im running haround this blooming town? 'E's worse nor the other, *hand* Gawd knows 'e was bad enough. 'E's a cold-*blooded* beggar, 'e *is*!"

"You missed yore chance," grunted the other. "Wish *I* had that gun you had."

"I was wishing to Gawd you *did*," retorted the proprietor. "It never looked so bloody big before, d—n 'is '*ide*!"

"Well, his cayuse is in Hawley's corral," said the first speaker. "If I ever finds Hawley kept him under cover I'll blow his head off. Come on; we'll get Harris first. He ought to be gettin' close to town if he got th' word I sent over to Tuxedo. He won't let us call him. He's a man of his word."

"He'll be here, all right. Fred an' Tom is watchin' his shack, an' we better take th' other end of town—there's no tellin' how he'll come in now," suggested Art Thomas. "But I wish I knowed where that cussed gun-man is."

As they went out, Bill, his chaps on and his boots in his hand, crept down the stairs, and stopped as he neared the hall door. The proprietor was coming back. The others were outside, going to their stations, and did not hear the choking gasp that the proprietor made as a pair of strong hands reached out and throttled him. When he came to he was lying face down on a bed, gagged and bound by a rope that cut into his flesh with every movement. Bill, waiting a moment, slipped into the darkness and was swallowed up. He was looking for Mr. Harris, and looking eagerly.

The moon arose and bathed the dusty street and its crude shacks in silver, cunningly and charitably hiding its ugliness; and passed on as the skirmishing rays of the sun burst into the sky in close and eternal pursuit. As the dawn spread swiftly and long, thin shadows sprang across the sandy street, there arose from the dissipated darkness close to the wall of a building an armed man, weary and slow from a tiresome vigil. Another emerged from behind a pile of boards that faced the marshal's abode, while down the street another crept over the edge of a dried-out water course and swore softly as he stood up slowly to flex away the stiffness of cramped limbs. Of vain speculation he was empty; he had exhausted all the whys and hows long before and now only muttered discontentedly as he reviewed the hours of fruitless waiting. And he was uneasy; it was not like Harris to take a dare and swallow his own threats without a struggle. He looked around apprehensively, shrugged his shoulders and stalked behind the shacks across from the two hotels.

Another figure crept from the protection of Hawley's corral like a slinking coyote, gun in hand and nervously alert. He was just in time to escape the challenge that would have been hurled at him by Hawley, himself, had that gentleman seen the skulker as he grouchily opened one shutter and scowled sleepily at the kindling eastern sky. Mr. Hawley was one of those who go to bed with regret and get up with remorse, and his temper was always easily disturbed before breakfast. The skulker, safe from the remorseful gentleman's eyes, and gun, kept close to the building as he walked and was again fortu-

nate, for he had passed when Mr. Hawley strode heavily into his kitchen to curse the cold, rusty stove, a rite he faithfully performed each morning. Across the street George and Art Thomas walked to meet each other behind the row of shacks and stopped near the harness shop to hold a consultation. The subject was so interesting that for a few moments they were oblivious to all else.

A man softly stepped to the door of the Victoria and watched the two across the street with an expression on his face that showed his smiling contempt for them and their kind. He was a small man, so far as physical measurements go, but he was lithe, sinewy and compact. On his opened vest, hanging slovenly and blinking in the growing light as if to prepare itself for the blinding glare of midday, glinted a five-pointed star of nickel, a lowly badge that every rural community knows and holds in an awe far above the metal or design. Swinging low on his hip gleamed the ivory butt of a silver-plated Colt, the one weakness that his vanity seized upon. But under the silver and its engraving, above and before the cracked and stained ivory handles, lay the power of a great force. Under the casing of that small body lay a virile manhood, strong in courage and determination. Toby Harris watched, smilingly; he loved the dramatic and found keen enjoyment in the situation. Out of the corner of his eye he saw a carelessly dressed cow-puncher slouching indolently along close to the buildings on the other side of the street with the misleading sluggishness of a panther. The red hair, kissed by the slanting rays of the sun where it showed beneath the soiled sombrero, seemed to be a flaming warning; the half-closed eyes, squinting under the brim of the big hat, missed nothing as they darted from point to point.

The marshal stepped silently to the porch and then onto the ground, his back to the rear of the hotel, waiting to be discovered. He had been in sight perhaps a minute. The cow-puncher made a sudden, eye-baffling movement and smoke whirled about his hips. Fred, turning the corner behind the marshal, dropped his gun with a scream of rage and pain and crashed against the window in sudden sickness, his gun-hand hanging by a tendon from his wrist. The marshal stepped quickly forward at the shot and for an instant gazed deeply into the eyes of the startled rustlers. Then his Colt leaped out and crashed a fraction of a second before the brothers fired. George Thomas reeled, caught sight of the puncher and fired by instinct. Bill, leaving Harris to watch the other side of the street, was watching the rear corner of the Victoria and was unprepared for the shot. He crumpled and dropped and then the marshal, enraged, ended the rustler's earthy career in a stream of flame and smoke. Tom, turning into the street further down, wheeled and dashed for his horse, and Art, having leaped behind the harness shop, turned and fled for his life. He had nearly reached his horse and was going at top speed with great leaps when the prostrate man in the street, raising on his elbow, emptied his gun after him, the five shots sounding almost as one. Art Thomas arose convulsively and dove head-long under the horse he had tried to gain. Harris looked hastily down the street and saw a cloud of dust racing northward, and grunted, "Let him go—*he* won't never come back no more." Running to the cow-puncher he raised him after a hurried examination of the wounded thigh. "Hop along, Cassidy," he smiled in encouragement. "You'll be a better man with one good laig than th' whole gang was all put together."

The puncher smiled faintly as Hawley, running to them, helped him toward his hotel. "Th' bone is plumb smashed. I reckon I'll hop along through life. It'll be hop along, Cassidy, for me, all right. That's *my* name, all right. Huh! Hopalong Cassidy! But I didn't hop into h—l, did I, Harris?" he grinned bravely.

And thus was born a nickname that found honor and fame in the cow-country—a name that stood for loyalty, courage and most amazing gun-play. I have Red's word for this, and the endorsement of those who knew him at the time. And from this on, up to the time he died, and after, we will know him and speak of him as Hopalong Cassidy, a cow-puncher.

RAY CUMMINGS

RAYMOND KING CUMMINGS (1887–1957), often described as the American H. G. Wells and one of the founders of the science-fiction pulp story, was born in New York City to wealthy parents. The only job he ever held was that of a technical writer and editor for Thomas A. Edison from 1914 to 1919, after which he resigned to become a full-time writer. His first story, "The Girl in the Golden Atom," was published in 1919 and was spectacularly successful, finding its way into a hardcover book by 1922—a prestigious occurrence for any American writer of science fiction of the era. The story introduced what soon became a cliché of the genre: the likening of atoms to tiny suns and planets that are the homes of tiny life forms. Such stories parallel, but in a more outré fashion, those "lost race" novels in which civilizations—sometimes primitive, sometimes far advanced—are discovered within the earth's core, under the sea, in a deep tropical forest, or inside caves or mountains. Enormously successful, Cummings's story cried out for a sequel, which he wrote the following year: a long novel titled *The People of the Golden Atom*, first published as a six-part serial in *All-Story Weekly* (January 24–February 28, 1920). Cummings returned to the same plot, with minor variations, numerous times over the course of a prodigious career that produced about 750 short stories, novellas, and novels, mainly in the science-fiction and fantasy genres. His *Beyond the Stars* (1963), for example, is about a scientist who is convinced that the universe is merely one atom in a much larger cosmos. While Cummings's tired repetition of the same theme eventually doomed his reputation, his first effort stands as a major cornerstone of science fiction, and remains fresh and readable today—more so than many works of his more heralded contemporaries.

"The Girl in the Golden Atom" was first published in the March 15, 1919, issue of *All-Story Weekly*. Its first book appearance was in *The Girl in the Golden Atom*, published in Britain by Metheun in 1922, and in the United States by Harper & Brothers in 1923.

THE GIRL IN THE GOLDEN ATOM

RAY CUMMINGS

I

A UNIVERSE IN AN ATOM

"**THEN YOU MEAN** to say there is no such thing as the *smallest* particle of matter?" asked the Doctor.

"You can put it that way if you like," the Chemist replied. "In other words, what I believe is that things can be infinitely small just as well as they can be infinitely large. Astronomers tell us of the immensity of space. I have tried to imagine space as finite. It is impossible. How can you conceive the edge of space? Something must be beyond—something or nothing, and even that would be more space, wouldn't it?"

"Gosh," said the Very Young Man, and lighted another cigarette.

The Chemist resumed, smiling a little. "Now, if it seems probable that there is no limit to the immensity of space, why should we make its smallness finite? How can you say that the atom cannot be divided? As a matter of fact, it already has been. The most powerful microscope will show you realms of smallness to which you can penetrate no other way. Multiply that power a thousand times, or ten thousand times, and who shall say what you will see?"

The Chemist paused, and looked at the intent little group around him.

He was a youngish man, with large features and horn-rimmed glasses, his rough English-cut clothes hanging loosely over his broad, spare frame. The Banker drained his glass and rang for the waiter.

"Very interesting," he remarked.

"Don't be an ass, George," said the Big Business Man. "Just because you don't understand, doesn't mean there is no sense to it."

"What I don't get clearly—" began the Doctor.

"None of it's clear to me," said the Very Young Man.

The Doctor crossed under the light and took an easier chair. "You intimated you had discovered something unusual in these realms of the infinitely small," he suggested, sinking back luxuriously. "Will you tell us about it?"

"Yes, if you like," said the Chemist, turning from one to the other. A nod of assent followed his glance, as each settled himself more comfortably.

"Well, gentlemen, when you say I have discovered something unusual in another world—in the world of the infinitely small—you are right in a way. I have seen something and lost it. You won't believe me, probably." He glanced at the Banker an instant. "But that is not important. I am going to tell you the facts, just as they happened."

The Big Business Man filled up the glasses all around, and the Chemist resumed:

"It was in 1910 that this problem first came to interest me. I had never gone in for microscopic work very much, but now I let it absorb all my attention. I secured larger, more powerful instruments—I spent most of my money"—he smiled ruefully—"but never could I come to the end of the space into which I was looking. Something was always hidden beyond—something I could almost, but not quite, distinguish.

"Then I realized that I was on the wrong track. My instrument was not merely of insufficient power, it was not one-thousandth the power I needed.

"So I began to study the laws of optics and lenses. In 1913 I went abroad, and with one of the most famous lens-makers of Europe I produced a lens of an entirely different quality, a lens that I hoped would give me what I wanted. So I returned here and fitted up my microscope that I knew would prove vastly more powerful than any yet constructed.

"It was finally completed and set up in my laboratory, and one night I went in alone to look through it for the first time. It was in the fall of 1914, I remember.

"I can recall now my feelings at that moment. I was about to see into another world, to behold what no man had ever looked on before. What would I see? What new realms was I, first of all our human race, to enter? With furiously beating heart, I sat down before the huge instrument and carefully adjusted the eyepiece.

"Then I glanced around for some object to examine. On my finger I had a ring, my mother's wedding ring, and I decided to use that. I have it here." He took a plain gold band from his little finger and laid it on the table.

"You will see a slight mark on the outside. That is the place into which I looked."

His friends crowded around the table and examined a scratch on one side of the band.

"What did you see?" asked the Very Young Man eagerly.

"Gentlemen," resumed the Chemist, "what I saw staggered even my own imagination. With trembling hands I put the ring in place, looking directly down into that scratch. For a moment I saw nothing. I was like a person coming suddenly out of the sunlight into a darkened room. I knew there was something visible in my view, but my eyes did not seem able to receive the impressions. I realize now they were not yet adjusted to the new form of light. Gradually, as I looked, objects of definite shape began to emerge from the blackness.

"Gentlemen, I want to make clear to you now—as clear as I can—the peculiar aspect of everything that I saw under this microscope. I seemed to be inside an immense cave. One side, near at hand, I could now make out quite clearly. The walls were extraordinarily rough and indented, with a peculiar phosphorescent light on the projections and blackness in the hollows. I say phosphorescent light, for that is the nearest word I can find to describe it—a curious radiation, quite different from the reflected light to which we are accustomed.

"I said that the hollows inside of the cave were blackness. But not blackness—the absence of light—as we know it. It was a blackness that seemed also to radiate light, if you can imagine such a condition; a blackness that seemed not empty, but merely withholding its contents just beyond my vision.

"Except for a dim suggestion of roof over the cave, and its floor, I could distinguish nothing. After a moment this floor became clearer. It seemed to be—well, perhaps I might call it black marble—smooth, glossy, yet somewhat translucent. In the foreground the floor was apparently liquid. In no way did it differ in appearance from the solid part, except that its surface seemed to be in motion.

"Another curious thing was the outlines of all the shapes in view. I noticed that no outline held steady when I looked at it directly; it seemed to quiver. You see something like it when looking at an object through water—only, of course, there was no distortion. It was also like looking at something with the radiation of heat between.

"Of the back and other side of the cave, I

could see nothing, except in one place, where a narrow effulgence of light drifted out into the immensity of the distance behind.

"I do not know how long I sat looking at this scene; it may have been several hours. Although I was obviously in a cave, I never felt shut in—never got the impression of being in a narrow, confined space.

"On the contrary, after a time I seemed to feel the vast immensity of the blackness before me. I think perhaps it may have been that path of light stretching out into the distance. As I looked, it seemed like the reversed tail of a comet, or the dim glow of the Milky Way, and penetrating to equally remote realms of space.

"Perhaps I fell asleep, or at least there was an interval of time during which I was so absorbed in my own thoughts I was hardly conscious of the scene before me.

"Then I became aware of a dim shape in the foreground—a shape merged with the outlines surrounding it. And as I looked, it gradually assumed form, and I saw it was the figure of a young girl, sitting beside the liquid pool. Except for the same waviness of outline and phosphorescent glow, she had quite the normal aspect of a human being of our own world. She was beautiful, according to our own standards of beauty; her long braided hair a glowing black, her face, delicate of feature and winsome in expression. Her lips were a deep red, although I felt rather than saw the color.

"She was dressed only in a short tunic of a substance I might describe as gray opaque glass, and the pearly whiteness of her skin gleamed with iridescence.

"She seemed to be singing, although I heard no sound. Once she bent over the pool and plunged her hand into it, laughing gaily.

"Gentlemen, I cannot make you appreciate my emotions, when all at once I remembered I was looking through a microscope. I had forgotten entirely my situation, absorbed in the scene before me. And then, all at once, a great realization came upon me—the realization that everything I saw was inside that ring. I was un-nerved for the moment at the importance of my discovery.

"When I looked again, after the few moments my eye took to become accustomed to the new form of light, the scene showed itself as before, except that the girl had gone.

"For over a week, each night at the same time I watched that cave. The girl came always, and sat by the pool as I had first seen her. Once she danced with the wild grace of a wood nymph, whirling in and out the shadows, and falling at last in a little heap beside the pool.

"It was on the tenth night after I had first seen her that the accident happened. I had been watching, I remember, an unusually long time before she appeared, gliding out of the shadows. She seemed in a different mood, pensive and sad, as she bent down over the pool, staring into it intently. Suddenly there was a tremendous cracking sound, sharp as an explosion, and I was thrown backward upon the floor."

"When I recovered consciousness—I must have struck my head on something—I found the microscope in ruins. Upon examination I saw that its larger lens had exploded—flown into fragments scattered around the room. Why I was not killed I do not understand. The ring I picked up from the floor; it was unharmed and unchanged in any way.

"Can I make you understand how I felt at this loss? Because of the war in Europe I knew I could never replace my lens—for many years, at any rate. And then, gentlemen, came the most terrible feeling of all; I knew at last that the scientific achievement I had made and lost counted for little with me. It was the girl. I realized then that the only being I ever could care for was living out her life with her world, and, indeed, her whole universe, in an atom of that ring."

The Chemist stopped talking and looked from one to the other of the tense faces of his companions.

"It's almost too big an idea to grasp," murmured the Doctor.

"What caused the explosion?" asked the Very Young Man.

"I do not know." The Chemist addressed his reply to the Doctor, as the most understanding of the group. "I can appreciate, though, that through that lens I was magnifying tremendously those peculiar light-radiations that I have described. I believe the molecules of the lens were shattered by them—I had exposed it longer to them that evening than any of the others."

The Doctor nodded his comprehension of this theory.

Impressed in spite of himself, the Banker took another drink and leaned forward in his chair. "Then you really think that there is a girl now inside the gold of that ring?" he asked.

"He didn't say that necessarily," interrupted the Big Business Man.

"Yes, he did."

"As a matter of fact, I do believe that to be the case," said the Chemist earnestly. "I believe that every particle of matter in our universe contains within it an equally complex and complete a universe, which to its inhabitants seems as large as ours. I think, also, that the whole realm of our interplanetary space, our solar system and all the remote stars of the heavens are contained within the atom of some other universe as gigantic to us as we are to the universe in that ring."

"Gosh!" said the Very Young Man.

"It doesn't make one feel very important in the scheme of things, does it?" remarked the Big Business Man dryly.

The Chemist smiled. "The existence of no individual, no nation, no world, nor any one universe is of the least importance."

"Then it would be possible," said the Doctor, "for this gigantic universe that contains us in one of its atoms, to be itself contained within the atom of another universe, still more gigantic than it is, and so on."

"That is my own theory," said the Chemist.

"And in each of the atoms of the rocks of that cave there may be other worlds proportionately minute?"

"I can see no reason to doubt it."

"Well, there is no proof, anyway," said the Banker. "We might as well believe it."

"I intend to get the proof," said the Chemist.

"Do you believe all these innumerable universes, both larger and smaller than ours, are inhabited?" the Doctor asked him.

"I should think probably most of them are. The existence of life, I believe, is as fundamental as the existence of matter without life."

"How do you suppose that girl got in there?" asked the Very Young Man, coming out of a brown study.

"What puzzled me," resumed the Chemist, ignoring the question, "is why the girl should so resemble our own race. I have thought about it a good deal, and I have reached the conclusion that the inhabitants of any universe in the next smaller or larger plane to ours probably resemble us fairly closely. That ring, you see, is in the same—shall we say—environment as ourselves. The same forces control it that control us. Now, if the ring had been created on Mars, for instance, I believe that the universes within its atoms would be inhabited by beings like the Martians—if Mars has any inhabitants. Of course, in planes beyond those next to ours, either smaller or larger, changes would probably occur, becoming greater as you go in or out from our own universe."

"Good Lord! It makes one dizzy to think of it," said the Big Business Man excitedly.

"I wish I knew how that girl got in there," sighed the Very Young Man, looking at the ring.

"She probably didn't," retorted the Doctor. "Very likely she was created there, the same as you were here."

"I think that is probably so," said the Chemist. "And yet, sometimes I am not at all sure. She was very human." The Very Young Man looked at him sympathetically.

"How are you going to prove your theories?" asked the Banker, in his most irritatingly practical way.

The Chemist picked up the ring and put it on his finger. "Gentlemen," he said, "I have tried to tell you facts, not theories. What I saw through that ultramicroscope was not an unproven theory, but a fact. My theories you have brought out by your questions."

"You are quite right," said the Doctor, "but you did mention yourself that you hoped to provide proof."

The Chemist hesitated a moment, then made his decision. "I will tell you the rest," he said.

"After the destruction of the microscope, I was quite at a loss how to proceed. I thought about the problem for many weeks. Finally I decided to work along another altogether different line—a theory about which I am surprised you have not already questioned me."

He paused, but no one spoke.

"I am hardly ready with proof to-night," he resumed after a moment. "Will you all take dinner with me here at the club one week from to-night?" He read affirmation in the glance of each.

"Good. That's settled," he said, rising. "At seven, then."

"But what was the theory you expected us to question you about?" asked the Very Young Man.

The Chemist leaned on the back of his chair.

"The only solution I could see to the problem," he said slowly, "was to find some way of making myself sufficiently small to be able to enter that other universe. I have found such a way, and one week from to-night, gentlemen, with your assistance, I am going to enter the surface of that ring at the point where it is scratched!"

II
INTO THE RING

The cigars were lighted and dinner over before the Doctor broached the subject uppermost in the minds of every member of the party.

"A toast, gentlemen," he said, raising his glass. "To the greatest research chemist in the world. May he be successful in his adventure to-night."

The Chemist bowed his acknowledgment.

"You have not heard me yet," he said smiling.

"But we want to," said the Very Young Man impulsively.

"And you shall." He settled himself more comfortably in his chair. "Gentlemen, I am going to tell you, first, as simply as possible, just what I have done in the past two years. You must draw your own conclusions from the evidence I give you.

"You will remember that I told you last week of my dilemma after the destruction of the microscope. Its loss, and the impossibility of replacing it, led me into still bolder plans than merely the visual examination of this minute world. I reasoned, as I have told you, that because of its physical proximity, its similar environment, so to speak, this other world should be capable of supporting life identical with our own.

"By no process of reasoning can I find adequate refutation of this theory. Then, again, I had the evidence of my own eyes to prove that a being I could not tell from one of my own kind was living there. That this girl, other than in size, differs radically from those of our race, I cannot believe.

"I saw then but one obstacle standing between me and this other world—the discrepancy of size. The distance separating our world from this other is infinitely great or infinitely small, according to the viewpoint. In my present size it is only a few feet from here to the ring on that plate. But to an inhabitant of that other world, we are as remote as the faintest stars of the heavens, diminished a thousand times."

He paused a moment, signing the waiter to leave the room.

"This reduction of bodily size, great as it is, involves no deeper principle than does a light contraction of tissue, except that it must be carried further. The problem, then, was to find a chemical, sufficiently unharmful to life, that would so act upon the body cells as to cause a reduction in bulk, without changing their shape. I had to secure a uniform and also a proportionate rate of contraction of each cell, in order not to have the body shape altered.

"After a comparatively small amount of research work, I encountered an apparently insurmountable obstacle. As you know, gentlemen, our living human bodies are held together by the power of the central intelligence we call the mind. Every instant during your lifetime your subconscious mind is commanding and directing the individual life of each cell that makes up your body. At death this power is withdrawn; each cell is thrown under its own individual command, and dissolution of the body takes place.

"I found, therefore, that I could not act upon the cells separately, so long as they were under control of the mind. On the other hand, I could not withdraw this power of the subconscious mind without causing death.

"I progressed no further than this for several months. Then came the solution. I reasoned that after death the body does not immediately disintegrate; far more time elapses than I expected to need for the cell-contraction. I devoted my time, then, to find a chemical that would temporarily withhold, during the period of cell-contraction, the power of the subconscious mind, just as the power of the conscious mind is withheld by hypnotism."

"I am not going to weary you by trying to lead you through the maze of chemical experiments into which I plunged. Only one of you"—he indicated the Doctor—"has the technical bases of knowledge to follow me. No one had been before me along the path I traversed. I pursued the method of pure theoretical deduction, drawing my conclusions from the practical results obtained.

"I worked on rabbits almost exclusively. After a few weeks I succeeded in completely suspending animation in one of them for several hours. There was no life apparently existing during that period. It was not a trance or coma, but the complete simulation of death. No harmful results followed the revivifying of the animal. The contraction of the cells was far more difficult to accomplish; I finished my last experiment less than six months ago."

"Then you really have been able to make an animal infinitely small?" asked the Big Business Man.

The Chemist smiled. "I sent four rabbits into the unknown last week," he said.

"What did they look like going?" asked the Very Young Man. The Chemist signed him to be patient.

"The quantity of diminution to be obtained bothered me considerably. Exactly how small that other universe is, I had no means of knowing, except by the computations I made of the magnifying power of my lens. These figures, I know, must necessarily be very inaccurate. Then, again, I have no means of judging by the visual rate of diminution of these rabbits, whether this contraction is at a uniform rate or accelerated. Nor can I tell how long it is prolonged, or the quantity of drug administered, as only a fraction of the diminution has taken place when the animal passes beyond the range of any microscope I now possess.

"These questions were overshadowed, however, by a far more serious problem that encompassed them all.

"As I was planning to project myself into this unknown universe and to reach the exact size proportionate to it, I soon realized such a result could not be obtained were I in an unconscious state. Only by successive doses of the drug, or its retardant about which I will tell you later, could I hope to reach the proper size. Another necessity is that I place myself on the exact spot on that ring where I wish to enter and to climb down among its atoms when I have become sufficiently small to do so. Obviously, this would be impossible to one not possessing all his faculties and physical strength."

"And did you solve that problem, too?" asked

the Banker. "I'd like to see it done," he added, reading his answer in the other's confident smile.

The Chemist produced two small paper packages from his wallet. "These drugs are the result of my research," he said. "One of them causes contraction, and the other expansion, by an exact reversal of the process. Taken together, they produce no effect, and a lesser amount of one retards the action of the other." He opened the papers, showing two small vials. "I have made them as you see, in the form of tiny pills, each containing a minute quantity of the drug. It is by taking them successively in unequal amounts that I expect to reach the desired size."

"There's one point that you do not mention," said the Doctor. "Those vials and their contents will have to change size as you do. How are you going to manage that?"

"By experimentation I have found," answered the Chemist, "that any object held in close physical contact with the living body being contracted is contracted itself at an equal rate. I believe that my clothes will be affected also. These vials I will carry strapped under my armpits."

"Suppose you should die, or be killed, would the contraction cease?" asked the Doctor.

"Yes, almost immediately," replied the Chemist. "Apparently, though I am acting through the subconscious mind while its power is held in abeyance, when this power is permanently withdrawn by death, the drug no longer affects the individual cells. The contraction or expansion ceases almost at once."

The Chemist cleared a space before him on the table. "In a well-managed club like this," he said, "there should be no flies, but I see several around. Do you suppose we can catch one of them?"

"I can," said the Very Young Man, and forthwith he did.

The Chemist moistened a lump of sugar and laid it on the table before him. Then, selecting one of the smallest of the pills, he ground it to powder with the back of a spoon and sprinkled this powder on the sugar.

"Will you give me the fly, please?"

The Very Young Man gingerly did so. The Chemist held the insect by its wings over the sugar. "Will someone lend me one of his shoes?"

The Very Young Man hastily slipped off one of his shoes.

"Thank you," said the Chemist, placing it on the table with a quizzical smile.

The rest of the company rose from their chairs and gathered around, watching with interested faces what was about to happen.

"I hope he is hungry," remarked the Chemist, and placed the fly gently down on the sugar, still holding it by the wings. The insect, after a moment, ate a little.

Silence fell upon the group as each watched intently. For a few moments nothing happened. Then, almost imperceptibly at first, the fly became larger. In another minute it was the size of a large horse-fly, struggling to release its wings from the Chemist's grasp. A minute more and it was the size of a beetle. No one spoke. The Banker moistened his lips, drained his glass hurriedly and moved slightly farther away. Still the insect grew; now it was the size of a small chicken, the multiple lens of its eyes presenting a most terrifying aspect, while its ferocious droning reverberated through the room. Then suddenly the Chemist threw it upon the table, covered it with a napkin, and beat it violently with the shoe. When all movement had ceased he tossed its quivering body into a corner of the room.

"Good God!" ejaculated the Banker, as the white-faced men stared at each other. The quiet voice of the Chemist brought them back to themselves. "That, gentlemen, you must understand, was only a fraction of the very first stage of growth. As you may have noticed, it was constantly accelerated. This acceleration attains a speed of possibly fifty thousand times that you observed. Beyond that, it is my theory, the change is at a uniform rate." He looked at the body of the fly, lying inert on the floor. "You can appreciate now, gentlemen, the importance of having this growth cease after death."

"Good Lord, I should say so!" murmured the Big Business Man, mopping his forehead. The Chemist took the lump of sugar and threw it into the open fire.

"Gosh!" said the Very Young Man, "suppose when we were not looking, another fly had—"

"Shut up!" growled the Banker.

"Not so skeptical now, eh, George?" said the Big Business Man.

"Can you catch me another fly?" asked the Chemist. The Very Young Man hastened to do so. "The second demonstration, gentlemen," said the Chemist, "is less spectacular, but far more pertinent than the one you have just witnessed." He took the fly by the wings, and prepared another lump of sugar, sprinkling a crushed pill from the other vial upon it.

"When he is small enough I am going to try to put him on the ring, if he will stay still," said the Chemist.

The Doctor pulled the plate containing the ring forward until it was directly under the light, and everyone crowded closer to watch; already the fly was almost too small to be held. The Chemist tried to set it on the ring, but could not; so with his other hand he brushed it lightly into the plate, where it lay, a tiny black speck against the gleaming whiteness of the china.

"Watch it carefully, gentlemen," he said, as they bent closer.

"It's gone," said the Big Business Man.

"No, I can still see it," said the Doctor. Then he raised the plate closer to his face. "Now it's gone," he said.

The Chemist sat down in his chair. "It's probably still there, only too small for you to see. In a few minutes, if it took a sufficient amount of the drug, it will be small enough to fall between the molecules of the plate."

"Do you suppose it will find another inhabited universe down there?" asked the Very Young Man.

"Who knows," said the Chemist. "Very possibly it will. But the one we are interested in is here," he added, touching the ring.

"Is it your intention to take this stuff yourself, to-night?" asked the Big Business Man.

"If you will give me your help, I think so, yes. I have made all arrangements. The club has given us this room in absolute privacy for forty-eight hours. Your meals will be served here when you want them, and I am going to ask you, gentlemen, to take turns watching and guarding the ring during that time. Will you do it?"

"I should say we would!" cried the Doctor, and the others nodded assent.

"It is because I wanted you to be convinced of my entire sincerity that I have taken you so thoroughly into my confidence. Are those doors locked?" The Very Young Man locked them.

"Thank you," said the Chemist, starting to disrobe. In a moment he stood before them attired in a woolen bathing-suit of pure white. Over his shoulders was strapped tightly a narrow leather harness, supporting two silken pockets, one under each armpit. Into each of these he placed one of the vials, first laying four pills from one of them upon the table.

At this point the Banker rose from his chair and selected another in the farther corner of the room. He sank into it a crumpled heap and wiped the beads of perspiration from his face with a shaking hand.

"I have every expectation," said the Chemist, "that this suit and harness will contract in size uniformly with me. If the harness should not, then I shall have to hold the vials in my hand."

On the table, directly under the light, he spread a large silk handkerchief, upon which he placed the ring. He then produced a teaspoon, which he handed to the Doctor.

"Please listen carefully," he said, "for perhaps the whole success of my adventure, and my life itself, may depend upon your actions during the next few minutes. You will realize, of course, that when I am still large enough to be visible to you, I shall be so small that my voice may be inaudible. Therefore, I want you to know, now, just what to expect.

"When I am something under a foot high, I shall step upon that handkerchief, where you will see my white suit plainly against its black surface. When I become less than an inch in height, I shall run over to the ring and stand beside it. When I have diminished to about a quarter of an inch, I shall climb upon it, and, as I get smaller, will follow its surface until I come to the scratch."

"I want you to watch me very closely. I may miscalculate the time and wait until I am too small to climb upon the ring. Or I may fall off. In either case, you will place that spoon beside me and I will climb into it. You will then do your best to help me get on the ring. Is all this quite clear?"

The Doctor nodded assent.

"Very well, watch me as long as I remain visible. If I have an accident, I shall take the other drug and endeavor to return to you at once. This you must expect at any moment during the next forty-eight hours. Under all circumstances, if I am alive, I shall return at the expiration of that time.

"And, gentlemen, let me caution you most solemnly, do not allow that ring to be touched until that length of time has expired. Can I depend on you?"

"Yes," they answered breathlessly.

"After I have taken the pills," the Chemist continued, "I shall not speak unless it is absolutely necessary. I do not know what my sensations will be, and I want to follow them as closely as possible." He then turned out all the lights in the room with the exception of the center electrolier that shone down directly on the handkerchief and ring.

The Chemist looked about him. "Good-by, gentlemen," he said, shaking hands all around. "Wish me luck." And without hesitation he placed the four pills in his mouth and washed them down with a swallow of water.

Silence fell on the group as the Chemist seated himself and covered his face with his hands. For perhaps two minutes the tenseness of the silence was unbroken, save by the heavy breathing of the Banker as he lay huddled in his chair.

"Oh, my God! He *is* growing smaller!" whispered the Big Business Man in a horrified tone to the Doctor. The Chemist raised his head and smiled at them. Then he stood up, steadying himself against a chair. He was less than four feet high. Steadily he grew smaller before their horrified eyes. Once he made as if to speak, and the Doctor knelt down beside him. "It's all right, good-by," he said in a tiny voice.

Then he stepped upon the handkerchief. The Doctor knelt on the floor beside it, the wooden spoon ready in his hand, while the others, except the Banker, stood behind him. The figure of the Chemist, standing motionless near the edge of the handkerchief, seemed now like a little white wooden toy, hardly more than one inch in height.

Waving his hand and smiling, he suddenly started to walk and then ran swiftly over to the ring. By the time he reached it, somewhat out of breath, he was little more than twice as high as the width of its band. Without pausing, he leaped up, and sat astraddle, leaning over and holding to it tightly with his hands. In another moment he was on his feet, on the upper edge of the ring, walking carefully along its circumference toward the scratch.

The Big Business Man touched the Doctor on the shoulder and tried to smile. "He's making it," he whispered. As if in answer the little figure turned and waved its arms. They could just distinguish its white outline against the gold surface underneath.

"I don't see him," said the Very Young Man in a scared voice.

"He's right near the scratch," answered the Doctor, bending closer. Then, after a moment, "He's gone." He rose to his feet. "Good Lord! Why haven't we a microscope!" he added.

"I never thought of that," said the Big Business Man, "we could have watched him for a long time yet."

"Well, he's gone now," returned the Doctor, "and there is nothing for us to do but wait."

"I hope he finds that girl," sighed the Very Young Man, as he sat chin in hand beside the handkerchief.

The Banker snored stertorously from his mattress in a corner of the room. In an easy-chair near by, with his feet on the table, lay the Very Young Man, sleeping also.

The Doctor and the Big Business Man sat by the handkerchief conversing in low tones.

"How long has it been now?" asked the latter.

"Just forty hours," answered the Doctor, "and he said that forty-eight hours was the limit. He should come back at about ten to-night."

"I wonder if he *will* come back," questioned the Big Business Man nervously. "Lord, I wish *he* wouldn't snore so loud," he added irritably, nodding in the direction of the Banker.

They were silent for a moment, and then he went on: "You'd better try to sleep awhile," he said to the Doctor. "You're worn out. I'll watch here."

"I suppose I should," answered the Doctor wearily. "Wake up that kid: he's sleeping most of the time."

"No, I'll watch," repeated the Big Business Man; "You lie down over there."

The Doctor did so while the other settled himself more comfortably on a cushion beside the handkerchief, and prepared for his lonely watching.

The Doctor apparently dropped off to sleep at once, for he did not speak again. The Big Business Man sat staring steadily at the ring, bending nearer to it occasionally. Every ten or fifteen minutes he looked at his watch.

Perhaps an hour passed in this way, when the Very Young Man suddenly sat up and yawned. "Haven't they come back yet?" he asked in a sleepy voice.

The Big Business Man answered in a much lower tone. "What do you mean—they?" he said.

"I dreamed that he brought the girl back with him," said the Very Young Man.

"Well, if he did, they have not arrived," answered the Big Business Man. "You'd better go back to sleep. We've got six or seven hours yet."

The Very Young Man rose and crossed the room. "No, I'll watch awhile," he said, seating himself on the floor. "What time is it?"

"Quarter of three."

"He said he'd be back by ten to-night. I'm crazy to see that girl."

The Big Business Man rose and went over to a dinner-tray, standing near the door. "Lord, I'm hungry, I must have forgotten to eat to-day." He lifted up one of the silver covers. What he saw evidently encouraged him, for he drew up a chair and began his lunch.

The Very Young Man lighted a cigarette. "It will be the tragedy of my life," he said, "if he never comes back."

The Big Business Man smiled. "How about *his* life?" he answered, but the Very Young Man had fallen into a reverie and did not reply.

The Big Business Man finished his lunch in silence and was just about to light a cigar when a sharp exclamation brought him hastily to his feet.

"Come here, quick, I see something." The Very Young Man had his face close to the ring and was trembling violently.

The other pushed him back. "Let me see. Where?"

"There by the scratch; he's lying there; I can see him."

The Big Business Man looked and then hurriedly woke the Doctor.

"He's come back," he said briefly; "you can see him there." The Doctor bent down over the ring while the others woke up the Banker.

"He doesn't seem to be getting any bigger," said the Very Young Man; "he's just lying there. Maybe he's dead."

"What shall we do?" asked the Big Business Man, and made as if to pick up the ring. The Doctor shoved him away. "Don't do that!" he said sharply. "Do you want to kill him?"

"He's sitting up," cried the Very Young Man. "He's all right."

"He must have fainted," said the Doctor. "Probably he's taking more of the drug now."

"He's much larger," said the Very Young Man; "look at him!"

The tiny figure was sitting sideways on the ring, with its feet hanging over the outer edge. It was growing perceptibly larger each instant, and in a moment it slipped down off the ring and sank in a heap on the handkerchief.

"Good Heavens! Look at him!" cried the Big Business Man. "He's all covered with blood."

The little figure presented a ghastly sight. As it steadily grew larger they could see and recognize the Chemist's haggard face, his cheek and neck stained with blood, and his white suit covered with dirt.

"Look at his feet," whispered the Big Business Man. They were horribly cut and bruised and greatly swollen.

The Doctor bent over and whispered gently, "What can I do to help you?" The Chemist shook his head. His body, lying prone upon the handkerchief, had torn it apart in growing. When he was about twelve inches in length he raised his head. The Doctor bent closer. "Some brandy, please," said a wraith of the Chemist's voice. It was barely audible.

"He wants some brandy," called the Doctor. The Very Young Man looked hastily around, then opened the door and dashed madly out of the room. When he returned, the Chemist had grown to nearly four feet. He was sitting on the floor with his back against the Doctor's knees. The Big Business Man was wiping the blood off his face with a damp napkin.

"Here!" cried the Very Young Man, thrusting forth the brandy. The Chemist drank a little of it. Then he sat up, evidently somewhat revived.

"I seem to have stopped growing," he said. "Let's finish it up now. God! How I want to be the right size again," he added fervently.

The Doctor helped him extract the vials from under his arm, and the Chemist touched one of the pills to his tongue. Then he sank back, closing his eyes. "I think that should be about enough," he murmured.

No one spoke for nearly ten minutes. Gradually the Chemist's body grew, the Doctor shifting his position several times as it became larger. It seemed finally to have stopped growing, and was apparently nearly its former size.

"Is he asleep?" whispered the Very Young Man.

The Chemist opened his eyes.

"No," he answered. "I'm all right now, I think." He rose to his feet, the Doctor and the Big Business Man supporting him on either side.

"Sit down and tell us about it," said the Very Young Man. "Did you find the girl?"

The Chemist smiled wearily.

"Gentlemen, I cannot talk now. Let me have a bath and some dinner. Then I will tell you all about it."

The Doctor rang for an attendant, and led the Chemist to the door, throwing a blanket around him as he did so. In the doorway the Chemist paused and looked back, with a wan smile, over the wreck of the room.

"Give me an hour," he said. "And eat something yourselves while I am gone." Then he left, closing the door after him.

When he returned, fully dressed in clothes that were ludicrously large for him, the room had been straightened up, and his four friends were finishing their meal. He took his place among them quietly and lighted a cigar.

"Well, gentlemen, I suppose that you are interested to hear what happened to me," he began. The Very Young Man asked his usual question.

"Let him alone," said the Doctor.

"Was it all as you expected?" asked the Banker.

It was his first remark since the Chemist returned.

"To a great extent, yes," answered the Chemist. "But I had better tell you just what happened." The Very Young Man nodded his eager agreement.

"When I took those first four pills," began the Chemist in a quiet, even tone, "my immediate sensation was a sudden reeling of the senses, combined with an extreme nausea. This latter feeling passed after a moment.

"You will remember that I seated myself upon the floor and closed my eyes. When I opened them my head had steadied itself somewhat, but I was oppressed by a curious feeling of drowsiness, impossible to shake off.

"My first mental impression was one of wonderment when I saw you all begin to increase in size. I remember standing up beside the chair, which was then half again its normal size, and you"—indicating the Doctor—"towered beside me as a giant of nine or ten feet high.

"Steadily upward, with a curious crawling motion, grew the room and all its contents. Except for the feeling of sleep that oppressed me, I felt quite my usual self. No change appeared happening to me, but everything else seemed growing to gigantic and terrifying proportions.

"Can you imagine a human being a hundred feet high? That is how you looked to me as I stepped upon that huge expanse of black silk and shouted my last good-by to you!

"Over to my left lay the ring, apparently fifteen or twenty feet away. I started to walk toward it, but although it grew rapidly larger, the distance separating me from it seemed to increase rather than lessen. Then I ran, and by the time I arrived it stood higher than my waist—a beautiful, shaggy, golden pit.

"I jumped upon its rim and clung to it tightly. I could feel it growing beneath me as I sat. After a moment I climbed upon its top surface and started to walk toward the point where I knew the scratch to be.

"I found myself now, as I looked about, walking upon a narrow, though ever broadening, curved path. The ground beneath my feet appeared to be a rough, yellowish quartz. This path grew rougher as I advanced. Below the bulging edges of the path, on both sides, lay a shining black plain, ridged and indented, and with a sunlike sheen on the higher portions of the ridges. On the one hand this black plain stretched in an unbroken expanse to the horizon. On the other, it appeared as a circular valley, enclosed by a shining yellow wall.

"The way had now become extraordinarily rough. I bore to the left as I advanced, keeping close to the outer edge. The other edge of the path I could not see. I clambered along hastily, and after a few moments was confronted by a row of rocks and boulders lying directly across my line of progress. I followed their course for a short distance, and finally found a space through which I could pass.

"This transverse ridge was perhaps a hundred feet deep. Behind it and extending in a parallel direction lay a tremendous valley. I knew then I had reached my first objective.

"I sat down upon the brink of the precipice and watched the cavern growing ever wider and deeper. Then I realized that I must begin my descent if ever I was to reach the bottom. For perhaps six hours I climbed steadily downward. It was a fairly easy descent after the first little while, for the ground seemed to open up before me as I advanced, changing its contour so constantly that I was never at a loss for an easy downward path.

"My feet suffered cruelly from the shaggy, metallic ground, and I soon had to stop and rig a sort of protection for the soles of them from a portion of the harness over my shoulder. According to the stature I was when I reached the bottom, I had descended perhaps twelve thousand feet during this time.

"The latter part of this journey found me nearing the bottom of the cañon. Objects around me no longer seemed to increase in size, as had been constantly the case before, and I reasoned that probably my stature was remaining constant.

"I noticed, too, as I advanced, a curious alteration in the form of light around me. The glare from above (the sky showed only a narrow dull ribbon of blue) barely penetrated to the depths of the cañon's floor. But all about me there was a soft radiance, seeming to emanate from the rocks themselves."

"The sides of the cañon were shaggy and rough, beyond anything I had ever seen. Huge boulders, hundreds of feet in diameter, were embedded in them. The bottom also was strewn with similar gigantic rocks.

"I surveyed this lonely waste for some time in dismay, not knowing in what direction lay my goal. I knew that I was at the bottom of the scratch, and by the comparison of its size I realized I was well started on my journey.

"I have not told you, gentlemen, that at the time I marked the ring I made a deeper indentation in one portion of the scratch and focused the microscope upon that. This indentation I now searched for. Luckily I found it, less than half a mile away—an almost circular pit, perhaps five miles in diameter, with shining walls extending downward into blackness. There seemed no possible way of descending into it, so I sat down near its edge to think out my plan of action.

"I realized now that I was faint and hungry, and whatever I did must be done quickly. I could turn back to you, or I could go on. I decided to risk the latter course, and took twelve more of the pills—three times my original dose."

The Chemist paused for a moment, but his auditors were much too intent to question him. Then he resumed in his former matter-of-fact tone.

"After my vertigo had passed somewhat—it was much more severe this time—I looked up and found my surroundings growing at a far more rapid rate than before. I staggered to the edge of the pit. It was opening up and widening out at an astounding rate. Already its sides were becoming rough and broken, and I saw many places where a descent would be possible.

"The feeling of sleep that had formerly merely oppressed me, combined now with my physical fatigue and the larger dose of the drug I had taken, became almost intolerable. I yielded

to it for a moment, lying down on a crag near the edge of the pit. I must have become almost immediately unconscious, and remained so for a considerable time. I can remember a horrible sensation of sliding headlong for what seemed like hours. I felt that I was sliding or falling downward. I tried to rouse but could not. Then came absolute oblivion.

"When I recovered my senses I was lying partly covered by a mass of smooth, shining pebbles. I was bruised and battered from head to foot—in a far worse condition than you first saw me in when I returned.

"I sat up and looked around. Beside me, sloped upward at an apparently increasing angle, a tremendous glossy plane. This extended, as far as I could see, both to the right and left and upward into the blackness of the sky overhead. It was this plane that had evidently broken my fall, and I had been sliding down it, bringing with me a considerable mass of rocks and boulders.

"As my senses became clearer I saw I was lying on a fairly level floor. I could see perhaps two miles in each direction. Beyond that there was only darkness. The sky overhead was unbroken by stars or light of any kind. I should have been in total darkness except, as I have told you before, that everything, even the blackness itself, seemed to be self-luminous.

"The incline down which I had fallen was composed of some smooth substance suggesting black marble. The floor underfoot was quite different—more of a metallic quality with a curious corrugation. Before me, in the dim distance, I could just make out a tiny range of hills.

"I rose, after a time, and started weakly to walk toward these hills. Though I was faint and dizzy from my fall and the lack of food, I walked for perhaps half an hour, following closely the edge of the incline. No change in my visual surroundings occurred, except that I seemed gradually to be approaching the line of hills. My situation at this time, as I turned it over in my mind, appeared hopelessly desperate, and I admit I neither expected to reach my destination nor to be able to return to my own world.

"A sudden change in the feeling of the ground underfoot brought me to myself; I bent down and found I was treading on vegetation—a tiny forest extending for quite a distance in front and to the side of me. A few steps ahead a little silver ribbon threaded its way through the trees. This I judged to be water.

"New hope possessed me at this discovery. I sat down at once and took a portion of another of the pills.

"I must again have fallen asleep. When I awoke, somewhat refreshed, I found myself lying beside the huge trunk of a fallen tree. I was in what had evidently once been a deep forest, but which now was almost utterly desolated. Only here and there were the trees left standing. For the most part they were lying in a crushed and tangled mass, many of them partially embedded in the ground.

"I cannot express adequately to you, gentlemen, what an evidence of tremendous superhuman power this scene presented. No storm, no lightning, nor any attack of the elements could have produced more than a fraction of the destruction I saw all around me.

"I climbed cautiously upon the fallen tree-trunk, and from this elevation had a much better view of my surroundings. I appeared to be near one end of the desolated area, which extended in a path about half a mile wide and several miles deep. In front, a thousand feet away, perhaps, lay the unbroken forest.

"Descending from the tree-trunk I walked in this direction, reaching the edge of the woods after possibly an hour of the most arduous traveling of my whole journey.

"During this time almost my only thought was the necessity of obtaining food. I looked about me as I advanced, and on one of the fallen tree-trunks I found a sort of vine growing. This vine bore a profusion of small gray berries, much like our huckleberries. They proved similar in taste, and I sat down and ate a quantity.

"When I reached the edge of the forest I felt somewhat stronger. I had seen up to this time no sign of animal life whatever. Now, as I stood silent, I could hear around me all the multitudinous tiny voices of the woods. Insect life stirred underfoot, and in the trees above an occasional bird flitted to and fro.

"Perhaps I am giving you a picture of our own world. I do not mean to do so. You must remember that above me there was no sky, just blackness. And yet so much light illuminated the scene that I could not believe it was other than what we would call daytime. Objects in the forest were as well lighted—better probably than they would be under similar circumstances in our own familiar world.

"The trees were of huge size compared to my present stature; straight, upstanding trunks, with no branches until very near the top. They were bluish-gray in color, and many of them well covered with the berry-vine I have mentioned. The leaves overhead seemed to be blue—in fact the predominating color of all the vegetation was blue, just as in our world it is green. The ground was covered with dead leaves, mold, and a sort of gray moss. Fungus of a similar color appeared, but of this I did not eat.

"I had penetrated perhaps two miles into the forest when I came unexpectedly to the bank of a broad, smooth-flowing river, its silver surface seeming to radiate waves of the characteristic phosphorescent light. I found it cold, pure-tasting water, and I drank long and deeply. Then I remember lying down upon the mossy bank, and in a moment, utterly worn out, I again fell asleep."

III

LYLDA

"I was awakened by the feel of soft hands upon my head and face. With a start I sat up abruptly; I rubbed my eyes confusedly for a moment, not knowing where I was. When I collected my wits I found myself staring into the face of a girl, who was kneeling on the ground before me. I recognized her at once—she was the girl of the microscope.

"To say I was startled would be to put it mildly, but I read no fear in her expression, only wonderment at my springing so suddenly into life. She was dressed very much as I had seen her before. Her fragile beauty was the same, and at this closer view infinitely more appealing, but I was puzzled to account for her older, more mature look. She seemed to have aged several years since the last evening I had seen her through the microscope. Yet, undeniably, it was the same girl.

"For some moments we sat looking at each other in wonderment. Then she smiled and held out her hand, palm up, speaking a few words as she did so. Her voice was soft and musical, and the words of a peculiar quality that we generally describe as liquid, for want of a better term. What she said was wholly unintelligible, but whether the words were strange or the intonation different from anything I knew, I could not tell.

"Afterward, during my stay in this other world, I found that the language of its people resembled English quite closely, so far as the words themselves went. But the intonation with which they were given, and the gestures accompanying them, differed so widely from our own that they conveyed no meaning.

"The gap separating us, however, was very much less than you would imagine. Strangely enough, though, it was not I who learned to speak her tongue, but she who mastered mine."

The Very Young Man sighed contentedly.

"We became quite friendly after this greeting," resumed the Chemist, "and it was apparent from her manner that she had already conceived her own idea of who and what I was.

"For some time we sat and tried to communicate with each other. My words seemed almost as unintelligible to her as hers to me, except that occasionally she would divine my meaning, clapping her hands in childish delight. I made out that she lived at a considerable distance, and that her name was Lylda. Finally she pulled me by the hand and led me away with a proprietary air that amused and, I must admit to you, pleased me tremendously.

"We had progressed through the woods in this way, hardly more than a few hundred yards, when suddenly I found that she was taking me into the mouth of a cave or passageway, sloping downward at an angle of perhaps twenty degrees. I noticed now, more graphically than ever before, a truth that had been gradually forcing itself upon me. Darkness was impossible in this new world. We were now shut in between narrow walls of crystalline rock, with a roof hardly more than fifty feet above.

"No artificial light of any kind was in evidence, yet the scene was lighted quite brightly. This, I have explained, was caused by the phosphorescent radiation that apparently emanated from every particle of mineral matter in this universe.

"As we advanced, many other tunnels crossed the one we were traveling. And now, occasionally, we passed other people, the men dressed similarly to Lylda, but wearing their hair chopped off just above the shoulder line.

"Later, I found that the men were generally about five and a half feet in stature: lean, muscular, and with a grayer, harder look to their skin than the iridescent quality that characterized the women.

"They were fine-looking chaps these we encountered. All of them stared curiously at me, and several times we were held up by chattering groups. The intense whiteness of my skin, for it looked in this light the color of chalk, seemed to both awe and amuse them. But they treated me with great deference and respect, which I afterward learned was because of Lylda herself, and also what she told them about me.

"At several of the intersections of the tunnels there were wide open spaces. One of these we now approached. It was a vast amphitheater, so broad its opposite wall was invisible, and it seemed crowded with people. At the side, on a rocky niche in the wall, a speaker harangued the crowd.

"We skirted the edge of this crowd and plunged into another passageway, sloping downward still more steeply. I was so much interested in the strange scenes opening before me that I remarked little of the distance we traveled. Nor did I question Lylda very often. I was absorbed in the complete similarity between this and my own world in its general characteristics, and yet its complete strangeness in details.

"I felt not the slightest fear. Indeed the sincerity and kindliness of these people seemed absolutely genuine, and the friendly, naïve manner of my little guide put me wholly at my ease. Toward me Lylda's manner was one of childish delight at a new-found possession. Toward those of her own people with whom we talked, I found she preserved a dignity they profoundly respected.

"We had hardly more than entered this last tunnel when I heard the sound of drums and a weird sort of piping music, followed by shouts and cheers. Figures from behind us scurried past, hastening toward the sound. Lylda's clasp on my hand tightened, and she pulled me forward eagerly. As we advanced the crowd became denser, pushing and shoving us about and paying little attention to me.

"In close contact with these people I soon found I was stronger than they, and for a time I had no difficulty in shoving them aside and opening a path for us. They took my rough handling all in good part; in fact, never have I met a more even-tempered, good-natured people than these."

"After a time the crowd became so dense we could advance no more. At this Lylda signed me to bear to the side. As we approached the wall of the cavern she suddenly clasped her hands high over her head and shouted something in a clear, commanding voice. Instantly the crowd fell back, and in a moment I found myself being pulled up a narrow flight of stone steps in the wall and out upon a level space some twenty feet above the heads of the people.

"Several dignitaries occupied this platform. Lylda greeted them quietly, and they made place for us beside the parapet. I could see now that we were at the intersection of a transverse passageway, much broader than the one we had been traversing. And now I received the greatest surprise I had had in this new world, for down this latter tunnel was passing a broad line of men who obviously were soldiers.

"The uniformly straight lines they held; the glint of light on the spears they carried upright before them; the weird, but rhythmic, music that passed at intervals, with which they kept step; and, above all, the cheering enthusiasm of the crowd, all seemed like an echo of my own great world above.

"This martial ardor and what it implied came as a distinct shock. All I had seen before showed the gentle kindliness of a people whose life seemed far removed from the struggle for existence to which our race is subjected. I had come gradually to feel that this new world, at least, had attained the golden age of security, and that fear, hate, and wrongdoing had long since passed away, or had never been born.

"Yet here, before my very eyes, made wholesome by the fires of patriotism, stalked the grim God of War. Knowing nothing yet of the motives that inspired these people, I could feel no enthusiasm, but only disillusionment at this discovery of the omnipotence of strife.

"For some time I must have stood in silence. Lylda, too, seemed to divine my thoughts, for she did not applaud, but pensively watched the cheering throng below. All at once, with an impulsively appealing movement, she pulled me down toward her, and pressed her pretty cheek to mine. It seemed almost as if she was asking me to help.

"The line of marching men seemed now to have passed, and the crowd surged over into the open space and began to disperse. As the men upon the platform with us prepared to leave, Lylda led me over to one of them. He was nearly as tall as I, and dressed in the characteristic tunic that seemed universally worn by both sexes. The upper part of his body was hung with beads, and across his chest was a thin, slightly convex stone plate.

"After a few words of explanation from Lylda, he laid his hands on my shoulders near the base of the neck, smiling with his words of greeting. Then he held one hand before me, palm up, as Lylda had done, and I laid mine in it, which seemed the correct thing to do.

"I repeated this performance with two others who joined us, and then Lylda pulled me away. We descended the steps and turned into the broader tunnel, finding near at hand a sort of sleigh, which Lylda signed me to enter. It was constructed evidently of wood, with a pile of leaves, or similar dead vegetation, for cushions. It was balanced upon a single runner of polished stone, about two feet broad, with a narrow, slightly shorter outrider on each side.

"Harnessed to the shaft were two animals, more resembling our reindeer than anything else, except that they were gray in color and had no horns. An attendant greeted Lylda respectfully as we approached, and mounted a seat in front of us when we were comfortably settled.

"We drove in this curious vehicle for over an hour. The floor of the tunnel was quite smooth, and we glided down its incline with little effort and at a good rate. Our driver preserved the balance of the sleigh by shifting his body from side to side so that only at rare intervals did the side-runners touch the ground.

"Finally, we emerged into the open, and I found myself viewing a scene of almost normal, earthly aspect. We were near the shore of a smooth, shining lake. At the side a broad stretch of rolling country, dotted here and there with trees, was visible. Near at hand, on the lake shore, I saw a collection of houses, most of them low and flat, with one much larger on a promontory near the lake.

"Overhead arched a gray-blue, cloudless sky, faintly star-studded, and reflected in the lake before me I saw that familiar, gleaming trail of stardust, hanging like a huge straightened rainbow overhead, and ending at my feet."

The Chemist paused and relighted his cigar. "Perhaps you have some questions," he suggested.

The Doctor shifted in his chair.

"Did you have any theory at this time"—he wanted to know—"about the physical conformation of this world? What I mean is, when you came out of this tunnel, were you on the inside or the outside of the world?"

"Was it the same sky you saw overhead when you were in the forest?" asked the Big Business Man.

"No, it was what he saw in the microscope, wasn't it?" said the Very Young Man.

"One at a time, gentlemen." The Chemist laughed. "No, I had no particular theory at this time—I had too many other things to think of. But I do remember noticing one thing which gave me the clue to a fairly complete understanding of this universe. From it I formed a definite explanation, which I found was the belief held by the people themselves."

"What was that?" asked the Very Young Man.

"I noticed, as I stood looking over this broad expanse of country before me, one vital thing that made it different from any similar scene I had ever beheld. If you will stop and think a moment, gentlemen, you will realize that in our world here the horizon is caused by a curvature of the earth below the straight line of vision. We are on a convex surface. But as I gazed over this landscape—and even with no appreciable light from the sky, I could see a distance of several miles—I saw at once that quite the reverse was true. I seemed to be standing in the center of a vast shallow bowl. The ground curved upward into the distance. There was no distinct horizon line, only the gradual fading into shadow of the visual landscape. I was standing, obviously, on a concave surface, on the inside, not the outside of the world.

"The situation, as I now understand it, was this: According to the smallest stature I reached, and calling my height at that time roughly six feet, I had descended into the ring at the time I met Lylda several thousand miles, at least. By the way, where is the ring?"

"Here it is," said the Very Young Man, handing it to him. The Chemist replaced it on his finger. "It's pretty important to me now," he said, smiling.

"You bet!" agreed the Very Young Man.

"You can readily understand how I descended such a distance, if you consider the comparative immensity of my stature during the first few hours I was in the ring. It is my understanding that this country through which I passed is a barren waste—merely the atoms of the mineral we call gold.

"Beyond that I entered the hitherto unexplored regions within the atom. The country at that point where I found the forest, I was told later, is habitable for several hundred miles. Around it on all sides lies a desert, across which no one has ever penetrated.

"This surface is the outside of the Oroid world, for so they call their earth. At this point the shell between the outer and inner surface is only a few miles in thickness. The two surfaces do not parallel each other here, so that in descending these tunnels we turned hardly more than an eighth of a complete circle.

"At the city of Arite, where Lylda first took me, and where I had my first view of the inner surface, the curvature is slightly greater than that of our own earth, although, as I have said, in the opposite direction."

"And the space within this curvature—the heavens you have mentioned—how great do you estimate it to be?" asked the Doctor.

"Based on the curvature at Arite it would be about six thousand miles in diameter."

"Has this entire inner surface been explored?" asked the Big Business Man.

"No, only a small portion. The Oroids are not an adventurous people. There are only two nations, less than twelve million people altogether, on a surface nearly as extensive as our own."

"How about those stars?" suggested the Very Young Man.

"I believe they comprise a complete universe similar to our own solar system. There is a central sun-star, around which many of the others revolve. You must understand, though, that these other worlds are infinitely tiny compared to the Oroids, and, if inhabited, support beings nearly as much smaller than the Oroids, as they are smaller than you."

"Great Caesar!" ejaculated the Banker. "Don't let's go into that any deeper!"

"Tell us more about Lylda," prompted the Very Young Man.

"You are insatiable on that point," said the Chemist, laughing. "Well, when we left the sleigh, Lylda took me directly into the city of Arite. I found it an orderly collection of low houses, seemingly built of uniformly cut, highly polished gray blocks. As we passed through the streets, some of which were paved with similar blocks, I was reminded of nothing so much as the old jingles of Spotless Town. Everything was immaculately, inordinately clean. Indeed, the whole city seemed built of some curious form of opaque glass, newly scrubbed and polished.

"Children crowded from the doorways as we advanced, but Lylda dispersed them with a gentle, though firm, command. As we approached the sort of castle I have mentioned, the reason for Lylda's authoritative manner dawned upon me. She was, I soon learned, daughter of one of the most learned men of the nation and was—hand-maiden, do you call it?—to the queen."

"So it was a monarchy?" interrupted the Big Business Man. "I should never have thought that."

"Lylda called their leader a king. In reality he was the president, chosen by the people, for a period of about what we would term twenty years; I learned something about this republic during my stay, but not as much as I would have liked. Politics was not Lylda's strong point, and I had to get it all from her, you know."

"For several days I was housed royally in the castle. Food was served me by an attendant who evidently was assigned solely to look after my needs. At first I was terribly confused by the constant, uniform light, but when I found certain hours set aside for sleep, just as we have them, when I began to eat regularly, I soon fell into the routine of this new life.

"The food was not greatly different from our own, although I found not a single article I could identify. It consisted principally of vegetables and fruits, the latter of an apparently inexhaustible variety.

"Lylda visited me at intervals, and I learned I was awaiting an audience with the king. During these days she made rapid progress with my language—so rapid that I shortly gave up the idea of mastering hers.

"And now, with the growing intimacy between us and our ability to communicate more readily, I learned the simple, tragic story of her race—new details, of course, but the old, old tale of might against right, and the tragedy of a trusting, kindly people, blindly thinking others as just as themselves.

"For thousands of years, since the master life-giver had come from one of the stars to populate the world, the Oroid nation had dwelt in peace and security. These people cared nothing for adventure. No restless thirst for knowledge led them to explore deeply the limitless land surrounding them. Even from the earliest times no struggle for existence, no doctrine of the survival of the fittest, hung over them as with us. No wild animals harassed them; no savages menaced them. A fertile boundless land, a perfect climate, nurtured them tenderly.

"Under such conditions they developed only the softer, gentler qualities of nature. Many laws among them were unnecessary, for life was so simple, so pleasant to live, and the attainment of all the commonly accepted standards of wealth so easy, that the incentive to wrongdoing was almost non-existent.

"Strangely enough, and fortunately, too, no individuals rose among them with the desire for power. Those in command were respected and loved as true workers for the people, and they accepted their authority in the same spirit with which it was given. Indolence, in its highest sense the wonderful art of doing nothing gracefully, played the greatest part in their life.

"Then, after centuries of ease and peaceful security, came the awakening. Almost without warning another nation had come out of the unknown to attack them.

"With the hurt feeling that comes to a child unjustly treated, they all but succumbed to this first onslaught. The abduction of numbers of their women, for such seemed the principal purpose of the invaders, aroused them sufficiently to repel this first crude attack. Their manhood challenged, their anger as a nation awakened for the first time, they sprang as one man into the horror we call war.

"With the defeat of the Malites came another period of ease and security. They had learned no lesson, but went their indolent way, playing through life like the kindly children they were. During this last period some intercourse between them and the Malites took place. The latter people, whose origin was probably nearly opposite them on the inner surface, had by degrees pushed their frontiers closer and closer to the Oroids. Trade between the two was carried on to some extent, but the character of the Malites, their instinctive desire for power, for its own sake, their consideration for themselves as superior beings, caused them to be distrusted and feared by their more simple-minded companion nation.

"You can almost guess the rest, gentlemen. Lylda told me little about the Malites, but the loathing disgust of her manner, her hesitancy even to bring herself to mention them, spoke more eloquently than words.

"Four years ago, as they measure time, came the second attack, and now, in a huge arc, only a few hundred miles from Arite, hung the opposing armies."

The Chemist paused. "That's the condition I found, gentlemen," he said. "Not a strikingly original or unfamiliar situation, was it?"

"By Jove!" remarked the Doctor thoughtfully. "What a curious thing that the environment of our earth should so affect that world inside the ring. It does make you stop and think, doesn't it, to realize how those infinitesimal creatures are actuated now by the identical motives that inspire us?"

"Yet it does seem very reasonable, I should say," the Big Business Man put in.

"Let's have another round of drinks," suggested the Banker. "This is dry work!"

"As a scientist you'd make a magnificent plumber, George!" retorted the Big Business Man. "You're about as helpful in this little gathering as—as an oyster!"

The Very Young Man rang for a waiter.

"I've been thinking—" began the Banker, and stopped at the smile of his companion. "Shut up!" he finished. "That's cheap wit, you know!"

"Go on, George," encouraged the other, "you've been thinking—"

"I've been tremendously interested in this extraordinary story"—he addressed himself to the Chemist—"but there's one point I don't get at all. How many days were you in that ring do you make out?"

"I believe about seven, all told," returned the Chemist.

"But you were only away from us some forty hours. I ought to know, I've been right here." He looked at his crumpled clothes somewhat ruefully.

"The change of time-progress was one of the surprises of my adventure," said the Chemist. "It is easily explained in a general way, although I cannot even attempt a scientific theory of its cause. But I must confess that before I started, the possibility of such a thing never even occurred to me."

"To get a conception of this change you must analyze definitely what time is. We measure and mark it by years, months, and so forth, down to minutes and seconds, all based upon the movements of our earth around its sun. But that is the measurement of time, not time itself. How would you describe time?"

The Big Business Man smiled. "Time," he said, "is what keeps everything from happening at once."

"Very clever," said the Chemist, laughing.

•   •   •

The Doctor leaned forward earnestly. "I should say," he began, "that time is the rate at which we live—the speed at which we successively pass through our existence from birth to death. It's very hard to put intelligibly, but I think I know what I mean," he finished somewhat lamely.

"Exactly so. Time is a rate of life-progress, different for every individual, and only made standard because we take the time-duration of the earth's revolution around the sun, which is constant, and arbitrarily say: 'That is thirty-one million five hundred and thirty-six thousand seconds.' "

"Is time different for every individual?" asked the Banker argumentatively.

"Think a moment," returned the Chemist. "Suppose your brain were to work twice as fast as mine. Suppose your heart beat twice as fast, and all the functions of your body were accelerated in a like manner. What we call a second would certainly seem to you twice as long. Further than that, it actually would be twice as long, so far as you were concerned. Your digestion, instead of taking perhaps four hours, would take two. You would eat twice as often. The desire for sleep would overtake you every twelve hours instead of twenty-four, and you would be satisfied with four hours of unconsciousness instead of eight. In short, you would soon be living a cycle of two days every twenty-four hours. Time then, as we measure it, for you at least, would have doubled—you would be progressing through life at twice the rate that I am through mine."

"That may be theoretically true," the Big Business Man put in. "Practically, though, it has never happened to anyone."

"Of course not, to such a great degree as the instance I put. No one, except in disease, has ever doubled our average rate of life-progress, and lived it out as a balanced, otherwise normal existence. But there is no question that to some much smaller degree we all of us differ one from the other. The difference, however, is so comparatively slight that we can each one reconcile it to the standard measurement of time. And so, outwardly, time is the same for all of us. But inwardly, why, we none of us conceive a minute or an hour to be the same. How do you know how long a minute is to me? More than that, time is not constant even in the same individual. How many hours are shorter to you than others? How many days have been almost interminable? No, instead of being constant, there is nothing more inconstant than time."

"Haven't you confused two different issues?" suggested the Big Business Man. "Granted what you say about the slightly different rate at which different individuals live, isn't it quite another thing, how long time seems to you? A day when you have nothing to do seems long, or, on the other hand, if you are very busy it seems short. But mind, it only *seems* short or long, according to the preoccupation of your mind. That has nothing to do with the speed of your progress through life."

"Ah, but I think it has!" cried the Chemist. "You forget that none of us have all of the one thing to the exclusion of the other. Time seems short; it seems long; and in the end it all averages up, and makes our rate of progress what it is. Now if any of us were to go through life in a calm, deliberate way, making time seem as long as possible, he would live more years, as we measure them, than if he rushed headlong through the days, accomplishing always as much as possible. I mean in neither case to go to the extremes, but only so far as would be consistent with the maintenance of a normal standard of health. How about it?" He turned to the Doctor. "You ought to have an opinion on that."

"I rather think you are right," said the latter thoughtfully, "although I doubt very much if the man who took it easy would do as much during his longer life as the other with his energy would accomplish in the lesser time that had been allotted to him."

"Probably he wouldn't," said the Chemist; "but that does not alter the point we are discussing."

"How does this apply to the world in the ring?" ventured the Very Young Man, somewhat timidly.

"I believe there is a very close relationship between the dimensions of length, breadth, and thickness, and time. Just what connection with them it has, I have no idea. Yet, when size changes, time-rate changes; you have only to look at our own universe to discover that."

"How do you mean?" asked the Very Young Man.

"Why, all life on our earth, in a general way, illustrates the fundamental fact that the larger a thing is, the slower its time-progress is. An elephant, for example, lives more years than we humans. Yet a fly is born, matured, and aged in a few months. There are exceptions, of course; but in a majority of cases it is true.

"So fundamental is this fact that the same condition holds with the heavenly bodies. Mercury, smallest of the planets, travels the fastest. Venus, slower, but faster than the earth, and so on throughout the solar system.

"So I believe that as I diminished in stature, my time-progress became faster and faster. I am seven days older than when I left you day before yesterday. I have lived those seven days, gentlemen, there is no way of getting around that fact."

"This is all tremendously interesting," sighed the Big Business Man; "but not very comprehensible."

IV

STRATEGY AND KISSES

"It was the morning of my third day in the castle," began the Chemist again, "that I was taken by Lylda before the king. We found him seated alone in a little anteroom, overlooking a large courtyard, which we could see was crowded with an expectant, waiting throng. I must explain to you now, that I was considered by Lylda somewhat in the light of a Messiah, come to save her nation from the destruction that threatened it.

"She believed me a supernatural being, which, indeed, if you come to think of it, gentlemen, is exactly what I was. I tried to tell her something of myself and the world I had come from, but the difficulties of language and her smiling insistence and faith in her own conception of me, soon caused me to desist. Thereafter I let her have her own way, and did not attempt any explanation again for some time.

"For several weeks before Lylda found me sleeping by the river's edge, she had made almost a daily pilgrimage to that vicinity. A maidenly premonition, a feeling that had first come to her several years before, told her of my coming, and her father's knowledge and scientific beliefs had led her to the outer surface of the world as the direction in which to look. A curious circumstance, gentlemen, lies in the fact that Lylda clearly remembered the occasion when this first premonition came to her. And in the telling, she described graphically the scene in the cave, where I saw her through the microscope." The Chemist paused an instant and then resumed.

"When we entered the presence of the king, he greeted me quietly, and made me sit by his side, while Lylda knelt on the floor at our feet. The king impressed me as a man about fifty years of age. He was smooth-shaven, with black, wavy hair, reaching his shoulders. He was dressed in the usual tunic, the upper part of his body covered by a quite similar garment, ornamented with a variety of metal objects. His feet were protected with a sort of buskin; at his side hung a crude-looking metal spear.

"The conversation that followed my entrance, lasted perhaps fifteen minutes. Lylda interpreted for us as well as she could, though I must confess we were all three at times completely at a loss. But Lylda's bright, intelligent little face, and the resourcefulness of her gestures, always managed somehow to convey her meaning. The charm and grace of her manner, all during the talk, her winsomeness, and the almost spiritual kindness and tenderness that characterized her, made me feel that she embodied all those qualities with which we of this earth idealize our own womanhood.

"I found myself falling steadily under the spell of her beauty, until—well, gentlemen, it's childish for me to enlarge upon this side of my adventure, you know; but—Lylda means everything to me now, and I'm going back for her just as soon as I possibly can."

"Good for you!" cried the Very Young Man. "Why didn't you bring her with you this time?"

"Let him tell it his own way," remonstrated the Doctor. The Very Young Man subsided with a sigh.

"During our talk," resumed the Chemist, "I learned from the king that Lylda had promised him my assistance in overcoming the enemies that threatened his country. He smilingly told me that our charming little interpreter had assured him I would be able to do this. Lylda's blushing face, as she conveyed this meaning to me, was so thoroughly captivating, that before I knew it, and quite without meaning to, I pulled her up toward me and kissed her.

"The king was more surprised by far than Lylda, at this extraordinary behavior. Obviously neither of them had understood what a kiss meant, although Lylda, by her manner, evidently comprehended pretty thoroughly.

"I told them then, as simply as possible to enable Lylda to get my meaning, that I could, and would gladly aid in their war. I explained, then, that I had the power to change my stature, and could make myself grow very large or very small in a short space of time.

"This, as Lylda evidently told it to him, seemed quite beyond the king's understanding. He comprehended finally, or at least he agreed to believe my statement.

"This led to the consideration of practical questions of how I was to proceed in their war. I had not considered any details before, but now they appeared of the utmost simplicity. All I had to do was to make myself a hundred or two hundred feet high, walk out to the battle lines, and scatter the opposing army like toys."

"What a quaint idea!" said the Banker. "A modern 'Gulliver.'"

The Chemist did not heed this interruption.

"Then like three children we plunged into a discussion of exactly how I was to perform these wonders, the king laughing heartily as we pictured the attack on my tiny enemies.

"He then asked me how I expected to accomplish this change of size, and I very briefly told him of our larger world, and the manner in which I had come from it into his. Then I showed the drugs that I still carried carefully strapped to me. This seemed definitely to convince the king of my sincerity. He rose abruptly to his feet, and strode through a doorway onto a small balcony overlooking the courtyard below.

"As he stepped out into the view of the people, a great cheer arose. He waited quietly for them to stop, and then raised his hand and began speaking. Lylda and I stood hand in hand in the shadow of the doorway, out of sight of the crowd, but with it and the entire courtyard plainly in our view.

"It was a quadrangular enclosure, formed by the four sides of the palace, perhaps three hundred feet across, packed solidly now with people of both sexes, the gleaming whiteness of the upper parts of their bodies, and their upturned faces, making a striking picture.

"For perhaps ten minutes the king spoke steadily, save when he was interrupted by applause. Then he stopped abruptly, and turning, pulled Lylda and me out upon the balcony. The enthusiasm of the crowd doubled at our appearance. I was pushed forward to the balcony rail, where I bowed repeatedly to the cheering throng.

"Just after I left the king's balcony, I met Lylda's father. He was a kindly-faced old gentleman, and took a great interest in me and my story. He it was who told me about the physical conformation of his world, and he seemed to comprehend my explanation of mine.

"That night it rained—a heavy, torrential downpour, such as we have in the tropics. Lylda and I had been talking for some time, and, I must confess, I had been making love to her ardently. I broached now the principal object of my entrance into her world, and, with an eloquence I did not believe I possessed, I pictured the wonders of our own great earth above, begging her to come back with me and live out her life with mine in my world.

"Much of what I said, she probably did not understand, but the main facts were intelligible without question. She listened quietly. When I had finished, and waited for her decision, she reached slowly out and clutched my shoulders, awkwardly making as if to kiss me. In an instant she was in my arms, with a low, happy little cry."

"The clattering fall of rain brought us to ourselves. Rising to her feet, Lylda pulled me over to the window-opening, and together we stood and looked out into the night. The scene before us was beautiful, with a weirdness almost impossible to describe. It was as bright as I had ever seen this world, for even though very heavy clouds hung overhead, the light from the stars was never more than a negligible quantity.

"We were facing the lake—a shining expanse of silver radiation, its surface shifting and crawling, as though a great undulating blanket of silver mist lay upon it. And coming down to meet it from the sky were innumerable lines of silver—a vast curtain of silver cords that broke apart into great strings of pearls when I followed their downward course.

"And then, as I turned to Lylda, I was struck with the extraordinary weirdness of her beauty as never before. The reflected light from the rain had something the quality of our moonlight. Shining on Lylda's body, it tremendously enhanced the iridescence of her skin. And her face, upturned to mine, bore an expression of radiant happiness and peace such as I had never seen before in a woman's countenance."

The Chemist paused, his voice dying away into silence as he sat lost in thought. Then he pulled himself together with a start. "It was a sight, gentlemen, the memory of which I shall cherish all my life.

"The next day was that set for my entrance into the war. Lylda and I had talked nearly all night, and had decided that she was to return with me to my world. By morning the rain had stopped, and we sat together in the window-opening, silenced with the thrill of the wonderful new joy that had come into our hearts.

"The country before us, under the cloudless, starry sky, stretched gray-blue and beautiful into the quivering obscurity of the distance. At our feet lay the city, just awakening into life. Beyond, over the rolling meadows and fields, wound the road that led out to the battle-front, and coming back over it now, we could see an endless line of vehicles. These, as they passed through the street beneath our window, I found were loaded with soldiers, wounded and dying. I shuddered at the sight of one cart in particular, and Lylda pressed closer to me, pleading with her eyes for my help for her stricken people.

"My exit from the castle was made quite a ceremony. A band of music and a guard of several hundred soldiers ushered me forth, walking beside the king, with Lylda a few paces behind. As we passed through the streets of the city, heading for the open country beyond, we were cheered continually by the people who thronged the streets and crowded upon the house-tops to watch us pass.

"Outside Arite I was taken perhaps a mile, where a wide stretch of country gave me the necessary space for my growth. We were standing upon a slight hill, below which, in a vast semicircle, fully a hundred thousand people were watching.

"And now, for the first time, fear overtook me. I realized my situation—saw myself in a de-tached sort of way—a stranger in this extraordinary world, with only the power of my drug to raise me out of it. This drug you must remember, I had not as yet taken. Suppose it were not to act? Or were to act wrongly?

"I glanced around. The king stood before me, quietly waiting my pleasure. Then I turned to Lylda. One glance at her proud, happy little face, and my fear left me as suddenly as it had come. I took her in my arms and kissed her there before that multitude. Then I set her down, and signified to the king I was ready.

"I took a minute quantity of one of the drugs, and as I had done before, sat down with my eyes covered. My sensations were fairly similar to those I have already described. When I looked up after a moment, I found the landscape dwindling to tiny proportions in quite as astonishing a way as it had grown before. The king and Lylda stood now hardly above my ankle.

"A great cry arose from the people—a cry wherein horror, fear, and applause seemed equally mixed. I looked down and saw thousands of them running away in terror.

"Still smaller grew everything within my vision, and then, after a moment, the landscape seemed at rest. I kneeled now upon the ground, carefully, to avoid treading on any of the people around me. I located Lylda and the king after a moment; tiny little creatures less than an inch in height. I was then, I estimated, from their viewpoint, about four hundred feet tall.

"I put my hand flat upon the ground near Lylda, and after a moment she climbed into it, two soldiers lifting her up the side of my thumb as it lay upon the ground. In the hollow of my palm, she lay quite securely, and very carefully I raised her up toward my face. Then, seeing that she was frightened, I set her down again.

"At my feet, hardly more than a few steps away, lay the tiny city of Arite and the lake. I could see all around the latter now, and could make out clearly a line of hills on the other side. Off to the left the road wound up out of sight in the distance. As far as I could see, a line of soldiers was passing out along this road—marching four abreast, with carts at intervals, loaded evidently with supplies; only occasionally, now, vehicles passed in the other direction. Can I make it plain to you, gentlemen, my sensations in changing stature? I felt at first as though I were tremendously high in the air, looking down as from a balloon upon the familiar territory beneath me.

"That feeling passed after a few moments, and I found that my point of view had changed. I no longer felt that I was looking down from a balloon, but felt as a normal person feels. And again I conceived myself but six feet tall, standing above a dainty little toy world. It is all in the viewpoint, of course, and never, during all my changes, was I for more than a moment able to feel of a different stature than I am at this present instant. It was always everything else that changed."

"According to the directions I had received from the king, I started now to follow the course of the road. I found it difficult walking, for the country was dotted with houses, trees, and cultivated fields, and each footstep was a separate problem.

"I progressed in this manner perhaps two miles, covering what the day before I would have called about a hundred and thirty or forty miles. The country became wilder as I advanced, and now was in places crowded with separate collections of troops.

"I have not mentioned the commotion I made in this walk over the country. My coming must have been told widely by couriers the night before, to soldiers and peasantry alike, or the sight of me would have caused utter demoralization. As it was, I must have been terrifying to a tremendous degree. I think the careful way in which I picked my course, stepping in the open as much as possible, helped reassure the people. Behind me, whenever I turned, they seemed rather more curious than fearful, and once or twice when I stopped for a few moments they approached my feet closely. One athletic young soldier caught the loose end of the string of one of my buskins, as it hung over my instep close to the ground, and pulled himself up hand over hand, amid the enthusiastic cheers of his admiring comrades.

"I had walked nearly another mile, when almost in front of me, and perhaps a hundred yards away, I saw a remarkable sight that I did not at first understand. The country here was crossed by a winding river running in a general way at right angles to my line of progress. At the right, near at hand, and on the nearer bank of the river, lay a little city, perhaps half the size of Arite; with its back up against a hill.

"What first attracted my attention was that, from a dark patch across the river which seemed to be woods, pebbles appeared to pop up at intervals, traversing a little arc perhaps as high as my knees, and falling into the city. I watched for a moment and then I understood. There was a siege in progress, and the catapults of the Malites were bombarding the city with rocks.

"I went up a few steps closer, and the pebbles stopped coming. I stood now beside the city, and as I bent over it, I could see by the battered houses the havoc the bombardment had caused. Inert little figures lay in the streets, and I bent lower and inserted my thumb and forefinger between a row of houses and picked one up. It was the body of a woman, partly mashed. I set it down again hastily.

"Then as I stood up, I felt a sting on my leg. A pebble had hit me on the shin and dropped at my feet. I picked it up. It was the size of a small walnut—a huge boulder six feet or more in diameter it would have been in Lylda's eyes. At the thought of her I was struck with a sudden fit of anger. I flung the pebble violently down into the wooded patch and leaped over the river in one bound, landing squarely on both feet in the woods. It was like jumping into a patch of ferns.

"I stamped about me for a moment until a large part of the woods was crushed down. Then I bent over and poked around with my finger. Underneath the tangled wreckage of tiny tree-trunks, lay numbers of the Malites. I must have trodden upon a thousand or more, as one would stamp upon insects.

"The sight sickened me at first, for after all, I could not look upon them as other than men, even though they were only the length of my thumb-nail. I walked a few steps forward, and in all directions I could see swarms of the little creatures running. Then the memory of my coming departure from the world with Lylda, and my promise to the king to rid his land once and for all from these people, made me feel again that they, like vermin, were to be destroyed.

"Without looking directly down, I spent the next two hours stamping over this entire vicinity. Then I ran two or three miles directly toward the country of the Malites, and returning I stamped along the course of the river for a mile or so in both directions. Then I walked back to Arite, again picking my way carefully among crowds of the Oroids, who now feared me so little that I had difficulty in moving without stepping upon them.

"When I had regained my former size, which needed two successive doses of the drug, I found myself surrounded by a crowd of the Oroids, pushing and shoving each other in an effort to get close to me. The news of my success over their enemy had been divined by them, evidently. Lord knows it must have been obvious enough what I was going to do, when they saw me stride away, a being four hundred feet tall.

"Their enthusiasm and thankfulness now was so mixed with awe and reverent worship of me as a divine being, that when I advanced toward Arite they opened a path immediately. The king, accompanied by Lylda, met me at the edge of the city. The latter threw herself into my arms at once, crying with relief to find me the proper size for her world once more.

"I need not go into details of the ceremonies of rejoicing that took place this afternoon. These people seemed little given to pomp and public demonstration. The king made a speech from his balcony, telling them all I had done, and the city was given over to festivities and preparations to receive suitably the returning soldiers."

The Chemist pushed his chair back from the table, and moistened his dry lips with a swallow of water. "I tell you, gentlemen," he continued, "I felt pretty happy that day. It's a wonderful feeling to find yourself the actual savior of a nation."

At that the Doctor jumped to his feet, overturning his chair, and striking the table a blow with his fist that made the glasses dance.

"By God!" he fairly shouted. "That's just what you can be here to us."

The Banker looked startled, while the Very Young Man pulled the Chemist by the coat in his eagerness to be heard. "A few of those pills," he said in a voice that quivered with excitement, "when you are standing near enemy country, and you can kick the houses apart with the toe of your boot."

"Why not?" said the Big Business Man, and silence fell on the group as they stared at each other, awed by the possibilities that suddenly opened up before them.

V

"I MUST GO BACK!"

The tremendous plan for the salvation of their own suffering world through the Chemist's discovery occupied the five friends for some time. Then laying aside this subject, that now had become of the most vital importance to them all, the Chemist resumed his narrative.

"My last evening in the world of the ring, I spent with Lylda, discussing our future, and making plans for the journey. I must tell you now, gentlemen, that never for a moment during my stay in Arite was I once free from an awful dread of this return trip. I tried to conceive what it would be like, and the more I thought about it, the more hazardous it seemed.

"You must realize, when I was growing smaller, coming in, I was able to climb down, or fall or slide down, into the spaces as they opened up. Going back, I could only imagine the world as closing in upon me, crushing me to death unless I could find a larger space immediately above into which I could climb.

"And as I talked with Lylda about this and tried to make her understand what I hardly understood myself, I gradually was brought to realize the full gravity of the danger confronting us. If only I had made the trip out once before, I could have ventured it with her. But as I looked at her fragile little body, to expose it to the terrible possibilities of such a journey was unthinkable.

"There was another question, too, that troubled me. I had been gone from you nearly a week, and you were only to wait for me two days. I believed firmly that I was living at a faster rate, and that probably my time with you had not expired. But I did not know. And suppose, when I had come out on to the surface of the ring, one of you had had it on his finger walking along the street? No, I did not want Lylda with me in that event.

"And so I told her—made her understand—that she must stay behind, and that I would come back for her. She did not protest. She said nothing—just looked up into my face with wide, staring eyes and a little quiver of her lips. Then she clutched my hand and fell into a low, sobbing cry.

"I held her in my arms for a few moments, so little, so delicate, so human in her sorrow, and yet almost superhuman in her radiant beauty. Soon she stopped crying and smiled up at me bravely.

"Next morning I left. Lylda took me through the tunnels and back into the forest by the river's edge where I had first met her. There we parted. I can see, now, her pathetic, drooping little figure as she trudged back to the tunnel.

"When she had disappeared, I sat down to plan out my journey. I resolved now to reverse as nearly as possible the steps I had taken coming in. Acting on this decision, I started back to that portion of the forest where I had trampled it down.

"I found the place without difficulty, stopping once on the way to eat a few berries, and some of the food I carried with me. Then I took a small amount of one of the drugs, and in a few moments the forest-trees had dwindled into tiny twigs beneath my feet.

"I started now to find the huge incline down which I had fallen, and when I reached it, after some hours of wandering, I followed its bottom edge to where a pile of rocks and dirt marked my former landing place. The rocks were much larger than I remembered them, and so I knew I was not so large, now, as when I was here before.

"Remembering the amount of the drug I had taken coming down, I took now twelve of the pills. Then, in a sudden panic, I hastily took two of the others. The result made my head swim most horribly. I sat or lay down, I forget which. When I looked up I saw the hills beyond the river and forest coming toward me, yet dwindling away beneath my feet as they approached. The incline seemed folding up upon itself like a telescope. As I watched, its upper edge came into view, a curved, luminous line against the blackness above. Every instant it crawled down closer, more sharply curved, and its inclined surface grew steeper.

"All this time, as I stood still, the ground beneath my feet seemed to be moving. It was crawling toward me, and folding up underneath where I was standing. Frequently I had to move to avoid rocks that came at me and passed under my feet into nothingness.

"Then, all at once, I realized that I had been stepping constantly backward, to avoid the inclined wall as it shoved itself toward me. I turned to see what was behind, and horror made my flesh creep at what I saw. A black, forbidding wall, much like the incline in front, entirely encircled me. It was hardly more than half a mile away, and towered four or five thousand feet overhead.

"And as I stared in terror, I could see it closing in, the line of its upper edge coming steadily closer and lower. I looked wildly around with an overpowering impulse to run. In every direction towered this rocky wall, inexorably swaying in to crush me.

"I think I fainted. When I came to myself the scene had not greatly changed. I was lying at the bottom and against one wall of a circular pit, now about a thousand feet in diameter and nearly twice as deep. The wall all around I could see was almost perpendicular, and it seemed impossible to ascend its smooth, shining sides. The action of the drug had evidently worn off, for everything was quite still.

"My fear had now left me, for I remembered this circular pit quite well. I walked over to its center, and looking around and up to its top, I estimated distance carefully. Then I took two more of the pills.

"Immediately the familiar, sickening, crawling sensation began again. As the walls closed in upon me, I kept carefully in the center of the pit. Steadily they crept in. Now only a few hundred feet away! Now only a few paces—and then I reached out and touched both sides at once with my hands.

"I tell you, gentlemen, it was a terrifying sensation to stand in that well (as it now seemed) and feel its walls closing up with irresistible force. But now the upper edge was within reach of my fingers. I leaped upward and hung for a moment, then pulled myself up and scrambled out, tumbling in a heap on the ground above. As I recovered myself, I looked again at the hole out of which I had escaped; it was hardly big enough to contain my fist.

"I knew, now, I was at the bottom of the scratch. But how different it looked than before. It seemed this time a long, narrow cañon, hardly more than sixty feet across. I glanced up and saw the blue sky overhead that I knew was the space of this room above the ring.

"The problem now was quite a different one than getting out of the pit, for I saw that the scratch was so deep in proportion to its width that if I let myself get too big, I would be crushed by its walls before I could jump out. It would be necessary, therefore, to stay comparatively small and climb up its side.

"I selected what appeared to be an especially rough section, and took a portion of another of the pills. Then I started to climb. After an hour the buskins on my feet were torn to fragments, and I was bruised and battered as you saw me. I see, now, how I could have made both the descent into the ring, and my journey back, with comparatively little effort, but I did the best I knew at the time."

"When the cañon was about ten feet in width, and I had been climbing arduously for several hours, I found myself hardly more than fifteen or twenty feet above its bottom. And I was still almost that far from the top. With the stature I had then attained, I could have climbed the remaining distance easily, but for the fact that the wall above had grown too smooth to afford foothold. The effects of the drug had again worn off, and I sat down and prepared to take another dose. I did so—the smallest amount I could—and held ready in my hand a pill of the other kind in case of emergency. Steadily the walls closed in.

"A terrible feeling of dizziness now came over me. I clutched the rock beside which I was sitting, and it seemed to melt like ice beneath my grasp. Then I remembered seeing the edge of the cañon within reach above my head, and with my last remaining strength, I pulled myself up, and fell upon the surface of the ring. You know the rest. I took another dose of the powder, and in a few minutes was back among you."

The Chemist stopped speaking, and looked at his friends. "Well," he said, "you've heard it all. What do you think of it?"

"It is a terrible thing to me," sighed the Very Young Man, "that you did not bring Lylda with you."

"It would have been a terrible thing if I had brought her. But I am going back for her."

"When do you plan to go back?" asked the Doctor after a moment.

"As soon as I can—in a day or two," answered the Chemist.

"Before you do your work here? You must not," remonstrated the Big Business Man. "Our war here needs you, our nation, the whole cause of liberty and freedom needs you. You cannot go."

"Lylda needs me, too," returned the Chemist. "I have an obligation toward her now, you know, quite apart from my own feelings. Understand me, gentlemen," he continued earnestly, "I do not mean to place myself and mine before the great fight for democracy and justice being waged in this world. That would be absurd. But it is not quite that way, actually; I can go back for Lylda and return here in a week. That week will make little difference to the war. On the other hand, if I go to Europe first, it may take me a good many months to complete my task, and during that time Lylda will be using up her life several times faster than I do. No, gentlemen, I am going to her first."

Two days later the company met again in the privacy of the clubroom. When they had finished dinner, the Chemist began in his usual quiet way:

"I am going to ask you this time, gentlemen, to give me a full week. There are four of you— six hours a day of watching for each. It need not be too great a hardship. You see," he continued, as they nodded in agreement, "I want to spend a longer period in the ring world this time. I may never go back, and I want to learn, in the interest of science, as much about it as I can. I was there such a short time before, and it was all so strange and remarkable, I confess I learned practically nothing.

"I told you all I could of its history. But of its art, its science, and all its sociological and economic questions, I got hardly more than a glimpse. It is a world and a people far less advanced than ours, yet with something we have not, and probably never will have—the universally distributed milk of human kindness. Yes, gentlemen, it is a world well worth studying."

The Banker came out of a brown study. "How about your formulas for these drugs?" he asked abruptly; "where are they?" The Chemist tapped his forehead smilingly. "Well, hadn't

you better leave them with us?" the Banker pursued. "The hazards of your trip—you can't tell, you know—"

"Don't misunderstand me, gentlemen," broke in the Chemist, "I wouldn't give you those formulas if my life and even Lylda's depended on it. There again you do not differentiate between the individual and the race. These drugs are the most powerful thing for good in the world today. But they are equally as powerful for evil. I would stake my life on what you would do, but I will not stake the life of a nation."

"I know what I'd do if I had the formulas," began the Very Young Man.

"Yes, but I don't know what you'd do," laughed the Chemist. "Don't you see I'm right?"

They admitted they did, though the Banker acquiesced very grudgingly.

"The time of my departure is at hand. Is there anything else, gentlemen, before I leave you?" asked the Chemist, beginning to disrobe.

"Please tell Lylda I want very much to meet her," said the Very Young Man earnestly, and they all laughed.

When the room was cleared, and the handkerchief and the ring in place once more, the Chemist turned to them again. "Good-by, my friends," he said, holding out his hands. "One week from to-night, at most." Then he took the pills.

No unusual incident marked his departure. The last they saw of him he was sitting on the ring near the scratch.

Then passed the slow days of watching, each taking his turn for the allotted six hours.

By the fifth day, they began to hourly expect the Chemist, but it passed through its weary length, and he did not come. The sixth day dragged by, and then came the last—the day he had promised would end their watching. Still he did not come, and in the evening they gathered, and all four watched together, each unwilling to miss the return of the adventurer and his woman from another world.

But the minutes lengthened into hours, and midnight found the white-faced little group,

THE GIRL IN THE GOLDEN ATOM

hopeful yet hopeless, with fear tugging at their hearts. A second week passed, and still they watched, explaining with an optimism they could none of them feel, the non-appearance of their friend. At the end of the second week they met again to talk the situation over, a dull feeling of fear and horror possessing them. The Doctor was the first to voice what now each of them was forced to believe. "I guess it's all useless," he said. "He's not coming back."

"I don't hardly dare give him up," said the Big Business Man.

"Me, too," agreed the Very Young Man sadly.

The Doctor sat for some time in silence, thoughtfully regarding the ring. "My friends," he began finally, "this is too big a thing to deal with in any but the most careful way. I can't imagine what is going on inside that ring, but I do know what is happening in our world, and what our friend's return means to civilization here. Under the circumstances, therefore, I cannot, I will not give him up.

"I am going to put that ring in a museum and pay for having it watched indefinitely. Will you join me?" He turned to the Big Business Man as he spoke.

"Make it a threesome," said the Banker gruffly. "What do you take me for?" and the Very Young Man sighed with the tragedy of youth.

And so to-day, if you like, you may go and see the ring. It lies in the Museum of the American Society for Biological Research. You will find it near the center of the third gallery, lying on its black silk handkerchief, and covered by a glass bell. The air in the bell is renewed constantly, and near at hand sit two armed guards, watching day and night. And as you stand before it, thinking of the wonderful world within its atoms, you well may shudder at your infinite unimportance as an individual and yet glow with pride at your divine omnipotence as a fragment of human life.

TO SERVE MAN

DAMON KNIGHT

DAMON FRANCIS KNIGHT (1922–2002) hitchhiked from his native Oregon to New York City when he was nineteen and joined the Futurians, a collective of science-fiction fans, professionals, and authors (including Isaac Asimov, Frederik Pohl, and Donald Wollheim). He sold his first story, "Resilience," the same year. In addition to writing science fiction, Knight became the genre's leading reviewer and critic, attempting to bring the same standards to science fiction that other critics brought to literary fiction. His essays and reviews were collected in *In Search of Wonder* (1956), often cited as the first major critical study of modern science fiction. He also founded the Science Fiction Writers of America in 1965 and served as its first president. In 1994, the organization named him a Grand Master for lifetime achievement, and renamed it the Damon Knight Memorial Grand Master Award in his honor upon his death in 2002. A noted anthologist and editor, Knight is known for discovering Frank Herbert's *Dune* in 1965—though he lost his job due to the book's high production costs and poor sales.

Knight's most famous work is the short story "To Serve Man," which was adapted as one of the most popular episodes of Rod Serling's *The Twilight Zone*. It first aired on March 2, 1962, in the third season of the successful series with a script by Serling. Directed by Richard L. Bare, it starred Lloyd Bochner and Susan Cummings, with Richard Kiel as the leader of the Kanamits; Kiel later starred as the steel-toothed giant Jaws in the James Bond movies *The Spy Who Loved Me* (1977) and *Moonraker* (1979).

"To Serve Man" was first published in the November 1950 issue of *Galaxy Science Fiction;* over five decades later, it was given a Retro Hugo Award as the best short story of its year. In a poignant prefatory note to the story in its publication in *The Best of Damon Knight* (New York: Pocket, 1976), Knight writes: " 'To Serve Man' was written in 1950, when I was living in Greenwich Village and my unhappy first marriage was breaking up. I wrote it in one afternoon, while my wife was out with another man."

TO SERVE MAN

DAMON KNIGHT

THE KANAMIT were not very pretty, it's true. They looked something like pigs and something like people, and that is not an attractive combination. Seeing them for the first time shocked you; that was their handicap. When a thing with the countenance of a fiend comes from the stars and offers a gift, you are disinclined to accept.

I don't know what we expected interstellar visitors to look like—those who thought about it at all, that is. Angels, perhaps, or something too alien to be really awful. Maybe that's why we were all so horrified and repelled when they landed in their great ships and we saw what they really were like.

The Kanamit were short and very hairy— thick, bristly brown-gray hair all over their abominably plump bodies. Their noses were snoutlike and their eyes small, and they had thick hands of three fingers each. They wore green leather harness and green shorts, but I think the shorts were a concession to our notions of public decency. The garments were quite modishly cut, with slash pockets and half-belts in the back. The Kanamit had a sense of humor, anyhow.

There were three of them at this session of the U.N., and, lord, I can't tell you how queer it looked to see them there in the middle of a solemn plenary session—three fat piglike creatures in green harness and shorts, sitting at the long table below the podium, surrounded by the packed arcs of delegates from every nation.

They sat correctly upright, politely watching each speaker. Their flat ears drooped over the earphones. Later on, I believe, they learned every human language, but at this time they knew only French and English.

They seemed perfectly at ease—and that, along with their humor, was a thing that tended to make me like them. I was in the minority; I didn't think they were trying to put anything over.

The delegate from Argentina got up and said that his government was interested in the demonstration of a new cheap power source, which the Kanamit had made at the previous session, but that the Argentine government could not commit itself as to its future policy without a much more thorough examination.

It was what all the delegates were saying, but I had to pay particular attention to Señor Valdes, because he tended to sputter and his diction was bad. I got through the translation all right, with only one or two momentary hesitations, and then switched to the Polish–English line to hear how Grigori was doing with Janciewicz. Janciewicz was the cross Grigori had to bear, just as Valdes was mine.

Janciewicz repeated the previous remarks with a few ideological variations, and then the Secretary-General recognized the delegate from France, who introduced Dr. Denis Lévêque, the criminologist, and a great deal of complicated equipment was wheeled in.

Dr. Lévêque remarked that the question in many people's minds had been aptly expressed by the delegate from the U.S.S.R. at the preceding session, when he demanded, "What is the motive of the Kanamit? What is their purpose in offering us these unprecedented gifts, while asking nothing in return?"

The doctor then said, "At the request of several delegates and with the full consent of our guests, the Kanamit, my associates and I have made a series of tests upon the Kanamit with the equipment which you see before you. These tests will now be repeated."

A murmur ran through the chamber. There was a fusillade of flashbulbs, and one of the TV cameras moved up to focus on the instrument board of the doctor's equipment. At the same time, the huge television screen behind the podium lighted up, and we saw the blank faces of two dials, each with its pointer resting at zero, and a strip of paper tape with a stylus point resting against it.

The doctor's assistants were fastening wires to the temples of one of the Kanamit, wrapping a canvas-covered rubber tube around his forearm, and taping something to the palm of his right hand.

In the screen, we saw the paper tape begin to move while the stylus traced a slow zigzag pattern along it. One of the needles began to jump rhythmically; the other flipped halfway over and stayed there, wavering slightly.

"These are the standard instruments for testing the truth of a statement," said Dr. Lévêque. "Our first object, since the physiology of the Kanamit is unknown to us, was to determine whether or not they react to these tests as human beings do. We will now repeat one of the many experiments which were made in the endeavor to discover this."

He pointed to the first dial. "This instrument registers the subject's heartbeat. This shows the electrical conductivity of the skin in the palm of his hand, a measure of perspiration, which increases under stress. And this—" pointing to the tape-and-stylus device—"shows the pattern and intensity of the electrical waves emanating from his brain. It has been shown, with human subjects, that all these readings vary markedly depending upon whether the subject is speaking the truth."

He picked up two large pieces of cardboard, one red and one black. The red one was a square about three feet on a side; the black was a rectangle three and a half feet long. He addressed himself to the Kanama.

"Which of these is longer than the other?"

"The red," said the Kanama.

Both needles leaped wildly, and so did the line on the unrolling tape.

"I shall repeat the question," said the doctor. "Which of these is longer than the other?"

"The black," said the creature.

This time the instruments continued in their normal rhythm.

"How did you come to this planet?" asked the doctor.

"Walked," replied the Kanama.

Again the instruments responded, and there was a subdued ripple of laughter in the chamber.

"Once more," said the doctor. "How did you come to this planet?"

"In a spaceship," said the Kanama, and the instruments did not jump.

The doctor again faced the delegates. "Many such experiments were made," he said, "and my colleagues and myself are satisfied that the mechanisms are effective. Now—" he turned to the Kanama—"I shall ask our distinguished guest to reply to the question put at the last session by the delegate of the U.S.S.R.—namely, what is the motive of the Kanamit people in offering these great gifts to the people of Earth?"

The Kanama rose. Speaking this time in English, he said, "On my planet there is a saying, 'There are more riddles in a stone than in a philosopher's head.' The motives of intelligent beings, though they may at times appear obscure, are simple things compared to the complex workings of the natural universe. Therefore I hope that the people of Earth will understand, and believe, when I tell you that our mission upon your planet is simply this—to bring to you the peace and plenty which we ourselves enjoy, and which we have in the past brought to other races throughout the galaxy. When your world has no more hunger, no more war, no more needless suffering, that will be our reward."

And the needles had not jumped once.

The delegate from the Ukraine jumped to his feet, asking to be recognized, but the time was up and the Secretary-General closed the session.

I met Grigori as we were leaving the chamber. His face was red with excitement. "Who promoted that circus?" he demanded.

"The tests looked genuine to me," I told him.

"A circus!" he said vehemently. "A second-rate farce! If they were genuine, Peter, why was debate stifled?"

"There'll be time for debate tomorrow, surely."

"Tomorrow the doctor and his instruments will be back in Paris. Plenty of things can happen before tomorrow. In the name of sanity, man, how can anybody trust a thing that looks as if it ate the baby?"

I was a little annoyed. I said, "Are you sure you're not more worried about their politics than their appearance?"

He said, "Bah," and went away.

The next day reports began to come in from government laboratories all over the world where the Kanamit's power source was being tested. They were wildly enthusiastic. I don't understand such things myself, but it seemed that those little metal boxes would give more electrical power than an atomic pile, for next to nothing and nearly forever. And it was said that they were so cheap to manufacture that everybody in the world could have one of his own. In the early afternoon there were reports that seventeen countries had already begun to set up factories to turn them out.

The next day the Kanamit turned up with plans and specimens of a gadget that would increase the fertility of any arable land by 60 to 100 per cent. It speeded the formation of nitrates in the soil, or something. There was nothing in the

newscasts any more but stories about the Kanamit. The day after that, they dropped their bombshell.

"You now have potentially unlimited power and increased food supply," said one of them. He pointed with his three-fingered hand to an instrument that stood on the table before him. It was a box on a tripod, with a parabolic reflector on the front of it. "We offer you today a third gift which is at least as important as the first two."

He beckoned to the TV men to roll their cameras into closeup position. Then he picked up a large sheet of cardboard covered with drawings and English lettering. We saw it on the large screen above the podium; it was all clearly legible.

"We are informed that this broadcast is being relayed throughout your world," said the Kanama. "I wish that everyone who has equipment for taking photographs from television screens would use it now."

The Secretary-General leaned forward and asked a question sharply, but the Kanama ignored him.

"This device," he said, "generates a field in which no explosive, of whatever nature, can detonate."

There was an uncomprehending silence.

The Kanama said, "It cannot now be suppressed. If one nation has it, all must have it." When nobody seemed to understand, he explained bluntly, "There will be no more war."

That was the biggest news of the millennium, and it was perfectly true. It turned out that the explosions the Kanama was talking about included gasoline and Diesel explosions. They had simply made it impossible for anybody to mount or equip a modern army.

We could have gone back to bows and arrows, of course, but that wouldn't have satisfied the military. Besides, there wouldn't be any reason to make war. Every nation would soon have everything.

Nobody ever gave another thought to those lie-detector experiments, or asked the Kanamit what their politics were. Grigori was put out; he had nothing to prove his suspicions.

I quit my job with the U.N. a few months later, because I foresaw that it was going to die under me anyhow. U.N. business was booming at the time, but after a year or so there was going to be nothing for it to do. Every nation on Earth was well on the way to being completely self-supporting; they weren't going to need much arbitration.

I accepted a position as translator with the Kanamit Embassy, and it was there that I ran into Grigori again. I was glad to see him, but I couldn't imagine what he was doing there.

"I thought you were on the opposition," I said. "Don't tell me you're convinced the Kanamit are all right."

He looked rather shamefaced. "They're not what they look, anyhow," he said.

It was as much of a concession as he could decently make, and I invited him down to the embassy lounge for a drink. It was an intimate kind of place, and he grew confidential over the second daiquiri.

"They fascinate me," he said. "I hate them instinctively still—that hasn't changed—but I can evaluate it. You were right, obviously; they mean us nothing but good. But do you know—" he leaned across the table—"the question of the Soviet delegate was never answered."

I am afraid I snorted.

"No, really," he said. "They told us what they wanted to do—'to bring to you the peace and plenty which we ourselves enjoy.' But they didn't say *why*."

"Why do missionaries—"

"Missionaries be damned!" he said angrily. "Missionaries have a religious motive. If these creatures have a religion, they haven't once mentioned it. What's more, they didn't send a missionary group; they sent a diplomatic delegation—a group representing the will and policy of their whole people. Now just what have the Kanamit, as a people or a nation, got to gain from our welfare?"

I said, "Cultural—"

"Cultural cabbage soup! No, it's something less obvious than that, something obscure that belongs to their psychology and not to ours. But trust me, Peter, there is no such thing as a completely disinterested altruism. In one way or another, they have something to gain."

"And that's why you're here," I said. "To try to find out what it is."

"Correct. I wanted to get on one of the ten-year exchange groups to their home planet, but I couldn't; the quota was filled a week after they made the announcement. This is the next best thing. I'm studying their language, and you know that language reflects the basic assumptions of the people who use it. I've got a fair command of the spoken lingo already. It's not hard, really, and there are hints in it. Some of the idioms are quite similar to English. I'm sure I'll get the answer eventually."

"More power," I said, and we went back to work.

I saw Grigori frequently from then on, and he kept me posted about his progress. He was highly excited about a month after that first meeting; said he'd got hold of a book of the Kanamit's and was trying to puzzle it out. They wrote in ideographs, worse than Chinese, but he was determined to fathom it if it took him years. He wanted my help.

Well, I was interested in spite of myself, for I knew it would be a long job. We spent some evenings together, working with material from Kanamit bulletin boards and so forth, and with the extremely limited English–Kanamit dictionary they issued to the staff. My conscience bothered me about the stolen book, but gradually I became absorbed by the problem. Languages are my field, after all. I couldn't help being fascinated.

We got the title worked out in a few weeks. It was *How to Serve Man*, evidently a handbook they were giving out to new Kanamit members of the embassy staff. They had new ones in, all the time now, a shipload about once a month;

they were opening all kinds of research laboratories, clinics and so on. If there was anybody on Earth besides Grigori who still distrusted those people, he must have been somewhere in the middle of Tibet.

It was astonishing to see the changes that had been wrought in less than a year. There were no more standing armies, no more shortages, no unemployment. When you picked up a newspaper you didn't see H-BOMB or SATELLITE leaping out at you; the news was always good. It was a hard thing to get used to. The Kanamit were working on human biochemistry, and it was known around the embassy that they were nearly ready to announce methods of making our race taller and stronger and healthier—practically a race of supermen—and they had a potential cure for heart disease and cancer.

I didn't see Grigori for a fortnight after we finished working out the title of the book; I was on a long-overdue vacation in Canada. When I got back, I was shocked by the change in his appearance.

"What on earth is wrong, Grigori?" I asked. "You look like the very devil."

"Come down to the lounge."

I went with him, and he gulped a stiff Scotch as if he needed it.

"Come on, man, what's the matter?" I urged.

"The Kanamit have put me on the passenger list for the next exchange ship," he said. "You, too, otherwise I wouldn't be talking to you."

"Well," I said, "but—"

"They're not altruists."

I tried to reason with him. I pointed out they'd made Earth a paradise compared to what it was before. He only shook his head.

Then I said, "Well, what about those lie-detector tests?"

"A farce," he replied, without heat. "I said so at the time, you fool. They told the truth, though, as far as it went."

"And the book?" I demanded, annoyed. "What about that—*How to Serve Man*? That wasn't put there for you to read. They *mean* it. How do you explain that?"

"I've read the first paragraph of that book," he said. "Why do you suppose I haven't slept for a week?"

I said, "Well?" and he smiled a curious, twisted smile.

"It's a cookbook," he said.

ARMAGEDDON—2419 A.D.

PHILIP FRANCIS NOWLAN

THE MOST influential science-fiction character of all time is Anthony "Buck" Rogers, the creation of a relatively ordinary writer named Philip Francis Nowlan (1888–1940), who produced little other work of significance. The first appearance of Rogers was in an unsuccessful and now apparently lost play produced in 1927. The first of two short novels featuring him, "Armageddon—2419 A.D.," ran in the pulp magazine *Amazing Stories* the following year, and its sequel, "The Airlords of Han," in March of 1929.

Anthony Rogers, formerly an American pilot in World War I, is exploring an abandoned coal mine for the American Radioactive Gas Corporation when a sudden cave-in traps him in a state of deep hibernation in a pocket of radioactive gas. Released by a seismic shift, he awakens 492 years later to learn that China has conquered most of the world, including the United States. The Chinese, known as the Han Airlords, now live in sophisticated luxury in fifteen large U.S. cities such as Nu-Yok and Bah-flo, while the surviving Americans live as scattered tribes (called "gangs"), trying to avoid extermination by the Mongolians while planning to retake the country from their cruel but increasingly dissolute Han Airlord oppressors. This important story and its sequel anticipated numerous scientific and military developments, including the bazooka, walkie-talkies, jet planes, and infrared guns for night fighting.

The author quickly saw the potential for a juvenile version and created (with artist Dick Calkins) the first science-fiction comic strip, *Buck Rogers 2429 A.D.*, which premiered on January 7, 1929, and continued until 1968. The title changed annually to keep it exactly five hundred years in the future, finally becoming simply *Buck Rogers in the 25th Century* in 1933. The strip heavily influenced Alex Raymond as he was developing his similar Flash Gordon strip (which would become more successful because of its superior art and better story lines). Nowlan's strip was also the basis for the radio series *Buck Rogers in the 25th Century*, which aired from 1931 to 1939; the serial film *Buck Rogers* (1939), which lived on in reedited incarnations such as *Planet Outlaws* (1953) and *Buck Rogers: Destination Saturn* (1965); and two television series, one from 1950 to 1951 and the other from 1979 to 1981. Strangely, one of the two most famous science-fiction heroes of all time (along with Flash Gordon) was named

Anthony Rogers in his pulp appearances; the shorter and more familiar "Buck" was a product of the comic strip.

"Armageddon—2419 A.D." was first published in the November 1928 issue of *Amazing Stories;* it was lightly revised and first published in book form along with its sequel as *Armageddon 2419* (New York: Avalon, 1962).

ARMAGEDDON—2419 A.D.

PHILIP FRANCIS NOWLAN

*Seen upon the ultroscope view plate, the battle looked as though
it were being fought in daylight, perhaps on a cloudy day,
while the explosions of the rockets appeared as flashes of extra
brilliance.*

ELSEWHERE I HAVE set down, for whatever interest they have in this, the 25th Century, my personal recollections of the 20th Century.

Now it occurs to me that my memoirs of the 25th Century may have an equal interest five hundred years from now—particularly in view of that unique perspective from which I have seen the 25th Century, entering it as I did, in one leap across a gap of 492 years.

This statement requires elucidation. There are still many in the world who are not familiar with my unique experience. Five centuries from now there may be many more, especially if civilization is fated to endure any worse convulsions than those which have occurred between 1975 A.D. and the present time.

I should state, therefore, that I, Anthony Rogers, am, so far as I know, the only man alive whose normal span of eighty-one years of life has been spread over a period of 573 years. To be precise, I lived the first twenty-nine years of my life between 1898 and 1927; the other fifty-two since 2419. The gap between these two, a period of nearly five hundred years, I spent in a state of suspended animation, free from the ravages of catabolic processes, and without any apparent effect on my physical or mental faculties.

When I began my long sleep, man had just begun his real conquest of the air in a sudden series of trans-oceanic flights in airplanes driven by internal combustion motors. He had barely begun to speculate on the possibilities of harnessing sub-atomic forces, and had made no further practical penetration into the field of ethereal pulsations than the primitive radio and television of that day. The United States of America was the most powerful nation in the world, its political, financial, industrial and scientific influence being supreme; and in the arts also it was rapidly climbing into leadership.

I awoke to find the America I knew a total wreck—to find Americans a hunted race in their own land, hiding in the dense forests that covered the shattered and leveled ruins of their once magnificent cities, desperately preserving, and struggling to develop in their secret retreats, the remnants of their culture and science—and the undying flame of their sturdy independence.

World domination was in the hands of Mongolians and the center of world power lay in inland China, with Americans one of the few races of mankind unsubdued—and it must be admitted, in fairness to the truth, not worth the trouble of subduing in the eyes of the Han Airlords who ruled North America as titular tributaries of the Most Magnificent.

For they needed not the forests in which the Americans lived, nor the resources of the vast territories these forests covered. With the perfection to which they had reduced the synthetic production of necessities and luxuries, their remarkable development of scientific processes and mechanical accomplishment of work, they had no economic desire for the enslaved labor of an unruly race.

They had all they needed for their magnificently luxurious and degraded scheme of civilization within the walls of the fifteen cities of sparkling glass they had flung skyward on the sites of ancient American centers, into the bowels of the earth underneath them, and with relatively small surrounding areas of agriculture.

Complete domination of the air rendered communication between these centers a matter of ease and safety. Occasional destructive raids on the waste lands were considered all that was necessary to keep the "wild" Americans on the run within the shelter of their forests, and prevent their becoming a menace to the Han civilization.

But nearly three hundred years of easily maintained security, the last century of which had been nearly sterile in scientific, social and economic progress, had softened and devitalized the Hans.

It had likewise developed, beneath the protecting foliage of the forest, the growth of a vigorous new American civilization, remarkable in the mobility and flexibility of its organization, in its conquest of almost insuperable obstacles, in the development and guarding of its industrial and scientific resources, all in anticipation of that "Day of Hope" to which it had been looking forward for generations, when it would be strong enough to burst from the green chrysalis of the forests, soar into the upper air lanes and destroy the Yellow Incubus.

At the time I awoke, the "Day of Hope" was almost at hand. I shall not attempt to set forth a detailed history of the Second War of Independence, for that has been recorded already by better historians than I am. Instead I shall confine myself largely to the part I was fortunate enough to play in this struggle and in the events leading up to it.

It all resulted from my interest in radioactive gases. During the latter part of 1927 my company, the American Radioactive Gas Corporation, had been keeping me busy investigating reports of unusual phenomena observed in certain abandoned coal mines near the Wyoming Valley, in Pennsylvania.

With two assistants and a complete equipment of scientific instruments, I began the exploration of a deserted working in a mountainous district, where several weeks before, a number of mining engineers had reported traces of carnotite* and what they believed to be radioactive gases. Their report was not without foundation, it was apparent from the outset, for in our examination of the upper levels of the mine, our instruments indicated a vigorous radioactivity.

On the morning of December 15th, we descended to one of the lowest levels. To our surprise, we found no water there. Obviously it had drained off through some break in the strata. We noticed too that the rock in the side walls of the shaft was soft, evidently due to the radioactivity, and pieces crumbled under foot rather easily. We made our way cautiously down the shaft, when suddenly the rotted timbers above us gave way.

I jumped ahead, barely escaping the avalanche of coal and soft rock, but my companions, who

*A hydrovanadate of uranium, and other metals; used as a source of radium compounds.

were several paces behind me, were buried under it, and undoubtedly met instant death.

I was trapped. Return was impossible. With my electric torch I explored the shaft to its end, but could find no other way out. The air became increasingly difficult to breathe, probably from the rapid accumulation of the radioactive gas. In a little while my senses reeled and I lost consciousness.

When I awoke, there was a cool and refreshing circulation of air in the shaft. I had no thought that I had been unconscious more than a few hours, although it seems that the radioactive gas had kept me in a state of suspended animation for something like 500 years. My awakening, I figured out later, had been due to some shifting of the strata which reopened the shaft and cleared the atmosphere in the working. This must have been the case, for I was able to struggle back up the shaft over a pile of debris, and stagger up the long incline to the mouth of the mine, where an entirely different world, overgrown with a vast forest and no visible sign of human habitation, met my eyes.

I shall pass over the days of mental agony that followed in my attempt to grasp the meaning of it all. There were times when I felt that I was on the verge of insanity. I roamed the unfamiliar forest like a lost soul. Had it not been for the necessity of improvising traps and crude clubs with which to slay my food, I believe I should have gone mad.

Suffice it to say, however, that I survived this psychic crisis. I shall begin my narrative proper with my first contact with Americans of the year 2419 A.D.

FLOATING MEN

My first glimpse of a human being of the 25th Century was obtained through a portion of woodland where the trees were thinly scattered with a dense forest beyond.

I had been wandering along aimlessly, and hopelessly, musing over my strange fate, when I noticed a figure that cautiously backed out of the dense growth across the glade. I was about to call out joyfully, but there was something furtive about the figure that prevented me. The boy's attention (for it seemed to be a lad of fifteen or sixteen) was centered tensely on the heavy growth of trees from which he had just emerged.

He was clad in rather tight-fitting garments entirely of green, and wore a helmet-like cap of the same color. High around his waist he wore a broad thick belt, which bulked up in the back across the shoulders, into something of the proportions of a knapsack.

As I was taking in these details, there came a vivid flash and heavy detonation, like that of a hand grenade, not far to the left of him. He threw up an arm and staggered a bit in a queer, gliding way; then he recovered himself and slipped cautiously away from the place of the explosion, crouching slightly, and still facing the denser part of the forest. Every few steps he would raise his arm, and point into the forest with something he held in his hand. Wherever he pointed there was a terrific explosion, deeper in among the trees. It came to me then that he was shooting with some form of pistol, though there was neither flash nor detonation from the muzzle of the weapon.

After firing several times, he seemed to come to a sudden resolution, and turning in my general direction, leaped—to my amazement sailing through the air between the sparsely scattered trees in such a jump as I had never in my life seen before. That leap must have carried him a full fifty feet, although at the height of his arc, he was not more than ten or twelve feet from the ground.

When he alighted, his foot caught in a projecting root, and he sprawled gently forward. I say "gently" for he did not crash down as I expected him to do. The only thing I could compare it with was a slow-motion cinema, although I had never seen one in which horizontal motions were registered at normal speed and only the vertical movements were slowed down.

Due to my surprise, I suppose my brain did not function with its normal quickness, for I gazed at the prone figure for several seconds before I saw the blood that oozed out from under the tight green cap. Regaining my power of action, I dragged him out of sight back of a big tree. The wound was not a deep one. My companion was more dazed than hurt. But what of the pursuers?

I took the weapon from his grasp and examined it hurriedly. It was not unlike the automatic pistol to which I was accustomed, except that it apparently fired with a button instead of a trigger. I inserted several fresh rounds of ammunition into its magazine from my companion's belt, as rapidly as I could, for I soon heard near us, the suppressed conversation of his pursuers.

There followed a series of explosions round about us, but none very close. They evidently had not spotted our hiding place, and were firing at random.

I waited tensely, balancing the gun in my hand, to accustom myself to its weight and probable throw.

Then I saw a movement in the green foliage of a tree not far away, and the head and face of a man appeared. Like my companion, he was clad entirely in green, which made his figure difficult to distinguish. But his face could be seen clearly. It was an evil face, and had murder in it.

That decided me. I raised the gun and fired. My aim was bad, for there was no kick in the gun, as I had expected, and I hit the trunk of the tree several feet below him. It blew him from his perch like a crumpled bit of paper, and he floated down to the ground, like some limp, dead thing, gently lowered by an invisible hand. The tree, its trunk blown apart by the explosion, crashed down.

There followed another series of explosions around us. These guns we were using made no sound in the firing, and my opponents were evidently as much at sea as to my position as I was to theirs. So I made no attempt to reply to their fire, contenting myself with keeping a sharp lookout in their general direction. And patience had its reward.

Very soon I saw a cautious movement in the top of another tree. Exposing myself as little as possible, I aimed carefully at the tree trunk and fired again. A shriek followed the explosion. I heard the tree crash down; then a groan.

There was silence for awhile. Then I heard a faint sound of boughs swishing. I shot three times in its direction, pressing the button as rapidly as I could. Branches crashed down where my shells had exploded, but there was no body.

Then I saw one of them. He was starting one of those amazing leaps from the bough of one tree to another, about forty feet away.

I threw up my gun impulsively and fired. By now I had gotten the feel of the weapon, and my aim was good. I hit him. The "bullet" must have penetrated his body and exploded. For one moment I saw him flying through the air. Then the explosion, and he had vanished. He never finished his leap. It was annihilation.

How many more of them there were I don't know. But this must have been too much for them. They used a final round of shells on us, all of which exploded harmlessly, and shortly after I heard them swishing and crashing away from us through the tree tops. Not one of them descended to earth.

Now I had time to give some attention to my companion. She was, I found, a girl, and not a boy. Despite her bulky appearance, due to the peculiar belt strapped around her body high up under the arms, she was very slender, and very pretty.

There was a stream not far away, from which I brought water and bathed her face and wound.

Apparently the mystery of these long leaps, the monkey-like ability to jump from bough to bough, and of the bodies that floated gently down instead of falling lay in that belt. The thing was some sort of anti gravity belt that almost balanced the weight of the wearer, thereby tremendously multiplying the propulsive power of the leg muscles, and the lifting power of the arms.

•   •   •

When the girl came to, she regarded me as curiously as I did her, and promptly began to quiz me. Her accent and intonation puzzled me a lot, but nevertheless we were able to understand each other fairly well, except for certain words and phrases. I explained what had happened while she lay unconscious, and she thanked me simply for saving her life.

"You are a strange exchange," she said, eying my clothing quizzically. Evidently she found it mirth-provoking by contrast with her own neatly efficient garb. "Don't you understand what I mean by 'exchange'? I mean ah—let me see—a stranger, somebody from some other gang. What gang do you belong to?" (She pronounced it "gan," with only a suspicion of a nasal sound.)

I laughed. "I'm not a gangster," I said. But she evidently did not understand this word. "I don't belong to any gang," I explained, "and never did. Does everybody belong to a gang nowadays?"

"Naturally," she said, frowning. "If you don't belong to a gang, where and how do you live? Why have you not found and joined a gang? How do you eat? Where do you get your clothing?"

"I've been eating wild game for the past two weeks," I explained, "and this clothing I—er—ah—." I paused, wondering how I could explain that it must be many hundred years old.

In the end I saw I would have to tell my story as well as I could, piecing it together with my assumptions as to what had happened. She listened patiently; incredulously at first, but with more confidence as I went on. When I had finished, she sat thinking for a long time.

"That's hard to believe," she said, "but I believe it." She looked me over with frank interest.

"Were you married when you slipped into unconsciousness down in that mine?" she asked me suddenly. I assured her I had never married. "Well, that simplifies matters," she continued. "You see, if you were technically classed as a family man, I could take you back only as an invited exchange and I, being unmarried, and no relation of yours, couldn't do the inviting."

THE FOREST GANGS

She gave me a brief outline of the very peculiar social and economic system under which her people lived. At least it seemed very peculiar from my 20th Century viewpoint.

I learned with amazement that exactly 492 years had passed over my head as I lay unconscious in the mine.

Wilma, for that was her name, did not profess to be a historian, and so could give me only a sketchy outline of the wars that had been fought, and the manner in which such radical changes had come about. It seemed that another war had followed the First World War, in which nearly all the European nations had banded together to break the financial and industrial power of America. They succeeded in their purpose, though they were beaten, for the war was a terrific one, and left America, like themselves, gasping, bleeding and disorganized, with only the hollow shell of a victory.

This opportunity had been seized by the Russian Soviets, who had made a coalition with the Chinese, to sweep over all Europe and reduce it to a state of chaos.

America, industrially geared to world production and the world trade, collapsed economically, and there ensued a long period of stagnation and desperate attempts at economic reconstruction. But it was impossible to stave off war with the Mongolians, who by now had subjugated the Russians, and were aiming at a world empire.

In about 2109, it seems, the conflict was finally precipitated. The Mongolians, with overwhelming fleets of great airships, and a science that far outstripped that of crippled America, swept in over the Pacific and Atlantic Coasts, and down from Canada, annihilating American air craft, armies and cities with their terrific *disintegrator* rays. These rays were projected from a machine not unlike a searchlight in appearance, the reflector of which, however, was not material substance, but a complicated balance of interacting electronic forces. This resulted in a terribly destructive beam. Under its influence, material substance melted into "nothingness"; i.e., into electronic vibrations. It destroyed all then known substances, from air to the most dense metals and stone.

They settled down to the establishment of what became known as the Han dynasty in America, as a sort of province in their world empire.

Those were terrible days for the Americans. They were hunted like wild beasts. Only those survived who finally found refuge in mountains, canyons and forests. Government was at an end among them. Anarchy prevailed for several generations. Most would have been eager to submit to the Hans, even if it meant slavery. But the Hans did not want them, for they themselves had marvelous machinery and scientific processes by which all difficult labor was accomplished.

Ultimately they stopped their active search for, and annihilation of, the widely scattered groups of now savage Americans. So long as they remained hidden in their forests, and did not venture near the great cities the Hans had built, little attention was paid to them.

Then began the building of the new American civilization. Families and individuals gathered together in clans or "gangs" for mutual protection. For nearly a century they lived a nomadic and primitive life, moving from place to place, in desperate fear of the casual and occasional Hans air raids, and the terrible disintegrator ray. As the frequency of these raids decreased, they began to stay permanently in given localities, organizing upon lines which in many respects were similar to those of the military households of the Norman feudal barons, except that instead of gathering together in castles, their defense tactics necessitated a certain scattering of living quarters for families and individuals. They lived virtually in the open air, in the forests, in green tents, resorting to camouflage tactics that would conceal their presence from air observers. They dug underground factories and laboratories, that they might better be shielded from the electrical detectors of the Hans. They tapped the radio communication lines of the Hans, with crude instruments at first; better ones later on. They bent every effort toward the redevelopment of science. For many generations they labored as unseen, unknown scholars of the Hans, picking up their knowledge piecemeal, as fast as they were able to.

During the earlier part of this period, there were many deadly wars fought between the various gangs, and occasional courageous but childishly futile attacks upon the Hans, followed by terribly punitive raids.

But as knowledge progressed, the sense of American brotherhood redeveloped. Reciprocal arrangements were made among the gangs over constantly increasing areas. Trade developed to a certain extent, as between one gang and another. But the interchange of knowledge became more important than that of goods, as skill in the handling of synthetic processes developed.

Within the gang, an economy was developed that was a compromise between individual liberty and a military socialism. The right of private property was limited practically to personal possessions, but private privileges were many, and sacredly regarded. Stimulation to achievement lay chiefly in the winning of various kinds of leadership and prerogatives, and only in a very limited degree in the hope of owning anything that might be classified as "wealth," and nothing that might be classified as "resources." Resources of every description, for military safety and efficiency, belonged as a matter of public interest to the community as a whole.

In the meantime, through these many generations, the Hans had developed a luxury economy, and with it the perfection of gilded vice and degradation. The Americans were regarded as "wild men of the woods." And since they neither needed nor wanted the woods or the wild men, they treated them as beasts and were conscious of no human brotherhood with them. As time went on, and synthetic processes of producing foods and materials were further developed, less and less ground was needed by the Hans for the purposes of agriculture, and finally, even the working of mines was abandoned when it became cheaper to build up metals from electronic vibrations than to dig them out of the ground.

The Han race, devitalized by its vices and luxuries, with machinery and scientific processes to satisfy its every want, with virtually no necessity to labor, began then to assume a defensive attitude toward the Americans.

And quite naturally, the Americans regarded the Hans with a deep, grim hatred. Conscious of individual superiority as men, knowing that latterly they were outstripping the Hans in science and civilization, they longed desperately for the day when they should be powerful enough to rise and annihilate the Yellow Blight that lay over the continent.

At the time of my awakening, the gangs were rather loosely organized, but were considering the establishment of a special military force, whose special business it would be to harry the Hans and bring down their airships whenever possible without causing general alarm among the Mongolians. This force was destined to become the nucleus of the national force, when the Day of Retribution arrived. But that, however, did not happen for ten years, and is another story.

Wilma told me she was a member of the Wyoming Gang, which claimed the entire Wyoming Valley as its territory, under the leadership of Boss Hart. Her mother and father were dead, and she was unmarried, so she was not a "family member." She lived in a little group of tents known as Camp 17, under a woman Camp Boss, with seven other girls.

Her duties alternated between military or police scouting and factory work. For the two-week period which would end the next day, she had been on "air patrol." This did not mean, as I first imagined, that she was flying, but rather that she was on the lookout for Han ships over this outlying section of the Wyoming territory, and had spent most of her time perched in the tree tops scanning the skies. Had she seen one she would have fired a "drop flare" several miles off to one side, which would ignite when it was floating vertically toward the earth, so that the direction or point from which it had been fired might not be guessed by the airship and bring a blasting play of the disintegrator ray in her vicinity. Other members of the air patrol would send up rockets on seeing hers, until finally a scout equipped with an ultrophone, which, unlike the ancient radio, operated on the ultronic ethereal vibrations, would pass the warning simultaneously to the headquarters of the Wyoming Gang and other communities with a radius of several hundred miles, not to mention the few American rocketships that might be in the air, and which instantly would duck to cover either through forest clearings or by flattening down to earth in green fields where their coloring would probably protect them from observation. The favorite American method of propulsion was known as "*rocketing.*" The *rocket* is what I would describe, from my 20th Century comprehension of the matter, as an extremely powerful gas blast, atomically produced through the stimulation of chemical action. Scientists of today regard it as a childishly simple reaction, but by that very virtue, most economical and efficient.

But tomorrow, she explained, she would go back to work in the cloth plant, where she would take charge of one of the synthetic processes by which those wonderful substitutes for woven fabrics of wool, cotton and silk are produced. At the end of another two weeks, she would be back on military duty again, perhaps at the same work, or maybe as a "contact guard," on duty

where the territory of the Wyomings merged with that of the Delawares, or the "Susquannas" (Susquehannas) or one of the half dozen other "gangs" in that section of the country which I knew as Pennsylvania and New York States.

Wilma cleared up for me the mystery of those flying leaps which she and her assailants had made, and explained in the following manner, how the inertron belt balances weight:

"*Jumpers*" were in common use at the time I "awoke," though they were costly, for at that time *inertron* had not been produced in very great quantity. They were very useful in the forest. They were belts, strapped high under the arms, containing an amount of inertron adjusted to the wearer's weight and purposes. In effect they made a man weigh as little as he desired; two pounds if he liked.

"*Floaters*" are a later development of "*jumpers*"—rocket motors encased in *inertron* blocks

On the left a Han girl; on the right an American girl, who is equipped with an inertron belt and rocket gun.

and strapped to the back in such a way that the wearer floats, when drifting, facing slightly downward. With his motor in operation, he moves like a diver, head-foremost, controlling his direction by twisting his body and by movements of his outstretched arms and hands. Ballast weights locked in the front of the belt adjust weight and lift. Some men prefer a few ounces of weight in floating, using a slight motor thrust to overcome this. Others prefer a buoyance balance of a few ounces. The inadvertent dropping of weight is not a serious matter. The motor thrust always can be used to descend. But as an extra precaution, in case the motor should fail, for any reason, there are built into every belt a number of detachable sections, one or more of which can be discarded to balance off any loss in weight.

"But who were your assailants," I asked, "and why were you attacked?"

Her assailants, she told me, were members of an outlaw gang, referred to as "Bad Bloods," a group which for several generations had been under the domination of conscienceless leaders who tried to advance the interests of their clan by tactics which their neighbors had come to regard as unfair, and who in consequence had been virtually boycotted. Their purpose had been to slay her near the Delaware frontier, making it appear that the crime had been committed by Delaware scouts and thus embroil the Delawares and Wyomings in acts of reprisal against each other, or at least cause suspicions.

Fortunately they had not succeeded in surprising her, and she had been successful in dodging them for some two hours before the shooting began, at the moment when I arrived on the scene.

"But we must not stay here talking," Wilma concluded. "I have to take you in, and besides I must report this attack right away. I think we had better slip over to the other side of the mountain. Whoever is on that post will have a phone, and I can make a direct report. But you'll have to have a belt. Mine alone won't help much against our combined weights, and there's little to be gained by jumping heavy. It's almost as bad as walking."

After a little search, we found one of the men I had killed, who had floated down among the trees some distance away and whose belt was not badly damaged. In detaching it from his body, it nearly got away from me and shot up in the air. Wilma caught it, however, and though it reinforced the lift of her own belt so that she had to hook her knee around a branch to hold herself down, she saved it. I climbed the tree, and with my weight added to hers, we floated down easily.

LIFE IN THE 25TH CENTURY

We were delayed in starting for quite awhile since I had to acquire a few crude ideas about the technique of using these belts. I had been sitting down, for instance, with the belt strapped about me, enjoying an ease similar to that of a comfortable armchair; when I stood up with a natural exertion of muscular effort, I shot ten feet into the air, with a wild instinctive thrashing of arms and legs that amused Wilma greatly.

But after some practice, I began to get the trick of gauging muscular effort to a minimum of vertical and a maximum of horizontal. The correct form, I found, was in a measure comparable to that of skating. I found, also, that in forest work particularly the arms and hands could be used to great advantage in swinging along from branch to branch, so prolonging leaps almost indefinitely at times.

In going up the side of the mountain, I found that my 20th Century muscles did have an advantage, in spite of lack of skill with the belt, and since the slopes were very sharp, and most of our leaps were upward, I could have distanced Wilma easily. But when we crossed the ridge and descended, she outstripped me with her superior technique. Choosing the steepest slopes, she would crouch in the top of a tree, and propel herself outward, literally diving until, with the loss of horizontal momentum, she would assume a more upright position and float downward. In this manner she would sometimes cover as much as a quarter of a mile in a single leap, while I leaped and scrambled clumsily behind, thoroughly enjoying the novel sensation.

Halfway down the mountain, we saw another green-clad figure leap out above the tree tops toward us. The three of us perched on an outcropping of rock from which a view for many miles around could be had, while Wilma hastily explained her adventure and my presence to her fellow guard, whose name was Alan. I learned later that this was the modern form of Helen.

"You want to report by phone then, don't you?" Alan took a compact packet about six inches square from a holster attached to her belt and handed it to Wilma.

So far as I could see, it had no special receiver for the ear. Wilma merely threw back a lid, as though she were opening a book, and began to talk. The voice that came back from the machine was as audible as her own.

She was queried closely as to the attack upon her, and at considerable length as to myself, and I could tell from the tone of that voice that its owner was not prepared to take me at my face value as readily as Wilma had. For that matter, neither was the other girl. I could realize it from the suspicious glances she threw my way, when she thought my attention was elsewhere, and the manner in which her hand hovered constantly near her gun holster.

Wilma was ordered to bring me in at once, and informed that another scout would take her place on the other side of the mountain. So she closed down the lid of the phone and handed it back to Alan, who seemed relieved to see us departing over the tree tops in the direction of the camps.

We had covered perhaps ten miles, in what still seemed to me a surprisingly easy fashion, when Wilma explained that from here on we would have to keep to the ground. We were nearing the camps, she said, and there was always the possibility that some small Han scoutship, invisible high in the sky, might catch sight of us through a projectoscope and thus find the general location of the camps.

Wilma took me to the Scout office, which proved to be a small building of irregular shape, conforming to the trees around it, and substantially constructed of green sheet-like material.

I was received by the assistant Scout Boss, who reported my arrival at once to the historical office, and to officials he called the Psycho Boss and the History Boss, who came in a few minutes later. The attitude of all three men was at first polite but skeptical, and Wilma's ardent advocacy seemed to amuse them secretly.

For the next two hours I talked, explained and answered questions. I had to explain, in detail, the manner of my life in the 20th Century and my understanding of customs, habits, business, science and the history of that period, and about developments in the centuries that had elapsed. Had I been in a classroom, I would have come through the examination with a very poor mark, for I was unable to give any answer to fully half of their questions. But before long I realized that the majority of these questions were designed as traps. Objects, of whose purpose I knew nothing, were casually handed to me, and I was watched keenly as I handled them.

In the end I could see both amazement and belief begin to show in the faces of my inquisitors, and at last the History and Psycho Bosses agreed openly that they could find no flaw in my story or reactions, and that, unbelievable as it seemed, my story must be accepted as genuine.

They took me at once to Big Boss Hart. He was a portly man with a "poker face." He would probably have been the successful politician even in the 20th Century.

They gave him a brief outline of my story and a report of their examination of me. He made no comment other than to nod his acceptance of it. Then he turned to me.

"How does it feel?" he asked. "Do we look funny to you?"

"A bit strange," I admitted. "But I'm beginning to lose that dazed feeling, though I can see I have an awful lot to learn."

"Maybe we can learn some things from you, too," he said. "So you fought in the First World War. Do you know, we have very little left in the way of records of the details of that war—that is, the precise conditions under which it was fought, and the tactics employed. We forgot many things during the Han terror, and—well, I think you might have a lot of ideas worth thinking over for our raid masters. By the way, now that you're here, and can't go back to your own century, so to speak, what do you want to do? You're welcome to become one of us. Or perhaps you'd just like to visit with us for awhile, and then look around among other gangs. Maybe you'd like some of the others better. Don't make up your mind now. We'll put you down as an exchange for a while. Let's see. You and Bill Hearn ought to get along well together. He's Camp Boss of Number 34 when he isn't acting as Raid Boss or Scout Boss. There's a vacancy in his camp. Stay with him and think things over as long as you want to. As soon as you make up your mind to anything, let me know."

We all shook hands, for that was one custom that had not died out in five hundred years, and I set out with Bill Hearn.

Bill, like all the others, was clad in green. He was a big man. That is, he was about my own height, five feet eleven. This was considerably above the average now, for the race had lost something in stature, it seemed, through the vicissitudes of five centuries. Most of the women were a bit below five feet, and the men only a trifle above this height.

For a period of two weeks Bill was to confine himself to camp duties, so I had a good chance to familiarize myself with the community life. It was not easy. There were so many marvels to absorb. I never ceased to wonder at the strange combination of rustic social life and feverish industrial activity. At least, it was strange to me. For in my experience, industrial development meant crowded cities, tenements, paved streets, profusion of vehicles, noise, hurrying men and women with strained or dull faces, vast structures and ornate public works.

Here, however, was rustic simplicity, apparently isolated families and groups, living in the heart of the forest, with a quarter of a mile or more between households, a total absence of crowds, no means of conveyance other than the belts called jumpers, almost constantly worn by everybody, and an occasional rocket ship, used only for longer journeys, and underground plants or factories that were to my mind more like laboratories and engine rooms; many of them were excavations as deep as mines, with well-finished, lighted and comfortable interiors. These people were adepts at camouflage against air observations. Not only would their activity have been unsuspected by an airship passing over the center of the community, but even by an enemy who might happen to drop through the screen of the upper branches to the floor of the forest. The camps, or household structures, were all irregular in shape and of colors that blended with the great trees among which they were hidden.

There were 724 dwellings or "camps" among the Wyomings, located within an area of about fifteen square miles. The total population was 8,688, every man, woman and child, whether member or "exchange," being listed.

The plants were widely scattered through the territory also. Nowhere was anything like congestion permitted. So far as possible, families and individuals were assigned to living quarters not too far from the plants or offices in which their work lay.

All able-bodied men and women alternated in two-week periods between military and industrial service, except those who were needed for household work. Since working conditions in the plants and offices were ideal, and everybody thus had plenty of healthy outdoor activity in addition, the population was sturdy and active. Laziness was regarded as nearly the greatest of social offences. Hard work and general merit were variously rewarded with extra privileges, advancement to positions of authority, and with various items of personal equipment for convenience and luxury.

In leisure moments, I got great enjoyment from sitting outside the dwelling in which I was quartered with Bill Hearn and ten other men, watching the occasional passers-by, as with leisurely, but swift movements, they swung up and down the forest trail, rising from the ground in long almost-horizontal leaps, occasionally swinging from one convenient branch overhead to another before "sliding" back to the ground farther on. Normal traveling pace, where these trails were straight enough, was about twenty miles an hour. Such things as automobiles and railroad trains (the memory of them not more than a month old in my mind) seemed inexpressibly silly and futile compared with such convenience as these belts or jumpers offered.

Bill suggested that I wander around for several days, from plant to plant, to observe and study what I could. The entire community had been apprised of my coming, my rating as an "exchange" reaching every building and post in the community, by means of ultronic broadcast. Everywhere I was welcomed in an interested and helpful spirit.

I visited the plants where ultronic vibrations were isolated from the ether and through slow processes built up into sub-electronic, electronic and atomic forms into the two great synthetic elements, ultron and inertron. I learned something, superficially at least, of the processes of combined chemical and mechanical action through which were produced the various forms of building materials. But I was particularly interested in the munitions plant and the rocket-ship shops.

Ultron is a solid of great molecular density and moderate elasticity, which has the property of being 100 percent conductive to those pulsations known as light, electricity and heat. Since it is completely permeable to light vibrations, it is therefore *absolutely invisible and non-reflective*. Its magnetic response is almost, but not quite, 100 percent also. It is therefore very heavy under normal conditions but extremely responsive to

the *repellor* or anti-gravity rays, such as the Hans use as "legs" for their airships.

Inertron is the second great triumph of American research and experimentation with ultronic forces. It was developed just a few years before my awakening in the abandoned mine. It is a synthetic element, built up, through a complicated heterodyning of ultronic pulsations, from "infra balanced" subionic forms. It is completely inert to both electric and magnetic forces in all the order above the *ultronic*; that is to say, the *sub-electronic*, the *electronic*, the *atomic* and the *molecular*. In consequence it has a number of amazing and valuable properties. One of these is *the total lack of weight*. Another is a total lack of heat. It has no molecular vibration whatever. It reflects 100 percent of the heat and light impinging upon it. It does not feel cold to the touch, of course, since it will not absorb the heat of the hand. It is a solid, very dense in molecular structure despite its lack of weight, of great strength and considerable elasticity. It is a perfect shield against the disintegrator rays.

Rocket guns are very simple contrivances so far as the mechanism of launching the bullet is concerned. They are simple light tubes, closed at the rear end, with a trigger-actuated pin for piercing the thin skin at the base of the cartridge. This piercing of the skin starts the chemical and atomic reaction. The entire cartridge leaves the tube under its own power, at a very easy initial velocity, just enough to insure accuracy of aim; so the tube does not have to be of heavy construction. The bullet increases in velocity as it goes. It may explode on contact or on time, or a combination of these two.

Bill and I talked mostly of weapons, military tactics and strategy. Strangely enough he had no idea whatever of the possibilities of the barrage, though the tremendous effect of a "curtain of fire" with such high-explosive projectiles as these modern rocket guns used was obvious to me. But the barrage idea, it seemed, has been lost track of completely in the air wars that followed the First World War, and in the peculiar guerilla tactics developed by Americans in the later period of operations from the ground against Han airships, and in the gang wars which until a few generations ago, I learned, had been almost continuous.

"I wonder," said Bill one day, "if we couldn't work up some form of barrage to spring on the Bad Bloods. The Big Boss told me today that he's been in communication with the other gangs, and all are agreed that the Bad Bloods might as well be wiped out for good. That attempt on Wilma Deering's life and their evident desire to make trouble among the gangs has stirred up every community east of the Alleghenies. The Boss says that none of the others will object if we go after them. So I imagine that before long we will. Now show me again how you worked that business in the Argonne forest. The conditions ought to be pretty much the same."

I went over it with him in detail, and gradually we worked out a modified plan that would be better adapted to our more powerful weapons, and the use of jumpers.

"It will be easy," Bill exulted. "I'll slide down and talk it over with the Boss tomorrow."

During the first two weeks of my stay with the Wyomings, Wilma Deering and I saw a great deal of each other. I naturally felt a little closer friendship for her, in view of the fact that she was the first human being I saw after waking from my long sleep; her appreciation of my saving her life, though I could not have done otherwise than I did in that matter; and most of all my own appreciation of the fact that she had not found it as difficult as the others to believe my story, operated in the same direction. I could easily imagine my story must have sounded incredible.

It was natural enough too, that she should feel an unusual interest in me. In the first place, I was her personal discovery. In the second, she was a girl of studious and reflective turn of mind. She never got tired of my stories and descriptions of the 20th Century.

The others of the community, however, seemed to find our friendship a bit amusing. It seemed that Wilma had a reputation for being cold toward the opposite sex, and so others, not being able to appreciate some of her fine qualities as I did, misinterpreted her attitude, much to their delight. Wilma and I, however, ignored this as much as we could.

A HAN AIR RAID

There was a girl in Wilma's camp named Gerdi Mann, with whom Bill Hearn was desperately in love, and the four of us used to go around a lot together. Gerdi was a distinct type. Whereas Wilma had the usual dark brown hair and hazel eyes that marked nearly every member of the community, Gerdi had red hair, blue eyes and very fair skin. She has been dead many years now, but I remember her vividly because she was a throwback in physical appearance to a certain 20th Century type which I have found rare among modern Americans; also because the four of us were engaged one day in a discussion of this very point, when I obtained my first experience of a Han air raid.

We were sitting high on the side of a hill overlooking the valley that teemed with human activity, invisible beneath its blanket of foliage.

The other three, who knew of the Irish but vaguely and indefinitely, as a race on the other side of the globe, which, like ourselves, had succeeded in maintaining a precarious and fugitive existence in rebellion against the Mongolian domination of the earth, were listening with interest to my theory that Gerdi's ancestors of several hundred years ago must have been Irish. I explained that Gerdi was an Irish type, evidently a throwback, and that her surname might well have been McMann, or McMahan, and still more anciently "mac Mathghamhain." They were interested too in my surmise that "Gerdi" was the same name as that which had been "Gerty" or "Gertrude" in the 20th Century.

In the middle of our discussion, we were startled by an alarm rocket that burst high in the air, far to the north, spreading a pall of red smoke that drifted like a cloud. It was followed by others at scattered points in the northern sky.

"A Han raid!" Bill exclaimed in amazement. "The first in seven years!"

"Maybe it's just one of their ships off its course," I ventured.

"No" said Wilma in some agitation. "That would be green rockets. Red means only one thing, Tony. They're sweeping the countryside with their dis beams. Can you see anything, Bill?"

"We had better get under cover," Gerdi said nervously. "The four of us are bunched here in the open. For all we know they may be twelve miles up, out of sight, yet looking at us with a projecto."

Bill had been sweeping the horizon hastily with his glass, but apparently saw nothing.

"We had better scatter, at that," he said finally. "It's orders, you know. See!" He pointed to the valley.

Here and there a tiny human figure shot for a moment above the foliage of the tree tops.

"That's bad," Wilma commented, as she counted the jumpers. "No less than fifteen people visible, and all clearly radiating from a central point. Do they want to give away our location?"

The standard orders covering air raids were that the population was to scatter individually. There should be no grouping, or even pairing, in view of the destructiveness of the disintegrator rays. Experience of generations had proved that if this were done, and everybody remained hidden beneath the tree screens, the Hans would have to sweep mile after mile of territory, foot by foot, to catch more than a small percentage of the community.

Gerdi, however, refused to leave Bill, and Wilma developed an equal obstinacy against quitting my side. I was inexperienced at this sort of thing, she explained, quite ignoring the fact that she was too; she was only thirteen or fourteen years old at the time of the last air raid.

However, since I could not argue her out of it, we leaped together about a quarter of a mile to the right, while Bill and Gerdi disappeared down the hillside among the trees.

Wilma and I both wanted a point of vantage from which we might overlook the valley and the sky to the north, and we found it near the top of the ridge, where, protected from visibility by thick branches, we could look out between the tree trunks, and get a good view of the valley.

No more rockets went up. Except for a few of those warning red clouds, drifting lazily in a blue sky, there was no visible indication of man's past or present existence anywhere in the sky or on the ground.

Then Wilma gripped my arm and pointed. I saw it, away off in the distance; looking like a phantom dirigible airship, in its coat of low-visibility paint, a bare spectre.

"Seven thousand feet up," Wilma whispered, crouching close to me. "Watch."

The ship was about the same shape as the great dirigibles of the 20th Century that I had seen, but without the suspended control car, engines, propellors, rudders or elevating planes. As it loomed rapidly nearer, I saw that it was wider and somewhat flatter than I had supposed.

Now I could see the repellor rays that held the ship aloft, like searchlight beams faintly visible in the bright daylight (and still faintly visible to the human eye at night). Actually, I had been informed by my instructors, there were two rays: the visible one generated by the ship's apparatus, and directed toward the ground as a beam of "carrier" impulses; and the true repellor ray, the complement of the other in one sense, induced by the action of the "carrier" and reacting in a concentrating upward direction from the mass of the earth, becoming successively electronic, atomic and finally molecular in its nature, according to various ratios of distance between earth mass and "carrier" source, until in the last analysis, the ship itself actually is supported on an upward rushing column of air, like a ball supported on a fountain jet.

The raider neared with incredible speed. Its rays were both slanted astern at a sharp angle, so that it slid forward with tremendous momentum.

The ship was operating two disintegrator rays, though only in a casual, intermittent fashion. But whenever they flashed downward with blinding brilliancy, forest, rocks and ground melted instantaneously into nothing where they played upon them.

When later I inspected the scars left by these rays I found them some five feet deep and thirty feet wide, the exposed surfaces being lava-like in texture, but of a pale, iridescent, greenish hue.

No systematic use of the rays was made by the ship, however, until it reached a point over the center of the valley—the center of the community's activities. There it came to a sudden stop by shooting its repellor beams sharply forward and easing them back gradually to the vertical, holding the ship floating and motionless. Then the work of destruction began systematically.

Back and forth traveled the destroying rays, ploughing parallel furrows from hillside to hillside. We gasped in dismay, Wilma and I, as time after time we saw it plough through sections where we knew camps or plants were located.

"This is awful" she moaned, a terrified question in her eyes. "How could they know the location so exactly, Tony? Did you see? They were never in doubt. They stalled at a predetermined spot—and—and it was exactly the right spot."

We did not talk of what might happen if the rays were turned in our direction. We both knew. We would simply disintegrate in a split second into mere scattered electronic vibrations. Strangely enough, it was this self-reliant girl of the 25th Century who clung to me, a relatively primitive man of the 20th, less familiar than she with the thought of this terrifying possibility, for moral support.

We knew that many of our companions must have been whisked into absolute non-existence before our eyes in these few moments. The whole thing paralyzed us into mental and physical immobility for I do not know how long.

It couldn't have been long, however, for the rays had not ploughed more than thirty of their twenty-foot furrows or so across the valley, when I regained control of myself, and brought Wilma to herself by shaking her roughly.

"How far will this rocket gun shoot, Wilma?" I demanded.

"It depends on your rocket, Tony. It will take even the longest-range rocket, but you could shoot more accurately from a longer tube. But why? You couldn't penetrate the shell of that ship with rocket force, even if you could reach it."

I fumbled clumsily with my rocket pouch, for I was excited. I had an idea I wanted to try; a "hunch" I called it, forgetting that Wilma could not understand my ancient slang. But finally, with her help, I selected the longest-range explosive rocket in my pouch, and fitted it to my pistol.

"It won't carry seven thousand feet, Tony," Wilma objected. But I took aim carefully. It was another thought that I had in my mind. The supporting repellor ray, I had been told, became molecular in character at what was called a logarithmic level of five (below that it was a purely electronic "flow" or pulsation between the source of the "carrier" and the average mass of the earth). Below that level, if I could project my explosive bullet into this stream where it began to carry material substance upward, might it not rise with the air column, gathering speed and hitting the ship with enough impact to carry it through the shell? It was worth trying anyhow. Wilma became greatly excited, too, when she grasped the nature of my inspiration.

Feverishly I looked around for some formation of branches against which I could rest the pistol, for I had to aim most carefully. At last I found one. Patiently I sighted on the hulk of the ship far above us, aiming at the far side of it, at such an angle as would, so far as I could estimate, bring my bullet path through the forward repellor beam. At last the sights wavered across the point I sought and I pressed the button gently.

For a moment we gazed breathlessly.

Suddenly the ship swung bow down, as on a pivot, and swayed like a pendulum. Wilma screamed in her excitement.

"Oh Tony, you hit it! You hit it! Do it again; bring it down."

We had only one more rocket of extreme range between us, and we dropped it three times

in our excitement in inserting it in my gun. Then, forcing myself to be calm by sheer will power, while Wilma stuffed her little fist into her mouth to keep from shrieking, I sighted carefully again and fired. In a flash, Wilma had grasped the hope that this discovery of mine might lead to the end of the Han domination.

The elapsed time of the rocket's invisible flight seemed an age.

Then we saw the ship falling. It seemed to plunge lazily, but actually it fell with terrific acceleration, turning end over end, its disintegrator rays, out of control, describing vast, wild arcs, and once cutting a gash through the forest less than two hundred feet from where we stood.

The crash with which the heavy craft hit the ground reverberated from the hill—the momentum of eighteen or twenty thousand tons, in a sheer drop of seven thousand feet. A mangled mass of metal, it buried itself in the ground, with poetic justice, in the middle of the smoking, semi-molten field of destruction it had been so deliberately ploughing.

The silence, the vacuity of the landscape, was oppressive, as the last echoes died away.

Then far down the hillside, a single figure leaped exultantly above the foliage screen. And in the distance another, and another.

In a moment the sky was punctured by signal rockets. One after another the little red puffs became drifting clouds.

"Scatter! Scatter!" Wilma exclaimed. "In half an hour there'll be an entire Han fleet here from Nu-Yok, and another from Bahflo. They'll get this instantly on their recordographs and location finders. They'll blast the whole valley and the country for miles beyond. Come, Tony. There's no time for the gang to rally. See the signals. We've got to jump."

Over the ridge we went, in long leaps toward the east, the country of the Delawares.

From time to time signal rockets puffed in the sky. Most of them were the "red warnings," the "scatter" signals. But from certain of the others, which Wilma identified as Wyoming rockets, she gathered that whoever was in command (we did not know whether the Boss was alive or not) was ordering an ultimate rally toward the south, and so we changed our course.

It was a great pity, I thought, that the clan had not been equipped throughout its membership with ultrophones, but Wilma explained to me, that not enough of these had been built for distribution as yet, although general distribution had been contemplated within a couple of months.

We traveled far before nightfall overtook us, trying only to put as much distance as possible between ourselves and the valley.

When gathering dusk made jumping too dangerous we sought a comfortable spot beneath the trees, and consumed part of our emergency rations. It was the first time I had tasted the stuff—a highly nutritive synthetic substance called "concentro," which was, however, a bit bitter and unpalatable. But as only a mouthful or so was needed, it did not matter.

Neither of us had a cloak, but we were both thoroughly tired and happy, so we curled up together for warmth. I remember Wilma making some sleepy remark about our mating, as she cuddled up, as though the matter were all settled, and my surprise at my own instant acceptance of the idea, for I had not consciously thought of her that way before. But we both fell asleep at once.

In the morning we found little time for love making. The practical problem facing us was too great. Wilma felt that the Wyoming plan must be to rally in the Susquanna territory, but she had her doubts about the wisdom of this plan. In my elation at my success in bringing down the Han ship, and my newly found interest in my charming companion, who was, from my viewpoint of another century, at once more highly civilized and yet more primitive than myself, I had forgotten the ominous fact that the Han ship

I had destroyed must have known the exact location of the Wyoming Works.

This meant, to Wilma's logical mind, either that the Hans had perfected new instruments as yet unknown to us, or that somewhere, among the Wyomings or some other nearby gang, there were traitors so degraded as to commit that unthinkable act of trafficking in information with the Hans. In either contingency, she argued, other Han raids would follow, and since the Susquannas had a highly developed organization and more than usually productive plants, the next raid might be expected to strike them.

But at any rate it was clearly our business to get in touch with the other fugitives as quickly as possible, so in spite of muscles that were sore from the excessive leaping of the day before, we continued on our way.

We had traveled for only a couple of hours when we saw a multicolored rocket in the sky, some ten miles ahead of us.

"Bear to the left, Tony," Wilma said, "and listen for the whistle."

"Why?" I asked.

"Haven't they given you the rocket code yet?" she replied. "That's what the green, followed by yellow and purple means; to concentrate five miles east of the rocket position. You know the rocket position itself might draw a play of disintegrator beams."

It did not take us long to reach the neighborhood of the indicated rallying, though we were now traveling beneath the trees, with but an occasional leap to a top branch to see if any more rocket smoke was floating above. And soon we heard a distant whistle.

We found about half the Gang already there, in a spot where the trees met high above a little stream. The Big Boss and Raid Bosses were busy reorganizing the remnants.

We reported to Boss Hart at once. He was silent, but interested, when he heard our story.

"You two stick close to me," he said, adding grimly, "I'm going back to the valley at once with a hundred picked men, and I'll need you."

SETTING THE TRAP

Inside of fifteen minutes we were on our way. A certain amount of caution was sacrificed for the sake of speed, and the men leaped away either across the forest top, or over open spaces of ground, but concentration was forbidden. The Big Boss named the spot on the hillside as the rallying point.

"We'll have to take a chance on being seen, so long as we don't group," he declared, "at least until within five miles of the rallying spot. From then on I want every man to disappear from sight and to travel under cover. And keep your ultrophones open, and tuned on ten-four-seven-six."

Wilma and I had received our battle equipment from the Gear Boss. It consisted of a long-gun, a hand-gun, with a special case of ammunition constructed of inertron, which made the load weigh but a few ounces, and a short sword. This gear we strapped over each other's shoulders, on top of our jumping belts. In addition, we each received an ultrophone, and a light inertron blanket rolled into a cylinder about six inches long by two or three in diameter. This fabric was exceedingly thin and light, but it had considerable warmth, because of the mixture of inertron in its composition.

"This looks like business," Wilma remarked to me with sparkling eyes. (And I might mention a curious thing here. The word "business" had survived from the 20th Century American vocabulary, but not with any meaning of "industry" or "trade," for such things, being purely community activities, were spoken of as "work" and "clearing." Business simply meant fighting, and that was all.)

"Did you bring all this equipment from the valley?" I asked the Gear Boss.

"No," he said. "There was no time to gather anything. All this stuff we cleared from the Susquannas a few hours ago. I was with the Boss on the way down, and he had me jump on ahead and arrange it. But you two had better be moving. He's beckoning you now."

Hart was about to call us on our phones when we looked up. As soon as we did so, he leaped away, waving us to follow close by.

He was a powerful man, and he darted ahead in long, swift, low leaps up the banks of the stream, which followed a fairly straight course at this point. By extending ourselves, however, Wilma and I were able to catch up to him.

As we gradually synchronized our leaps with his, he outlined to us, between the grunts that accompanied each leap, his plan of action.

"We have to start the big business—unh—sooner or later," he said. "And if—unh—the Hans have found any way of locating our positions—unh—it's time to start now, although the Council of Bosses—unh—had intended waiting a few years until enough rocket ships have been—unh—built. But no matter what the sacrifice—unh—we can't afford to let them get us on the run—unh—. We'll set a trap for the yellow devils in the—unh—valley if they come back for their wreckage—unh—and if they don't, we'll go rocketing for some of their liners—unh—on the Nu-Yok, Clee-lan, Ski-ka-ga course. We can use—unh—that idea of yours of shooting up the repellor—unh—beams. Want you to give us a demonstration."

With further admonition to follow him closely, he increased his pace, and Wilma and I were taxed to our utmost to keep up with him. It was only in ascending the slopes that my tougher muscles overbalanced his greater skill, and I was able to set the pace for him, as I had for Wilma.

We slept in greater comfort that night, under our inertron blankets, and were off with the dawn, leaping cautiously to the top of the ridge overlooking the valley which Wilma and I had left.

The Boss scanned the sky with his ultroscope, patiently taking some fifteen minutes to the task, and then swung his phone into use, calling the roll and giving the men their instructions.

His first order was for us all to slip our ear and chest discs into permanent position.

These ultrophones were quite different from the one used by Wilma's companion scout the day I saved her from the vicious attack of the bandit Gang. That one was contained entirely in a small pocket case. These, with which we were now equipped, consisted of a pair of ear discs, each a separate and self-contained receiving set. They slipped into little pockets over our ears in the fabric helmets we wore, and shut out virtually all extraneous sounds. The chest discs were likewise self-contained sending sets, strapped to the chest a few inches below the neck and actuated by the vibrations from the vocal cords through the body tissues. The total range of these sets was about eighteen miles. Reception was remarkably clear, quite free from the static that so marked the 20th Century radios, and of a strength in direct proportion to the distance of the speaker.

The Boss's set was triple powered, so that his orders would cut in on any local conversations, which were indulged in, however, with great restraint, and only for the purpose of maintaining contacts.

I marveled at the efficiency of this modern method of battle communication in contrast to the clumsy signaling devices of more ancient times; and also at other military contrasts in which the 20th and 25th Century methods were the reverse of each other in efficiency. These modern Americans, for instance, knew little of hand-to-hand fighting, and nothing, naturally, of trench warfare. Of barrages they were quite ignorant, although they possessed weapons of terrific power. And until my recent flash of inspiration, no one among them, apparently, had even thought of the scheme of shooting a rocket into a repellor beam and letting the beam itself hurl it upward into the most vital part of the Han ship.

Hart patiently placed his men, first giving his instructions to the campmasters, and then remaining silent, while they placed the individuals.

In the end, the hundred men were ringed about the valley, on the hillsides and tops, each in a position from which he had a good view of the wreckage of the Han ship. But not a man had come in view, so far as I could see, in the whole process.

The Boss explained to me that it was his idea that he, Wilma and I should investigate the wreck. If Han ships should appear in the sky, we would leap for the hillsides.

I suggested to him to have the men set up their long-guns trained on an imaginary circle surrounding the wreck. He busied himself with this after the three of us leaped down to the Han ship, serving as a target himself, while he called on the men individually to aim their pieces and lock them in position.

In the meantime Wilma and I climbed into the wreckage, but did not find much. Practically all of the instruments and machinery had been twisted out of all recognizable shape, or utterly destroyed by the ship's disintegrator rays, which apparently had continued to operate in the midst of its warped remains for some moments after the crash.

It was unpleasant work searching the mangled bodies of the crew. But it had to be done. The Han clothing, I observed, was quite different from that of the Americans, and in many respects more like the garb to which I had been accustomed in the earlier part of my life. It was made of synthetic fabrics like silks, loose and comfortable trousers of knee length, and sleeveless shirts.

No protection, except that against drafts, was needed, Wilma explained to me, for the Han cities were entirely enclosed, with splendid arrangements for ventilation and heating. These arrangements, of course, were equally adequate in their airships. The Hans, indeed, had quite a distaste for unshaded daylight, since their lighting apparatus diffused a controlled amount of violet rays, making the unmodified sunlight unnecessary for health, and undesirable for comfort. Since the Hans did not have the secret of inertron, none of them wore anti-gravity belts. Yet in spite of the fact that they had to bear their own full weights at all times, they were physically far inferior to the Americans, for they lived lives of degenerative physical inertia, having machinery of every description for the performance of all labor, and convenient conveyances for any movement of more than a few steps.

Even from the twisted wreckage of this ship I could see that seats, chairs and couches played an extremely important part in their scheme of existence.

But none of the bodies were overweight. They seemed to have been the bodies of men in good health, but muscularly much underdeveloped. Wilma explained to me that they had mastered the science of gland control, and of course dietetics, to the point where men and women among them not uncommonly reached the age of a hundred years with arteries and general health in splendid condition.

I did not have time to study the ship and its contents as carefully as I would have liked, however. Time pressed, and it was our business to discover some clue to the deadly accuracy with which the ship had spotted the Wyoming Works.

The Boss had hardly finished his arrangements for the ring barrage, when one of the scouts on an eminence to the north, announced the approach of seven Han ships, spread out in a great semicircle.

Hart leaped for the hillside, calling to us to do likewise, but Wilma and I had raised the flaps of our helmets and switched off our "speakers" for conversation between ourselves, and by the time we discovered what had happened, the ships were clearly visible, so fast were they approaching.

"Jump!" we heard the Boss order, "Deering to the north. Rogers to the east."

But Wilma looked at me meaningly and pointed to where the twisted plates of the ship, projecting from the ground, offered a shelter.

"Too late, Boss," she said. "They'd see us.

Besides, I think there's something here we ought to look at. It's probably their magnetic graph."

"You're signing your death warrant," Hart warned.

"We'll risk it," said Wilma and I together.

"Good for you," replied the Boss. "Take command then, Rogers, for the present. Do you all know his voice, boys?"

A chorus of assent rang in our ears, and I began to do some fast thinking as the girl and I ducked into the twisted mass of metal.

"Wilma, hunt for that record," I said, knowing that by the simple process of talking I could keep the entire command continuously informed as to the situation. "On the hillsides, keep your guns trained on the circle and stand by. On the hilltops, how many of you are there? Speak in rotation from Bald Knob around to the east, north, west."

In turn the men called their names. There were twenty of them.

I assigned them by name to cover the various Han ships, numbering the latter from left to right.

"Train your rockets on their repellor rays about three-quarters of the way up between ships and ground. Aim is more important than elevation. Follow those rays with your aim continuously. Shoot when I tell you, not before. Deering has the record. The Hans probably have not seen us, or at least think there are but two of us in the valley, since they're settling without opening up disintegrators. Any opinions?"

My ear discs remained silent.

"Deering and I remain here until they land and debark. Stand by and keep alert."

Rapidly and easily the largest of the Han ships settled to the earth. Three scouted sharply to the south, rising to a higher level. The others floated motionless about a thousand feet above.

Peeping through a small fissure between two plates, I saw the vast hulk of the ship come to rest full on the line of our prospective ring barrage. A door clanged open a couple of feet from the ground, and one by one the crew emerged.

THE "WYOMING MASSACRE"

"They're coming out of the ship." I spoke quietly, with my hand over my mouth, for fear they might hear me. "One—two—three—four—five—six—seven—eight—nine. That seems to be all. Who knows how many men a ship like that is likely to carry?"

"About ten, if there are no passengers," replied one of my men, probably one of those on the hillside.

"How are they armed?"

"Just knives," came the reply. "They never permit hand-rays on the ships. Afraid of accidents. Have a ruling against it."

"Leave them to us then," I said, for I had a hastily formed plan in my mind. "You, on the hillsides, take the ships above. Abandon the ring target. Divide up in training on those repellor rays. You on the hilltops, all train on the repellors of the ships to the south. Shoot at the word, but not before.

"Wilma, crawl over to your left where you can make a straight leap for the door in that ship. These men are all walking around the wreck in a bunch. When they're on the far side, I'll give the word and you leap through that door in one bound. I'll follow. Maybe we won't be seen. We'll overpower the guard inside, but don't shoot. We may escape being seen by both this crew and ships above. They can't see over this wreck."

It was so easy that it seemed too good to be true. The Hans who had emerged from the ship walked round the wreckage lazily, talking in guttural tones, keenly interested in the wreck, but quite unsuspicious.

At last they were on the far side. In a moment they would be picking their way into the wreck.

"Wilma, leap!" I almost whispered the order.

The distance between Wilma's hiding place and the door in the side of the Han ship was not more than fifteen feet. She was already crouched with her feet braced against a metal beam. Taking the lift of that wonderful inertron belt into her calculation, she dove headforemost, like a

green projectile, through the door. I followed in a split second, more clumsily, but no less speedily, bruising my shoulder painfully as I ricocheted from the edge of the opening and brought up sliding against the unconscious girl; for she evidently had hit her head against the partition within the ship into which she had crashed.

We had made some noise within the ship. Shuffling footsteps were approaching down a well-lit gangway.

"Any signs we have been observed?" I asked my men on the hillsides.

"Not yet," I heard the Boss reply. "Ships overhead still standing. No beams have been broken out. Men on ground absorbed in wreck. Most of them have crawled into it out of sight."

"Good," I said quickly. "Deering hit her head. Knocked out. One or more members of the crew approaching. We're not discovered yet. I'll take care of them. Stand a bit longer, but be ready."

I think my last words must have been heard by the man who was approaching, for he stopped suddenly.

I crouched at the far side of the compartment, motionless. I would not draw my sword if there were only one of them. He would be a weakling, I figured, and I should easily overcome him with my bare hands.

Apparently reassured at the absence of any further sound, a man came around a sort of bulkhead—and I leaped.

I swung my legs up in front of me as I did so, catching him full in the stomach, and knocked him cold.

I ran forward along the keel gangway, searching for the control room. I found it well up in the nose of the ship. And it was deserted. What could I do to jam the controls of the ships that would not register on the recording instruments of the other ships? I gazed at the mass of controls. Levers and wheels galore. In the center of the compartment, on a massively braced universal joint mounting, was what I took for the repellor generator. A dial on it glowed and a faint hum came from within its shielding metallic case. But I had no time to study it.

Above all else, I was afraid that some automatic telephone apparatus existed in the room, through which I might be heard on the other ships. The risk of trying to jam the controls was too great. I abandoned the idea and withdrew softly. I would have to take a chance that there was no other member of the crew aboard.

I ran back to the entrance compartment. Wilma still lay where she had slumped down. I heard the voices of the Hans approaching. It was time to act. The next few seconds would tell whether the ships in the air would try or be able to melt us into nothingness. I spoke.

"Are you boys all ready?" I asked, creeping to a position opposite the door and drawing my hand-gun.

There was a chorus of assent.

"Then on the count of three, shoot up those repellor rays—all of them—and for God's sake, don't miss." And I counted.

I think my "three" was a bit weak. I know it took all the courage I had to utter it.

For an agonizing instant nothing happened, except that the landing party from the ship strolled into my range of vision.

Then, startled, they turned their eyes upward. For an instant they stood frozen with horror at whatever they saw.

One hurled his knife at me. It grazed my cheek. Then a couple of them made a break for the doorway. The rest followed. But I fired pointblank with my hand-gun, pressing the button as fast as I could and aiming at their feet to make sure my explosive rockets would make contact and do their work.

The detonations of my rockets were deafening. The spot on which the Hans stood flashed into a blinding glare. Then there was nothing there except their torn and mutilated corpses. They had been fairly bunched, and I got them all.

I ran to the door, expecting any instant to be hurled into infinity by the sweep of a disintegrator ray.

Some eighth of a mile away I saw one of the ships crash to earth. A disintegrator ray came into my line of vision, wavered uncertainly for a moment and then began to sweep directly toward the ship in which I stood. But it never reached it. Suddenly, like a light switched off, it shot to one side and a moment later another vast hulk crashed to earth. I looked out, then stepped out on the ground.

The only Han ships in the sky were two of the scouts to the south, which were hanging perpendicularly, and sagging slowly down. The

The American leaped and swung his legs out, catching the Han full in the stomach.

others must have crashed down while I was deafened by the sound of the explosion of my own rockets.

Somebody hit the other repellor ray of one of the two remaining ships and it fell out of sight beyond a hilltop. The other, farther away, drifted down diagonally, its disintegrator ray playing viciously over the ground below it.

I shouted with exultation and relief.

"Take back the command, Boss!" I yelled.

His commands, sending out jumpers in pursuit of the descending ship, rang in my ears, but I paid no attention to them. I leaped back into my compartment of the Han ship and knelt beside my Wilma. Her padded helmet had absorbed much of the blow, I thought; otherwise, her skull might have been fractured.

"Oh, my head!" she groaned, coming to as I lifted her gently in my arms and strode out in the open with her. "We must have won, dearest; did we?"

"We most certainly did," I reassured her. "All but one crashed and that one is drifting down toward the south; we've captured this one we're in intact. There was only one member of the crew aboard when we dove in."

Less than an hour afterward the Big Boss ordered the outfit to tune in ultrophones on three-twenty-three to pick up a translated broadcast of the Han intelligence office in Nu-Yok from the Susquanna station. It was in the form of a public warning and news item, and read as follows:

"This is Public Intelligence Office, Nu-Yok, broadcasting warning to navigators of private ships, and news of public interest. The squadron of seven ships which left Nu-Yok this morning to investigate the recent destruction of the GK-984 in the Wyoming Valley, has been destroyed by a series of mysterious explosions similar to those which wrecked the GK-984.

"The phones, viewplates and all other signaling devices of five of the seven ships ceased operating suddenly at approximately the same moment, about seven-four-nine." (According to the Han system of reckoning time, seven and forty-nine one hundredths after midnight.) "After violent disturbances the location finders went out of operation. Electroactivity registers applied to the territory of the Wyoming Valley remain dead.

"The Intelligence Office has no indication of the kind of disaster which overtook the squadron except certain evidences of explosive phenomena similar to those in the case of the GK-984, which recently went dead while beaming the valley in a systematic effort to wipe out the works and camps of the tribesmen. The Office

considers, as obvious, the deduction that the tribesmen have developed a new, and as yet undetermined, technique of attack on airships, and has recommended to the Heaven-Born that immediate and unlimited authority be given the Navigation Intelligence Division to make an investigation of this technique and develop a defense against it.

"In the meantime it urges that private navigators avoid this territory in particular, and in general hold as closely as possible to the official inter-city routes, which now are being patrolled by the entire force of the Military Office, which is beaming the routes generously to a width of ten miles. The Military Office reports that it is at present considering no retaliatory raids against the tribesmen. With the Navigation Intelligence Division, it holds that unless further evidence of the nature of the disaster is developed in the near future, the public interest will be better served, and at smaller cost of life, by a scientific research than by attempts at retaliation, which may bring destruction on all ships engaging therein. So unless further evidence actually is developed, or the Heaven-Born orders to the contrary, the Military will hold to a defensive policy.

"Unofficial intimations from Lo-Tan are to the effect that the Heaven-Council has the matter under consideration.

"The Navigation Intelligence Office broadcasts the following detailed observations:

"The squadron proceeded to a position above the Wyoming Valley where the wreck of the GK-984 was known to be, from the record of its location finder before it went dead recently. There the bottom projectoscope relays of all ships registered the wreck of the GK-984. Teleprojectoscope views of the wreck and the bowl of the valley showed no evidence of the presence of tribesmen. Neither ship registers nor base registers showed any indication of electroactivity except from the squadron itself. On orders from the Base Squadron Commander, the LD-248, LK-745 and LG-25 scouted southward at 3,000 feet. The GK-43, GK-981 and GK-220 stood above at 2,500 feet, and the GK-

18 landed to permit personal inspection of the wreck by the science committee. The party debarked, leaving one man on board in the control cabin. He set all projectoscopes at universal focus except RB-3," (this meant the third projectoscope from the bow of the ship, on the right-hand side of the lower deck) "with which he followed the landing group as it walked around the wreck."

"The first abnormal phenomenon recorded by any of the instruments at Base was that relayed automatically from projectoscope RB-4 of the GK-18, which, as the party disappeared from view in back of the wreck, recorded two green missiles of roughly cylindrical shape, projected from the wreckage into the landing compartment of the ship. At such close range these were not clearly defined, owing to the universal focus at which the projectoscope was set. The Base Captain of GK-18 at once ordered the man in the control room to investigate, and saw him leave the control room in compliance with this order. An instant later confused sounds reached the control-room electrophone, such as might be made by a man falling heavily, and footsteps reapproached the control room, a figure entering and leaving the control room hurriedly. The Base Captain now believes, and the stills of the photorecord support his belief, that this was not the crew member who had been left in the control room. Before the Base Captain could speak to him he left the room, nor was any response given to the attention signal the Captain flashed throughout the ship.

"At this point projectoscope RB-3 of the ship, now out of focus control, dimly showed the landing party walking back toward the ship. RB-4 showed it more clearly. Then on both these instruments, a number of blinding explosives in rapid succession were seen and the electrophone relays registered terrific concussions; the ship's electronic apparatus and projectoscopes apparatus went dead.

"Reports of the other ships' Base Observers and Executives, backed by the photorecords, show the explosions as taking place in the midst of the landing party as it returned, evidently unsuspicious, to the ship. Then in rapid succession they indicate that terrific explosions occurred inside and outside the three ships standing above close to their rep-ray generators, and all signals from these ships thereupon went dead.

"Of the three ships scouting to the south, the LD-248 suffered an identical fate, at the same moment. Its records add little to the knowledge of the disaster. But with the LK-745 and the LG-25 it was different.

"The relay instruments of the LK-745 indicated the destruction by an explosion of the rear rep-ray generator, and that the ship hung stern down for a short space, swinging like a pendulum. The forward viewplates and indicators did not cease functioning, but their records are chaotic, except for one projectoscope still, which shows the bowl of the valley, and the GK-981 falling, but no visible evidence of tribesmen. The control-room viewplate is also a chaotic record of the ship's crew tumbling and falling to the rear wall. Then the forward rep-ray generator exploded, and all signals went dead.

"The fate of the LG-25 was somewhat similar, except that this ship hung nose down, and drifted on the wind southward as it descended out of control.

"As its control room was shattered, verbal report from its Action Captain was precluded. The record of the interior rear viewplate shows members of the crew climbing toward the rear rep-ray generator in an attempt to establish manual control of it, and increase the lift. The projectoscope relays, swinging in wide arcs, recorded little of value except at the ends of their swings. One of these, from a machine which happened to be set in telescopic focus, shows several views of great value in picturing the falls of the other ships, and all of the rear projectoscope records enable the reconstruction in detail of the pendulum and torsional movements of the ship, and its sag toward the earth. But none of the views showing the forest below contain any indication of tribesmen's presence. A final explosion put this ship out of commission at a height of 1,000 feet, and at a point four miles S. by E. of the center of the valley."

The message ended with a repetition of the warning to other airmen to avoid the valley.

INCREDIBLE TREASON

After receiving this report, and reassurances of support from the Big Bosses of the neighboring gangs, Hart determined to reestablish the Wyoming Valley community.

A careful survey of the territory showed that it was only the northern sections and slopes that had been "beamed" by the first Han ship.

The synthetic fabrics plant had been partially wiped out, though the lower levels underground had not been reached by the dis ray. The forest screen above it, however, had been annihilated, and it was determined to abandon it, after removing all usable machinery and evidences of the processes that might be of interest to the Han scientists, should they return to the valley in the future.

The ammunition plant, and the rocket-ship plant, which had just been about to start operation at the time of the raid, were intact, as were the other important plants.

Hart brought the Camboss up from the Susquanna Works, and laid out new camp locations, scattering them farther to the south, and avoiding ground which had been seared by the Han beams and the immediate locations of the Han wrecks.

During this period, a sharp check was kept upon Han messages, for the phone plant had been one of the first to be put in operation, and when it became evident that the Hans did not intend any immediate reprisals, the entire membership of the community was summoned back, and normal life was resumed.

Wilma and I had been married the day after the destruction of the ships, and spent this intervening period in a delightful honeymoon, camping high in the mountains. On our return, we had a camp of our own, of course. We were assigned to location 1017. And as might be expected, we had a great deal of banter over which one of us was Camp Boss. The title stood after my name on the Big Boss's records and those of the Big Camboss, of course, but Wilma airily held that this meant nothing at all—and generally succeeded in making me admit it whenever she chose.

I found myself a full-fledged member of the Gang now, for I had elected to search no farther for a permanent alliance, much as I would have liked to familiarize myself with this 25th Century life in other sections of the country. The Wyomings had a high morale, and had prospered under the rule of Big Boss Hart for many years. But many of the gangs, I found, were badly organized, lacked strong hands in authority, and were rife with intrigue. On the whole, I thought I would be wise to stay with a group which had already proved its friendliness, and in which I seemed to have prospects of advancement. Under these modern social and economic conditions, the kind of individual freedom to which I had been accustomed in the 20th Century was impossible. I would have been as much of a nonentity in every phase of human relationship by attempting to avoid alliances, as any man of the 20th Century would have been politically, who aligned himself with no political party.

This entire modern life, it appeared to me, judging from my ancient viewpoint, was organized along what I called "political" lines. And in this connection, it amused me to notice how universal had become the use of the word "boss." The leader, the person in charge or authority over anything, was a "boss." There was as little formality in his relations with his followers as there was in the case of the 20th Century political boss, and the same high respect paid him by his followers as well as the same high consideration by him of their interests. He was just as much of an autocrat, and just as much dependent upon the general popularity of his actions for the ability to maintain his autocracy.

The sub-boss who could not command the

loyalty of his followers was as quickly deposed, either by them or by his superiors, as the ancient ward leader of the 20th Century who lost control of his votes.

As society was organized in the 20th Century, I do not believe the system could have worked in anything but politics. I tremble to think what would have happened, had the attempt been made to handle the A.E.F. this way during the First World War, instead of by that rigid military discipline and complete assumption of the individual as a mere standardized cog in the machine.

But owing to the centuries of desperate suffering the people had endured at the hands of the Hans, there developed a spirit of self-sacrifice and consideration for the common good that made the scheme applicable and efficient in all forms of human cooperation.

I have a little heresy about all this, however. My associates regard the thought with as much horror as many worthy people of the 20th Century felt in regard to any heretical suggestion that the original outline of government as laid down in the First Constitution did not apply as well to 20th Century conditions as to those of the early 19th.

In later years, I felt that there was a certain softening of moral fiber among the people, since the Hans had been finally destroyed with all their works; and Americans have developed a new luxury economy. I have seen signs of the reawakening of greed, of selfishness. The eternal cycle seems to be at work. I fear that slowly, though surely, private wealth is reappearing, codes of inflexibility are developing; they will be followed by corruption, degradation; and in the end some cataclysmic event will end this era and usher in a new one.

All this, however, is wandering afar from my story, which concerns our early battles against the Hans, and not our more modern problems of self-control.

Our victory over the seven Han ships had set the country ablaze. The secret had been carefully communicated to the other gangs, and the country was agog, from one end to the other. There was feverish activity in the ammunition plants, and the hunting of stray Han ships became an enthusiastic sport. The results were disastrous to our hereditary enemies.

From the Pacific Coast came the report of a great Transpacific liner of 75,000 tons "lift" being brought to earth from a position of invisibility above the clouds. A dozen Sacramentos had caught the hazy outlines of its rep rays approaching them, head-on, in the twilight, like ghostly pillars reaching into the sky. They had fired rockets into it with ease, whereas they would have had difficulty in hitting it if it had been moving at right angles to their position. They got one rep ray. The other was not strong enough to hold it up. It floated to earth, nose down, and since it was unarmed and unarmored, they had no difficulty in shooting it to pieces and massacring its crew and passengers. It seemed barbarous to me. But then I did not have centuries of bitter persecution in my blood.

From the Jersey Beaches we received news of the destruction of a Nu-Yok–A-lan-a liner. The Sandsnipers, practically invisible in their sand-colored clothing, and half buried along the beaches, lay in wait for days, risking the play of dis beams along the route, and finally registering four hits within a week. The Hans discontinued their service along this route, and as evidence that they were badly shaken by our success, sent no raiders down the Beaches.

It was a few weeks later that Big Boss Hart sent for me.

"Tony," he said, "there are two things I want to talk to you about. One of them will become public property in a few days, I think. We aren't going to get any more Han ships by shooting up their repellor rays unless we use much larger rockets. They are wise to us now. They're putting armor of great thickness in the hulls of their ships below the rep-ray machines. Near

Bah-flo this morning a party of Eries shot one without success. The explosions staggered her, but did not penetrate. As near as we can gather from their reports, their laboratories have developed a new alloy of great tensile strength and elasticity which nevertheless lets the rep rays through like a sieve. Our reports indicate that the Eries's rockets bounced off harmlessly. Most of the party was wiped out as the dis rays went into action on them.

"This is going to mean real business for all of the gangs before long. The Big Bosses have just held a national ultrophone council. It was decided that America must organize on a national basis. The first move is to develop sectional organization by Zones. I have been made Superboss of the Midatlantic Zone.

"We're in for it now. The Hans are sure to launch reprisal expeditions. If we're to save the race we must keep them away from our camps and plants. I'm thinking of developing a permanent field force, along the lines of the regular armies of the 20th Century you told me about. Its business will be twofold: to carry the warfare as much as possible to the Hans, and to serve as a decoy, to keep their attention from our plants. I'm going to need your help in this.

"The other thing I wanted to talk to you about is this: Amazing and impossible as it seems, there is a group, or perhaps an entire gang, somewhere among us, that is betraying us to the Hans. It may be the Bad Bloods, or it may be one of those gangs who live near one of the Han cities. You know, a hundred and fifteen or twenty years ago there were certain of these people's ancestors who actually degraded themselves by mating with the Hans, sometimes even serving them as slaves, in the days before they brought all their service machinery to perfection.

"There is such a gang, called the Nagras, up near Bah-flo, and another in Mid-Jersey that men call the Pineys. But I hardly suspect the Pineys. There is little intelligence among them. They wouldn't have the information to give the Hans, nor would they be capable of imparting it. They're absolute savages."

"Just what evidence is there that anybody has been clearing information to the Hans?" I asked.

"Well," he replied, "first of all there was that raid upon us. That first Han ship knew the location of our plants exactly. You remember it floated directly into position above the valley and began a systematic beaming. Then, the Hans quite obviously have learned that we are picking up their electrophone waves, for they've gone back to their old, but extremely accurate, system of directional control. But we've been getting them for the past week by installing automatic rebroadcast units along the scar paths. This is what the Americans called those strips of country directly under the regular ship routes of the Hans, who as a matter of precaution frequently blasted them with their dis beams to prevent the growth of foliage which might give shelter to the Americans. But they've been beaming those paths so hard, it looks as though they even had information of this strategy. And in addition, they've been using code. Finally, we've picked up three messages in which they discuss, with some nervousness, the existence of our 'mysterious' ultrophone."

"But they still have no knowledge of the nature and control of ultronic activity?" I asked.

"No," said the Big Boss thoughtfully, "they don't seem to have a bit of information about it."

"Then it's quite clear," I ventured, "that whoever is 'clearing' us to them is doing it piecemeal. It sounds like a bit of occasional barter, rather than an out and out alliance. They're holding back as much information as possible for future bartering, perhaps."

"Yes," Hart said, "and it isn't information the Hans are giving in return, but some form of goods, or privilege. The trick would be to locate the goods. I guess I'll have to make a personal trip around among the Big Bosses."

THE HAN CITY

This conversation set me thinking. All of the Han electrophone inter-communication had been an open record to the Americans for a good many years, and the Hans were just finding it out. For centuries they had not regarded us as any sort of a menace. Unquestionably it had never occurred to them to secrete their own records. Somewhere in Nu-Yok or Bah-flo, or possibly in Lo-Tan itself, the record of this traitorous transaction would be more or less openly filed. If we could only get at it! I wondered if a raid might not be possible.

Bill Hearn and I talked it over with our Han-Affairs Boss and his experts. There ensued several days of research, in which the Han records of the entire decade were scanned and analyzed. In the end they picked out a mass of detail, and fitted it together into a very definite picture of the great central filing office of the Hans in Nu-Yok, where the entire mass of official records was kept, constantly available for instant projectoscoping to any of the city's offices, and of the system by which the information was filed.

The attempt began to look feasible, though Hart instantly turned the idea down when I first presented it to him. It was unthinkable, he said. Sheer suicide. But in the end I persuaded him.

"I will need," I said, "Blash, who is thoroughly familiar with the Han library system; Bert Gaunt, who for years has specialized on their military offices; Bill Barker, the ray specialist, and the best swooper pilot we have." *Swoopers* are one-man and two-man ships, developed by the Americans, with skeleton backbones of inertron (during the war painted green for invisibility against the green forests below) and "bellies" of clear ultron.

"That will be Mort Gibbons," said Hart. "We've only got three swoopers left, Tony, but I'll risk one of them if you and the others will voluntarily risk your existences. But mind, I won't urge or order one of you to go. I'll spread the word to every Plant Boss at once to give you anything and everything you need in the way of equipment."

When I told Wilma of the plan, I expected her to raise violent and tearful objections, but she didn't. She was made of far sterner stuff

than the women of the 20th Century. Not that she couldn't weep as copiously or be just as whimsical on occasion; but she wouldn't weep for the same reasons.

She just gave me an unfathomable look, in which there seemed to be a bit of pride, and asked eagerly for the details. I confess I was somewhat disappointed that she could so courageously risk my loss, even though I was amazed at her fortitude. But later I was to learn how little I knew her then.

We were ready to slide off at dawn the next morning. I had kissed Wilma good-bye at our camp, and after a final conference over our plans, we boarded our craft and gently glided away over the tree tops on a course which, after crossing three routes of the Han ships, would take us out over the Atlantic, off the Jersey coast, whence we would come up on Nu-Yok from the ocean.

Twice we had to nose down and lie motionless on the ground near a route while Han ships passed. Those were tense moments. Had the green back of our ship been observed, we would have been disintegrated in a second. But it wasn't.

Once over the water, however, we climbed in a great spiral, ten miles in diameter, until our altimeter registered ten miles. Here Gibbons shut off his rocket motor, and we floated, far above the level of the Atlantic liners, whose course was well to the north of us anyhow, and waited for nightfall.

Then Gibbons turned from his control long enough to grin at me.

"I have a surprise for you, Tony," he said, throwing back the lid of what I had supposed was a big supply case. And with a sigh of relief, Wilma stepped out of the case.

"If you 'go into zero' (a common expression of the day for being annihilated by the disintegrator ray), you don't think I'm going to let you go alone, do you, Tony? I couldn't believe my ears last night when you spoke of going without me, until I realized that you are still five hundred years behind the times in lots of ways. Don't you know, dear heart, that you offered me the greatest insult a husband could give a wife? You didn't, of course."

The others, it seemed, had all been in on the secret, and now they would have kidded me unmercifully, except that Wilma's eyes blazed dangerously.

At nightfall, we maneuvered to a position directly above the city. This took some time and calculation on the part of Bill Barker, who explained to me that he had to determine our point by ultronic bearings. The slightest resort to an electronic instrument, he feared, might be detected by our enemies' locaters. In fact, we did not dare bring our swooper any lower than five miles for fear that its capacity might be reflected in their instruments.

Finally, however, he succeeded in locating above the central tower of the city.

"If my calculations are as much as ten feet off," he remarked with confidence, "I'll eat the tower. Now the rest is up to you, Mort. See what you can do to hold her steady. No—here, watch this indicator—the red beam, not the green one. See—if you keep it exactly centered on the needle, you're O.K. The width of the beam represents seventeen feet. The tower platform is fifty feet square, so we've got a good margin to work on."

For several moments we watched as Gibbons bent over his levers, constantly adjusting them with deft touches of his fingers. After a bit of wavering, the beam remained centered on the needle.

"Now," I said, "let's drop."

I opened the trap and looked down, but quickly shut it again when I felt the air rushing out of the ship into the rarefied atmosphere in a torrent. Gibbons literally yelled a protest from his instruction board.

"I forgot," I mumbled. "Silly of me. Of course, we'll have to drop out of compartment."

The compartment, to which I referred, was similar to those in some of the 20th Century submarines. We all entered it. There was barely room for us to stand, shoulder to shoulder. With some struggles, we got into our special air helmets and adjusted the pressure. At our signal, Gibbons exhausted the air in the compartment, pumping it into the body of the ship, and as the little signal light flashed, Wilma threw open the hatch.

Setting the ultron wire reel, I climbed through, and began to slide down gently.

We all had our belts on, of course, adjusted to a weight balance of but a few ounces. And the five-mile reel of ultron wire that was to be our guide was of gossamer fineness, though, anyway, I believe it would have lifted the full weight of the five of us, so strong and tough was the invisible metal. As an extra precaution, since the wire was of the purest metal, and therefore totally invisible, even in daylight, we all had our belts hooked on small rings that slid down the wire.

I went down with the end of the wire. Wilma followed a few feet above me, then Barker, Gaunt and Blash. Gibbons, of course, stayed behind to hold the ship in position and control the paying out of the line. We all had our ultrophones in place inside our air helmets, and so could converse with one another and with Gibbons. But at Wilma's suggestion, although we would have liked to let the Big Boss listen in, we kept them adjusted to short-range work, for fear that those who had been clearing with the Hans, and against whom we were on a raid for evidence, might also pick up our conversation. We had no fear that the Hans would hear us. In fact, we had the added advantage that, even after we landed, we could converse freely without danger of their hearing our voices through our air helmets.

For a while I could see nothing below but utter darkness. Then I realized, from the feel of the air as much as from anything, that we were sinking through a cloud layer. We passed through two more cloud layers before anything was visible to us.

Then there came under my gaze, about two miles below, one of the most beautiful sights I have ever seen: the soft, yet brilliant, radiance of the great Han city of Nu-Yok. Every foot of its structural members seemed to glow with a wonderful incandescence, tower piled up on tower, and all built on the vast base-mass of the city, which, so I had been told, sheered upward from the surface of the rivers to a height of 728 levels.

The city, I noted with some surprise, did not cover anything like the same area as the New York of the 20th Century. It occupied, as a matter of fact, only the lower half of Manhattan Island, with one section straddling the East River and spreading out sufficiently over what once had been Brooklyn, to provide berths for the great liners and other air craft.

Straight beneath my feet was a tiny dark patch. It seemed the only spot in the entire city that was not aflame with radiance. This was the central tower, in the top floors of which were housed the vast library of record files and the main projectoscope plant.

"You can shoot the wire now," I ultro-phoned Gibbons, and let go the little weighted knob. It dropped like a plummet, and we followed with considerable speed, but braking our descent with gloved hands sufficiently to see whether the knob, on which a faint light glowed as a signal for ourselves, might be observed by any Han guard or night prowler. Apparently it was not, and we again shot down with accelerated speed.

We landed on the roof of the tower without any mishap, and fortunately for our plan, in darkness. Since there was nothing above it on which it would have been worthwhile to shed illumination, or from which there was any need to observe it, the Hans had neglected to light the tower roof, or indeed to occupy it at all. This was the reason we had selected it.

As soon as Gibbons had our word, he extinguished the knob light, and the knob, as well as the wire, became totally invisible. At our ultro-phoned word, he would light it again.

"No gun play now," I warned. "Swords only, and then only if absolutely necessary."

Closely bunched, and treading as lightly as only inertron-belted people could, we made our way cautiously through a door and down an inclined plane to the floor below, where Gaunt and Blash assured us the military offices were located.

Twice Barker cautioned us to stop as we were about to pass in front of mirror-like "windows" in the passage wall, and flattening ourselves to the floor, we crawled past them.

"Projectoscopes," he said. "Probably on automatic record only, at this time of night. Still, we don't want to leave any records for them to study after we're gone."

"Were you ever here before?" I asked.

"No," he replied, "but I haven't been studying their electrophone communications for seven years without being able to recognize these machines when I run across them."

THE FIGHT IN THE TOWER

So far we had not laid eyes on a Han. The tower seemed deserted. Blash and Gaunt, however, assured me that there would be at least one man on "duty" in the military offices, though he would probably be asleep, and two or three in the library proper and the projectoscope plant.

"We've got to put them out of commission," I said. "Did you bring the 'dope' cans, Wilma?"

"Yes," she said, "two for each."

We were now two levels below the roof, and at the point where we were to separate.

I did not want to let Wilma out of my sight, but it was necessary.

According to our plan, Barker was to make his way to the projectoscope plant, Blash and I to the library, and Wilma and Gaunt to the military office.

Blash and I traversed a long corridor, and paused at the green arched doorway of the library. Cautiously we peered in. Seated at three great switchboards were library operatives. Occasionally one of them would reach lazily for a lever, or sleepily push a button, as little numbered lights winked on and off. They were answering calls for electrograph and viewplate records on all sorts of subjects from all sections of the city.

I apprised my companions of the situation.

"Better wait a bit," Blash added. "The calls will lessen shortly."

Wilma reported an officer in the military office sound asleep.

"Give him the can, then," I said.

Barker was to do nothing more than keep watch in the projectoscope plant, and a few moments later he reported himself well concealed, with a splendid view of the floor.

"I think we can take a chance now," Blash said to me, and at my nod, he opened the lid of his dope can. Of course, the fumes did not affect us, through our helmets. They were absolutely without odor or visibility, and in a few seconds the librarians were unconscious. We stepped into the room.

There ensued considerable cautious observation and experiment on the part of Gaunt, working from the military office, and Blash in the library; while Wilma and I, with drawn swords and sharply attuned ultroscopes, stood guard, and occasionally patrolled nearby corridors.

"I hear something approaching," Wilma said after a bit, with excitement in her voice. "It's a soft, gliding sound."

"That's an elevator somewhere," Barker cut in from the projectoscope floor. "Can you locate it? I can't hear it."

"It's to the east of me," she replied.

"And to my west," said I, faintly catching it. "It's between us, Wilma, and nearer you than me. Be careful. Have you got any information yet, Blash and Gaunt?"

"Getting it now," one of them replied. "Give us two minutes more."

"Keep at it then," I said. "We'll guard."

The soft, gliding sound ceased.

"I think it's very close to me," Wilma almost whispered. "Come closer, Tony, I have a feeling something is going to happen. I've never known my nerves to get taut like this without reason."

In some alarm, I launched myself down the corridor in a great leap toward the intersection whence I knew I could see her.

In the middle of my leap my ultrophone registered her gasp of alarm. The next instant I glided to a stop at the intersection to see Wilma backing toward the door of the military office, her sword red with blood, and an inert form on the corridor floor. Two other Hans were circling to either side of her with wicked-looking knives, while a third, evidently a high officer, judging by the resplendence of his garb, tugged desperately to get an electrophone instrument out of a bulky pocket. If he ever gave the alarm, there was no telling what might happen to us.

I was at least seventy feet away, but I crouched low and sprang with every bit of strength in my legs. It would be more correct to say that I dived, for I reached the fellow head-on, with no attempt to draw my legs beneath me.

Some instinct must have warned him, for he turned suddenly as I hurtled close to him. But by this time I had sunk to the floor, and had stiffened myself rigidly, lest a dragging knee or foot might just prevent my reaching him. I brought my blade upward and over. It was a vicious slash that laid him open, bisecting him from groin to chin, and his dead body toppled down on me, as I slid to a tangled stop.

The other two startled, turned. Wilma leaped at one and struck him down with a side slash; I looked up at this instant, and the dazed fear on his face at the length of her leap registered vividly. The Hans knew nothing of our inertron belts, it seemed, and these leaps and dives of ours filled them with terror.

As I rose to my feet, a gory mess, Wilma, with a poise and speed which I found time to admire even in this crisis, again leaped. This time she dove head first as I had done, and with a beautifully executed thrust, ran the last Han through the throat.

Uncertainly, she scrambled to her feet, staggered queerly, and then sank gently prone on the corridor. She had fainted.

At this juncture, Blash and Gaunt reported with elation that they had the record we wanted.

"Back to the roof, everybody!" I ordered, as I picked Wilma up in my arms. With her inertron belt, she felt as light as a feather.

Gaunt joined me at once from the military office, and at the intersection of the corridor, we came upon Blash waiting for us. Barker, however, was not in evidence.

"Where are you, Barker?" I called.

"Go ahead," he replied. "I'll be with you on the roof at once."

We came out in the open without any further mishap, and I instructed Gibbons in the ship to light the knob on the end of the ultron wire. It flashed dully a few feet away from us. Just how he had maneuvered the ship to keep our end of the line in position, without its swinging in a tremendous arc, I have never been able to understand. Had not the night been an unusually still one, he could not have checked the initial pendulum-like movements. As it was, there was considerable air current at certain of the levels, and in different directions too. But Gibbons was an expert of rare ability and sensitivity in the handling of a rocket ship, and he managed, with the aid of his delicate instruments, to sense the drifts almost before they affected the fine ultron wire, and to neutralize them with little shifts in the position of the ship.

Blash and Gaunt fastened their rings to the wire, and I hooked my own and Wilma's on, too. But on looking around, I found Barker was still missing.

"Barker, come!" I called. "We're waiting."

"Coming!" he replied, and indeed, at that instant, his figure appeared up the ramp. He chuckled as he fastened his ring to the wire and said something about a little surprise he had left for the Hans.

"Don't reel in the wire more than a few hundred feet," I instructed Gibbons. "It will take too long to wind it in. We'll float up, and when we're aboard, we can drop it."

In order to float up, we had to dispense with a pound or two of weight apiece. We hurled our

swords from us, and kicked off our shoes as Gibbons reeled up the line a bit, and then, letting go of the wire, began to hum upward on our rings with increasing velocity.

The rush of air brought Wilma to, and I hastily explained to her that we had been successful. Receding far below us now, I could see our dully shining knob swinging to and fro in an ever widening arc, as it crossed and recrossed the black square of the tower roof. As an extra precaution, I ordered Gibbons to shut off the light, and to show one from the belly of the ship, for so great was our speed now, that I began to fear we would have difficulty in checking ourselves. We were literally falling upward, and with terrific acceleration.

Fortunately, we had several minutes in which to solve this difficulty, which none of us, strangely enough, had foreseen. It was Gibbons who found the answer.

"You'll be all right if all of you grab the wire tight when I give the word," he said. "First I'll start reeling it in at full speed. You won't get much of a jar, and then I'll decrease its speed again gradually, and its weight will hold you back. Are you ready? One—two—three!"

We all grabbed tightly with our gloved hands as he gave the word. We must have been rising a good bit faster than he figured, however, for it wrenched our arms considerably, and the maneuver set up a sickening pendulum motion.

For a while all we could do was swing there in an arc that may have been a quarter of a mile across, about three and a half miles above the city, and still more than a mile away from our ship.

Gibbons skillfully took up the slack as our momentum pulled up the line. Then at last we had ourselves under control again, and continued our upward journey, checking our speed somewhat with our gloves.

There was not one of us who did not breathe a big sigh of relief when we scrambled through the hatch safely into the ship again, cast off the ultron line and slammed the trap shut.

Little realizing that we had a still more terrible experience to go through, we discussed the information Blash and Gaunt had between them extracted from the Han records, and the advisability of ultrophoning our findings to Hart at once.

THE WALLS OF HELL

The traitors were, it seemed, a degenerate gang of Americans, located a few miles north of Nu-Yok on the wooded banks of the Hudson, the Sinsings. They had exchanged scraps of information to the Hans in return for several old repellor ray machines, and the privilege of tuning in on the Han electronic power broadcast for their operation, provided their ships agreed to subject themselves to the orders of the Han traffic office, while aloft.

The rest wanted to ultrophone their news at once, since there was always danger that we might never get back to the Gang with it.

I objected, however. The Sinsings would be likely to pick up our message. Even if we used the directional projector, they might have scouts out to the west and south in the big inter-gang stretches of country. They would flee to Nu-Yok and escape the punishment they merited. It seemed to be vitally important that they should not, for the sake of example to other weak groups among the American gangs, as well as to prevent a crisis in which they might clear more vital information to the enemy.

"Out to sea again," I ordered Gibbons. "They'll be less likely to look for us in that direction."

"Easy, Boss, easy," he replied. "Wait until we get up a mile or two more. They must have discovered evidences of our raid by now, and their dis ray wall may go in operation any moment."

Even as he spoke, the ship lurched downward and to one side.

"There it is!" he shouted. "Hang on, every-body. We're going to nose straight up!" And he flipped the rocket motor control wide open.

Looking through one of the rear ports, I could see a nebulous, luminous ring, and on all sides the atmosphere took on a faint iridescence.

We were almost over the destructive range of the disintegrator ray wall, a hollow cylinder of annihilation shooting upward from a solid ring of generators surrounding the city. It was the main defense system of the Hans, which had never been used except in periodic tests. They may or may not have suspected that an American rocket ship was within the cylinder; probably they had turned on their generators more as a precaution to prevent any reaching a position above the city.

But even at our present great height, we were in great danger. It was a question how much we might have been harmed by the rays themselves, for their effective range was not much more than seven or eight miles. The greater danger lay in the terrific downward rush of air within the cylinder to replace that which was being burned into nothingness by the continual play of the disintegrators. The air fell into the cylinder with the force of a gale. It would be rushing toward the wall from the outside with terrific force also, but, naturally, the effect was intensified on the interior.

Our ship vibrated and trembled. We had only one chance of escape—to fight our way well above the current. To drift down with it meant ultimately, and inevitably, to be sucked into the destruction wall at some lower level.

But very gradually and jerkily our upward movement, as shown on the indicators, began to increase, and after an hour of desperate struggle we were free of the maelstrom and into the rarefied upper levels. The terror beneath us was now invisible through several layers of cloud formations.

Gibbons brought the ship back to an even keel, and drove her eastward into one of the most brilliantly gorgeous sunrises I have ever seen.

We described a great circle to the south and west, in a long easy dive, for he had cut out his rocket motors to save them as much as possible. We had drawn terrifically on their fuel reserves in our battle with the elements. For the moment, the atmosphere below cleared, and we could see the Jersey coast far beneath, like a great map.

"We're not through yet," remarked Gibbons suddenly, pointing at his periscope, and adjusting it to telescopic focus. "A Han ship, and a 'drop ship' at that—and he's seen us. If he whips that beam of his on us, we're done."

I gazed, fascinated, at the viewplate. What I saw was a cigar-shaped ship not dissimilar to our own in design, and from the proportional size of its ports, of about the same size as our swoopers. We learned later that they carried crews, for the most part of not more than three or four men. They had streamlined hulls and trails that embodied universal-jointed double fish-tail rudders. In operation they rose to great heights on their powerful repellor rays, then gathered speed either by a straight nose dive, or an inclined dive in which they sometimes used the repellor ray slanted at a sharp angle. He was already above us, though several miles to the north. He could, of course, try to get on our tail and "spear" us with his beam as he dropped at us from a great height.

Suddenly his beam blazed forth in a blinding flash, whipping downward slowly to our right. He went through a peculiar corkscrew-like evolution, evidently maneuvering to bring his beam to bear on us with a spiral motion.

Gibbons instantly sent our ship into a series of evolutions that must have looked like those of a frightened hen. Alternately, he used the forward and the reverse rocket blasts, and in varying degree. We fluttered, we shot suddenly to right and left, and dropped like a plummet in uncertain movements. But all the time the Han scout dropped toward us, determinedly whipping the air around us with his beam. Once it sliced across beneath us, not more than a hundred feet, and we dropped with a jar into the pockets formed by the destruction of the air.

He had dropped to within a mile of us, and was coming with the speed of a projectile, when the end came. Gibbons always swore it was sheer luck. Maybe it was, but I like pilots who are lucky that way.

In the midst of a dizzy, fluttering maneuver of our own, with the Han ship enlarging to our gaze with terrifying rapidity, and its beam slowly slicing toward us in what looked like certain destruction within the second, I saw Gibbon's fingers flick at the lever of his rocket gun and a split second later the Han ship flew apart like a clay pigeon.

We staggered, and fluttered crazily for several moments while Gibbons struggled to bring our ship into balance, and a section of about four square feet in the side of the ship near the stern slowly crumbled like rusted metal. His beam actually had touched us, but our explosive rocket had got him a thousandth of a second sooner.

Part of our rudder had been annihilated, and our motor damaged. But we were able to swoop gently back across Jersey, fortunately crossing the ship lanes without sighting any more Han craft, and finally settling to rest in the little glade beneath the trees, near Hart's camp.

THE NEW BOSS

We had ultrophoned our arrival and the Big Boss himself, surrounded by the Council, was on hand to welcome us and learn our news. In turn we were informed that during the night a band of raiding Bad Bloods, disguised under the insignia of Altoonas, a gang some distance to the west of us, had destroyed several of our camps before our people had rallied and driven them off. Their purpose, evidently, had been to embroil us with the Altoonas, but fortunately, one of our exchanges recognized the Bad Blood leader, who had been slain.

The Big Boss had mobilized the full raiding force of the Gang, and was on the point of heading an expedition for the extermination of the Bad Bloods.

I looked around the grim circle of the sub-bosses, and realized the fate of America, at this moment, lay in their hands. Their temper demanded the immediate expenditure of our full effort in revenging ourselves for this raid. But the strategic exigencies, to my mind, quite clearly demanded the instant and absolute extermination of the Sinsings. It might be only a matter of hours, for all we knew, before these degraded people would barter clues to the American ultronic secrets to the Hans.

"How large a force have we?" I asked Hart.

"Every man and maid who can be spared," he replied. "That gives us seven hundred married and unmarried men, and three hundred girls, more than the entire Bad Blood Gang. Everyone is equipped with belts, ultrophones, rocket guns and swords, and all fighting mad."

I meditated how I might put the matter to these determined men, and was vaguely conscious that they were awaiting my words.

Finally I began to speak. I do not remember to this day just what I said. I talked calmly, with due regard for their passion, but with deep conviction. I went over the information we had collected, point by point, building my case logically, and painting a lurid picture of the danger impending in that half-alliance between the Sinsings and the Hans of Nu-Yok. I became impassioned, culminating, I believe, with a vow to proceed single-handed against the hereditary enemies of our race, "if the Wyomings were blindly set on placing a gang feud ahead of honor and duty and the hopes of all America."

As I concluded, a great calm came over me, as of one detached. I had felt much the same way during several crises in the First World War. I gazed from face to face, striving to read their expressions, and in a mood to make good my threat without any further heroics, if the decision was against me.

But it was Hart who sensed the temper of the Council more quickly then I did, and looked beyond it into the future.

He arose from the tree trunk on which he had been sitting.

"That settles it," he said, looking around the ring. "I have felt this thing coming on for some time now. I'm sure the Council agrees with me that there is among us a man more capable than I to boss the Wyoming Gang, despite his handicap of having had all too short a time in which to familiarize himself with our modern ways and facilities. Whatever I can do to support his effective leadership, at any cost, I pledge myself to do."

As he concluded, he advanced to where I stood, and taking from his head the green-crested helmet that constituted his badge of office, to my surprise he placed it in my mechanically extended hand.

The roar of approval that went up from the Council members left me dazed. Somebody ultrophoned the news to the rest of the Gang, and even though the earflaps of my helmet were turned up, I could hear the cheers with which my invisible followers greeted me, from near and distant hillsides, camps and plants.

My first move was to make sure that the Phone Boss, in communicating this news to the members of the Gang, had not re-broadcast my talk nor mentioned my plan of shifting the attack from the Bad Bloods to the Sinsings. I was relieved by his assurance that he had not, for it would have wrecked the whole plan. Everything depended upon our ability to surprise the Sinsings.

So I pledged the Council and my companions to secrecy, and allowed it to be believed that we were about to take to the air and the trees against the Bad Bloods.

That outfit must have been badly scared, the way they were "burning" the ether with ultrophone alibis and propaganda for the benefit of the more distant gangs. It was their old game, and the only method by which they had avoided extermination long ago from their immediate neighbors—these appeals to the spirit of American brotherhood, addressed to gangs too far away to have had the sort of experience with them that had fallen to our lot.

I chuckled. Here was another good reason for the shift in my plans. Were we actually to undertake the extermination of the Bad Bloods at once, it would have been a hard job to convince some of the gangs that we had not been precipitate and unjustified. Jealousies and prejudices existed. There were gangs which would give the benefit of the doubt to the Bad Bloods, rather than to ourselves, and the issue was now hopelessly beclouded with the clever lies that were being broadcast in an unceasing stream.

But the extermination of the Sinsings would be another thing. In the first place, there would be no warning of our action until it was all over, I hoped. In the second place, we would have indisputable proof, in the form of their rep-ray ships and other paraphernalia, of their traffic with the Hans; and the state of American prejudice, at the time of which I write, held trafficking with the Hans a far more heinous thing than even a vicious gang feud.

I called an executive session of the Council at once. I wanted to inventory our military resources.

I created a new office on the spot, that of "Control Boss," and appointed Ned Garlin to the post, turning over his former responsibility as Plants Boss to his assistant. I needed someone, I felt, to tie in the records of the various functional activities of the campaign, and take over from me the task of keeping the records of them up to the minute.

I received reports from the bosses of the ultrophone unit, and those of food, transportation, fighting gear, chemistry, electronic activity and electrophone intelligence, ultroscopes, air patrol and contact guard.

My ideas for the campaign, of course, were somewhat tinged with my 20th Century experience, and I found myself faced with the task of working out a staff organization that was a composite of the best and most easily applied principles of business and military efficiency, as I knew them from the viewpoint of immediate practicality.

What I wanted was an organization that would be specialized, functionally, not as that indicated above, but from the angles of: intelligence as to the Sinsings activities; intelligence as to Han activities; perfection of communication with my own units; co-operation of field command; and perfect mobilization of emergency supplies and resources.

It took several hours of hard work with the Council to map out the plan. First we assigned functional experts and equipment to each "Division" in accordance with its needs. Then these in turn were reassigned by the new Division Bosses to the Field Commands as needed, or as Independent or Headquarters Units. The two intelligence divisions were named the White and the Yellow, indicating that one specialized on the American enemy and the other on the Mongolians.

The division in charge of our own communications, the assignment of ultrophone frequencies and strengths, and the maintenance of operators and equipment, I called "Communications."

I named Bill Hearn to the post of Field Boss, in charge of the main or undetached fighting units, and to the Resources Division, I assigned all responsibility for what few air craft we had; and all transportation and supply problems, I assigned to "Resources." The functional bosses stayed with this division.

We finally completed our organization with the assignment of liaison representatives among the various divisions as needed.

Thus I had a "Headquarters Staff" composed of the Division Bosses who reported directly to Ned Garlin as Control Boss, or to Wilma as my personal assistant. And each of the Division Bosses had his own small staff.

In the final summing up of our personnel and resources, I found we had roughly a thousand "troops," of whom some three hundred and fifty were in what I called the Service Divisions, the rest being in Bill Hearn's Field Division. This latter number, however, was cut down somewhat by the assignment of numerous small units to detached service. Altogether, the actual available fighting force, I figured, would number about five hundred, by the time we actually went into action.

We had only six small swoopers, but I had an ingenious plan in my mind, as the result of our little raid on Nu-Yok, that would make this sufficient, since the reserves of inertron blocks were larger than I expected to find them. The Resources Division, by packing its supply cases a bit tight, or by slipping in extra blocks of inertron, was able to reduce each to a weight of a few ounces. These easily could be floated and towed by the swoopers in any quantity. Hitched to ultron lines, it would be a virtual impossibility for them to break loose.

The entire personnel, of course, was supplied with jumpers, and if each man and girl was careful to adjust balances properly, the entire number could also be towed along through the air, grasping wires of ultron, swinging below the swoopers, or stringing out behind them.

There would be nothing tiring about this, because the strain would be no greater than that of carrying a one- or two-pound weight in the hand, except for air friction at high speeds. But to make doubly sure that we should lose none of our personnel, I gave strict orders that the belts and two lines should be equipped with rings and hooks.

So great was the efficiency of the fundamental organization and discipline of the Gang, that we got under way at nightfall.

One by one the swoopers eased into the air, each followed by its long train or "kite tail" of humanity and supply cases hanging lightly from its tow line. For convenience, the two lines were made of an alloy of ultron which, unlike the metal itself, is visible.

At first these "tails" hung downward, but as the ships swung into formation and headed eastward toward the Bad Blood territory, gathering speed, they began to string out behind. And swinging low from each ship on heavily weighted

lines, ultroscope, ultrophone and straight-vision observers keenly scanned the countryside, while intelligence men in the swoopers above bent over their instrument boards and view-plates.

Leaving Control Boss Ned Garlin temporarily in charge of affairs, Wilma and I dropped a weighted line from our ship, and slid down about halfway to the under lookouts, that is to say, about a thousand feet. The sensation of floating swiftly through the air like this, in the absolute security of one's confidence in the inertron belt, was one of never-ending delight to me.

We reascended into the swooper as the expedition approached the territory of the Bad Bloods, and directed the preparations for the bombardment. It was part of my plan to appear to carry out the attack as originally planned.

About fifteen miles from their camps our ships came to a halt and maintained their positions for a while with the idling blasts of their rocket motors, to give the ultroscope operators a chance to make a thorough examination of the territory below us, for it was very important that this next step in our program should be carried out with all secrecy.

At length they reported the ground below us entirely clear of any appearance of human occupation, and a gun unit of long-range specialists was lowered with a dozen rocket guns, equipped with special automatic devices that the Resources Division had developed at my request, a few hours before our departure. These were aiming and timing devices. After calculating the range, elevation and rocket charges carefully, the guns were left, concealed in a ravine, and the men were hauled up into the ship again. At the predetermined hour, those unmanned rocket guns would begin automatically to bombard the Bad Bloods' hillsides, shifting their aim and elevation slightly with each shot, as did many of our artillery pieces in the First World War.

In the meantime, we turned south about twenty miles, and grounded, waiting for the bombardment to begin before we attempted to sneak across the Han ship lane. I was relying for security on the distraction that the bombardment might furnish the Han observers.

It was tense work waiting, but the affair went through as planned, our squadron drifting across the route high enough to enable the ships' tails of troops and supply cases to clear the ground.

In crossing the second ship route, out along the Beaches of Jersey, we were not so successful in escaping observation. A Han ship came speeding along at a very low elevation. We caught it on our electronic location and direction finders, and also located it with our ultroscopes, but it came so fast and so low that I thought it best to remain where we had grounded the second time, and lie quiet, rather than get under way and cross in front of it.

The point was this. While the Hans had no such devices as our ultroscopes, with which we could see in the dark (within certain limitations of course), and their electronic instruments would be virtually useless in uncovering our presence, since all but natural electronic activities were carefully eliminated from our apparatus, except electrophone receivers (which are not easily spotted), the Hans did have some very highly sensitive sound devices which operated with great efficiency in calm weather, so far as sounds emanating from the air were concerned. But the "ground roar" greatly confused their use of these instruments in the location of specific sounds floating up from the surface of the earth.

This ship must have caught some slight noise of ours, however, in its sensitive instruments, for we heard its electronic devices go into play, and picked up the routine report of the noise to its Base Ship Commander. But from the nature of the conversation, I judged they had not identified it, and were, in fact, more curious about the detonations they were picking up now from the Bad Bloods' lands some sixty miles or so to the west.

Immediately after this ship had shot by, we took the air again, and following much the same route that I had taken the previous night, climbed in a long semicircle out over the ocean, swung toward the north and finally the west. We set our course, however, for the Sinsings' land north of Nu-Yok, instead of for the city itself.

THE FINGER OF DOOM

As we crossed the Hudson River, a few miles north of the city, we dropped several units of the Yellow Intelligence Division, with full instrumental equipment. Their apparatus cases were nicely balanced at only a few ounces' weight each, and the men used their chute capes to ease their drops.

We recrossed the river a little distance above and began dropping White Intelligence units and a few long- and short-range gun units. Then we held our position until we began to get reports. Gradually we ringed the territory of the Sinsings, our observation units working busily and patiently at their locaters and scopes, both aloft and aground, until Garlin finally turned to me with the remark:

"The map circle is complete now, Boss. We've got clear locations all the way around them."

"Let me see it," I replied, and studied the illuminated viewplate map, with its little overlapping circles of light that indicated spots proved clear of the enemy by ultroscopic observation.

I nodded to Bill Hearn. "Go ahead now, Hearn," I said, "and place your barrage men."

He spoke into his ultrophone, and three of the ships began to glide in a wide ring around the enemy territory. Every few seconds, at the word from his Unit Boss, a gunner would drop off the wire, and slipping the clasp of his chute cape, drift down into the darkness below.

Bill formed two lines, parallel to and facing the river, and enclosing the entire territory of the enemy between them. Above and below, straddling the river, were two defensive lines. These latter were merely to hold their positions.

The others were to close in toward each other, pushing a high-explosive barrage five miles ahead of them. When the two barrages met, both lines were to switch to short-vision-range barrage and continue to close in on any of the enemy who might have drifted through the previous curtain of fire.

In the meantime Bill kept his reserves, a picked corps of a hundred men (the same that had accompanied Hart and myself in our fight with the Han squadron) in the air, divided about equally among the "kite tails" of our ships.

A final roll call, by units, companies, divisions and functions, established the fact that all our forces were in position. No Han activity was reported, and no Han broadcasts indicated any suspicion of our expedition. Nor was there any indication that the Sinsings had any knowledge of the fate in store for them. The idling of rep-ray generators was reported from the center of their camp, obviously those of the ships the Hans had given them—the price of their treason to their race.

Again I gave the word, and Hearn passed on the order to his subordinates. Far below us, and several miles to the right and left, the two barrage lines made their appearance. From the great height to which we had risen, they appeared like lines of brilliant, winking lights, and the detonations were muffled by the distances into a sort of rumbling, distant thunder. Hearn and his assistants were very busy; measuring, calculating and snapping out ultrophone orders to unit commanders that resulted in the straightening of lines and the closing of gaps in the barrage.

The White Division Boss reported the utmost confusion in the Sinsing organization— they were, as might be expected, an inefficient, loosely disciplined gang—and repeated broadcasts for help to neighboring gangs. Ignoring the fact that the Mongolians had not used explosives for many generations, they nevertheless jumped at the conclusion that they were being raided by the Hans. Their frantic broadcasts persisted in this thought, despite the nervous electrophonic inquiries of the Hans themselves, to whom the sound of the battle was evidently audible, and who were trying to locate the trouble.

At this point, the swooper I had sent south toward the city went into action as a diversion, to keep the Hans at home. Its "kite tail" loaded with long-range gunners, using the most highly explosive rockets we had, hung invisible in the darkness of the sky and bombarded the city from a distance of about five miles. With an entire city to shoot at, and the object of creating as much commotion therein as possible, regardless of actual damage, the gunners had no difficulty in hitting the mark. I could see the glow of the city and the stabbing flashes of exploding rockets. In the end, the Hans, uncertain as to what was going on, fell back on a defensive policy, and shot their "hell cylinder," or wall of upturned disintegrator rays, into operation. That, of course, ended our bombardment of them. The rays were a perfect defense, disintegrating our rockets as they were reached.

If they had not sent out ships before turning on the rays, and if they had none within sufficient radius already in the air, all would be well.

I queried Garlin on this, but he assured me Yellow Intelligence reported no indication of Han ships nearer than 800 miles. This would probably give us a free hand for a while, since most of their instruments recorded only imperfectly or not at all, through the death wall.

Requisitioning one of the viewplates of the headquarters ship, and the services of an expert operator, I instructed him to focus on our lines below. I wanted a close-up of the men in action.

He began to manipulate his controls and chaotic shadows moved rapidly across the plate, fading in and out of focus, until he reached an adjustment that gave me a picture of the forest floor, apparently 100 feet wide, with the intervening branches and foliage of the trees appearing like shadows that melted into reality a few feet above the ground.

I watched one man setting up his long-gun with skillful speed. His lips pursed slightly as though he were whistling, as he adjusted the tall tripod on which the long tube was balanced. Swiftly he twirled the knobs controlling the aim and elevation of his piece. Then, lifting a belt of

Setting the rocket gun for a long-distance shot.

ammunition from the big box, which itself looked heavy enough to break down the spindly tripod, he inserted the end of it in the lock of his tube and touched the proper combination of buttons.

Then he stepped aside, and occupied himself with peering carefully through the trees ahead. Not even a tremor shook the tube, but I knew that at intervals of something less than a second, it was discharging small projectiles which, traveling under their own continuously reduced power, were arching into the air, to fall precisely five miles ahead and explode with the force of eight-inch shells, such as we used in the First World War.

Another gunner, fifty feet to the right of him, waved a hand and called out something to him. Then, picking up his own tube and tripod, he gauged the distance between the trees ahead of him, and the height of their lowest branches, and bending forward a bit, flexed his muscles and

leaped lightly, some twenty feet or so, where he set up his piece.

I ordered my observer then to switch to the barrage itself. He got a close focus on it, but this showed little except a continuous series of blinding flashes, which, from the viewplate, lit up the entire interior of the ship. An eight-hundred-foot focus proved better. I had thought that some of our French and American artillery of the 20th Century had achieved the ultimate in mathematical precision of fire, but I had never seen anything to equal the accuracy of that line of terrific explosions as it moved steadily forward, mowing down trees as a scythe cuts grass (or used to 500 years ago), literally churning up the earth and the splintered, blasted remains of the forest giants, to a depth of from ten to twenty feet.

By now the two curtains of fire were nearing each other, lines of vibrant, shimmering, continuous, brilliant destruction, inevitably squeezing the panic-stricken Sinsings between them.

Even as I watched, a group of them, who had been making a futile effort to get their three repray machines into the air, abandoned their efforts, and rushed forth into the milling mob.

I queried the Control Boss sharply on the futility of this attempt of theirs, and learned that the Hans, apparently in doubt as to what was going on, had continued to "play safe," and broken off their power broadcast, after ordering all their own ships east of the Alleghenies to the ground, for fear these ships they had traded to the Sinsings might be used against them.

Again I turned to my viewplate, which was still focused on the central section of the Sinsing works. The confusion of the traitors was entirely that of fear, for our barrage had not yet reached them.

Some of them set up their long-guns and fired at random over the barrage line, then gave it up. They realized that they had no target to shoot at, no way of knowing whether our gunners were a few hundred feet or several miles beyond it.

Their ultrophone men, of whom they did not have many, stood around in tense attitudes, their helmet phones strapped around their ears, nervously fingering the tuning controls at their belts. Unquestionably they must have located some of our frequencies, and overheard many of our reports and orders. But they were confused and disorganized. If they had an Ultrophone Boss they evidently were not reporting to him in an organized way.

They were beginning to draw back now before our advancing fire. With intermittent desperation, they began to shoot over our barrage again, and the explosions of their rockets flashed at widely scattered points beyond. A few took distance "potshots."

Oddly enough it was our own forces that suffered the first casualties in the battle. Some of these distance shots by chance registered hits, while our men were under strict orders not to exceed their barrage distances.

Seen upon the ultroscope viewplate, the battle looked as though it were being fought in daylight, perhaps on a cloudy day, while the explosions of the rockets appeared as flashes of extra brilliance.

The two barrage lines were not more than five hundred feet apart when the Sinsings resorted to tactics we had not foreseen. We noticed first that they began to lighten themselves by throwing away extra equipment. A few of them in their excitement threw away too much, and shot suddenly into the air. Then a scattering few floated up gently, followed by increasing numbers, while still others, preserving a weight balance, jumped toward the closing barrages and leaped high, hoping to clear them. Some succeeded. We saw others blown about like leaves in a windstorm, to crumple and drift slowly down, or else to fall into the barrage, their belts blown from their bodies.

However, it was not part of our plan to allow a single one of them to escape and find his way to the Hans. I quickly passed the word to Bill Hearn to have the alternate men in his line raise their barrages and heard him bark out a mathematical formula to the Unit Bosses.

We backed off our ships as the explosions climbed into the air in stagger formation until they reached a height of three miles. I don't believe any of the Sinsings who tried to float away to freedom succeeded.

But we did know later, that a few who leaped the barrage got away and ultimately reached Nu-Yok.

It was those who managed to jump the barrage who gave us the most trouble. With half of our long-guns turned aloft, I foresaw we would not have enough to establish successive ground barrages and so ordered the barrage back two miles, from which positions our "curtains" began to close in again, this time, however, gauged to explode, not on contact, but thirty feet in the air. This left little chance for the Sinsings to leap either over or under it.

Gradually, the two barrages approached each other until they finally met, and in the gray dawn the battle ended.

Our own casualties totaled one hundred and nine. Since nearly every member of the Sinsing Gang had, so far as we knew, been killed, we considered the raid a great success.

It had, however, a far greater significance than this. To all of us, who took part in the expedition, the effectiveness of our barrage tactics definitely established a confidence in our ability to overcome the Hans.

As I pointed out to Wilma:

"It has been my belief all along, dear, that the American explosive rocket is a far more efficient weapon than the disintegrator ray of the Hans, once we can train all our gangs to use it systematically and in co-ordinated fashion. As a weapon in the hands of a single individual, shooting at a mark in direct line of vision, the rocket gun is inferior in destructive power to the dis ray, except as its range may be a little greater. The trouble is that to date it has been used only as we used our rifles and shotguns in the 20th Century. The possibilities of its use as artillery, in laying barrages that advance along the ground, or climb into the air, are tremendous.

"The dis ray inevitably reveals its source of emanation. The rocket gun does not. The dis ray can reach its target only in a straight line. The rocket can travel in an arc, over intervening obstacles, to an unseen target.

"Nor must we forget that our ultronists now are promising us a perfect shield against the dis ray in inertron."

"I tremble though, Tony dear, when I think of the horrors that are ahead of us. The Hans are clever. They will develop defenses against our new tactics. And they are sure to mass against us not only the full force of their power in America, but the united forces of the World Empire. They are ruthless and clever."

"Nevertheless," I prophesied, "the Finger of Doom points squarely at them today, and unless you and I are killed in the struggle, we shall live to see America blast the Yellow Blight from the face of the earth."

GEOFFREY HOUSEHOLD

GEOFFREY EDWARD WEST HOUSEHOLD (1900–1988) was born in Bristol, England. After graduating from Oxford with a degree in English literature, he laid the foundation for his future career as an author of international adventure fiction by taking jobs in Romania, Spain, the United States, and various other countries in the Middle East, South America, and Europe. When World War II erupted, he served with distinction as a member of the British intelligence corps.

Household's first published short story, "The Salvation of Pisco Gabar," was published in the prestigious *Atlantic Monthly* and later served as the title story for his first collection of short fiction. He went on to pen six more collections, as well as twenty-eight novels, most of which were international thrillers packed with exciting chases. His most famous work, and probably his best, is his third novel, *Rogue Male* (1939), a nonstop action story set shortly before England's involvement in World War II. The novel follows a wealthy young Englishman who, while on a hunting trip in Europe, manages to get a clean shot at an unnamed dictator into his rifle sight (the cover of nearly every edition of the book depicts Adolf Hitler). The hunter is caught, tortured, and thrown over a cliff, apparently to his death. He survives and returns to England, where he is pursued by agents intent on finishing him off, until he turns the tables on his pursuers and returns to the Continent, this time to hunt the dictator in earnest. *Rogue Male* was superbly adapted by Fritz Lang in 1941 as the classic chase film *Man Hunt*, starring Walter Pidgeon, Joan Bennett, and George Sanders. Peter O'Toole later starred in a 1976 British television movie that restored the original title of *Rogue Male*, and which O'Toole described as his favorite of all his films in a BBC radio interview in 2007.

"Woman in Love" was first published as "Secret Information" in *This Week* magazine in 1952; its first publication in book form was in the author's short-story collection *Tales of Adventurers* (London: Joseph, 1952).

WOMAN IN LOVE

GEOFFREY HOUSEHOLD

IT WAS the nearest he had ever come to sending an agent to his death. Her death, rather. He admitted that he shouldn't have taken the risk, that a man with his experience of women should have known better; but there he was with the enemy order of battle—or ally's peaceful deployment, according to how you look at it—all along the southern fringe of the Iron Curtain from Bratislava to the Black Sea. The list was complete, and accurate up to the previous Saturday; and there wasn't a chance of getting it out to the West. No handy secret wireless. No landing grounds. Not a trustworthy agent who had the remotest hope of being given a passport in time to be of use. Theotaki had found his job much easier when operating under the noses of the Gestapo.

He was a Roumanian of Greek origin, with all a Greek's hungry passion for the ideal freedom which had never in practical politics existed, and never could. He had also the Greek's love of adventurous intrigue for its own sake. One gets used to the trade, he would say. Steeple jacks, for example. They couldn't be thinking all the time about risk. They took, he supposed, meticulous care with all their preparations—blocks and tackle, scaffolding, belts—and then got on with the job. It was only when a man had scamped the preliminaries that he need worry about risks.

Normally there was no need to scamp them, no disastrous demand for hurry. Cold war wasn't like hot war, and there weren't any impa-

tient generals howling for immediate results. So caution, caution, caution, all the time. It was a bit dull, he said, but the main objective had to be to keep his organization alive.

He admitted, however, that this had been an occasion for desperate measures. The only chance he could see of getting that enemy order of battle into hands that would appreciate it was D 17. D 17 was going the very next day to Stockholm to be married. She would never have been allowed to leave for less neutral territory; but it was hard, even for Communist bureaucrats, to think up a really valid excuse for preventing a citizen—an entirely useless citizen whose parents were living on the proceeds of their jewelry and furniture—from taking herself off to Sweden and matrimony, when a firm request for her had been passed through diplomatic channels.

Alexia—D 17—was a very minor agent: somewhat too enthusiastic, said Theotaki, for her sister had been mishandled by the Russian advance guards when they entered Bucharest and had died the following week. The unfortunate incident had had some effect on Theotaki's ideals of freedom, too. But he never confessed to emotion. To judge by his jowled, dead, decadent face, you wouldn't have thought him capable of feeling any.

Since he had moved before the war in the social circle of the parents and their two daughters, he knew Alexia very well. She had, of course, no idea that he was in any way responsible for the occasional orders received by D 17. She couldn't have given away more than the three names of the other members of her cell—at least she couldn't up to the time when Theotaki was forced into gambling against his better judgment.

He kept her under observation all the morning. She was shopping for a few clothes and necessary trifles that she could much better have bought abroad. But she didn't know that. Alexia visualized the outside world as seething with unemployment and economic distress. Of course she did, of course she did, exclaimed Theotaki, defending this absurd shopping. Even when you are aware that all your news is tainted, you have to believe some of it. For all Alexia knew, the shops of Stockholm might well have been looted by starving rioters or bought out by dollar-waving American troops.

She was obviously happy. Well, why wouldn't she be? She was a tense and luminous woman in her middle twenties escaping to her lover and doing a bit of buying to please his eyes. When, however, she sat down, alone, in the huge barren hall of a cheap café, she was ashamed of herself. Theotaki guessed it from her bearing, from the uncertainty of her eyes. He was clever as any woman at guessing mood when not a word had passed. To be ashamed of yourself for being happy was, he explained, one of the most damnable, minor, nagging aches of political tyranny. Your personal tastes and joys could not be altered by the common discontent, yet you felt they should be. Love and the flighting of duck at first light and the relish of wine to a man and the feel of a dress to a woman—they don't come to an end because your country is enslaved and terrorized.

So that was the position—D 17 sitting in a café, thinking of her beloved with one half of her mind, and with the other her duty to hate; and Theotaki moving behind her to find a table, not too far away, where she couldn't see and greet him.

He took one of the café's illustrated papers in its cane frame, and began abstractedly to write a poem across the blank spaces of an advertise-

ment. When he had finished his drink and his casual scribbling, he paid his bill and sent the waiter to Alexia with the paper. He then vanished from his table and stood talking to a casual acquaintance by the door, whence he could watch in a mirror the effect of his inspiration.

The waiter suspected nothing. It was a quite normal act to send a paper to a customer who had asked for it—especially if the customer were a pretty girl. At least it appeared quite normal when Theotaki did it. That he was alive at all was largely due to his naturalness of manner.

Alexia received the paper as if it were expected. Theotaki approved her presence of mind, and well he might. Any gesture of surprise could have led—if the waiter earned a little extra money by giving information to the police—to prolonged questioning of both of them. He admitted that he had been apprehensive. He hadn't been able to arrange much training for her and her like.

She glanced idly through the coarse rotogravures of factory openings and parades, and found the doodling of some previous reader. There were girls' heads, and jottings for a very commonplace love poem to sweet seventeen. Among the half lines, the blanks to be filled in, the notes for promising rhymes, was a phrase *your garden at three in the morning* continually repeated, toyed with and crossed out because no order of the words could be made to scan. Then came a row of capital D's, as if the lovesick doodler, failing to succeed as a poet, had tried to design the most decorative letter with which to begin his work.

D 17's garden at 3 a.m.—the message would have been instantly clear to Theotaki who never read anything that was misplaced, even a printer's error, without wondering why it was misplaced. But he didn't expect the same alertness from D 17; he only hoped. As a man of imagination he had, he insisted, the keenest sympathy for romance, and therefore thought it more than likely that Alexia would be too absorbed by justifiable dreams to notice his vulgar scribblings. He was very pleased with her indeed when her hand began to fiddle with ashtray, saucer and saltcellar, arranging them into a group of three to show, if there were anyone watching her, that she had read and understood.

D 17's garden—or rather her parents'—was a reasonably safe spot for a rendezvous. A high but climbable wall separated its overgrown shrubbery from the state-disciplined bushes of a public park. In happier days Alexia and her sister had been very well aware of its advantages.

High-spirited young ladies, said Theotaki. Yes, and they had had their own uproarious methods of discouraging unwelcome suitors. When he dropped over the wall that night, for the second time in his life, he remembered that ten years earlier there had been a cunning arrangement of glass and empty cans to receive him, and a crash that woke the uneasy summer sleepers in four blocks of flats that faced the park.

This time there were only silence and soft leaf mold. Theotaki in a whisper reminded the darkness of his last visit and of the two excitable policemen who had burst with Alexia's father into the garden. Even in those days he had been skilled at evading policemen.

The darkness did not answer. Very rightly. This might be a trap. D 17 had not received her orders through the usual channels.

Theotaki sat down with his back against the wall and waited. After a while he again addressed the dark shapes of the bushes. He warned them that if they were not alone they had better say so, for he was about to speak of the relationship—the 1951 relationship, that is—between himself and Alexia.

Alexia detached herself from her background, and assured him that she was alone. As proof of his authority, he told her the names and numbers of the other members of her cell and what their recent activities had been.

"Will that do?" he asked. "Or do you want more details, D 17?"

She murmured that she couldn't know . . . that she would never have believed it possible . . . that never in all her life had she respected him—or anyone—so much. . . .

Theotaki apologized for being desperate. Caution—caution, he told her, was the only road to success. There was no hurry, no room for either risks or enthusiasm. Still, sometimes—regretfully—one had to improvise. Where was it safe to talk?

She led him away from the wall into a tunnel of green darkness, and begged him to say what he wanted from her. Always that dangerous feminine enthusiasm. Yet it was a little forced. Theotaki could tell by her voice that she was uneasy at the unexpected mixture of her social life—such as it was—with her very secret service.

He apologized again for his inefficiency, for the urgency—there should never be any urgency—which had compelled him to appeal to her directly.

"It isn't fair to any of us," he said.

"Whatever happens to me, I shall not talk," Alexia assured him in a passionate whisper.

Theotaki considered the eager, small-boned body with the pitying eye of a professional. It would be capable of exquisite suffering, but he was inclined to share Alexia's faith in its resistance. Torture had little effect upon a flame. Better technique was to confine it closely and have patience until it went out. He reckoned that about three months would be enough to draw out full confession from an Alexia who by then would be Alexia no longer.

Three months. Or much less, if she were caught without possibility of blank denials. Good God, when he thought, afterwards, how nearly it had happened, how but for the most amazing luck . . .

"You are in love?" he asked.

"Doesn't it stand to reason?"

Theotaki quickly answered that he hadn't doubted it for a moment. Nor had he. She wasn't the type of woman to marry, just to escape from the country, without love. No, he wanted to know what she would answer—to hear, as it were, the worst from her own lips.

He remembered the man who taught him his trade. He liked to remember him very carefully, for, since the man was dead, there was no other method of consultation. This teacher of his used to say that a female agent was every bit as good as any male. What she lacked in attack, she made up in human understanding. But never, the dead man had insisted, never choose a woman in love!

Something of this, by way of warning, he repeated to D 17.

"I think your friend did not understand women," she answered.

Theotaki explained that his friend had been talking only of women of character, who worked for patriotism, not money. He had not implied that such a woman's devotion would be any less because she was in love, nor that she would be likely to sacrifice the cause to her private happiness. No, he had only meant that any woman of outstanding intensity was, when in love, Love Itself. She became possessed by hormones and happiness, and ceased to bother with details.

"And I wouldn't choose any woman but a woman in love," Alexia laughed. "Because until she is, she's only half alive."

Theotaki admitted there was something in that. The will of a woman in love dominated her environment; though it couldn't, perhaps, burn its way through armor plate, it would certainly try.

"But don't forget my friend's experience," he warned her. "He was a man of very wide experience. And so be a little more careful over details than you would be ordinarily. Just to compensate."

He gave her the precious sheet of foolscap, closely typed over with the positions, the strengths, the armor of corps, divisions and independent brigades.

"Learn that by heart," he said, "and then burn it. Burn it and crush the ashes. When you get to Stockholm, make an excuse, as soon as you reasonably can, to be alone, and go straight to the address you will read at the bottom of the sheet. Say you come from me, and recite your lesson. That's all. Then you can be happy with a good conscience. I, your leader, tell you so."

When she had vanished silently into the house, Theotaki flowed, inch by careful inch, like the battered tom-cat he resembled, back over the wall. He walked from the park to his flat through streets deserted by all but the police. Several times during the journey he showed his papers. He was a privileged person, kept rather contemptuously by the Ministry of the Interior for the sake of his general usefulness. Nobody could possibly have suspected Theotaki of any idealism.

D 17—well, what D 17 did when she was alone in her bedroom could only be reconstructed from his knowledge of her and the story that reached him weeks later. She had a quick, reliable memory, and in the gray hour before dawn she learned those dull military numerals as conscientiously as she had learned poetry for school examinations. She would remember, said Theotaki—who had practiced, earlier in his career, the same exact and desperate memorizing—every fact and figure for the rest of her life. That done, she would have been relaxed and beautifully at ease. The last service had been asked of her; she had an honorable discharge. She could give her whole attention to dreaming of the joy that would begin next day.

She must have sat down about sunrise, in the last of her spare time, too excited to sleep, to write to her fiancé. That was like her. She was rich in forethought and expedients. Her departure might still be delayed by some incalculable change in the official mind. If it were, her lover would have a letter to comfort him. If it were not, they would read the two pages together, and laugh for relief from their common fears which had not come true.

Then, when the letter was in its envelope and stamped, came all the fuss of leaving, the weeping mother, the insistence that she should have enough breakfast, the last-minute closing of her four suitcases, the drive to the station.

At the frontier Theotaki took up direct observation again, for, if D 17 should walk into trouble, he wanted to have first news of it. He was astonished at the ease, the gallantry of her departure. The Roumanian officials searched two of her cases and left the rest unopened. It was the starry-eyedness of her and youth and her own infectious certainty that no one could stop so innocently blissful a girl which carried her through. A perfect example, Theotaki pointed out, of the woman in love dominating her environment. That grim frontier post, on both sides of the line, was all bows and smiles.

Theotaki could go no farther. That he had been allowed to come so far, and on the flimsiest of excuses, was a severe test of his nuisance value to his Ministry. He hastened back to Bucharest, very relieved but unable to get rid of an aching nervousness. He put it down to his dislike of breaking the rules of the trade. By short-circuiting his own organization, he had hopelessly committed its safety to the hands of D 17. He assured himself that she could have no further difficulties, but she had still to cross a frontier between Budapest and Prague; and at Prague, before she took the plane to Stockholm, there would be a last, thorough and envious examination of her papers and her baggage.

Theotaki spoke of Alexia's journey as if he had been on the train with her. In thought, hour after hour, so he was. He knew to the minute—though that of course was mere calculation of schedules—when the blinds of the train would be pulled down so that no passenger might see the possible presence and activities of Russian troops. Thirtieth Assault Division, she would say to herself, and inevitably her mind would run over the bare details of its strength and its experimental bridging equipment. She wouldn't be able to help this silent recitation, and would try to stop herself forming the mental words lest they might be magically overheard.

All that was true enough. Nevertheless Alexia, as he heard afterwards, had passed most of the journey in a dream of romantic confidence. It had been broken, while she sat in the train, by moments of vague inexplicable worry; but whenever she and her baggage were in contact with the enemy, she treated officials as if they were as gay and careless as she herself, in twelve hours more, hoped to be. She turned the future into the present with an audacity that no mere man could have imitated and which she didn't even recognize as unreal—with the result that when police and customs and their informers on the train gave her a look, they saw only a girl neither immorally rich nor suspiciously poor, and much too happy to have anything in their line of business upon her conscience.

At Prague, however, the solid and bad-tempered Czechs turned her inside out. They flung the upper layers of her bags aside and angrily rummaged the bottom for antisocial contraband. They interrogated her. They gave her a fresh batch of forms to sign. And when they had punished her so far as they could for wanting to leave the Russian orbit at all, they had to allow her to leave it.

After that it was all plain sailing. She was met by her fiancé on arrival, and Swedish smiles passed her straight into their country, and let her loose in a blue and white Stockholm which sparkled like her mood. No, not sentimentalists, Theotaki explained. They had merely done their investigation of Alexia at the proper time, and once her visa had been issued there was no further point in annoying her. That was the mark of a civilized country. Communists hadn't yet learned to make up their minds and stand by the decision.

It must have been very difficult for D 17 to shake off fiancé and future parents-in-law and the odd score of hospitable friends who were determined to cherish her; but she did it. She had, after all, long experience in concealing her intentions. Somehow she established her right to a moment of privacy, and claimed it. She delivered her message, word perfect, and kept the taxi waiting and was back in her bedroom in half an hour.

Then she started, said Theotaki, to unpack. He heard of that unpacking when he met his Stockholm correspondent in the quiet course of their business, and even then they couldn't laugh. He was right. He had never come nearer to sending an agent to certain death. On the top of the first case Alexia opened was her writing pad, just where she had hastily thrown it in the unworldly light of dawn, after finishing that last letter, that all-absorbing letter, to her fiancé. The bag was the only one of the four that had never been examined by Roumanians or Hungarians, and the Czechs had gone like burrowing dogs for the bottom while scattering out the top between their legs. In the writing pad, hidden only by its flimsy cardboard cover, was the sheet of foolscap, gloriously forgotten, not crushed at all to ashes, not even burned, which Theotaki had given her with such delicate precautions.

MACHINERY AND THE CAULIFLOWERS

ALISTAIR MacLEAN

ALISTAIR STUART MacLEAN (1922–1987) was a native of Glasgow, Scotland, and spoke Scottish Gaelic as a young man; English, his second language, was forbidden at home. When he was eighteen, he joined the Royal Navy, serving chiefly as a torpedo man until the end of World War II. After the war, he went to Glasgow University and earned an English degree with honors, thereafter becoming a teacher and writing short stories in his spare time. His experiences in the navy gave him a great sense of the sea, which he used as background for many of his stories and, later, his adventure and war novels. MacLean's first novel, *H.M.S. Ulysses* (1955), was immediately successful and was quickly followed by the thrilling tales for which he is remembered today. The first of these was *The Guns of Navarone* (1957), which was made into a film in 1961, with an international all-star cast that included Gregory Peck and David Niven. MacLean later wrote a sequel, *Force 10 from Navarone* (1968), with a similar plot (a group of patriots on a mission to destroy an important element of the German war effort: two giant guns in the first book, a bridge in the second), which also became a movie, this time starring Robert Shaw and Edward Fox, in 1977. Among the author's other bestsellers are *South of Java Head* (1958), *The Last Frontier* (1959), and *Ice Station Zebra* (1963), the latter of which became a 1968 film of the same name with Rock Hudson. In addition, *When Eight Bells Toll* (1966) inspired a 1971 film starring Anthony Hopkins; *Where Eagles Dare* (1967) led to a 1969 film with Clint Eastwood and Richard Burton; and *Bear Island* (1971) came to the screen in 1980 with Vanessa Redgrave and Donald Sutherland. MacLean accurately described himself as a storyteller, acknowledging his rudimentary style and characterizations. His women are usually beautiful, noble, and brave; his men strong, attractive, charming, adept at fighting and other useful skills, and also courageous. The narratives have a powerful moral sense, with the good guys (see the men and women described above) very good, and the bad guys devoid of redeeming value. One of his heroes explains why he did what he felt he had to do: "All I do is exterminate vermin. To me, all crooks, armed or not, are vermin." As one of the leading action-adventure writers of his day, MacLean never allowed the pace to flag, bringing millions of avid readers and filmgoers to his work.

"MacHinery and the Cauliflowers" was first published in *The Lonely Sea: Collected Short Stories* (London: Collins, 1985).

MacHINERY AND THE CAULIFLOWERS

ALISTAIR MacLEAN

"I FIND YOU WELL, Mr. MacHinery?" Ah Wong asked courteously. He pronounced the name as "Mackinelli" and although ten years in the Far East had accustomed MacHinery to this heathenish mispronunciation of a legendary Scottish clan name that ranked in antiquity with anything the Almanac de Gotha had to offer, nevertheless his proud Celtic soul winced whenever he heard it. Still, he reflected charitably, it was hardly Ah Wong's fault. Some parts of the world were still emerging from the caves, so to speak. Primitive, barbaric—in fact, MacHinery conceded generously to himself, very like the MacHinerys of a few centuries ago when the more pressing business activities of cattle-thieving and hacking opposing clansmen to pieces had left them little time for the more cultural pursuits of life. But twenty intervening generations had had their civilizing effect . . .

MacHinery fingered a beer bottle scar received in a political debate in Glasgow many years previously, and smiled tolerantly.

"I'm weel enough, Mr. Wong. Fair to middling, you ken."

"You do not look it," Ah Wong said slowly. "You are pale but you perspire freely. You perspire but you shiver and shake. And your eyes are not the eyes of a well man." He turned to a wall cabinet and poured amber liquid into a tumbler. "A well-tried specific from your own homeland, Mr. MacHinery."

"Och, man, it was chust what I was needing." MacHinery drank deeply, shuddered violently and coughed until the tears rolled down his cheeks. Ah Wong looked at him with suddenly narrowed eyes. Less than a month had elapsed since two sailors had inconsiderately dropped dead after drinking, in one of his emporiums, a bottle of what had purported to be proprietary Scotch, and had it not been for the prompt midnight transfer of a couple of barrels of wood alcohol to the go-down of a cherished enemy and the sending to the authorities of a letter signed "Pro Bono Publico," he might have been in trouble indeed. As it was, any adverse reaction to his Scotch now struck deep at Ah Wong's sensitive soul.

"You do not like my whisky, Mr. MacHinery?" he asked slowly.

"Not like it?" MacHinery coughed. "Hoots, mon, it's perfect, chust perfect." MacHinery had, in fact, the misfortune to be allergic to any type of whisky but the part of the hard-drinking Clydeside engineer was no more difficult to sustain than the phoney accent that went with it. "Chust a touch of fever, Mr. Wong, that's all." Experience had long shown him that no one cared whether the fever in question was chicken-pox or the Black Plague.

"So." Ah Wong relaxed a minute fraction, the most he ever permitted himself to relax. "And you are the new chief engineer of the *Grasshopper,* Mr. MacHinery?"

"For ma sins," MacHinery said bitterly. "A filthier, rustier, auld bucket of bolts—"

"Beggars cannot be choosers, Mr. MacHinery," Ah Wong said coldly. He waved a piece of paper. "And you are a beggar. According to this letter of introduction from my good friend Benabi, you'd been in the Djakarta gutters for weeks before he gave you this job. Even your chief engineer's ticket is a forgery—your real one was taken from you."

"Aye, and a grosser miscarriage of justice—"

"Be quiet," Ah Wong said contemptuously. "The *Grasshopper*'s cargo has been unloaded and cleared through customs?"

"Aye. Not thirty minutes ago." MacHinery shivered again and stirred restlessly in his seat. Sweat poured down his face. Ah Wong affected not to notice.

"Good. You will have been given a private copy of the manifest." He stretched out his hand. "Let me see it."

"Well noo, chust wait a minute," MacHinery said cunningly. "You ken who I am. The letter tells you. But I don't ken who *you* are. How do I know you ken one another? You and Benabi, I mean?"

"Fool," Ah Wong said shortly. "I, one of the biggest food importers in Malaya? Benabi, of Benabi Tjitarum's truck farms, the biggest suppliers in Indonesia? Not know each other? Idiot!"

"There's nae call to be personal," MacHinery said doggedly. "I hae ma orders, Mr. Wong. From Mr. Benabi himself. You must match this, he says." He drew a piece of rice paper from his wallet and showed Ah Wong a curious ink marking, smaller than a thumbnail.

"Of course," Ah Wong smiled. He twisted a signet ring on his middle finger, pressed it on an ink pad and made an identical mark on the paper. "The seal of the broken junk. We have the only two such signet rings in the world. Benabi and I—we are brothers."

"You wouldna think it," MacHinery said candidly. "He's a tall, well built, good-looking cove, whereas you—"

"I spoke metaphorically," Ah Wong said coldly. "The manifest, Mr. MacHinery."

"Aye." MacHinery rose, opened the Glad-

stone bag he'd left in the middle of the floor of Ah Wong's sumptuous apartment, fished out a manifest and handed it over.

"Why the bag?" Ah Wong asked in idle curiosity.

"Why the bag?" MacHinery echoed bitterly. "The *Grasshopper*'s two nights in Singapore and if you think I'm going to spend them aboard yon bloody flea-ridden, cockroach-infested hellhole, you—"

"Silence!" Ah Wong opened the manifest. "Ah, yes. Sides of beef, one hundred. Of pork, two hundred. Bananas, onions, beans, peppers, eggplants, butter. Yes, yes, all seems there. Best Bandung cauliflowers, eighty crates. Lettuce, fifty. Yes, all in order." He broke off, looked thoughtfully at MacHinery and said in Cantonese: "I am going to kill you, my friend."

"Whit was that?" MacHinery asked blankly.

"Nothing." Ah Wong smiled. "I thought you might be a linguist." He picked up a telephone and spoke quickly in Cantonese, referring to the manifest from time to time and ticking off items with a pencil, then replaced the phone. He smiled again. "Just ordering up some meat and vegetables from my go-down, Mr. MacHinery. From your own cargo."

"And the very cream of the crop, I'll be bound," MacHinery said bitterly. "Nae bloody flies on you Chinese."

Ah Wong smiled yet again. The kind of smile, MacHinery thought grimly, that you might expect to see on the face of a spider when a particularly juicy fly landed on its web. Ah Wong, for his part, thought it unnecessary to inform MacHinery that he was of pure Armenian stock and had changed his name partly for business reasons in a Chinese-dominated field of commerce, but mainly because he regarded the honourable name of his ancestors as sullied beyond redemption by its frequent inclusion in Interpol files throughout the world.

"No need to be bitter, Mr. MacHinery," Ah Wong said pleasantly. "I thought you might like to stay for dinner with me."

"Dinner?" After a brief struggle, a conciliatory smile appeared on MacHinery's face. "Well, noo, Mr. Wong, that is kind of you. Very, very kind. I'll be honoured to accept." MacHinery hadn't sat down again, and now he paced the room restlessly, the sheen of sweat bathing his entire face. He was shivering more violently than ever and one side of his face had begun to twitch.

"You are not well, I'm afraid," Ah Wong said again.

"I'm fine." A pause. "Dammit, no, I'm no'. I'll hae to go oot for a minute to get some medicine. I—I know the cure for this." He gulped. "I feel sick, Mr. Wong, awful sick. Where's your bathroom? Quick."

"Through that door there."

MacHinery left abruptly and closed the door behind him. He turned on both basin taps, pulled the lever that operated the toilet cistern and used the sound of running water to drown the slight clicking noise made as he lifted the Venetian blind that shut out the hot Malayan sun.

Parked on the opposite side of the street below was a dark van with blue-tinted side windows and a ventilator on top. The ventilator was motionless. MacHinery thrust out a hand, waved briefly, withdrew his hand, waited until he saw the ventilator revolve just once, then lowered the blind as cautiously as he had raised it. He turned off the taps and went back into Ah Wong's apartment.

"You feel better, Mr. MacHinery?" It was no light task for Ah Wong to get concern into both voice and face but he made it after a struggle.

"I feel bloody awful," MacHinery said candidly. He was shaking now like a broken bedspring and his teeth were beginning to chatter. "I must go oot, Mr. Wong. I must. Ma medicine. I'll no be but minutes."

"Any medicine you care to name, Mr. MacHinery, I have it. Among other things, I'm the wholesale supplier to many chemists' shops."

"You'll no' find the medicine I need in any bloody chemist's shop," MacHinery said violently. "A jiffy, Mr. Wong. That's all I'll be."

He headed for the doorway, then stopped abruptly. There was a man standing there. By courtesy definition, MacHinery thought, he might be called a man. He looked more like the early prototype of the Neanderthal caveman, only bigger. Much bigger. He had shoulders like a bull, hands like two bunches of bananas and a brutalized moronic face that might have been carved from granite by a power-chisel.

"John," Ah Wong introduced him. "My secretary. I don't think he wants you to leave, Mr. MacHinery."

"Aye. Your secretary. No mistaking the intellectual type, is there?" MacHinery shuddered violently again and dropped his voice. "One side, laddie."

"Don't be foolish," Ah Wong said sharply. "He can break you in half. Come now, Mr. MacHinery. Just sit down and take your coat off. Madness to wear it in this heat and sweating as you are."

"I'm allergic to sunlight," MacHinery said between clamped teeth. "Never take it off. One side, you."

"There's no sunlight in here," Ah Wong said softly.

"I must get oot," MacHinery shouted. "I must. Damn you, Wong, you don't know what you're doing to me." He made a bull rush for the doorway and tried to dive under John's outstretched arms. His head and shoulders smashed into a five-barred gate. At least, it felt like a five-barred gate. A couple of power shovels closed over MacHinery's upper arms, lifted him effortlessly off his feet and bore him back to the armchair in the centre of the room.

"You are extremely foolish," Ah Wong said sadly. "I want to be your friend, Mr. MacHinery. And I want you to be mine. I think, Mr. MacHinery, that you can offer me what a man in my position so very rarely acquires—an unswerving allegiance that neither money nor oaths could buy."

MacHinery struggled futilely in the grip of giant hands. He said in a strangled voice: "I'll kill you for this, Wong."

"Kill me? Kill your doctor? Kill the one man who can give you the medicine you need?" Ah Wong smiled. "You are singularly lacking in intelligence. Take his jacket off, John."

John removed MacHinery's jacket. He did it by the simple process of ripping the white lining down the back middle seam and pulling off the two separate halves.

"Now the shirt sleeves," Ah Wong murmured.

John twitched his fingers, the buttons burst from their moorings and the sleeves were pulled up beyond MacHinery's elbows. For a long moment all three men stared down at the inside of MacHinery's forearms. Both of them were covered by a mass of pale-purplish spots, none of them more than half an inch distant from its fellows. Ah Wong's face remained as immobile as ever. He bent over MacHinery's Gladstone bag, flung a shirt to one side and picked up a narrow rectangular box. He slid a catch, opened the wooden lid and extracted a hypodermic syringe, holding it by the plunger.

"So very conveniently to hand," he said gently. "Your medicine goes in this, doesn't it, MacHinery? And there's hardly a place left in your arms for you to use it, is there? A junky, Mr. MacHinery. A dope addict. And now you're climbing the walls, as they say, because you're overdue your next shot. Isn't that it, Mr. MacHinery?"

"I'll kill you for this, Ah Wong." MacHinery's voice was weak, mechanical. He was jerking violently in his seat. "So help me God, I'll kill you." He arched himself stiffly in his armchair, his eyes showing white, his mouth strained open. "I'll kill you," he croaked.

"Kill me?" Ah Wong asked quietly. "Kill the goose that lays the golden eggs? Kill your doctor, as I said before? Kill the doctor who not only recognizes all the symptoms but can prescribe the medicine for it? Prescribe it and supply it. Supply it now. Heroin, is it not, Mr. MacHinery?"

John's grip eased. MacHinery struggled to his feet and gripped Ah Wong by the arms.

"You have the stuff?" he whispered. "God, you have the stuff? You have it here?"

"I have it here." Ah Wong looked into the stricken eyes. "My friend Benabi. He is even more brilliant than I had thought. Always the weak link in our organization was the courier from Djakarta to here. But not any more. You will have as much of the white powder, Mr. MacHinery, as often as you like, whenever you like, for the remainder of your days."

"You mean—you mean I'll never have to worry aboot it again? Never have to lie or beg or cheat or steal to get it? It will always be there?"

"While you remain in the employment of Benabi and myself, it will always be there."

"I'm your man for life," MacHinery said simply.

"I don't doubt it." Ah Wong looked at him in distaste, shook off his hands, picked up the phone and spoke rapidly. He replaced the phone and said: "One minute. No more."

"My God!" MacHinery said stupidly. "When I think of the number of times I've chased roond Singapore, near screaming ma head off for the stuff, wondering where I could lay ma hands on it, where the source of supply was, I could—"

"You're at the source now, Mr. MacHinery. No need to wonder any more."

"You—you supply the whole town?"

"Much of it."

"But—but have you never worried aboot whit you're doing? Have you ever seen a man, a far gone junky, who canna get the stuff? Or a man trying to dry oot? Both going mad. Insane screaming mad. Have you never seen it?"

"Don't be so naive, Mr. MacHinery. Of course I've seen it. The sensible ones stick to a pellet of opium. But the sophisticates—" his lips curled— "must have it straight. If I don't supply it, others will." He smiled contemptuously. "Now perhaps you'd like to inform the police?"

"I'll cut ma throat," MacHinery whispered. "I'll blow ma brains oot. But I'll never, never tell."

"I know you won't," Ah Wong said drily. "Ah, here it comes." A servant crossed to the table and dumped a crate of vegetables on top of it.

"Cauliflowers?" MacHinery said stupidly.

"Best Bandung," Ah Wong agreed. He lifted one, gingerly slit the heart with a knife, extracted a twist of cellophane and poured a little white powder into MacHinery's trembling hand. "Try it."

MacHinery placed it on his tongue, tasted it, tasted it again, then whispered: "Dear God. This is it. This is it. And—and this is the way it comes into Singapore?"

"For years," Ah Wong said calmly. "An ordinary cauliflower, the heart carefully parted, the heroin inserted, shellac for preservative and to glue the stems together, then carried in the crates. Three times the customs have searched the *Grasshopper* from stem to stern—but who would ever think of cauliflowers?"

"Damn the cauliflowers," MacHinery said hoarsely. His voice shook, his hands trembled more violently than ever. "Mix it up for me, for God's sake!"

Ah Wong nodded, went to the bathroom and returned in a minute with a small vial of milky liquid. He nodded to the syringe lying on the table. "Your medicine, Mr. MacHinery."

"For pity's sake fill the hypo for me," MacHinery begged. "My hands—"

"I can see them," Ah Wong said. "Unsteady, we might say." He lifted the hypodermic, depressed the plunger and inserted the needle in the vial. "Sufficient, I should say, Mr. MacHinery?"

"Aye, aye, that'll do." MacHinery grabbed the hypodermic by the plunger, hesitated, then blurted out: "God alone knows I'm just a junky, but a man still has his pride. Even a junky. The—the bathroom. And I feel sick again."

"You make *me* sick," Ah Wong said dispassionately. "Go on."

MacHinery hurried into the bathroom, pulled the cistern lever, opened the Venetian blind and thrust the hypodermic out of the window. Five men came swarming out of the van below. MacHinery withdrew his arm and, still holding the

hypodermic gingerly by the plunger, laid it carefully on the windowsill. He waited twenty seconds, then walked back into Ah Wong's apartment just as the outer door crashed open and the five men from the van, uniformed policemen with guns, burst into the room. MacHinery nodded towards John.

"Watch the big lad," he advised. "If he twitches an eyebrow, shoot five or six bullets into him. Not at his head—they'd bounce off."

Ah Wong stood stock-still, his face inscrutable. After a moment or two he said softly: "What is the meaning of this outrage?"

"Inspector Hanbro," the leading policeman introduced himself. "Warrant for your arrest, Mr. Wong. Receiving, being in illegal possession of and distributing knowingly proscribed narcotics. I have to warn you—"

"What tomfoolery is this?" Ah Wong's face had gone very stiff, very watchful. "What wild rubbish—narcotics, you said?"

"Narcotics, I said." Hanbro turned towards MacHinery. "This man will testify—"

"This man," Ah Wong said incredulously. "This derelict Scots engineer—"

"Curiously enough, he was an engineer once," Hanbro said. "Also Scots. Hardly derelict. Changed his profession years ago. Mr. Wong, may I introduce Inspector Donald MacHinery of the Hong Kong Vice Squad? Seconded to Singapore for—ah—special duties. The faces of my own men are too well known in those parts."

"You can take him away, Inspector Hanbro," MacHinery said tiredly. "I don't know how many wrecked lives and suicides lie at his door and it doesn't matter any more. We have enough on him to put him away for life."

"I'm innocent of all charges," Ah Wong said dully. "As one of the biggest merchants and most influential citizens in—"

"Shut up," MacHinery said shortly. "You were right, Mr. Wong. Your former courier, the previous chief engineer on the *Grasshopper, was* your weak link. He got drunk one night in Djakarta and talked too much in the presence of a plain-clothes man. Just enough for a lead, no more. We knew he wouldn't talk—men who talk in your business invariably die before the night is out—so we let him be while I established myself on the waterfront as a drunken junky engineer. When the time was right the Djakarta cops picked him up and held him incommunicado and there I was waiting, the ideal substitute. Your pal Benabi wasn't even smart, far less brilliant."

"You can't prove a thing. You can't—"

"We can prove everything. Ten years in Hong Kong and I talk Cantonese as well as you do. Better—you Armenians have difficulty with some vowel sounds. Yes, Armenian, Mr. Wong—we know all about you. I heard you give the numbers to your go-down—they will correspond exactly to the numbers on the crate."

"It's only your word—"

"The police had your line tapped, for good measure."

"Tapping is inadmissible evidence—"

"And," MacHinery went on remorselessly, "every word of our conversation is preserved for posterity. The bottom half of that Gladstone bag of mine—a very efficient recorder, I can tell you. Further, the marks you made on that manifest will match the crate numbers removed from your go-down. Graphite tests will show that it was the pencil on that table that made the marks and fingerprint tests will show that you were the last to handle that pencil. That signet seal shared by yourself and Benabi—any court in the East will recognize the significance of that. That crate there, lying on your own floor, with dope in every cauliflower head—how are you going to explain that away? Good lord, man, there's even enough evidence in the bathroom to have you put away for life—a hypo full of heroin with your fingerprints all over the glass cylinder."

"You're a junky yourself." Ah Wong's voice was a dazed whisper. "Narcotics addicts can't testify. I—I know all the symptoms. You—"

"Symptoms?" MacHinery smiled. "I've already stopped shivering. No bother. And as soon as I remove the three jerseys under my shirt I'll stop sweating, too. Pale face—makeup. Junky's eyes—didn't you know red peppers give exactly the same effect?"

"But your arms," Ah Wong said desperately. "Look at them. Riddled with punctures. How—"

"Sharpened knitting needle sterilized and dipped in aniline dye. Don't ever try it, Mr. Wong. It's most damnably painful."

WHEELS WITHIN WHEELS

H. C. McNEILE

HERMAN CYRIL McNEILE (1888–1937) served in the British Army Corps of Engineers for twelve years, retiring as a lieutenant colonel shortly after the end of World War I. During his years of service, he wrote numerous military adventure stories, but it was the creation of Bulldog Drummond in 1920 that made him one of the most popular writers in England. For his works published in Britain, McNeile used the pseudonym "Sapper"—a word derived from the military slang term for an engineer. Most of his fiction is fast-paced, with cliffhangers, romance, and action in long supply, while stylistic nuance and characterization are not.

Partially based on McNeile's friend Gerard Fairlie (who continued the Drummond adventures when McNeile died of a war-related illness), Captain Hugh Drummond finds himself bored after the war and runs a newspaper advertisement that reads:

> Demobilized officer, finding peace incredibly tedious, would welcome diversion. Legitimate, if possible; but crime, if of a comparatively humourous description, no objection. Excitement essential. Would be prepared to consider permanent job if suitably impressed by applicant for his services. Reply at once Box X10.

The fiercely patriotic Drummond sniffs out England's enemies everywhere, especially among Germans and Russians, and will risk his life (as well as those of his wife, Phyllis, and his valet, Algy) to do so. His greatest adversary is Carl Peterson, a super-villain who cares nothing about national loyalties as long as his allies aid his selfish goals. McNeile wrote ten novels about Drummond, Fairlie wrote seven, and more than twenty films have been based on the hero's exploits, featuring such stars as Ronald Colman, John Howard, Ralph Richardson, Ray Milland, Tom Conway, and Walter Pidgeon. The heroic Englishman also starred in a somewhat inauthentic U.S. radio series from 1941 to 1954, which opened with: "Out of the fog, out of the night, and into his American adventures, steps Bulldog Drummond . . ."

"Wheels Within Wheels" was first published in the November 1937 issue of the *Strand* magazine.

WHEELS WITHIN WHEELS

H. C. McNEILE

THE FRONT DOOR of No. 3, Bridgewater Square opened suddenly, and from it there issued a discordant volume of sound and a large man in evening clothes. At any hour of the day or night such a thing was unusual in that ultra-respectable locality; at two a.m. it was not only unusual but a definite outrage. And yet what else was to be expected when the Dowager Countess of Betterby had been unwise enough to let her house for the season to Mrs. van Ranton of Baltimore, U.S.A.?

Mrs. van Ranton was a young and vivacious American, whose husband, as was only proper, was cornering something in his native town in order to supply the wife of his bosom with the means to keep her end up in London. And since the dear fellow was succeeding most admirably, Mrs. van Ranton decided to give a party which was a party. It was to be a party which would linger in the memory of the guests as a knock-out, and to do the little lady justice she had succeeded. It was a wow from the word go.

Now it is not my intention to describe the performance in any detail, since, save as a foundation, it has nothing to do with what follows. But even the most unintelligent reader will demand some reason for Hugh Drummond's presence in Bridgewater Square in the middle of a fine July night, wearing a large false nose of crimson hue. He will demand even more reason when it has to be truthfully stated that Drummond was quite unaware of his adornment.

To say that hardy warrior was "sewn" would be an exaggeration. Possessing, as he did, a head of teak, even Mrs. van Ranton could not accomplish that miracle. But honesty compels the narrator to admit that he was not in a condition where his presence would have been welcomed at the mid-term celebrations in a girls' school. Let us leave it at that.

The door closed behind him; the noise died down. And for a while he stood there contemplating the row of empty cars and wondering why he had left the party. A slight indiscretion during a game of sardines, inaugurated by Algy Longworth, had passed off better than he had anticipated; the trouble was he could not remember who the girl was or where he had asked her to lunch. And now, with the cool air beating on his brow, he wondered whether he ought not to return and settle these two trifling points. But it was difficult. Eighty wenches: betting seventy-nine to one against sotting the winner. Not good enough.

A cat joined him, a friendly cat—and at two a.m. in Bridgewater Square a man needs friendship. It proves that life is still extant in an apparently dead world. And Drummond was on the verge of stroking the new arrival when there came from the distance a most unexpected sound. He straightened up and listened. There was no doubt about it: someone was running, and running fast. And the next moment the runner came in sight.

The cat vanished; alone Drummond awaited the onslaught. It came with an abruptness that left him bewildered. He had a fleeting vision of a white-faced man whose breath was coming in great sobs; he felt a paper thrust into his hands; he heard a gasped-out sentence—"Take it to Scotland Yard"—and he was alone again. The runner had disappeared round the other end of the Square.

Drummond blinked thoughtfully. The matter required consideration. From inside No. 3 there still came bursts of hilarity, but his mind no longer toyed with the seventy-nine to one chance. Why should a man run in a condition of great distress through Bridgewater Square in the middle of the night? And to do him justice there is but little doubt that, given sufficient time, he would have solved the problem correctly had it been necessary. It was not; the solution appeared almost at once in the shape of three more men running swiftly towards him.

He put the paper in his pocket and again awaited the onslaught.

"Hey, you!" cried the first. "Has a guy passed running this way?"

"Why," said Drummond solemnly, "should I reveal the secrets of my heart to a complete stranger?"

"Aw! cut it out, Bill," muttered one of the others. "The bloke's tight. Let's get on."

"An extremely offensive utterance," remarked Drummond as a window above was flung up, and the voices of happy revellers came to their ears. "Almost libellous. Dear me! How distressing."

It was a charlotte russe that descended from the stratosphere, and it burst, by superb chance, on the first speaker's head.

"An albatross without a doubt," said Drummond sympathetically. "How true it is that the rain it raineth upon the just and the unjust alike. However, as I think it is more than likely that there will be an encore, I will wish you all a hearty good night."

"Have you seen a man running?" snarled the leader, plucking macaroons from his ears.

"You remind me of the old song, 'Have you ever seen a dream walking?' " said Drummond

reminiscently. "Have you a moment? If so, I will sing it to you. No? Well, perhaps you're right."

He watched them vanish round the corner, and waited till the sound of their footsteps had died away. Then, his hands thrust deep in his trousers pockets, he started to saunter homewards. What story lay behind the runners of Bridgewater Square? Who were the pursuers and who the pursued?

Suddenly it struck him that he had not yet looked at the paper, and he paused under a street lamp. It was a dirty little fragment torn hurriedly from a cheap notebook, and on it three words were scrawled in pencil: "Rest House, Aldmersham." And having examined both sides, and satisfied himself that there was nothing more, he replaced it in his pocket and walked on.

On the face of it a harmless enough communication in all conscience. And yet a man with bursting lungs, running for his life, had deemed it of sufficient importance for Scotland Yard. At which stage of his reflections he frowned.

Running for his life! If he was any judge of men and matters that was no exaggeration, and he had done nothing about it. It was true that until the pursuers appeared on the scene it had not struck him that way. It was true that the man had come and gone so quickly that there had been no time to do anything. But for all that, Drummond had an uneasy twinge of conscience that his performance had not been too good; that the brain had not functioned with that speed which he had a right to expect. And why?

Came the measured tread of a policeman; he would make inquiries.

"Officer," he remarked as they met, "I would hold converse with you. And what, may I ask," he continued, "are you laughing at?"

"Your nose, sir. Most refreshing."

"An unusual epithet to apply to the organ in question," said Drummond with dignity. "It is a poor thing doubtless, but . . ."

He paused as his hand encountered the obstruction.

"I perceive the cause of your hilarity," he remarked. "I appear to be wearing a false one."

"I should hope so, sir."

"What do you mean—you hope so?"

"Only, sir, that if that was real you'd better stick to milk for a bit."

"I take your meaning," said Drummond, removing the offence. "And to tell you the truth I am constrained to cry—*touché*. As man to man would you say I was tight?"

"Oh, no, sir! Slightly oiled, if I may say so."

"That accounts for it," remarked Drummond with great relief. "I feared it might be softening of the brain. Listen, my trusty rozzer: unless I'm much mistaken there's some dirty work afoot. Some five minutes ago a man raced through Bridgewater Square, with three others hard on his heels. I detained the pursuers for a space, but I should think the betting is that they caught him. And I don't think they wanted to kiss him good night."

"Your name, sir?" said the policeman curtly, pulling out his notebook.

"Hugh Drummond: 87, Half Moon Street."

"Which way were they going?"

"From north to south."

"Would you know them again?"

"I should know the man they were after and at any rate one of the other three."

"Thank you, sir. Good night. I know where to get you if I want you."

The constable disappeared almost at a run, and Drummond resumed his way.

"Slightly oiled," he murmured sorrowfully to himself. "Slightly oiled. And at my time of life. Disgraceful. It must have been the orange juice in that Bronx. Very dangerous fruit."

It was at ten o'clock the following morning that his servant Denny awoke him with his early tea, and the news that a couple of cops were in the sitting-room.

"One of 'em's an ordinary peeler," he added. "The other is that inspector bloke we've worked with in the past."

"Give them something to smoke and drink," said Drummond. "I'll be with them as soon as I've shaved."

Fate had been kind: his hangover was of the mildest. And five minutes later he stepped into the sitting-room to find Inspector McIver and his friend of last night. Moreover, their faces were grave.

"Good morning, boys," he remarked. "Sherlock Holmes deduces that developments have occurred."

"Murder, Captain Drummond," said McIver quietly, and Drummond paused with a cigarette half-way to his mouth.

"Is that so?" He stared at the inspector. "And the victim is the runner of Bridgewater Square?"

"That must, of course, be confirmed later," said McIver. "On the face of what you told Constable Baxter it seems more than likely, but you will be able to settle it definitely. I will now tell you what has happened. Following your information, Baxter went through Bridgewater Square, and along Taunton Street into Milverton Square. Not a soul was in sight, and he was beginning to be afraid that the trail was cold when he saw something sticking out from an area gate. He walked up to it to find that it was a man's leg: the man was on the steps inside— dead. Across the pavement lay a trail of blood. It was obvious that the body had been dragged from near the gutter to where it was then lying."

"How had he been killed?" asked Drummond quietly.

"Stabbed in three or four places. He was only just dead: the blood was still flowing. And of his assailants there was no trace; the Square was quite deserted. So Baxter summoned assistance; took the body to the station, and here we are. For *if* the dead man is your runner of last night—and it seems almost certain that he must be—you are the only man who has seen the murderers. Now can you give us any further details? And then I will ask you to get dressed and come with us to view the body, which, incidentally, I have not yet seen myself."

Drummond was frowning.

"I'm sorry about this," he said at length. "I blame myself very considerably. Whoever the poor devil is I feel I ought to have prevented it. But, as Baxter has doubtless mentioned in his report, I was a bit on last night. And the brain didn't function with its usual lucidity. I'd been to a party at Mrs. van Ranton's—No. 3. And it was just as I left that it happened. The pursued man dashed up to me—and gave me a bit of paper with instructions to take it to Scotland Yard. . . ."

"Hold hard," cried McIver. "Have you got it?"

In silence Drummond handed it over. "I was coming to see you this morning about it," he remarked. "Hullo, McIver—you seem excited!"

"Aldmersham," muttered the inspector. "I wonder if it is possible. Go on, Captain Drummond, and cut it as short as possible. The sooner we see the dead man the sooner I'll know."

"There's not much more to tell," said Drummond. "I had barely recovered from the hare's arrival when the hounds hove into sight, who paused to demand if I had seen a man running."

"You would recognize them?"

"As I told Baxter, the leader is the only one I'd swear to. A swarthy, powerfully built man of about my height. I'd know him again at once, even though his features were obliterated almost immediately. You see," he explained, "we were still just outside the house, and the party was in great heart. At any rate someone bunged a charlotte russe out of an upstairs window, and by the mercy of Allah it burst on the leader's head."

"Charlotte russe!" cried Baxter excitedly. "Is that one of them things full of cream?"

"Very," said Drummond. "And sponge fingers and things."

"Proof, sir," said Baxter to the inspector. "There was a great smear of white cream on the dead man's coat."

McIver nodded. "Go on, Captain Drummond."

"That's all. They departed at speed, and Baxter knows the rest."

"I see," said McIver. "Could you come with us at once?"

"Give me ten minutes to get dressed and I'm at your service. Got any line on it, McIver?"

"Just this," answered the inspector. "If the dead man is the man who gave you this paper, which I think almost certain, and if the dead man is the man I believe he is, which I think very possible, we're on to one of the biggest things we've tackled for some months."

"Excellent," said Drummond. "You'll find beer in the sideboard."

The body had been placed in a small mortuary attached to the district police station, and one glance at the dead man's face was sufficient for Drummond. It was the runner of the previous night.

"Is that your man?" asked McIver.

"It is," said Drummond.

"And mine too. So I was right, Captain Drummond: we're on to something very big. Did you find anything in his pockets?" he continued, turning to the sergeant in charge.

"Nothing, sir, of the slightest importance. Some loose money, and a cheap watch. Do you know his name, sir?" he added curiously.

"I do," said McIver. "Or one of 'em. At the moment, however, he had better remain an unknown man, at any rate so far as those gentlemen are concerned."

He glanced through the window at a couple of youths, metaphorically sucking their pencils, with reporter written all over them.

"It's a pity, Captain Drummond," he continued thoughtfully, "that the man who did this job last night saw you. They had to, naturally, as you saw them, but I'd give a lot to have 'em pointed out to me without their smelling a rat."

"A rather tall order, McIver," said Drummond. "Like looking for a needle in a bundle of hay."

"No, sir, that's where you're wrong. The location, sooner or later, of the needle is clear—the Rest House, Aldmersham. But if you spot them, they'll spot you, and that's what I want to avoid. Not that I mind you being recognized," he went on cheerfully. "You're quite capable of looking after yourself. But it will show we're after 'em."

"I'll guarantee to disguise myself," began Drummond, only to pause as he saw a grin spreading over Baxter's face. "Good Lord!" he cried, "I'd forgotten that. Listen, McIver, the wicket's good. As I told you, last night was a little damp. Now when I saw these blokes, I was standing under a lamp with an opera hat on, so that my face was in shadow. In addition to that I was wearing a large false nose, of which Baxter is more qualified to speak than I."

"I'll bank on it, sir," said the constable. "They wouldn't recognize the captain again. They only saw him for a second, and he won't be in evening clothes next time."

"You're sure of that?" snapped McIver.

"Dead sure."

"And are you willing to help, Captain Drummond?"

"More than willing," said Drummond quietly. "It's true I don't know that poor devil in there, but I have a very definite feeling that if I had acted differently he wouldn't be dead. Wherefore I would like to play."

"Good. Then we must have a little talk. Come in here."

He led the way into an inner office and closed the door.

"It's the age-old story of drug trafficking," began McIver, "but on an unprecedentedly large scale. You probably haven't followed matters, but since the Geneva commission was set up, facts and figures have come to light which prove that far from diminishing the trade is increasing. Cocaine and heroin particularly. The price of the stuff is decreasing in order to get more addicts, but they can still make enormous profits because it's being manufactured secretly all over the East and Near East.

"Six months ago Paris got in touch with us: they were trying to get on to the western European gang of distributors. And since the Paris and London underworld are far more closely interlocked than most people think, we worked together. It soon became obvious that a new and very dangerous crowd were at work—new, because all the usuals were accounted for; danger-

ous, because of the vast amount of stuff that was coming through, and because of the skill with which they covered their traces.

"But three months ago they made one slip. A tiny one, it's true—but it narrowed our field of search for their headquarters down considerably. From a possibility of anywhere in England, we became tolerably certain that we could concentrate on the eastern counties. But nearer than that we couldn't get, though we caught some of the smaller fry and pumped 'em dry. Honestly, I don't believe they knew themselves.

"And then he appeared on the scene." McIver jerked his thumb towards the mortuary. "Half French, half English—he spoke both languages fluently. He was wished on to me by the Sûreté, and we took him for what he was worth. Name of Esmer, which was as good as any other, but what his motive was we didn't inquire. Not, I venture to think, a very exalted one: he was a gentleman with a sultry past if I'm any judge. But he offered to help us, and we didn't say no. It was his funeral—and that's what it's turned out to be.

"Evidently he knew the gang and managed to link up with them. I should say he'd been mixed up in the dope traffic himself in the past, so he had no difficulty over that. And consequently he got in with the men at the top, sufficiently to get information he passed to you."

"Where is Aldmersham?" asked Drummond.

"Suffolk. About ten miles from the coast. But it wasn't only that that made me suspect before I saw the body. I thought I recognized the writing, even though it was a mere scrawl. In any event, we now know where we stand. The Rest House at Aldmersham is a red spot on the map. Whether it's *the* red spot remains to be seen."

"By me?" said Drummond.

McIver nodded.

"If you're on," he said. "Though of course we shall be in the vicinity; very much so. But in view of their record up to date I'm under no delusions about these gentlemen. They're a swift crowd, and although we don't know them, I'm pretty certain they know the classic features of most of the Yard. And if they saw me at the Rest House, it would be a case of goodbye for ever. We've got to have 'em pointed out to us without their knowing it. And if in addition to that we can catch 'em with the stuff on 'em, we're home. So, once again, are you on?"

"You bet I'm on," said Drummond. "I haven't had any fun for a long while. What are your ideas on the plan of campaign?"

McIver rang a bell and the sergeant entered.

"Find out at once full particulars of the Rest House at Aldmersham," he said. "And when we know those we'll decide, Captain Drummond."

"Will you be able to run these swine for murder?" asked Drummond.

McIver shrugged his shoulders and lit a cigarette.

"Not much to go on up to date," he said. "But one never knows. I should have liked to have seen the charlotte russe episode," he added irrelevantly.

"You would," agreed Drummond as the sergeant came back.

"Eight bedrooms, sir. Fully licensed," he announced. "Good reputation and crowded at this time of the year with cyclists and hikers."

"Excellent," said McIver. "What about a bicycle tour, Captain Drummond?"

"Great Scot!" cried Drummond. "I hadn't bargained for that."

"Or you can hike," said McIver kindly. "Shorts and a nice knapsack. However, I leave it to you."

"Thanks awfully, old boy."

"Not at all, not at all. Having arrived there you will engage a room and make it your headquarters."

"Hiking every day?"

"But never going far from the Rest House. You might be an artist. However," he continued hurriedly, "once again I leave that to you. I will arrange for some youngster of ours to be there too. He will make himself known to you by asking you for a match. If and when our birds turn up you will let him know by asking him for one. And he will pass that on to me. After that events

must shape themselves. But I want to catch 'em, Captain Drummond—with the stuff."

"So do I, McIver. And we will."

The Rest House at Aldmersham was certainly crowded when Drummond and Algy Longworth arrived at six o'clock that evening. Quite rightly contending that the cause of the whole affair was Mrs. van Ranton's party, his attendance at which was directly due to Algy, Drummond had insisted on that young gentleman accompanying him.

"Variety, you scourge, is the salt of life," he had remarked. "After the caviare of Bridgewater Square, we go to the ham and eggs of great open spaces in Suffolk. So put on your shorts, if you own any, and we will join the great army of hikers. It's all right," he added consolingly. "We do all but the last mile by train."

They found an empty table in a corner of the verandah, and proceeded to take stock of their surroundings. And it would have been hard to imagine a setting less likely to harbour crime. Young men and maidens clad in varying degrees of shorts were taking nourishment. Strange noises from an open window proclaimed that the Hosh-Bosh sextette had jumped a claim on Regional. And in one corner two very dreadful women in plus fours were eating boiled eggs. Just a little bit of unspoiled England. . . .

"Beer," said Algy faintly. "Beer at all costs. It isn't," he went on plaintively, "that I dislike legs. Far from it. But a permanent diet of this would send any man into a monastery screaming for mercy. There should be a law passed on the matter. The wearing of shorts and other dangerous practices related thereto. No woman having a knee of greater circumference than a yard is ever to be permitted to show it in public: penalty imprisonment. If said knee is scalded red in the sun the penalty to be amputation."

A waiter brought them their beer, and at the same moment a pleasant-looking youth rose from a neighbouring table and came over.

"Excuse me, sir," he said to Drummond. "I

wonder if I could trouble you for a match. Thank you. You'll hold him if he comes, won't you, sir. Until the inspector has seen him."

"Our ally, Algy," remarked Drummond as the youth sat down again. "And there, I take it, is the proprietor."

A stout and smiling man was standing in the doorway leading into the house, regarding the scene complacently. Aesthetic quibbles on legs concerned him not. His mental range began and ended with the capacity of the human stomach for food. And on that standard all was well.

He caught Drummond's eye and came over to the table. A room? Certainly. He could manage that for them with ease. And if they had a car there was a garage attached to the house, with a competent man in charge. Just been opened.

He strolled away and Drummond lit a cigarette.

"Lower your beer, Algy," he said, "and we'll do our little tour of inspection. On the face of it," he continued as they threaded their way through the tables, "mine host has no appearance of a criminal. One cannot quite visualize him as the centre of a dope gang."

"They probably use the place unknown to him," answered Algy. "One can hardly think of an atmosphere that would afford a better blind."

They rounded a corner. In front of them stood the garage. It was, as the landlord had said, evidently a new addition, and they walked over to the entrance. Three baby cars were in the yard, and a small empty van with the back axle jacked up and minus its rear wheels. And they were just turning away again when a man emerged from a workshop at the back carrying a spare wheel. He stared at them for a moment; then he stood the wheel up against the running-board of the van and came towards them.

"Looking for anything, gents?" he remarked.

"No, thank you," said Drummond affably. "This is new since my friend and I were last here."

"Opened last May," answered the man, shading his eyes with his hand and staring up the road.

"Pretty busy?" continued Drummond.

"So-so," said the man. "Varies, you know; it varies. Good evening."

With a nod he turned away and went back to his workshop, to come out again shortly with another spare wheel which he placed by the first. Then, apparently conscious of arduous work well done, he sat down on the running-board of the van and lit a cigarette.

"Nothing doing here," said Drummond, swinging on his heels. "Let's go and sample the bar."

"Anything you like," said Algy cheerfully, "so long as I don't see those female plus fours again."

"You'll see something a damned sight more interesting," said Drummond curtly. "Here's our man."

A big Bentley had drawn up by the petrol pump, and the garage attendant had appeared hurriedly.

"That big fellow driving," continued Drummond, "know him a mile off. MFF236. So far, so good. Let's get hold of McIver's warrior."

The young plain-clothes man was still at the same table, and he glanced up as Drummond approached.

"Just getting out of that Bentley," said Drummond quietly. "The tall, dark man."

He strolled on towards the bar, followed by Algy. McIver's man promptly vanished, and the driver of the Bentley, with passenger, was evidently bound barwards also.

"So we've got to keep him for a while, Algy, until McIver has given him the once over. Now, as I get it, if there's anything in this place at all, he'll either be picking the stuff up here or dropping it. Otherwise there's no meaning to the performance, since no one would come here for fun."

"Which means that there's a confederate in the house," said Algy.

"Probably. Steady the Buffs! Here he comes."

The first thing that became apparent was that the visitor had been there before. He called the barman "George," and was greeted as Mr. Margiter in reply. And having given Drummond and Algy one brief uncompromising stare, in which no shadow of recognition lurked, Mr. Margiter ordered two double whiskies.

"Trade good?" he asked in a harsh domineering voice which was obviously natural.

"Very, sir," answered George. "Nothing to complain of."

"Then you're luckier than most of us," said Margiter with a laugh, which turned into a snarl of anger as Drummond bumped accidentally against his arm and spilled his drink. "Confound you, sir! Don't be so infernally clumsy."

Drummond turned round very slowly.

"Are you speaking to me, my good man?" he said in a drawl so offensive that it would have provoked sudden death at a pacifist meeting.

Mr. Margiter put the remains of his drink on the counter, and his face turned a full red.

"Did you call me 'my good man'?" he remarked softly.

"Gentlemen, gentlemen!" George was dancing up and down in his agitation, but he might have been a fly on the wall for all the notice anyone paid him. His companion was plucking at Margiter's coat. Algy, wise to the ways of Drummond, suppressed a happy grin. And at the same time felt the tingle in his veins which is born of murder in the air.

"I did," said Drummond casually. "But now that I've seen you more closely, I withdraw the phrase in its literal sense."

The veins stood out on Margiter's forehead. A vicious back-hander nearly knocked over his friend, who was muttering feverishly in his ear. Margiter was dead to caution. So dead that there was nothing real in his universe save a yokel in grey flannel trousers and an old tweed coat, who had deliberately gone out of his way to insult him. He failed to notice the watchful glint that had come into the yokel's eyes; and when a vicious left-hander missed its objective by a foot he failed to read the writing on the wall.

He swung a right haymaker, and then something that felt like a pile driver hit him straight in the mouth, so that he staggered back, spitting blood, into the arms of his friend just as the door opened and a stern official voice rang out.

"Now then—what's all this?"

Inspector McIver was standing there, giving Drummond a glance without a trace of recognition.

"Can't have brawling here, gentlemen. Stop it you, sir," he roared, as Margiter showed further signs of wanting to go on, "or I'll take you in charge. I'm an Inspector of Police."

With a gigantic effort Margiter pulled himself together.

"Yes," continued McIver, staring at him thoughtfully. "And I'm just wondering where I've seen you before."

"Professionally?" cried Drummond happily. "Has he murdered his wife?"

And through half-closed eyes, he saw that the second man had turned very white.

"I don't understand you," said Margiter, now completely in control of himself. "Why should you have seen me before?"

He lit a cigarette with a perfectly steady hand, and Drummond wondered. Was McIver bluffing, or did he really recognize the man? In either case, what was the idea? If he wanted to catch them actually with the stuff, why warn them to start with?

"Why should you have seen me before?" repeated Margiter with rising warmth. "Put as you put it, it seems to me a damned libellous remark."

"In fact, I'd like to question both you gentlemen," continued McIver unperturbed, and his gaze shifted to Drummond.

"I trust you haven't seen me before," said Drummond in alarm.

"Maybe not. But if my suspicions are correct we shan't be strangers in the future. What were you two men fighting about?"

"I accidentally upset his drink, Inspector," remarked Drummond, and McIver snorted.

"Don't play the fool with me, sir," he said

sternly. "It won't pay you. Now where's the stuff?"

"The stuff?" echoed Drummond blankly.

"The dope. You're running a load of it between you, and that's what you were fighting about. Moreover, I'm going to find it."

"I think, Inspector," said Margiter solicitously, "that the Suffolk sun must have gone to your head. My friend and I arrived here ten minutes ago: our car is outside. If you wish to, you are at perfect liberty to search us and the car."

Drummond still failed to get McIver's idea: did he really imagine the stuff *was* in the car? Or on Margiter? And the humorous point was that Margiter was now treating him as an ally. "Well, Inspector," he said. "Are you ready?"

Margiter began to turn out his pockets, until McIver stopped him.

"We'll have a look at your car," he said curtly. "You stay where you are, sir." He turned to Drummond, who bowed.

"Your slightest wish is law, Inspector," he remarked amiably. "I'll have a look for the hiding-place in here."

He watched the three men troop out; then he crossed to the window which opened on to the garage. And having got there he paused, an unlighted cigarette half-way to his mouth.

"Come here, Algy," he said curtly. "Another van has arrived."

"What of it?" remarked Algy as he joined Drummond.

It was true: another van, identical with the one that had been in the yard, was now there. And the back wheels were being changed. It was one of those vans that had double wheels on the rear axle, and against the running-boards they could see three wheels propped up on each side.

"Most interesting," said Drummond thoughtfully. "Our friend in charge of the garage must be a prophet. How," he continued even more thoughtfully as Algy stared at him, "did he guess that the two spare wheels he brought out while we were watching him would be required? You note that they no longer adorn the side of the original van, and they are just being put on

van number two. Let us see what happens to the two wheels that have just come off van number two."

For a few minutes they watched in silence, and Drummond's frown grew more pronounced.

"Is this a new game?" he said, as the van, the change completed, drove away, leaving its own two wheels behind. "Is it conceivable?" he went on half to himself, "that . . . Come on," he cried suddenly. "It's sheer guess work, but it's worth following up. We will jape with them, Algy, and see if we strike a bull."

He strode over to a table and picked up a large bowl of castor sugar. Then he left the bar, followed by a completely bewildered Algy Longworth, and walked towards the Bentley.

"Are you satisfied now, Inspector," Margiter was saying with a sneer. "Or would you like me to have the engine taken down?"

"Don't worry," cried Drummond. "I know where the dope is."

For the fraction of a second Margiter's face grew strained. Then as Drummond produced the sugar-bowl from behind his back he laughed heartily.

"In the bar, Chief Constable," continued Drummond. "Right under our noses. Snow, my dear fellah: cocaine by the pound. Have some."

He offered the bowl to McIver, and Margiter laughed even more heartily.

"Do you good, Inspector," he said jovially. "And now, if you don't mind, I'll be getting along. How much was that petrol?" he called out, and the garage man approached.

"Twelve and eight, sir. I suppose you aren't by any chance going past Durnover's garage just this side of Ipswich?"

"I am. Why?"

"I was wondering, sir, if you would mind dropping these two spare wheels there. They were lent to a van, and . . ."

"Put 'em in the back," said Margiter, getting into the driving-seat. "And another time, Inspector, I think it would be better if you didn't jump to such farcical conclusions."

"Quaite," remarked Drummond, emerging from behind the car. "Quaite. In fact, McIver, it was most reprehensible of you," he continued as the car drove off. "What are you going to do now?"

"Search this place for the stuff."

"I'll bet you a well-earned pint it's not here," said Drummond with a grin. "And I'll bet you another that I know where it is."

"Where?" snapped McIver.

"In the car. Summon the Baby Austin, old sleuth hound, and we will chase the Bentley."

"Don't be a fool, Captain Drummond," said McIver. "How can we possibly overtake it?"

"Yet a third pint is now on," grinned Drummond. "I'll bet you we find the Bentley stationary by the road within three miles."

"Whereabouts in the car is it?" said McIver as their driver drew up beside them.

"Those two spares," answered Drummond. They boarded the car and started in pursuit.

"Not a place one would think of looking when they were actually on the van wheels. The inside one of each pair: always changed at the Rest House. And I'll bet that Durnover's garage would be a bit surprised if they were handed in. . . . What did I tell you, McIver?" He was pointing ahead. "The third pint is OK. There's the Bentley."

"How the deuce did you do it?" asked McIver curiously.

"A little jest of my own," said Drummond. "Never known to fail."

They drew up behind the stationary car, as Margiter, white with rage, emerged from under the bonnet.

"What the hell do you want now?" he snarled.

"Those two spare wheels," said McIver calmly, and things moved.

Margiter's hand shot to his pocket, but he was up against two past-masters in a scrap. A few seconds later, his hands handcuffed behind him and his gun in McIver's pocket, he was leaning up against the car panting, with his companion by his side.

"It's there all right," he said sullenly. "But if only this damned car hadn't died on me you'd never have got it."

"I know," remarked Drummond sympathetically. "That's what I wanted the castor sugar for. Incidentally, I didn't really think it was snow," he went on brightly. "In fact, I don't suppose cocaine would have acted. But castor sugar in the petrol tank is wonderful. Gums up the jets marvellously. Stops any car within a mile or two, and it's funny how few people know it."

"So that was it," said Margiter softly, staring at Drummond with a look of recognition dawning in his eyes. "Where the devil have I seen you before today?"

Drummond grinned happily.

"An albatross, without a doubt," he murmured.

BARONESS ORCZY

BARONESS "EMMUSKA" ORCZY (1865–1947), whose full name was Emma Magdolina Rozália Jozefa Borbála Orczy, was born in Hungary and spoke no English until she was fifteen and her family had moved to London, though all her novels, plays, and short stories were written in English. To detective-fiction aficionados she is best known as the creator of The Old Man in the Corner, a detective who relies entirely on his cerebral faculties to solve crimes. The character that brought her worldwide popularity, however, was Sir Percy Blakeney, a.k.a. The Scarlet Pimpernel, an effete English gentleman who secretly acts as a courageous espionage agent during the French Revolution, daringly saving the lives of countless French aristocrats who have been condemned to the guillotine. Baroness Orczy was initially unsuccessful in selling her novel about Sir Percy, so she and her husband converted it into a stage play that opened in London in 1905; reviewers were unenthusiastic, but audiences loved it. *The Scarlet Pimpernel* was also published as a novel of the same title in the same year, to become the first of numerous adventures about the thorn in the side of the bloodthirsty citizens of the Committee of Public Safety and the Committee of General Security and the *gendarmerie*. As Sir Percy says of his alter ego: "We seek him here, we seek him there/Those Frenchies seek him everywhere./Is he in heaven?—Is he in hell?/That demmed, elusive Pimpernel?" Other books include *I Will Repay* (1906), *The Elusive Pimpernel* (1908), *Eldorado* (1913), *The League of the Scarlet Pimpernel* (1919), and *The Triumph of the Scarlet Pimpernel* (1922), and *Adventures of the Scarlet Pimpernel* (1929). There have also been numerous screen versions of the Pimpernel saga, beginning with the 1917 silent film, *The Scarlet Pimpernel;* the 1934 version starring Leslie Howard is perhaps the classic. The Scarlet Pimpernel takes his name from a wildflower that blossoms and dies in a single night.

"A Question of Passports" was first published in *The League of the Scarlet Pimpernel* (London: Cassell, 1919).

A QUESTION OF PASSPORTS

BARONESS ORCZY

BIBOT WAS very sure of himself. There never was, never had been, there never would be again another such patriotic citizen of the Republic as was citizen Bibot of the Town Guard.

And because his patriotism was so well known among the members of the Committee of Public Safety, and his uncompromising hatred of the aristocrats so highly appreciated, citizen Bibot had been given the most important military post within the city of Paris.

He was in command of the Porte Montmartre, which goes to prove how highly he was esteemed, for, believe me, more treachery had been going on inside and out of the Porte Montmartre than in any other quarter of Paris. The last commandant there, citizen Ferney, was guillotined for having allowed a whole batch of aristocrats—traitors to the Republic, all of them—to slip through the Porte Montmartre and to find safety outside the walls of Paris. Ferney pleaded in his defence that these traitors had been spirited away from under his very nose by the devil's agency, for surely that meddlesome Englishman who spent his time in rescuing aristocrats—traitors, all of them—from the clutches of Madame la Guillotine must be either the devil himself, or at any rate one of his most powerful agents.

"*Nom de Dieu!* just think of his name! The Scarlet Pimpernel they call him! No one knows him by any other name! and he is preternaturally tall and strong and superhumanly cunning! And the power which he has of being transmuted into various personalities—rendering himself quite unrecognisable to the eyes of the most sharp-seeing patriot of France, must of a surety be a gift of Satan!"

But the Committee of Public Safety refused to listen to Ferney's explanations. The Scarlet Pimpernel was only an ordinary mortal—an exceedingly cunning and meddlesome personage it is true, and endowed with a superfluity of wealth which enabled him to break the thin crust of patriotism that overlay the natural cupidity of many Captains of the Town Guard—but still an ordinary man for all that! and no true lover of the Republic should allow either superstitious terror or greed to interfere with the discharge of his duties which at the Porte Montmartre consisted in detaining any and every person—aristocrat, foreigner, or otherwise traitor to the Republic—who could not give a satisfactory reason for desiring to leave Paris. Having detained such persons, the patriot's next duty was to hand them over to the Committee of Public Safety, who would then decide whether Madame la Guillotine would have the last word over them or not.

And the guillotine did nearly always have the last word to say, unless the Scarlet Pimpernel interfered.

The trouble was, that that same accursed Englishman interfered at times in a manner which was positively terrifying. His impudence, *certes*, passed all belief. Stories of his daring and of his impudence were abroad which literally made the lank and greasy hair of every patriot curl with wonder. 'Twas even whispered—not too loudly, forsooth—that certain members of the Committee of Public Safety had measured their skill and valour against that of the Englishman and emerged from the conflict beaten and humiliated, vowing vengeance which, of a truth, was still slow in coming.

Citizen Chauvelin, one of the most implacable and unyielding members of the Committee, was known to have suffered overwhelming shame at the hands of that daring gang, of whom the so-called Scarlet Pimpernel was the accredited chief. Some there were who said that citizen Chauvelin had for ever forfeited his prestige, and even endangered his head by measuring his well-known astuteness against that mysterious League of spies.

But then Bibot was different!

He feared neither the devil, nor any Englishman. Had the latter the strength of giants and the protection of every power of evil, Bibot was ready for him. Nay! he was aching for a tussle, and haunted the purlieus of the Committees to obtain some post which would enable him to come to grips with the Scarlet Pimpernel and his League.

Bibot's zeal and perseverance were duly rewarded, and anon he was appointed to the command of the guard at the Porte Montmartre.

A post of vast importance as aforesaid; so much so, in fact, that no less a person than citizen Jean-Paul Marat himself came to speak with Bibot on that third day of Nivose in the year I of the Republic, with a view to impressing upon him the necessity of keeping his eyes open, and of suspecting every man, woman, and child indiscriminately until they had proved themselves to be true patriots.

"Let no one slip through your fingers, citizen Bibot," Marat admonished with grim earnestness. "That accursed Englishman is cunning and resourceful, and his impudence surpasses that of the devil himself."

"He'd better try some of his impudence on me!" commented Bibot with a sneer, "he'll soon find out that he no longer has a Ferney to deal with. Take it from me, citizen Marat, that if a batch of aristocrats escape out of Paris within the next few days, under the guidance of the d——d Englishman, they will have to find some other way than the Porte Montmartre."

"Well said, citizen!" commented Marat. "But be watchful to-night . . . to-night especially. The Scarlet Pimpernel is rampant in Paris just now."

"How so?"

"The *ci-devant* Duc and Duchesse de Montreux and the whole of their brood—sisters, brothers, two or three children, a priest, and several servants—a round dozen in all, have been condemned to death. The guillotine for them to-morrow at daybreak! Would it could have been to-night," added Marat, whilst a demoniacal leer contorted his face which already exuded lust for blood from every pore. "Would it could have been to-night. But the guillotine has been busy; over four hundred executions to-day . . . and the tumbrils are full—the seats bespoken in advance—and still they come. . . . But to-morrow morning at daybreak Madame la Guillotine will have a word to say to the whole of the Montreux crowd!"

"But they are in the Conciergerie prison surely, citizen! out of the reach of that accursed Englishman?"

"They are on their way, and I mistake not, to the prison at this moment. I came straight on here after the condemnation, to which I listened with true joy. Ah, citizen Bibot! the blood of these hated aristocrats is good to behold when it drips from the blade of the guillotine. Have a care, citizen Bibot, do not let the Montreux crowd escape!"

"Have no fear, citizen Marat! But surely there is no danger! They have been tried and condemned! They are, as you say, even now on their way—well guarded, I presume—to the Conciergerie prison!—to-morrow at daybreak, the guillotine! What is there to fear?"

"Well! well!" said Marat, with a slight tone of hesitation, "it is best, citizen Bibot, to be over-careful these times."

Even whilst Marat spoke his face, usually so cunning and so vengeful, had suddenly lost its look of devilish cruelty which was almost super-human in the excess of its infamy, and a greyish hue—suggestive of terror—had spread over the sunken cheeks. He clutched Bibot's arm, and leaning over the table he whispered in his ear:

"The Public Prosecutor had scarce finished his speech to-day, judgment was being pro-nounced, the spectators were expectant and still, only the Montreux woman and some of the fe-males and children were blubbering and moan-ing, when suddenly, it seemed from nowhere, a small piece of paper fluttered from out the as-sembly and alighted on the desk in front of the Public Prosecutor. He took the paper up and glanced at its contents. I saw that his cheeks had paled, and that his hand trembled as he handed the paper over to me."

"And what did that paper contain, citizen Marat?" asked Bibot, also speaking in a whisper, for an access of superstitious terror was gripping him by the throat.

"Just the well-known accursed device, citi-zen, the small scarlet flower, drawn in red ink, and the few words: 'To-night the innocent men and women now condemned by this infamous tribunal will be beyond your reach!'"

"And no sign of a messenger?"

"None."

"And when did—"

"Hush!" said Marat peremptorily, "no more of that now. To your post, citizen, and remem-ber—all are suspect! let none escape!"

The two men had been sitting outside a small tavern, opposite the Porte Montmartre, with a bottle of wine between them, their elbows rest-ing on the grimy top of a rough wooden table. They had talked in whispers, for even the walls of the tumble-down cabaret might have had ears.

Opposite them the city wall—broken here by the great gate of Montmartre—loomed threat-eningly in the fast-gathering dusk of this win-ter's afternoon. Men in ragged red shirts, their unkempt heads crowned with Phrygian caps adorned with a tricolour cockade, lounged against the wall, or sat in groups on the top of piles of refuse that littered the street, with a rough deal plank between them and a greasy pack of cards in their grimy fingers. Guns and bayonets were propped against the wall. The gate itself had three means of egress; each of these was guarded by two men with fixed bayo-nets at their shoulders, but otherwise dressed like the others, in rags—with bare legs that looked blue and numb in the cold—the sans-culottes of revolutionary Paris.

Bibot rose from his seat, nodding to Marat, and joined his men.

From afar, but gradually drawing nearer, came the sound of a ribald song, with chorus ac-companiment sung by throats obviously sur-feited with liquor.

For a moment—as the sound approached—Bibot turned back once more to the Friend of the People.

"Am I to understand, citizen," he said, "that my orders are not to let anyone pass through these gates to-night?"

"No, no, citizen," replied Marat, "we dare not do that. There are a number of good patriots in the city still. We cannot interfere with their liberty or—"

And the look of fear of the demagogue—himself afraid of the human whirlpool which he has let loose—stole into Marat's cruel, piercing eyes.

"No, no," he reiterated more emphatically, "we cannot disregard the passports issued by the Committee of Public Safety. But examine each passport carefully, citizen Bibot! If you have any reasonable ground for suspicion, detain the holder, and if you have not—"

The sound of singing was quite near now. With another wink and a final leer, Marat drew back under the shadow of the cabaret, and Bibot swaggered up to the main entrance of the gate.

"*Qui va là?*" he thundered in stentorian tones as a group of some half-dozen people lurched towards him out of the gloom, still shouting hoarsely their ribald drinking song.

The foremost man in the group paused opposite citizen Bibot, and with arms akimbo, and legs planted well apart tried to assume a rigidity of attitude which apparently was somewhat foreign to him at this moment.

"Good patriots, citizen," he said in a thick voice which he vainly tried to render steady.

"What do you want?" queried Bibot.

"To be allowed to go on our way unmolested."

"What is your way?"

"Through the Porte Montmartre to the village of Barency."

"What is your business there?"

This query delivered in Bibot's most pompous manner seemed vastly to amuse the rowdy crowd. He who was the spokesman turned to his friends and shouted hilariously:

"Hark at him, citizens! He asks me what is our business. *Ohé*, citizen Bibot, since when have you become blind? A dolt you've always been, else you had not asked the question."

But Bibot, undeterred by the man's drunken insolence, retorted gruffly:

"Your business, I want to know."

"Bibot! my little Bibot!" cooed the bibulous orator now in dulcet tones, "dost not know us, my good Bibot? Yet we all know thee, citizen— Captain Bibot of the Town Guard, eh, citizens! Three cheers for the citizen captain!"

When the noisy shouts and cheers from half a dozen hoarse throats had died down, Bibot, without more ado, turned to his own men at the gate.

"Drive these drunken louts away!" he commanded; "no one is allowed to loiter here."

Loud protest on the part of the hilarious crowd followed, then a slight scuffle with the bayonets of the Town Guard. Finally the spokesman, somewhat sobered, once more appealed to Bibot.

"Citizen Bibot! you must be blind not to know me and my mates! And let me tell you that you are doing yourself a deal of harm by interfering with the citizens of the Republic in the proper discharge of their duties, and by disre-

garding their rights of egress through this gate, a right confirmed by passports signed by two members of the Committee of Public Safety."

He had spoken now fairly clearly and very pompously. Bibot, somewhat impressed and remembering Marat's admonitions, said very civilly:

"Tell me your business then, citizen, and show me your passports. If everything is in order you may go your way."

"But you know me, citizen Bibot?" queried the other.

"Yes, I know you—unofficially, citizen Durand."

"You know that I and the citizens here are the carriers for citizen Legrand, the market gardener of Barency?"

"Yes, I know that," said Bibot guardedly, "unofficially."

"Then, unofficially, let me tell you, citizen, that unless we get to Barency this evening, Paris will have to do without cabbages and potatoes tomorrow. So now you know that you are acting at your own risk and peril, citizen, by detaining us."

"Your passports, all of you," commanded Bibot.

He had just caught sight of Marat still sitting outside the tavern opposite, and was glad enough, in this instance, to shelve his responsibility on the shoulders of the popular "Friend of the People." There was general searching in ragged pockets for grimy papers with official seals thereon, and whilst Bibot ordered one of his men to take the six passports across the road to citizen Marat for his inspection, he himself, by the last rays of the setting winter sun, made close examination of the six men who desired to pass through the Porte Montmartre.

As the spokesman had averred, he—Bibot— knew every one of these men. They were the carriers to citizen Legrand, the Barency market gardener. Bibot knew every face. They passed with a load of fruit and vegetables in and out of Paris every day. There was really and absolutely no cause for suspicion, and when citizen Marat returned the six passports, pronouncing them to be genuine, and recognising his own signature at the bottom of each, Bibot was at last satisfied, and the six bibulous carriers were allowed to pass through the gate, which they did, arm in arm, singing a wild *carmagnole,* and vociferously cheering as they emerged out into the open.

But Bibot passed an unsteady hand over his brow. It was cold, yet he was in a perspiration. That sort of thing tells on a man's nerves. He rejoined Marat, at the table outside the drinking booth, and ordered a fresh bottle of wine.

The sun had set now, and with the gathering dusk a damp mist descended on Montmartre. From the wall opposite, where the men sat playing cards, came occasional volleys of blasphemous oaths. Bibot was feeling much more like himself. He had half forgotten the incident of the six carriers, which had occurred nearly half an hour ago.

Two or three other people had, in the meanwhile, tried to pass through the gates, but Bibot had been suspicious and had detained them all.

Marat having commended him for his zeal took final leave of him. Just as the demagogue's slouchy, grimy figure was disappearing down a side street there was the loud clatter of hoofs from that same direction, and the next moment a detachment of the mounted Town Guard, headed by an officer in uniform, galloped down the ill-paved street.

Even before the troopers had drawn rein the officer had hailed Bibot.

"Citizen," he shouted, and his voice was breathless, for he had evidently ridden hard and fast, "this message to you from the citizen Chief Commissary of the Section. Six men are wanted by the Committee of Public Safety. They are disguised as carriers in the employ of a market gardener, and have passports for Barency! . . . The passports are stolen: the men are traitors— escaped aristocrats—and their spokesman is that d——d Englishman, the Scarlet Pimpernel."

Bibot tried to speak; he tugged at the collar of his ragged shirt; an awful curse escaped him.

"Ten thousand devils!" he roared.

"On no account allow these people to go through," continued the officer. "Keep their passports. Detain them! . . . Understand?"

Bibot was still gasping for breath even whilst the officer, ordering a quick "Turn!" reeled his horse round, ready to gallop away as far as he had come.

"I am for the St. Denis Gate—Grosjean is on guard there!" he shouted. "Same orders all round the city. No one to leave the gates! . . . Understand?"

His troopers fell in. The next moment he would be gone, and those cursed aristocrats well in safety's way.

"Citizen Captain!"

The hoarse shout at last contrived to escape Bibot's parched throat. As if involuntarily, the officer drew rein once more.

"What is it? Quick!—I've no time. That confounded Englishman may be at the St. Denis Gate even now!"

"Citizen Captain," gasped Bibot, his breath coming and going like that of a man fighting for his life. "Here! . . . at this gate! . . . not half an hour ago . . . six men . . . carriers . . . market gardeners . . . I seemed to know their faces. . . ."

"Yes! yes! market gardener's carriers," exclaimed the officer gleefully, "aristocrats all of them . . . and that d——d Scarlet Pimpernel. You've got them? You've detained them? . . . Where are they? . . . Speak, man, in the name of hell! . . ."

"Gone!" gasped Bibot. His legs would no longer bear him. He fell backwards on to a heap of street debris and refuse, from which lowly vantage ground he contrived to give away the whole miserable tale.

"Gone! half an hour ago. Their passports were in order! . . . I seemed to know their faces! Citizen Marat was here. . . . He, too—"

In a moment the officer had once more swung his horse round, so that the animal reared, with wild forefeet pawing the air, with champing of bit, and white foam scattered around.

"A thousand million curses!" he exclaimed. "Citizen Bibot, your head will pay for this treachery. Which way did they go?"

A dozen hands were ready to point in the direction where the merry party of carriers had disappeared half an hour ago; a dozen tongues gave rapid, confused explanations.

"Into it, my men!" shouted the officer; "they were on foot! They can't have gone far. Remember the Republic has offered ten thousand francs for the capture of the Scarlet Pimpernel."

Already the heavy gates had been swung open, and the officer's voice once more rang out clear through a perfect thunder-clap of fast galloping hoofs:

"Ventre a terre! Remember!—ten thousand francs to him who first sights the Scarlet Pimpernel!"

The thunder-clap died away in the distance, the dust of four score hoofs was merged in the fog and in the darkness; the voice of the captain was raised again through the mist-laden air. One shout . . . a shout of triumph . . . then silence once again.

Bibot had fainted on the heap of debris.

His comrades brought him wine to drink. He gradually revived. Hope came back to his heart; his nerves soon steadied themselves as the heavy beverage filtrated through into his blood.

"Bah!" he ejaculated as he pulled himself together, "the troopers were well-mounted . . . the officer was enthusiastic; those carriers could not have walked very far. And, in any case, I am free from blame. Citizen Marat himself was here and let them pass!"

A shudder of superstitious terror ran through him as he recollected the whole scene: for surely he knew all the faces of the six men who had gone through the gate. The devil indeed must have given the mysterious Englishman power to transmute himself and his gang wholly into the bodies of other people.

More than an hour went by. Bibot was quite himself again, bullying, commanding, detaining everybody now.

At that time there appeared to be a slight altercation going on, on the farther side of the gate. Bibot thought it his duty to go and see what the noise was about. Someone wanting to get into Paris instead of out of it at this hour of the night was a strange occurrence.

Bibot heard his name spoken by a raucous voice. Accompanied by two of his men he crossed the wide gates in order to see what was happening. One of the men held a lanthorn, which he was swinging high above his head. Bibot saw standing there before him, arguing with the guard by the gate, the bibulous spokesman of the band of carriers.

He was explaining to the sentry that he had a message to deliver to the citizen commanding at the Porte Montmartre.

"It is a note," he said, "which an officer of the mounted guard gave me. He and twenty troopers were galloping down the great North Road not far from Barency. When they overtook the six of us they drew rein, and the officer gave me this note for citizen Bibot and fifty francs if I would deliver it tonight."

"Give me the note!" said Bibot calmly.

But his hand shook as he took the paper; his face was livid with fear and rage.

The paper had no writing on it, only the outline of a small scarlet flower done in red—the device of the cursed Englishman, the Scarlet Pimpernel.

"Which way did the officer and the twenty troopers go," he stammered, "after they gave you this note?"

"On the way to Calais," replied the other, "but they had magnificent horses, and didn't spare them either. They are a league and more away by now!"

All the blood in Bibot's body seemed to rush up to his head, a wild buzzing was in his ears. . . .

And that was how the Duc and Duchesse de Montreux, with their servants and family, escaped from Paris on that third day of Nivose in the year I of the Republic.

INTELLIGENCE

RAFAEL SABATINI

ONE OF THE most successful writers of adventure fiction who ever lived, Rafael Sabatini (1875–1950) was born in Italy to an English mother and an Italian father. The family moved frequently, so young Rafael learned numerous languages, which he put to good use as a translator for the British during World War I. At seventeen, he went to work in business but, yearning to write fiction, he began selling short stories in the 1890s to such major English magazines as *Pearson's, Grand,* and *London.* His first novel, *The Suitors of Yvonne,* was published in 1902 and he was soon producing a book a year, along with numerous short stories. Nonetheless, great success eluded him until the 1921 publication of *Scaramouche,* with its famed opening lines: "He was born with a gift of laughter and a sense that the world was mad. And that was his only patrimony." The novel became an international bestseller and was followed the next year by an even greater success, *Captain Blood.* Both were made into highly popular motion pictures, the former in 1952 with Stewart Granger and Eleanor Parker, and the latter in 1935 with Errol Flynn and Olivia de Havilland; Flynn also starred in a 1940 adaptation of Sabatini's *The Sea Hawk* (1915), a novel inspired by the exploits of Sir Francis Drake.

Although best known for his seafaring novels, Sabatini wrote in numerous genres, including those of romance, mystery, historical fiction, and, as in the following story, the international espionage game.

"Intelligence" was originally published in the January 1918 issue of the *Grand* magazine; it has never before been published in book form.

INTELLIGENCE

RAFAEL SABATINI

FOR AN HOUR Professor Kauffmann had been deep in the slumber that is common alike to just and unjust provided that physical conditions are healthy, when he was aroused, first subconsciously, then consciously, by the loud insistent trilling of the electric bell.

Professor Kauffmann sat up in bed, switched on the light, and verified that it was ten minutes past two. A little while he sat quite still, an oddly intent alertness in the grey eyes that looked so very light by contrast with his swarthy black-bearded face and the black hair, cut *en brosse,* that rose stiffly above it. At last, moving leisurely, he left the bed, and from a chair-back near at hand he took up a heavy quilted dressing-gown. He was a tall, active man of about forty, who did not look as if he were an easy prey to fear. Yet he trembled a little as he put on that garment. But then the night was cold, for the month was December—December of that fateful year 1914. From a small table near the bed he picked up a life-preserver, a slight weapon of lead and whipcord, and he thrust it together with the hand that held it into the roomy pocket of his gown.

Then—the bell still ringing—he left his bedroom, passed down the heavily-carpeted stairs of that choicely appointed little house in Mayfair, and went to open the door. As it swung back, the light from the hall behind the professor fell upon a slim pale young gentleman in a fur-lined coat over evening clothes.

Professor Kauffmann's relief showed itself a moment, to give place almost at once to surprise and irritation.

"Elphinstone!" he exclaimed. "What the devil . . . ? Do you realise that it is after two o'clock?"

His English was so fluent and colloquial that he might easily have passed for an Englishman. It was only occasionally that a too guttural note proclaimed his real origin.

The young gentleman lounged in without waiting to be invited.

"Awfully sorry, Kauff, to drag you out of bed. But I never imagined you would answer the bell yourself."

The professor grunted, and closed the door. "I am all alone in the house. My man is away ill," he explained. And he added without cordiality—"Come along in. There may still be a fire in the study."

He led the way upstairs, opened a door, touched a switch, and lighted up a spacious lofty room, the air of which was pleasantly warm and tobacco-laden. In the fireplace the remains of a fire still smouldered under an ashen crust. The professor went to stir it into life, and as he passed the massive writing-table that occupied the middle of the room he put down the life-preserver which the event had proved to be unnecessary.

Elphinstone removed his opera hat and loosened his heavy coat. His hands trembled a little. He was very pale and rather breathless. Uneasiness was stamped upon his weak face and haunted the restless eyes that took stock of the room, from the gleaming bookcases flanking a blank-faced mahogany press to the heavy purple curtains masking the French windows of the balcony above the porch.

"I'm a dreadful nuisance, Kauff, I know," he was apologising. "But I certainly shouldn't have knocked you up at this time of night if the matter hadn't been urgent." He paused nervously, to add a moment later—"I'm in trouble rather."

Kauffmann came upright again and looked round calmly, still grasping the poker. "Have a drink," he invited, and pointed to a side-table and a tray bearing decanters, glasses, and a syphon.

"Thanks."

The visitor crossed, poured himself a half-tumbler of whiskey, squirted a tablespoonful of soda into it, and gulped it down.

The professor's light eyes watched him inscrutably.

"Been playing bridge again, I suppose," he hazarded. "I've told you before that you ought to give it up. You know that you're not lucky, and everybody else knows that you can't play. You haven't the temperament."

"Oh, shut up," was the peevish answer. "It isn't bridge this time."

Elphinstone flung himself into the padded chair at the writing-table and looked across it at his host. "As a matter of fact, it isn't chiefly about myself that I'm troubled. It's about you."

"About me? Oh! What about me?"

Watching the man's calm assurance Elphinstone's lip curled in a deprecatory smile. He half shrugged.

"What do you suppose? Do you think a man can go on behaving as you do in such times as these—with the country excited about spies?"

Very quietly the professor put down the poker. In silence he crossed the room, and came to lean upon the writing-table, facing Elphinstone at close quarters.

"I don't know what you mean," he said in a very level voice.

"Oh, yes, you do. I mean that your damned

mysterious ways of life have brought you under the notice of the Home Office. I don't know whether there's occasion for it or not, and I don't want to know. I've got troubles enough of my own. But you've behaved rather decently to me, Kauff, and . . . well, there it is. I thought you'd like to know that you're being watched."

"You thought I'd like to know it?" Kauffmann smiled. "Of course it gives me the liveliest pleasure. And who is watching me?"

"The Government, of course. Have you ever heard of Scott-Drummond?"

The light eyes flickered, and a keen ear might have detected the faintest change in the voice that asked—"Scott-Drummond? Do you mean Scott-Drummond of the Intelligence?"

"Do I mean . . . ? What other Scott-Drummond should I mean? What other Scott-Drummond is there?"

"Ha!" Kauffmann stood upright again, his hands in the pockets of his dressing-gown. "I know of him—yes," he answered easily. "What about him?"

"I have good reason to believe that he is in charge of your case. He is having you shadowed—or whatever they call it. That's what I came to tell you, so that you may take your precautions."

The professor laughed outright, a thought too heartily perhaps.

"That's very kind of you, Elphinstone—very kind. But what precautions need I take? Good Heavens, if Scott-Drummond chooses to waste his time over my affairs, the more fool he. Have another drink?"

But Elphinstone ignored the invitation. His weak mouth was sullen, and it was an impatient hand that thrust back the rumpled fair hair from his brow. "It's not very generous of you to pretend that my warning is of no value," he complained. "I don't suppose they'd suspect you without good reason. And I can tell you that I've come here at considerable risk to myself."

The professor smiled at him tolerantly as one smiles at a foolish child.

"You really believe that, do you? Well, well!"

He sat on the edge of the writing-table. "Tell me, anyhow: Where did you pick up this priceless piece of gossip?"

"It's more than gossip. I happened to overhear something from a talkative young undersecretary at Flynn's this evening. And from what he said I should clear the country quick if I were you, Kauff. That's all."

"Bah! You've stumbled on a mare's nest."

"You know best, of course." There was vexation in the thin voice. "But at least you'll admit that I've acted as a friend to you—that I've taken a good deal of risk in coming here."

"Not much risk, really," laughed the professor. "Still you are very kind, and I am grateful to you for your friendly intentions."

"Oh, that's all right. I think I'll be going." He rose slowly. The uneasiness that had marked his manner throughout became more manifest. "That's all right," he repeated, faltering. Then he paused. "There's another matter I wanted to talk to you about," he said. And then, speaking quickly, like a man who, resolved, takes things at the rush—"Fact is, I am in a bit of a mess," he confessed. "I absolutely must have a hundred pounds by morning. Do you think you could . . . I mean, I should be most awfully grateful to you if you would . . ."

He left the sentence there, glancing self-consciously at his host.

Kauffmann's eyes considered the weedy degenerate with frank contempt. He even laughed shortly, through closed lips.

"I thought we should come to that sooner or later," said he.

Elphinstone made a movement of indignant protest. His cheeks flushed faintly.

"You don't suppose," he cried, "that I am asking you to pay me for the information I have . . ."

"Are you quite sure," Kauffmann cut in, "that you didn't manufacture the information for the express purpose of placing me in your debt?"

"Kauffmann!"

"Are you quite sure," the other continued,

his light eyes almost hypnotic in their steady glance, "that you are not simply making capital out of silly suspicions of your own, and that this story about Scott-Drummond is not a pure fabrication?"

"What do you take me for?" was the resentful question.

"For a young gentleman who plays bridge for stakes far beyond his means, who loses persistently, and who is reduced by his losses to perpetual borrowing."

The flush deepened in Elphinstone's cheeks; then it ebbed again, leaving them paler than ever. With a great show of dignity he buttoned his coat and reached for his hat. "It's no use being angry with you . . ." he was beginning.

"No use at all," Kauffmann agreed.

Elphinstone shrugged, put on his hat, and turned to go. But his need was greater than his pride. He paused again.

"Kauffmann," he said seriously, "I only wish for your own sake that I could confess that you are right. But I haven't said a word that isn't absolutely true. From what I overheard I'll lay fifty to one that if you remain in England until tomorrow night you will spend it in prison."

"Don't be a fool." There was a note of irritation creeping into the voice that hitherto had been so smooth. "A man can't be arrested in this country without some sort of evidence against him, and there's not a scrap of evidence against me; not a scrap."

"If Scott-Drummond makes it his business to find evidence that you are in the pay of Germany—naturalised British subject though you may be—he'll find it."

"Not if it doesn't exist; and it doesn't exist; it can't exist. I tell you," the professor added vehemently, "that I am not in the pay of Germany. In fact, you would be insulting me if you weren't boring me, and after all you're obviously only half sober. It's very late, Elphinstone, and I want to go to bed."

"All right," was the sullen answer. "I am going."

But it was one thing to announce the resolve,

and another to find the courage to carry it out. Far, indeed, from doing so, Elphinstone broke down utterly. Quite suddenly the lingering remains of reserve fell from him.

"Kauff, old man," he exclaimed desperately, "I'm in the very devil of a mess. If I don't get a hundred pounds before morning I don't know what will happen."

"Pooh! Creditors can wait."

"It isn't creditors—not an ordinary creditor. It . . . it's a case of borrowed money."

"As one who has frequently lent, I confess I don't perceive the difference."

Hoping to move him, Elphinstone was driven to make a full and humiliating confession. "This money was borrowed without asking permission. If I don't put it back before it is discovered it will look like . . . Oh, you know what it will look like. I shall be ruined. I don't know what'll happen to me. Kauff, for God's sake . . ."

But the professor remained entirely unmoved, unless it were to a deeper contempt.

"Do you know how much money you owe me already?" he asked coldly. "Do you realise that it amounts to close upon a thousand pounds?"

"I know. But I shall be able to pay you back very shortly."

There was a whine in the pleading voice.

"I am glad to hear it. But until you do I'm afraid I can't help you any further."

"Not after what I've told you?"

Elphinstone was overcome with horrified amazement.

"It's no use, my boy. You must get it from someone else. I can't afford it at the moment."

Elphinstone's lips tightened. His weak face became ghastly.

"You absolutely refuse me, then?"

"Sorry, of course." The professor's blandness savoured of contempt. "But I can't afford it."

"You can't afford it?" Elphinstone looked at him, and sneered. At bay, his manner assumed a certain truculence. "What about all this German gold you are receiving?"

The professor eyed him stonily a moment.

Then—"Drop that, Elphinstone," he said shortly. "It won't pay you."

"Won't it?" Elphinstone's angry excitement was rising; his voice grew shriller. "I am not so sure. You think I am a fool, Kauffmann. If I've kept my mouth shut it's because you've been kind to me and helped me when I was in trouble. But it doesn't follow that I've kept my eyes shut, too. I know more than you think. I could tell Scott-Drummond something that would . . ."

And then Kauffmann became really angry.

"Get out of my house," he ordered. "Do you think I am the man to submit to blackmail? Get out at once."

The tall vigorous figure and grim swarthy face became oddly menacing. Elphinstone was scared.

"Wait a minute, Kauffmann." He was cringing again. "I didn't mean it. I really didn't. I am up against it. I . . ."

"I don't care whether you meant it or not. Go to Scott-Drummond and tell him anything you like. But don't forget that he may have some questions to ask you. Don't forget that it will come out that you have had about a thousand pounds from me, and that a jury of your countrymen will certainly want to know what it was for."

"What it was for?" Elphinstone stared in amazement. "I never intended . . ."

"No. But I did," Kauffmann answered dryly. "I don't pay a thousand pounds to seal a man's lips without taking good care to see that the seal is going to hold. My dear Elphinstone, when you realise that you are a fool you will have taken the first great step towards wisdom. Meanwhile, I have had enough of you. Get out before I throw you out."

"For God's sake, Kauffmann . . ." Elphinstone was beginning desperately.

Kauffmann advanced upon him round the table. "Get out, I tell you." He seized the young man by the shoulders to thrust him towards the door. But Elphinstone squirmed and twisted in his grasp.

"Take your hands off me, you damned German spy!" he cried, thoroughly enraged at this indignity. He wrenched himself from those compelling hands and sprang away, round the table. With an oath Kauffmann turned to follow him; and then the thing happened.

By purest chance Elphinstone's hand had found the wicked little life-preserver that lay among the professor's papers. Fierce now as a cornered rat he snatched it up, and in his blind unreflecting fury brought it down upon the head of his aggressor.

There was an ominous squelching crack. Kauffmann's hands were jerked violently up to the level of his shoulders with the mechanical action of an automaton, and he collapsed in a heap at Elphinstone's feet.

Standing over him, still clutching the weapon, Elphinstone apostrophised the fallen man, breathlessly, almost hysterically.

"That will teach you better manners, you dirty spy. That will teach you to keep your hands to yourself. If you thought I was going to let myself be man-handled by a . . ."

He broke off. There was something ominous about the utter stillness of the body and the red viscous fluid slowly oozing from his head and spreading to the Persian carpet.

"Kauffmann!" His voice shrilled up and cracked. "Kauffmann!"

In shuddering, slobbering terror he went down beside the professor, and shook him.

"Kauffmann!"

The body sank limply down again as Elphinstone relaxed his grip of it and it lay still and unresponsive as before. A sudden horrible realisation was borne in upon the young man's senses. With a whimpering sound he shrank back, still kneeling. "Oh my God!" he gasped, and covered his white face with trembling hands.

The next moment he almost screamed aloud, for somewhere in the room behind him something—someone—had moved. He whipped round in a frenzy of terror.

The heavy curtains masking the French windows had parted, and on the near side of them stood now a slight man in a shabby suit of tweeds, a faded scarf round his neck, an old tweed cap on his head. He had a keen, hungry-looking hatchet face and dark eyes which were considering Elphinstone and his work with almost inhuman emotionlessness.

For a long moment they stared at each other in silence. Then the newcomer spoke, his voice so quiet and self-contained as to sound almost mocking.

"Well?" he asked. "What are you going to do about it?"

Elphinstone sprang up. "Who are you?" he asked mechanically.

"Just a burglar," said the other, indicating the window behind him, from which a square of glass had been cut.

"A thief!"

The burglar let the curtains fall back into place, and moved forward soundlessly. "You needn't be so superior," said he. "I'm not a murderer, anyhow."

"A murd . . . ! My God! He's not . . . he can't be dead!"

"Not if his head is made of cast iron."

There was something almost revolting in the cynicism with which the newcomer accepted the fact. He knelt beside the professor, and made a swift examination.

"Dead as mutton," he pronounced nonchalantly. "You've smashed his skull."

Elphinstone sank limply against the desk, and clutched it to steady himself. Breath seemed to fail him.

"I didn't mean it," he whimpered. "I swear I didn't. I . . . I did it in self-defence. You must have seen how it happened. It was an accident."

"Oh, I saw how it happened all right," the other answered, rising. "But you don't suppose my evidence would help either of us very much. This may be very nasty for you."

The burglar met the stare of the young man's dilating eyes, and saw purpose suddenly kindle in them, saw the hand that still held the life-preserver tighten its grip. But he was swifter of purpose and action than Elphinstone, and on the instant the latter found himself contemplating the nozzle of a pistol.

"Drop that weapon! Drop it at once," the burglar commanded, and there was steel in the voice that had been so languid.

Elphinstone's nerveless hand let fall the life-preserver.

"You didn't think . . ."

"No. But you might have been tempted, and one broken skull is enough in one evening." He slipped his pistol back into his pocket. "Well?" he asked again. "Have you made up your mind what you're going to do about it?"

"Do about it?" Elphinstone echoed dully. There was a gleam of perspiration on his brow. "You'll not give me away," he was beginning to plead, then suddenly he realised the situation as it affected the other, and from that derived a confidence that rendered him aggressive. "You daren't," he announced. "It would look pretty black against you, my friend. If anyone were to find us now, which way do you think appearances would point? Who's to say that it wasn't you who killed him?"

"No one—unless you do."

"Exactly," said Elphinstone, and he almost sneered. He had fancied that the burglar winced under that last question of his, as well he might. Far from being disastrous, it began to be clear to him that the advent of the thief was providential; that he, himself, was entirely master of the situation. In this comforting persuasion he recovered his nerve almost as swiftly as he had lost it.

"You had better not attempt to keep me here, or it may be the worse for you. You can get away as you came, and there's nothing to prevent you taking whatever you came for. There's no one in the house. His man is away ill."

"I know. I informed myself of that before I came."

"Very well, then. He's got a collection of jewels in there that is worth a fortune," and Elphinstone pointed to the blind face of the mahogany press standing between the bookcases.

"I know," said the burglar again. "That's what I came for."

"Then let me get out of this, and you can help yourself."

"Who's keeping you?" the other asked him in that uncannily cool, matter-of-fact voice of his. "I'm certainly not. In your place I should have cleared already. So long as you don't interfere with my job I don't care whether you go or stay."

He swung round with that, crossed to the press, turned the key, and threw open the double doors, revealing a safe immediately behind them. He knelt down to examine the lock. Then from one of his pockets he took a chamois-skin bundle. He unrolled it and placed it on the floor beside him, displaying an array of bright steel implements. From another pocket he took a bunch of skeleton keys, and proceeded to make a selection.

For a moment, Elphinstone stood watching the man's cool, expert address in amazement. At last he roused himself, shuddered again as his eye fell upon that thing on the floor, and he sidled away towards the door.

"I think I'll be going," he said. With his hand on the knob he checked. "Someone may have seen me come in, and may see me going out again."

"That'll be all right," said the burglar, without turning. "They'll know nothing about this until morning." By a jerk of the thumb over his shoulder he indicated the body. "And it'll look like burglary by then. It'll look uncommonly like burglary by the time I'm through. You needn't make a secret of having visited him. No one can say that this didn't happen after you had left. It will certainly look like it. You're quite safe. Good night!"

"Ah!" said Elphinstone, and on that he went out.

To his terrified, conscience-stricken imagination the night seemed alive with watching eyes. He dared not shut the front door of that house lest the bang should draw attention to his departure. Leaving it ajar, he slunk fearfully away, and as he went his panic so grew upon him that by the time he had turned the corner into

Piccadilly he was persuaded that by leaving as he had done he had determined his own doom, walked into some trap unperceived by himself but quite clear to that incredibly cool burglar whom he had left behind. Already he saw himself arraigned and sentenced for the murder of Kauffmann. A sick giddiness of terror overtook him; his teeth chattered and his legs so trembled that he was scarcely able to walk. And then suddenly, upon the utter stillness of the night, rang a loud metallic sound that brought him shuddering to a standstill. It was the ring of a police inspector's baton, striking the pavement to call the constable of the beat.

For a moment Elphinstone's disordered mind connected the summons with himself and the thing he had left behind him. Then inspiration flashed upon his mind. There was a clear course that by definitely fastening the guilt elsewhere would make him absolutely safe. That burglar must be caught in the act by the police.

He ran forward in the direction whence the sound had reached him, and a moment later he was breathlessly delivering himself to a stalwart inspector.

". . . Over there, in Park Gardens," he heard himself saying, "a house is being burgled. I saw a man entering a window from the balcony over the porch."

Two constables joined them as he was speaking. There was a brief exchange of question and answer, and then the four of them went back together at the double. Elphinstone pointed out the house, and the inspector was intrigued to find the door ajar.

"Looks as if we were too late already," he commented, and ordering his men to go up with Elphinstone, himself remained there to keep an eye upon the street.

They went softly upstairs to the study, burst into it and surprised the burglar still at his work. The safe was standing open, and there was a litter of its contents on the floor; among these were half-a-dozen small showcases containing the collection of jewels of which Kauffmann had been so proud. One of the constables shouted to the inspector below before the pair of them sprang at the burglar and overpowered him. Even as they did so, and the man offered no resistance, Elphinstone moving round the table almost fell over the professor's body.

The policemen heard his outcry; they saw him reel back, appalled. He was really acting very well.

"Look here!" he called to them, and dropped on his knees beside the dead man. "Lord! He's dead! Dead!" He looked up at them blankly. "We're too late," he said.

"We've got the murderer, anyhow," he was gruffly answered by one of the constables, who, leaving the handcuffed man in the care of his colleague, came round himself to view the body at closer quarters.

Elphinstone looked at the burglar, and the burglar's eyes met the glance. The fellow appeared to have lost none of his cool masterfulness and none of his cynicism, for as his eyes met Elphinstone's, his lip curled in contempt of the fellow who had made him a defenceless scapegoat.

"I had the idea," he said without resentment, "that this was what you would do."

And then the inspector came in. "What's this?" he asked as he entered.

"Murder," cried Elphinstone stridently, "that's what it is—robbery and murder. And there's the murderer. Caught absolutely red-handed. Caught in the very act."

"In the act of burgling—not murdering," was all the prisoner said, quite gently.

The inspector stooped over the body. He met the eye of the constable who had been making an examination, and the subordinate nodded with ominous eloquence.

"A clear case," said the inspector. "Fetch him along, and . . ."

The inspector looked full at the burglar, and quite suddenly he checked, stiffened, and stood to attention.

"Beg pardon, sir," said he with a quite extraordinary deference. "Didn't know as how it was you. What's this, sir?" indicating the body. "Had an accident?"

"No. It's murder all right as that fellow says, and he should know, for he's the murderer. It was he who killed Professor Kauffmann. I saw the whole thing from behind those curtains. I gave him his chance to get away. Very wrong of me, of course; but I didn't want any publicity on my own methods. Besides," he added slyly, "I thought it very likely he would come back with the police, and so save me all trouble. He would naturally imagine that a burglar could have nothing to say in his own defence."

"I see, Mr. Scott-Drummond. Very good, sir," was the inspector's respectful answer, and he came forward with quick concern to remove the handcuffs from the prisoner.

It was then that Elphinstone roused himself at last from his horrified amazement.

"Scott-Drummond! Scott-Drummond!" he repeated, foolishly.

The burglar stooped to pick up a slender case of japanned tin, which he had dropped when the constables seized him. The lid had been wrenched off and the edges of a sheaf of blue tracing papers protruded.

"We had good reason," he said, "to suspect Professor Kauffmann of being an agent of the German Government, and I came to get hold of evidence. I've found what I was looking for—more even than I expected—so I'll be going."

He glanced across at the stricken Elphinstone standing limply between the two constables.

"You'd better take that fellow to Vine Street," he said quietly. "I'll forward my report. Good night, inspector."

GEORGE FIELDING ELIOT

BORN IN BROOKLYN, George Fielding Eliot (1894–1971) moved with his family to Australia when he was eight, and he was studying at Melbourne University when World War I broke out. He fought in the Australian army at Gallipoli in 1915, then at the battles of the Somme, Passchendaele, Arras, and Amiens; after the war he joined the U.S. Army Reserves as an officer and studied military history. In 1926, while working as an accountant, he read an issue of the pulp *War Stories*, and decided he could earn extra money by selling the magazine a narrative of his own wartime experiences, thus beginning Eliot's career as a full-time writer, albeit only intermittently for the pulps. He took a job writing for the *Infantry Journal* in 1928, and also produced the full-length novels *The Eagles of Death* (1930) and *Federal Bullets* (1936), a G-Man adventure. The first of his many nonfiction books about the military, *If War Comes* (1937), written with Major Richard Ernest Dupuy, was a well-received survey of war zones; his *The Ramparts We Watch* (1938) was a prescient warning that the U.S. should prepare to defend itself and its neighbors against an Axis attack. With the outbreak of war in 1939, Eliot became a military writer for the *New York Herald Tribune*, and also worked as a correspondent for CBS Radio. He was then a columnist for the *New York Post*, before syndicating his own column in 1950.

The straightforward analysis on display in Eliot's highly regarded military books can hardly prepare the reader for the extremities, both of language and subject, of his pulp fiction. Even the insidious Dr. Fu Manchu pales a bit in comparison to the evil mandarin Yuan Li in this famous Yellow Peril story.

"The Copper Bowl" was originally published in the December 1928 issue of *Weird Tales*.

THE COPPER BOWL

GEORGE FIELDING ELIOT

YUAN LI, the mandarin, leaned back in his rose-wood chair.

"It is written," he said softly, "that a good servant is a gift of the gods, whilst a bad one—"

The tall, powerfully built man standing humbly before the robed figure in the chair bowed thrice, hastily, submissively.

Fear glinted in his eye, though he was armed, and moreover was accounted a brave soldier. He could have broken the little smooth-faced mandarin across his knee, and yet . . .

"Ten thousand pardons, beneficent one," he said. "I have done all—having regard to your honourable order to slay the man not nor do him permanent injury—I have done all that I can. But—"

"But he speaks not!" murmured the mandarin. "And you come to me with a tale of failure? I do not like failures, Captain Wang!"

The mandarin toyed with a little paper knife on the low table beside him. Wang shuddered.

"Well, no matter for this time," the mandarin said after a moment. Wang breathed a sigh of most heartfelt relief, and the mandarin smiled softly, fleetingly. "Still," he went on, "our task is yet to be accomplished. We have the man—he has the information we require; surely some way may be found. The servant has failed; now the master must try his hand. Bring the man to me."

Wang bowed low and departed with considerable haste.

The mandarin sat silent for a moment, looking across the wide, sunlit room at a pair of singing birds in a wicker cage hanging in the farther window. Presently he nodded—one short, satisfied nod—and struck a little silver bell which stood on his beautifully inlaid table.

Instantly a white-robed, silent-footed servant entered, and stood with bowed head awaiting his master's pleasure. To him Yuan Li gave certain swift, incisive orders.

The white-robed one had scarcely departed when Wang, captain of the mandarin's guard, reentered the spacious apartment.

"The prisoner, Benevolent!" he announced.

The mandarin made a slight motion with his slender hand; Wang barked an order, and there entered, between two heavily muscled, half-naked guardsmen, a short, sturdily built man, barefooted, clad only in a tattered shirt and khaki trousers, but with fearless blue eyes looking straight at Yuan Li under the tousled masses of his blonde hair.

A white man!

"Ah!" said Yuan Li, in his calm way, speaking faultless French. "The excellent Lieutenant Fournet! Still obstinate?"

Fournet cursed him earnestly, in French and three different Chinese dialects.

"You'll pay for this, Yuan Li!" he wound up. "Don't think your filthy brutes can try the knuckle torture and their other devil's tricks on a French officer and get away with it!"

Yuan Li toyed with his paper knife, smiling.

"You threaten me, Lieutenant Fournet," he answered, "yet your threats are but as rose petals wafted away on the morning breeze—unless you return to your post to make your report."

"Why, damn you!" answered the prisoner. "You needn't try that sort of thing—you know better than to kill me! My commandant is perfectly aware of my movements—he'll be knocking on your door with a company of the Legion at his back if I don't show up by tomorrow at reveille!"

Yuan Li smiled again.

"Doubtless—and yet we still have the better part of the day before us," he said. "Much may be accomplished in an afternoon and evening."

Fournet swore again.

"You can torture me and be damned," he answered. "I know and you know that you don't dare to kill me or to injure me so that I can't get back to Fort Deschamps. For the rest, do your worst, you yellow-skinned brute!"

"A challenge!" the mandarin exclaimed. "And I, Lieutenant Fournet, pick up your glove! Look you—what I require from you is the strength and location of your outpost on the Mephong River. So—"

"So that your cursed bandits, whose murders and lootings keep you here in luxury, can rush the outpost some dark night and open the river route for their boats," Fournet cut in. "I know you, Yuan Li, and I know your trade—mandarin of thieves! The military governor of Tonkin sent a battalion of the Foreign Legion here to deal with such as you, and to restore peace and order on the frontier, not to yield to childish threats! That is not the Legion's way, and you should know it. The best thing you can do is to send in your submission, or I can assure you that within a fortnight your head will be rotting over the North Gate of Hanoi, as a warning to others who might follow your bad example."

The mandarin's smile never altered, though well he knew that this was no idle threat. With Tonkinese tirailleurs, even with Colonial infantry, he could make some sort of headway, but these thrice-accursed Legionnaires were devils from the very pit itself. He—Yuan Li, who had ruled as king in the valley of the Mephong, to whom half a Chinese province and many a square mile of French Tonkin had paid tribute humbly—felt his throne of power tottering beneath him. But one hope remained: down the river, beyond the French outposts, were boats filled with men and with the loot of a dozen villages—the most successful raiding party he had ever sent out. Let these boats come through, let him have back his men (and they were his best), get his hands on the loot, and perhaps something might be done. Gold, jewels, jade—and though the soldiers of France were terrible, there were in Hanoi certain civilian officials not wholly indifferent to these things. But on the banks of the Mephong, as though they knew his hopes, the Foreign Legion had established an outpost—he must know exactly where, he must know exactly how strong; for till this river post was gone, the boats could never reach him.

And now Lieutenant Fournet, staff officer to the commandant, had fallen into his hands. All night his torturers had reasoned with the stubborn young Norman, and all morning they had never left him for a minute. They had marked him in no way, nor broken bones, nor so much as cut or bruised the skin—yet there are ways! Fournet shuddered all over at the thought of what he had gone through, that age-long night and morning.

To Fournet, his duty came first; to Yuan Li, it was life or death that Fournet should speak. And he had taken measures which now marched to their fulfilment.

He dared not go to extremes with Fournet; nor yet could French justice connect the mandarin Yuan Li with the bandits of the Mephong.

They might suspect, but they could not prove; and an outrage such as the killing or maiming of a French officer in his own palace was more than Yuan Li dared essay. He walked on thin ice indeed those summer days, and walked warily.

Yet—he had taken measures.

"My head is still securely on my shoulders," he replied to Fournet. "I do not think it will decorate your gate spikes. So you will not speak?"

"Certainly not!"

Lieutenant Fournet's words were as firm as his jaw.

"Ah, but you will. Wang!"

"Magnanimous!"

"Four more guards. Make the prisoner secure."

Wang clapped his hands.

Instantly four additional half-naked men sprang into the room: two, falling on their knees, seized Fournet round the legs; another threw his corded arms round the lieutenant's waist; another stood by, club in hand, as a reserve in case of—what?

The two original guards still retained their grip on Fournet's arms.

Now, in the grip of those sinewy hands, he was held immobile, utterly helpless, a living statue.

Yuan Li, the mandarin, smiled again. One who did not know him would have thought his smile held an infinite tenderness, a divine compassion.

He touched the bell at his side.

Instantly, in the farther doorway, appeared two servants, conducting a veiled figure—a woman, shrouded in a dark drapery.

A word from Yuan Li—rough hands tore the veil aside, and there stood drooping between the impassive servants a vision of loveliness, a girl scarce out of her teens, dark-haired, slender, with the great appealing brown eyes of a fawn: eyes which widened suddenly as they rested on Lieutenant Fournet.

"Lily!" exclaimed Fournet, and his five guards had their hands full to hold him as he struggled to be free.

"You fiend!" he spat at Yuan Li. "If a hair of this girl's head is touched, by the Holy Virgin of Yvetot I will roast you alive in the flames of your own palace! My God, Lily, how—"

"Quite simply, my dear Lieutenant," the mandarin's silky voice interrupted. "We knew, of course—every house-servant in North Tonkin is a spy of mine—that you had conceived an affection for this woman; and when I heard you were proving obdurate under the little attentions of my men, I thought it well to send for her. Her father's bungalow is far from the post—indeed, it is in Chinese and not French territory, as you know—and the task was not a difficult one. And now—"

"André! André!" the girl was crying, struggling in her turn with the servants. "Save me, André—these beasts—"

"Have no fear, Lily," André Fournet replied. "They dare not harm you, any more than they dare to kill me. They are bluffing—"

"But have you considered well, Lieutenant?" asked the mandarin gently. "You, of course, are a French officer. The arm of France—and it is a long and unforgiving arm—will be stretched out to seize your murderers. The gods forbid I should set that arm reaching for me and mine. But this girl—ah, that is different!"

"Different? How is it different? The girl is a French citizen—"

"I think not, my good Lieutenant Fournet. She is three-quarters French in blood, true; but her father is half Chinese, and is a Chinese subject; she is a resident of China—I think you will find that French justice will not be prepared to avenge her death quite so readily as your own. At any rate, it is a chance I am prepared to take."

Fournet's blood seemed to turn to ice in his veins. The smiling devil was right! Lily—his lovely white Lily, whose only mark of Oriental blood was the rather piquant slant of her great eyes—was not entitled to the protection of the tricolour.

God! What a position! Either betray his flag, his regiment, betray his comrades to their deaths—or see his Lily butchered before his eyes!

"So now, Lieutenant Fournet, we understand each other," Yuan Li continued after a brief pause to let the full horror of the situation grip the other's soul. "I think you will be able to remember the location and strength of that outpost for me—now?"

Fournet stared at the man in bitter silence, but the words had given the quick-minded Lily a key to the situation, which she had hardly understood at first.

"No, no, André!" she cried. "Do not tell him. Better that I should die than that you should be a traitor! See—I am ready."

Fournet threw back his head, his wavering resolution reincarnate.

"The girl shames me!" he said. "Slay her if you must, Yuan Li—and if France will not avenge her, I will! But traitor I will not be!"

"I do not think that is your last word, Lieutenant," the mandarin purred. "Were I to strangle the girl, yes—perhaps. But first she must cry to you for help, and when you hear her screaming in agony, the woman you love, perhaps then you will forget these noble heroics!"

Again he clapped his hands; and again silent servants glided into the room. One bore a small brazier of glowing charcoal; a second had a little cage of thick wire mesh, inside of which something moved horribly; a third bore a copper bowl with handles on each side, to which was attached a steel band that glittered in the sunlight.

The hair rose on the back of Fournet's neck. What horror impended now? Deep within him some instinct warned that what was now to follow would be fiendish beyond the mind of mortal man to conceive. The mandarin's eyes seemed suddenly to glow with infernal fires. Was he in truth man—or demon?

A sharp word in some Yunnan dialect unknown to Fournet—and the servants had flung the girl upon her back on the floor, spreadeagled in pitiful helplessness, upon a magnificent peacock rug.

Another word from the mandarin's thin lips—and roughly they tore the clothing from the upper half of the girl's body. White and silent she lay upon that splendid rug, her eyes still on Fournet's: silent, lest words of hers should impair the resolution of the man she loved.

Fournet struggled furiously with his guards, but they were five strong men, and they held him fast.

"Remember, Yuan Li!" he panted. "You'll pay! Damn your yellow soul—"

The mandarin ignored the threat.

"Proceed," he said to the servants. "Note carefully, Monsieur le Lieutenant Fournet, what we are doing. First, you will note, the girl's wrists and ankles are lashed to posts and to heavy articles of furniture, suitably placed so that she cannot move. You wonder at the strength of the rope, the number of turns we take to hold so frail a girl? I assure you, they will be required. Under the copper bowl, I have seen a feeble old man tear his wrist free from an iron chain."

The mandarin paused; the girl was now bound so tightly that she could scarce move a muscle of her body.

Yuan Li regarded the arrangements.

"Well done," he approved. "Yet if she tears any limb free, the man who bound that limb shall have an hour under the bamboo rods. Now—the bowl! Let me see it."

He held out a slender hand. Respectfully a servant handed him the bowl, with its dangling band of flexible steel. Fournet, watching with eyes full of dread, saw that the band was fitted with a lock, adjustable to various positions. It was like a belt, a girdle.

"Very well." The mandarin nodded, turning the thing over and over in fingers that almost seemed to caress it. "But I anticipate—perhaps the lieutenant and the young lady are not familiar with this little device. Let me explain, or rather, demonstrate. Put the bowl in place, Kan-su. No, no—just the bowl, this time."

Another servant, who had started forward, stepped back into his corner. The man addressed as Kan-su took the bowl, knelt at the side of the girl, passed the steel band under her body and placed the bowl, bottom up, on her naked abdomen, tugging at the girdle till the rim of the bowl bit into the soft flesh. Then he snapped the lock fast, holding the bowl thus firmly in place by the locked steel belt attached to its two handles and passing round the girl's waist. He rose, stood silent with folded arms.

Fournet felt his flesh crawling with horror—and all this time Lily had said not one word, though the tight girdle, the pressure of the circular rim of the bowl, must have been hurting her cruelly.

But now she spoke, bravely.

"Do not give way, André," she said. "I can bear it—it does—it does not hurt!"

"God!" yelled André Fournet, still fighting vainly against those clutching yellow hands.

"It does not hurt!" the mandarin echoed the girl's last words. "Well, perhaps not. But we will take it off, notwithstanding. We must be merciful."

At his order the servant removed the bowl and girdle. An angry red circle showed on the white skin of the girl's abdomen where the rim had rested.

"And still I do not think you understand, Mademoiselle and Monsieur," he went on. "For presently we must apply the bowl again—and when we do, under it we will put—this!"

With a swift movement of his arm he snatched from the servant in the corner the wire cage and held it up to the sunlight.

The eyes of Fournet and Lily fixed themselves upon it in horror. For within, plainly seen now, moved a great grey rat—a whiskered, beady-eyed, restless, scabrous rat, its white chisel-teeth shining through the mesh.

"*Dieu de Dieu!*" breathed Fournet. His mind refused utterly to grasp the full import of the dreadful fate that was to be Lily's; he could only stare at the unquiet rat—stare—stare . . .

"You understand now, I am sure," purred the mandarin. "The rat under the bowl—observe the bottom of the bowl, note the little flange. Here we put the hot charcoal—the copper becomes heated—the heat is overpowering—the rat cannot support it—he has but one means of escape: he gnaws his way out through the lady's body! And now about that outpost, Lieutenant Fournet?"

"No—no—no!" cried Lily. "They will not do it—they are trying to frighten us—they are human; men cannot do a thing like that. Be silent, André, be silent, whatever happens; don't

let them beat you! Don't let them make a traitor of you! Ah—"

At a wave from the mandarin, the servant with the bowl again approached the half-naked girl. But this time the man with the cage stepped forward also. Deftly he thrust in a hand, avoided the rat's teeth, jerked the struggling vermin out by the scruff of the neck.

The bowl was placed in position. Fournet fought desperately for freedom—if only he could get one arm clear, snatch a weapon of some sort!

Lily gave a sudden little choking cry.

The rat had been thrust under the bowl.

Click! The steel girdle was made fast—and now they were piling the red-hot charcoal on the upturned bottom of the bowl, while Lily writhed in her bonds as she felt the wriggling, pattering horror of the rat on her bare skin, under that bowl of fiends.

One of the servants handed a tiny object to the impassive mandarin.

Yuan Li held it up in one hand.

It was a little key.

"This key, Lieutenant Fournet," he said, "unlocks the steel girdle which holds the bowl in place. It is yours—as a reward for the information I require. Will you not be reasonable? Soon it will be too late!"

Fournet looked at Lily. The girl was quiet now, had ceased to struggle; her eyes were open, or he would have thought she had fainted.

The charcoal glowed red on the bottom of the copper bowl. And beneath its carved surface, Fournet could imagine the great grey rat stirring restlessly, turning around, seeking escape from the growing heat, at last sinking his teeth in that soft white skin, gnawing, burrowing desperately . . .

God!

His duty—his flag—his regiment—France! Young Sous-lieutenant Pierre Desjardins—gay young Pierre—and twenty men, to be surprised and massacred horribly, some saved for the torture, by an overwhelming rush of bandit-devils, through his treachery? He knew in his heart that he could not do it.

He must be strong—he must be firm.

If only he might suffer for Lily—gentle, loving little Lily, brave little Lily who had never harmed a soul.

Loud and clear through the room rang a terrible scream.

André, turning in fascinated horror, saw that Lily's body, straining upward in an arc from the rug, was all but tearing asunder the bonds which held it. He saw, what he had not before noticed, that a little nick had been broken from one edge of the bowl—and through this nick and across the white surface of the girl's heaving body was running a tiny trickle of blood!

The rat was at work.

Then something snapped in André's brain. He went mad.

With the strength that is given to madmen, he tore loose his right arm from the grip that held it—tore loose, and dashed his fist into the face of the guard. The man with the club sprang forward unwarily; the next moment André had the weapon, and was laying about him with berserk fury. Three guards were down before Wang drew his sword and leaped into the fray.

Wang was a capable and well-trained soldier. It was cut, thrust, and parry for a moment, steel against wood—then Wang, borne back before that terrible rush, had the reward of his strategy.

The two remaining guards, to whom he had signalled, and a couple of the servants flung themselves together on Fournet's back and bore him roaring to the floor.

The girl screamed again, shattering the coarser sounds of battle.

Fournet heard her—even in his madness he heard her. And as he heard, a knife hilt in a servant's girdle met his hand. He caught at it, thrust upward savagely: a man howled; the weight on Fournet's back grew less; blood gushed over his neck and shoulders. He thrust

again, rolled clear of the press, and saw one man sobbing out his life from a ripped-open throat, while another, with both hands clasped over his groin, writhed in silent agony upon the floor.

André Fournet, gathering a knee under him, sprang like a panther straight at the throat of Wang the captain.

Down the two men went, rolling over and over on the floor. Wang's weapons clashed and clattered—a knife rose, dripping blood, and plunged home.

With a shout of triumph André Fournet sprang to his feet, his terrible knife in one hand, Wang's sword in the other.

Screaming, the remaining servants fled before that awful figure.

Alone, Yuan Li the mandarin faced incarnate vengeance.

"The key!"

Hoarsely Fournet spat out his demand; his reeling brain had room for but one thought:

"The key, you yellow demon!"

Yuan Li took a step backward into the embrasured window, through which the jasmine-scented afternoon breeze still floated sweetly.

The palace was built on the edge of a cliff; below that window ledge, the precipice fell a sheer fifty feet down to the rocks and shallows of the upper Mephong.

Yuan Li smiled once more, his calm unruffled.

"You have beaten me, Fournet," he said, "yet I have beaten you, too. I wish you joy of your victory. Here is the key." He held it up in his hand; and as André sprang forward with a shout, Yuan Li turned, took one step to the window ledge, and without another word was gone into space, taking the key with him.

Far below he crashed in red horror on the rocks, and the waters of the turbulent Mephong closed forever over the key to the copper bowl.

Back sprang André—back to Lily's side. The blood ran no more from under the edge of the bowl; Lily lay very still, very cold . . .

God! She was dead!

Her heart was silent in her tortured breast.

André tore vainly at the bowl, the steel girdle—tore with bleeding fingers, with broken teeth, madly—in vain.

He could not move them.

And Lily was dead.

Or was she? What was that?

In her side a pulse beat—beat strongly and more strongly . . .

Was there still hope?

The mad Fournet began chafing her body and arms.

Could he revive her? Surely she was not dead—could not be dead!

The pulse still beat—strange it beat only in one place, on her soft white side, down under her last rib.

He kissed her cold and unresponsive lips.

When he raised his head the pulse had ceased to beat. Where it had been, blood was flowing sluggishly—dark venous blood, flowing in purple horror.

And from the midst of it, out of the girl's side, the grey, pointed head of the rat was thrusting, its muzzle dripping gore, its black eyes glittering beadily at the madman who gibbered and frothed above it.

So, an hour later, his comrades found André Fournet and Lily his beloved—the tortured maniac keening over the tortured dead.

But the grey rat they never found.

THE HAND OF THE MANDARIN QUONG

SAX ROHMER

ARTHUR HENRY SARSFIELD WARD (1883–1959), using the pseudonym Sax Rohmer, wrote more than fifty books, but is best known for creating one of the greatest villains in literature, the insidious Dr. Fu Manchu. Ward's early interest in the occult and Egyptology influenced his writing and caused him to join the Hermetic Order of the Golden Dawn, alongside other literary figures such as Arthur Machen, Aleister Crowley, and W. B. Yeats. Many of his books and stories are set in the mysterious East, including *Brood of the Witch Queen* (1918), *Tales of Secret Egypt* (1918), *The Golden Scorpion* (1919), and *Tales of East and West* (1932).

A newspaper assignment sent Ward to Limehouse, London's Chinatown, an area so forbidding that few white people ventured into it even in daylight. For months, he sought a mysterious "Mr. King," who was said to rule all the criminal elements of the district. King, who would become the inspiration for Fu Manchu, is mentioned by name in *Yellow Shadows* (1925), which, along with *Dope* (1919), helped clean up Limehouse and bring about government action on the drug trade.

The Boxer Rebellion at the turn of the century had aroused fears of a Yellow Peril and convinced Ward that an Oriental arch-villain would be successful, so he began writing stories about sinister Chinese characters, notably the Devil Doctor. The first of fourteen novels about the sinister Fu Manchu was *The Mystery of Dr. Fu-Manchu* (1913). Ward deliberately gave his character an impossible name, both *Fu* and *Manchu* being Chinese surnames; it was hyphenated in the first three books. The only Fu Manchu short stories were written very late in Ward's life and are dramatically inferior to the novels and most of his other short tales.

"The Hand of the Mandarin Quong" was originally published in London in the December 1920 issue of *Cassell's Magazine* in a somewhat different form. Using an Egyptian/Arabian background, it was titled "The Hand of the White Sheikh." For the story's first American magazine appearance in the February 1922 issue of *Munsey's Magazine*, Ward rewrote the story, retaining the same plot, to give it a background of Chinatown, and it was retitled "The Mystery of the Shriveled Hand." It was retitled yet again for its first book publication in *Tales of Chinatown* (London: Cassell, 1922).

THE HAND OF THE MANDARIN QUONG

SAX ROHMER

I
THE SHADOW ON THE CURTAIN

"SINGAPORE IS by no means herself again," declared Jennings, looking about the lounge of the Hôtel de l'Europe. "Don't you agree, Knox?"

Burton fixed his lazy stare upon the speaker.

"Don't blame poor old Singapore," he said. "There is no spot in this battered world that I have succeeded in discovering which is not changed for the worse."

Dr. Matheson flicked ash from his cigar and smiled in that peculiarly happy manner which characterizes a certain American type and which lent a boyish charm to his personality.

"You are a pair of pessimists," he pronounced. "For some reason best known to themselves Jennings and Knox have decided upon a Busman's Holiday. Very well. Why grumble?"

"You are quite right, Doctor," Jennings admitted. "When I was on service here in the Straits Settlements I declared heaven knows how often that the country would never see me again once I was demobbed. Yet here you see I am; Burton belongs here; but here's Knox, and we are all as fed up as we can be!"

"Yes," said Burton slowly. "I may be a bit tired of Singapore. It's a queer thing, though, that you fellows have drifted back here again. The call of the East is no fable. It's a call that one hears for ever."

The conversation drifted into another chan-nel, and all sorts of topics were discussed, from racing to the latest feminine fashions, from ball-room dances to the merits and demerits of coali-tion government. Then suddenly:

"What became of Adderley?" asked Jennings.

There were several men in the party who had been cronies of ours during the time that we were stationed in Singapore, and at Jennings's words a sort of hush seemed to fall on those who had known Adderley. I cannot say if Jennings noticed this, but it was perfectly evident to me that Dr. Matheson had perceived it, for he glanced swiftly across in my direction in an oddly significant way.

"I don't know," replied Burton, who was an engineer. "He was rather an unsavoury sort of character in some ways, but I heard that he came to a sticky end."

"What do you mean?" I asked with curiosity, for I myself had often wondered what had become of Adderley.

"Well, he was reported to his C.O., or something, wasn't he, just before the time for his de-mobilization? I don't know the particulars; I thought perhaps you did, as he was in your regi-ment."

"I have heard nothing whatever about it," I replied.

"You mean Sidney Adderley, the man who was so indecently rich?" someone interjected. "Had a place at Katong, and was always talking about his father's millions?"

"That's the fellow."

"Yes," said Jennings, "there was some scandal, I know, but it was after my time here."

"Something about an old mandarin out Johore Bahru way, was it not?" asked Burton. "The last thing I heard about Adderley was that he had disappeared."

"Nobody would have cared much if he had," declared Jennings. "I know of several who would have been jolly glad. There was a lot of the brute about Adderley, apart from the fact that he had more money than was good for him. His culture was a veneer. It was his check-book that spoke all the time."

"Everybody would have forgiven Adderley his vulgarity," said Dr. Matheson, quietly, "if the man's heart had been in the right place."

"Surely an instance of trying to make a silk purse out of a sow's ear," someone murmured.

Burton gazed rather hard at the last speaker.

"So far as I am aware," he said, "the poor devil is dead, so go easy."

"Are you sure he is dead?" asked Dr. Matheson, glancing at Burton in that quizzical, amused way of his.

"No, I am not sure; I am merely speaking from hearsay. And now I come to think of it, the information was rather vague. But I gathered that he had vanished, at any rate, and remembering certain earlier episodes in his career, I was led to suppose that this vanishing meant—"

He shrugged his shoulders significantly.

"You mean the old mandarin?" suggested Dr. Matheson.

"Yes."

"Was there really anything in that story, or was it suggested by the unpleasant reputation of Adderley?" Jennings asked.

"I can settle any doubts upon that point," said I; whereupon I immediately became a focus of general attention.

"What! were you ever at that place of Adderley's at Katong?" asked Jennings with intense curiosity.

I nodded, lighting a fresh cigarette in a manner that may have been unduly leisurely.

"Did you see her?"

Again I nodded.

"Really!"

"I must have been peculiarly favoured, but certainly I had that pleasure."

"You speak of seeing *her*," said one of the party, now entering the conversation for the first time. "To whom do you refer?"

"Well," replied Burton, "it's really a sort of fairy tale—unless Knox"—glancing across in my direction—"can confirm it. But there was a story current during the latter part of Adderley's stay in Singapore to the effect that he had made the acquaintance of the wife, or some member of the household, of an old gentleman out Johore Bahru way—sort of mandarin or big pot among the Chinks."

"It was rumoured that he had bolted with her," added another speaker.

"I think it was more than a rumour."

"Why do you say so?"

"Well, representations were made to the authorities, I know for an absolute certainty, and I have an idea that Adderley was kicked out of the Service as a consequence of the scandal which resulted."

"How is it one never heard of this?"

"Money speaks, my dear fellow," cried Burton, "even when it is possessed by such a peculiar outsider as Adderley. The thing was hushed up. It was a very nasty business. But Knox was telling us that he had actually seen the lady. Please carry on, Knox, for I must admit that I am intensely curious."

"I can only say that I saw her on one occasion."

"With Adderley?"

"Undoubtedly."

"Where?"

"At his place at Katong."

"I even thought his place at that resort was something of a myth," declared Jennings. "He never asked *me* to go there, but, then, I took that as a compliment. Pardon the apparent innuendo, Knox," he added, laughing. "But you say you actually visited the establishment?"

"Yes," I replied slowly, "I met him here in this very hotel one evening in the winter of '15, after the natives' attempt to mutiny. He had been drinking rather heavily, a fact which he was quite unable to disguise. He was never by any means a real friend of mine; in fact, I doubt that he had a true friend in the world. Anyhow, I could see that he was lonely, and as I chanced to be at a loose end I accepted an invitation to go over to what he termed his 'little place at Ka-tong.'

"His little place proved to be a veritable palace. The man privately, or rather, secretly, to be exact, kept up a sort of pagan state. He had any number of servants. Of course he became practically a millionaire after the death of his father, as you will remember; and given more congenial company, I must confess that I might have spent a most enjoyable evening there.

"Adderley insisted upon priming me with champagne, and after a while I may as well admit that I lost something of my former reserve, and began in a fashion to feel that I was having a fairly good time. By the way, my host was not quite frankly drunk. He got into that objectionable and dangerous mood which some of you will recall, and I could see by the light in his eyes that there was mischief brewing, although at the time I did not know its nature.

"I should explain that we were amusing ourselves in a room which was nearly as large as the lounge of this hotel, and furnished in a somewhat similar manner. There were carved pillars and stained glass domes, a little fountain, and all those other peculiarities of an Eastern household.

"Presently, Adderley gave an order to one of his servants, and glanced at me with that sort of mocking, dare-devil look in his eyes which I loathed, which everybody loathed who ever met the man. Of course I had no idea what all this portended, but I was very shortly to learn.

"While he was still looking at me, but stealing side-glances at a doorway before which was draped a most wonderful curtain of a sort of flamingo colour, this curtain was suddenly pulled aside, and a girl came in.

"Of course, you must remember that at the time of which I am speaking the scandal respecting the mandarin had not yet come to light. Consequently I had no idea who the girl could be. I saw she was a Eurasian. But of her striking beauty there could be no doubt whatever. She was dressed in magnificent robes, and she literally glittered with jewels. She even wore jewels upon the toes of her little bare feet. But the first thing that struck me at the moment of her appearance was that her presence there was contrary to her wishes and inclinations. I have never seen a similar expression in any woman's eyes. She looked at Adderley as though she would gladly have slain him!

"Seeing this look, his mocking smile in which there was something of triumph—of the joy of possession—turned to a scowl of positive brutality. He clenched his fists in a way that set me bristling. He advanced toward the girl—and although the width of the room divided them, she recoiled—and the significance of expression and gesture was unmistakable. Adderley paused.

" 'So you have made up your mind to dance after all?' he shouted.

"The look in the girl's dark eyes was pitiful, and she turned to me with a glance of dumb entreaty.

" 'No, no!' she cried. 'No, no! Why do you bring me here?'

" 'Dance!' roared Adderley. 'Dance! That's what I want you to do.'

"Rebellion leapt again to the wonderful eyes, and she started back with a perfectly splendid gesture of defiance. At that my brutal and drunken host leapt in her direction. I was on my feet now, but before I could act the girl said a thing which checked him, sobered him, which pulled him up short, as though he had encountered a stone wall.

" 'Ah, God!' she said. (She was speaking, of course, in her native tongue.) 'His hand! His hand! Look! *His hand!*'

"To me her words were meaningless, naturally, but following the direction of her positively agonized glance I saw that she was watching what seemed to me to be the shadow of someone moving behind the flame-like curtain which produced an effect not unlike that of a huge, outstretched hand, the fingers crooked, claw-fashion.

" 'Knox, Knox!' whispered Adderley, grasping me by the shoulder.

"He pointed with a quivering finger toward this indistinct shadow upon the curtain, and:

" 'Do you see it—do you see it?' he said huskily. 'It is his hand—it is his hand!'

"Of the pair, I think, the man was the more frightened. But the girl, uttering a frightful shriek, ran out of the room as though pursued by a demon. As she did so whoever had been moving behind the curtain evidently went away. The shadow disappeared, and Adderley, still staring as if hypnotized at the spot where it had been, continued to hold my shoulder as in a vise. Then, sinking down upon a heap of cushions beside me, he loudly and shakily ordered more champagne.

"Utterly mystified by the incident, I finally left him in a state of stupor, and returned to my quarters, wondering whether I had dreamed half of the episode or the whole of it, whether he did really possess that wonderful palace, or whether he had borrowed it to impress me."

I ceased speaking, and my story was received in absolute silence, until:

"And that is all you know?" said Burton.

"Absolutely all. I had to leave about that time, you remember, and afterward went to France."

"Yes, I remember. It was while you were away that the scandal arose respecting the mandarin. Extraordinary story, Knox. I should like to know what it all meant, and what the end of it was."

Dr. Matheson broke his long silence.

"Although I am afraid I cannot enlighten you respecting the end of the story," he said quietly, "perhaps I can carry it a step further."

"Really, Doctor? What do you know about the matter?"

"I accidentally became implicated as follows," replied the American: "I was, as you know, doing voluntary surgical work near Singapore at the time, and one evening, presumably about the same period of which Knox is speaking, I was returning from the hospital at Katong, at which I acted sometimes as anaesthetist, to my quarters in Singapore; just drifting along, leisurely by the edge of the gardens admiring the beauty of the mangroves and the deceitful peace of the Eastern night.

"The hour was fairly late and not a soul was about. Nothing disturbed the silence except those vague sibilant sounds which are so characteristic of the country. Presently, as I rambled on with my thoughts wandering back to the dim ages, I literally fell over a man who lay in the road.

"I was naturally startled, but I carried an electric pocket torch, and by its light I discovered that the person over whom I had fallen was a dignified-looking Chinaman, somewhat past middle age. His clothes, which were of good quality, were covered with dirt and blood, and he bore all the appearance of having recently been engaged in a very tough struggle. His face was notable only for its possession of an unusually long jet-black moustache. He had swooned from loss of blood."

"Why, was he wounded?" exclaimed Jennings.

"His hand had been nearly severed from his wrist!"

"Merciful heavens!"

"I realized the impossibility of carrying him so far as the hospital, and accordingly I extemporized a rough tourniquet and left him under a palm tree by the road until I obtained assistance. Later, at the hospital, following a consultation, we found it necessary to amputate."

"I should say he objected fiercely?"

"He was past objecting to anything, otherwise I have no doubt he would have objected furiously. The index finger of the injured hand had one of those preternaturally long nails, protected by an engraved golden case. However, at least I gave him a chance of life. He was under my care for some time, but I doubt if ever he was properly grateful. He had an iron constitution, though, and I finally allowed him to depart. One queer stipulation he had made—that the severed hand, with its golden nail-case, should be given to him when he left hospital. And this bargain I faithfully carried out."

"Most extraordinary," I said. "Did you ever learn the identity of the old gentleman?"

"He was very reticent, but I made a number of inquiries, and finally learned with absolute certainty, I think, that he was the Mandarin Quong Mi Su from Johore Bahru, a person of great repute among the Chinese there, and rather a big man in China. He was known locally as the Mandarin Quong."

"Did you learn anything respecting how he had come by his injury, Doctor?"

Matheson smiled in his quiet fashion, and selected a fresh cigar with great deliberation. Then:

"I suppose it is scarcely a case of betraying a professional secret," he said, "but during the time that my patient was recovering from the effects of the anaesthetic he unconsciously gave me several clues to the nature of the episode. Putting two and two together I gathered that someone, although the name of this person never once passed the lips of the mandarin, had abducted his favourite wife."

"Good heavens! truly amazing," I exclaimed.

"Is it not? How small a place the world is. My old mandarin had traced the abductor and presumably the girl to some house which I gathered to be in the neighbourhood of Katong. In an attempt to force an entrance—doubtless with the amiable purpose of slaying them both—he had been detected by the prime object of his hatred. In hurriedly descending from a window he had been attacked by some weapon, possibly a

sword, and had only made good his escape in the condition in which I found him. How far he had proceeded I cannot say, but I should imagine that the house to which he had been was no great distance from the spot where I found him."

"Comment is really superfluous," remarked Burton. "He was looking for Adderley."

"I agree," said Jennings.

"And," I added, "it was evidently after this episode that I had the privilege of visiting that interesting establishment."

There was a short interval of silence; then:

"You probably retain no very clear impression of the shadow which you saw," said Dr. Matheson, with great deliberation. "At the time perhaps you had less occasion particularly to study it. But are you satisfied that it was really caused by someone moving behind the curtain?"

I considered his question for a few moments.

"I am not," I confessed. "Your story, Doctor, makes me wonder whether it may not have been due to something else."

"What else can it have been due to?" exclaimed Jennings contemptuously—"unless to the champagne?"

"I won't quote Shakespeare," said Dr. Matheson, smiling in his odd way. "The famous lines, though appropriate, are somewhat overworked. But I will quote Kipling: 'East is East, and West is West.'"

II

THE LADY OF KATONG

Fully six months had elapsed, and on returning from Singapore I had forgotten all about Adderley and the unsavoury stories connected with his reputation. Then, one evening as I was strolling aimlessly along St. James's Street, wondering how I was going to kill time—for almost everyone I knew was out of town, including Paul Harley, and London can be infinitely more lonely under such conditions than any desert—I saw a thick-set figure approaching along the other side of the street.

The swing of the shoulders, the aggressive turn of the head, were vaguely familiar, and while I was searching my memory and endeavouring to obtain a view of the man's face, he stared across in my direction.

It was Adderley.

He looked even more debauched than I remembered him, for whereas in Singapore he had had a tanned skin, now he looked unhealthily pallid and blotchy. He raised his hand, and:

"Knox!" he cried, and ran across to greet me.

His boisterous manner and a sort of coarse geniality which he possessed had made him popular with a certain set in former days, but I, who knew that this geniality was forced, and assumed to conceal a sort of appalling animalism, had never been deceived by it. Most people found Adderley out sooner or later, but I had detected the man's true nature from the very beginning. His eyes alone were danger signals for any amateur psychologist. However, I greeted him civilly enough:

"Bless my soul, you are looking as fit as a fiddle!" he cried. "Where have you been, and what have you been doing since I saw you last?"

"Nothing much," I replied, "beyond trying to settle down in a reformed world."

"Reformed world!" echoed Adderley. "More like a ruined world it has seemed to me."

He laughed loudly. That he had already explored several bottles was palpable.

We were silent for a while, mentally weighing one another up, as it were. Then:

"Are you living in town?" asked Adderley.

"I am staying at the Carlton at the moment," I replied. "My chambers are in the hands of the decorators. It's awkward. Interferes with my work."

"Work!" cried Adderley. "Work! It's a nasty word, Knox. Are you doing anything now?"

"Nothing, until eight o'clock, when I have an appointment."

"Come along to my place," he suggested, "and have a cup of tea, or a whisky-and-soda if you prefer it."

Probably I should have refused, but even as he spoke I was mentally translated to the lounge of the Hôtel de l'Europe, and prompted by a very human curiosity I determined to accept his invitation. I wondered if Fate had thrown an opportunity in my way of learning the end of the peculiar story which had been related on that occasion.

I accompanied Adderley to his chambers, which were within a stone's throw of the spot where I had met him. That this gift for making himself unpopular with all and sundry, high and low, had not deserted him, was illustrated by the attitude of the liftman as we entered the hall of the chambers. He was barely civil to Adderley and even regarded myself with marked disfavour.

We were admitted by Adderley's man, whom I had not seen before, but who was some kind of foreigner, I think a Portuguese. It was characteristic of Adderley. No Englishman would ever serve him for long, and there had been more than one man in his old Company who had openly avowed his intention of dealing with Adderley on the first available occasion.

His chambers were ornately furnished; indeed, the room in which we sat more closely resembled a scene from an Oscar Asche production than a normal man's study. There was something unreal about it all. I have since thought that this unreality extended to the person of the man himself. Grossly material, he yet possessed an aura of mystery, mystery of an unsavoury sort. There was something furtive, secretive, about Adderley's entire mode of life.

I had never felt at ease in his company, and now as I sat staring wonderingly at the strange and costly ornaments with which the room was overladen I bethought me of the object of my visit. How I should have brought the conversation back to our Singapore days I know not, but a suitable opening was presently offered by Adderley himself.

"Do you ever see any of the old gang?" he inquired.

"I was in Singapore about six months ago," I replied, "and I met some of them again."

"What! Had they drifted back to the East after all?"

"Two or three of them were taking what Dr. Matheson described as a Busman's Holiday."

At mention of Dr. Matheson's name Adderley visibly started.

"So you know Matheson," he murmured. "I didn't know you had ever met him."

Plainly to hide his confusion he stood up, and crossing the room drew my attention to a rather fine silver bowl of early Persian ware. He was displaying its peculiar virtues and showing a certain acquaintance with his subject when he was interrupted. A door opened suddenly and a girl came in. Adderley put down the bowl and turned rapidly as I rose from my seat.

It was the lady of Katong!

I recognized her at once, although she wore a very up-to-date gown. While it did not suit her dark good looks so well as the native dress which she had worn at Singapore, yet it could not conceal the fact that in a barbaric way she was a very beautiful woman. On finding a visitor in the room she became covered with confusion.

"Oh," she said, speaking in Hindustani. "Why did you not tell me there was someone here?"

Adderley's reply was characteristically brutal.

"Get out," he said. "You fool."

I turned to go, for I was conscious of an intense desire to attack my host. But:

"Don't go, Knox, don't go!" he cried. "I am sorry, I am damned sorry, I—"

He paused, and looked at me in a queer sort of appealing way. The girl, her big eyes widely open, retreated again to the door, with curious lithe steps, characteristically Oriental. The door regained, she paused for a moment and extended one small hand in Adderley's direction.

"I hate you," she said slowly, "hate you! Hate you!"

She went out, quietly closing the door behind her. Adderley turned to me with an embarrassed laugh.

"I know you think I am a brute and an outsider," he said, "and perhaps I am. Everybody says I am, so I suppose there must be something in it. But if ever a man paid for his mistakes I have paid for mine, Knox. Good God, I haven't a friend in the world."

"You probably don't deserve one," I retorted.

"I know I don't, and that's the tragedy of it," he replied. "You may not believe it, Knox; I don't expect anybody to believe me; but for more than a year I have been walking on the edge of Hell. Do you know where I have been since I saw you last?"

I shook my head in answer.

"I have been half round the world, Knox, trying to find peace."

"You don't know where to look for it," I said.

"If only you knew," he whispered, "if only you knew," and sank down upon the settee, ruffling his hair with his hands and looking the picture of haggard misery. Seeing that I was still set upon departure:

"Hold on a bit, Knox," he implored. "Don't go yet. There is something I want to ask you, something very important."

He crossed to a sideboard and mixed himself a stiff whisky-and-soda. He asked me to join him, but I refused.

"Won't you sit down again?"

I shook my head.

"You came to my place at Katong once," he began abruptly. "I was damned drunk, I admit it. But something happened, do you remember?"

I nodded.

"This is what I want to ask you: Did you, or did you not, see that *shadow*?"

I stared him hard in the face.

"I remember the episode to which you refer," I replied. "I certainly saw a shadow."

"But what sort of shadow?"

"To me it seemed an indefinite, shapeless thing, as though caused by someone moving behind the curtain."

"It didn't look to you like—the shadow of a *hand*?"

"It might have been, but I could not be positive."

Adderley groaned.

"Knox," he said, "money is a curse. It has been a curse to me. If I have had my fun, God knows I have paid for it."

"Your idea of fun is probably a peculiar one," I said dryly.

Let me confess that I was only suffering the man's society because of an intense curiosity which now possessed me on learning that the lady of Katong was still in Adderley's company.

Whether my repugnance for his society would have enabled me to remain any longer I cannot say. But as if Fate had deliberately planned that I should become a witness of the concluding phases of this secret drama, we were now interrupted a second time, and again in a dramatic fashion.

Adderley's nondescript valet came in with letters and a rather large brown paper parcel sealed and fastened with great care.

As the man went out:

"Surely that is from Singapore," muttered Adderley, taking up the parcel.

He seemed to become temporarily oblivious of my presence, and his face grew even more haggard as he studied the writing upon the wrapper. With unsteady fingers he untied it, and I lingered, watching curiously. Presently out from the wrappings he took a very beautiful casket of ebony and ivory, cunningly carved and standing upon four claw-like ivory legs.

"What the devil's this?" he muttered.

He opened the box, which was lined with sandal-wood, and thereupon started back with a great cry, recoiling from the casket as though it had contained an adder. My former sentiments forgotten, I stepped forward and peered into the interior. Then I, in turn, recoiled.

In the box lay a shrivelled yellow hand—with long tapering and well-manicured nails—neatly severed at the wrist!

The nail of the index finger was enclosed in a tiny, delicately fashioned case of gold, upon which were engraved a number of Chinese characters.

Adderley sank down again upon the settee.

"My God!" he whispered, "his hand! His hand! *He has sent me his hand!*"

He began laughing. Whereupon, since I could see that the man was practically hysterical because of his mysterious fears:

"Stop that," I said sharply. "Pull yourself together, Adderley. What the deuce is the matter with you?"

"Take it away!" he moaned, "take it away. Take the accursed thing away!"

"I admit it is an unpleasant gift to send to anybody," I said, "but probably you know more about it than I do."

"Take it away," he repeated. "Take it away, for God's sake, take it away, Knox!"

He was quite beyond reason, and therefore:

"Very well," I said, and wrapped the casket in the brown paper in which it had come. "What do you want me to do with it?"

"Throw it in the river," he answered. "Burn it. Do anything you like with it, but take it out of my sight!"

III
THE GOLD-CASED NAIL

As I descended to the street the liftman regarded me in a curious and rather significant way. Finally, just as I was about to step out into the hall:

"Excuse me, sir," he said, having evidently decided that I was a fit person to converse with, "but are you a friend of Mr. Adderley's?"

"Why do you ask?"

"Well, sir, I hope you will excuse me, but at times I have thought the gentleman was just a little bit queer, like."

"You mean insane?" I asked sharply.

"Well, sir, I don't know, but he is always asking me if I can see shadows and things in the lift, and sometimes when he comes in late of a night he absolutely gives me the cold shivers, he does."

I lingered, the box under my arm, reluctant to obtain confidences from a servant, but at the same time keenly interested. Thus encouraged:

"Then there's that lady friend of his who is always coming here," the man continued. "*She's* haunted by shadows, too." He paused, watching me narrowly.

"There's nothing better in this world than a clean conscience, sir," he concluded.

Having returned to my room at the hotel, I set down the mysterious parcel, surveying it with much disfavour. That it contained the hand of the Mandarin Quong I could not doubt, the hand which had been amputated by Dr. Matheson. Its appearance in that dramatic fashion confirmed Matheson's idea that the mandarin's injury had been received at the hands of Adderley. What did all this portend, unless that the Mandarin Quong was dead? And if he were dead why was Adderley more afraid of him dead than he had been of him living?

I thought of the haunting shadow, I thought of the night at Katong, and I thought of Dr. Matheson's words when he had told us of his discovery of the Chinaman lying in the road that night outside Singapore.

I felt strangely disinclined to touch the relic, and it was only after some moments' hesitation that I undid the wrappings and raised the lid of the casket. Dusk was very near and I had not yet lighted the lamps; therefore at first I doubted the evidence of my senses. But having lighted up and peered long and anxiously into the sandal-wood lining of the casket I could doubt no longer.

The casket was empty!

It was like a conjuring trick. That the hand had been in the box when I had taken it up from Adderley's table I could have sworn before any jury. When and by whom it had been removed was a puzzle beyond my powers of unravelling. I

stepped toward the telephone—and then remembered that Paul Harley was out of London. Vaguely wondering if Adderley had played me a particularly gruesome practical joke, I put the box on a sideboard and again contemplated the telephone doubtfully for a moment. It was in my mind to ring him up. Finally, taking all things into consideration, I determined that I would have nothing further to do with the man's unsavoury and mysterious affairs.

It was in vain, however, that I endeavoured to dismiss the matter from my mind; and throughout the evening, which I spent at a theatre with some American friends, I found myself constantly thinking of Adderley and the ivory casket, of the mandarin of Johore Bahru, and of the mystery of the shrivelled yellow hand.

I had been back in my room about half an hour, I suppose, and it was long past midnight, when I was startled by a ringing of my telephone bell. I took up the receiver, and:

"Knox! Knox!" came a choking cry.

"Yes, who is speaking?"

"It is I, Adderley. For God's sake come round to my place at once!"

His words were scarcely intelligible. Undoubtedly he was in the grip of intense emotion.

"What do you mean? What is the matter?"

"It is here, Knox, it is here! It is knocking on the door! Knocking! Knocking!"

"You have been drinking," I said sternly. "Where is your man?"

"The cur has bolted. He bolted the moment he heard that damned knocking. I am all alone; I have no one else to appeal to." There came a choking sound, then: "My God, Knox, it is getting in! I can see . . . the shadow on the blind . . ."

Convinced that Adderley's secret fears had driven him mad, I nevertheless felt called upon to attend to his urgent call, and without a moment's delay I hurried around to St. James's Street. The liftman was not on duty, the lower hall was in darkness, but I raced up the stairs and found to my astonishment that Adderley's door was wide open.

"Adderley!" I cried. "Adderley!"

There was no reply, and without further ceremony I entered and searched the chambers. They were empty. Deeply mystified, I was about to go out again when there came a ring at the door-bell. I walked to the door and a policeman was standing upon the landing.

"Good evening, sir," he said, and then paused, staring at me curiously.

"Good evening, constable," I replied.

"You are not the gentleman who ran out a while ago," he said, a note of suspicion coming into his voice.

I handed him my card and explained what had occurred, then:

"It must have been Mr. Adderley I saw," muttered the constable.

"You saw—when?"

"Just before you arrived, sir. He came racing out into St. James's Street and dashed off like a madman."

"In which direction was he going?"

"Toward Pall Mall."

The neighbourhood was practically deserted at that hour. But from the guard on duty before the palace we obtained our first evidence of Adderley's movements. He had raced by some five minutes before, frantically looking back over his shoulder and behaving like a man flying for his life. No one else had seen him. No one else ever did see him alive. At two o'clock there was no news, but I had informed Scotland Yard and official inquiries had been set afoot.

Nothing further came to light that night, but as all readers of the daily press will remember, Adderley's body was taken out of the pond in St. James's Park on the following day. Death was due to drowning, but his throat was greatly discoloured as though it had been clutched in a fierce grip.

It was I who identified the body, and as many people will know, in spite of the closest inquiries, the mystery of Adderley's death has not been properly cleared up to this day. The identity of the lady who visited him at his chambers was never discovered. She completely disappeared.

The ebony and ivory casket lies on my table at this present moment, visible evidence of an invisible menace from which Adderley had fled around the world.

Doubtless the truth will never be known now. A significant discovery, however, was made some days after the recovery of Adderley's body.

From the bottom of the pond in St. James's Park a patient Scotland Yard official brought up the gold nail-case with its mysterious engravings—and it contained, torn at the root, the incredibly long finger-nail of the Mandarin Quong!

IN DARKEST AFRICA

JOHN BUCHAN

JOHN BUCHAN, first Baron Tweedsmuir (1875–1940), was a Scottish diplomat, journalist, and publisher, as well as an author of both historical works and espionage and adventure fiction. Although more than half of his literary output was nonfiction, including his first book, a biography titled *Sir Quixote of the Moors* (1895), published when he was only twenty years old, Buchan is most remembered today for his thrillers, particularly those involving his hero Richard Hannay and his activities for British Intelligence. Modeled after one of Buchan's military idols, General Edmund "Tiny" Ironside, Hannay embarks on his first adventure in the classic *The Thirty-Nine Steps* (1915), set just before the outbreak of World War I. The success of this novel spurred the sequels *Greenmantle* (1916), *Mr. Standfast* (1919), *The Three Hostages* (1924), and *The Island of Sheep* (1936). The enduring popularity of *The Thirty-Nine Steps* is partially due to the outstanding 1935 film version directed by Alfred Hitchcock, which starred Robert Donat as Hannay, and Madeleine Carroll. The motion picture is considerably tightened from the novel: it is largely a chase film, with the British police after Hannay because they believe he killed an American spy, and foreign spies in pursuit because they believe he has sensitive information that he will turn over to the British government. The film was remade in a forgettable 1960 production with Kenneth More and Taina Elg.

"The Green Wildebeest" is Buchan's only short story about Hannay. It was first published in the September 1927 issue of *Pall Mall Magazine;* its first book publication was in the short-story collection *The Runagates Club* (London: Hodder, Stoughton, 1928).

THE GREEN WILDEBEEST

JOHN BUCHAN

> We carry with us the wonders we seek without us; there is all Africa and her prodigies in us.
> —SIR THOMAS BROWNE: *Religio Medici.*

WE WERE TALKING about the persistence of race qualities—how you might bury a strain for generations under fresh graftings but the aboriginal sap would some day stir. The obvious instance was the Jew, and Pugh had also something to say about the surprises of a tincture of hill blood in the Behari. Peckwether, the historian, was inclined to doubt. The old stock, he held, could disappear absolutely as if by a chemical change, and the end be as remote from the beginnings as—to use his phrase—a ripe Gorgonzola from a bucket of new milk.

"I don't believe you're ever quite safe," said Sandy Arbuthnot.

"You mean that an eminent banker may get up one morning with a strong wish to cut himself shaving in honour of Baal?"

"Maybe. But the tradition is more likely to be negative. There are some things that for no particular reason he won't like, some things that specially frighten him. Take my own case. I haven't a scrap of real superstition in me, but I hate crossing a river at night. I fancy a lot of my blackguard ancestors got scuppered at moonlight fords. I believe we're all stuffed full of atavistic fears, and you can't tell how or when a man will crack till you know his breeding."

"I think that's about the truth of it," said Hannay, and after the discussion had rambled on for a while he told us this tale.

Just after the Boer War (he said) I was on a prospecting job in the north-eastern Transvaal. I was a mining engineer, with copper as my speciality, and I had always a notion that copper might be found in big quantities in the Zoutpansberg foothills. There was of course Messina at the west end, but my thoughts turned rather to the north-east corner, where the berg breaks down to the crook of the Limpopo. I was a young man then, fresh from two years' campaigning with the Imperial Light Horse, and I was thirsty for better jobs than trying to drive elusive burghers up against barbed wire and blockhouses. When I started out with my mules from Pietersburg on the dusty road to the hills, I think I felt happier than ever before in my life.

I had only one white companion, a boy of twenty-two called Andrew Du Preez. Andrew, not Andries, for he was named after the Reverend Andrew Murray, who had been a great Pope among the devout Afrikanders. He came of a rich Free State farming family, but his particular branch had been settled for two generations in the Wakkerstroom region along the upper

Pongola. The father was a splendid old fellow with a head like Moses, and he and all the uncles had been on commando, and most of them had had a spell in Bermuda or Ceylon. The boy was a bit of a freak in that stock. He had been precociously intelligent, and had gone to a good school in the Cape and afterwards to a technical college in Johannesburg. He was as modern a product as the others were survivals, with none of the family religion or family politics, very keen on science, determined to push his way on the Rand—which was the Mecca of all enterprising Afrikanders—and not very sorry that the War should have found him in a place from which it was manifestly impossible to join the family banner. In October '99 he was on his first job in a new mining area in Rhodesia, and as he hadn't much health he was wise enough to stick there till peace came.

I had known him before, and when I ran across him on the Rand I asked him to come with me, and he jumped at the offer. He had just returned from the Wakkerstroom farm, to which the rest of his clan had been repatriated, and didn't relish the prospect of living in a tin-roofed shanty with a father who read the Bible most of the day to find out why exactly he had merited such misfortunes. Andrew was a hard young sceptic, in whom the family piety produced acute exasperation. . . . He was a good-looking boy, always rather smartly dressed, and at first sight you would have taken him for a young American, because of his heavy hairless chin, his dull complexion, and the way he peppered his ordinary speech with technical and business phrases. There was a touch of the Mongol in his face, which was broad, with high cheek bones, eyes slightly slanted, short thick nose and rather full lips. I remembered that I had seen the same thing before in young Boers, and I thought I knew the reason. The Du Preez family had lived for generations close up to the Kaffir borders, and somewhere had got a dash of the tar-brush.

We had a light wagon with a team of eight mules, and a Cape-cart drawn by four others; five boys went with us, two of them Shangaans, and three Basutos from Malietsie's location north of Pietersburg. Our road was over the Wood Bush, and then north-east across the two Letabas to the Pufuri river. The countryside was amazingly empty. Beyer's commandos had skirmished among the hills, but the war had never reached the plains; at the same time it had put a stop to all hunting and prospecting and had scattered most of the native tribes. The place had become in effect a sanctuary, and I saw more varieties of game than I had ever seen before south of the Zambesi, so that I wished I were on a hunting trip instead of on a business job. Lions were plentiful, and every night we had to build a *scherm* for our mules and light great fires, beside which we listened to their eerie serenades.

It was early December, and in the Wood Bush it was the weather of an English June. Even in the foothills, among the wormwood and wild bananas, it was pleasant enough, but when we got out into the plains it was as hot as Tophet. As far as the eye could reach the bushveld rolled its scrub like the scrawled foliage a child draws on a slate, with here and there a baobab swimming unsteadily in the glare. For long stretches we were away from water, and ceased to see big game—only Kaffir queens and tick-birds, and now and then a wild ostrich. Then on the sixth day out from Pietersburg we raised a blue line of mountains on the north, which I knew to be the eastern extension of the Zoutpansberg. I had never travelled this country before, and had never met a man who had, so we steered by compass, and by one of the old bad maps of the Transvaal Government. That night we crossed the Pufuri, and next day the landscape began to change. The ground rose, so that we had a sight of the distant Lebombo hills to the east, and mopani bushes began to appear—a sure sign of a healthier country.

That afternoon we were only a mile or two from the hills. They were the usual type of berg which you find everywhere from Natal to the

Zambesi—cut sheer, with an overhang in many places, but much broken up by kloofs and fissures. What puzzled me was the absence of streams. The ground was as baked as the plains, all covered with aloe and cactus and thorn, with never a sign of water. But for my purpose the place looked promising. There was that unpleasant metallic green that you find in a copper country, so that everything seemed to have been steeped in a mineral dye—even the brace of doves which I shot for luncheon.

We turned east along the foot of the cliffs, and presently saw a curious feature. A promontory ran out from the berg, connected by a narrow isthmus with the main *massif*. I suppose the superficial area of the top might have been a square mile or so; the little peninsula was deeply cut into by ravines, and in the ravines tall timber was growing. Also we came to well-grassed slopes, dotted with mimosa and syringa bushes. This must mean water at last, for I had never found yellowwoods and stinkwoods growing far from a stream. Here was our outspan for the night, and when presently we rounded a corner and looked down into a green cup I thought I had rarely seen a more habitable place. The sight of fresh green herbage always intoxicated me, after the dust and heat and the ugly greys and umbers of the bushveld. There was a biggish kraal in the bottom, and a lot of goats and leggy Kaffir sheep on the slopes. Children were bringing in the cows for the milking, smoke was going up from the cooking fires, and there was a cheerful evening hum in the air. I expected a stream, but could see no sign of one: the cup seemed to be as dry as a hollow of the Sussex Downs. Also, though there were patches of mealies and Kaffir corn, I could see no irrigated land. But water must be there, and after we had fixed a spot for our outspan beside a clump of olivewoods, I took Andrew and one of our boys and strolled down to make inquiries.

I daresay many of the inhabitants of that kraal had never seen a white man before, for our arrival made a bit of a sensation. I noticed that there were very few young men about the place, but an inordinate number of old women. The first sight of us scattered them like plovers, and we had to wait for half an hour, smoking patiently in the evening sun, before we could get into talk with them. Once the ice was broken, however, things went well. They were a decent peaceable folk, very shy and scared and hesitating, but with no guile in them. Our presents of brass and copper wire and a few tins of preserved meat made a tremendous impression. We bought a sheep from them at a ridiculously small price, and they threw in a basket of green mealies. But when we raised the water question we struck a snag.

There was water, good water, they said, but it was not in any pan or stream. They got it morning and evening from up there—and they pointed to the fringe of a wood under the cliffs where I thought I saw the roof of a biggish *rondavel*. They got it from their Father; they were Shangaans, and the word they used was not the ordinary word for chief, but the name for a great priest and medicine-man.

I wanted my dinner, so I forbore to inquire further. I produced some more Kaffir truck, and begged them to present it with my compliments to their Father, and to ask for water for two white strangers, five of their own race, and twelve mules. They seemed to welcome the proposition, and a string of them promptly set off uphill with their big calabashes. As we walked back I said something foolish to Andrew about having struck a Kaffir Moses who could draw water from the rock. The lad was in a bad temper. "We have struck an infernal rascal who has made a corner in the water supply and bleeds these poor devils. He's the kind of grafter I would like to interview with a sjambok."

In an hour we had all the water we wanted. It stood in a row of calabashes, and beside it the presents I had sent to the provider. The villagers had deposited it and then vanished, and our boys who had helped them to carry it were curiously quiet and solemnised. I was informed that the Father sent the water as a gift to the strangers without payment. I tried to cross-examine one of our Shangaans, but he would tell me nothing except that the water had come from a sacred place into which no man could penetrate. He also muttered something about a wildebeest which I couldn't understand. Now the Kaffir is the most superstitious of God's creatures. All the way from Pietersburg we had been troubled by the vivid imaginations of our outfit. They wouldn't sleep in one place because of a woman without a head who haunted it; they dared not go a yard along a particular road after dark because of a spook that travelled it in the shape of a rolling ball of fire. Usually their memories were as short as their fancies were quick, and five minutes after their protest they would be laughing like baboons. But that night they seemed to have been really impressed by something. They did not chatter or sing over their supper, but gossiped in undertones, and slept as near Andrew and myself as they dared.

Next morning the same array of gourds stood before our outspan, and there was enough water for me to have a tub in my collapsible bath. I don't think I ever felt anything colder.

I had decided to take a holiday and go shooting. Andrew would stay in camp and tinker up one of the wheels of the mule-wagon which had suffered from the bush roads. He announced his intention of taking a walk later and interviewing the water-merchant.

"For Heaven's sake, be careful," I said. "Most likely he's a priest of sorts, and if you're not civil to him we'll have to quit this country. I make a point of respecting the gods of the heathen."

"All you English do," he replied tartly. "That's why you make such a damned mess of handling Kaffirs. . . . But this fellow is a business man with a pretty notion of cornering public utilities. I'm going to make his acquaintance."

I had a pleasant day in that hot scented wilderness. First I tried the low ground, but found nothing there but some old spoor of kudu, and a paauw, which I shot. Then I tried the skirts of the berg to the east of the village, and found that the kloofs, which from below looked

climbable, had all somewhere a confounded overhang which checked me. I saw no way of getting to the top of the plateau, so I spent the afternoon in exploring the tumbled glacis. There was no trace of copper here, for the rock was a reddish granite, but it was a jolly flowery place, with green dells among the crags, and an amazing variety of birds. But I was glad that I had brought a water-bottle, for I found no water; it was there all right, but it was underground. I stalked a bushbuck ram and missed him, but I got one of the little buck-like chamois which the Dutch call *klipspringer*. With it and the paauw strung round my neck I sauntered back leisurely to supper.

As soon as I came in sight of the village I saw that something had played the deuce with it. There was a great hubbub going on, and all the folk were collected at the end farthest away from our camp. The camp itself looked very silent. I could see the hobbled mules, but I could see nothing of any of our outfit. I thought it best in these circumstances to make an inconspicuous arrival, so I bore away to my left, crossed the hollow lower down where it was thick with scrub, and came in on the outspan from the south. It was very silent. The cooking fires had been allowed to go out, though the boys should have been getting ready the evening meal, and there seemed to be not a single black face on the premises. Very uneasy, I made for our sleeping tent, and found Andrew lying on his bed, smoking.

"What on earth has happened?" I demanded. "Where are Coos and Klemboy and . . ."

"Quit," he said shortly. "They've all quit."

He looked sulky and tired and rather white in the face, and there seemed to be more the matter with him than ill temper. He would lay down his pipe, and press his hand on his forehead like a man with a bad headache. Also he never lifted his eyes to mine. I daresay I was a bit harsh, for I was hungry, and there were moments when I thought he was going to cry. However at last I got a sort of story out of him.

He had finished his job on the wagon wheel in

the morning, and after luncheon had gone for a walk to the wood above the village at the foot of the cliffs. He wanted to see where the water came from and to have a word with the man who controlled it. Andrew, as I have told you, was a hard young realist and, by way of reaction from his family, a determined foe of superstition, and he disliked the notion of this priest and his mumbo-jumbo. Well, it seemed that he reached the priest's headquarters—it was the big *rondavel* we had seen from below, and there was a kind of stockade stretching on both sides, very strongly fenced, so that the only entrance was through the *rondavel*. He had found the priest at home, and had, according to his account, spoken to him civilly and had tried to investigate the water problem. But the old man would have nothing to say to him, and peremptorily refused his request to be allowed to enter the enclosure. By and by Andrew lost his temper, and forced his way in. The priest resisted and there was a scuffle; I daresay Andrew used his sjambok, for a backveld Dutchman can never keep his hands off a Kaffir.

I didn't like the story, but it was no use being angry with a lad who looked like a sick dog.

"What is inside? Did you find the water?" I asked.

"I hadn't time. It's a thick wood and full of beasts. I tell you I was scared out of my senses and had to run for my life."

"Leopards?" I asked. I had heard of native chiefs keeping tame leopards.

"Leopards be damned. I'd have faced leopards. I saw a wildebeest as big as a house—an old brute, grey in the nozzle and the rest of it green—green, I tell you. I took a pot shot at it and ran. . . . When I came out the whole blasted kraal was howling. The old devil must have roused them. I legged it for home. . . . No, they didn't follow, but in half an hour all our outfit had cut their stick . . . didn't wait to pick up their duds. . . . Oh, hell, I can't talk. Leave me alone."

I had laughed in spite of myself. A wildebeest is not ornamental at the best, but a green one

must be a good recipe for the horrors. All the same I felt very little like laughing. Andrew had offended the village and its priest, played havoc with the brittle nerves of our own boys, and generally made the place too hot to hold us. He had struck some kind of native magic, which had frightened him to the bone, for all his scepticism. The best thing I could do seemed to be to try and patch up a peace with the water-merchant. So I made a fire and put on a kettle to boil, stayed my hunger with a handful of biscuits, and started out for the *rondavel*. But first I saw that my revolver was loaded, for I fancied that there might be trouble. It was a calm bright evening, but up from the hollow where the kraal lay there rose a buzz like angry wasps.

No one interfered with me; indeed, I met no one till I presented myself at the *rondavel* door. It was a big empty place, joined to the stockades on both sides, and opposite the door was another which opened on to a dull green shade. I never saw a *scherm* so stoutly built. There was a palisade of tall pointed poles, and between them a thick wall of wait-a-bit thorns interlaced with a scarlet-flowered creeper. It would have taken a man with an axe half a day to cut a road through. The only feasible entrance was by the *rondavel*.

An old man was squatted on an earthen floor, which had been so pounded and beaten that it looked like dark polished stone. His age might have been anything above seventy from the whiteness of his beard, but there seemed a good deal of bodily strength left in him, for the long arms which rested on his knees were muscular. His face was not the squat face of the ordinary Kaffir, but high-boned and regular, like some types of well-bred Zulu. Now that I think of it, there was probably Arab blood in him. He lifted his head at the sound of my steps, and by the way he looked at me I knew that he was blind.

There he sat without a word, every line of his body full of dejection and tragedy. I had suddenly a horrible feeling of sacrilege. That that young fool Andrew should have lifted his hand upon an old man and a blind man and outraged some harmless *tabu* seemed to me an abominable thing. I felt that some holiness had been violated, something ancient and innocent cruelly insulted. At that moment there was nothing in the world I wanted so much as to make restitution.

I spoke to him, using the Shangaan word which means both priest and king. I told him that I had been away hunting and had returned to find that my companion had made bad mischief. I said that Andrew was very young, and that his error had been only the foolishness and hot-headedness of youth. I said—and my voice must have shown him that I meant it—that I was cut to the heart by what had happened, that I bowed my head in the dust in contrition, and that I asked nothing better than to be allowed to make atonement. . . . Of course I didn't offer money. I would as soon have thought of offering a tip to the Pope.

He never lifted his head, so I said it all over again, and the second time it was genuine pleading. I had never spoken like that to a Kaffir before, but I could not think of that old figure as a Kaffir, but as the keeper of some ancient mystery which a rude hand had outraged.

He spoke at last. "There can be no atonement," he said. "Wrong has been done, and on the wrong-doer must fall the penalty."

The words were wholly without menace; rather he spoke as if he were an unwilling prophet of evil. He was there to declare the law, which he could not alter if he wanted.

I apologised, I protested, I pled, I fairly grovelled; I implored him to tell me if there was no way in which the trouble could be mended; but if I had offered him a million pounds I don't believe that that old fellow would have changed his tone. He seemed to feel, and he made me feel it too, that a crime had been committed against the law of nature, and that it was nature, not man, that would avenge it. He wasn't in the least unfriendly; indeed, I think he rather liked the serious way I took the business and realised how sorry I was; his slow sentences came out without a trace of bitterness. It was this that impressed me so horribly—he was like an old stone oracle repeating the commands of the god he served.

I could make nothing of him, though I kept at it till the shadows had lengthened outside, and it was almost dark within the *rondavel*. I wanted to ask him at least to help me to get back my boys, and to make our peace with the village, but I simply could not get the words out. The atmosphere was too solemn to put a practical question like that. . . .

I was turning to go away, when I looked at the door on the far side. Owing to the curious formation of the cliffs the sinking sun had only now caught the high tree-tops, and some ricochet of light made the enclosure brighter than when I first arrived. I felt suddenly an overwhelming desire to go inside.

"Is it permitted, Father," I said, "to pass through that door?"

To my surprise he waved me on. "It is permitted," he said, "for you have a clean heart." Then he added a curious thing. "What was there is there no more. It has gone to the fulfilling of the law."

It was with a good deal of trepidation that I entered that uncanny *enceinte*. I remembered Andrew's terror, and I kept my hand on my revolver, for I had a notion that there might be some queer fauna inside. There was light in the upper air, but below it was a kind of olive-green dusk. I was afraid of snakes, also of tiger-cats, and there was Andrew's green wildebeest!

The place was only a couple of acres in extent, and though I walked very cautiously I soon had made the circuit of it. The *scherm* continued in a half-moon on each side till it met the sheer wall of the cliffs. The undergrowth was not very thick, and out of it grew tall straight trees, so that the wood seemed like some old pagan grove. When one looked up the mulberry sunset sky showed in patches between the feathery tops, but where I walked it was very dark.

There was not a sign of life in it, not a bird or beast, not the crack of a twig or a stir in the bushes; all was as quiet and dead as a crypt. Having made the circuit I struck diagonally across, and presently came on what I had been looking for—a pool of water. The spring was nearly circular, with a diameter of perhaps six yards, and what amazed me was that it was surrounded by a parapet of hewn stone. In the centre of the grove there was a little more light, and I could see that that stonework had never been made by Kaffir hands. Evening is the time when water comes to its own; it sleeps in the day but it has its own strange life in the darkness. I dipped my hand in it and it was as cold as ice. There was no bubbling in it, but there seemed to be a slow rhythmical movement, as if fresh currents were always welling out of the deeps and always returning. I have no doubt that it would have been crystal clear if there had been any light, but, as I saw it, it was a surface of darkest jade, opaque, impenetrable, swaying to some magic impulse from the heart of the earth.

It is difficult to explain just the effect it had on me. I had been solemnised before, but this grove and fountain gave me the abject shapeless fear of a child. I felt that somehow I had strayed beyond the reasonable world. The place was clean against nature. It was early summer, so these dark aisles should have been alive with moths and flying ants and all the thousand noises of night. Instead it was utterly silent and lifeless, dead as a stone except for the secret pulsing of the cold waters.

I had had quite enough. It is an absurd thing to confess, but I bolted—shuffled through the undergrowth and back into the *rondavel,* where the old man still sat like Buddha on the floor.

"You have seen?" he asked.

"I have seen," I said—"but I do not know what I have seen. Father, be merciful to foolish youth."

He repeated again the words that had chilled me before. "What was there has gone to fulfil the law."

I ran all the way back to our outspan, and took some unholy tosses on the road, for I had got it into my head that Andrew was in danger. I don't think I ever believed in his green wildebeest, but he had been positive that the place was full of animals, and I knew for a fact that it was empty. Had some fearsome brute been unloosed on the world?

I found Andrew in our tent, and the kettle I had put on to boil empty and the fire out. The boy was sleeping heavily with a flushed face, and I saw what had happened. He was practically a teetotaller, but he had chosen to swallow a good third of one of our four bottles of whisky. The compulsion must have been pretty strong which drove him to drink.

After that our expedition went from bad to worse. In the morning there was no water to be had, and I didn't see myself shouldering a calabash and going back to the grove. Also our boys did not return, and not a soul in the kraal would come near us. Indeed, all night they had kept up a most distressing racket, wailing and beating little drums. It was no use staying on, and, for myself, I had a strong desire to get out of the neighbourhood. The experience of the night before had left an aftertaste of disquiet in my mind, and I wanted to flee from I knew not what. Andrew was obviously a sick man. We did not carry clinical thermometers in those days, but he certainly had fever on him.

So we inspanned after breakfast, and a heavy job trekking is when you have to do all the work yourself. I drove the wagon and Andrew the Cape-cart, and I wondered how long he would be able to sit on his seat. My notion was that by going east we might be able to hire fresh boys, and start prospecting in the hill-country above the bend of the Limpopo.

But the word had gone out against us. You know the way in which Kaffirs send news for a hundred miles as quick as the telegraph—by drum-taps or telepathy—explain it any way you like. Well, we struck a big kraal that afternoon, but not a word would they say to us. Indeed, they were actually threatening, and I had to show my revolver and speak pretty stiffly before we got off. It was the same next day, and I grew nervous about our provisions, for we couldn't buy anything—not a chicken or an egg or a mealie-cob. Andrew was a jolly companion. He had relapsed into the primeval lout, and his manners were those of a cave-man. If he had not been patently suffering, I would have found it hard to keep my temper.

Altogether it was a bright look-out, and to crown all, on the third morning Andrew went down like a log with the worst bout of malaria I have ever seen. That fairly put the lid on it. I thought it was going to be black-water, and all my irritation at the boy vanished in my anxiety. There was nothing for it but to give up the expedition and make the best speed possible to the coast. I made for Portuguese territory, and that evening got to the Limpopo. Happily we struck a more civil brand of native, who had not heard of our performances, and I was able to make a bargain with the headman of the village, who undertook to take charge of our outfit till it was sent for, and sold us a big native boat. I hired four lusty fellows as rowers and next morning we started down the river.

We spent a giddy five days before I planted Andrew in hospital at Lourenço Marques. The sickness was not black-water, thank God, but it was a good deal more than ordinary malaria; indeed, I think there was a touch of brain fever in it. Curiously enough I was rather relieved when it came. I had been scared by the boy's behaviour the first two days. I thought that the old priest had actually laid some curse on him; I remembered how the glade and the well had solemnised even me, and I considered that Andrew, with a Kaffir strain somewhere in his ancestry, was probably susceptible to something which left me cold. I had knocked too much about Africa to be a dogmatic sceptic about the mysteries of the heathen. But this fever seemed to explain it. He had been sickening for it; that was why he had behaved so badly to the old man, and had come back babbling about a green wildebeest. I knew that the beginnings of fever often make a man light-headed so that he loses all self-control and gets odd fancies. . . . All the same I didn't quite convince myself. I couldn't get out of my head the picture of the old man and his ominous words, or that empty grove under the sunset.

I did my best for the boy, and before we reached the coast the worst had passed. A bed was made for him in the stern, and I had to watch him by night and day to prevent him going overboard among the crocodiles. He was apt to be violent, for in his madness he thought he was being chased, and sometimes I had all I could do to keep him in the boat. He would scream like a thing demented, and plead, and curse, and I noticed as a queer thing that his ravings were never in Dutch but always in Kaffir—mostly the Sesutu which he had learnt in his childhood. I expected to hear him mention the green wildebeest, but to my comfort he never uttered the name. He gave no clue to what frightened him, but it must have been a full-sized terror, for every nerve in his body seemed to be quivering, and I didn't care to look at his eyes.

The upshot was that I left him in bed in hospital, as weak as a kitten, but with the fever gone and restored to his right mind. He was again the good fellow I had known, very apologetic and grateful. So with an easy conscience I arranged for the retrieving of my outfit and returned to the Rand.

Well, for six months I lost sight of Andrew. I had to go to Namaqualand, and then up to the copper country of Barotseland, which wasn't as easy a trek as it is to-day. I had one letter from him, written from Johannesburg—not a very satisfactory epistle, for I gathered that the boy was very unsettled. He had quarrelled with his family, and he didn't seem to be contented with the job he had got in the goldfields. As I had known him he had been a sort of school-book industrious apprentice, determined to get on in the world, and not in the least afraid of a dull job and uncongenial company. But this letter was full of small grouses. He wanted badly to have a talk with me—thought of chucking his work and making a trip north to see me; and he ended with an underlined request that I should telegraph when I was coming down-country. As it happened I had no chance just then of sending a telegram, and later I forgot about it.

By and by I finished my tour and was at the Falls, where I got a local Rhodesian paper. From it I had news of Andrew with a vengeance. There were columns about a murder in the bushveld—two men had gone out to look for Kruger's treasure and one had shot the other, and to my horror I found that the one who was now lying in Pretoria gaol under sentence of death was my unhappy friend.

You remember the wild yarns after the Boer War about a treasure of gold which Kruger in his flight to the coast had buried somewhere in the Selati country. That, of course, was all nonsense: the wily ex-President had long before seen the main funds safe in a European bank. But I daresay some of the officials had got away with Treasury balances, and there may have been bullion cached in the bushveld. Anyhow, every scallywag south of the Zambesi was agog about the business, and there were no end of expeditions which never found a single Transvaal sovereign. Well, it seemed that two months before Andrew and a Dutchman called Smit had started out to try their luck, and somewhere on the Olifants the two had gone out one evening and only one had returned. Smit was found by the native boys with a hole in his head, and it was proved that the bullet came from Andrew's rifle, which he had been carrying when the two set out. After that the story became obscure. Andrew had been very excited when he returned and declared that he had "done it at last," but when Smit's body was found he denied that he had shot him. But it was clear that Smit had been killed by Andrew's sporting .303, and the natives swore that the men had been constantly quarrelling and that Andrew had always shown a very odd temper. The Crown prosecutor argued that the two believed they had found treasure, and that Andrew had murdered Smit in cold blood to prevent his sharing. The defence seemed to be chiefly the impossibility of a guilty man behaving as Andrew had behaved, and the likelihood of his having fired at a beast in the dark and killed his companion. It sounded to me very thin, and the jury did not believe it, for their verdict was wilful murder.

I knew that it was simply incredible that Andrew could have committed the crime. Men are queer cattle, and I wouldn't have put even murder past certain fairly decent fellows I knew, but this boy was emphatically not one of them. Unless he had gone stark mad I was positive that he could never have taken human life. I knew him intimately, in the way you know a fellow you have lived alone with for months, and that was one of the things I could bank on. All the same it seemed clear that he had shot Smit. . . . I sent the longest telegram I ever sent in my life to a Scotch lawyer in Johannesburg called Dalgleish whom I believed in, telling him to move heaven and earth to get a reprieve. He was to see Andrew and wire me details about his state of mind. I thought then that temporary madness was probably our best line, and I believed myself that that was the explanation. I longed to take the train forthwith to Pretoria, but I was tied by the heels till the rest of my outfit came in. I was tortured by the thought that the hanging might have already taken place, for that wretched newspaper was a week old.

In two days I got Dalgleish's reply. He had seen the condemned man, and had told him that he came from me. He reported that Andrew was curiously peaceful and apathetic, and not very willing to talk about the business except to declare his innocence. Dalgleish thought him not quite right in his mind, but he had been already examined, and the court had rejected the plea of insanity. He sent his love to me and told me not to worry.

I stirred up Dalgleish again, and got a further reply. Andrew admitted that he had fired the rifle, but not at Smit. He had killed something, but what it was he would not say. He did not seem to be in the least keen to save his neck.

When I reached Bulawayo, on my way south, I had a brain-wave, but the thing seemed so preposterous that I could hardly take it seriously. Still I daren't neglect any chance, so I wired again to Dalgleish to try to have the execution postponed, until he got hold of the priest who lived in the berg above the Pufuri. I gave him full directions how to find him. I said that the old man had laid some curse on Andrew, and that that might explain his state of mind. After all, demoniacal possession must be equivalent in law to insanity. But by this time I had become rather hopeless. It seemed a futile thing to be wiring this rigmarole when every hour was bringing the gallows nearer.

I left the railroad at Mafeking, for I thought I could save the long circuit by De Aar by trekking across country. I would have done better to stick to the train, for everything went wrong with me. I had a breakdown at the drift of the Selous river and had to wait a day in Rustenburg, and I had trouble again at Commando Nek, so that it was the evening of the third day before I reached Pretoria. . . . As I feared, it was all over. They told me in the hotel that Andrew had been hanged that morning.

I went back to Johannesburg to see Dalgleish with a cold horror at my heart and complete mystification in my head. The Devil had taken an active hand in things and caused a hideous miscarriage of justice. If there had been anybody I could blame I would have felt better, but the fault seemed to lie only with the crookedness of fate. . . . Dalgleish could tell me little. Smit had been the ordinary scallywag, not much of a fellow and no great loss to the world; the puzzle was why Andrew wanted to go with him. The boy in his last days had been utterly apathetic—bore no grudge against anybody—appeared at peace with the world, but didn't seem to want to live. The predikant who visited him daily could make nothing of him. He appeared to be sane enough, but, beyond declaring his innocence, was not inclined to talk, and gave no assistance to those who were trying to get a reprieve . . . scarcely took any interest in it. . . . He had asked repeatedly for me, and had occupied his last days in writing me a long letter, which was to be delivered unopened into my hand. Dalgleish gave me the thing, seven pages in Andrew's neat calligraphy, and in the evening on his stoep I read it.

It was like a voice speaking to me out of the grave, but it was not the voice I knew. Gone was the enlightened commercially-minded young man, who had shed all superstition, and had a dapper explanation for everything in heaven and earth. It was a crude boy who had written those pages, a boy in whose soul old Calvinistic terrors had been awakened, and terrors older still out of primordial African shadows.

He had committed a great sin—that was the point he insisted upon, and by this sin he had set free something awful to prey on the world. . . . At first it seemed sheer raving mania to me, but as I mused on it I remembered my own feelings in that empty grove. I had been solemnised, and this boy, with that in his blood which was not in mine, had suffered a cataclysmic spiritual experience. He did not dwell on it, but his few sentences were eloquent in their harsh intensity. He had struggled, he had tried to make light of it, to forget it, to despise it; but it rode him like a nightmare. He thought he was going mad. I had been right about that touch of brain fever.

As far as I could make it out, he believed that from that outraged sanctuary something real and living had gone forth, something at any rate of flesh and blood. But this idea may not have come to him till later, when his mind had been for several months in torture, and he had lost the power of sleep. At first, I think, his trouble was only an indefinite haunting, a sense of sin and impending retribution. But in Johannesburg the *malaise* had taken concrete form. He believed that through his act something awful was at large, with infinite power for evil—evil not only against the wrongdoer himself but against the world. And he believed that it might still be stopped, that it was still in the eastern bush. So crude a fancy showed how his normal intelligence had gone to bits. He had tumbled again into the backveld world of his childhood.

He decided to go and look for it. That was where the tough white strain in him came out. He might have a Kaffir's blind terrors, but he had the frontier Boer's cast-iron courage. If you think of it, it needed a pretty stout heart to set out to find a thing the thought of which set every nerve quivering. I confess I didn't like to contemplate that lonely, white-faced, tormented boy. I think he knew that tragedy must be the end of it, but he had to face up to that and take the consequences.

He heard of Smit's expedition, and took a half share in it. Perhaps the fact that Smit had a baddish reputation was part of the attraction. He didn't want as companion a man with whom he had anything in common, for he had to think his own thoughts and follow his own course.

Well, you know the end of it. In his letter he said nothing about the journey, except that he had found what he sought. I can readily believe that the two did not agree very well—the one hungry for mythical treasure, the other with a problem which all the gold in Africa could not solve. . . . Somewhere, somehow, down in the Selati bushveld his incubus took bodily form, and he met—or thought he met—the thing which his impiety had released. I suppose we must call it madness. He shot his comrade, and thought he had killed an animal. "If they had looked next morning they would have found the spoor," he wrote. Smit's death didn't seem to trouble him at all—I don't think he quite realised it. The thing that mattered for him was that he had put an end to a terror and in some way made atonement. "Good-bye, and don't worry about me," were the last words, "I am quite content."

I sat a long time thinking, while the sun went down over the Magaliesberg. A gramophone was grinding away on an adjacent stoep, and the noise of the stamps on the Rand came like faraway drums. People at that time used to quote some Latin phrase about a new thing always coming out of Africa. I thought that it was not the new things in Africa that mattered so much as the old things.

I proposed to revisit that berg above the Pufuri and have a word with the priest, but I did not get a chance till the following summer, when I trekked down the Limpopo from Main Drift. I didn't like the job, but I felt bound to have it out with that old man for Andrew's sake. You see, I wanted something more to convince the Wakkerstroom household that the boy had not been guilty, as his father thought, of the sin of Cain.

I came round the corner of the berg one January evening after a day of blistering heat, and looked down on the cup of green pasture. One glance showed me that there was not going to be any explanation with the priest. . . . A bit of the cliff had broken away, and the rock fall had simply blotted out the grove and the *rondavel*. A huge mass of debris sloped down from half-way up the hill, and buried under it were the tall trees through which I had peered up at the sky. Already it was feathered with thorn-bush and grasses. There were no patches of crops on the sides of the cup, and crumbling mud walls were all that remained of the kraal. The jungle had flowed over the village, and, when I entered it, great moon flowers sprawled on the rubble, looking in the dusk like ghosts of a vanished race.

There was one new feature in the place. The landslip must have released the underground water, for a stream now flowed down the hollow. Beside it, in a meadow full of agapanthus and arum lilies, I found two Australian prospectors. One of them—he had been a Melbourne bank-clerk—had a poetic soul. "Nice little place," he said. "Not littered up with black fellows. If I were on a homesteading job, I reckon I'd squat here."

THE SLAVE BRAND OF SLEMAN BIN ALI

JAMES ANSON BUCK

IN THE MIDST OF her long and eventful life as a comic-book heroine, Sheena briefly appeared in the pulps, beginning with a one-off issue of *Stories of Sheena, Queen of the Jungle* in 1951. The magazine contained three long stories, all written by unknown writers under the house name James Anson Buck. Not only are these stories written in disparate styles, but details change as well, including the status of Sheena's pet ape, Chim, who becomes a small monkey after the first story. In addition to her own stories in the pulps, Sheena made a comeback in a single story in the Spring 1954 issue of *Jungle Stories.*

Sheena was created by the legendary comic artists Will Eisner and S. M. "Jerry" Iger, though which of them deserved the lion's share of credit for her remained in dispute their entire lives. Eisner has said that Sheena, in addition to being modeled on Tarzan, was also a natural extension of the queen (often referred to as "She-who-must-be-obeyed") in H. Rider Haggard's 1887 novel *She.* Sheena's first appearance was in a comic strip in the European tabloid *Wags,* in 1937; the following year she came to America in *Jumbo Comics.* She soon became the primary character in that comic book, appearing in all 167 issues before it expired in 1953. She also had her own comic for eighteen issues between 1942 and 1952. In addition to comics and pulps, Sheena was featured in twenty-six half-hour episodes of the syndicated television series *Sheena, Queen of the Jungle* (1955–1956) with Irish McCalla; a 1984 motion picture, *Sheena,* starring Tanya Roberts; and a more contemporary syndicated television series, *Sheena,* starring Gena Lee Nolin (2000–2002).

Each medium changed Sheena's background story a little, but certain elements are reasonably similar: Like Tarzan, she is an orphan in the jungles of Africa (okay, the film puts her in South America), she has a pet primate (variously an ape, a monkey, and a chimpanzee), and she is regarded as a "great white goddess," wise woman, queen, and protector who can make herself understood by both jungle animals and the various tribes of her region (the Belgian Congo in the pulps). Sheena's adversaries have included slave traders, rapacious white hunters or diamond smugglers, violent predatory tribes, ferocious jungle creatures, and natural disasters.

"The Slave Brand of Sleman Bin Ali" was first published in the first and only issue of the pulp magazine *Stories of Sheena, Queen of the Jungle,* in the spring of 1951.

THE SLAVE BRAND OF SLEMAN BIN ALI

JAMES ANSON BUCK

SHEENA STEPPED out of the pool. She shook out the wet veil of her golden hair and stood, statuesque, her bronzed beauty glowing in a shaft of amber sunlight. The warm ray caressed her, and swiftly drank the moisture from the shimmering veil. Then she flashed across the little clearing to the hut which stood on stilts, five feet above the crawling earth. Quickly she shrugged into leopard skin, and then came to stand in the doorway of the hut, looking out across the pool.

How still it was on these idle days under the thatched eaves of the little house. The pale fruit hung high on the ajap tree before the door, and, higher still, Chim, her pet ape, swung from branch to branch, performing amazing gymnastic feats, and scolding because she did not laugh and shout her approval. The twelve-hour tyranny of the sun was at its ebb, its violence done to the yellow earth of the clearing, and the arras of the forest hung breathless over its secret; for here, deep in the African Congo, was the holy dwelling place of Sheena, the Golden Goddess of the Jungle and all its tribesmen. Here no man had ever set foot, not even those whose escutcheon was white skin and who boasted the title, Bwana. Wise men knew better than to flaunt tribal taboos, and fools die quickly on the forbidden trails of the Congo jungle.

The rainy season was overdue, the heat oppressive in the little clearing even after sundown. Lightning flashed around the horizon, the thunder rolled like distant drums, and all nature waited in breathless suspense. But no rain fell and, though Sheena knew that it must make her forest home damp and depressing, she longed for it to come and break this brooding stillness, this tense waiting for something to happen.

It was a strange, new feeling that had beset her in this season, a feeling that incessantly grew out of her inner heart. She could no longer believe that it was entirely due to the weather. It was linked with the young trader who had come up to the Kuango post as surely as it was linked with his black, bearded companion.

Though no white man had set eyes upon Sheena, not one who came into her domain escaped her scrutiny. Always she liked to look closely into their faces when sleep had removed the mask of consciousness and showed the naked soul. Through their camps she stole, like a ghost in the dead of night. The trader, the hunter, explorer and missionary—she knew them all. Some were wise in the ways of exile, and came and went their ways; others went into the forest with a backward look, and came out with secret and stricken countenance. Sometimes one or another lingered too long in the jungle, and then, as the Abamas said: "He sent his heart into the dark," and built out of his lonely horror and the license of solitude a perverse habitation for his soul. Such men were dangerous, as deadly as the mamba.

And such a man was the Black-Bearded One, with gold rings in his ears. An evil face was his, with a cruel twist to the mouth even in repose.

But the young one, flung out on his canvas cot, bronzed chest and muscular limbs thinly veiled by mosquito netting, had not been hard to look at. Black curls against the white of his pillow, a strong face softened by some dream that made him smile in his sleep. Not so tall, perhaps, as Ekoti, chief of the Abamas, but then Ekoti was a giant of a man.

Was it the evil she had seen in the face of the one, or was it the disturbing which came when she thought of the other, that kept her in idleness beside this jungle pool?

She could not tell. The uncertainty made her moody and reawakened in her a craving for the trails long familiar to her—the trails that ever coiled and wound mysteriously around the mountains, down into the valleys, and through the dark forest. Chim dropped to the ground and then bounced up onto the floor beside her. She ran her hand through his black hair, and spoke softly what was in her mind:

"Soon the rain must come, little one. Tomorrow we will leave this place for the cave in the mountains."

Chim grimaced at her. They had never stayed in this place for so long before. He sensed his mistress's moodiness, and it made him feel bad. He could not keep still. He swung up into the ajap tree again, and sat scolding her in his comical way.

The sun sank behind the mountains, and shadows overflowed the clearing. The surrounding jungle was windless, yet full of hurried noises, and the sweet, lingering song of the bush cuckoos. Soon the drums, in the deep, absorbing silence of the forest so like the clicking of a giant telegraph, began to talk. At this hour, everywhere, the villages gave ear to the gossip of the jungle.

The drums were not of equal power, nor were their voices more alike than the voices of people are. Sheena never failed to locate a drum by its voice. In the old, primeval code all the facts of life had their phrases, all the adventures

and misadventures of the day their announcements; and no sovereign, despite the white man's magic, knew more of the hopes and fears of his people, or knew them sooner, than did Sheena, Queen of the Jungle.

"Your wife has borne a son!" one drum said. And somewhere on the veldt, or deep in the forest, a lone hunter paused to build a ritual fire, and give thanks to his gods. Then out of the darkness, as swift as an arrow aimed at her heart, Sheena heard her own ndan, her own drum name, and coupled with it was this phrase:

"Aku is dead. The Bearded One killed him. Come, cross his hands on his breast!"

And then there was a crying in the wilderness as one drum, and then another, and another, sobbed out the old, poignant call to mourning.

Under the immediate thrust of it all life in the clearing seemed to be arrested, and Sheena's heart was like a cold stone in her breast. Then, suddenly, she jumped to her feet, her hands clenched, her blue eyes blazing. So, they had dared to kill one of her people, a hunter brave and good. This was the thing her unquiet spirit had tried to warn her against. But she had not listened to the small voice within her. She had seen the evil in the face of the Bearded One, yet she had not sent Ekoti and his warriors to drive him out. No, she had not done that, because—because, in her heart there lurked a hidden wish to talk with the young one! Ah, but she was not deaf to the small voice now. Let the white men beware, soon they would meet Sheena face to face!

From a peg above her bed she snatched her quiver and bow; then sped down the moon-dappled trail to the Abama village, as light as dust, as swift as a cloud shadow over the veldt. From his perch in the ajap tree Chim saw her flash down the trail, and shrieked out his protest. To keep off the jungle trails at night was just plain monkey-sense.

At sunrise Sheena stood on a rocky eminence, looking toward the distant mountains, a superb figure with her hair streaming out in the hot wind from the southeast. The rippling veldt ran out to the foothills, and there were dark pools of shadow under the euphobia trees which pointed milky-jade fingers against the serene blue of the sky. But Sheena looked upon the familiar panorama, frowning, undeceived by its beauty. The creeks that wiggled across the plain were showing ripples of sun-baked mud, and there was the stench of decaying fish in the wind. The land was drying up under the furnace-heat of the sun, and the blistering wind from the desert. All the game was drifting south—the eland and the zebra in flashing stampede to avoid the lion and the leopard slinking on their flanks. If the rain did not come soon, it would be bad for her people who hunted and pastured their herds on this plain.

In the far distance the huts of the Abama village released smoke to smudge the blue of the sky. Swiftly she sped on.

The village surrounded a hill and straggled along the fast-drying river which looped around it like a great python. Sheena had been born among the Abamas, but not in this village. All she knew of her past had come to her from the lips of old N'bid Ela, the witch-woman of the tribe. And that was so long ago that it was hard to remember what the old woman had said. But sometimes, as now when she drew near to the village, a vivid picture of N'bid Ela would arise in her mind, and she would see the old woman strike the earth with her staff and drone:

"This and I—we are very old! Soon I go to the Black Kloof. Before I go, I have words for you. Your father and your mother were of the Tribe of God. Your skin is white, little one. You, too, are of the Tribe of God, and it is not good for you to play with black children. I will tell the people to build a hut for us in the forest. I will teach you my craft. Then, when I am gone, you will be their mata-yenda, their wise-woman, and they will obey you."

And so it had come to pass. For a long time she had lived in the forest, drinking of N'bid Ela's dark wisdom until she had sucked the fountain dry. And more beautiful and glowing in her youth she grew under the African sun every day. More than once N'bid Ela had taken her to the village, on the Day of Testing when the young men of the Abama clans gathered to prove their fitness for war and wedlock. In those contests no man had proved himself swifter on foot, or more deadly in his aim with the spear and the bow. The tale of her prowess and wisdom had been carried from kraal to kraal, so that now there were few village headmen who would have thought to venture upon any undertaking without having first consulted her.

At times she wondered at N'bid Ela's strange words. Since the Abamas called all missionaries Men of the Tribe of God, she supposed that her father had been a missionary. Beyond this she could not think. It was foolish to try, like tugging at a vine to which there was no fruit attached.

No one was moving on the dusty trails that criss-crossed the village. Goats lay panting in the shade of a grove of ironwood trees, and the birds perched above them held their wings fanwise to catch the air. The mushroom houses, shaggy with the thickest of palm-leaf thatch, crouched under the burden of sunlight, but in the palavar-house there was permanent dusk. The sudden glitter of copper ornaments was there, and the glitter of spear heads. Brilliant eyes set in dark faces, fantastic headdresses studded with buttons and shells and beads. The tumult and vehement gestures of controversy were there also—and then silence when Sheena came to stand among them.

Her eyes picked out Ekoti, the young chief of the Abamas. "My ears are open, Ekoti," she said.

"The white men sent a runner to our village," the chief said as he got to his feet, "because they wanted to trade with us. As you know, Sheena, we are great hunters and there is an ivory under every man's bed in this village. It seemed good to me that we should trade some of it for guns. And—"

"Why did you ask for guns?" Sheena interposed sharply.

Ekoti looked around him uneasily, then he took a deep breath and at length: "Nothing can be hidden from Sheena. I want the guns to go against the Arab's town. Long ago he drove our people. He drove our brothers, the M'Bama, stole many of their women and made slaves of their young men. If I think to make war against him, is it a bad thing?"

Sheena gave him a cold-eyed stare. "Perhaps," she said softly, "Ekoti thinks too much of war. Perhaps it is not good for him to be Chief of the Abamas."

A low murmur ran around the circle of elders, and Ekoti looked down at the ground. Not until the Jungle Queen smiled on him again would his grasp on the chieftainship be firm. For a time Sheena kept him in an agony of suspense, then suddenly she smiled:

"It is good for a man to speak his heart even though it betray his folly. Because your chief did this without fear, I am pleased with him. But in your fathers' time the Abamas, like foolish young bulls, rushed against the Arab's walls, and they broke their horns. Even if you had guns, the Arab would be too strong for you, Ekoti. Think no more of war with him. Now, go on with your story."

"I sent my uncle, Aku, with two hands of teeth to the trader's kraal," Ekoti took up his story. "I did this because once Aku was on safari with the Bearded One, and he knows the Swahili speech which the traders use. I sent only as many men as were needed to carry the ivory. Truly, my head was sick when I did that! The Bearded One would not give Aku guns. No, he cheated Aku. He offered only cloth and beads. This made Aku angry because he knew that the trader offered less for ten teeth—big teeth, I say—than a coast trader would give for one." He paused for breath, then went on:

"Then Aku would have left the trader's kraal, but the Bearded One would not let his men touch the ivory. There was a fight. The trader drove our people. Aku ran for the bush, but the Bearded One fired his gun and Aku fell. Then the trader's people rushed out and seized five of ours,

and took them into their kraal. Aku they took also. Doubtless, he is dead. Doubtless, too, the trader will kill the others if we go against him. Now, we ask you what we should do about this thing." He sat down, and all eyes were turned upon Sheena. She was silent for some time, then:

"Ekoti, you spoke only of the Bearded One. Where was the young Bwana when this evil was done?"

"We do not know, Sheena." He swept out his arm and muscles rippled under his black, satin skin. "All who came back sit here now. And they say that the young, white man was not there."

Sheena's smile came and went quickly.

Just for a moment it made her dark eyes shine in the dim light. It was a fleeting glimpse of the real woman behind the taboo which was always before her like a shield. Ekoti saw it and, shrewdly guessing what had prompted it, frowned darkly, and spoke a thought fathered by the wish:

"Perhaps he has gone down the river to the coast."

Sheena shook her head. "The drums would have spoken of it," she said, and then fell silent, her eyes clouded with thought. Minutes passed without a sound but the labored breathing of the old men. Then:

"The trader must be shown that he cannot shoot and cheat our people," she said. "We will drive him."

"Good! Good!" the elders approved in one voice. Only Ekoti looked dubious.

"How can we drive them, Sheena?" he asked. "Their kraal is strong. They have guns. Also, they have five of our people behind their fence."

The Jungle Queen smiled. "You are a warrior, Ekoti, and you have nothing in your head but spears and guns. Hear me now. You have much ivory, also. The Bearded One wants ivory, so you will make a big safari and take all your ivory to his place."

Ekoti's jaw sagged. For a long moment he stared at her in complete bewilderment. At last he gasped out: "Is it in your mind to give him the ivory in trade for our captured ones?"

Sheena laughed softly. "It is in my mind," she said, "to teach him, and you, a lesson, Ekoti. Obey me, and all will be well. Be ready to march at sunrise. Leave your spears behind. Let no man carry more than his knife. I have spoken."

"I hear, and obey," said Ekoti.

At the door of the palavar-house she turned suddenly and asked: "Do your wives still sew well, Ekoti?"

"Truly, Sheena."

"Good! I would talk with them now." Wearing an expression of profound puzzlement, Ekoti followed her out into the sunlight.

II

Tough trader and hunter that he was, Rick Thorne felt out of his depth in this isolated trading post on the Portuguese side of the Kuango river. It was not the heat, or the loneliness that bothered him—he was used to both. It was Lazaro Pero who had given him a bad case of the jitters. The Portuguese had a hair-trigger temper, and his bald head, inflamed by the African sun, his beady eyes, his hooked nose, combined to give him a predatory look, strongly suggestive of the bald-headed eagles that as a boy Rick had watched circling the buttes in far-off Montana. The worst of it was, he'd been warned against Pero's blind fits of rage before he had left the coast two months ago. And Pero was about through as senior agent up on the Kuango, according to the Chief Factor of the Companhia do Nayanda.

"His record is not good," Freire had told him when he had taken the job. "I will be frank. Senhor Pero has not asked for an assistant but I am sending you up to him. I want to know what is wrong up there, and I expect you to find out. And I will give you fair warning. Look out for yourself, senhor. Watch Pero, he is a devil of a man."

The Chief Factor had made it plain enough that he believed Pero was trading with the Company's goods on his own account. And, cer-

tainly, there was much in Pero's talk to justify that suspicion. From the first day of his arrival, it seemed to Rick, Pero had been sounding him out, hinting darkly at some clever scheme he'd worked out, a scheme that would make a bright young fellow who knew how to keep his mouth shut a rich man in a very short time.

And now there was this trouble with the Abamas. Why the devil had he chosen this day to go hunting? If the old Abama headman kicked off, there'd be hell to pay.

The post was quiet now, dozing in the late afternoon heat. The sky was cloudless, a shimmering, cobalt bowl, pouring withering fire down on the red earth of the compound. Pero was lounging in a cane chair, drinking gin.

"Where did you put that fellow?" Rick asked suddenly.

Pero pushed his glass out in the direction of one of the huts that faced the bungalow across the compound. "In there," he answered, and then added callously:

"He will die at sundown. They always do."

A muscle in Rick's jaw tightened, but he said evenly: "We're sitting on a powder keg, senhor. You'd better send those other fellows back to their village before—"

"I heard you the first time!" Pero snapped. "And I tell you again that I am in charge here. I give the orders." He touched the butt of his revolver. "If a black talks back, whip him; if he puts his hand on a weapon, shoot him. That's my rule. And when I give orders I make no distinction between white men and black men. Remember this, senhor, and you will not get hurt."

Rick's mouth was shaped to an oath as he turned on his heel and went into the main room of the bungalow. He went straight to the big medicine chest which stood over against the wall from the door. From it he took out his own first aid kit. When he straightened up Pero was standing in the doorway, his eyes narrowed to slits.

"What are you going to do with that?" he demanded.

"What I can for that poor devil you plugged," Rick told him calmly.

"Holy Saints!" Pero's face became charged with blood. "Did you not hear me tell you to keep away from him?"

Rick put the case down on the floor with slow deliberation. He considered Pero thoughtfully for a moment before he said: "I'm not a doctor, but I took a course in first aid at Luanda. And I'm not going to sit here and let that poor devil die just to please you."

"So!" Pero spat on the floor, then: "Just now I told you that I give the orders here." His hand went down to his holster, and then jerked up as he started back against the wall and froze to it. "Holy Saints!" he gasped.

At the first downward movement of his hand Rick's Colt had flashed from its holster as if by magic. Its muzzle pointed skyward, and the light glinting on its bright metal was reflected by his gray eyes.

"Any cowhand where I come from could teach you gunplay, senhor," he said quietly. "I don't know what you've got against that Abama out there, and I don't know why you blasted him. I do know that you'd better get rid of that gun. If you're packing it when I come back I'll take it to mean that you want to shoot it out."

The colt spun on his finger, and plopped snugly back into its holster. He picked up his case and walked across the room. The bravado had been shocked out of Pero. He kept his hands shoulder high and backed out of Rick's path.

The wounded Abama was stretched out on the dirt floor of the hut, with his face turned to the wall. Gently Rick rolled him onto his back and knelt to examine the wound. The native was badly hurt, unconscious. At a glance Rick saw that the deltoid muscle had been torn clean across near the right shoulder joint. The ends of the sinew had contracted, and if the man was to have the use of his right arm again the torn ends of the muscle must be pulled together expertly. It was a job beyond Rick's skill. The Abama groaned and opened his eyes as Rick probed and cleansed the wound. Fear came into his eyes, but faded as Rick patted his shoulder and smiled. Rick made things easier for him with a little opium and, as he bandaged the wound, the native said faintly in Swahili:

"It is hard to die so far from my village, Bwana."

"You will not die," Rick told him. "I will take you downriver to the mission station. What is your name?"

"Aku, Bwana."

"You speak good Swahili, Aku. Perhaps you have traded with Bwana Pero before?"

"Even so. Once I was his headman. I showed him the way to Kilma, the Arab's town."

Rick started so violently that the roll of bandage fell from his hand. He let it roll across the dirt floor, and asked: "You took ivory there, Aku?"

"Oh yes, Bwana! Big teeth we took there."

With a grunt of satisfaction Rick crawled after the roll of bandage. He saw it all now. Pero was selling ivory to Sleman bin Ali who could ship it down the Congo to the Belgian ports without arousing suspicion. He chuckled softly. Sleman bin Ali was a freebooter of the old school. He should have known from the start that if there was a crooked dollar to be made in the Congo the old sinner would be reaching for it. No wonder Pero had not wanted him to talk to Aku! At the thought his face sobered, and he said:

"Let no one know that you have told me this, Aku. You will not leave this place alive if you do." Then he thought that he'd better make sure of it, and he gave Aku a knockout dose of opium. "Rest now," he said. "I will come for you soon."

Pero was sitting on the rail of the verandah when Rick came back. If he had a gun it was nowhere to be seen. He tugged at his beard nervously as Rick came up the steps. Rick dropped into a cane chair and, tilting it back, rolled a cigarette with aggravating slowness.

"Well?" demanded Pero.

"He's got a good chance if he gets proper care. With your permission I'll take him down to São Vincente."

Sudden fear came into Pero's eyes. "So—to the mission, eh? What did he tell you?"

Rick shrugged, and said, "I doped him, and I'll have to keep him that way until he's over the shock. Besides, what could he tell me? I don't speak his dialect."

A gleam of satisfaction came into Pero's eyes. "Nothing, senhor—nothing!" he said with obvious relief. "I thought that perhaps you would blame me. Well, I am to blame. You see, I am just. I have a heart, too. Take him to São Vincente, my friend. Yes, and tell the good fathers that I will pay for everything."

Rick's slow smile quirked the corners of his mouth. "Well, that's generous," he said. "It won't be safe to move for a couple of days, though."

"Do not delay too long, my friend. Holy Saints, I have never known the rain to hold off for so long. In another week there will be enough water in the river to float a canoe, and it may be that you will have to come back on foot."

"Well, I'll have to take that chance," said Rick, frowning. "Right now the trip would kill the poor devil."

"You know best," said Pero. "When you are ready to go take Benji and five of my Swahilis. They know the river and will make a quick trip for you."

Rick was not particularly happy in the choice of Benji. Pero's headman was a civilisado, and his exaggerated idea of the privileges of Portuguese citizenship sometimes pushed him into downright insolence. But he wanted to keep Pero unsuspicious until he had Aku safe in the mission hospital, and raised no objection.

During the two days that followed two things began to worry Rick. One was the vague feeling of uneasiness that Pero's changed attitude gave him. There was something more than the fear of his Colt behind the Portuguese's sudden affability—something he couldn't fathom. The other worry was equally intangible, but so strong in its suggestion of brooding menace that it kept him pacing the verandah of the bungalow for long hours. It was the unnatural silence that had

come to the jungle. Not a drum throbbed at night, and not a native came in his canoe to barter his fish on the bamboo float which jutted out into the broad river. The post was isolated, the natives avoiding it as if it were the center of a plague.

On the morning of the third day he stood on the verandah looking upstream. The river was falling, and from the exposed ooze, baking in the sun, came the effluvia of decay and corruption. Beyond the first bend of the river there was no vista, only the unlimited expanse of the jungle, looking more gray than green, without form or perspective, silent, foreboding. The bamboo jetty was still afloat, but he doubted that it would be tomorrow. He decided to leave for São Vincente at sundown.

He went into the bungalow to announce his decision to Pero, but before he could get the words out of his mouth a sudden commotion broke out in the compound. Then Benji came running to the veranda steps.

"Safari, Bwana!" he shouted at Pero. "Big safari!"

Both white men ran out onto the verandah and saw many paddles flashing in the sun. Soon the black shapes of a dozen big dugouts could be seen moving rapidly downstream, the beat of a drum timing the rhythmical stroke of the paddles. Strung out in a long, slanting line they came lurching toward the float. As the first canoe slid alongside, three big natives leaped out of it. Four others immediately began to pass out the canoe's cargo into the hands of their fellows on the float. In a moment a half-dozen prime tusks lay at their feet. Another canoe shot alongside, and another, and another, and the same process was repeated. Pero's eyes bulged as the pile of coffee-brown tusks grew larger and larger.

"Holy Saints!" he cried out at last. "Not one under forty pounds!" In his excitement he slapped Rick on the back, "Senhor," he exclaimed, "all my life I have dreamed that something like this might happen to me! Ho, Benji! Open the gates! Break out a keg of rum for our guests! Don't stand there gaping, you black scum, jump to it!" Again he slapped Rick's back. "That's the trick of it, senhor, all there is to it! Get 'em dead drunk, treat 'em like fidalgos and they'll trade a prime tusk for a coil of copper wire."

"They'll catch up with you one of these days," Rick told him with a shake of his head.

A long file of blacks was moving up the steep trail to the gates; not all of them shouldered an ivory, but Rick counted thirty-six. He did a little mental arithmetic, and whistled at the total. There was close to a hundred thousand dollars walking up that trail, or he didn't know a prime tusk when he saw one! Then his attention was drawn to the last canoe to reach the float. Four big blacks, one of them a gigantic fellow wearing the headdress of a chief, were lifting something out of it—something sewn up in a hammock of skins. With a puzzled expression he watched the four set the hammock down on the float carefully and run a stout bamboo pole through the lashings looped around it. Then they lifted it shoulder high, and came jogging up the trail.

"What d'you suppose they've got there, Pero?" he wondered. But the Portuguese was out in the compound, driving his crew of Swahilis to work. The doors of the big trade shed were swung open. Soon every man was rolling out kegs, breaking open bales of cloth and stacking them on the shelves that lined three sides of the huge shed. They moved fast under the lash of Pero's tongue and the sting of Benji's cane.

III

As the leading files of the safari passed into the compound Pero came back to the verandah to receive its headman. There was none of the clamor and excitement that usually turned the post into a pandemonium upon the arrival of a caravan. The bearers quietly deposited their ivories on the ground in front of the bungalow; then, as if at an unseen signal, as quietly they all trooped across the compound to form a solid phalanx before the open doors of the trade shed, and stood silently watching the busy, sweating Swahilis within. Observing this maneuver, Rick's eyes widened in sudden alarm. He touched Pero's arm and said quietly:

"We've got trouble. These fellows aren't porters, they're warriors!"

But Pero could not take his eyes from the ivory. "Nonsense!" he muttered. "There's not a spear among them, and—Holy Saints, what is this?" He broke off pointing as Ekoti and his warriors set their burden down at the foot of the verandah steps.

As if in answer to his question the Abama chief drew his knife, and threw a quick look around the compound. Then he ripped open the seam of the skin bundle, and Sheena burst from it, like a gorgeous butterfly from its chrysalis.

Bow in hand, poised to draw and shoot, she faced the two dumbfounded white men. At a nod of her golden head, Ekoti bellowed out a command. The Abamas near the shed dashed forward, threw their weight against the doors and swung them shut, trapping every man the post could muster within.

Sheena's blonde beauty held Rick spellbound. Pero was the first to recover from the shock of it all. He gasped:

"A raid! Your gun, senhor! Holy Saints—" He started to run for the door of the bungalow, evidently with his own gun in mind.

"Hold!" said Sheena, in a clear ringing voice. At the same instant her bow twanged. The arrow plunged into the door post just ahead of Pero, and he pulled up with his hooked nose touching the quivering shaft.

"Be still!" commanded the Jungle Queen. With her eyes fixed on the young trader she notched another arrow. He appeared to be shaking the stupefaction that had taken possession. He passed his hand before his eyes, shook his head, and muttered something in a tongue she did not know. He was almost as tall as Ekoti, and his eyes were very bold when open. There was no fear in them, but something else was there— a gleam that pleased her and yet made it hard to give him stare for stare. He seemed to sense her discomfiture; for a slow smile came to his lips, and he said in Swahili:

"Lady, I have seen many strange things, but never a thing as strange as your coming—or a thing as beautiful as I see now. It cannot be that you have come to steal like a bushman."

"Why like a bushman?" she flashed at him. "Why not like a white trader? They are the great thieves. Your friend has killed one of my people, and he has taken five others. I know that you were not here when this was done, and that is well for you, Brass Eyes!" She shifted her gaze to the Bearded One, and her blue eyes snapped at him. "Are you as ready to die as you are to kill?" she asked.

He made a queer animal noise in his throat, and his fear oozed out of him like a smelly sweat. His eyes darted frantically around the compound, but could find no way of escape. He could not speak, so great was his fear; and his eyes held the dumb pleading look of a sick dog when he turned them on his young companion. Brass Eyes spoke for him:

"Aku is not dead, Lady. This man has done evil, but he is sorry for it. Is it not the custom of these—of your people to hold a palaver when a wrong has been done to them? My friend is willing to talk, to pay whatever you ask."

Sheena regarded him steadily for a time. He was not afraid, this one, and it was only fear that made men lie.

"Where is Aku?" she demanded.

He pointed to one of the huts. And, at a nod of her head, Ekoti sped across the compound to it. Not a word was spoken until he returned.

"He speaks the truth, Sheena," Ekoti reported in a low voice. "Aku speaks well of the young Bwana. There is some trouble between him and the other, but Aku does not know what it is."

"Good!" said Sheena. "Seize the Bearded One, and then search all the huts for guns."

The Bearded One shrank back as Ekoti mounted the verandah steps, and the young one looked as if he would show fight. She laughed

softly, and then said: "Be still, Brass Eyes. We are too many for you, and it is no longer in my mind to kill your friend. We will talk now, you and I."

Pero yelped as Ekoti took hold of him. He struggled, trying to pull away from the Abama chief's iron grasp.

"Senhor!" he appealed to Rick. "Help me— Holy Saints, you cannot let this she-devil—"

"Better go quietly, Pero," Rick told him. "You've been asking for something like this for—"

"Speak Swahili!" Sheena told him sharply.

Then Ekoti lost patience with the twisting and screaming Portuguese. He hit him once, then heaved Pero's limp body over his shoulder like a dead buck. He stepped aside as Sheena came up the steps and went into the bungalow.

The young one followed her in. She was conscious of his eyes. They never left her as she glided across the room and sat in one of the cane chairs. He came to a stand, looking down at her, his gaze disconcertingly warm.

"Lady," he said with his slow smile, "when I saw you first I thought that I was dreaming. Even now I am not sure that I am awake."

"Are women with white skins so strange to you?" She held his gaze as the snake holds the bird's that it will soon devour. And suddenly she knew that she had power over this man, and yet there was a recklessness, a wildness in him that she could not help but see. Here was a spirit as strong and free as her own. She had the power to stir him, even to control him with her smiles, but he would not tremble at her frown as Ekoti did. To make this one her slave she would have to share the burden of his chains.

"Who are you?" he asked in his wonderment. "Where do you come from?"

"I am Sheena. That is enough for you, Brass Eyes."

"Brass Eyes is not my name," he told her, frowning. "I am Richard Thorne, hunter, trader, anything so long as it keeps me on the move. Call me Rick, it will make it easier for me to believe my eyes."

"Rick—Rick," she repeated the name and smiled, then: "It is a little name to give such a big man." Then her face sobered, and she asked: "Tell me why I should not take all the trade goods here and give them to my people? The Bearded One has wronged and cheated them. Would it not be just?"

"No!" he answered promptly. "It would not because the goods do not belong to the Bearded One. Lazaro Pero is his name. The goods belong to the Company I work for, and taking them will do Pero no harm. Listen, Lady—"

"Sheena."

"Well then, Sheena. Now I will tell you about Pero . . ."

She listened to all he had to say, and liked the deep, resonant tones of his voice. When he stopped talking she was silent, turning it all over in her mind. Suddenly she asked:

"This man you hunt for, he will think well of you if you send all the ivory my people brought in down the river to the coast?"

He gave her a startled look, then his slow smile came. "Truly, he would think well of me," he said. "He would think me a prince among traders."

"Good! Then I will tell Ekoti to make fair trade with you. I do this because of what you will do for Aku."

"I would do it for any man," he said. "We leave at sundown, as I have said." Then his eyes became troubled, and he asked: "What about Pero?"

"Have no fear for him. As you say, it is best to give him up to his own people for punishment. He knows nothing, and Ekoti will make fair trade with him while you are downriver. Also, Ekoti will watch this place until you come back. Do as you will with Pero then. Now, I go." She rose in a swift, lithe movement and moved to the door. He sprang to intercept her.

"Where are you going?" he asked, and caught hold of her arm. "You can't walk in and out of my life like this!"

At the touch of his hand she felt her heart jump, then she stiffened and thrust him back. "Are you weary of life?" she lashed at him. "No man may touch me. If my people saw your hand on me their spears would drink your blood!"

The unexpected strength behind the thrust of her arm had thrown him back several paces, and the look that came to his face was almost funny in its expression of complete astonishment.

"What are—who—what the devil—" He gulped, and stared at her, speechless. She laughed softly, then turned and left him, still staring.

At sundown, from behind a screen of bush, she watched Rick and his men carry Aku down to the river on a mat of woven grass.

When the canoe was an amorphous blur on the yellow water, in a mood compounded of nameless yearnings and a strange feeling of emptiness, she took the trail back to her forest sanctuary.

Rick made good time downriver, arriving at São Vincente a little before sundown two days later. The town was typical of the Portuguese frontier—a cluster of flat-roofed, pink-and-whitewashed adobe houses, clinging to the river bank with the indefatigable jungle pushing at them from behind. The mission of Carmelite friars was a stone building with castellated walls, and cool arched corridors shaded by palms.

While Aku was installed in the hospital, Rick chatted with a plump, worldly-looking brother of the order.

"Christian charity is rare in these parts," said the monk. "You have done an act of mercy for which God will reward you, my son."

"Well," smiled Rick, "there are a lot of black marks against me up there, Father. I'll be lucky if I get a cancellation on this. And, by the way, have you ever heard any talk of a white woman—a sort of goddess—up on the Kuango?"

"Oh, yes! The natives are full of such tales.

But it is wise to believe in such marvels only when we see them, my son."

"And it is not always wise to talk of the marvels we see, eh, Father?"

"Not if we wish to be thought truthful, my son."

"That's how I figure it," murmured Rick. Then: "Well, I must leave tonight. It is my wish to pay for Aku's care now."

The monk chuckled. "Ah, you are a jewel. Nothing is asked, nothing is expected, but a gift is always thrice blessed," he added as Rick pressed a small bag of coins into his hand. "God go with you, my son!"

The Kuango was falling rapidly now. A few miles above the town Rick, Benji and his four Swahilis were forced to abandon their heavy canoe. They continued the trek on foot, through the scented cedar forest and across the burnt veldt.

Herds of zebra thundered southward, the scent of greener pastures strong in their nostrils. The natives were leaving their villages, trekking for São Vincente in anticipation of famine.

Short rations forced Rick to shoot for the pot, and the heat forced him to short, night marches. A trek of no more than three marches under normal conditions dragged out to six, and it was near noon on that day when he marched into the Kuango factory.

The post was deserted. The compound empty.

After the first shock of it was over, Rick soothed the fears of his jabbering Swahilis.

"There has been no fighting, Benji. Bwana Pero must have marched downriver with the ivory."

"Doubtless he has marched with the ivory!" The headman spat on the ground. "But not down to São Vincente," he added with a vehemence that caused Rick to give him a sharp look. But the Swahilis were crowding around them with bulging eyes, and he only said:

"Come to the bungalow, Benji. We will talk of this."

Papers littered the floor of the main room, and the storeroom had been rifled. Pero had taken all his small safari could carry, plus the ivory. But there were several cases of canned food left. Also a dozen muskets stood in the rack, and there was powder and shot. Looking around, Rick wondered vaguely why Pero hadn't set fire to the post. He supposed that it was because Pero had wanted to get away quietly without attracting the attention of the native villages. But what had happened to the Abamas and Sheena who had said they would watch the post?

Then a crushing sense of defeat twisted his mouth awry with a grimace of self-deprecation, and drove everything else from his mind. Freire had sent him up to watch Pero, and Pero had walked out of Kuango with a hundred thousand dollars' worth of ivory—taken it right from under his nose! He could hear the old timers chuckling over it—"Did you hear about the fast one that dango, Pero, pulled on young Thorne up at Kuango—" No, not that!

No man could make a monkey out of Rick Thorne and get clean away. Anger so intense that it whitened his lips and made his hands shake swept over him. By thunder, he'd get that ivory back. He'd get it back if he had to turn the Congo jungle upside down and shake it out! He swung around to face Benji.

"You know where Bwana Pero has taken the ivory!"

Benji's insolent eyes became fixed on a square bottle of gin which stood on a table under the window. Rick poured out a brimmer and the headman swallowed it in a gulp.

"Well?" Rick prompted him.

"Bwana," Benji began, "before you came I counted the teeth. Sometimes the number that came in and the number that went downriver was not the same. But when I told Bwana Pero about it he only cursed me for a fool and said I could not count right. Once he flogged me, so I spoke of it no more. But I am not stupid, and I have eyes."

"Are they sharp enough to find the road to Kilma, Benji?"

"I know the road, Bwana. But we are only six. What can we do against Sleman bin Ali?"

"I'll think of that when I get there. All I want you to do is show me the road." He unslung his rifle and handed it to Benji. "Is this a good gun?" he asked.

"Oh yes, Bwana!" said Benji, handling the rifle lovingly.

"It is yours, if you show me the road to Kilma. Also, I will give a musket to each of your men, and powder and shot. Will they go?"

"Oh yes! They will march with me. What else can they do?"

"At sundown then, Benji."

"At sundown, Bwana!"

IV

Up in the hills, far beyond the village, Sheena paused to listen to an Abama drummer. She frowned as the drum spoke her ndan, and then split into accurate lengths of tumult the quiet of the jungle. In less time than it would have taken to speak the words she knew what had happened to Rick Thorne, knew that he was already two marches beyond the Kuango. Her first reaction was anger, and her wrath was turned against Ekoti who had dared to disobey her, who had failed to watch the post until Rick's return, as she had told him to do. Her next thought was of Rick. Truly, he was a reckless young fool, yet splendid in his folly marching against Sleman bin Ali and all his guns with only six men!

And Ekoti's fault was hers. She had promised Rick that she would watch the post and his enemy. A fool he surely was, but she could not let him march to his death because of Ekoti's disobedience. It was unthinkable. She must help Rick. But how? She could not overtake him. Another day's march would take him deep into Sleman bin Ali's country. And the half-Arab understood drum-talk, and he would send out men to capture Rick. Well then, Sleman bin Ali had been a thorn in the Abamas' side for a long

time. Perhaps now was the time to deal with him. Surely there was a way.

She sat down on a rock to think about it and Chim was suddenly quiet. He came to sit beside her, his chin cupped in his hands, imitating his mistress's pose—a grotesque caricature of blonde beauty wrapped in thought.

It was a long time before Sheena's eyes brightened and a faint smile of satisfaction came to her lips. There was a way, there was always a way if she thought about it long enough. But first she must punish Ekoti. With feline grace she rose and spoke to Chim:

"Fill your belly, little one. We must travel far and fast."

When the heat waves slid down to evening and the sunlight lay in broken fragments on the village trails, Sheena's call summoned Ekoti from his hut. Alone in the semi-dark of the palavar-house, Sheena confronted him.

"You did not obey me!" she accused him at once.

But Ekoti did not look down at the ground, nor did he squirm under the cold, angry glare of her blue eyes. His face maintained an expression of impassive innocence. And presently he said:

"Do not be angry with me, Sheena. I obeyed. I watched the trader's kraal until I could stay no longer. Four days I watched, but the young Bwana did not come, and—"

"Why did you leave? Why?" the furious girl demanded.

"Because the game left the country, Sheena. Our cooking pots were empty. We are hunters. We must follow the game. Soon I must lead my people south because of this. We cannot stay in this place. Turn your anger against the Arogi, against the witches who hold back the rain. Am I to be blamed for what they do?"

There was a long pause, and then a deep sigh of relief came from Ekoti's lips as he saw the angry light in the Jungle Queen's eyes slowly fade.

"You are not to be blamed," she said. And Ekoti's strong, filed teeth flashed in a broad grin. "Now I will speak of another thing," she went on. "Tomorrow we march south against the Arab's town."

The grin faded from Ekoti's face and his expression settled into one of utter bewilderment. Presently he gave tongue to it: "It is a thing unheard of!"

"Are you afraid, Ekoti?"

"No!" roared the exasperated chief. "I do not fear the Arab, and well you know it! But when I would have gone against him with guns you called it foolish. And now you would go against him with spears. And at such a time."

"Have I said that I will go against him with spears only!"

"Truly, you did not say so. But without guns or spears the thing cannot be done."

"Do not say of the ajap tree in fruit," she told him quietly, "that it bears nothing but leaves. Did you not think the same thing when I said I would drive the Bearded One? Do as I say now and all will be well."

Ekoti was silent for a long time, his face set in grave lines; then: "Always the Abamas have obeyed you, Sheena. It is well for us to obey. We would be nothing without you, our enemies would have eaten us up long ago. We will obey you now. But for my people I ask why we must do this thing?"

"Because Sleman bin Ali is our enemy, and because I fear that he will do harm to the young Bwana who is our friend."

"Aie, aie!" rumbled Ekoti. "It is as I thought. I think back to the village where we were born, Sheena. My heart sings at the memory of the days when we played together, and learned to shoot with the bow. Aie, they were good days! I speak of them now because there is a thing that troubles my mind, and when I say what is in my mind I know that it will make you angry."

"Truly, they were good days, Ekoti. I have not forgotten them. Speak and do not fear my anger."

A dubious smile changed the young chief's eyes. Then, as when a man is about to plunge into a cold mountain stream, he took a deep breath and said, "I speak of a thing I saw in the young Bwana's eyes when he looked at you, Sheena. If we find him alive it will be a good thing for him to leave this country."

"So!" Her blue eyes kindled.

"Even so, because if he tries to take you away the Abamas will kill him. They would do so because they love you, also because of the taboo of N'bid Ela. It is strong magic. Even stronger than you, Sheena. You could not save the young Bwana, if my people thought that you would go away with him." And, having spoken his mind like a man, Ekoti braced himself, as if he expected the roof of the palavar-house to fall on his head.

But the storm did not break. No one knew better than Sheena the fatal power of imagination working through superstitious fear. It was taboo that gave her the power to command. And something more she had. The love of these simple jungle folk who, during her helpless infancy, had cherished her as one of their own. Never had she felt the sting of a blow, never an unkind rebuke. Her hand fell lightly on Ekoti's shoulder.

"You have spoken well, Ekoti," she said softly. "Now I tell you: I will leave the Abamas and this forest when the leaves of the majuti trees fall."

The saying caught Ekoti's fancy. He left the palavar-house chuckling over it deeply, for no man ever had seen the leaves of a majuti tree fall. It was evergreen.

Rick and his little band toiled upward onto the parklands of the M'bama plateau, following the dry bed of a river that stank like a sewer in the sun. It was undulating country with wild and fantastically broken scenery—deep kloofs and granite kopjies alternating with wooded hills, some densely covered with mimosa bush.

That night Rick's tent was pitched in a little clearing overlooking the south-curving valley of the Silma. The dry spell had reduced even this considerable tributary of the Kuango to a miserable thread of water, meandering through cracks in the sun-baked clay of its bed. Soon cooking fires flared against the black velvet of the night. The silence of the surrounding jungle was compounded of sounds seldom separately recognizable, but for the droning of the cicadas, which came rasping through the aisles of the trees, and gave a knife edge to the heat.

When the late meal was over Benji left his companions and came to squat at Rick's fire. Rick watched him fill his wide nostrils with snuff, his eyes narrowed with thought. From little things Benji had let drop, Rick had drawn the conclusion his headman knew more of Pero's activities than he chose to tell. Moreover, he suspected that Benji was working toward some dark end of his own, or he surely would have quit after the first day of this hard, dry trek.

"Kilma is one day's march from here, Bwana," Benji announced suddenly. "Its chief is a half-Arab called Sleman bin Ali."

"That I know," said Rick.

"In the old days," Benji went on as if he had not heard Rick, "Sleman bin Ali came into this country with a big caravan. A Zanzibari merchant sent him, but Sleman did not come back with ivory, or with the merchant's goods. No, he drove the M'bamas who lived here. He killed many and made slaves of others. Then he made them build Kilma, and he made himself chief of this country. He has many men and many guns. I tell you this, Bwana, because, now that we are close to his town, I wonder what you are going to do."

"You might well wonder," said Rick with a wry smile.

Benji chuckled. "So you have thought of nothing. I wonder, also, what you would do with the ivory if you got it back, Bwana."

"The Company would pay well, Benji."

The headman spat into the fire. "The Company would pat you on the shoulder and say, 'Good boy! Good boy!' I know the Company! Truly, they would not give you as much as we could sell it for across the border at Bampo."

Rick smiled. So that was it! Pero had an apt pupil in Benji. And Benji needed him for some-

thing or he would have kept his plans to himself. He said: "First we must get the ivory. How are we to do that?"

Benji grinned insolently. "For half of it I will tell you that."

You're in bad company, young feller! Rick told himself. One gun against five. Better take it slow and easy, shake this jasper down for all he's got. Aloud he said:

"It is agreed, Benji. For half of it."

"Good. You do well to agree, Bwana, as you will see." He leaned forward. "Listen now. When the rain comes and Pero can get porters he will make a caravan and march for Bampo. It is five marches from Kilma, and we—"

"We cannot ambush a caravan with six guns," Rick interposed with quick comprehension.

"True, Bwana. But there is a M'bama village nearby. They do not love Sleman bin Ali. They will make a trap for the caravan if one of the Company's Bwanas tells them to do so. Oh yes, it will be easy—" He broke off suddenly, straightened up, and stood looking from right to left.

"What is it?" asked Rick.

Benji motioned him to silence. There was a faint rustling sound which might have been taken by a careless ear for the wind passing through the grass. But to Benji's quick ear it was something else. He was reaching for his rifle when flame spurted out of the surrounding darkness.

Benji pitched forward across the fire without a cry. Rick's Colt roared a split second after the report of the musket. He had fired at the flash of the gun, and a yelp and the sound of a body crashing through the bush told him that he had not missed. He flung himself on the ground and rolled out of the firelight. He could see nothing, but there was the rustle of movement all around him. Benji's men stood bathed in the light of their fire, motionless, fearing to move lest a volley be poured into them by the invisible raiders.

Lazaro Pero's voice came harshly out of the

blackness. "You are surrounded! Throw down your gun, senhor!"

Rick threw down his gun. Dark shapes crept out of the bush, hemming him in. Pero pushed through them into the pool of firelight. He rolled Benji's body over with his foot, and said:

"I knew this fool would follow me but I did not think you would be so stupid, senhor. Holy Saints, what a man you would be if you were as quick with your brain as you are with your gun. Perhaps you came to shoot it out with me, eh, Senhor Cowboy?"

"All right," said Rick from between clenched teeth. "You can shoot when you damn well please, and—"

"Kill you?" Pero shook his head. "I see no reason to kill you. No, I will take you to Kilma. My good friend Sleman bin Ali will keep you there until I am clear of this cursed country. Then he will send you down to the coast, and you can tell that fat pig, Friere, what happened to his ivory. A good joke on him, eh? I deeply regret that I shall not be there to see his face when you do tell him. Holy Saints!" He slapped his thigh, and laughed until the tears ran down his cheeks.

Rick wondered if it was worth risking a blast from the guns that bristled around him just to hit Pero once.

Pero wiped his eyes with the back of his hand. "And they sent you to watch me," he gasped. "How such people get rich, I do not understand. Ah, but I see that all this is very painful for you, senhor. Forgive me for making a fool of you also. But enough." He gave a sharp order.

His Swahilis closed around Rick. His hands were bound, a rope was looped around his neck. The order to march was given and, cursing fluently, he stumbled through the darkness on the heels of the man who tugged at the rope about his neck.

V

It was a long weary trek up onto the M'bama country. Day after day the Abamas padded their way along the old, tribal trails. Lean, hungry warriors ranged on the flanks of the long, straggling line of old men, women and children. And it was a lucky man who brought in meat for his wife to roast. The game was far south. The villages along their route were deserted: a cluster of huts and gardens with the dry stalks of the guinea-corn crackling in the hot wind, the true forest, a deserted clearing, a stretch of true forest again. In the clearings the sunlight was a river of fire between the walls of the forest. The jungle was not strong but it was close, the way narrow, and broken light and broken color beat up into their eyes, so that the women and children and the old ones were weary after a short time of such going. The pace was slow.

There was corn and cassava to be gleaned from the neglected gardens, but such sop did not sit well on Abama stomachs. They were hunters and warriors, and jilo, the meat hunger, gnawed hard at their bellies.

Far ahead of the main body Sheena, Ekoti and Chim stood on a kopji, overlooking the valley of the Silma.

"It is bad," said Ekoti. "Soon there will be no water. We should follow the game to the lake, I think."

"There is water and meat in Kilma," Sheena told him.

"There are walls and guns at Kilma also," growled Ekoti. "It cannot be that you think the Arab will open his gates to the Abama."

"He will open them," said the Jungle Queen confidently. Suddenly she tensed, peering ahead into the heat haze which danced and shimmered before her, rendering visibility close to zero. A group of vultures wheeled in perfect grace over the painted woods. A copper armband flashed in the sun as she pointed and said:

"See yonder!"

"Aie, meat!" exclaimed Ekoti, uttering the thought uppermost in his mind.

But another thought had flashed into Sheena's mind at first sight of the scavenger birds. With an involuntary cry of mingled fear and anger, she sped down the hillside, her golden hair streaming in the wind behind her. Chim went bounding after her, the Abama chief in his wake. But neither could match the flashing speed of the Jungle Queen. Both were soon left far behind.

At any other time Sheena would have approached the spot with utmost care, knowing well that some beast must have driven the vultures from their obscene feast. But in her fear for Rick, in her anxiety to be rid of it, or to know the worst, she forgot caution and burst suddenly into the clearing. She got a fleeting glimpse of the leopard crouched over the remains of Benji's body, and then spotted, snarling fury came hurtling at her. But in Sheena the incredible swiftness of the feline beast was combined with the intelligence of man, with a brain as swift and clear as a mountain stream. For Sheena knew no fear of man or beast.

Unlike the hunted creatures of the jungle whose survival depends on the split-second response to the impulse of flight, she did not swerve in her stride but launched herself in a dive under the leopard's white belly. The beast struck downward with one paw as it flashed over her. Its razor-edged claws combed her hair, and her quiver of arrows was torn from her right shoulder. The leopard's spring carried it halfway across the clearing and, as its forepaws touched the earth, Sheena sprang to her feet and whirled to face it.

The baffled beast crouched, tail lashing the ground, yellow eyes fixed on the blonde goddess in an unwinking glare. Sheena's leopard skin had been ripped from her shoulder. The beast's claws had grazed her flesh, and a thin trickle of blood ran down her exposed right breast. Her bow was in her hand, but her quiver lay on the ground, out of reach. She dared not move, or take her eyes from the half-starved animal which, flat on its belly, was now edging toward her, inch by inch. Her hand slid down to her knife, the leopard's lean flanks quivered, and a snarl bared its fangs as it prepared to spring. And just then Chim came bouncing into the

clearing. He came in behind the leopard, saw it, and let out an almost human scream, then leaped for the nearest tree.

Startled by the cry the leopard whirled around to confront the new foe. In that instant, in one fluid motion the Jungle Queen pounced on her quiver. The beast sensed, rather than saw, the movement. As quick as a flash it turned, a tawny blur in a swirl of dust and dry leaves, and sprang. Sheena's bow twanged just as it left the ground. She leaped aside as the big cat twisted in the air, then fell on its back, rolling over and over, snarling and biting at the arrow driven into its chest. Then Ekoti came panting into the clearing and a thrust from his leaf-bladed spear put a swift end to the beast's struggle.

When he looked around Sheena was moving up wind from the grisly remains of Benji's body, the beauty of her face marred by a grimace of disgust.

"Enough is left," she said, "to tell that his skin was black."

"Many men camped here," Ekoti observed, looking over the ground. "The spoor is not cold, see!" He squatted, pointing to boot-prints on a patch of sandy soil. "Two white men and many black fellows."

They followed the spoor until Sheena was satisfied that it would lead them to Kilma; then she said:

"I go on. You go back to your people. Tell your warriors that Sheena says that there is meat for them at Kilma."

Ekoti rubbed his wooly head. He was a warrior, and he was no man's fool, but for the life of him he could not see how his spearmen could break into Kilma, and his puzzlement was profound. But what Sheena said could not be doubted. Though he had played with her as a child, and though, outwardly, she appeared to be as other women, he had never doubted that she was something more than mortal, and possessed of powers quite beyond his comprehension. There was conviction and awe in his face when he said:

"I think that I will see a great magic at Kilma."

Famine and death surrounded Kilma. The rinderpest had come in the wake of the prolonged drouth, and on the plains vultures gorged themselves on the carcasses of dead cattle, spreading their wings as they reached their ugly heads into the fetid mass, their wing tips and breast feathers greasy with fat. But within the mud-walled town itself there was plenty. Its stilted, thatched-roofed silos were full of grain, and a subterranean stream bubbled into its wells, and fed the fountain in the sequestered gardens of Sleman bin Ali's house.

Like most native African towns, all of which seemed to have the Zulu kraal, with its boma of thorn-bush as impenetrable as a barbed-wire entanglement for their prototype, Kilma had two gates, one facing the other at opposite ends of a broad, central road. The walls encompassed an area of not more than five acres, and into this space was crowded, haphazardly, an unbelievable number of adobe houses with a maze of narrow lanes twisting among them. Sleman bin Ali's house fronted on the main road, and its high-walled garden, with its pond and fountain, green grass and heavy-scented hibiscus and jasmine, was like an oasis in a desert of smells that made Rick shudder whenever he set foot outside the arched gate which gave onto the dusty road.

He was allowed the freedom of the town. Famine was his gaoler, and it was Lazaro Pero's gaoler also; for until the rain came the long trek across the border to Bampo was an impossible undertaking. Sleman bin Ali had given Rick a room in his own house, and often he took his meals with the venerable half-Arab who looked more like a saint than the old rogue he undoubtedly was. After his fashion, Ali was a devout man, strict in his observance of the letter, if not spirit, of the precepts set forth in the Koran; and his long white beard, the spotless, white robe and the austerity he affected were so strongly suggestive of the Biblical patriarch that Rick doubted that it was wholly unconscious. He was a courteous and generous host, and that made it easy to forget his crimes and cruelties.

As the days wore on and still the rain did not come, Pero fumed and fretted. Rick avoided him; for whenever they met the Portuguese never failed to jibe at him, to remind him that soon he must go back to the coast and tell Freire how Lazaro Pero had so cleverly tricked him out of a small fortune in ivory.

The whereabouts of the ivory had puzzled Rick from the first day of his arrival in Kilma. There was no building in the town large enough to hold it. He knew that it had long been the custom of native chiefs to bury their hoards to protect them from the rapacity of well-armed raiders; and, finally, he came to the conclusion that the ivory must be cached somewhere out in the hills surrounding the town.

Toward sundown on the fifth day of his stay at Kilma a tribe of natives swarmed down from the hills onto the plain. From the flat roof of Sleman bin Ali's house Rick watched them pour out of a narrow gap in the hills and debouch onto the veldt to cut a black swath through the tall, feathery spear-grass. Pero stood beside Sleman bin Ali, who had an old, brass telescope clamped to one eye. Suddenly the Arab exclaimed:

"Merciful Allah! It is that daughter of Shaitan, Sheena."

"Sheena! Surely you are mistaken, my friend!" said Pero. "What would she want of us? Not the ivory. The trade was fair."

Sleman bin Ali's eyes slanted in Rick's direction as he handed the telescope to Pero. "Wallai," he said, "you are a great fool if you cannot guess what she has come for!"

"Holy Saints, who would have thought of that!" muttered Pero in his beard; then: "They have no guns, a volley will drive them off."

"No!" said the Arab sharply. "If they do not attack, we do no shooting. It may be that she wants only our young friend here. By Allah, if that be all, she can have him! I want no trouble with that she-devil. See, they make camp." He turned, shouting for one of his slaves. A M'bama boy answered his call, and Sleman said: "Go tell Ahmed to double all guards. Let him report to me when it is done." To Pero he said: "Those goat-skin water bags you see on the poles will soon be empty. We will know what she wants before long and, Allah willing, she will be gone in the morning."

Out in the Abama camp Sheena called Ekoti to her fire.

"There is much to do before the sun sets," she told him, and then swept out her arm in a gesture that took in the surrounding hills. "Somewhere out there the Arab has hidden his ivory. Let all the people, even the women, if need be, go out into the hills to look for it."

"What good is ivory?" growled Ekoti. "We cannot eat it." Then his face brightened and his deep laugh rumbled up from the pit of his stomach. "Ho, ho!" he said. "I think I see what is in your mind now, Sheena. You will make the Arab trade meat for his own ivory! Ho, that is good!"

"Perchance he will trade his town for it, Ekoti."

The chief's laughter ended in a grunt of incredulity. "He is not so big a fool, Sheena."

"We will see," the Jungle Queen told him with a smile. "When you find the ivory do not bring it into camp. Leave it where you find it. Now there is another thing. I go into the town tonight. When it is dark you will take your warriors close to the gate yonder. Let them make much noise so that the Arab will think that you are about to attack him."

Ekoti looked across the plain to the high walls of the town and the thatch-roofed watchtowers standing on them. He shook his head. All this talk of trading towns for ivory was very bewildering, and he refused to perplex himself with it any further. Silent, and wooden-faced, he went to organize the search for the ivory.

Soon the Abamas were leaving the camp in small groups to scour the hills. Sheena remained in the camp, watching the town. Presently, two figures came to stand on the roof of Sleman bin Ali's house, and the sun flashed on the brass of the tube one held to his eyes. She watched them, a faint smile on her lips. The Arab, she knew, would guess what her people were looking for; and the Bearded One would fume and sweat, because he was a man who could not control his passions. He would want to rush out and attack the Abamas. But not Sleman bin Ali. He was cautious, and he would wait until he knew the result of the search.

A woman brought her a pot of bangu, a mess of native corn and greens. She accepted it gratefully, ate, and then slept until the noise of the Abama hunters returning to camp aroused her. The sun was down, and the shadow of the western hills was reaching across the veldt, like a black, open hand with six long fingers. The two figures had returned to the roof of the house to watch the incoming search parties. Ekoti's face was sour when he came to report:

"The Arab is a fox, and he does not hide everything in one hole. We have found some teeth. We left them where we found them, as you told us to do."

"How many, Ekoti?"

"Only two hands, Sheena. But they are big teeth," he added defensively.

"It is enough. You have done well. Now, rest your warriors until the middle of the night."

There was a bright moon that night, and it made a ghost town of Kilma. Starving jackals, driven from the carrion stinking on the plain, howled dismally on the fringe of the bush, and occasionally a dog within the town yelped a half-hearted answer to the challenge of the veldt. When the moon was overhead, flooding the plain with the abundance of its light, Ekoti and his warriors left the camp.

VI

Amid a great ostentation of guns and horns they advanced across the open space, in plain view of the guards in the watchtowers. A gun flashed, and another, and then the sleeping town awoke to the deep, booming alarm of a big drum. Soon many guns were snapping on the walls. The Abamas continued their noisy advance upon the west gate until bullets began to whistle all around them; then, at a shout from Ekoti, they sank into the sea of grass, and fanned out. And where there had been shouting and tumult and the glint of moonlight on spears a moment before, there was now nothing to be seen, and no sound but the rustle of movement through the tall grass.

Meanwhile, Sheena and Chim crouched in an area of shadow on the opposite side of the town. The shadow was cast by one of the watchtowers. Its wooden platform, supported by angle-beams sunk into the adobe, overhung the wall. A bright rectangle of moonlight showed between the peaked roof and the breast-high fence of bamboo which enclosed the square space within. The silhouette of the guard's head and shoulders showed black against the sky. The man's attention was drawn to the west gate by a sudden burst of musketry, his back turned to Sheena. Swiftly she darted forward to within twenty paces of the wall. There she stood for an instant, poised with drawn bow-string touching her ear. At the twang of the string winged peril sped true to her aim. The arrow pierced the guard's gun-arm, and the shock sent him slumping against the bamboo rail, knocking him out.

Under the platform Sheena uncoiled a long length of woven-grass rope and tied it around Chim's waist.

"Up, little one!" she commanded, patting the wall with her hand.

There were cracks in the sun-baked adobe, but it was a hard climb even for an ape, and Chim nearly fell twice before he grasped and swung from one of the angle-beams under the platform. Holding one end of the rope, Sheena quickly ran to the other side of the beam, and patted the wall again, calling Chim down. Chim started to come down the same way as he had gone up, but a sharp word from below stopped him. He swung back onto the beam and jumped up and down, scolding Sheena. He was very an-gry. The night was full of loud and terrifying noises. He was in no mood to play this silly game and felt safer where he was. But when he saw his mistress turn as if to go he came down in a hurry and bounded after her. He was a very surprised and frightened ape when the rope, which he had unwittingly looped over the beam, suddenly tightened and jerked him from his feet.

"Good, little one! Good!" Sheena petted and soothed him as she untied the rope. "Go now!" she hissed. And just then a volley of gunfire crashed on the walls, and Chim went like a black streak through the grass.

A moment later the Jungle Queen swung her long, shapely legs over the rail of the platform. A ladder, a tree trunk with slats bound across it, made easy her descent into the town.

It was in the dead of that night that Rick awoke with the report of a musket singing in his ears. By the time he had dressed and made his way through the garden and out onto the central road, calamity was on the loose in Kilma. As he came out of the arched gate a group of half-naked Swahilis raced by, yelling like fiends. Others came rushing, muskets in hand, from the huts that flanked the road, and the screams of their women rose to a shrill crescendo as a ragged volley crashed out on the wall near the west gate.

With his back flat again the wall of Sleman bin Ali's garden, with every man in the town capable of bearing arms running for the west gate, Rick's mind jumped to the obvious conclusion. The Abamas were attacking it in force. His first thought was of escape and, hugging the shadow of the wall, he started to move against the tide, heading for the east gate of the town. At the back of his mind there was the dim idea that if he could get out of the town the Abamas might help him to carry out the plan Benji had suggested. But escape was the dominant idea at the moment—escape from Pero's mockery and the nagging sense of defeat that kept flicking at his high spirit like the lash of a vorslaag.

Darkness closed all the lanes which opened onto the main road. The firing on the walls had slackened, and only the occasional flash of a gun tore a path under the starlit sky. The defenders had evidently gotten to their posts in time to beat back the first onslaught. And now silence, breathless, expectant, settled on the town. He was crossing the black opening of one of the lanes when he heard a hiss, and then his name spoken softly.

"Sheena!" He turned quickly and saw her shadowy outline against the wall of a hut.

Sheena beckoned to him, and he stepped into the shadows, and stood very close to her. His eyes were very bright and he asked in a husky voice:

"You came to help me?"

"I have come to settle an old quarrel with Sleman bin Ali," she told him coldly. "He has killed many of my people and made slaves of others. It may be that we can help each other."

"I see," he said. But the disappointed look that brought a slight frown to his face told her that he saw nothing and understood less. She smiled inwardly and said:

"The attack is a trick to keep the fools looking the other way while we leave this place. If you want to go we must go quickly. You will have to run fast. Even so, a bullet may find you."

"I'll take that chance," he said. Then he pointed to the east gate. "There is a small door in the big gate. It is the easiest way out if I can creep up on the guard."

She smiled in the darkness. He was more used to giving orders than taking them. She said: "We go by the same way as I came. Come!" And she turned and ran swiftly down the lane.

Straight to the watchtower she led him and went up the ladder in a quick dash that made Rick stare for a moment. As he heaved himself up onto the platform the Swahilis on the far wall were shouting taunts at the Abamas, calling them women because they would not show themselves. Out on the plain the Abama camp fires winked.

Rick went to the rail of the platform and looked down. Sheena saw his puzzlement and there was faint mockery in her soft laugh.

"Sometimes I follow where an ape leads," she told him. He gave her an odd, startled look. Then he saw the stunned guard with the arrow through his arm. Sheena swung from the platform at arm's length, caught the dangling rope with her feet, and quickly slid to the ground. Rick was very nimble, and soon dropped lightly to the ground beside her.

"Run for the fires!" she told him.

"You first," said he.

She looked at him closely. Was he afraid? No, there was not a shadow of fear to dim the brightness of his eyes, now shining with excitement. And suddenly she knew what was in his mind. He wanted to shield her with his body, to protect Sheena, Queen of the Jungle! Was there no end to his folly? Did he think she was like one of the pale-faced coast women, a ninny to be petted and pampered by men? Truly he had much to learn. But now was not the time to teach him. Without another word she sprang forward and went flashing across the open space from which the grass had been cleared for more than a hundred yards.

Again Rick stood staring for a moment, then with a muttered prayer, he started to run. There was a shot. A bullet plucked the dirt close to his flying feet. With a thrill of fear he realized that his white topee and shirt must show like a flare against the black of the ground. Hot lead was sizzling about his ears as he plunged into the grass and, panting for breath, dropped to all fours. He crawled the rest of the way into the Abama camp.

Sheena was waiting for him beside one of the fires. Standing there straight and tall, with the firelight highlighting the bronzed perfection of her body, she looked like a goddess indeed. Several native women were grouped about her, naked but for a few tufts of grass. At Rick's approach they withdrew.

"Lady, you are swifter than the wind," he said.

She gave him an enigmatic smile, but did not speak. He tried to interest himself in the contents of a pot bubbling on the fire. But his mind was not on food. Always his eyes came back to her. She found herself wishing that she had not told the other women to leave the fire. She moved back into the shadows. There was no telling what his youthful folly might prompt him to do next.

But soon Ekoti and his warriors came straggling back from the sham attack. Hungry-looking warriors they still were, armed with leaf-bladed spears and painted shields. Some had never seen a white man before, and came to point and stare at Rick. Then a drum began to throb, and the bystanders were drawn away to join in the dancing.

"I know you, Bwana," Ekoti greeted Rick in his deep basso.

"I know you, Chief," Rick returned. "It is in my heart to hope that none of your warriors fell in the fight."

The chieftain chuckled. "There was no fight, Bwana. Those Swahili dogs made much noise with their guns, but not a bullet touched us." Then he looked at Sheena and added: "Perchance, tomorrow it will be different. Tell me, Sheena, do we play at war tomorrow, or do we drive them?"

"We drive them," she answered, and glanced up at the sky, now gray with the false dawn! "Rest now, Ekoti. You, Rick, must come with me."

They left the camp and moved swiftly through the grass. It was light when they climbed a wooded hill and looked down on the west gate of the town. Vast banks of clouds, red-bellied with the first rays of the sun, hid the peaks of the distant mountains, and rolled northward on the wings of a freshening wind. It was the first real hope of rain, and the freshness of the breeze bathed them, wiping out memories of heat, hunger and fatigue. Sheena stood beside Rick, her breasts rising and falling as she drank deeply of the freshness of the morning. She said:

"You must help me now, because I do not think that Ekoti would understand what is in my mind." She pointed to the gap in the hills. "Look well at the country before you."

They stood upon a trail that led down to the west gate. Rick's eyes followed the path through the town and across the veldt to where it entered the gap in the hills. There it joined the old caravan road to Bampo, and appeared again like a red welt on the shoulder of a low hill to the northeast of the town, and then it dropped out of sight into a densely wooded kloof.

Again Sheena directed his attention to the narrow gap. "I will give you twenty men," she said. "They will carry the ivory we found across that gap. You must make them march slowly, *slowly*, so that the first man will have time to run back through the bush and come out onto the road again before the last man has crossed the gap. Then—"

A sharp exclamation from Rick interrupted her. And he said something in his own tongue, but she saw the light of understanding come into his eyes. She went on:

"Sleman bin Ali will think that we have found all his ivory. He will think that you are marching to Bampo with it, and he will send out his men to attack you. Then Ekoti and his warriors, who will be hidden near this spot, will rush down and break into the town."

Again Rick studied the landscape carefully, checking its features against his memory of the scene as he had seen it from the roof of Sleman bin Ali's house. His level was above that of the flat roof; yet, through the gap in the hills, he could see only that section of the Bampo road which arched over the low hill. From the roof of Ali's house even less of it could be seen. It was a perfect setup for what Sheena had in mind. He said:

"It is like dragging a buck to catch a lion."

"Truly," she said, and then added with a faint smile: "Now you see why I had to bring you out of the town." His awestruck expression somehow reminded her of Ekoti, and did not please her at all. Then his slow smile came and went as he said:

"And a monk, a holy man, told me not to believe in miracles."

"There is no miracle," she told him with a frown. "Men reach for what they want. In this country it is ivory they want most of all, so the Arab will reach out to grasp his ivory. Elsewhere it may be different, I cannot tell." And with that she led the way back to camp.

VII

On the following morning Sheena watched the dawn break over the eastern hills. The Abamas had broken camp and, under cover of night, had hidden their women and children in a wooded valley far from the town. Rick was on the Bampo road with his twenty porters, waiting for the sun to come out of the earth. Behind Sheena, in the bush which bordered the trail, crouched Ekoti and his warriors, looking down upon the sleeping town with hungry eyes.

As the sun came to stand on the hills like a huge copper disc on edge, Sheena's attention became fixed on the gap in the hills. Suddenly metal caught the rays of the sun; then figures, black against the red sky, appeared on the road. Rick was leading his men with the ivory over the arch of the road. A gap appeared in the slowly moving line of linked, black dots, and Sheena's pulse quickened with alarm. But soon other dots appeared behind them. It looked exactly as if a large caravan was moving off in the direction of Bampo. The Abamas behind Sheena pointed and uttered soft exclamations of wonderment. Truly, their mata-yenda was possessed of powers beyond all other wizards.

"Behold!" they murmured. "She sent but two hands of us into the hills, and now they are as many as the stars! It is a great magic!"

Then the report of a musket shattered the silence of the morning. After a time two figures appeared on the roof of Sleman bin Ali's house. The white of Pero's topee and of Sleman's robes flared against the burnt brown of the hills. Their movements were quick, agitated, and in a mo-

ment they were gone. Sheena smiled. The buck was dragging, and the lion had the wind of it.

Then drums began to throb in many-tongued panic. As their urgent, incessant clamor went echoing and re-echoing among the hills, she saw many white-robed Swahilis massing on the central road of the town. Then a great shout went up as the eastern gate was thrown open, and they went streaming out across the veldt, with Sleman bin Ali and Pero in the van. Straight as an arrow the column headed for the gap in the hills.

Ekoti struck the trunk of the majuti tree, which his men had felled and trimmed, with the butt of his spear, and looked around at his warriors, grim-visaged and impatient to swoop down on the now weakly defended town.

"Ho, my children! Do you smell the flesh pots of Kilma?" his deep voice boomed.

A low growl answered him and a dozen men jumped forward to lift the log shoulder high. Sheena waited until Sleman's column entered the gap and vanished from sight. Then with the Abama war-cry on her lips she sprang forward. The Abamas echoed the cry, and went charging down the slope on the heels of the Jungle Queen.

Like a black wave they swept across the veldt, and the noise of their going through the tall, dry grass was like a strong wind in the jungle. A few muskets flashed as they neared the gate. Bullets slapped into their close-packed ranks. Several warriors fell but nothing could stop the meat-hungry Abamas. They swept on to mass before the gate. More men fell as the log was driven against the split-log barrier. A log splintered, then another. The gate burst open under the sheer weight of their numbers as, at a shout from Sheena, they hurled themselves against it.

The few Swahilis left behind made a stand on the road. A volley was poured into the Abamas as they surged over the debris of the gate. They wavered, but Ekoti's bull-like roars rallied them; and they charged, and swept over the Swahilis before they could reload their guns and discharge another volley.

After a few minutes of sharp hand-to-hand fighting those of the Swahilis who had not been speared in the first onrush threw down their muskets—and Sheena was mistress of Kilma. And it was well for the Swahilis that Ekoti was not their conqueror, for he was lusting to wreck bloody vengeance on the hated slavers, and it took all of Sheena's power and prestige to prevent a general massacre.

Meanwhile, at the first alarm, Rick and his little band had taken to the bush, and were now circling around the town to lead the Abama women and children to the safety of its walls. Sleman bin Ali and his column had advanced several miles along the Bampo road in hot pursuit of the elusive caravan which seemed to have melted into the dust before his eyes. Even at the sound of gunfire he did not grasp immediately what had happened. And when he did turn back, and again looked upon his stronghold, it was to see Rick and the Abama women and children streaming into the town through the western gate.

"Merciful Allah!" he gasped. "That daughter of Shaitan—may she burn in hell!" And then he was seized by a paroxysm of rage that left him in a state of collapse before it was spent.

At sundown Sleman bin Ali encamped on the plain within gunshot of the town's walls. And then began a siege which, if not unique in the annals of warfare, was a strange and rare inversion of classical examples—for while the besieged gorged themselves on the biltong in the town's storerooms and drank of clear fountains, the besiegers starved and thirsted on the sun-scorched veldt. Sleman bin Ali had the guns, but not enough powder and shot to risk an assault upon the town, and Sheena did not have the manpower to risk a pitched battle on the plain. And it was not necessary that she should, since it was not in the nature of things that the siege could last long.

Calmly she awaited Sleman bin Ali's inevitable submission to her will. In the Arab's garden she lay, full length on her belly in a patch of moonlight. Outside of the enclosing walls the night was filled with the rumble of drums and the victory chant of the Abamas. She appeared to be asleep, and no sleeping jungle cat could have been more still. Her hair fell in shimmering waves over her shoulders and face, but through the golden veil she was watching Rick, who sat on a stone slab near the pool where the fountain gurgled and the lotus shone with the lustre of pearls in the moonlight.

The Jungle Queen's eyebrows were drawn together by a frown. Something had changed Rick's attitude toward her. Ever since the attack on the town he had been strangely silent, and he did not look at her as he had been wont to do. Even now, when he might feast his eyes in secret, he was not looking at her, but kept his eyes steadfastly fixed on the stars. His aloofness was like the prick of a knife point. Her brain told her that there was an unspoken reproach behind it, but her woman's heart whispered that it might be something else, and became strangely tumultuous at the thought. Impulsively, she decided to put both mind and heart at rest, and got to her feet in a swift, lithe movement.

He rose from his seat as she came swaying toward him. She smiled and asked softly:

"Why are you angry with me, Rick?"

He looked surprised and answered quickly, "I am not angry, Sheena."

"Then why do you not look at me?"

The slow smile came to his lips, and he clasped his hands behind his back. "You should know without asking, Sheena. Did you not say that men reach for what they want?"

She smiled. No, she had not lost her power over him. It was very strong now; the gleam in his eyes and his tightly compressed lips told her that. She felt his power too, wondered how strong it was, and her heart seemed to jump into her throat and take her breath with its wild beating. Suddenly she was conscious only of his nearness, and the primitive paeon of the drums pounding in her blood. As in a dream she heard herself say:

"So! But you keep your hands behind your back, Brass Eyes. Is that to say that you do not want me?"

She saw the startled look come into his eyes, and then his arms were about her, his kiss hot on her lips. For a moment she clung to him, forgetful of all else. Then suddenly it flashed into her mind that this man's power to stir her was as great as her own to stir him. In sudden alarm she stiffened in his arms and tried to push him off. But he only tightened his grip about her waist, and his arms were strong, crushing her to him. She felt the will to resist slipping from her; and, half in anger, half in terror, she snatched her knife from her belt and drove the point into the fleshy part of his forearm. With a startled cry he released her. She jumped back and stood glaring at him.

He was very angry, so angry that he could not speak for a moment. Then he said in a low, tense voice:

"You, you witch! You asked for that, and I'll tame you if it's the last thing I do on earth!"

"Stand back from me!" she warned.

For a long moment they stood glaring at each other. Gradually his anger died. He pulled a rag from his pocket and bound it around his forearm.

"I am sorry for that," she told him. "But you would not let me go."

He looked down at the spreading, red stain on the rag, shook his head and said: "In a jungle garden I plucked a flower and a thorn drew my blood. That's an old Swahili saying."

"Do not try to pluck another," she told him. "Abama spears are sharper than thorns. Leave this country soon."

He looked at her steadily, his eyes very bright. "I'll leave," he said. "But I'll be gone just as long as it takes me to get that damned ivory down to the coast. Then I'll come back for you, Sheena."

She tossed her golden head. "Truly there is no end to your folly!" she said. "And I tell you now, as I told Ekoti, that I will mate with you, or

any man, when the leaves of the majuti trees fall. That is my own saying."

"And I've heard others say much the same thing," said he.

"Others? What others—who—" She checked herself as she saw the slow smile come to his lips. Furious with herself she turned away.

"I'll tell you about them, my girl," Rick muttered as she passed swiftly from sight under the arched doorway to the garden. "Someday when we're nice and cozy—and you haven't got that knife."

A little before noon on the second day of the siege Rick was called to the roof of Sleman bin Ali's house. Sheena was there looking out across the plain. She pointed and Rick saw the Arab and Pero advancing to the gate. They carried a white rag on a pole.

"We go to meet them," Sheena told him coldly.

She led the way down. Rick ran to his room and snatched up his gunbelt, and hurried after Sheena, buckling the belt about his waist as he went.

Together they passed out of the gate, and came to a halt about fifty paces from it, and waited for Pero and the Arab to come up to them. The sun in its full meridian vigor beat down on the plain. Distant objects were blurred by the heat waves, so that the hill tops seemed to be disconnected from their bases and to hang trembling in space.

Sleman bin Ali's bearing was dignified, his expression calm. Pero smiled, but the suppressed anger in his eyes was as hot as the ground under Sheena's feet. He was the first to speak. He addressed himself to Rick.

"It is a clever trick that you have turned, senhor. I made a joke of your wits but I am not laughing now."

"I never had what it takes to pull any thing like that," Rick told him with a grin. "I'm just lucky enough to be on the right side of the fence."

Sleman bin Ali was silent, pulling at his beard, and regarding Sheena with black, intelligent eyes.

"We are reasonable men, Sleman and I," Pero went on. "We offer twenty fraslas of ivory, and safe conduct to the coast."

"The ivory is not yours to give," Sheena told him coldly. "And Rick will leave this country when he is ready. Doubtless he will take you with him to the coast where your own people will punish you."

"Holy Saints, the cock is silent while the hen cackles!" Pero exclaimed with a malicious grin.

"Be silent!" Sleman's voice cut in sharply. "Sheena, I am not a fool like this one. I know when I am beaten. What is your will?"

"You will free your slaves, you will give up the ivory this man stole, and you will give up your guns so that you can raid no more villages."

"Wallai!" exclaimed the Arab, and lifted his eyes to heaven. "To the first two conditions I agree. To the last I cannot agree. I cannot leave my people unarmed among savages. Do what you will with me, but in the name of Allah I ask mercy for the women and children who call me chief."

Rick touched Sheena's arm and whispered a few words. She nodded her head and said aloud: "I will do as you ask, Rick, to show that there is no anger in my heart now." Then to Sleman she said: "My friend says that if you swear on your sacred book you will keep your word. Swear that you will not raid another kraal, and you may keep your guns."

Again Sleman bin Ali lifted his eyes to heaven and spread wide his arms. "Allah is all-wise, all-knowing!" he intoned piously. "In sha Allah! I will swear on the Koran, Sheena."

"Then let it be so," said Sheena coolly. "Ekoti's warriors will stay in the town until Rick has made two marches to the coast, then we will go in peace. Food and water will be sent out to your camp. I have spoken."

Just as she turned to go Pero dodged behind the Arab, his teeth bared by a snarl of rage and hate. Out of the tail of his eyes Rick saw his hand flash down to his gun butt. He whirled around, and the roar of his Colt blended with the report of Pero's big revolver. The Portuguese staggered, clutched at Sleman's robe, and dragged the old man down as he fell.

"Allah be praised!" gasped Sleman as Rick helped him to his feet. "Your bullet might have struck me, did He not know his own!" He looked down at Pero. "Dog of a Nazarani. Fool." He lifted his foot to kick the body but Sheena's voice stopped him.

"Speak softly of the dead!" said she.

"The peace of Allah be with him, and with you, Sheena!" Sleman bin Ali said hastily. "And may the withering hand of old age never touch thy beauty." To which, under his breath, Rick added a fervent, "Amen!"

At long last the rain came, and on the following day Rick marched out of Kilma. From the roof of Sleman bin Ali's house Sheena watched until his caravan vanished into the rain-mist that now hung over the Bampo road. Then she went slowly down to the garden.

Again the strange feeling of emptiness assailed her. His parting words had been: "Until we meet again!" And truly, he was fool enough to dare anything. Absently, she pulled a flower from a bush as she moved toward the fountain, and started with a sharp intake of breath as a thorn pricked her finger. Smiling faintly, she drew the thorn out, and watched a drop of blood ooze from the tiny wound. At a faint sound she looked around.

Ekoti had come to stand guard over her. Near the gateway he leaned on his spear, his eyes watchful, his dark face impassive. The Jungle Queen's hand tightened on the flower she still held. A tremulous sigh parted her lips, and she tossed the crushed blossom into the pond.

L. PATRICK GREENE

BORN LOUIS MONTAGUE GREENE, Lewis Patrick Greene (1891–?) grew up in England, then spent several years in Rhodesia as a civil servant before being sidelined by a back injury. By 1913, he had settled in the U.S. and become a citizen. Although Greene's stories and novellas number in the hundreds, his most popular works by a wide margin are those about Aubrey St. John Major, known to everyone in Greene's South Africa as the Major. This strange figure, who looks and speaks like P. G. Wodehouse's Bertie Wooster, is both a shrewd rogue and a heroic character. His success stems from his ability to make others think of him as a fool—not difficult to do, as he sports a monocle, dresses foppishly even in the desert and the heart of the jungle, and is given to such expressions as "old thing" and "'pon my word." The Major makes his living (sometimes a good one and sometimes not) as an illicit diamond buyer who purchases and sells diamonds to those without permits which, in the area controlled by the de Beers syndicate, makes him a criminal. The police know him and play at chasing him, while he plays at eluding them; but he would have to be caught absolutely red-handed to be arrested, for the authorities admire his sense of honor and his unselfish willingness to help others. The Major's stories feature a rarity in pulp fiction: a black sidekick, a Hottentot named Jim, with whom the Major shares a relationship of mutual care and respect. Nonetheless, the modern reader should be warned not to bring a twenty-first-century expectation of political correctness to stories written more than eighty years ago, when white people living in Africa referred to natives as "niggers" without a second thought, the casual epithet implying neither racism nor villainy, merely common, if unattractive, usage.

The first story about the Major, "No Evidence," was published in the November 3, 1919, issue of *Adventure* magazine. Nearly a hundred additional stories followed in the 1920s and '30s, mostly in the pages of *Short Stories,* and almost all were collected in books published in England. Oddly, since the stories were enormously popular in American pulp magazines, only one volume, *The Major—Diamond Buyer,* found an American publisher (Doubleday, 1924).

"Fire" was first published in the June 10, 1930, issue of *Short Stories;* its first publication in book form was in *Major Developments* (London: Hamilton, 1931).

FIRE

L. PATRICK GREENE

THE MAJOR was sitting in a deck chair which Jim, the Hottentot, had placed for him in the shade of a tree, yawning contentedly, stretching himself, filling his lungs with the clean sweet air of the high veld.

The Hottentot was seated on the ground, a little distant from his *baas,* cleaning the dishes and pans used for the midday meal.

Presently, that task completed, he stored the things neatly away in the place allotted them in the light, tent-topped trek wagon, looked to see that the four mules had not strayed too far from the outspan, then returned to his former place, sat down completely relaxed, and sighed contentedly.

"*Au-a, baas!*" he exclaimed. "Now we are back in our own country. And it is good! I can rest now in a land where there is no evil."

Jim's voice died away; and then he was slumbering, composedly.

The Major looked about him. North, south, east and west stretched the undulating veld. Open country, it seemed; flat and innocent of guile. Here and there patches of mimosa scrub broke the monotony of tall, sun-browned grass. The southern horizon was lined with a ridge of distant blue hills.

The Major lighted another cigarette.

"By Jove," he murmured, "Jim's absolutely right. The scene is quite a pastoral one, utterly peaceful."

He let the cigarette drop to the ground, auto- matically extinguishing it under his heel. His eyes closed and, presently, he was sleeping as soundly as the Hottentot.

And then of a sudden, both men awakened at the same instant. For the silence and vast empti- ness of the veld was destroyed. It had become, all at once, full of latent danger.

The Hottentot looked meaningly at his *baas,* rose to his feet and climbed up into the wagon. Emerging again he handed his *baas* the revolver and rifle he had taken from their storage place. He retained a sharp, stabbing *assagai.*

The Major buckled the revolver about his waist and opened the magazine cut-off of his ri- fle.

And then both men were listening intently for a repetition of the sound which had awak- ened them from sleep.

Their keen eyes continually searched the sur- rounding landscape; nothing that was within their field of vision escaped notice. And they saw nothing suspicious! It seemed as if they stood in the center of a large, level plain in which there was no life.

But they had been warned through their sense of hearing and, knowing Africa, had no thought of disregarding that warning. Men who do—die.

Presently Jim spoke, very quietly. "A man rides fast."

The Major nodded. He too had heard the

The Major dismounted and started "burns" in a number of places.

dull thud of a horse's feet on the iron hard veld.

"And I think," the Hottentot continued after a short interval, "the man is lost."

The Major's eyebrows twitched in doubt at that.

"He *is* lost, *baas*," the Hottentot now said definitely, and relaxing, sat down on the ground. "There is nothing to be feared from a man who is lost."

The Major looked down at him and chuckled softly. Then he, too, relaxed, and waited to see what would happen.

A faint shot brought them back to their alertness. Jim leaped to his feet and climbed to the top of a nearby termite heap.

Another shot, then two in quick succession. And the Major answered them with shots from his revolver.

Jim climbed down from the termite heap.

"He comes, *baas*," he said in tones of smug complacency. "He comes this way."

As he spoke the Major saw a horseman ride into view, mounting the crest of the land wave which had hitherto hidden him. He was still too far away for them to distinguish anything about him—not even Jim's keen eyes could do that and the Major's field-glasses helped very little here.

"When he fired the shot which awakened us, Jim, he was much nearer than he is now," said the Major wonderingly.

"He has ridden in a circle, *baas*. I said that he was lost."

The Major nodded.

"That would explain things, Jim," he admitted, "if it *was* his shot we heard."

"And it was, *baas*. There is no one else."

"No, Jim?" the Major bantered.

"No, *baas*," Jim said positively. Then, "I think no, *baas*," he added with rather less assurance and assumed an intent, listening attitude.

Then they saw the horseman pull to a halt and, standing up in the stirrups, gaze all around. It seemed impossible that he should not see the outspan: the white-tented top of the wagon; the blue coil of smoke from the fire; the mules and Jim—he had climbed the termite heap again—who shouted and waved his arms like one gone mad.

But a man lost on the veld is a man completely devoid of all sense. And this man was no exception. Apparently he saw nothing and heard nothing, for he dropped back into his saddle and urged his jaded mount to a gallop continuing in the southward direction.

The Major sighed.

"I'm going after him, Jim," he said. "Catch one of the mules."

The Hottentot lost no time in obeying his *baas*'s orders.

"You will be careful, *baas*," he said when he brought the strongest and fastest of the four mules up to the Major.

"I'll have to be, Jim," the Major said dryly as he vaulted on to the mule's bony back. "Phew! It is like sitting on the edge of a spear blade, Jim."

Jim grinned and the Major rode off at a sharp canter. He presented a somewhat ludicrous figure. Picture! An immaculately attired white man: white silk shirt, snowy, and very baggy, riding breeches, brown polo boots golden-spurred, and a white pith helmet. In his right eye a monocle glistened. And he was so tall that his feet nearly touched the ground. And to cap it all he was mounted, bareback at that, on a scraggy, squint-eyed mule.

But when one looked closer there was no further cause for laughter. It was evident that the surface indications were only illusion; that the foppish exterior was merely a thin veneer which protected the man it covered. Just as the dudish clothes disguised strong, supple muscles; so the inane, silly ass grin disguised the keen brain which directed those muscles.

Jim seated himself on the top of the termite heap, the field-glasses in his hands and looked in the direction of the lost horseman.

That man was swinging around in another circle, inclining now toward the outspan once again.

Jim watched him keenly, a puzzled expression on his face.

"He can't have seen the *baas*," Jim decided, "so it must be that he has seen some landmark he knows, or someone who is outspanned near the patch of mimosa scrub."

Jim focused the Major's glasses on the patch of thorn scrub to which the horseman was approaching. Seeing nothing, he shifted his attention to the horseman. The distance was still too great for him to discern a great deal. But he nodded sagely.

"He has seen someone, I think," he concluded. "He is no longer afraid of being lost, and he lets his horse walk. *Wo-we!* But what now?"

The horseman—he was very near to the thorn scrub—suddenly changed his course again, heading directly for the Major's outspan, urging his tired horse to a gallop, his right arm rising and falling as if he were wielding a *sjambok*.

Swiftly Jim focused the glasses once again on

the mimosa patch and, as he did so, he saw a little puff of white smoke, and then another spurted out from the bush and rose lazily into the air. A few moments later he heard two faint reports.

"Wo-we!" Jim exclaimed, trembling with excitement. He looked again to where he had last seen the horseman—and saw only a riderless horse standing abjectly on the veld.

"Wo-we!" Jim said again and thoughtfully scratched his grizzled head. "And now what? I think he who was lost saw an outspan hidden in the scrub and rode toward it. Then he saw that an enemy was hidden there and he turned away. But he was too late. Truly he was too late. And my *baas*—where is he? Ah!"

The Major had suddenly come into view, riding up from a deep *donga*. He too saw the riderless horse—that was evident to Jim by the way in which the Major urged his obstinate mount to a better speed. Jim thought, too, that his *baas* could probably see the fallen rider.

"If," Jim mused, "the man who was lost is now dead, my *baas* can bring him in alone. But if he is wounded—*au-a!* Then—the *baas* will need help."

And Jim scrambled down from the termite heap, intending to inspan the mules and drive over the veld after his *baas*.

Then, suddenly, he acted like one gone mad or at least like a native who knows there is no one at hand to chide him and who, therefore, takes all manner of childish liberties with his *baas*'s possessions.

He capered about the outspan, his steps strangely unsteady because he was looking at the ground through the wrong end of the field-glasses. Tiring of this, he climbed up into the wagon and vanished for a little while under the tented cover.

When he emerged again, he wore an old coat of the Major's, a helmet on his head, and he was smoking a large black cigar.

He climbed down from the wagon and with a swaggering gait he went to the deck chair and lowered himself into it. And there he sat, smoking furiously, laughing boisterously at times. One would have said he was the native servant of a man who does not know how to treat natives and who has forfeited their respect.

But despite an outer appearance of contentment, and the snatches of ribald songs he sang between puffs at the cigar, Jim's eyes did not laugh; beads of sweat stood out on his forehead.

The mules had stopped grazing and, bunched together, were staring suspiciously before them.

And then, presently, at a point in the bush behind the Hottentot's chair, three men appeared, grinning to themselves at the success of their "be-creeping."

They each carried a rifle and one, a sandy-haired colossus of a man, a wicked-looking *sjambok*.

They were dressed in the free and easy costume adopted by the back veld Boer: shapeless baggy trousers, an equally shapeless coat, a slouch hat and stout, homemade *veld-schoen*.

Soft-footed, very slowly, the three men crept nearer and nearer to the Hottentot.

Jim yawned, stretched himself, then burst into song, the words of which were the reverse of complimentary to white men, and especially insulting to his own *baas*.

The three men looked at each other significantly. The sandy-haired man tightened his hold on the *sjambok*.

The next moment he brought the cutting lash down across the Hottentot's shoulders, splitting open the tunic and drawing blood. And, as Jim jumped to his feet with a wild cry of pain and surprised terror, more blows followed the first.

Jim ducked and ran in an endeavor to escape, but the enraged Boer followed him, his arms rising and falling with an automatic regularity.

Round and round they went, Jim shouting tearful protests; the sandy-haired Boer cursing and panting, egged on by the other two.

Presently Jim dived under the wagon and there the Boer did not attempt to follow him.

His fury had spent itself and he turned with a brutal laugh to his companions.

"That will teach the good-for-nothing Kaffir not to sing his insulting songs of white men! Not?"

The youngest man—his name was Anders—nodded.

"Yes, Pete," he agreed. "Your hand is very heavy. But what does it matter what this Totty thinks or says? So be gentle with him. He may be useful to us. At least he has no love for his *baas*. That is evident from the song he was singing."

"*Ou!*" Jim called timidly. "Did you beat me because I mocked the man I call *baas*? *Ou,* I tell you, he is no man. He is only a *verdoemte* fool of a *roinek*."

The man with the *sjambok* turned angrily on Jim, threatening to go under the wagon after him.

"So you speak the Taal, do you, Hottentot?"

"*Ja!*" Jim replied glibly. "And, if you please, no more beating. *Wo-we!* How it hurt."

"There will be no more beatings," the sandy-haired man said, "if you behave yourself, Hottentot. Tell us now something, of this *baas* of yours."

Jim shrugged his shoulders.

"I only know that he is altogether a fool."

"He speaks the *Taal*?"

"*Ja! Vrachtig!*"

"And he speaks your tongue?"

"*Ja!*"

"And he is a *roinek*, you say?"

"Truly."

"Then he cannot be altogether a fool," Anders exclaimed. "Whoever heard of a *roinek*, who was a fool, speaking the *Taal* and the language of Kaffirs. I know these *roinek* fools; they shout in their own tongue and expect all others to understand them. So you lie, Hottentot, when you say your *baas* is a fool."

But Jim protested stolidly.

"I say he is a fool, *baas,* as you shall see when he comes."

"And where is your *baas* now?" asked Anders.

Jim grinned impudently.

"We saw a man riding a horse. He was lost. And my *baas* went out to get him. Presently, it may be, my *baas* will lose himself. He is *that* sort of a fool."

The three men considered this thoughtfully.

One of them picked up the field-glasses Jim had dropped when he ran to escape from the *sjamboking*.

"And what, Hottentot," he asked, "did you see through these when you watched from the top of the termite heap?"

Jim grinned.

"*Ou, baas,* what should I see? They are magic glasses. They make things which are near seem very far. Give me, that I may put them back before my *baas* returns."

The man who had the field-glasses put them to his eyes.

"Not that way, *baas,*" Jim said somewhat patronizingly. "The big end you hold to your eyes."

The three looked at each other and laughed. They had reached the conclusion that the Hottentot was a guileless fool.

The man who had the glasses—it was Anders—climbed the termite heap and looked back over the veld.

Rejoining his companions he nodded assurance.

"All goes well," he said.

"Could you see Oom Piet?"

Anders shook his head.

"He's *slim* that one," he exclaimed admiringly.

The three conversed together in whispers looking frequently at the Hottentot who shifted his weight uneasily from one foot to the other.

"Listen now, Hottentot," Anders said abruptly. "We suspect your *baas* of evil-doing, so we are going to hide in the bush about the outspan in order to trap him."

Jim grunted.

"Truly," he said contemptuously, "my *baas* can do no evil because he is too big a fool."

But Anders continued, ignoring the Hottentot's interruption: "So I say, Hottentot, that we will hide in the bush and see to it that you play no tricks."

"Tricks, *baas*," Jim exclaimed, incredulously. "I know no tricks."

"Maybe not, Hottentot, but I think that you are a liar like all the people of your color, and so we take no chances. Although when we are hidden in the bush you will not see us, yet we will see you, and our guns will be pointed at your heart. If you give your *baas*, when he returns, any sign that we are in hiding, then the bullets from our guns will enter your body."

He looked keenly at Jim then added softly: "No, I think not into your body, but into the body of your *baas*, because something tells me that you are, perhaps, playing a game with us. I think, perhaps, that you love your *baas* and would risk death in order to warn him. You Totties are like that sometimes."

"*Au-a!*" Jim protested. "Am I a fool that I should risk my life for a fool? And my *baas* is that, I tell you."

"Maybe," Anders said, "but we take no chances, so remember that I have warned you."

"What then must I do?" Jim asked.

"You will sit in the chair," Anders said, "not moving its position until your *baas* comes. And no tricks, remember!"

"I know no tricks," Jim said sulkily as he sat down in the chair. He stretched himself and yawned loudly. "And I am tired so I will sleep until my *baas* comes." He folded his arms across his chest, his head dropped forward.

The three men watched him for a little while, then backed softly and slowly away. A few moments later they had vanished into the bush and Jim was apparently alone. But he did not move, did not open his eyes. Presently he snored.

II

Meanwhile the Major had come to that place on the veld where the riderless horse stood beside the body of its master. The Major dismounted stiffly from his mule and approached the prostrate form.

Gently he turned the man over and looked into wide-open black eyes which stared sightlessly at him. He put his head down on the man's chest and listened, but the heart had ceased pumping.

Taking off the dead man's jacket he found a bullet wound on the shoulder. It was little more than a flesh wound. Of itself, it would not have caused death, but a closer examination disclosed another wound close to the base of the dead man's spine. The bullet which made it had passed through the man's body, but had been halted by the buckle of the man's wide belt.

The Major pulled it out, wiped it carefully and put it in his pocket. He rose slowly to his feet and looked down at the dead man. "Only a youngster," he mused. "Barely out of his teens. I wonder who shot him and why?" He looked round the veld but could see nothing.

"But," he muttered, "the fact that I can see no one proves nothing. I wish Jim were here. Perhaps he could see, where I am blind. There must be someone hidden within shooting range, and, because of that, I must act cautiously. Oh, very.

"I rather fancy I have a little job on my hands," he continued muttering to himself. "I have got to find and bring to justice—veld justice maybe—the man who murdered this poor chap. But certainly I am not going to ride aimlessly about the veld looking for a murderer. I'd rather that he came to me—and I think he'll do that."

He shrugged his shoulders and lighted a cigarette. Then stooping over, the Major picked up the dead man and put him carefully, reverentially, onto the horse, climbed up into the saddle behind him and rode slowly back across the veld in the direction of his camp, followed dutifully by his mule.

It would have been very difficult for the closest observer to have detected any movement in the Major, other than that imparted by the gait of his horse. But, nevertheless, the long fingers of his capable hands were continually busy. They fluttered over the dead man's body. One by one they explored his pockets, exposing their contents to the Major's keen scrutiny. Neither did the Major give any outward indication of surprise when he finally brought to light a small piece of dirty paper on which a map was crudely sketched.

It was a scrap of paper which had been folded and unfolded so many times that it was almost falling apart. It was covered with grease spots and it gave the Major food for much grave thought.

"By Jove," he muttered. "One would say that piece of paper has gone through the wars. Oh, quite! And it must be valuable. Perhaps the map on it shows the way to a sort of Tom Tiddler's ground. A gold reef maybe. Or a spot where diamonds are to be found. Yes, I think it must be something like that, because this poor laddie had it wrapped up very carefully and tucked away in a place where no chance seeker would find it." He looked thoughtfully at the piece of paper.

"I am quite convinced," he continued presently, "that if this paper could talk, it would tell a story of bloodshed and whatnot."

The Major came presently to a deep *donga* and rode carefully down the steep bank, holding firmly on to the dead body before him. And then, when he was at the very bottom of the *donga,* he halted for a little while among the jumble of rocks which littered the ground and examined the map closely, memorizing its features.

When he rode on again he was smoking a cigarette. A crude, clumsily rolled cigarette. And that crudeness was not entirely due to the fact that it was foreign to the Major's custom to roll his own cigarettes, but chiefly to the fact that the paper which contained the tobacco, forming the shell of the cigarette, was the dirty piece of paper on which the map was sketched.

He came at last to his camp, surprised and not a little angry that Jim had not come to meet him. And then a look of perplexity for a moment passed across his face, for the Hottentot was lounging in a deck chair, a helmet on his head, between his lips a large black cigar which, judging by the clouds of smoke which rose almost continuously into the air, the Hottentot was smoking frantically.

It was almost as if those puffs of smoke formed a signal, for the look of perplexity passed from the Major's face. For a moment his eyes flashed with stern suspicion and his whole body tensed as if to meet the shock of some hidden danger. Then he relaxed, and in some miraculous way appeared to be only a soft, foolish dude of a man, utterly incapable of sustained effort— mental or physical. He reined in his horse.

"Hi, Jim!" he shouted angrily. "Come here, you lazy misbegotten ape." And, despite his self-control, he could scarcely refrain from chuckling when Jim replied in the Hottentot vernacular:

"You are a fool, my *baas.* Talking to me in a language you know I do not understand! Speak the language of us black ones. Then maybe I will do your bidding, or not, as it pleases me."

The Major, feigning great anger, exclaimed harshly in the vernacular: "You dog! You dare to speak to me like that. I will thrash the hide off your back. Come here, I tell you, and give me aid with this dead one I found out there on the veld."

Jim turned his head so that he could see his *baas,* otherwise he did not move. For a short, silent moment the eyes of white man and black servant met, asking and answering questions. Then said Jim with a careless shrug of his shoulders:

"What is it to me that you find dead men on the veld. You went against my counsel to rescue a man who was lost, and that man is now dead." And, with a shrug of his shoulders, Jim turned his back once again on the Major.

That man rubbed his chin reflectively, spat out the stub of his cigarette and rode forward again. Coming to the wagon, he dismounted and lowered the dead body to the ground. Then he stood, his back against the wagon, his legs astraddle, his hands resting on his hips—his right hand was not far from the butt of his revolver.

"Jim," he called in helpless accents, "what am I to do with this dead one?"

"It is all of one to me, *baas,* what you do with him, as long as you do not ask me to dig a hole in which to bury him."

"I was thinking of that, Jim," the Major admitted.

"That I will not do," the Hottentot replied flatly.

"Well, I think this laddie should be buried. And we shall see. Rather!"

Then, like lightning, the Major's revolver seemed to leap of its own volition from the holster into his hand. Suddenly he had become conscious of the peril which menaced him. For a moment he stood, tensed; he relaxed somewhat as a sneering voice said:

"None of that, *roinek;* we've got you covered. Drop your gun and no tricks unless you want a bullet through your fat head."

Adding emphasis to the command, a shot sounded viciously, and a bullet, passing through the Major's helmet, whipped that dazzlingly white head-gear from his head, exposing his sleek, immaculately groomed black hair.

The Major's revolver fell from his hand with a thud to the ground, his hand dropped listlessly to his sides, his mouth gaped wide open and he looked scared to the point of petrification. And yet, like a damning symbol of his utter inanity, his monocle still gleamed in his eye.

"I say," the Major drawled in a protesting voice. "This sort of thing isn't done, you know. Really it isn't. Shooting at a chappie like that! Most dangerous; you might have killed me. As it is, you've ruined a perfectly good helmet. Come out, my man, come out. And you'll either apologize or I'll—er—I'll write to the papers about it. As true as my name's Aubrey St. John Major, I will."

He waited expectantly, but no one appeared, no one spoke. He looked meaningly at Jim and saw that, despite the leering grin which contorted the Hottentot's pleasantly ugly face, that man was laboring under a great strain.

The Major whistled softly. This was unlike Jim. Jim was the last man in the world he would expect to give way to fear. And Jim was, if the Major judged correctly, very near the breaking point.

He called aloud in a querulous voice:

"I say, Mister Hide-in-the-Grass. Why don't you show yourself? I'm unarmed and I raise my hands above my head."

His actions fitted his words.

There was a short pause, a low chuckle. "We are coming," a voice said.

And then, from three widely separated points, the three Boers rose to their feet, rifles at the ready, and converged on the Major.

He scrutinized them sharply as they came toward him and halted within an arm's length. Between them, on the ground, was the body of the dead man.

"Well?" the Major questioned.

"Almighty!" exclaimed the sandy-haired man. "Well, you say! And this *younker* lies dead at your feet!"

He knelt down, affecting great sorrow, beside the corpse. The other two kept the Major covered with their rifles, laughing at the hypocritical grief of the kneeling man.

The Major yawned.

"My arms ache," he said. "May I take them down? After all there can be no danger. You have me covered and I am unarmed."

The sandy-haired man looked up. "Yep! Take them down," he growled, "but no tricks, mind." To his companions he said, "Watch him closely, I do not think he is the fool he would have us believe, and see to it that he keeps his hands away from his pockets."

"Ach sis!" retorted one of the other men angrily. "You talk to us as if we were children, or your slaves. Truly we are no fools, we do not have to be told what to do; we will watch him. You—you get on with your mourning."

The sandy-haired man scowled and was on the point of making a heated retort, thought better of it, then applied himself to an industrious search of the dead man's pockets, putting all their contents in a little heap on the ground.

The pockets emptied, he removed the man's garments one by one, examining each piece thoroughly. The other two Boers watched him carefully, but not once did the muzzles of their rifles waver; and the Major knew that, though their attention was apparently upon their companion, any suspicious move on his part would be the signal for the pressure of fingers upon the triggers, the report of two rifles and the smash of heavy bullets through his body. So he did not move. Instead, he watched the search with the air of a disinterested spectator.

But he saw things that the three Boers did not see. The sandy-haired man was too engrossed with his search; the other two were too concerned in watching their partner, evidently suspicious that he might trick them. They had completely forgotten Jim, the Hottentot! But then, they were so sure that there was no need to watch Jim. He had shown himself to be only an impudent nigger who had no love for his *baas* and would certainly do nothing to rescue him from the predicament into which he had fallen. And so they had ignored him.

But now that the three Boers had turned their backs on him and their attentions were busily occupied elsewhere, Jim's quickness of mind and action was beginning to assert itself. He made his way stealthily to the wagon, took from its socket the long driving whip—the pole was all of eighteen feet long, the lash of even greater length—and now, carrying the whip in his two hands, he was approaching within good striking distance of the three Boers. The whip, wielded as Jim knew how to wield it, would make an effective weapon. But he could not afford to make a mistake. If his first blow failed, then the situation was lost. Before he could strike again, their rifles would speak death.

And it was in order to give Jim the chance to maneuver into the best position for his task, that the Major taunted the three Boers, ridiculing their distrust of each other and trapping them into oral indiscretions.

They were slow-witted and, because they were confident of themselves, rose easily to his taunts, giving him the information which he sought.

No, the *younker* was not a friend of theirs. Almighty no! He was only a young fool of a *roinek*. Besides being a fool, he was also a liar and a thief. Truly he was an ungrateful *skellum*. They found him when he was lost on the veld. He had been prospecting with three other *roineks,* and they had died. But before they died they had discovered where there was much gold. They had made a map of the place and this young fool of a *roinek* had that map. It was only right that the men who found him, the Boers, should share it and his wealth. Had they not saved him from death? But mark his ingratitude: he fled from them. But death punished his ingratitude, and now they looked for the map that they might take the gold for themselves.

And from this, the Major at last discovered why the youngster was shot, although he was fully convinced that he had *not* yet been told the whole truth of the matter. He glanced up swiftly and saw that Jim was almost prepared to strike. He must hold the Boers a moment longer.

"You tell me a lot," he said easily, "but not the whole truth, I think. And so, I shall tell the truth to you. I think perhaps you killed the companions of this dead one. Perhaps you met them on the veld, and they drank a lot, celebrating their good fortune, and they told you things which, had they been sober, they would not have told. You killed them because of the gold they had discovered. And you would have killed this one too, only you were clever, and so perhaps he was warned and he fled from you."

The man Anders grinned. "You are *verdoemte* clever, *roinek*. Maybe it is as you say. And if it is, what matter? You have no proof, and even if you had it would avail you nothing. It is only your word against our word. Besides, I think you will not live to give your word; I think you are going to die, just as this young fool died, and no one will know."

The Major shrugged his shoulders. "Have it your own way," he said drawlingly, "but what have you gained by this one's death? What will you gain by my death unless, perhaps, you have found this map of which you speak?"

"I have not found it," said the sandy-haired man, "and you know I have not found it."

"Oh, but I don't know," the Major said airily, "and I am sure your friends do not know that either." He looked at them appealingly.

"No," Anders growled. "We do not know. We have had to watch the *roinek* as well as you, Pete, and maybe you have found the paper and put it in your pocket."

"You talk like a fool," the sandy-haired man retorted. "I tell you I have found no paper on him. If you do not believe me you may search me."

"We will do that in good time, and in our own way. But first we will search the *roinek*. Maybe he has taken the paper. After we have searched him I do not think he will live very long; he knows too much."

"I know nothing at all," the Major hastened to assure them, "and I don't want to die yet— and I don't think I will.' "

As the Major concluded on a triumphant note, Jim struck. The long lash of the driving whip snaked forward with a vicious report and coiled round the barrels of the two rifles, whipping them from the hands of the two Boers. They had relaxed somewhat during their conversation with the Major, but not entirely off guard. Neither did the Hottentot's sudden attack completely unnerve them. For at the very instant that the whip snatched the rifles from the hands of the two Boers, their fingers jerked convulsively on the triggers and two shots sounded, the bullets from their rifles going perilously near the Major's head. But that was all. Before either of the two Boers could recover, or the kneeling man rise and draw his revolver, the Major had

recovered his own weapon and was in command of the situation.

"I think, Jim," he said, smiling mockingly at the three men who, with loud cursing and mutual recriminations, stood with their hands above their heads, "that we will truss up these three gentlemen. Then I will ask them questions which, because they are fond of life, they will be glad to answer."

"Yes, indeed," the Major continued, reverting to his English drawl, "we will have quite a pleasant confab. For now the dude *roinek* rides in the saddle and—"

Further speech was interrupted by a harsh voice shouting, "Hands up, *roinek*! I've got you covered."

Swiftly the Major pivoted, ready to fire at sight. He saw no one.

Again came the command and, adding emphasis to it, a bullet ploughed into the ground at the Major's feet, spraying the red dust of the veld over his riding boots.

The three Boers guffawed loudly as the Major, a look of chagrin on his face, dropped his revolver and, for the second time that day, raised his hands above his head in abject surrender.

Again the harsh voice gave an order; this time to the three Boers.

"Bind the dude *and* the nigger!"

Quickly and with no gentle hands the three Boers obeyed.

A moment later a horseman rode up to the wagon and clumsily dismounted.

He was a rat of a man, little over five feet in height, his shoulders so badly rounded that they looked like a deformed hump. His black eyes, set close together, squinted malevolently; his batlike ears were overlarge and almost lobeless.

He carried a rifle in the crook of his right arm. The hand which closed over the stock was small and very white, almost like a woman's. The diamonds set into the large rings he wore sparkled in the sunlight. He was neatly, soberly dressed. The chief feature about him, and the one which aroused the Major's interest, was his vindictive slit of a mouth, the pale lips pressed firmly together—the mouth of a killer. Evidently the three Boers, despite their immense physical superiority, were afraid of him.

He looked down coldly at the dead body, and then at the little pile of things which the sandy-haired man had taken from the dead man's pockets.

"So you searched him, did you?" the newcomer asked.

"Yes, Gregson," Anders replied. "We did not know where you were and so—"

"Oh, shut up," Gregson snapped. "I don't want to hear your excuses. Did you find anything?" Although it was Anders he was questioning, he looked now at the other two Boers.

"No, Gregson," Anders replied. "He has nothing on him."

"No?" the little man's eyes came back to Anders. There was a long pause, and then he said slowly: "No, I see you have found nothing. But next time do not take so much upon yourselves. You will search when I tell you to search, and not until. You see, you clodhopper?" And there was venom and suppressed wrath in his voice, although it did not change in tone or raise in pitch. "Well, you big hulks," Gregson shouted at the three Boers, "what have you to say for yourselves?"

They shuffled uneasily; they hung their heads like scolded schoolboys.

"We were wrong, Gregson," Anders muttered at last. "We should have waited for you, we see that now."

Anders's voice was humble, but the Major, watching him closely, noted the look of resentment which came into his eyes.

"Well," Gregson said with a smirk of complacency, "now you can search the dude, Anders."

Quickly, expertly, Anders obeyed, Gregson watching him very closely. But the search brought nothing of interest to light. A handful of gold and silver coins, a cigarette case and the Major's spare monocle. That was all; save that from the breast pocket of the Major's tunic Anders extracted a bullet—the bullet which had killed the youngster lying dead at their feet.

Anders looked at it curiously, turning it round and round between his fingers. Then he exclaimed wonderingly:

"Almighty, Gregson, how came the dude by this? It came from your gun; I'd know it anywhere. That notch there—"

A snarl from Gregson interrupted him.

"You talk too much," he said, and striding forward he snatched the bullet from Anders's fingers.

"Why," Anders began wonderingly. "I only—"

"Shut up," Gregson snapped, and he struck Anders in the face with the palm of his hand.

"*Ach sis!*" Anders roared and he raised one hamlike fist, threatening to smash the little man to the ground.

There was a loud report and Anders wheeled round, blindly clawing at the air, finally collapsing, with a bullet hole drilled in the center of his forehead. For a moment a hard light came into the Major's eyes. It quickly vanished. It was replaced by one of bored indifference. The other two Boers looked wonderingly, frightenedly, from the dead body of Anders to Gregson.

"That was murder, ma-an!" one of them exclaimed. "Why did you do that?"

But Gregson only smiled as he opened the breach of his rifle and blew down the barrel. For a little while he seemed to be fully occupied with his gun.

"And that's that," he said finally. "Anders, now. He talked too much; he wasn't safe. It was best that he should die. Besides," he laughed at the other two, "there will be more for us. His share shall be ours."

"There is something in that," the two Boers admitted dubiously. "But now what? It looks as if we have done all this for nothing."

Gregson laughed.

"I think not. I think the dude will be able to tell us a great deal. You see," and he was addressing his remarks to the Major, "I know who he is. He calls himself Aubrey St. John Major; folks generally call him the Major. He's got a reputation of being damned smart. He can ride and he can shoot, and he knows the niggers, and he's clever. And so, although we could find nothing on him, I think he knows where the little piece of paper is we want so badly; or perhaps—" he looked slyly at the Major—"perhaps he has destroyed that paper. But yes! I think he memorized all that it said on it."

"By Jove, but you *are* clever!" the Major exclaimed in tones of mock admiration. "But I think you are too fond of killing to be really and truly clever. You have committed two murders this morning. Cold-blooded murders, too, and somehow I think you will have to pay."

Gregson laughed at that.

"Two men killed," he said. "Why not? It's as easy to kill a man as a jackal. Easier, because a jackal is harder to chase. My conscience doesn't bother me any. And if you are thinking of yourself as an instrument of vengeance, you had better forget it. You are not going to live long enough to be a danger to anyone—you or your nigger. Very soon, I think, you are going to die."

"Maybe, maybe not," the Major said, lightly. "But at least I don't think you will kill me, or Jim, until you have discovered for sure whether I know what you want to know."

"You'd be surprised," Gregson said, "how quickly I can make a man tell me things." He looked just then like a personification of cruelty. "I should say," he continued, "that by noon tomorrow I shall have found out all that you or your nigger can tell me. At the present I am not interested. There are other things to be done."

He set the two Boers to work digging a shallow grave into which the bodies of the two men were placed; and covered them with boulders.

"No one can accuse me," Gregson remarked to the Major, "of being callous. You see I give them a Christian burial."

"And that," the Major drawled, "is more than you, friend Gregson, are likely to get."

Gregson spat in his face and turned away to give other orders to his sycophantic followers.

Half an hour later the mules were inspanned. Then the Major and Jim were gagged so that they could not hold speech with each other and were rudely thrown into the trek wagon. One of the Boers held the reins, the other, the long driving whip. Their horses, as well as the horses of the two dead men, were tethered to the tailboard.

"Now we'll trek," said Gregson as he mounted his own horse.

The long whip cracked loudly and the mules broke into a canter, heading across the veld toward the distant blue hills.

III

An hour later they outspanned again by the side of a wide, slowly flowing river. Here the bush was very thick; so thick that a man might walk within a dozen feet of the outspan and yet not be aware of its presence.

The Major and Jim were both taken from the wagon, their gags removed.

"And now," said Gregson with a smirk, "we will get down to business. You took a paper from that youngster, didn't you? Well, where is it?"

"I haven't got it," the Major replied sadly.

"You know where it is?"

The Major shook his head.

"I am afraid not," he said slowly. "You see I had no idea of its importance and I made a cigarette of it, and smoked it all up."

Gregson chuckled.

"That's a bad move, Major," he said. "You are not in the habit of rolling your own cigarettes. Besides, why should you roll a cigarette when your case is full of them?"

The Major looked sheepish.

"If you destroyed the paper in the way you say," Gregson continued, "then you did so because you knew the paper was valuable. Well now, because it was valuable I feel quite sure that you know all that was on it, and so I propose that you tell me what you know."

"Why *should* I tell you?" the Major said. "What do I gain by telling you? It is not my habit to give something for nothing."

"If you tell, man," Gregson said, "I promise you and your nigger an easy death. And if you don't tell, then you will die, both of you, a very unpleasant death."

"I will tell you nothing," the Major said firmly.

Gregson laughed. He gave an order to the two Boers. There was an ant hill near by, full of hard-biting, poison-injecting crawlers. The Boers cut off the top of this ant hill, leveling it off to make a space large enough for a man to stand on. They then unbound Jim, removed all his clothes, and ordered him to stand on the top of the ant hill.

"Listen, Hottentot," said Gregson, and he spoke the vernacular fluently. "If you move any part of you, I'll send a bullet through it. If you want to live, you will stand as if you were made of stone, while I ask questions of your *baas*."

The two guards sat down on the veld about twenty yards from the ant hill. They had their guns with them, and they were crack marksmen.

"There's no need for this!" the Major exclaimed, anticipating the torture in store for Jim.

"I'm not ready to hear you yet," Gregson replied roughly.

The sun shone down in savage mockery upon Jim. The heat beat into the unprotected interior of the ant hill. The ants swarmed out in their thousands, ready to kill. Their home had been robbed of the protection they had raised and they wanted vengeance. They crawled over Jim's feet, they ran up his legs, biting, biting, biting. Up Jim's hips, round his legs, round his waist, up his spine, until he was covered with ants, each one digging his tiny prongs into the burning, itching Hottentot who stood on the top of their hill.

There was agony in Jim's eyes; his face was contorted. He moved his leg a fraction of an inch. One of the Boers fired, and a bullet creased the flesh of Jim's thigh, drawing blood.

Gregson turned with a laugh to the Major. "Now," he said, "I am ready to hear you talk. If you are ready to talk."

"I have been ready for a long time," the Major said coldly. "Let Jim go."

"It's all right, Hottentot, you may get down now," Gregson shouted.

"*Baas*," Jim gasped to the Major, "there is no need for you to talk if you wish to remain silent."

"I will talk, Jim," the Major said. "Get down quickly."

And then Jim descended from the ant hill. He brushed a thousand ants off his body and then ran in a panic for the river and dived into its cooling depths. The Boers followed him to see that he did not go too far.

Meanwhile the Major was telling Gregson all that he had learnt from the scrap of paper.

Again and again Gregson questioned him. Again and again the Major gave the same replies.

"And now," Gregson said, freeing the Major's right hand and giving him a pencil, "now you shall draw me the map as you saw it."

He held a piece of paper while the Major traced the outline of a map and filled in the names which had been on the paper.

Just then the two Boers returned, escorting Jim; a miserable, itching Jim.

"Gag the Hottentot," Gregson ordered.

The two Boers obeyed. Then both of them came and stood truculently before their leader.

"Did the *roinek* tell you, Gregson?" they asked eagerly.

He nodded.

"Yes."

They grinned happily.

"Then what now; what are you going to do with the *roinek* and his nigger?"

"Shoot 'em," Gregson said.

"Almighty!" the younger of the Boers exclaimed. "Is there to be yet more killing?"

"And if you kill them," the other one exclaimed, "and then find that the *roinek* has lied to you—what then?"

Gregson rubbed his chin thoughtfully.

"Sometimes," he said grudgingly, "you are not altogether a fool, Pete. These two shall live a little while longer. We will go to this place he speaks of. And if he has lied, there will still be time to make him tell the truth."

"I have not lied," the Major said hastily.

But Gregson ignored him. He was walking thoughtfully up and down. Presently he turned abruptly on the two Boers, who were watching him eagerly.

"Yes," he said patronizingly. "You have exposed the weakness of my plan, and so I must improve it. This is what I will do. I will now go to the place the Major spoke of. It is not far from here, and he has drawn me a map of the place. You will stay here and guard the Major and the nigger. If the Major has lied, then I'll return here and will deal with him properly."

The sandy-haired Boer, Pete, laughed. "And if the Major has not lied," he said sarcastically, "then you will *not* return here. Almighty! We may be fools, but we are not big fools like that, Gregson. No, I say we go together, or we stay together."

Gregson's face was convulsed with wrath, and the two Boers flinched before the killing light in his eyes. But his rifle was leaning against a tree a few yards away. His revolver was in its holster, and the two Boers covered him with their guns. So he said mildly, "You ought to trust me. We are in this together."

"As for that," said the younger Boer, "I am not so sure. At least, so far we have done no killing. And," he added after a pause, "will not."

Gregson ignored that.

"It would be folly," he said presently, "for us all to go to this place together. Here we are safe. It is not likely that anyone will see us. But if we trek further, who knows who may run across our trail. It is best that you let me go alone."

The two Boers shook their heads. On that one point, at least, they were firm and united.

"We do not trust you, Gregson," said Pete, the sandy-haired one. "If you go, we go, and there is an end to it."

Gregson frowned.

"Then one of you shall go," he said. "How does that suit you?"

They looked at each other doubtfully, thinking that some dark plan was behind Gregson's words. They shook their heads.

"You mean that you would send one of us off on a wild-goose chase and then you'd kill the other," said Pete. "No, we do not like it."

"You are fools," Gregson snapped. "You do not trust me, neither then do I trust you. Yet listen: both of you shall go, for you cannot cheat me. You shall go, and if you are not back by sundown I shall come after you and—" he smiled grimly—"I do not think you will live very long."

But still the Boers were not satisfied.

"It will not do, Gregson," Pete said. "I say we all go together, or we all stay together. Together we sink or swim."

"Or," the young Boer added, "I will go, if the dude will go with me. Then I shall be sure that, whatever happens, I will know at least as much as you know."

Gregson considered this for a moment. Then he nodded.

"Yes, that might do it. The Major shall lead you to the place. He shall ride my horse and his hands shall be bound to a rope which you will hold, and whatever happens to you I have no fear about his not returning, because if he doesn't, then the nigger will know what torture really is. You hear that, Major?"

The Major nodded.

"If I go," he said, "I will return. I give you my word of honor."

"And this further," Gregson continued to the young Boer. "You will go unarmed. I'm not going to have you sneak up behind my back and shoot me."

They argued this point, heatedly, but at last Gregson—he was backed up by Pete, the sandy-haired Boer—won his point.

And so it was settled.

Five minutes later the Major and the young Boer rode off at a fast pace.

IV

It was half an hour later. At the sound of a crisp report which had echoed faintly over the veld, the young Boer reined in his horse with a violent oath, stopping the Major's horse so suddenly, by yanking at the reins which he held, that the Major, bound as he was, was almost unseated.

"What was that?" the Boer asked anxiously. "Did you hear it?"

The Major looked at him curiously. "Yes, I heard it," he said, "but—"

"What was it?" the Boer repeated again.

"Don't you know?" the Major asked. "It was a revolver shot. I think our friend Gregson has decided that it is better to divide the loot into two shares rather than three. I think he has killed your countryman."

"Almighty," the Boer exclaimed, "if I thought that—" he broke off with a curse; his eyes blazed angrily.

"Yes," the Major said, "if you thought that—"

"I'd go back and kill the killer," the Boer concluded fiercely. "With my two hands I'd kill him."

"Then shall we go back," the Major suggested. "And perhaps it would be better if you untied my hands." He held them out to the Boer. His wrists were lashed together by stout *reim*—thongs of hippo hide—one end of which the Boer held. "Four hands are better than two," he continued. "And we are unarmed. Had you forgotten that?"

A look of slow comprehension came to the Boer's face. "Almighty," he exclaimed slowly. "I had not thought of that. Truly that one Gregson is very *slim*. And so—" He shrugged his shoulders, and pursed his lips thoughtfully.

"Let us go back," the Major said again. "Together I think that we can deal with Gregson as he should be dealt with."

The Boer shivered.

"No!" he said dully. "We must go on, I must do as Gregson ordered. I am sorry for you, *roinek*. I am sorry for myself, but he is an evil man and I cannot escape him. Truly I have been a fool. And for my folly I must pay. Now we will trek."

The Major sighed and the two men resumed the trek, heading for a sugarloaf-shaped *kopje* which was their goal. They rode in silence, each man concerned with his own thoughts.

From time to time the Major looked curiously at his companion. That man rode like one in a dream, apparently forgetful of his prisoner. He had scarcely any grip on the rope he held in his hand and it hung loosely between the two horses.

Cautiously the Major worked his hands trying to get them free. After a time he succeeded to the extent of being able to move his wrists apart several inches. More than that he could not do. The hide rope held firm and it was wet now with the blood which welled up from his lacerated wrists. But at least he could grip something with his hands.

He toyed with the suggestion of making a grab for the reins and galloping for safety. But such a maneuver, although it would mean his own personal freedom, would not help Jim. On the contrary, it would be Jim's death warrant, for undoubtedly the Boer would ride back to Gregson and notify him of the Major's escape.

So they rode on, the Major still working on his bound wrists, the Boer brooding over the folly of his ways.

It was the Major who broke the long silence.

"We should go faster," he said, "if we are to reach the place before sundown."

The Boer grunted in agreement, dug his spurs into his shaggy-coated horse, and their pace increased to a canter. Suddenly the Major threw himself sideways and fell from his horse with a wild cry.

The Boer halted the two horses, turned and rode back to where the Major sprawled, face downward, on the veld. A worried look came into his eyes.

"Almighty," he muttered, "is he dead too?" And in a loud voice he shouted, "Come on, *roinek*, stop shamming. You are not a girl to be killed by such a little tumble."

But the man stretched out on the veld made no reply, and there seemed to be no movement in his body.

The Boer scratched his head. And then with an oath he dismounted and stooped over the Major, gripping him by the shoulder and shaking him. He knelt down and turned the Major over on to his back. The Major's face seemed very white, his eyes were closed, his mouth gaped open, his face was smeared with blood.

"Almighty," the Boer breathed softly, and bent over, his head to the Major's chest, listening for the beating of his heart. As he did so two strong hands closed about his throat, squeezing.

The Boer struggled violently, he lashed out with his hands, but the grip about his throat tightened. The Major's legs pinioned his and presently his struggles ceased. The darkness of night seemed to fall very swiftly upon him.

When he opened his eyes again he saw the Major sitting beside him, and the Major was no longer bound. There was no blood on his face.

"Almighty," the Boer groaned. His hands were tied behind his back, and his feet were bound together so he could not move. "Almighty," he said again, "I thought you were dead, *roinek*."

The Major laughed softly. "I was a little winded," he confessed, "that was all."

"But the blood on your face? There was blood on your face, *roinek*!"

"It came from my wrists," the Major said, chuckling softly. "I must have looked a pretty ghastly sight. It was a child's trick I played on you, but it worked."

"And you are free!" the Boer exclaimed, his slow mind being unable to grasp all things quickly.

The Major nodded. "Truly. First I worked my hands free, just a little. Just enough so that I

could close them about your throat. And then, when you were unconscious—well, there was a knife in your belt and the rest was easy."

The Boer groaned.

"Not so easy, *roinek*. The end is not yet. There is still Gregson."

The Major nodded; his eyes were very stern. "I have not forgotten," he said, softly. "I have not forgotten Gregson."

They were silent for a while. The Boer's eyes closed as a protection from the strong light of the sun.

"What are you going to do, *roinek*?" he asked.

"I am waiting for darkness," the Major replied, "and then I am going back to deal with Gregson."

"Unarmed!" the Boer exclaimed. "Truly you are a fool."

"You forget I have your knife," the Major reminded him. "And besides, Mister Gregson will be unprepared for what I am planning for him. Oh quite!"

"What do you intend to do with me?" the Boer asked.

The Major frowned. "You are somewhat of a problem," he admitted. "If I thought I could trust you, I would take you as a partner, but . . ." He shook his head.

"You are right, *roinek*," the Boer said. "You cannot trust me. I might give you my word, but once I got near Gregson . . ." He shivered. "I tell you he is an evil man. I am afraid of him. And so I would rather be on his side than against him."

"Quite," the Major said casually. "So I think I shall have to leave you here, bound as you are. I don't like doing it, really. Anything might happen to a man bound on the veld, alone, at night."

The Boer grunted, but made no protest. He gazed moodily at the distant *kopje*.

"*Ach sis!*" he exclaimed in sudden anger. "The *verdoemte* fools. Look at them!"

"What is it?" the Major asked.

The Boer nodded in the direction of the *kopje*. From its lower slopes coils of black smoke mounted into the air.

"The niggers are out setting fire to the brush."

"What of it?" the Major asked. "It is a common thing they do. In that way they get fresh green grass for their cattle."

"True," the Boer agreed. "But they are fools. They do not learn. They light a little fire and in a little while it gets out of hand. You—have you not seen bush fires?"

The Major looked thoughtful.

"But there is no danger," he expostulated. "There is no wind."

"There will be a wind, when the sun sets," the Boer insisted harshly. "And almighty, *roinek*," there was something suspiciously like tears in his voice, "if a wind blows one way it does not matter; if it blows the other way . . . Listen, *roinek:* I have a homestead, not ten miles from here. And if the fire goes that way—*ach sis,* man! I tell you that my *vrow* is ill, and there are two little *kinder*."

The Major looked at him thoughtfully.

"I do not think you are lying," he said slowly, "and so . . ." He cut the Boer free.

That man murmured incoherent words of thanks. He mounted his horse and rode rapidly away, following a course which would take him some distance to the eastward of the sugarloaf-shaped *kopje*.

V

The sun had long since set. The Major rode slowly back through the darkness toward the outspan at the river. The night air was still. Behind him the sugarloaf-shaped *kopje* was blazing like a mountain of fire. The Major reined in to watch the spectacle it presented. And then, with a suddenness that is Africa, a wind sprang up, blowing from the *kopje* toward the Major. And, following its course, a wide tongue of flame leaped out from the base of the mountain, like a red, fiery finger, pointing toward the white man. Quickly the flames spread, east and west. Quickly they advanced.

There was smoke in the air. It became thicker with every passing moment. Birds were flying down past the Major, and insects and locusts. The Major heard the thunder of animals' hoofs. The bush suddenly became alive with sound.

The wind increased. The day's hot sun had evaporated all the dew and moisture from the grass. On the wings of the wind came the fire and before it fled every living creature. A stream of terrified creatures fled past the Major, hardly swerving their flight, unconscious of his presence. A herd of *kudu*, a mass of moving gray; then *wildebeeste*, heads lowered, like cavalry heading a forlorn hope. A herd of zebra galloped by. Birds and beasts. And, a malignant sight, hardly seen in the red glow of the fire, a black *momba*, the deadly South African snake, passed within three feet of the Major's horse, half of its twelve-foot body suspended above the ground. It went past effortlessly, seeming to flow over the ground.

The Major dismounted, and started "burns" in a number of places. In a few moments each little flame became a violent conflagration, sweeping on before the wind, leaving behind it blackened ground, inches deep in ashes, and glowing cinders.

The Major mounted again and waited; waited until the scorching breath of the fire behind him was almost upon him. The heat was unbearable; sparks and live brands blew through the air. Many fell upon the Major, burning his clothing, blistering his back.

And then, when it seemed that human flesh and blood could stand no more, the fire divided at the "burn" the Major had made, and splitting, swept onward on either side.

A little while longer the Major waited before he rode onward, following the course of the fire.

VI

Gregson awoke from a pleasant dream of wealth worklessly acquired, to a foretaste of hell. The bush about the outspan echoed to the sound of stampeding animals. The air was filled with red sparks. The blackness of the night was painted red by the bush fire. The tented top of the Major's wagon was already ablaze. The mules had stampeded. The two horses which were tethered to the tailboard of the wagon were neighing in deadly terror.

Gregson cursed, but did not lose his presence of mind. Nearby, the river ran placidly, a haven of refuge, and he ran for it, deaf to the terrified neighs of the horses and the cries of Jim, the Hottentot, who was bound to one of the wheels of the wagon. But he was not alone in his flight to the river. A herd of *impala* rushed by him. A wart hog sow with her litter brushed against his legs, nearly knocking him off his balance. He hit out viciously at the animals which crowded about him with a stick he had picked up while running from the outspan.

A black *momba* passed very close to him. He struck at it, missing, and the snake, which otherwise would have passed him by, turned incensed at the human who had broken the truce which all animals hold in the face of mutual peril. It struck once and passed on.

Gregson screamed his terror. He gashed the wound with his knife—that was all he could do—and then, blood streaming from his thigh, struggled on.

By the time he reached the river, strength failed Gregson and he fell face downward into the mire at the verge. He died a horrible death there while panic-stricken animals trampled over his body.

Back at the camp, the fire was checked. The trodden ground about the cleared ground of the outspan provided little fuel for the onrushing bush fire. The grass flamed up and as quickly died down, but the heat in that tiny space, as the fire roared about it on all sides, was like that of a mighty oven. The two horses, plunging and rearing, at last broke away, dashing madly about the clearing, looking for an opening in the wall of fire. At last the flames passed on, and after them, calling frantically, came the Major. He was streaming with sweat, his body blistered and caked with ash.

"Jim," he called, "Jim!"

And the Hottentot found somewhere strength enough to reply, "I am here, *baas*. Be quick. The flame grows hot."

The Major spurred up to the blazing wagon, dismounted, and in a few moments he had cut Jim loose from the wheel to which he had been lashed, just as the wagon collapsed, shooting up a shower of sparks and blazing brands.

Then the Major tenderly helped Jim up into the saddle of his frightened horse, and mounting behind him rode away from that scene of evil and destruction. They had lost all of their possessions, their wagon and all its contents, their mules; but the one thing the bush fire could not take away from them was the secret of the gold buried in the sugarloaf-shaped *kopje*, the secret which the Major had so carefully committed to memory and which the killer Gregson would now never be able to make use of.

So Jim and the Major rode across the desolation of black scorched veld, sorry figures. But they had within their grasp the means to buy a new wagon and mules and guns, and with those they could trek to new adventures.

H. RIDER HAGGARD

THE NAME OF no writer is more closely or affectionately connected to adventure fiction than that of Sir Henry Rider Haggard (1856–1925), whose novels and stories, although written for adults, are avidly read by adolescents as well. Like so many Englishmen of the Victorian era, Haggard was a solid imperialist with a great interest in politics, and was regarded as an expert on British colonialism. Born in Norfolk, he was sent at the age of nineteen to South Africa to be an assistant to the lieutenant governor of Natal. When the Transvaal was annexed by Great Britain, he served in its government, but resigned in 1880 to take up ostrich farming. The following year, the area was given back to the Dutch, and Haggard returned to England, where he married, studied law, and, in 1884, became a barrister. With the publication of *King Solomon's Mines* in the following year, however, Haggard's financial security was assured, and he never practiced law again. He followed this enormously successful novel with many others, predominantly set in Africa, that have become classics still read with pleasure today. Haggard's notable adventures include *She* (1887), *Allan Quatermain* (1887), and *Maiwa's Revenge* (1888). In these and other thrilling stories, enterprising British explorers, most frequently the famous Quatermain, along with their heroic African guides, discover lost cities and tribes and confront astonishing figures—such as Ayesha, the mysterious white queen of *She*. Known as "She-who-must-be-obeyed," Haggard's imposing creation has given a popular phrase to the English language: John Mortimer's acerbic London barrister, for one, refers to his wife in this manner in the television series *Rumpole of the Bailey* (1978–1992). Although Haggard wrote more than forty novels, romantic thrillers filled with breathtaking action in which all women are beautiful and all heroes courageous and strong, he received his knighthood for expert treatises on agriculture, immigration, labor colonies, and colonial emigration.

Allan Quatermain is a British outdoorsman who earns his living as a big-game hunter in Africa, which he much prefers to the crowded cities of his native land—though he feels it his duty to help bring Western (i.e., British) civilization to the Dark Continent. The hunter appears in fifteen novels by Haggard, but, like Sherlock Holmes, he has also found new life in works by other writers, particularly the graphic novel series *The League of Extraordinary Gentlemen* (1999–).

"Hunter Quatermain's Story" was first published in a rare anthology produced for charity, *In a Good Cause,* in 1885; it was later collected in Haggard's *Allan's Wife and Other Tales* (London: Spencer, Blackett, 1889).

HUNTER QUATERMAIN'S STORY

H. RIDER HAGGARD

SIR HENRY CURTIS, as everybody acquainted with him knows, is one of the most hospitable men on earth. It was in the course of the enjoyment of his hospitality at his place in Yorkshire the other day that I heard the hunting story which I am now about to transcribe. Many of those who read it will no doubt have heard some of the strange rumours that are flying about to the effect that Sir Henry Curtis and his friend Captain Good, R.N., recently found a vast treasure of diamonds out in the heart of Africa, supposed to have been hidden by the Egyptians, or King Solomon, or some other antique person. I first saw the matter alluded to in a paragraph in one of the society papers the day before I started for Yorkshire to pay my visit to Curtis, and arrived, needless to say, burning with curiosity; for there is something very fascinating to the mind in the idea of hidden treasure. When I reached the Hall, I at once asked Curtis about it, and he did not deny the truth of the story; but on my pressing him to tell it he would not, nor would Captain Good, who was also staying in the house.

"You would not believe me if I did," Sir Henry said, with one of the hearty laughs which seem to come right out of his great lungs. "You must wait till Hunter Quatermain comes; he will arrive here from Africa to-night, and I am not going to say a word about the matter, or Good either, until he turns up. Quatermain was with us all through; he has known about the business for years and years, and if it had not been for him

we should not have been here to-day. I am going to meet him presently."

I could not get a word more out of him, nor could anybody else, though we were all dying of curiosity, especially some of the ladies. I shall never forget how they looked in the drawing-room before dinner when Captain Good produced a great rough diamond, weighing fifty carats or more, and told them that he had many larger than that. If ever I saw curiosity and envy printed on fair faces, I saw them then.

It was just at this moment that the door was opened, and Mr. Allan Quatermain announced, whereupon Good put the diamond into his pocket, and sprang at a little man who limped shyly into the room, convoyed by Sir Henry Curtis himself.

"Here he is, Good, safe and sound," said Sir Henry, gleefully. "Ladies and gentlemen, let me introduce you to one of the oldest hunters and the very best shot in Africa, who has killed more elephants and lions than any other man alive."

Everybody turned and stared politely at the curious-looking little lame man, and though his size was insignificant, he was quite worth staring at. He had short grizzled hair, which stood about an inch above his head like the bristles of a brush, gentle brown eyes, that seemed to notice everything, and a withered face, tanned to the colour of mahogany from exposure to the weather. He spoke, too, when he returned Good's enthusiastic greeting, with a curious little accent, which made his speech noticeable.

It so happened that I sat next to Mr. Allan Quatermain at dinner, and, of course, did my best to draw him; but he was not to be drawn. He admitted that he had recently been a long journey into the interior of Africa with Sir Henry Curtis and Captain Good, and that they had found treasure, and then politely turned the subject and began to ask me questions about England, where he had never been before—that is, since he came to years of discretion. Of course, I did not find this very interesting, and so cast about for some means to bring the conversation round again.

Now, we were dining in an oak-panelled vestibule, and on the wall opposite to me were fixed two gigantic elephant tusks, and under them a pair of buffalo horns, very rough and knotted, showing that they came off an old bull, and having the tip of one horn split and chipped. I noticed that Hunter Quatermain's eyes kept glancing at these trophies, and took an occasion to ask him if he knew anything about them.

"I ought to," he answered, with a little laugh; "the elephant to which those tusks belonged tore one of our party right in two about eighteen months ago, and as for the buffalo horns, they were nearly my death, and were the end of a servant of mine to whom I was much attached. I gave them to Sir Henry when he left Natal some months ago;" and Mr. Quatermain sighed and turned to answer a question from the lady whom he had taken down to dinner, and who, needless to say, was also employed in trying to pump him about the diamonds.

Indeed, all round the table there was a simmer of scarcely suppressed excitement, which, when the servants had left the room, could no longer be restrained.

"Now, Mr. Quatermain," said the lady next him, "we have been kept in an agony of suspense by Sir Henry and Captain Good, who have persistently refused to tell us a word of this story about the hidden treasure till you came, and we simply can bear it no longer; so, please, begin at once."

"Yes," said everybody, "go on, please."

Hunter Quatermain glanced round the table apprehensively; he did not seem to appreciate finding himself the object of so much curiosity.

"Ladies and gentlemen," he said at last, with a shake of his grizzled head, "I am very sorry to disappoint you, but I cannot do it. It is this way. At the request of Sir Henry and Captain Good I have written down a true and plain account of King Solomon's Mines and how we found them, so you will soon all be able to learn all about that wonderful adventure for yourselves; but until then I will say nothing about it, not from any wish to disappoint your curiosity, or to make myself important, but simply because the whole story partakes so much of the marvellous, that I am afraid to tell it in a piecemeal, hasty fashion, for fear I should be set down as one of those common fellows of whom there are so many in my profession, who are not ashamed to narrate things they have not seen, and even to tell wonderful stories about wild animals they have never killed. And I think that my companions in adventure, Sir Henry Curtis and Captain Good, will bear me out in what I say."

"Yes, Quatermain, I think you are quite right," said Sir Henry. "Precisely the same considerations have forced Good and myself to hold our tongues. We did not wish to be bracketed with—well, with other famous travellers."

There was a murmur of disappointment at these announcements.

"I believe you are all hoaxing us," said the young lady next to Mr. Quatermain, rather sharply.

"Believe me," answered the old hunter, with a quaint courtesy and a little bow of his grizzled head; "though I have lived all my life in the wilderness, and amongst savages, I have neither the heart, nor the want of manners, to wish to deceive one so lovely."

Whereat the young lady, who was pretty, looked appeased.

"This is very dreadful," I broke in. "We ask for bread and you give us a stone, Mr. Quatermain. The least that you can do is to tell us the story of the tusks opposite and the buffalo horns underneath. We won't let you off with less."

"I am but a poor story-teller," put in the old hunter, "but if you will forgive my want of skill, I shall be happy to tell you, not the story of the tusks, for it is part of the history of our journey to King Solomon's Mines, but that of the buffalo horns beneath them, which is now ten years old."

"Bravo, Quatermain!" said Sir Henry. "We shall all be delighted. Fire away! Fill up your glass first."

The little man did as he was bid, took a sip of claret, and began:—"About ten years ago I was hunting up in the far interior of Africa, at a place called Gatgarra, not a great way from the Chobe River. I had with me four native servants, namely, a driver and voorlooper, or leader, who were natives of Matabeleland, a Hottentot called Hans, who had once been the slave of a Transvaal Boer, and a Zulu hunter, who for five years had accompanied me upon my trips, and whose name was Mashune. Now near Gatgarra I found a fine piece of healthy, park-like country, where the grass was very good, considering the time of year; and here I made a little camp or headquarter settlement, from whence I went expeditions on all sides in search of game, especially elephant. My luck, however, was bad; I got but little ivory. I was therefore very glad when some natives brought me news that a large herd of elephants were feeding in a valley about thirty miles away. At first I thought of trekking down to the valley, waggon and all, but gave up the idea on hearing that it was infested with the deadly 'tsetse' fly, which is certain death to all animals, except men, donkeys, and wild game. So I reluctantly determined to leave the waggon in the charge of the Matabele leader and driver, and to start on a trip into the thorn country, accompanied only by the Hottentot Hans, and Mashune.

"Accordingly on the following morning we started, and on the evening of the next day reached the spot where the elephants were reported to be. But here again we were met by ill luck. That the elephants had been there was evident enough, for their spoor was plentiful, and

so were other traces of their presence in the shape of mimosa trees torn out of the ground, and placed topsy-turvy on their flat crowns, in order to enable the great beasts to feed on their sweet roots; but the elephants themselves were conspicuous by their absence. They had elected to move on. This being so, there was only one thing to do, and that was to move after them, which we did, and a pretty hunt they led us. For a fortnight or more we dodged about after those elephants, coming up with them on two occasions, and a splendid herd they were—only, however, to lose them again. At length we came up with them a third time, and I managed to shoot one bull, and then they started off again, where it was useless to try and follow them. After this I gave it up in disgust, and we made the best of our way back to the camp, not in the sweetest of tempers, carrying the tusks of the elephant I had shot.

"It was on the afternoon of the fifth day of our tramp that we reached the little koppie overlooking the spot where the waggon stood, and I confess that I climbed it with a pleasurable sense of home-coming, for his waggon is the hunter's home, as much as his house is that of the civilized person. I reached the top of the koppie, and looked in the direction where the friendly white tent of the waggon should be, but there was no waggon, only a black burnt plain stretching away as far as the eye could reach. I rubbed my eyes, looked again, and made out on the spot of the camp, not my waggon, but some charred beams of wood. Half wild with grief and anxiety, followed by Hans and Mashune, I ran at full speed down the slope of the koppie, and across the space of plain below to the spring of water, where my camp had been. I was soon there, only to find that my worst suspicions were confirmed.

"The waggon and all its contents, including my spare guns and ammunition, had been destroyed by a grass fire.

"Now before I started, I had left orders with the driver to burn off the grass round the camp, in order to guard against accidents of this nature, and here was the reward of my folly: a very proper illustration of the necessity, especially where natives are concerned, of doing a thing one's self if one wants it done at all. Evidently the lazy rascals had not burnt round the waggon; most probably, indeed, they had themselves carelessly fired the tall and resinous tambouki grass near by; the wind had driven the flames on to the waggon tent, and there was quickly an end of the matter. As for the driver and leader, I know not what became of them: probably fearing my anger, they bolted, taking the oxen with them. I have never seen them from that hour to this.

"I sat down on the black veldt by the spring, and gazed at the charred axles and disselboom of my waggon, and I can assure you, ladies and gentlemen, I felt inclined to weep. As for Mashune and Hans they cursed away vigorously, one in Zulu and the other in Dutch. Ours was a pretty position. We were nearly 300 miles away from Bamangwato, the capital of Khama's country, which was the nearest spot where we could get any help, and our ammunition, spare guns, clothing, food, and everything else, were all totally destroyed. I had just what I stood in, which was a flannel shirt, a pair of 'veldt-schoons,' or shoes of raw hide, my eight-bore rifle, and a few cartridges. Hans and Mashune had also each a Martini rifle and some cartridges, not many. And it was with this equipment that we had to undertake a journey of 300 miles through a desolate and almost uninhabited region. I can assure you that I have rarely been in a worse position, and I have been in some queer ones. However, these things are the natural incidents of a hunter's life, and the only thing to do was to make the best of them.

"Accordingly, after passing a comfortless night by the remains of my waggon, we started next morning on our long journey towards civilization. Now if I were to set to work to tell you all the troubles and incidents of that dreadful journey I should keep you listening here till midnight; so I will, with your permission, pass on to the particular adventure of which the pair of buffalo horns opposite are the melancholy memento.

"We had been travelling for about a month, living and getting along as best we could, when one evening we camped some forty miles from Bamangwato. By this time we were indeed in a melancholy plight, footsore, half starved, and utterly worn out; and, in addition, I was suffering from a sharp attack of fever, which half blinded me and made me weak as a babe. Our ammunition, too, was exhausted; I had only one cartridge left for my eight-bore rifle, and Hans and Mashune, who were armed with Martini Henrys, had three between them. It was about an hour from sundown when we halted and lit a fire—for luckily we had still a few matches. It was a charming spot to camp, I remember. Just off the game track we were following was a little hollow, fringed about with flat-crowned mimosa trees, and at the bottom of the hollow, a spring of clear water welled up out of the earth, and formed a pool, round the edges of which grew an abundance of watercresses of an exactly similar kind to those which were handed round the table just now. Now we had no food of any kind left, having that morning devoured the last remains of a little oribe antelope, which I had shot two days previously. Accordingly Hans, who was a better shot than Mashune, took two of the three remaining Martini cartridges, and started out to see if he could not kill a buck for supper. I was too weak to go myself.

"Meanwhile Mashune employed himself in dragging together some dead boughs from the mimosa trees to make a sort of 'skerm,' or shelter for us to sleep in, about forty yards from the edge of the pool of water. We had been greatly troubled with lions in the course of our long tramp, and only on the previous night had very nearly been attacked by them, which made me nervous, especially in my weak state. Just as we had finished the skerm, or rather something which did duty for one, Mashune and I heard a shot apparently fired about a mile away.

" 'Hark to it!' sung out Mashune in Zulu, more, I fancy, by way of keeping his spirits up than for any other reason—for he was a sort of black Mark Tapley, and very cheerful under difficulties. 'Hark to the wonderful sound with which the "Maboona" (the Boers) shook our fathers to the ground at the battle of the Blood River. We are hungry now, my father; our stomachs are small and withered up like a dried ox's paunch, but they will soon be full of good meat. Hans is a Hottentot, and an "umfagozan," that is, a low fellow, but he shoots straight—ah! he certainly shoots straight. Be of a good heart, my father, there will soon be meat upon the fire, and we shall rise up men.'

"And so he went on talking nonsense till I told him to stop, because he made my head ache with his empty words.

"Shortly after we heard the shot the sun sank in his red splendour, and there fell upon earth and sky the great hush of the African wilderness. The lions were not up as yet, they would probably wait for the moon, and the birds and beasts were all at rest. I cannot describe the intensity of the quiet of the night: to me in my weak state, and fretting as I was over the non-return of the Hottentot Hans, it seemed almost ominous—as though Nature were brooding over some tragedy which was being enacted in her sight.

"It was quiet—quiet as death, and lonely as the grave.

" 'Mashune,' I said at last, 'where is Hans? My heart is heavy for him.'

" 'Nay, my father, I know not; mayhap he is weary, and sleeps, or mayhap he has lost his way.'

" 'Mashune, art thou a boy to talk folly to me?' I answered. 'Tell me, in all the years thou hast hunted by my side, didst thou ever know a Hottentot to lose his path or to sleep upon the way to camp?'

" 'Nay, Macumazahn' (that, ladies, is my native name, and means the man who 'gets up by night,' or who 'is always awake'), 'I know not where he is.'

"But though we talked thus, we neither of us liked to hint at what was in both our minds, namely, that misfortune had overtaken the poor Hottentot.

" 'Mashune,' I said at last, 'go down to the water and bring me of those green herbs that grow there. I am hungered, and must eat something.'

" 'Nay, my father; surely the ghosts are there; they come out of the water at night, and sit upon the banks to dry themselves. An Isanusi* told it me.'

"Mashune was, I think, one of the bravest men I ever knew in the daytime, but he had a more than civilized dread of the supernatural.

" 'Must I go myself, thou fool?' I said, sternly.

" 'Nay, Macumazahn, if thy heart yearns for strange things like a sick woman, I go, even if the ghosts devour me.'

"And accordingly he went, and soon returned with a large bundle of watercresses, of which I ate greedily.

" 'Art thou not hungry?' I asked the great Zulu presently, as he sat eyeing me eating.

" 'Never was I hungrier, my father.'

" 'Then eat,' and I pointed to the watercresses.

" 'Nay, Macumazahn, I cannot eat those herbs.'

" 'If thou dost not eat thou wilt starve: eat, Mashune.'

"He stared at the watercresses doubtfully for a while, and at last seized a handful and crammed them into his mouth, crying out as he did so, 'Oh, why was I born that I should live to feed on green weeds like an ox? Surely if my mother could have known it she would have killed me when I was born!' and so he went on lamenting between each fistful of watercresses till all were finished, when he declared that he was full indeed of stuff, but it lay very cold on his stomach, 'like snow upon a mountain.' At any other time I should have laughed, for it must be admitted he had a ludicrous way of putting things. Zulus do not like green food.

"Just after Mashune had finished his watercress, we heard the loud 'woof! woof!' of a lion, who was evidently promenading much nearer to

---

Isanusi, witch-finder.

our little skerm than was pleasant. Indeed, on looking into the darkness and listening intently, I could hear his snoring breath, and catch the light of his great yellow eyes. We shouted loudly, and Mashune threw some sticks on the fire to frighten him, which apparently had the desired effect, for we saw no more of him for a while.

"Just after we had had this fright from the lion, the moon rose in her fullest splendour, throwing a robe of silver light over all the earth. I have rarely seen a more beautiful moonrise. I remember that sitting in the skerm I could with ease read faint pencil notes in my pocket-book. As soon as the moon was up game began to trek down to the water just below us. I could, from where I sat, see all sorts of them passing along a little ridge that ran to our right, on their way to the drinking place. Indeed, one buck—a large eland—came within twenty yards of the skerm, and stood at gaze, staring at it suspiciously, his beautiful head and twisted horns standing out clearly against the sky. I had, I recollect, every mind to have a pull at him on the chance of providing ourselves with a good supply of beef; but remembering that we had but two cartridges left, and the extreme uncertainty of a shot by moonlight, I at length decided to refrain. The eland presently moved on to the water, and a minute or two afterwards there arose a great sound of splashing, followed by the quick fall of galloping hoofs.

" 'What's that, Mashune?' I asked.

" 'That dam lion; buck smell him,' replied the Zulu in English, of which he had a very superficial knowledge.

"Scarcely were the words out of his mouth before we heard a sort of whine over the other side of the pool, which was instantly answered by a loud coughing roar close to us.

" 'By Jove!' I said, 'there are two of them. They have lost the buck; we must look out they don't catch us.' And again we made up the fire, and shouted, with the result that the lions moved off.

" 'Mashune,' I said, 'do your watch till the

moon gets over that tree, when it will be the middle of the night. Then wake me. Watch well, now, or the lions will be picking those worthless bones of yours before you are three hours older. I must rest a little, or I shall die.'

" 'Koos!' (chief), answered the Zulu. 'Sleep, my father, sleep in peace; my eyes shall be open as the stars; and like the stars watch over you.'

"Although I was so weak, I could not at once follow his advice. To begin with, my head ached with fever, and I was torn with anxiety as to the fate of the Hottentot Hans; and, indeed, as to our own fate, left with sore feet, empty stomachs, and two cartridges, to find our way to Bamangwato, forty miles off. Then the mere sensation of knowing that there are one or more hungry lions prowling round you somewhere in the dark is disquieting, however well one may be used to it, and, by keeping the attention on the stretch, tends to prevent one from sleeping. In addition to all these troubles, too, I was, I remember, seized with a dreadful longing for a pipe of tobacco, whereas, under the circumstances, I might as well have longed for the moon.

"At last, however, I fell into an uneasy sleep as full of bad dreams as a prickly pear is of points, one of which, I recollect, was that I was setting my naked foot upon a cobra which rose upon its tail and hissed my name, 'Macumazahn,' into my ear. Indeed, the cobra hissed with such persistency that at last I roused myself.

" '*Macumazahn, nanzia, nanzia!*' (there, there!) whispered Mashune's voice into my drowsy ears. Raising myself, I opened my eyes, and I saw Mashune kneeling by my side and pointing towards the water. Following the line of his outstretched hand, my eyes fell upon a sight that made me jump, old hunter as I was even in those days. About twenty paces from the little skerm was a large ant-heap, and on the summit of the ant-heap, her four feet rather close together, so as to find standing space, stood the massive form of a big lioness. Her head was towards the skerm, and in the bright moonlight I saw her lower it and lick her paws.

"Mashune thrust the Martini rifle into my hands, whispering that it was loaded. I lifted it and covered the lioness, but found that even in that light I could not make out the foresight of the Martini. As it would be madness to fire without doing so, for the result would probably be that I should wound the lioness, if, indeed, I did not miss her altogether, I lowered the rifle; and, hastily tearing a fragment of paper from one of the leaves of my pocket-book, which I had been consulting just before I went to sleep, I proceeded to fix it on to the front sight. But all this took a little time, and before the paper was satisfactorily arranged, Mashune again gripped me by the arm, and pointed to a dark heap under the shade of a small mimosa tree which grew not more than ten paces from the skerm.

" 'Well, what is it?' I whispered; 'I can see nothing.'

" 'It is another lion,' he answered.

" 'Nonsense! thy heart is dead with fear, thou seest double;' and I bent forward over the edge of the surrounding fence, and stared at the heap.

"Even as I said the words, the dark mass rose and stalked out into the moonlight. It was a magnificent, black-maned lion, one of the largest I had ever seen. When he had gone two or three steps he caught sight of me, halted, and stood there gazing straight towards us;—he was so close that I could see the firelight reflected in his wicked, greenish eyes.

" 'Shoot, shoot!' said Mashune. 'The devil is coming—he is going to spring!'

"I raised the rifle, and got the bit of paper on the foresight, straight on to a little path of white hair just where the throat is set into the chest and shoulders. As I did so, the lion glanced back over his shoulder, as, according to my experience, a lion nearly always does before he springs. Then he dropped his body a little, and I saw his big paws spread out upon the ground as he put his weight on them to gather purchase. In haste I pressed the trigger of the Martini, and not an instant too soon; for, as I did so, he was in the act of springing. The report of the rifle rang out sharp and clear on the intense silence of the night, and in another second the great brute had landed on his head within four feet of us, and rolling over and over towards us, was sending the bushes which composed our little fence flying with convulsive strokes of his great paws. We sprang out of the other side of the skerm, and he rolled on to it and into it and then right through the fire. Next he raised himself and sat upon his haunches like a great dog, and began to roar. Heavens! how he roared! I never heard anything like it before or since. He kept filling his lungs with air, and then emitting it in the most heart-shaking volumes of sound. Suddenly, in the middle of one of the loudest roars, he rolled over on to his side and lay still, and I knew that he was dead. A lion generally dies upon his side.

"With a sigh of relief I looked up towards his mate upon the ant-heap. She was standing there apparently petrified with astonishment, looking over her shoulder, and lashing her tail; but to our intense joy, when the dying beast ceased roaring, she turned, and, with one enormous bound, vanished into the night.

"Then we advanced cautiously towards the prostrate brute, Mashune droning an improvised Zulu song as he went, about how Macumazahn, the hunter of hunters, whose eyes are open by night as well as by day, put his hand down the lion's stomach when it came to devour him and pulled out his heart by the roots, &c., &c., by way of expressing his satisfaction, in his hyperbolical Zulu way, at the turn events had taken.

"There was no need for caution; the lion was as dead as though he had already been stuffed with straw. The Martini bullet had entered within an inch of the white spot I had aimed at, and travelled right through him, passing out at the right buttock, near the root of the tail. The Martini has wonderful driving power, though the shock it gives to the system is, comparatively speaking, slight, owing to the smallness of the hole it makes. But fortunately the lion is an easy beast to kill.

"I passed the rest of that night in a profound

slumber, my head reposing upon the deceased lion's flank, a position that had, I thought, a beautiful touch of irony about it, though the smell of his singed hair was disagreeable. When I woke again the faint primrose lights of dawn were flushing in the eastern sky. For a moment I could not understand the chill sense of anxiety that lay like a lump of ice at my heart, till the feel and smell of the skin of the dead lion beneath my head recalled the circumstances in which we were placed. I rose, and eagerly looked round to see if I could discover any signs of Hans, who, if he had escaped accident, would surely return to us at dawn, but there were none. Then hope grew faint, and I felt that it was not well with the poor fellow. Setting Mashune to build up the fire I hastily removed the hide from the flank of the lion, which was indeed a splendid beast, and cutting off some lumps of flesh, we toasted and ate them greedily. Lions' flesh, strange as it may seem, is very good eating, and tastes more like veal than anything else.

"By the time that we had finished our much-needed meal the sun was getting up, and after a drink of water and a wash at the pool, we started to try and find Hans, leaving the dead lion to the tender mercies of the hyaenas. Both Mashune and myself were, by constant practice, pretty good hands at tracking, and we had not much difficulty in following the Hottentot's spoor, faint as it was. We had gone on in this way for half-an-hour or so, and were, perhaps, a mile or more from the site of our camping-place, when we discovered the spoor of a solitary bull buffalo mixed up with the spoor of Hans, and were able, from various indications, to make out that he had been tracking the buffalo. At length we reached a little glade in which there grew a stunted old mimosa thorn, with a peculiar and overhanging formation of root, under which a porcupine, or an ant-bear, or some such animal, had hollowed out a wide-lipped hole. About ten or fifteen paces from this thorn-tree there was a thick patch of bush.

" 'See, Macumazahn! see!' said Mashune, excitedly, as we drew near the thorn; 'the buffalo

has charged him. Look, here he stood to fire at him; see how firmly he planted his feet upon the earth; there is the mark of his crooked toe.' (Hans had one bent toe.) 'Look! here the bull came like a boulder down the hill, his hoofs turning up the earth like a hoe. Hans had hit him: he bled as he came; there are the blood spots. It is all written down there, my father—there upon the earth.'

" 'Yes,' I said; 'yes; but *where is Hans?*'

"Even as I said it Mashune clutched my arm, and pointed to the stunted thorn just by us. Even now, gentlemen, it makes me feel sick when I think of what I saw.

"For fixed in a stout fork of the tree some eight feet from the ground was Hans himself, or rather his dead body, evidently tossed there by the furious buffalo. One leg was twisted round the fork, probably in a dying convulsion. In the side, just beneath the ribs, was a great hole, from which the entrails protruded. But this was not all. The other leg hung down to within five feet of the ground. The skin and most of the flesh were gone from it. For a moment we stood aghast, and gazed at this horrifying sight. Then I understood what had happened. The buffalo, with that devilish cruelty which distinguishes the animal, had, after his enemy was dead, stood underneath his body, and licked the flesh off the pendant leg with his file-like tongue. I had heard of such a thing before, but had always treated the stories as hunters' yarns; but I had no doubt about it now. Poor Hans's skeleton foot and ankle were an ample proof.

"We stood aghast under the tree, and stared and stared at this awful sight, when suddenly our cogitations were interrupted in a painful manner. The thick bush about fifteen paces off burst asunder with a crashing sound, and uttering a series of ferocious pig-like grunts, the bull buffalo himself came charging out straight at us. Even as he came I saw the blood mark on his side where poor Hans's bullet had struck him, and also, as is often the case with particularly savage buffaloes, that his flanks had recently been terribly torn in an encounter with a lion.

"On he came, his head well up (a buffalo does

not generally lower his head till he does so to strike); those great black horns—as I look at them before me, gentlemen, I seem to see them come charging at me as I did ten years ago, silhouetted against the green bush behind;—on, on!

"With a shout Mashune bolted off sideways towards the bush. I had instinctively lifted my eight-bore, which I had in my hand. It would have been useless to fire at the buffalo's head, for the dense horns must have turned the bullet; but as Mashune bolted, the bull slewed a little, with the momentary idea of following him, and as this gave me a ghost of a chance, I let drive my only cartridge at his shoulder. The bullet struck the shoulder-blade and smashed it up, and then travelled on under the skin into his flank; but it did not stop him, though for a second he staggered.

"Throwing myself on to the ground with the energy of despair, I rolled under the shelter of the projecting root of the thorn, crushing myself as far into the mouth of the ant-bear hole as I could. In a single instant the buffalo was after me. Kneeling down on his uninjured knee—for one leg, that of which I had broken the shoulder, was swinging helplessly to and fro—he set to work to try and hook me out of the hole with his crooked horn. At first he struck at me furiously, and it was one of the blows against the base of the tree which splintered the tip of the horn in the way that you see. Then he grew more cunning, and pushing his head as far under the root as possible, made long semicircular sweeps at me, grunting furiously, and blowing saliva and hot steamy breath all over me. I was just out of reach of the horn, though every stroke, by widening the hole and making more room for his head, brought it closer to me, but every now and again I received heavy blows in the ribs from his muzzle. Feeling that I was being knocked silly, I made an effort and seizing his rough tongue, which was hanging from his jaws, I twisted it with all my force. The great brute bellowed with pain and fury, and jerked himself backwards so strongly, that he dragged me some inches further from the mouth of the hole, and again made a sweep at me, catching me this time round the shoulder-joint in the hook of his horn.

"I felt that it was all up now, and began to holloa.

" 'He has got me!' I shouted in mortal terror. '*Gwasa, Mashune, gwasa!*' ('Stab, Mashune, stab!')

"One hoist of the great head, and out of the hole I came like a periwinkle out of his shell. But even as I did so, I caught sight of Mashune's stalwart form advancing with his 'bangwan,' or broad stabbing assegai, raised above his head. In another quarter of a second I had fallen from the horn, and heard the blow of the spear, followed by the indescribable sound of steel shearing its way through flesh. I had fallen on my back, and, looking up, I saw that the gallant Mashune had driven the assegai a foot or more into the carcass of the buffalo, and was turning to fly.

"Alas! it was too late. Bellowing madly, and spouting blood from mouth and nostrils, the devilish brute was on him, and had thrown him up like a feather, and then gored him twice as he lay. I struggled up with some wild idea of affording help, but before I had gone a step the buffalo gave one long sighing bellow, and rolled over dead by the side of his victim.

"Mashune was still living, but a single glance at him told me that his hour had come. The buffalo's horn had driven a great hole in his right lung, and inflicted other injuries.

"I knelt down beside him in the uttermost distress, and took his hand.

" 'Is he dead, Macumazahn?' he whispered. 'My eyes are blind; I cannot see.'

" 'Yes, he is dead.'

" 'Did the black devil hurt thee, Macumazahn?'

" 'No, my poor fellow, I am not much hurt.'

" 'Ow! I am glad.'

"Then came a long silence, broken only by the sound of the air whistling through the hole in his lung as he breathed.

" 'Macumazahn, art thou there? I cannot feel thee.'

" 'I am here, Mashune.'

" 'I die, Macumazahn—the world flies round and round. I go—I go out into the dark! Surely, my father, at times in days to come—thou wilt think of Mashune who stood by thy side—when thou killest elephants, as we used—as we used—'

"They were his last words, his brave spirit passed with him. I dragged his body to the hole under the tree, and pushed it in, placing his broad assegai by him, according to the custom of his people, that he might not go defenceless on his long journey; and then, ladies—I am not ashamed to confess—I stood alone there before it, and wept like a woman."

BOSAMBO OF MONROVIA

EDGAR WALLACE

DURING THE HEIGHT of his popularity in the 1920s as the most successful thriller writer who had ever lived, Edgar Wallace (1875–1932) is reputed to have been the author of one of every four books sold in his native England. After dropping out of school at an early age, Wallace had joined the army and was sent to South Africa, where he wrote war poems and later worked as a journalist during the Boer War. He returned to England with a desire to write fiction, and self-published *The Four Just Men* in 1905; it was a financial disaster, but Wallace would go on to produce at least 173 books and seventeen plays. His "just men" are wealthy dilettantes who set out to administer justice when the law is unable, or unwilling, to do the job; there were five sequels in what became one of Wallace's two most successful series. His other famous series follows Commissioner Sanders, a representative of the Foreign Office of Great Britain whose job is to keep the king's peace in Africa's River Territories (unnamed, but generally assumed to be Congo country). This entails dispensing justice by punishing the wicked, and protecting the West African natives from one another as well as from traveling swindlers, purveyors of liquor, and slave traders. Sanders, called Sandi by the River people, is assisted by Captain Hamilton, commander of the Ninth Regiment, which enforces the law, and Lieutenant Tibbetts, an intellectually challenged bumbler known as "Bones." He is also aided by Bosambo, the chief of the Ochori tribe, a relentless liar and thief but a loyal and good-natured partner to Sanders in maintaining peace in the territory.

Because of Wallace's intimate knowledge of Africa, magazine editors asked him to write some stories set on the Dark Continent, which he did, the most popular featuring Sanders. The first appeared in 1909 in the British magazine the *Weekly Tale-Teller*. In the early 1910s, Wallace's African-set pieces found American publication in the high-paying *McClure's, Metropolitan,* and *Harper's Weekly;* stories later appeared in such pulps as *Adventure, Blue Book,* and *All-Story Weekly*. There were about 150 Sanders stories in all.

"Bosambo of Monrovia" was first published in the March 19, 1910, issue of the *Weekly Tale-Teller;* it was first published in the United States in the August 26, 1911, issue of *Harper's Weekly*. Its first book publication was in *Sanders of the River* (London: Ward, Lock, 1911); the collection was published in the U.S. by Doubleday, Doran in 1930.

BOSAMBO OF MONROVIA

EDGAR WALLACE

FOR MANY YEARS have the Ochori people formed a sort of grim comic relief to the tragedy of African colonisation. Now it may well be that we shall laugh at the Ochori no more. Nor, in the small hours of the night, when conversation flags in the little circle about the fires in fishing camps, shall the sleepy-eyed be roused to merriment by stories of Ochori meekness. All this has come about by favour of the Liberian Government, though at present the Liberian Government is not aware of the fact.

With all due respect to the Republic of Liberia, I say that the Monrovians are naturally liars and thieves.

Once upon a time, that dignity might be added to the State, a warship was acquired—if I remember aright it was presented by a disinterested shipowner. The Government appointed three admirals, fourteen captains, and as many officers as the ship would hold, and they all wore gorgeous but ill-fitting uniforms. The Government would have appointed a crew also, but for the fact that the ship was not big enough to hold any larger number of people than its officers totalled.

This tiny man-of-war of the black republic went to sea once, the admirals and captains taking it in turn to stoke and steer—a very pleasing and novel sensation, this latter.

Coming back into the harbour, one of the admirals said—

"It is my turn to steer now," and took the wheel.

The ship struck a rock at the entrance of the harbour and went down. The officers escaped easily enough, for your Monrovian swims like a fish, but their uniforms were spoilt by the sea water. To the suggestion that salvage operations should be attempted to refloat the warship, the Government very wisely said no, they thought not.

"We know where she is," said the President—he was sitting on the edge of his desk at Government House, eating sardines with his fingers—"and if we ever want her, it will be comforting to know she is so close to us."

Nothing more would have been done in the matter but for the fact that the British Admiralty decided that the wreck was a danger to shipping, and issued orders forthwith for the place where it lay to be buoyed.

The Liberian Government demurred on account of expense, but on pressure being applied (I suspect the captain of H.M.S. *Dwarf*, who was a man with a bitter tongue) they agreed, and the bell-buoy was anchored to the submerged steamer.

It made a nice rowdy, clanging noise, did that bell, and the people of Monrovia felt they were getting their money's worth.

But all Monrovia is not made up of the freed American slaves who were settled there in 1821. There are people who are described in a lordly fashion by the true Monrovians as "indigenous natives," and the chief of these are the Kroomen, who pay no taxes, defy the Government, and at intervals tweak the official nose of the Republic.

The second day after the bell was in place, Monrovia awoke to find a complete silence reigning in the bay, and that in spite of a heavy swell. The bell was still, and two ex-admirals, who were selling fish on the foreshore, borrowed a boat and rowed out to investigate. The explanation was simple—the bell had been stolen.

"Now!" said the President of the Liberian Republic in despair, "may Beelzebub, who is the father and author of all sin, descend upon these thieving Kroomen!"

Another bell was attached. The same night it was stolen. Yet another bell was put to the buoy, and a boat-load of admirals kept watch. Throughout the night they sat, rising and falling with the swell, and the monotonous "clang-jangle-clong" was music in their ears. All night it sounded, but in the early morning, at the dark hour before the sun comes up, it seemed that the bell, still tolling, grew fainter and fainter.

"Brothers," said an admiral, "we are drifting away from the bell."

But the explanation was that the bell had drifted away from them, for, tired of half measures, the Kroomen had come and taken the buoy, bell and all, and to this day there is no mark to show where a sometime man-of-war rots in the harbour of Monrovia.

The ingenious soul who planned and carried out this theft was one Bosambo, who had three wives, one of whom, being by birth Congolaise, and untrustworthy, informed the police, and with some ceremony Bosambo was arrested and tried at the Supreme Court, where he was found guilty of "theft and high treason" and sentenced to ten years' penal servitude.

They took Bosambo back to prison, and Bosambo interviewed the black gaoler.

"My friend," he said, "I have a big ju-ju in the forest, and if you do not release me at once you and your wife shall die in great torment."

"Of your ju-ju I know nothing," said the gaoler philosophically, "but I receive two dollars a week for guarding prisoners, and if I let you escape I shall lose my job."

"I know a place where there is much silver hidden," said Bosambo with promptitude. "You and I will go to this place, and we shall be rich."

"If you knew where there was silver, why did you steal bells, which are of brass and of no particular value?" asked his unimaginative guard.

"I see that you have a heart of stone," said Bosambo, and went away to the forest settlement to chop down trees for the good of the State.

Four months after this, Sanders, Chief Commissioner for the Isisi, Ikeli, and Akasava countries, received, *inter alia*, a communication of a stereotyped description:

TO WHOM IT MAY CONCERN

WANTED—on a warrant issued by H. E. the President of Liberia, Bosambo Krooboy, who escaped from the penal settlement near Monrovia, after killing a guard. He is believed to be making for your country.

A description followed.

Sanders put the document away with other such notices—they were not infrequent in their occurrence—and gave his mind to the eternal problem of the Ochori.

Now, as ever, the Ochori people were in sad trouble. There is no other tribe in the whole of Africa that is as defenceless as the poor Ochori. The Fingoes, slaves as they are by name and tradition, were ferocious as the Masai, compared with the Ochori.

Sanders was a little impatient, and a deputation of three, who had journeyed down to headquarters to lay the grievances of the people before him, found him unsympathetic.

He interviewed them on his verandah.

"Master, no man leaves us in peace," said one. "Isisi folk, N'Gombi people from far-away countries, they come to us demanding this and that, and we give, being afraid."

"Afraid of what?" asked Sanders wearily.

"We fear death and pain, also burning and the taking of our women," said the other.

"Who is chief of you?" asked Sanders, wilfully ignorant.

"I am chief, lord," said an elderly man, clad in a leopard skin.

"Go back to your people, chief, if indeed chief you are, and not some old woman without shame; go back and bear with you a fetish—a most powerful fetish—which shall be, as me, watching your interest and protecting you. This fetish you shall plant on the edge of your village that faces the sun at noon. You shall mark the place where it shall be planted, and at midnight, with proper ceremony, and the sacrifice of a young goat, you shall set my fetish in its place. And after that whosoever ill-treats you or robs you shall do so at some risk."

Sanders said this very solemnly, and the men of the deputation were duly impressed. More impressed were they when, before starting on their homeward journey, Sanders placed in their hands a stout pole, to the end of which was attached a flat board inscribed with certain marks.

They carried their trophy six days' journey through the forest, then four days' journey by canoe along the Little River, until they came to Ochori. There, by the light of the moon, with the sacrifice of two goats (to make sure), the pole was planted so that the board inscribed with mystic characters would face the sun at noon.

News travels fast in the back lands, and it came to the villages throughout the Isisi and the Akasava country that the Ochori were particularly protected by white magic. Protected they had always been, and many men had died at the white man's hand because the temptation to kill the Ochori folk had proved irresistible.

"I do not believe that Sandi has done this thing," said the chief of the Akasava. "Let us go across the river and see with our own eyes, and if they have lied we shall beat them with sticks, though let no man kill, because of Sandi and his cruelty."

So across the water they went, and marched until they came within sight of the Ochori city, and the Ochori people, hearing that the Akasava people were coming, ran away into the woods and hid, in accordance with their custom.

The Akasava advanced until they came to the pole stuck in the ground and the board with the devil marks.

Before this they stood in silence and in awe, and having made obeisance to it and sacrificed a chicken (which was the lawful property of the Ochori) they turned back.

After this came a party from Isisi, and they must come through the Akasava country.

They brought presents with them and lodged with the Akasava for one night.

"What story is this of the Ochori?" asked the Isisi chief in command; so the chief of the Akasava told him.

"You may save yourself the journey, for we have seen it."

"That," said the Isisi chief, "I will believe when I have seen."

"That is bad talk," said the Akasava people, who were gathered at the palaver; "these dogs of Isisi call us liars."

Nevertheless there was no bloodshed, and in the morning the Isisi went on their way.

The Ochori saw them coming, and hid in the woods, but the precaution was unnecessary, for the Isisi departed as they came.

Other folk made a pilgrimage to the Ochori, N'Gombi, Bokeli, and the Little People of the Forest, who were so shy that they came by night, and the Ochori people began to realise a sense of their importance.

Then Bosambo, a Krooman and an adventurer at large, appeared on the scene, having crossed eight hundred miles of wild land in the earnest hope that time would dull the memory of the Liberian Government and incidentally bring him to a land of milk and honey.

Now Bosambo had in his life been many things. He had been steward on an Elder Dempster boat, he had been scholar at a mission school—he was the proud possessor of a bound copy of *The Lives of the Saints,* a reward of industry—and among his accomplishments was a knowledge of English.

The hospitable Ochori received him kindly, fed him with sweet manioc and sugar-cane, and told him about Sandi's magic. After he had eaten, Bosambo walked down to the post and read the inscription: TRESPASSERS BEWARE.

He was not impressed, and strolled back again thinking deeply.

"This magic," he said to the chief, "is good magic. I know, because I have white man's blood in my veins."

In support of this statement he proceeded to libel a perfectly innocent British official at Sierra Leone.

The Ochori were profoundly moved. They poured forth the story of their persecutions, a story which began in remote ages, when Tiganobeni, the great king, came down from the north and wasted the country as far south as the Isisi.

Bosambo listened—it took two nights and the greater part of a day to tell the story, because the official story-teller of the Ochori had only one method of telling—and when it was finished Bosambo said to himself—

"This is the people I have long sought. I will stay here."

Aloud he asked:

"How often does Sandi come to you?"

"Once every year, master," said the chief, "on the twelfth moon, and a little after."

"When came he last?"

"When this present moon is at full, three moons since; he comes after the big rains."

"Then," said Bosambo, again to himself, "for nine months I am safe."

They built him a hut and planted for him a banana grove and gave him seed. Then he demanded for wife the daughter of the chief, and although he offered nothing in payment the girl came to him. That a stranger lived in the chief village of the Ochori was remarked by the other tribes, for news of this kind spreads, but since he was married, and into the chief's family at that, it was accepted that the man must be of the Ochori folk, and such was the story that came to headquarters. Then the chief of the Ochori died. He died suddenly in some pain; but such deaths are common, and his son ruled in his place. Then the son died after the briefest reign, and Bosambo called the people together, the elders, the wise men, and the headmen of the country.

"It appears," he said, "that the many gods of the Ochori are displeased with you, and it has been revealed to me in a dream that I shall be chief of the Ochori. Therefore, O chiefs and wise men and headmen, bow before me, as is the custom, and I will make you a great people."

It is characteristic of the Ochori that no man said "nay" to him, even though in the assembly were three men who by custom might claim the chieftainship.

Sanders heard of the new chief and was puzzled.

"Etabo?" he repeated—this was how Bosambo called himself—"I do not remember the man—yet if he can put backbone into the people I do not care who he is."

Backbone or cunning, or both, Bosambo was certainly installed.

"He has many strange practices," reported a native agent to Sanders. "Every day he assembles the men of the village and causes them to walk past a *pelebi* (table) on which are many eggs. And it is his command that each man as he passes shall take an egg so swiftly that no eye may see him take it. And if the man bungle or break the egg, or be slow, this new chief puts shame upon him, whipping him."

"It is a game," said Sanders; but for the life of him he could not see what game it was. Report after report reached him of the new chief's madness. Sometimes he would take the unfortunate Ochori out by night, teaching them such things as they had never known before. Thus he instructed them in what manner they might seize upon a goat so that the goat could not cry. Also how to crawl on their bellies inch by inch so that they made no sound or sign. All these things the Ochori did, groaning aloud at the injustice and the labour of it.

"I'm dashed if I can understand it!" said Sanders, knitting his brows, when the last report came in. "With anybody but the Ochori this would mean war. But the Ochori!"

Notwithstanding his contempt for their fighting qualities, he kept his Police Houssas ready.

But there was no war. Instead, there came complaint from the Akasava that "many leopards were in the woods."

Leopards will keep, thought Sanders, and, anyway, the Akasava were good enough hunters to settle that palaver without outside help. The next report was alarming. In two weeks these leopards had carried off three score of goats, twenty bags of salt, and much ivory.

Leopards eat goats; there might conceivably be fastidious leopards that cannot eat goats without salt; but a leopard does not take ivory tusks even to pick his teeth with. So Sanders made haste to journey up the river, because little things were considerable in a country where people strain at gnats and swallow whole caravans.

"Lord, it is true," said the chief of the Akasava, with some emotion, "these goats disappear night by night, though we watch them; also the salt and ivory, because that we did not watch."

"But no leopard could take these things," said Sanders irritably. "These are thieves."

The chief's gesture was comprehensive.

"Who could thieve?" he said. "The N'Gombi people live very far away; also the Isisi. The Ochori are fools, and, moreover, afraid."

Then Sanders remembered the egg games, and the midnight manoeuvres of the Ochori.

"I will call on this new chief," he said; and crossed the river that day.

Sending a messenger to herald his coming, he waited two miles out of the city, and the councillors and wise men came out to him with offerings of fish and fruit.

"Where is your chief?" he asked.

"Lord, he is ill," they said gravely. "This day there came to him a feeling of sickness, and he fell down moaning. We have carried him to his hut."

Sanders nodded.

"I will see him," he said grimly.

They led him to the door of the chief's hut, and Sanders went in. It was very dark, and in the darkest corner lay a prostrate man. Sanders bent over him, touched his pulse lightly, felt gingerly for the swelling on the neck behind the ears for a sign of sleeping sickness. No symptom could he find; but on the bare shoulder, as his fingers passed over the man's flesh, he felt a scar of singular regularity; then he found another, and traced their direction. The convict brand of the Monrovian Government was familiar to him.

"I thought so," said Sanders, and gave the moaning man a vigorous kick.

"Come out into the light, Bosambo of Monrovia," he said; and Bosambo rose obediently and followed the Commissioner into the light.

They stood looking at one another for several minutes; then Sanders, speaking in the dialect of the Pepper Coast, said—

"I have a mind to hang you, Bosambo."

"That is as your Excellency wishes," said Bosambo.

Sanders said nothing, tapping his boot with his walking-stick and gazing thoughtfully downward.

"Having made thieves, could you make men of these people?" he said, after a while.

"I think they could fight now, for they are puffed with pride because they have robbed the Akasava," said Bosambo.

Sanders bit the end of his stick like a man in doubt.

"There shall be neither theft nor murder," he said. "No more chiefs or chiefs' sons shall die suddenly," he added significantly.

"Master, it shall be as you desire."

"As for the goats you have stolen, them you may keep, and the teeth (ivory) and the salt also. For if you hand them back to Akasava you will fill their stomachs with rage, and that would mean war."

Bosambo nodded slowly.

"Then you shall remain, for I see you are a clever man, and the Ochori need such as you. But if—"

"Master, by the fat of my heart I will do as you wish," said Bosambo; "for I have always desired to be a chief under the British."

Sanders was half-way back to headquarters before he missed his field-glasses, and wondered where he could have dropped them. At that identical moment Bosambo was exhibiting the binoculars to his admiring people.

"From this day forth," said Bosambo, "there shall be no lifting of goats nor stealing of any kind. This much I told the great Sandi, and as a sign of his love, behold, he gave me these things of magic that eat up space."

"Lord," said a councillor in awe, "did you know the Great One?"

"I have cause to know him," said Bosambo modestly, "for I am his son."

Fortunately Sanders knew nothing of this interesting disclosure.

CORNELL WOOLRICH

ALTHOUGH HE IS known as the greatest writer of suspense fiction of the twentieth century, Cornell George Hopley Woolrich (1903–1968) embraced many kinds of fiction in his long and prolific career. His first novel, *Cover Charge* (1926) was a romance, as was his second, *Children of the Ritz* (1927); the latter won a $10,000 prize (a staggering sum at that time) jointly offered by *College Humor* magazine and First National Pictures, which produced a film based on the book two years later. Woolrich's next four books were also romantic novels, and were so well received that critics compared him to F. Scott Fitzgerald. In the 1920s and '30s, he found magazines eager to buy his varied output of humor, western, and adventure fiction—and, finally, in 1934, his true forte, the noir stories for which he is properly revered today. Many of Woolrich's greatest works, written either as himself or under his pen names, William Irish and George Hopley, have been adapted for motion pictures. These include *The Bride Wore Black* (1940), filmed by François Truffaut in 1967; *Phantom Lady* (1942), filmed in 1944; "It Had to Be Murder" (1942), filmed by Alfred Hitchcock as *Rear Window* in 1954; *Black Alibi* (1942), filmed as *The Leopard Man* in 1943; *The Black Angel* (1943), filmed in 1946; and *Night Has a Thousand Eyes* (1945), filmed in 1948.

Upholding the conventions of their time, Woolrich's adventure stories are generally set in exotic locales and assume the superiority of white characters in confrontations with Mexicans, South Americans, Asians, and Africans. In "Black Cargo," however, Woolrich provides a counterpoint to the standard bigotry by introducing a female character who recoils at the actions of the slave traders with whom she comes into contact. Set in the eighteenth century, the story depicts in powerful detail the horrific treatment of captured slaves in transit to America, yet still has an overriding attitude of white supremacy to the almost subhuman creatures with whom the hero of the story engages in virtually mythic combat.

"Black Cargo" was first published in the July 31, 1937, issue of *Argosy;* this is its first appearance in book form.

BLACK CARGO

CORNELL WOOLRICH

I

AT SUNDOWN the longboat made its last trip out from the shore, bringing the captain, Matthews, and Goodblood, the coastal interpreter, back to the *Sea-Wolf*.

Pritchard, the mate, his job of cramming one hundred and forty unfortunate blacks into the long narrow slave-hold at an end, leaned moodily over the gunwale watching their approach. This was his first trip on a slaver, and it would be his last; they'd ship a new mate next time. He'd

hoped for a brush with the Frenchies, a glimpse of the Spanish Main, something high and stirring like that. He had not, until they'd reached Barbados on the first leg of the triangular voyage, known what the actual purpose of the enterprise was. Glamor! Adventure! Was this it? *Pah!* The young Virginian spat into the turgid water overside to show what he thought of the undertaking.

"Cargo all stowed, Mr. Pritchard?" the captain asked, climbing over the side.

"All below, sir, and linked fast. I've left the hatch off for your inspection."

Matthews, pock-marked face glistening with sweat, peered down over the edge of the black chasm. Dozens of white eyeballs rolled fearfully upwards toward them. They could not, of course, stand erect down there; each sitter was chained to his neighbor, and every twelfth one fastened to a staple. There was no pain yet; that would come later with the rolling of the ship at sea and the draining of the oxygen in the air.

"Good enough," said Matthews. But then, noting a lane left down the center between the soles of their outstretched feet, he added regretfully, "There'd have been space for the few he had left on his hands. Could have had them cheap, too. Pity to waste them; he kills the ones he can't sell, y'know. Batten her down, Mr. Pritchard, and let's get under way before we all come down with a fever." Then, noting the disapproval in his mate's face as he relayed the order, "Smile, man, smile—this day's work's put money in all our pockets."

"There's better ways of making it," Pritchard said, giving him a hard look. "I'm new at this stuffing of live cargo."

"Aye, that's to be seen," agreed Matthews sarcastically, turning on his heel.

Under a vast white African moon, like a grinning skull shining above the water, they coursed slowly down the estuary, and by dawn were far out upon the bosom of the Guinea Gulf, sailing westward to round the vast snout of Africa that juts out into mid-Atlantic. The shoreline was out of sight, but the mud and silt that still discolored the water revealed its hidden presence. A full day and a night they sailed, and by midmorning of the second day hove to before the rotting Portuguese "factory" (trading-post) where they were to drop Goodblood. From the open roadstead where they rode at anchor, out beyond reach of the coastal rollers, it was nothing more than a huddle of shacks about a mildewed stone watchtower dating from Da Gama's day, one of a dozen such that strewed the road to India, and forgotten by the very nation that owned it.

To Pritchard's surprise, Matthews went ashore with the interpreter. There was nothing to be had here, not even fresh water. Slavers always brought out enough to last them both legs of the voyage, anyway. He asked no questions, however, and the captain gave no explanations. It had to do, obviously, with something he had learned from Goodblood.

In about an hour the longboat reappeared, riding the long rollers out like a dancing cork. There were now two other people in it with the captain, and one was—a woman! The mate strained his eyes at the figure bunched there in the prow, thinking the heat-haze over the glistening water must be playing him false. But no, it was a woman, and a European at that. Some light-lady of the town, perhaps, come out to satisfy a whim and look over the ship. The mate's face set stonily; he had no love for fancy-women thrusting in where they had no business to be.

And then when she stood upon the deck before him, he saw that he was wrong; she was no fancy-lady. She was little more than a girl, blue-eyed, holding her traveling-cloak to her affrightedly, a wisp or two of honey-colored hair escaping from beneath its hood. Her eyes dropped at his searching look, and her arm went solicitously about the wasted, malaria-ridden old man they were helping over the side. He was a very ill old man; he had the mark of death upon him. Matthews came last, smirking and scraping with great show of courtliness. And behind him, Pritchard saw, the men were already bringing up the dripping longboat.

"Surely, sir, these people are not taking passage with us?" he blurted out.

"Why not?" Matthews removed a small bag of gold from his waistband, tossed it, caught it lightly again. "Would you refuse two stranded fellow-countrymen a favor? Their ship was wrecked in these waters three full months ago and they've had no means of getting out ever since."

"And where are they to quarter?"

"Why, as to that," said Matthews softly, "there's naught for it but to give them up your quarters, and berth you with the men. Surely you will not begrudge so fair a creature and her father—" Then noting that the girl had led the tottering old man inside and out of earshot, he changed his tune subtly. "Especially when the old man will not last a fortnight by the looks of it." And he batted his eye and nudged Pritchard in the ribs.

"So that's the game, is it?" the latter said scathingly. "You'd better get them off the ship, sir, before we cast off."

Matthews turned ugly all at once. "We *are* casting off—at once, sir! Is this my ship or yours, Mr. Pritchard? She stays then!"

"I take no heed of superstitious nonsense," the mate said sharply, "but have you never heard a woman on a ship is an omen of ill-luck?"

"I'll chance it!" Matthews roared in his face. "What of the ten others below? Are you in command here or am I?"

He stepped closer until they were eye to eye, clenched his great ham of a fist, drew it back. Pritchard's own went back, as if both worked on a single tendon.

"You are, sir. But if you strike me once," he warned, "you'll not strike twice!"

They both stood their ground for a moment. Finally Matthews's hand came back to his side again, fell open. "See to your duties, Mr. Pritchard, or I'll report you for mutiny at Bridgetown," he said gruffly. "We weigh anchor at once."

II

After that they stood directly out to sea at last, helped by a land-breeze blowing off the coast of Guinea, headed due west for Bridgetown, halfway across the world. The heat didn't abate any, but at least it cleared itself of the fetid mists that clung to the shoreline of Africa. Their two passengers, whose names Pritchard learned were Dominick Lowrie and his daughter, Mary, remained secluded in his former quarters, the girl presumably spending her nights in a rug on the floor beside the ailing man's bunk, attending to his wants. Once Pritchard caught sight of her for a few moments at the bulwark, where she had come for a breath of air, her hair blowing prettily in the evening breeze. She turned at the sound of his tread, then seeing who it was, gave him a flashing look of indignation and turned away again. She had overheard his opposition to their coming aboard, evidently, and misunderstood its grounds.

An ironic smile formed at his mouth. "Good even, mistress," he greeted, and went on his way.

Her shoulders shrugged impatiently. Then when she thought him far enough away, she turned and stole a look after him. He looked back at the same moment, and she quickly gazed seaward again.

The third day out the seaman who fed them reported to him in the forecastle: "Two dead, mister; and one who won't open her eyes, though she still breathes."

Pritchard went down to inspect, then reported to Matthews, whom he had steered clear of as much as his duties would permit since they'd left the Bight. He found the captain at sodden ease in his quarters, a heavy odor of rum in the air. "Two dead, sir, one dying," he reported curtly.

"Easy to get at?" Matthews wanted to know indifferently.

"Furthest from the hatch. All females."

Matthews looked slightly relieved; they brought a lower price. "Aye, they always go first. Must have been defective to start with. Detach them then, Mr. Pritchard, and throw the three of them over. Hereafter just do the like, you needn't come to me each time."

The mate was staring at him. "All three, sir? But one isn't gone yet!"

"Do it anyway and have it over with!" Matthews snapped. "Any that fail this early, won't last the voyage, you'll only have your trouble over again." And then as Pritchard still stood there, undisguised repugnance on his face, he reared up suddenly and brought his fist down on the side of the bunk. "Those are my orders! Am I to give two for every one necessary on this ship?"

Pritchard turned and strode out and sent two seamen down with a mallet and chisel to free the "dead weight" from the others. He stood by while the three were brought up, propped side by side along the gunwale, the live one on the end. He then ordered the hatch replaced and left those below to their perpetual gloom.

The seamen picked up one between them, swung, let go—and there were only two left. Then the second. The ill one, meanwhile, had begun to revive, even after so short a space in the open air. Her chest rose and fell visibly as the seamen caught her up to throw her.

There was a sudden tap of hasty shoes upon the deck-planks, and the merchant's daughter flew at them. "Wait, let her be! She needs but air, it's easy to see. How can you do this?" She had whirled on Pritchard, in a fine moral rage. Her cheeks, he thought, looked better for the high crimson in them. Her blue eyes sparkled. "Why, this is murder! In England or the Colonies, you would be hanged for this, sir!"

Pritchard, who half agreed with her in his own mind, was irritated that she should make him the scapegoat. "We are at sea," he reminded her coldly, "and not in England or the Colonies"—and very much under his breath— "worse luck! The captain's word is law upon this ship, and I am only carrying out his orders."

She had half-flung herself upon the negro woman, meanwhile, and clung with both arms. "I will not permit you to destroy this poor soul's life!" she cried, in the stately phrases of the period. The seamen, balked, stood by uncertainly, looking at Pritchard for further orders.

Matthews came out to discover what the disturbance was, and saved him the necessity of giving any. "Sir, I beg of you!" the rescuing angel began heatedly, from where she crouched on the deck, skirts billowing about her, "let me keep this poor creature by me. I have tonics with which to restore her. Don't let these men do away with her."

Matthews coughed uncomfortably, avoiding the mate's accusing eyes. He squatted beside the prone woman, made a great show of pressing her eyes open with his thumb. "Aye, she can no doubt be brought around," he said judiciously. "Do as the young lady says, you men." And he helped her gallantly to her feet, as though they were pacing a minuet together.

"Thank you, sir. You are a gentleman," she murmured, not forgetting to cast a scathing look at Pritchard. The slave was carried into the already cramped quarters she shared with her father, and as she followed with the captain, Pritchard heard her say: "That man is a monster!"

He just stood there, arms akimbo, glaring quizzically after her and shaking his head at the knack of womankind for putting the blame on the wrong man. Finally he performed his favorite rite of spitting over the side, and thereby eased his soul.

Rising gently, dipping softly, the *Sea-Wolf* swam onward into the sun.

The experiment of opening the slave-hatch for a short period twice a day and letting a little air in, was tried from then on at Pritchard's suggestion. It was a sign, perhaps, that he was a novice at this business of slave-running, but Matthews, at first inclined to countermand it, finally gave his reluctant approval when he saw how it was keeping the death-rate down. After all, the fewer that died, the more money in his pocket. Even so, a score more, including all but two of the females, had died of suffocation and body-cramp before the end of the first week. This however was a vast improvement compared to the toll on most slavers, and Matthews had been in the trade long enough to realize that, although he did mutter sarcastically about his mate "pampering" them.

The girl's father had, as Matthews had foreseen, been removed from the fever-ridden coast too late; he died the fifth day after they sailed. And at the brief burial service that was conducted, before the body in its makeshift shroud was thrown unceremoniously over, Pritchard could not help noting how the captain's roving eye wandered to the girl's bowed head even in the act of reading the service. She bore herself well, showing no tears, only a wistful resignation. She was alone now, on a ship at sea, full of rough men, with the protection of the ill old man gone, little as it had been worth.

Pritchard knocked on her door that night, soon after the quick tropic twilight had faded, making sure that no one saw him. She opened it unhesitatingly, still unaware she had anything to fear. But at sight of the one man on board from whom she had least to fear, she drew herself up coldly. A lantern was lit upon the wall within, and by its wavering light Pritchard could make out the negress whose life she had saved, restored to health now, sitting off in a corner jabbering like a jungle monkey.

"Have you anything to tell me?" she inquired haughtily, as he stood stricken speechless with sudden embarrassment.

For answer, he thrust a small firing-piece he had brought aboard with him. "Keep this with you," he said gruffly. "And remain within at nights." Without asking leave, he tested the bolts on the door. "Keep it fast, and do not open at the first-comer's knock, as you did just now. They are not all angels on this ship with you. If—if aught's amiss, just call to me. My name's Pritchard."

She kept looking at him, rather than the weapon he had provided her with. Far from being alarmed, she seemed secretly amused, as though at some private joke of her own. "I know that," she answered. "Davey Pritchard, is it not?"

He turned away self-consciously and would have stalked off, but she laid a detaining hand on his arm. For the first time since she had come aboard, he saw her smile a little. "You take great thought for my safety, Mr. Pritchard, for one who was so inhospitable when first I came on the ship."

He could feel himself flushing under his mahogany sunburn. "It is no fit ship for a woman, I still say so!" he muttered stubbornly.

Her eyes were laughing at him openly, if not her lips. "I do believe I have misjudged you, Mr. Pritchard. I do believe your bark is worse than your bite." She closed the door, but not too quickly for him to see that the smile had spread to her lips, too.

He moved away, scratching the back of his neck awkwardly, and feeling ten thousand kinds of a fool.

He felt less of one, though, when her muffled cry of "Oh, Mr. Pritchard! Oh, Davey Pritchard!" sounded in the night-silence of eight-bells. He leaped from his hammock, ran out on deck barefooted. Matthews, drunk as a lord, was shouldering the fastened door of her quarters with great heaves. It was a stout barrier, for they built their ships well in those days. Pritchard had no fear for it. He folded his arms, and suddenly was lounging there at ease alongside the scowling captain, looking on with an acid smile.

"What's amiss?" he drawled. "You wake our passenger, sir."

Matthews stepped back at the unexpected apparition, and fell to chafing his shoulder to cover his confusion. Whatever he was physically, he was a coward morally. "I—I but wanted to speak to her, of a certain matter," he stammered.

Pritchard raised his voice. "The captain would like to speak to you, Mistress Lowrie," he called mockingly. "Can you hear from where you are? Then remain there. Put your ear close to the panel."

Matthews looked guiltily toward the forecastle once or twice, as though loath to be caught by his men in this discomfiting position. "It can wait," he growled, and shambled off.

"The captain has changed his mind, Mistress Lowrie," announced Pritchard cheerfully. And, could a man be killed by a look, he would have dropped at the baleful glare Matthews sent back at him when he turned off the deck.

There was a pause, then the slightest of whispers came through the door. "I thank you, Mr. Pritchard."

Pritchard only found courage to say it because the bolted door was safely between them. "Davey's my name," he breathed back, and looked up at the moon, with something of the expression of a calf that has the colic.

The first week slipped uneventfully into the second, and they were well out into the South Atlantic now, without a sight of a prowling Frenchman, without a storm, to mar the even course of the voyage. Only two incidents, and those barely worth noting, occurred in all that time. Both had to do with the black woman whom Mary Lowrie had attached to her. Bangi was her name, or perhaps Bangi-Bangi. At least when her new mistress pointed at her and asked her how she was called, she chattered "Bangi-bangi-bangi." So it was either her name, or the name of the country from which she had been stolen.

She had recovered completely, with the resiliency of a forest-animal, and as soon as she lost her fear of the ship's motion and the sight of the water, Mary began sending her out to fetch back her food and water. She found it more comfortable to eat unwatched in her quarters than at the board with Matthews, devoured by his greedy eyes, subject to his hypocritical gallantries that only stayed within the bounds of decorum because Pritchard was present.

Matthews, when she began sending Bangi with a platter, filled it from his own helpings. The first few times the food never reached its destination; the negress made away with it herself en route. A good caning, however, cured her of this, and she became more dependable. Then one day, as she was returning the empty platter while Matthews was still at table, the captain caught her to him. She had long untended nails, and like a flash had struck and raked him down his already pock-marked face.

Pritchard, at the yelp Matthews gave, and at sight of the five reddening streaks that appeared, lowered his head and laughed soundlessly into his plate. Matthews, beside himself, chased her out, caught her on the deck, held her fast by both wrists, and bellowed loudly to the carpenter to bring him a file. "Scratch me, will she, the jungle cat!" he barked when the implement had been brought. "We'll have no more of that! File her fingers down to the quick!"

Bangi, finding she was not to be put to death then and there, ceased howling and caterwaul-

ing, and watched the operation with dilated eyes. Even after the grinning seaman had pitched the file down and released her, she cowered there, eying it curiously as though it were some kind of a fetish. Matthews went inside again, swearing, to sop rum to his smarting face. Pritchard, still chuckling to himself at the poor figure the captain always seemed to cut at passages of love, went about his duties. When next he looked that way, both the negress and the file were gone. He did not miss the latter, for he had failed to notice it in the first place. Or rather, forgot that he had.

The very next day, passing the reeking half-open hatch during one of the airing periods, he caught sight of Bangi squatted there by its rim, chattering down like a monkey. She had never dared approach it before, for fear of being returned to it herself. As his shadow fell athwart her, she straightened with a squeak and ran back to the protection of her mistress. He bent his arm threateningly after her, then jumped down into the midst of the slaves to see what she had been up to. Those nearest the hatch were hastily wolfing scraps of food she had evidently stolen from Matthews's table. Pritchard picked his way among the captives, examining their bound hands and the few scraps of rags they wore, to see if any weapon or instrument had been smuggled to them. He could find nothing. He didn't compel them to hoist their bodies off the planks and look under them, because there was scarcely room to do so in the jammed place, and he had no hankering to remain in the stench-filled place. He climbed back to the deck and ordered the hatch battened down. He didn't tell Matthews on the girl, because it seemed a small enough thing to get her a whipping for. There was no love lost between them anyway; let the slaves eat the scraps from his table for all he cared.

He did however speak of it to Mary Lowrie when next he saw her standing in the doorway looking out, and immediately regretted doing so. It set them at cross-purposes again, as they had been in the beginning.

"It is best you keep her away from the hatch, lest she throw them something with which to try to free themselves. I would not tell Matthews for your sake, for she gives you company, and he would return her there at once."

She was what a later age would have called a humanitarian. "And would it be a crime if they did free themselves? What right have you and the others to carry them away from their homes into slavery?"

He took a patient breath at this typical bit of feminine logic. "If these savages were freed, ma'm, you realize what their first act would be, I trust?"

"Why," she said defiantly, "they would do what anyone would do in their place, and who could blame them? They would make off in the small boats and escape back whence they have been so unjustly taken."

His sigh was a heave this time. "No ma'm," he said severely, "they would cut all our throats, yours included. We ride the seas with a powder-mine beneath our feet. So long as no spark is put to it."

"You see evil in all men's hearts, Mr. Pritchard. You are just like all the others, and I had begun to think you different. You do not ev-idently believe, like Rousseau, in the true nobil-ity of the savage."

Poor Pritchard, who had never heard of Rousseau in his life, had a feeling he was getting the worst of the argument, through no fault of his own. "Is he in the slave-running business?" he asked uncertainly. For answer she gave him a look and slammed the door in his face.

III

On the thirteenth night after they had left Africa, in the dark of the moon, the man at the wheel suddenly screamed out just once, in the stillness. Pritchard, startled awake, leaned up in his hammock, listening. It had been the scream of a man in his death agony, suddenly cut short. On top of it came a splash, a heavier one than the incessant heaving of the water at the ship's sides. A faint rustling as of dry leaves stirred by the wind came to his ears; it might have been the stealthy tread of countless bare feet sweeping over the decks. Then at last the belated boom of a firing-piece, and a voice calling out in conster-nation: "God have mercy! The devils are loose!"

But by that time Pritchard was already bounding out of the forecastle, shouting a need-less warning to the crew members straggling out after him.

The watch had already been cut to pieces, in silence but for the helmsman. Not for nothing had they stalked Africa's jungles, these blacks. The war-cry, seeming to split the ship in half, sounded just as he reached the deck, from half-a-hundred throats at once, from everywhere, from fore and aft, from port, from starboard, from above-deck and below, where some had not yet freed themselves. They were swarming all over the doomed ship like ants; bigger than ants, like death-dealing maniac apes.

He snatched at a belaying pin, cracked at the nearest one. The skull gave a horrid gourd-like sound. The firing-piece, or another like it, went off a second time, in the narrow gangway leading aft from the quarterdeck. The red flash illu-mined Matthews's pitted face there for an in-stant, surrounded by them, and, forgetting their enmity, Pritchard made toward him, striking out right and left, tearing off clutching hands like barnacles.

He could make him out faintly in the starlight, struggling in the center of all of them there, in the narrow lane he had been trapped in, unable to fire again without reloading, for this was the eighteenth century. And unable to re-load for the sheer weight of bodies that pressed upon him. Pritchard bawled: "Hold your feet! Hold your feet, man! I'm coming!" Hands caught at his throat from behind and he was pulling something after him along the deck bodily. They were strong; they found his windpipe. He flung his pin up overhead, backhand, and they let go.

A faint whiteness before him, about the size of an egg in the starlight, was Matthews's face—the last time he was to see it. It went down in all its ugliness into final oblivion, into a pit of living black bodies. The pistol he had just fired shot out from under the squirming mass, along the deck. Pritchard stooped to snatch at it, went down himself with somebody athwart him in an ape-like leap. He rolled over on him, broke the grip, twisted, kneed him in the belly. His assailant was half-starved; his ribs stood out like those of a skinny, plucked bird. Pritchard smashed down on them with the pistol-butt, and he could hear them crack like twigs.

He found his feet, started edging away with his back to the bulwark, to extricate himself from that narrow place. It was too late to do anything for Matthews, he had been torn to pieces, but Pritchard was given a moment's breathing spell while they occupied themselves with the obsequies. He could see Bangi, the cause of all their misfortunes, for it must have been she who had unbattened the hatch from above, so that they could push their way up from below. He could see her standing over the place where Matthews had disappeared into their midst. She was anointing her face with Matthews's blood, screeching her revenge to the stars.

Pritchard thought of the girl then, of Mary Lowrie, alone in her quarters with just a pistol and a handful of lead—no, dead by now, murdered in her sleep, for surely that female panther had done her to death before she ever crept forth to free the others. "Oh spare her, have it not so!" he choked, and wondered at the added wrench this gave in the midst of so much other death and violence.

The band of Matthews's killers were between him and her; he could perhaps have tried to hack his way through, but that was the slower way.

He thrust his chargeless gun into his bellyband, leaped upward, caught at the deck-house roof with both his hands, and somehow scrambled up on it. He ran past, unnoticed above their heads, to drop down again beside her door.

They were here, too, but not in any numbers. He struck down two that made at him, then turned and hammered on the panel with his gun-butt. "Mary! Mary, do you live?" And yet he knew she must, for the door was fastened on the inside.

The answer was instant. She must have been waiting there on the other side for death to come and get her. "Oh, Davey—wait, I'll open!"

"No!" he hissed furiously. "Stay as you are! They're all loose. The bolts will guard you, once you open you are lost. Make no sound, they'll know not that you're in there!"

"*She* knows!" came her frightened breath. "I woke and the door was ajar, she had watched and learned how it was opened—I quickly made it fast again—"

"She'll not have the chance to tell them!" he vowed. "Mary, Mary Lowrie, will you do as I say? Open it not, though the Recording Angel himself summon you!"

A form leaped at him through the air, bare-handed. They grappled, fell together, the filed-off loosened remnant of the slave's manacle clinked against the door. Even in the throes of the struggle, Pritchard knew a stabbing fear lest she come out in her fright, and undo herself. The thought made him a fiend incarnate. He caught at the kinky pate, battered it against the boards. The man fell still with the suddenness of a crumpled balloon.

He found his feet, wiping blood—not his own—from over his eye and rested his shoulder-blades against the door. For a moment he was left in peace, unseen there in the shadow of the deck-house.

"What was that?"

"Naught," he panted. He took a step away, knowing he endangered her by lingering here. Her heart must have heard the sound of his going, for her ears could not have.

"No, wait—don't leave me!"

"I'll be back, I promise you. Wait for me within, as you are." He turned suddenly, put both hands outspread upon the door. "And if— perhaps—I'm not, then let me tell you now. I love you."

He swerved and ran forward again, into the narrow lane where Matthews had met his death. They had dispersed from there, in the pursuit of new quarry. What had been Matthews still lay there though, and over him, swaying like a co- bra, blood-drunk, was the woman, Bangi. She knew and could tell them there was a white woman aboard, if she had not done so already.

He struck no blow at her, just caught her head in the crook of one bulging arm, the shank of her leg with the other, swayed with her to the side, and heaved her across. Thrashing, bleat- ing, she spun and vanished in a silver tulip-cup of upthrust spray.

Three of them came running at him from the aft-end of the gangway, and for the first time that night, he turned and made off from their onset. He knew what he wanted to do, while he still could, before his own approaching death overtook him. There was a small brass cannon up by the very bow, meant only for signaling in case of distress, but loaded with grapeshot. It faced outward, true, but was mounted on a swivel. If he could only reach it, the odds might be made more to a man's liking.

The quarterdeck was a shambles, slippery with blood. The death cries of the crew were ebbing now, for few were alive. Torn to pieces, most of them had been, by sheer weight of numbers. The thudding of bare feet on wood, the musical clash and tinkle of splintered shackles, sounded now here, now there, as the slave horde hunted down their prey in troops.

A voice called thinly down above the uproar, from somewhere high up the rigging: "This way! Up, men! They're afraid to climb!" Pritchard wasted not a look; he had a job to do here below.

A man named Johnson, red-bearded, all clothing torn from him, huge muscles swelling like Vulcan's, was fighting his way backwards step by step over at the opposite gunwale, wield- ing a cutlass like a rapier and holding a whole pack of them at bay.

"The gun! The signal-gun!" Pritchard bel- lowed at him, and pointed to show what he meant. They both turned and fled simultane- ously along the opposite gunwales, converging where the ship narrowed to its prow, leaping up on the raised bulkhead that held the gun, their attackers in full cry after them. They faced about again, water on three sides, death on the fourth.

"Can you cover me a moment till I march it around?" Pritchard panted hoarsely.

Johnson swooped down low, cutting, hack- ing, thrusting. Pritchard hugged the snub-nosed little thing with both arms, swung it back on it- self so that it swept the swarming deck behind it. There was flint there in a box, with oil-soaked waste, kept in readiness. He struck a spark and held the lighted rag above the touch-hole.

"Back, man!" he warned Johnson, and plunged the burning wick.

"My arms ache," was the last thing Johnson said, "I'll take mine this way!" and leaped off sideways into the sea.

Then the gun boomed out like thunder, with a sudden orange furnace-glow that instantly went out again, and a curtain of acrid vapor that veiled Pritchard where he stood alone, outlined against the stars. Through it sounded the spat of grapeshot falling far and near like hail. When it cleared the quarterdeck before him was a grave- yard of prone shapes, some still, some squirm- ing, writhing, screaming. A few by the bulwarks, whether hit or not, suddenly climbed up on them and leaped off in sheer fright at this sud- den apparition of the fire-god in their midst. There was a scuttling away of the unhurt, and the whole fore part of the ship was Pritchard's— and the dead's.

But the gun was empty now, there was noth- ing at hand to reload it with, nor could he get be- low to where the small supply of powder and shot they carried was kept. Thus it was only a matter of time, for no terror lasts forever, even with primitives.

Already Pritchard could hear them in the shadows far astern, gibbering, rallying one another, creeping slowly back upon him. He turned and shook his fist down at the sea, for Johnson had played the coward; together they might have regained command of the entire ship. And the quiet, the lack of strife throughout the ship now, told him plainly no one was left alive any more, but himself, that craven up in the halyards, and the girl imprisoned in her quarters.

A horizontal salmon bar seared the horizon—but off to starboard now, at their stern, for the wheel had been unmanned half the night and they were drifting unguided wherever the wind chose to push them. And as another and another joined it, like the rungs of a fiery ladder up the sky, the bloody night was at last at an end.

They came creeping out of the two gangways in the early light, joined across the quarterdeck in a thin unbroken line, and advanced upon him with a slowness horrible to bear. Some crouched double, some were flat on their bellies, undulating like the Indians of his own country in their warfare. Step by step, ready to turn and fly back again at necessity—as though they could have outraced powder and shot had there been any!

His eye ran over their numbers, and he saw that if all were gathered together here to set upon him, then the murdered crew had died hard and his gun had done its work well. There were less than two-score of them left, out of a hundred that had stolen out of the hole a few hours ago. But forty-to-one were no odds to be managed, and if Johnson's arms had ached, his own were lost to feeling; he could not tell where they ended, or where they began. He wanted to lie down on his face and let them have him. Still that was no way to die. So he leaned there over the gun, bent double at his waist, staring out at them across its brass barrel, hands folded beneath his chin.

He let them come on until they were close as the first time, baleful, guttural sounds coming from their throats. Then he raised his head, parted his hands, and they stopped motionless. Then, at the first return of motion, he clapped his hand to the brass of the gun with a stinging smack.

They broke and fled, spilling back over the deck into the gangways. He sent raucous laughter, harsh, stinging curses after them. But now the spell was broken, and he was undone. No fire, no smoke, from the white man's tubular fetish; it lacked food.

Instantly they reformed, came back-tracking again, with less awe this time. Pritchard, tired of waiting for death, suddenly ended the thing himself. He left the gun, leaped down off the bulkhead, and dashed raging into their midst, swinging Johnson's cutlass all about him like a scythe. They closed about him like a sort of flesh trap, one that held his weapon fast in the very wounds it made before he could extricate it. They pulled him down flat upon the deck by sheer weight of numbers, and their bodies atop him hid the sun.

The time that comes once to every man, the time for dying, was at hand. . . .

IV

And yet Pritchard still lived, and he could only blink in wonderment. For the morning sun was still in the sky, and the white sails of the *Sea-Wolf* still over him, and the blue slop of the sea still washed high, now on this side, now on that. He was on his feet, too, pressed back against the bulwark, a patina of red glaze like a copper statue all over his body, a dozen arms holding him fast. They were ringed about him, holding a palaver. His own cutlass pointed at his throat, ready to be plunged in.

One among them, a sculpturesque buck, was gesturing, holding forth in the jabber of the Niger jungles. To the sails he pointed, and to the wheel; to the limitless horizon, and to the sun overhead, and to Pritchard himself. Angry denials rose in the throats of the others, but still some nodded their heads in affirmation.

It was easy to make out the pantomime, as it was repeated a second, a third, a fourth time. They were free now, yes. But this great white bird must be made to carry them back to their homeland. Only the white men knew how to make it obey them. Therefore this last one must be left alive to guide it; he alone knew in which direction lay the shores of this vast lake; he alone could bring them back whence they had come. Kill him later, when he had done so; but not until then, or their native villages would never see them again.

But why he, Pritchard wondered dully; hadn't there been a man up in the crow's nest? He looked and it was empty. Fallen—or perhaps a toothless cur like Johnson, leaping over when he saw Pritchard go down and knew there was no more hope. "But had I been up there where he was," thought the Virginian scornfully, "I'd have thought I owned the world. And even here where I am, I am not dead yet—nor propose to be!"

There was Mary yet, cached in the cabin. He had an obligation to stay alive. And since might could not contend with them, strategy must do it.

The voices of dissent died down; the one among them who had taken thought for their future, had his way. Pritchard was dragged stumbling to the wheel, thrust over it. They crowded threateningly about him, pointing to the dancing needle within the boxed compass, telling him to cast his spells upon it, to make the white man's juju do as they wished; they patted the planks with the palms of their hands. Africa, back to Mother Africa!

He nodded grimly and he took the wheel, half-dead as he was. She was without food or water in there, and venture forth she dare not. And stay very long she could not. Some passing ship might come within hail; even the dungeons of French St. Nazaire would be a heaven to this. By dint of long, patient gesturing he finally managed to have them fetch him out Matthews's

charts and log-book, and he kept these by him as a mystic, all-powerful juju in reserve. They had, the night before, before the holocaust occurred, reached Longitude 26′ 2″ W., he saw. How far out of their course they had drifted since then, he had no means of knowing. Still, due north of that position, lay the little English "factory" of Bathhurst, in Gambia. And somewhere between was the great trade route all ships took, rounding the horn of Africa to go down to the Cape.

He brought her around, west-west-by-north, west-by-north, but the strong easterly wind that had been tailing them for days keeled her over dangerously, her masthead slanted down until it seemed her sails would dip into the sea, and half of them tumbled howling across the deck, and some went in. He had to bring her back again, and made signs to them the sails would have to be furled. They misunderstood, started chipping and hacking at the mast with their knives and the late carpenter's axe. He shook his head violently, to make them desist, whereupon they began sawing at the ropes, and before he could stop them the sheets had fallen like a great blanket; the white bird had folded its wings and was crippled now, at the mercy of every gust that blew.

Still to them, who knew no better, it was as though he had succeeded; these tokens of his might impressed them with superstitious terror. Some, when she had righted herself again, fell down upon the deck before him and worshipped him—or the wheel and compass, he could not be sure which. Yet when he made a move to leave the wheel, their knives flashed out and growls of warning came from their throats. He made signs to his mouth, and they brought him food and water—they had located the ship's storeroom by now and were making the most of it—and he kept some by him for the hidden girl, letting them think it was an offering to the needle.

As the afternoon waned, they set two guards by him to see that he kept by the wheel (useless task that that now was!) and the rest commenced a great orgy out on the quarterdeck in full sight of him, gorging on the ship's supplies, swilling the rum and brandy they had unearthed in Matthews's quarters, nursing their wounds and gashes, dancing and chanting their freedom and victory. They rolled out a cask that had held biscuits, and used it for a war-drum, thumping it with the flats of their hands.

As the sun dipped, they even made preparations for building a fire on the deck-planks, as though they were ashore! Pritchard had to warn and threaten them, showing by signs that they would go up in flames and down to the bottom. They compromised finally by dragging out a great copper cauldron from the galley, and building a small one in the depths of that. He had them wet the planks under it with sea-water, and buttress it with staves thrust into the deck, to keep it from shifting with the ship's motion; at that it was a constant menace. The dim, red glow its mouth cast up illumined their faces weirdly as darkness came on and they huddled about it, shivering in the night-air. One by one, befuddled with drink and doped with the unaccustomed quantities of food, they fell asleep, until they lay sprawled all over the deck.

Pritchard, with a face like stone, stood there wearily hugging the useless wheel, as though unaware. Behind him, the head of the second of his two guards at last dropped heavily onto his chest, and both slept, huddled.

Pritchard turned slowly, stretched his numbed arms out wide, like a cross-bar, to cause the blood to course through them once more. Then he stooped, picked up the food and water left to placate the needle, and moving through their huddled bodies with a seaman's dexterity, stole aft like a wraith, toward the famished, thirsty girl hidden away in the cabin.

When he appeared again out of the shadows, the food and water was gone. A knife was tied now to one leg, under his shredded trousers, a loaded pistol lashed to the other. But his hands were bare. He brooded there above them all, the only upright form on the deck.

. . .

In the morning when they stirred, it was he who was motionless, asleep over the wheel, in full sight of all. But more than one, waking, missed the face of his nearest neighbor, who had been stretched beside him the night before—found only a blank space of deck instead. Yet each one no doubt thought the missing one was elsewhere about the ship, and being self-centered as children or animals, their interest stopped there.

The sun waxed and waned, and the shipload of helpless humanity pitched this way and that on their wooden crate, at the caprice of the wind and glittering waves, all day long. Again, during the long watches of the night, came muffled splashes overside from time to time, a quickly-stifled intake of breath, the flop of an arm or leg against the planks. In the morning there would again be those gaps among the sleepers, always at their outermost fringes, nearest the bulwark. A name or two was called, and its owner did not answer, and was not to be found for the rest of the day. Beyond that, they failed to inquire or understand.

Another night, another day, and then suddenly the knowledge of what it was was in their midst, kindled like a spark, leaping from one to the next like flame to tinder. Oncoming night now brought terror to them they had not known before, for who could be sure, when he lay down to sleep, that he would be among those to awaken again? Whom would the powerful juju of the needle choose to sweep up into the sky without a trace tonight? Vainly they tried to halt the sun in its setting by chants and lamentations, vainly they tried to propitiate the juju by offerings and sacrifices. Purple-black shadows of night swallowed them up none the less. They lay huddled closer to the protective fire-pot now, like spokes of a contracting wheel, squabbling and bickering for the comparative safety of the innermost places, thrusting the weaker ones to the outside to be their living shields against—they knew not what.

Set guards against the terror they could not, for none would risk staying awake alone, lest they meet the evil spirit face to face in the dark, and all could not stay awake together. They slept contorted, arms thrown over their heads to ward off the sight of the juju, or with heads and shoulders burrowed under gunny-sacks and rags, like ostriches; and the merciless blue eyes that saw them thus, might have pitied and relented—had there been less at stake. And more than one, waking to the first warning tug of his own body along the deck, the stifling pressure of a demon's hand at his mouth or throat, would still have had time to cry out and rouse the rest, but failed to do so out of sheer fright.

On the third day they discovered the girl's presence before the sun had gone very high. She had made some slight noise within, perhaps, as one was passing. A warning shout brought them all running. But Pritchard had expected this sooner or later. They had scarcely any knives left now to hack at the door, and, although her terror must be great, she was safe if she but kept her presence of mind and made no move. There was always the juju.

Pritchard made a great shout and called them back again. Then pointing to the quivering needle that was their greatest object of fear and veneration, he made signs to show that it was the spirit of this that was dwelling behind that fastened door, and they must not disturb or anger it, or it would wreak a terrible revenge. And Bangi was no longer among them to give him the lie.

They gave her hiding-place a wide berth after this, and he had the satisfaction of knowing that she was safe enough for the present. Tomorrow would see an end to all this; but he was haggard, and his strength was going fast.

The second night they slept less deeply. There had been less rum left to stupefy them, less food to share that day. A strangled scream sounded in their midst, just as the helmsman's scream had

wakened Pritchard that other, fatal night. A head or two was raised inquiringly, fearfully; the juju must be at work in their midst again, for their numbers had been thinned once more. A motionless white form, crouched in the shadow of the bulwark, went unnoticed. The seeking heads dropped back again.

But the great black buck who had been the cause of sparing Pritchard and who was something of a leader among them now, peered craftily out between half-lidded eyes. The white form moved again at last, picked something up that lay there still, and threw it over. A splash sounded over the side.

The negro was crawling soundlessly now on hands and feet toward the white form that stood there looking over the side with its back to him, a knife between his teeth. Slowly he crept nearer, took the knife in his hand at last, reared and swept his arm back to strike.

The new moon struck at the blade, sent a gleam up the bulwark like a feeble mirror-flash in the sun. Pritchard twisted around snake-like at the waist, caught the blow with his thick forearm just as it fell. The blade skewered through, peered out at the other end. He hissed through his locked teeth with pain, staggered, brought his legs around in line with the upper part of his body, tried to reach down to the freshly-sheathed knife at his own leg. But there was no room, no time.

The negro's hand was at his throat, forcing his head back while it strangled. His backbone slowly curved under the weight of the onslaught. The bulwark held his legs there rigid, unable to give ground. He tried desperately to squirm sideways and loop out of the vise; the African clung like bark to a tree-trunk, gave him no egress.

He was already veering over at a dangerous angle; the deck seemed to be keeling away from him. To stiffen and go with it meant a broken back. And not to—

His legs shot out from under him as gravity had its way, kicking the other's foothold loose, too. His unwounded arm caught the back of the negro's neck to him, closed like a vise, and the two of them went over together locked in a death-grip, a tangled tarantula of four arms and legs plunging to its own destruction. Their double death-yell sounded as one.

But the shock of the water broke the grip, and they came up apart. Pritchard's one arm was useless, bubbling blood where the knife had bitten, and the negro couldn't swim. They floundered there a yard apart, while the looming black hulk of the ship slowly drifted by them.

There was a warning phosphorescence, a pale gleam caught by the starlight and the crescent moon just under the surface of the water, as an upturned silver belly made its way at them with the swiftness of an arrow. They must have been following the ship for days, and feeding well from it latterly. Churning water blotted out his late opponent's bouncing head and he went under in a creaming froth. Something rough-edged like a hacksaw knocked Pritchard against the ship's side—the lash of the shark's tail as it veered in to the bite. Farther off there was another gleaming belly-flash, a triangular fin slicing the water, as a second one came on with the deadly certainty of a slingshot.

Something slimy dragged across his bobbing shoulder like a snake, and he caught at it despairingly with both hands, pulled himself along the slack length of a rope trailing overside from the ship. It tautened in a moment, so it was not loose upon the deck. His shoulders and waist came clear of the water as he climbed up on it hand over hand, forcing a grip from his wounded arm that he had not thought it could give. He found the ship's side with one leg, and thrust it out for a brake.

A flash of lightning exploded at the end of the other one, as something raked his foot, then coursed up his body to burst a second time in his brain. He was pulled out flat away from the ship for a moment, without letting go the rope—then

the pull stopped and he was free to come in again. There was a coating of icy, painless shock all over his system, that he knew must thaw soon. But first he must get up that rope.

Spiraling loosely like a corpse upon a gibbet, he did it somehow, one arm nearly useless, one foot—a black jelly now, trailing after him. His head came up over the side at last, and he clung to the slippery bulwark by the pits of his arms and his outthrust jaw, unable to summon up the little added strength that would take him over. He could feel consciousness slowly draining out of him, like something squeezed from a sponge. Pain was coming on in, in white-hot surges traveling upward from his foot, with a pause between each one, but a pause that grew less each time.

And on the deck before him was a ring of black faces, drawing in closer, closer, about those two splayed arms and pain-masked face that showed above the side. The odds had climbed too high again; a man could do so much single-handed, and then do no more.

Scarcely realizing what he did, he raised his voice and called feebly in the tense, waiting silence: "Mary. Mary, come forth or I perish!"

Impossible that she should hear the weak bleat, or realize its urgency in time. Yet without the sound of a released bolt or an opening door, a pistol suddenly cracked somewhere at the back of them, and one fell down upon his face and clawed the deck. They broke and fled away into the shadows, and he saw her standing there in the gloom, a feather of smoke dancing before her.

The pistol hit the deck and quickly she had stepped across the prone figure had caught him by the arms, was pulling at him. He would not have thought she had that much strength, nor would she herself perhaps. Strange creatures, women! For somehow he was rolling over at her feet upon the deck, so love must have strong arms.

There was no pause now between the pain-surges. His eyes dimming as he lay there on his back looking up at her, he had only time to breathe: "Reload it, before they close in again—"

She reached for the pistol, looked down at it, uncocked it. "I've killed a man!" she said in a horrified whisper. "I—I've killed a fellow human being!"

"And I," he wanted to say, "have killed a half-a-hundred, and the ship is ours," but darkness swept in and her face floated away into the night.

The beating of a tom-tom roused him in glaring noonday sunlight, and he thought at first the savages were in command again and having their war-dance. But the beating was a pounding coming up his leg, and he saw Mary Lowrie crouched tenderly beside him, laving his head from a bucket filled with salt-water. His mouth was parched, and his head seemed to dance high above the deck, like a kite. There was silence on the ship, no living things but the two of them.

"They haven't come back?" he whispered. "Where do they lurk?"

"I drove them back before me into the hold," she said simply. "They thought me some ghost or spirit, in my flowing dresses. I refired but once, up into the air, and motioned them in. Some I had to chase and ferret out. It was hard to close the hatch upon them unaided, yet somehow I did." Her hands and face were streaked and tarred like any seaman's, her gown was rent, and her nails were split. Yet he thought he had never seen anyone so beautiful before, not even in a painting.

She held fresh water to his lips, and he drank, choking.

Pain soon forced him erect again, for it would not let him lie still, and he looked down at his foot, where the shark's teeth had raked it. It was puffed and flaming, and there was no doubt infection was beginning. The tom-tom that he heard beat therein unceasingly.

"Mary," he said, "the carpenter's axe, that I took from them in the night, bring it out here.

And search below Matthews's bunk, perhaps there is some brandy left."

"But they are safely shut up below," she said, not understanding. "They are too frightened of me to come forth even if they could—" Nevertheless she brought the axe and found a little rum.

"Now dip it in the sea-water," he said, "to cleanse it. Then bring goods and tear it into rags."

Her face blanched. "What are you about?"

He looked at his foot. "There is death in this. It must come off. And you must help me." He was offering the axe to her haft-first.

She screamed and dropped the implement. "Sever it? No, I can't! I can't!"

"Then I must, while I still have my reason. Else I'll be dead by morning." He took the rags and tied them tightly at his ankle. "Fetch me some thin piece of wood to thrust in and pull it tighter still. This is to staunch the flow. Now look away, and when you hear the axe fall discarded, empty sea-water over—it." He tilted the bottle, drained it; struggled up on his one foot, thrust the mortified one out before him so that the gunwale caught it under the arch. But, unable to sustain the position, he toppled weakly back again upon the deck.

The axe was suddenly in her hands again and she was white-lipped. "God give me strength," she pleaded. "Make no move, Davey—for a moment."

He saw the blade flash down, heard its chunk into the deck-plank, but felt no lightest blow. So she had missed the mark—but the darkness rolled in again, more quickly than in the quickest tropic storm.

Oh, many times he woke, and waking dreamed that she was by him laving his head with cool sea-water, or pressing even cooler more refreshing lips to his, or applying brandy-soaked bandages to a board-like stiffness that was his leg, without fire in it now or the beat of drums. But once when

he awoke she was not by him, and when he whispered her name, a thunderclap answered him
and pungent wisps of powder-smoke floated past
him, coming from the bow where there was that
signal gun. Then presently she was beside him
again, gaunt, hollow-cheeked, breathing: "Oh, it
was so hard to turn upon its swivel, and they are
so far from us, so small a speck of white!"

Like an echo, the merest breath of sound,
came a far-off clap of sound. Her head fell forward on his chest and she lay without moving.

Then it was dark, and there was a lantern
coming up over the side, and another, and a
third, and presently ghosts ringed them about,
the ghosts of white men.

Pritchard stared up unblinkingly from where
he lay, unafraid of them, knowing they would
soon melt away. Then they were putting brandy
to her lips and to his, and he reached weakly
forth and touched one's face, and it was warm
and living.

They were propped up, and over the side
nearby he could see lights that rose and fell, yellow and green and red, and an upthrust blackness that blotted out the stars. "What lights are
those?" he whispered. "Are they real?"

"They are the lights of His Majesty's frigate
Hercules," said one pityingly, "and they are real
enough, as many a Frenchman has found to his
cost! What has befallen here?"

And when a gasping word or two had told the
story, the lieutenant in command among them
rapped his sword down on the deck and said to
those about him: "Sink me, sirs! This ship is a
veritable charnel-house! What an ill-starred
voyage!"

Pritchard smiled up at them in feeble contra-
diction. "For the others perhaps, not for me.
I've lost my foot, but what's a foot? I found the
fighting and the doing that I craved," His hand
sought hers. "I found my true love too. What
more does a man ask of but a single voyage?"

TARZAN THE TERRIBLE

EDGAR RICE BURROUGHS

EDGAR RICE BURROUGHS (1875–1950) had a brief military career, followed by a string of brief and relatively insignificant jobs, until he decided to write stories for the pulps. He introduced his first character, the valiant John Carter of Mars, in the serialized novel *Under the Moons of Mars,* which ran in *All-Story Weekly* from February to July of 1912. He quickly followed this success with *Tarzan of the Apes,* which was published as a complete novel in the October 1912 issue of *All-Story;* the novel reached book form in 1914. Although Burroughs found staggering success in the pulps with his tales of Mars, Venus, and lost civilizations, as well as with western and historical fiction, nothing compared to the popularity of Tarzan—now justly considered one of the most famous fictional characters of all time. As the star of over two dozen novels by Burroughs, and many by other writers (some authorized and some not), as well as films (at least eighty-nine), radio and television series, comic books, and even a Broadway musical, Tarzan has been a ubiquitous presence around the world for nearly a century.

The son of a British lord and lady marooned on the west coast of Africa, John Clayton, Lord Greystoke, is only a baby when his mother dies of natural causes and his father is killed by Kerchak, the leader of a tribe of apes unknown to science. Kerchak and his mate, Kala, adopt and raise the orphan, giving him the name Tarzan, which means "White-Skin." Later, as an adult, Tarzan falls in love with Jane Porter, an American woman recently marooned in the same place he had been twenty years earlier. Tarzan eventually follows Jane to her own country and they marry, but he is unhappy with civilization; Jane, Tarzan, and their son, Jack (later named Korak the Killer), return to live on an estate in Africa, which becomes the starting base for many of their adventures. Among Tarzan's exploits are journeys to Opar, a lost outpost of Atlantis; the City of Gold, whose inhabitants hunt their prey with lions; Pellucidar, a land of eternal daylight located at the center of the earth; and, in *Tarzan the Terrible,* the land of Pal-ul-Don, where dinosaurs and upright manlike creatures live side by side.

Tarzan the Terrible first appeared as seven parts in *Argosy All-Story Weekly* in 1921. The same year, it was published as a book by A. C. McClurg of Chicago.

TARZAN THE TERRIBLE

EDGAR RICE BURROUGHS

I

THE PITHECANTHROPUS

SILENT AS THE shadows through which he moved, the great beast slunk through the midnight jungle, his yellow-green eyes round and staring, his sinewy tail undulating behind him, his head lowered and flattened, and every muscle vibrant to the thrill of the hunt. The jungle moon dappled an occasional clearing which the great cat was always careful to avoid. Though he moved through thick verdure across a carpet of innumerable twigs, broken branches, and leaves, his passing gave forth no sound that might have been apprehended by dull human ears.

Apparently less cautious was the hunted thing moving even as silently as the lion a hundred paces ahead of the tawny carnivore, for instead of skirting the moon-splashed natural clearings it passed directly across them, and by the tortuous record of its spoor it might indeed be guessed that it sought these avenues of least resistance, as well it might, since, unlike its grim stalker, it walked erect upon two feet—it walked upon two feet and was hairless except for a black thatch upon its head; its arms were well shaped and muscular; its hands powerful and slender with long tapering fingers and thumbs reaching almost to the first joint of the index fingers. Its legs too were shapely but its feet departed from the standards of all races of men, except possibly a few of the lowest races, in that the great toes protruded at right angles from the foot.

Pausing momentarily in the full light of the gorgeous African moon the creature turned an attentive ear to the rear and then, his head lifted, his features might readily have been discerned in the moonlight. They were strong, clean cut, and regular—features that would have attracted attention for their masculine beauty in any of the great capitals of the world. But was this thing a man? It would have been hard for a watcher in the trees to have decided as the lion's prey resumed its way across the silver tapestry that Luna had laid upon the floor of the dismal jungle, for from beneath the loin cloth of black fur that girdled its thighs there depended a long hairless, white tail.

In one hand the creature carried a stout club, and suspended at its left side from a shoulder belt was a short, sheathed knife, while a cross belt supported a pouch at its right hip. Confining these straps to the body and also apparently supporting the loin cloth was a broad girdle which glittered in the moonlight as though encrusted with virgin gold, and was clasped in the center of the belly with a huge buckle of ornate design that scintillated as with precious stones.

Closer and closer crept Numa, the lion, to his intended victim, and that the latter was not entirely unaware of his danger was evidenced by the increasing frequency with which he turned his ear and his sharp black eyes in the direction of the cat upon his trail. He did not greatly increase his speed, a long swinging walk where the open places permitted, but he loosened the knife in its scabbard and at all times kept his club in readiness for instant action.

Forging at last through a narrow strip of dense jungle vegetation the man-thing broke through into an almost treeless area of considerable extent. For an instant he hesitated, glancing quickly behind him and then up at the security of the branches of the great trees waving overhead, but some greater urge than fear or caution influenced his decision apparently, for he moved off again across the little plain leaving the safety of the trees behind him. At greater or less intervals leafy sanctuaries dotted the grassy expanse ahead of him and the route he took, leading from one to another, indicated that he had not entirely cast discretion to the winds. But after the second tree had been left behind the distance to the next was considerable, and it was then that Numa walked from the concealing cover of the jungle and, seeing his quarry apparently helpless before him, raised his tail stiffly erect and charged.

Two months—two long, weary months filled with hunger, with thirst, with hardships, with disappointment, and, greater than all, with gnawing pain—had passed since Tarzan of the Apes learned from the diary of the dead German captain that his wife still lived. A brief investigation in which he was enthusiastically aided by the Intelligence Department of the British East African Expedition revealed the fact that an attempt had been made to keep Lady Jane in hiding in the interior, for reasons of which only the German High Command might be cognizant.

In charge of Lieutenant Obergatz and a detachment of native German troops she had been sent across the border into the Congo Free State.

Starting out alone in search of her, Tarzan had succeeded in finding the village in which she had been incarcerated only to learn that she had escaped months before, and that the German officer had disappeared at the same time. From there on the stories of the chiefs and the warriors whom he quizzed, were vague and often contradictory. Even the direction that the fugitives had taken Tarzan could only guess at by piecing together bits of fragmentary evidence gleaned from various sources.

Sinister conjectures were forced upon him by various observations which he made in the village. One was incontrovertible proof that these people were man-eaters; the other, the presence in the village of various articles of native German uniforms and equipment. At great risk and in the face of surly objection on the part of the chief, the ape-man made a careful inspection of every hut in the village, from which at least a little ray of hope resulted from the fact that he found no article that might have belonged to his wife.

Leaving the village he had made his way toward the southwest, crossing, after the most appalling hardships, a vast waterless steppe covered for the most part with dense thorn, coming at last into a district that had probably never been previously entered by any white man and which was known only in the legends of the tribes whose country bordered it. Here were precipitous mountains, well-watered plateaus, wide plains, and vast swampy morasses, but neither the plains, nor the plateaus, nor the mountains were accessible to him until after weeks of arduous effort he succeeded in finding a spot where he might cross the morasses—a hideous stretch infested by venomous snakes and other larger dangerous reptiles. On several occasions he glimpsed at distances or by night what might have been titanic reptilian monsters, but as there were hippopotami, rhinoceri, and elephants in great numbers in and about the marsh he was never positive that the forms he saw were not of these.

When at last he stood upon firm ground after crossing the morasses he realized why it was that for perhaps countless ages this territory had defied the courage and hardihood of the heroic races of the outer world that had, after innumerable reverses and unbelievable suffering penetrated to practically every other region, from pole to pole.

From the abundance and diversity of the game it might have appeared that every known species of bird and beast and reptile had sought here a refuge wherein they might take their last stand against the encroaching multitudes of men that had steadily spread themselves over the surface of the earth, wresting the hunting grounds from the lower orders, from the moment that the first ape shed his hair and ceased to walk upon his knuckles. Even the species with which Tarzan was familiar showed here either the results of a divergent line of evolution or an unaltered form that had been transmitted without variation for countless ages.

Too, there were many hybrid strains, not the least interesting of which to Tarzan was a yellow and black striped lion. Smaller than the species with which Tarzan was familiar, but still a most formidable beast, since it possessed in addition to sharp saber-like canines the disposition of a devil. To Tarzan it presented evidence that tigers had once roamed the jungles of Africa, possibly giant saber-tooths of another epoch, and these apparently had crossed with lions with the resultant terrors that he occasionally encountered at the present day.

The true lions of this new, Old World differed but little from those with which he was familiar; in size and conformation they were almost identical, but instead of shedding the leopard spots of cubhood, they retained them through life as definitely marked as those of the leopard.

Two months of effort had revealed no slightest evidence that she he sought had entered this beautiful yet forbidding land. His investigation, however, of the cannibal village and his questioning of other tribes in the neighborhood had convinced him that if Lady Jane still lived it must be in this direction that he seek her, since by a process of elimination he had reduced the direction of her flight to only this possibility. How she had crossed the morass he could not guess and yet something within seemed to urge upon him belief that she had crossed it, and that if she still lived it was here that she must be sought. But this unknown, untraversed wild was of vast extent; grim, forbidding mountains blocked his way, torrents tumbling from rocky fastnesses impeded his progress, and at every turn he was forced to match wits and muscles with the great carnivora that he might procure sustenance.

Time and again Tarzan and Numa stalked the same quarry and now one, now the other bore off the prize. Seldom, however, did the ape-man go hungry for the country was rich in game animals and birds and fish, in fruit and the countless other forms of vegetable life upon which the jungle-bred man may subsist.

Tarzan often wondered why in so rich a country he found no evidences of man and had at last come to the conclusion that the parched, thorn-covered steppe and the hideous morasses had formed a sufficient barrier to protect this country effectively from the inroads of mankind.

After days of searching he had succeeded finally in discovering a pass through the mountains and, coming down upon the opposite side, had found himself in a country practically identical with that which he had left. The hunting was good and at a water hole in the mouth of a canon where it debouched upon a tree-covered plain Bara, the deer, fell an easy victim to the ape-man's cunning.

It was just at dusk. The voices of great four-footed hunters rose now and again from various directions, and as the canon afforded among its trees no comfortable retreat the ape-man shouldered the carcass of the deer and started downward onto the plain. At its opposite side rose lofty trees—a great forest which suggested to his practiced eye a mighty jungle. Toward this the ape-man bent his step, but when midway of the plain he discovered standing alone such a tree as best suited him for a night's abode, swung lightly to its branches and, presently, a comfortable resting place.

Here he ate the flesh of Bara and when satisfied carried the balance of the carcass to the opposite side of the tree where he deposited it far above the ground in a secure place. Returning to his crotch he settled himself for sleep and in another moment the roars of the lions and the howlings of the lesser cats fell upon deaf ears.

The usual noises of the jungle composed rather than disturbed the ape-man but an unusual sound, however imperceptible to the awakened ear of civilized man, seldom failed to impinge upon the consciousness of Tarzan, however deep his slumber, and so it was that when the moon was high a sudden rush of feet across the grassy carpet in the vicinity of his tree brought him to alert and ready activity. Tarzan does not awaken as you and I with the weight of slumber still upon his eyes and brain, for did the creatures of the wild awaken thus, their awakenings would be few. As his eyes snapped open, clear and bright, so, clear and bright upon the nerve centers of his brain, were registered the various perceptions of all his senses.

Almost beneath him, racing toward his tree was what at first glance appeared to be an almost naked white man, yet even at the first instant of discovery the long, white tail projecting rearward did not escape the ape-man. Behind the fleeing figure, escaping, came Numa, the lion, in full charge. Voiceless the prey, voiceless the killer; as two spirits in a dead world the two moved in silent swiftness toward the culminating tragedy of this grim race.

Even as his eyes opened and took in the scene beneath him—even in that brief instant of perception, followed reason, judgment, and decision, so rapidly one upon the heels of the other that almost simultaneously the ape-man was in mid-air, for he had seen a white-skinned creature cast in a mold similar to his own, pursued by Tarzan's hereditary enemy. So close was the lion to the fleeing man-thing that Tarzan had no time carefully to choose the method of his attack. As a diver leaps from the springboard headforemost into the waters beneath, so Tarzan of the Apes dove straight for Numa, the lion; naked in his right hand the blade of his father that so many times before had tasted the blood of lions.

A raking talon caught Tarzan on the side, inflicting a long, deep wound and then the ape-man was on Numa's back and the blade was sinking again and again into the savage side. Nor was the man-thing either longer fleeing, or idle. He too, creature of the wild, had sensed on the instant the truth of the miracle of his saving, and turning in his tracks, had leaped forward with raised bludgeon to Tarzan's assistance and Numa's undoing. A single terrific blow upon the flattened skull of the beast laid him insensible and then as Tarzan's knife found the wild heart a few convulsive shudders and a sudden relaxation marked the passing of the carnivore.

Leaping to his feet the ape-man placed his foot upon the carcass of his kill and, raising his face to Goro, the moon, voiced the savage victory cry that had so often awakened the echoes of his native jungle.

As the hideous scream burst from the ape-man's lips the man-thing stepped quickly back as in sudden awe, but when Tarzan returned his hunting knife to its sheath and turned toward him the other saw in the quiet dignity of his demeanor no cause for apprehension.

For a moment the two stood appraising each other, and then the man-thing spoke. Tarzan realized that the creature before him was uttering articulate sounds which expressed in speech, though in a language with which Tarzan was unfamiliar, the thoughts of a man possessing to a greater or less extent the same powers of reason that he possessed. In other words, that though the creature before him had the tail and thumbs and great toes of a monkey, it was, in all other respects, quite evidently a man.

The blood which was now flowing down Tarzan's side caught the creature's attention. From the pocket-pouch at his side he took a small bag and approaching Tarzan indicated by signs that he wished the ape-man to lie down that he might treat the wound, whereupon, spreading the edges of the cut apart, he sprinkled the raw flesh with powder from the little bag. The pain of the wound was as nothing to the exquisite torture of the remedy but, accustomed to physical suffering, the ape-man withstood it stoically and in a few moments not only had the bleeding ceased but the pain as well.

In reply to the soft and far from unpleasant modulations of the other's voice, Tarzan spoke in various tribal dialects of the interior as well as in the language of the great apes, but it was evident that the man understood none of these. Seeing that they could not make each other understood, the pithecanthropus advanced toward Tarzan and placing his left hand over his own heart laid the palm of his right hand over the heart of the ape-man. To the latter the action appeared as a form of friendly greeting and, being versed in the ways of uncivilized races, he responded in kind as he realized it was doubtless intended that he should. His action seemed to satisfy and please his new-found acquaintance, who immediately fell to talking again and finally, with his head tipped back, sniffed the air in the direction of the tree above them and then suddenly pointing toward the carcass of Bara, the deer, he touched his stomach in a sign language which even the densest might interpret. With a wave of his hand Tarzan invited his guest to partake of the remains of his savage repast, and the other, leaping nimbly as a little monkey to the lower branches of the tree, made his way quickly to the flesh, assisted always by his long, strong sinuous tail.

The pithecanthropus ate in silence, cutting small strips from the deer's loin with his keen knife. From his crotch in the tree Tarzan watched his companion, noting the preponderance of human attributes which were doubtless accentuated by the paradoxical thumbs, great toes, and tail.

He wondered if this creature was representative of some strange race or if, what seemed more likely, but an atavism. Either supposition would have seemed preposterous enough did he not have before him the evidence of the creature's existence. There he was, however, a tailed man with distinctly arboreal hands and feet. His trappings, gold encrusted and jewel studded, could have been wrought only by skilled artisans; but whether they were the work of this individual or

of others like him, or of an entirely different race, Tarzan could not, of course, determine.

His meal finished, the guest wiped his fingers and lips with leaves broken from a nearby branch, looked up at Tarzan with a pleasant smile that revealed a row of strong white teeth, the canines of which were no longer than Tarzan's own, spoke a few words which Tarzan judged were a polite expression of thanks and then sought a comfortable place in the tree for the night.

The earth was shadowed in the darkness which precedes the dawn when Tarzan was awakened by a violent shaking of the tree in which he had found shelter. As he opened his eyes he saw that his companion was also astir, and glancing around quickly to apprehend the cause of the disturbance, the ape-man was astounded at the sight which met his eyes.

The dim shadow of a colossal form reared close beside the tree and he saw that it was the scraping of the giant body against the branches that had awakened him. That such a tremendous creature could have approached so closely without disturbing him filled Tarzan with both wonderment and chagrin. In the gloom the ape-man at first conceived the intruder to be an elephant; yet, if so, one of greater proportions than any he had ever before seen, but as the dim outlines became less indistinct he saw on a line with his eyes and twenty feet above the ground the dim silhouette of a grotesquely serrated back that gave the impression of a creature whose each and every spinal vertebra grew a thick, heavy horn. Only a portion of the back was visible to the ape-man, the rest of the body being lost in the dense shadows beneath the tree, from whence there now arose the sound of giant jaws powerfully crunching flesh and bones. From the odors that rose to the ape-man's sensitive nostrils he presently realized that beneath him was some huge reptile feeding upon the carcass of the lion that had been slain there earlier in the night.

As Tarzan's eyes, straining with curiosity, bored futilely into the dark shadows he felt a light touch upon his shoulder, and, turning, saw that his companion was attempting to attract his attention. The creature, pressing a forefinger to his own lips as to enjoin silence, attempted by pulling on Tarzan's arm to indicate that they should leave at once.

Realizing that he was in a strange country, evidently infested by creatures of titanic size, with the habits and powers of which he was entirely unfamiliar, the ape-man permitted himself to be drawn away. With the utmost caution the pithecanthropus descended the tree upon the opposite side from the great nocturnal prowler, and, closely followed by Tarzan, moved silently away through the night across the plain.

The ape-man was rather loath thus to relinquish an opportunity to inspect a creature which he realized was probably entirely different from anything in his past experience; yet he was wise enough to know when discretion was the better part of valor and now, as in the past, he yielded to that law which dominates the kindred of the wild, preventing them from courting danger uselessly, whose lives are sufficiently filled with danger in their ordinary routine of feeding and mating.

As the rising sun dispelled the shadows of the night, Tarzan found himself again upon the verge of a great forest into which his guide plunged, taking nimbly to the branches of the trees through which he made his way with the celerity of long habitude and hereditary instinct, but though aided by a prehensile tail, fingers, and toes, the man-thing moved through the forest with no greater ease or surety than did the giant ape-man.

It was during this journey that Tarzan recalled the wound in his side inflicted upon him the previous night by the raking talons of Numa, the lion, and examining it was surprised to discover that not only was it painless but along its edges were no indications of inflammation, the results doubtless of the antiseptic powder his strange companion had sprinkled upon it.

They had proceeded for a mile or two when Tarzan's companion came to earth upon a grassy slope beneath a great tree whose branches overhung a clear brook. Here they drank and Tarzan discovered the water to be not only deliciously pure and fresh but of an icy temperature that indicated its rapid descent from the lofty mountains of its origin.

Casting aside his loin cloth and weapons Tarzan entered the little pool beneath the tree and after a moment emerged, greatly refreshed and filled with a keen desire to breakfast. As he came out of the pool he noticed his companion examining him with a puzzled expression upon his face. Taking the ape-man by the shoulder he turned him around so that Tarzan's back was toward him and then, touching the end of Tarzan's spine with his forefinger, he curled his own tail up over his shoulder and, wheeling the ape-man about again, pointed first at Tarzan and then at his own caudal appendage, a look of puzzlement upon his face, the while he jabbered excitedly in his strange tongue.

The ape-man realized that probably for the first time his companion had discovered that he was tailless by nature rather than by accident, and so he called attention to his own great toes and thumbs to further impress upon the creature that they were of different species.

The fellow shook his head dubiously as though entirely unable to comprehend why Tarzan should differ so from him but at last, apparently giving the problem up with a shrug, he laid aside his own harness, skin, and weapons and entered the pool.

His ablutions completed and his meager apparel redonned he seated himself at the foot of the tree and motioning Tarzan to a place beside him, opened the pouch that hung at his right side taking from it strips of dried flesh and a couple of handfuls of thin-shelled nuts with which Tarzan was unfamiliar. Seeing the other break them with his teeth and eat the kernel, Tarzan followed the example thus set him, discovering the meat to be rich and well flavored. The dried flesh also was far from unpalatable, though it had evidently been jerked without salt, a commodity which Tarzan imagined might be rather difficult to obtain in this locality.

As they ate Tarzan's companion pointed to

the nuts, the dried meat, and various other nearby objects, in each instance repeating what Tarzan readily discovered must be the names of these things in the creature's native language. The ape-man could but smile at this evident desire upon the part of his new-found acquaintance to impart to him instructions that eventually might lead to an exchange of thoughts between them. Having already mastered several languages and a multitude of dialects the ape-man felt that he could readily assimilate another even though this appeared one entirely unrelated to any with which he was familiar.

So occupied were they with their breakfast and the lesson that neither was aware of the beady eyes glittering down upon them from above; nor was Tarzan cognizant of any impending danger until the instant that a huge, hairy body leaped full upon his companion from the branches above them.

II
"TO THE DEATH!"

In the moment of discovery Tarzan saw that the creature was almost a counterpart of his companion in size and conformation, with the exception that his body was entirely clothed with a coat of shaggy black hair which almost concealed his features, while his harness and weapons were similar to those of the creature he had attacked. Ere Tarzan could prevent it, the creature had struck the ape-man's companion a blow upon the head with his knotted club that felled him, unconscious, to the earth; but before he could inflict further injury upon his defenseless prey the ape-man had closed with him.

Instantly Tarzan realized that he was locked with a creature of almost superhuman strength. The sinewy fingers of a powerful hand sought his throat while the other lifted the bludgeon above his head. But if the strength of the hairy attacker was great, great too was that of his smooth-skinned antagonist. Swinging a single terrific blow with clenched fist to the point of the other's chin, Tarzan momentarily staggered his assailant and then his own fingers closed upon the shaggy throat, as with the other hand he seized the wrist of the arm that swung the club. With equal celerity he shot his right leg behind the shaggy brute and throwing his weight forward hurled the thing over his hip heavily to the ground, at the same time precipitating his own body upon the other's chest.

With the shock of the impact the club fell from the brute's hand and Tarzan's hold was wrenched from its throat. Instantly the two were locked in a deathlike embrace. Though the creature bit at Tarzan the latter was quickly aware that this was not a particularly formidable method of offense or defense, since its canines were scarcely more developed than his own. The thing that he had principally to guard against was the sinuous tail which sought steadily to wrap itself about his throat and against which experience had afforded him no defense.

Struggling and snarling the two rolled growling about the sward at the foot of the tree, first one on top and then the other but each more occupied at present in defending his throat from the other's choking grasp than in aggressive, offensive tactics. But presently the ape-man saw his opportunity and as they rolled about he forced the creature closer and closer to the pool, upon the banks of which the battle was progressing. At last they lay upon the very verge of the water and now it remained for Tarzan to precipitate them both beneath the surface but in such a way that he might remain on top.

At the same instant there came within range of Tarzan's vision, just behind the prostrate form of his companion, the crouching, devil-faced figure of the striped saber-tooth hybrid, eyeing him with snarling, malevolent face.

Almost simultaneously Tarzan's shaggy antagonist discovered the menacing figure of the great cat. Immediately he ceased his belligerent activities against Tarzan and, jabbering and chattering to the ape-man, he tried to disengage himself from Tarzan's hold but in such a way that indicated that as far as he was concerned their battle was over. Appreciating the danger to his unconscious companion and being anxious to protect him from the saber-tooth the ape-man relinquished his hold upon his adversary and together the two rose to their feet.

Drawing his knife Tarzan moved slowly toward the body of his companion, expecting that his recent antagonist would grasp the opportunity for escape. To his surprise, however, the beast, after regaining its club, advanced at his side.

The great cat, flattened upon its belly, remained motionless except for twitching tail and snarling lips where it lay perhaps fifty feet beyond the body of the pithecanthropus. As Tarzan stepped over the body of the latter he saw the eyelids quiver and open, and in his heart he felt a strange sense of relief that the creature was not dead and a realization that without his suspecting it there had arisen within his savage bosom a bond of attachment for this strange new friend.

Tarzan continued to approach the saber-tooth, nor did the shaggy beast at his right lag behind. Closer and closer they came until at a distance of about twenty feet the hybrid charged. Its rush was directed toward the shaggy manlike ape who halted in his tracks with upraised bludgeon to meet the assault. Tarzan, on the contrary, leaped forward and with a celerity second not even to that of the swift-moving cat, he threw himself headlong upon him as might a Rugby tackler on an American gridiron. His right arm circled the beast's neck in front of the right shoulder, his left behind the left foreleg, and so great was the force of the impact that the two rolled over and over several times upon the ground, the cat screaming and clawing to liberate itself that it might turn upon its attacker, the man clinging desperately to his hold.

Seemingly the attack was one of mad, senseless ferocity unguided by either reason or skill. Nothing, however, could have been farther from the truth than such an assumption since every muscle in the ape-man's giant frame obeyed the dictates of the cunning mind that long experience had trained to meet every exigency of such an encounter. The long, powerful legs, though seemingly inextricably entangled with the hind feet of the clawing cat, ever as by a miracle, escaped the raking talons and yet at just the proper instant in the midst of all the rolling and tossing they were where they should be to carry out the ape-man's plan of offense. So that on the instant that the cat believed it had won the mastery of its antagonist it was jerked suddenly upward as the ape-man rose to his feet, holding the striped back close against his body as he rose and forcing it backward until it could but claw the air helplessly.

Instantly the shaggy black rushed in with drawn knife which it buried in the beast's heart. For a few moments Tarzan retained his hold but when the body had relaxed in final dissolution he pushed it from him and the two who had formerly been locked in mortal combat stood facing each other across the body of the common foe.

Tarzan waited, ready either for peace or war. Presently two shaggy black hands were raised; the left was laid upon its own heart and the right extended until the palm touched Tarzan's breast. It was the same form of friendly salutation with which the pithecanthropus had sealed his alliance with the ape-man and Tarzan, glad of every ally he could win in this strange and savage world, quickly accepted the proffered friendship.

At the conclusion of the brief ceremony Tarzan, glancing in the direction of the hairless pithecanthropus, discovered that the latter had recovered consciousness and was sitting erect watching them intently. He now rose slowly and at the same time the shaggy black turned in his direction and addressed him in what evidently was their common language. The hairless one replied and the two approached each other slowly. Tarzan watched interestedly the outcome of their meeting. They halted a few paces apart, first one and then the other speaking rapidly but without apparent excitement, each occasionally glancing or nodding toward Tarzan, indicating that he was to some extent the subject of their conversation.

Presently they advanced again until they met, whereupon was repeated the brief ceremony of alliance which had previously marked the cessation of hostilities between Tarzan and the black. They then advanced toward the ape-man addressing him earnestly as though endeavoring to convey to him some important information. Presently, however, they gave it up as an unprofitable job and, resorting to sign language, conveyed to Tarzan that they were proceeding upon their way together and were urging him to accompany them.

As the direction they indicated was a route which Tarzan had not previously traversed he was extremely willing to accede to their request, as he had determined thoroughly to explore this unknown land before definitely abandoning search for Lady Jane therein.

For several days their way led through the foothills parallel to the lofty range towering above. Often were they menaced by the savage denizens of this remote fastness, and occasionally Tarzan glimpsed weird forms of gigantic proportions amidst the shadows of the nights.

On the third day they came upon a large natural cave in the face of a low cliff at the foot of which tumbled one of the numerous mountain brooks that watered the plain below and fed the morasses in the lowlands at the country's edge. Here the three took up their temporary abode where Tarzan's instruction in the language of his companions progressed more rapidly than while on the march.

The cave gave evidence of having harbored other manlike forms in the past. Remnants of a crude, rock fireplace remained and the walls and ceiling were blackened with the smoke of many fires. Scratched in the soot, and sometimes deeply into the rock beneath, were strange hieroglyphics and the outlines of beasts and birds and reptiles, some of the latter of weird form suggesting the extinct creatures of Jurassic times. Some of the more recently made hieroglyphics Tarzan's companions read with interest and commented upon, and then with the points

of their knives they too added to the possibly age-old record of the blackened walls.

Tarzan's curiosity was aroused, but the only explanation at which he could arrive was that he was looking upon possibly the world's most primitive hotel register. At least it gave him a further insight into the development of the strange creatures with which Fate had thrown him. Here were men with the tails of monkeys, one of them as hair covered as any fur-bearing brute of the lower orders, and yet it was evident that they possessed not only a spoken, but a written language. The former he was slowly mastering and at this new evidence of unlooked-for civilization in creatures possessing so many of the physical attributes of beasts, Tarzan's curiosity was still further piqued and his desire quickly to master their tongue strengthened, with the result that he fell to with even greater assiduity to the task he had set himself. Already he knew the names of his companions and the common names of the fauna and flora with which they had most often come in contact.

Ta-den, he of the hairless, white skin, having assumed the rôle of tutor, prosecuted his task with a singleness of purpose that was reflected in his pupil's rapid mastery of Ta-den's mother tongue. Om-at, the hairy black, also seemed to feel that there rested upon his broad shoulders a portion of the burden of responsibility for Tarzan's education, with the result that either one or the other of them was almost constantly coaching the ape-man during his waking hours. The result was only what might have been expected—a rapid assimilation of the teachings to the end that before any of them realized it, communication by word of mouth became an accomplished fact.

Tarzan explained to his companions the purpose of his mission but neither could give him any slightest thread of hope to weave into the fabric of his longing. Never had there been in their country a woman such as he described, nor any tailless man other than himself that they ever had seen.

"I have been gone from A-lur while Bu, the moon, has eaten seven times," said Ta-den. "Many things may happen in seven times twenty-eight days; but I doubt that your woman could have entered our country across the terrible morasses which even you found an almost insurmountable obstacle, and if she had, could she have survived the perils that you already have encountered beside those of which you have yet to learn? Not even our own women venture into the savage lands beyond the cities."

" 'A-lur,' Light-city, City of Light," mused Tarzan, translating the word into his own tongue. "And where is A-lur?" he asked. "Is it your city, Ta-den, and Om-at's?"

"It is mine," replied the hairless one; "but not Om-at's. The Waz-don have no cities—they live in the trees of the forests and the caves of the hills—is it not so, black man?" he concluded, turning toward the hairy giant beside him.

"Yes," replied Om-at, "We Waz-don are free—only the Ho-don imprison themselves in cities. I would not be a white man!"

Tarzan smiled. Even here was the racial distinction between white man and black man—Ho-don and Waz-don. Not even the fact that they appeared to be equals in the matter of intelligence made any difference—one was white and one was black, and it was easy to see that the white considered himself superior to the other—one could see it in his quiet smile.

"Where is A-lur?" Tarzan asked again. "You are returning to it?"

"It is beyond the mountains," replied Ta-den. "I do not return to it—not yet. Not until Ko-tan is no more."

"Ko-tan?" queried Tarzan.

"Ko-tan is king," explained the pithecanthropus. "He rules this land. I was one of his warriors. I lived in the palace of Ko-tan and there I met O-lo-a, his daughter. We loved, Like-star-light, and I; but Ko-tan would have none of me. He sent me away to fight with the men of the village of Dak-at, who had refused to pay his tribute to the king, thinking that I would

be killed, for Dak-at is famous for his many fine warriors. And I was not killed. Instead I returned victorious with the tribute and with Dak-at himself my prisoner; but Ko-tan was not pleased because he saw that O-lo-a loved me even more than before, her love being strengthened and fortified by pride in my achievement.

"Powerful is my father, Ja-don, the Lion-man, chief of the largest village outside of A-lur. Him Ko-tan hesitated to affront and so he could not but praise me for my success, though he did it with half a smile. But you do not understand! It is what we call a smile that moves only the muscles of the face and affects not the light of the eyes—it means hypocrisy and duplicity. I must be praised and rewarded. What better than that he reward me with the hand of O-lo-a, his daughter? But no, he saves O-lo-a for Bu-lot, son of Mo-sar, the chief whose great-grandfather was king and who thinks that he should be king. Thus would Ko-tan appease the wrath of Mo-sar and win the friendship of those who think with Mo-sar that Mo-sar should be king.

"But what reward shall repay the faithful Ta-den? Greatly do we honor our priests. Within the temples even the chiefs and the king himself bow down to them. No greater honor could Ko-tan confer upon a subject—who wished to be a priest, but I did not so wish. Priests other than the high priest must become eunuchs for they may never marry.

"It was O-lo-a herself who brought word to me that her father had given the commands that would set in motion the machinery of the temple. A messenger was on his way in search of me to summon me to Ko-tan's presence. To have refused the priesthood once it was offered me by the king would have been to have affronted the temple and the gods—that would have meant death; but if I did not appear before Ko-tan I would not have to refuse anything. O-lo-a and I decided that I must not appear. It was better to fly, carrying in my bosom a shred of hope, than to remain and, with my priesthood, abandon hope forever.

"Beneath the shadows of the great trees that grow within the palace grounds I pressed her to me for, perhaps, the last time and then, lest by ill-fate I meet the messenger, I scaled the great wall that guards the palace and passed through the darkened city. My name and rank carried me beyond the city gate. Since then I have wandered far from the haunts of the Ho-don but strong within me is the urge to return if even but to look from without her walls upon the city that holds her most dear to me and again to visit the village of my birth, to see again my father and my mother."

"But the risk is too great?" asked Tarzan.

"It is great, but not too great," replied Ta-den. "I shall go."

"And I shall go with you, if I may," said the ape-man, "for I must see this City of Light, this A-lur of yours, and search there for my lost mate even though you believe that there is little chance that I find her. And you, Om-at, do you come with us?"

"Why not?" asked the hairy one. "The lairs of my tribe lie in the crags above A-lur and though Es-sat, our chief, drove me out I should like to return again, for there is a she there upon whom I should be glad to look once more and who would be glad to look upon me. Yes, I will go with you. Es-sat feared that I might become chief and who knows but that Es-sat was right. But Pan-at-lee! it is she I seek first even before a chieftainship."

"We three, then, shall travel together," said Tarzan.

"And fight together," added Ta-den; "the three as one," and as he spoke he drew his knife and held it above his head.

"The three as one," repeated Om-at, drawing his weapon and duplicating Ta-den's act. "It is spoken!"

"The three as one!" cried Tarzan of the Apes. "To the death!" and his blade flashed in the sunlight.

"Let us go, then," said Om-at; "my knife is dry and cries aloud for the blood of Es-sat."

The trail over which Ta-den and Om-at led and which scarcely could be dignified even by the name of trail was suited more to mountain sheep, monkeys, or birds than to man; but the three that followed it were trained to ways which no ordinary man might essay. Now, upon the lower slopes, it led through dense forests where the ground was so matted with fallen trees and over-rioting vines and brush that the way held always to the swaying branches high above the tangle; again it skirted yawning gorges whose slippery-faced rocks gave but momentary foothold even to the bare feet that lightly touched them as the three leaped chamois-like from one precarious foothold to the next. Dizzy and terrifying was the way that Om-at chose across the summit as he led them around the shoulder of a towering crag that rose a sheer two thousand feet of perpendicular rock above a tumbling river. And when at last they stood upon comparatively level ground again Om-at turned and looked at them both intently and especially at Tarzan of the Apes.

"You will both do," he said. "You are fit companions for Om-at, the Waz-don."

"What do you mean?" asked Tarzan.

"I brought you this way," replied the black, "to learn if either lacked the courage to follow where Om-at led. It is here that the young warriors of Es-sat come to prove their courage. And yet, though we are born and raised upon cliff sides, it is considered no disgrace to admit that Pastar-ul-ved, the Father of Mountains, has defeated us, for of those who try it only a few succeed—the bones of the others lie at the feet of Pastar-ul-ved."

Ta-den laughed. "I would not care to come this way often," he said.

"No," replied Om-at; "but it has shortened our journey by at least a full day. So much the sooner shall Tarzan look upon the Valley of Jad-ben-Otho. Come!" and he led the way upward along the shoulder of Pastar-ul-ved until there lay spread below them a scene of mystery and of beauty—a green valley girt by towering cliffs of marble whiteness—a green valley dotted by deep blue lakes and crossed by the blue trail of a winding river. In the center a city of the whiteness of the marble cliffs—a city which even at so great a distance evidenced a strange, yet artistic architecture. Outside the city there were visible about the valley isolated groups of buildings—sometimes one, again two and three and four in a cluster—but always of the same glaring whiteness, and always in some fantastic form.

About the valley the cliffs were occasionally cleft by deep gorges, verdure-filled, giving the appearance of green rivers rioting downward toward a central sea of green.

"*Jad Pele ul Jad-ben-Otho*," murmured Tarzan in the tongue of the pithecanthropi; "The Valley of the Great God—it is beautiful!"

"Here, in A-lur, lives Ko-tan, the king, ruler over all Pal-ul-don," said Ta-den.

"And here in these gorges live the Waz-don," exclaimed Om-at, "who do not acknowledge that Ko-tan is the ruler over all the Land-of-man."

Ta-den smiled and shrugged. "We will not quarrel, you and I," he said to Om-at, "over that which all the ages have not proved sufficient time in which to reconcile the Ho-don and Waz-don; but let me whisper to you a secret, Om-at. The Ho-don live together in greater or less peace under one ruler so that when danger threatens them they face the enemy with many warriors, for every fighting Ho-don of Pal-ul-don is there. But you Waz-don, how is it with you? You have a dozen kings who fight not only with the Ho-don but with one another. When one of your tribes goes forth upon the fighting trail, even against the Ho-don, it must leave behind sufficient warriors to protect its women and its children from the neighbors upon either hand. When we want eunuchs for the temples or servants for the fields or the homes we march forth in great numbers upon one of your villages. You cannot even flee, for upon either side of you are enemies and though you fight bravely we come back with those who will presently be eunuchs in the temples and servants in our fields and homes. So long as the Waz-don are thus foolish the Ho-don will dominate and their king will be king of Pal-ul-don."

"Perhaps you are right," admitted Om-at. "It

is because our neighbors are fools, each thinking that his tribe is the greatest and should rule among the Waz-don. They will not admit that the warriors of my tribe are the bravest and our shes the most beautiful."

Ta-den grinned. "Each of the others presents precisely the same arguments that you present, Om-at," he said, "which, my friend, is the strongest bulwark of defense possessed by the Ho-don."

"Come!" exclaimed Tarzan; "such discussions often lead to quarrels and we three must have no quarrels. I, of course, am interested in learning what I can of the political and economic conditions of your land; I should like to know something of your religion; but not at the expense of bitterness between my only friends in Pal-ul-don. Possibly, however, you hold to the same god?"

"There indeed we do differ," cried Om-at, somewhat bitterly and with a trace of excitement in his voice.

"Differ!" almost shouted Ta-den; "and why should we not differ? Who could agree with the preposterous—"

"Stop!" cried Tarzan. "Now, indeed, have I stirred up a hornets' nest. Let us speak no more of matters political or religious."

"That is wiser," agreed Om-at; "but I might mention, for your information, that the one and only god has a long tail."

"It is sacrilege," cried Ta-den, laying his hand upon his knife; "Jad-ben-Otho has no tail!"

"Stop!" shrieked Om-at, springing forward; but instantly Tarzan interposed himself between them.

"Enough!" he snapped. "Let us be true to our oaths of friendship that we may be honorable in the sight of God in whatever form we conceive Him."

"You are right, Tailless One," said Ta-den. "Come, Om-at, let us look after our friendship and ourselves, secure in the conviction that Jad-ben-Otho is sufficiently powerful to look after himself."

"Done!" agreed Om-at, "but—"

"No 'buts,' Om-at," admonished Tarzan.

The shaggy black shrugged his shoulders and smiled. "Shall we make our way down toward the valley?" he asked. "The gorge below us is uninhabited; that to the left contains the caves of my people. I would see Pan-at-lee once more. Ta-den would visit his father in the valley below and Tarzan seeks entrance to A-lur in search of the mate that would be better dead than in the clutches of the Ho-don priests of Jad-ben-Otho. How shall we proceed?"

"Let us remain together as long as possible," urged Ta-den. "You, Om-at, must seek Pan-at-lee by night and by stealth, for three, even we three, may not hope to overcome Es-sat and all his warriors. At any time may we go to the village where my father is chief, for Ja-don always will welcome the friends of his son. But for Tarzan to enter A-lur is another matter, though there is a way and he has the courage to put it to the test—listen, come close for Jad-ben-Otho has keen ears and this he must not hear," and with his lips close to the ears of his companions Ta-den, the Tall-tree, son of Ja-don, the Lion-man, unfolded his daring plan.

And at the same moment, a hundred miles away, a lithe figure, naked but for a loin cloth and weapons, moved silently across a thorn-covered, waterless steppe, searching always along the ground before him with keen eyes and sensitive nostrils.

III
PAN-AT-LEE

Night had fallen upon uncharted Pal-ul-don. A slender moon, low in the west, bathed the white faces of the chalk cliffs presented to her, in a mellow, unearthly glow. Black were the shadows in Kor-ul-ja, Gorge-of-lions, where dwelt the tribe of the same name under Es-sat, their chief. From an aperture near the summit of the lofty escarpment a hairy figure emerged—the head and shoulders first—and fierce eyes scanned the cliff side in every direction.

It was Es-sat, the chief. To right and left and below he looked as though to assure himself that he was unobserved, but no other figure moved upon the cliff face, nor did another hairy body protrude from any of the numerous cave mouths, from the high-flung abode of the chief to the habitations of the more lowly members of the tribe nearer the cliff's base. Then he moved outward upon the sheer face of the white chalk wall. In the half-light of the baby moon it appeared that the heavy, shaggy black figure moved across the face of the perpendicular wall in some miraculous manner, but closer examination would have revealed stout pegs, as large around as a man's wrist protruding from holes in the cliff into which they were driven. Es-sat's four hand-like members and his long, sinuous tail permitted him to move with consummate ease whither he chose—a gigantic rat upon a mighty wall. As he progressed upon his way he avoided the cave mouths, passing either above or below those that lay in his path.

The outward appearance of these caves was similar. An opening from eight to as much as twenty feet long by eight high and four to six feet deep was cut into the chalklike rock of the cliff; in the back of this large opening, which formed what might be described as the front veranda of the home, was an opening about three feet wide and six feet high, evidently forming the doorway to the interior apartment or apartments. On either side of this doorway were smaller openings which it were easy to assume were windows through which light and air might find their way to the inhabitants. Similar windows were also dotted over the cliff face between the entrance porches, suggesting that the entire face of the cliff was honeycombed with apartments. From many of these smaller apertures small streams of water trickled down the escarpment, and the wall above others was blackened as by smoke. Where the water ran the wall was eroded to a depth of from a few inches to as much as a foot, suggesting that some of the tiny streams had been trickling downward to the green carpet of vegetation below for ages.

In this primeval setting the great pithecan-thropus aroused no jarring discord for he was as much a part of it as the trees that grew upon the summit of the cliff or those that hid their feet among the dank ferns in the bottom of the gorge.

Now he paused before an entrance-way and listened and then, noiselessly as the moonlight upon the trickling waters, he merged with the shadows of the outer porch. At the doorway leading into the interior he paused again, listen-ing, and then quietly pushing aside the heavy skin that covered the aperture he passed within a large chamber hewn from the living rock. From the far end, through another doorway, shone a light, dimly. Toward this he crept with utmost stealth, his naked feet giving forth no sound. The knotted club that had been hanging at his back from a thong about his neck he now re-moved and carried in his left hand.

Beyond the second doorway was a corridor running parallel with the cliff face. In this corri-dor were three more doorways, one at each end and a third almost opposite that in which Es-sat stood. The light was coming from an apartment at the end of the corridor at his left. A sputtering flame rose and fell in a small stone receptacle that stood upon a table or bench of the same ma-terial, a monolithic bench fashioned at the time the room was excavated, rising massively from the floor, of which it was a part.

In one corner of the room beyond the table had been left a dais of stone about four feet wide and eight feet long. Upon this were piled a foot or so of softly tanned pelts from which the fur had not been removed. Upon the edge of this dais sat a young female Waz-don. In one hand she held a thin piece of metal, apparently of hammered gold, with serrated edges, and in the other a short, stiff brush. With these she was oc-cupied in going over her smooth, glossy coat which bore a remarkable resemblance to plucked sealskin. Her loin cloth of yellow and black striped *jato*-skin lay on the couch beside her with the circular breastplates of beaten gold, re-vealing the symmetrical lines of her nude figure in all its beauty and harmony of contour, for even though the creature was jet black and en-tirely covered with hair yet she was undeniably beautiful.

That she was beautiful in the eyes of Es-sat, the chief, was evidenced by the gloating expres-sion upon his fierce countenance and the increased rapidity of his breathing. Moving quickly forward he entered the room and as he did so the young she looked up. Instantly her eyes filled with terror and as quickly she seized the loin cloth and with a few deft movements ad-justed it about her. As she gathered up her breastplates Es-sat rounded the table and moved quickly toward her.

"What do you want?" she whispered, though she knew full well.

"Pan-at-lee," he said, "your chief has come for you."

"It was for this that you sent away my father and my brothers to spy upon the Kor-ul-lul? I will not have you. Leave the cave of my ances-tors!"

Es-sat smiled. It was the smile of a strong and wicked man who knows his power—not a pleas-ant smile at all. "I will leave, Pan-at-lee," he said; "but you shall go with me—to the cave of Es-sat, the chief, to be the envied of the shes of Kor-ul-ja. Come!"

"Never!" cried Pan-at-lee. "I hate you. Sooner would I mate with a Ho-don than with you, beater of women, murderer of babes."

A frightful scowl distorted the features of the chief. "She-*jato*!" he cried. "I will tame you! I will break you! Es-sat, the chief, takes what he will and who dares question his right, or combat his least purpose, will first serve that purpose and then be broken as I break this," and he picked a stone platter from the table and broke it in his powerful hands. "You might have been first and most favored in the cave of the ances-tors of Es-sat; but now shall you be last and least and when I am done with you you shall belong to all of the men of Es-sat's cave. Thus for those who spurn the love of their chief!"

He advanced quickly to seize her and as he laid a rough hand upon her she struck him heavily upon the side of his head with her golden breastplates. Without a sound Es-sat, the chief, sank to the floor of the apartment. For a moment Pan-at-lee bent over him, her improvised weapon raised to strike again should he show signs of returning consciousness, her glossy breasts rising and falling with her quickened breathing. Suddenly she stooped and removed Es-sat's knife with its scabbard and shoulder belt. Slipping it over her own shoulder she quickly adjusted her breastplates and keeping a watchful glance upon the figure of the fallen chief, backed from the room.

In a niche in the outer room, just beside the doorway leading to the balcony, were neatly piled a number of rounded pegs from eighteen to twenty inches in length. Selecting five of these she made them into a little bundle about which she twined the lower extremity of her sinuous tail and thus carrying them made her way to the outer edge of the balcony. Assuring herself that there was none about to see, or hinder her, she took quickly to the pegs already set in the face of the cliff and with the celerity of a monkey clambered swiftly aloft to the highest row of pegs which she followed in the direction of the lower end of the gorge for a matter of some hundred yards. Here, above her head, were a series of small round holes placed one above another in three parallel rows. Clinging only with her toes she removed two of the pegs from the bundle carried in her tail and taking one in either hand she inserted them in two opposite holes of the outer rows as far above her as she could reach. Hanging by these new holds she now took one of the three remaining pegs in each of her feet, leaving the fifth grasped securely in her tail. Reaching above her with this member she inserted the fifth peg in one of the holes of the center row and then, alternately hanging by her tail, her feet, or her hands, she moved the pegs upward to new holes, thus carrying her stairway with her as she ascended.

At the summit of the cliff a gnarled tree exposed its time-worn roots above the topmost holes forming the last step from the sheer face of the precipice to level footing. This was the last avenue of escape for members of the tribe hard pressed by enemies from below. There were three such emergency exits from the village and it were death to use them in other than an emergency. This Pan-at-lee well knew; but she knew, too, that it were worse than death to remain where the angered Es-sat might lay hands upon her.

When she had gained the summit, the girl moved quickly through the darkness in the direction of the next gorge which cut the mountain-side a mile beyond Kor-ul-ja. It was the Gorge-of-water, Kor-ul-lul, to which her father and two brothers had been sent by Es-sat ostensibly to spy upon the neighboring tribe. There was a chance, a slender chance, that she might find them; if not there was the deserted Kor-ul-gryf several miles beyond, where she might hide indefinitely from man if she could elude the frightful monster from which the gorge derived its name and whose presence there had rendered its caves uninhabitable for generations.

Pan-at-lee crept stealthily along the rim of the Kor-ul-lul. Just where her father and brothers would watch she did not know. Sometimes their spies remained upon the rim, sometimes they watched from the gorge's bottom. Pan-at-lee was at a loss to know what to do or where to go. She felt very small and helpless alone in the vast darkness of the night. Strange noises fell upon her ears. They came from the lonely reaches of the towering mountains above her, from far away in the invisible valley and from the nearer foothills and once, in the distance, she heard what she thought was the bellow of a bull *gryf*. It came from the direction of the Kor-ul-gryf. She shuddered.

Presently there came to her keen ears another sound. Something approached her along the rim of the gorge. It was coming from above. She halted, listening. Perhaps it was her father, or a brother. It was coming closer. She strained her eyes through the darkness. She did not move— she scarcely breathed. And then, of a sudden, quite close it seemed, there blazed through the black night two yellow-green spots of fire.

Pan-at-lee was brave, but as always with the primitive, the darkness held infinite terrors for her. Not alone the terrors of the known but more frightful ones as well—those of the unknown. She had passed through much this night and her nerves were keyed to the highest pitch—raw, taut nerves, they were, ready to react in an exaggerated form to the slightest shock.

But this was no slight shock. To hope for a father and a brother and to see death instead glaring out of the darkness! Yes, Pan-at-lee was brave, but she was not of iron. With a shriek that reverberated among the hills she turned and fled along the rim of Kor-ul-lul and behind her, swiftly, came the devil-eyed lion of the mountains of Pal-ul-don.

Pan-at-lee was lost. Death was inevitable. Of this there could be no doubt, but to die beneath the rending fangs of the carnivore, congenital terror of her kind—it was unthinkable. But there was an alternative. The lion was almost upon her—another instant and he would seize her. Pan-at-lee turned sharply to her left. Just a few steps she took in the new direction before she disappeared over the rim of Kor-ul-lul. The baffled lion, planting all four feet, barely stopped upon the verge of the abyss. Glaring down into the black shadows beneath he mounted an angry roar.

Through the darkness at the bottom of Kor-ul-ja, Om-at led the way toward the caves of his people. Behind him came Tarzan and Ta-den. Presently they halted beneath a great tree that grew close to the cliff.

"First," whispered Om-at, "I will go to the cave of Pan-at-lee. Then will I seek the cave of my ancestors to have speech with my own blood. It will not take long. Wait here—I shall return soon. Afterward shall we go together to Ta-den's people."

He moved silently toward the foot of the cliff up which Tarzan could presently see him as-cending like a great fly on a wall. In the dim light the ape-man could not see the pegs set in the face of the cliff. Om-at moved warily. In the lower tier of caves there should be a sentry. His knowledge of his people and their customs told him, however, that in all probability the sentry was asleep. In this he was not mistaken, yet he did not in any way abate his wariness. Smoothly and swiftly he ascended toward the cave of Pan-at-lee while from below Tarzan and Ta-den watched him.

"How does he do it?" asked Tarzan. "I can see no foothold upon that vertical surface and yet he appears to be climbing with the utmost ease."

Ta-den explained the stairway of pegs. "You could ascend easily," he said, "although a tail would be of great assistance."

They watched until Om-at was about to enter the cave of Pan-at-lee without seeing any indication that he had been observed and then, simul-taneously, both saw a head appear in the mouth of one of the lower caves. It was quickly evident that its owner had discovered Om-at for imme-diately he started upward in pursuit. Without a word Tarzan and Ta-den sprang forward toward the foot of the cliff. The pithecanthropus was the first to reach it and the ape-man saw him spring upward for a handhold on the lowest peg above him. Now Tarzan saw other pegs roughly paralleling each other in zigzag rows up the cliff face. He sprang and caught one of these, pulled himself upward by one hand until he could reach a second with his other hand; and when he had ascended far enough to use his feet, discovered that he could make rapid progress. Ta-den was outstripping him, however, for these precarious ladders were no novelty to him and, further, he had an advantage in possessing a tail.

Nevertheless, the ape-man gave a good ac-count of himself, being presently urged to re-doubled efforts by the fact that the Waz-don above Ta-den glanced down and discovered his pursuers just before the Ho-don overtook him. Instantly a wild cry shattered the silence of the gorge—a cry that was immediately answered by hundreds of savage throats as warrior after warrior emerged from the entrance to his cave.

The creature who had raised the alarm had now reached the recess before Pan-at-lee's cave and here he halted and turned to give battle to Ta-den. Unslinging his club which had hung down his back from a thong about his neck he stood upon the level floor of the entrance-way effectually blocking Ta-den's ascent. From all directions the warriors of Kor-ul-ja were swarming toward the interlopers. Tarzan, who had reached a point on the same level with Ta-den but a little to the latter's left, saw that nothing short of a miracle could save them. Just at the ape-man's left was the entrance to a cave that either was deserted or whose occupants had not as yet been aroused, for the level recess remained unoccupied. Resourceful was the alert mind of Tarzan of the Apes and quick to respond were the trained muscles. In the time that you or I might give to debating an action he would accomplish it and now, though only seconds separated his nearest antagonist from him, in the brief span of time at his disposal he had stepped into the recess, unslung his long rope and leaning far out shot the sinuous noose, with the precision of long habitude, toward the menacing figure wielding its heavy club above Ta-den. There was a momentary pause of the rope-hand as the noose sped toward its goal, a quick movement of the right wrist that closed it upon its victim as it settled over his head and then a surging tug as, seizing the rope in both hands, Tarzan threw back upon it all the weight of his great frame.

Voicing a terrified shriek, the Waz-don lunged headforemost from the recess above Ta-den. Tarzan braced himself for the coming shock when the creature's body should have fallen the full length of the rope and as it did there was a snap of the vertebrae that rose sickeningly in the momentary silence that had followed the doomed man's departing scream. Unshaken by the stress of the suddenly arrested weight at the end of the rope, Tarzan quickly pulled the body to his side that he might remove the noose from about its neck, for he could not afford to lose so priceless a weapon.

During the several seconds that had elapsed since he cast the rope the Waz-don warriors had remained inert as though paralyzed by wonder or by terror. Now, again, one of them found his voice and his head and straightway, shrieking invectives at the strange intruder, started upward for the ape-man, urging his fellows to attack. This man was the closest to Tarzan. But for him the ape-man could easily have reached Ta-den's side as the latter was urging him to do. Tarzan raised the body of the dead Waz-don above his head, held it poised there for a moment as with face raised to the heavens he screamed forth the horrid challenge of the bull apes of the tribe of Kerchak, and with all the strength of his giant sinews he hurled the corpse heavily upon the ascending warrior. So great was the force of the impact that not only was the Waz-don torn from his hold but two of the pegs to which he clung were broken short in their sockets.

As the two bodies, the living and the dead, hurtled downward toward the foot of the cliff a great cry arose from the Waz-don. "Jad-guru-don! Jad-guru-don!" they screamed, and then: "Kill him! Kill him!"

And now Tarzan stood in the recess beside Ta-den. "Jad-guru-don!" repeated the latter, smiling—"The terrible man! Tarzan the Terrible! They may kill you, but they will never forget you."

"They shall not ki—What have we here?" Tarzan's statement as to what "they" should not do was interrupted by a sudden ejaculation as two figures, locked in deathlike embrace, stumbled through the doorway of the cave to the outer porch. One was Om-at, the other a creature of his own kind but with a rough coat, the hairs of which seemed to grow straight outward from the skin, stiffly, unlike Om-at's sleek covering. The two were quite evidently well matched and equally evident was the fact that each was bent upon murder. They fought almost in silence except for an occasional low growl as one or the other acknowledged thus some new hurt.

Tarzan, following a natural impulse to aid his ally, leaped forward to enter the dispute only to be checked by a grunted admonition from Om-at. "Back!" he said. "This fight is mine, alone."

The ape-man understood and stepped aside.

"It is a *gund-bar*," explained Ta-den, "a chief-battle. This fellow must be Es-sat, the chief. If Om-at kills him without assistance Om-at may become chief."

Tarzan smiled. It was the law of his own jungle—the law of the tribe of Kerchak, the bull ape—the ancient law of primitive man that needed but the refining influences of civilization to introduce the hired dagger and the poison cup. Then his attention was drawn to the outer edge of the vestibule. Above it appeared the shaggy face of one of Es-sat's warriors. Tarzan sprang to intercept the man; but Ta-den was there ahead of him. "Back!" cried the Ho-don to the newcomer. "It is *gund-bar*." The fellow looked scrutinizingly at the two fighters, then turned his face downward toward his fellows. "Back!" he cried, "it is *gund-bar* between Es-sat and Om-at." Then he looked back at Ta-den and Tarzan. "Who are you?" he asked.

"We are Om-at's friends," replied Ta-den.

The fellow nodded. "We will attend to you later," he said and disappeared below the edge of the recess.

The battle upon the ledge continued with unabated ferocity, Tarzan and Ta-den having difficulty in keeping out of the way of the contestants who tore and beat at each other with hands and feet and lashing tails. Es-sat was unarmed—Pan-at-lee had seen to that—but at Om-at's side swung a sheathed knife which he made no effort to draw. That would have been contrary to their savage and primitive code for the chief-battle must be fought with nature's weapons.

Sometimes they separated for an instant only to rush upon each other again with all the ferocity and nearly the strength of mad bulls. Presently one of them tripped the other but in that viselike embrace one could not fall alone—Es-sat dragged Om-at with him, toppling upon the brink of the niche. Even Tarzan held his breath. There they surged to and fro perilously for a moment and then the inevitable happened—the two, locked in murderous embrace, rolled over the edge and disappeared from the ape-man's view.

Tarzan voiced a suppressed sigh for he had liked Om-at and then, with Ta-den, approached the edge and looked over. Far below, in the dim light of the coming dawn, two inert forms should be lying stark in death; but, to Tarzan's amazement, such was far from the sight that met his eyes. Instead, there were the two figures still vibrant with life and still battling only a few feet below him. Clinging always to the pegs with two holds—a hand and a foot, or a foot and a tail, they seemed as much at home upon the perpendicular wall as upon the level surface of the vestibule; but now their tactics were slightly altered, for each seemed particularly bent upon dislodging his antagonist from his holds and precipitating him to certain death below. It was soon evident that Om-at, younger and with greater powers of endurance than Es-sat, was gaining an advantage. Now was the chief almost wholly on the defensive. Holding him by the cross belt with one mighty hand Om-at was forcing his foeman straight out from the cliff, and with the other hand and one foot was rapidly breaking first one of Es-sat's holds and then another, alternating his efforts, or rather punctuating them, with vicious blows to the pit of his adversary's stomach. Rapidly was Es-sat weakening and with the knowledge of impending death there came, as there comes to every coward and bully under similar circumstances, a crumbling of the veneer of bravado which had long masqueraded as courage and with it crumbled his code of ethics. Now was Es-sat no longer chief of Kor-ul-ja—instead he was a whimpering craven battling for life. Clutching at Om-at, clutching at the nearest pegs, he sought any support that would save him from that awful fall, and as he strove to push aside the hand of death, whose cold fingers he already felt upon his heart, his tail sought Om-at's side and the handle of the knife that hung there.

Tarzan saw and even as Es-sat drew the blade from its sheath he dropped catlike to the pegs beside the battling men. Es-sat's tail had drawn back for the cowardly fatal thrust. Now many others saw the perfidious act and a great cry of rage and disgust arose from savage throats; but as the blade sped toward its goal, the ape-man seized the hairy member that wielded it, and at the same instant Om-at thrust the body of Es-sat from him with such force that its weakened holds were broken and it hurtled downward, a brief meteor of screaming fear, to death.

IV

TARZAN-JAD-GURU

As Tarzan and Om-at clambered back to the vestibule of Pan-at-lee's cave and took their stand beside Ta-den in readiness for whatever eventuality might follow the death of Es-sat, the sun that topped the eastern hills touched also the figure of a sleeper upon a distant, thorn-covered steppe awakening him to another day of tireless tracking along a faint and rapidly disappearing spoor.

For a time silence reigned in the Kor-ul-ja. The tribesmen waited, looking now down upon the dead thing that had been their chief, now at one another, and now at Om-at and the two who stood upon his either side. Presently Om-at spoke. "I am Om-at," he cried. "Who will say that Om-at is not *gund* of Kor-ul-ja?"

He waited for a taker of his challenge. One or two of the larger young bucks fidgeted restlessly and eyed him; but there was no reply.

"Then Om-at is *gund*," he said with finality. "Now tell me, where are Pan-at-lee, her father, and her brothers?"

An old warrior spoke. "Pan-at-lee should be in her cave. Who should know that better than you who are there now? Her father and her brothers were sent to watch Kor-ul-lul; but neither of these questions arouse any tumult in our

breasts. There is one that does: Can Om-at be chief of Kor-ul-ja and yet stand at bay against his own people with a Ho-don and that terrible man at his side—that terrible man who has no tail? Hand the strangers over to your people to be slain as is the way of the Waz-don and then may Om-at be *gund*."

Neither Tarzan nor Ta-den spoke then, they but stood watching Om-at and waiting for his decision, the ghost of a smile upon the lips of the ape-man. Ta-den, at least, knew that the old warrior had spoken the truth—the Waz-don entertain no strangers and take no prisoners of an alien race.

Then spoke Om-at. "Always there is change," he said. "Even the old hills of Pal-ul-don appear never twice alike—the brilliant sun, a passing cloud, the moon, a mist, the changing seasons, the sharp clearness following a storm; these things bring each a new change in our hills. From birth to death, day by day, there is constant change in each of us. Change, then, is one of Jad-ben-Otho's laws.

"And now I, Om-at, your *gund*, bring another change. Strangers who are brave men and good friends shall no longer be slain by the Waz-don of Kor-ul-ja!"

There were growls and murmurings and a restless moving among the warriors as each eyed the others to see who would take the initiative against Om-at, the iconoclast.

"Cease your mutterings," admonished the new *gund*. "I am your chief. My word is your law. You had no part in making me chief. Some of you helped Es-sat to drive me from the cave of my ancestors; the rest of you permitted it. I owe you nothing. Only these two, whom you would have me kill, were loyal to me. I am *gund* and if there be any who doubts it let him speak—he cannot die younger."

Tarzan was pleased. Here was a man after his own heart. He admired the fearlessness of Om-at's challenge and he was a sufficiently good judge of men to know that he had listened to no idle bluff—Om-at would back up his words to the death, if necessary, and the chances were that he would not be the one to die. Evidently the majority of the Kor-ul-jaians entertained the same conviction.

"I will make you a good *gund*," said Om-at, seeing that no one appeared inclined to dispute his rights. "Your wives and daughters will be safe—they were not safe while Es-sat ruled. Go now to your crops and your hunting. I leave to search for Pan-at-lee. Ab-on will be *gund* while I am away—look to him for guidance and to me for an accounting when I return—and may Jad-ben-Otho smile upon you."

He turned toward Tarzan and the Ho-don. "And you, my friends," he said, "are free to go among my people; the cave of my ancestors is yours, do what you will."

"I," said Tarzan, "will go with Om-at to search for Pan-at-lee."

"And I," said Ta-den.

Om-at smiled. "Good!" he exclaimed. "And when we have found her we shall go together upon Tarzan's business and Ta-den's. Where first shall we search?" He turned toward his warriors. "Who knows where she may be?"

None knew other than that Pan-at-lee had gone to her cave with the others the previous evening—there was no clew, no suggestion as to her whereabouts.

"Show me where she sleeps," said Tarzan; "let me see something that belongs to her—an article of her apparel—then, doubtless, I can help you."

Two young warriors climbed closer to the ledge upon which Om-at stood. They were In-sad and O-dan. It was the latter who spoke.

"*Gund* of Kor-ul-ja," he said, "we would go with you to search for Pan-at-lee."

It was the first acknowledgment of Om-at's chieftainship and immediately following it the tenseness that had prevailed seemed to relax— the warriors spoke aloud instead of in whispers, and the women appeared from the mouths of caves as with the passing of a sudden storm. In-sad and O-dan had taken the lead and now all seemed glad to follow. Some came to talk with Om-at and to look more closely at Tarzan; oth-

ers, heads of caves, gathered their hunters and discussed the business of the day. The women and children prepared to descend to the fields with the youths and the old men, whose duty it was to guard them.

"O-dan and In-sad shall go with us," announced Om-at, "we shall not need more. Tarzan, come with me and I shall show you where Pan-at-lee sleeps, though why you should wish to know I cannot guess—she is not there. I have looked for myself."

The two entered the cave where Om-at led the way to the apartment in which Es-sat had surprised Pan-at-lee the previous night.

"All here are hers," said Om-at, "except the war club lying on the floor—that was Es-sat's."

The ape-man moved silently about the apartment, the quivering of his sensitive nostrils scarcely apparent to his companion who only wondered what good purpose could be served here and chafed at the delay.

"Come!" said the ape-man, presently, and led the way toward the outer recess.

Here their three companions were awaiting them. Tarzan passed to the left side of the niche and examined the pegs that lay within reach. He looked at them but it was not his eyes that were examining them. Keener than his keen eyes was that marvelously trained sense of scent that had first been developed in him during infancy under the tutorage of his foster mother, Kala, the she-ape, and further sharpened in the grim jungles by that master teacher—the instinct of self-preservation.

From the left side of the niche he turned to the right. Om-at was becoming impatient.

"Let us be off," he said. "We must search for Pan-at-lee if we would ever find her."

"Where shall we search?" asked Tarzan.

Om-at scratched his head. "Where?" he repeated. "Why all Pal-ul-don, if necessary."

"A large job," said Tarzan. "Come," he added, "she went this way," and he took to the pegs that led aloft toward the summit of the cliff. Here he followed the scent easily since none had passed that way since Pan-at-lee had fled. At the point at which she had left the permanent pegs and resorted to those carried with her Tarzan came to an abrupt halt. "She went this way to the summit," he called back to Om-at who was directly behind him; "but there are no pegs here."

"I do not know how you know that she went this way," said Om-at; "but we will get pegs. In-sad, return and fetch climbing pegs for five."

The young warrior was soon back and the pegs distributed. Om-at handed five to Tarzan and explained their use. The ape-man returned one. "I need but four," he said.

Om-at smiled. "What a wonderful creature you would be if you were not deformed," he said, glancing with pride at his own strong tail.

"I admit that I am handicapped," replied Tarzan. "You others go ahead and leave the pegs in place for me. I am afraid that otherwise it will be slow work as I cannot hold the pegs in my toes as you do."

"All right," agreed Om-at; "Ta-den, In-sad, and I will go first, you follow, and O-dan bring up the rear and collect the pegs—we cannot leave them here for our enemies."

"Can't your enemies bring their own pegs?" asked Tarzan.

"Yes; but it delays them and makes easier our defense and—they do not know which of all the holes you see are deep enough for pegs—the others are made to confuse our enemies and are too shallow to hold a peg."

At the top of the cliff beside the gnarled tree Tarzan again took up the trail. Here the scent was fully as strong as upon the pegs and the ape-man moved rapidly across the ridge in the direction of the Kor-ul-lul.

Presently he paused and turned toward Om-at. "Here she moved swiftly, running at top speed, and, Om-at, she was pursued by a lion."

"You can read that in the grass?" asked O-dan as the others gathered about the ape-man.

Tarzan nodded. "I do not think the lion got her," he added; "but that we shall determine quickly. No, he did not get her—look!" and he pointed toward the southwest, down the ridge.

Following the direction indicated by his finger, the others presently detected a movement in some bushes a couple of hundred yards away.

"What is it?" asked Om-at. "It is she?" and he started toward the spot.

"Wait," advised Tarzan. "It is the lion which pursued her."

"You can see him?" asked Ta-den.

"No, I can smell him."

The others looked their astonishment and incredulity; but of the fact that it was indeed a lion they were not left long in doubt. Presently the bushes parted and the creature stepped out in full view, facing them. It was a magnificent beast, large and beautifully maned, with the brilliant leopard spots of its kind well marked and symmetrical. For a moment it eyed them and then, still chafing at the loss of its prey earlier in the morning, it charged.

The Pal-ul-donians unslung their clubs and stood waiting the onrushing beast. Tarzan of the Apes drew his hunting knife and crouched in the path of the fanged fury. It was almost upon him when it swerved to the right and leaped for Om-at only to be sent to earth with a staggering blow upon the head. Almost instantly it was up and though the men rushed fearlessly in, it managed to sweep aside their weapons with its mighty paws. A single blow wrenched O-dan's club from his hand and sent it hurtling against Ta-den, knocking him from his feet. Taking advantage of its opportunity the lion rose to throw itself upon O-dan and at the same instant Tarzan flung himself upon its back. Strong, white teeth buried themselves in the spotted neck, mighty arms encircled the savage throat and the sinewy legs of the ape-man locked themselves about the gaunt belly.

The others, powerless to aid, stood breathlessly about as the great lion lunged hither and thither, clawing and biting fearfully and futilely at the savage creature that had fastened itself upon him. Over and over they rolled and now the onlookers saw a brown hand raised above the lion's side—a brown hand grasping a keen blade. They saw it fall and rise and fall again—each time with terrific force and in its wake they saw a crimson stream trickling down *ja*'s gorgeous coat.

Now from the lion's throat rose hideous screams of hate and rage and pain as he redoubled his efforts to dislodge and punish his tormentor; but always the tousled black head remained half buried in the dark brown mane and the mighty arm rose and fell to plunge the knife again and again into the dying beast.

The Pal-ul-donians stood in mute wonder and admiration. Brave men and mighty hunters they were and as such the first to accord honor to a mightier.

"And you would have had me slay him!" cried Om-at, glancing at In-sad and O-dan.

"Jad-ben-Otho reward you that you did not," breathed In-sad.

And now the lion lunged suddenly to earth and with a few spasmodic quiverings lay still. The ape-man rose and shook himself, even as might *ja*, the leopard-coated lion of Pal-ul-don, had he been the one to survive.

O-dan advanced quickly toward Tarzan. Placing a palm upon his own breast and the other on Tarzan's, "Tarzan the Terrible," he said, "I ask no greater honor than your friendship."

"And I no more than the friendship of Om-at's friends," replied the ape-man simply, returning the other's salute.

"Do you think," asked Om-at, coming close to Tarzan and laying a hand upon the other's shoulder, "that he got her?"

"No, my friend; it was a hungry lion that charged us."

"You seem to know much of lions," said In-sad.

"Had I a brother I could not know him better," replied Tarzan.

"Then where can she be?" continued Om-at.

"We can but follow while the spoor is fresh," answered the ape-man and again taking up his interrupted tracking he led them down the ridge and at a sharp turning of the trail to the left brought them to the verge of the cliff that dropped into the Kor-ul-lul. For a moment Tarzan examined the ground to the right and to the left, then he stood erect and looking at Om-at pointed into the gorge.

For a moment the Waz-don gazed down into the green rift at the bottom of which a tumultuous river tumbled downward along its rocky bed, then he closed his eyes as to a sudden spasm of pain and turned away.

"You—mean—she jumped?" he asked.

"To escape the lion," replied Tarzan. "He was right behind her—look, you can see where his four paws left their impress in the turf as he checked his charge upon the very verge of the abyss."

"Is there any chance—" commenced Om-at, to be suddenly silenced by a warning gesture from Tarzan.

"Down!" whispered the ape-man, "many men are coming. They are running—from down the ridge." He flattened himself upon his belly in the grass, the others following his example.

For some minutes they waited thus and then the others, too, heard the sound of running feet and now a hoarse shout followed by many more.

"It is the war cry of the Kor-ul-lul," whispered Om-at—"the hunting cry of men who hunt men. Presently shall we see them and if Jad-ben-Otho is pleased with us they shall not too greatly outnumber us."

"They are many," said Tarzan, "forty or fifty, I should say; but how many are the pursued and how many the pursuers we cannot even guess, except that the latter must greatly outnumber the former, else these would not run so fast."

"Here they come," said Ta-den.

"It is An-un, father of Pan-at-lee, and his two sons," exclaimed O-dan. "They will pass without seeing us if we do not hurry," he added looking at Om-at, the chief, for a sign.

"Come!" cried the latter, springing to his feet and running rapidly to intercept the three fugitives. The others followed him.

"Five friends!" shouted Om-at as An-un and his sons discovered them.

"*Adenen yo!*" echoed O-dan and In-sad.

The fugitives scarcely paused as these unexpected reinforcements joined them but they eyed Ta-den and Tarzan with puzzled glances.

"The Kor-ul-lul are many," shouted An-un. "Would that we might pause and fight; but first we must warn Es-sat and our people."

"Yes," said Om-at, "we must warn our people."

"Es-sat is dead," said In-sad.

"Who is chief?" asked one of An-un's sons.

"Om-at," replied O-dan.

"It is well," cried An-un. "Pan-at-lee said that you would come back and slay Es-sat."

Now the enemy broke into sight behind them.

"Come!" cried Tarzan, "let us turn and charge them, raising a great cry. They pursued but three and when they see eight charging upon them they will think that many men have come to do battle. They will believe that there are more even than they see and then one who is swift will have time to reach the gorge and warn your people."

"It is well," said Om-at. "Id-an, you are swift—carry word to the warriors of Kor-ul-ja that we fight the Kor-ul-lul upon the ridge and that Ab-on shall send a hundred men."

Id-an, the son of An-un, sped swiftly toward the cliff-dwellings of the Kor-ul-ja while the others charged the oncoming Kor-ul-lul, the war cries of the two tribes rising and falling in a certain grim harmony. The leaders of the Kor-ul-lul paused at sight of the reinforcements, waiting apparently for those behind to catch up with them and, possibly, also to learn how great a force confronted them. The leaders, swifter runners than their fellows, perhaps, were far in advance while the balance of their number had not yet emerged from the brush; and now as Om-at and his companions fell upon them with a ferocity born of necessity they fell back, so that when their companions at last came in sight of them they appeared to be in full rout. The natural result was that the others turned and fled.

Encouraged by this first success Om-at followed them into the brush, his little company charging valiantly upon his either side, and loud and terrifying were the savage yells with which they pursued the fleeing enemy. The brush, while not growing so closely together as to impede progress, was of such height as to hide the members of the party from one another when they became separated by even a few yards. The result was that Tarzan, always swift and always keen for battle, was soon pursuing the enemy far in the lead of the others—a lack of prudence which was to prove his undoing.

The warriors of Kor-ul-lul, doubtless as valorous as their foemen, retreated only to a more strategic position in the brush, nor were they long in guessing that the number of their pursuers was fewer than their own. They made a stand then where the brush was densest—an ambush it was, and into this ran Tarzan of the Apes. They tricked him neatly. Yes, sad as is the narration of it, they tricked the wily jungle lord. But then they were fighting on their own ground, every foot of which they knew as you know your front parlor, and they were following their own tactics, of which Tarzan knew nothing.

A single black warrior appeared to Tarzan a laggard in the rear of the retreating enemy and thus retreating he lured Tarzan on. At last he turned at bay confronting the ape-man with bludgeon and drawn knife and as Tarzan charged him a score of burly Waz-don leaped from the surrounding brush. Instantly, but too late, the giant Tarmangani realized his peril. There flashed before him a vision of his lost mate and a great and sickening regret surged through him with the realization that if she still lived she might no longer hope, for though she might never know of the passing of her lord the fact of it must inevitably seal her doom.

And consequent to this thought there enveloped him a blind frenzy of hatred for these creatures who dared thwart his purpose and menace the welfare of his wife. With a savage growl he threw himself upon the warrior before him twisting the heavy club from the creature's hand as if he had been a little child, and with his left fist backed by the weight and sinew of his giant frame, he crashed a shattering blow to the center of the Waz-don's face—a blow that crushed the bones and dropped the fellow in his tracks. Then he swung upon the others with their fallen comrade's bludgeon striking to right and left mighty, unmerciful blows that drove down their own weapons until that wielded by the ape-man was splintered and shattered. On either hand they fell before his cudgel; so rapid the delivery of his blows, so catlike his recovery that in the first few moments of the battle he seemed invulnerable to their attack; but it could not last—he was outnumbered twenty to one and his undoing came from a thrown club. It struck him upon the back of the head. For a moment he stood swaying and then like a great pine beneath the woodsman's ax he crashed to earth.

Others of the Kor-ul-lul had rushed to engage the balance of Om-at's party. They could be heard fighting at a short distance and it was evident that the Kor-ul-ja were falling slowly back and as they fell Om-at called to the missing one: "Tarzan the Terrible! Tarzan the Terrible!"

"*Jad-guru,* indeed," repeated one of the Kor-ul-lul rising from where Tarzan had dropped him. "Tarzan-jad-guru! He was worse than that."

V

IN THE KOR-UL-GRYF

As Tarzan fell among his enemies a man halted many miles away upon the outer verge of the morass that encircles Pal-ul-don. Naked he was except for a loin cloth and three belts of cartridges, two of which passed over his shoulders, crossing upon his chest and back, while the third encircled his waist. Slung to his back by its leathern sling-strap was an Enfield, and he carried too a long knife, a bow and a quiver of arrows. He had come far, through wild and savage lands, menaced by fierce beasts and fiercer men, yet intact to the last cartridge was the ammunition that had filled his belts the day that he set out.

The bow and the arrows and the long knife had brought him thus far safely, yet often in the face of great risks that could have been minimized by a single shot from the well-kept rifle at his back. What purpose might he have for conserving this precious ammunition? in risking his life to bring the last bright shining missile to his unknown goal? For what, for whom were these death-dealing bits of metal preserved? In all the world only he knew.

When Pan-at-lee stepped over the edge of the cliff above Kor-ul-lul she expected to be dashed to instant death upon the rocks below; but she had chosen this in preference to the rending fangs of *ja.* Instead, chance had ordained that she make the frightful plunge at a point where the tumbling river swung close beneath the overhanging cliff to eddy for a slow moment in a deep pool before plunging madly downward again in a cataract of boiling foam, and water thundering against rocks.

Into this icy pool the girl shot, and down and down beneath the watery surface until, half choked, yet fighting bravely, she battled her way once more to air. Swimming strongly she made the opposite shore and there dragged herself out upon the bank to lie panting and spent until the approaching dawn warned her to seek concealment, for she was in the country of her people's enemies.

Rising, she moved into the concealment of the rank vegetation that grows so riotously in the well-watered *kors*[1] of Pal-ul-don.

Hidden amidst the plant life from the sight of any who might chance to pass along the well-beaten trail that skirted the river Pan-at-lee

[1] I have used the Pal-ul-don word for "gorge" with the English plural, which is not the correct native plural form. The latter, it seems to me, is awkward for us and so I have generally ignored it throughout my manuscript, permitting, for example, Kor-ul-ja to answer for both singular and plural. However, for the benefit of those who may be interested in such things I may say that the plurals are formed simply for all words in the Pal-ul-don language by doubling the initial letter of the word, as *k'kor,* "gorges," pronounced as though written "kakor," the *a* having the sound of *a* in *sofa.* "Lions," then, would be *j'ja,* or men *d'don.*

sought rest and food, the latter growing in abundance all about her in the form of fruits and berries and succulent tubers which she scooped from the earth with the knife of the dead Es-sat.

Ah! if she had but known that he was dead! What trials and risks and terrors she might have been saved; but she thought that he still lived and so she dared not return to Kor-ul-ja. At least not yet while his rage was at white heat. Later, perhaps, her father and brothers returned to their cave, she might risk it; but not now—not now. Nor could she for long remain here in the neighborhood of the hostile Kor-ul-lul and somewhere she must find safety from beasts before the night set in.

As she sat upon the bole of a fallen tree seeking some solution of the problem of existence that confronted her, there broke upon her ears from up the gorge the voices of shouting men— a sound that she recognized all too well. It was the war cry of the Kor-ul-lul. Closer and closer it approached her hiding place. Then, through the veil of foliage she caught glimpses of three figures fleeing along the trail, and behind them the shouting of the pursuers rose louder and louder as they neared her. Again she caught sight of the fugitives crossing the river below the cataract and again they were lost to sight. And now the pursuers came into view—shouting Kor-ul-lul warriors, fierce and implacable. Forty, perhaps fifty of them. She waited breathless; but they did not swerve from the trail and passed her, unguessing that an enemy she lay hid within a few yards of them.

Once again she caught sight of the pursued— three Waz-don warriors clambering the cliff face at a point where portions of the summit had fallen away presenting a steep slope that might be ascended by such as these. Suddenly her attention was riveted upon the three. Could it be? O Jad-ben-Otho! had she but known a moment before. When they passed she might have joined them, for they were her father and two brothers. Now it was too late. With bated breath and tense muscles she watched the race. Would they reach the summit? Would the Kor-ul-lul overhaul

them? They climbed well, but, oh, so slowly. Now one lost his footing in the loose shale and slipped back! The Kor-ul-lul were ascending— one hurled his club at the nearest fugitive. The Great God was pleased with the brother of Pan-at-lee, for he caused the club to fall short of its target, and to fall, rolling and bounding, back upon its owner carrying him from his feet and precipitating him to the bottom of the gorge.

Standing now, her hands pressed tight above her golden breastplates, Pan-at-lee watched the race for life. Now one, her older brother, reached the summit and clinging there to something that she could not see he lowered his body and his long tail to the father beneath him. The latter, seizing this support, extended his own tail to the son below—the one who had slipped back—and thus, upon a living ladder of their own making, the three reached the summit and disappeared from view before the Kor-ul-lul overtook them. But the latter did not abandon the chase. On they went until they too had disappeared from sight and only a faint shouting came down to Pan-at-lee to tell her that the pursuit continued.

The girl knew that she must move on. At any moment now might come a hunting party, combing the gorge for the smaller animals that fed or bedded there.

Behind her were Es-sat and the returning party of Kor-ul-lul that had pursued her kin; before her, across the next ridge, was the Kor-ul-gryf, the lair of the terrifying monsters that brought the chill of fear to every inhabitant of Pal-ul-don; below her, in the valley, was the country of the Ho-don, where she could look for only slavery, or death; here were the Kor-ul-lul, the ancient enemies of her people; and everywhere were the wild beasts that eat the flesh of man.

For but a moment she debated and then turning her face toward the southeast she set out across the gorge of water toward the Kor-ul-gryf—at least there were no men there. As it is now, so it was in the beginning, back to the primitive progenitor of man which is typified by Pan-at-lee and her kind today: of all the hunters that woman fears, man is the most relentless, the most terrible. To the dangers of man she preferred the dangers of the *gryf*.

Moving cautiously she reached the foot of the cliff at the far side of Kor-ul-lul and here, toward noon, she found a comparatively easy ascent. Crossing the ridge she stood at last upon the brink of Kor-ul-gryf—the horror place of the folklore of her race. Dank and mysterious grew the vegetation below; giant trees waved their plumed tops almost level with the summit of the cliff; and over all brooded an ominous silence.

Pan-at-lee lay upon her belly and stretching over the edge scanned the cliff face below her. She could see caves there and the stone pegs which the ancients had fashioned so laboriously by hand. She had heard of these in the firelight tales of her childhood and of how the *gryfs* had come from the morasses across the mountains and of how at last the people had fled after many had been seized and devoured by the hideous creatures, leaving their caves untenanted for no man living knew how long. Some said that Jad-ben-Otho, who has lived forever, was still a little boy. Pan-at-lee shuddered; but there were caves and in them she would be safe even from the *gryfs*.

She found a place where the stone pegs reached to the very summit of the cliff, left there no doubt in the final exodus of the tribe when there was no longer need of safeguarding the deserted caves against invasion. Pan-at-lee clambered slowly down toward the uppermost cave. She found the recess in front of the doorway almost identical with those of her own tribe. The floor of it, though, was littered with twigs and old nests and the droppings of birds, until it was half choked. She moved along to another recess and still another, but all were alike in the accumulated filth. Evidently there was no need in looking further. This one seemed large and commodious. With her knife she fell to work cleaning away the debris by the simple expedient of pushing it over the edge, and always her eyes turned constantly toward the silent gorge where lurked the fearsome creatures of Pal-ul-don.

And other eyes there were, eyes she did not see, but that saw her and watched her every move—fierce eyes, greedy eyes, cunning and cruel. They watched her, and a red tongue licked flabby, pendulous lips. They watched her, and a half-human brain laboriously evolved a brutish design.

As in her own Kor-ul-ja, the natural springs in the cliff had been developed by the long-dead builders of the caves so that fresh, pure water trickled now, as it had for ages, within easy access to the cave entrances. Her only difficulty would be in procuring food and for that she must take the risk at least once in two days, for she was sure that she could find fruits and tubers and perhaps small animals, birds, and eggs near the foot of the cliff, the last two, possibly, in the caves themselves. Thus might she live on here indefinitely. She felt now a certain sense of security imparted doubtless by the impregnability of her high-flung sanctuary that she knew to be safe from all the more dangerous beasts, and this one from men, too, since it lay in the abjured Kor-ul-gryf.

Now she determined to inspect the interior of her new home. The sun, still in the south, lighted the interior of the first apartment. It was similar to those of her experience—the same beasts and men were depicted in the same crude fashion in the carvings on the walls—evidently there had been little progress in the race of Waz-don during the generations that had come and departed since Kor-ul-gryf had been abandoned by men. Of course Pan-at-lee thought no such thoughts, for evolution and progress existed not for her, or her kind. Things were as they had always been and would always be as they were.

That these strange creatures have existed thus for incalculable ages it can scarce be doubted, so marked are the indications of antiquity about their dwellings—deep furrows worn by naked feet in living rock; the hollow in the jamb of a stone doorway where many arms have touched in passing; the endless carvings that cover, ofttimes, the entire face of a great cliff and all the walls and ceilings of every cave and each carving wrought by a different hand, for each is the coat of arms, one might say, of the adult male who traced it.

And so Pan-at-lee found this ancient cave homelike and familiar. There was less litter within than she had found without and what there was was mostly an accumulation of dust. Beside the doorway was the niche in which wood and tinder were kept, but there remained nothing now other than mere dust. She had, however, saved a little pile of twigs from the debris on the porch. In a short time she had made a light by firing a bundle of twigs and lighting others from this fire she explored some of the inner rooms. Nor here did she find aught that was new or strange nor any relic of the departed owners other than a few broken stone dishes. She had been looking for something soft to sleep upon, but was doomed to disappointment as the former owners had evidently made a leisurely departure, carrying all their belongings with them. Below, in the gorge were leaves and grasses and fragrant branches, but Pan-at-lee felt no stomach for descending into that horrid abyss for the gratification of mere creature comfort—only the necessity for food would drive her there.

And so, as the shadows lengthened and night approached she prepared to make as comfortable a bed as she could by gathering the dust of ages into a little pile and spreading it between her soft body and the hard floor—at best it was only better than nothing. But Pan-at-lee was very tired. She had not slept since two nights before and in the interval she had experienced many dangers and hardships. What wonder then that despite the hard bed, she was asleep almost immediately she had composed herself for rest.

She slept and the moon rose, casting its silver light upon the cliff's white face and lessening the gloom of the dark forest and the dismal gorge. In the distance a lion roared. There was a long silence. From the upper reaches of the gorge came a deep bellow. There was a movement in the trees at the cliff's foot. Again the bellow, low and ominous. It was answered from below the deserted village. Something dropped from the foliage of a tree directly below the cave in which Pan-at-lee slept—it dropped to the ground among the dense shadows. Now it moved, cautiously. It moved toward the foot of the cliff, taking form and shape in the moonlight. It moved like the creature of a bad dream—slowly, sluggishly. It might have been a huge sloth—it might have been a man, with so grotesque a brush does the moon paint—master cubist.

Slowly it moved up the face of the cliff—like a great grubworm it moved, but now the moonbrush touched it again and it had hands and feet and with them it clung to the stone pegs and raised itself laboriously aloft toward the cave where Pan-at-lee slept. From the lower reaches of the gorge came again the sound of bellowing, and it was answered from above the village.

Tarzan of the Apes opened his eyes. He was conscious of a pain in his head, and at first that was about all. A moment later grotesque shadows, rising and falling, focused his arousing perceptions. Presently he saw that he was in a cave. A dozen Waz-don warriors squatted about, talking. A rude stone cresset containing burning oil lighted the interior and as the flame rose and fell the exaggerated shadows of the warriors danced upon the walls behind them.

"We brought him to you alive, *gund*," he heard one of them saying, "because never before was Ho-don like him seen. He has no tail—he was born without one, for there is no scar to mark where a tail had been cut off. The thumbs upon his hands and feet are unlike those of the races of Pal-ul-don. He is more powerful than many men put together and he attacks with the fearlessness of *ja*. We brought him alive, that you might see him before he is slain."

The chief rose and approached the ape-man, who closed his eyes and feigned unconsciousness. He felt hairy hands upon him as he was turned over, none too gently. The *gund* examined him from head to foot, making comments, especially upon the shape and size of his thumbs and great toes.

"With these and with no tail," he said, "it cannot climb."

"No," agreed one of the warriors, "it would surely fall even from the cliff pegs."

"I have never seen a thing like it," said the chief. "It is neither Waz-don nor Ho-don. I wonder from whence it came and what it is called."

"The Kor-ul-ja shouted aloud, 'Tarzan-jad-guru!' and we thought that they might be calling this one," said a warrior. "Shall we kill it now?"

"No," replied the chief, "we will wait until its life returns into its head that I may question it. Remain here, In-tan, and watch it. When it can again hear and speak call me."

He turned and departed from the cave, the others, except In-tan, following him. As they moved past him and out of the chamber Tarzan caught snatches of their conversation which indicated that the Kor-ul-ja reinforcements had fallen upon their little party in great numbers and driven them away. Evidently the swift feet of Id-an had saved the day for the warriors of Om-at. The ape-man smiled, then he partially opened an eye and cast it upon In-tan. The warrior stood at the entrance to the cave looking out—his back was toward his prisoner. Tarzan tested the bonds that secured his wrists. They seemed none too stout and they had tied his hands in front of him! Evidence indeed that the Waz-don took few prisoners—if any.

Cautiously he raised his wrists until he could examine the thongs that confined them. A grim smile lighted his features. Instantly he was at work upon the bonds with his strong teeth, but ever a wary eye was upon In-tan, the warrior of Kor-ul-lul. The last knot had been loosened and Tarzan's hands were free when In-tan turned to cast an appraising eye upon his ward. He saw that the prisoner's position was changed—he no longer lay upon his back as they had left him, but upon his side, and his hands were drawn up against his face. In-tan came closer and bent down. The bonds seemed very loose upon the prisoner's wrists. He extended his hand to examine them with his fingers and instantly the two hands leaped from their bonds—one to seize his

own wrist, the other his throat. So unexpected the catlike attack that In-tan had not even time to cry out before steel fingers silenced him. The creature pulled him suddenly forward so that he lost his balance and rolled over upon the prisoner and to the floor beyond to stop with Tarzan upon his breast. In-tan struggled to release himself—struggled to draw his knife; but Tarzan found it before him. The Waz-don's tail leaped to the other's throat, encircling it—he too could choke; but his own knife, in the hands of his antagonist, severed the beloved member close to its root.

The Waz-don's struggles became weaker—a film was obscuring his vision. He knew that he was dying and he was right. A moment later he was dead. Tarzan rose to his feet and placed one foot upon the breast of his dead foe. How the urge seized him to roar forth the victory cry of his kind! But he dared not. He discovered that they had not removed his rope from his shoulders and that they had replaced his knife in its sheath. It had been in his hand when he was felled. Strange creatures! He did not know that they held a superstitious fear of the weapons of a dead enemy, believing that if buried without them he would forever haunt his slayers in search of them and that when he found them he would kill the man who killed him. Against the wall leaned his bow and quiver of arrows.

Tarzan stepped toward the doorway of the cave and looked out. Night had just fallen. He could hear voices from the nearer caves and there floated to his nostrils the odor of cooking food. He looked down and experienced a sensation of relief. The cave in which he had been held was in the lowest tier—scarce thirty feet from the base of the cliff. He was about to chance an immediate descent when there occurred to him a thought that brought a grin to his savage lips—a thought that was born of the name the Waz-don had given him—Tarzan-jad-guru—Tarzan the Terrible—and a recollection of the days when he had delighted in baiting the blacks of the distant jungle of his birth. He turned back into the cave where lay the dead body of In-tan. With his knife he severed the warrior's head and carrying it to the outer edge of the recess tossed it to the ground below, then he dropped swiftly and silently down the ladder of pegs in a way that would have surprised the Kor-ul-lul who had been so sure that he could not climb.

At the bottom he picked up the head of In-tan and disappeared among the shadows of the trees carrying the grisly trophy by its shock of shaggy hair. Horrible? But you are judging a wild beast by the standards of civilization. You may teach a lion tricks, but he is still a lion. Tarzan looked well in a Tuxedo, but he was still a Tarmangani and beneath his pleated shirt beat a wild and savage heart.

Nor was his madness lacking in method. He knew that the hearts of the Kor-ul-lul would be filled with rage when they discovered the thing that he had done and he knew, too, that mixed with the rage would be a leaven of fear and it was fear of him that had made Tarzan master of many jungles—one does not win the respect of the killers with bonbons.

Below the village Tarzan returned to the foot of the cliff searching for a point where he could make the ascent to the ridge and thus back to the village of Om-at, the Kor-ul-ja. He came at last to a place where the river ran so close to the rocky wall that he was forced to swim it in search of a trail upon the opposite side and here it was that his keen nostrils detected a familiar spoor. It was the scent of Pan-at-lee at the spot where she had emerged from the pool and taken to the safety of the jungle.

Immediately the ape-man's plans were changed. Pan-at-lee lived, or at least she had lived after the leap from the cliff's summit. He had started in search of her for Om-at, his friend, and for Om-at he would continue upon the trail he had picked up thus fortuitously by accident. It led him into the jungle and across the gorge and then to the point at which Pan-at-lee had commenced the ascent of the opposite cliffs. Here Tarzan abandoned the head of In-tan, tying it to the lower branch of a tree, for he knew that it would handicap him in his ascent of the steep escarpment. Apelike he ascended, follow-

ing easily the scent spoor of Pan-at-lee. Over the summit and across the ridge the trail lay, plain as a printed page to the delicate senses of the jungle-bred tracker.

Tarzan knew naught of the Kor-ul-gryf. He had seen, dimly in the shadows of the night, strange, monstrous forms and Ta-den and Om-at had spoken of great creatures that all men feared; but always, everywhere, by night and by day, there were dangers. From infancy death had stalked, grim and terrible, at his heels. He knew little of any other existence. To cope with danger was his life and he lived his life as simply and as naturally as you live yours amidst the dangers of the crowded city streets. The black man who goes abroad in the jungle by night is afraid, for he has spent his life since infancy surrounded by numbers of his own kind and safeguarded, especially at night, by such crude means as lie within his powers. But Tarzan had lived as the lion lives and the panther and the elephant and the ape—a true jungle creature dependent solely upon his prowess and his wits, playing a lone hand against creation. Therefore he was surprised at nothing and feared nothing and so he walked through the strange night as undisturbed and unapprehensive as the farmer to the cow lot in the darkness before the dawn.

Once more Pan-at-lee's trail ended at the verge of a cliff; but this time there was no indication that she had leaped over the edge and a moment's search revealed to Tarzan the stone pegs upon which she had made her descent. As he lay upon his belly leaning over the top of the cliff examining the pegs his attention was suddenly attracted by something at the foot of the cliff. He could not distinguish its identity, but he saw that it moved and presently that it was ascending slowly, apparently by means of pegs similar to those directly below him. He watched it intently as it rose higher and higher until he was able to distinguish its form more clearly, with the result that he became convinced that it more nearly resembled some form of great ape than a lower order. It had a tail, though, and in other respects it did not seem a true ape.

Slowly it ascended to the upper tier of caves, into one of which it disappeared. Then Tarzan took up again the trail of Pan-at-lee. He followed it down the stone pegs to the nearest cave and then further along the upper tier. The ape-man raised his eyebrows when he saw the direction in which it led, and quickened his pace. He had almost reached the third cave when the echoes of Kor-ul-gryf were awakened by a shrill scream of terror.

VI

THE TOR-O-DON

Pan-at-lee slept—the troubled sleep, of physical and nervous exhaustion, filled with weird dreamings. She dreamed that she slept beneath a great tree in the bottom of the Kor-ul-gryf and that one of the fearsome beasts was creeping upon her but she could not open her eyes nor move. She tried to scream but no sound issued from her lips. She felt the thing touch her throat, her breast, her arm, and there it closed and seemed to be dragging her toward it. With a superhuman effort of will she opened her eyes. In the instant she knew that she was dreaming and that quickly the hallucination of the dream would fade—it had happened to her many times before. But it persisted. In the dim light that filtered into the dark chamber she saw a form beside her, she felt hairy fingers upon her and a hairy breast against which she was being drawn. Jad-ben-Otho! this was no dream. And then she screamed and tried to fight the thing from her; but her scream was answered by a low growl and another hairy hand seized her by the hair of the head. The beast rose now upon its hind legs and dragged her from the cave to the moonlit recess without and at the same instant she saw the figure of what she took to be a Ho-don rise above the outer edge of the niche.

The beast that held her saw it too and growled ominously but it did not relinquish its hold upon her hair. It crouched as though waiting an attack, and it increased the volume and frequency of its growls until the horrid sounds reverberated through the gorge, drowning even the deep bellowings of the beasts below, whose mighty thunderings had broken out anew with the sudden commotion from the high-flung cave. The beast that held her crouched and the creature that faced it crouched also, and growled—as hideously as the other. Pan-at-lee trembled. This was no Ho-don and though she feared the Ho-don she feared this thing more, with its catlike crouch and its beastly growls. She was lost—that Pan-at-lee knew. The two things might fight for her, but whichever won she was lost. Perhaps, during the battle, if it came to that, she might find the opportunity to throw herself over into the Kor-ul-gryf.

The thing that held her she had recognized now as a Tor-o-don, but the other thing she could not place, though in the moonlight she could see it very distinctly. It had no tail. She could see its hands and its feet, and they were not the hands and feet of the races of Pal-ul-don. It was slowly closing upon the Tor-o-don and in one hand it held a gleaming knife. Now it spoke and to Pan-at-lee's terror was added an equal weight of consternation.

"When it leaves go of you," it said, "as it will presently to defend itself, run quickly behind me, Pan-at-lee, and go to the cave nearest the pegs you descended from the cliff top. Watch from there. If I am defeated you will have time to escape this slow thing; if I am not I will come to you there. I am Om-at's friend and yours."

The last words took the keen edge from Pan-at-lee's terror; but she did not understand. How did this strange creature know her name? How did it know that she had descended the pegs by a certain cave? It must, then, have been here when she came. Pan-at-lee was puzzled.

"Who are you?" she asked, "and from whence do you come?"

"I am Tarzan," he replied, "and just now I came from Om-at, *gund* of Kor-ul-ja, in search of you."

Om-at, *gund* of Kor-ul-ja! What wild talk was this? She would have questioned him further, but now he was approaching the Tor-o-don and the latter was screaming and growling so loudly as to drown the sound of her voice. And then it did what the strange creature had said that it would do—it released its hold upon her hair as it prepared to charge. Charge it did and in those close quarters there was no room to fence for openings. Instantly the two beasts locked in deadly embrace, each seeking the other's throat. Pan-at-lee watched, taking no advantage of the opportunity to escape which their preoccupation gave her. She watched and waited, for into her savage little brain had come the resolve to pin her faith to this strange creature who had un-locked her heart with those four words—"I am Om-at's friend!" And so she waited, with drawn knife, the opportunity to do her bit in the van-quishing of the Tor-o-don. That the newcomer could do it unaided she well knew to be beyond the realms of possibility, for she knew well the prowess of the beastlike man with whom it fought. There were not many of them in Pal-ul-don, but what few there were were a terror to the women of the Waz-don and the Ho-don, for the old Tor-o-don bulls roamed the mountains and the valleys of Pal-ul-don between rutting sea-sons and woe betide the women who fell in their paths.

With his tail the Tor-o-don sought one of Tarzan's ankles, and finding it, tripped him. The two fell heavily, but so agile was the ape-man and so quick his powerful muscles that even in falling he twisted the beast beneath him, so that Tarzan fell on top and now the tail that had tripped him sought his throat as had the tail of In-tan, the Kor-ul-lul. In the effort of turning his antagonist's body during the fall Tarzan had had to relinquish his knife that he might seize the shaggy body with both hands and now the weapon lay out of reach at the very edge of the recess. Both hands were occupied for the mo-ment in fending off the clutching fingers that sought to seize him and drag his throat within reach of his foe's formidable fangs and now the tail was seeking its deadly hold with a formidable persistence that would not be denied.

Pan-at-lee hovered about, breathless, her dagger ready, but there was no opening that did not also endanger Tarzan, so constantly were the two duelists changing their positions. Tarzan felt the tail slowly but surely insinuating itself about his neck though he had drawn his head down between the muscles of his shoulders in an effort to protect this vulnerable part. The battle seemed to be going against him for the giant beast against which he strove would have been a fair match in weight and strength for Bolgani, the gorilla. And knowing this he suddenly ex-erted a single superhuman effort, thrust far apart the giant hands and with the swiftness of a striking snake buried his fangs in the jugular of the Tor-o-don. At the same instant the crea-ture's tail coiled about his own throat and then commenced a battle royal of turning and twist-ing bodies as each sought to dislodge the fatal hold of the other, but the acts of the ape-man were guided by a human brain and thus it was that the rolling bodies rolled in the direction that Tarzan wished—toward the edge of the recess.

The choking tail had shut the air from his lungs, he knew that his gasping lips were parted and his tongue protruding; and now his brain reeled and his sight grew dim; but not before he reached his goal and a quick hand shot out to seize the knife that now lay within reach as the two bodies tottered perilously upon the brink of the chasm.

With all his remaining strength the ape-man drove home the blade—once, twice, thrice, and then all went black before him as he felt himself, still in the clutches of the Tor-o-don, topple from the recess.

Fortunate it was for Tarzan that Pan-at-lee had not obeyed his injunction to make good her escape while he engaged the Tor-o-don, for it was to this fact that he owed his life. Close be-side the struggling forms during the brief mo-ments of the terrific climax she had realized every detail of the danger to Tarzan with which the emergency was fraught and as she saw the two rolling over the outer edge of the niche she seized the ape-man by an ankle at the same time throwing herself prone upon the rocky floor. The muscles of the Tor-o-don relaxed in death with the last thrust of Tarzan's knife and with its hold upon the ape-man released it shot from sight into the gorge below.

It was with infinite difficulty that Pan-at-lee retained her hold upon the ankle of her protector, but she did so and then, slowly, she sought to drag the dead weight back to the safety of the niche. This, however, was beyond her strength and she could but hold on tightly, hoping that some plan would suggest itself before her powers of endurance failed. She wondered if, after all, the creature was already dead, but that she could not bring herself to believe—and if not dead how long it would be before he regained consciousness. If he did not regain it soon he never would regain it, that she knew, for she felt her fingers numbing to the strain upon them and slipping, slowly, slowly, from their hold. It was then that Tarzan regained consciousness. He could not know what power upheld him, but he felt that whatever it was it was slowly releasing its hold upon his ankle. Within easy reach of his hands were two pegs and these he seized upon just as Pan-at-lee's fingers slipped from their hold.

As it was he came near to being precipitated into the gorge—only his great strength saved him. He was upright now and his feet found other pegs. His first thought was of his foe. Where was he? Waiting above there to finish him? Tarzan looked up just as the frightened face of Pan-at-lee appeared over the threshold of the recess.

"You live?" she cried.

"Yes," replied Tarzan. "Where is the shaggy one?"

Pan-at-lee pointed downward. "There," she said, "dead."

"Good!" exclaimed the ape-man, clambering to her side. "You are unharmed?" he asked.

"You came just in time," replied Pan-at-lee; "but who are you and how did you know that I was here and what do you know of Om-at and where did you come from and what did you mean by calling Om-at, *gund*?"

"Wait, wait," cried Tarzan; "one at a time. My, but you are all alike—the shes of the tribe of Kerchak, the ladies of England, and their sisters of Pal-ul-don. Have patience and I will try to tell you all that you wish to know. Four of us set out with Om-at from Kor-ul-ja to search for you. We were attacked by the Kor-ul-lul and separated. I was taken prisoner, but escaped. Again I stumbled upon your trail and followed it, reaching the summit of this cliff just as the hairy one was climbing up after you. I was coming to investigate when I heard your scream—the rest you know."

"But you called Om-at, *gund* of Kor-ul-ja," she insisted. "Es-sat is *gund*."

"Es-sat is dead," explained the ape-man. "Om-at slew him and now Om-at is *gund*. Om-at came back seeking you. He found Es-sat in your cave and killed him."

"Yes," said the girl, "Es-sat came to my cave and I struck him down with my golden breast-plates and escaped."

"And a lion pursued you," continued Tarzan, "and you leaped from the cliff into Kor-ul-lul, but why you were not killed is beyond me."

"Is there anything beyond you?" exclaimed Pan-at-lee. "How could you know that a lion pursued me and that I leaped from the cliff and not know that it was the pool of deep water below that saved me?"

"I would have known that, too, had not the Kor-ul-lul come then and prevented me continuing upon your trail. But now I would ask you a question—by what name do you call the thing with which I just fought?"

"It was a Tor-o-don," she replied. "I have seen but one before. They are terrible creatures with the cunning of man and the ferocity of a beast. Great indeed must be the warrior who slays one single-handed." She gazed at him in open admiration.

"And now," said Tarzan, "you must sleep, for tomorrow we shall return to Kor-ul-ja and Om-at, and I doubt that you have had much rest these two nights."

Pan-at-lee, lulled by a feeling of security, slept peacefully into the morning while Tarzan stretched himself upon the hard floor of the recess just outside her cave.

The sun was high in the heavens when he awoke; for two hours it had looked down upon another heroic figure miles away—the figure of a godlike man fighting his way through the hideous morass that lies like a filthy moat defending Pal-ul-don from the creatures of the outer world. Now waist deep in the sucking ooze, now menaced by loathsome reptiles, the man advanced only by virtue of Herculean efforts gaining laboriously by inches along the devious way that he was forced to choose in selecting the least precarious footing. Near the center of the morass was open water—slimy, green-hued water. He reached it at last after more than two hours of such effort as would have left an ordinary man spent and dying in the sticky mud, yet he was less than halfway across the marsh. Greasy with slime and mud was his smooth, brown hide, and greasy with slime and mud was his beloved Enfield that had shone so brightly in the first rays of the rising sun.

He paused a moment upon the edge of the open water and then throwing himself forward struck out to swim across. He swam with long, easy, powerful strokes calculated less for speed than for endurance, for his was, primarily, a test of the latter, since beyond the open water was another two hours or more of gruelling effort between it and solid ground. He was, perhaps, halfway across and congratulating himself upon the ease of the achievement of this portion of his task when there arose from the depths directly in his path a hideous reptile, which, with wide-distended jaws, bore down upon him, hissing shrilly.

Tarzan arose and stretched, expanded his great chest and drank in deep draughts of the fresh morning air. His clear eyes scanned the wondrous beauties of the landscape spread out before them. Directly below lay Kor-ul-gryf, a dense, somber green of gently moving tree tops. To Tarzan it was neither grim, nor forbidding— it was jungle, beloved jungle. To his right there spread a panorama of the lower reaches of the Valley of Jad-ben-Otho, with its winding streams and its blue lakes. Gleaming whitely in the sunlight were scattered groups of dwellings—the feudal strongholds of the lesser chiefs of the Ho-don. A-lur, the City of Light, he could not see as it was hidden by the shoulder of the cliff in which the deserted village lay.

For a moment Tarzan gave himself over to that spiritual enjoyment of beauty that only the man-mind may attain and then Nature asserted herself and the belly of the beast called aloud that it was hungry. Again Tarzan looked down at Kor-ul-gryf. There was the jungle! Grew there a jungle that would not feed Tarzan? The ape-man smiled and commenced the descent to the gorge. Was there danger there? Of course. Who knew it better than Tarzan? In all jungles lies death, for life and death go hand in hand and where life teems death reaps his fullest harvest. Never had Tarzan met a creature of the jungle with which he could not cope—sometimes by virtue of brute strength alone, again by a combination of brute strength and the cunning of the man-mind; but Tarzan had never met a *gryf*.

He had heard the bellowings in the gorge the night before after he had lain down to sleep and he had meant to ask Pan-at-lee this morning what manner of beast so disturbed the slumbers of its betters. He reached the foot of the cliff and strode into the jungle and here he halted, his keen eyes and ears watchful and alert, his sensitive nostrils searching each shifting air current for the scent spoor of game. Again he advanced deeper into the wood, his light step giving forth no sound, his bow and arrows in readiness. A light morning breeze was blowing from up the gorge and in this direction he bent his steps. Many odors impinged upon his organs of scent. Some of these he classified without effort, but others were strange—the odors of beasts and of birds, of trees and shrubs and flowers with which he was unfamiliar. He sensed faintly the reptilian odor that he had learned to connect with the strange, nocturnal forms that had loomed dim and bulky on several occasions since his introduction to Pal-ul-don.

And then, suddenly he caught plainly the strong, sweet odor of Bara, the deer. Were the belly vocal, Tarzan's would have given a little cry of joy, for it loved the flesh of Bara. The ape-man moved rapidly, but cautiously forward. The prey was not far distant and as the hunter approached it, he took silently to the trees and still in his nostrils was the faint reptilian odor that spoke of a great creature which he had never yet seen except as a denser shadow among the dense shadows of the night; but the odor was of such a faintness as suggests to the jungle bred the distance of absolute safety.

And now, moving noiselessly, Tarzan came within sight of Bara drinking at a pool where the stream that waters Kor-ul-gryf crosses an open place in the jungle. The deer was too far from the nearest tree to risk a charge, so the ape-man must depend upon the accuracy and force of his first arrow, which must drop the deer in its tracks or forfeit both deer and shaft. Far back came the right hand and the bow, that you or I might not move, bent easily beneath the muscles of the forest god. There was a singing twang and Bara, leaping high in air, collapsed upon the ground, an arrow through his heart. Tarzan dropped to earth and ran to his kill, lest the animal might even yet rise and escape; but Bara was safely dead. As Tarzan stooped to lift it to his shoulder there fell upon his ears a thunderous bellow that seemed almost at his right elbow, and as his eyes shot in the direction of the sound, there broke upon his vision such a creature as paleontologists have dreamed as having possibly existed in the dimmest vistas of Earth's infancy—a gigantic creature, vibrant with mad rage, that charged, bellowing, upon him.

When Pan-at-lee awoke she looked out upon the niche in search of Tarzan. He was not there. She sprang to her feet and rushed out, looking down into Kor-ul-gryf guessing that he had gone down in search of food and there she caught a glimpse of him disappearing into the forest. For an instant she was panic-stricken. She knew that he was a stranger in Pal-ul-don and that, so, he might not realize the dangers that lay in that gorge of terror. Why did she not call to him to return? You or I might have done so, but no Pal-ul-don, for they know the ways of the *gryf*—they know the weak eyes and the keen ears, and that at the sound of a human voice they come. To have called to Tarzan, then, would but have been to invite disaster and so she did not call. Instead, afraid though she was, she descended into the gorge for the purpose of overhauling Tarzan and warning him in whispers of his danger. It was a brave act, since it was performed in the face of countless ages of inherited fear of the creatures that she might be called upon to face. Men have been decorated for less.

Pan-at-lee, descended from a long line of hunters, assumed that Tarzan would move up wind and in this direction she sought his tracks, which she soon found well marked, since he had made no effort to conceal them. She moved rapidly until she reached the point at which Tarzan had taken to the trees. Of course she knew what had happened, since her own people were semi-arboreal; but she could not track him through the trees, having no such well-developed sense of scent as he.

She could but hope that he had continued on up wind and in this direction she moved, her heart pounding in terror against her ribs, her eyes glancing first in one direction and then another. She had reached the edge of a clearing when two things happened—she caught sight of Tarzan bending over a dead deer and at the same instant a deafening roar sounded almost beside her. It terrified her beyond description, but it brought no paralysis of fear. Instead it galvanized her into instant action with the result that Pan-at-lee swarmed up the nearest tree to the very loftiest branch that would sustain her weight. Then she looked down.

The thing that Tarzan saw charging him

when the warning bellow attracted his surprised eyes loomed terrifically monstrous before him—monstrous and awe-inspiring; but it did not terrify Tarzan, it only angered him, for he saw that it was beyond even his powers to combat and that meant that it might cause him to lose his kill, and Tarzan was hungry. There was but a single alternative to remaining for annihilation and that was flight—swift and immediate. And Tarzan fled, but he carried the carcass of Bara, the deer, with him. He had not more than a dozen paces' start, but on the other hand the nearest tree was almost as close. His greatest danger lay, he imagined, in the great, towering height of the creature pursuing him, for even though he reached the tree he would have to climb high in an incredibly short time as, unless appearances were deceiving, the thing could reach up and pluck him down from any branch under thirty feet above the ground, and possibly from those up to fifty feet, if it reared up on its hind legs.

But Tarzan was no sluggard and though the *gryf* was incredibly fast despite its great bulk, it was no match for Tarzan, and when it comes to climbing, the little monkeys gaze with envy upon the feats of the ape-man. And so it was that the bellowing *gryf* came to a baffled stop at the foot of the tree and even though he reared up and sought to seize his prey among the branches, as Tarzan had guessed he might, he failed in this also. And then, well out of reach, Tarzan came to a stop and there, just above him, he saw Pan-at-lee sitting, wide-eyed and trembling.

"How came you here?" he asked.

She told him. "You came to warn me!" he said. "It was very brave and unselfish of you. I am chagrined that I should have been thus surprised. The creature was up wind from me and yet I did not sense its near presence until it charged. I cannot understand it."

"It is not strange," said Pan-at-lee. "That is one of the peculiarities of the *gryf*—it is said that man never knows of its presence until it is upon him—so silently does it move despite its great size."

"But I should have smelled it," cried Tarzan, disgustedly.

"Smelled it!" ejaculated Pan-at-lee. "Smelled it?"

"Certainly. How do you suppose I found this deer so quickly? And I sensed the *gryf*, too, but faintly as at a great distance." Tarzan suddenly ceased speaking and looked down at the bellowing creature below them—his nostrils quivered as though searching for a scent. "Ah!" he exclaimed. "I have it!"

"What?" asked Pan-at-lee.

"I was deceived because the creature gives off practically no odor," explained the ape-man. "What I smelled was the faint aroma that doubtless permeates the entire jungle because of the long presence of many of the creatures—it is the sort of odor that would remain for a long time, faint as it is.

"Pan-at-lee, did you ever hear of a triceratops? No? Well this thing that you call a *gryf* is a triceratops and it has been extinct for hundreds of thousands of years. I have seen its skeleton in the museum in London and a figure of one restored. I always thought that the scientists who did such work depended principally upon an overwrought imagination, but I see that I was wrong. This living thing is not an exact counterpart of the restoration that I saw; but it is so similar as to be easily recognizable, and then, too, we must remember that during the ages that have elapsed since the paleontologist's specimen lived many changes might have been wrought by evolution in the living line that has quite evidently persisted in Pal-ul-don."

"Triceratops, London, paleo—I don't know what you are talking about," cried Pan-at-lee.

Tarzan smiled and threw a piece of dead wood at the face of the angry creature below them. Instantly the great bony hood over the neck was erected and a mad bellow rolled upward from the gigantic body. Full twenty feet at the shoulder the thing stood, a dirty slate-blue in color except for its yellow face with the blue bands encircling the eyes, the red hood with the yellow lining and the yellow belly. The three parallel lines of bony protuberances down the back gave a further touch of color to the body, those following the line of the spine being red, while those on either side are yellow. The five- and three-toed hoofs of the ancient horned dinosaurs had become talons in the *gryf,* but the three horns, two large ones above the eyes and a median horn on the nose, had persisted through all the ages. Weird and terrible as was its appearance Tarzan could not but admire the mighty creature looming big below him, its seventy-five feet of length majestically typifying those things which all his life the ape-man had admired— courage and strength. In that massive tail alone was the strength of an elephant.

The wicked little eyes looked up at him and the horny beak opened to disclose a full set of powerful teeth.

"Herbivorous!" murmured the ape-man. "Your ancestors may have been, but not you," and then to Pan-at-lee: "Let us go now. At the cave we will have deer meat and then—back to Kor-ul-ja and Om-at."

The girl shuddered. "Go?" she repeated. "We will never go from here."

"Why not?" asked Tarzan.

For answer she but pointed to the *gryf.*

"Nonsense!" exclaimed the man. "It cannot climb. We can reach the cliff through the trees and be back in the cave before it knows what has become of us."

"You do not know the *gryf,*" replied Pan-at-lee gloomily. "Wherever we go it will follow and always it will be ready at the foot of each tree when we would descend. It will never give us up."

"We can live in the trees for a long time if necessary," replied Tarzan, "and sometime the thing will leave."

The girl shook her head. "Never," she said, "and then there are the Tor-o-don. They will come and kill us and after eating a little will throw the balance to the *gryf*—the *gryf* and Tor-o-don are friends, because the Tor-o-don shares his food with the *gryf.*"

"You may be right," said Tarzan; "but even

so I don't intend waiting here for someone to come along and eat part of me and then feed the balance to that beast below. If I don't get out of this place whole it won't be my fault. Come along now and we'll make a try at it," and so saying he moved off through the tree tops with Pan-at-lee close behind. Below them, on the ground, moved the horned dinosaur and when they reached the edge of the forest where there lay fifty yards of open ground to cross to the foot of the cliff he was there with them, at the bottom of the tree, waiting.

Tarzan looked ruefully down and scratched his head.

VII
JUNGLE CRAFT

Presently he looked up and at Pan-at-lee. "Can you cross the gorge through the trees very rapidly?" he questioned.

"Alone?" she asked.

"No," replied Tarzan.

"I can follow wherever you can lead," she said then.

"Across and back again?"

"Yes."

"Then come, and do exactly as I bid." He started back again through the trees, swiftly, swinging monkey-like from limb to limb, following a zigzag course that he tried to select with an eye for the difficulties of the trail beneath. Where the underbrush was heaviest, where fallen trees blocked the way, he led the footsteps of the creature below them; but all to no avail. When they reached the opposite side of the gorge the *gryf* was with them.

"Back again," said Tarzan, and, turning, the two retraced their high-flung way through the upper terraces of the ancient forest of Kor-ul-gryf. But the result was the same—no, not quite; it was worse, for another *gryf* had joined the first and now two waited beneath the tree in which they stopped.

The cliff looming high above them with its

innumerable cave mouths seemed to beckon and to taunt them. It was so near, yet eternity yawned between. The body of the Tor-o-don lay at the cliff's foot where it had fallen. It was in plain view of the two in the tree. One of the *gryfs* walked over and sniffed about it, but did not offer to devour it. Tarzan had examined it casually as he had passed earlier in the morning. He guessed that it represented either a very high order of ape or a very low order of man— something akin to the Java man, perhaps; a truer example of the pithecanthropi than either the Ho-don or the Waz-don; possibly the precursor of them both. As his eyes wandered idly over the scene below his active brain was working out the details of the plan that he had made to permit Pan-at-lee's escape from the gorge. His thoughts were interrupted by a strange cry from above them in the gorge.

"Whee-oo! Whee-oo!" it sounded, coming closer.

The *gryfs* below raised their heads and looked in the direction of the interruption. One of them made a low, rumbling sound in its throat. It was not a bellow and it did not indicate anger. Immediately the "Whee-oo!" responded. The *gryfs* repeated the rumbling and at intervals the "Whee-oo!" was repeated, coming ever closer.

Tarzan looked at Pan-at-lee. "What is it?" he asked.

"I do not know," she replied. "Perhaps a strange bird, or another horrid beast that dwells in this frightful place."

"Ah," exclaimed Tarzan; "there it is. Look!"

Pan-at-lee voiced a cry of despair. "A Tor-o-don!"

The creature, walking erect and carrying a stick in one hand, advanced at a slow, lumbering gait. It walked directly toward the *gryfs*, who moved aside, as though afraid. Tarzan watched intently. The Tor-o-don was now quite close to one of the triceratops. It swung its head and snapped at him viciously. Instantly the Tor-o-don sprang in and commenced to belabor the huge beast across the face with his stick. To the

ape-man's amazement the *gryf*, that might have annihilated the comparatively puny Tor-o-don instantly in any of a dozen ways, cringed like a whipped cur.

"Whee-oo! Whee-oo!" shouted the Tor-o-don and the *gryf* came slowly toward him. A whack on the median horn brought it to a stop. Then the Tor-o-don walked around behind it, clambered up its tail and seated himself astraddle of the huge back. "Whee-oo!" he shouted and prodded the beast with a sharp point of his stick. The *gryf* commenced to move off.

So rapt had Tarzan been in the scene below him that he had given no thought to escape, for he realized that for him and Pan-at-lee time had in these brief moments turned back countless ages to spread before their eyes a page of the dim and distant past. They two had looked upon the first man and his primitive beasts of burden.

And now the ridden *gryf* halted and looked up at them, bellowing. It was sufficient. The creature had warned its master of their presence. Instantly the Tor-o-don urged the beast close beneath the tree which held them, at the same time leaping to his feet upon the horny back. Tarzan saw the bestial face, the great fangs, the mighty muscles. From the loins of such had sprung the human race—and only from such could it have sprung, for only such as this might have survived the horrid dangers of the age that was theirs.

The Tor-o-don beat upon his breast and growled horribly—hideous, uncouth, beastly. Tarzan rose to his full height upon a swaying branch—straight and beautiful as a demigod— unspoiled by the taint of civilization—a perfect specimen of what the human race might have been had the laws of man not interfered with the laws of nature.

The Present fitted an arrow to his bow and drew the shaft far back. The Past basing its claims upon brute strength sought to reach the other and drag him down; but the loosed arrow sank deep into the savage heart and the Past sank back into the oblivion that had claimed his kind.

"Tarzan-jad-guru!" murmured Pan-at-lee, unknowingly giving him out of the fullness of her admiration the same title that the warriors of her tribe had bestowed upon him.

The ape-man turned to her. "Pan-at-lee," he said, "these beasts may keep us treed here indefinitely. I doubt if we can escape together, but I have a plan. You remain here, hiding yourself in the foliage, while I start back across the gorge in sight of them and yelling to attract their attention. Unless they have more brains than I suspect they will follow me. When they are gone you make for the cliff. Wait for me in the cave not longer than today. If I do not come by tomorrow's sun you will have to start back for Kor-ul-ja alone. Here is a joint of deer meat for you." He had severed one of the deer's hind legs and this he passed up to her.

"I cannot desert you," she said simply; "it is not the way of my people to desert a friend and ally. Om-at would never forgive me."

"Tell Om-at that I commanded you to go," replied Tarzan.

"It is a command?" she asked.

"It is! Good-bye, Pan-at-lee. Hasten back to Om-at—you are a fitting mate for the chief of Kor-ul-ja." He moved off slowly through the trees.

"Good-bye, Tarzan-jad-guru!" she called after him. "Fortunate are my Om-at and his Pan-at-lee in owning such a friend."

Tarzan, shouting aloud, continued upon his way and the great *gryfs*, lured by his voice, followed beneath. His ruse was evidently proving successful and he was filled with elation as he led the bellowing beasts farther and farther from Pan-at-lee. He hoped that she would take advantage of the opportunity afforded her for escape, yet at the same time he was filled with concern as to her ability to survive the dangers which lay between Kor-ul-gryf and Kor-ul-ja. There were lions and Tor-o-dons and the unfriendly tribe of Kor-ul-lul to hinder her progress, though the distance in itself to the cliffs of her people was not great.

He realized her bravery and understood the resourcefulness that she must share in common with all primitive people who, day by day, must contend face to face with nature's law of the survival of the fittest, unaided by any of the numerous artificial protections that civilization has thrown around its brood of weaklings.

Several times during this crossing of the gorge Tarzan endeavored to outwit his keen pursuers, but all to no avail. Double as he would he could not throw them off his track and ever as he changed his course they changed theirs to conform. Along the verge of the forest upon the southeastern side of the gorge he sought some point at which the trees touched some negotiable portion of the cliff, but though he traveled far both up and down the gorge he discovered no such easy avenue of escape. The ape-man finally commenced to entertain an idea of the hopelessness of his case and to realize to the full why the Kor-ul-gryf had been religiously abjured by the races of Pal-ul-don for all these many ages.

Night was falling and though since early morning he had sought diligently a way out of this cul-de-sac he was no nearer to liberty than at the moment the first bellowing *gryf* had charged him as he stooped over the carcass of his kill: but with the falling of night came renewed hope for, in common with the great cats, Tarzan was, to a greater or lesser extent, a nocturnal beast. It is true he could not see by night as well as they, but that lack was largely recompensed for by the keenness of his scent and the highly developed sensitiveness of his other organs of perception. As the blind follow and interpret their Braille characters with deft fingers, so Tarzan reads the book of the jungle with feet and hands and eyes and ears and nose; each contributing its share to the quick and accurate translation of the text.

But again he was doomed to be thwarted by one vital weakness—he did not know the *gryf*, and before the night was over he wondered if the things never slept, for wheresoever he moved they moved also, and always they barred his road to liberty. Finally, just before dawn, he relinquished his immediate effort and sought rest in a friendly tree crotch in the safety of the middle terrace.

Once again was the sun high when Tarzan awoke, rested and refreshed. Keen to the necessities of the moment he made no effort to locate his jailers lest in the act he might apprise them of his movements. Instead he sought cautiously and silently to melt away among the foliage of the trees. His first move, however, was heralded by a deep bellow from below.

Among the numerous refinements of civilization that Tarzan had failed to acquire was that of profanity, and possibly it is to be regretted since there are circumstances under which it is at least a relief to pent emotion. And it may be that in effect Tarzan resorted to profanity if there can be physical as well as vocal swearing, since immediately the bellow announced that his hopes had been again frustrated, he turned quickly and seeing the hideous face of the *gryf* below him seized a large fruit from a nearby branch and hurled it viciously at the horned snout. The missile struck full between the creature's eyes, resulting in a reaction that surprised the ape-man; it did not arouse the beast to a show of revengeful rage as Tarzan had expected and hoped; instead the creature gave a single vicious side snap at the fruit as it bounded from his skull and then turned sulkily away, walking off a few steps.

There was that in the act that recalled immediately to Tarzan's mind similar action on the preceding day when the Tor-o-don had struck one of the creatures across the face with his staff, and instantly there sprung to the cunning and courageous brain a plan of escape from his predicament that might have blanched the cheek of the most heroic.

The gambling instinct is not strong among creatures of the wild; the chances of their daily life are sufficient stimuli for the beneficial excitement of their nerve centers. It has remained for civilized man, protected in a measure from the natural dangers of existence, to invent artificial stimulants in the form of cards and dice and roulette wheels. Yet when necessity bids there are no greater gamblers than the savage denizens of the jungle, the forest, and the hills, for as lightly as you roll the ivory cubes upon the green cloth they will gamble with death—their own lives the stake.

And so Tarzan would gamble now, pitting the seemingly wild deductions of his shrewd brain against all the proofs of the bestial ferocity of his antagonists that his experience of them had adduced—against all the age-old folklore and legend that had been handed down for countless generations and passed on to him through the lips of Pan-at-lee.

Yet as he worked in preparation for the greatest play that man can make in the game of life, he smiled; nor was there any indication of haste or excitement or nervousness in his demeanor.

First he selected a long, straight branch about two inches in diameter at its base. This he cut from the tree with his knife, removed the smaller branches and twigs until he had fashioned a pole about ten feet in length. This he sharpened at the smaller end. The staff finished to his satisfaction he looked down upon the triceratops.

"Whee-oo!" he cried.

Instantly the beasts raised their heads and looked at him. From the throat of one of them came faintly a low rumbling sound.

"Whee-oo!" repeated Tarzan and hurled the balance of the carcass of the deer to them.

Instantly the *gryfs* fell upon it with much bellowing, one of them attempting to seize it and keep it from the other: but finally the second obtained a hold and an instant later it had been torn asunder and greedily devoured. Once again they looked up at the ape-man and this time they saw him descending to the ground.

One of them started toward him. Again Tarzan repeated the weird cry of the Tor-o-don. The *gryf* halted in his track, apparently puzzled, while Tarzan slipped lightly to the earth and advanced toward the nearer beast, his staff raised menacingly and the call of the first-man upon his lips.

Would the cry be answered by the low rumbling of the beast of burden or the horrid bellow of the man-eater? Upon the answer to this question hung the fate of the ape-man.

Pan-at-lee was listening intently to the sounds of the departing *gryfs* as Tarzan led them cunningly from her, and when she was sure that they were far enough away to insure her safe retreat she dropped swiftly from the branches to the ground and sped like a frightened deer across the open space to the foot of the cliff, stepped over the body of the Tor-o-don who had attacked her the night before and was soon climbing rapidly up the ancient stone pegs of the deserted cliff village. In the mouth of the cave near that which she had occupied she kindled a fire and cooked the haunch of venison that Tarzan had left her, and from one of the trickling streams that ran down the face of the escarpment she obtained water to satisfy her thirst.

All day she waited, hearing in the distance, and sometimes close at hand, the bellowing of the *gryfs* which pursued the strange creature that had dropped so miraculously into her life. For him she felt the same keen, almost fanatical loyalty that many another had experienced for Tarzan of the Apes. Beast and human, he had held them to him with bonds that were stronger than steel—those of them that were clean and courageous, and the weak and the helpless; but never could Tarzan claim among his admirers the coward, the ingrate or the scoundrel; from such, both man and beast, he had won fear and hatred.

To Pan-at-lee he was all that was brave and noble and heroic and, too, he was Om-at's friend—the friend of the man she loved. For any one of these reasons Pan-at-lee would have died

for Tarzan, for such is the loyalty of the simple-minded children of nature. It has remained for civilization to teach us to weigh the relative rewards of loyalty and its antithesis. The loyalty of the primitive is spontaneous, unreasoning, unselfish and such was the loyalty of Pan-at-lee for the Tarmangani.

And so it was that she waited that day and night, hoping that he would return that she might accompany him back to Om-at, for her experience had taught her that in the face of danger two have a better chance than one. But Tarzan-jad-guru had not come, and so upon the following morning Pan-at-lee set out upon her return to Kor-ul-ja.

She knew the dangers and yet she faced them with the stolid indifference of her race. When they directly confronted and menaced her would be time enough to experience fear or excitement or confidence. In the meantime it was unnecessary to waste nerve energy by anticipating them. She moved therefore through her savage land with no greater show of concern than might mark your sauntering to a corner drug-store for a sundae. But this is your life and that is Pan-at-lee's and even now as you read this Pan-at-lee may be sitting upon the edge of the recess of Om-at's cave while the *ja* and *jato* roar from the gorge below and from the ridge above, and the Kor-ul-lul threaten upon the south and the Ho-don from the Valley of Jad-ben-Otho far below, for Pan-at-lee still lives and preens her silky coat of jet beneath the tropical moonlight of Pal-ul-don.

But she was not to reach Kor-ul-ja this day, nor the next, nor for many days after though the danger that threatened her was neither Waz-don enemy nor savage beast. She came without misadventure to the Kor-ul-lul and after descending its rocky southern wall without catching the slightest glimpse of the hereditary enemies of her people, she experienced a renewal of confidence that was little short of practical assurance that she would successfully terminate her venture and be restored once more to her own people and the lover she had not seen for so many long and weary moons.

She was almost across the gorge now and moving with an extreme caution abated no wit by her confidence, for wariness is an instinctive trait of the primitive, something which cannot be laid aside even momentarily if one would survive. And so she came to the trail that follows the windings of Kor-ul-lul from its uppermost reaches down into the broad and fertile Valley of Jad-ben-Otho.

And as she stepped into the trail there arose on either side of her from out of the bushes that border the path, as though materialized from thin air, a score of tall, white warriors of the Ho-don. Like a frightened deer Pan-at-lee cast a single startled look at these menacers of her freedom and leaped quickly toward the bushes in an effort to escape; but the warriors were too close at hand. They closed upon her from every side and then, drawing her knife she turned at bay, metamorphosed by the fires of fear and hate from a startled deer to a raging tiger-cat. They did not try to kill her, but only to subdue and capture her; and so it was that more than a single Ho-don warrior felt the keen edge of her blade in his flesh before they had succeeded in overpowering her by numbers. And still she fought and scratched and bit after they had taken the knife from her until it was necessary to tie her hands and fasten a piece of wood between her teeth by means of thongs passed behind her head.

At first she refused to walk when they started off in the direction of the valley but after two of them had seized her by the hair and dragged her for a number of yards she thought better of her original decision and came along with them, though still as defiant as her bound wrists and gagged mouth would permit.

Near the entrance to Kor-ul-lul they came upon another body of their warriors with which were several Waz-don prisoners from the tribe of Kor-ul-lul. It was a raiding party come up from a Ho-don city of the valley after slaves. This Pan-at-lee knew for the occurrence was by no means unusual. During her lifetime the tribe

to which she belonged had been sufficiently fortunate, or powerful, to withstand successfully the majority of such raids made upon them, but yet Pan-at-lee had known of friends and relatives who had been carried into slavery by the Ho-don and she knew, too, another thing which gave her hope, as doubtless it did to each of the other captives—that occasionally the prisoners escaped from the cities of the hairless whites.

After they had joined the other party the entire band set forth into the valley and presently, from the conversation of her captors, Pan-at-lee knew that she was headed for A-lur, the City of Light; while in the cave of his ancestors, Om-at, chief of the Kor-ul-ja, bemoaned the loss of both his friend and she that was to have been his mate.

VIII

A-LUR

As the hissing reptile bore down upon the stranger swimming in the open water near the center of the morass on the frontier of Pal-ul-don it seemed to the man that this indeed must be the futile termination of an arduous and danger-filled journey. It seemed, too, equally futile to pit his puny knife against this frightful creature. Had he been attacked on land it is possible that he might as a last resort have used his Enfield, though he had come thus far through all these weary, danger-ridden miles without recourse to it, though again and again had his life hung in the balance in the face of the savage denizens of forest, jungle, and steppe. For whatever it may have been for which he was preserving his precious ammunition he evidently held it more sacred even than his life, for as yet he had not used a single round and now the decision was not required of him, since it would have been impossible for him to have unslung his Enfield, loaded and fired with the necessary celerity while swimming.

Though his chance for survival seemed slender, and hope at its lowest ebb, he was not minded therefore to give up without a struggle. Instead he drew his blade and awaited the oncoming reptile. The creature was like no living thing he ever before had seen although possibly it resembled a crocodile in some respects more than it did anything with which he was familiar.

As this frightful survivor of some extinct progenitor charged upon him with distended jaws there came to the man quickly a full consciousness of the futility of endeavoring to stay the mad rush or pierce the armor-coated hide with his little knife. The thing was almost upon him now and whatever form of defense he chose must be made quickly. There seemed but a single alternative to instant death, and this he took at almost the instant the great reptile towered directly above him.

With the celerity of a seal he dove headforemost beneath the oncoming body and at the same instant, turning upon his back, he plunged his blade into the soft, cold surface of the slimy belly as the momentum of the hurtling reptile carried it swiftly over him; and then with powerful strokes he swam on beneath the surface for a dozen yards before he rose. A glance showed him the stricken monster plunging madly in pain and rage upon the surface of the water behind him. That it was writhing in its death agonies was evidenced by the fact that it made no effort to pursue him, and so, to the accompaniment of the shrill screaming of the dying monster, the man won at last to the farther edge of the open water to take up once more the almost superhuman effort of crossing the last stretch of clinging mud which separated him from the solid ground of Pal-ul-don.

A good two hours it took him to drag his now weary body through the clinging, stinking muck, but at last, mud-covered and spent, he dragged himself out upon the soft grasses of the bank. A hundred yards away a stream, winding its way down from the distant mountains, emptied into the morass, and, after a short rest, he made his way to this and seeking a quiet pool, bathed himself and washed the mud and slime from his weapons, accouterments, and loin cloth. Another hour was spent beneath the rays of the hot sun in wiping, polishing, and oiling his Enfield though the means at hand for drying it consisted principally of dry grasses. It was afternoon before he had satisfied himself that his precious weapon was safe from any harm by dirt, or dampness, and then he arose and took up the search for the spoor he had followed to the opposite side of the swamp.

Would he find again the trail that had led into the opposite side of the morass, to be lost there, even to his trained senses? If he found it not again upon this side of the almost impassable barrier he might assume that his long journey had ended in failure. And so he sought up and down the verge of the stagnant water for traces of an old spoor that would have been invisible to your eyes or mine, even had we followed directly in the tracks of its maker.

As Tarzan advanced upon the *gryfs* he imitated as closely as he could recall them the methods and mannerisms of the Tor-o-don, but up to the instant that he stood close beside one of the huge creatures he realized that his fate still hung in the balance, for the thing gave forth no sign, either menacing or otherwise. It only stood there, watching him out of its cold, reptilian eyes and then Tarzan raised his staff and with a menacing "Whee-oo!" struck the *gryf* a vicious blow across the face.

The creature made a sudden side snap in his direction, a snap that did not reach him, and then turned sullenly away, precisely as it had when the Tor-o-don commanded it. Walking around to its rear as he had seen the shaggy first-man do, Tarzan ran up the broad tail and seated himself upon the creature's back, and then again imitating the acts of the Tor-o-don he prodded it with the sharpened point of his staff, and thus goading it forward and guiding it with blows, first upon one side and then upon the other, he started it down the gorge in the direction of the valley.

At first it had been in his mind only to deter-

mine if he could successfully assert any authority over the great monsters, realizing that in this
possibility lay his only hope of immediate escape
from his jailers. But once seated upon the back
of his titanic mount the ape-man experienced
the sensation of a new thrill that recalled to him
the day in his boyhood that he had first clambered to the broad head of Tantor, the elephant,
and this, together with the sense of mastery that
was always meat and drink to the lord of the
jungle, decided him to put his newly acquired
power to some utilitarian purpose.

Pan-at-lee he judged must either have already reached safety or met with death. At least,
no longer could he be of service to her, while below Kor-ul-gryf, in the soft green valley, lay A-
lur, the City of Light, which, since he had gazed
upon it from the shoulder of Pastar-ul-ved, had
been his ambition and his goal.

Whether or not its gleaming walls held the
secret of his lost mate he could not even guess
but if she lived at all within the precincts of Pal-
ul-don it must be among the Ho-don, since the
hairy black men of this forgotten world took no
prisoners. And so to A-lur he would go, and how
more effectively than upon the back of this grim
and terrible creature that the races of Pal-ul-don
held in such awe?

A little mountain stream tumbles down from
Kor-ul-gryf to be joined in the foothills with that
which empties the waters of Kor-ul-lul into the
valley, forming a small river which runs southwest, eventually entering the valley's largest lake
at the city of A-lur, through the center of which
the stream passes. An ancient trail, well marked
by countless generations of naked feet of man
and beast, leads down toward A-lur beside the
river, and along this Tarzan guided the *gryf*.
Once clear of the forest which ran below the
mouth of the gorge, Tarzan caught occasional
glimpses of the city gleaming in the distance far
below him.

The country through which he passed was
resplendent with the riotous beauties of tropical
verdure. Thick, lush grasses grew waist high
upon either side of the trail and the way was broken now and again by patches of open park-like
forest, or perhaps a little patch of dense jungle
where the trees overarched the way and trailing
creepers depended in graceful loops from
branch to branch.

At times the ape-man had difficulty in commanding obedience upon the part of his unruly
beast, but always in the end its fear of the relatively puny goad urged it on to obedience. Late
in the afternoon as they approached the conflu-
ence of the stream they were skirting and another
which appeared to come from the direction of
Kor-ul-ja the ape-man, emerging from one of the
jungle patches, discovered a considerable party
of Ho-don upon the opposite bank. Simultaneously they saw him and the mighty creature he
bestrode. For a moment they stood in wide-eyed
amazement and then, in answer to the command
of their leader, they turned and bolted for the
shelter of the nearby wood.

The ape-man had but a brief glimpse of them
but it was sufficient indication that there were
Waz-don with them, doubtless prisoners taken
in one of the raids upon the Waz-don villages of
which Ta-den and Om-at had told him.

At the sound of their voices the *gryf* had bellowed terrifically and started in pursuit even
though a river intervened, but by dint of much
prodding and beating, Tarzan had succeeded in
heading the animal back into the path though
thereafter for a long time it was sullen and more
intractable than ever.

As the sun dropped nearer the summit of the
western hills Tarzan became aware that his plan
to enter A-lur upon the back of a *gryf* was likely
doomed to failure, since the stubbornness of the
great beast was increasing momentarily, doubtless due to the fact that its huge belly was crying
out for food. The ape-man wondered if the Tor-
o-dons had any means of picketing their beasts
for the night, but as he did not know and as no
plan suggested itself, he determined that he
should have to trust to the chance of finding it
again in the morning.

There now arose in his mind a question as to
what would be their relationship when Tarzan

had dismounted. Would it again revert to that of hunter and quarry or would fear of the goad continue to hold its supremacy over the natural instinct of the hunting flesh-eater? Tarzan wondered but as he could not remain upon the *gryf* forever, and as he preferred dismounting and putting the matter to a final test while it was still light, he decided to act at once.

How to stop the creature he did not know, as up to this time his sole desire had been to urge it forward. By experimenting with his staff, however, he found that he could bring it to a halt by reaching forward and striking the thing upon its beaklike snout. Close by grew a number of leafy trees, in any one of which the ape-man could have found sanctuary, but it had occurred to him that should he immediately take to the trees it might suggest to the mind of the *gryf* that the creature that had been commanding him all day feared him, with the result that Tarzan would once again be held a prisoner by the triceratops.

And so, when the *gryf* halted, Tarzan slid to the ground, struck the creature a careless blow across the flank as though in dismissal and walked indifferently away. From the throat of the beast came a low rumbling sound and without even a glance at Tarzan it turned and entered the river where it stood drinking for a long time.

Convinced that the *gryf* no longer constituted a menace to him the ape-man, spurred on himself by the gnawing of hunger, unslung his bow and selecting a handful of arrows set forth cautiously in search of food, evidence of the near presence of which was being borne up to him by a breeze from down river.

Ten minutes later he had made his kill, again one of the Pal-ul-don specimens of antelope, all species of which Tarzan had known since childhood as Bara, the deer, since in the little primer that had been the basis of his education the picture of a deer had been the nearest approach to the likeness of the antelope, from the giant eland to the smaller bushbuck of the hunting grounds of his youth.

Cutting off a haunch he cached it in a nearby tree, and throwing the balance of the carcass across his shoulder trotted back toward the spot at which he had left the *gryf.* The great beast was just emerging from the river when Tarzan, seeing it, issued the weird cry of the Tor-o-don. The creature looked in the direction of the sound voicing at the same time the low rumble with which it answered the call of its master. Twice Tarzan repeated his cry before the beast moved slowly toward him, and when it had come within a few paces he tossed the carcass of the deer to it, upon which it fell with greedy jaws.

"If anything will keep it within call," mused the ape-man as he returned to the tree in which he had cached his own portion of his kill, "it is the knowledge that I will feed it." But as he finished his repast and settled himself comfortably for the night high among the swaying branches of his eyrie he had little confidence that he would ride into A-lur the following day upon his prehistoric steed.

When Tarzan awoke early the following morning he dropped lightly to the ground and made his way to the stream. Removing his weapons and loin cloth he entered the cold waters of the little pool, and after his refreshing bath returned to the tree to breakfast upon another portion of Bara, the deer, adding to his repast some fruits and berries which grew in abundance nearby.

His meal over he sought the ground again and raising his voice in the weird cry that he had learned, he called aloud on the chance of attracting the *gryf,* but though he waited for some time and continued calling there was no response, and he was finally forced to the conclusion that he had seen the last of his great mount of the preceding day.

And so he set his face toward A-lur, pinning his faith upon his knowledge of the Ho-don tongue, his great strength and his native wit.

Refreshed by food and rest, the journey toward A-lur, made in the cool of the morning along the bank of the joyous river, he found delightful in the extreme. Differentiating him from his fellows of the savage jungle were many characteristics other than those physical and mental. Not the least of these were in a measure spiritual, and one that had doubtless been as strong as another in influencing Tarzan's love of the jungle had been his appreciation of the beauties of nature. The apes cared more for a grub-worm in a rotten log than for all the majestic grandeur of the forest giants waving above them. The only beauties that Numa acknowledged were those of his own person as he paraded them before the admiring eyes of his mate, but in all the manifestations of the creative power of nature of which Tarzan was cognizant he appreciated the beauties.

As Tarzan neared the city his interest became centered upon the architecture of the outlying buildings which were hewn from the chalklike limestone of what had once been a group of low hills, similar to the many grass-covered hillocks that dotted the valley in every direction. Taden's explanation of the Ho-don methods of house construction accounted for the ofttimes remarkable shapes and proportions of the buildings which, during the ages that must have been required for their construction, had been hewn from the limestone hills, the exteriors chiseled to such architectural forms as appealed to the eyes of the builders while at the same time following roughly the original outlines of the hills in an evident desire to economize both labor and space. The excavation of the apartments within had been similarly governed by necessity.

As he came nearer Tarzan saw that the waste material from these building operations had been utilized in the construction of outer walls about each building or group of buildings resulting from a single hillock, and later he was to learn that it had also been used for the filling of inequalities between the hills and the forming of paved streets throughout the city, the result, possibly, more of the adoption of an easy method of disposing of the quantities of broken limestone than by any real necessity for pavements.

There were people moving about within the city and upon the narrow ledges and terraces that broke the lines of the buildings and which seemed to be a peculiarity of Ho-don architec-ture, a concession, no doubt, to some inherent instinct that might be traced back to their early cliff-dwelling progenitors.

Tarzan was not surprised that at a short distance he aroused no suspicion or curiosity in the minds of those who saw him, since, until closer scrutiny was possible, there was little to distinguish him from a native either in his general conformation or his color. He had, of course, formulated a plan of action and, having decided, he did not hesitate in the carrying out of his plan.

With the same assurance that you might venture upon the main street of a neighboring city Tarzan strode into the Ho-don city of A-lur. The first person to detect his spuriousness was a little child playing in the arched gateway of one of the walled buildings. "No tail! no tail!" it shouted, throwing a stone at him, and then it suddenly grew dumb and its eyes wide as it sensed that this creature was something other than a mere Ho-don warrior who had lost his tail. With a gasp the child turned and fled screaming into the courtyard of its home.

Tarzan continued on his way, fully realizing that the moment was imminent when the fate of his plan would be decided. Nor had he long to wait since at the next turning of the winding street he came face to face with a Ho-don warrior. He saw the sudden surprise in the latter's eyes, followed instantly by one of suspicion, but before the fellow could speak Tarzan addressed him.

"I am a stranger from another land," he said; "I would speak with Ko-tan, your king."

The fellow stepped back, laying his hand upon his knife. "There are no strangers that come to the gates of A-lur," he said, "other than as enemies or slaves."

"I come neither as a slave nor an enemy," replied Tarzan. "I come directly from Jad-ben-Otho. Look!" and he held out his hands that the Ho-don might see how greatly they differed from his own, and then wheeled about that the other might see that he was tailless, for it was upon this fact that his plan had been based, due to his recollection of the quarrel between Ta-den and Om-at, in which the Waz-don had claimed that Jad-ben-Otho had a long tail while the Ho-don had been equally willing to fight for his faith in the taillessness of his god.

The warrior's eyes widened and an expression of awe crept into them, though it was still tinged with suspicion. "Jad-ben-Otho!" he murmured, and then, "It is true that you are neither Ho-don nor Waz-don, and it is also true that Jad-ben-Otho has no tail. Come," he said, "I will take you to Ko-tan, for this is a matter in which no common warrior may interfere. Follow me," and still clutching the handle of his knife and keeping a wary side glance upon the ape-man he led the way through A-lur.

The city covered a large area. Sometimes there was a considerable distance between groups of buildings, and again they were quite close together. There were numerous imposing groups, evidently hewn from the larger hills, often rising to a height of a hundred feet or more. As they advanced they met numerous warriors and women, all of whom showed great curiosity in the stranger, but there was no attempt to menace him when it was found that he was being conducted to the palace of the king.

They came at last to a great pile that sprawled over a considerable area, its western front facing upon a large blue lake and evidently hewn from what had once been a natural cliff. This group of buildings was surrounded by a wall of considerably greater height than any that Tarzan had before seen. His guide led him to a gateway before which waited a dozen or more warriors who had risen to their feet and formed a barrier across the entrance-way as Tarzan and his party appeared around the corner of the palace wall, for by this time he had accumulated such a following of the curious as presented to the guards the appearance of a formidable mob.

The guide's story told, Tarzan was conducted into the courtyard where he was held while one of the warriors entered the palace, evidently with the intention of notifying Ko-tan. Fifteen minutes later a large warrior appeared, followed by several others, all of whom examined Tarzan with every sign of curiosity as they approached.

The leader of the party halted before the ape-man. "Who are you?" he asked, "and what do you want of Ko-tan, the king?"

"I am a friend," replied the ape-man, "and I have come from the country of Jad-ben-Otho to visit Ko-tan of Pal-ul-don."

The warrior and his followers seemed impressed. Tarzan could see the latter whispering among themselves.

"How come you here," asked the spokesman, "and what do you want of Ko-tan?"

Tarzan drew himself to his full height. "Enough!" he cried. "Must the messenger of Jad-ben-Otho be subjected to the treatment that might be accorded to a wandering Waz-don? Take me to the king at once lest the wrath of Jad-ben-Otho fall upon you."

There was some question in the mind of the ape-man as to how far he might carry his unwarranted show of assurance, and he waited therefore with amused interest the result of his demand. He did not, however, have long to wait for almost immediately the attitude of his questioner changed. He whitened, cast an apprehensive glance toward the eastern sky and then extended his right palm toward Tarzan, placing his left over his own heart in the sign of amity that was common among the peoples of Pal-ul-don.

Tarzan stepped quickly back as though from a profaning hand, a feigned expression of horror and disgust upon his face.

"Stop!" he cried, "who would dare touch the sacred person of the messenger of Jad-ben-Otho? Only as a special mark of favor from Jad-ben-Otho may even Ko-tan himself receive this honor from me. Hasten! Already now have I waited too long! What manner of reception the Ho-don of A-lur would extend to the son of my father!"

At first Tarzan had been inclined to adopt the rôle of Jad-ben-Otho himself but it occurred to him that it might prove embarrassing and considerable of a bore to be compelled constantly to portray the character of a god, but with the growing success of his scheme it had suddenly occurred to him that the authority of the son of Jad-ben-Otho would be far greater than that of an ordinary messenger of a god, while at the same time giving him some leeway in the matter of his acts and demeanor, the ape-man reasoning that a young god would not be held so strictly accountable in the matter of his dignity and bearing as an older and greater god.

This time the effect of his words was immediately and painfully noticeable upon all those near him. With one accord they shrank back, the spokesman almost collapsing in evident terror. His apologies, when finally the paralysis of his fear would permit him to voice them, were so abject that the ape-man could scarce repress a smile of amused contempt.

"Have mercy, O Dor-ul-Otho," he pleaded, "on poor old Dak-lot. Precede me and I will show you to where Ko-tan, the king, awaits you, trembling. Aside, snakes and vermin," he cried pushing his warriors to right and left for the purpose of forming an avenue for Tarzan.

"Come!" cried the ape-man peremptorily, "lead the way, and let these others follow."

The now thoroughly frightened Dak-lot did as he was bid, and Tarzan of the Apes was ushered into the palace of Ko-tan, King of Pal-ul-don.

IX
BLOOD-STAINED ALTARS

The entrance through which he caught his first glimpse of the interior was rather beautifully carved in geometric designs, and within the walls were similarly treated, though as he proceeded from one apartment to another he found also the figures of animals, birds, and men taking their places among the more formal figures of the mural decorator's art. Stone vessels were much in evidence as well as ornaments of gold and the skins of many animals, but nowhere did he see an indication of any woven fabric, indicating that in that respect at least the Ho-don were still low in the scale of evolution, and yet the proportions and symmetry of the corridors and apartments bespoke a degree of civilization.

The way led through several apartments and long corridors, up at least three flights of stone stairs and finally out upon a ledge upon the western side of the building overlooking the blue lake. Along this ledge, or arcade, his guide led him for a hundred yards, to stop at last before a wide entrance-way leading into another apartment of the palace.

Here Tarzan beheld a considerable concourse of warriors in an enormous apartment, the domed ceiling of which was fully fifty feet above the floor. Almost filling the chamber was a great pyramid ascending in broad steps well up under the dome in which were a number of round apertures which let in the light. The steps of the pyramid were occupied by warriors to the very pinnacle, upon which sat a large, imposing figure of a man whose golden trappings shone brightly in the light of the afternoon sun, a shaft of which poured through one of the tiny apertures of the dome.

"Ko-tan!" cried Dak-lot, addressing the resplendent figure at the pinnacle of the pyramid. "Ko-tan and warriors of Pal-ul-don! Behold the honor that Jad-ben-Otho has done you in sending as his messenger his own son," and Dak-lot, stepping aside, indicated Tarzan with a dramatic sweep of his hand.

Ko-tan rose to his feet and every warrior within sight craned his neck to have a better view of the newcomer. Those upon the opposite side of the pyramid crowded to the front as the words of the old warrior reached them. Skeptical were the expressions on most of the faces; but theirs was a skepticism marked with caution. No matter which way fortune jumped they wished to be upon the right side of the fence. For a moment all eyes were centered upon Tarzan and then gradually they drifted to Ko-tan, for from his attitude would they receive the cue that would determine theirs. But Ko-tan was evidently in the same quandary as they—the very attitude of his body indicated it—it was one of indecision and of doubt.

The ape-man stood erect, his arms folded upon his broad breast, an expression of haughty disdain upon his handsome face; but to Dak-lot there seemed to be indications also of growing anger. The situation was becoming strained. Dak-lot fidgeted, casting apprehensive glances at Tarzan and appealing ones at Ko-tan. The silence of the tomb wrapped the great chamber of the throneroom of Pal-ul-don.

At last Ko-tan spoke. "Who says that he is Dor-ul-Otho?" he asked, casting a terrible look at Dak-lot.

"He does!" almost shouted that terrified noble.

"And so it must be true?" queried Ko-tan.

Could it be that there was a trace of irony in the chief's tone? Otho forbid! Dak-lot cast a side glance at Tarzan—a glance that he intended should carry the assurance of his own faith; but that succeeded only in impressing the ape-man with the other's pitiable terror.

"O Ko-tan!" pleaded Dak-lot, "your own eyes must convince you that indeed he is the son of Otho. Behold his godlike figure, his hands, and his feet, that are not as ours, and that he is entirely tailless as is his mighty father."

Ko-tan appeared to be perceiving these facts for the first time and there was an indication that his skepticism was faltering. At that moment a young warrior who had pushed his way forward from the opposite side of the pyramid to where he could obtain a good look at Tarzan raised his voice.

"Ko-tan," he cried, "it must be even as Dak-lot says, for I am sure now that I have seen Dor-ul-Otho before. Yesterday as we were returning with the Kor-ul-lul prisoners we beheld him seated upon the back of a great *gryf*. We hid in the woods before he came too near, but I saw enough to make sure that he who rode upon the great beast was none other than the messenger who stands here now."

This evidence seemed to be quite enough to convince the majority of the warriors that they indeed stood in the presence of deity—their faces showed it only too plainly, and a sudden modesty that caused them to shrink behind their neighbors. As their neighbors were attempting to do the same thing, the result was a sudden melting away of those who stood nearest the ape-man, until the steps of the pyramid directly before him lay vacant to the very apex and to Ko-tan. The latter, possibly influenced as much by the fearful attitude of his followers as by the evidence adduced, now altered his tone and his manner in such a degree as might comport with the requirements if the stranger was indeed the Dor-ul-Otho while leaving his dignity a loophole of escape should it appear that he had entertained an impostor.

"If indeed you are the Dor-ul-Otho," he said, addressing Tarzan, "you will know that our doubts were but natural since we have received no sign from Jad-ben-Otho that he intended honoring us so greatly, nor how could we know, even, that the Great God had a son? If you are he, all Pal-ul-don rejoices to honor you; if you are not he, swift and terrible shall be the punishment of your temerity. I, Ko-tan, King of Pal-ul-don, have spoken."

"And spoken well, as a king should speak," said Tarzan, breaking his long silence, "who fears and honors the god of his people. It is well that you insist that I indeed be the Dor-ul-Otho before you accord me the homage that is my due. Jad-ben-Otho charged me specially to ascertain if you were fit to rule his people. My first experience of you indicates that Jad-ben-Otho chose well when he breathed the spirit of a king into the babe at your mother's breast."

The effect of this statement, made so casually, was marked in the expressions and excited whispers of the now awe-struck assemblage. At last they knew how kings were made! It was decided by Jad-ben-Otho while the candidate was still a suckling babe! Wonderful! A miracle! and this divine creature in whose presence they stood knew all about it. Doubtless he even discussed such matters with their god daily. If there had been an atheist among them before, or an agnostic, there was none now, for had they not looked with their own eyes upon the son of god?

"It is well then," continued the ape-man, "that you should assure yourself that I am no impostor. Come closer that you may see that I am not as are men. Furthermore it is not meet that you stand upon a higher level than the son of your god." There was a sudden scramble to reach the floor of the throneroom, nor was Ko-tan far behind his warriors, though he managed to maintain a certain majestic dignity as he descended the broad stairs that countless naked feet had polished to a gleaming smoothness through the ages. "And now," said Tarzan as the king stood before him, "you can have no doubt that I am not of the same race as you. Your priests have told you that Jad-ben-Otho is tailless. Tailless, therefore, must be the race of gods that spring from his loins. But enough of such proofs as these! You know the power of Jad-ben-Otho; how his lightnings gleaming out of the sky carry death as he wills it; how the rains come at his bidding, and the fruits and the berries and the grains, the grasses, the trees and the flowers spring to life at his divine direction; you have witnessed birth and death, and those who honor their god honor him because he controls these things. How would it fare then with an impostor who claimed to be the son of this all-powerful god? This then is all the proof that you require, for as he would strike you down should you deny me, so would he strike down one who wrongfully claimed kinship with him."

This line of argument being unanswerable must needs be convincing. There could be no questioning of this creature's statements without the tacit admission of lack of faith in the omnipotence of Jad-ben-Otho. Ko-tan was satisfied that he was entertaining deity, but as to just what form his entertainment should take he was rather at a loss to know. His conception of god had been rather a vague and hazy affair, though in common with all primitive people his god was a personal one as were his devils and demons. The pleasures of Jad-ben-Otho he had assumed to be

the excesses which he himself enjoyed, but devoid of any unpleasant reaction. It therefore occurred to him that the Dor-ul-Otho would be greatly entertained by eating—eating large quantities of everything that Ko-tan liked best and that he had found most injurious; and there was also a drink that the women of the Ho-don made by allowing corn to soak in the juices of succulent fruits, to which they had added certain other ingredients best known to themselves. Ko-tan knew by experience that a single draught of this potent liquor would bring happiness and surcease from worry, while several would cause even a king to do things and enjoy things that he would never even think of doing or enjoying while not under the magical influence of the potion, but unfortunately the next morning brought suffering in direct ratio to the joy of the preceding day. A god, Ko-tan reasoned, could experience all the pleasure without the headache, but for the immediate present he must think of the necessary dignities and honors to be accorded his immortal guest.

No foot other than a king's had touched the surface of the apex of the pyramid in the throneroom at A-lur during all the forgotten ages through which the kings of Pal-ul-don had ruled from its high eminence. So what higher honor could Ko-tan offer than to give place beside him to the Dor-ul-Otho? And so he invited Tarzan to ascend the pyramid and take his place upon the stone bench that topped it. As they reached the step below the sacred pinnacle Ko-tan continued as though to mount to his throne, but Tarzan laid a detaining hand upon his arm.

"None may sit upon a level with the gods," he admonished, stepping confidently up and seating himself upon the throne. The abashed Ko-tan showed his embarrassment, an embarrassment he feared to voice lest he incur the wrath of the king of kings.

"But," added Tarzan, "a god may honor his faithful servant by inviting him to a place at his side. Come, Ko-tan; thus would I honor you in the name of Jad-ben-Otho."

The ape-man's policy had for its basis an attempt not only to arouse the fearful respect of Ko-tan but to do it without making of him an enemy at heart, for he did not know how strong a hold the religion of the Ho-don had upon them, for since the time that he had prevented Ta-den and Om-at from quarreling over a religious difference the subject had been utterly taboo among them. He was therefore quick to note the evident though wordless resentment of Ko-tan at the suggestion that he entirely relinquish his throne to his guest. On the whole, however, the effect had been satisfactory as he could see from the renewed evidence of awe upon the faces of the warriors.

At Tarzan's direction the business of the court continued where it had been interrupted by his advent. It consisted principally in the settling of disputes between warriors. There was present one who stood upon the step just below the throne and which Tarzan was to learn was the place reserved for the higher chiefs of the allied tribes which made up Ko-tan's kingdom. The one who attracted Tarzan's attention was a stalwart warrior of powerful physique and massive, lion-like features. He was addressing Ko-tan on a question that is as old as government and that will continue in unabated importance until man ceases to exist. It had to do with a boundary dispute with one of his neighbors.

The matter itself held little or no interest for Tarzan, but he was impressed by the appearance of the speaker and when Ko-tan addressed him as Ja-don the ape-man's interest was permanently crystallized, for Ja-don was the father of Ta-den. That the knowledge would benefit him in any way seemed rather a remote possibility since he could not reveal to Ja-don his friendly relations with his son without admitting the falsity of his claims to godship.

When the affairs of the audience were concluded Ko-tan suggested that the son of Jad-ben-Otho might wish to visit the temple in which were performed the religious rites coincident to the worship of the Great God. And so the ape-man was conducted by the king himself, followed by the warriors of his court, through the corridors of the palace toward the northern end of the group of buildings within the royal enclosure.

The temple itself was really a part of the palace and similar in architecture. There were several ceremonial places of varying sizes, the purposes of which Tarzan could only conjecture. Each had an altar in the west end and another in the east and were oval in shape, their longest diameter lying due east and west. Each was excavated from the summit of a small hillock and all were without roofs. The western altars invariably were a single block of stone the top of which was hollowed into an oblong basin. Those at the eastern ends were similar blocks of stone with flat tops and these latter, unlike those at the opposite ends of the ovals were invariably stained or painted a reddish brown, nor did Tarzan need to examine them closely to be assured of what his keen nostrils already had told him—that the brown stains were dried and drying human blood.

Below these temple courts were corridors and apartments reaching far into the bowels of the hills, dim, gloomy passages that Tarzan glimpsed as he was led from place to place on his tour of inspection of the temple. A messenger had been dispatched by Ko-tan to announce the coming visit of the son of Jad-ben-Otho with the result that they were accompanied through the temple by a considerable procession of priests whose distinguishing mark of profession seemed to consist in grotesque headdresses; sometimes hideous faces carved from wood and entirely concealing the countenances of their wearers; or again, the head of a wild beast cunningly fitted over the head of a man. The high priest alone wore no such headdress. He was an old man with close-set, cunning eyes and a cruel, thin-lipped mouth.

At first sight of him Tarzan realized that here lay the greatest danger to his ruse, for he saw at a glance that the man was antagonistic toward him and his pretensions, and he knew too that doubtless of all the people of Pal-ul-don the high priest was most likely to harbor the truest estimate of Jad-ben-Otho, and, therefore, would look with suspicion on one who claimed to be the son of a fabulous god.

No matter what suspicion lurked within his crafty mind, Lu-don, the high priest of A-lur, did not openly question Tarzan's right to the title of Dor-ul-Otho, and it may be that he was restrained by the same doubts which had originally restrained Ko-tan and his warriors—the doubt that is at the bottom of the minds of all blasphemers even and which is based upon the fear that after all there may be a god. So, for the time being at least Lu-don played safe. Yet Tarzan knew as well as though the man had spoken aloud his inmost thoughts that it was in the heart of the high priest to tear the veil from his imposture.

At the entrance to the temple Ko-tan had relinquished the guidance of the guest to Lu-don and now the latter led Tarzan through those portions of the temple that he wished him to see. He showed him the great room where the votive offerings were kept, gifts from the barbaric chiefs of Pal-ul-don and from their followers. These things ranged in value from presents of dried fruits to massive vessels of beaten gold, so that in the great main storeroom and its connecting chambers and corridors was an accumulation of wealth that amazed even the eyes of the owner of the secret of the treasure vaults of Opar.

Moving to and fro throughout the temple were sleek black Waz-don slaves, fruits of the Ho-don raids upon the villages of their less civilized neighbors. As they passed the barred entrance to a dim corridor, Tarzan saw within a great company of pithecanthropi of all ages and of both sexes, Ho-don as well as Waz-don, the majority of them squatted upon the stone floor in attitudes of utter dejection while some paced back and forth, their features stamped with the despair of utter hopelessness.

"And who are these who lie here thus unhappily?" he asked of Lu-don. It was the first question that he had put to the high priest since entering the temple, and instantly he regretted

that he had asked it, for Lu-don turned upon him a face upon which the expression of suspicion was but thinly veiled.

"Who should know better than the son of Jad-ben-Otho?" he retorted.

"The questions of Dor-ul-Otho are not with impunity answered with other questions," said the ape-man quietly, "and it may interest Lu-don, the high priest, to know that the blood of a false priest upon the altar of his temple is not displeasing in the eyes of Jad-ben-Otho."

Lu-don paled as he answered Tarzan's question. "They are the offerings whose blood must refresh the eastern altars as the sun returns to your father at the day's end."

"And who told you," asked Tarzan, "that Jad-ben-Otho was pleased that his people were slain upon his altars? What if you were mistaken?"

"Then countless thousands have died in vain," replied Lu-don.

Ko-tan and the surrounding warriors and priests were listening attentively to the dialogue. Some of the poor victims behind the barred gateway had heard and rising, pressed close to the barrier through which one was conducted just before sunset each day, never to return.

"Liberate them!" cried Tarzan with a wave of his hand toward the imprisoned victims of a cruel superstition, "for I can tell you in the name of Jad-ben-Otho that you are mistaken."

X

THE FORBIDDEN GARDEN

Lu-don paled. "It is sacrilege," he cried; "for countless ages have the priests of the Great God offered each night a life to the spirit of Jad-ben-Otho as it returned below the western horizon to its master, and never has the Great God given sign that he was displeased."

"Stop!" commanded Tarzan. "It is the blindness of the priesthood that has failed to read the messages of their god. Your warriors die beneath the knives and clubs of the Waz-don; your hunters are taken by *ja* and *jato;* no day goes by but witnesses the deaths of few or many in the villages of the Ho-don, and one death each day of those that die is the toll which Jad-ben-Otho has exacted for the lives you take upon the eastern altar. What greater sign of his displeasure could you require, O stupid priest?"

Lu-don was silent. There was raging within him a great conflict between his fear that this indeed might be the son of god and his hope that it was not, but at last his fear won and he bowed his head. "The son of Jad-ben-Otho has spoken," he said, and turning to one of the lesser priests: "Remove the bars and return these people from whence they came."

He thus addressed did as he was bid and as the bars came down the prisoners, now all fully aware of the miracle that had saved them, crowded forward and throwing themselves upon their knees before Tarzan raised their voices in thanksgiving.

Ko-tan was almost as staggered as the high priest by this ruthless overturning of an age-old religious rite. "But what," he cried, "may we do that will be pleasing in the eyes of Jad-ben-Otho?" turning a look of puzzled apprehension toward the ape-man.

"If you seek to please your god," he replied, "place upon your altars such gifts of food and apparel as are most welcome in the city of your people. These things will Jad-ben-Otho bless, when you may distribute them among those of the city who need them most. With such things are your storerooms filled as I have seen with mine own eyes, and other gifts will be brought when the priests tell the people that in this way they find favor before their god," and Tarzan turned and signified that he would leave the temple.

As they were leaving the precincts devoted to the worship of their deity, the ape-man noticed a small but rather ornate building that stood entirely detached from the others as though it had been cut from a little pinnacle of limestone which had stood out from its fellows. As his interested glance passed over it he noticed that its door and windows were barred.

"To what purpose is that building dedicated?" he asked of Lu-don. "Who do you keep imprisoned there?"

"It is nothing," replied the high priest nervously, "there is no one there. The place is vacant. Once it was used but not now for many years," and he moved on toward the gateway which led back into the palace. Here he and the priests halted while Tarzan with Ko-tan and his warriors passed out from the sacred precincts of the temple grounds.

The one question which Tarzan would have asked he had feared to ask for he knew that in the hearts of many lay a suspicion as to his genuineness, but he determined that before he slept he would put the question to Ko-tan, either directly or indirectly—as to whether there was, or had been recently within the city of A-lur a female of the same race as his.

As their evening meal was being served to them in the banquet hall of Ko-tan's palace by a part of the army of black slaves upon whose shoulders fell the burden of all the heavy and menial tasks of the city, Tarzan noticed that there came to the eyes of one of the slaves what was apparently an expression of startled recognition, as he looked upon the ape-man for the first time in the banquet hall of Ko-tan. And again later he saw the fellow whisper to another slave and nod his head in his direction. The ape-man did not recall ever having seen this Waz-don before and he was at a loss to account for an explanation of the fellow's interest in him, and presently the incident was all but forgotten.

Ko-tan was surprised and inwardly disgusted to discover that his godly guest had no desire to gorge himself upon rich foods and that he would not even so much as taste the villainous brew of the Ho-don. To Tarzan the banquet was a dismal and tiresome affair, since so great was the interest of the guests in gorging themselves with food and drink that they had no time for conversation, the only vocal sounds being confined to a continuous grunting which, together with their table manners reminded Tarzan of a visit he had once made to the famous Berkshire herd of His Grace, the Duke of Westminster at Woodhouse, Chester.

One by one the diners succumbed to the stupefying effects of the liquor with the result that the grunting gave place to snores, so presently Tarzan and the slaves were the only conscious creatures in the banquet hall.

Rising, the ape-man turned to a tall black who stood behind him. "I would sleep," he said, "show me to my apartment."

As the fellow conducted him from the chamber the slave who had shown surprise earlier in the evening at sight of him, spoke again at length to one of his fellows. The latter cast a half-frightened look in the direction of the departing ape-man. "If you are right," he said, "they should reward us with our liberty, but if you are wrong, O Jad-ben-Otho, what will be our fate?"

"But I am not wrong!" cried the other.

"Then there is but one to tell this to, for I have heard that he looked sour when this Dor-ul-Otho was brought to the temple and that while the so-called son of Jad-ben-Otho was there he gave this one every cause to fear and hate him. I mean Lu-don, the high priest."

"You know him?" asked the other slave.

"I have worked in the temple," replied his companion.

"Then go to him at once and tell him, but be sure to exact the promise of our freedom for the proof."

And so a black Waz-don came to the temple gate and asked to see Lu-don, the high priest, on a matter of great importance, and though the hour was late Lu-don saw him, and when he had heard his story he promised him and his friend not only their freedom but many gifts if they could prove the correctness of their claims.

And as the slave talked with the high priest in the temple at A-lur the figure of a man groped its way around the shoulder of Pastar-ul-ved and the moonlight glistened from the shiny barrel of an Enfield that was strapped to the naked back, and brass cartridges shed tiny rays of reflected light from their polished cases where they hung in the bandoliers across the broad brown shoulders and the lean waist.

Tarzan's guide conducted him to a chamber overlooking the blue lake where he found a bed similar to that which he had seen in the villages of the Waz-don, merely a raised dais of stone upon which was piled great quantities of furry pelts. And so he lay down to sleep, the question that he most wished to put still unasked and unanswered.

With the coming of a new day he was awake and wandering about the palace and the palace grounds before there was sign of any of the inmates of the palace other than slaves, or at least he saw no others at first, though presently he stumbled upon an enclosure which lay almost within the center of the palace grounds surrounded by a wall that piqued the ape-man's curiosity, since he had determined to investigate as fully as possible every part of the palace and its environs.

This place, whatever it might be, was apparently without doors or windows but that it was at least partially roofless was evidenced by the sight of the waving branches of a tree which spread above the top of the wall near him. Finding no other method of access, the ape-man uncoiled his rope and throwing it over the branch of the tree where it projected beyond the wall, was soon climbing with the ease of a monkey to the summit.

There he found that the wall surrounded an enclosed garden in which grew trees and shrubs and flowers in riotous profusion. Without waiting to ascertain whether the garden was empty or contained Ho-don, Waz-don, or wild beasts, Tarzan dropped lightly to the sward on the inside and without further loss of time commenced a systematic investigation of the enclosure.

His curiosity was aroused by the very evident

fact that the place was not for general use, even by those who had free access to other parts of the palace grounds and so there was added to its natural beauties an absence of mortals which rendered its exploration all the more alluring to Tarzan since it suggested that in such a place might he hope to come upon the object of his long and difficult search.

In the garden were tiny artificial streams and little pools of water, flanked by flowering bushes, as though it all had been designed by the cunning hand of some master gardener, so faithfully did it carry out the beauties and contours of nature upon a miniature scale.

The interior surface of the wall was fashioned to represent the white cliffs of Pal-ul-don, broken occasionally by small replicas of the verdure-filled gorges of the original.

Filled with admiration and thoroughly enjoying each new surprise which the scene offered, Tarzan moved slowly around the garden, and as always he moved silently. Passing through a miniature forest he came presently upon a tiny area of flower-studded sward and at the same time beheld before him the first Ho-don female he had seen since entering the palace. A young and beautiful woman stood in the center of the little open space, stroking the head of a bird which she held against her golden breastplate with one hand. Her profile was presented to the ape-man and he saw that by the standards of any land she would have been accounted more than lovely.

Seated in the grass at her feet, with her back toward him, was a female Waz-don slave. Seeing that she he sought was not there and apprehensive that an alarm be raised were he discovered by the two women, Tarzan moved back to hide himself in the foliage, but before he had succeeded the Ho-don girl turned quickly toward him as though apprised of his presence by that unnamed sense, the manifestations of which are more or less familiar to us all.

At sight of him her eyes registered only her surprise though there was no expression of terror reflected in them, nor did she scream or even raise her well-modulated voice as she addressed him.

"Who are you," she asked, "who enters thus boldly the Forbidden Garden?"

At sound of her mistress's voice the slave maiden turned quickly, rising to her feet. "Tarzan-jad-guru!" she exclaimed in tones of mingled astonishment and relief.

"You know him?" cried her mistress turning toward the slave and affording Tarzan an opportunity to raise a cautioning finger to his lips lest Pan-at-lee further betray him, for it was Pan-at-lee indeed who stood before him, no less a source of surprise to him than had his presence been to her.

Thus questioned by her mistress and simultaneously admonished to silence by Tarzan, Pan-at-lee was momentarily silenced and then haltingly she groped for a way to extricate herself from her dilemma. "I thought—" she faltered, "but no, I am mistaken—I thought that he was one whom I had seen before near the Kor-ul-gryf."

The Ho-don looked first at one and then at the other, an expression of doubt and questioning in her eyes. "But you have not answered me," she continued presently; "who are you?"

"You have not heard then," asked Tarzan, "of the visitor who arrived at your king's court yesterday?"

"You mean," she exclaimed, "that you are the Dor-ul-Otho?" And now the erstwhile doubting eyes reflected naught but awe.

"I am he," replied Tarzan; "and you?"

"I am O-lo-a, daughter of Ko-tan, the king," she replied.

So this was O-lo-a, for love of whom Ta-den had chosen exile rather than priesthood. Tarzan had approached more closely the dainty barbarian princess. "Daughter of Ko-tan," he said, "Jad-ben-Otho is pleased with you and as a mark of his favor he has preserved for you through many dangers him whom you love."

"I do not understand," replied the girl but the flush that mounted to her cheek belied her words. "Bu-lat is a guest in the palace of Ko-tan, my father. I do not know that he has faced any danger. It is to Bu-lat that I am betrothed."

"But it is not Bu-lat whom you love," said Tarzan.

Again the flush and the girl half turned her face away. "Have I then displeased the Great God?" she asked.

"No," replied Tarzan; "as I told you he is well satisfied and for your sake he has saved Ta-den for you."

"Jad-ben-Otho knows all," whispered the girl, "and his son shares his great knowledge."

"No," Tarzan hastened to correct her lest a reputation for omniscience might prove embarrassing. "I know only what Jad-ben-Otho wishes me to know."

"But tell me," she said, "I shall be reunited with Ta-den? Surely the son of god can read the future."

The ape-man was glad that he had left himself an avenue of escape. "I know nothing of the future," he replied, "other than what Jad-ben-Otho tells me. But I think you need have no fear for the future if you remain faithful to Ta-den and Ta-den's friends."

"You have seen him?" asked O-lo-a. "Tell me, where is he?"

"Yes," replied Tarzan, "I have seen him. He was with Om-at, the *gund* of Kor-ul-ja."

"A prisoner of the Waz-don?" interrupted the girl.

"Not a prisoner but an honored guest," replied the ape-man.

"Wait," he exclaimed, raising his face toward the heavens; "do not speak. I am receiving a message from Jad-ben-Otho, my father."

The two women dropped to their knees, covering their faces with their hands, stricken with awe at the thought of the awful nearness of the Great God. Presently Tarzan touched O-lo-a on the shoulder.

"Rise," he said. "Jad-ben-Otho has spoken. He has told me that this slave girl is from the tribe of Kor-ul-ja, where Ta-den is, and that she is betrothed to Om-at, their chief. Her name is Pan-at-lee."

O-lo-a turned questioningly toward Pan-at-lee. The latter nodded, her simple mind unable to determine whether or not she and her mistress were the victims of a colossal hoax. "It is even as he says," she whispered.

O-lo-a fell upon her knees and touched her forehead to Tarzan's feet. "Great is the honor that Jad-ben-Otho has done his poor servant," she cried. "Carry to him my poor thanks for the happiness that he has brought to O-lo-a."

"It would please my father," said Tarzan, "if you were to cause Pan-at-lee to be returned in safety to the village of her people."

"What cares Jad-ben-Otho for such as she?" asked O-lo-a, a slight trace of hauteur in her tone.

"There is but one god," replied Tarzan, "and he is the god of the Waz-don as well as of the Ho-don; of the birds and the beasts and the flowers and of everything that grows upon the earth or beneath the waters. If Pan-at-lee does right she is greater in the eyes of Jad-ben-Otho than would be the daughter of Ko-tan should she do wrong."

It was evident that O-lo-a did not quite understand this interpretation of divine favor, so contrary was it to the teachings of the priesthood of her people. In one respect only did Tarzan's teachings coincide with her belief—that there was but one god. For the rest she had always been taught that he was solely the god of the Ho-don in every sense, other than that other creatures were created by Jad-ben-Otho to serve some useful purpose for the benefit of the Ho-don race. And now to be told by the son of god that she stood no higher in divine esteem than the black handmaiden at her side was indeed a shock to her pride, her vanity, and her faith. But who could question the word of Dor-ul-Otho, especially when she had with her own eyes seen him in actual communion with god in heaven?

"The will of Jad-ben-Otho be done," said O-lo-a meekly, "if it lies within my power. But it would be best, O Dor-ul-Otho, to communicate your father's wish directly to the king."

"Then keep her with you," said Tarzan, "and see that no harm befalls her."

O-lo-a looked ruefully at Pan-at-lee. "She

was brought to me but yesterday," she said, "and never have I had slave woman who pleased me better. I shall hate to part with her."

"But there are others," said Tarzan.

"Yes," replied O-lo-a, "there are others, but there is only one Pan-at-lee."

"Many slaves are brought to the city?" asked Tarzan.

"Yes," she replied.

"And many strangers come from other lands?" he asked.

She shook her head negatively. "Only the Ho-don from the other side of the Valley of Jad-ben-Otho," she replied, "and they are not strangers."

"Am I then the first stranger to enter the gates of A-lur?" he asked.

"Can it be," she parried, "that the son of Jad-ben-Otho need question a poor ignorant mortal like O-lo-a?"

"As I told you before," replied Tarzan, "Jad-ben-Otho alone is all-knowing."

"Then if he wished you to know this thing," retorted O-lo-a quickly, "you would know it."

Inwardly the ape-man smiled that this little heathen's astuteness should beat him at his own game, yet in a measure her evasion of the question might be an answer to it.

"There have been other strangers here then recently?" he persisted.

"I cannot tell you what I do not know," she replied. "Always is the palace of Ko-tan filled with rumors, but how much fact and how much fancy how may a woman of the palace know?"

"There has been such a rumor then?" he asked.

"It was only rumor that reached the Forbidden Garden," she replied.

"It described, perhaps, a woman of another race?" As he put the question and awaited her answer he thought that his heart ceased to beat, so grave to him was the issue at stake.

The girl hesitated before replying, and then: "No," she said, "I cannot speak of this thing, for if it be of sufficient importance to elicit the interest of the gods then indeed would I be subject to the wrath of my father should I discuss it."

"In the name of Jad-ben-Otho I command you to speak," said Tarzan. "In the name of Jad-ben-Otho in whose hands lies the fate of Ta-den!"

The girl paled. "Have mercy!" she cried, "and for the sake of Ta-den I will tell you all that I know."

"Tell what?" demanded a stern voice from the shrubbery behind them. The three turned to see the figure of Ko-tan emerging from the foliage. An angry scowl distorted his kingly features but at sight of Tarzan it gave place to an expression of surprise not unmixed with fear. "Dor-ul-Otho!" he exclaimed, "I did not know that it was you," and then, raising his head and squaring his shoulders he said, "but there are places where even the son of the Great God may not walk and this, the Forbidden Garden of Ko-tan, is one."

It was a challenge but despite the king's bold front there was a note of apology in it, indicating that in his superstitious mind there flourished the inherent fear of man for his Maker. "Come, Dor-ul-Otho," he continued, "I do not know all this foolish child has said to you but whatever you would know Ko-tan, the king, will tell you. O-lo-a, go to your quarters immediately," and he pointed with stern finger toward the opposite end of the garden.

The princess, followed by Pan-at-lee, turned at once and left them.

"We will go this way," said Ko-tan and preceding, led Tarzan in another direction. Close to that part of the wall which they approached Tarzan perceived a grotto in the miniature cliff into the interior of which Ko-tan led him, and down a rocky stairway to a gloomy corridor the opposite end of which opened into the palace proper. Two armed warriors stood at this entrance to the Forbidden Garden, evidencing how jealously were the sacred precincts of the place guarded.

In silence Ko-tan led the way back to his own quarters in the palace. A large chamber just outside the room toward which Ko-tan was leading his guest was filled with chiefs and warriors awaiting the pleasure of their ruler. As the two entered, an aisle was formed for them the length of the chamber, down which they passed in silence.

Close to the farther door and half hidden by the warriors who stood before him was Lu-don, the high priest. Tarzan glimpsed him but briefly but in that short period he was aware of a cunning and malevolent expression upon the cruel countenance that he was subconsciously aware boded him no good, and then with Ko-tan he passed into the adjoining room and the hangings dropped.

At the same moment the hideous headdress of an under priest appeared in the entrance of the outer chamber. Its owner, pausing for a moment, glanced quickly around the interior and then having located him whom he sought moved rapidly in the direction of Lu-don. There was a whispered conversation which was terminated by the high priest.

"Return immediately to the quarters of the princess," he said, "and see that the slave is sent to me at the temple at once." The under priest turned and departed upon his mission while Lu-don also left the apartment and directed his footsteps toward the sacred enclosure over which he ruled.

A half-hour later a warrior was ushered into the presence of Ko-tan. "Lu-don, the high priest, desires the presence of Ko-tan, the king, in the temple," he announced, "and it is his wish that he come alone."

Ko-tan nodded to indicate that he accepted the command which even the king must obey. "I will return presently, Dor-ul-Otho," he said to Tarzan, "and in the meantime my warriors and my slaves are yours to command."

XI
THE SENTENCE OF DEATH

But it was an hour before the king re-entered the apartment and in the meantime the ape-man had occupied himself in examining the carvings upon the walls and the numerous specimens of the handicraft of Pal-ul-donian artisans which combined to impart an atmosphere of richness and luxury to the apartment.

The limestone of the country, close-grained and of marble whiteness yet worked with comparative ease with crude implements, had been wrought by cunning craftsmen into bowls and urns and vases of considerable grace and beauty. Into the carved designs of many of these virgin gold had been hammered, presenting the effect of a rich and magnificent cloisonné. A barbarian himself the art of barbarians had always appealed to the ape-man to whom they represented a natural expression of man's love of the beautiful to even a greater extent than the studied and artificial efforts of civilization. Here was the real art of old masters, the other the cheap imitation of the chromo.

It was while he was thus pleasurably engaged that Ko-tan returned. As Tarzan, attracted by the movement of the hangings through which the king entered, turned and faced him he was almost shocked by the remarkable alteration of the king's appearance. His face was livid; his hands trembled as with palsy, and his eyes were wide as with fright. His appearance was one apparently of a combination of consuming anger and withering fear. Tarzan looked at him questioningly.

"You have had bad news, Ko-tan?" he asked.

The king mumbled an unintelligible reply. Behind there thronged into the apartment so great a number of warriors that they choked the entrance-way. The king looked apprehensively to right and left. He cast terrified glances at the ape-man and then raising his face and turning his eyes upward he cried: "Jad-ben-Otho be my witness that I do not this thing of my own accord." There was a moment's silence which was again broken by Ko-tan. "Seize him," he cried to the warriors about him, "for Lu-don, the high priest, swears that he is an impostor."

To have offered armed resistance to this great concourse of warriors in the very heart of the palace of their king would have been worse than fatal. Already Tarzan had come far by his wits and now that within a few hours he had had his hopes and his suspicions partially verified by the vague admissions of O-lo-a he was impressed with the necessity of inviting no mortal risk that he could avoid.

"Stop!" he cried, raising his palm against them. "What is the meaning of this?"

"Lu-don claims he has proof that you are not the son of Jad-ben-Otho," replied Ko-tan. "He demands that you be brought to the throne-room to face your accusers. If you are what you claim to be none knows better than you that you need have no fear in acquiescing to his demands, but remember always that in such matters the high priest commands the king and that I am only the bearer of these commands, not their author."

Tarzan saw that Ko-tan was not entirely convinced of his duplicity as was evidenced by his palpable design to play safe.

"Let not your warriors seize me," he said to Ko-tan, "lest Jad-ben-Otho, mistaking their intention, strike them dead." The effect of his words was immediate upon the men in the front rank of those who faced him, each seeming suddenly to acquire a new modesty that compelled him to self-effacement behind those directly in his rear—a modesty that became rapidly contagious.

The ape-man smiled. "Fear not," he said, "I will go willingly to the audience chamber to face the blasphemers who accuse me."

Arrived at the great throneroom a new complication arose. Ko-tan would not acknowledge the right of Lu-don to occupy the apex of the pyramid and Lu-don would not consent to occupying an inferior position while Tarzan, to remain consistent with his high claims, insisted that no one should stand above him, but only to the ape-man was the humor of the situation apparent.

To relieve the situation Ja-don suggested that all three of them occupy the throne, but this suggestion was repudiated by Ko-tan who argued that no mortal other than a king of Pal-ul-don

had ever sat upon the high eminence, and that furthermore there was not room for three there.

"But who," said Tarzan, "is my accuser and who is my judge?"

"Lu-don is your accuser," explained Ko-tan.

"And Lu-don is your judge," cried the high priest.

"I am to be judged by him who accuses me then," said Tarzan. "It were better to dispense then with any formalities and ask Lu-don to sentence me." His tone was ironical and his sneering face, looking straight into that of the high priest, but caused the latter's hatred to rise to still greater proportions.

It was evident that Ko-tan and his warriors saw the justice of Tarzan's implied objection to this unfair method of dispensing justice. "Only Ko-tan can judge in the throneroom of his palace," said Ja-don, "let him hear Lu-don's charges and the testimony of his witnesses, and then let Ko-tan's judgment be final."

Ko-tan, however, was not particularly enthusiastic over the prospect of sitting in trial upon one who might after all very possibly be the son of his god, and so he temporized, seeking for an avenue of escape. "It is purely a religious matter," he said, "and it is traditional that the kings of Pal-ul-don interfere not in questions of the church."

"Then let the trial be held in the temple," cried one of the chiefs, for the warriors were as anxious as their king to be relieved of all responsibility in the matter. This suggestion was more than satisfactory to the high priest who inwardly condemned himself for not having thought of it before.

"It is true," he said, "this man's sin is against the temple. Let him be dragged thither then for trial."

"The son of Jad-ben-Otho will be dragged nowhere," cried Tarzan. "But when this trial is over it is possible that the corpse of Lu-don, the high priest, will be dragged from the temple of the god he would desecrate. Think well, then, Lu-don before you commit this folly."

His words, intended to frighten the high

priest from his position failed utterly in consummating their purpose. Lu-don showed no terror at the suggestion the ape-man's words implied.

"Here is one," thought Tarzan, "who, knowing more of his religion than any of his fellows, realizes fully the falsity of my claims as he does the falsity of the faith he preaches."

He realized, however, that his only hope lay in seeming indifference to the charges. Ko-tan and the warriors were still under the spell of their belief in him and upon this fact must he depend in the final act of the drama that Lu-don was staging for his rescue from the jealous priest whom he knew had already passed sentence upon him in his own heart.

With a shrug he descended the steps of the pyramid. "It matters not to Dor-ul-Otho," he said, "where Lu-don enrages his god, for Jad-ben-Otho can reach as easily into the chambers of the temple as into the throneroom of Ko-tan."

Immeasurably relieved by this easy solution of their problem the king and the warriors thronged from the throneroom toward the temple grounds, their faith in Tarzan increased by his apparent indifference to the charges against him. Lu-don led them to the largest of the altar courts.

Taking his place behind the western altar he motioned Ko-tan to a place upon the platform at the left hand of the altar and directed Tarzan to a similar place at the right.

As Tarzan ascended the platform his eyes narrowed angrily at the sight which met them. The basin hollowed in the top of the altar was filled with water in which floated the naked corpse of a new-born babe. "What means this?" he cried angrily, turning upon Lu-don.

The latter smiled malevolently. "That you do not know," he replied, "is but added evidence of the falsity of your claim. He who poses as the son of god did not know that as the last rays of the setting sun flood the eastern altar of the temple the lifeblood of an adult reddens the white stone for the edification of Jad-ben-Otho, and that when the sun rises again from the body of its maker it looks first upon this western altar and

rejoices in the death of a new-born babe each day, the ghost of which accompanies it across the heavens by day as the ghost of the adult returns with it to Jad-ben-Otho at night.

"Even the little children of the Ho-don know these things, while he who claims to be the son of Jad-ben-Otho knows them not; and if this proof be not enough, there is more. Come, Waz-don," he cried, pointing to a tall slave who stood with a group of other blacks and priests on the temple floor at the left of the altar.

The fellow came forward fearfully. "Tell us what you know of this creature," cried Lu-don, pointing to Tarzan.

"I have seen him before," said the Waz-don. "I am of the tribe of Kor-ul-lul, and one day recently a party of which I was one encountered a few of the warriors of the Kor-ul-ja upon the ridge which separates our villages. Among the enemy was this strange creature whom they called Tarzan-jad-guru; and terrible indeed was he for he fought with the strength of many men so that it required twenty of us to subdue him. But he did not fight as a god fights, and when a club struck him upon the head he sank unconscious as might an ordinary mortal.

"We carried him with us to our village as a prisoner but he escaped after cutting off the head of the warrior we left to guard him and carrying it down into the gorge and tying it to the branch of a tree upon the opposite side."

"The word of a slave against that of a god!" cried Ja-don, who had shown previously a friendly interest in the pseudo godling.

"It is only a step in the progress toward truth," interjected Lu-don. "Possibly the evidence of the only princess of the house of Ko-tan will have greater weight with the great chief from the north, though the father of a son who fled the holy offer of the priesthood may not receive with willing ears any testimony against another blasphemer."

Ja-don's hand leaped to his knife, but the warriors next him laid detaining fingers upon his arms. "You are in the temple of Jad-ben-Otho, Ja-don," they cautioned and the great chief was forced to swallow Lu-don's affront though it left in his heart bitter hatred of the high priest.

And now Ko-tan turned toward Lu-don. "What knoweth my daughter of this matter?" he asked. "You would not bring a princess of my house to testify thus publicly?"

"No," replied Lu-don, "not in person, but I have here one who will testify for her." He beckoned to an under priest. "Fetch the slave of the princess," he said.

His grotesque headdress adding a touch of the hideous to the scene, the priest stepped forward dragging the reluctant Pan-at-lee by the wrist.

"The Princess O-lo-a was alone in the Forbidden Garden with but this one slave," explained the priest, "when there suddenly appeared from the foliage nearby this creature who claims to be the Dor-ul-Otho. When the slave saw him the princess says that she cried aloud in startled recognition and called the creature by name—Tarzan-jad-guru—the same name that the slave from Kor-ul-lul gave him. This woman is not from Kor-ul-lul but from Kor-ul-ja, the very tribe with which the Kor-ul-lul says the creature was associating when he first saw him. And further the princess said that when this woman, whose name is Pan-at-lee, was brought to her yesterday she told a strange story of having been rescued from a Tor-o-don in the Kor-ul-gryf by a creature such as this, whom she spoke of then as Tarzan-jad-guru; and of how the two were pursued in the bottom of the gorge by two monster *gryfs,* and of how the man led them away while Pan-at-lee escaped, only to be taken prisoner in the Kor-ul-lul as she was seeking to return to her own tribe."

"Is it not plain now," cried Lu-don, "that this creature is no god. Did he tell you that he was the son of god?" he almost shouted, turning suddenly upon Pan-at-lee.

The girl shrank back terrified. "Answer me, slave!" cried the high priest.

"He seemed more than mortal," parried Pan-at-lee.

"Did he tell you that he was the son of god? Answer my question," insisted Lu-don.

"No," she admitted in a low voice, casting an appealing look of forgiveness at Tarzan who returned a smile of encouragement and friendship.

"That is no proof that he is not the son of god," cried Ja-don. "Dost think Jad-ben-Otho goes about crying 'I am god! I am god!' Hast ever heard him Lu-don? No, you have not. Why should his son do that which the father does not do?"

"Enough," cried Lu-don. "The evidence is clear. The creature is an impostor and I, the head priest of Jad-ben-Otho in the city of A-lur, do condemn him to die." There was a moment's silence during which Lu-don evidently paused for the dramatic effect of his climax. "And if I am wrong may Jad-ben-Otho pierce my heart with his lightnings as I stand here before you all."

The lapping of the wavelets of the lake against the foot of the palace wall was distinctly audible in the utter and almost breathless silence which ensued. Lu-don stood with his face turned toward the heavens and his arms outstretched in the attitude of one who bares his breast to the dagger of an executioner. The warriors and the priests and the slaves gathered in the sacred court awaited the consuming vengeance of their god.

It was Tarzan who broke the silence. "Your god ignores you Lu-don," he taunted, with a sneer that he meant to still further anger the high priest, "he ignores you and I can prove it before the eyes of your priests and your people."

"Prove it, blasphemer! How can you prove it?"

"You have called me a blasphemer," replied Tarzan, "you have proved to your own satisfaction that I am an impostor, that I, an ordinary mortal, have posed as the son of god. Demand then that Jad-ben-Otho uphold his godship and the dignity of his priesthood by directing his consuming fires through my own bosom."

Again there ensued a brief silence while the onlookers waited for Lu-don to thus consummate the destruction of this presumptuous impostor.

"You dare not," taunted Tarzan, "for you

know that I would be struck dead no quicker than were you."

"You lie," cried Lu-don, "and I would do it had I not but just received a message from Jad-ben-Otho directing that your fate be different."

A chorus of admiring and reverential "Ah"s arose from the priesthood. Ko-tan and his warriors were in a state of mental confusion. Secretly they hated and feared Lu-don, but so ingrained was their sense of reverence for the office of the high priest that none dared raise a voice against him.

None? Well, there was Ja-don, fearless old Lion-man of the north. "The proposition was a fair one," he cried. "Invoke the lightnings of Jad-ben-Otho upon this man if you would ever convince us of his guilt."

"Enough of this," snapped Lu-don. "Since when was Ja-don created high priest? Seize the prisoner," he cried to the priests and warriors, "and on the morrow he shall die in the manner that Jad-ben-Otho has willed."

There was no immediate movement on the part of any of the warriors to obey the high priest's command, but the lesser priests on the other hand, imbued with the courage of fanaticism leaped eagerly forward like a flock of hideous harpies to seize upon their prey.

The game was up. That Tarzan knew. No longer could cunning and diplomacy usurp the functions of the weapons of defense he best loved. And so the first hideous priest who leaped to the platform was confronted by no suave ambassador from heaven, but rather a grim and ferocious beast whose temper savored more of hell.

The altar stood close to the western wall of the enclosure. There was just room between the two for the high priest to stand during the performance of the sacrificial ceremonies and only Lu-don stood there now behind Tarzan, while before him were perhaps two hundred warriors and priests.

The presumptuous one who would have had the glory of first laying arresting hands upon the blasphemous impersonator rushed forward with outstretched hand to seize the ape-man. Instead it was he who was seized; seized by steel fingers that snapped him up as though he had been a dummy of straw, grasped him by one leg and the harness at his back and raised him with giant arms high above the altar. Close at his heels were others ready to seize the ape-man and drag him down, and beyond the altar was Lu-don with drawn knife advancing toward him.

There was no instant to waste, nor was it the way of the ape-man to fritter away precious moments in the uncertainty of belated decision. Before Lu-don or any other could guess what was in the mind of the condemned, Tarzan with all the force of his great muscles dashed the screaming hierophant in the face of the high priest, and, as though the two actions were one, so quickly did he move, he had leaped to the top of the altar and from there to a handhold upon the summit of the temple wall. As he gained a footing there he turned and looked down upon those beneath. For a moment he stood in silence and then he spoke.

"Who dare believe," he cried, "that Jad-ben-Otho would forsake his son?" and then he dropped from their sight upon the other side.

There were two at least left within the enclosure whose hearts leaped with involuntary elation at the success of the ape-man's maneuver, and one of them smiled openly. This was Ja-don, and the other, Pan-at-lee.

The brains of the priest that Tarzan had thrown at the head of Lu-don had been dashed out against the temple wall while the high priest himself had escaped with only a few bruises, sustained in his fall to the hard pavement. Quickly scrambling to his feet he looked around in fear, in terror and finally in bewilderment, for he had not been a witness to the ape-man's escape. "Seize him," he cried; "seize the blasphemer," and he continued to look around in search of his victim with such a ridiculous expression of bewilderment that more than a single warrior was compelled to hide his smiles beneath his palm.

The priests were rushing around wildly, exhorting the warriors to pursue the fugitive but these awaited now stolidly the command of their king or high priest. Ko-tan, more or less secretly pleased by the discomfiture of Lu-don, waited for that worthy to give the necessary directions which he presently did when one of his acolytes excitedly explained to him the manner of Tarzan's escape.

Instantly the necessary orders were issued and priests and warriors sought the temple exit in pursuit of the ape-man. His departing words, hurled at them from the summit of the temple wall, had had little effect in impressing the majority that his claims had not been disproven by Lu-don, but in the hearts of the warriors was admiration for a brave man and in many the same unholy gratification that had risen in that of their ruler at the discomfiture of Lu-don.

A careful search of the temple grounds revealed no trace of the quarry. The secret recesses of the subterranean chambers, familiar only to the priesthood, were examined by these while the warriors scattered through the palace and the palace grounds without the temple. Swift runners were dispatched to the city to arouse the people there that all might be upon the lookout for Tarzan the Terrible. The story of his imposture and of his escape, and the tales that the Waz-don slaves had brought into the city concerning him were soon spread throughout A-lur, nor did they lose aught in the spreading, so that before an hour had passed the women and children were hiding behind barred doorways while the warriors crept apprehensively through the streets expecting momentarily to be pounced upon by a ferocious demon who, bare-handed, did victorious battle with huge *gryfs* and whose lightest pastime consisted in tearing strong men limb from limb.

XII
THE GIANT STRANGER

And while the warriors and the priests of A-lur searched the temple and the palace and the city for the vanished ape-man there entered the head of Kor-ul-ja down the precipitous trail from the mountains, a naked stranger bearing an Enfield upon his back. Silently he moved downward toward the bottom of the gorge and there where the ancient trail unfolded more levelly before him he swung along with easy strides, though always with the utmost alertness against possible dangers. A gentle breeze came down from the mountains behind him so that only his ears and his eyes were of value in detecting the presence of danger ahead. Generally the trail followed along the banks of the winding brooklet at the bottom of the gorge, but in some places where the waters tumbled over a precipitous ledge the trail made a detour along the side of the gorge, and again it wound in and out among rocky outcroppings, and presently where it rounded sharply the projecting shoulder of a cliff the stranger came suddenly face to face with one who was ascending the gorge.

Separated by a hundred paces the two halted simultaneously. Before him the stranger saw a tall white warrior, naked but for a loin cloth, cross belts, and a girdle. The man was armed with a heavy, knotted club and a short knife, the latter hanging in its sheath at his left hip from the end of one of his cross belts, the opposite belt supporting a leathern pouch at his right side. It was Ta-den hunting alone in the gorge of his friend, the chief of Kor-ul-ja. He contemplated the stranger with surprise but no wonder, since he recognized in him a member of the race with which his experience of Tarzan the Terrible had made him familiar and also, thanks to his friendship for the ape-man, he looked upon the newcomer without hostility.

The latter was the first to make outward sign of his intentions, raising his palm toward Ta-den in that gesture which has been a symbol of peace from pole to pole since man ceased to walk upon his knuckles. Simultaneously he advanced a few paces and halted.

Ta-den, assuming that one so like Tarzan the Terrible must be a fellow-tribesman of his lost friend, was more than glad to accept this overture of peace, the sign of which he returned in kind as he ascended the trail to where the other stood. "Who are you?" he asked, but the newcomer only shook his head to indicate that he did not understand.

By signs he tried to carry to the Ho-don the fact that he was following a trail that had led him over a period of many days from some place beyond the mountains and Ta-den was convinced that the newcomer sought Tarzan-jad-guru. He wished, however, that he might discover whether as friend or foe.

The stranger perceived the Ho-don's prehensile thumbs and great toes and his long tail with an astonishment which he sought to conceal, but greater than all was the sense of relief that the first inhabitant of this strange country whom he had met had proven friendly, so greatly would he have been handicapped by the necessity for forcing his way through a hostile land.

Ta-den, who had been hunting for some of the smaller mammals, the meat of which is especially relished by the Ho-don, forgot his intended sport in the greater interest of his new discovery. He would take the stranger to Om-at and possibly together the two would find some way of discovering the true intentions of the newcomer. And so again through signs he apprised the other that he would accompany him and together they descended toward the cliffs of Om-at's people.

As they approached these they came upon the women and children working under guard of the old men and the youths—gathering the wild fruits and herbs which constitute a part of their diet, as well as tending the small acres of growing crops which they cultivate. The fields lay in small level patches that had been cleared of trees and brush. Their farm implements consisted of metal-shod poles which bore a closer resemblance to spears than to tools of peaceful agriculture. Supplementing these were others with flattened blades that were neither hoes nor spades, but instead possessed the appearance of an unhappy attempt to combine the two implements in one.

At first sight of these people the stranger halted and unslung his bow for these creatures were black as night, their bodies entirely covered with hair. But Ta-den, interpreting the doubt in the other's mind, reassured him with a gesture and a smile. The Waz-don, however, gathered around excitedly jabbering questions in a language which the stranger discovered his guide understood though it was entirely unintelligible to the former. They made no attempt to molest him and he was now sure that he had fallen among a peaceful and friendly people.

It was but a short distance now to the caves and when they reached these Ta-den led the way aloft upon the wooden pegs, assured that this creature whom he had discovered would have no more difficulty in following him than had Tarzan the Terrible. Nor was he mistaken for the other mounted with ease until presently the two stood within the recess before the cave of Om-at, the chief.

The latter was not there and it was midafternoon before he returned, but in the meantime many warriors came to look upon the visitor and in each instance the latter was more thoroughly impressed with the friendly and peaceable spirit of his hosts, little guessing that he was being entertained by a ferocious and warlike tribe who never before the coming of Ta-den and Tarzan had suffered a stranger among them.

At last Om-at returned and the guest sensed intuitively that he was in the presence of a great man among these people, possibly a chief or king, for not only did the attitude of the other black warriors indicate this but it was written also in the mien and bearing of the splendid creature who stood looking at him while Ta-den explained the circumstances of their meeting. "And I believe, Om-at," concluded the Ho-don, "that he seeks Tarzan the Terrible."

At the sound of that name, the first intelligible word that had fallen upon the ears of the stranger since he had come among them, his face lightened. "Tarzan!" he cried, "Tarzan of the Apes!" and by signs he tried to tell them that it was he whom he sought.

They understood, and also they guessed from the expression of his face that he sought Tarzan from motives of affection rather than the reverse, but of this Om-at wished to make sure. He pointed to the stranger's knife, and repeating Tarzan's name, seized Ta-den and pretended to stab him, immediately turning questioningly toward the stranger.

The latter shook his head vehemently and then first placing a hand above his heart he raised his palm in the symbol of peace.

"He is a friend of Tarzan-jad-guru," exclaimed Ta-den.

"Either a friend or a great liar," replied Om-at.

"Tarzan," continued the stranger, "you know him? He lives? O God, if I could only speak your language." And again reverting to sign language he sought to ascertain where Tarzan was. He would pronounce the name and point in different directions, in the cave, down into the gorge, back toward the mountains, or out upon the valley below, and each time he would raise his brows questioningly and voice the universal "eh?" of interrogation which they could not fail to understand. But always Om-at shook his head and spread his palms in a gesture which indicated that while he understood the question he was ignorant as to the whereabouts of the ape-man, and then the black chief attempted as best he might to explain to the stranger what he knew of the whereabouts of Tarzan.

He called the newcomer Jar-don, which in the language of Pal-ul-don means "stranger," and he pointed to the sun and said *as*. This he repeated several times and then he held up one hand with the fingers outspread and touching them one by one, including the thumb, repeated the word *adenen* until the stranger understood that he meant five. Again he pointed to the sun and describing an arc with his forefinger starting at the eastern horizon and terminating at the western, he repeated again the words *as adenen*. It was plain to the stranger that the words meant that the sun had crossed the heavens five times. In other words, five days had passed. Om-at then pointed to the cave where they stood, pronouncing Tarzan's name and imitating a walk-

ing man with the first and second fingers of his right hand upon the floor of the recess, sought to show that Tarzan had walked out of the cave and climbed upward on the pegs five days before, but this was as far as the sign language would permit him to go.

This far the stranger followed him and, indicating that he understood he pointed to himself and then indicating the pegs leading above announced that he would follow Tarzan.

"Let us go with him," said Om-at, "for as yet we have not punished the Kor-ul-lul for killing our friend and ally."

"Persuade him to wait until morning," said Ta-den, "that you may take with you many warriors and make a great raid upon the Kor-ul-lul, and this time, Om-at, do not kill your prisoners. Take as many as you can alive and from some of them we may learn the fate of Tarzan-jad-guru."

"Great is the wisdom of the Ho-don," replied Om-at. "It shall be as you say, and having made prisoners of all the Kor-ul-lul we shall make them tell us what we wish to know. And then we shall march them to the rim of Kor-ul-gryf and push them over the edge of the cliff."

Ta-den smiled. He knew that they would not take prisoner all the Kor-ul-lul warriors—that they would be fortunate if they took one and it was also possible that they might even be driven back in defeat, but he knew too that Om-at would not hesitate to carry out his threat if he had the opportunity, so implacable was the hatred of these neighbors for each other.

It was not difficult to explain Om-at's plan to the stranger or to win his consent since he was aware, when the great black had made it plain that they would be accompanied by many warriors, that their venture would probably lead them into a hostile country and every safeguard that he could employ he was glad to avail himself of, since the furtherance of his quest was the paramount issue.

He slept that night upon a pile of furs in one of the compartments of Om-at's ancestral cave, and early the next day following the morning meal they sallied forth, a hundred savage warriors swarming up the face of the sheer cliff and out upon the summit of the ridge, the main body preceded by two warriors whose duties coincided with those of the point of modern military maneuvers, safeguarding the column against the danger of too sudden contact with the enemy.

Across the ridge they went and down into the Kor-ul-lul and there almost immediately they came upon a lone and unarmed Waz-don who was making his way fearfully up the gorge toward the village of his tribe. Him they took prisoner which, strangely, only added to his terror since from the moment that he had seen them and realized that escape was impossible, he had expected to be slain immediately.

"Take him back to Kor-ul-ja," said Om-at, to one of his warriors, "and hold him there unharmed until I return."

And so the puzzled Kor-ul-lul was led away while the savage company moved stealthily from tree to tree in its closer advance upon the village. Fortune smiled upon Om-at in that it gave him quickly what he sought—a battle royal, for they had not yet come in sight of the caves of the Kor-ul-lul when they encountered a considerable band of warriors headed down the gorge upon some expedition.

Like shadows the Kor-ul-ja melted into the concealment of the foliage upon either side of the trail. Ignorant of impending danger, safe in the knowledge that they trod their own domain where each rock and stone was as familiar as the features of their mates, the Kor-ul-lul walked innocently into the ambush. Suddenly the quiet of that seeming peace was shattered by a savage cry and a hurled club felled a Kor-ul-lul.

The cry was a signal for a savage chorus from a hundred Kor-ul-ja throats with which were soon mingled the war cries of their enemies. The air was filled with flying clubs and then as the two forces mingled, the battle resolved itself into a number of individual encounters as each warrior singled out a foe and closed upon him. Knives gleamed and flashed in the mottling sunlight that filtered through the foliage of the trees above. Sleek black coats were streaked with crimson stains.

In the thick of the fight the smooth brown skin of the stranger mingled with the black bodies of friend and foe. Only his keen eyes and his quick wit had shown him how to differentiate between Kor-ul-lul and Kor-ul-ja since with the single exception of apparel they were identical, but at the first rush of the enemy he had noticed that their loin cloths were not of the leopard-matted hides such as were worn by his allies.

Om-at, after dispatching his first antagonist, glanced at Jar-don. "He fights with the ferocity of *jato*," mused the chief. "Powerful indeed must be the tribe from which he and Tarzan-jad-guru come," and then his whole attention was occupied by a new assailant.

The fighters surged to and fro through the forest until those who survived were spent with exhaustion. All but the stranger who seemed not to know the sense of fatigue. He fought on when each new antagonist would have gladly quit, and when there were no more Kor-ul-lul who were not engaged, he leaped upon those who stood pantingly facing the exhausted Kor-ul-ja.

And always he carried upon his back the peculiar thing which Om-at had thought was some manner of strange weapon but the purpose of which he could not now account for in view of the fact that Jar-don never used it, and that for the most part it seemed but a nuisance and needless encumbrance since it banged and smashed against its owner as he leaped, catlike, hither and thither in the course of his victorious duels. The bow and arrows he had tossed aside at the beginning of the fight but the Enfield he would not discard, for where he went he meant that it should go until its mission had been fulfilled.

Presently the Kor-ul-ja, seemingly shamed by the example of Jar-don closed once more with the enemy, but the latter, moved no doubt to terror by the presence of the stranger, a tireless demon who appeared invulnerable to their attacks, lost heart and sought to flee. And then it was that at Om-at's command his warriors surrounded a half-dozen of the most exhausted and made them prisoners.

It was a tired, bloody, and elated company that returned victorious to the Kor-ul-ja. Twenty of their number were carried back and six of these were dead men. It was the most glorious and successful raid that the Kor-ul-ja had made upon the Kor-ul-lul in the memory of man, and it marked Om-at as the greatest of chiefs, but that fierce warrior knew that advantage had lain upon his side largely because of the presence of his strange ally. Nor did he hesitate to give credit where credit belonged, with the result that Jar-don and his exploits were upon the tongue of every member of the tribe of Kor-ul-ja and great was the fame of the race that could produce two such as he and Tarzan-jad-guru.

And in the gorge of Kor-ul-lul beyond the ridge the survivors spoke in bated breath of this second demon that had joined forces with their ancient enemy.

Returned to his cave Om-at caused the Kor-ul-lul prisoners to be brought into his presence singly, and each he questioned as to the fate of Tarzan. Without exception they told him the same story—that Tarzan had been taken prisoner by them five days before but that he had slain the warrior left to guard him and escaped, carrying the head of the unfortunate sentry to the opposite side of Kor-ul-lul where he had left it suspended by its hair from the branch of a tree. But what had become of him after, they did not know; not one of them, until the last prisoner was examined, he whom they had taken first—the unarmed Kor-ul-lul making his way from the direction of the Valley of Jad-ben-Otho toward the caves of his people.

This one, when he discovered the purpose of their questioning, bartered with them for the lives and liberty of himself and his fellows. "I can tell you much of this terrible man of whom you ask, Kor-ul-ja," he said. "I saw him yesterday and I know where he is, and if you will promise to let me and my fellows return in safety

to the caves of our ancestors I will tell you all, and truthfully, that which I know."

"You will tell us anyway," replied Om-at, "or we shall kill you."

"You will kill me anyway," retorted the prisoner, "unless you make me this promise; so if I am to be killed the thing I know shall go with me."

"He is right, Om-at," said Ta-den, "promise him that they shall have their liberty."

"Very well," said Om-at. "Speak Kor-ul-lul, and when you have told me all, you and your fellows may return unharmed to your tribe."

"It was thus," commenced the prisoner. "Three days since I was hunting with a party of my fellows near the mouth of Kor-ul-lul not far from where you captured me this morning, when we were surprised and set upon by a large number of Ho-don who took us prisoners and carried us to A-lur where a few were chosen to be slaves and the rest were cast into a chamber beneath the temple where are held for sacrifice the victims that are offered by the Ho-don to Jad-ben-Otho upon the sacrificial altars of the temple at A-lur.

"It seemed then that indeed was my fate sealed and that lucky were those who had been selected for slaves among the Ho-don, for they at least might hope to escape—those in the chamber with me must be without hope.

"But yesterday a strange thing happened. There came to the temple, accompanied by all the priests and by the king and many of his warriors, one whom all did great reverence, and when he came to the barred gateway leading to the chamber in which we wretched ones awaited our fate, I saw to my surprise that it was none other than that terrible man who had so recently been a prisoner in the village of Kor-ul-lul—he whom you call Tarzan-jad-guru but whom they addressed as Dor-ul-Otho. And he looked upon us and questioned the high priest and when he was told of the purpose for which we were imprisoned there he grew angry and cried that it was not the will of Jad-ben-Otho that his people be thus sacrificed, and he commanded the high priest to liberate us, and this was done.

"The Ho-don prisoners were permitted to return to their homes and we were led beyond the city of A-lur and set upon our way toward Kor-ul-lul. There were three of us, but many are the dangers that lie between A-lur and Kor-ul-lul and we were only three and unarmed. Therefore none of us reached the village of our people and only one of us lives. I have spoken."

"That is all you know concerning Tarzan-jad-guru?" asked Om-at.

"That is all I know," replied the prisoner, "other than that he whom they call Lu-don, the high priest at A-lur, was very angry, and that one of the two priests who guided us out of the city said to the other that the stranger was not Dor-ul-Otho at all; that Lu-don had said so and that he had also said that he would expose him and that he should be punished with death for his presumption. That is all they said within my hearing.

"And now, chief of Kor-ul-ja, let us depart."

Om-at nodded. "Go your way," he said, "and Ab-on, send warriors to guard them until they are safely within the Kor-ul-lul.

"Jar-don," he said beckoning to the stranger, "come with me," and rising he led the way toward the summit of the cliff, and when they stood upon the ridge Om-at pointed down into the valley toward the city of A-lur gleaming in the light of the western sun.

"There is Tarzan-jad-guru," he said, and Jar-don understood.

XIII
THE MASQUERADER

As Tarzan dropped to the ground beyond the temple wall there was in his mind no intention to escape from the city of A-lur until he had satisfied himself that his mate was not a prisoner there, but how, in this strange city in which every man's hand must be now against him, he was to live and prosecute his search was far from clear to him.

There was only one place of which he knew that he might find even temporary sanctuary and that was the Forbidden Garden of the king. There was thick shrubbery in which a man might hide, and water and fruits. A cunning jungle creature, if he could reach the spot unsuspected, might remain concealed there for a considerable time, but how he was to traverse the distance between the temple grounds and the garden unseen was a question the seriousness of which he fully appreciated.

"Mighty is Tarzan," he soliloquized, "in his native jungle, but in the cities of man he is little better than they."

Depending upon his keen observation and sense of location he felt safe in assuming that he could reach the palace grounds by means of the subterranean corridors and chambers of the temple through which he had been conducted the day before, nor any slightest detail of which had escaped his keen eyes. That would be better, he reasoned, than crossing the open grounds above where his pursuers would naturally immediately follow him from the temple and quickly discover him.

And so a dozen paces from the temple wall he disappeared from sight of any chance observer above, down one of the stone stairways that led to the apartments beneath. The way that he had been conducted the previous day had followed the windings and turnings of numerous corridors and apartments, but Tarzan, sure of himself in such matters, retraced the route accurately without hesitation.

He had little fear of immediate apprehension here since he believed that all the priests of the temple had assembled in the court above to witness his trial and his humiliation and his death, and with this idea firmly implanted in his mind he rounded the turn of the corridor and came face to face with an under priest, his grotesque headdress concealing whatever emotion the sight of Tarzan may have aroused.

However, Tarzan had one advantage over the masked votary of Jad-ben-Otho in that the moment he saw the priest he knew his intention concerning him, and therefore was not compelled to delay action. And so it was that before the priest could determine on any suitable line of conduct in the premises a long, keen knife had been slipped into his heart.

As the body lunged toward the floor Tarzan caught it and snatched the headdress from its shoulders, for the first sight of the creature had suggested to his ever-alert mind a bold scheme for deceiving his enemies.

The headdress saved from such possible damage as it must have sustained had it fallen to the floor with the body of its owner, Tarzan relinquished his hold upon the corpse, set the headdress carefully upon the floor and stooping down severed the tail of the Ho-don close to its root. Near by at his right was a small chamber from which the priest had evidently just emerged and into this Tarzan dragged the corpse, the headdress, and the tail.

Quickly cutting a thin strip of hide from the loin cloth of the priest, Tarzan tied it securely about the upper end of the severed member and then tucking the tail under his loin cloth behind him, secured it in place as best he could. Then he fitted the headdress over his shoulders and stepped from the apartment, to all appearances a priest of the temple of Jad-ben-Otho unless one examined too closely his thumbs and his great toes.

He had noticed that among both the Ho-don and the Waz-don it was not at all unusual that the end of the tail be carried in one hand, and so he caught his own tail up thus lest the lifeless appearance of it dragging along behind him should arouse suspicion.

Passing along the corridor and through the various chambers he emerged at last into the palace grounds beyond the temple. The pursuit had not yet reached this point though he was conscious of a commotion not far behind him. He met now both warriors and slaves but none gave him more than a passing glance, a priest being too common a sight about the palace.

And so, passing the guards unchallenged, he came at last to the inner entrance to the Forbidden Garden and there he paused and scanned quickly that portion of the beautiful spot that lay before his eyes. To his relief it seemed unoccupied and congratulating himself upon the ease with which he had so far outwitted the high powers of A-lur he moved rapidly to the opposite end of the enclosure. Here he found a patch of flowering shrubbery that might safely have concealed a dozen men.

Crawling well within he removed the uncomfortable headdress and sat down to await whatever eventualities fate might have in store for him the while he formulated plans for the future. The one night that he had spent in A-lur had kept him up to a late hour, apprising him of the fact that while there were few abroad in the temple grounds at night, there were yet enough to make it possible for him to fare forth under cover of his disguise without attracting the unpleasant attention of the guards, and, too, he had noticed that the priesthood constituted a privileged class that seemed to come and go at will and unchallenged throughout the palace as well as the temple. Altogether then, he decided, night furnished the most propitious hours for his investigation—by day he could lie up in the shrubbery of the Forbidden Garden, reasonably free from detection. From beyond the garden he heard the voices of men calling to one another both far and near, and he guessed that diligent was the search that was being prosecuted for him.

The idle moments afforded him an opportunity to evolve a more satisfactory scheme for attaching his stolen caudal appendage. He arranged it in such a way that it might be quickly assumed or discarded, and this done he fell to examining the weird mask that had so effectively hidden his features.

The thing had been very cunningly wrought from a single block of wood, very probably a section of a tree, upon which the features had been carved and afterward the interior hollowed out until only a comparatively thin shell remained. Two semicircular notches had been rounded out from opposite sides of the lower edge. These fitted snugly over his shoulders, aprons of wood extending downward a few inches upon his chest and back. From these aprons hung long tassels or switches of hair tapering from the outer edges toward the center which reached below the bottom of his torso. It required but the most cursory examination to indicate to the ape-man that these ornaments consisted of human scalps, taken, doubtless, from the heads of the sacrifices upon the eastern altars. The headdress itself had been carved to depict in formal design a hideous face that suggested both man and *gryf*. There were the three white horns, the yellow face with the blue bands encircling the eyes and the red hood which took the form of the posterior and anterior aprons.

As Tarzan sat within the concealing foliage of the shrubbery meditating upon the hideous priest-mask which he held in his hands he became aware that he was not alone in the garden. He sensed another presence and presently his trained ears detected the slow approach of naked feet across the sward. At first he suspected that it might be one stealthily searching the Forbidden Garden for him but a little later the figure came within the limited area of his vision which was circumscribed by stems and foliage and flowers. He saw then that it was the princess O-lo-a and that she was alone and walking with bowed head as though in meditation—sorrowful meditation for there were traces of tears upon her lids.

Shortly after his ears warned him that others had entered the garden—men they were and their footsteps proclaimed that they walked neither slowly nor meditatively. They came directly toward the princess and when Tarzan could see them he discovered that both were priests.

"O-lo-a, Princess of Pal-ul-don," said one, addressing her, "the stranger who told us that he was the son of Jad-ben-Otho has but just fled from the wrath of Lu-don, the high priest, who

exposed him and all his wicked blasphemy. The temple, and the palace, and the city are being searched and we have been sent to search the Forbidden Garden, since Ko-tan, the king, said that only this morning he found him here, though how he passed the guards he could not guess."

"He is not here," said O-lo-a. "I have been in the garden for some time and have seen nor heard no other than myself. However, search it if you will."

"No," said the priest who had before spoken, "it is not necessary since he could not have entered without your knowledge and the connivance of the guards, and even had he, the priest who preceded us must have seen him."

"What priest?" asked O-lo-a.

"One passed the guards shortly before us," explained the man.

"I did not see him," said O-lo-a.

"Doubtless he left by another exit," remarked the second priest.

"Yes, doubtless," acquiesced O-lo-a, "but it is strange that I did not see him." The two priests made their obeisance and turned to depart.

"Stupid as Buto, the rhinoceros," soliloquized Tarzan, who considered Buto a very stupid creature indeed. "It should be easy to outwit such as these."

The priests had scarce departed when there came the sound of feet running rapidly across the garden in the direction of the princess to an accompaniment of rapid breathing as of one almost spent, either from fatigue or excitement.

"Pan-at-lee," exclaimed O-lo-a, "what has happened? You look as terrified as the doe for which you were named!"

"O Princess of Pal-ul-don," cried Pan-at-lee, "they would have killed him in the temple. They would have killed the wondrous stranger who claimed to be the Dor-ul-Otho."

"But he escaped," said O-lo-a. "You were there. Tell me about it."

"The head priest would have had him seized and slain, but when they rushed upon him he hurled one in the face of Lu-don with the same ease that you might cast your breastplates at me; and then he leaped upon the altar and from there to the top of the temple wall and disappeared below. They are searching for him, but, O Princess, I pray that they do not find him."

"And why do you pray that?" asked O-lo-a. "Has not one who has so blasphemed earned death?"

"Ah, but you do not know him," replied Pan-at-lee.

"And you do, then?" retorted O-lo-a quickly. "This morning you betrayed yourself and then attempted to deceive me. The slaves of O-lo-a do not such things with impunity. He is then the same Tarzan-jad-guru of whom you told me? Speak woman and speak only the truth."

Pan-at-lee drew herself up very erect, her little chin held high, for was not she too among her own people already as good as a princess? "Pan-at-lee, the Kor-ul-ja does not lie," she said, "to protect herself."

"Then tell me what you know of this Tarzan-jad-guru," insisted O-lo-a.

"I know that he is a wondrous man and very brave," said Pan-at-lee, "and that he saved me from the Tor-o-don and the *gryf* as I told you, and that he is indeed the same who came into the garden this morning; and even now I do not know that he is not the son of Jad-ben-Otho for his courage and his strength are more than those of mortal man, as are also his kindness and his honor: for when he might have harmed me he protected me, and when he might have saved himself he thought only of me. And all this he did because of his friendship for Om-at, who is *gund* of Kor-ul-ja and with whom I should have mated had the Ho-don not captured me."

"He was indeed a wonderful man to look upon," mused O-lo-a, "and he was not as are other men, not alone in the conformation of his hands and feet or the fact that he was tailless, but there was that about him which made him seem different in ways more important than these."

"And," supplemented Pan-at-lee, her savage little heart loyal to the man who had befriended her and hoping to win for him the consideration of the princess even though it might not avail him; "and," she said, "did he not know all about Ta-den and even his whereabouts. Tell me, O Princess, could mortal know such things as these?"

"Perhaps he saw Ta-den," suggested O-lo-a.

"But how would he know that you loved Ta-den," parried Pan-at-lee. "I tell you, my Princess, that if he is not a god he is at least more than Ho-don or Waz-don. He followed me from the cave of Es-sat in Kor-ul-ja across Kor-ul-lul and two wide ridges to the very cave in Kor-ul-gryf where I hid, though many hours had passed since I had come that way and my bare feet left no impress upon the ground. What mortal man could do such things as these? And where in all Pal-ul-don would virgin maid find friend and protector in a strange male other than he?"

"Perhaps Lu-don may be mistaken—perhaps he is a god," said O-lo-a, influenced by her slave's enthusiastic championing of the stranger.

"But whether god or man he is too wonderful to die," cried Pan-at-lee. "Would that I might save him. If he lived he might even find a way to give you your Ta-den, Princess."

"Ah, if he only could," sighed O-lo-a, "but alas it is too late for tomorrow I am to be given to Bu-lot."

"He who came to your quarters yesterday with your father?" asked Pan-at-lee.

"Yes; the one with the awful round face and the big belly," exclaimed the Princess disgustedly. "He is so lazy he will neither hunt nor fight. To eat and to drink is all that Bu-lot is fit for, and he thinks of naught else except these things and his slave women. But come, Pan-at-lee, gather for me some of these beautiful blossoms. I would have them spread around my couch tonight that I may carry away with me in the morning the memory of the fragrance that I love best and which I know that I shall not find in the village of Mo-sar, the father of Bu-lot. I will help you, Pan-at-lee, and we will gather armfuls of them, for I love to gather them as I love nothing else—they were Ta-den's favorite flowers."

The two approached the flowering shrubbery where Tarzan hid, but as the blooms grew plentifully upon every bush the ape-man guessed there would be no necessity for them to enter the patch far enough to discover him. With little exclamations of pleasure as they found particularly large or perfect blooms the two moved from place to place upon the outskirts of Tarzan's retreat.

"Oh, look, Pan-at-lee," cried O-lo-a presently; "there is the king of them all. Never did I see so wonderful a flower—No! I will get it myself—it is so large and wonderful no other hand shall touch it," and the princess wound in among the bushes toward the point where the great flower bloomed upon a bush above the ape-man's head.

So sudden and unexpected her approach that there was no opportunity to escape and Tarzan sat silently trusting that fate might be kind to him and lead Ko-tan's daughter away before her eyes dropped from the high-growing bloom to him. But as the girl cut the long stem with her knife she looked down straight into the smiling face of Tarzan-jad-guru.

With a stifled scream she drew back and the ape-man rose and faced her.

"Have no fear, Princess," he assured her. "It is the friend of Ta-den who salutes you," raising her fingers to his lips.

Pan-at-lee came now excitedly forward. "O Jad-ben-Otho, it is he!"

"And now that you have found me," queried Tarzan, "will you give me up to Lu-don, the high priest?"

Pan-at-lee threw herself upon her knees at O-lo-a's feet. "Princess! Princess!" she beseeched, "do not discover him to his enemies."

"But Ko-tan, my father," whispered O-lo-a fearfully, "if he knew of my perfidy his rage would be beyond naming. Even though I am a princess Lu-don might demand that I be sacrificed to appease the wrath of Jad-ben-Otho, and between the two of them I should be lost."

"But they need never know," cried Pan-at-lee, "that you have seen him unless you tell them

yourself for as Jad-ben-Otho is my witness I will never betray you."

"Oh, tell me, stranger," implored O-lo-a, "are you indeed a god?"

"Jad-ben-Otho is not more so," replied Tarzan truthfully.

"But why do you seek to escape then from the hands of mortals if you are a god?" she asked.

"When gods mingle with mortals," replied Tarzan, "they are no less vulnerable than mortals. Even Jad-ben-Otho, should he appear before you in the flesh, might be slain."

"You have seen Ta-den and spoken with him?" she asked with apparent irrelevancy.

"Yes, I have seen him and spoken with him," replied the ape-man. "For the duration of a moon I was with him constantly."

"And—" she hesitated—"he—" she cast her eyes toward the ground and a flush mantled her cheek—"he still loves me?" and Tarzan knew that she had been won over.

"Yes," he said, "Ta-den speaks only of O-lo-a and he waits and hopes for the day when he can claim her."

"But tomorrow they give me to Bu-lot," she said sadly.

"May it be always tomorrow," replied Tarzan, "for tomorrow never comes."

"Ah, but this unhappiness will come, and for all the tomorrows of my life I must pine in misery for the Ta-den who will never be mine."

"But for Lu-don I might have helped you," said the ape-man. "And who knows that I may not help you yet?"

"Ah, if you only could, Dor-ul-Otho," cried the girl, "and I know that you would if it were possible for Pan-at-lee has told me how brave you are, and at the same time how kind."

"Only Jad-ben-Otho knows what the future may bring," said Tarzan. "And now you two go your way lest someone should discover you and become suspicious."

"We will go," said O-lo-a, "but Pan-at-lee will return with food. I hope that you escape and that Jad-ben-Otho is pleased with what I have done." She turned and walked away and Pan-at-lee followed while the ape-man again resumed his hiding.

At dusk Pan-at-lee came with food and having her alone Tarzan put the question that he had been anxious to put since his conversation earlier in the day with O-lo-a.

"Tell me," he said, "what you know of the rumors of which O-lo-a spoke of the mysterious stranger which is supposed to be hidden in A-lur. Have you too heard of this during the short time that you have been here?"

"Yes," said Pan-at-lee, "I have heard it spoken of among the other slaves. It is something of which all whisper among themselves but of which none dares to speak aloud. They say that there is a strange she hidden in the temple and that Lu-don wants her for a priestess and that Ko-tan wants her for a wife and that neither as yet dares take her for fear of the other."

"Do you know where she is hidden in the temple?" asked Tarzan.

"No," said Pan-at-lee. "How should I know? I do not even know that it is more than a story and I but tell you that which I have heard others say."

"There was only one," asked Tarzan, "whom they spoke of?"

"No, they speak of another who came with her but none seems to know what became of this one."

Tarzan nodded. "Thank you Pan-at-lee," he said. "You may have helped me more than either of us guess."

"I hope that I have helped you," said the girl as she turned back toward the palace.

"And I hope so too," exclaimed Tarzan emphatically.

XIV
THE TEMPLE OF THE GRYF

When night had fallen Tarzan donned the mask and the dead tail of the priest he had slain in the vaults beneath the temple. He judged that it would not do to attempt again to pass the guard, especially so late at night as it would be likely to arouse comment and suspicion, and so he swung into the tree that overhung the garden wall and from its branches dropped to the ground beyond.

Avoiding too grave risk of apprehension the ape-man passed through the grounds to the court of the palace, approaching the temple from the side opposite to that at which he had left it at the time of his escape. He came thus it is true through a portion of the grounds with which he was unfamiliar but he preferred this to the danger of following the beaten track between the palace apartments and those of the temple. Having a definite goal in mind and endowed as he was with an almost miraculous sense of location he moved with great assurance through the shadows of the temple yard.

Taking advantage of the denser shadows close to the walls and of what shrubs and trees there were he came without mishap at last to the ornate building concerning the purpose of which he had asked Lu-don only to be put off with the assertion that it was forgotten—nothing strange in itself but given possible importance by the apparent hesitancy of the priest to discuss its use and the impression the ape-man had gained at the time that Lu-don lied.

And now he stood at last alone before the structure which was three stories in height and detached from all the other temple buildings. It had a single barred entrance which was carved from the living rock in representation of the head of a *gryf,* whose wide-open mouth constituted the doorway. The head, hood, and front paws of the creature were depicted as though it lay crouching with its lower jaw on the ground between its outspread paws. Small oval windows, which were likewise barred, flanked the doorway.

Seeing that the coast was clear, Tarzan stepped into the darkened entrance where he tried the bars only to discover that they were ingeniously locked in place by some device with which he was unfamiliar and that they also were probably too strong to be broken even if he could have risked the noise which would have resulted. Nothing was visible within the darkened interior and so, momentarily baffled, he sought the windows. Here also the bars refused to yield up their secret, but again Tarzan was not dismayed since he had counted upon nothing different.

If the bars would not yield to his cunning they would yield to his giant strength if there proved no other means of ingress, but first he would assure himself that this latter was the case. Moving entirely around the building he examined it carefully. There were other windows but they were similarly barred. He stopped often to look and listen but he saw no one and the sounds that he heard were too far away to cause him any apprehension.

He glanced above him at the wall of the building. Like so many of the other walls of the city, palace, and temple, it was ornately carved and there were too the peculiar ledges that ran sometimes in a horizontal plane and again were tilted at an angle, giving ofttimes an impression of irregularity and even crookedness to the buildings. It was not a difficult wall to climb, at least not difficult for the ape-man.

But he found the bulky and awkward headdress a considerable handicap and so he laid it aside upon the ground at the foot of the wall. Nimbly he ascended to find the windows of the second floor not only barred but curtained within. He did not delay long at the second floor since he had in mind an idea that he would find the easiest entrance through the roof which he had noticed was roughly dome shaped like the throneroom of Ko-tan. Here there were apertures. He had seen them from the ground, and if the construction of the interior resembled even slightly that of the throneroom, bars would not be necessary upon these apertures, since no one could reach them from the floor of the room.

There was but a single question: would they be large enough to admit the broad shoulders of the ape-man.

He paused again at the third floor, and here, in spite of the hangings, he saw that the interior was lighted and simultaneously there came to his nostrils from within a scent that stripped from him temporarily any remnant of civilization that might have remained and left him a fierce and terrible bull of the jungles of Kerchak. So sudden and complete was the metamorphosis that there almost broke from the savage lips the hideous challenge of his kind, but the cunning brute-mind saved him this blunder.

And now he heard voices within—the voice of Lu-don he could have sworn, demanding. And haughty and disdainful came the answering words though utter hopelessness spoke in the tones of this other voice which brought Tarzan to the pinnacle of frenzy.

The dome with its possible apertures was forgotten. Every consideration of stealth and quiet was cast aside as the ape-man drew back his mighty fist and struck a single terrific blow upon the bars of the small window before him, a blow that sent the bars and the casing that held them clattering to the floor of the apartment within.

Instantly Tarzan dove headforemost through the aperture carrying the hangings of antelope hide with him to the floor below. Leaping to his feet he tore the entangling pelt from about his head only to find himself in utter darkness and in silence. He called aloud a name that had not passed his lips for many weary months. "Jane, Jane," he cried, "where are you?" But there was only silence in reply.

Again and again he called, groping with outstretched hands through the Stygian blackness of the room, his nostrils assailed and his brain tantalized by the delicate effluvia that had first assured him that his mate had been within this very room. And he had heard her dear voice combatting the base demands of the vile priest. Ah, if he had but acted with greater caution! If he had but continued to move with quiet and stealth he might even at this moment be holding her in his arms while the body of Lu-don, beneath his foot, spoke eloquently of vengeance achieved. But there was no time now for idle self-reproaches.

He stumbled blindly forward, groping for he knew not what till suddenly the floor beneath

814

him tilted and he shot downward into a darkness even more utter than that above. He felt his body strike a smooth surface and he realized that he was hurtling downward as through a polished chute while from above there came the mocking tones of a taunting laugh and the voice of Ludon screamed after him: "Return to thy father, O Dor-ul-Otho!"

The ape-man came to a sudden and painful stop upon a rocky floor. Directly before him was an oval window crossed by many bars, and beyond he saw the moonlight playing on the waters of the blue lake below. Simultaneously he was conscious of a familiar odor in the air of the chamber, which a quick glance revealed in the semidarkness as of considerable proportion.

It was the faint, but unmistakable odor of the *gryf*, and now Tarzan stood silently listening. At first he detected no sounds other than those of the city that came to him through the window overlooking the lake; but presently, faintly, as though from a distance he heard the shuffling of padded feet along a stone pavement, and as he listened he was aware that the sound approached.

Nearer and nearer it came, and now even the breathing of the beast was audible. Evidently attracted by the noise of his descent into its cavernous retreat it was approaching to investigate. He could not see it but he knew that it was not far distant, and then, deafeningly there reverberated through those gloomy corridors the mad bellow of the *gryf*.

Aware of the poor eyesight of the beast, and his own eyes now grown accustomed to the darkness of the cavern, the ape-man sought to elude the infuriated charge which he well knew no living creature could withstand. Neither did he dare risk the chance of experimenting upon this strange *gryf* with the tactics of the Tor-o-don that he had found so efficacious upon that other occasion when his life and liberty had been the stakes for which he cast. In many respects the conditions were dissimilar. Before, in broad daylight, he had been able to approach the *gryf* under normal conditions in its natural state, and the *gryf* itself was one that he had seen subjected to

the authority of man, or at least of a manlike creature; but here he was confronted by an imprisoned beast in the full swing of a furious charge and he had every reason to suspect that this *gryf* might never have felt the restraining influence of authority, confined as it was in this gloomy pit to serve likely but the single purpose that Tarzan had already seen so graphically portrayed in his own experience of the past few moments.

To elude the creature, then, upon the possibility of discovering some loophole of escape from his predicament seemed to the ape-man the wisest course to pursue. Too much was at stake to risk an encounter that might be avoided—an encounter the outcome of which there was every reason to apprehend would seal the fate of the mate that he had just found, only to lose again so harrowingly. Yet high as his disappointment and chagrin ran, hopeless as his present estate now appeared, there tingled in the veins of the savage lord a warm glow of thanksgiving and elation. She lived! After all these weary months of hopelessness and fear he had found her. She lived!

To the opposite side of the chamber, silently as the wraith of a disembodied soul, the swift jungle creature moved from the path of the charging Titan that, guided solely in the semidarkness by its keen ears, bore down upon the spot toward which Tarzan's noisy entrance into its lair had attracted it. Along the further wall the ape-man hurried. Before him now appeared the black opening of the corridor from which the beast had emerged into the larger chamber. Without hesitation Tarzan plunged into it. Even here his eyes, long accustomed to darkness that would have seemed total to you or to me, saw dimly the floor and the walls within a radius of a few feet—enough at least to prevent him plunging into any unguessed abyss, or dashing himself upon solid rock at a sudden turning.

The corridor was both wide and lofty, which indeed it must be to accommodate the colossal proportions of the creature whose habitat it was, and so Tarzan encountered no difficulty in moving with reasonable speed along its winding trail. He was aware as he proceeded that the trend of the passage was downward, though not steeply, but it seemed interminable and he wondered to what distant subterranean lair it might lead. There was a feeling that perhaps after all he might better have remained in the larger chamber and risked all on the chance of subduing the *gryf* where there was at least sufficient room and light to lend to the experiment some slight chance of success. To be overtaken here in the narrow confines of the black corridor where he was assured the *gryf* could not see him at all would spell almost certain death and now he heard the thing approaching from behind. Its thunderous bellows fairly shook the cliff from which the cavernous chambers were excavated. To halt and meet this monstrous incarnation of fury with a futile "whee-oo!" seemed to Tarzan the height of insanity and so he continued along the corridor, increasing his pace as he realized that the *gryf* was overhauling him.

Presently the darkness lessened and at the final turning of the passage he saw before him an area of moonlight. With renewed hope he sprang rapidly forward and emerged from the mouth of the corridor to find himself in a large circular enclosure the towering white walls of which rose high upon every side—smooth perpendicular walls upon the sheer face of which was no slightest foothold. To his left lay a pool of water, one side of which lapped the foot of the wall at this point. It was, doubtless, the wallow and the drinking pool of the *gryf*.

And now the creature emerged from the corridor and Tarzan retreated to the edge of the pool to make his last stand. There was no staff with which to enforce the authority of his voice, but yet he made his stand for there seemed naught else to do. Just beyond the entrance to the corridor the *gryf* paused, turning its weak eyes in all directions as though searching for its prey. This then seemed the psychological moment for his attempt and raising his voice in peremptory command the ape-man voiced the weird "whee-oo!" of the Tor-o-don. Its effect upon the *gryf* was instantaneous and complete—

with a terrific bellow it lowered its three horns and dashed madly in the direction of the sound.

To right nor to left was any avenue of escape, for behind him lay the placid waters of the pool, while down upon him from before thundered annihilation. The mighty body seemed already to tower above him as the ape-man turned and dove into the dark waters.

Dead in her breast lay hope. Battling for life during harrowing months of imprisonment and danger and hardship it had fitfully flickered and flamed only to sink after each renewal to smaller proportions than before and now it had died out entirely leaving only cold, charred embers that Jane Clayton knew would never again be rekindled. Hope was dead as she faced Lu-don, the high priest, in her prison quarters in the Temple of the Gryf at A-lur. Both time and hardship had failed to leave their impress upon her physical beauty—the contours of her perfect form, the glory of her radiant loveliness had defied them, yet to these very attributes she owed the danger which now confronted her, for Lu-don desired her. From the lesser priests she had been safe, but from Lu-don she was not safe, for Lu-don was not as they, since the high priestship of Pal-ul-don may descend from father to son.

Ko-tan, the king, had wanted her and all that had so far saved her from either was the fear of each for the other, but at last Lu-don had cast aside discretion and had come in the silent watches of the night to claim her. Haughtily had she repulsed him, seeking ever to gain time, though what time might bring her of relief or renewed hope she could not even remotely conjecture. A leer of lust and greed shone hungrily upon his cruel countenance as he advanced across the room to seize her. She did not shrink nor cower, but stood there very erect, her chin up, her level gaze freighted with the loathing and contempt she felt for him. He read her expression and while it angered him, it but increased his desire for possession. Here indeed was a queen, perhaps a goddess; fit mate for the high priest.

"You shall not!" she said as he would have touched her. "One of us shall die before ever your purpose is accomplished."

He was close beside her now. His laugh grated upon her ears. "Love does not kill," he replied mockingly.

He reached for her arm and at the same instant something clashed against the bars of one of the windows, crashing them inward to the floor, to be followed almost simultaneously by a human figure which dove headforemost into the room, its head enveloped in the skin window hangings which it carried with it in its impetuous entry.

Jane Clayton saw surprise and something of terror too leap to the countenance of the high priest and then she saw him spring forward and jerk upon a leather thong that depended from the ceiling of the apartment. Instantly there dropped from above a cunningly contrived partition that fell between them and the intruder, effectively barring him from them and at the same time leaving him to grope upon its opposite side in darkness, since the only cresset the room contained was upon their side of the partition.

Faintly from beyond the wall Jane heard a voice calling, but whose it was and what the words she could not distinguish. Then she saw Lu-don jerk upon another thong and wait in evident expectancy of some consequent happening. He did not have long to wait. She saw the thong move suddenly as though jerked from above and then Lu-don smiled and with another signal put in motion whatever machinery it was that raised the partition again to its place in the ceiling.

Advancing into that portion of the room that the partition had shut off from them, the high priest knelt upon the floor, and down tilting a section of it, revealed the dark mouth of a shaft leading below. Laughing loudly he shouted into the hole: "Return to thy father, O Dor-ul-Otho!"

Making fast the catch that prevented the trapdoor from opening beneath the feet of the unwary until such time as Lu-don chose the high priest rose again to his feet.

"Now, Beautiful One!" he cried, and then, "Ja-don! what do you here?"

Jane Clayton turned to follow the direction of Lu-don's eyes and there she saw framed in the entrance-way to the apartment the mighty figure of a warrior, upon whose massive features sat an expression of stern and uncompromising authority.

"I come from Ko-tan, the king," replied Ja-don, "to remove the beautiful stranger to the Forbidden Garden."

"The king defies me, the high priest of Jad-ben-Otho?" cried Lu-don.

"It is the king's command—I have spoken," snapped Ja-don, in whose manner was no sign of either fear or respect for the priest.

Lu-don well knew why the king had chosen this messenger whose heresy was notorious, but whose power had as yet protected him from the machinations of the priest. Lu-don cast a surreptitious glance at the thongs hanging from the ceiling. Why not? If he could but maneuver to entice Ja-don to the opposite side of the chamber!

"Come," he said in a conciliatory tone, "let us discuss the matter," and moved toward the spot where he would have Ja-don follow him.

"There is nothing to discuss," replied Ja-don, yet he followed the priest, fearing treachery.

Jane watched them. In the face and figure of the warrior she found reflected those admirable traits of courage and honor that the profession of arms best develops. In the hypocritical priest there was no redeeming quality. Of the two then she might best choose the warrior. With him there was a chance—with Lu-don, none. Even the very process of exchange from one prison to another might offer some possibility of escape. She weighed all these things and decided, for Lu-don's quick glance at the thongs had not gone unnoticed nor uninterpreted by her.

"Warrior," she said, addressing Ja-don, "if

you would live enter not that portion of the room."

Lu-don cast an angry glance upon her. "Silence, slave!" he cried.

"And where lies the danger?" Ja-don asked of Jane, ignoring Lu-don.

The woman pointed to the thongs. "Look," she said, and before the high priest could prevent she had seized that which controlled the partition which shot downward separating Lu-don from the warrior and herself.

Ja-don looked inquiringly at her. "He would have tricked me neatly but for you," he said; "kept me imprisoned there while he secreted you elsewhere in the mazes of his temple."

"He would have done more than that," replied Jane, as she pulled upon the other thong. "This releases the fastenings of a trapdoor in the floor beyond the partition. When you stepped on that you would have been precipitated into a pit beneath the temple. Lu-don has threatened me with this fate often. I do not know that he speaks the truth, but he says that a demon of the temple is imprisoned there—a huge *gryf*."

"There is a *gryf* within the temple," said Ja-don. "What with it and the sacrifices, the priests keep us busy supplying them with prisoners, though the victims are sometimes those for whom Lu-don has conceived hatred among our own people. He has had his eyes upon me for a long time. This would have been his chance but for you. Tell me, woman, why you warned me. Are we not all equally your jailers and your enemies?"

"None could be more horrible than Lu-don," she replied; "and you have the appearance of a brave and honorable warrior. I could not hope, for hope has died and yet there is the possibility that among so many fighting men, even though they be of another race than mine, there is one who would accord honorable treatment to a stranger within his gates—even though she be a woman."

Ja-don looked at her for a long minute. "Ko-tan would make you his queen," he said. "That he told me himself and surely that were honor-

able treatment from one who might make you a slave."

"Why, then, would he make me queen?" she asked.

Ja-don came closer as though in fear his words might be overheard. "He believes, although he did not tell me so in fact, that you are of the race of gods. And why not? Jad-ben-Otho is tailless, therefore it is not strange that Ko-tan should suspect that only the gods are thus. His queen is dead leaving only a single daughter. He craves a son and what more desirable than that he should found a line of rulers for Pal-ul-don descended from the gods?"

"But I am already wed," cried Jane. "I cannot wed another. I do not want him or his throne."

"Ko-tan is king," replied Ja-don simply as though that explained and simplified everything.

"You will not save me then?" she asked.

"If you were in Ja-lur," he replied, "I might protect you, even against the king."

"What and where is Ja-lur?" she asked, grasping at any straw.

"It is the city where I rule," he answered. "I am chief there and of all the valley beyond."

"Where is it?" she insisted, and, "Is it far?"

"No," he replied, smiling, "it is not far, but do not think of that—you could never reach it. There are too many to pursue and capture you. If you wish to know, however, it lies up the river that empties into Jad-ben-lul whose waters kiss the walls of A-lur—up the western fork it lies with water upon three sides. Impregnable city of Pal-ul-don—alone of all the cities it has never been entered by a foeman since it was built there while Jad-ben-Otho was a boy."

"And there I would be safe?" she asked.

"Perhaps," he replied.

Ah, dead Hope; upon what slender provocation would you seek to glow again! She sighed and shook her head, realizing the inutility of Hope—yet the tempting bait dangled before her mind's eye—Ja-lur!

"You are wise," commented Ja-don interpreting her sigh. "Come now, we will go to the quarters of the princess beside the Forbidden

Garden. There you will remain with O-lo-a, the king's daughter. It will be better than this prison you have occupied."

"And Ko-tan?" she asked, a shudder passing through her slender frame.

"There are ceremonies," explained Ja-don, "that may occupy several days before you become queen, and one of them may be difficult of arrangement." He laughed, then.

"What?" she asked.

"Only the high priest may perform the marriage ceremony for a king," he explained.

"Delay!" she murmured; "blessed delay!" Tenacious indeed of life is Hope even though it be reduced to cold and lifeless char—a veritable phoenix.

XV
"THE KING IS DEAD!"

As they conversed Ja-don had led her down the stone stairway that leads from the upper floors of the Temple of the Gryf to the chambers and the corridors that honeycomb the rocky hills from which the temple and the palace are hewn and now they passed from one to the other through a doorway upon one side of which two priests stood guard and upon the other two warriors. The former would have halted Ja-don when they saw who it was that accompanied him for well known throughout the temple was the quarrel between king and high priest for possession of this beautiful stranger.

"Only by order of Lu-don may she pass," said one, placing himself directly in front of Jane Clayton, barring her progress. Through the hollow eyes of the hideous mask the woman could see those of the priest beneath gleaming with the fires of fanaticism. Ja-don placed an arm about her shoulders and laid his hand upon his knife.

"She passes by order of Ko-tan, the king," he said, "and by virtue of the fact that Ja-don, the chief, is her guide. Stand aside!"

The two warriors upon the palace side pressed forward. "We are here, *gund* of Ja-lur,"

said one, addressing Ja-don, "to receive and obey your commands."

The second priest now interposed. "Let them pass," he admonished his companion. "We have received no direct commands from Lu-don to the contrary and it is a law of the temple and the palace that chiefs and priests may come and go without interference."

"But I know Lu-don's wishes," insisted the other.

"He told you then that Ja-don must not pass with the stranger?"

"No—but—"

"Then let them pass, for they are three to two and will pass anyway—we have done our best."

Grumbling, the priest stepped aside. "Lu-don will exact an accounting," he cried angrily.

Ja-don turned upon him. "And get it when and where he will," he snapped.

They came at last to the quarters of the Princess O-lo-a where, in the main entrance-way, loitered a small guard of palace warriors and several stalwart black eunuchs belonging to the princess, or her women. To one of the latter Ja-don relinquished his charge.

"Take her to the princess," he commanded, "and see that she does not escape."

Through a number of corridors and apartments lighted by stone cressets the eunuch led Lady Greystoke halting at last before a doorway concealed by hangings of *jato*-skin, where the guide beat with his staff upon the wall beside the door.

"O-lo-a, Princess of Pal-ul-don," he called, "here is the stranger woman, the prisoner from the temple."

"Bid her enter," Jane heard a sweet voice from within command.

The eunuch drew aside the hangings and Lady Greystoke stepped within. Before her was a low-ceiled room of moderate size. In each of the four corners a kneeling figure of stone seemed to be bearing its portion of the weight of the ceiling upon its shoulders. These figures were evidently intended to represent Waz-don slaves and were not without bold artistic beauty. The ceiling itself was slightly arched to a central dome which was pierced to admit light by day, and air. Upon one side of the room were many windows, the other three walls being blank except for a doorway in each. The princess lay upon a pile of furs which were arranged over a low stone dais in one corner of the apartment and was alone except for a single Waz-don slave girl who sat upon the edge of the dais near her feet.

As Jane entered O-lo-a beckoned her to approach and when she stood beside the couch the girl half rose upon an elbow and surveyed her critically.

"How beautiful you are," she said simply.

Jane smiled, sadly; for she had found that beauty may be a curse.

"That is indeed a compliment," she replied quickly, "from one so radiant as the Princess O-lo-a."

"Ah!" exclaimed the princess delightedly; "you speak my language! I was told that you were of another race and from some far land of which we of Pal-ul-don have never heard."

"Lu-don saw to it that the priests instructed me," explained Jane; "but I am from a far country, Princess; one to which I long to return—and I am very unhappy."

"But Ko-tan, my father, would make you his queen," cried the girl; "that should make you very happy."

"But it does not," replied the prisoner; "I love another to whom I am already wed. Ah, Princess, if you had known what it was to love and to be forced into marriage with another you would sympathize with me."

The Princess O-lo-a was silent for a long moment. "I know," she said at last, "and I am very sorry for you; but if the king's daughter cannot save herself from such a fate who may save a slave woman? for such in fact you are."

The drinking in the great banquet hall of the palace of Ko-tan, king of Pal-ul-don had commenced earlier this night than was usual, for the king was celebrating the morrow's betrothal of his only daughter to Bu-lot, son of Mo-sar, the chief, whose great-grandfather had been king of Pal-ul-don and who thought that he should be king, and Mo-sar was drunk and so was Bu-lot, his son. For that matter nearly all of the warriors, including the king himself, were drunk. In the heart of Ko-tan was no love either for Mo-sar, or Bu-lot, nor did either of these love the king. Ko-tan was giving his daughter to Bu-lot in the hope that the alliance would prevent Mo-sar from insisting upon his claims to the throne, for, next to Ja-don, Mo-sar was the most powerful of the chiefs and while Ko-tan looked with fear upon Ja-don, too, he had no fear that the old Lion-man would attempt to seize the throne, though which way he would throw his influence and his warriors in the event that Mo-sar declare war upon Ko-tan, the king could not guess.

Primitive people who are also warlike are seldom inclined toward either tact or diplomacy even when sober; but drunk they know not the words, if aroused. It was really Bu-lot who started it.

"This," he said, "I drink to O-lo-a," and he emptied his tankard at a single gulp. "And this," seizing a full one from a neighbor, "to her son and mine who will bring back the throne of Pal-ul-don to its rightful owners!"

"The king is not yet dead!" cried Ko-tan, rising to his feet; "nor is Bu-lot yet married to his daughter—and there is yet time to save Pal-ul-don from the spawn of the rabbit breed."

The king's angry tone and his insulting reference to Bu-lot's well-known cowardice brought a sudden, sobering silence upon the roistering company. Every eye turned upon Bu-lot and Mo-sar, who sat together directly opposite the king. The first was very drunk though suddenly he seemed quite sober. He was so drunk that for an instant he forgot to be a coward, since his reasoning powers were so effectually paralyzed by the fumes of liquor that he could not intelligently weigh the consequences of his acts. It is reasonably conceivable that a drunk and angry rabbit might commit a rash deed. Upon no other hypothesis is the thing that Bu-lot now did explicable. He rose suddenly from the seat to which he had sunk after delivering his toast and seizing the knife from the sheath of the warrior upon his right hurled it with terrific force at Ko-tan. Skilled in the art of throwing both their knives and their clubs are the warriors of Pal-ul-don and at this short distance and coming as it did without warning there was no defense and but one possible result—Ko-tan, the king, lunged forward across the table, the blade buried in his heart.

A brief silence followed the assassin's cowardly act. White with terror, now, Bu-lot fell slowly back toward the doorway at his rear, when suddenly angry warriors leaped with drawn knives to prevent his escape and to avenge their king. But Mo-sar now took his stand beside his son.

"Ko-tan is dead!" he cried. "Mo-sar is king! Let the loyal warriors of Pal-ul-don protect their ruler!"

Mo-sar commanded a goodly following and these quickly surrounded him and Bu-lot, but there were many knives against them and now Ja-don pressed forward through those who confronted the pretender.

"Take them both!" he shouted. "The warriors of Pal-ul-don will choose their own king after the assassin of Ko-tan has paid the penalty of his treachery."

Directed now by a leader whom they both respected and admired those who had been loyal to Ko-tan rushed forward upon the faction that had surrounded Mo-sar. Fierce and terrible was the fighting, devoid, apparently, of all else than the ferocious lust to kill and while it was at its height Mo-sar and Bu-lot slipped unnoticed from the banquet hall.

To that part of the palace assigned to them during their visit to A-lur they hastened. Here were their servants and the lesser warriors of their party who had not been bidden to the feast of Ko-tan. These were directed quickly to gather together their belongings for immediate departure. When all was ready, and it did not take long, since the warriors of Pal-ul-don require but little impedimenta on the march, they moved toward the palace gate.

Suddenly Mo-sar approached his son. "The princess," he whispered. "We must not leave the city without her—she is half the battle for the throne."

Bu-lot, now entirely sober, demurred. He had had enough of fighting and of risk. "Let us get out of A-lur quickly," he urged, "or we shall have the whole city upon us. She would not come without a struggle and that would delay us too long."

"There is plenty of time," insisted Mo-sar. "They are still fighting in the *pal-e-don-so*. It will be long before they miss us and, with Ko-tan dead, long before any will think to look to the safety of the princess. Our time is now—it was made for us by Jad-ben-Otho. Come!"

Reluctantly Bu-lot followed his father, who first instructed the warriors to await them just inside the gateway of the palace. Rapidly the two approached the quarters of the princess. Within the entrance-way only a handful of warriors were on guard. The eunuchs had retired.

"There is fighting in the *pal-e-don-so*," Mo-sar announced in feigned excitement as they entered the presence of the guards. "The king desires you to come at once and has sent us to guard the apartments of the princess. Make haste!" he commanded as the men hesitated.

The warriors knew him and that on the morrow the princess was to be betrothed to Bu-lot, his son. If there was trouble what more natural than that Mo-sar and Bu-lot should be intrusted with the safety of the princess. And then, too, was not Mo-sar a powerful chief to whose orders disobedience might prove a dangerous thing? They were but common fighting men disciplined in the rough school of tribal warfare, but they had learned to obey a superior and so they departed for the banquet hall—the place-where-men-eat.

Barely waiting until they had disappeared Mo-sar crossed to the hangings at the opposite end of the entrance-hall and followed by Bu-lot made his way toward the sleeping apartment of O-lo-a and a moment later, without warning, the two men burst in upon the three occupants of the room. At sight of them O-lo-a sprang to her feet.

"What is the meaning of this?" she demanded angrily.

Mo-sar advanced and halted before her. Into his cunning mind had entered a plan to trick her. If it succeeded it would prove easier than taking her by force, and then his eyes fell upon Jane Clayton and he almost gasped in astonishment and admiration, but he caught himself and returned to the business of the moment.

"O-lo-a," he cried, "when you know the urgency of our mission you will forgive us. We have sad news for you. There has been an uprising in the palace and Ko-tan, the king, has been slain. The rebels are drunk with liquor and now on their way here. We must get you out of A-lur at once—there is not a moment to lose. Come, and quickly!"

"My father dead?" cried O-lo-a, and suddenly her eyes went wide. "Then my place is here with my people," she cried. "If Ko-tan is dead I am queen until the warriors choose a new ruler—that is the law of Pal-ul-don. And if I am queen none can make me wed whom I do not wish to wed—and Jad-ben-Otho knows I never wished to wed thy cowardly son. Go!" She pointed a slim forefinger imperiously toward the doorway.

Mo-sar saw that neither trickery nor persuasion would avail now and every precious minute counted. He looked again at the beautiful woman who stood beside O-lo-a. He had never before seen her but he well knew from palace gossip that she could be no other than the godlike stranger whom Ko-tan had planned to make his queen.

"Bu-lot," he cried to his son, "take you your own woman and I will take—mine!" and with that he sprang suddenly forward and seizing Jane about the waist lifted her in his arms, so that before O-lo-a or Pan-at-lee might even guess his purpose he had disappeared through the hangings near the foot of the dais and was gone with the stranger woman struggling and fighting in his grasp.

And then Bu-lot sought to seize O-lo-a, but O-lo-a had her Pan-at-lee—fierce little tiger-girl of the savage Kor-ul-ja—Pan-at-lee whose name belied her—and Bu-lot found that with the two of them his hands were full. When he would have lifted O-lo-a and borne her away Pan-at-lee seized him around the legs and strove to drag him down. Viciously he kicked her, but she would not desist, and finally, realizing that he might not only lose his princess but be so delayed as to invite capture if he did not rid himself of this clawing, scratching she-*jato*, he hurled O-lo-a to the floor and seizing Pan-at-lee by the hair drew his knife and—

The curtains behind him suddenly parted. In two swift bounds a lithe figure crossed the room and before ever the knife of Bu-lot reached its goal his wrist was seized from behind and a terrific blow crashing to the base of his brain dropped him, lifeless, to the floor. Bu-lot, coward, traitor, and assassin, died without knowing who struck him down.

As Tarzan of the Apes leaped into the pool in the *gryf* pit of the temple at A-lur one might have accounted for his act on the hypothesis that it was the last blind urge of self-preservation to delay, even for a moment, the inevitable tragedy in which each some day must play the leading rôle upon his little stage; but no—those cool, gray eyes had caught the sole possibility for escape that the surroundings and the circumstances offered—a tiny, moonlit patch of water glimmering through a small aperture in the cliff at the surface of the pool upon its farther side. With swift, bold strokes he swam for speed alone knowing that the water would in no way deter his pursuer. Nor did it. Tarzan heard the great splash as the huge creature plunged into the pool behind him; he heard the churning waters as it forged rapidly onward in his wake. He was nearing the opening—would it be large enough to permit the passage of his body? That portion of it which showed above the surface of the water most certainly would not. His life, then, depended upon how much of the aperture was submerged. And now it was directly before him and the *gryf* directly behind. There was no alternative—there was no other hope. The apeman threw all the resources of his great strength into the last few strokes, extended his hands before him as a cutwater, submerged to the water's level and shot forward toward the hole.

Frothing with rage was the baffled Lu-don as he realized how neatly the stranger she had turned his own tables upon him. He could of course escape the Temple of the Gryf in which her quick wit had temporarily imprisoned him; but during the delay, however brief, Ja-don would find time to steal her from the temple and deliver her to Ko-tan. But he would have her yet—that the high priest swore in the names of Jad-ben-Otho and all the demons of his faith. He hated Ko-tan. Secretly he had espoused the cause of Mo-sar, in whom he would have a willing tool. Perhaps, then, this would give him the opportunity he had long awaited—a pretext for inciting the revolt that would dethrone Ko-tan and place Mo-sar in power—with Lu-don the real ruler of Pal-ul-don. He licked his thin lips as he sought the window through which Tarzan had entered and now Lu-don's only avenue of escape. Cautiously he made his way across the floor, feeling before him with his hands, and when they discovered that the trap was set for him an ugly snarl broke from the priest's lips. "The she-devil!" he muttered; "but she shall pay, she shall pay—ah, Jad-ben-Otho; how she shall pay for the trick she has played upon Lu-don!"

He crawled through the window and climbed easily downward to the ground. Should he pursue Ja-don and the woman, chancing an encounter with the fierce chief, or bide his time until treachery and intrigue should accomplish his design? He chose the latter solution, as might have been expected of such as he.

Going to his quarters he summoned several of his priests—those who were most in his confidence and who shared his ambitions for absolute power of the temple over the palace—all men who hated Ko-tan.

"The time has come," he told them, "when the authority of the temple must be placed definitely above that of the palace. Ko-tan must make way for Mo-sar, for Ko-tan has defied your high priest. Go then, Pan-sat, and summon Mo-sar secretly to the temple, and you others go to the city and prepare the faithful warriors that they may be in readiness when the time comes."

For another hour they discussed the details of the coup d'état that was to overthrow the government of Pal-ul-don. One knew a slave who, as the signal sounded from the temple gong, would thrust a knife into the heart of Ko-tan, for the price of liberty. Another held personal knowledge of an officer of the palace that he could use to compel the latter to admit a number of Lu-don's warriors to various parts of the palace. With Mo-sar as the cat's paw, the plan seemed scarce possible of failure and so they separated, going upon their immediate errands to palace and to city.

As Pan-sat entered the palace grounds he was aware of a sudden commotion in the direction of the *pal-e-don-so* and a few minutes later Lu-don was surprised to see him return to the apartments of the high priest, breathless and excited.

"What now, Pan-sat?" cried Lu-don. "Are you pursued by demons?"

"O master, our time has come and gone while we sat here planning. Ko-tan is already dead and Mo-sar fled. His friends are fighting with the warriors of the palace but they have no head, while Ja-don leads the others. I could learn but little from frightened slaves who had fled at the outburst of the quarrel. One told me that Bu-lot had slain the king and that he had seen Mo-sar and the assassin hurrying from the palace."

"Ja-don," muttered the high priest. "The fools will make him king if we do not act and act quickly. Get into the city, Pan-sat—let your feet fly and raise the cry that Ja-don has killed the king and is seeking to wrest the throne from O-lo-a. Spread the word as you know best how to spread it that Ja-don has threatened to destroy the priests and hurl the altars of the temple into Jad-ben-lul. Rouse the warriors of the city and urge them to attack at once. Lead them into the temple by the secret way that only the priests know and from here we may spew them out upon the palace before they learn the truth. Go, Pan-sat, immediately—delay not an instant.

"But stay," he called as the under priest turned to leave the apartment; "saw or heard you anything of the strange white woman that Ja-don stole from the Temple of the Gryf where we have had her imprisoned?"

"Only that Ja-don took her into the palace where he threatened the priests with violence if they did not permit him to pass," replied Pan-sat. "This they told me, but where within the palace she is hidden I know not."

"Ko-tan ordered her to the Forbidden Garden," said Lu-don, "doubtless we shall find her there. And now, Pan-sat, be upon your errand."

In a corridor by Lu-don's chamber a hideously masked priest leaned close to the curtained aperture that led within. Were he listening he must have heard all that passed between Pan-sat and the high priest, and that he had listened was evidenced by his hasty withdrawal to the shadows of a nearby passage as the lesser priest moved across the chamber toward the doorway. Pan-sat went his way in ignorance of the near presence that he almost brushed against as he hurried toward the secret passage that leads from the temple of Jad-ben-Otho, far beneath the palace, to the city beyond, nor did he sense the silent creature following in his footsteps.

XVI
THE SECRET WAY

It was a baffled *gryf* that bellowed in angry rage as Tarzan's sleek brown body cutting the moonlit waters shot through the aperture in the wall of the *gryf* pool and out into the lake beyond. The ape-man smiled as he thought of the comparative ease with which he had defeated the purpose of the high priest but his face clouded again at the ensuing remembrance of the grave danger that threatened his mate. His sole object now must be to return as quickly as he might to the chamber where he had last seen her on the third floor of the Temple of the Gryf, but how he was to find his way again into the temple grounds was a question not easy of solution.

In the moonlight he could see the sheer cliff rising from the water for a great distance along the shore—far beyond the precincts of the temple and the palace—towering high above him, a seemingly impregnable barrier against his return. Swimming close in, he skirted the wall searching diligently for some foothold, however slight, upon its smooth, forbidding surface. Above him and quite out of reach were numerous apertures, but there were no means at hand by which he could reach them. Presently, however, his hopes were raised by the sight of an opening level with the surface of the water. It lay just ahead and a few strokes brought him to it—cautious strokes that brought forth no sound from the yielding waters. At the nearer side of the opening he stopped and reconnoitered. There was no one in sight. Carefully he raised his body to the threshold of the entrance-way, his smooth brown hide glistening in the moonlight as it shed the water in tiny sparkling rivulets.

Before him stretched a gloomy corridor, unlighted save for the faint illumination of the diffused moonlight that penetrated it for but a short distance from the opening. Moving as rapidly as reasonable caution warranted, Tarzan followed the corridor into the bowels of the cave. There was an abrupt turn and then a flight of steps at the top of which lay another corridor running parallel with the face of the cliff. This passage was dimly lighted by flickering cressets set in niches in the walls at considerable distances apart. A quick survey showed the ape-man numerous openings upon each side of the corridor and his quick ears caught sounds that indicated that there were other beings not far distant—priests, he concluded, in some of the apartments letting upon the passageway.

To pass undetected through this hive of enemies appeared quite beyond the range of possibility. He must again seek disguise and knowing from experience how best to secure such he crept stealthily along the corridor toward the nearest doorway. Like Numa, the lion, stalking a wary prey he crept with quivering nostrils to the hangings that shut off his view from the interior of the apartment beyond. A moment later his head disappeared within; then his shoulders, and his lithe body, and the hangings dropped quietly into place again. A moment later there filtered to the vacant corridor without a brief, gasping gurgle and again silence. A minute passed; a second, and a third, and then the hangings were thrust aside and a grimly masked priest of the temple of Jad-ben-Otho strode into the passageway.

With bold steps he moved along and was about to turn into a diverging gallery when his attention was aroused by voices coming from a room upon his left. Instantly the figure halted and crossing the corridor stood with an ear close to the skins that concealed the occupants of the room from him, and him from them. Presently he leaped back into the concealing shadows of the diverging gallery and immediately thereafter the hangings by which he had been listening parted and a priest emerged to turn quickly down the main corridor. The eavesdropper waited until the other had gained a little distance and then stepping from his place of concealment followed silently behind.

The way led along the corridor which ran parallel with the face of the cliff for some little distance and then Pan-sat, taking a cresset from one of the wall niches, turned abruptly into a small apartment at his left. The tracker followed cautiously in time to see the rays of the flickering light dimly visible from an aperture in the floor before him. Here he found a series of steps, similar to those used by the Waz-don in scaling the cliff to their caves, leading to a lower level.

First satisfying himself that his guide was continuing upon his way unsuspecting, the other descended after him and continued his stealthy stalking. The passageway was now both narrow and low, giving but bare headroom to a tall man, and it was broken often by flights of steps leading always downward. The steps in each unit seldom numbered more than six and sometimes there was only one or two but in the aggregate the tracker imagined that they had descended between fifty and seventy-five feet from the level of the upper corridor when the passageway terminated in a small apartment at one side of which was a little pile of rubble.

Setting his cresset upon the ground, Pan-sat commenced hurriedly to toss the bits of broken stone aside, presently revealing a small aperture at the base of the wall upon the opposite side of which there appeared to be a further accumulation of rubble. This he also removed until he had a hole of sufficient size to permit the passage of his body, and leaving the cresset still burning upon the floor the priest crawled through the opening he had made and disappeared from the sight of the watcher hiding in the shadows of the narrow passageway behind him.

No sooner, however, was he safely gone than the other followed, finding himself, after passing through the hole, on a little ledge about halfway between the surface of the lake and the top of the cliff above. The ledge inclined steeply upward, ending at the rear of a building which stood upon the edge of the cliff and which the second priest entered just in time to see Pan-sat pass out into the city beyond.

As the latter turned a nearby corner the other emerged from the doorway and quickly surveyed his surroundings. He was satisfied the priest who had led him hither had served his purpose in so far as the tracker was concerned. Above him, and perhaps a hundred yards away, the white walls of the palace gleamed against the northern sky. The time that it had taken him to acquire definite knowledge concerning the secret passageway between the temple and the city he did not count as lost, though he begrudged every instant that kept him from the prosecution of his main objective. It had seemed to him, however, necessary to the success of a bold plan that he had formulated upon overhearing the conversation between Lu-don and Pan-sat as he stood without the hangings of the apartment of the high priest.

Alone against a nation of suspicious and half-savage enemies he could scarce hope for a successful outcome to the one great issue upon which hung the life and happiness of the creature he loved best. For her sake he must win allies and it was for this purpose that he had sacrificed these precious moments, but now he lost no further time in seeking to regain entrance to the palace grounds that he might search out whatever new prison they had found in which to incarcerate his lost love.

He found no difficulty in passing the guards at the entrance to the palace for, as he had guessed, his priestly disguise disarmed all suspicion. As he approached the warriors he kept his hands behind him and trusted to fate that the sickly light of the single torch which stood beside the doorway would not reveal his un-Pal-ul-donian feet. As a matter of fact so accustomed were they to the comings and goings of the priesthood that they paid scant attention to him and he passed on into the palace grounds without even a moment's delay.

His goal now was the Forbidden Garden and this he had little difficulty in reaching though he elected to enter it over the wall rather than to chance arousing any suspicion on the part of the guards at the inner entrance, since he could imagine no reason why a priest should seek entrance there thus late at night.

He found the garden deserted, nor any sign

of her he sought. That she had been brought hither he had learned from the conversation he had overheard between Lu-don and Pan-sat, and he was sure that there had been no time or opportunity for the high priest to remove her from the palace grounds. The garden he knew to be devoted exclusively to the uses of the princess and her women and it was only reasonable to assume therefore that if Jane had been brought to the garden it could only have been upon an order from Ko-tan. This being the case the natural assumption would follow that he would find her in some other portion of O-lo-a's quarters.

Just where these lay he could only conjecture, but it seemed reasonable to believe that they must be adjacent to the garden, so once more he scaled the wall and passing around its end directed his steps toward an entrance-way which he judged must lead to that portion of the palace nearest the Forbidden Garden.

To his surprise he found the place unguarded and then there fell upon his ear from an interior apartment the sound of voices raised in anger and excitement. Guided by the sound he quickly traversed several corridors and chambers until he stood before the hangings which separated him from the chamber from which issued the sounds of altercation. Raising the skins slightly he looked within. There were two women battling with a Ho-don warrior. One was the daughter of Ko-tan and the other Pan-at-lee, the Kor-ul-ja.

At the moment that Tarzan lifted the hangings, the warrior threw O-lo-a viciously to the ground and seizing Pan-at-lee by the hair drew his knife and raised it above her head. Casting the encumbering headdress of the dead priest from his shoulders the ape-man leaped across the intervening space and seizing the brute from behind struck him a single terrible blow.

As the man fell forward dead, the two women recognized Tarzan simultaneously. Pan-at-lee fell upon her knees and would have bowed her head upon his feet had he not, with an impatient gesture, commanded her to rise. He had no time to listen to their protestations of gratitude or an-

swer the numerous questions which he knew
would soon be flowing from those two feminine
tongues.

"Tell me," he cried, "where is the woman of
my own race whom Ja-don brought here from
the temple?"

"She is but this moment gone," cried O-lo-a.
"Mo-sar, the father of this thing here," and she
indicated the body of Bu-lot with a scornful finger, "seized her and carried her away."

"Which way?" he cried. "Tell me quickly, in
what direction he took her."

"That way," cried Pan-at-lee, pointing to the
doorway through which Mo-sar had passed.
"They would have taken the princess and the
stranger woman to Tu-lur, Mo-sar's city by the
Dark Lake."

"I go to find her," he said to Pan-at-lee, "she
is my mate. And if I survive I shall find means to
liberate you too and return you to Om-at."

Before the girl could reply he had disappeared behind the hangings of the door near the
foot of the dais. The corridor through which he
ran was illy lighted and like nearly all its kind in
the Ho-don city wound in and out and up and
down, but at last it terminated at a sudden turn
which brought him into a courtyard filled with
warriors, a portion of the palace guard that had
just been summoned by one of the lesser palace
chiefs to join the warriors of Ko-tan in the battle
that was raging in the banquet hall.

At sight of Tarzan, who in his haste had forgotten to recover his disguising headdress, a
great shout arose. "Blasphemer!" "Defiler of
the temple!" burst hoarsely from savage throats,
and mingling with these were a few who cried,
"Dor-ul-Otho!" evidencing the fact that there
were among them still some who clung to their
belief in his divinity.

To cross the courtyard armed only with a
knife, in the face of this great throng of savage
fighting men seemed even to the giant ape-man a
thing impossible of achievement. He must use
his wits now and quickly too, for they were closing upon him. He might have turned and fled
back through the corridor but flight now even in

the face of dire necessity would but delay him in
his pursuit of Mo-sar and his mate.

"Stop!" he cried, raising his palm against
them. "I am the Dor-ul-Otho and I come to you
with a word from Ja-don, who it is my father's
will shall be your king now that Ko-tan is slain.
Lu-don, the high priest, has planned to seize the
palace and destroy the loyal warriors that Mo-sar
may be made king—Mo-sar who will be the tool
and creature of Lu-don. Follow me. There is no
time to lose if you would prevent the traitors
whom Lu-don has organized in the city from entering the palace by a secret way and overpowering Ja-don and the faithful band within."

For a moment they hesitated. At last one
spoke. "What guarantee have we," he demanded,
"that it is not you who would betray us and by
leading us now away from the fighting in the
banquet hall cause those who fight at Ja-don's
side to be defeated?"

"My life will be your guarantee," replied
Tarzan. "If you find that I have not spoken the
truth you are sufficient in numbers to execute
whatever penalty you choose. But come, there is
not time to lose. Already are the lesser priests
gathering their warriors in the city below," and
without waiting for any further parley he strode
directly toward them in the direction of the gate
upon the opposite side of the courtyard which
led toward the principal entrance to the palace
grounds.

Slower in wit than he, they were swept away
by his greater initiative and that compelling
power which is inherent to all natural leaders.
And so they followed him, the giant ape-man
with a dead tail dragging the ground behind
him—a demigod where another would have
been ridiculous. Out into the city he led them
and down toward the unpretentious building
that hid Lu-don's secret passageway from the
city to the temple, and as they rounded the last
turn they saw before them a gathering of warriors which was being rapidly augmented from
all directions as the traitors of A-lur mobilized at
the call of the priesthood.

"You spoke the truth, stranger," said the

chief who marched at Tarzan's side, "for there are the warriors with the priests among them, even as you told us."

"And now," replied the ape-man, "that I have fulfilled my promise I will go my way after Mo-sar, who has done me a great wrong. Tell Ja-don that Jad-ben-Otho is upon his side, nor do you forget to tell him also that it was the Dor-ul-Otho who thwarted Lu-don's plan to seize the palace."

"I will not forget," replied the chief. "Go your way. We are enough to overpower the traitors."

"Tell me," asked Tarzan, "how I may know this city of Tu-lur?"

"It lies upon the south shore of the second lake below A-lur," replied the chief, "the lake that is called Jad-in-lul."

They were now approaching the band of traitors, who evidently thought that this was another contingent of their own party since they made no effort either toward defense or retreat. Suddenly the chief raised his voice in a savage war cry that was immediately taken up by his followers, and simultaneously, as though the cry were a command, the entire party broke into a mad charge upon the surprised rebels.

Satisfied with the outcome of his suddenly conceived plan and sure that it would work to the disadvantage of Lu-don, Tarzan turned into a side street and pointed his steps toward the outskirts of the city in search of the trail that led southward toward Tu-lur.

XVII

BY JAD-BAL-LUL

As Mo-sar carried Jane Clayton from the palace of Ko-tan, the king, the woman struggled incessantly to regain her freedom. He tried to compel her to walk, but despite his threats and his abuse she would not voluntarily take a single step in the direction in which he wished her to go. Instead she threw herself to the ground each time he sought to place her upon her feet, and so of necessity he was compelled to carry her though at last he tied her hands and gagged her to save himself from further lacerations, for the beauty and slenderness of the woman belied her strength and courage. When he came at last to where his men had gathered he was glad indeed to turn her over to a couple of stalwart warriors, but these too were forced to carry her since Mo-sar's fear of the vengeance of Ko-tan's retainers would brook no delays.

And thus they came down out of the hills from which A-lur is carved, to the meadows that skirt the lower end of Jad-ben-lul, with Jane Clayton carried between two of Mo-sar's men. At the edge of the lake lay a fleet of strong canoes, hollowed from the trunks of trees, their bows and sterns carved in the semblance of grotesque beasts or birds and vividly colored by some master in that primitive school of art, which fortunately is not without its devotees today.

Into the stern of one of these canoes the warriors tossed their captive at a sign from Mo-sar, who came and stood beside her as the warriors were finding their places in the canoes and selecting their paddles.

"Come, Beautiful One," he said, "let us be friends and you shall not be harmed. You will find Mo-sar a kind master if you do his bidding," and thinking to make a good impression on her he removed the gag from her mouth and the thongs from her wrists, knowing well that she could not escape surrounded as she was by his warriors, and presently, when they were out on the lake, she would be as safely imprisoned as though he held her behind bars.

And so the fleet moved off to the accompaniment of the gentle splashing of a hundred paddles, to follow the windings of the rivers and lakes through which the waters of the Valley of Jad-ben-Otho empty into the great morass to the south. The warriors, resting upon one knee, faced the bow and in the last canoe Mo-sar tiring of his fruitless attempts to win responses from his sullen captive, squatted in the bottom of the canoe with his back toward her and resting his head upon the gunwale sought sleep.

Thus they moved in silence between the verdure-clad banks of the little river through which the waters of Jad-ben-lul emptied—now in the moonlight, now in dense shadow where great trees overhung the stream, and at last out upon the waters of another lake, the black shores of which seemed far away under the weird influence of a moonlight night.

Jane Clayton sat alert in the stern of the last canoe. For months she had been under constant surveillance, the prisoner first of one ruthless race and now the prisoner of another. Since the long-gone day that Hauptmann Fritz Schneider and his band of native German troops had treacherously wrought the Kaiser's work of rapine and destruction on the Greystoke bungalow and carried her away to captivity she had not drawn a free breath. That she had survived unharmed the countless dangers through which she had passed she attributed solely to the beneficence of a kind and watchful Providence.

At first she had been held on the orders of the German High Command with a view of her ultimate value as a hostage and during these months she had been subjected to neither hardship nor oppression, but when the Germans had become hard pressed toward the close of their unsuccessful campaign in East Africa it had been determined to take her further into the interior and now there was an element of revenge in their motives, since it must have been apparent that she could no longer be of any possible military value.

Bitter indeed were the Germans against that half-savage mate of hers who had cunningly annoyed and harassed them with a fiendishness of persistence and ingenuity that had resulted in a noticeable loss in morale in the sector he had chosen for his operations. They had to charge against him the lives of certain officers that he had deliberately taken with his own hands, and one entire section of trench that had made possible a disastrous turning movement by the British. Tarzan had out-generaled them at every point. He had met cunning with cunning and cruelty with cru-

elties until they feared and loathed his very name. The cunning trick that they had played upon him in destroying his home, murdering his retainers, and covering the abduction of his wife in such a way as to lead him to believe that she had been killed, they had regretted a thousand times, for a thousandfold had they paid the price for their senseless ruthlessness, and now, unable to wreak their vengeance directly upon him, they had conceived the idea of inflicting further suffering upon his mate.

In sending her into the interior to avoid the path of the victorious British, they had chosen as her escort Lieutenant Erich Obergatz who had been second in command of Schneider's company, and who alone of its officers had escaped the consuming vengeance of the ape-man. For a long time Obergatz had held her in a native village, the chief of which was still under the domination of his fear of the ruthless German oppressors. While here only hardships and discomforts assailed her, Obergatz himself being held in leash by the orders of his distant superior but as time went on the life in the village grew to be a veritable hell of cruelties and oppressions practiced by the arrogant Prussian upon the villagers and the members of his native command—for time hung heavily upon the hands of the lieutenant and with idleness combining with the personal discomforts he was compelled to endure, his none too agreeable temper found an outlet first in petty interference with the chiefs and later in the practice of absolute cruelties upon them.

What the self-sufficient German could not see was plain to Jane Clayton—that the sympathies of Obergatz's native soldiers lay with the villagers and that all were so heartily sickened by his abuse that it needed now but the slightest spark to detonate the mine of revenge and hatred that the pig-headed Hun had been assiduously fabricating beneath his own person.

And at last it came, but from an unexpected source in the form of a German native deserter from the theater of war. Footsore, weary, and spent, he dragged himself into the village late one afternoon, and before Obergatz was even aware of his presence the whole village knew that the power of Germany in Africa was at an end. It did not take long for the lieutenant's native soldiers to realize that the authority that held them in service no longer existed and that with it had gone the power to pay them their miserable wage. Or at least, so they reasoned. To them Obergatz no longer represented aught else than a powerless and hated foreigner, and short indeed would have been his shrift had not a native woman who had conceived a doglike affection for Jane Clayton hurried to her with word of the murderous plan, for the fate of the innocent white woman lay in the balance beside that of the guilty Teuton.

"Already they are quarreling as to which one shall possess you," she told Jane.

"When will they come for us?" asked Jane. "Did you hear them say?"

"Tonight," replied the woman, "for even now that he has none to fight for him they still fear the white man. And so they will come at night and kill him while he sleeps."

Jane thanked the woman and sent her away lest the suspicion of her fellows be aroused against her when they discovered that the two whites had learned of their intentions. The woman went at once to the hut occupied by Obergatz. She had never gone there before and the German looked up in surprise as he saw who his visitor was.

Briefly she told him what she had heard. At first he was inclined to bluster arrogantly, with a great display of bravado but she silenced him peremptorily.

"Such talk is useless," she said shortly. "You have brought upon yourself the just hatred of these people. Regardless of the truth or falsity of the report which has been brought to them, they believe in it and there is nothing now between you and your Maker other than flight. We shall both be dead before morning if we are unable to escape from the village unseen. If you go to them

now with your silly protestations of authority you will be dead a little sooner, that is all."

"You think it is as bad as that?" he said, a noticeable alteration in his tone and manner.

"It is precisely as I have told you," she replied. "They will come tonight and kill you while you sleep. Find me pistols and a rifle and ammunition and we will pretend that we go into the jungle to hunt. That you have done often. Perhaps it will arouse suspicion that I accompany you but that we must chance. And be sure my dear Herr Lieutenant to bluster and curse and abuse your servants unless they note a change in your manner and realizing your fear know that you suspect their intention. If all goes well then we can go out into the jungle to hunt and we need not return.

"But first and now you must swear never to harm me, or otherwise it would be better that I called the chief and turned you over to him and then put a bullet into my own head, for unless you swear as I have asked I were no better alone in the jungle with you than here at the mercies of these degraded blacks."

"I swear," he replied solemnly, "in the names of my God and my Kaiser that no harm shall befall you at my hands, Lady Greystoke."

"Very well," she said, "we will make this pact to assist each other to return to civilization, but let it be understood that there is and never can be any semblance even of respect for you upon my part. I am drowning and you are the straw. Carry that always in your mind, German."

If Obergatz had held any doubt as to the sincerity of her word it would have been wholly dissipated by the scathing contempt of her tone. And so Obergatz, without further parley, got pistols and an extra rifle for Jane, as well as bandoliers of cartridges. In his usual arrogant and disagreeable manner he called his servants, telling them that he and the white *kali* were going out into the brush to hunt. The beaters would go north as far as the little hill and then circle back to the east and in toward the village. The gun carriers he directed to take the extra pieces and precede himself and Jane slowly toward the east, waiting for them at the ford about half a mile distant. The blacks responded with greater alacrity than usual and it was noticeable to both Jane and Obergatz that they left the village whispering and laughing.

"The swine think it is a great joke," growled Obergatz, "that the afternoon before I die I go out and hunt meat for them."

As soon as the gun bearers disappeared in the jungle beyond the village the two Europeans followed along the same trail, nor was there any attempt upon the part of Obergatz's native soldiers, or the warriors of the chief to detain them, for they too doubtless were more than willing that the whites should bring them in one more mess of meat before they killed them.

A quarter of a mile from the village, Obergatz turned toward the south from the trail that led to the ford and hurrying onward the two put as great a distance as possible between them and the village before night fell. They knew from the habits of their erstwhile hosts that there was little danger of pursuit by night since the villagers held Numa, the lion, in too great respect to venture needlessly beyond their stockade during the hours that the king of beasts was prone to choose for hunting.

And thus began a seemingly endless sequence of frightful days and horror-laden nights as the two fought their way toward the south in the face of almost inconceivable hardships, privations, and dangers. The east coast was nearer but Obergatz positively refused to chance throwing himself into the hands of the British by returning to the territory which they now controlled, insisting instead upon attempting to make his way through an unknown wilderness to South Africa where, among the Boers, he was convinced he would find willing sympathizers who would find some way to return him in safety to Germany, and the woman was perforce compelled to accompany him.

And so they had crossed the great thorny, waterless steppe and come at last to the edge of the morass before Pal-ul-don. They had reached this point just before the rainy season when the waters of the morass were at their lowest ebb. At this time a hard crust is baked upon the dried surface of the marsh and there is only the open water at the center to materially impede progress. It is a condition that exists perhaps not more than a few weeks, or even days at the termination of long periods of drought, and so the two crossed the otherwise almost impassable barrier without realizing its latent terrors. Even the open water in the center chanced to be deserted at the time by its frightful denizens which the drought and the receding waters had driven southward toward the mouth of Pal-ul-don's largest river which carries the waters out of the Valley of Jad-ben-Otho.

Their wanderings carried them across the mountains and into the Valley of Jad-ben-Otho at the source of one of the larger streams which bears the mountain waters down into the valley to empty them into the main river just below the great lake on whose northern shore lies A-lur. As they had come down out of the mountains they had been surprised by a party of Ho-don hunters. Obergatz had escaped while Jane had been taken prisoner and brought to A-lur. She had neither seen nor heard aught of the German since that time and she did not know whether he had perished in this strange land, or succeeded in successfully eluding its savage denizens and making his way at last into South Africa.

For her part, she had been incarcerated alternately in the palace and the temple as either Ko-tan or Lu-don succeeded in wresting her temporarily from the other by various strokes of cunning and intrigue. And now at last she was in the power of a new captor, one whom she knew from the gossip of the temple and the palace to be cruel and degraded. And she was in the stern of the last canoe, and every enemy back was toward her, while almost at her feet Mo-sar's loud snores gave ample evidence of his unconsciousness to his immediate surroundings.

The dark shore loomed closer to the south as

Jane Clayton, Lady Greystoke, slid quietly over the stern of the canoe into the chill waters of the lake. She scarcely moved other than to keep her nostrils above the surface while the canoe was yet discernible in the last rays of the declining moon. Then she struck out toward the southern shore.

Alone, unarmed, all but naked, in a country overrun by savage beasts and hostile men, she yet felt for the first time in many months a sensation of elation and relief. She was free! What if the next moment brought death, she knew again, at least a brief instant of absolute freedom. Her blood tingled to the almost forgotten sensation and it was with difficulty that she restrained a glad triumphant cry as she clambered from the quiet waters and stood upon the silent beach.

Before her loomed a forest, darkly, and from its depths came those nameless sounds that are a part of the night life of the jungle—the rustling of leaves in the wind, the rubbing together of contiguous branches, the scurrying of a rodent, all magnified by the darkness to sinister and awe-inspiring proportions; the hoot of an owl, the distant scream of a great cat, the barking of wild dogs, attested the presence of the myriad life she could not see—the savage life, the free life of which she was now a part. And then there came to her, possibly for the first time since the giant ape-man had come into her life, a fuller realization of what the jungle meant to him, for though alone and unprotected from its hideous dangers she yet felt its lure upon her and an exaltation that she had not dared hope to feel again.

Ah, if that mighty mate of hers were but by her side! What utter joy and bliss would be hers! She longed for no more than this. The parade of cities, the comforts and luxuries of civilization held forth no allure half as insistent as the glorious freedom of the jungle.

A lion moaned in the blackness to her right, eliciting delicious thrills that crept along her spine. The hair at the back of her head seemed to stand erect—yet she was unafraid. The muscles bequeathed her by some primordial ancestor reacted instinctively to the presence of an ancient enemy—that was all. The woman moved slowly and deliberately toward the wood. Again the lion moaned; this time nearer. She sought a low-hanging branch and finding it swung easily into the friendly shelter of the tree. The long and perilous journey with Obergatz had trained her muscles and her nerves to such unaccustomed habits. She found a safe resting place such as Tarzan had taught her was best and there she curled herself, thirty feet above the ground, for a night's rest. She was cold and uncomfortable and yet she slept, for her heart was warm with renewed hope and her tired brain had found temporary surcease from worry.

She slept until the heat of the sun, high in the heavens, awakened her. She was rested and now her body was well as her heart was warm. A sensation of ease and comfort and happiness pervaded her being. She rose upon her gently swaying couch and stretched luxuriously; her naked limbs and lithe body mottled by the sunlight filtering through the foliage above combined with the lazy gesture to impart to her appearance something of the leopard. With careful eye she scrutinized the ground below and with attentive ear she listened for any warning sound that might suggest the near presence of enemies, either man or beast. Satisfied at last that there was nothing close of which she need have fear she clambered to the ground. She wished to bathe but the lake was too exposed and just a bit too far from the safety of the trees for her to risk it until she became more familiar with her surroundings. She wandered aimlessly through the forest searching for food which she found in abundance. She ate and rested, for she had no objective as yet. Her freedom was too new to be spoiled by plannings for the future. The haunts of civilized man seemed to her now as vague and unattainable as the half-forgotten substance of a dream. If she could but live on here in peace, waiting, waiting for—*him*. It was the old hope revived. She knew that he would come some day, if he lived. She had always known that, though recently she had believed that he would come too late. If he lived! Yes, he would come if he lived, and if he did not live she were as well off here as elsewhere, for then nothing mattered, only to wait for the end as patiently as might be.

Her wanderings brought her to a crystal brook and there she drank and bathed beneath an overhanging tree that offered her quick asylum in the event of danger. It was a quiet and beautiful spot and she loved it from the first. The bottom of the brook was paved with pretty stones and bits of glassy obsidian. As she gathered a handful of the pebbles and held them up to look at them she noticed that one of her fingers was bleeding from a clean, straight cut. She fell to searching for the cause and presently discovered it in one of the fragments of volcanic glass which revealed an edge that was almost razor-like. Jane Clayton was elated. Here, God-given to her hands, was the first beginning with which she might eventually arrive at both weapons and tools—a cutting edge. Everything was possible to him who possessed it—nothing without.

She sought until she had collected many of the precious bits of stone—until the pouch that hung at her right side was almost filled. Then she climbed into the great tree to examine them at leisure. There were some that looked like knife blades, and some that could easily be fashioned into spear heads, and many smaller ones that nature seemed to have intended for the tips of savage arrows.

The spear she would essay first—that would be easiest. There was a hollow in the bole of the tree in a great crotch high above the ground. Here she cached all of her treasure except a single knifelike sliver. With this she descended to the ground and searching out a slender sapling that grew arrow-straight she hacked and sawed until she could break it off without splitting the wood. It was just the right diameter for the shaft of a spear—a hunting spear such as her beloved Waziri had liked best. How often had she watched them fashioning them, and they had

taught her how to use them, too—them and the heavy war spears—laughing and clapping their hands as her proficiency increased.

She knew the arborescent grasses that yielded the longest and toughest fibers and these she sought and carried to her tree with the spear shaft that was to be. Clambering to her crotch she bent to her work, humming softly a little tune. She caught herself and smiled—it was the first time in all these bitter months that song had passed her lips or such a smile.

"I feel," she sighed, "I almost feel that John is near—my John—my Tarzan!"

She cut the spear shaft to the proper length and removed the twigs and branches and the bark, whittling and scraping at the nubs until the surface was all smooth and straight. Then she split one end and inserted a spear point, shaping the wood until it fitted perfectly. This done she laid the shaft aside and fell to splitting the thick grass stems and pounding and twisting them until she had separated and partially cleaned the fibers. These she took down to the brook and washed and brought back again and wound tightly around the cleft end of the shaft, which she had notched to receive them, and the upper part of the spear head which she had also notched slightly with a bit of stone. It was a crude spear but the best that she could attain in so short a time. Later, she promised herself, she should have others—many of them—and they would be spears of which even the greatest of the Waziri spear-men might be proud.

XVIII
THE LION PIT OF TU-LUR

Though Tarzan searched the outskirts of the city until nearly dawn he discovered nowhere the spoor of his mate. The breeze coming down from the mountains brought to his nostrils a diversity of scents but there was not among them the slightest suggestion of her whom he sought. The natural deduction was therefore that she had been taken in some other direction. In his search he had many times crossed the fresh tracks of many men leading toward the lake and these he concluded had probably been made by Jane Clayton's abductors. It had only been to minimize the chance of error by the process of elimination that he had carefully reconnoitered every other avenue leading from A-lur toward the southeast where lay Mo-sar's city of Tu-lur, and now he followed the trail to the shores of Jad-ben-lul where the party had embarked upon the quiet waters in their sturdy canoes.

He found many other craft of the same description moored along the shore and one of these he commandeered for the purpose of pursuit. It was daylight when he passed through the lake which lies next below Jad-ben-lul and paddling strongly passed within sight of the very tree in which his lost mate lay sleeping.

Had the gentle wind that caressed the bosom of the lake been blowing from a southerly direction the giant ape-man and Jane Clayton would have been reunited then, but an unkind fate had willed otherwise and the opportunity passed with the passing of his canoe which presently his powerful strokes carried out of sight into the stream at the lower end of the lake.

Following the winding river which bore a considerable distance to the north before doubling back to empty into the Jad-in-lul, the ape-man missed a portage that would have saved him hours of paddling.

It was at the upper end of this portage where Mo-sar and his warriors had debarked that the chief discovered the absence of his captive. As Mo-sar had been asleep since shortly after their departure from A-lur, and as none of the warriors recalled when she had last been seen, it was impossible to conjecture with any degree of accuracy the place where she had escaped. The consensus of opinion was, however, that it had been in the narrow river connecting Jad-ben-lul with the lake next below it, which is called Jad-bal-lul, which freely translated means the lake of gold. Mo-sar had been very wroth and having himself been the only one at fault he naturally

sought with great diligence to fix the blame upon another.

He would have returned in search of her had he not feared to meet a pursuing company dispatched either by Ja-don or the high priest, both of whom, he knew, had just grievances against him. He would not even spare a boatload of his warriors from his own protection to return in quest of the fugitive but hastened onward with as little delay as possible across the portage and out upon the waters of Jad-in-lul.

The morning sun was just touching the white domes of Tu-lur when Mo-sar's paddlers brought their canoes against the shore at the city's edge. Safe once more behind his own walls and protected by many warriors, the courage of the chief returned sufficiently at least to permit him to dispatch three canoes in search of Jane Clayton, and also to go as far as A-lur if possible to learn what had delayed Bu-lot, whose failure to reach the canoes with the balance of the party at the time of the flight from the northern city had in no way delayed Mo-sar's departure, his own safety being of far greater moment than that of his son.

As the three canoes reached the portage on their return journey the warriors who were dragging them from the water were suddenly startled by the appearance of two priests, carrying a light canoe in the direction of Jad-in-lul. At first they thought them the advance guard of a larger force of Lu-don's followers, although the correctness of such a theory was belied by their knowledge that priests never accepted the risks or perils of a warrior's vocation, nor even fought until driven into a corner and forced to do so. Secretly the warriors of Pal-ul-don held the emasculated priesthood in contempt and so instead of immediately taking up the offensive as they would have had the two men been warriors from A-lur instead of priests, they waited to question them.

At sight of the warriors the priests made the sign of peace and upon being asked if they were alone they answered in the affirmative.

The leader of Mo-sar's warriors permitted

them to approach. "What do you here," he asked, "in the country of Mo-sar, so far from your own city?"

"We carry a message from Lu-don, the high priest, to Mo-sar," explained one.

"Is it a message of peace or of war?" asked the warrior.

"It is an offer of peace," replied the priest.

"And Lu-don is sending no warriors behind you?" queried the fighting man.

"We are alone," the priest assured him. "None in A-lur save Lu-don knows that we have come upon this errand."

"Then go your way," said the warrior.

"Who is that?" asked one of the priests suddenly, pointing toward the upper end of the lake at the point where the river from Jad-bal-lul entered it.

All eyes turned in the direction that he had indicated to see a lone warrior paddling rapidly into Jad-in-lul, the prow of his canoe pointing toward Tu-lur. The warriors and the priests drew into the concealment of the bushes on either side of the portage.

"It is the terrible man who called himself the Dor-ul-Otho," whispered one of the priests. "I would know that figure among a great multitude as far as I could see it."

"You are right, priest," cried one of the warriors who had seen Tarzan the day that he had first entered Ko-tan's palace. "It is indeed he who has been rightly called Tarzan-jad-guru."

"Hasten priests," cried the leader of the party. "You are two paddles in a light canoe. Easily can you reach Tu-lur ahead of him and warn Mo-sar of his coming, for he has but only entered the lake."

For a moment the priests demurred for they had no stomach for an encounter with this terrible man, but the warrior insisted and even went so far as to threaten them. Their canoe was taken from them and pushed into the lake and they were all but lifted bodily from their feet and put aboard it. Still protesting they were shoved out upon the water where they were immediately in full view of the lone paddler above them. Now

there was no alternative. The city of Tu-lur offered the only safety and bending to their paddles the two priests sent their craft swiftly in the direction of the city.

The warriors withdrew again to the concealment of the foliage. If Tarzan had seen them and should come hither to investigate there were thirty of them against one and naturally they had no fear of the outcome, but they did not consider it necessary to go out upon the lake to meet him since they had been sent to look for the escaped prisoner and not to intercept the strange warrior, the stories of whose ferocity and prowess doubtless helped them to arrive at their decision to provoke no uncalled-for quarrel with him.

If he had seen them he gave no sign, but continued paddling steadily and strongly toward the city, nor did he increase his speed as the two priests shot out in full view. The moment the priests' canoe touched the shore by the city its occupants leaped out and hurried swiftly toward the palace gate, casting affrighted glances behind them. They sought immediate audience with Mo-sar, after warning the warriors on guard that Tarzan was approaching.

They were conducted at once to the chief, whose court was a smaller replica of that of the king of A-lur. "We come from Lu-don, the high priest," explained the spokesman. "He wishes the friendship of Mo-sar, who has always been his friend. Ja-don is gathering warriors to make himself king. Throughout the villages of the Ho-don are thousands who will obey the commands of Lu-don, the high priest. Only with Lu-don's assistance can Mo-sar become king, and the message from Lu-don is that if Mo-sar would retain the friendship of Lu-don he must return immediately the woman he took from the quarters of the Princess O-lo-a."

At this juncture a warrior entered. His excitement was evident. "The Dor-ul-Otho has come to Tu-lur and demands to see Mo-sar at once," he said.

"The Dor-ul-Otho!" exclaimed Mo-sar.

"That is the message he sent," replied the

warrior, "and indeed he is not as are the people of Pal-ul-don. He is, we think, the same of whom the warriors that returned from A-lur today told us and whom some call Tarzan-jad-guru and some Dor-ul-Otho. But indeed only the son of god would dare come thus alone to a strange city, so it must be that he speaks the truth."

Mo-sar, his heart filled with terror and indecision, turned questioningly toward the priests.

"Receive him graciously, Mo-sar," counseled he who had spoken before, his advice prompted by the petty shrewdness of his defective brain which, under the added influence of Lu-don's tutorage leaned always toward duplicity. "Receive him graciously and when he is quite convinced of your friendship he will be off his guard, and then you may do with him as you will. But if possible, Mo-sar, and you would win the undying gratitude of Lu-don, the high priest, save him alive for my master."

Mo-sar nodded understandingly and turning to the warrior commanded that he conduct the visitor to him.

"We must not be seen by the creature," said one of the priests. "Give us your answer to Lu-don, Mo-sar, and we will go our way."

"Tell Lu-don," replied the chief, "that the woman would have been lost to him entirely had it not been for me. I sought to bring her to Tu-lur that I might save her for him from the clutches of Ja-don, but during the night she escaped. Tell Lu-don that I have sent thirty warriors to search for her. It is strange you did not see them as you came."

"We did," replied the priests, "but they told us nothing of the purpose of their journey."

"It is as I have told you," said Mo-sar, "and if they find her, assure your master that she will be kept unharmed in Tu-lur for him. Also tell him that I will send my warriors to join with his against Ja-don whenever he sends word that he wants them. Now go, for Tarzan-jad-guru will soon be here."

He signaled to a slave. "Lead the priests to the temple," he commanded, "and ask the high priest of Tu-lur to see that they are fed and permitted to return to A-lur when they will."

The two priests were conducted from the apartment by the slave through a doorway other than that at which they had entered, and a moment later Tarzan-jad-guru strode into the presence of Mo-sar, ahead of the warrior whose duty it had been to conduct and announce him. The ape-man made no sign of greeting or of peace but strode directly toward the chief who, only by the exertion of his utmost powers of will, hid the terror that was in his heart at sight of the giant figure and the scowling face.

"I am the Dor-ul-Otho," said the ape-man in level tones that carried to the mind of Mo-sar a suggestion of cold steel; "I am Dor-ul-Otho, and I come to Tu-lur for the woman you stole from the apartments of O-lo-a, the princess."

The very boldness of Tarzan's entry into this hostile city had had the effect of giving him a great moral advantage over Mo-sar and the savage warriors who stood upon either side of the chief. Truly it seemed to them that no other than the son of Jad-ben-Otho would dare so heroic an act. Would any mortal warrior act thus boldly, and alone enter the presence of a powerful chief and, in the midst of a score of warriors, arrogantly demand an accounting? No, it was beyond reason. Mo-sar was faltering in his decision to betray the stranger by seeming friendliness. He even paled to a sudden thought—Jad-ben-Otho knew everything, even our inmost thoughts. Was it not therefore possible that this creature, if after all it should prove true that he was the Dor-ul-Otho, might even now be reading the wicked design that the priests had implanted in the brain of Mo-sar and which he had entertained so favorably? The chief squirmed and fidgeted upon the bench of hewn rock that was his throne.

"Quick," snapped the ape-man, "Where is she?"

"She is not here," cried Mo-sar.

"You lie," replied Tarzan.

"As Jad-ben-Otho is my witness, she is not in

Tu-lur," insisted the chief. "You may search the palace and the temple and the entire city but you will not find her, for she is not here."

"Where is she, then?" demanded the ape-man. "You took her from the palace at A-lur. If she is not here, where is she? Tell me not that harm has befallen her," and he took a sudden threatening step toward Mo-sar, that sent the chief shrinking back in terror.

"Wait," he cried, "if you are indeed the Dor-ul-Otho you will know that I speak the truth. I took her from the palace of Ko-tan to save her for Lu-don, the high priest, lest with Ko-tan dead Ja-don seize her. But during the night she escaped from me between here and A-lur, and I have but just sent three canoes full-manned in search of her."

Something in the chief's tone and manner assured the ape-man that he spoke in part the truth, and that once again he had braved incalculable dangers and suffered loss of time futilely.

"What wanted the priests of Lu-don that preceded me here?" demanded Tarzan chancing a shrewd guess that the two he had seen paddling so frantically to avoid a meeting with him had indeed come from the high priest at A-lur.

"They came upon an errand similar to yours," replied Mo-sar; "to demand the return of the woman whom Lu-don thought I had stolen from him, thus wronging me as deeply, O Dor-ul-Otho, as have you."

"I would question the priests," said Tarzan. "Bring them hither." His peremptory and arrogant manner left Mo-sar in doubt as to whether to be more incensed, or terrified, but ever as is the way with such as he, he concluded that the first consideration was his own safety. If he could transfer the attention and the wrath of this terrible man from himself to Lu-don's priests it would more than satisfy him and if they should conspire to harm him, then Mo-sar would be safe in the eyes of Jad-ben-Otho if it finally developed that the stranger was in reality the son of god. He felt uncomfortable in Tarzan's presence and this fact rather accentuated his doubt, for thus indeed

would mortal feel in the presence of a god. Now he saw a way to escape, at least temporarily.

"I will fetch them myself, Dor-ul-Otho," he said, and turning, left the apartment. His hurried steps brought him quickly to the temple, for the palace grounds of Tu-lur, which also included the temple as in all of the Ho-don cities, covered a much smaller area than those of the larger city of A-lur. He found Lu-don's messengers with the high priest of his own temple and quickly transmitted to them the commands of the ape-man.

"What do you intend to do with him?" asked one of the priests.

"I have no quarrel with him," replied Mo-sar. "He came in peace and he may depart in peace, for who knows but that he is indeed the Dor-ul-Otho?"

"We know that he is not," replied Lu-don's emissary. "We have every proof that he is only mortal, a strange creature from another country. Already has Lu-don offered his life to Jad-ben-Otho if he is wrong in his belief that this creature is not the son of god. If the high priest of A-lur, who is the highest priest of all the high priests of Pal-ul-don is thus so sure that the creature is an impostor as to stake his life upon his judgment then who are we to give credence to the claims of this stranger? No, Mo-sar, you need not fear him. He is only a warrior who may be overcome with the same weapons that subdue your own fighting men. Were it not for Lu-don's command that he be taken alive I would urge you to set your warriors upon him and slay him, but the commands of Lu-don are the commands of Jad-ben-Otho himself, and those we may not disobey."

But still the remnant of a doubt stirred within the cowardly breast of Mo-sar, urging him to let another take the initiative against the stranger.

"He is yours then," he replied, "to do with as you will. I have no quarrel with him. What you may command shall be the command of Lu-don, the high priest, and further than that I shall have nothing to do in the matter."

The priests turned to him who guided the destinies of the temple at Tu-lur. "Have you no plan?" they asked. "High indeed will he stand in the counsels of Lu-don and in the eyes of Jad-ben-Otho who finds the means to capture this impostor alive."

"There is the lion pit," whispered the high priest. "It is now vacant and what will hold *ja* and *jato* will hold this stranger if he is not the Dor-ul-Otho."

"It will hold him," said Mo-sar; "doubtless too it would hold a *gryf*, but first you would have to get the *gryf* into it."

The priests pondered this bit of wisdom thoughtfully and then one of those from A-lur spoke. "It should not be difficult," he said, "if we use the wits that Jad-ben-Otho gave us instead of the worldly muscles which were handed down to us from our fathers and our mothers and which have not even the power possessed by those of the beasts that run about on four feet."

"Lu-don matched his wits with the stranger and lost," suggested Mo-sar. "But this is your own affair. Carry it out as you see best."

"At A-lur, Ko-tan made much of this Dor-ul-Otho and the priests conducted him through the temple. It would arouse in his mind no suspicion were you to do the same, and let the high priest of Tu-lur invite him to the temple and gathering all the priests make a great show of belief in his kinship to Jad-ben-Otho. And what more natural then than that the high priest should wish to show him through the temple as did Lu-don at A-lur when Ko-tan commanded it, and if by chance he should be led through the lion pit it would be a simple matter for those who bear the torches to extinguish them suddenly and before the stranger was aware of what had happened, the stone gates could be dropped, thus safely securing him."

"But there are windows in the pit that let in light," interposed the high priest, "and even though the torches were extinguished he could still see and might escape before the stone door could be lowered."

"Send one who will cover the windows tightly with hides," said the priest from A-lur.

"The plan is a good one," said Mo-sar, seeing an opportunity for entirely eliminating himself from any suspicion of complicity, "for it will require the presence of no warriors, and thus with only priests about him his mind will entertain no suspicion of harm."

They were interrupted at this point by a messenger from the palace who brought word that the Dor-ul-Otho was becoming impatient and if the priests from A-lur were not brought to him at once he would come himself to the temple and get them. Mo-sar shook his head. He could not conceive of such brazen courage in mortal breast and glad he was that the plan evolved for Tarzan's undoing did not necessitate his active participation.

And so, while Mo-sar left for a secret corner of the palace by a roundabout way, three priests were dispatched to Tarzan and with whining words that did not entirely deceive him, they acknowledged his kinship to Jad-ben-Otho and begged him in the name of the high priest to honor the temple with a visit, when the priests from A-lur would be brought to him and would answer any questions that he put to them.

Confident that a continuation of his bravado would best serve his purpose, and also that if suspicion against him should crystallize into conviction on the part of Mo-sar and his followers that he would be no worse off in the temple than in the palace, the ape-man haughtily accepted the invitation of the high priest.

And so he came into the temple and was received in a manner befitting his high claims. He questioned the two priests of A-lur from whom he obtained only a repetition of the story that Mo-sar had told him, and then the high priest invited him to inspect the temple.

They took him first to the altar court, of which there was only one in Tu-lur. It was almost identical in every respect with those at A-lur. There was a bloody altar at the east end and the drowning basin at the west, and the grizzly fringes upon the headdresses of the priests attested the fact that the eastern altar was an active force in the rites of the temple. Through the chambers and corridors beneath they led him, and finally, with torch bearers to light their steps, into a damp and gloomy labyrinth at a low level and here in a large chamber, the air of which was still heavy with the odor of lions, the crafty priests of Tu-lur encompassed their shrewd design.

The torches were suddenly extinguished. There was a hurried confusion of bare feet moving rapidly across the stone floor. There was a loud crash as of a heavy weight of stone falling upon stone, and then surrounding the ape-man naught but the darkness and the silence of the tomb.

XIX
DIANA OF THE JUNGLE

Jane had made her first kill and she was very proud of it. It was not a very formidable animal—only a hare; but it marked an epoch in her existence. Just as in the dim past the first hunter had shaped the destinies of mankind so it seemed that this event might shape hers in some new mold. No longer was she dependent upon the wild fruits and vegetables for sustenance. Now she might command meat, the giver of the strength and endurance she would require successfully to cope with the necessities of her primitive existence.

The next step was fire. She might learn to eat raw flesh as had her lord and master; but she shrank from that. The thought even was repulsive. She had, however, a plan for fire. She had given the matter thought, but had been too busy to put it into execution so long as fire could be of no immediate use to her. Now it was different— she had something to cook and her mouth watered for the flesh of her kill. She would grill it above glowing embers. Jane hastened to her tree. Among the treasures she had gathered in the bed

of the stream were several pieces of volcanic glass, clear as crystal. She sought until she had found the one in mind, which was convex. Then she hurried to the ground and gathered a little pile of powdered bark that was very dry, and some dead leaves and grasses that had lain long in the hot sun. Near at hand she arranged a supply of dead twigs and branches—small and large.

Vibrant with suppressed excitement she held the bit of glass above the tinder, moving it slowly until she had focused the sun's rays upon a tiny spot. She waited breathlessly. How slow it was! Were her high hopes to be dashed in spite of all her clever planning? No! A thin thread of smoke rose gracefully into the quiet air. Presently the tinder glowed and broke suddenly into flame. Jane clasped her hands beneath her chin with a little gurgling exclamation of delight. She had achieved fire!

She piled on twigs and then larger branches and at last dragged a small log to the flames and pushed an end of it into the fire which was crackling merrily. It was the sweetest sound that she had heard for many a month. But she could not wait for the mass of embers that would be required to cook her hare. As quickly as might be she skinned and cleaned her kill, burying the hide and entrails. That she had learned from Tarzan. It served two purposes. One was the necessity for keeping a sanitary camp and the other the obliteration of the scent that most quickly attracts the man-eaters.

Then she ran a stick through the carcass and held it above the flames. By turning it often she prevented burning and at the same time permitted the meat to cook thoroughly all the way through. When it was done she scampered high into the safety of her tree to enjoy her meal in quiet and peace. Never, thought Lady Greystoke, had aught more delicious passed her lips. She patted her spear affectionately. It had brought her this toothsome dainty and with it a feeling of greater confidence and safety than she had enjoyed since that frightful day that she and

Obergatz had spent their last cartridge. She would never forget that day—it had seemed one hideous succession of frightful beast after frightful beast. They had not been long in this strange country, yet they thought that they were hardened to dangers, for daily they had had encounters with ferocious creatures; but this day—she shuddered when she thought of it. And with her last cartridge she had killed a black and yellow striped lion-thing with great saber teeth just as it was about to spring upon Obergatz who had futilely emptied his rifle into it—the last shot—his final cartridge. For another day they had carried the now useless rifles; but at last they had discarded them and thrown away the cumbersome bandoliers, as well. How they had managed to survive during the ensuing week she could never quite understand, and then the Ho-don had come upon them and captured her. Obergatz had escaped—she was living it all over again. Doubtless he was dead unless he had been able to reach this side of the valley which was quite evidently less overrun with savage beasts.

Jane's days were very full ones now, and the daylight hours seemed all too short in which to accomplish the many things she had determined upon, since she had concluded that this spot presented as ideal a place as she could find to live until she could fashion the weapons she considered necessary for the obtaining of meat and for self-defense.

She felt that she must have, in addition to a good spear, a knife, and bow and arrows. Possibly when these had been achieved she might seriously consider an attempt to fight her way to one of civilization's nearest outposts. In the meantime it was necessary to construct some sort of protective shelter in which she might feel a greater sense of security by night, for she knew that there was a possibility that any night she might receive a visit from a prowling panther, although she had as yet seen none upon this side of the valley. Aside from this danger she felt comparatively safe in her aerial retreat.

The cutting of the long poles for her home occupied all of the daylight hours that were not engaged in the search for food. These poles she carried high into her tree and with them constructed a flooring across two stout branches binding the poles together and also to the branches with fibers from the tough arboraceous grasses that grew in profusion near the stream. Similarly she built walls and a roof, the latter thatched with many layers of great leaves. The fashioning of the barred windows and the door were matters of great importance and consuming interest. The windows, there were two of them, were large and the bars permanently fixed; but the door was small, the opening just large enough to permit her to pass through easily on hands and knees, which made it easier to barricade. She lost count of the days that the house cost her; but time was a cheap commodity—she had more of it than of anything else. It meant so little to her that she had not even any desire to keep account of it. How long since she and Obergatz had fled from the wrath of the Negro villagers she did not know and she could only roughly guess at the seasons. She worked hard for two reasons; one was to hasten the completion of her little place of refuge, and the other a desire for such physical exhaustion at night that she would sleep through those dreaded hours to a new day. As a matter of fact the house was finished in less than a week—that is, it was made as safe as it ever would be, though regardless of how long she might occupy it she would keep on adding touches and refinements here and there.

Her daily life was filled with her house building and her hunting, to which was added an occasional spice of excitement contributed by roving lions. To the woodcraft that she had learned from Tarzan, that master of the art, was added a considerable store of practical experience derived from her own past adventures in the jungle and the long months with Obergatz, nor was any day now lacking in some added store of useful knowledge. To these facts was attributable her apparent immunity from harm, since they told her when *ja* was approaching before he crept close enough for a successful charge and, too, they kept her close to those never-failing havens of retreat—the trees.

The nights, filled with their weird noises, were lonely and depressing. Only her ability to sleep quickly and soundly made them endurable. The first night that she spent in her completed house behind barred windows and barricaded door was one of almost undiluted peace and happiness. The night noises seemed far removed and impersonal and the soughing of the wind in the trees was gently soothing. Before, it had carried a mournful note and was sinister in that it might hide the approach of some real danger. That night she slept indeed.

She went further afield now in search of food. So far nothing but rodents had fallen to her spear—her ambition was an antelope, since beside the flesh it would give her, and the gut for her bow, the hide would prove invaluable during the colder weather that she knew would accompany the rainy season. She had caught glimpses of these wary animals and was sure that they always crossed the stream at a certain spot above her camp. It was to this place that she went to hunt them. With the stealth and cunning of a panther she crept through the forest, circling about to get up wind from the ford, pausing often to look and listen for aught that might menace her—herself the personification of a hunted deer. Now she moved silently down upon the chosen spot. What luck! A beautiful buck stood drinking in the stream. The woman wormed her way closer. Now she lay upon her belly behind a small bush within throwing distance of the quarry. She must rise to her full height and throw her spear almost in the same instant and she must throw it with great force and perfect accuracy. She thrilled with the excitement of the minute, yet cool and steady were her swift muscles as she rose and cast her missile. Scarce by the width of a finger did the point strike from the spot at which it had been directed. The buck leaped high, landed upon the bank of the stream, and fell dead. Jane Clayton sprang quickly forward toward her kill.

"Bravo!" A man's voice spoke in English

from the shrubbery upon the opposite side of the stream. Jane Clayton halted in her tracks—stunned, almost, by surprise. And then a strange, unkempt figure of a man stepped into view. At first she did not recognize him, but when she did, instinctively she stepped back.

"Lieutenant Obergatz!" she cried. "Can it be you?"

"It can. It is," replied the German. "I am a strange sight, no doubt; but still it is I, Erich Obergatz. And you? You have changed too, is it not?"

He was looking at her naked limbs and her golden breastplates, the loin cloth of *jato*-hide, the harness and ornaments that constitute the apparel of a Ho-don woman—the things that Lu-don had dressed her in as his passion for her grew. Not Ko-tan's daughter, even, had finer trappings.

"But why are you here?" Jane insisted. "I had thought you safely among civilized men by this time, if you still lived."

"Gott!" he exclaimed. "I do not know why I continue to live. I have prayed to die and yet I cling to life. There is no hope. We are doomed to remain in this horrible land until we die. The bog! The frightful bog! I have searched its shores for a place to cross until I have entirely circled the hideous country. Easily enough we entered; but the rains have come since and now no living man could pass that slough of slimy mud and hungry reptiles. Have I not tried it! And the beasts that roam this accursed land! They hunt me by day and by night."

"But how have you escaped them?" she asked.

"I do not know," he replied gloomily. "I have fled and fled and fled. I have remained hungry and thirsty in tree tops for days at a time. I have fashioned weapons—clubs and spears—and I have learned to use them. I have slain a lion with my club. So even will a cornered rat fight. And we are no better than rats in this land of stupendous dangers, you and I. But tell me about yourself. If it is surprising that I live, how much more so that you still survive."

Briefly she told him and all the while she was

wondering what she might do to rid herself of him. She could not conceive of a prolonged existence with him as her sole companion. Better, a thousand times better, to be alone. Never had her hatred and contempt for him lessened through the long weeks and months of their constant companionship, and now that he could be of no service in returning her to civilization, she shrank from the thought of seeing him daily. And, too, she feared him. Never had she trusted him; but now there was a strange light in his eye that had not been there when last she saw him. She could not interpret it—all she knew was that it gave her a feeling of apprehension—a nameless dread.

"You lived long then in the city of A-lur?" he said, speaking in the language of Pal-ul-don.

"You have learned this tongue?" she asked. "How?"

"I fell in with a band of half-breeds," he replied, "members of a proscribed race that dwells in the rock-bound gut through which the principal river of the valley empties into the morass. They are called Waz-ho-don and their village is partly made up of cave dwellings and partly of houses carved from the soft rock at the foot of the cliff. They are very ignorant and superstitious and when they first saw me and realized that I had no tail and that my hands and feet were not like theirs they were afraid of me. They thought that I was either god or demon. Being in a position where I could neither escape them nor defend myself, I made a bold front and succeeded in impressing them to such an extent that they conducted me to their city, which they call Bu-lur, and there they fed me and treated me with kindness. As I learned their language I sought to impress them more and more with the idea that I was a god, and I succeeded, too, until an old fellow who was something of a priest among them, or medicine-man, became jealous of my growing power. That was the beginning of the end and came near to being the end in fact. He told them that if I was a god I would not bleed if a knife was stuck into me—if I did bleed it would prove conclusively that I was not a god.

Without my knowledge he arranged to stage the ordeal before the whole village upon a certain night—it was upon one of those numerous occasions when they eat and drink to Jad-ben-Otho, their pagan deity. Under the influence of their vile liquor they would be ripe for any bloodthirsty scheme the medicine-man might evolve. One of the women told me about the plan—not with any intent to warn me of danger, but prompted merely by feminine curiosity as to whether or not I would bleed if stuck with a dagger. She could not wait, it seemed, for the orderly procedure of the ordeal—she wanted to know at once, and when I caught her trying to slip a knife into my side and questioned her she explained the whole thing with the utmost naïveté. The warriors already had commenced drinking—it would have been futile to make any sort of appeal either to their intellects or their superstitions. There was but one alternative to death and that was flight. I told the woman that I was very much outraged and offended at this reflection upon my godhood and that as a mark of my disfavor I should abandon them to their fate.

" 'I shall return to heaven at once!' I exclaimed.

"She wanted to hang around and see me go, but I told her that her eyes would be blasted by the fire surrounding my departure and that she must leave at once and not return to the spot for at least an hour. I also impressed upon her the fact that should any other approach this part of the village within that time not only they, but she as well, would burst into flames and be consumed.

"She was very much impressed and lost no time in leaving, calling back as she departed that if I were indeed gone in an hour she and all the village would know that I was no less than Jad-ben-Otho himself, and so they must think me, for I can assure you that I was gone in much less than an hour, nor have I ventured close to the neighborhood of the city of Bu-lur since," and he fell to laughing in harsh, cackling notes that sent a shiver through the woman's frame.

As Obergatz talked Jane had recovered her spear from the carcass of the antelope and commenced busying herself with the removal of the hide. The man made no attempt to assist her, but stood by talking and watching her, the while he continually ran his filthy fingers through his matted hair and beard. His face and body were caked with dirt and he was naked except for a torn greasy hide about his loins. His weapons consisted of a club and knife of Waz-don pattern, that he had stolen from the city of Bu-lur; but what more greatly concerned the woman than his filth or his armament were his cackling laughter and the strange expression in his eyes.

She went on with her work, however, removing those parts of the buck she wanted, taking only as much meat as she might consume before it spoiled, as she was not sufficiently a true jungle creature to relish it beyond that stage, and then she straightened up and faced the man.

"Lieutenant Obergatz," she said, "by a chance of accident we have met again. Certainly you would not have sought the meeting any more than I. We have nothing in common other than those sentiments which may have been engendered by my natural dislike and suspicion of you, one of the authors of all the misery and sorrow that I have endured for endless months. This little corner of the world is mine by right of discovery and occupation. Go away and leave me to enjoy here what peace I may. It is the least that you can do to amend the wrong that you have done me and mine."

The man stared at her through his fishy eyes for a moment in silence, then there broke from his lips a peal of mirthless, uncanny laughter.

"Go away! Leave you alone!" he cried. "I have found you. We are going to be good friends. There is no one else in the world but us. No one will ever know what we do or what becomes of us and now you ask me to go away and live alone in this hellish solitude." Again he laughed, though neither the muscles of his eyes or his mouth reflected any mirth—it was just a hollow sound that imitated laughter.

"Remember your promise," she said.

"Promise! Promise! What are promises? They are made to be broken—we taught the world that at Liège and Louvain. No, no! I will not go away. I shall stay and protect you."

"I do not need your protection," she insisted. "You have already seen that I can use a spear."

"Yes," he said; "but it would not be right to leave you here alone—you are but a woman. No, no; I am an officer of the Kaiser and I cannot abandon you."

Once more he laughed. "We could be very happy here together," he added.

The woman could not repress a shudder, nor, in fact, did she attempt to hide her aversion.

"You do not like me?" he asked. "Ah, well; it is too sad. But some day you will love me," and again the hideous laughter.

The woman had wrapped the pieces of the buck in the hide and this she now raised and threw across her shoulder. In her other hand she held her spear and faced the German.

"Go!" she commanded. "We have wasted enough words. This is my country and I shall defend it. If I see you about again I shall kill you. Do you understand?"

An expression of rage contorted Obergatz's features. He raised his club and started toward her.

"Stop!" she commanded, throwing her spear-hand backward for a cast. "You saw me kill this buck and you have said truthfully that no one will ever know what we do here. Put these two facts together, German, and draw your own conclusions before you take another step in my direction."

The man halted and his club-hand dropped to his side. "Come," he begged in what he intended as a conciliatory tone. "Let us be friends, Lady Greystoke. We can be of great assistance to each other and I promise not to harm you."

"Remember Liège and Louvain," she reminded him with a sneer. "I am going now—be sure that you do not follow me. As far as you can walk in a day from this spot in any direction you may consider the limits of my domain. If ever again I see you within these limits I shall kill you."

There could be no question that she meant what she said and the man seemed convinced for he but stood sullenly eyeing her as she backed from sight beyond a turn in the game trail that crossed the ford where they had met, and disappeared in the forest.

XX

SILENTLY IN THE NIGHT

In A-lur the fortunes of the city had been tossed from hand to hand. The party of Ko-tan's loyal warriors that Tarzan had led to the rendezvous at the entrance to the secret passage below the palace gates had met with disaster. Their first rush had been met with soft words from the priests. They had been exhorted to defend the faith of their fathers from blasphemers. Ja-don was painted to them as a defiler of temples, and the wrath of Jad-ben-Otho was prophesied for those who embraced his cause. The priests insisted that Lu-don's only wish was to prevent the seizure of the throne by Ja-don until a new king could be chosen according to the laws of the Ho-don.

The result was that many of the palace warriors joined their fellows of the city, and when the priests saw that those whom they could influence outnumbered those who remained loyal to the palace, they caused the former to fall upon the latter with the result that many were killed and only a handful succeeded in reaching the safety of the palace gates, which they quickly barred.

The priests led their own forces through the secret passageway into the temple, while some of the loyal ones sought out Ja-don and told him all that had happened. The fight in the banquet hall had spread over a considerable portion of the palace grounds and had at last resulted in the temporary defeat of those who had opposed Ja-

don. This force, counseled by under priests sent for the purpose by Lu-don, had withdrawn within the temple grounds so that now the issue was plainly marked as between Ja-don on the one side and Lu-don on the other.

The former had been told of all that had occurred in the apartments of O-lo-a to whose safety he had attended at the first opportunity and he had also learned of Tarzan's part in leading his men to the gathering of Lu-don's warriors.

These things had naturally increased the old warrior's former inclinations of friendliness toward the ape-man, and now he regretted that the other had departed from the city.

The testimony of O-lo-a and Pan-at-lee was such as to strengthen whatever belief in the godliness of the stranger Ja-don and others of the warriors had previously entertained, until presently there appeared a strong tendency upon the part of this palace faction to make the Dor-ul-otho an issue of their original quarrel with Lu-don. Whether this occurred as the natural sequence to repeated narrations of the ape-man's exploits, which lost nothing by repetition, in conjunction with Lu-don's enmity toward him, or whether it was the shrewd design of some wily old warrior such as Ja-don, who realized the value of adding a religious cause to their temporal one, it were difficult to determine; but the fact remained that Ja-don's followers developed bitter hatred for the followers of Lu-don because of the high priest's antagonism to Tarzan.

Unfortunately however Tarzan was not there to inspire the followers of Ja-don with the holy zeal that might have quickly settled the dispute in the old chieftain's favor. Instead, he was miles away and because their repeated prayers for his presence were unanswered, the weaker spirits among them commenced to suspect that their cause did not have divine favor. There was also another and a potent cause for defection from the ranks of Ja-don. It emanated from the city where the friends and relatives of the palace warriors, who were largely also the friends and relatives of Lu-don's forces, found the means, urged on by the priesthood, to circulate throughout the palace pernicious propaganda aimed at Ja-don's cause.

The result was that Lu-don's power increased while that of Ja-don waned. Then followed a sortie from the temple which resulted in the defeat of the palace forces, and though they were able to withdraw in decent order withdraw they did, leaving the palace to Lu-don, who was now virtually ruler of Pal-ul-don.

Ja-don, taking with him the princess, her women, and their slaves, including Pan-at-lee, as well as the women and children of his faithful followers, retreated not only from the palace but from the city of A-lur as well and fell back upon his own city of Ja-lur. Here he remained, recruiting his forces from the surrounding villages of the north which, being far removed from the influence of the priesthood of A-lur, were enthusiastic partisans in any cause that the old chieftain espoused, since for years he had been revered as their friend and protector.

And while these events were transpiring in the north, Tarzan-jad-guru lay in the lion pit at Tu-lur while messengers passed back and forth between Mo-sar and Lu-don as the two dickered for the throne of Pal-ul-don. Mo-sar was cunning enough to guess that should an open breach occur between himself and the high priest he might use his prisoner to his own advantage, for he had heard whisperings among even his own people that suggested that there were those who were more than a trifle inclined to belief in the divinity of the stranger and that he might indeed be the Dor-ul-Otho. Lu-don wanted Tarzan himself. He wanted to sacrifice him upon the eastern altar with his own hands before a multitude of people, since he was not without evidence that his own standing and authority had been lessened by the claims of the bold and heroic figure of the stranger.

The method that the high priest of Tu-lur had employed to trap Tarzan had left the ape-man in possession of his weapons though there seemed little likelihood of their being of any service to him. He also had his pouch, in which were the various odds and ends which are the natural accumulation of all receptacles from a gold meshbag to an attic. There were bits of obsidian and choice feathers for arrows, some pieces of flint and a couple of steel, an old knife, a heavy bone needle, and strips of dried gut. Nothing very useful to you or me, perhaps; but nothing useless to the savage life of the ape-man.

When Tarzan realized the trick that had been so neatly played upon him he had awaited expectantly the coming of the lion, for though the scent of *ja* was old he was sure that sooner or later they would let one of the beasts in upon him. His first consideration was a thorough exploration of his prison. He had noticed the hide-covered windows and these he immediately uncovered, letting in the light, and revealing the fact that though the chamber was far below the level of the temple courts it was yet many feet above the base of the hill from which the temple was hewn. The windows were so closely barred that he could not see over the edge of the thick wall in which they were cut to determine what lay close in below him. At a little distance were the blue waters of Jad-in-lul and beyond, the verdure-clad farther shore, and beyond that the mountains. It was a beautiful picture upon which he looked—a picture of peace and harmony and quiet. Nor anywhere a slightest suggestion of the savage men and beasts that claimed this lovely landscape as their own. What a paradise! And some day civilized man would come and—spoil it! Ruthless axes would raze that age-old wood; black, sticky smoke would rise from ugly chimneys against that azure sky; grimy little boats with wheels behind or upon either side would churn the mud from the bottom of Jad-in-lul, turning its blue waters to a dirty brown; hideous piers would project into the lake from squalid buildings of corrugated iron, doubtless, for of such are the pioneer cities of the world.

But would civilized man come? Tarzan hoped

not. For countless generations civilization had ramped about the globe; it had dispatched its emissaries to the North Pole and the South; it had circled Pal-ul-don once, perhaps many times, but it had never touched her. God grant that it never would. Perhaps He was saving this little spot to be always just as He had made it, for the scratching of the Ho-don and the Waz-don upon His rocks had not altered the fair face of Nature.

Through the windows came sufficient light to reveal the whole interior to Tarzan. The room was fairly large and there was a door at each end—a large door for men and a smaller one for lions. Both were closed with heavy masses of stone that had been lowered in grooves running to the floor. The two windows were small and closely barred with the first iron that Tarzan had seen in Pal-ul-don. The bars were let into holes in the casing, and the whole so strongly and neatly contrived that escape seemed impossible. Yet within a few minutes of his incarceration Tarzan had commenced to undertake his escape. The old knife in his pouch was brought into requisition and slowly the ape-man began to scrape and chip away the stone from about the bars of one of the windows. It was slow work but Tarzan had the patience of absolute health.

Each day food and water were brought him and slipped quickly beneath the smaller door which was raised just sufficiently to allow the stone receptacles to pass in. The prisoner began to believe that he was being preserved for something beside lions. However, that was immaterial. If they would but hold off for a few more days they might select what fate they would—he would not be there when they arrived to announce it.

And then one day came Pan-sat, Lu-don's chief tool, to the city of Tu-lur. He came ostensibly with a fair message for Mo-sar from the high priest at A-lur. Lu-don had decided that Mo-sar should be king and he invited Mo-sar to come at once to A-lur and then Pan-sat, having delivered the message, asked that he might go to the temple of Tu-lur and pray, and there he sought the high priest of Tu-lur to whom was the true message that Lu-don had sent. The two were closeted alone in a little chamber and Pan-sat whispered into the ear of the high priest.

"Mo-sar wishes to be king," he said, "and Lu-don wishes to be king. Mo-sar wishes to retain the stranger who claims to be the Dor-ul-Otho and Lu-don wishes to kill him, and now," he leaned even closer to the ear of the high priest of Tu-lur, "if you would be high priest at A-lur it is within your power."

Pan-sat ceased speaking and waited for the other's reply. The high priest was visibly affected. To be high priest at A-lur! That was almost as good as being king of all Pal-ul-don, for great were the powers of him who conducted the sacrifices upon the altars of A-lur.

"How?" whispered the high priest. "How may I become high priest at A-lur?"

Again Pan-sat leaned close: "By killing the one and bringing the other to A-lur," replied he. Then he rose and departed knowing that the other had swallowed the bait and could be depended upon to do whatever was required to win him the great prize.

Nor was Pan-sat mistaken other than in one trivial consideration. This high priest would indeed commit murder and treason to attain the high office at A-lur; but he had misunderstood which of his victims was to be killed and which to be delivered to Lu-don. Pan-sat, knowing himself all the details of the plannings of Lu-don, had made the quite natural error of assuming that the other was perfectly aware that only by publicly sacrificing the false Dor-ul-Otho could the high priest at A-lur bolster his waning power and that the assassination of Mo-sar, the pretender, would remove from Lu-don's camp the only obstacle to his combining the offices of high priest and king. The high priest at Tu-lur thought that he had been commissioned to kill Tarzan and bring Mo-sar to A-lur. He also thought that when he had done these things he would be made high priest at A-lur; but he did not know that already the priest had been selected who was to murder him within the hour that he arrived at A-lur, nor did he know that a secret grave had been prepared for him in the floor of a subterranean chamber in the very temple he dreamed of controlling.

And so when he should have been arranging the assassination of his chief he was leading a dozen heavily bribed warriors through the dark corridors beneath the temple to slay Tarzan in the lion pit. Night had fallen. A single torch guided the footsteps of the murderers as they crept stealthily upon their evil way, for they knew that they were doing the thing that their chief did not want done and their guilty consciences warned them to stealth.

In the dark of his cell the ape-man worked at his seemingly endless chipping and scraping. His keen ears detected the coming of footsteps along the corridor without—footsteps that approached the larger door. Always before had they come to the smaller door—the footsteps of a single slave who brought his food. This time there were many more than one and their coming at this time of night carried a sinister suggestion. Tarzan continued to work at his scraping and chipping. He heard them stop beyond the door. All was silence broken only by the scrape, scrape, scrape of the ape-man's tireless blade.

Those without heard it and listening sought to explain it. They whispered in low tones making their plans. Two would raise the door quickly and the others would rush in and hurl their clubs at the prisoner. They would take no chances, for the stories that had circulated in A-lur had been brought to Tu-lur—stories of the great strength and wonderful prowess of Tarzan-jad-guru that caused the sweat to stand upon the brows of the warriors, though it was cool in the damp corridor and they were twelve to one.

And then the high priest gave the signal—the door shot upward and ten warriors leaped into the chamber with poised clubs. Three of the heavy weapons flew across the room toward a darker shadow that lay in the shadow of the opposite wall, then the flare of the torch in the priest's hand lighted the interior and they saw that the thing at which they had flung their clubs was a pile of skins torn from the windows and that except for themselves the chamber was vacant.

One of them hastened to a window. All but a single bar was gone and to this was tied one end of a braided rope fashioned from strips cut from the leather window hangings.

To the ordinary dangers of Jane Clayton's existence was now added the menace of Obergatz's knowledge of her whereabouts. The lion and the panther had given her less cause for anxiety than did the return of the unscrupulous Hun, whom she had always distrusted and feared, and whose repulsiveness was now immeasurably augmented by his unkempt and filthy appearance, his strange and mirthless laughter, and his unnatural demeanor. She feared him now with a new fear as though he had suddenly become the personification of some nameless horror. The wholesome, outdoor life that she had been leading had strengthened and rebuilt her nervous system yet it seemed to her as she thought of him that if this man should ever touch her she should scream, and, possibly, even faint. Again and again during the day following their unexpected meeting the woman reproached herself for not having killed him as she would *ja* or *jato* or any other predatory beast that menaced her existence or her safety. There was no attempt at self-justification for these sinister reflections—they needed no justification. The standards by which the acts of such as you or I may be judged could not apply to hers. We have recourse to the protection of friends and relatives and the civil soldiery that upholds the majesty of the law and which may be invoked to protect the righteous weak against the unrighteous strong; but Jane Clayton comprised within herself not only the righteous weak but all the various agencies for the protection of the weak. To her, then, Lieutenant Erich Obergatz presented no different a problem than did *ja,* the lion, other than that she considered the former the more dangerous animal. And so she determined that should he ignore her warning there would be no temporizing upon the occasion of their next meeting—the same swift spear that would meet *ja*'s advances would meet his.

That night her snug little nest perched high in the great tree seemed less the sanctuary that it had before. What might resist the sanguinary intentions of a prowling panther would prove no great barrier to man, and influenced by this thought she slept less well than before. The slightest noise that broke the monotonous hum of the nocturnal jungle startled her into alert wakefulness to lie with straining ears in an attempt to classify the origin of the disturbance, and once she was awakened thus by a sound that seemed to come from something moving in her own tree. She listened intently—scarce breathing. Yes, there it was again. A scuffing of something soft against the hard bark of the tree. The woman reached out in the darkness and grasped her spear. Now she felt a slight sagging of one of the limbs that supported her shelter as though the thing, whatever it was, was slowly raising its weight to the branch. It came nearer. Now she thought that she could detect its breathing. It was at the door. She could hear it fumbling with the frail barrier. What could it be? It made no sound by which she might identify it. She raised herself upon her hands and knees and crept stealthily the little distance to the doorway, her spear clutched tightly in her hand. Whatever the thing was, it was evidently attempting to gain entrance without awakening her. It was just beyond the pitiful little contraption of slender boughs that she had bound together with grasses and called a door—only a few inches lay between the thing and her. Rising to her knees she reached out with her left hand and felt until she found a place where a crooked branch had left an opening a couple of inches wide near the center of the barrier. Into this she inserted the point of her spear. The thing must have heard her move

within for suddenly it abandoned its efforts for stealth and tore angrily at the obstacle. At the same moment Jane thrust her spear forward with all her strength. She felt it enter flesh. There was a scream and a curse from without, followed by the crashing of a body through limbs and foliage. Her spear was almost dragged from her grasp, but she held to it until it broke free from the thing it had pierced.

It was Obergatz; the curse had told her that. From below came no further sound. Had she, then, killed him? She prayed so—with all her heart she prayed it. To be freed from the menace of this loathsome creature were relief indeed. During all the balance of the night she lay there awake, listening. Below her, she imagined, she could see the dead man with his hideous face bathed in the cold light of the moon—lying there upon his back staring up at her.

She prayed that *ja* might come and drag it away, but all during the remainder of the night she heard never another sound above the drowsy hum of the jungle. She was glad that he was dead, but she dreaded the gruesome ordeal that awaited her on the morrow, for she must bury the thing that had been Erich Obergatz and live on there above the shallow grave of the man she had slain.

She reproached herself for her weakness, repeating over and over that she had killed in self-defense, that her act was justified; but she was still a woman of today, and strong upon her were the iron mandates of the social order from which she had sprung, its interdictions and its superstitions.

At last came the tardy dawn. Slowly the sun topped the distant mountains beyond Jad-in-lul. And yet she hesitated to loosen the fastenings of her door and look out upon the thing below. But it must be done. She steeled herself and untied the rawhide thong that secured the barrier. She looked down and only the grass and the flowers looked up at her. She came from her shelter and examined the ground upon the opposite side of the tree—there was no dead man there, nor anywhere as far as she could see. Slowly she descended, keeping a wary eye and an alert ear ready for the first intimation of danger.

At the foot of the tree was a pool of blood and a little trail of crimson drops upon the grass, leading away parallel with the shore of Jad-bal-lul. Then she had not slain him! She was vaguely aware of a peculiar, double sensation of relief and regret. Now she would be always in doubt. He might return; but at least she would not have to live above his grave.

She thought some of following the bloody spoor on the chance that he might have crawled away to die later, but she gave up the idea for fear that she might find him dead nearby, or, worse yet badly wounded. What then could she do? She could not finish him with her spear— no, she knew that she could not do that, nor could she bring him back and nurse him, nor could she leave him there to die of hunger or of thirst, or to become the prey of some prowling beast. It were better then not to search for him for fear that she might find him.

That day was one of nervous starting to every sudden sound. The day before she would have said that her nerves were of iron; but not today. She knew now the shock that she had suffered and that this was the reaction. Tomorrow it might be different, but something told her that never again would her little shelter and the patch of forest and jungle that she called her own be the same. There would hang over them always the menace of this man. No longer would she pass restful nights of deep slumber. The peace of her little world was shattered forever.

That night she made her door doubly secure with additional thongs of rawhide cut from the pelt of the buck she had slain the day that she met Obergatz. She was very tired for she had lost much sleep the night before; but for a long time she lay with wide-open eyes staring into the darkness. What saw she there? Visions that brought tears to those brave and beautiful eyes— visions of a rambling bungalow that had been home to her and that was no more, destroyed by the same cruel force that haunted her even now in this remote, uncharted corner of the earth; vi-sions of a strong man whose protecting arm would never press her close again; visions of a tall, straight son who looked at her adoringly out of brave, smiling eyes that were like his father's. Always the vision of the crude simple bungalow rather than of the stately halls that had been as much a part of her life as the other. But *he* had loved the bungalow and the broad, free acres best and so she had come to love them best, too.

At last she slept, the sleep of utter exhaustion. How long it lasted she did not know; but suddenly she was wide awake and once again she heard the scuffing of a body against the bark of her tree and again the limb bent to a heavy weight. He had returned! She went cold, trembling as with ague. Was it he, or, O God! had she killed him then and was this—? She tried to drive the horrid thought from her mind, for this way, she knew, lay madness.

And once again she crept to the door, for the thing was outside just as it had been last night. Her hands trembled as she placed the point of her weapon to the opening. She wondered if it would scream as it fell.

XXI
THE MANIAC

The last bar that would make the opening large enough to permit his body to pass had been removed as Tarzan heard the warriors whispering beyond the stone door of his prison. Long since had the rope of hide been braided. To secure one end to the remaining bar that he had left for this purpose was the work of but a moment, and while the warriors whispered without, the brown body of the ape-man slipped through the small aperture and disappeared below the sill.

Tarzan's escape from the cell left him still within the walled area that comprised the palace and temple grounds and buildings. He had reconnoitered as best he might from the window after he had removed enough bars to permit him to pass his head through the opening, so that he knew what lay immediately before him—a winding and usually deserted alleyway leading in the direction of the outer gate that opened from the palace grounds into the city.

The darkness would facilitate his escape. He might even pass out of the palace and the city without detection. If he could elude the guard at the palace gate the rest would be easy. He strode along confidently, exhibiting no fear of detection, for he reasoned that thus would he disarm suspicion. In the darkness he easily could pass for a Ho-don and in truth, though he passed several after leaving the deserted alley, no one accosted or detained him, and thus he came at last to the guard of a half-dozen warriors before the palace gate. These he attempted to pass in the same unconcerned fashion and he might have succeeded had it not been for one who came running rapidly from the direction of the temple shouting: "Let no one pass the gates! The prisoner has escaped from the *pal-ul-ja*!"

Instantly a warrior barred his way and simultaneously the fellow recognized him. "*Xot tor!*" he exclaimed: "Here he is now. Fall upon him! Fall upon him! Back! Back before I kill you."

The others came forward. It cannot be said that they rushed forward. If it was their wish to fall upon him there was a noticeable lack of enthusiasm other than that which directed their efforts to persuade someone else to fall upon him. His fame as a fighter had been too long a topic of conversation for the good of the morale of Mo-sar's warriors. It were safer to stand at a distance and hurl their clubs and this they did, but the ape-man had learned something of the use of this weapon since he had arrived in Pal-ul-don. And as he learned great had grown his respect for this most primitive of arms. He had come to realize that the black savages he had known had never appreciated the possibilities of their knob sticks, nor had he, and he had discovered, too, why the Pal-ul-donians had turned their ancient spears into plowshares and pinned their faith to the heavy-ended club alone. In deadly execution it was far more effective than a spear and it answered, too, every purpose of a shield, combining the two in one and thus

reducing the burden of the warrior. Thrown as they throw it, after the manner of the hammer-throwers of the Olympian games, an ordinary shield would prove more a weakness than a strength while one that would be strong enough to prove a protection would be too heavy to carry. Only another club, deftly wielded to deflect the course of an enemy missile, is in any way effective against these formidable weapons and, too, the war club of Pal-ul-don can be thrown with accuracy a far greater distance than any spear.

And now was put to the test that which Tarzan had learned from Om-at and Ta-den. His eyes and his muscles trained by a lifetime of necessity moved with the rapidity of light and his brain functioned with an uncanny celerity that suggested nothing less than prescience, and these things more than compensated for his lack of experience with the war club he handled so dexterously. Weapon after weapon he warded off and always he moved with a single idea in mind—to place himself within reach of one of his antagonists. But they were wary for they feared this strange creature to whom the superstitious fears of many of them attributed the miraculous powers of deity. They managed to keep between Tarzan and the gateway and all the time they bawled lustily for reinforcements. Should these come before he had made his escape the ape-man realized that the odds against him would be unsurmountable, and so he redoubled his efforts to carry out his design.

Following their usual tactics two or three of the warriors were always circling behind him collecting the thrown clubs when Tarzan's attention was directed elsewhere. He himself retrieved several of them which he hurled with such deadly effect as to dispose of two of his antagonists, but now he heard the approach of hurrying warriors, the patter of their bare feet upon the stone pavement and then the savage cries which were to bolster the courage of their fellows and fill the enemy with fear.

There was no time to lose. Tarzan held a club in either hand and, swinging one he hurled it at a warrior before him and as the man dodged he rushed in and seized him, at the same time casting his second club at another of his opponents. The Ho-don with whom he grappled reached instantly for his knife but the ape-man grasped his wrist. There was a sudden twist, the snapping of a bone and an agonized scream, then the warrior was lifted bodily from his feet and held as a shield between his fellows and the fugitive as the latter backed through the gateway. Beside Tarzan stood the single torch that lighted the entrance to the palace grounds. The warriors were advancing to the succor of their fellow when the ape-man raised his captive high above his head and flung him full in the face of the foremost attacker. The fellow went down and two directly behind him sprawled headlong over their companion as the ape-man seized the torch and cast it back into the palace grounds to be extinguished as it struck the bodies of those who led the charging reinforcements.

In the ensuing darkness Tarzan disappeared in the streets of Tu-lur beyond the palace gate. For a time he was aware of sounds of pursuit but the fact that they trailed away and died in the direction of Jad-in-lul informed him that they were searching in the wrong direction, for he had turned south out of Tu-lur purposely to throw them off his track. Beyond the outskirts of the city he turned directly toward the northwest, in which direction lay A-lur.

In his path he knew lay Jad-bal-lul, the shore of which he was compelled to skirt, and there would be a river to cross at the lower end of the great lake upon the shores of which lay A-lur. What other obstacles lay in his way he did not know but he believed that he could make better time on foot than by attempting to steal a canoe and force his way up stream with a single paddle. It was his intention to put as much distance as possible between himself and Tu-lur before he slept for he was sure that Mo-sar would not lightly accept his loss, but that with the coming of day, or possibly even before, he would dispatch warriors in search of him.

A mile or two from the city he entered a for-est and here at last he felt such a measure of safety as he never knew in open spaces or in cities. The forest and the jungle were his birthright. No creature that went upon the ground upon four feet, or climbed among the trees, or crawled upon its belly had any advantage over the ape-man in his native heath. As myrrh and frankincense were the dank odors of rotting vegetation in the nostrils of the great Tarmangani. He squared his broad shoulders and lifting his head filled his lungs with the air that he loved best. The heavy fragrance of tropical blooms, the commingled odors of the myriad-scented life of the jungle went to his head with a pleasurable intoxication far more potent than aught contained in the oldest vintages of civilization.

He took to the trees now, not from necessity but from pure love of the wild freedom that had been denied him so long. Though it was dark and the forest strange yet he moved with a surety and ease that bespoke more a strange uncanny sense than wondrous skill. He heard *ja* moaning somewhere ahead and an owl hooted mournfully to the right of him—long-familiar sounds that imparted to him no sense of loneliness as they might to you or to me, but on the contrary one of companionship for they betokened the presence of his fellows of the jungle, and whether friend or foe it was all the same to the ape-man.

He came at last to a little stream at a spot where the trees did not meet above it so he was forced to descend to the ground and wade through the water and upon the opposite shore he stopped as though suddenly his godlike figure had been transmuted from flesh to marble. Only his dilating nostrils bespoke his pulsing vitality. For a long moment he stood there thus and then swiftly, but with a caution and silence that were inherent in him he moved forward again, but now his whole attitude bespoke a new urge. There was a definite and masterful purpose in every movement of those steel muscles rolling softly beneath the smooth brown hide. He moved now toward a certain goal that quite evidently filled him with far greater enthusiasm than had the possible event of his return to A-lur.

And so he came at last to the foot of a great tree and there he stopped and looked up above him among the foliage where the dim outlines of a roughly rectangular bulk loomed darkly. There was a choking sensation in Tarzan's throat as he raised himself gently into the branches. It was as though his heart were swelling either to a great happiness or a great fear.

Before the rude shelter built among the branches he paused listening. From within there came to his sensitive nostrils the same delicate aroma that had arrested his eager attention at the little stream a mile away. He crouched upon the branch close to the little door.

"Jane," he called, "heart of my heart, it is I."

The only answer from within was as the sudden indrawing of a breath that was half gasp and half sigh, and the sound of a body falling to the floor. Hurriedly Tarzan sought to release the thongs which held the door but they were fastened from the inside, and at last, impatient with further delay, he seized the frail barrier in one giant hand and with a single effort tore it completely away. And then he entered to find the seemingly lifeless body of his mate stretched upon the floor.

He gathered her in his arms; her heart beat; she still breathed, and presently he realized that she had but swooned.

When Jane Clayton regained consciousness it was to find herself held tightly in two strong arms, her head pillowed upon the broad shoulder where so often before her fears had been soothed and her sorrows comforted. At first she was not sure but that it was all a dream. Timidly her hand stole to his cheek.

"John," she murmured, "tell me, is it really you?"

In reply he drew her more closely to him. "It is I," he replied. "But there is something in my throat," he said haltingly, "that makes it hard for me to speak."

She smiled and snuggled closer to him. "God has been good to us, Tarzan of the Apes," she said.

For some time neither spoke. It was enough that they were reunited and that each knew that the other was alive and safe. But at last they found their voices and when the sun rose they were still talking, so much had each to tell the other; so many questions there were to be asked and answered.

"And Jack," she asked, "where is he?"

"I do not know," replied Tarzan. "The last I heard of him he was on the Argonne Front."

"Ah, then our happiness is not quite complete," she said, a little note of sadness creeping into her voice.

"No," he replied, "but the same is true in countless other English homes today, and pride is learning to take the place of happiness in these."

She shook her head. "I want my boy," she said.

"And I too," replied Tarzan, "and we may have him yet. He was safe and unwounded the last word I had. And now," he said, "we must plan upon our return. Would you like to rebuild the bungalow and gather together the remnants of our Waziri or would you rather return to London?"

"Only to find Jack," she said. "I dream always of the bungalow and never of the city, but John, we can only dream, for Obergatz told me that he had circled this whole country and found no place where he might cross the morass."

"I am not Obergatz," Tarzan reminded her, smiling. "We will rest today and tomorrow we will set out toward the north. It is a savage country, but we have crossed it once and we can cross it again."

And so, upon the following morning, the Tarmangani and his mate went forth upon their journey across the Valley of Jad-ben-Otho, and ahead of them were fierce men and savage beasts, and the lofty mountains of Pal-ul-don; and beyond the mountains the reptiles and the morass, and beyond that the arid, thorn-covered steppe, and other savage beasts and men and weary, hostile miles of untracked wilderness between them and the charred ruins of their home.

Lieutenant Erich Obergatz crawled through the grass upon all fours, leaving a trail of blood behind him after Jane's spear had sent him crashing to the ground beneath her tree. He made no sound after the one piercing scream that had acknowledged the severity of his wound. He was quiet because of a great fear that had crept into his warped brain that the devil woman would pursue and slay him. And so he crawled away like some filthy beast of prey, seeking a thicket where he might lie down and hide.

He thought that he was going to die, but he did not, and with the coming of the new day he discovered that his wound was superficial. The rough obsidian-shod spear had entered the muscles of his side beneath his right arm inflicting a painful, but not a fatal wound. With the realization of this fact came a renewed desire to put as much distance as possible between himself and Jane Clayton. And so he moved on, still going upon all fours because of a persistent hallucination that in this way he might escape observation. Yet though he fled his mind still revolved muddily about a central desire—while he fled from her he still planned to pursue her, and to his lust of possession was added a desire for revenge. She should pay for the suffering she had inflicted upon him. She should pay for rebuffing him, but for some reason which he did not try to explain to himself he would crawl away and hide. He would come back though. He would come back and when he had finished with her, he would take that smooth throat in his two hands and crush the life from her.

He kept repeating this over and over to himself and then he fell to laughing out loud, the cackling, hideous laughter that had terrified Jane. Presently he realized his knees were bleeding and that they hurt him. He looked cautiously behind. No one was in sight. He listened. He could hear no indications of pursuit and so he rose to his feet and continued upon his way a sorry sight—covered with filth and blood, his beard and hair tangled and matted and filled with burrs and dried mud and unspeakable filth. He kept no track of time. He ate fruits and berries and tubers that he dug from the earth with his fingers. He followed the shore of the lake and the river that he might be near water, and when *ja* roared or moaned he climbed a tree and hid there, shivering.

And so after a time he came up the southern shore of Jad-ben-lul until a wide river stopped his progress. Across the blue water a white city glimmered in the sun. He looked at it for a long time, blinking his eyes like an owl. Slowly a recollection forced itself through his tangled brain. This was A-lur, the City of Light. The association of ideas recalled Bu-lur and the Waz-ho-don. They had called him Jad-ben-Otho. He commenced to laugh aloud and stood up very straight and strode back and forth along the shore. "I am Jad-ben-Otho," he cried, "I am the Great God. In A-lur is my temple and my high priests. What is Jad-ben-Otho doing here alone in the jungle?"

He stepped out into the water and raising his voice shrieked loudly across toward A-lur. "I am Jad-ben-Otho!" he screamed. "Come hither slaves and take your god to his temple." But the distance was great and they did not hear him and no one came, and the feeble mind was distracted by other things—a bird flying in the air, a school of minnows swimming around his feet. He lunged at them trying to catch them, and falling upon his hands and knees he crawled through the water grasping futilely at the elusive fish.

Presently it occurred to him that he was a sea lion and he forgot the fish and lay down and tried to swim by wriggling his feet in the water as though they were a tail. The hardships, the privations, the terrors, and for the past few weeks the lack of proper nourishment had reduced Erich Obergatz to little more than a gibbering idiot.

A water snake swam out upon the surface of the lake and the man pursued it, crawling upon his hands and knees. The snake swam toward the shore just within the mouth of the river where tall reeds grew thickly and Obergatz followed, making grunting noises like a pig. He lost the snake within the reeds but he came upon something else—a canoe hidden there close to the bank. He examined it with cackling laughter. There were two paddles within it which he took and threw out into the current of the river. He watched them for a while and then he sat down beside the canoe and commenced to splash his hands up and down upon the water. He liked to hear the noise and see the little splashes of spray. He rubbed his left forearm with his right palm and the dirt came off and left a white spot that drew his attention. He rubbed again upon the now thoroughly soaked blood and grime that covered his body. He was not attempting to wash himself; he was merely amused by the strange results. "I am turning white," he cried. His glance wandered from his body now that the grime and blood were all removed and caught again the white city shimmering beneath the hot sun.

"A-lur—City of Light!" he shrieked and that reminded him again of Bu-lur and by the same process of associated ideas that had before suggested it, he recalled that the Waz-ho-don had thought him Jad-ben-Otho.

"I am Jad-ben-Otho!" he screamed and then his eyes fell again upon the canoe. A new idea came and persisted. He looked down at himself, examining his body, and seeing the filthy loin cloth, now water soaked and more bedraggled than before, he tore it from him and flung it into the lake. "Gods do not wear dirty rags," he said aloud. "They do not wear anything but wreaths and garlands of flowers and I am a god—I am Jad-ben-Otho—and I go in state to my sacred city of A-lur."

He ran his fingers through his matted hair and beard. The water had softened the burrs but had not removed them. The man shook his head. His hair and beard failed to harmonize with his other godly attributes. He was commencing to think more clearly now, for the great idea had taken hold of his scattered wits and concentrated them upon a single purpose, but he was still a maniac. The only difference being that he was now a maniac with a fixed intent. He went out on the shore and gathered flowers and ferns and wove them in his beard and hair—blazing blooms of different colors—green ferns that trailed about his ears or rose bravely upward like the plumes in a lady's hat.

When he was satisfied that his appearance would impress the most casual observer with his evident deity he returned to the canoe, pushed it from shore and jumped in. The impetus carried it into the river's current and the current bore it out upon the lake. The naked man stood erect in the center of the little craft, his arms folded upon his chest. He screamed aloud his message to the city: "I am Jad-ben-Otho! Let the high priest and the under priests attend upon me!"

As the current of the river was dissipated by the waters of the lake the wind caught him and his craft and carried them bravely forward. Sometimes he drifted with his back toward A-lur and sometimes with his face toward it, and at intervals he shrieked his message and his commands. He was still in the middle of the lake when someone discovered him from the palace wall, and as he drew nearer, a crowd of warriors and women and children were congregated there watching him and along the temple walls were many priests and among them Lu-don, the high priest. When the boat had drifted close enough for them to distinguish the bizarre figure standing in it and for them to catch the meaning of his words Lu-don's cunning eyes narrowed. The high priest had learned of the escape of Tarzan and he feared that should he join Ja-don's forces, as seemed likely, he would attract many recruits who might still believe in him, and the Dor-ul-Otho, even if a false one, upon the side of the enemy might easily work havoc with Lu-don's plans.

The man was drifting close in. His canoe would soon be caught in the current that ran close to shore here and carried toward the river that emptied the waters of Jad-ben-lul into Jad-bal-lul. The under priests were looking toward Lu-don for instructions.

"Fetch him hither!" he commanded. "If he is Jad-ben-Otho I shall know him."

The priests hurried to the palace grounds and summoned warriors. "Go, bring the stranger to Lu-don. If he is Jad-ben-Otho we shall know him."

And so Lieutenant Erich Obergatz was brought before the high priest at A-lur. Lu-don looked closely at the naked man with the fantastic headdress.

"Where did you come from?" he asked.

"I am Jad-ben-Otho," cried the German. "I came from heaven. Where is my high priest?"

"I am the high priest," replied Lu-don.

Obergatz clapped his hands. "Have my feet bathed and food brought to me," he commanded.

Lu-don's eyes narrowed to mere slits of crafty cunning. He bowed low until his forehead touched the feet of the stranger. Before the eyes of many priests, and warriors from the palace he did it.

"Ho, slaves," he cried, rising; "fetch water and food for the Great God," and thus the high priest acknowledged before his people the god-hood of Lieutenant Erich Obergatz, nor was it long before the story ran like wildfire through the palace and out into the city and beyond that to the lesser villages all the way from A-lur to Tu-lur.

The real god had come—Jad-ben-Otho himself, and he had espoused the cause of Lu-don, the high priest. Mo-sar lost no time in placing himself at the disposal of Lu-don, nor did he mention aught about his claims to the throne. It was Mo-sar's opinion that he might consider himself fortunate were he allowed to remain in peaceful occupation of his chieftainship at Tu-lur, nor was Mo-sar wrong in his deductions.

But Lu-don could still use him and so he let him live and sent word to him to come to A-lur with all his warriors, for it was rumored that Ja-don was raising a great army in the north and might soon march upon the City of Light.

Obergatz thoroughly enjoyed being a god. Plenty of food and peace of mind and rest partially brought back to him the reason that had been so rapidly slipping from him; but in one respect he was madder than ever, since now no power on earth would ever be able to convince him that he was not a god. Slaves were put at his disposal and these he ordered about in godly fashion. The sane portion of his naturally cruel mind met upon common ground the mind of Lu-don, so that the two seemed always in accord. The high priest saw in the stranger a mighty force wherewith to hold forever his power over all Pal-ul-don and thus the future of Obergatz was assured so long as he cared to play god to Lu-don's high priest.

A throne was erected in the main temple court before the eastern altar where Jad-ben-Otho might sit in person and behold the sacrifices that were offered up to him there each day at sunset. So much did the cruel, half-crazed mind enjoy these spectacles that at times he even insisted upon wielding the sacrificial knife himself and upon such occasions the priests and the people fell upon their faces in awe of the dread deity.

If Obergatz taught them not to love their god more he taught them to fear him as they never had before, so that the name of Jad-ben-Otho was whispered in the city and little children were frightened into obedience by the mere mention of it. Lu-don, through his priests and slaves, circulated the information that Jad-ben-Otho had commanded all his faithful followers to flock to the standard of the high priest at A-lur and that all others were cursed, especially Ja-don and the base impostor who had posed as the Dor-ul-Otho. The curse was to take the form of early death following terrible suffering, and Lu-don caused it to be published abroad that the name of any warrior who complained of a pain should be brought to him, for such might be deemed to be under suspicion, since the first effects of the curse would result in slight pains attacking the unholy. He counseled those who felt pains to look carefully to their loyalty. The result was remarkable and immediate—half a nation without a pain, and recruits pouring into A-lur to offer their services to Lu-don while secretly hoping that the little pains they had felt in arm or leg or belly would not recur in aggravated form.

XXII

A JOURNEY ON A *GRYF*

Tarzan and Jane skirted the shore of Jad-bal-lul and crossed the river at the head of the lake. They moved in leisurely fashion with an eye to comfort and safety, for the ape-man, now that he had found his mate, was determined to court no chance that might again separate them, or delay or prevent their escape from Pal-ul-don. How they were to recross the morass was a matter of little concern to him as yet—it would be time enough to consider that matter when it became of more immediate moment. Their hours were filled with the happiness and content of reunion after long separation; they had much to talk of, for each had passed through many trials and vicissitudes and strange adventures, and no important hour might go unaccounted for since last they met.

It was Tarzan's intention to choose a way above A-lur and the scattered Ho-don villages below it, passing about midway between them and the mountains, thus avoiding, in so far as possible, both the Ho-don and Waz-don, for in this area lay the neutral territory that was uninhabited by either. Thus he would travel northwest until opposite the Kor-ul-ja where he planned to stop to pay his respects to Om-at and give the *gund* word of Pan-at-lee, and a plan Tarzan had for insuring her safe return to her people. It was upon the third day of their journey and they had almost reached the river that passes through A-lur when Jane suddenly clutched Tarzan's arm and pointed ahead toward the edge of a forest that they were approaching. Beneath the shadows of the trees loomed a great bulk that the ape-man instantly recognized.

"What is it?" whispered Jane.

"A *gryf*," replied the ape-man, "and we have met him in the worst place that we could possibly have found. There is not a large tree within a quarter of a mile, other than those among which he stands. Come, we shall have to go back, Jane; I cannot risk it with you along. The best we can do is to pray that he does not discover us."

"And if he does?"

"Then I shall have to risk it."

"Risk what?"

"The chance that I can subdue him as I subdued one of his fellows," replied Tarzan. "I told you—you recall?"

"Yes, but I did not picture so huge a creature. Why, John, he is as big as a battleship."

The ape-man laughed. "Not quite, though I'll admit he looks quite as formidable as one when he charges."

They were moving away slowly so as not to attract the attention of the beast.

"I believe we're going to make it," whispered the woman, her voice tense with suppressed excitement. A low rumble rolled like distant thunder from the wood. Tarzan shook his head.

" 'The big show is about to commence in the main tent,' " he quoted, grinning. He caught the woman suddenly to his breast and kissed her. "One can never tell, Jane," he said. "We'll do our best—that is all we can do. Give me your spear, and—don't run. The only hope we have lies in that little brain more than in us. If I can control it—well, let us see."

The beast had emerged from the forest and was looking about through his weak eyes, evidently in search of them. Tarzan raised his voice in the weird notes of the Tor-o-don's cry; "Whee-oo! Whee-oo! Whee-oo!" For a moment the great beast stood motionless, his attention riveted by the call. The ape-man advanced straight toward him, Jane Clayton at his elbow. "Whee-oo!" he cried again peremptorily. A low rumble rolled from the *gryf*'s cavernous chest in answer to the call, and the beast moved slowly toward them.

"Fine!" exclaimed Tarzan. "The odds are in our favor now. You can keep your nerve?—but I do not need to ask."

"I know no fear when I am with Tarzan of the Apes," she replied softly, and he felt the pressure of her soft fingers on his arm.

And thus the two approached the giant monster of a forgotten epoch until they stood close in the shadow of a mighty shoulder. "Whee-oo!" shouted Tarzan and struck the hideous snout with the shaft of the spear. The vicious side snap that did not reach its mark—that evidently was not intended to reach its mark—was the hoped-for answer.

"Come," said Tarzan, and taking Jane by the hand he led her around behind the monster and up the broad tail to the great, horned back. "Now will we ride in the state that our forebears knew, before which the pomp of modern kings pales into cheap and tawdry insignificance. How would you like to canter through Hyde Park on a mount like this?"

"I am afraid the Bobbies would be shocked by our riding habits, John," she cried, laughingly.

Tarzan guided the *gryf* in the direction that they wished to go. Steep embankments and rivers proved no slightest obstacle to the ponderous creature.

"A prehistoric tank, this," Jane assured him, and laughing and talking they continued on their way. Once they came unexpectedly upon a dozen Ho-don warriors as the *gryf* emerged suddenly into a small clearing. The fellows were lying about in the shade of a single tree that grew alone. When they saw the beast they leaped to their feet in consternation and at their shouts the *gryf* issued his hideous, challenging bellow and charged them. The warriors fled in all directions while Tarzan belabored the beast across the snout with his spear in an effort to control him, and at last he succeeded, just as the *gryf* was almost upon one poor devil that it seemed to have singled out for its special prey. With an angry grunt the *gryf* stopped and the man, with a single backward glance that showed a face white with terror, disappeared in the jungle he had been seeking to reach.

The ape-man was elated. He had doubted that he could control the beast should it take it into its head to charge a victim and had intended abandoning it before they reached the Kor-ul-ja. Now he altered his plans—they would ride to the very village of Om-at upon the *gryf,* and the Kor-ul-ja would have food for conversation for many generations to come. Nor was it the theatric instinct of the ape-man alone that gave favor to this plan. The element of Jane's safety entered into the matter for he knew that she would be safe from man and beast alike so long as she rode upon the back of Pal-ul-don's most formidable creature.

As they proceeded slowly in the direction of the Kor-ul-ja, for the natural gait of the *gryf* is far from rapid, a handful of terrified warriors came panting into A-lur, spreading a weird story of the Dor-ul-Otho, only none dared call him the Dor-ul-Otho aloud. Instead they spoke of him as Tarzan-jad-guru and they told of meeting him mounted upon a mighty *gryf* beside the beautiful stranger woman whom Ko-tan would have made queen of Pal-ul-don. This story was brought to Lu-don who caused the warriors to be hailed to his presence, when he questioned them closely until finally he was convinced that they spoke the truth and when they had told him the direction in which the two were traveling, Lu-don guessed that they were on their way to Ja-lur to join Ja-don, a contingency that he felt must be prevented at any cost. As was his wont in the stress of emergency, he called Pan-sat into consultation and for long the two sat in close conference. When they arose a plan had been developed. Pan-sat went immediately to his own quarters where he removed the headdress and trappings of a priest to don in their stead the harness and weapons of a warrior. Then he returned to Lu-don.

"Good!" cried the latter, when he saw him. "Not even your fellow-priests or the slaves that wait upon you daily would know you now. Lose no time, Pan-sat, for all depends upon the speed with which you strike and—remember! Kill the man if you can; but in any event bring the woman to me here, alive. You understand?"

"Yes, master," replied the priest, and so it was that a lone warrior set out from A-lur and made his way northwest in the direction of Ja-lur.

The gorge next above Kor-ul-ja is uninhabited and here the wily Ja-don had chosen to mobilize his army for its descent upon A-lur. Two considerations influenced him—one being the fact that could he keep his plans a secret from the enemy he would have the advantage of delivering a surprise attack upon the forces of Lu-don from a direction that they would not expect attack, and in the meantime he would be able to keep his men from the gossip of the cities where strange tales were already circulating relative to the coming of Jad-ben-Otho in person to aid the high priest in his war against Ja-don. It took stout hearts and loyal ones to ignore the implied threats of divine vengeance that these tales suggested. Already there had been desertions and the cause of Ja-don seemed tottering to destruction.

Such was the state of affairs when a sentry posted on the knoll in the mouth of the gorge sent word that he had observed in the valley below what appeared at a distance to be nothing less than two people mounted upon the back of a *gryf*. He said that he had caught glimpses of them, as they passed open spaces, and they seemed to be traveling up the river in the direction of the Kor-ul-ja.

At first Ja-don was inclined to doubt the veracity of his informant; but, like all good generals, he could not permit even palpably false information to go uninvestigated and so he determined to visit the knoll himself and learn precisely what it was that the sentry had observed through the distorting spectacles of fear. He had scarce taken his place beside the man ere the fellow touched his arm and pointed. "They are closer now," he whispered, "you can see them

plainly." And sure enough, not a quarter of a mile away Ja-don saw that which in his long experience in Pal-ul-don he had never before seen—two humans riding upon the broad back of a *gryf*.

At first he could scarce credit even this testimony of his own eyes, but soon he realized that the creatures below could be naught else than they appeared, and then he recognized the man and rose to his feet with a loud cry.

"It is he!" he shouted to those about him. "It is the Dor-ul-Otho himself."

The *gryf* and his riders heard the shout though not the words. The former bellowed terrifically and started in the direction of the knoll, and Ja-don, followed by a few of his more intrepid warriors, ran to meet him. Tarzan, loath to enter an unnecessary quarrel, tried to turn the animal, but as the beast was far from tractable it always took a few minutes to force the will of its master upon it; and so the two parties were quite close before the ape-man succeeded in stopping the mad charge of his furious mount.

Ja-don and his warriors, however, had come to the realization that this bellowing creature was bearing down upon them with evil intent and they had assumed the better part of valor and taken to trees, accordingly. It was beneath these trees that Tarzan finally stopped the *gryf*. Ja-don called down to him.

"We are friends," he cried. "I am Ja-don, Chief of Ja-lur. I and my warriors lay our foreheads upon the feet of Dor-ul-Otho and pray that he will aid us in our righteous fight with Lu-don, the high priest."

"You have not defeated him yet?" asked Tarzan. "Why I thought you would be king of Pal-ul-don long before this."

"No," replied Ja-don. "The people fear the high priest and now that he has in the temple one whom he claims to be Jad-ben-Otho many of my warriors are afraid. If they but knew that the Dor-ul-Otho had returned and that he had blessed the cause of Ja-don I am sure that victory would be ours."

Tarzan thought for a long minute and then

he spoke. "Ja-don," he said, "was one of the few who believed in me and who wished to accord me fair treatment. I have a debt to pay to Ja-don and an account to settle with Lu-don, not alone on my own behalf, but principally upon that of my mate. I will go with you Ja-don to mete to Lu-don the punishment he deserves. Tell me, chief, how may the Dor-ul-Otho best serve his father's people?"

"By coming with me to Ja-lur and the villages between," replied Ja-don quickly, "that the people may see that it is indeed the Dor-ul-Otho and that he smiles upon the cause of Ja-don."

"You think that they will believe in me more now than before?" asked the ape-man.

"Who will dare doubt that he who rides upon the great *gryf* is less than a god?" returned the old chief.

"And if I go with you to the battle at A-lur," asked Tarzan, "can you assure the safety of my mate while I am gone from her?"

"She shall remain in Ja-lur with the Princess O-lo-a and my own women," replied Ja-don. "There she will be safe for there I shall leave trusted warriors to protect them. Say that you will come, O Dor-ul-Otho, and my cup of happiness will be full, for even now Ta-den, my son, marches toward A-lur with a force from the northwest and if we can attack, with the Dor-ul-Otho at our head, from the northeast our arms should be victorious."

"It shall be as you wish, Ja-don," replied the ape-man; "but first you must have meat fetched for my *gryf*."

"There are many carcasses in the camp above," replied Ja-don, "for my men have little else to do than hunt."

"Good," exclaimed Tarzan. "Have them brought at once."

And when the meat was brought and laid at a distance the ape-man slipped from the back of his fierce charger and fed him with his own hand. "See that there is always plenty of flesh for him," he said to Ja-don, for he guessed that his mastery might be short-lived should the vicious beast become over-hungry.

It was morning before they could leave for Ja-lur, but Tarzan found the *gryf* lying where he had left him the night before beside the carcasses of two antelope and a lion; but now there was nothing but the *gryf*.

"The paleontologists say that he was herbivorous," said Tarzan as he and Jane approached the beast.

The journey to Ja-lur was made through the scattered villages where Ja-don hoped to arouse a keener enthusiasm for his cause. A party of warriors preceded Tarzan that the people might properly be prepared, not only for the sight of the *gryf* but to receive the Dor-ul-Otho as became his high station. The results were all that Ja-don could have hoped and in no village through which they passed was there one who doubted the deity of the ape-man.

As they approached Ja-lur a strange warrior joined them, one whom none of Ja-don's following knew. He said he came from one of the villages to the south and that he had been treated unfairly by one of Lu-don's chiefs. For this reason he had deserted the cause of the high priest and come north in the hope of finding a home in Ja-lur. As every addition to his forces was welcome to the old chief he permitted the stranger to accompany them, and so he came into Ja-lur with them.

There arose now the question as to what was to be done with the *gryf* while they remained in the city. It was with difficulty that Tarzan had prevented the savage beast from attacking all who came near it when they had first entered the camp of Ja-don in the uninhabited gorge next to the Kor-ul-ja, but during the march to Ja-lur the creature had seemed to become accustomed to the presence of the Ho-don. The latter, however, gave him no cause for annoyance since they kept as far from him as possible and when he passed through the streets of the city he was viewed from the safety of lofty windows and roofs. However tractable he appeared to have become there would have been no enthusiastic seconding of a suggestion to turn him loose within the city. It was finally suggested that he be turned into a walled enclosure within the palace grounds and this was done, Tarzan driving him in after Jane had dismounted. More meat was thrown to him and he was left to his own devices, the awe-struck inhabitants of the palace not even venturing to climb upon the walls to look at him.

Ja-don led Tarzan and Jane to the quarters of the Princess O-lo-a who, the moment that she beheld the ape-man, threw herself to the ground and touched her forehead to his feet. Pan-at-lee was there with her and she too seemed happy to see Tarzan-jad-guru again. When they found that Jane was his mate they looked with almost equal awe upon her, since even the most skeptical of the warriors of Ja-don were now convinced that they were entertaining a god and a goddess within the city of Ja-lur, and that with the assistance of the power of these two, the cause of Ja-don would soon be victorious and the old Lion-man set upon the throne of Pal-ul-don.

From O-lo-a Tarzan learned that Ta-den had returned and that they were to be united in marriage with the weird rites of their religion and in accordance with the custom of their people as soon as Ta-den came home from the battle that was to be fought at A-lur.

The recruits were now gathering at the city and it was decided that the next day Ja-don and Tarzan would return to the main body in the hidden camp and immediately under cover of night the attack should be made in force upon Lu-don's forces at A-lur. Word of this was sent to Ta-den where he awaited with his warriors upon the north side of Jad-ben-lul, only a few miles from A-lur.

In the carrying out of these plans it was necessary to leave Jane behind in Ja-don's palace at Ja-lur, but O-lo-a and her women were with her and there were many warriors to guard them, so Tarzan bid his mate good-bye with no feelings of apprehension as to her safety, and again seated upon the *gryf* made his way out of the city with Ja-don and his warriors.

At the mouth of the gorge the ape-man abandoned his huge mount since it had served its purpose and could be of no further value to him in their attack upon A-lur, which was to be made just before dawn the following day when, as he could not have been seen by the enemy, the effect of his entry to the city upon the *gryf* would have been totally lost. A couple of sharp blows with the spear sent the big animal rumbling and growling in the direction of the Kor-ul-gryf nor was the ape-man sorry to see it depart since he had never known at what instant its short temper and insatiable appetite for flesh might turn it upon some of his companions.

Immediately upon their arrival at the gorge the march on A-lur was commenced.

XXIII
TAKEN ALIVE

As night fell a warrior from the palace of Ja-lur slipped into the temple grounds. He made his way to where the lesser priests were quartered. His presence aroused no suspicion as it was not unusual for warriors to have business within the temple. He came at last to a chamber where several priests were congregated after the evening meal. The rites and ceremonies of the sacrifice had been concluded and there was nothing more of a religious nature to make call upon their time until the rites at sunrise.

Now the warrior knew, as in fact nearly all Pal-ul-don knew, that there was no strong bond between the temple and the palace at Ja-lur and that Ja-don only suffered the presence of the priests and permitted their cruel and abhorrent acts because of the fact that these things had been the custom of the Ho-don of Pal-ul-don for countless ages, and rash indeed must have been the man who would have attempted to interfere with the priests or their ceremonies. That Ja-don never entered the temple was well known, and that his high priest never entered the palace, but the people came to the temple with their votive offerings and the sacrifices were made night and morning as in every other temple in Pal-ul-don.

The warrior knew these things, knew them better perhaps than a simple warrior should have known them. And so it was here in the temple that he looked for the aid that he sought in the carrying out of whatever design he had.

As he entered the apartment where the priests were he greeted them after the manner which was customary in Pal-ul-don, but at the same time he made a sign with his finger that might have attracted little attention or scarcely been noticed at all by one who knew not its meaning. That there were those within the room who noticed it and interpreted it was quickly apparent, through the fact that two of the priests rose and came close to him as he stood just within the doorway and each of them, as he came, returned the signal that the warrior had made.

The three talked for but a moment and then the warrior turned and left the apartment. A little later one of the priests who had talked with him left also and shortly after that the other.

In the corridor they found the warrior waiting, and led him to a little chamber which opened upon a smaller corridor just beyond where it joined the larger. Here the three remained in whispered conversation for some little time and then the warrior returned to the palace and the two priests to their quarters.

The apartments of the women of the palace at Ja-lur are all upon the same side of a long, straight corridor. Each has a single door leading into the corridor and at the opposite end several windows overlooking a garden. It was in one of these rooms that Jane slept alone. At each end of the corridor was a sentinel, the main body of the guard being stationed in a room near the outer entrance to the women's quarters.

The palace slept for they kept early hours there where Ja-don ruled. The *pal-e-don-so* of the great chieftain of the north knew no such wild orgies as had resounded through the palace of the king at A-lur. Ja-lur was a quiet city by comparison with the capital, yet there was al-

ways a guard kept at every entrance to the chambers of Ja-don and his immediate family as well as at the gate leading into the temple and that which opened upon the city.

These guards, however, were small, consisting usually of not more than five or six warriors, one of whom remained awake while the others slept. Such were the conditions then when two warriors presented themselves, one at either end of the corridor, to the sentries who watched over the safety of Jane Clayton and the Princess O-lo-a, and each of the newcomers repeated to the sentinels the stereotyped words which announced that they were relieved and these others sent to watch in their stead. Never is a warrior loath to be relieved of sentry duty. Where, under different circumstances he might ask numerous questions he is now too well satisfied to escape the monotonies of that universally hated duty. And so these two men accepted their relief without question and hastened away to their pallets.

And then a third warrior entered the corridor and all of the newcomers came together before the door of the ape-man's slumbering mate. And one was the strange warrior who had met Ja-don and Tarzan outside the city of Ja-lur as they had approached it the previous day; and he was the same warrior who had entered the temple a short hour before, but the faces of his fellows were unfamiliar, even to one another, since it is seldom that a priest removes his hideous headdress in the presence even of his associates.

Silently they lifted the hangings that hid the interior of the room from the view of those who passed through the corridor, and stealthily slunk within. Upon a pile of furs in a far corner lay the sleeping form of Lady Greystoke. The bare feet of the intruders gave forth no sound as they crossed the stone floor toward her. A ray of moonlight entering through a window near her couch shone full upon her, revealing the beautiful contours of an arm and shoulder in cameo-distinctness against the dark furry pelt beneath which she slept, and the perfect profile that was turned toward the skulking three.

But neither the beauty nor the helplessness of the sleeper aroused such sentiments of passion or pity as might stir in the breasts of normal men. To the three priests she was but a lump of clay, nor could they conceive aught of that passion which had aroused men to intrigue and to murder for possession of this beautiful American girl, and which even now was influencing the destiny of undiscovered Pal-ul-don.

Upon the floor of the chamber were numerous pelts and as the leader of the trio came close to the sleeping woman he stooped and gathered up one of the smaller of these. Standing close to her head he held the rug outspread above her face. "Now," he whispered and simultaneously he threw the rug over the woman's head and his two fellows leaped upon her, seizing her arms and pinioning her body while their leader stifled her cries with the furry pelt. Quickly and silently they bound her wrists and gagged her and during the brief time that their work required there was no sound that might have been heard by occupants of the adjoining apartments.

Jerking her roughly to her feet they forced her toward a window but she refused to walk, throwing herself instead upon the floor. They were very angry and would have resorted to cruelties to compel her obedience but dared not, since the wrath of Lu-don might fall heavily upon whoever mutilated his fair prize.

And so they were forced to lift and carry her bodily. Nor was the task any sinecure since the captive kicked and struggled as best she might, making their labor as arduous as possible. But finally they succeeded in getting her through the window and into the garden beyond where one of the two priests from the Ja-lur temple directed their steps toward a small barred gateway in the south wall of the enclosure.

Immediately beyond this a flight of stone stairs led downward toward the river and at the foot of the stairs were moored several canoes. Pan-sat had indeed been fortunate in enlisting aid from those who knew the temple and the palace so well, or otherwise he might never have escaped from Ja-lur with his captive. Placing the woman in the bottom of a light canoe Pan-sat entered it and took up the paddle. His companions unfastened the moorings and shoved the little craft out into the current of the stream. Their traitorous work completed they turned and retraced their steps toward the temple, while Pan-sat, paddling strongly with the current, moved rapidly down the river that would carry him to the Jad-ben-lul and A-lur.

The moon had set and the eastern horizon still gave no hint of approaching day as a long file of warriors wound stealthily through the darkness into the city of A-lur. Their plans were all laid and there seemed no likelihood of their miscarriage. A messenger had been dispatched to Ta-den whose forces lay northwest of the city. Tarzan, with a small contingent, was to enter the temple through the secret passageway, the location of which he alone knew, while Ja-don, with the greater proportion of the warriors, was to attack the palace gates.

The ape-man, leading his little band, moved stealthily through the winding alleys of A-lur, arriving undetected at the building which hid the entrance to the secret passageway. This spot being best protected by the fact that its existence was unknown to others than the priests, was unguarded. To facilitate the passage of his little company through the narrow winding, uneven tunnel, Tarzan lighted a torch which had been brought for the purpose and preceding his warriors led the way toward the temple.

That he could accomplish much once he reached the inner chambers of the temple with his little band of picked warriors the ape-man was confident since an attack at this point would bring confusion and consternation to the easily overpowered priests, and permit Tarzan to attack the palace forces in the rear at the same time that Ja-don engaged them at the palace gates, while Ta-den and his forces swarmed the northern walls. Great value had been placed by Ja-don on the moral effect of the Dor-ul-Otho's mysterious appearance in the heart of the temple and he had urged Tarzan to take every advantage of the old chieftain's belief that many of Lu-don's warriors still wavered in their allegiance between the high priest and the Dor-ul-Otho, being held to the former more by the fear which he engendered in the breasts of all his followers than by any love or loyalty they might feel toward him.

There is a Pal-ul-donian proverb setting forth a truth similar to that contained in the old Scotch adage that "The best laid schemes o' mice and men gang aft a-gley." Freely translated it might read, "He who follows the right trail sometimes reaches the wrong destination," and such apparently was the fate that lay in the footsteps of the great chieftain of the north and his godlike ally.

Tarzan, more familiar with the windings of the corridors than his fellows and having the advantage of the full light of the torch, which at best was but a dim and flickering affair, was some distance ahead of the others, and in his keen anxiety to close with the enemy he gave too little thought to those who were to support him. Nor is this strange, since from childhood the ape-man had been accustomed to fight the battles of life single-handed so that it had become habitual for him to depend solely upon his own cunning and prowess.

And so it was that he came into the upper corridor from which opened the chambers of Lu-don and the lesser priests far in advance of his warriors, and as he turned into this corridor with its dim cressets flickering somberly, he saw another enter it from a corridor before him—a warrior half carrying, half dragging the figure of a woman. Instantly Tarzan recognized the gagged and fettered captive whom he had thought safe in the palace of Ja-don at Ja-lur.

The warrior with the woman had seen Tarzan at the same instant that the latter had discovered him. He heard the low beastlike growl that broke from the ape-man's lips as he sprang forward to wrest his mate from her captor and wreak upon him the vengeance that was in the Tarmangani's savage heart. Across the corridor from Pan-sat

was the entrance to a smaller chamber. Into this he leaped carrying the woman with him.

Close behind came Tarzan of the Apes. He had cast aside his torch and drawn the long knife that had been his father's. With the impetuosity of a charging bull he rushed into the chamber in pursuit of Pan-sat to find himself, when the hangings dropped behind him, in utter darkness. Almost immediately there was a crash of stone on stone before him followed a moment later by a similar crash behind. No other evidence was necessary to announce to the ape-man that he was again a prisoner in Lu-don's temple.

He stood perfectly still where he had halted at the first sound of the descending stone door. Not again would he easily be precipitated to the *gryf* pit, or some similar danger, as had occurred when Lu-don had trapped him in the Temple of the Gryf. As he stood there his eyes slowly grew accustomed to the darkness and he became aware that a dim light was entering the chamber through some opening, though it was several minutes before he discovered its source. In the roof of the chamber he finally discerned a small aperture, possibly three feet in diameter and it was through this that what was really only a lesser darkness rather than a light was penetrating the Stygian blackness of the chamber in which he was imprisoned.

Since the doors had fallen he had heard no sound though his keen ears were constantly strained in an effort to discover a clue to the direction taken by the abductor of his mate. Presently he could discern the outlines of his prison cell. It was a small room, not over fifteen feet across. On hands and knees, with the utmost caution, he examined the entire area of the floor. In the exact center, directly beneath the opening in the roof, was a trap, but otherwise the floor was solid. With this knowledge it was only necessary to avoid this spot in so far as the floor was concerned. The walls next received his attention. There were only two openings. One the doorway through which he had entered, and upon the opposite side that through which the warrior had borne Jane Clayton. These were both closed by the slabs of stone which the fleeing warrior had released as he departed.

Lu-don, the high priest, licked his thin lips and rubbed his bony white hands together in gratification as Pan-sat bore Jane Clayton into his presence and laid her on the floor of the chamber before him.

"Good, Pan-sat!" he exclaimed. "You shall be well rewarded for this service. Now, if we but had the false Dor-ul-Otho in our power all Pal-ul-don would be at our feet."

"Master, I have him!" cried Pan-sat.

"What!" exclaimed Lu-don, "you have Tarzan-jad-guru? You have slain him perhaps. Tell me, my wonderful Pan-sat, tell me quickly. My breast is bursting with a desire to know."

"I have taken him alive, Lu-don, my master," replied Pan-sat. "He is in the little chamber that the ancients built to trap those who were too powerful to take alive in personal encounter."

"You have done well, Pan-sat, I—"

A frightened priest burst into the apartment. "Quick, master, quick," he cried, "the corridors are filled with the warriors of Ja-don."

"You are mad," cried the high priest. "My warriors hold the palace and the temple."

"I speak the truth, master," replied the priest, "there are warriors in the corridor approaching this very chamber, and they come from the direction of the secret passage which leads hither from the city."

"It may be even as he says," exclaimed Pan-sat. "It was from that direction that Tarzan-jad-guru was coming when I discovered and trapped him. He was leading his warriors to the very holy of holies."

Lu-don ran quickly to the doorway and looked out into the corridor. At a glance he saw that the fears of the frightened priest were well founded. A dozen warriors were moving along the corridor toward him but they seemed confused and far from sure of themselves. The high priest guessed that deprived of the leadership of

Tarzan they were little better than lost in the unknown mazes of the subterranean precincts of the temple.

Stepping back into the apartment he seized a leathern thong that depended from the ceiling. He pulled upon it sharply and through the temple boomed the deep tones of a metal gong. Five times the clanging notes rang through the corridors, then he turned toward the two priests. "Bring the woman and follow me," he directed.

Crossing the chamber he passed through a small doorway, the others lifting Jane Clayton from the floor and following him. Through a narrow corridor and up a flight of steps they went, turning to right and left and doubling back through a maze of winding passageways which terminated in a spiral staircase that gave forth at the surface of the ground within the largest of the inner altar courts close beside the eastern altar.

From all directions now, in the corridors below and the grounds above, came the sound of hurrying footsteps. The five strokes of the great gong had summoned the faithful to the defense of Lu-don in his private chambers. The priests who knew the way led the less familiar warriors to the spot and presently those who had accompanied Tarzan found themselves not only leaderless but facing a vastly superior force. They were brave men but under the circumstances they were helpless and so they fell back the way they had come, and when they reached the narrow confines of the smaller passageway their safety was assured since only one foeman could attack them at a time. But their plans were frustrated and possibly also their entire cause lost, so heavily had Ja-don banked upon the success of their venture.

With the clanging of the temple gong Ja-don assumed that Tarzan and his party had struck their initial blow and so he launched his attack upon the palace gate. To the ears of Lu-don in the inner temple court came the savage war cries that announced the beginning of the battle. Leaving Pan-sat and the other priest to guard the woman he hastened toward the palace personally to direct his force and as he passed through the temple grounds he dispatched a messenger to learn the outcome of the fight in the corridors below, and other messengers to spread the news among his followers that the false Dor-ul-Otho was a prisoner in the temple.

As the din of battle rose above A-lur, Lieutenant Erich Obergatz turned upon his bed of soft hides and sat up. He rubbed his eyes and looked about him. It was still dark without.

"I am Jad-ben-Otho," he cried, "who dares disturb my slumber?"

A slave squatting upon the floor at the foot of his couch shuddered and touched her forehead to the floor. "It must be that the enemy have come, O Jad-ben-Otho." She spoke soothingly for she had reason to know the terrors of the mad frenzy into which trivial things sometimes threw the Great God.

A priest burst suddenly through the hangings of the doorway and falling upon his hands and knees rubbed his forehead against the stone flagging. "O Jad-ben-Otho," he cried, "the warriors of Ja-don have attacked the palace and the temple. Even now they are fighting in the corridors near the quarters of Lu-don, and the high priest begs that you come to the palace and encourage your faithful warriors by your presence."

Obergatz sprang to his feet. "I am Jad-ben-Otho," he screamed. "With lightning I will blast the blasphemers who dare attack the holy city of A-lur."

For a moment he rushed aimlessly and madly about the room, while the priest and the slave remained upon hands and knees with their foreheads against the floor.

"Come," cried Obergatz, planting a vicious kick in the side of the slave girl. "Come! Would you wait here all day while the forces of darkness overwhelm the City of Light?"

Thoroughly frightened as were all those who were forced to serve the Great God, the two arose and followed Obergatz toward the palace.

Above the shouting of the warriors rose constantly the cries of the temple priests: "Jad-ben-Otho is here and the false Dor-ul-Otho is a prisoner in the temple." The persistent cries

reached even to the ears of the enemy as it was intended that they should.

The sun rose to see the forces of Ja-don still held at the palace gate. The old warrior had seized the tall structure that stood just beyond the palace and at the summit of this he kept a warrior stationed to look toward the northern wall of the palace where Ta-den was to make his attack; but as the minutes wore into hours no sign of the other force appeared, and now in the full light of the new sun upon the roof of one of the palace buildings appeared Lu-don, the high priest, Mo-sar, the pretender, and the strange, naked figure of a man, into whose long hair and beard were woven fresh ferns and flowers. Behind them were banked a score of lesser priests who chanted in unison: "This is Jad-ben-Otho. Lay down your arms and surrender." This they repeated again and again, alternating it with the cry: "The false Dor-ul-Otho is a prisoner."

In one of those lulls which are common in battles between forces armed with weapons that require great physical effort in their use, a voice suddenly arose from among the followers of Ja-don: "Show us the Dor-ul-Otho. We do not believe you!"

"Wait," cried Lu-don. "If I do not produce him before the sun has moved his own width, the gates of the palace shall be opened to you and my warriors will lay down their arms."

He turned to one of his priests and issued brief instructions.

The ape-man paced the confines of his narrow cell. Bitterly he reproached himself for the stupidity which had led him into this trap, and yet was it stupidity? What else might he have done other than rush to the succor of his mate? He wondered how they had stolen her from Ja-lur, and then suddenly there flashed to his mind the features of the warrior whom he had just seen with her. They were strangely familiar. He racked his brain to recall where he had seen the man before and then it came to him. He was the strange warrior who had joined Ja-don's forces outside of Ja-lur the day that Tarzan had ridden upon the great *gryf* from the uninhabited gorge next to the Kor-ul-ja down to the capital city of the chieftain of the north. But who could the man be? Tarzan knew that never before that other day had he seen him.

Presently he heard the clanging of a gong from the corridor without and very faintly the rush of feet, and shouts. He guessed that his warriors had been discovered and a fight was in progress. He fretted and chafed at the chance that had denied him participation in it.

Again and again he tried the doors of his prison and the trap in the center of the floor, but none would give to his utmost endeavors. He strained his eyes toward the aperture above but he could see nothing, and then he continued his futile pacing to and fro like a caged lion behind its bars.

The minutes dragged slowly into hours. Faintly sounds came to him as of shouting men at a great distance. The battle was in progress. He wondered if Ja-don would be victorious and should he be, would his friends ever discover him in this hidden chamber in the bowels of the hill? He doubted it.

And now as he looked again toward the aperture in the roof there appeared to be something depending through its center. He came closer and strained his eyes to see. Yes, there was something there. It appeared to be a rope. Tarzan wondered if it had been there all the time. It must have, he reasoned, since he had heard no sound from above and it was so dark within the chamber that he might easily have overlooked it.

He raised his hand toward it. The end of it was just within his reach. He bore his weight upon it to see if it would hold him. Then he released it and backed away, still watching it, as

you have seen an animal do after investigating some unfamiliar object, one of the little traits that differentiated Tarzan from other men, accentuating his similarity to the savage beasts of his native jungle. Again and again he touched and tested the braided leather rope, and always he listened for any warning sound from above.

He was very careful not to step upon the trap at any time and when finally he bore all his weight upon the rope and took his feet from the floor he spread them wide apart so that if he fell he would fall astride the trap. The rope held him. There was no sound from above, nor any from the trap below.

Slowly and cautiously he drew himself upward, hand over hand. Nearer and nearer the roof he came. In a moment his eyes would be above the level of the floor above. Already his extended arms projected into the upper chamber and then something closed suddenly upon both his forearms, pinioning them tightly and leaving him hanging in mid-air unable to advance or retreat.

Immediately a light appeared in the room above him and presently he saw the hideous mask of a priest peering down upon him. In the priest's hands were leathern thongs and these he tied about Tarzan's wrists and forearms until they were completely bound together from his elbows almost to his fingers. Behind this priest Tarzan presently saw others and soon several lay hold of him and pulled him up through the hole.

Almost instantly his eyes were above the level of the floor he understood how they had trapped him. Two nooses had lain encircling the aperture into the cell below. A priest had waited at the end of each of these ropes and at opposite sides of the chamber. When he had climbed to a sufficient height upon the rope that had dangled into his prison below and his arms were well within the encircling snares the two priests had pulled quickly upon their ropes and he had been made an easy captive without any opportunity of defending himself or inflicting injury upon his captors.

And now they bound his legs from his ankles

to his knees and picking him up carried him from the chamber. No word did they speak to him as they bore him upward to the temple yard.

The din of battle had risen again as Ja-don had urged his forces to renewed efforts. Ta-den had not arrived and the forces of the old chieftain were revealing in their lessened efforts their increasing demoralization, and then it was that the priests carried Tarzan-jad-guru to the roof of the palace and exhibited him in the sight of the warriors of both factions.

"Here is the false Dor-ul-Otho," screamed Lu-don.

Obergatz, his shattered mentality having never grasped fully the meaning of much that was going on about him, cast a casual glance at the bound and helpless prisoner, and as his eyes fell upon the noble features of the ape-man, they went wide in astonishment and fright, and his pasty countenance turned a sickly blue. Once before had he seen Tarzan of the Apes, but many times had he dreamed that he had seen him and always was the giant ape-man avenging the wrongs that had been committed upon him and his by the ruthless hands of the three German officers who had led their native troops in the ravishing of Tarzan's peaceful home. Hauptmann Fritz Schneider had paid the penalty of his needless cruelties; Unter-lieutenant von Goss, too, had paid; and now Obergatz, the last of the three, stood face to face with the Nemesis that had trailed him through his dreams for long, weary months. That he was bound and helpless lessened not the German's terror—he seemed not to realize that the man could not harm him. He but stood cringing and jibbering and Lu-don saw and was filled with apprehension that others might see and seeing realize that this bewhiskered idiot was no god—that of the two Tarzan-jad-guru was the more godly figure. Already the high priest noted that some of the palace warriors standing near were whispering together and pointing. He stepped closer to Obergatz. "You are Jad-ben-Otho," he whispered, "denounce him!"

The German shook himself. His mind cleared of all but his great terror and the words of the high priest gave him the clue to safety.

"I am Jad-ben-Otho!" he screamed.

Tarzan looked him straight in the eye. "You are Lieutenant Obergatz of the German Army," he said in excellent German. "You are the last of the three I have sought so long and in your putrid heart you know that God has not brought us together at last for nothing."

The mind of Lieutenant Obergatz was functioning clearly and rapidly at last. He too saw the questioning looks upon the faces of some of those around them. He saw the opposing warriors of both cities standing by the gate inactive, every eye turned upon him, and the trussed figure of the ape-man. He realized that indecision now meant ruin, and ruin, death. He raised his voice in the sharp barking tones of a Prussian officer, so unlike his former maniacal screaming as to quickly arouse the attention of every ear and to cause an expression of puzzlement to cross the crafty face of Lu-don.

"I am Jad-ben-Otho," snapped Obergatz. "This creature is no son of mine. As a lesson to all blasphemers he shall die upon the altar at the hand of the god he has profaned. Take him from my sight, and when the sun stands at zenith let the faithful congregate in the temple court and witness the wrath of this divine hand," and he held aloft his right palm.

Those who had brought Tarzan took him away then as Obergatz had directed, and the German turned once more to the warriors by the gate. "Throw down your arms, warriors of Ja-don," he cried, "lest I call down my lightnings to blast you where you stand. Those who do as I bid shall be forgiven. Come! Throw down your arms."

The warriors of Ja-don moved uneasily, casting looks of appeal at their leader and of apprehension toward the figures upon the palace roof. Ja-don sprang forward among his men. "Let the cowards and knaves throw down their arms and enter the palace," he cried, "but never will

Ja-don and the warriors of Ja-lur touch their foreheads to the feet of Lu-don and his false god. Make your decision now," he cried to his followers.

A few threw down their arms and with sheepish looks passed through the gateway into the palace, and with the example of these to bolster their courage others joined in the desertion from the old chieftain of the north, but staunch and true around him stood the majority of his warriors and when the last weakling had left their ranks Ja-don voiced the savage cry with which he led his followers to the attack, and once again the battle raged about the palace gate.

At times Ja-don's forces pushed the defenders far into the palace grounds and then the wave of combat would recede and pass out into the city again. And still Ta-den and the reinforcements did not come. It was drawing close to noon. Lu-don had mustered every available man that was not actually needed for the defense of the gate within the temple, and these he sent, under the leadership of Pan-sat, out into the city through the secret passageway and there they fell upon Ja-don's forces from the rear while those at the gate hammered them in front.

Attacked on two sides by a vastly superior force the result was inevitable and finally the last remnant of Ja-don's little army capitulated and the old chief was taken a prisoner before Lu-don. "Take him to the temple court," cried the high priest. "He shall witness the death of his accomplice and perhaps Jad-ben-Otho shall pass a similar sentence upon him as well."

The inner temple court was packed with humanity. At either end of the western altar stood Tarzan and his mate, bound and helpless. The sounds of battle had ceased and presently the ape-man saw Ja-don being led into the inner court, his wrists bound tightly together before him. Tarzan turned his eyes toward Jane and nodded in the direction of Ja-don. "This looks like the end," he said quietly. "He was our last and only hope."

"We have at least found each other, John," she replied, "and our last days have been spent together. My only prayer now is that if they take you they do not leave me."

Tarzan made no reply for in his heart was the same bitter thought that her own contained—not the fear that they would kill him but the fear that they would not kill her. The ape-man strained at his bonds but they were too many and too strong. A priest near him saw and with a jeering laugh struck the defenseless ape-man in the face.

"The brute!" cried Jane Clayton.

Tarzan smiled. "I have been struck thus before, Jane," he said, "and always has the striker died."

"You still have hope?" she asked.

"I am still alive," he said as though that were sufficient answer. She was a woman and she did not have the courage of this man who knew no fear. In her heart of hearts she knew that he would die upon the altar at high noon for he had told her, after he had been brought to the inner court, of the sentence of death that Obergatz had pronounced upon him, and she knew too that Tarzan knew that he would die, but that he was too courageous to admit it even to himself.

As she looked upon him standing there so straight and wonderful and brave among his savage captors her heart cried out against the cruelty of the fate that had overtaken him. It seemed a gross and hideous wrong that that wonderful creature, now so quick with exuberant life and strength and purpose should be presently naught but a bleeding lump of clay—and all so uselessly and wantonly. Gladly would she have offered her life for his but she knew that it was a waste of words since their captors would work upon them whatever it was their will to do—for him, death; for her—she shuddered at the thought.

And now came Lu-don and the naked Obergatz, and the high priest led the German to his place behind the altar, himself standing upon the other's left. Lu-don whispered a word to Obergatz, at the same time nodding in the direction of

Ja-don. The Hun cast a scowling look upon the old warrior.

"And after the false god," he cried, "the false prophet," and he pointed an accusing finger at Ja-don. Then his eyes wandered to the form of Jane Clayton.

"And the woman, too?" asked Lu-don.

"The case of the woman I will attend to later," replied Obergatz. "I will talk with her tonight after she has had a chance to meditate upon the consequences of arousing the wrath of Jad-ben-Otho."

He cast his eyes upward at the sun. "The time approaches," he said to Lu-don. "Prepare the sacrifice."

Lu-don nodded to the priests who were gathered about Tarzan. They seized the ape-man and lifted him bodily to the altar where they laid him upon his back with his head at the south end of the monolith, but a few feet from where Jane Clayton stood. Impulsively and before they could restrain her the woman rushed forward and bending quickly kissed her mate upon the forehead. "Good-bye, John," she whispered.

"Good-bye," he answered, smiling.

The priests seized her and dragged her away. Lu-don handed the sacrificial knife to Obergatz. "I am the Great God," cried the German, "thus falleth the divine wrath upon all my enemies!" He looked up at the sun and then raised the knife high above his head.

"Thus die the blasphemers of God!" he screamed, and at the same instant a sharp staccato note rang out above the silent, spell-bound multitude. There was a screaming whistle in the air and Jad-ben-Otho crumpled forward across the body of his intended victim. Again the same alarming noise and Lu-don fell, a third and Mo-sar crumpled to the ground. And now the warriors and the people, locating the direction of this new and unknown sound turned toward the western end of the court.

Upon the summit of the temple wall they saw two figures—a Ho-don warrior and beside him an almost naked creature of the race of Tarzan-

jad-guru; across his shoulders and about his hips were strange broad belts studded with beautiful cylinders that glinted in the mid-day sun, and in his hands a shining thing of wood and metal from the end of which rose a thin wreath of blue-gray smoke.

And then the voice of the Ho-don warrior rang clear upon the ears of the silent throng. "Thus speaks the true Jad-ben-Otho," he cried, "through this his Messenger of Death. Cut the bonds of the prisoners. Cut the bonds of the Dor-ul-Otho and of Ja-don, King of Pal-ul-don, and of the woman who is the mate of the son of God."

Pan-sat, filled with the frenzy of fanaticism saw the power and the glory of the régime he had served crumpled and gone. To one and only one did he attribute the blame for the disaster that had but just overwhelmed him. It was the creature who lay upon the sacrificial altar who had brought Lu-don to his death and toppled the dreams of power that day by day had been growing in the brain of the under priest.

The sacrificial knife lay upon the altar where it had fallen from the dead fingers of Obergatz. Pan-sat crept closer and then with a sudden lunge he reached forth to seize the handle of the blade, and even as his clutching fingers were poised above it, the strange thing in the hands of the strange creature upon the temple wall cried out its crashing word of doom and Pan-sat the under priest, screaming, fell back upon the dead body of his master.

"Seize all the priests," cried Ta-den to the warriors, "and let none hesitate lest Jad-ben-Otho's messenger send forth still other bolts of lightning."

The warriors and the people had now witnessed such an exhibition of divine power as might have convinced an even less superstitious and more enlightened people, and since many of them had but lately wavered between the Jad-ben-Otho of Lu-don and the Dor-ul-Otho of Ja-don it was not difficult for them to swing quickly back to the latter, especially in view of the unanswerable argument in the hands of him whom Ta-den had described as the Messenger of the Great God.

And so the warriors sprang forward now with alacrity and surrounded the priests, and when they looked again at the western wall of the temple court they saw pouring over it a great force of warriors. And the thing that startled and appalled them was the fact that many of these were black and hairy Waz-don.

At their head came the stranger with the shiny weapon and on his right was Ta-den, the Ho-don, and on his left Om-at, the black *gund* of Kor-ul-ja.

A warrior near the altar had seized the sacrificial knife and cut Tarzan's bonds and also those of Ja-don and Jane Clayton, and now the three stood together beside the altar and as the newcomers from the western end of the temple court pushed their way toward them the eyes of the woman went wide in mingled astonishment, incredulity, and hope. And the stranger, slinging his weapon across his back by a leather strap, rushed forward and took her in his arms.

"Jack!" she cried, sobbing on his shoulder. "Jack, my son!"

And Tarzan of the Apes came then and put his arms around them both, and the King of Pal-ul-don and the warriors and the people kneeled in the temple court and placed their foreheads to the ground before the altar where the three stood.

XXV
HOME

Within an hour of the fall of Lu-don and Mo-sar, the chiefs and principal warriors of Pal-ul-don gathered in the great throneroom of the palace at A-lur upon the steps of the lofty pyramid and placing Ja-don at the apex proclaimed him king. Upon one side of the old chieftain stood Tarzan of the Apes, and upon the other Korak, the Killer, worthy son of the mighty ape-man.

And when the brief ceremony was over and the warriors with upraised clubs had sworn fealty to their new ruler, Ja-don dispatched a trusted company to fetch O-lo-a and Pan-at-lee and the women of his own household from Ja-lur.

And then the warriors discussed the future of Pal-ul-don and the question arose as to the administration of the temples and the fate of the priests, who practically without exception had been disloyal to the government of the king, seeking always only their own power and comfort and aggrandizement. And then it was that Ja-don turned to Tarzan. "Let the Dor-ul-Otho transmit to his people the wishes of his father," he said.

"Your problem is a simple one," said the ape-man, "if you but wish to do that which shall be pleasing in the eyes of God. Your priests, to increase their power, have taught you that Jad-ben-Otho is a cruel god, that his eyes love to dwell upon blood and upon suffering. But the falsity of their teachings has been demonstrated to you today in the utter defeat of the priesthood.

"Take then the temples from the men and give them instead to the women that they may be administered in kindness and charity and love. Wash the blood from your eastern altar and drain forever the water from the western.

"Once I gave Lu-don the opportunity to do these things but he ignored my commands, and again is the corridor of sacrifice filled with its victims. Liberate these from every temple in Pal-ul-don. Bring offerings of such gifts as your people like and place them upon the altars of your god. And there he will bless them and the priestesses of Jad-ben-Otho can distribute them among those who need them most."

As he ceased speaking a murmur of evident approval ran through the throng. Long had they been weary of the avarice and cruelty of the priests and now that authority had come from a high source with a feasible plan for ridding themselves of the old religious order without necessitating any change in the faith of the people they welcomed it.

"And the priests," cried one. "We shall put them to death upon their own altars if it pleases the Dor-ul-Otho to give the word."

"No," cried Tarzan. "Let no more blood be spilled. Give them their freedom and the right to take up such occupations as they choose."

That night a great feast was spread in the *pal-e-don-so* and for the first time in the history of ancient Pal-ul-don black warriors sat in peace and friendship with white. And a pact was sealed between Ja-don and Om-at that would ever make his tribe and the Ho-don allies and friends.

It was here that Tarzan learned the cause of Ta-den's failure to attack at the stipulated time. A messenger had come from Ja-don carrying instructions to delay the attack until noon, nor had they discovered until almost too late that the messenger was a disguised priest of Lu-don. And they had put him to death and scaled the walls and come to the inner temple court with not a moment to spare.

The following day O-lo-a and Pan-at-lee and the women of Ja-don's family arrived at the palace at A-lur and in the great throneroom Ta-den and O-lo-a were wed, and Om-at and Pan-at-lee.

For a week Tarzan and Jane and Korak remained the guests of Ja-don, as did Om-at and his black warriors. And then the ape-man announced that he would depart from Pal-ul-don. Hazy in the minds of their hosts was the location of heaven and equally so the means by which the gods traveled between their celestial homes and the haunts of men and so no questionings arose when it was found that the Dor-ul-Otho with his mate and son would travel overland across the mountains and out of Pal-ul-don toward the north.

They went by way of the Kor-ul-ja accompanied by the warriors of that tribe and a great contingent of Ho-don warriors under Ta-den. The king and many warriors and a multitude of people accompanied them beyond the limits of A-lur and after they had bid them good-bye and Tarzan had invoked the blessings of God upon them the three Europeans saw their simple, loyal friends prostrate in the dust behind them until the cavalcade had wound out of the city and disappeared among the trees of the nearby forest.

They rested for a day among the Kor-ul-ja while Jane investigated the ancient caves of these strange people and then they moved on, avoiding the rugged shoulder of Pastar-ul-ved and winding down the opposite slope toward the great morass. They moved in comfort and in safety, surrounded by their escort of Ho-don and Waz-don.

In the minds of many there was doubtless a question as to how the three would cross the great morass but least of all was Tarzan worried by the problem. In the course of his life he had been confronted by many obstacles only to learn that he who will may always pass. In his mind lurked an easy solution of the passage but it was one which depended wholly upon chance.

It was the morning of the last day that, as they were breaking camp to take up the march, a deep bellow thundered from a nearby grove. The ape-man smiled. The chance had come. Fittingly then would the Dor-ul-Otho and his mate and their son depart from unmapped Pal-ul-don.

He still carried the spear that Jane had made, which he had prized so highly because it was her handiwork that he had caused a search to be made for it through the temple in A-lur after his release, and it had been found and brought to him. He had told her laughingly that it should have the place of honor above their hearth as the ancient flintlock of her Puritan grandsire had held a similar place of honor above the fireplace of Professor Porter, her father.

At the sound of the bellowing the Ho-don warriors, some of whom had accompanied Tarzan from Ja-don's camp to Ja-lur, looked questioningly at the ape-man while Om-at's Waz-don looked for trees, since the *gryf* was the one creature of Pal-ul-don which might not be safely encountered even by a great multitude of warriors. Its tough, armored hide was impregnable to their knife thrusts while their thrown clubs rattled from it as futilely as if hurled at the rocky shoulder of Pastar-ul-ved.

"Wait," said the ape-man, and with his spear in hand he advanced toward the *gryf,* voicing the weird cry of the Tor-o-don. The bellowing ceased and turned to low rumblings and presently the huge beast appeared. What followed was but a repetition of the ape-man's previous experience with these huge and ferocious creatures.

And so it was that Jane and Korak and Tarzan rode through the morass that hems Pal-ul-don, upon the back of a prehistoric triceratops while the lesser reptiles of the swamp fled hissing in terror. Upon the opposite shore they turned and called back their farewells to Ta-den and Om-at and the brave warriors they had learned to admire and respect. And then Tarzan urged their titanic mount onward toward the north, aban-doning him only when he was assured that the Waz-don and the Ho-don had had time to reach a point of comparative safety among the craggy ravines of the foothills.

Turning the beast's head again toward Pal-ul-don the three dismounted and a sharp blow upon the thick hide sent the creature lumbering majestically back in the direction of its native haunts. For a time they stood looking back upon the land they had just quit—the land of Tor-o-don and *gryf;* of *ja* and *jato;* of Waz-don and Ho-don; a primitive land of terror and sudden death and peace and beauty; a land that they all had learned to love.

And then they turned once more toward the north and with light hearts and brave hearts took up their long journey toward the land that is best of all—home.

PERMISSIONS ACKNOWLEDGMENTS

Charles Ardai: "Nor Idolatry Blind the Eye" by Gabriel Hunt as told to Charles Ardai from *Hunt Through the Cradle of Fear*, originally published by Dorchester Publishing Co., Inc., in 2009. Copyright © 2009 by Winterfall LLC. Reprinted by permission of the author.

H. Bedford-Jones: "Peace Waits at Marokee" by H. Bedford-Jones, *Adventure* magazine, November 1940. Copyright © 1940 by Popular Publications, Inc. Copyright renewed 1968 and assigned to Argosy Communications, Inc. All rights reserved. Reprinted by permission of Argosy Communications, Inc.

Loring Brent: "The Master Magician" by Loring Brent, *Argosy* magazine, February 25, 1933. Copyright © 1933 by The Frank A. Munsey Company. Copyright renewed 1961 and assigned to Argosy Communications, Inc. All rights reserved. Reprinted by permission of Argosy Communications, Inc.

John Buchan: "The Green Wildebeest" by John Buchan, first published in *Pall Mall Magazine*, September 1927. Copyright © 1927 by John Buchan, copyright renewed. Reprinted by permission of A. P. Watt, Ltd., on behalf of Jean, Lady Tweedsmuir, The Lord Tweedsmuir and Sally, Lady Tweedsmuir.

Lester Dent: "Hell Cay" by Lester Dent. Copyright © 2011 by the Estate of Norma Dent. Reprinted by permission of Will Murray.

George Fielding Eliot: "The Copper Bowl" by George Fielding Eliot, first published in *Weird Tales*, December 1928. Copyright © 1928 by *Weird Tales*. Reprinted by permission of Weird Tales Ltd.

Philip José Farmer: "After King Kong Fell" by Philip José Farmer, from *Omega*, edited by Roger Elwood, originally published by Walker, New York, in 1973. Copyright © 1973 by Philip José Farmer. Reprinted by permission of Ralph M. Vicinanza, Ltd., as agent for the estate of Philip José Farmer.

Geoffrey Household: "Woman in Love" by Geoffrey Household, from *Tales of Adventure* originally published by Michael Joseph, London, in 1952. Copyright © 1952. Copyright renewed. Reprinted by permission of A. M. Heath & Co., Ltd.

Damon Knight: "To Serve Man" by Damon Knight, *Galaxy*, 1950. Copyright © 1950 by Damon Knight. Copyright renewed. Reprinted by permission of Kate Wilhelm.

Louis L'Amour: "Off the Mangrove Coast," from *The Collected Short Stories of Louis L'Amour: The Adventure Stories, Volume Four* by Louis L'Amour. Copyright © 2006 by Louis and Katherine L'Amour Trust. Reprinted by permission of Bantam Books, a division of Random House, Inc.

Fritz Leiber: "The Seven Black Priests" by Fritz Leiber. Copyright © 1952. Copyright renewed. Reprinted by permission of Richard Curtis Associates.

Alistair MacLean: "MacHinery and the Cauliflowers" by Alistair MacLean from *The Lonely Sea*. Copyright © 1985 by HarperCollins Publishers Limited. Reprinted by permission of HarperCollins Publishers Limited, London.

THE VAMPIRE ARCHIVES

*The Most Complete Volume of Vampire Tales
Ever Published*

The Vampire Archives is the biggest, hungriest, undeadliest collection of vampire stories, as well as the most comprehensive bibliography of vampire fiction ever assembled. Whether imagined by Bram Stoker or Anne Rice, vampires are part of the human lexicon and as old as blood itself. They are your neighbors, your friends, and they are always lurking. Now Otto Penzler has compiled the darkest, the scariest, and by far the most evil collection of vampire stories ever. With over eighty stories, including the works of Stephen King and D. H. Lawrence, alongside Lord Byron and Tanith Lee, not to mention Edgar Allan Poe and Harlan Ellison, it will drive a stake through the heart of any other collection out there.

Fiction

ALSO AVAILABLE IN MASS-MARKET VOLUMES:

BLOODSUCKERS
The Vampire Archives, Volume 1
Including stories by Stephen King, Dan Simmons, and
Bram Stoker

FANGS
The Vampire Archives, Volume 2
Including stories by Clive Barker, Anne Rice, and
Arthur Conan Doyle

COFFINS
The Vampire Archives, Volume 3
Including stories by Harlan Ellison, Robert Bloch, and
Edgar Allan Poe

ZOMBIES! ZOMBIES! ZOMBIES!

The legendary editor of *The Vampire Archives* now brings us *Zombies! Zombies! Zombies!*, an unstoppable anthology of the living dead. These superstars of horror are everywhere, storming the world of print and visual media. Their endless march will never be stopped. It's the Zombie Zeitgeist! Now, with his wide sweep of knowledge and keen eye for great storytelling, Otto Penzler offers a remarkable catalog of zombie literature. From world-renowned authors like Stephen King, Joe R. Lansdale, Robert McCammon, Robert E. Howard, and Richard Matheson to the writer who started it all, W. B. Seabrook, *Zombies! Zombies! Zombies!* is the darkest, the living-deadliest, scariest, and—dare we say—tasteful collection of the wandering zombie horde ever assembled. Its relentless pages will devour horror fans from coast to coast.

Fiction

Forthcoming from Vintage Crime/Black Lizard in Fall 2011

AGENTS OF TREACHERY

Never Before Published Spy Fiction from
Today's Most Exciting Writers

For the first time ever, Otto Penzler has handpicked some of the most respected and bestselling thriller writers working today for a riveting collection of spy fiction. From first to last, this stellar collection signals mission accomplished. Featuring: Lee Child with an incredible look at the formation of a special ops team; James Grady writing about an Arab undercover FBI agent with an active cell; Joseph Finder riffing on a Boston architect who's convinced that his Persian neighbors are up to no good; John Lawton concocting a Len Deighton-esque story about British intelligence; Stephen Hunter thrilling us with a tale about a WWII brigade; and much more.

Spy Fiction

VINTAGE CRIME/BLACK LIZARD
Available wherever books are sold.
www.randomhouse.com